The Mad Patagonian

Javier Pedro Zabala

Translated from The Spanish
and with an Introduction

by

Tomás García Guerrero

Peter Damian Bellis
Editor, English language edition

River Boat Books
St. Paul, MN

Translated from The Spanish by Tomás García Guerrero.

Printed in the United States of America.

Published by River Boat Books. St. Paul, MN.
First printing June 26, 2018.

ISBN: 978-0-9654756-7-9

Cover Illustration: Adaptation of "The Fair" by Maruja Mallo, 1927. Used with permission of the artist's estate.

Fonts used for cover: Twentieth Century MT, Garamond
Fonts used for title page: Moonbeam, Papyrus
Font used for heading text: Moonbeam
Font used for text: Palantino Linotype

All of the photographs used in "The Translator's Introductory Remarks" are part of the Zabala family collection and used with the expressed, written permission of the Heirs of Javier Pedro Zabala.

Javier Pedro Zabala's *The Mad Patagonian* is a literary supernova. From absolute silence, both the author and his 1,200-page book appeared suddenly and completely. Fans of William T. Vollmann, Roberto Bolaño, Julio Cortázar, and Alain Robbe-Grillett will find it a novel take on recognizable topics and themes. The cumulative effect of this polyphonic novel is akin to a kaleidoscope, each fragmented and embedded narrative falling over each other in an ever-expanding and ever-evolving narrative.

5 Stars

– Jacob Singer, Book Review Editor, *Entropy*

The Mad Patagonian was for me like capturing lightning in a bottle. It is a book that I'd want on whatever desert island I would be shipwrecked on, and to my mind easily comparable in range, multi-dimensionality and execution to my two favorite epics of Latin American fiction — Bolaño's *2666* and Mario Vargas Llosa's *Conversation in the Cathedral*. IMO it is a flat-out masterpiece and I would encourage anyone at all interested in reading great literature to go out and get him/herself a copy.

5 Stars

– Larry Riley, Early Reviewers, *Library Thing*

The Mad Patagonian is borderless unlike Vargas Llosa's masterpiece, *Conversations in the Cathedral,* which is self-contained; and at the same time it is more contained than Bolaño's false epic, *2666*. In this respect it is similar to Cervantes' *Don Quixote,* and also Gabriel García Márquez' *One Hundred Years of Solitude*. One could also say that in his use of language, Zabala also seems a worthy heir to James Joyce, writing each passage according to the dictates of the content.

Of course one other Spanish language comparison is to Borges, for the book's wealth of intricate, labyrinthine arcania—it is brimming with such…to the point that the reader no longer cares in the least what is true and what is not. We do know that there were Merovingian Kings, but was Diego Penalosa governor of Cuba in 1746? There are dozens of such details, all of which are available in the sweep of the language, none of which require a pause—though during my second read, which may not occur this year, I intend to do a great deal more digging, as the book is an extremely learned text that wears its genius lightly.

5 Stars

–Rick Harsch, author of *The Driftless Trilogy*

It's probably fair to say that Javier Pedro Zabala is the greatest Latin American writer you've never heard of, and his magnum opus *The Mad Patagonian* is the greatest novel in Spanish of the 21st century that you've never read. Zabala is acutely aware of the limitations of language, as aware as no other writer of his generation, except perhaps David Foster Wallace. He knows that language describes what is not as much as it describes what is: gun delineates a specific object as much as it rules out the possibility that the object is not something else, like nun or gum. Zabala knows that when a writer writes something as apparently innocuous as a description of the night, he is also drawing a line through other possibilities: *Outside the moon has set.* can also just as well refuse to be: *Outside the moon is glowing in the night sky.* or even *Outside it is twilight and the birds have stopped calling to each other.* Zabala gives us all three descriptions, as if asking us to choose, or to understand them as a radically telescoped sequence, or to consider their possibilities as palimpsest.

At 1,200 plus pages, the book is a daunting read. However Zabala's imagination is a fount of fecundity; a multitudinous world envelopes the reader, crowded with vivid characters and events, a great deal of salt, genuine feeling, irony and humour, and a kind of unstoppable energy. Mahler said of the symphony that it should embrace the world, and the really great novels of the 20th/21st centuries: *Gravity's Rainbow, Infinite Jest, Underworld, 2666,* seem to have also embraced this view. Zabala's novel should rightfully take its place alongside them.

5 Stars

– Tom Murr, Book Critic, *The Lectern*

You have wakened not out of sleep, but into a prior dream, and that dream lies within another, and so on, to infinity, which is the number of the grains of sand. The path that you are to take is endless, and you will die before you have truly awakened.
—Jorge Luis Borges

I know who I am and who I may be, if I choose.
— Miguel de Cervantes Saavedra

When life seems lunatic, who knows where madness lies? Perhaps to be too practical is madness. To surrender dreams — this may be madness. Too much sanity may be madness — and maddest of all, to see life as it is and not as it should be.
— Miguel de Cervantes Saavedra

A Note from the Publisher

It is with great sadness that I must announce the passing of Tomás García Guerrero, the translator of Zabala's masterpiece, The Mad Patagonian. Mr. Guerrero was born in San Pedrito, Mexico in 1937. He earned his Doctorate in Linguistics from UNAM in 1962 and taught at various institutions throughout Mexico. He retired in 1998 from the University of Tamaulipas, Mexico and moved to Toledo, Ohio to live with his daughter. This was his first translation. He died on January 9, 2016 of complications from pneumonia.

I cannot adequately put into words my gratitude to Mr. Guerrero for the time and effort he put into this English edition. I am certain that he felt about this book as a father might feel about a child. I possess a similar feeling, though in my case the word stepchild would be more accurate. But I would be remiss if I did not say that Mr. Guerrero's sudden absence robbed us of an essential voice during the latter stages of the editorial process. This is not to excuse any defects that may exist in the manuscript. It is to suggest instead that I alone, as the editor and publisher of the English edition of The Mad Patagonian, am responsible for any narrative or linguistic shortcomings of the book in its current form, shortcomings that are in all probability a result of my inadequate knowledge of the Spanish language in general, or of the remarkable history and culture of Spain, Cuba and the Americas in particular.

Peter Damian Bellis
Editor & Publisher
River Boat Books

The Translator's Introductory Remarks

Cuban writer Javier Pedro Zabala and Chilean writer Roberto Bolaño first crossed paths in Mexico City in the mid-seventies. Their very first meeting, recounted at some length in Zabala's diary, occurred in April of 1975. The meeting did not take place in Librería Gandhi or any other bookstore. It did not take place in that mysterious Mexican hangout known as Café La Habana, although that venue would have been appropriate on many levels, certainly because it was the haunt of writers and artists for generations, but also because it is supposedly the spot where Fidel Castro and Che Guevara drew up their plans for overthrowing the Batista regime and taking control of Cuba. No, the first meeting between Zabala and Bolaño was not imbued with such a heavy-handed sense of history and timing. Instead, the two writers, both young men who had not yet made a dent in the literary world, met by accident in a greasy spoon of a café called El Abrevadero on Calle de Tacuba, a few blocks east of the Palace of Fine Arts. It is now a McDonald's, but back then it was the kind of place where you could get a beer at any hour of the day or night. Bolaño was capping a thirty-six-hour stint of walking and writing by eating a large, overcooked breakfast before he went to bed. He was sitting alone, with his back to the window. 'He was a brightly shining shadow sitting in a pool of dark sunlight,' Zabala later wrote. Zabala was with a young woman, Blanca Barutti, a recent graduate of the Facultad de Medicina UNAM, who would later become Zabala's wife. She was originally from Santiago, Cuba, from the wealthy Vista Alegre neighborhood, but her family had left when Castro came to power. She was extraordinarily beautiful and was often mistaken for a movie star. She also had a reputation for a razor-sharp wit. Both qualities caught Bolaño's attention.

In his diary, which Zabala kept with religious diligence, he recorded that he and Bolaño soon struck up an uneasy conversation, precipitated by the presence of Blanca.

> *We spent half an hour sparring politely, an imaginary war between two young lions pacing back and forth in*

the same cage. Blanca was the prize. And then we forgot all about Blanca and talked about everything except the preposterous art of writing. Bolaño said Mexican politics was disheartening. Echeverría had only made things worse. Then he said Echeverría was why he had left Mexico in '72 and spent some time with leftist guerrillas in El Salvador. He said he had been a counter-revolutionary, a spy. He said he had then gone back to Chile to give his heart and soul to Allende's noble struggle to build a socialist state, but then Pinochet seized control. Pinochet is worse than Echeverría, he said. Didn't you know that Echeverría supported Allende? I asked him. How can you be against Echeverría and Pinochet both? But he seemed not to hear me. Of course I was only half serious. I mean who was I to comment on the labyrinthine complexities of Latin American politics? But I thought Bolaño was full of shit, to be frank. He sounded like a counterfeit Trotskyist who knew nothing about the deprivations and personal sacrifice that go along with revolution. Besides, he was too skinny for even the most resolute revolutionary. He seemed more like a refugee. Then he said when he had gone back to Chile the police picked him up because of his odd-sounding accent and tossed him in jail. Everyone around him was smeared with blood. Everyone was suffering from contagious amnesia. He said he spent nine days in a rat-infested swamp of a prison cell, waiting to be tortured like the other prisoners, before a guard he knew from high school recognized him, so they released him. It was at that point I knew he was a writer more than anything else, and I said so, and he laughed. He told me about a new poetry movement he had founded that would pick up the torch lit by Rimbaud. We ordered some beers. Then he said the oddest thing. He said he hoped one day to win the Casa de las Américas Award for a book of poetry. I think he said this to see if I was paying attention. Or maybe to irritate me. Or maybe he was back to flirting with Blanca and wanted to impress her. I looked at him over my glass of beer. What was the use of a literary award to a poet like Rimbaud, who abandoned poetry for a mercantile career in Africa? I asked him. He put his finger to his mouth to shush me, as if we were both collaborators on the verge of discovery, and then he started laughing and disappeared into his own beer, the morning light refracting through the dirty glass containing his amber colored ambrosia, producing a soft golden halo effect above his head.

Zabala later told his daughter, Cecilia, that he and Bolaño got along well enough. They met now and then over the course of the summer of 1975 and talked about poetry and what it meant to be a writer and whether or not you could call yourself a writer if you didn't write a single word. They talked about their disappointment with establishment writers like Octavio Paz and Juan Rulfo (though Zabala confesses at one point in his diary that their reasons were childish and more a reflection of their own as yet untested literary ambitions than anything else). They were both moved by the surrealistic impulses of Alfonso Reyes. They didn't bother to discuss Carlos Fuentes, except Zabala said he had enjoyed *La muerte de Artemio Cruz* immensely. They agreed about Cuban writer Norberto Fuentes. They disagreed about Gabriel García Marquez. On the whole they liked Mario Vargas Llosa's books. They could not praise enough the literary efforts of Miguel Ángel Asturias and Rómulo Gallegos and, of course, Borges. They tossed around the names of all sorts of eccentric poets. They joked about Carlos Pellicer, who looked like a butcher or a tenor in a barbershop quartet, according to Bolaño. They agreed it was easy to masturbate after reading the erotic poetry of Pierre Louÿs and next to impossible to masturbate after reading the sublime poetry of Sor Juana Inés de la Cruz. Zabala dismissed Luis Cernuda outright. He thought Cernuda would have been nothing at all if he hadn't flung open the doors of his homosexuality for the whole outraged world to see. Bolaño disagreed. Bolaño asked if Zabala had read the Chilean poet Carlos de Rokha and Zabala said he hadn't heard of him and Bolaño said he wasn't surprised because even the Chileans he grew up with hadn't heard of de Rokha. Zabala asked Bolaño if he had read the Mexican poet Sageuo Ruedas but Bolaño had not. Then Zabala asked if Bolaño had heard of the Peruvian activist and poet Eduardo de Jesús Montoyo, who ran in the same circle as the writer José Carlos Mariátegui before they had a falling out, but Bolaño said that except for Adán and Vallejo and Emilio Westphalen, and also Jorge Pimentel, the founder of Movimiento Hora Zero, who had discovered a way to evoke the natural beauty of everyday Peruvian life in his poetry, like in a ballad, and Tulio Moro and Juan Ramírez Ruis, who followed

Pimentel down Quilca street, and then there was César Moro, whose real name was Alfredo Quíspez Asín but he thought he would have better success if he hid his true identity so he used the name of a character by the writer Ramón Gómez de la Serna, but aside from all that the only thing he really knew about Peru was they made pretty good Pisco Sours there, but not as good as in Chile. They both respected the lyrical beauty of Emilio Ballagas. They talked intense trash about all sorts of sycophants and university snobs, the vultures waiting in the wings. 'Our opinions contained a great deal of adolescent posturing even though we were both in our twenties,' Zabala later wrote, 'but we had one hell of a time getting drunk.'

By 1976 Bolaño was fully immersed in the world of his infrarealist poetry movement. Zabala was not interested in becoming an infrarealist. He later confessed to his daughter that he thought the whole idea was just a thin disguise for surrealism, which had been around since the twenties. He didn't understand how you could create a movement that already existed. Eventually, the two men parted company. Bolaño published his first book of poetry, *Reinventar el amor*, and after that he fled to France, and then Africa, before settling in Spain. Zabala and Blanca left for Cuba. Bolaño was twenty-three. Zabala was twenty-six. They communicated sporadically with each other over the next thirteen years, always by letter, never by telephone. They did not see each other again until 1989.

Roberto Bolaño, Javier Zabala, and Bruno Montané, Mexico City, 1975.

To say Javier Pedro Zabala was a Cuban writer is to raise a series of questions about who he truly was and how he came to be that way. Zabala was unknown as a writer during his lifetime. He did not seek out other writers, although he did endeavor to maintain his strange, intermittent, secretive, somewhat conspiratorial relationship with Bolaño; but he did not cultivate a writer's persona; he did not live what we normally conceive as a writer's life, except for the fact that he was constantly writing. In truth, he was a private, as opposed to public, writer. He abandoned all of the pretensions that usually accompany literary pursuits. And though he stopped writing for a time when his wife disappeared in 1996, by 1998 he was back at his typewriter. He died at the age of fifty-two, two months after he had completed his novel, without fanfare, unnoticed by anyone save his daughter, in a tiny cinder block house with a tin roof and a view of the Caribbean Sea in La Boca, Cuba, a small seaside village in Sancti Spíritus province. Zabala lived in La Boca for the last twenty-six years of his life. His daughter was born there. But he himself had not been born in Cuba, nor were his parents Cuban. Thus, we are left with a series of questions regarding his personal identity, which is a by-product of his personal choices as much as his ethnic origins, but we are also forced to grapple with some more problematic questions, at least from a purely academic perspective, about his cultural and spiritual identity as well.

Zabala was in fact a product of the multicultural forces that have been shaping the Americas for over five-hundred years. His father, Miguel Octavio Cercas, was born in 1923 in Matamoros, a border town in northeastern Mexico. His mother, Anabelle Elizabeth Zabala (whose surname he ultimately kept) was from Miami, Florida. She herself was half-Spanish (Basque) and half-German, 'an enigmatic mixture of cold fire and sizzling ice,' according to Zabala. Anabelle Zabala's father, Alberto Diaz Zabala, had emigrated from San Sebastián, Spain in 1922. Her mother, Lucy Elizabeth Wilshusen, had emigrated from Bremervörde, Germany in 1926. They met in New York City in 1927, married, and moved to Florida. So what, then, is Zabala? What is his heritage? Is he Spanish? German? Mexican? American? And what is the relationship between his heritage and his writing? Given the complexities of his family tree, it is tempting to suggest that writing *The Mad Patagonian* was for Zabala a lifelong endeavor to weave a single tapestry from these many disparate threads, a tapestry that would express with unequivocal clarity who he was. But is this a fair assessment? What I think we can say is that the tension between competing cultures was a constant reminder for Zabala that he was always on the outside looking in. He was an exile not just in Miami; he was an exile wherever he went. Even as a small child he found himself wondering if he would ever find a home, a place to rest, to call his own. In a diary entry dated June 6, 1988 he writes:

> *I was a misfit from day one, an outcast, a fallen angel, neither Mexican nor American, neither Spanish nor German. I was the small, starving refugee kid, an exile, always hungry, at least in my imagination, standing outside a gleaming golden bakery or a deli or a diner, staring blankly at the bubble of happy, blank faces on the other side of the plate glass window, the people laughing with joyful, unconcerned, uncomprehending laughter, at least this is how I heard it in my mind, and as this laughter was swirling through my consciousness, a tiny part of me like a wandering hermit crab, a most insignificant part, was wondering when it would be my turn. But I was oblivious to the commotion my lingering presence outside these bakeries or delis or diners might cause until a waiter or a cashier or some other working class stiff would rush out the door to shoo me away. In those moments I had no home, no refuge. Where could I go? It seemed to me I could go nowhere. Every place would be the same. Every person I met would view me with either suspicion or pity. I don't know which I hated more. I guess it was pity because by the time I turned fourteen, I actively cultivated suspicion.*

One could argue that Zabala's flights of extreme childhood despair were in all likelihood a creation of an older Zabala looking back. This is not to say that he did not feel like an outcast or an exile while growing up. It is only to suggest that a thoughtful understanding of what it meant to be an exile came later. Moreover, Zabala's somewhat malleable sense of his own identity, at least in terms of how his adult self remembered his youthful self, was probably shaped more by growing up in a working-class household than it was by his parents' ethnic origins. From the little biographical information available on

Zabala, it would seem that his family life was fairly typical of immigrant working class families living in southern Florida in the fifties. Zabala's parents met in April 1949 in Galveston, Texas, where they were married on May 27, 1949 by a Justice of the Peace. Miguel wanted to move to Mexico, perhaps even Mexico City. Anabelle wanted to go back to Miami. After a four-day honeymoon on Padre Island, she convinced him that moving to Mexico would be a mistake. There was more opportunity living in the United States, she told him. Miguel reluctantly agreed, so they headed east. Zabala was born nine months later on February 6, 1950. His sister, Julia, was born in 1951, and his brother, Emidio, was born in 1953. From 1950 to 1964 the family lived in a modest five-room bungalow with a front porch and a cedar porch swing in Allapattah, a small neighborhood northwest of downtown Miami. They rarely strayed outside the social and economic boundaries of their tiny world. Once a year they made the three-week journey to Matamoros to visit relatives, but that was it for traveling. Zabala's father worked as an auto mechanic and his mother worked in a bakery. Neither were big readers. In fact there wasn't a single book in the house, a material absence which Zabala later recalled with some measure of pride. What they gave him instead of books was the gift of an unrestrained passion for living that did not need the inducements of material comfort. This is what shaped his attitude not only towards his life, but invariably towards his inexorable need to write. In a diary entry dated June 14, 1992 he wrote:

Javier Zabala and his father in Allapattah, Florida in 1957.

> *What others might see as disadvantages have always been my advantages. We grew up without money, without any apparent opportunity. We lived as all the working poor have always lived. There wasn't a single book anywhere in our house. My mother occasionally bought a copy of the magazine Vanidades. My*

father read the newspaper, but only the Sunday edition. We listened to the radio, but we owned no television. And our car was an old 1932 Studebaker, a Commander 8 that my father was always repairing. But none of this mattered. My parents always said life was short so I should find my happiness wherever I could, whenever I happened to stumble upon it, because it would most certainly vanish before the sun rose the next morning. Life was a gift that should not be taken for granted, they said. It was the experience that counted. So they encouraged me to do whatever I wanted, regardless of books or opportunities or any of the bourgeois accoutrements that most Americans take for granted. That is how I was able to proclaim myself a writer before I had written even a single word.

In 1964, the year Zabala turned fourteen, he experienced for himself the ephemeral nature of happiness. His father, who had become increasingly homesick for Mexico, decided in March to return to Matamoros. His mother did not try to dissuade him. Zabala was devastated by having to choose which parent to live with, and though he ultimately decided to go with his father ('my mother had Julia and Emidio for comfort, but who did my father have?' he wrote), the decision seemed to confirm what would become a central theme of his book, namely: how do we gain some measure of peace when nothing is permanent, not even love. In an entry dated October 11, 1995 he writes:

At the time I was struck by the impermanence of life, of all experience, even with something so elemental as human emotion. If love did not exist beyond this tiny existential dot we call a moment, then what was the point in cultivating the emotion? What was the point in cultivating any emotion? Of course I was not so philosophical in my musings at the tender age of fourteen. And I failed to consider that if love did not truly exist, then neither did hatred. If joy did not exist, then neither, ultimately, did frustration, and so on and so forth. All of humanity's dualities could be disposed of with a single stroke of an imaginary pen. I did not begin to think so deeply about such matters until much, much later. But the seed was sown the day my father and I left for Mexico.

During the journey from Miami to Matamoros, Zabala and his father stopped for a single night on Padre Island. For Zabala's father it was perhaps a fitting place to say goodbye to the memory of his wife. But for Zabala it marks the first time he began to think about writing as a way of exploring his own identity. They arrived early in the afternoon on Saturday, March 14. Zabala's father was finding temporary solace in a bottle of tequila, so Zabala went for a walk along the beach. He came to the beachfront of a very fancy hotel with a few guests hiding from the sun beneath heavy canvas umbrellas. It was only March, so the temperature was still comfortable, but the sun was very bright off the water. Zabala writes about that day in an entry dated November 14, 1995:

> *I was staring at a long line of blue umbrellas like so many teardrops glistening in the sun. It was so bright I almost couldn't see a thing. Then I was distracted by the sounds of a young woman screaming. She was forty yards or so offshore and she was thrashing about and her voice was vibrating at a very high pitch. She seemed to be tangled up in the sea, maybe a patch of seaweed or some abandoned fishing line, but I could not tell. She was clearly in a panic, and then suddenly it was much more than a panic. The sound of her voice became hundreds of tiny daggers of sound clawing at the air, thousands of daggers. Then a young man rushed into the waves and swam out a little ways towards her, but before he got very far she had stopped screaming. The next thing I remember was a white wooden boat pushing across the waves with four lifeguards with red flotation buoys, and then the boat finally reached the woman and the lifeguards dragged her into the boat and brought her back. They laid her out in the sand and the young man collapsed on top of her, and from what he was saying it was crystal clear that they had just been married, that this was their honeymoon, but nobody moved to comfort him. Nobody said a word. But what would they have said? There was nothing to say. So the lifeguards watched over the young man for a while, and then a small brown jeep came and two of the lifeguards loaded up the woman's lifeless body and helped the young man into the back seat and then they drove up towards the Red Cross station. I didn't ask anyone what had happened to the young woman, but somebody else went over to the*

other two lifeguards who had stayed behind. They were pulling the long wooden boat up away from the tide, which was rolling in. They said the woman had got tangled up in a patch of Portuguese Man-O-War. They had stung her pretty badly. It was rare to die from the venom, but it did happen. Besides, she must have been stung fifty times. Then the lifeguards went away, and so did everyone else, and I was staring at the spot in the sand where they had laid the woman's body. I could still see the indentation like a passing thought. I was affected by the woman's death in ways that I could not then describe, but strangely I was not sad. I remember staring at the soft mark where she had been, a blank stare, and then I was staring out at the sea. I could see tiny blue umbrellas floating in the water, like the umbrellas on the beach only much smaller, a tiny flotilla of teardrops, and then I realized they were not teardrops or tiny umbrellas, they were dozens and dozens of Portuguese Man-O-War. The tide was bringing them in. In fact the beach was already littered with their flimsy, insubstantial, but obviously deadly bodies. It was a surreal moment, but it was also very beautiful, and I remember wondering how was it that I could see this beauty in the face of the tragic death of this young woman on her honeymoon. I wondered what was wrong with me. But there was no denying how powerfully beautiful the whole moment was. Yes, it was a beauty shaped by the suddenness of the woman's death, but it was also shaped by love and the blue umbrellas and the blue umbrella-like Portuguese Man-O-War, and yes, there was a great sadness there that would linger until the end of time, but it was a surface sadness, an echo of the happiness the young woman had possessed during her lifetime, like the echo of a church bell. I had somehow gone beneath the waves of this sadness to the beauty that existed at a greater depth, a beauty that existed outside of time, outside of this imperfect realm we call the world, so it would always exist. How was this possible? I wondered.

That was the moment when I first knew I would be a writer. That I was already a writer. I also knew that I would spend the rest of my life exploring that strange aberration in my consciousness, my way of seeing the world, that allowed me to glimpse such beauty even in death.

Zabala lived in Mexico from 1964 thru the end of 1976. He lived for a time with his father in a small house in Matamoros, working alongside him in a small auto body shop on Galeana Street. He became interested in American movies, particularly hard-boiled detective movies. Anything film noir. His favorite actor was Humphrey Bogart. But he also admired Peter Lorre. But Zabala would not stay in Matamoros long. Though he had dropped out of high school, he suddenly became an avid reader of borrowed books. He does not share with us why he began to read, only that from that point forward he was consumed with reading. And because of the books he read, he began to look at the world through newborn eyes. He began to believe he had some control over the direction his life would take, that he had some say in what he might do, that he could in fact shape his own future. He also became politically aware, even angry, though it should be added that his anger at this point was probably modulated as much by a youthful desire to rebel against authority as by an awareness of the very real injustices committed by those in power against those without power in Mexico and elsewhere.

Javier Zabala in Matamoros, Mexico, 1965.

In October 1968, however, Zabala found for the first time a very real cause to anchor his anger. On the 2nd of October, the Mexican army, armed to the hilt with machine guns and tanks and orders to do whatever was necessary to keep the peace, fired randomly into a crowd of twenty-thousand students and other civilians, men, women, and even small children, who had gathered peacefully in the Plaza de las Tres Culturas in Mexico City to protest against the Gustavo Díaz Ordaz government, a protest defined in part by a call for democracy with the goal of forcing the government to honor the constitutional guarantees that already existed in the Mexican constitution. By some estimates as many as nine-hundred protestors were killed. Maybe more. No one knows the exact number. It was a tragedy. It became known as the Tlatelolco massacre, a sad, bloody monument in the history of Mexico to rival the Aztec massacre of the Spanish conquistadors and their Indian collaborators at Zultapec in 1520. Two weeks after Tlatelolco, this crime of the century, Zabala decided to move to the capital. He talks about why in his diary:

> *I couldn't explain to my father why I wanted to move to Mexico City in '68. But I was really troubled by the Tlatelolco massacre. I was overwhelmed by the sadness of La Noche Triste (the sad night), which hung over the entire country like a lingering cloud. There was no escaping it. But I felt I had to do something, so that's what I did. I guess I just had to be there. It was not a political statement at all. It was like an act of faith. Like leaping from a burning building. It was something a writer would do, and I knew at that point that everything I would ever do would be something a writer would do. The only thing I didn't know was what kind of a writer I was going to be. I knew that some writers wrote about politics, but I didn't want to be labeled a political writer. As I said, I wasn't making a political statement by moving to Mexico City. I didn't know a thing about politics. It was only years later that I realized that writing is by its very nature a political act.*

Upon arriving in Mexico City, Zabala had to struggle just to survive. He moved in with an uncle, Humberto Pedro Melina y Cercas. Pedro for short. Pedro worked for a Pontiac car dealership downtown. He had worked there for twenty years so he was able to get Zabala a job in the dealership's garage working on smaller cars, mostly Volkswagen Beetles. Only the more experienced mechanics were allowed to work on Pontiacs. But Zabala didn't mind. He had steady work. He had time to himself to think. And he began to understand the kind of writer he wanted to be. In an entry dated February 22, 1999 Zabala writes:

> *I spent my first three months in Mexico City just getting acclimated to the routine of working in the garage during the day and drinking with my friends during the evenings. Sure, we talked politics over a few beers, but so did everybody else. It's funny looking back on it now. I started telling people I was a writer, but I couldn't even*

tell a story. Thank God for my uncle. My uncle didn't teach me a thing about working on cars when I worked at the Pontiac dealership. I learned about cars from my father, not my uncle. But my uncle taught me the principle rules of storytelling, even though he probably didn't realize he was teaching me a thing. Every day during the lunch break the men would gather around a small picnic table next to an old electric fan in the back of the garage and tell stories. My uncle was the best of the lot. He was a great storyteller. Even though he told the same story over and over again, you could not help but listen. He liked to talk about driving in La Carrera Panamericana, the mythic two-thousand-mile road rally from Ciudad Juárez in the north to Ciudad Cuauhtémoc on the border with Guatemala. My uncle said he drove in the very first race in 1950. He said at that time the owner of the Pontiac dealership, Antonio Cornejo, was also the man in charge of the race. Cornejo put up a car for my uncle to drive. My uncle said over a thousand cars started the race, but only a handful finished. He said the road went through some of the most treacherous mountain terrain in Mexico. Hundreds of people died because they were terrible drivers or their cars were no good to begin with, so the slightest difficulty or chance encounter sent them spinning over the edge of a cliff in a freefall that ended in a fireball. He also said it was a race without any rules. Except there was one rule. If you stopped your car for any reason you were disqualified. I don't know if I believed him or not. Every time he told the story the details would change. Sometimes he was describing a moment when he was in a duel with another car for space on a narrow winding portion of the road, and the other car shoved him and he almost went over the edge, which was a five-hundred-foot drop and certain death, but then he regained control and shoved the other car the other way and it went careening into the mountain side and burst into flames, an incredible explosion, and my uncle said there was no hope for that driver, but he didn't know for sure because he lost sight of him going around a curve. At other times he recounted how he stopped to help a young woman who had been driving with her husband as if they were heading to a Sunday picnic in the country, but they had gone into a ditch because the husband had been eating an egg sandwich that his wife had prepared for him with great joy that morning and so he had lost sight of the road, this is how my uncle would tell the story, and so this husband was now bleeding, an artery in his leg had been severed, and the moment my uncle stopped his car and stepped out onto the pavement to help, he was disqualified by two race officials who materialized quite suddenly out of thin air, as if they had been suddenly beamed to earth from a distant star or an alien spaceship, waving their flags and shouting with energetic, rapid-fire mania about the one rule, or perhaps they had been driving a small white Fiat and had just happened by at precisely that moment, who could truly say, but if my uncle hadn't stopped when he did, the woman's husband would have surely died. My uncle never said if he finished the race. Not in any of the versions he told. But always he was caught up in the midst of a life or death struggle, which is why you could not pull yourself away from his tall tale. You were always on the edge of your seat. The lives of the people he encountered on that treacherous road in that terrifying race mattered more in those moments listening to his deep soothing voice than

Humberto Pedro Melina y Cercas and a friend standing in front of car #113, which 'Pedro' drove in La Carrera Panamericana in 1950. (Photograph taken in Ciudad Juárez the day before the race.)

anyone you actually knew. No matter how far-fetched the narrative, no matter how far removed from verifiable fact, the stories my uncle told rang out with the truth, in so far as any human experience can be called true. I learned the art of storytelling from my uncle.

In the spring of 1970, Zabala was supposedly recruited by members of the Liga Obrero Estudiantil, a radicalized student group that had appeared among a sea of political student groups at UNAM in the mid-sixties. This was a turbulent period for Zabala, as it was for everyone living in Mexico at the time. On the one hand, there was a sense of growing social unrest spurred by rumors of secret goon squad violence. On the other hand, there was the ever-present problem of the Mexican government capitulating without a second thought to the economic interests of the United States at the expense of Mexico's poor and working classes. The impoverished outnumbered the privileged fifty to one, a ratio that had not changed in any substantive way since the Mexican Revolution, and was not likely to change in the foreseeable future. In the face of such overwhelming disparity, Zabala saw no ethical alternative but to stand shoulder to shoulder with the powerless against those pulling the strings. He believed that change was possible, if only everyone worked together. So he joined the Liga Obrero Estudiantil, and then later he joined the Mexican Communist Party (PCM).

In an entry dated September 17, 1992 he writes about his optimistic state of mind:

We were hippies, of course. We had long hair. Many of us wore beards. We rarely bathed. We were almost always broke. And we were no different than anyone else. We were no different than the thousands of Mexican students who had been savagely eliminated by the army back in '68. We were no different than the Mexican police who had been trained to steal children and old women out of their beds in the middle of the night and murder them in secret. We were no different than the farmers and the factory workers and the bus drivers and the nurses and the auto mechanics and the grocers who bled away their lives for a few pesos. We were no different than the lawyers and the businessmen and the teachers and the doctors and the priests and the musicians and the television personalities and the writers and the ambassadors who turned a blind eye to whatever the government was doing or wanted to do. We were no better or worse than anyone else, anywhere in Mexico. We were all of us shadowy, imperfect reflections of each other. And all we wanted was a fair shake. We didn't even want a better life. We just wanted what was fair. That's why we stood up to the government. What other choice did we truly have? If we wanted to change things we had no other choice. We did what we had to do. We wanted these old politicians who had grown fat on the misery of an entire country to remember the ideals of their own youth. We wanted them to look into the fragile mirror of our young lives and see their own misplaced aspirations. This is what we hoped.

Zabala writes with great passion, great conviction, and in reading his diary, one wonders why he did not make a name for himself as a leader within the student community at UNAM, and then later within the crumbling mosaic of Mexican politics. He certainly had an intuitive grasp of the competing tensions that were pulling Mexican society apart. And he was more than able to capture this tension in eloquent, even poetic, yet absolutely precise language. So why is he unknown in Mexican intellectual circles?

Perhaps the answer lies in the simple fact that he was too good of a thinker and a writer to have gone unnoticed. Thus, one must conclude that either he did not share his thoughts with those around him, which given the collaborative nature of political activism in those days seems unlikely; or we must conclude that he did not actually participate in the protests and the demonstrations that he details with great compassion and ideological insight. In other words, Zabala filled his diary with compelling fictions about his life, fictions that expressed, perhaps, what he wished he had done or was capable of doing. When it comes right down to it, he had already begun to work on his craft.

Zabala claims in his diary that in July of 1970 he participated in a student march expressing solidarity with the workers of a local textile company. He claims that in August of 1970 he began accompanying PCM organizers in secret to various rural communities all over Mexico in support of thousands of unarmed peasants in their struggle to acquire land. He claims that in April of 1971 he drafted a UNAM petition for the amnesty of University professors who had been imprisoned for their political views by the government in '68. And he claims that he helped organize a mass demonstration in Mexico City of nearly ten thousand students who gathered near Santo Tomás, mainly on the Ribera de San Cosme, on June 10, 1971, to express their solidarity with the students of the Autonomous University of Nuevo León in Monterrey. At that time the students in Monterrey were engaged in a battle of wills with the Governor of Nuevo León, Eduardo Elizondo. Zabala also claims that he narrowly avoided becoming a casualty the afternoon of the demonstration as hundreds of men armed with cudgels and clubs and dressed in unassuming plain clothes descended upon the students, attacking them with ferocious, unrestrained zeal in what later became known as the Corpus Christi Massacre. What is more, Zabala claims all of this without batting an equivocal eye, in spite of the fact that he was never a student at UNAM, or at any university for that matter. In fact there is some evidence to suggest that Zabala did not even move to Mexico City until 1974, the year he met Blanca.

Is it possible that Zabala was involved in various student protests? Certainly. But whether he was or wasn't is irrelevant as far as his growth as a writer is concerned. What is clear from his diary, whether or not the details he records are accurate, is that Zabala's writing is infused with an indomitable revolutionary spirit. Zabala uses words to change reality. He even composed a variation of a popular but rather abusive anthem the students sang at every political rally during the summer of 1968:

Death to the monkey, Díaz Ordaz!
Come out on the balcony, with your big ass snout!
Come out on the balcony, monkey with a big ass snout!
Black monkey, to the fucking wall!
Black monkey, come out on the balcony!
Díaz Ordaz, motherfucker! motherfucker! motherfucker!

Contrary to his claim that he 'did not want a better life' quoted earlier, Zabala did want a better life, but not just for himself and those around him. He wanted a better life for everyone. Ironically, it was this desire, which possessed for Zabala the quality of an unspoken faith, which allowed him to live in a world torn apart by violence. In his diary he writes:

The world is constantly being destroyed by angry, purpose-driven men with guns. But that is only half of the picture, for with each act of unmitigated violence there is an equally powerful counter-insurgency of renewal and rebirth. It is part of the unseen machinery behind creation. It has been this way since the beginning of time.

One might be tempted to label Zabala an idealist, or perhaps a religious anti-intellectual, and certainly his position is a bit of an anachronism by postmodern standards, but these labels would be unfair as well as inaccurate. Zabala's brand of idealism was born of practical interactions with the oppressive tyrannies of modern life and so mirrors the pragmatic idealism of earlier political revolutionaries like Trotsky, whose books Zabala knew intimately, and Julio Antonio Mella, a journalist and the founder of the Communist Party of Cuba in the 1920s, who, according to Cecilia, was one of Zabala's ideological heroes. (Julio Mella had written numerous articles for such leftist publications as *El Libertador* and *Tren Blindado* when he lived in Mexico City, articles espousing equality for all men.) For Zabala, both Trotsky and Mella were symbols of the need to keep the struggle for absolute equality alive no matter the personal cost. Both Trotsky and Mella believed that when the world finally achieved equality for everyone, then everything else would be possible. The world would become a paradise. Zabala took their belief and transformed it into a personal quest to discover if happiness was even possible in a world in which the notion of absolute equality for everyone had been replaced by the notion of absolute liberty for some, which meant that everyone on the planet was unintentionally driving with ruthless efficiency towards unhappiness. This is the terrain Zabala is exploring in his book, *The Mad Patagonian*.

In 1974, Zabala met Blanca Barutti, and his charismatic revolutionary idealism and his evolving identity as a writer were reshaped by Blanca's intense sense of purpose. Blanca was a few years older than Zabala and her heritage was as varied as his. She was of Spanish, Italian, and German descent. Her father, Bruno Barutti, was born in 1920 in Villafranca Piemonte, a small Italian town in the province of Turin, but the family left Italy for Cuba in November 1922 one month after the Fascist blackshirts under Mussolini's direction stormed into the city of Rome. So Bruno Barutti grew up in Santiago, Cuba and then became a civil engineer, working on various municipal construction projects within a ten-block radius of Parque Céspedes, including the City Hall project on Francisco Vicente Aguilera from 1948 until the building was completed in 1950. Blanca's mother, Emily Duarte de Hernani y Arredondo, came from a well-to-do family that had emigrated from Barcelona in the latter half of the 19th century.

One year after Castro came to power, the Barutti family again took the path of exile and moved to Mexico City. They moved into an Art Nouveau style house in Colonia Condesa on a shady, tree-lined street a few blocks from Parque España. Bruno Barutti was seemingly unemployed for several years after moving to Mexico City, but in 1967 he took a position with a civil engineering firm named Ingenieros Civiles y Asociados, which was the lead engineering firm in the construction of the Mexico City Metro. He worked at Ingenieros Civiles y Asociados until he retired for health reasons in 1983.

From the day Blanca was born (July 5, 1947), her parents began grooming her for medical school, so it was no shock when she entered the Facultad de Medicina UNAM in 1970. She was an exemplary student, graduating with distinction in 1973. She met Zabala during her internship (1974) at the Hospital General de México. Supposedly he came into the emergency room with a variety of lacerations and bruises and a broken nose. Blanca was working with the attending physician.

Zabala never fully explained to her how he had acquired his injuries. But according to Cecilia in an interview in April 2015, her mother knew instantly that he had received them fighting for the cause of equality:

> *My mother said she first saw Papi at 11 o'clock on September 2, 1974. He was covered in dried blood and possessed a ruthlessly happy smile. Mother said he was also carrying a copy of Madera, one of the dozens of leftist, revolutionary publications circulating around Mexico City at that time. She took him for a passionate but inexperienced revolutionary, partly because of his bearded demeanor, but also because the attending physician, who openly expressed his sympathies for every student cause that made it into the papers and was himself a member of the PCM, seemed to know my father. The next day the*

attending physician approached my mother with a wink and a smile. He told her there had been a protest or a riot by some student groups during Echeverría's State of the Nation address. The protesters had been clubbed into silence. Some of them had sustained severe injuries, but thankfully, no one had been killed. From that point on, my mother was convinced that my father belonged to one of the groups that had been protesting. My father came back to the hospital one week later and asked my mother to dinner. She said she could not help herself. She had fallen madly in love with him that very first night because of the revolutionary ardor you could see burning in his eyes, and his unrestrained, revolutionary laughter that shook free the very dust from the ceiling. That was how my mother described it. They went to dinner the next evening.

So is Cecilia's somewhat romanticized story accurate? There is no record of the student protest she describes, but that in itself is not unusual, particularly since there were no deaths. The magazine Zabala carried into the emergency room, *Madera,* was in fact a leftist publication printed by Liga Comunista 23 de Septiembre (LC23S), a Marxist-Leninist group quite active in Mexico City during the seventies and eighties. It is certainly conceivable that Zabala provided articles and commentary for the magazine, perhaps under an assumed name. It is also worth noting that the LC23S had ties with the Liga Obrero Estudiantil, which Zabala had supposedly joined in 1970. But whether or not Zabala was affiliated with the LC23S is unimportant. What is important is the story establishes the degree to which Zabala's revolutionary idealism was visible to others, in this case Blanca. It also provides a subtext for understanding the relationship between Zabala and Blanca, why they fell in love with such apparent intensity, why they moved to Cuba, and why Zabala remained in Cuba after Blanca's disappearance. Cecilia comments on their love story:

My father had great passion, but he was undisciplined. He needed my mother's sense of direction, her firm belief in working to fulfill some unwritten destiny, and her unwavering, even ruthless commitment to achieving her goal. She always kept her eyes on her goal. But my mother would never have understood her destiny without my father. His passion helped her see precisely where she needed to go and what she needed to do. They were married almost one year after they first met on the 23rd of August, 1975, in a quiet civil ceremony. My mother made my father shave his beard and get a haircut for the occasion. She said her parents didn't trust him, but they trusted her. After a short honeymoon in the sleepy seaside village of Puerto Morelos, which looked out on the Caribbean Sea, they moved into a little apartment on Calle Soledad in the center of historic Mexico City. Their street was a street filled with vendors. They lived directly above a grocer who opened his stall at seven every morning except Sundays. It was my father's idea, of course. They were one block from the crumbling, antiquated glory (my father's words) of the Church of Santa Cruz y La Soledad. They were a short ten-minute walk from the Candelaria metro station. My mother said that every moment of every day you could feel the surging, seething, irrepressible lifeblood of Mexico City like an ocean swirling around you, carrying you forward with its unrepentant kinetic energy, there was no escaping it, she said, and no use trying, and then one day she realized she did not wish to escape 'this bubbling ocean of humanity,' as she put it. She realized that her value as a doctor would rise or fall in direct proportion to her commitment to easing the suffering of everyday people like the people that moved through the streets of Mexico City. I think my father knew my mother would come to this conclusion. I think he was teaching her, guiding her along the path to herself. My parents lived in their apartment on Soledad for one year so that my mother could finish her post-graduate internship at the General Hospital of Mexico. Then on the 22nd of October 1976, they left for Cuba. My mother decided that the people she felt the greatest connection to lived in Cuba. They were everyday people like the people swirling up and down Calle Soledad, but they were her people. The Cuban people were her first vocation. That is why my parents left for Cuba. But my mother would never have even thought of going to Cuba if my father had not first opened her eyes to the misery and despair of the disenfranchised in Mexico. My father had no choice but to go with her. He would have been lost without her, and he knew this. But then he did not care where he was so long as he was with her. He would have followed her to the moon and back.

Blanca Barutti and Javier Pedro Zabala in front of Blanca's car on their honeymoon in Puerto Morelos, Mexico in August 1975.

In November of 1976, Javier Pedro Zabala and Blanca Barutti moved into a tiny house in the small seaside community of La Boca, Cuba in Sancti Spíritus province. Blanca began working at the medical clinic in Trinidad, seven kilometers to the east. Zabala worked in the sugar cane fields as a cutter during *La Gran Zafra* (the Great Sugar Cane Harvest) that first year and every year after that until 1994. At first he worked in the fields because that is what he thought any good revolutionary and leftist writer would do, and indeed, many leftist writers and thinkers from other countries came to Cuba each year during the *zafra* to help the Cubans bring in Castro's symbolic if not altogether impossible ten million tons of sugar cane. But even as he grew older and became disillusioned with Castro's failed economic policies and the growing poverty of the country, Zabala continued to work in the fields because he 'enjoyed the pure simple escapism of physical exertion. It is not clear from Zabala's diary what he did when he was not working in the cane fields. But his daughter said that sometimes her father worked as a fisherman, sometimes he drove a truck, sometimes he drove one of those bright red tractors from Belarus, and on those days he was smiling from ear to ear, sometimes he did various odd jobs in the medical clinic in Trinidad, and during the last six years of his life he became a farmer and joined a small agricultural cooperative that grew vegetables, mainly beans and cassava, on a nine-acre plot in the Viñales Valley, a fertile but infamous valley that had once been home to over seventy cane sugar mills and fifty-thousand slaves.

It is perhaps one of the peculiarities of living in Cuba under Castro that Zabala could commit to living a full, robust life, even as he was aware of the irony of that life. He realized that Cuba's socialist experiment was a severe caricature of Trotsky's vision of Communism, even during his early years in La Boca, when the euphoria of a young newlywed couple moving to Cuba to make a difference was still palpable. And yet as late as 1994, he was also, somehow, still committed to the idealistic vision of absolute equality for everyone that lay at the foundation of the political thinking of both Trotsky and Mella. In an entry dated March 11, 1994, he saw better days ahead.

> *Our diseased, corrupt, parody of a state is a natural outgrowth of our dependence, both political and economic, upon the Soviet Union, which was itself an absurdist parody of Communism even as early as 1926, as Trotsky points out in The Revolution Betrayed. The death of the Soviet Union was inevitable. Why did we not see this? And what of Cuba? What did we really expect from Castro? But all that is past us. Now that the Soviets are no longer pulling the strings, I see a day when the people will once again reassert their right to govern their own lives. Castro will have no choice but to let them.*

That Zabala could maintain the integrity of his convictions living in a country whose leadership was constantly caught unprepared for the consequences of its own policy choices, to steal a line from Trotsky, is a testament to his creative, intellectual, and artistic temperament. But it is also worth remembering that Zabala had made a conscious choice to reject the materialism of the world at large. He lived the life of a modern ascetic. And he would have lived this life if he had lived in Cuba or New York City or Rome. Geography would have made no difference. His philosophy was an integral part of his make-up. As his daughter, Cecilia, said: "My father lived his life with one foot planted in the physical realities of this world, though barely, and the other foot firmly planted in the spiritual idealism of the next."

It was Zabala's ability to inhabit these two worlds simultaneously that allowed him to live in a state of balance in Castro's Cuba. It was this same ability, I might add, that allowed him to write his magnum opus.

***The Mad Patagonian* was the only book Zabala finished writing.** He spent his entire adult life working on the manuscript, drafting lengthy sections in longhand before transferring them to a more permanent state using an old 1940s Corona typewriter. He wrote most of the book in the small cinder block house in La Boca. He sat by a window with a view of the Caribbean Sea and wrote every day from four in the afternoon until one or two in the morning. Some evenings were more productive than others. Zabala writes:

> *Sometimes, not often, and always very late at night, I come to the conclusion that my only friend is the sound of the sea, the waves rolling in, breaking against the rocks, but even this friend exists only in my mind, for it is dark and I cannot see a thing that is out there. It is only in these moments, when I realize there is only an impenetrable darkness beyond my field of vision, a darkness, moreover, which extends to the edges of the universe, that I understand how completely and totally alone I am and must be. It is only in these moments that I can truly write.*

Many writers have had similar epiphanies, but few have embraced the writer's need for absolute isolation the way Zabala did. Even when he was not writing he had cut himself off from the world. As already noted, with the strange exception of Bolaño, Zabala did not know or communicate with any other writer in Cuba or anywhere else. But what is more astonishing is that none of Zabala's friends, neighbors or co-workers knew he was writing. Certainly his wife, Blanca, knew, and also his daughter, but no one else. To one living in the contemporary world where there is no privacy whatsoever, no matter where you live, and especially in a country like Cuba, where everyone is looking over everyone else's conspiratorial shoulder, it seems inconceivable that Zabala could shut himself away so completely. And yet this is what he did. It is a remarkable accomplishment, almost as remarkable as the book he wrote.

According to Cecilia, Zabala began working on his manuscript in the summer of 1983, but even as late as 1987 he himself wasn't sure what he was doing. He had no clear understanding of what he was trying to write. Indeed, in a letter he sent to Bolaño in August 1987 he confessed that he could not very well be a writer since he had not written anything worthy of publication, to which Bolaño replied:

> *Fear not, my friend, you have simply joined the ranks of those sublime writers who exist in every age who write with exemplary clarity without putting pen to paper. Better that than to be a hack who has written too many words without expressing a single intelligible thought.*

By mid-January 1988, however, Zabala had decided he was writing a grand, multi-generational epic with the majestic, historic sweep of Tolstoy. His book would follow the fortunes of Escolástica and Isabel Vda De Miranda, two sisters from Logroño, Spain, and their descendants. The younger sister, Escolástica, would emigrate from Spain to Cuba with her uncle in 1899 in search of the paradise of new beginnings. Her descendants would eventually make their way from Santiago, Cuba to Havana to Miami. The older sister, Isabel, would marry into a family from Vera de Bidasoa, Spain and move to the mountains and later fight against the Fascists. Her grandchildren would immigrate to the United States in 1939 and also eventually settle in Miami. Neither branch would know of the other. But the book soon became much more complex in conception than a realistic family saga. Zabala decided he would explore his own complex psychological and cultural heritage through the lives of this fictional family from Spain. In so doing, he hoped the book would provide an alternative view of reality that would stand against what he saw as the resounding failure of religion and traditional philosophy to provide a useful psychological framework for assigning value and hence meaning to the living of one's own life.

In this narrow sense, Zabala was an existentialist. But he himself would not have claimed this label. Indeed, his views are modulated by a subtle yet persistent faith in the existence of God, a faith which he could never quite shed. He firmly believed that if there were no conscious entities to recognize and validate creation, then creation itself would have no value. Thus, all value emanated from humanity's ability to apprehend the universe. But he also maintained a fundamental belief that God was part of the creation equation. God needed to create mankind to appreciate His handiwork,' he once wrote, 'otherwise there would be no meaning behind creation. But without God, mankind would serve no purpose. God needs mankind as much as mankind needs God. You cannot have one without the other.' Thus, *The Mad Patagonian* is also an implicit criticism of the existentialists for their inability to strike a balance between 'meaningful human activity in the temporal realm' (the world that we see with our eyes) and 'purposeful human activity in the mythic realm' (the world that we see with our hearts). In short, though certainly with a self-deprecating, tongue-in-cheek sense of the absurdity of life in general, Zabala wanted *The Mad Patagonian* to be all things to all readers.

Zabala decided that the book would be divided into nine separate but interconnected novellas of varying lengths. The stories begun in the earlier novellas would not be concluded until the later sections. Zabala described the first novella as a fictional rendering of his adolescent American self. (Its gently ironic tone and youthful idiomatic perspective are perhaps an echo of Salinger, but stylistically it is a curious blend of Hemingway, André Breton, and Enrique Vila-Matas.) The first novella would introduce the leitmotif of the eternal quest for true love, and then open up into the second novella (a literary nod to Henry Miller, Julio Cortázar, Alfonso Reyes, and again, Vila-Matas), which Zabala described as the beginning of his search for his Spanish roots. The second novella would open up into the third, the third into the fourth, and so on. The ninth novella would circle back to the narrative begun in the first novella. Zabala described this last section as an existential, quasi-objective rendering of reality from the perspective of an individual who must eventually, inevitably, choose between the world as it is and the world as it should be.

The guiding principle of the book is the idea that nothing is what it appears to be. Thus, the arc of the story through the nine novellas works its way backwards through time and history from Jacksonville, Florida and Miami and a quasi-familiar American landscape to the historical melting pot of Logroño, Spain in the 1890s and the mythic stories of Escolástica and Isabel Escoraz Vda De Miranda. From Spain we head to

Santiago, Cuba, circa 1900-1907, a tumultuous period in Cuban history when forgotten poets lingered in the shadows before descending into oblivion, the determined followers of José Martí were still seeking liberty and equality for every Cuban citizen, and *brujería* magic was a force to be reckoned with. From Santiago we then travel to a film nourish 1950s Havana, with swanky, exclusive nightclubs overflowing with the sounds of sultry danzón singers; and corrupt government officials and remorseless gangsters who read Pirandello find themselves in a battle to the death with anarchists from Germany, who believe they are working for a sinister, alien (as in outer space) race intent on subjugating the Earth; and then we find ourselves in a contemporary parallel universe America (with one Kafkaesque detour thru parts of France, Germany, and the city of Prague) where an aging Basque immigrant who fought Franco, a World War One tank commander, Latin-American revolutionaries, CIA operatives, FBI agents, ex-poets, ex-priests, atheists, an internationally acclaimed porn star, an expert on Nazi mysticism and the occult, a modern-day saint, a Hollywood movie director who was nominated for an Academy Award, and a hairdresser from Buenos Aires who once cut the hair of Jorge Borges in a hotel room in New York City, all take their turn on center stage, and the hope of finding paradise takes on profoundly spiritual dimensions.

Zabala wanted to blur the lines between history and fiction, and between religion and science, and so create a mythic realm where 'God is granted the power to create, but creation itself is only visible through the prism of the human imagination.' But he soon realized that his epic tale was in fact taking him into the abyss, but he saw the abyss as a temporary construct of delusional thinking that one needed to confront before one could find true happiness. He believed, like Dante, that if you wanted to reach paradise, you first had to go through Hell. But he also felt that Dante's pre-existential view of human freedom, a view that firmly placed on human shoulders the responsibility for one's actions, was limited by Dante's reliance on the framework of Catholic orthodoxy, which Zabala viewed as a form of Fascism. So T*he Mad Patagonian* goes far beyond the scope of a generational epic and becomes in the final analysis a psychological, even surreal exploration of the mythic power of the imagination, of human consciousness itself, to lift us out of the darkness that threatens to swallow the universe at any given moment, and that in fact does so from time to time. In this respect, Zabala's notion of both our relation to the abyss and our responsibility when we recognize the abyss is closer to Camus than to Kafka, and closer still to Michel Foucault, (or at least an interpretation of Foucault by various contemporary philosophers) who suggested that 'an interrogation of the limit (the abyss) and of transgression' (moving beyond this limit in the hope of recovering the 'sacred,' as Bataille defined it, from the grave of Nietzsche's dead god) would result in 'a return of the self' (a self free from the limits superimposed on the self not only by society, but by the self itself, so to transgress these limits would be the ultimate paradise, if you will, though Foucault would not have used the word, except, perhaps, to describe the nostalgic symbolism of an Oriental garden).

Thus, Zabala takes us on a journey into his own troubled psyche, which is also a journey into Hell, or at least a symbolic representation of Hell that our collective unconscious would recognize. But he does not leave us there. (It is this aspect of *The Mad Patagonian* that provides a stark counterpoint to the darker vision of much of Roberto Bolaño's work and is, perhaps, an effort on the part of Zabala to engage Bolaño in a metaliterary conversation about the nature of the world and our role in that world. Moreover, the subtextual interplay between these two competing visions is perhaps crucial to understanding Zabala's novel.) In an entry in his diary dated August 24, 1998, Zabala wrote about the journey through Hell:

> *Hell is that place where consciousness vies with itself for supremacy over creation. It is a place created by the mind to keep us trapped within the spatial and temporal boundaries superimposed on the mind by the mind itself. But it is an illusion. It is a labyrinth with darkly gleaming mirrors at every turn. And once we recognize this truth, we are free to continue our journey towards paradise. In fact we are more than free to continue. We have an ethical responsibility to do so, not just for ourselves, but so others might follow. Hell is but the midpoint of our journey.*

But if Hell for Zabala was a product of our mind, then paradise was a product of what Zabala thought of as the anti-mind, what the Buddhists would call the place of no-mind. Zabala believed that paradise was beyond our comprehension because it existed outside of time and space. He also believed that we could and in fact should claim paradise as our birthright. His beliefs were a reflection of his understanding of the transcendence of the human soul, not as the result of religious conviction, nor as the result of glimpsing the horror of the abyss and retreating to the relative safety and hypocritical respectability of a normative or intellectually pacifying notion of what it means to be human, as Nietzsche seems to have accused most philosophers of doing. For Zabala, a belief in both the transcendence of the human soul and paradise is also a belief in humanity's ability to explore without limits the breadth and depth of human experience and so free us from the 'dark, firm net of custom and habit' (Foucault). Thus, the paradise which the characters in *The Mad Patagonian* hope for, that they are chasing after, the paradise they imagine at the beginning of their separate journeys, is not the paradise they eventually discover because the very act of searching for paradise, however tentatively, changes its composition.

So what then is going on in *The Mad Patagonian*? The journeys that Zabala's characters are taking in search of a real paradise are also for Zabala symbolic representations of the journeys we all are in the process of taking. What his characters must learn, we also must learn. The choices they are faced with mirror our own. Thus, one can read *The Mad Patagonian* as a critique of human evil, but also, more importantly, as a testament to the enduring strength and beauty of the human spirit as humanity itself is consumed by the eternal struggle to reach the shores of paradise. Moreover, Zabala is quite clear in his assertion that not only are we responsible for whether or not we eventually reach these shores (Dante's notion of responsibility), but that ultimately paradise would not exist except that we as creative agents are mysteriously and unconsciously involved in its creation. Unfortunately, Zabala's explanation of how we are mysteriously and unconsciously involved in creating paradise is not so clear. God may be the ultimate source of the creative power of the universe, a belief that Zabala can never quite bring himself to reject, and we may be the unconscious translators of that power into something real, something visible, so we can think of ourselves as co-creators, but Zabala only alludes to the mechanics of this process in cryptic terms. Indeed, one gets the impression from reading both Zabala's diary and his novel that for him God both exists and does not exist, so the question of whether or not paradise actually exists is part of an ongoing debate that can only be determined on a case-by-case basis.

Zabala gets tangled up in the labyrinth of his own metaphysical thinking.

To be fair, we must keep in mind that Zabala is not a philosopher. He is not writing a philosophical treatise. He is not engaged in an intellectual debate, except, perhaps, with himself. *The Mad Patagonian* is, after all, a work of fiction. The philosophical foundation of the novel is not so much a solid foundation as it is a sandy beach in constant flux and serves only as a backdrop (a temporary, ever-changing, shifting-sands backdrop) to illuminate the struggles of his characters. In the end, Zabala provides no definitive answer to the philosophical questions he raises, and so to use his diary as a means for interpreting his novel is to perhaps misjudge his intent. He is a poet more than a philosopher, and uses the language of metaphor to express what cannot be rendered in precise, analytical prose. Yes, there is plenty of room in the novel for broad-stroke philosophical interpretations. One can also zoom in on seemingly trivial details and debate their quasi-philosophical implications. For example, what is one to make of the fact that the word 'time' makes 517 appearances in the first five novellas of *The Mad Patagonian,* which on both a psychological and a symbolic level represent the descent into Hell, but the word disappears completely in the last four novellas, which are focused on the ascent towards paradise? The novel is riddled with such riddles, large and small. Indeed, there are so many veiled ironic references to one philosophical position or another that one begins to suspect that Zabala is simply having some fun. (And who does not like to poke fun at philosophy now and then?) But Zabala's focus is not on critiquing the philosophers of any particular age or expressing some particular philosophical message. As any good novelist would, he focuses squarely on the lives of his characters and on the choices they face as they attempt to discover their truest selves in a world where many lose their way. And because Zabala's characters never quite succumb to the darkness of their world, there is always the possibility that they may indeed find happiness, and if not happiness, at least some measure of contentment. Who could reasonably ask for anything more?

Zabala and Bolaño saw each other for the second and last time in November 1989 in Caracas, Venezuela. Zabala had accompanied Blanca, who had been part of a team of doctors from Cuba sent to help the Venezuelans with an outbreak of Dengue fever. They had arrived in September and took up residence in one of the dormitories on the campus of the University of Caracas. Zabala saw very little of Blanca during the four months they were in Venezuela. He took the time to write and read and explore the city. He was particularly interested in the almost mythic blindness of the politicians to the continual economic hardships of the people of Caracas. As he wrote in his dairy in an entry dated January 6, 1990:

I went up into the barrios, those ramshackle shanty towns encroaching on the city limits, neighborhoods without a proper sewer system or even the possibility of electricity. I spoke with survivors of the Caracazo, men and women who had taken to the streets in late February and early March 1989 to protest the neoliberal economic policies of Pérez. Buses were burned. Traffic ground to a halt. And then the people from the barrios began looting and burning stores. A grocery store with a bright blue exterior went up in flames. So did a pasta factory. Some people were carrying cans of evaporated milk and chocolate bars and packages of spaghetti back to their families. In other areas, the looting became more intense. Radios, color television sets, even refrigerators were carted away. The police went up into the barrios and began firing at shadows. Bodies began tumbling down steps. Then the army came in with tanks and machine guns and canisters of tear gas and the will to attack indiscriminately. More tumbling bodies. As many as three thousand civilians were murdered over the ten days of the massacre and the dead bodies were loaded into trucks by shadowy, faceless men and driven to abandoned construction sites along the edge of this ever-expanding city on the edge of paradise. The faceless men tossed the bodies into great, gaping ditches as if no one had died, as if they were simply tossing stones to the ground, as the poet Neruda once wrote, and then the bodies were covered over quickly with lime and dirt. It was an act of erasure. The government did not want anyone to know how many people had died, so the dead were simply erased. But you could still feel their unmentionable deaths lingering over the city like a hemorrhagic haze. I have not felt so closely connected to such an unspeakable, horrific atrocity since '68. It was just as we felt in Mexico City. The same overwhelming, unending, suffocating sadness. Before the February massacre in Caracas, the poor of the barrios had covered the walls of their shanty towns with graffiti that said 'El pueblo está bravo ('the people are angry') or 'Se han burlado de nosotros' ('an end to deception') or El pueblo tiene hambre' ('the people are hungry'). Afterwards the graffiti simply said: 'We are the children of '89.' They will be calling themselves the children of '89 for the rest of their lives. What was Pérez thinking? So many dead, so many orphaned children, so many Venezuelans struggling to stay afloat in an ocean of poverty superimposed from above, and all so the Americans can buy Venezuelan goods at dirt cheap prices as part of a deal with the World Bank.

At the time, Zabala told his wife that the real plague in Caracas was not Dengue fever. The real plague was the propagation of a privileged class at the expense of everyone else. It didn't matter if you were neoliberal or anti-neoliberal. It didn't matter if you were left or right. As soon as you found yourself in a position of power, you worked as hard as you could to become a class unto yourself. Zabala felt quite strongly about the nature of this evil. 'It is like the Nazis all over again,' he wrote, 'though on a smaller scale. But small scales can quickly become large scales, so there is really no substantive difference.'

But Zabala did not spend all of his time in Caracas contemplating the injustice and violence perpetrated on the Venezuelan people by their government. In his diary he notes that he visited the National Pantheon and knelt before the tomb of Rufino Blanco-Fombona, who was nominated for the Nobel prize in literature but never won. He also visited the tombs of Renato Beluche, a sailor and pirate who was Simón Bolívar's favorite admiral, and Rómulo Gallegos, a better writer perhaps than Blanco-Fombona, and also the first Venezuelan elected president without a controversy, who was also nominated for the Nobel prize in literature, and also never won.

On another day Zabala sat in a pew near the back of the Caracas Cathedral and later wrote that 'the gleaming white and golden brilliance of the interior of this baroque enclave left me dazzled and virtually blind.' He visited the Bellas Artes and split his time between the Latin American collection and the Egyptian collection. Later, by accident, he found himself in Parque Carabobo and stumbled upon a statue of Pedro Camejo, a slave, 'The First Black,' who fought first for the royal army against the rebels but then later switched sides in the Venezuelan War of Independence (1811-1823) and fought at the Battle of Carabobo against Calixto García de Luna e Izquierdo (who, according to Zabala, also switched sides, 'but only after the war had ended, which is why the new government put him in prison, where he languished for almost ten years before he was mysteriously set free, at which point he left his wife and young son and Venezuela altogether and went to Cuba to prove himself against the Spanish').

Zabala also writes that in the first week of October he met a burn victim at the Carabobo metro station, a man who had been a bus driver and had suffered first degree burns on his arms and legs and third degree burns on his neck and face. This chance meeting made quite an impression on Zabala. The man's injuries had happened during the Caracazo. He told Zabala that his bus had been overwhelmed by a maniac crowd and set on fire and he had stupidly (his word) rushed into the flames to do something, put the fire out, save his lunch, he didn't remember, and had caught fire himself. He had lost his job as a bus driver because most people couldn't stomach the reality of a burn victim driving their bus. Zabala noted that the ex-bus driver's skin on the left side of his face all the way down the left side of his neck was leathery and black, almost a charcoal color. It looked like he was suffering from some malignant form of cancer or leprosy. Zabala went back to the Carabobo station several times to talk with the man, but never saw him again. Zabala also notes in his diary that he spent many lonely hours wandering along Avenida Lincoln during the afternoon in search of tiny cafes where he could smoke and drink coffee and watch the people flow back and forth. On a bright sunny day sitting outside a small café near the Sabana Grande metro station he wrote:

> *Caracas is a violent, dangerous, bustling modern city; it is a city of swirling ghosts and lost bullets; it is a city of enormous privilege standing on the shoulders of an incomprehensible poverty; it is a city of Americanized bureaucrats and drug addicts and leftist insurgents; it is a city suffocating beneath the ever-expanding black cloud of big oil; it is a city of operettas on every street corner and prostitutes lurking in the shadows of every hotel; it is*

an eternal city of vagabond poets and unrepentant, self-absorbed dictators who arrive with scorn, proclaiming the void and annihilating the competition; it is a city of pirates and writers and visiting bullfighters and international race car drivers who are kidnapped and held for a king's ransom and ambassadors who have outlived their usefulness, all of them now dancing the Joropo by candlelight; it is a city where the flames of the revolution burn brightly each and every night, only to be snuffed out at dawn; it is a city that wakes every morning to the pestilent stench of diesel fumes and ancient church bells tolling for the newly dead; it is a city of fornicating and thievery and angry laughter and Indian families living in makeshift homes made from cardboard boxes and plywood crates and children carrying guns and swift farewells; it is a smoldering powder keg ready to combust; it is an urban jungle where the scent of wild violets and orange blossoms from centuries ago has been replaced by the smells of rotting corpses drifting up through the Metro vents; and the smell of almond trees and the murmur of the ocean's millenary waves have been replaced by the Parisian perfumes of high-priced models and the tinkling of their laughter as they run in and out of shops along Avenida Lincoln looking to buy handbags and shoes; a city where everything is ultimately fatal and vultures pick at the skeletal remains of revolutionaries from a century ago; but all this makes it a writer's paradise.

Zabala was quite taken with Caracas, so it is no wonder that he also wrote Bolaño, the only other writer he knew, and invited him to come to Caracas and share in his discoveries. Bolaño wrote back that he would, and on Wednesday, November 22, 1989, at some point in the evening, they met in the once elegant lobby of Hotel El Conde, an iconic hotel in the historic section of downtown Caracas one block west of Plaza Bolívar. Zabala recorded his thoughts of Bolaño's visit in an entry in his diary dated November 26, 1989:

Bolaño left yesterday. I am only now just recovering. We spent sixty-some hours in a raging, drunken brawl with every preconceived notion about life we have ever held, all in a mad effort to see what would remain standing after we were finished. It was a dismantling of reality of the first order, and then a reassembling of that reality. It was a philosophical maelstrom, but it was also a poetic, anti-poetic, revolutionary, idealistic, paranoid, adolescent, obsessive, religious, atheistic, sexual, anti-sexual, bluesy, jazzy jam session. We crammed in every duality we could think of. And it began the moment Bolaño walked into the lobby of the hotel. I cannot think of a better venue from where to embark on a journey such as we took than Hotel El Conde. It is a modern hotel of iron and concrete, a fairly recent addition (1948) to a city that seems determined to replace the decaying, baroque elegance of the past with the ultra-modernity of the future, and yet the hotel itself is an odd portal that gives us a glimpse of the very past the city wishes to escape. When you first walk into the lobby you are instantly confronted with a few iconic pieces of artwork depicting the stylized faces of dead Venezuelan heroes, and you are almost overwhelmed by the musty odor like incense of the heavy blue drapes that admit into the lobby only surreptitious flashes of sunlight or starlight like vagabond ghosts that have wandered down from the mountains. It is a place where history is constantly whispering even though the architecture is barely forty years old. But a hell of a lot has happened within these walls in those forty years. Politicians and poet ambassadors and bullfighters and rising journalists have slept with society divas in the rooms above the lobby. Decadent drug lords have held court downstairs. International porn stars have tiptoed down the hallways late at night seeking out ritual comfort in one room or another. Murders have been committed here, carnival atrocities. New revolutions have been planned but then the plans have been shelved on the advice of foreign agents. The great writer Rómulo Gallegos himself lived in this hotel for a few months after he was elected President in February 1948 until he was thrown out of the country in November of that same year. It is said you could hear him typing away late at night, supposedly working on new sections of his great novel, Doña Bárbara. Was he ever finished with that book? Is he still hoping to add a chapter or two even in death? How amazing to think that he had only been in San Fernando de Apure for a single week doing research, and to read Doña Bárbara you would have thought he had been born there! The people who actually live in San Fernando say as much. Or perhaps Gallegos was working on something else when he called Hotel El Conde his home. Some say you can still hear him typing away madly. At any rate, this is where we had decided to meet. Hotel El Conde became our jumping off point, our crossroads between the past and the future. Of course the moment Bolaño walked into the lobby he breathed in the intoxicating, beguiling, surreal atmosphere of this hotel caught between two worlds. I was sitting in one of two red leather chairs near the hotel entrance, with a potted fern on one side. But he stopped as soon as he saw me and raised his hand as if to ask for silence. It was a bit dramatic. He just stood there for a while, his face submerged in the glare of a well-placed floor lamp, listening to some unseen music, and for a moment it was almost as if he had vanished. All I could see where he stood was the pulsating aura of the lamp light, as if he had been absorbed into the light itself, beamed up into oblivion by an alien spacecraft. Then he stepped out of the glare and sat down, smiling, a ludicrous smile, and asked me if I thought all that much about immortality, and I laughed and said what does it matter, madness is madness is madness, and sadness too, and he started laughing and said yes, yes, we are all children of Caliban, and I remember how astonished I was that he said that because I was thinking exactly the same thing, and then he asked me if I could feel the unappeased literary genius of Gallegos swirling about the lobby like smoke seeking escape, and I said I could, I said I had suggested Hotel El Conde for precisely that reason, and then we were both laughing hysterically. I think Bolaño and I were cut from the same cloth, though perhaps from opposite ends of the ragged bolt. We would agree and disagree in the same breath. I don't know how long we stayed at the hotel. We did not stay long. The hotel has a small, dingy bar, again a vision of faded, surreal elegance, where we downed a few beers, and then we hit the streets, which is to say we roamed all over the city that first night, searching out hidden bars and cafés tucked away in the crevices of Venezuelan culture, riding the gleaming silver bullet trains of the Metro in search of the burn victim I had discovered back in October, but the further we traveled by train, the further my burn victim retreated into the majesty of my own myth-making. We lingered over midnight snacks and pre-dawn breakfasts and pestilent, sun-blazing, late afternoon lunches, or maybe we ate nothing at all, maybe we only drank, and it is impossible to calculate how much we drank, beer, tequila, wine, whiskey, rum, all sorts of mixed drinks, even Kahlúa and cream, which I absolutely detest, but I drank it anyway. I don't know what we were thinking. I guess we were thinking we were back in Mexico City in 1975. But what does that even mean? What does it mean to think back on a Mexico that existed fourteen years ago, a Mexico that no longer exists? Time lifts us with ancient cymbals, as the poet Gerbasi says, but not quite in the way he imagined it. The distant thunderstorms no longer agonize me. I am no longer stuffed with ashes. The hard geometries of my youth have swiftly bled away. So who cares what we were doing or why oh so many years ago? No one can tell your political sympathies by looking at your bones. The time of our youth was past. We had both moved on. And now we were drinking to the memory of that youth, or to something else. It did not matter. It was an endless night of drinking. The drinking is what mattered. That fact is indisputable. And we talked while we drank. We talked the way I had always imagined writers would talk. That fact is also indisputable. We spoke of the slippery nature of reality, the interconnectedness of things, the intertextuality of all history. We talked at length about Paul Kammerer, who said that history was the serial repetition of a singular event, an idea which he quite properly called seriality, but which Jung later stole and called synchronicity and now nobody knows about Paul Kammerer. We talked about the impossibility of defeating the Fascism of time, especially since we were armed only with the arrows of mortal ambition, which are easily turned aside. We wondered if in fact any writer could truly achieve immortality since the fate of all books, with no exceptions, is that sooner or later they are used for kindling. This is a practical reality. I remember that I talked about my Big Spanish book and Bolaño talked about his German book, which was almost finished, except for the polishing. It was a book which he said wasn't really about Germany, it was more about the intellectual games we all play trying to justify the violence of existence, or the nature of existence in a violent world, or something like that. Germany was just a front, Bolaño said, and he was laughing subversively as he spoke so I knew he was being ironic, but it was more than ironic, there was a smaller seriousness embedded in his irony, but that seriousness was also folded over into irony, with an even smaller seriousness embedded in that, and so on, like a series of opposing mirrors stretching with exquisite precision towards infinity. You never knew how far Bolaño would go when he was being ironic. I told him I would need to read the book to see what he was getting at. Then he talked about an idea he had for another book, a book that would be an encyclopedia of right-wing writers living in Latin America, and he was almost laughing as he talked about this book, but not quite, it was more like he was posing for the future. He said none of the writers would be real writers, they wouldn't actually exist in the world, he would make it all up, but he was convinced that people reading the book would think the writers were real. And then he did burst out laughing. Actually, it seemed pretty funny when he was talking about it, and Bolaño's laughter was certainly infectious, and it did break the monotony of sitting in a foul-smelling Metro station with the fluorescent lights flickering and buzzing at three in the morning, waiting for the train to Pérez Bonalde, though why we going to Pérez Bonalde I am not quite sure, but I seem to remember that we had heard a lot of gunfire at one point during the afternoon, I don't know where the hell we were, some café or bar or restaurant in Catia, just off Calle El Cristo, or maybe it was closer to Parque del Oeste, I don't really remember, but the gunfire sounded pretty close wherever we were, and there was a lot of it, and Bolaño was convinced there was another riot going on and people were dying right and left, but then the gunfire stopped and the owner of the café came over and smiled with great enthusiasm, a gleaming, hopeful smile like a burning sun that most certainly masked the invincible melancholy of a defeated people, and he said they were working on some of the transformers down at the electricity company, which was only a few blocks away, that was why we had heard all those popping sounds, it sounded like that sometimes, so there was no need to worry, and then he brought us another round of beers, perhaps to disguise the fact that his explanation seemed unconvincing, because the very air of Caracas is saturated with an unthinking and unrepentant violence, because in the streets of Caracas the hope of Baudelaire is erased by the certain knowledge that everything is fatal, even chance, but who were we to contradict the owner's great enthusiasm and his hopeful generosity and so expose the truth behind the mask, so we went back to our drinking, so I think that's why we were going to Pérez Bonalde, because there was a hospital a few blocks from the station and if there were any survivors from the massacre that afternoon, that's where they would have been, except there was no fucking hospital, how we got this idea into our heads I can't imagine, and there probably hadn't been a massacre either, but what the fuck, in retrospect the whole damn thing was fucking hilarious, the whole sequence was rather like something out of an absurdist play by Fernando Arrabal, Bolaño talking about his idea for a new book at three in the morning, the two of us bathed in the erratic glow of festering, fluorescent lights in a deserted Metro station in lonely, mythic Caracas without even rats scratching about, somewhere beyond the known boundaries of reality, I suspect, and then Bolaño out of the blue remembering about the imagined gunfire from before, no warning, just bam! and then he became obsessed with the need to talk to a survivor of the imaginary riot that had taken place only in our collective brain that afternoon, this need surging through his arteries like a bolt of lightning, the fluorescent lights flickering with a more visible intensity as his obsession grew, and then bam! just like that the lights went out, also without warning, the two of us now waiting in a hazy, humid darkness backlit by the faint red glow of half-a-dozen emergency lights floating in the blackness of the Metro tunnel like the eyes of Cerberus guarding the black Gates of Hell, the two of us waiting for the train to Pérez Bonalde so we could go to a hospital that did not exist, so our plan was pretty much fucked from the start, but like I said, we didn't know. I'm pretty sure that was the reason, but we were both fairly drunk by then. I'm not even sure if we made it to Pérez Bonalde. I guess we must have made it because how else would I know the hospital didn't exist, but I don't remember. But while we were waiting in the darkness for the goddamn train I told Bolaño I wanted to see his right-wing writers' encyclopedia when he was done, and he said he'd send me a copy. After that we didn't talk any more about literature. We were too tired to talk about something so heady and yet so insubstantial, so unreal as literature. To tell you the truth, I think we were just plain exhausted. And then all of a sudden it was Friday night and we had arrived at the last stop on our whirlwind journey through this terrifying yet seductive landscape of dark nights and even darker treachery. We were sitting in a seedy dive on Calle Los Apamates, a stone's throw from yet another Metro station, a café where humanity's darkest intentions were made visible. It was the kind of place that served horrible dinners until nine or ten, and anything you wanted to drink until five in the morning. The patrons were mostly prostitutes sitting on the laps of drunken, overweight, mid-level businessmen, the prostitutes playfully tugging at ties and rubbing with surreptitious skill the bulges that had started to grow and spoon-feeding the hungry businessmen until their plates were empty and then the girls whispering words that promised a night of unending joy coupled with eternal absolution (¿Pendiente de una vuelta?) and the businessmen whispering back words that echoed with the hope of unrestrained passion (¡Chévere!) and then two by two the newly formed couples would begin heading for the door and the crystallized obscurity of the dark Venezuelan night, only to be replaced by more playful prostitutes and more eager businessmen. There were also a few out-of-place University students who had abandoned their studies days earlier and were now teetering on the brink, hoping for table scraps, perhaps, their eyes glazed over with the luminous, impenetrable anxiety of drug addiction, certain to end up the victims of some unspeakable crime. Bolaño and I were sitting at a small, triangular table next to a narrow aquarium that had been shoved into the back corner. Our tiny table was partially illuminated by the dim light from the hallway that led to the bathroom. The aquarium was supposedly filled with all sorts of tropical fish, though it was hard to see, perhaps it was only a few half-starved piranhas, and every now and then someone on their way back from the bathroom would toss a few coins into the aquarium and stop and stare for a while at the murky darkness of the water and the faint, greenish glow of a tiny light bulb lodged inside a porcelain deep sea diver. Everyone who tossed a few coins into the aquarium seemed hypnotized by the tiny deep sea diver. Then they would shudder and shake their heads and the spell would be broken. They would mutter a small prayer for good luck, or maybe they were cursing someone under their breath, hoping to cast the evil eye on an enemy, and then head back to their tables. I think we were the last ones to order dinner. We were eating pabellón, a meal that consists of carne mechada, black beans, sweet fried plantains, and queso blanco. We were also drinking a spicy, dry, dark rum, Pampero Anniversario, glass after glass after glass. We ate in absolute silence because we were very hungry, but once we finished eating, we began talking with the same fervor we possessed at the beginning of our journey. We talked about the ever-expanding galaxy, and we wondered at mankind's insufferable egotism to suppose that our star alone of all the stars in the sky possessed planets that supported sentient life. We lamented the lost beauty and obscured significance of those unheralded beings from distant planets whom we would never know. We wondered if they were flesh and blood creatures like we were, or if perhaps they were instead made of gas or water or frozen light and simply floated like nebulas or clouds from one place to another. We cursed our inability to soar through the heavens, except by using our puny, febrile imaginations, towards the unfathomable purity of those unreachable stars. We talked about the technology of spaceships. We talked about time travel. Who will be left far behind? I asked Bolaño. We all will, he replied. Then we talked about Simón Bolívar and Venezuela's struggle for independence. We talked about Bolívar's relationship with the famous German explorer Alexander von Humboldt. Why is it the Europeans, especially the Germans, but also a few Venezuelan myth-makers, insist on perpetuating the story that Humboldt gave Bolívar the idea of a free Venezuela when they met in Paris in November 1804? Wasn't Bolívar a bit too young and inexperienced to absorb such weighty advice at that point? Isn't it more likely that their first meeting was a bit more frivolous in nature, that perhaps all Bolívar wanted to know was the name of a good restaurant? Isn't it more likely that the political intent of El Libertador was stamped upon his psyche after his return to Venezuela, where he was ultimately confronted with the inescapable tragedy of life as a bonded servant to Spain? Wouldn't this realization have been enough to spur his political ambition? And what of Bolívar's strange, almost legendary meeting with José de San Martín, the great Argentine General, the Protector of Peruvian Freedom, who had liberated not only Peru but also Chile and what is now Argentina? What actually happened at that fateful conference in Guayaquil? Who was the puppet master? Why did San Martin accept the defeat of his political hopes to install a new monarchy in Peru (or was this hope also a fabrication of later historians) in favor of Simón Bolívar's dream of a series of republics? Was the banquet and ball given in honor of San Martin a political demonstration of Bolívar's complete victory? Is this why San Martin soon abdicated, leaving South America for good in 1829 for the shores of idyllic France and a life of quiet retreat? Can the riddle of Guayaquil only be pierced by two historians whose very existence is limited to the pages of a short story of the same name written by Borges? Is all reality suspect? Does the successive, ordered use of language by its very nature tend to exaggerate the importance of what we are saying? And what of Bolívar's own claim that he was in Milan in 1805 and attended the coronation of Napoleon? We were both fascinated by the swirling eddies of myth and deception that surrounded Bolívar. We wondered if his lover, Manuela Sáenz, a patriot and hero of the revolution in her own right, minded all that much that her beloved was taken from his initial resting place in the Cathedral of Santa Marta and put on permanent display, so to speak, in the National Pantheon in 1842, becoming thus a symbol of the impervious commitment to the competing ideals of liberty and equality, while she herself died in 1856 of diphtheria and was dumped with unceremonious disdain, and no small measure of fear due to the possibility of contagion, into a mass grave. We wondered who actually created these fantastic stories that we now take for history. We wondered if we ourselves could create such stories. Who will be left far behind? Bolaño said. We all will, I said. We were filled with sudden troubling premonitions. Or perhaps we were having simultaneous attacks of gastroenteritis. Then we were talking about Venezuela under Pérez and how it was a ticking time bomb. The day that shook the country had only exposed the problem for the whole world to see. There was no brutal rupture with the past, no collapsing sky, no need to invent a new metanarrative to superimpose upon the universe. It was the same story that had plagued Venezuela since the days of the Spanish Empire, the same story that plagued all of Latin America. Everyone with eyes to see could see that the gap between the rich and the poor remained, and so did the frustration that fragments the lives of those living at the bottom. The streets of Caracas were still home to thousands and thousands of 'buhoneros' (vendors) who continued to scratch and claw with desperate enthusiasm just to stay alive, selling everything and anything from Rolex watches to rock-and-roll t-shirts to handbags to empanadas to raw oysters to pistols to drugs. The upper crust still hid out in their fortified castles, protected by barbed wire and surveillance cameras and German mercenary bodyguards armed to the teeth with fully serrated army knives and semi-automatic machine guns. And all over the city, in the slums of Caucaguita and San Agustin and Monte Piedad and Sierra Maestra, dozens of hastily built, ramshackle apartment buildings and burnt-red ranchos were still washed away in the muddy torrential rivers that followed on the heels of severe thunderstorms, in spite of the tangled black net of cables and wires that seemed to hold the barrios in place when it wasn't raining. The tears that were shed only months earlier for those who had died in the name of freedom had already evaporated like desert raindrops. But Pérez cannot wash his hands of that blood, nor the blood that is to come, I said. He cannot forever blame the leftist guerrillas and criminals and drug lords and counter-revolutionaries from Cuba and other politically undesirable elements for the plague that has already arrived on his doorstep. And it is not just a Venezuelan issue. It is a global issue. We must focus on helping everyone meet their basic needs, I said. It is time to put Marcel Duchamp's urinal back on the wall. And Bolaño naturally agreed. Then we talked about the explosive violence of the Caracazo itself and the burning buses and the looting that had spread like an Egyptian pestilence, like a fucking plague of locusts, and the government declaring marital law, and just like that Bolaño wanted to know all about the burn victim I had met in October, in fact it was more like an interrogation, like he was pumping me for information, what was his name? said Bolaño (Ernesto Peralta, I said) and where did he live before the riots? (in the neighborhood called El Marques just off Avenida Boyaca in the shadow of Cerro El Avila, the lungs of Caracas because of all the greenery) and where did he now live? (I did not know, I had not seen him since that first time) and how extensive were his injuries? (the entire left side of his face and neck and shoulder were burned very badly, I could not see the skin beneath his shirt, but the skin that was exposed was still very black, almost a charcoal color, and it was leathery, I mean it seemed like his skin was actually a piece of leather that had been left to rot in the elements, and it was also cracked in many places, and it was clear that his arms and his legs from the knees down had also been burned, but not as badly, but the overall impression was of someone with a rare, festering, malignant form of cancer or someone suffering from leprosy, he didn't look human at all from a certain angle, in fact in the dim light of the Metro station where I met him he looked more like a creature from outer space) and did he possess any unusual smell? (an unusual smell?) yes, like formaldehyde or rubbing alcohol or ammonium chloride? (I do not know, I do not remember any unusual smell) and did he seem to have an aversion to direct sunlight? (that is difficult to determine, one could argue that was the case, since I stumbled upon him at the deepest level of the Metro station, but I only met him the one time, so it is impossible to perceive a pattern) and did he seem to have come to terms with his deformity? (you mean psychologically?) yes, or emotionally, or did it seem like he possessed a violent, sinister streak just below the surface? (yes, now that you mention it, he most definitely possessed an aura of maladjustment, the tremulous tremors that lull us to sleep, as if he were just waiting for the right moment to slit someone's throat) good, very good, said Bolaño, and there were many more precise, journalistic, though slightly bizarre questions after that, nitty-gritty questions, an attempt to get at the hidden psychology of what it means to live out one's days as a burn victim, and I did my best to answer every question he put to me, it was actually kind of fun, like we were two detectives comparing notes, that is the impression I had, as if Bolaño had come face to face with numerous burn victims since he had left Mexico City and was cataloguing how each had responded to their deformity in the hopes of answering certain fundamental questions about the nature of identity and whether or not you could indeed remain yourself if the face you had been born with no longer existed. Yes, it was an interesting conversation. And then just like that it was over, but not because we had exhausted its possibilities. Bolaño was just about to ask me what might have been the most profound question he had asked all evening (that was certainly the look in his eyes sparkling with mischief), when we were savagely interrupted by two immaculately dressed local gangsters engaged in a furious discussion about a recent epidemic of UFO sightings in the skies above Caracas. I say gangsters because each gentleman possessed a small pocket gun, a Beistegui Brothers Libia 6.35 mm originally manufactured in Spain but purchased only God knew where. With a flair for theatric gestures, they had placed their guns on their table while they were arguing. These were not the kind of guns police detectives would have carried. Yes, they were deadly enough, but a Libia is more for show, a collector's item, more for the prestige of owning such a gun, more to announce to the world that the man who possesses it is a man of some stature, more the kind of gun a gangster on the rise would possess. What was more intriguing than their tiny showcase pistols, however, was that their argument seemed less like an actual argument than it did an occasion for arguing. It was soon apparent that both men believed in the existence of UFOs, and that their comments about the sightings and the possibility of being visited by aliens or even abducted were aimed at disarming the paranoid vigilance of their opponent, thus creating an opportunity to get off a quick potshot. We were in fact witnessing a rarely seen ritual dance between two second-tier egomaniacs vying for power (and a chance to gain market share in gangsterland) in the dim, bluish, cavernous light of this seedy dive on Calle Los Apamates south of Solano. Both men seemed to be frothing at the mouth. What about the story of Emelino Gonzales, the truck driver? said the one. Ah, my friend, why do you need to go back to 1954? said the other. We are talking about alien encounters, are we not? What better example than Gonzales, who was forced to exit his truck because a nine-foot wide spherical craft was hovering six feet off the ground, blocking the road to Petare? said the one. Ah, yes, but some say Gonzales was a deranged drug addict. Who else would claim he was attacked by hairy dwarves? said the other. But you do not dispute the fact that his assailants emerged from the craft and sent him flying backwards some fifteen feet with a concentrated beam of light? said the one. No, no. But Gonzales did say his astral assailants were covered with hair and they were wearing loincloths. I dispute that. And he also said some of these hairy dwarves were off gathering rocks when he surprised them. I dispute that as well. What aliens wear loincloths? And why did they need rocks from the road to Petare? said the other. What of the story of Lorenzo Paz and Alberto Rosales? said the one. You mean Rosales the shoe salesman and amateur photographer and not Rosales the philosopher? said the other. Yes, certainly, the one who along with Paz took the pictures of a luminous oval craft zooming back and forth in the skies over Carora, with great orange flames shooting out from its underbelly, incinerating the landscape. Who could deny the truth of the pictures? said the one. Yes, that is certainly a truthful account. But it is also an old, old story. And it does not take place in Caracas, said the other. Very well then, let us return to the recent sightings. What do you say about the craft Mrs. Regina Rivero said she saw from the plaza just outside the Chacaito subway station? said the one. Yes, yes, this report has been on the news on every channel. A whitish blue light of great size and luminosity, much brighter than any other heavenly body in the sky. The light appearing stationary for five or ten minutes, and then accelerating at great speed and vanishing in the hazy, urban glow of the city and the darkness beyond. But a whitish blue light is hardly a spacecraft, said the other. What then of the small, circular black object seen in the skies above La Pastora, an object that was most definitely an alien spacecraft according to the witnesses, and there were thousands of reputable witnesses who said the ship crisscrossed the heavens, looking for unsuspecting victims to snatch away, slicing up the sky in odd, bewildering geometric patterns before it zoomed away at the speed of light and was lost in the clouds surrounding Cerro El Avila? What of that, my friend? But instead of responding with another criticism, the other gangster picked up his Libia in a motion so quick and easy it was difficult to believe the gun had not always been a part of his hand, and without even a backward glance at his friend, he fired in quick succession at three hanging lamps hanging directly over the darkly stained bar. There was an explosion of glass particles and shards of darkness as the lights were extinguished one by one, and then a roar of jubilant laughter followed by a competing roar, and then the voice of the first gangster saying watch this! as the light from several more hanging lamps (these were hanging above various tables) was extinguished, and then there was more roaring, robust, jubilant laughter, and then for some strange, unfathomable, possibly psychotic reason, the men turned their Libias on the poor forgotten aquarium nestled in the back corner and emptied their weapons in unison, an amazing feat of synchronous skill which suggested, among other things, that these two gangsters were connected telepathically, twins of body, mind and soul. The aquarium glass shattered with the impact of the bullets, and then there was a rush of murky, aquarium water, and soon after that you could hear the fish flopping about on the tiled floor. The gangsters started congratulating themselves on their marksmanship. Their laughter swelled with their joy. Then one of them (it was difficult to see who was who) tossed a large bill to the table. For the damage, he said. And then they were gone. Just like that. We barely had any time to reflect on what had happened. We were like fugitives, too tired from running to think, rubbing our sore feet, lost in the second desert of our delusions. We just sat there numbly, absorbed by the darkness. And it was very dark indeed. The interior of this seedy dive on Calle Los Apamates had been plunged into what I can only describe as a primeval darkness. A couple of hanging lanterns had survived, and there was still the dim glow from the hallway that led to the bathroom. And remarkably, the tiny porcelain deep sea diver was still intact, still standing on the pebbly though unwatery bottom of his domain like an exposed skeleton, and he was still glowing faintly with a soft, surreal greenish light. But that was it for illumination. It was almost like the world had been suddenly transformed into a grainy film noir gangster movie from the forties, except there was no femme fatale. So we sat there for a while. I don't remember how long. I do remember it was dark enough that I had trouble making out even the face of Bolaño, who couldn't have been more than two feet away. Then I heard Bolaño's voice swimming towards me through that ocean of darkness. Who will be left far behind? Bolaño asked. We all will, I replied. And then we were laughing hysterically, arm in arm with death, that impertinent lover who whispers only bitter stories. That's what it seemed like. That's the last thing I remember.

One would be hard pressed to find a more compelling portrait of two writers on a two-day bender. But the passage is so neatly developed, so charged with purpose-driven, kinetic energy, that it seems more like a fictionalized account of what should have happened (an ideal version of reality) than what actually did happen (plain old boring reality). Both the obvious details and those hidden beneath the luminescent surface of the prose dovetail in ways that seem crafted, as opposed to accidental. The hotel where Zabala says he and Bolaño met is a case in point. Hotel El Conde is located on the very corner where the house of the Count of San Javier lived with his wife and extended family during the 18th century. That the name Javier lay at the historic foundation of the hotel where he and Bolaño began their epic journey must surely have appealed to Zabala's sense of irrefutable destiny. Likewise, the looming presence of Rómulo Gallegos as a one-time resident of the hotel carries a similar prophetic weight when one considers that Bolaño was virtually unknown as a writer until he won the Rómulo Gallegos Prize for his novel, *The Savage Detectives,* in 1999. The irony of this fact may indeed be a coincidence, given that the second meeting between Zabala and Bolaño supposedly took place ten years earlier, but this small but significant detail could just as easily have been inserted into Zabala's narrative after 1999 and we would be none the wiser.

Of course two questions emerge from this line of thinking. First, when was this particular passage actually composed? And why would Zabala engage in yet another deception, particularly since it seems unlikely that he ever intended for his diary to be published? To answer these questions, it is perhaps instructive to examine the texture of the passage as a whole. Zabala gives us dozens of clues that as a writer he is interested in blurring the lines between history and myth, between fact and fiction. He declares at the very beginning of this passage that he and Bolaño were engaged in 'a dismantling of reality of the first order, and then a reassembling of that reality.' Then Zabala comments on Gallegos' great novel, *Doña Bárbara,* which is a mythic exploration of the life of a cattle rustler and petty tyrant from Venezuela (who also happens to be a witch), whose sense of reality, which is shaped by the violent nature of existence on the plains of Venezuela, deteriorates over the course of the novel as a consequence of both her struggle to find peace and love for herself and her struggle against the legitimate government of Venezuela. For Zabala, Hotel El Conde and Gallegos' novel are each an ideal 'jumping off point,' a trampoline, if you will, for the journey Zabala and Bolaño are about to make into unknown territory, and thus they also serve as appropriate symbols of the 'crossroads between the past and the future.' Reality is thus ever malleable. Bolaño listens to 'unseen music' and vanishes in the glare of the lamp light. They talk about the nature of reality and the meaning of existence. Bolaño describes a book he hopes to write that will be an encyclopedia of fake writers but everyone who reads it will think they are real. They go to 'some café or bar or restaurant in Catia, just off Calle El Cristo, or maybe it was closer to Parque del Oeste.' Zabala doesn't really remember. They imagine they hear gunfire outside this café and assume a riot is taking place, or at least Bolaño makes this assumption. The owner of the café wears a 'mask' to hide his melancholy disposition. Nothing in this account is precisely located either in memory or, seemingly, in actual fact. Zabala and Bolaño wait for the train to Pérez Bonalde in a Metro station 'somewhere beyond the known boundaries of reality' so they can 'go to a hospital that [does] not exist.' Zabala compares their experiences to something that might exist in the world of an absurdist play by the Spanish writer Fernando Arrabal. They curse the limitations of their imaginations, limitations which make it impossible to comprehend the 'unfathomable purity of [the] unreachable stars.' They talk about the myth and deception that surrounds the life of Simón Bolívar. They wonder if the riddle of Guayaquil can 'only be pierced by two historians whose very existence is limited to the pages of a short story of the same name written by Borges,' a writer who was himself a master of blurring the lines between myth and history. They talk about 'the hidden psychology of what it means to live out one's days as a burn victim' in an attempt to answer 'certain fundamental questions about the nature of identity and whether or not you [can] indeed remain yourself if the face you [have] been born with no longer [exists].' They witness a lively debate between two local gangsters about the truth of various UFO sightings in and around Caracas, but the sophisticated intellectual tenor of this debate seems well beyond what we would normally expect from gangsters, especially with its half-buried reference to Alberto Rosales, a Venezuelan philosopher and an expert in both Kant and Heidegger who was particularly interested in Heidegger's distinction between the notion of Being (*Sein*) and being (*Seiende*). Finally, everywhere Zabala and Bolaño go during their epic two-day journey, light does not truly illuminate. More often than not the two writers are surrounded by a hazy, murky, mythic, at times primordial darkness, as if the 'world had [indeed] been transformed into a grainy film noir gangster movie from the forties.' In short, Zabala seems to be saying that what we understand as reality is not reality, what we think of as our identity is perhaps something else. Everything is up for grabs. Of course many writers have tackled such themes. Understanding the nature of reality and identity have become the cornerstone themes of the post-modern era. What distinguishes Zabala from most other post-modern writers, however, is that he seems to embrace the joy of not knowing (as opposed to wallowing in the swamp of confusion and despair) because he is seeking spiritual enlightenment rather than intellectual certainty, which he viewed as something of a red herring. Zabala makes the search for identity and the search to understand reality the same search, but in the end he abandons both because, as he writes in his diary in an entry dated April 14, 2001: 'to search to the exclusion of all else for something that changes before our very eyes is a waste of breath and prevents us from experiencing the incalculable joy and ephemeral beauty of life.'

In May of 1996 Blanca Barutti went to South Africa with a group of one-hundred Cuban doctors as part of Cuba's ongoing commitment to share the country's medical personnel

and medical expertise with countries in need. Blanca spent several months in the KwaZulu-Natal region of South Africa working in a rural clinic that had been abandoned since 1993. But by August of 1996, Blanca had disappeared. What happened to her is anyone's guess. Her name does appear on a list of doctors working at the Médecins Sans Frontières mission in Kigali, Rwanda from September to November 1996. The list contained the names of perhaps thirty Cuban doctors. But many of the doctors who worked with Médecins Sans Frontières ultimately went to the refugee camps that had sprung up along the border between Zaire and Rwanda as a result of the First Congo War, so their precise movements are difficult to track. There was also an unconfirmed report that the body of a woman matching Blanca's description was found among the bodies of several hundred Rwandan refugees that had been massacred by members of the Rwandese army near the temporary refugee camp at Chimanga, some forty miles west of Bukavu in the Kivu region of Zaire. But whether Blanca was at Chimanga or not is probably irrelevant. In all likelihood she just happened to be in the wrong place at the wrong time and so fell victim to the unrestrained violence that had become an indelible part of the African landscape.

News of Blanca's disappearance had an immediate effect on Zabala. He simply stopped writing. For two years he did not work on his book. And while he did manage an occasional entry in his journal, these were mostly copied excerpts from poets he admired, poetry that spoke to his unarticulated grief.

According to his daughter, Cecilia, Zabala lived the life of a zombie for those two years, struggling to come to terms with Blanca's absence. She said he was up at all hours of the night, wandering through the tiny, vacant rooms of the house in La Boca, a ghost without anywhere to go. Sometimes during the day he would sit beneath an Acacia tree near the water and stare out at the Caribbean Sea for hours without moving a muscle. She would follow him, fearing for his safety, but he would just sit by the water and stare out at the sea. 'I did the best I could for him during those two years,' Cecilia said. 'I made sure he had enough to eat. I brought him books to read. I made his bed. I washed his clothes. But I could not go where he had gone. And I could not help him get back.'

Eventually, Zabala did begin writing again, and he did so with a renewed sense of purpose, a renewed vigor. It was almost as if he believed he would see his beloved Blanca again, but only after he had finished his masterpiece. This was Cecilia's opinion. The end came quickly. In April 2002, he finished writing *The Mad Patagonian.* In May, he told his daughter that when he left this world he wished to be cremated and have his ashes scattered out in the Caribbean. That way, he said, they would perhaps find their way to Africa. He also asked that Cecilia burn his manuscript and mingle its ashes with his. 'We are the same thing,' he told her. 'My life and the book are the same thing. We are both seeking to return to Blanca.'

One month later, on June 26th, Zabala died when an undiagnosed cerebral aneurysm suddenly burst. Cecilia found him sitting up against the same Acacia tree where he had spent hours staring at the sea in the wake of Blanca's absence. 'He seemed to be at peace,' she said. 'And then I realized that he was with my mother, and they were in whatever paradise he had spent his life imagining.'

It is one of those quirks of history that *The Mad Patagonian* survived beyond the death of Zabala. To begin with, Cecilia was unable to fulfill either of her father's wishes. She could not bring herself to cremate his body. Instead she had him buried in Circuito Sur cemetery near Trinidad. And she could not burn his great book either. Then in 2003, with the help of a friend, she managed to get a copy of the manuscript to the editors of a now defunct literary press (Ediciones Pequeña Luna) in Caracas, Venezuela, and they agreed to publish it, but in 2004 the press went out of business, a casualty of the riots that rocked Caracas in February of that year. So the novel was never officially published and seemed destined for oblivion. Then in 2011 fate intervened. In January of that year, the unthinkable began to happen: relations between the United States and Cuba began to thaw. Cecilia began to communicate with her uncle, Emidio, who had moved from Miami to Pensacola, Florida and worked at the Naval Air Station there. It was Emidio who suggested they try again to get the novel published, but he suggested they publish it in English, not Spanish. Six months later, in June 2011, I received a letter from Emidio and Cecilia asking me to translate the book. How Zabala's masterpiece actually ended up in my hands and the challenges I faced during the four years I spent on the project is the subject of the Afterword to the current edition. Let me just say here that I have endeavored to preserve Zabala's vision as faithfully as possible. I have also endeavored in this introduction to give the reader some sense of who Zabala was by quoting generously from his diary because I believe the glimpses they provide of Zabala's soul are useful anchors for appreciating his novel. If the English edition fails to live up to the spectacular, audacious, linguistic brilliance of the original Spanish, then it is the fault of my ability as a translator. But I do believe the essence of the novel has been preserved. Zabala himself believed that all books were ghosts of some greater reality, so a translation is in fact a ghost of a ghost. But like any ghost worthy of recognition, *The Mad Patagonian* lingers in your imagination long after you have set it down.

Tomás García Guerrero,
Adjunct Professor of Linguistics, Emeritus
Communications Department, University of Tamaulipas, Mexico
August 24, 2015

The Mad Patagonian

Escoraz Family descended from Andres and Ana

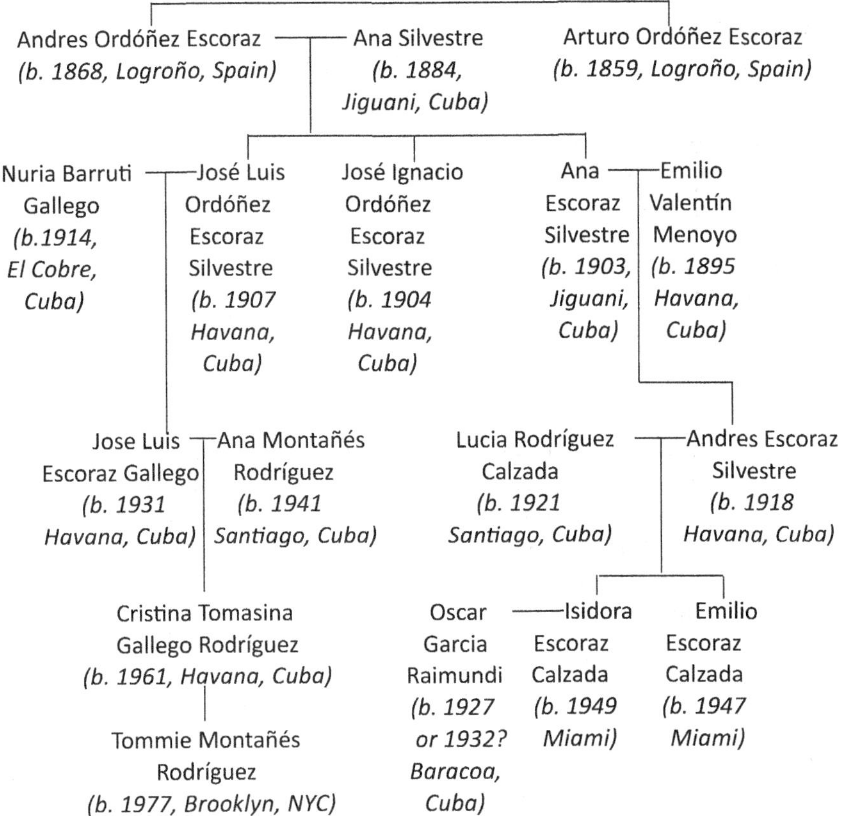

Escoraz Family descended from Arturo and Verona

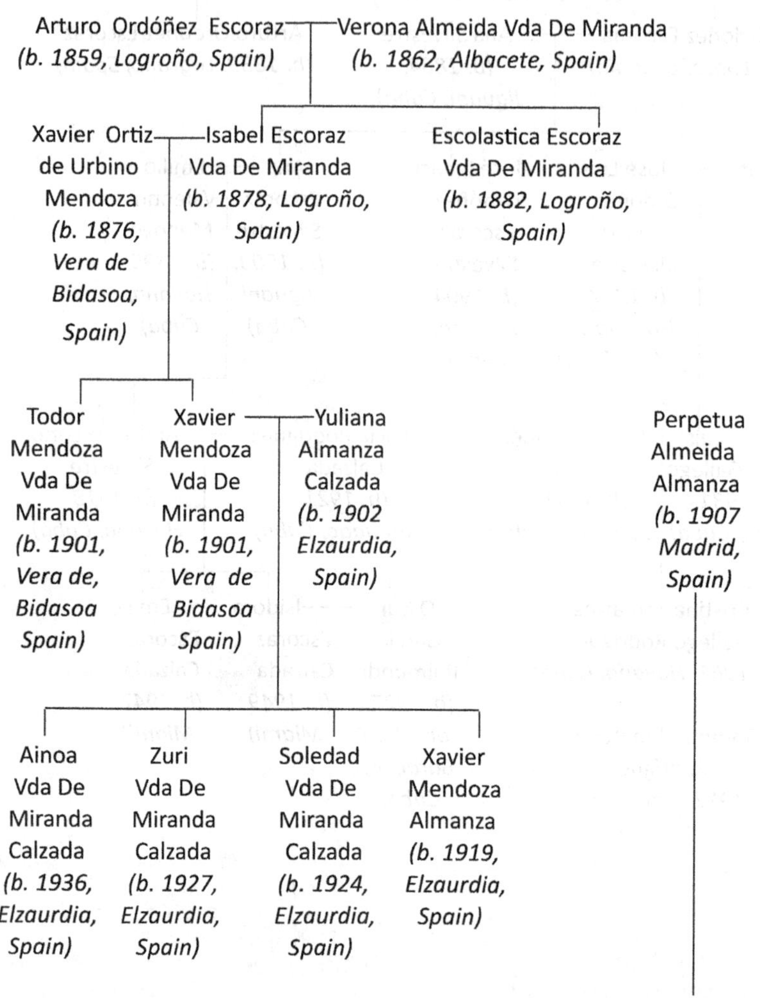

PART ONE

(an echo of paradise)

Tout est vol, tout est concussion dans la nature; le désir de s'emparer du bien d'autrui est la première... la plus légitime passion que nous ayons reçue d'elle. Ce sont les premières lois que sa main grave en nous, c'est le premier penchant de tous les êtres et, sans doute, le plus agréable.

De Sade, L'Histoire de Juliette, ou les Prospérités du Vice

BOOK ONE

the house at the beach

-1-

Three weeks after my dad died I headed south to Florida. I was heading to Jacksonville to be a teacher. It was my first job. I don't remember what I was thinking on the ride down. To tell the truth, I have never been so disconnected from myself in my whole life. I drove a junky white Toyota and the air conditioning wasn't working, so the choices were either you boiled your brains with the windows rolled up, or you left the windows open and you couldn't hear the radio with the wind flapping in your ears.

That's about all I remember. The whole trip was one gigantic blur. Except I do remember I picked up a hitchhiker. He was too old to be hitchhiking, but there he was, a damn lunatic, standing by the side of the road, along the edge of the shoulder where the road sloped away, a duffel bag by his feet. He didn't look like he even knew where he was, like maybe he might just walk out into the middle of the highway and get hit by a semi. So what else could I do? He was holding a metal detector by the handle and he was wearing a fisherman's hat to keep off the sun. I picked him up somewhere in Georgia. He said he was heading down to Miami, he had heard the beaches down there were real good for treasure hunting, he wanted to try his luck, and then he smiled a ridiculous smile and held up his metal detector so I could see, but I didn't care.

I don't think we spoke again till I turned off the Interstate and let him out at a gas station. He said I seemed like a nice enough fellow but I shouldn't let that go to my head. There was already too much insanity in the world. Then he wanted me to remember that nothing was ever what it seemed to be, but I didn't say anything. You sort of expect old guys to say clichéd shit like that. Then we got out of the car and I started filling up and he walked over to a tanker that had just dropped off its load and he started talking with the trucker like they were old friends. They shook hands after that and the trucker helped the old guy climb into the cab, but I swear, just before he got in, he turned to me and waved and smiled, and then I heard him speak, which he was fifty feet away so I shouldn't have been able to hear him speak. I mean he wasn't shouting. He was just talking in a normal tone. He said 'Life is a lingering fever' in this hoarse, raspy voice. It was almost like his voice was coming out of one of the metal boxes you use to talk to the gas station attendant when your pump isn't working. Then he climbed up into the tanker and they pulled out. That was the last I saw of him. I don't know. Maybe I made the whole thing up. Like I said, the whole trip down was one gigantic blur.

The next thing I remember is standing in the auditorium of this fairly glitzy prep school with a floor-to-ceiling window like you see in the churches of those lunatic television evangelists. The window looked out on a grassy lawn and some live oaks, and then there was a tangled mess of vegetation and the St. John's River beyond that. You couldn't really see the river, partly because of the vegetation, but mostly because of the way the sun slashed through the glass. The Dean of the Faculty was saying how glad he was to be back to start the new year, and then he was introducing the new faculty to the old faculty. Since I was one of the new ones, I had to parade myself across a red-velvet platform stage. Then I sat down at a round table up against the television evangelist window.

There were only three of us sitting at the table, me and two doe-eyed, help-me-cause-I'm-caught-in-the-blinding-glare-of-oncoming-traffic bombshells who were going to teach intermediate Spanish. Everyone else was sitting away from the window, so the glare and the heat weren't too bad, but where we were it was pretty awful. The sun was just pouring in. It was the middle of the afternoon in the middle of one of the hottest Augusts on record. Wave after wave of relentless heat pouring through the glass. I was certain the air conditioning wasn't working, and after a while I was sure I was hallucinating. It felt like I was back in my junky Toyota with the windows rolled up, driving across the Deep South, but no matter how much time passed, I wasn't getting anywhere. It felt like the sun was stuck in the sky. I was drunk with the heat and I nearly passed out. There wasn't even a pitcher of water or bottles or anything. One of the Spanish teachers kept saying "it'll be all right, Travis, it can't be much longer," but the other one gave us a look, and with that the first one sort of swallowed the sound of her own voice and sat back, blinking.

Then the introductions were over and the Dean was done with his stories and the faculty had been dismissed. I must have been pretty dehydrated from the sun pouring in through that window because the next few hours vanished just like that. I felt like I was choking on dust. I was trying to remember what water tasted like. Then the dust settled and I could breathe more easily, but we were nowhere near the school. We were standing inside a small Japanese restaurant in downtown Jacksonville, me and the two Spanish teachers. It was kind of surreal. It was like we were the only people left on the planet. Like we were stuck in an episode of *The Twilight Zone*. Our restaurant was squeezed in between a discount tanning salon on one side and a Christian Scientist's Reading Room on the other, but they were both closed. The street outside was deserted, except for our cars. We were waiting for a couple of other teachers, a stocky, ex-marine named Ed Glaser, who taught Junior English, and Mick Haggerty, an ex-hippie who taught Senior Honors World History.

It was a pretty nice restaurant. I had never been to a Japanese restaurant before. There was a goldfish pond when you first went in and several bloated fish lolling about in the water with these lazy, unhappy eyes, poking their mouths up at the surface and blowing air and then bubbling back down, all of them with scaly, whitish, discolored patches, like they were going bald, except it was their color. They looked like the victims of some slaggy, tropical fish disease. There was also a short, rugged-looking bamboo bridge that went over the pond, and on the other side there was a fake bamboo hut, which is where they kept the cash register, but there was no one there. Japanese lanterns hung everywhere, purple, blue, lavender, dozens of them, and a few orange ones way in the back, which gave the place a smoky, festival look.

After a while a woman in a blue kimono tiptoed across the bridge and asked if we wanted a table and we said we did but we were waiting on two more and she smiled and said "Okay, okay, but you sit now please," and then she waved for us to follow. All of the tables were about two feet off the ground with flat pillows scattered all around so you didn't have to sit on the floor. The tables had a nice cherry finish. We were the only ones in the whole place. She took us all the way to the back, I guess because it was closer to the kitchen. But she was very nice about it and brought us ice water with lemon and menus and then disappeared out front.

By the time Mick and Ed got there we had already ordered, but they didn't care. They said they had stopped off for a quick drink at a place on Beach Boulevard and had lost track of the time, but they were there now. Then Mick started talking about the good old days when he had been a hippie and how he had crisscrossed the country with Abbie Hoffman and his psychedelic entourage. I don't know if I believed him or not. Abbie Hoffman was a pretty long time ago. But just the possibility that Mick might have known old Abbie impressed the two Spanish teachers. And you could not deny that Mick actually looked like an ex-hippie. Or what I had always imagined an ex-hippie should look like. He was gaunt and gangly, with tangled threads of reddish-brown, beach-smelling hair that stretched halfway down his back, like seaweed or snakes or something, a Pancho-Villa style moustache that he liked to twirl, and a tiny pair of pale blue eyes, impetuous, unrelenting eyes that stared out at you from the dark of two cavernous sockets. I had never met anyone quite like him.

We ate dinner at that Japanese restaurant pretty much every Friday for the next nine months, the five of us. At first we talked very little and we ate tons of sushi. We commiserated over the long, interminably long, gloomy hours behind a teacher's desk and the gloomy smallness of our bank accounts. The dippy kids we taught spent more on clothes in a week than we made in a month. They drove BMWs and Mercedes convertibles and flew to Buenos Aires or Madrid for long weekends, and we drove around in junky damn Toyotas and old beat up Chevrolets and went to Baltimore or Tuscaloosa or Birmingham just to say we had been somewhere. But then we talked about other things. The two Spanish teachers were from Brooklyn. They had read a great deal about Cuba and the stultifying oppression of the Cuban people. They wanted to fly down to Cuba with Pastors for Peace and bring food and clothes and build houses. They wanted to *destultify* the Cubans, I guess. That was why they had come down to Florida. Then there was the stocky, ex-Marine from Charleston, South Carolina. His full name was Edward Saxton Glaser. He had been to Vietnam. He said he had been in a shithole he called Da Nang. He'd been in the Engineering Corp and done three tours and would have done a fourth, but by then the war was over. Ed didn't really talk a whole lot about the war except to say he'd "rather eat goddamn sushi than end up looking like it." The two Spanish teachers squirmed with weak, persecuted looks on their faces when he said that and stared down at their plates. Ed talked like that a lot. Man, he sure didn't think too much of those girls and their high-minded fixation with Cuba. He smirked gloomily whenever they opened their mouths.

And then there was Mick. The first thing that caught your eye about Mick was his smile. He smiled carelessly, effortlessly, without provocation, and often, and when he did you could see that several of his teeth were chipped. He said his teeth had collided with a Billy club one summer in Chicago during a week-long rally he had set up with old Abbie. Nobody could afford a hotel room, so they started hanging out in some park along Lake Michigan. Pretty soon there were thousands of hippies sleeping on the grass or on top of these ratty old Mexican blankets. Some were doing it right out in the open, but the rest didn't care. And every night the cops would try to roust them. There were cops everywhere. Hundreds of cops in their shiny, silver helmets like you see on *The Jetsons*, all of them with Billy clubs and talking into their walkie-talkies and some of them were even wearing gas masks. You could tell they were preparing for a major assault, and then all of a sudden they would let loose, not everywhere, the park was too big for that, so the cops picked their spots, they would appear here and there, a flurry of spastic motion followed by furious bursts of clubbing and shouting and screaming, and every once in a while a few gunshots. You never knew when they were coming. They just sort of materialized right out of the air, like they were jumping from black helicopters and sliding down ropes in the dark. The next thing you knew people were running into the streets, looking for anywhere to hide, even a garbage can. The cops were grabbing everyone they could and throwing them into trucks and hauling them away. But there weren't enough trucks. And some of the hippies were fighting back, throwing rocks, bottles, anything they could find. But most were running for their lives and shouting "pigs are whores" and "hell no we won't go" and shit like that. You didn't know what to expect, like one night an old man carrying a Marshall Field's bag got his head caved in for jaywalking. Another time a twenty-something mother and two little kiddies were pulled from their car and hauled off to jail because the kids were saying bam, bam, bam and pointing their fingers at the cops and the mother was laughing. Cars were stopped all over the fucking place because of the riot, but none of them belonged to the hippies from the hippie camp. Then there were the camera guys from the TV news, and they were just taking pictures, trying to capture a few good shots of democracy in action for good old Walter

Cronkite, but then they were getting clubbed by the cops like everybody else, and one of them even got punched in the stomach right on national television. Then the cops let loose a couple hundred German Shepherds, and they would go right for your throat, and then somebody said there were tanks coming down Michigan Avenue. That was the coup de grâce for Mick's teeth. Mick tossed a ragged old American flag over his shoulders like a cape and raced into the street shouting "Death to the fucking Fascists!" That's when he got smacked right in the mouth with a Billy club. That's how he got his teeth chipped. He didn't say how it felt getting smacked like that. I guess maybe he didn't remember from being unconscious. But he said he made the six o'clock national news.

I think the reason why Mick smiled so much was because he was kind of proud of his chipped teeth. Just about everybody loved his smile. The two Spanish teachers were in love with him. So was practically every teenage girl in the school. But you could tell old Ed didn't love him. You could tell old Ed secretly wanted to take a Billy club of his own to Mick's teeth. But he didn't. There was something about Mick. You just couldn't say anything against him. Even the Reverend Dubois, the Dean of the Faculty, even he kind of swallowed his tongue when Mick was around, which was pretty damn odd if you think about it. Mick lived in a brown-shingled house at the beach, a confirmed bachelor during the school year. But every summer a couple of girls who had been in his Senior Honors World History class moved in with him. Two new girls every summer. But whenever this was brought up to the Reverend Dubois, however damn tactfully, his tongue would half fall out of the side of his mouth, like you see in cartoons of people getting hung, and then he would start turning a purplish blue color and the veins in his forehead and neck would start quivering uncontrollably, wriggling like tiny eels, and then he'd be waving his arms in the air in erratic, angular fashion, and strange, drowning, gurgling noises would come popping out of his mouth the whole time, like he was really, truly getting hung. You never saw anything like it in your life. But the Reverend never said a word to Mick about his rotating harem, not that anybody ever heard anyway. When I told Mick I had been born in Chicago, he invited me over.

"So, you were born in Chicago, is that right Lauterbach?"

My full name is Travis Everet Lauterbach. A lawyer's

name, maybe, I'm pretty sure that's what my parents had in mind, but not a teacher's, at least not the Travis part, which might have been the reason Mick just called me Lauterbach. It was the last week of May, one week after graduation. We were standing on the rugged bamboo bridge in the Japanese restaurant, looking down at those slaggy, lazy, diseased goldfish. The middle-aged woman wearing the silky, blue kimono was standing behind the register in the bamboo hut, but she wasn't looking at us. She was changing the register tape, her body sort of twisted awkwardly to one side to avoid getting ink on the silk. Then she clacked the little door shut and sat back on a stool. There was no one else in the restaurant. It was too early for dinner. We were the first ones there.

"Do you know what Chicago is all about?" Mick asked.

I wasn't sure. I was born there. But we had moved pretty early.

"Do you know about the Black Panthers?"

We looked up at each other. I had heard of them.

"The Chicago Seven?"

I had heard of them too. But beyond a few names I didn't know much. Mick smiled, and several chipped teeth flashed against the darkness of his mouth, and his whole being flashed against the smoky dim light from the Japanese lanterns, the softly glowing purples and blues and lavenders and oranges. I looked again at the fish, and there, suddenly, was Mick's face as well, on top of the fish, among them, now half-submerged, now rising again, wavering, a watery face looking up at me, still bright and smiling, almost laughing. "Your knowledge about your own city, my innocent Lauterbach, is sadly, fucking deficient," the watery face said. "You come out to my place tomorrow afternoon and we'll fill in the gaps."

-2-

Mick's brown-shingled beach house was at 17 Shell Street, a narrow street with cracked pavement and sandy patches and shells scattered about. The street ended at Mick's house. On the northeast corner there were a couple of scraggly, ornamental trees with flutey wind-chimes hanging from thick, brittle branches, like the outlaws in old Westerns after they've been caught and lynched. There was a small, iron gate directly out front, a rusty greenish color. The gate was attached to a partially finished stone wall that went several yards and ended in a bunch of palmetto. The front yard was covered with red cobblestone bricks, though you could see the sandy soil between the cracks, and in some places there were patches of spongey grass sprouting up. Mick also had some ferns growing out of these Pueblo Indian style clay pots, and they were all over the damn place, so you could hardly walk. If you wanted to go down to the water, there was a narrow macadam path that went from the sidewalk out front down along the side of the house and disappeared into the dunes and the sea oats and the afternoon sun shining on the sand. No matter where you were, you could hear the Atlantic smacking up against the beach.

Filling in the gaps of my knowledge about Chicago started with drinking margaritas. Mick came out almost to the gate as I was getting out of my car, bright and smiling and his chipped teeth catching the rays of the sun. Then he kicked the gate open and grabbed hold of my arm and hauled me inside. Mick was a pretty impulsive type. The margaritas were waiting on a small Formica counter with the kitchen on one side and the living room on the other. The next thing I knew I was sitting on a bar stool, my back to the counter top, a frosty strawberry margarita in my hands. Mick was standing in front of a sliding-glass door, looking out at the sun and the sea oats shimmering on the dunes in the distance. Man, you should have seen him. He was like a damn guru or something. He was wearing a striped T-shirt and baggy string shorts with the strings untied, dangling, and his scraggly old hair hanging down like it was, and he was twirling his moustache and then gulping down some of his drink and then lecturing about the travesty and absolute injustice of a culture, any damn culture, dominated by the idea of sin. Mick had a thing about sin. He didn't mention The Black Panthers or The Chicago Seven. I think he forgot why I'd come out to his house in the first place. Then again, I wasn't really listening too closely to what he was saying. He could have been saying anything. I really wasn't paying attention, if you want to know the truth. I was sitting there with this Paleolithic grin plastered across my face, drinking my drink and looking at the two recently graduated girls who were now living with Mick for the summer, and thinking some pretty raunchy, self-indulgent thoughts.

The girls were curled up on a maroon colored sofa on the other side of the living room, sipping their margaritas. They were wearing these flimsy, yellow bikinis, though with their legs pulled up off the floor and the sexy angle of their hips against the curve of the sofa, it looked like maybe they were wearing just the tops. Above them was an oil painting of a mermaid lounging about on the edge of a weather-beaten dock, a brunette with starfish and shells in her hair, and a sea gull standing on one of the posts and a couple of drunken sailors in the background leering at her. It was the kind of painting you can pick up for twenty greasy simoleons in the parking lot of an abandoned Denny's with thirty or forty Persian rugs strewn about on the asphalt and a rusted Winnebago pulled off to one side. I remember thinking how Mick's two girls looked exactly like that mermaid the way they were sitting, except for the starfish and the shells, but which had come first, the mermaid or the girls, I didn't know.

When the girls finished their drinks, they set their glasses on the floor. They were looking at Mick with an unashamed, devoted kind of awe. But Mick was still looking out at the dunes and the sun and sighing, pretty much ignoring them, talking and twirling his moustache and gulping and gesticulating wildly, like any would-be guru would. He seemed absolutely oblivious to the effect he was having. "It's nothing but fucking Fascism in a robe," he was saying. "Now you look at the indigenous peoples of South America. They don't drape their adult insecurities all over their kids. They let 'em run around naked. The boys in one group, running around with their miniature bows and arrows, chasing after green iguanas and their little wee wees dangling and they don't even know," Mick turning from the sliding-glass door and smiling his bright smile at the girls and his margarita sloshing up over the rim and onto his bare feet, "and the girls, they're too busy with their little girl stuff, making baskets and going down to the river with their mothers to fish and shit like that. And they're not thinking about the boys, not about doing it, anyway," Mick slipping into the kitchen, still blabbing away. "Not until they're older. Not until it's time to make babies," Mick drinking the last of his drink and then sliding his glass onto the counter. "And then that's what they do. They make babies. And they don't give a goddamn fucking crap who the father is or how many of their kids have different fathers, what the fuck, everybody is everybody's father, even their gods have a collective ancestry," Mick opening the refrigerator door, pulling out a pitcher, "it's all communal," then refilling his glass, nodding the pitcher at my own half-empty glass, and then at the sagging maroon sofa and the mermaids sitting there, "you want some more, Lauterbach, girls?" and then my glass appearing on the counter and Mick pouring and then the two girls appearing on either side of me, suddenly, like in *Star Trek* or something, their empty glasses next to mine and Mick still pouring and then "girls, this is a dear friend of mine, a dear friend and classroom compatriot, Lauterbach, dear, sweet, innocent Lauterbach of the Chicago Lauterbachs," the girls turning as if only then did they notice me, as if Mick's speaking my name and directing their attention had suddenly brought me to life, the two girls now smiling in imitation of Mick, wedging me in with their curt, approving nods and their flirty, vulnerable, mermaid smiles and their flimsy, loosely tied, ready-to-be untied yellow bikinis, and then the two of them laughing and blowing questions into my face and the spicy, strawberry smell of the margaritas like a fog welling up and my eyes itching and watering, so I couldn't tell who was saying what, "Hello Mr. Lauterbach are you really from Chicago Mr. Lauterbach what brought you to Florida Mr. Lauterbach say you're pretty quiet Mr. Lauterbach cat got your tongue Mr. Lauterbach we can do something about that if you like, say how old are you Mr. Lauterbach do you have a girlfriend Mr. Lauterbach would you like a girlfriend Mr. Lauterbach we're old enough Mr. Lauterbach we're way past eighteen, if that's what you were wondering Mr. Lauterbach, say what kind of name is Lauterbach anyway, where's your swimsuit Mr. Lauterbach, you did bring one didn't you or did you think did you think you could borrow one of Mick's, well Mick doesn't believe in swimsuits Mr. Lauterbach, do you Mick, and neither do neither do we," and then some dippy, giggly, girlish laughter, and then Mick was standing over by the sliding-glass door, as if he had been there the whole time, "come on you three, let's go down to the beach," and then Mick and the girls were gone and the sliding-glass door was open and a warm, salty breeze was blowing in. I left my empty margarita glass on the counter top next to the others and ran down the macadam path.

The following September we decided to limit our Japanese dinners to every other Friday. We said it was because of money.

But it wasn't. The truth is you can get pretty damn apathetic if you see the same people every single Friday. What can I say? But there were other reasons as well. One of the Spanish teachers had married a banker named Walter over the summer, and since they only had the one car, a mostly blue Chevy Citation (the two front fenders were painted black from two separate accidents), and since her husband was one of those vigorous holier-than-thou, self-motivated, nut jobs (he had been promoted to Assistant Vice-President at the age of twenty-four, an achievement which he had supposedly earned for bringing in the business of a large boat manufacturer, but which was more probably the result of his having caddied for the bank's Grand Pooh-bah when he was a boy), she had to sacrifice every other Friday and pick him up from the office. Then he would drive them both over to one of those festively decorated meet-and-greet beer bashes sponsored by the Downtowners, which was mostly a group of twenty-something, neo-Nazi bankers like Walter, with a couple of restaurant managers and a girl who had started her own nail salon thrown in for diversity, and maybe get some shrimp and pasta afterwards.

Once she brought him along, but all he could do with his sushi was move it aimlessly about his plate with the chopsticks until it was time to go. But he did make one, sort of reluctant, obviously distasteful stab at joining the conversation. During the middle of the meal he looked up somewhat uncertainly at his wife, and then at the rest of us, and then he said that he had met with the owner of some small bakery out in San Marco about lending him some money, and we shouldn't say anything just yet because he needed to get the loan approved, but boy, they sure made some pretty tasty croissants, we should try some. But he didn't get a chance to say anything else because that right there really ticked off old Ed. You see Ed had been trying to get a car loan for seven months, but they wouldn't give him one. Ed said they wanted him to fill out a truckload of these bogus personal history forms, and he did that, and then they had some more forms they forgot the first time, which you know they don't forget procedural stuff like that, and then they wanted to know did he have any kids and where could they reach his ex-wife and were his parents still living and what did they do and who should they contact in case he died, the kind of intimate, bathroom revelations nobody has a right to demand, and, well, right there, Ed decided he'd had enough of all the rigmarole, it didn't look like they were going to give him the money anyway, so he dumped the whole mess of forms in a metal wastepaper basket and lit a match and watched his car loan burn right there in the bank. That's what he told us happened. Sometimes Ed was a damn lunatic. He sure didn't have any use for banks.

"Is that what you do, then," he asked the young banker husband. You just knew Ed had been waiting since he sat down to light into the guy, and drinking Takara Sake while he waited. His face seemed red and swollen. "You go around eating fucking croissants and if you like them you go give the guy some money. Fuck. That's fucked."

Then Ed got up slowly, rubbing his bow-legged, ex-marine legs to work out the cramps from sitting on pillows for so long, and then he stood there a moment, sort of teetering, looking down at the table and a second bottle of Sake the waitress had just brought out and the clump of uneaten sushi on Walter's plate and him pushing it around some more, and then not pushing it.

You could see in Ed's eyes the fierce, unthinking, animal viciousness of his Vietnam years coming back. We all thought for sure he was going to pick up the inarticulate, young banker and hurl the poor, dippy bastard head first into the glass-case counter out front by the pond. But he didn't. He said "just fuck it" a couple of times, but under his breath, as if he were suddenly embarrassed. Then he swooped up the waiting bottle of Sake and carried it off to the bar in the back and plopped himself down on a stool, and there the smoky, orangeish light of half-a-dozen Japanese lanterns descended upon him, gloomily.

No one said a word in the suddenness of this angry departure, or for many minutes afterwards. Then Mick started twirling his moustache, and then he smiled his careless, bright, mischievous smile, and his tiny pale blue eyes had this drunken sailor's glint to them. He pointed out that such raging outbursts were not uncommon in vets suffering from posttraumatic paralysis of the brain, which was clearly Ed's problem, and this sparked some embarrassed laughter, and then a feverish, pretty juvenile debate about the actual causes of such a malady, how many deaths you had to see and torturings and such, and if your childhood mattered, and really, what in the world had happened to Ed in the city of Da Nang anyway, which was the only place we had ever heard him mention, it must have been horrible. Even the newly married Spanish teacher wanted to root out the cause of Ed's distemper, and then, maybe, she said, we can cure him. Of course her banker husband didn't offer an opinion. He had succumbed once again to the aimless misery of maneuvering his sushi about his plate. Every so often he looked at his watch. When it was finally time to go, he took off two steps in front of his wife. He left without even a look at the goldfish.

That was it for excitement as far as our dinners went until Mick invited a couple of students to join us, a couple of wiggly, brainless girls, kind of like the two mermaid look-alikes who had been living with Mick the summer before and who had moved out in August to go north to school, or maybe west. Mick was never absolutely clear about where.

So there we were sitting on the bench up against the wall opposite the cash register. Me, the two Spanish teachers, and Ed. It was early October and warm enough outside so you didn't even need a sweater. Mick marched in wearing rope sandals and shorts and the hair on his legs beaded with sweat. He wore a fraying poncho out of old Mexico with blue and yellow and orange stripes instead of a shirt, and a straw hat with a string. He stomped over the bamboo bridge, his tiny blue eyes bouncing up to the rim of his hat and then down. The two girls bounced after him, looking with these dippy looks at the goldfish as they crossed and then looking away somewhat abruptly, like they had never seen diseased fish before. They were wearing jeans and plain cotton shirts. Modest shirts. Tucked-in shirts with black belts around their waists. Their names were Laurie and Sonya. I figured they were auditioning for next summer. I was somewhat surprised they weren't wearing bikinis.

"Buenas tardes, señoritas, muchachos," Mick said. *"Viva la revolución! Viva la revolucionario!"*

Laughing as if he hadn't a care in the world, he stopped in front of the bench and looked down at the four of us still sitting there silent and bewildered in the glint of his pleasant buffoonery. "What the hell are you people waiting for?" he said. "Let's eat some raw fish."

All through dinner I stared secretly at Laurie and Sonya, but I wasn't really looking at them. I was looking through them, back to that day at Mick's from the spring before. We had been all afternoon on the beach. It was a perfect day. The water was a bright, sparkling blue, like you see in postcards. There was a clothesline strung up between two poles and we played volleyball, boys against girls. Mick had a thing about boys against girls. He had been alternately savage and then charming, but in a playful, campy, theatrical way, spiking the ball at their smooth, girlish knees and watching them flop down in the sand, giggling, their flimsy tops slipping, and then Mick rushing to their aid if they took too long getting up, which they almost always did, and him apologizing, smiling softly, shyly, trying to help them with their straps, the sunlight bouncing off their nipples, but them pushing him away as they got to their feet, but they were still giggling. I couldn't believe what I was seeing. It was pretty erotic, like a pornographic version of *Beach Blanket Bingo.*

Later, when they were paddling around on a couple of dolphin floats, he ran up to the house and came back with some more margaritas. He waded into the water and they were laughing at him and calling him 'Grandpa Joe,' but in a cute way, and they grabbed the drinks and drank from a sitting, half-sinking position, and when they were done Mick tipped them over and it was his turn to laugh, and then he fled to the safety of the towels on the beach, which is where I had been since the volleyball because I didn't have a swimsuit.

"Ain't those two something, Lauterbach," he said, and there was an invigorating, trembling admiration in his voice. "You should get yourself a couple."

Then he sat there a while watching them. Like he was standing outside of time or something. I couldn't help thinking about what he said. I mean I'd only had two dates since coming down to Jacksonville. But you had to wonder what he was doing with a couple of giggly teenagers. He was over three times their age, which you have to admit sounds pretty damn suspicious, a little too much like something out of the pages of *Lolita.* But maybe it was the rest of us poor, dippy bastards that didn't get it. I mean both those girls were over eighteen, and they didn't have any trouble with him. They seemed happy enough. Maybe you couldn't really be happy until you gave in to your animal side. Maybe happiness wasn't something you thought about. You just had to experience it, instinctively. You ate when you were hungry and you slept when you were tired and you did it with girls whenever you could and you didn't worry about it later because it was all just a matter of animal magnetism anyway, and if it was warm enough you didn't wear any clothes, like those South American kids Mick knew about. Maybe if you thought about your own happiness at all, you couldn't ever really be happy, which I guess would mean that everything they said about God and self-sacrifice and the good of the country was just a lot of damn hype.

Then Mick had laughed and raced back into the noisy, splashing surf, and there was some shouting and the voices getting mixed together, and a couple of yellow bikini tops came flying off and they got mixed in with the spray and all you could see were naked arms and naked legs, and just like that I decided to go for a walk.

I started walking along the beach. I was headed in a generally southerly direction. After a while, the houses along the water gave way to a boardwalk with an arcade every two blocks and hotdog stands and souvenir shops and kids slurping down ice cream, and in the distance I could see the shimmering cloud of a couple of hotels, like an oasis in the desert. I was thinking it looked a little like paradise, not the kind Mick had, but the way you see it in those MasterCard commercials and you're sitting in a lounge chair beneath some palm trees, some exotic island somewhere in the Caribbean or the South China Sea, only with fake coconuts all over the place (it is a commercial after all), and then a waiter in a tuxedo comes with one of those ice cream drinks with a blue parasol and he smiles and you smile back and you slap your plastic on the tray and off he goes. That's what I was thinking, but when I got to the hotels, it was already turning dark, and the hotels didn't seem quite so shimmery, and I didn't even have a gas credit card, so I turned around and headed north. By the time I got back to Mick's place, Mick and the girls had gone up, but I didn't blame them. It had been a long day. I don't know how late it was, but it must have been pretty late because the house was dark.

They must have thought I'd come back sooner or later because the sliding-glass door was open. But I didn't go in. I just stood there in the dark, listening to the wind chimes when the breeze came up and the silence when there was nothing but the dark, shimmering heat, and then I thought I heard Mick murmuring something and the girls murmuring back. I listened to their voices for a while. Then I went around to the front and got in my car and drove home.

-3-

It's hard to believe I had only two dates that first year down in Jacksonville. It sure does sound terrible, like I'm disfigured or speak with a lisp or have lice. But the truth is I don't know why. August to April of that first year was a steamy, rainy, suffocating blur of dippy, school-kid faces looking at me to teach them something they didn't already know and lost homework by the truckload and weekly chapel services in that television evangelist style auditorium and the goldfish at the Japanese restaurant and the bright smile of Mick and the gloominess of Ed and the bubbly, sensitive, relentless vulnerability of the two Spanish teachers. I can't even put the months in order.

But then it was April and the blur of those first months was gone, and there I was out on this date, which I guess you'd have to call it a date since there was just the two of us, but I have to tell you it was pretty much a fiasco from the word go. I don't remember the girl's name. Maybe I didn't even know it to begin with. I sometimes have problems with names.

I met her by accident late one Saturday afternoon down at the Jacksonville Landing. I was looking at the murky, dark blue river and the blue bridge that went across, and there were four or five dolphins jetting along, making their way back to the Atlantic, and the way they were going through the water, first two arcing up into the air and their wet milky-gray skin flashing in the sunlight and the spray and then both of them splashing down, and then two more and then one more and then back again to two, well, it wasn't at all like you see in the tourist shows with the dolphins jumping through red plastic hula hoops and ringing a bell twenty feet above the surface of the pool and the tourists thinking they're getting a privileged glimpse of this sandy, sunny, palm-covered mecca called Florida. It was just unadulterated, unthinking, relentless joy out there in the river. You couldn't help but watch. Then the dolphins were gone and I pushed back from the green iron railing and whammed right back into this girl. She sort of flipped back from the physics of it and landed on her rear guard, and two of the bags she was carrying spilled out all over the boardwalk, but the third bag sort of flipped itself up over the railing and spilled itself into the river. I guess maybe she hadn't seen me standing there. I guess maybe she had too many bags in her way.

I helped her pick up the bags from the boardwalk, and then we were both standing at the railing, looking helplessly at the third bag floating on the surface, slowly filling with water, and beneath the bag you could see the boxes or packages that had spilled out, a shadowy brownish blur in the blueish-brownish water, making its way towards the bottom. There wasn't anything we could do. It was really pretty scummy where the water came up to the boardwalk and the brown foamy bubbles smearing the cement and the brownish-green algae that grows there, which meant you knew there was no use trying to climb down and salvage a damn thing. We stepped back from the railing, and you could see she wasn't happy, so I apologized and offered to buy her back everything she'd lost. She accepted my offer, but she still wasn't smiling, but later, after she had a brand new third bag in her hands, and after I had apologized a second time and told her my name was Travis, after all that she was smiling like she hadn't lost a thing.

I must have been absolutely out-of-my-mind possessed. She had this toothy sort of gummy horse-mouthed kind of smile, and she wasn't a whole lot better with her mouth shut, but all the same the next thing I knew we were going out on a date. We drove in separate cars because she had hers from shopping. She gave me directions where to meet her, and she was in a desperate, almost lunging kind of hurry, like we should have been there already, which should have been my first clue. My second clue should have been where we went, which was a country and western bar, the kind just off the highway with a big red neon cowboy boot dancing out front and lights blinking all around. The sun was just beginning to set and the parking lot was almost full. Everybody there was wearing designer boots and Stetsons and silky shirts studded with rhinestones, except me, and there was smoke all over the place so it was difficult to see, which meant you were always getting bumped, except where the DJ sat, but he was behind some Plexiglass. The main drinks were beer and whiskey, which I didn't mind so much, not at all in fact. We listened to some old Waylon Jennings songs while we drank, and then some Tammy Wynette, and then a bunch of others I'd never heard of, which after you've been drinking beer and whiskey a while you can hardly tell the difference. I drank a goddamn truckload of beer and whiskey, which made the waitresses pretty happy. Then the DJ said he was putting on a new somebody called Travis something, and we listened to some song about a girl in a pick-up truck driving to Durango, and all the while we were listening, this girl I'd whammed into at the river was squealing and squeezing my arm, and her fingernails dug in so hard she gave me a couple of scars. I figured this Travis guy was maybe why she had wanted to go out with me in the first place. That's how it seemed to me, anyway, after the Durango song and my date had gone off to the Little Cowgirls room to powder her nose. I was standing along a rail that overlooked the dance floor of that smoky barn. I was just standing there rubbing my sore arm and wondering how many other guys my date had lured to this spot. Maybe she figured since my name was Travis, I had a country and western fetish just like her. How else could it be with a name like Travis? I bet that's what she thought. People are always trying to squeeze you into their own personal fictions.

I never saw her again after that. I left her at the bar. They started doing some line dancing, and she was right there in the middle of the dance floor with the rest, about a hundred counterfeit cowboys and cowgirls with their happy horse faces and their too-happy rodeo smiles and their silk shirts studded with sequins and their designer boots clomping all over the parquet. If you've ever seen wild horses going loco, stomping around a corral and snorting and kicking up dust, which maybe you've only seen it in television westerns like me, well that's what it looked like. I paid for one last beer, but as soon as the waitress came I changed my mind. I left the beer on the rail and pushed my way through the smoke and didn't look back. Only once on the way home did I even think about leaving that girl like that, but it wasn't a big deal, I told myself. She had her own car. She was probably a lot happier without me.

The next date I had was on another Saturday, one month later. It wasn't as bad as the first, but that's not saying a whole lot. To begin with, it was arranged by the two Spanish teachers. The one who was eventually going to marry the banker, her name was Emily Lavigne, she thought it would be a good idea if I went out with the other Spanish teacher, Tommie Rodriguez. It was a Tuesday when I found out about the whole thing. The Tuesday before the Saturday. It was already extremely hot, in the nineties, which isn't all that unusual for

Florida in May. But it was pretty damn hot for me. I was sitting in the teacher's lounge in a ratty, old lounge chair someone had dug out of their grandmother's garage; it was cloth-covered, a dirty pinkish color with the fuzz beading up. A couple of other teachers were sitting at the glossy, greenish Formica-topped work table on the other side of the room. One was Janet Rainey, a shriveled-up raisin of a woman, from too much sun, who taught Religion part time, and who snapped her teeth like a cancer-stricken Doberman whenever you said or did something she didn't like. The other was Harvey Collins, an aging, too-fleshy math teacher with age spots on his wrists and neck, and stringy, white hair that he combed ear to ear. Harvey had the reputation, whether he deserved it or not, for pinching unsuspecting female behinds whenever he was waiting in a grocery checkout line or roaming around a Laundromat, waiting for a machine to open up. He was supposedly able to do this even with his arms full of milk and razor blades and cans of Campbell's Soup, or even a basket of dirty laundry and a box of Tide. Supposedly, Harvey only went after the really curvy ones.

So I was just sitting there. I had pushed the chair up against the air conditioner, which had been working when I came in, but then it had sputtered and whined and there was a shudder and it had started blowing dust and then it had stopped working altogether. Harvey Collins looked up and said something I didn't hear and then laughed. Janet Rainey didn't look up at all. I was still sitting there, half-glancing at a couple of memos and half-looking out the window and the glimmering, suffocating heat outside. I was just beginning to perspire when Emily Lavigne came in.

"Travis, Travis, Travis," she said. "What in the world have you been doing with yourself?"

She was wearing a clingy, yellow sweater dress, and when you looked at her you couldn't help but think about peeling bananas. She sat down on the arm of the chair.

"Travis, you are impossible, my dear," she said. "We've been looking for you everywhere!"

"What?"

"We tried calling you last night. Where were you? And then you didn't show up for first hour. Travis, Travis."

"I was late."

"You're a very naughty boy," she said.

Then Emily scooted herself a little bit closer, even as she

looked away towards the work table. I just stared at her. If she had scooted any closer she would have been in my lap, which I have to admit I wouldn't have minded. I could see little bits of pinkish fuzz stuck to her dress from the chair. I thought that in spite of her upcoming marriage to the neo-Nazi banker Walter Dooley, she was still very much a girl. What did she see in Walter Dooley anyway?

"We decided it was time you and Tommie went out."

"Who decided?" I said.

"Why, Tommie and I," she said.

I started to feel dizzy with that, even though I was just sitting there, and it seemed like the world was losing its color, like a photograph that has been overexposed. For a moment it was like I was somebody else.

"Oh don't worry, Travis. She likes you just as much as you like her. It's written all over her face. We thought we'd all go somewhere on Saturday night. You know. You and Tommie and me and Walter."

There was very little I could say against the bubbly, self-assured almost blinding brightness of Emily Lavigne, with her shimmering, dark brown hair flopping about her head as she spoke, and her flirty, familiar, gesturing eyes. But I gave it a try, one try, to be precise. I guess maybe her pounding away at me like that was a little more than I could take. In spite of the way she looked. I mean it didn't matter what a woman looked like if she didn't leave you alone. It kind of felt like getting slugged in the nose.

"Will you tell Tommie I can't make it?" I said.

"I most certainly will not."

"Why not?"

"Because you are being absolutely, unforgivably absurd, Travis Lauterbach. For eight months now we've been going to that dull, chintzy little Japanese restaurant of Mick's, and for eight months you've been mooning uncontrollably over that girl, and she's been behaving the same way about you. My God, the two of you can't even have a decent conversation you're both so thunderstruck, and it's been that way since the day you met. You almost passed out when the Dean introduced us to the faculty, if you remember, and it wasn't from the heat. I keep expecting one of you or both of you to jump in the river. I don't know which would make me happier."

Then Janet Rainey spoke up from the work table. She

spoke with a kind of veiled contempt, without inflection, without even her lips moving. At least that's how it looked.

"Would you two kindly be quiet," she said. "People are trying to work."

"Lighten up there, Janet. You be quiet yourself," said Harvey Collins. He had probably stopped working when Emily came in. He had probably been thinking for the last five minutes about Emily and grocery store checkout lines or Laundromats. "Go on there, Travis. Go out with the girl for God's sake. She's just a little bitty thing. She won't bite your head off like this one here," and he nodded at Janet.

This was followed by a moment of embarrassed silence. At least I was embarrassed. It was a pretty rude thing to say. And then I was thinking that Emily couldn't possibly have been right about Tommie Rodriguez and me. If I had been mooning over anyone, I said to myself, it would have been sweet Emily herself. She was the pretty one. Or prettier. Then Harvey and Janet returned to their work, and Emily was giving me a stern, dark probing look, as if she had guessed by my silence what I was thinking. She was pretty even in her displeasure. Then the look vanished and Emily nodded politely, a curt but categorical nod, and smiled.

"Well, then," she said. "It's all settled."

"Sure," I said. "It's settled."

"We'll pick you up at seven-thirty, give or take. Walter is driving, so you won't have to worry about a thing."

The next thing I knew I was going out with Tommie Rodriguez. She was my second date. And when Saturday came we went bowling. Me and Tommie and Emily and Walter. I don't know who the hell picked bowling. Probably Walter. We were all pretty rotten bowlers, but Walter was the worst. I think maybe he was looking for a little sympathy from Emily because of them having to go out with me and Tommie. But he didn't get any. But you could tell he sure wanted to be somewhere else from the minute they picked me up, him and Emily driving up in their black and blue Chevy Citation, sitting stiffly in the front seat like they'd just had an argument, Emily then turning to the window as I hurried out to the car, glistening and red-eyed and you could see the streaks on her face but she was smiling bravely anyway and out popped a "Hello Travis sweetie," and then me getting in and the dark shadow of Walter hunched over the wheel, sullen and composed and superior.

"Well, well, if it isn't Travis Lauterbach," he said. "I wouldn't have known you." Then he hit the gas, barely giving me time to shut the door.

Maybe Walter thought if he was going to be miserable he might as well make everybody else miserable too. He didn't say boo the rest of the night except to order watery rum and Cokes from the bowling alley waitress and make rude comments whenever one of us threw a gutter ball, which seemed inevitable every time one of us stepped to the line. But the girls pretty much ignored him. They talked for a while about Cuba, and then they started rambling on about their own personal shortcomings as far as bringing food to the poor and building homes for the homeless. Yes, of course they'd done some good. A group of them had flown down to Havana during Easter break, that was a good thing, wasn't it? They had brought canned goods, pineapples and beans mostly, which is kind of funny if you think about it because the place is loaded with pineapples and beans without the cans, but they also brought some Campbell's Chicken Soup, which I guess you can't get there, and some Easter chocolate for the children. They had built fourteen houses, each house with a fence, but then again they weren't so sure if the people were better off. One of those poor Cubans had tried to climb aboard their plane when they were leaving, his daughter supposedly lived in Miami, but he had been discovered by the police and they had cuffed him and taken him away. The rumor was he had been dragged behind one of those portable airport latrines and shot and then stuffed in a garbage bag. Emily and Tommie didn't know for sure. Nobody knew anything for sure. The truth was maybe nobody wanted to know, that's what Tommie said. What was the good of building houses if it ended up they didn't want to live in them, and what good was flying down there for a week or two if it meant that somebody would get killed?

I tried to break into their conversation a couple of times, but since I'd never been to Cuba, to build houses in Havana or for any other reason, I couldn't very well share in their misery. And I sure as hell didn't want to share in Walter's misery. He was sitting behind me and the girls, sitting stiffly, brazenly, like he was glued to the aquamarine molded-plastic bowler's bench, still trying to make his discomfort known, glaring icily at the lanes. He was a goddamn nut job if you asked me. I could have socked him a good one. I could have maybe broken his nose.

I mean I was almost angry enough to do it. But that wouldn't have looked too good with Tommie and Emily there.

So I drank bottled beer and bowled gutter balls and watched the two girls bowling and watched their curvy, unsuspecting, Harvey-Collins-type behinds, which almost made up for the rest of it. But I know if I had gone in my own car, I would have left just like the first time.

Emily Lavigne fixed me up one more time after that, but that was after I started going to Mick's house. It was in the middle of October during my second year. It was with the sister of one of Walter's friends, and it's funny, but I don't remember her name either. She was wearing so much blue eye shadow she kind of looked like a drunken, demented raccoon. And she had on this chintzy white blouse with ruffles, like maybe she had always dreamed of being a go-go girl and now was her chance. She was also wearing a pair of silver stilettos with a spiral loop that wrapped around her ankles, which meant she had trouble walking three feet without grabbing onto something, and a pair of designer jeans with glittery rhinestones down the sides, but the jeans were a little too tight so the rhinestones looked like rivets about to pop.

First we went out to dinner. Then we saw a movie I don't remember. Then we ended up at some glitzy night club in the corner of a grocery store parking lot. The place was overloaded with hype. The building was a square, cement block with a narrow strip of sidewalk along two sides, but there were strings of blinking lights hanging down from the roof, yellow and purple and green, to jazz it up, and a couple of fake palm trees just inside the door. A heavy-set bearded guy in a blue Hawaiian shirt was letting the girls go in for free, but he made me cough up a ten-dollar cover.

I think they called it The Paradise Club, or something exotic like that, but for ten dollars it didn't come even close. Everywhere you looked you saw guys in pin-striped shirts and khakis or jeans standing in fours and fives and these overly boisterous grins on their faces and talking big and extra loud and drinking frosty banana daiquiris, and there were girls flitting from group to group and accidentally bumping their hips up against these grinning big-talkers and giggling when they did it and the guys looking at each other and smirking and their boisterous grins becoming more boisterous, if you can believe that, like you wouldn't think a face could normally stretch that far, and then they were buying the girls drinks, and then the girls would be flitting off to somewhere else. Man, everybody in that place was drinking like mad.

As soon as we got to the bar, my date waved at a couple of the big-grinners, you could tell she knew them, and they came over and then they all started talking. I ordered a couple of beers and fished out a twenty and paid the man, and then I started looking around. I have to say I was pretty bored. They were playing some early Elvis Costello or something, but nobody was dancing. They had the stage set up for a Midnight Karaoke Contest with red and blue floodlights lit up so you couldn't see the audience, and a couple of bar stools for the singers and a couple of glittery microphones with long black cords, like the kind you see on reruns of *Star Search*. Any minute I was expecting Ed McMahon himself to come waltzing out and start the show. Not the older Ed McMahon who lost a fortune trying to prop up his wife's clothing company, but the younger one who kept bouncing around the country with that million-dollar check. But nothing happened right away, so I finished my beer and ordered another. My date was still talking with the two big-grinners, and I remember thinking if she ever did want another beer, they could be the ones to buy it. First they were talking about college and how they had cheated on this exam or that one and who they'd been going out with, and then it was about going down to Key West for a week at some place called the Blue Parrot, or maybe jetting off to Cancun, they were going to have a real good time. They had the kind of faces you wanted to just haul off and hit. You knew it was bound to happen one day. Simpering, snub-nosed baboon faces with fat red cheeks and fat, glittery eyes sort of just stuck there. It made you sick just to look at them.

Then the karaoke contest started. I couldn't see who it was very well on account of the floodlights, but you had to say the guy was absolutely terrible. I mean with his croaky old voice it sounded like he was drowning in radio static. But then the simpering, snub-nosed baboon faces started laughing, and one of them said they should toss the drunken jerk in the dumpster with the rest of the night's garbage and put a girl on instead, which it kind of ticked me off he said that. Not so much because of what he said. I mean his sense of the aesthetic was absolutely dead on the mark. I guess I just didn't like the way he said it, like they were having the damn karaoke contest just so he could screw up his simpering baboon face and make rude comments about the contestants.

So I was thinking what to say to him, because you really should try and talk with these big-grinning bastards before you go breaking their noses, but I couldn't think of a thing to say. Then I felt my fingers curling up and my arm pulling back, and I swear I was just about to let one fly, when a hell of a scramble broke out on the karaoke stage, and my arm relaxed. You wouldn't have believed it. The guy on the stage wouldn't leave. He was standing there, still croaking out his song, and when they tried to usher him off politely, he grabbed hold of the cord and swung the microphone at them. He was actually kind of whipping it around like he was in a god damn kung-fu movie or something. Then some dippy drunk leaned in too close and got clobbered on the forehead, and then everybody rolled back from the stage. You never saw a space clear out so fast. It was like Charlton Heston rolling back the Red Sea. And right there in the middle of all that emptiness and the red and blue floodlights and the sound of that microphone whipping around, well, like I said before, you wouldn't have believed it. It was surreal. I could hardly believe it myself. It was good old ex-Marine Ed standing there on the stage.

You could see plain enough he was drunk. The way he was swinging that microphone around and there wasn't anybody even near him. I don't think he even knew where he was. He probably thought he was back in Da Nang. He was probably looking out on a sea of Viet Cong faces. Then these three bouncers rushed him from behind, and poor old Ed, he couldn't do a thing. Bouncers are always these big, truculent nut jobs, six-foot-six and three hundred pounds and always they started out playing linebacker in the NFL and then they got kicked out for knifing some guy at the bottom of the pile and ended up in prison, and when they got out they became bouncers. One of them was the bearded guy from the door, and he had Ed in a Chinese choke hold. Another nearly ripped off Ed's arm to get that microphone. Then the third came around and gave Ed a swift chop in the stomach, I guess because there was nothing else left to do. It was damn cowardly, if you ask me, but you should have heard those snub-noses cheer when he did it. You could tell they wanted to get in on the action. Then the bouncers dragged Ed from the stage, but only a couple of steps at a time, because Ed still didn't want to go. Then he got one of his arms free and started swinging it, but he couldn't connect, and the bouncers kept grabbing hold of that arm, but old Ed kept shaking it loose, which was probably because of his all-purpose, martial-arts, jungle marine training.

Of course the whole time they were grappling with Ed they were closing in on those palm trees and the front door, and you knew they were going to toss him out. All the big-grinners in the place were cheering like mad, waiting for it to happen. But not me. I got to the door first, and I was trying to tell those bouncers I knew the guy and if they let him alone it would be all right, he was suffering from a paralyzed brain, but they just pushed me back.

Then Ed finally did connect, and it was one hell of a punch for being smothered by all those grappling-hook arms. Hell, it would have been a hell of a punch if he had been standing by himself. But it didn't land where he wanted it to. Ed connected with one of those fake palm trees instead, which I guess were probably made of cement, and he pretty much quieted down after that. It was like all the rage and persecution he had felt a moment before had been sucked out of him. To tell you the truth, I think he must have broken his hand. Then one of the bouncers held open the door and they threw Ed out and everybody cheered and laughed, and some even clapped. Poor old Ed, he must have sailed fifteen feet through the air. Then they turned on me, the bouncers, all three of them. I guess I was still trying to tell them Ed would be all right if only they left him alone.

"We'll leave him alone all right," they said. "We'll leave him alone right on his fucking ass."

They all seemed pretty pissed.

Then the cowardly bouncer, the one who had chopped Ed in the stomach, said I had better watch myself or they'd toss me out just like Ed. It was actually kind of funny because you could hardly understand a word he was saying the way he mumbled. It was like listening to the way they talk in those old 1930s Popeye cartoons. Then I guess I must have said something about that cartoonish resemblance because the next thing I knew I was sailing out the door myself.

I landed on the sidewalk, maybe two feet from Ed, but I don't think he noticed. He sure didn't look up. He was just sitting there on the curb, not moving, holding his broken hand up close to his chest, and with the other he was picking at bits of glass stuck in the pavement. You could see he was still pretty drunk. The act of getting tossed hadn't sobered him up any. But there was really nothing else to do but sit there with him. Even with a broken hand you wouldn't want to startle old Ed. If he didn't know you were there you just left him alone. I mean it took three damn bouncers to throw him out. So we sat there. The lights from The Paradise Club were blinking yellow and purple and green, and we just sat there. A couple of cars pulled up and a cab and they let some people out and drove off, and we sat there, still.

Then Ed looked over at me and broke into a sort of gloomy, maniacal grin. I think he had just realized it was me sitting there across from him.

"You all right Ed?"

He grunted something. "Yeah, I'm all right," he said. He stopped picking at the glass and held onto his broken hand. "Are you all right? How about you, Travis fucking Lauterbach? Are you all right?"

"Sure, Ed. I'm all right."

"Well me too. I never felt any better in my goddamn life."

I'll tell you one thing about old Ed, he could be a raging lunatic at times. There I was sitting on the curb outside a grocery store parking lot nightclub at one o'clock in the morning and thinking maybe he might all of a sudden forget it was me sitting there and smack me like he did that fake palm tree. Even if I didn't do anything he might smack me, right? But he didn't. He got real quiet for a while, like he was embarrassed, and I was thinking he sure embarrassed himself a lot. Then he started telling me about Vietnam, which I guess had something to do with him getting thrown out of The Paradise Club. Maybe once he had this idea about paradise, and he'd been looking for it, and maybe he thought Vietnam was going to be it. I mean before he got there. I mean Vietnam's pretty hot and there are jungles and beaches and the South China Sea, which is paradise to some people. But when he got there it wasn't like he had thought, which it almost never is. Maybe.

"I'll tell you something about Vietnam, Travis," he said. "Vietnam was one fucked-up place to be. Maybe not as fucked-up as here," and then he laughed. "But it sure was fucked. It was a goddamn cluster-fuck. You really didn't know what the fuck you were doing. You just did it. I remember one time they dropped us in the middle of the jungle, I don't know where exactly. It was south of Da Nang, I know that much. But I don't know how far. They flew us in one night, and then they flew in some trucks and graders and bulldozers and told us to build some roads. Now you tell me where in the fuck were we going to build roads to? But that's what they wanted. But the truth was you couldn't build roads there anyway. It was too damn hot, for one thing. We'd cut a path through the trees and pour concrete at night, but it was still too damn hot, you could see it in the morning, the road, bubbling up in places, all over, hell, it looked like some drunken bastard had poured some goddamn pancake batter all over the fucking ground. And then there was the rain, and maybe we had us a couple hundred yards of road, but the rain would wash it away, piece by fucking piece, and then you'd be standing in water up to your waist and the whole fucking jungle looking like one big VC bathtub that had been blown to bits, and after the rain there was the mud, and that was the worst, like the plagues of fucking Egypt, that goddamn mud could suck you under faster than anything, cows, dogs, trucks, marines. I heard it got a Lieutenant Colonel once, which would have been all right by me. And on top of all that shit you had the fucking Viet Cong trying to blow your ass to hell. They said it was a secure area, but every fucking night the VC would lob in a few mortars. If that's secure I'm the goddamn fucking Pope, but what were you going to do, somebody wanted a goddamn road in the middle of the jungle, so that's what we set out to do, and to keep us happy they'd send in some girls every couple of weeks, and then there'd be a lot of fucking and drinking beer, but there were never enough girls to go around, so you had to wait your turn, and some of the guys didn't like that, and some of the guys didn't want to stop once they started. I remember this one guy, he had this pretty little piece by the ass, she was strutting around in this blue silk bathrobe with the flaps wide open and a pair of cowgirl boots with white fur, and he was fucking the hell out of her from behind and that blue silk bathrobe was flapping and she was laughing some and then moaning, and then just like that she said her time was up, she had another appointment, and then she was gone, but this guy, that really pissed him off. He picked up his M-16 and followed her, and he didn't see which hooch it was exactly, but he started firing anyway, and he kept on firing till that goddamn rifle jammed, fucking M-16s were a piece of shit, and when the MP's came for him he was swinging that M-16 like a club. But that's the way it was, Travis. It was fucked-up."

Then he stopped talking. The Paradise Club closed at two, but I guess the karaoke contest was over because people were already spilling out into the night, mostly big-grinners in pin-stripes, but some girls, too. I thought about my date and wondered if she knew I'd been tossed and if she cared and if she had done any karaoke or just watched and if maybe she had thrown me over for one of those two snub-noses. I didn't care if she had. I figured by then they had probably bought her a truckload of beer, which meant that they were the ones who had to drive her home.

"Come on, Ed. Let's get going." I grabbed hold underneath his shoulders. He was pretty heavy. He was a lot heavier than he looked. "Come on you drunk."

Ed grunted something, but he didn't resist when I helped him up. I probably would have asked him where he had parked, since he lives out by the airport, but he was basically inert. So I lugged him over to my car and shoved him into the back. He sort of flopped over head first, and then he lay there on the seat, a lunatic grin pasted on his face. Then I got in the front and turned the key and gunned us out of the lot.

-4-

By the first week in November that second year I had become a native Floridian, at least in my appreciation of subtle changes in the weather. I could smell a faint, salty coolness in the air, and I remembered thinking that the year before I hadn't noticed any change, the whole of Florida had been one suffocating, steamy, brownish-greenish, sultry eternal summer. But there it was now, the coolness, and a sense that life was about to change, my life, perhaps. The feeling was pretty damn invigorating.

We were at the Japanese restaurant as usual. Mick and I were sitting on one side of the table and Laurie and Sonya were on the other side. They were both taking Mick's World History class, and they were both still living with their parents. I remember wondering if they were still auditioning or if they had already passed. Tommie Rodriguez was stuffed unhappily in between them. Emily wasn't there and neither was Ed. Emily had gone with Walter to some tennis tournament out in Ponte Vedra, or maybe it was golf, and Ed had gone home early. He said his hand was hurting from the cast, like he just wanted to chew himself free, that's how bad the pain was. Not even a bottle of Sake had helped. He said he was going to go home and drink till he passed out.

"So you had a good time, then," Mick was saying.

He had just opened a second bottle of Kirin beer.

"Sure we did."

It was Sonya. She was wearing a pale blue lambswool sweater, and her shoulders were turned slightly towards Tommie as she spoke, it looked sort of like they were mirror images of each other, but her eyes were squarely on me and there was nothing I could do. With the soft, smoky light of the lavender Japanese lantern on her, illuminating her, highlighting her youthful, unconscious beauty, and the way she was showing herself off, it looked like she was up on a stage.

"But I know if there'd been more of us along, it would have been a lot more fun," Sonya said.

"Sure," I said. I looked over at Mick but he just ignored me. "Where was it you two went exactly?"

"Oh, Mr. Lauterbach, you weren't listening."

It was the other one, Laurie. She had this bubble gum bounciness with her blond ponytail and the flash of a pink ribbon and a pink Minnie Mouse sweatshirt that was just a little too tight and an un-Disney-like button that said Kiss Me Mickey, I'm a Mouseketeer. I wondered just how many Mickeys she had kissed, and how many Micks.

"We went on a tour of some college."

"She never would have got back without me," Sonya said.

"Oh, good God! That's not true. I just wasn't ready to go home when she said."

"She means she wasn't ready to pass on all the free beer."

"Well I do like beer. So do you. Why I bet even Miss Rodriguez has a beer every once in a while. Do you Miss Rodriguez? Do you have a beer every now and then?"

"You would have been sick yourself just to see how much she drank," Sonya said. "And then she passed out and I dumped her in the car and drove home."

"Touché!" Mick said, finishing off half of his Kirin and

looking me square in the eye. "That's what friends are for. Isn't that so Lauterbach?"

"Is that what you think, Mr. Lauterbach?" Laurie asked.

"Sure he does. Mr. Lauterbach's a genuine sweetie."

"Would you have done the same thing as Sonya?" said Laurie. "Would you have dumped me like that in the back seat of your car and then taken me home?"

"Sure he would have," Sonya said. "And then he would have dumped you on your own front lawn."

"Is that what you'd do, Lauterbach?" Mick said. "Who the hell taught you about driving a girl home?"

"Me? No one taught me."

"Man, I can see that."

"Don't let them get to you, Travis," said Tommie. "All you need is some practice."

"Well now," Mick said. "I do believe the young lady is making a pass at you." Then a leering, drunken sailor's glint came to his eyes and he started twirling his moustache and then he started to grin. "Yes, it is most definitely a pass. Ah, my friend. My poor, dear, lonely, Travis Lauterbach. He will go off with this Tommie Rodriguez and then he will be lost to us *por siempre y para siempre,*" him picking up his half-empty bottle of Kirin, "of course he will be missed," looking at the beer inside, "*Si,*" looking at us through the glass of the bottle, "*nadie sabe lo que vale el agua hasta que falta,*" and then back at the beer, swirling it around, "but we will not grieve, for this Tommie Rodriguez is a very pretty girl, deliciously pretty, why, if it were not for our dear friend Travis Lauterbach, we would have a go at her ourselves." Mick polished off the rest of the bottle and set it deliberately, delicately on the table. "*Este, tambien, es paraíso, eh?*" he said.

"What?" Laurie asked.

Then Mick was laughing a loud, boisterous laugh because he was drunk and because he thought he had made a joke, and Tommie was laughing from absolute embarrassment, but kind of like she was coughing, but whether it was from Mick's comment about her being delicious or Mick having a go at her or for the way he spoke Spanish, I didn't know, and I was laughing because it's pretty hard not to laugh when Mick starts acting like an idiot, and the two Mouseketeers were laughing these giggly little piggly-wiggly laughs, probably because they didn't understand a word of Spanish and they thought he'd said something dirty. Then the waitress came and the sudden breezy, rustling of her silky blue kimono sort of hushed us and we stopped laughing. She was the same one from behind the register. Mick ordered another beer and I ordered one and the girls and Tommie had Cokes.

"Mick, something happens to you when you drink beer," I said. "I swear all of a sudden you think you're Pancho Villa taking pot shots at the Federales."

"Who is Pancho Villa?" Laurie asked.

"A Mexican revolutionary," Mick said.

"So it was Spanish you were speaking,' Sonya said.

Sonya started to giggle.

"I could hardly understand a word you were saying."

"Ah, you are saying I mangled my Spanish."

"It sounded like Spanish to me," Laurie said.

"I learned my Spanish in the streets."

"What streets?"

"Ah, I am not permitted to speak about this. A good revolutionary abandons the past completely once it is past."

"Go on," Sonya said. "What streets?"

"Come on now, Mick," I said. "You've provoked their interest. You might as well make up something."

"Yes," Tommie said. "I'd like to hear about the streets and this secret, revolutionary past of yours."

Mick looked directly at Tommie and smiled and the light from the lanterns was bouncing off his teeth.

"It is mostly about why I learned Spanish in the first place."

"Why is fine."

"Okay then. I'll tell you. It was in the sixties."

"Oh, God no," Sonya said.

"Not another boring sixties story," said Laurie.

Mick just smiled.

"We had gone up to New York City," he said, "to help Abbie set up these free stores. We were living in this rat-trap of an apartment building on the Lower East Side, and I have to tell you it was like living in goddamn fucking South America. Like in Bolivia. Nobody spoke any English. Even the goddamn signs. It was all *"hombre!"* this and *"hombre!"* that and *"El cuarto de baño está al final del pasillo,"* which usually meant there was a hell of a party going on in somebody's apartment. But when we first moved in we didn't know jack! We couldn't even buy rice without thumbing through a dictionary. But the kicker was this one night. I'd been going all over the place that evening handing out leaflets and stopping sometimes to talk and pass around a joint, and I guess that went on for hours. But then I must have passed out or fallen asleep or something because the next thing I knew I was stretched out on the floor of some vacant room in a bombed-out looking apartment building. I had no idea where I was, but the sun was just coming up, so I headed over to the window. There was group of people setting up a street market. Old men in butcher's aprons and old women in scarves were setting up fruit carts and vegetable carts, right there in the middle of the street, and there were more people waiting for the market to open, they were leaning against the buildings or standing under the trees, not saying much, nothing I could hear, a sort of low, far-away murmuring. Well right then I knew I was in exactly the right place. These were the people we had come for, this is what we were about, feeding the people. It was a goddamn beautiful realization. It was like some sort of Robert Altman vision of hippies helping all of God's children find their way back to Eden. Fucking beautiful. But the moment I had that thought, I realized I wasn't wearing a goddamn thing, which isn't all that unusual for me, but the floor in that apartment was a cold, linoleum floor, and I don't even want to mention the stains and the rat droppings. I must have been blitzed. Then I realized somebody had stolen everything I owned. They had stolen my leaflets and my joints. They had stolen my watch, a gift from my grandfather, and a gold chain that Abbie had given me. And they had stolen all of my clothes, all the way down to my socks. The fuckers cleaned me out. They even took my underwear."

Mick took a swig from his beer.

"Oh my God," Laurie said. "What did you do?"

"What do you think I did?"

"God, I don't even want to guess."

"Ladies, there's not much you can do when the Universe is jerking you around. I wrapped myself up in a pair of orange curtains from the window. I was hoping somebody else still lived in the building and maybe I could borrow some pants and a shirt. So I went across the hall and knocked on the door. Pretty funny, right? I'm standing in the hall in these orange curtains and they won't stay up unless I hold them, and they're pretty sheer to begin with, like you can almost see right through them, and I hadn't even taken a piss yet so I was pretty hard to boot, hell, I was about to burst. So I'm knocking on this door and then it opens and I'm looking at this fairly sexy *chiquita* wearing a t-shirt that's just a little too tight. She was holding a spatula in her hand and you could smell eggs or something from the kitchen. We just stared at each for I don't how long. Man, she didn't even blink. Then I started to say something about how I was embarrassed and did she have any pants I could borrow, but my Spanish wasn't so good and I used the word *embarazar,* which means to make pregnant. It's incredible the noise a simple misunderstanding can cause. She started screaming with *mucho disgusto* and waving that spatula in my face, but she didn't shut the door. She was just standing in the doorway screaming and shaking that spatula, and the next thing I knew I was running down the stairs, trying to keep those orange curtains from flapping up too high or falling off."

Mick finished off his beer.

"Hell, I wasn't about to wait around and see if maybe she had a husband with a baseball bat. I took off and never looked back."

And with that we knew the story was over and it was okay to laugh, which we all did a little bit, except Tommie, who was more or less groaning.

"Mick, I've heard that joke a hundred times," Tommie said. "And it's not any better now than it ever was."

"He was joking?" Laurie said.

"I was not," Mick said. "Maybe it sounds like a joke to the jaded and pretentious among us. But I swear it's the goddamn fucking truth. Mucho fucking."

"What did you think when she was screaming?" Laurie said.

"I was thinking, my dear, unjaded little girl, that if she hadn't been screaming, the two of us could have had ourselves a very nice little party. She was a very good looking *chiquita.*"

"Jesus!" Tommie said. "That's all you men ever think about."

Laurie and Sonya looked at each other and burst out laughing.

We left soon after that. Mick and I each with a bottle of Kirin in hand, and the girls without. The two Mouseketeers were parked right outside and Tommie a few spaces in front of them. The street rose sharply after that and came to a crest at a stop light. It was pretty late, and the stores and other businesses were all dark except for the glow of the stoplight reflected in the windows. A bus went by and stopped at the top of the hill and several people edged away from the darkness of the buildings and got on, and as the bus pulled away you could see them plainly in the yellow light of the inside looking for just the right seat among all the empty seats. Then Tommie got in her car and drove away. The two Mouseketeers talked with Mick a moment, and at first they were looking very serious, but then they brightened and Laurie laughed, and then they were in their car and Laurie leaned out and waved good-bye.

"Come on," Mick said.

We crossed the street and walked half a block down the hill to an alley parking lot overlaid with a whitish, powdery, concrete rubble. There was a harsh, white security light up on a telephone pole near the entrance to the lot and another light fixed to the side of a brown-brick building in the back, but it was broken. There were four tinny-looking cars in the lot and a two-tone pickup truck, gold with a white stripe, which was parked under the broken light. You could see a man and a woman were in the pick-up, or maybe it was just kids. You couldn't really tell. They were groping each other, squirming on the seat and slipping and regaining their balance, and the window was rolled halfway down, it was probably stuck, so you could hear them murmuring softly and moaning and him telling her to move her legs this way or that way because the buckles were in the way or he needed to shift himself to get a better grip.

Mick started laughing when he heard them, and by the time we got to our cars, a dull orange Datsun for Mick and the same old dirty white Toyota for me, the two in the pick-up had roared out of the lot. We had parked next to each other. Mick was leaning back against his own car, laughing again, waving away the whitish dust and drinking from his bottle of Kirin. I was sitting in my car with the window rolled down. I was drinking too.

"You going home?" Mick said.

"Yeah. I'm pretty tired."

Mick started to grin. He took a quick swig and his beer started to bubble up.

"Listen, next week I'm giving a little party, and you're going to be there, right?"

"Sure, Mick."

"It's sort of a farewell party."

"For you?"

"This one's going to be wild. Beach bums, bikers, a couple of jazz musicians I know, a couple of ex-Catholic priests, some girls in bikinis. It's going to be one hell of an eclectic bunch, with plenty of existentialism and margaritas and Bob Marley, and a joint or two if you're into that."

"You know where you're going this time?"

"Not yet. Maybe South America. Maybe all the way to Patagonia. But it doesn't matter. I've just got to get away from the strip-center, shopping-mall mentality that dominates this wonderful fucking paradise we've made for ourselves."

"How long?"

"As long as it takes. I told Dubois I'd be gone the rest of the school year."

"Damn, Mick. You're out there on the lunatic fringe."

"Hell, Lauterbach. Why don't you come with me?"

"Sure, Mick. And what'll I do for cash?"

Mick started tapping his almost empty bottle of beer against the side of the Datsun. He was smiling now and his teeth flashed in the glare from the one working security light. You could never tell if Mick was serious or not.

"Forget it, man. You don't have a reason to go yet."

"Did you tell the Mouseketeers you're going?" I said.

"The what?"

"Sonya and Laurie. The Mouseketeers."

"Man, you're all right, Lauterbach. No. I told them about the party. That's all they really care about anyway. There's not much else in their heads. They're pretty aimless. They're even worse than you, if you can believe that."

We laughed.

"At least think about it, Lauterbach."

"Sure, Mick, I'll think about it."

We finished our beers. Then Mick got in his car and drove off. He'd put on his straw hat with the string for the drive. I drove home in my dirty white Toyota. The coolness in the air had become a motionless, brittle kind of cool, like ice, except it was probably in the fifties. I drove along Riverside Avenue, and through the trees you could maybe catch a glimpse of the heavy blue St. John's River and the short choppy waves glinting in the moonlight. There weren't any boats out at this hour. Sometimes

I liked to sit along the river at night and watch the waves rolling across and it was like I was the only person alive on the planet. But this only seemed true if you looked south, where the river seemed to disappear into the cloudy, mottled darkness of the sky. If you looked north, you could see the downtown lights, the neon blues and greens, the shimmery whiteness of the Jacksonville Landing, and you knew you weren't alone. Downtown there were always people out and about, maybe heading back from dinner or shopping or a movie, whatever people do anywhere, and there were all sorts of drunks and boozers and homeless guys shuffling around Hemming Plaza, even at two in the morning you could see them, and maybe a couple of guys in raincoats or an oddball gap-toothed prostitute now and then hanging around the restrooms at the bus station, and always there were the cops.

Looking south or looking north was the difference between where you had come from and where you were going. But to tell you the truth, it didn't matter all that much to me. I took the job in Jacksonville after my dad died so I wouldn't have to focus on shit like that. He was always telling me to look where I was going, keep my eyes open, opportunity only knocks once or twice, you've got to grab the bull by the horns, close only counts in horseshoes and hand grenades, it's not enough to know how to ride, pretty much every cliché in the book. I guess he didn't want me to end up like him. My dad was a clerk in the army, a career man who spent his career counting inventory. My mom gave up on him pretty early, which sort of proves that life is a cliché, if you think about it. When he got transferred to Fort Dix, she stayed in Chicago. In a way, I guess my dad never left Chicago. He was stuck between coming and going the rest of his life. But I wasn't thinking about any of that shit the night Mick told me about the party. I was tired. The alcohol had worn off. I just wanted to get home.

I lived in a pinkish, orangeish cement block apartment building with an aqua-marine colored roof about five blocks from St. Vincent's hospital. It was pretty much a dump, without even a view of the river, but it was cheap. I pulled into the parking lot and walked up the path and up the outside stairs. I lived on the second floor. You could look out through the sliding glass doors of the porch and see a row of one-story bungalows on the other side of the street. The houses were surrounded by oaks and magnolias with their waxy green leaves, and masses of overgrown azalea bushes. Above the houses you could see the spire of a Baptist church two blocks away.

I went inside and flicked on the hall light and the kitchen light, and suddenly I wasn't tired. I grabbed a bag of pretzels and a couple of Cokes and sat down in front of the TV and turned on some western I was sure I'd seen before, and then the western faded and I was watching MTV and the first thing that came on was a Depeche Mode video. They were dressed in black and wearing black cowboy hats, it sort of looked like they were gunfighters, or maybe they were Mexican revolutionaries, it was hard to say, and then I was watching the news, and then some other movie I didn't know, some damn love story or something like that. I watched television all night, but I don't remember what I saw. I don't even remember turning the channels. Mostly I was thinking, and the television would sort of drift in and out of my mind while I thought, and after a while it was like my thoughts were right there on the screen, in living color.

The first thing I was thinking was about Mick going to some South American country to join the revolution, it didn't matter which country since it was one big revolution no matter where you went, and Pancho Villa was heading down from Mexico to help out, which I know is one big impossibility since Pancho Villa was assassinated in 1923, but in my imagination anything was possible, so there he was, the Pancho Villa of my imagination, slapping old Mick on the back and handing him a rifle and a few straps of ammunition, and then the two of them, Pancho and Mick, smiling at each other, and they both had these crazy, jagged, chipped teeth, like you could only be part of the revolution if you had once had your face smashed in with a Billy club. You could feel the excitement in the air. And then Mick was in Mexico fighting against the Federales, and then he was back at his beach house telling war stories to a couple of brand new baby Mouseketeers and then fucking the hell out of them.

I couldn't help but think that Mick was a lousy goddamn hypocrite. If he didn't like the shopping malls and all the theme park commercialism, why the hell didn't he stay and fight. Wasn't there plenty to fight about right here in the good old USA? Why did he have to leave the country to do his damn revolutionary thing? He was a damn hippie, after all. Well, an ex-hippie at least. Isn't that what they did in the sixties? They stood up and fought for what they believed in because that's what the founding fathers said they should do. But then maybe you couldn't do that anymore. We had created a sprawling, rotting, festering urban ecosystem of video outlets and airfare price wars and happy, smiley-faced concrete clowns handing out burgers at drive-through windows, and everything was so tangled up in everything else that if you attacked one thing, you attacked everything. Maybe there was no place any more for revolutionaries in America. They either ended up in jail or dead, a footnote on the national news. Maybe people like Mick had to go somewhere else, at least for a while, so their brains wouldn't rot away.

Then I was thinking about why I didn't want to go with Mick, which I have to admit sounded pretty damn appealing. But I could see myself getting abandoned in some South American city because Mick had gone north with Pancho Villa to fight for the peasants, and all Mick would have said before he left was 'you need to find your own fucking cause to fight for, Lauterbach, whatever gets you pissed, that's the only way you'll ever grow up,' but he would have been smiling with his gleaming, chipped-tooth smile and clapping me on the back like finding a cause to fight for was the easiest thing in the world, so it would been hard to gainsay his advice, and then I could see myself wandering up some hilly back alley and smack dab into some guerrilla outfit that didn't know Pancho or Mick or anyone else north of the equator, a dozen grisly-faced, toothless bastards, gringo-eating deviants with tattoos on their arms and the backs of their necks and riding mules and empty ammunition belts slung around their waists, and all of them bloody from fighting the night before, and then I could see my dead body on some bricked-over back alley road because they didn't like gringos who couldn't speak Spanish. I could see it all on the six o'clock news, only they wouldn't know who it was, just some poor, dippy American tourist who didn't have a MasterCard. That's why I wouldn't go with Mick. It wasn't like going all the way to South America would make me any happier. Who said South America was paradise?

Then the love story came on and I was thinking about Tommie Rodriguez and the bowling date and her curvey behind, the kind Harvey Collins liked, and then I was thinking about those other two dates, and God what a mess they were. And then I was thinking maybe I hadn't given Tommie a chance. Mick thought she was delicious looking. And I guess maybe she was. A guy could do a hell of a lot worse than Tommie Rodriguez. Maybe it had been so long since I had felt normal that I didn't even know my own mind. Maybe I just didn't like everybody I knew trying to push me and Tommie together. It had been practically non-stop since Emily Lavigne had tried. And now there was Mick and the party to think about, and I was pretty damn sure Tommie was going. What Mick had said at the restaurant about me and Tommie going off together, well, if he hadn't told her about the party yet, he was sure as hell going to. There was something perverse about Mick. But maybe Tommie and me wasn't such a bad idea. I had to admit I liked Tommie. I mean maybe Tommie was just what I needed.

Then the love story was over and some cartoons came on. You could see the sun coming up through the window and the dewy green of the trees and the gleaming white spire of the Baptist church. I still wasn't tired, but I was kind of numb from thinking so much. I went into the kitchen and dumped the empty pretzel bag in the garbage and the empty Coke cans. Then I fixed a bowl of cereal and went back to the TV.

-5-

The party at Mick's was one hell of a party. It was supposed to start at four in the afternoon, but I must have got the time wrong. I got there at quarter to and had to park three blocks away. I couldn't imagine Mick's little beach house with its matchbox living room holding three blocks worth of people. But there was no other explanation for all the cars. Man, they were everywhere. Beat up Chevy trucks and perky little red Ford Escorts and several BMWs, which meant students, and then there was a Volkswagen van and a bunch of regular bugs, a couple of blues and a yellow and a lime green convertible. And then about a block away someone had set up three sawhorse roadblocks, and on one side there were half a dozen Harley's, and then a few more cars, and then smack in the middle of the street was a stolen road construction sign which had been painted over. It said: "Warning! Party Ahead. Proceed At Your Own Risk." But Mick didn't need the sign.

Already you could hear people laughing and talking loudly and shouting, and underneath it all was the steady reggae hum of Bob Marley.

The first thing you saw when you actually got to Mick's house was a farewell banner hung over the front door, and a couple of loudspeakers set up on the roof with wires running down into the house through one of the windows and reggae music pouring out like rain. I have to say one thing: Mick sure had a thing for his music. There was no getting away from it either. He had two more speakers inside the house and two more on a rotting redwood picnic table down at the beach. And everywhere you looked there were people having a good time. In the front yard there were several groups of people scattered among the potted ferns, a few sitting on the sandy, cobblestone brick or on folding chairs, and some on a wooden Swiss Miss-style bench shoved up against the house. Or maybe it was just the one group with the ferns getting in the way. But either way there were several different conversations going on at once and girls running in and out through the front door with beers and banana daiquiris and margaritas, like they were waitresses or something. Two bikers were arguing with some ditzy redhead about a bike trip they took out to Rapid City, South Dakota the summer before, all the way out to Sturgis on their Harleys for some bike rally, there must have been a million bikers, they said, roaring through the Black Hills for a fucking week, it was something to see, it was a goddamn millennial event, and she was saying if they had really gone, then where were the t-shirts to prove it, and they didn't seem to know how to handle that, but then one of them mumbled something about they didn't sell any goddamn t-shirts at the rally, the rally didn't have any shit like that, it wasn't infected with any goddamn commercialistic assholes, Jesus fucking Christ, but you could see he wasn't telling the whole truth.

Inside it was just as crowded as the front yard, maybe more, and a hell of a lot noisier. People were sitting on the sofa and over by the kitchen counter and leaning against the walls and drinking and listening to the music and talking and smoking, and I thought it was pretty damn rude them smoking indoors like that instead of out, but I guess they thought they were in some Spanish biker bar out on U. S. Highway 1 or somewhere like that. I have to admit it felt like a bar with those waitress girls running around with drinks and getting flirty with the guests and then wiggling their rear ends up to the kitchen counter and then back out to the front yard, and behind the counter there was this guy named Rinaldo wearing cheap sunglasses and his hair slicked back, a tuxedo t-shirt top, swim trunks and Roman style sandals. He was mixing drinks in a blender and handing out beers, and just for a joke people started tipping him nickels and dimes and pennies, all of which went into a Mickey Mouse coffee mug or bowl or something right there on the counter. I guess after a while people forgot he wasn't really a bartender.

Mick wasn't around the house so I grabbed a margarita and tossed a couple of quarters into the Mickey Mouse mug and went back out through the sliding glass doors. Down at the beach there was about a truckload of people. Some were playing volleyball and some were watching and they were all drinking mostly beer because there was a keg half-buried in the sand next to the net, and every now and then some girl got picked up and carried to the water, laughing and screaming and wiggling with welcome hysteria, and then she'd get dumped in, and then everybody had these dippy looking grins on their faces, even the girl. But Mick wasn't with the volleyballers either, so I headed back up and there was Ed with his hand still in the cast and next to him was his ex-wife, Joyce, who had this shrill, flutey voice which kind of stabbed at your brain, and three others I didn't know. I guess they had just got there. They were sitting on a makeshift patio in the middle of Mick's sandy, grassy backyard, just before you got to the dunes. They were sitting in these white molded plastic chairs, which Mick must have borrowed or stolen because they hadn't been there before, and they weren't exactly the kind of chairs Mick would buy anyway. Mick wasn't into plastic. There was a pile of chairs stacked up against a scraggly old palmetto. I nodded a hello and pulled a chair off the top and sat down.

Everybody but Ed was smiling these easy-going vacuous smiles, as if they'd been drinking for days and were happy just to have chairs to sit in. They broke off their conversation just long enough for the unknowns to introduce themselves. First there was Iggy and Imants, both ex-priests, ex-Catholic priests, with shiny bald heads and viciously red necks from where they'd been shaving too closely for years, and next to them was this girl with hair that kind of looked like Spanish moss hanging from her head, and she was Joyce's sister, which I couldn't help thinking maybe she meant ex-sister, since everybody else there was an ex, but I didn't say anything.

So I sat there in that plastic white chair and the sun splattering down, listening to these people talk, and except for Ed, and Joyce, whom I had met once before, and except for Mick's farewell banner hanging over the front door, I would have sworn I'd gone to the wrong house. I had never seen the rest of these people before, at least that's what it seemed like, not Joyce's sister or the ex-priests, and certainly not the bikers or Rinaldo the bartender in his tuxedo top or the dippy looking volleyballers at the beach, which was by no means exclusive proof that Mick didn't know them. But it was a little weird all the same, a slow motion *Twilight Zone* kind of weird where the people are talking in low, garbled voices and then the sound goes out completely and it feels like you're stuck in quick sand and then all of a sudden you can't see a goddamn thing and then you hear Rod Serling's voice, only it sounds like the voice of God, and old Rod he's saying "Ladies and gentlemen, you have just witnessed what happens when the aimless, hopped-up hope of youth is overwhelmed by the frenetic despair of an over-urbanized and mechanized society, a clash of opposite energies that pushes us beyond the limits of our imagination, a beach party somewhere on the outskirts of what we call the modern world, an unexplainable sojourn between the here and now and what we might call the edge of tomorrow. You have just entered *The Twilight Zone*."

That's how it felt. But who can say for sure? Maybe most of these people had just seen the stolen construction sign and come off the street. Or maybe they'd heard about the party from some of Mick's friends. I guess it didn't really matter. I drank some of my margarita and tried to focus on the slow-motion conversation.

"Oh I went with a priest once," Joyce was saying. "He was an older one, I'd say. Nearer sixty than fifty. But he was absolutely ferocious in bed. I never saw a man like that. I guess abstinence makes the throbbing stronger." Both Joyce and her sister laughed, and Iggy and Imants sort of half-snickered, each of them grabbing and rubbing the red of their closely shaved necks. Ed sat back in his chair looking vaguely troubled. Then Joyce leaned away from Ed and touched her sister delicately on the knee. "Let me tell you something sweetie, if you're ever thinking about a priest, go after one of the older ones. They've been abstaining the absolute longest."

Joyce and her sister laughed again.

Old ex-husband Ed stared at Joyce, a look of bewildered disbelief becoming one of comprehension.

"You mean Father Adleman?" he said.

"Yes. Father Adleman. Who else would it be?" Joyce said.

"Was this before or after we got divorced?"

"Before, of course."

"Shit," Ed said.

You could tell Ed wanted to lash out at someone. He looked squarely at Iggy, who was still rubbing his neck. "That's pretty rich, aint it, Iggy," he said. "You goddamn horny priests."

"Horny ex-priests," Iggy said.

"Or ex-horny priests," Imants joked.

"Oh, I wouldn't go that far," Iggy said.

Joyce laughed, and then everybody else was laughing, except Ed, and then nobody said anything for a while. Probably it was only a couple of seconds, but it seemed a hell of a lot longer. The sun was warm against my face and I drank from my margarita. The others drank from their drinks. From where I was sitting I could see a sliver of the beach through the dunes and the bright wild blue of the Atlantic and the surf kicking up. The volleyballers had stopped playing and were heading down en masse to the water with another ultra girly-girl victim struggling playfully above their heads, and then there was a burst of gleeful, giddy, pseudo-sacrificial laughter, and then the volleyball girl was floating in the surf and the rest of them went back to their game. Good old Bob Marley was singing *Stir It Up.*

"Do you guys know this fucking Father Adleman?"

Old ex-husband Ed was shifting about in his white plastic chair, trying to get comfortable. The chair didn't seem all that sturdy with Ed in it. His face was turning red from the sun and from drinking and from being embarrassed and angry, all at the same time. It was pretty damn red. It was about as red as it could get.

"The fucking who?" Iggy said.

"It's a stage name," Imants said. "Like the Singing Nun or the Beef-Eating Bishop."

"Oh," Iggy said. "The Fucking Father. I remember. Yes, I knew him. But vaguely, vaguely. He didn't seem the type."

"What type? He was banging my wife."

"Your ex-wife," Joyce said.

"Shit," Ed said.

Ed sank back into the white plastic chair. He didn't know what else to say. He finished his beer, and with a flick of his wrist he sent the empty bottle spinning some ten feet through the air towards a Rubbermaid trash can on the grassy, sandy edge next to the stack of chairs. The bottle fell short and kicked up a poof of sand, but Ed didn't care. Brushing the wrinkles out of his shirt and pants, he headed down to watch the volleyballers, who were playing again. The others barely noticed Ed leaving. Joyce and her sister popped up from their chairs and happily flounced their way to the house to get refills. Iggy and Imants turned on me with these mockingly grave, ex-priestly eyes.

"So, Travis," Iggy said. "If you were this Father Adleman character, what would you have done?"

"What do you mean?"

"He means," Imants said, "if you were a priest and you wanted this woman, or any woman for that matter, would you quit being a priest just so you could have her, or would you stay a priest and screw her when you could?"

"Did Father Adleman quit?"

"I don't know. It doesn't matter. What would you do?"

"Well, I guess if I wanted her," I paused. "Do I love her?"

"Love, want. It's all the same thing in the end."

"So I love her."

"Sure, you love her."

"Then I guess I'd have to quit. I mean if I loved her I shouldn't be a priest, right?"

"Right," Iggy said. "You see?" He was laughing and then poking at Imants with his beer and sloshing some on Imants's shirt. "That's the moral point of view of young America speaking there."

"Christ, Iggy," said Imants. The sun was glinting off the spilled beer and also off Imants's bald head, and for a moment all I could see was Imants's grave glinting eyes coming at me through the glare. "Suppose that you loved being a priest as much as you loved this woman," he said.

"Can you do that?" I said. You could see that Imants was getting a little irritated with my clichéd bewilderment. I thought I'd have some fun with him. "If you're Catholic."

"Sure, you can do it. So what would you do then?"

"You mean I have to give up something. Like a sacrifice?"

"No, no, no" Imants said. "You don't have to give up a thing."

"Well, I don't know," I said. "I don't see how I could marry her if I were a priest. Not a Catholic priest anyway. I mean I suppose if they changed their minds and said priests could marry. I mean if they issued a formal edict or a Papal bulletin or something like that, then it would be different. But the way it is now, I guess I'd have to join the Episcopal Church."

Iggy started laughing.

I drank some more of my margarita and watched Imants pretty much choke on my words. I'm not like a lot of Catholics. I wouldn't hold it against you if you wanted to be an Episcopalian. I mean I teach at an Episcopal school, for God's sake.

"Good God, Iggy. What's the matter with these people?"

"Face it, Imants, yours is a morally untenable position."

"Ahhhg!" Imants coughed on the last of his beer and then tossed his empty bottle after Ed's and reached below his chair and brought up another one. He had a stash of three or four bottles in the shade of the chair. He had apparently decided to waste as little energy as possible in his efforts to get drunk. He would avoid going back and forth between Mick's house and this circle of white plastic, sun-splattered chairs for as long as his stash held out. He opened the second bottle and started drinking and immediately started coughing again. Laughing, Iggy clapped him on the back a few times and the coughing stopped. The girls came flouncing back from the house. Joyce plopped down in her chair and began scolding Iggy and Imants for their obviously misguided reliance on beer, holding up her very own strawberry margarita as proof of a reliable alternative. Joyce's sister scooted her chair next to mine.

"So which type are you?" she asked.

She was sitting with her shoulders turned slightly away from her sister, but her head seemed to be floating directly above the arm of my chair, like it was detached from the rest of her body, and her Spanish moss hair was dripping down my arm. At first I couldn't tell if she was talking or not. She spoke in a soft, eager, whispery voice, and she was holding up her strawberry margarita as if to ward off interruption. The others were arguing playfully about whether to drink beer or margaritas.

"How's that?" I said.

"Which type? Joyce and I figured as soon as we left Iggy and Imants would pounce. They're always after people to settle this debate of theirs. They're both a little loony. They both think it's perfectly natural for priests and women to, you know, to do it. But Iggy thinks they should leave the priesthood if they want to and Imants doesn't. I think Imants has been losing the argument more than winning recently. At least he's been getting ticked off at Iggy a little too easily lately. It's pretty funny."

"Yeah. He got so mad before he started choking on his beer."

Joyce's sister sipped her drink and leaned her Spanish-moss covered head even closer.

"So what did you say?"

"I said I'd have to become an Episcopal priest."

"Oh, good. I like that. It's kind of romantic."

She sat back in her white plastic chair and her hair went with her, and then she was smiling at Iggy and Imants and her sister, a happy, contented smile, and it seemed like her smile was reflected in her margarita. Or maybe her margarita was reflected in her smile.

"They're gay, you know," she said. "That's the really funny part. The whole thing is just theoretical to them."

Joyce's sister started to laugh, and Iggy and Imants and Joyce were laughing also, but probably for a different reason, and while they were laughing they traded drinks and Joyce started guzzling Iggy's beer and Iggy started sipping from Joyce's strawberry margarita, and then Imants had a turn, and then they were laughing some more. These people laughed a hell of a lot.

Then old ex-husband Ed came back from the volleyballers and stood squarely behind his chair.

"You all just have to see this," he said.

"See what?" Iggy said.

"There's a dolphin washed up on the beach."

"A live dolphin?" Joyce's sister said.

"I don't know. I think it might be dead. But it's a god-damn beautiful animal anyway."

"What do you want see a crummy old dead dolphin for?" Joyce asked. "Good God, Ed. You must be drunk."

"Sure, Joyce."

Grinning fiercely, Ed headed back to the beach. He was

pumped up by the dolphin and not even Joyce could take away his joy. He walked through the opening in the dunes and the salty, fishy smell of the ocean coming up with the wind and the glaring, burning sunlight fluttering in the wake of a few cloud puffs moving across the sky, and you could see a sudden tallness about Ed, as if he had grown three inches. He now seemed to possess a fierce, energetic, wide-angled brightness, like you see in the movies, which suggested, among other things, the absolute, religious, even mythic importance of looking at a dead dolphin.

"Come on everybody," Iggy said. "Let's go see it."

"I'm game," Imants said. "It sounds goddamn existential."

So that's what we did, all of us except Joyce. She sat there in rigid, damning defiance of the very idea that we should bother with anything that had washed up on the beach. She sat there silently in her white plastic chair, drinking her margarita, and also Iggy's beer. But the rest of us ran after Ed, and we caught up to him at the dolphin itself. There was a whole crowd of eager onlookers, mostly volleyballers, but also a few retiree-type beach-walkers up from Atlantic Beach, and one old sea-captain bum with a metal detector who looked like the kind of bum you might see anywhere. Everybody was sort of encircling the poor animal, leaning over it, leering, poking at it with their fingers, which they'd probably tell you not to do if it were some old lady passed out on the street from a heart attack, but it's different with a dead dolphin right there in front of you. I don't really know why we came down to look at it. But you know, I have to admit Ed was right. It was a beautiful animal, even in death, with its milky-grayish skin glistening in the sunlight and the brownish-yellowish hard-packed sand beneath it and the purple strands of seaweed and the sudsy wavelets coming in from the blue Atlantic. It sure didn't look dead, but it was. You couldn't really see why it had died. You could see it had scars all over the place, like purplish-gray welts, but they were old scars from old dolphin battles and were long ago healed, so why this animal had died was a mystery. It didn't seem that an animal like that would just give up. Then I started thinking of it as a living, breathing animal. I could see it churning through the cool depths of the Atlantic, slicing this way and that in search of adventure, calling out to his dolphin buddies to join him and then all of them shooting up towards the glimmery surface, unthinking in their animal joy, their unrestrained lust for life, and then arcing up into the warm, sunny, salt-sprayed air. And when I thought of that I remembered the dolphins I had seen in the St. John's River. I wondered if this dolphin was one of them, and then I was sure that he was. And then I started thinking some slightly weird thoughts. Some very weird thoughts, if you want to know the truth. All of a sudden I could see in this dead dolphin the happiness that had been its life and I started thinking that maybe this dolphin was a message to me. Like maybe God was trying to tell me that there was indeed happiness out there, my happiness, if only I looked in the right place.

"Here comes Mick," somebody said.

"Hey, Mick, where the hell have you been?" shouted one of the volleyballers. "Do you know about this dolphin? You can't play volleyball with a dead dolphin on the beach."

"Why not?" the volleyballer's girlfriend said.

"Look, will you. It's too distracting."

I don't think Mick really heard what anybody said. He came down from the house, his chipped-tooth smile beaming a soft rosy glow in the late afternoon sun, and he was wearing his straw hat with the string, but not on his head, it was bouncing against his back with the string tight around his neck, like he was a bandit in *The Magnificent Seven*. Mick bent down and looked at the dolphin and patted it a couple of times on the flank and then he looked up at the crowd.

"I came to tell you sun gods and goddesses it's time to eat."

Mick looked down at the dolphin again.

"What, you mean the dolphin?"

It was the one volleyballer's girlfriend.

"Jesus, Lilly. Think about it."

Mick ignored the volleyballer and his girlfriend, patted the flank one last time and stood up.

"There's plenty of burgers and hot dogs," he said. "And there's tofu for all you vegetarian freaks. And the drinks are still on the house."

Then Mick headed towards the savory, sizzling meat smell of the grill, which only then did we notice, and man did that smell just open you up. I mean snap, just like that, I could hardly keep from running I was so hungry, and it seemed that everybody else was feeling the same kind of hunger the way we all of a sudden forgot about that dead dolphin. So we followed Mick up to the house, all of us except the retiree-type beach walkers, and a couple of overly zealous volleyballers who went back to the net and started batting the ball back and forth some more, and the sea-captain bum with the metal detector, who gave the dolphin a slow going over and that little box was beeping a steady, slow beep, I guess because he wanted to make sure it hadn't swallowed any quarters or something.

By the time we got back to the house, it was a maddening jumble of people with plates and drinks, trying to keep themselves from spilling. You had to squirm your way through to the grill, which was against the back wall of the house, right next to the sliding-glass doors, and then it was inside to the kitchen counter-top bar if you were thirsty, and if you wanted to eat anywhere near the house you had to stand because there wasn't anywhere to sit, but nobody except maybe Ed seemed to mind with all the food and people joking and laughing. Some were even dancing to Bob Marley while they ate. Mick liked Bob Marley a hell of a lot. I fixed a Paper Mate plate with a couple of burgers and some potato salad, grabbed a beer and sat down with Ed. We sat down where we were before, but the plastic white chairs were gone so we sat on the ground. I didn't know what happened to Iggy and Joyce and the others, and I guess Ed didn't care. He didn't talk about them and I didn't ask. The truth was Ed didn't seem too interested in talking at all. So we ate our burgers in a sort of gloomy silence and watched the others eating and laughing and dancing some, and then Mick came bursting out through the sliding-glass doors with two guys in short-sleeved khaki style uniforms with baseball caps and black Vandemere sunglasses and green patches on their shoulders with a deer and a bird and a fish like some kind of merit badge, like these guys were a cross between the Secret Service and the Boy Scouts. They were both carrying shiny, metallic kits with the letters FWC marked on them. It was about the dolphin. Mick said something and was pointing towards the beach and the Boy Scouts nodded and took off, and then you couldn't really see them, but you could see the glare of the sun bouncing off their metallic kits, but almost immediately they were back jabbering by the sliding glass doors. They were telling Mick the dolphin was dead, they only handled injured animals, live ones, he had called the wrong people. But Mick only smiled his chipped-tooth smile and his pale blue eyes were bouncing around in the dark of his stubbly face and he said, "Come on, man. You can see we're having a hell of a party here. Couldn't you do us a favor?"

You just knew the Boy Scouts were going to give in, they were Boy Scouts for God's sake, probably trying to earn the next badge to add to their shirts. Mick gave them a couple of beers and they headed around to the front. Ten minutes later they were driving down the macadam path in this official looking silver colored truck with blue lights on top and the same green and white patch with the deer and the fish on the doors. They drove through the opening in the dunes and the sand spitting up behind them and then they disappeared down the beach. You could see them drinking the beers and laughing as they went by, which it got me thinking some more about the dead dolphin and how happy it had looked, but when those two Boy Scouts came back you could see him, or it, or whatever, stretched out in the back of the truck on some kind of dark blue leathery, aquatic-type gurney, and it was tied down with about a dozen white nylon ropes crisscrossed like shoelaces, to keep it from falling out if they hit a bump. It sure didn't look happy any more. It was like the happiness of that dolphin was connected to the ocean and the rivers where it swam, and when the two Boy Scouts scooped it up, the happiness part just kind of drained away into the sand. They were left with nothing but a dead animal carcass.

After dinner, the sun started to set and the sky turned a bright tangerine color, except way out over the water where it was a dull, heavy blue. Mick said it was time to build the bonfire before we couldn't see a thing. He took us around to the corner of the house to a pile of driftwood. I have to say there was a hell of lot of driftwood there. It looked like Mick had been collecting driftwood for months. We carried some of it down to the beach, me and Mick and a few bikers and Iggy (but not Imants, who was rummaging through various abandoned coolers in search of a beer), and then Iggy and Mick started digging a pit in the sand and the rest of us went for more wood (at which point Imants joined us with a bottle for himself and another for Iggy).

By the time we got the last of the driftwood down to the pit, Mick had a pretty good blaze going, and it was dark too, the sky was pretty much black all over, and the water was especially dark, except for the running lights of a few shrimp boats off shore.

The bonfire was a good time. People came down with their drinks and stood around it and watched the sparks and cinders fly up into the night sky. If you stared long enough at the shimmering heat of the fire it looked like the whole world was melting. Then a few people lit up cigarettes or maybe some joints and started passing them around. There wasn't much talking and laughing at that point. There was a quieter, more sensual feeling about the day and the beach and the night unfolding, opening itself up to us. You could see people dancing slowly along the edge of the firelight, moving into the shadows, almost like they were shadows themselves, and the happy, redemptive sound of Bob Marley mingling with the faint, swishy sound of the surf.

I don't know how long I stood there just watching and listening and breathing in the smoky smell of that fire. I don't remember thinking a single thought in the smoky, surreal serenity of being there. But then all of a sudden it was like the movie version of myself standing there and the light glinting off my face, but I wasn't looking at the bonfire any more. I was looking up towards the house and the redwood picnic table with the speakers, and there was Tommie Rodriguez. She was walking towards me, walking, hell, it looked like she was gliding, like she was one of those angels in a junior high Christmas play and they were moving her through the air on strings.

Tommie waved and then smiled, and then she held up a margarita to show me and then drank some, and then just like that she was standing next to me.

"Hi stranger," she said. "I've been looking all over for you. Where've you been?"

"I guess I've been here," I said, nodding at the bonfire. "What about you? I didn't see you before."

"I came late. I even missed the barbecue."

"You didn't miss much."

She drank some more of her drink, and the next thing I knew she was holding on to my arm and we were both of us looking at the fire and listening to the reggae. I didn't have a drink so she gave me some of hers, and then we were sharing back and forth and laughing and squirming. I don't know what happened to the empty glass. Then I guess we must have got tired of standing because we were sitting in the sand and the bonfire wasn't quite so bright any more, or hot, and you could feel the cool, salt breeze blowing in, which felt pretty good, and after a while we were talking about some pretty weird late-night stuff. Theoretical, Iggy and Imants kind of stuff. At least I was. I must have been out of my mind.

I think Tommie thought I was drunk. But she was real nice about it. She laughed a couple of times, but all the while she kept holding on to my arm.

"Tommie, did you ever wonder about dolphins?"

"Mmmmm? No. Not recently," she said.

"Did you ever think that maybe dolphins have souls?"

"No," she said, and she laughed softly. "I don't think I've ever had that thought. But who knows?"

"People have souls, right? So why not dolphins?"

"You know you're very sweet when you're drunk."

"No, no. There was a dead dolphin washed up on the beach this afternoon. Before you came."

"And you were wondering if it had a soul?"

"Yes. I was. We were looking at it before they carted it away, and it looked so happy even though it was dead. Then the Boy Scouts came and it didn't look happy after that. It was just a dead thing in the back of their truck."

"Boy Scouts?"

"Yeah, I mean they weren't really Boy Scouts. They were two fish and game guys I guess."

"So where does the soul come in?"

"Well, I've got a theory about that. Maybe that dolphin wasn't quite dead when we saw it. Maybe that happiness I saw was the dolphin's soul. But when the Boy Scouts got to it, it really was dead. Its soul had left."

"That sounds terribly mystical," Tommie said.

She snuggled some closer to me.

"Yeah, I guess it does. But that's how it seemed."

"Very mystical."

We must have sat there in the sand for almost an hour, looking at the dying bonfire and talking softly and the smoke drifting up into the sky. I felt like I had known her my whole life. I don't remember the rest of what we talked about, but there was a lot of giggly, squirmy laughter and Tommie going "shshshsh" and putting her free hand over her mouth because her other one had my arm, but she was still giggling anyway.

Then Mick came down, but he didn't see us. He had a shovel or something and he started shoving the larger pieces of driftwood around, and then there was a burst of cinders and the bonfire grew suddenly brighter and warmer, and then Mick went down to the surf and you couldn't see him. The reggae was still going, only it didn't seem as loud as before, and nobody was dancing anymore, but you could see maybe five or six couples stretched out in the sand or sitting, at least you could see their shadows all mixed up with each other, sort of like me and Tommie with her holding on to my arm. Then Tommie and I were just staring at each other, like I was falling into her eyes and she was falling into mine, it was like being in *Vertigo* or something, being at the top of that church tower and nowhere to go but down and then that black and white pinwheel thing starting to spin, and right then Bob Marley was singing about the shelter of a single bed and all I wanted to do was kiss Tommie as hard as I damn well could, right on the mouth, and then not so hard, a softer kiss, which she seemed to want the same thing. But we didn't move. Neither of us. We just stared at each other like two dippy high-school idiots. And then a dozen pairs of running legs went by on their way to the water and the sand skidding up into our laps, and that pretty much broke the moment. We both turned as they went past and watched until you couldn't really see them, but you could still hear them, laughing and murmuring and joking around and then splashing in the waves. Then we heard Mick's voice booming out from somewhere in the darkness. "Buckle up boys and girls," Mick said. "This show's just getting started." And then: "If you're going to get wet you might as well get naked."

Then the laughter and the splashing seemed to move on down the beach. It was very dark. All you could see were the tiny green lights of the shrimp boats.

"Come on," Tommie said. "Walk me to my car."

"You're going?"

"I have to go. Come."

She grabbed both my hands and somehow we pulled each other up and headed towards the house. But we didn't bother going inside. Dozens of people were still going in and out through the sliding glass doors. Mick had strung these yellow and blue and purple lights around the back so it looked like you were on a cruise ship to Jamaica or somewhere. Everyone was still drinking their beers or their margaritas and slipping off into the shadows and then back into the yellow and blue and purple streams of light and these sexy coy smiles on their faces. But Tommie had to go, so what was I going to say, don't go, I've fallen madly in love with you and if you go I'm going to jump into the Atlantic and drown myself, which it may have been a pretty fair approximation of my feelings at the time, but it didn't seem too practical a thing to put into words. So we followed the macadam path around to the front of the house, past the bikers sitting among the ferns, past the stolen construction sign and the sawhorse and the Volkswagen Beetles parked at odd angles. We weren't walking all that fast either. I kept thinking I'm going to do it, I'm going to kiss her when we get to her car, an opportunity like this doesn't come along every day. But there really wasn't a chance. For one thing, there were way too many people around. Some were running back and forth between the bright, tinny, festival frenzy of Mick's beach house and the parking lot of their cars and motorcycles and the hazy, whitish glare of the street lamps and the swirl of insects pooling around the light. Others were sitting with legs hanging out of the windows of nearby houses, as if the party had somehow migrated to the whole neighborhood, and they were smoking cigarettes or joints. And everybody was jabbering away, laughing, calling out to us as we went by, a bewildering melee of late-night voices, drunken or sleepy or angry or surprised or merely curious, and everywhere there was the sexy, serene inescapable hum of Bob Marley and The Wailers.

"I had fun," Tommie said.

We were standing next to her car, somewhat awkwardly. Tommie was sort of half-leaning back against the front door and I was standing sideways, straddling the curb, but it was like I didn't have any control of my hands. My one hand was fumbling with my belt buckle and the other one was flopping around on the hood and then fiddling with the antennae and then back on the hood, but all the while I was hoping I looked roguish and tough and worldly and likable, all at the same time, like Humphrey Bogart in *To Have and Have Not*.

"I wish I had come sooner," Tommie said.

"Me too."

"Are you going to stay long?"

"No. I'm going to try and find Mick though. I haven't really seen him since I got here. I better at least say good night. I bet he's still swimming.

"And naked, too!" Tommie laughed.

Then Tommie leaned forward and gave me a quick, darty kiss on the cheek, and before I had even the slightest chance to react, she was sitting behind the steering wheel and the window rolled down.

"Good night, Travis Lauterbach," Tommie said.

"Good night, Tommie. See ya."

And that was that. Tommie drove away and I headed off in search of Mick. Of course I didn't find him right away. I spent the better part of the next hour searching for him, mostly down along the beach where I had last heard his voice. But he wasn't there. Nobody was. There was nothing but the grayish water and the waves coming in. Even the shrimp boats had left. But not finding Mick didn't really bother me. I mean not at all. I was so pumped up from Tommie kissing me like she did, even though it was the exact opposite of the way I had wanted to kiss her, that I felt like I was going to explode, like I was some kind of comet streaking across the sky. Tommie's kiss was all I could think about. I breathed in the salt water air and felt in myself a reckless, unrelenting joy. It was goddamn poetic.

So I walked until I couldn't hear Mick's party, and then I walked some more. I could see a few of those blue bug lights from the other beach houses, the light filtering out through the trees and an occasional zap when an insect got too close. I decided to cut through by one of the bug lights and head back by way of First Avenue. By the time I got back to Mick's house it seemed that most everybody had left. The string of yellow, blue and purple lights had been disconnected. Bob Marley was barely a whisper. The sawhorse roadblocks and the construction sign were gone. Only a few cars were left. The front yard was empty except for the ferns, but there were maybe a dozen people inside. I finally found Mick, fully dressed, sitting in the sand by the bonfire. He was staring at the charred pieces of driftwood and the orange flecks of fire deep within.

"Hey, Mick," I said.

"Hey there, Lauterbach," Mick said. He did not look up. He was twirling his moustache and contemplating the stillness of the beach and the almost dead bonfire.

"Man, I didn't see you hardly at all today," I said. "It was a hell of a party, wasn't it?"

"Yeah, Lauterbach. It was one hell of a party. One hell of a hairy shindig, that's what Abbie would've said."

Mick flipped his head back and gave me his chipped-tooth smile. Even in the dim, orangey glow of the fire you could see his teeth glinting.

"Say, Lauterbach, how would you like a beach house?"

"You mean look after it while you're gone?"

"No, man. I'm giving it to you. I'm heading down to Patagonia and I'm not coming back. I'm going to find me some Patagonian girls and fuck them till my balls fall off."

"What if I don't want it?"

"Then I don't know. I guess it'll just rot on the beach, and it'll be on your conscience, Lauterbach. Don't forget!"

"Okay, Mick. But when you get back it's all yours."

"Yeah. Sure. If that's the way you want it. But I'm really not coming back, Lauterbach. There's this little voice inside my head that says it's time to move on. So I'm moving."

"So maybe it'll tell you someday to come back?"

"Maybe, Lauterbach. Maybe I'm dancing this little dance all by myself. Maybe it's all just one goddamn eternal circle and no matter what I do I'm going to end up right back where I started. Is that it, Lauterbach?"

Mick started to laugh, but it was a strange kind of laughter. I couldn't tell if he was laughing because he thought something was funny or for some other reason.

"If that happens I'll be dancing my eternal circles in jail."

"Jail?"

"Sure, Lauterbach. Fucking j-a-i-l! Do you know how I paid for this farewell frolic at the beach?"

"No."

"I sold my car, and boxes and boxes of old books, and the stereo equipment is going too. And then I maxed out my credit cards. I'm fucking twenty thousand dollars in debt, Lauterbach. I've got a one-way bus ticket to Miami and a suitcase full of cash like a goddamn bandito, and I'm twenty thousand in the fucking hole, and I don't give two goddamns about it because I'm leaving for good. The sky is opening up right in front of me. The Universe is saying it's time to go. So why would I come back?"

"But you didn't sell the house."

"It wasn't mine to sell. The guy who built it was a friend of mine, one of the few. He didn't believe in owning property, just like he didn't believe in banks or in any of that bullshit. He said we were all just renting space for a while and then we died or moved on and somebody else took over. He left fifteen years ago for Mexico, just one day he hopped on his motorcycle and took off. He was the real Pancho Villa, Lauterbach, a goddamn demagogue. He even had a carbine strapped to his back. Not like me and my costumey gringo lingo. He gave me the house. He told me to pay the taxes. That would be my way of paying rent. He told me to give it away before I left. If you want, Lauterbach, I'll toss in a couple of girls, too, with or without their bikinis."

I must have smiled because Mick laughed and clapped me on the back. It was a real laugh this time. You could tell. But Mick didn't know why I was smiling. I was still pretty psyched about Tommie, and now with Mick abandoning his beach house that very minute because the Universe was calling, well, all of a sudden it was like I was diving headlong into the surf and then popping back up with the shimmery brightness of the sun on my back, and I realized everyone was exactly where they were supposed to be. Everything that was happening, everything that was going to happen, it was all supposed to happen. It was a hell of a feeling. So why wouldn't I be smiling? Then we got up and raced towards the dunes and beyond that the soft yellow glow of the sliding-glass doors and the people inside. Mick beat me by a step, and then we stopped just outside and we were laughing and breathing heavy and each of us with a hand on the side of the house, and it sounded like Mick was actually wheezing. Then some girl came out and whispered something to Mick. It looked like one of the teenage Mouseketeers. It looked like Laurie. She and Mick stepped into the shadows for a moment, and you could hear Mick saying something in a low whisper, but it wasn't clear what, and then Laurie was giggling, and then they stepped back into the glow of the light coming through the sliding-glass doors. "Say, Lauterbach," Mick said. "Can you do us a favor? Laurie has been abandoned by her ride. Jilted, in the vernacular. Can you take her home? She's looking for a knight in shining armor."

"Sure, Mick," I said.

"Thanks, Mr. Lauterbach. I could just kill that Sonya."

We went inside, Mick first, and he went directly behind the kitchen counter and grabbed a beer, and then me and Laurie followed him. It seemed pretty warm in the house with everybody just sitting around on the floor and on the bar stools and squished together on the maroon colored sofa beneath the mermaid and all of them looking at us with these pleasant, slightly puzzled expressions, as if their brains had melted and they couldn't quite comprehend who we were or where we had come from. I said a couple of goodbyes to people I didn't really know, and then a voice piped up from the sofa.

It was Joyce's sister.

"So that's your type, eh, Travis?"

Then she started laughing and spilling some of her frothy strawberry margarita on the people next to her. I didn't say anything. I was suddenly conscious of Laurie sort of hovering there right by my elbow. I didn't even look at her. Then Laurie and I were out the door.

I don't think I said a word to Laurie all the way to her house. She lived in a development about fifty minutes away. We drove along this lonely stretch along Butler Boulevard where there's nothing but trees and this sort of grassy, swampy nothingness and these thin, wiry highway lamps that glow with a strange soft pinkish glow, like radiation or something. It's a pretty lonely, eerie stretch of road, desolate. Like alien abduction desolate. But I didn't say a word to Laurie the whole time we were in the car. I could feel her squirmy, teenage Mouseketeer presence there on the seat next to me. She kicked off her sandals and curled her legs up on the seat so her skirt was riding up along her thighs, high enough so you could see her bikini bottoms. It seemed like she was trying to get my attention. But I didn't really have anything to say. What would I say, thanks but no thanks Laurie, I'm madly in love with someone else, which was the absolute truth, but there was no need to share my intimate bathtub secrets with this girl.

I'm not sure what time it was when we pulled into Laurie's driveway. Laurie lived on the river on the San Marco side. You couldn't really see the house in the darkness, just this heavy lush shadow and trees all over the place and heavy, thick bushes, but you could feel the richness of the place. It was sort of like being chloroformed. The only light was coming from this seventeenth century Spanish-style cast iron lantern fixed to one side of the front door, and it was glowing a soft green light and it cast these shimmery greenish shadows down a narrow brick walk, and then the walk widening and a marble fountain with sculpted laurel leaves all around and a Greek god or goddess or something in the middle, but the water was off, and then the walk narrowing again. It looked like something from *Twenty Thousand Leagues Under the Sea.* I kept the motor running, but Laurie didn't get out of the car right away.

"Do you want to come in, Mr. Lauterbach?" she said.

And then: "My parents won't be home for a week."

Then she kissed me.

I was sitting there sort of stunned by her question and I wasn't even sure if I had heard her right, and then she kissed me. Or maybe I kissed her. I don't really know how it happened. But the truth is I really wasn't kissing her at all. I mean my body was. But my mind was kissing Tommie Rodriguez. I know that sounds pretty lame, but it's the truth. I was so pumped up from Tommie and the party at Mick's house and then I was kissing Laurie but I was thinking it was Tommie and my body just sort of took over. This was the kiss I had wanted to give to Tommie. I was Humphrey Bogart in body, mind, and soul, and I wasn't going to let Tommie escape so easily a second time, even if it wasn't really Tommie, so I wrapped my arms around Laurie and kissed her hard and long until she gave this breezy, moaning sigh, and then it was a softer kiss, our lips barely touching, feathery, moist, like clouds floating by, floating away, dissolving, and then her whole body shuddered and her moaning sigh from before became a cooing sort of sound, and then it was quiet. I don't know how long we sat there with the motor running. Then Laurie invited me in a second time, but I said no. I couldn't. I hadn't even meant to kiss her. But Laurie just sort of giggled and said, "It's all right Mr. Lauterbach. Don't worry about it."

And just like that Laurie slipped out of the car, her sandals dangling in her hand, and ran up the narrow brick walk with her blond ponytail bouncing and her whole lithe body moving effortlessly through the soft, hazy greenish underwater glow of the lantern, the way dolphins move through water, and then she disappeared inside. I watched her go, and after she was gone I stared at the soft green light of the lantern for a while. Then I left.

-6-

You always hear old guys talking about how time just keeps slipping away, faster and faster, and you don't really believe them because you think it's all just sour grapes now that they're old and can't get around like they used to. But it's true. Before I knew it, Thanksgiving was over and the kids were back in class with these dippy, bloated smiles from too much turkey and stuffing and cranberry sauce, and their brains were turned off by then because there were only two weeks left and then finals and then Christmas. It was all pretty much a blur. I tried calling Tommie a couple of times, but she was busy one night with grading Spanish papers, and the other night I guess she was out. We were supposed to have Thanksgiving at the beach house, just her and me, if you can believe that, and you just knew it was going to be one of those clear bright days when you feel that everything is possible, clear and bright like a photograph, and you knew there was going to be a warm breeze blowing up from the water and the sliding glass doors would be open so we could breathe in the salt spray, and maybe we would even eat our turkey outside on the makeshift patio so we could watch the waves coming in, but then Tommie's grandmother got sick and Tommie had to head up to Brooklyn because her grandmother was at that age when you wake up one morning with a cough and the next morning someone calls a priest. She headed up there the Wednesday before, and she was supposed to be back for classes on Monday, but she was gone almost three weeks. So it was me and Ed for Thanksgiving, but Ed didn't want to come out to the beach, and neither of us felt like cooking anyway, so we went out. The only place that was open was the Japanese restaurant downtown.

I have to say Ed was pretty damn gloomy. He had been in a pretty gloomy state ever since he found out about the affair between his ex-wife and Father Adleman. It didn't matter that it was from years ago or that he wasn't married anymore and he didn't even like his ex-wife to begin with. It went deeper than that. It was like he had just found out that God didn't exist, that the whole thing with Christ and walking on water and heaven when you die was a sham cooked up by some guys drinking whiskey in the back room of some seedy bar called Gus's down in Miami and laughing their heads off at the rest of us. You had to feel sorry for old Ed. When Catholics slide off the map they've got nowhere to go. So there we were sitting on pillows and our legs cramping because even after a year and a half of eating sushi we still weren't used to sitting cross-legged on the floor, or trying to. The silk pillows they gave us were no help. And poor old gloomy Ed was drinking Takara Sake by the gallon and leaning across the table and leering at me and pushing a shot glass of Sake across and watching me drink and then laughing and sitting back. This went on for a while, an endless loop. But at one point Ed seemed to sober up for a few minutes, like he was suddenly back in the Marines, and he said, "I'll tell you what, Travis, everybody gets fucked sooner or later, especially if you don't play along, then you get fucked before you know what hit you, and if you do play along, well, you get fucked then too, it just takes a little longer, but there's no way around it, so what the hell."

I was staring at Ed's face while he was talking, and the blue and orange light from a couple of lanterns was washing over him, and maybe it was the Sake, I don't really remember how many I'd had by then, not as much as Ed, but it must have been more than enough because all of a sudden old Ed reminded me of one of those slaggy, diseased goldfish in the pond out front blowing bubbles. His mouth was moving, but it was like he was under water or something because you could hardly understand him. Wave after wave of orange and blue light washing across his face and him waving his arms and his mouth moving but you could only make out a word or two, like he was drowning, and the more I focused on I trying to hear what he was saying, the worse it got, until I couldn't hear a thing except this sort of gargling sound way off in the distance. Then Ed seemed to forget I was even there and he was back at the Sake. I don't know how many bottles we put away. It was one hell of a Thanksgiving dinner. The woman from behind the register kept bringing us Sake, and every once in a while she brought out a tray of sushi and we gobbled it up while she was standing right there, smiling in her silky blue kimono and bowing slightly and then shuffling off the way those geisha girls do in the old Japanese movies, back and forth with trays even when we didn't ask and jabbering her broken English and smiling some more. After a while she became sort of a blue blur, like a ghost or something that you can only see out of the corner of your eye. I guess we were the only customers in the place. I guess Thanksgiving wasn't one of their big nights. Then the trays stopped and you could hear she was back at the register ringing something up and then the sound of the drawer banging shut, but you couldn't see her because of the fake bamboo hut.

Sometimes I think Ed knew all along what was going to happen, but he didn't know how to tell me. That's why he started in on the Sake like he did. Nothing much matters after a couple of bottles of Sake. You feel like a god damn samurai warrior after a couple of bottles, like you are mother fucking invincible, and even when you sober up the next day the glow of that feeling lingers a while, sometimes for days, even longer, depending upon the weather. For me, I was feeling invincible up until eleven a.m. on Friday, December 17th. It was the last day of the term. I had just given my last final and was walking across the courtyard. I was almost skipping across, like I was one of my dippy-faced kids heading down to Disney World. Glassy-eyed aimless kids drinking up the soma of the modern world. But I guess I was just like them. I had no clue what I really wanted or how to get it. I wanted to believe that my very own happiness was out there somewhere, if only I just looked in the right place. I wanted to believe in the unadulterated joy of dolphins and the search for paradise and two souls spinning across the universe. I guess I was glassy-eyed in my belief. I had talked to Tommie the night before on the phone and she said she was coming back on Saturday, her grandmother was much better. She said she had a lot of Christmas shopping to do and decorating the apartment and baking cookies and she wanted a tree and a whole bunch of Christmas-type stuff, and everything she wanted to do included me.

I have to say now that whole day and the next two weeks afterwards keep spinning through my mind like a slow-motion movie, especially that first day. I try to slow things down, freeze the frames, reverse everything, but it just goes on and on, and when it gets to the end it loops back to the beginning, all the way back to the very first day I started teaching, and then I have to live through everything all over again.

So there I was practically skipping across the courtyard, and the gloomy smallness of my bank account and the eternal oppressive heat of the Florida sun was washed away because I would see Tommie the next day. I remember thinking I could live in that moment forever, with hope stretching out beyond the horizon. There was no other place I would rather be. I crossed the one courtyard and then zigzagged between classrooms and across another courtyard. I breathed in the scent of pine trees. The school was a series of oblong red brick one-story buildings, some going north to south, some east to west, all of them connected by a maze of roofed walkways. There were courtyards all over the damn place with scraggly aspen trees propped up by stakes and cedar benches with plaques that said

Alumni Gift Class of Whatever where you could sit, but the outer edge of the school was surrounded by towering pine trees. Pine needles covered the ground. I once told Mick the school looked like a rat's maze, which made him laugh. First hour would end and the bell would ring and the dippy-faced kids would scurry out of their classrooms and down the walkways, and for five minutes it was like rats trying to escape the water in a sinking ship, and then the bell would ring a second time and you could see through the windows of each classroom, the kids once again trapped behind their desks, their bewildered dippy rat faces looking out at the pine trees and the patches of sky and the pine needles and the courtyards and the benches and wishing they were somewhere else. But today was different. I didn't notice anybody. I breathed in the scent of the pine trees and I felt the world opening up before me, and then it felt like I was standing outside of time. I felt a sense of freedom and pure joy I had felt only once before, that day at the Jacksonville Landing when I had watched those dolphins swimming up the St. John's River. I was going to see Tommie the very next day. Nothing else mattered.

The next thing I knew I was standing in the middle of the teacher's lounge. The place was already deserted. You could tell everybody had been anxious to get out of there. The mailboxes were mostly empty and the wastebasket was crammed full of extra exams and pens that didn't work, and there were half-drunk mugs of coffee all over the work table, and someone had left a perfectly good lunch in the microwave. The only other somebody in the lounge was Harvey Collins, but he was asleep in the fuzzy pink lounge chair. The air conditioner was on the fritz again and it was so damn hot that Harvey's white scalp was streaked with perspiration, and the few strands of white hair he had combed across his head were pasted to his skin. It was probably his lunch in the microwave, but he didn't seem to care. He was in short sleeves and his arms were covered in pink fuzzy beads and he was just snoring away, blissfully unconcerned with the real world, a ludicrous smile plastered across his face, like he was dreaming about grocery store lines and Laundromats and big beautiful curvy behinds. When I think back on everything, I'm not really sure why I went to the teacher's lounge anyway. When I think back on everything, I try to stop myself from going in. I guess a part of me thinks that if I hadn't gone in, if I hadn't noticed a small white envelope in my mailbox, then things would have turned out differently. I know it's a foolish thought, but I was a glassy-eyed aimless, dippy-faced kid same as the students I taught, like I already said. I didn't know what I didn't know. So there I was, standing in front of an avalanche of empty mailboxes with a small white envelope in my hand and my name scrawled across the middle in black ink, and then in parenthesis it said "urgent."

My first thought was it was from Tommie. My second thought was if it was from Tommie, how did it get there? My third thought was why was it marked urgent, and did I really want to find out? I don't remember what I was thinking after that. The letter wasn't from Tommie. It wasn't even a letter. It was a memo from the desk of The Very Reverend Richard Dubois, and it said I was to report to his office immediately, it was a very urgent matter, underlined twice for emphasis.

I read the memo three times just to be sure, and then I looked at the clock on the wall, one of those old fashioned General Electric clocks with the heavy black trim, and I knew it was eleven a.m., or close to it, but I couldn't make out the numbers. I thought maybe I was going suddenly blind, like I had been stricken with some strange, alien disease. It sort of felt like the fabric of reality was melting, like maybe I had slipped into an alternative reality universe like in *Blade Runner* and I was a replicant and Harrison Ford was gunning for me. A wave of nausea swept over me, through me. It seemed like my eyeballs were beginning to bleed. My teeth started to ache. I could hear Harvey Collins from the fuzzy pink lounge chair and he was laughing in his sleep, but it was a slightly hysterical, robotic kind of laughter, and then he wasn't sleeping any more, he was calling out to me, he was asking me if I was going to the faculty Christmas party on Saturday and was I still dating that little Spanish spitfire, Tommie Rodriguez, but his voice was distorted, thin, it had a tinny sound to it, it sounded staticky and very far away, like his voice was coming out of an old RCA Victor FM radio from the 1940s, like when my dad was a kid.

Then Harvey fell back asleep, or maybe he got up and went over to the microwave. I don't know. I was just standing there in front of the empty mailboxes, unable to move, staring at the memo. Probably it was only a few minutes, but it seemed a hell of a lot longer. After that a couple of happy, goofball teachers came in. They sounded as happy as clams, if you can imagine clams telling private jokes and then twittering away like no one else was around, but I didn't recognize them, which was pretty damn odd, if you want to know the truth, because there were only about a hundred teachers in the whole damn school, which I guess was just one more example that I had lost my grip. A couple more goofballs came in, as happy as clams like the other two, and I didn't recognize them either, and about then it felt like the whole goddamn world was closing in. I could hardly breathe. My eyesight had gotten worse. It was like looking through gauze. I could feel a tightening in my chest, and then a relaxing, and then a tightening again. My shirt was pretty much soaked through from perspiring. I was sweating bullets. I could tell the four happy-as-clam-types were looking at me with the memo in my hand like they were trying to read it over my shoulder. They were swirling around me, acting like they wanted to get to their own mailboxes, which even in the delirium of my going blind I could see were empty, I was close enough to see that, but they kept on swirling, and all the while they were laughing about their students and how many had failed their exams, and pretty much sounding like every other happy-as-a-clam teacher talking politely about the dippy kids they had to teach. Then there was a snapping sensation, like the frame of the universe had been tilted and some janitor had come along and grabbed hold of the frame and snapped it back into place, and just like that I could see again, only I was looking down at myself this time, like I had become detached from my body. I was sort of floating just above the mailboxes and the four teachers still swirling and still jabbering, and I was looking down at myself looking at the memo and blinking and the sweat still rolling down my back. I wondered if I was dead. I wondered if I had had a heart attack from one of those congenital conditions nobody knows about until it's too late, which you have to admit is an understandable reaction when you are floating above yourself, but if it had been a heart attack, my other self would have collapsed to the floor and the four goofball teachers would have switched to good Samaritan mode, and one of them would have started CPR, and another would have called for an ambulance, and the other two would have stood there, hunched over, looking at an almost dead body with eager, horrified expressions on their faces because most likely this would have been their first experience with death. But this did not happen because it wasn't a heart attack. I had not died. I think it was just the shock of the moment replayed a thousand times in my mind, which after a while you sort of detach yourself from what really happened and you start watching the events of your own life like you're watching a movie. That's why I see it now like I do. Sometimes I can even hear my own voice narrating the sequence of events.

Harvey Collins had retrieved his lunch and was sitting at the worktable spooning in macaroni stew, and he was talking to the other four and they were answering him back, but I still couldn't make out what they were saying. Probably some more about the Christmas party. I watched my other self head for the door, but then the door whooshed open and Amy Baxter whooshed in with a basket of last minute holiday announcements, and Amy almost knocked my other self over on account of she's one of those impulsive types that never look where they're going, which I have to say makes her the perfect secretary for the Reverend Dubois, but she caught herself at the last moment and just sort of bounced to one side. She started to say excuse me and was looking up with these two fiery green eyes that always look like they are about to explode and her red hair tossed about in a tangled mess, but when she saw it was me, which is to say when she saw my other self with the wrinkled memo in his hands and the blood dripping from his eyes, she swallowed her words and her eyes went dark with disapproval and she whirled away and began stuffing white envelopes with little green Christmas wreaths on the front into the mailboxes, one after another, like she was punching tickets. My other self didn't say a word. My other self headed out the door. But I stayed behind for a few moments, floating above the mailboxes, watching Amy Baxter and the other four and the pink-faced Harvey Collins with his arms still covered in pink fuzzy beads shoveling in macaroni stew. The next thing I knew everyone was reading their last minute holiday announcements, apparently Amy Baxter thought they should read them right away, only they weren't about the holidays, they were about me, both myself and my other self, and then the four teachers were shaking their heads and saying it was hard to believe, a nice fellow like him, how does something like that happen, you think you know people, but you never know people, not really, and then Amy Baxter piping up how she knew all along, there was something peculiar about that one, you could see it in his eyes, and the other four nodding in reluctant agreement, and Harvey Collins not saying much of anything, just sitting there blinking at Amy and the four happy-as-clam-types, and then back to his stew.

I didn't wait around after that. I floated up through the ceiling and headed outside. It was a cool, sunny bright day, but not too cool, which surprised me, I have to admit. You always imagine bad news arriving on rainy days, but that's not the case. Bad news almost always comes on the sunniest, brightest day there is, which I guess means the universe doesn't really bother about what happens to anyone. The universe could care less. I mean why should the universe care one way or the other, no matter what happens, life goes on. Of course I wasn't thinking all this back then. I wasn't thinking much of anything. I looked around to get my bearings. I was pretty high up by then and could see the whole campus. The red brick buildings were clumped together on one end, and beyond that there was a paved parking lot full of Datsuns and small, tinny Toyotas and old Chevys and dented Buicks for the teachers, and then a sandy parking lot beneath the pine trees for the students and Mercedes convertibles and BMWs pulling out, kicking up little puffs of dust and tires screeching when they hit the pavement, and on the other end of the campus there was a grassy stretch and the television evangelist style auditorium and the live oaks and the ground sloping away and then the heavy dark blue of the St. John's River. It almost looked like a painting, like the kind they sell in grocery store parking lots at the beach for the tourists. I could see a few students still hanging out in the courtyards below, and a few teachers trudging about with boxes of exams to grade, all of them heading for the teacher's lounge before they left for the day. My other self was heading for the office of The Very Reverend Richard Dubois, but I had no interest in joining him. I preferred the open air and the sunshine. From my vantage point above the trees the horizon seemed to stretch to infinity. I lost myself in the infinity of the moment. I lost myself in the silence of floating above the world. But it didn't last. After a while, I don't know how long, I heard the Reverend's voice, a faint, slightly nasal, squirrelly voice pricking at my ears. "I'm afraid you don't realize how serious this is Mr. Lauterbach, it is quite serious, and while it is not criminal, and believe me, Mr. Lauterbach, our investigation of the matter was quite exhaustive, if there had been even the barest hint of criminality, we would be having this conversation down at the police station, a statement, I think, which Ms. Daly and Ms. Pearsons sitting here beside me can both heartily endorse, but all that aside, Mr. Lauterbach, your actions are an irreparable breach of your moral responsibilities as a teacher at this educational institution, you were supposed to hold the interests of the students above your own at all times, which is to say that you were to understand what is in the best interest of the students at all times, there can be no exceptions, no excuses, did you not imagine, Mr. Lauterbach, what would happen, did you think the girl in question would remain unprovoked by her emotions, if you did you were naïve, she recorded every thought, every hope and dream in a diary, a diary, Mr. Lauterbach, which her mother found and read and brought to our attention in a state of panic not seen since the Chicago riots of the sixties when the police were armed with tear gas and assault rifles, yes, Mr. Lauterbach, that was the effect you had upon this young girl and upon her mother, unwittingly or no, you have brought this upon yourself, and it does not matter that most of what she wrote is a fabrication, it does not matter if the only crime was a single kiss, no indeed, the fact of the kiss is not the issue, and we have gone around this point for some time now, Ms. Daly and Ms. Pearsons and myself, no, the crime was that you put the girl in question into a situation where such a crime could occur, you assaulted her imagination with your presence, and you did this when her parents were away on an extended vacation, your abandonment of strict moral principles is quite extraordinary, Mr. Lauterbach, by which we mean to say it is totally unacceptable, we cannot tolerate this kind of behavior in our school, not under any circumstances, and so we have no choice, Mr. Lauterbach, but to terminate your employment, said termination to be effective immediately, the faculty and staff have already been notified, yes, Mr. Lauterbach, yes, the white envelopes with the Christmas wreaths on the front, yes, I suppose it is ironic at that, no, no, the announcement to the faculty merely states that you were terminated for unprofessional conduct, it does not define the nature of that conduct, no, Mr. Lauterbach, there are no mitigating circumstances, no, Mr. Lauterbach, what the faculty chooses to believe about what happened is entirely up to them, no, no, please, Mr. Lauterbach, no hysterics, the time for hysterics has passed, please take this box and gather up your things, you have one hour to vacate your classroom, after which time if you are still here we will call the police, what was that Mr. Lauterbach, why yes, of course, we are not without compassion, we are, after all, a Christian school founded on Christian principles, but remember, Mr. Lauterbach, you are to have no contact with this girl under any circumstances from this day forward, she is still a minor, or if she isn't, well, she is still a student at this school, so if you do try to contact her, well, that would be unfortunate, we would have to consider such behavior harassment and you would be charged under the law, and to the fullest extent of the law, do you understand what I am saying, Mr. Lauterbach, do I make myself clear, Mr. Lauterbach, yes, yes, good, very good."

Then the nasally, squirrelly voice of the good Reverend faded completely. It was almost as if it had been a figment of my imagination. But the silence of floating above the world did not return. At least that's how I remember it. I continued to float above the school for a while, but the silence from before was gone. I heard some kids shouting in the student parking lot and then some laughter and then the sound of someone leaning on a horn and then a couple more horns blaring away and then more laughter and then they drove off. I heard the heavy thud of a door slammed shut and then I saw my other self emerge from the shadows of the administration building, frowning a pinched-face frown, clutching an empty box. I saw my other self cut across the grass by the flagpole and then disappear into the maze of roofed walkways. From somewhere there was the sound of a bell. I could see a dozen or so colleagues at various points around the campus, some of them heading to the faculty parking lot, some of them cutting across courtyards or heading back to their classrooms. Some of them were murmuring to themselves, a low steady rumble that drifted up into the air. But all of them were reading the holiday announcement of my sudden termination, some of them reading as they walked, some of them walking and reading and then sitting down on one of the many alumni gift benches to catch their breath. You could tell some of them didn't know what to think. You could also tell that some of them had their own ideas from the very beginning, from before even the very first sentence.

I closed my eyes and tried to forget what was happening. I knew I wasn't dead. I knew if I waited long enough, everything would settle. I had seen enough documentaries on the Sci-Fi channel to know how out-of-body experiences worked. But it sure as hell made you think. Maybe when you died you were floating above yourself same as I was, and you could go anywhere you wanted to, take a look at any moment from your life, but after a while you would forget what you were looking at, and that's when you really died. Maybe that's how it had been with that dolphin. Maybe when I was looking at that dolphin on the beach, maybe it was floating in the air just above me, maybe its soul was still close enough that I could see its reflection in the body it was leaving behind, like one was a mirror to the other, and since the dolphin's other self, its soul, was brimming with happiness, that's what I saw.

I guess you can't say for sure about anything. My own experience didn't come close to what I thought might have happened to that dolphin. For one thing, I wasn't dead. I sure as hell knew that. I was floating above everything with my eyes closed, but at the same time I was rooted to the earth. I breathed in deeply. I heard the distant wavering cry of a blue jay. I heard the dull incessant whoosh of traffic moving along Atlantic Boulevard. Then I heard the sound of a car starting up. It was my own dirty white Toyota Corolla. I opened my eyes and watched my other self drive away, a flash of white through the dark green foliage of the pine trees. But I wasn't ready to descend just yet. I wanted to linger a while longer in the pure clean sunshine that existed beyond the naked ache of my dismissal. I wanted to float away on the breeze of my future. I wanted to know, at least for a moment, that the horizon, my horizon, stretched beyond the shadows of my imagination to the bright edge of infinity. I know that sounds pretty god damn lame, a bit too poetic. I don't usually go in for poetry. But that's pretty close to what it felt like. It's as close as I can get to it.

-7-

I no longer lived in the pinkish, orangeish cement apartment building five blocks from St. Vincent's hospital. I no longer lived in Jacksonville proper. After Mick left I took over his bungalow at the beach, and I stayed there through the end of December. I think it was the warmest December on record, that's what the paper said.

Mostly I didn't do a hell of a lot. Either I moped around the house drinking beer and eating cereal, or I walked up and down the beach thinking about Tommie and the dolphin and dolphins in general and that night by the bonfire. Sometimes I would get bored and head out to the beach with a couple of buckets of crushed seashells and toss handfuls to the seagulls and watch them scramble, thinking it was food. Sometimes I would watch the tourists from New York or Michigan take a dip in the ocean because they were the only ones who didn't think the water was cold and their kids screaming bloody murder all the way down to the edge and then laughing when they got wet and then they didn't want to leave.

That very first Saturday night, when the rest of the faculty was whooping it up at the faculty Christmas party at the Reverend Dubois' house, I was sitting in a white plastic chair wedged into the sand watching a handful of shrimp boats heading south along the horizon, dark shadows against the fading blue sky, and then it was just their green running lights winking in the darkness. I had brought down a cooler stuffed with beer. I was thinking some about Tommie and wondering if I would ever see her again. I didn't even get a chance to tell her what had happened. I hadn't really even talked to her since Mick's party. And now there was no chance. I was sure of that. I was pretty sure Emily Lavigne and Walter had filled her head with all sorts of crap, they were just the type. I could see old Walter hunched over the steering wheel of that goddamn black and blue Chevy Citation when they picked Tommie up from the airport and Walter smirking as he told her all about my depraved nature and everything I had done. I bet he told her I had raped the girl but the girl wouldn't talk and not even her mother or her aunt, who flew up from Miami, could get her to open up, and so they couldn't prove a thing, which was the only reason I wasn't in jail. I'm pretty sure Walter said something like that. I was pretty pissed about that. I was pretty pissed about Emily and Walter in general, but I didn't know what to do. So I sat in my white plastic chair and looked out at the swirling darkness where the sky meets the sea and I let my mind wander. I still felt kind of disoriented. I certainly wasn't happy about the way things had turned out, but then again, I was exactly unhappy either. The shrimp boats had moved down the coast a mile or so. It was hard to tell exactly how far. You had to really strain to see their green lights, and even then, it could have been your imagination. I gave up after a while and drank another beer.

I drank beer until I couldn't see a thing.

The next Monday Ed came out to the house. I guess he came out to see how I was doing, but he didn't want to come inside. I don't know why. Maybe he felt guilty about not telling me the trouble I was in when we were at the Japanese restaurant. Or maybe he thought I had a couple of mermaids stashed inside like Mick and the less he knew the better for him. Ed was funny like that sometimes. So I brought out my last four beers, even if it was only ten in the morning, and we stood outside in the middle of the street. We were close enough to the beach that parts of the street were covered with sand. The air was still cool, but the sky was a bright, warm, robin's egg blue, so you knew it was going to be a real scorcher.

For a while we didn't say anything. We just drank our beers and looked up at the sky or out at the beach, shading our eyes because of the brightness of the sun.

Then Ed started to open up.

"They're a bunch of fuckers," Ed said.

I grunted some into my beer.

"All of them," Ed said. "Every last goddamn one."

I still didn't know just what to say, and with Ed, well, you have to be careful. I began to think Ed had started his drinking for the day a few hours earlier.

"You know it's all anybody who works at that goddamn school can talk about," Ed said. "Hell, it's probably all over the goddamn town already."

"What's all over?" I said.

Ed glared down at his beer.

"Ah, just fuck it," he said. "Fuck everything."

"Yeah," I said. "That pretty much sums it up."

He drank some more of his beer.

"I hope to God you fucked the hell out of her," Ed said. "All of those girls, that's all they want anyway, the way they wiggle their tight little teenage asses so you can't help but stare at them and pushing their titties right into your face and looking up at you and their eyes getting bigger and you can almost taste it. They know exactly what they're doing."

Ed took another swig.

"Goddamn teases," he said. "What do they expect you to do?"

"Yeah, well, nothing happened, if that's what you're asking."

"What do you mean nothing happened?"

"I mean nothing happened. I mean I drove the girl home and then she leaned over and kissed me and said her parents were away and I said no thanks and that was that. She went inside and I went home. Nothing happened."

"But that doesn't make any sense."

"Nothing makes any sense."

Ed looked like he wanted to hit something, but he didn't.

"Fuck it," he said. "I guess you're right."

There wasn't much left to say between me and Ed after that. I was leaning up against my Toyota Corolla, which was parked sort of crooked, half on the sidewalk about two steps from the front of the house and the gate and the cobblestone walk and the potted ferns. The potted ferns were a dry brown color and you could tell they were pretty much dead. The next thing I knew I was looking at Ed's shadow. I wasn't looking directly at him. I was sort of looking at his shadow there in one of the sandy stretches on the street, but I wasn't feeling gloomy or anything like that. There was a slight breeze blowing across the street and Ed's shadow was sort of shimmering and I was looking at his shadow and thinking maybe our souls were like shadows and you could only see them in bright sunlight, but even then they were sort of shimmery, like Ed's shadow was, and the moment you realized you were looking at someone's soul it would disappear. I guess it was probably the beers doing all that thinking. I don't usually go in for beer at ten in the morning. Then Ed shifted himself away from the sun and his shadow was gone and he was leaning up against the Toyota, same as me. It was starting to get hot. We didn't speak for a long time. We looked out at the beach. There were a few Northerners running down to the water and a couple of beachcomber types wearing khaki bucket hats and sweeping the beach with metal detectors, sifting through the sand for loose change, and a few seagulls flying up into the air and flapping a while and then settling back down. We finished our beers, but we didn't move. We were hanging on to our empty bottles, the sun flashing against the bottle glass, but we didn't wince. We kept looking out at the beach and the salt water and the waves flashing silver and then curling and the sand pipers running up and then back out.

That was the last time I saw old Ed. He said maybe we should get together for New Year's, and then he said we would definitely get together, he would be out on the 31st with a couple of cases of beer, and we would drink until the moon fell into the fucking sea. Ed was a lunatic like that sometimes, but I couldn't tell if he really meant it or not. People are funny about things like that. They say they want to get together just to be polite but inside they're squirming like eels because all they want is to be let off the hook. I don't know if Ed was on the hook or not, but I let him off anyway. A couple of days before New Year's Eve I packed up my dirty white Toyota and headed south for Miami. Mick was in Miami. Or at least he had been. About one week after the party, I got a postcard from Mick. It had a Miami postmark. It was one of those vintage postcards from the 1930s with a picture of some kind of 18th century Spanish estate somewhere in Miami, somewhere overlooking a causeway with a couple of three-story stone buildings with red tile roofs and old-style iron lanterns fixed to the outside walls, and the water was a greenish, aquamarine blue and the sun setting in the background, and there was a flagstone walkway and a couple of steps up and then a small stone bridge arching over the water, the kind of bridge with an iron railing. There were about a dozen palm trees all over the place. At the top, printed in a very fancy type, were the words: *Venetian Casino, Coral Gables, Florida.* I guess it was supposed to be the Florida version of Venice. On the back Mick wrote: "I'll be here a few weeks. Can't say after that." He didn't say exactly where 'here' was. Maybe he had just been passing through Miami and was shacked up somewhere in the Keys drinking New Orleans-style Hurricanes night after night, drinking himself blind. Or maybe he really was going to Patagonia and he had already boarded a steamer and he was halfway there. It didn't matter. I was going to head south and find Mick no matter where he was and start my life completely fucking over, and at the same time I was going to let Ed off the hook whether that's what he wanted or not. That's pretty much what I was thinking. So I packed up my car, which didn't take all that long because I didn't have that much stuff anyway, a worn-out green army issue duffel bag that my dad gave me, filled to the brim with shirts and underwear and shorts and a few rolled up pairs of jeans; a shaving kit, a couple of pairs of khakis and three white shirts and two good jackets, preppy jackets, the kind I had to wear in the classroom, three boxes of books, everything from Kafka to Rod Serling to Hemingway, and a bunch of cassettes and a boom box. Then I scribbled a note to Ed and told him about the house and how I was giving it to him and he could do what he wanted just so long as he paid the taxes but if he didn't want it he could let it rot but then it would be his fault. I taped the keys and the note to the front door and started up the car, but then I just sat there for a while, looking at the reflection of the beach and the sky in the rear view mirror. It was a cloudy morning but you could see the sun sort of shimmering behind the clouds. I don't know how long I sat there. It was like my brain was trapped inside the clouds and I was waiting for the sun to burn them away. I thought about Ed and I wasn't sure if Ed wanted anything to do with an ex-hippie beach house. Then again, I wasn't even sure if Ed would get the note. It almost seemed like a joke, like stuffing a message into a bottle and chucking the bottle into the sea. But I didn't care. There was this little voice inside my head and it was telling me it was time to move. I think it was probably Mick's voice inside my head, but I guess that didn't matter too much. I was already moving in a direction that went beyond Mick. With my sudden termination I was now moving beyond anything and everything I could possibly have imagined. I was once again floating high above the world, higher even than the clouds, hardly able to breathe in the cold, thin atmosphere, dazzled by the sun. That's how it felt. That's how I saw myself. I was moving towards a limitless horizon. I was moving towards the bright edge of infinity. Then I leaned closer to the rear view mirror and saw my own reflection. I hadn't shaved in two weeks and the stubbly hair that grows on my face was pretty thick. My face looked almost black, except for these two brightly glowing eyes staring back at me from two sunken eye sockets. It was like the eyes of someone with radiation sickness. I was almost smiling, but it was a strange, twisted smile. I almost didn't recognize myself. I smiled back. Still smiling, I shifted the car into drive and hit the gas. I don't remember a thing after that.

BOOK TWO

the heart and soul of Calle Ocho

-8-

We are standing on a small stone bridge looking at tinted water. Across the water there are palm trees and an immaculate stone building with a red-tiled roof. We are waiting to see what we will do. It is almost like waiting for a funeral. I am beginning to think we are already dead.

We have never been here before. Correction. I have never been here before. The two teachers were here before. That's what they said. The one showed me a postcard. Venetian Casino, Coral Gables, it said. That's why I went with them. I wanted to see this Venetian Casino in south Florida. A taste of Europe with the barest hint of happy, unrepentant sex, like a spice, raw decadence, uncrushed, waiting to be crushed, the rush of breathing it in, the blood boiling, one brief hour of madness and joy. It has been a long time since I have been in Europe.

But the postcard was an illusion. It was a charlatan's ruse. There is no casino. It is a swimming pool instead. The Venetian canal so elegantly captured on the postcard is in reality a swimming pool. The stone building across from the stone bridge contains changing rooms and showers, a counter where you can buy hot dogs and sodas, a gift shop where you can buy suntan lotion and swimsuits, and a window where you pay to get in. If only I could have stepped into the painting on the postcard. There's a second stone building in the foreground, a Spanish style building like the first one, just before the bridge, with an old-time iron lantern fixed to the wall. The lantern is glowing in the postcard. It is sunset. The sky is streaked with a salmon pink color and the clouds float across, white wispy clouds, like white lace, virgin lace, the white lace dissipating, evaporating, leaving the naked, virgin, salmon pink sky to fend for itself. It is a delicious sky. It is the perfect sky for having sex. I am certain with the sky like it is that the stone building in the foreground is a bordello. I can smell a bordello a mile off, at least a mile. The whiff is unmistakable. That and the color of the sky. But I am getting ahead of myself here. To make sense of what happens next, I need to go back to before I even knew the Venetian Casino existed. Before I first crossed paths with the two teachers.

We live in Little Havana where Calle Ocho vanishes into

the glare of the midday sun, a good thirty-minute walk to Domino Park, at least for me. By "we" I am referring to myself, Xavier Mendoza, and Soledad, who has been with me since before I care to remember. We live on a bright, clean street in a bright, clean neighborhood. The buildings are painted bright pink and bright yellow and there are bars on the windows. It is always midday where we live, even in the middle of the night. We own a small café called The Patagonian Café and we live on the second floor. I do not remember if we chose the name, if my beautiful and resilient Soledad chose the name, or if it has always been The Patagonian Café.

We employ eight beautiful *chicas jóvenes* to serve plates of roast chicken and rice and red pimentos and sweet potato pudding for desert, or cornbread and chunks of fried pork and ripe plantains, which I don't care for myself, or black bean soup, or spicy beef hash and fried potatoes. There is always plenty to eat. No one complains. And always we are serving drinks, mojitos and caipirinhas and Cuba Libres and mango martinis, and also beer and wine, plenty of wine. We make most of our money on the drinks. After the drinks the girls are on their own.

One Friday night last year the police poured into our café and lined up all the men on one side and all the girls on the other side. We wondered if they were looking for someone in particular, or if anyone would do. It is not always easy to tell who is a criminal and who is not, especially with the men. Some of them were wearing white shirts and thin yellow ties and brown suits off the rack and suede saddle shoes, like they were accountants from downtown. Some of the others were a bit greasier in appearance with ratty leather jackets and shirts with sequins and dirty jeans and moccasins or maybe black boots, and always lice crawling through greasy hair, their hair is dripping with grease, like bacon grease, and always they have a knife or two or three up their sleeves. But for some reason these *greasy gamberros* never seem to carry guns. It is the well-dressed accountants who carry the guns. But the police were not overly concerned with the men. Their primary focus was the girls. They made the girls spread their legs wide like so, so they could make sure nothing was hidden, and the girls were giggling with their breezy chiffon skirts riding high and their meaty brown assess pushed out away from the wall and wiggling with the promise of something juicy, and some of them wearing only thongs underneath, and some of them wearing nothing at all. Later they said it would have been fun, except it was the police. The police said there was a lot of crime in the neighborhood, a lot of whores looking to score, a lot of johns with loose change ready to plug a nickel or a dime or a quarter into any open slot, any moist, wet, titillating crevice. They searched everyone's pockets and purses, but they didn't keep track of what came out of whose pocket or which purse. They dumped everything on a table in the middle of the cafe. Knives, pocket books, wallets, rosaries, keys, money clips overflowing with crisp new greenbacks, old photographs with yellow around the edges, doodads, loose change, dice, cigarettes, bottles of aspirin, condoms, rings, bracelets, an ivory handled revolver, a couple of pipes, a couple of dime bags. But they didn't find what they were looking for. After they left, the men and the girls rushed the table. A few girls got scratched, clawed was more like it, an earring pulled from a lobe, the flesh dangling, a budding black eye. A few men got punched in the stomach, clocked in the back of the head with the ivory handled revolver, a few missing teeth, a few broken noses and the blood gushing out. Pools of blood on the floor. But nobody got shot. Nobody was hauled off to jail.

The next day we swept the sidewalk out front as if nothing had happened. It is a clean street we live on. We sweep the sidewalk once in the morning, once every afternoon, and again in the evenings. It is good for business to keep the sidewalks swept. And business is good. We are filled to the gills with Cubans from around the corner and Nicaraguans from over by the cemetery and Dominicans and Hondurans who come down from Allapattah and a few Rastafarians mixed in. People come and go and we can hardly keep track. The night is over before we know it. We have forgotten to eat and drink ourselves. We end up eating raw oysters at six am and washing everything down with warm beer and then we go to bed and we sleep in the raw. We slip inside of each other and dream of raw oysters. We become raw oysters, wet, moist, slippery. This is not just how I remember it. This is how it is. We live in an eerie and seductive neighborhood, a festival atmosphere, Spanish trilling in the air, guitars strumming, the music flying about, troubadours with flutes and bangles and maracas, mystics, ghosts parading their pain, gigolos, prostitutes, drag queens, divas, drug dealers with neon running hot through their veins, hypnotists, palm readers, ex-priests, ex-nuns, Zen Buddhists, clairvoyants, clowns, all of history exists in this tiny enclave, this irrepressible paradise, this dot on the map, this broken landscape where men and women gather naked and unashamed and howl at the moon, all of eternity gasping its last gasp on this sun-burnt grid of asphalt and strip malls and abandoned churches and doughnut shops and chain-link fences and palm trees and children splashing in the urine-streaked fountains in the park, a seemingly endless progression of brightly painted streets and brightly painted streetwalkers between the airport in the west and the bright blue sun-sparkling bay in the east. It is the past, the present and the future all mingling together.

-9-

I confess this is more difficult than I thought. I am not a storyteller. What I mean by that is my stories are for Soledad. My stories erupt from the depth of my bowels, unbidden, unasked for, and to get rid of them, to purge myself, I tilt my head back and howl at the moon. That is what my stories sound like. A dog howling at the moon. Where they go after that I do not know. Who else hears this howling dog? Who else can capture the meaning and the chaos? Who else can share it with the world? Who would even dare do such a thing? I do not know. Perhaps I do not care. Perhaps I do not even give a fuck. Who can say? I am used to howling at the moon with Soledad spread eagle beneath me on the bed or on the floor and only a roughly woven braided rug to prevent splinters. It is only when I am inside Soledad and I am howling at the moon, or when I have just finished and then I am howling at the moon with greater intensity, it is only in these moments that I remember I have stories left to tell. That is where the past, the present and the future come together for me. Or sometimes we open the window and the moonlight is streaming in and from somewhere you can hear the sounds of a merengue floating on the wind, the rhythmic push and pull of sex, steamy and hard and then steamy and soft, the music then fading, a single note from a single moaning saxophone hanging in the air, wavering, lingering, then barely a whisper, barely a breath, and then from somewhere else it is a bolero, and a bolero is for hard, slow fucking, very hard, and very slow, so Soledad braces herself against the window sill and arches her hips to meet me and I plunge into her heaving, steaming, dripping *conejo*, a sliver of pink flashing in the moonlight, pink and fresh and bright with juice like a freshly peeled grapefruit, and then I pull out for a moment to feel the cool night air against my foreskin, swirling like silk, my shaft stiffening, my greedy, thirsty tongue lapping up the perspiration rolling down Soledad's moonchild of an ass, a luxurious ass, the fragrance of musk oil and lavender pricking my nostrils, and then again I plunge in and howl with glee. But I do not howl in all my fury even then, and I tell her this, I might send her through the window, I say, if I really let loose, and without her plush ass to hang on to, I wouldn't be far behind, the two of us hurtling through the window into the dark void, it would be inevitable, I tell her this also, and there are a few patches of weedy, spongey grass in the backyard, but not enough, it is mostly cracked cement down there, it would be a very long, hard fall with nothing to cushion the severity of the impact, one can only imagine how many cracked bones, but she only laughs and says she is strong enough for anything I can dish out. My Soledad says her big beautiful ass would cushion the fall for me. Then she smiles and says her big beautiful ass cushions every fall. Then she says I wouldn't be able to knock her out of the window anyway, even if I had a running start. I suspect she is right. And then I am sure she is. I am just past eighty, after a while it is hard to know how old you are, skin like dried leather and bones that you can see cracking and creaking beneath wax paper skin and flat feet and flabby arms and a flat ass like a boy of ten. My face is covered with so many wrinkles I sometimes think the mirror must be cracked. But Soledad is perfection. She is a curvaceous, meaty, goddess of the Pyrenees. She is my goddess. She will always be my goddess, with her curly brown hair pulled back tight and her greenish-gray eyes the color of a stormy sea and her smooth as porcelain, sun-washed skin. She flashes me a superior, haughty, indifferent smile now and then, especially when her juices are flowing and she is feeling good and my tiny explosion has come and gone and I am flaccid and shriveled and useless, a sun-dried fig, the eunuch of my deepest fears. It is then that I howl at the moon as loudly as I can, and she, like a priestess who has renounced her vows, flashes me her haughty, indifferent, superior smile, but then it is not so indifferent after all, for she is howling right there with me, beside me, the two of us looking up at the moon and howling, and she is holding on to me, playing with me, caressing me, until I grow again. So it is Soledad I am thinking of as I tell this story.

Let me begin by saying that they did not look like teachers. But this thought only came to me later. When I first saw them, they looked like everybody else who sat at the tables by the plate glass window and ate pork and cornbread or bean soup and drank beer and whistled at the beautiful *chicas jóvenes* and grabbed at their plump brown asses peeking through, the girls laughing and whisking away plates. So I gave them no thought at all. They were the kind of men you easily forget because they were like everybody else, especially if you did not see them again.

That first evening it was the usual assortment of Cubans and Nicaraguans and Dominicans and Hondurans. The air was thick and heavy from cigarette smoke. The sun had set. Darkness fell quickly in south Florida. A few street lights popped on, which gave the street outside a hazy, grainy quality, like an old photograph. The fluorescent lights inside the café crackled and hissed, but nobody cared. Everyone was eating black bean soup and drinking beer that night because it was the Wednesday night special. No one bothered the two teachers. The one teacher looked like a crazy Mexican with his hair all wild and flaming like the snakes of Medusa, and he wore a tattered Mexican blanket for a shawl and his teeth flashed like diamonds through the smoke. The other teacher was a lumbering mad dog it seemed, a mastiff foaming at the mouth with a beard that covered half his face and continued all the way down his neck, and there were bits of bean soup and foam from the beer caught in the hairs. So the Cubans and Nicaraguans and the Dominicans and the Hondurans left them alone, and you could not blame them, especially with people you didn't know, especially because these two had wild, crazy, dancing eyes, lunatic eyes filled with a psychotic kind of charisma that promised an immediate and violent death if you had not been initiated into their inner sanctum. At least that's how it seemed. But even as the teachers were left alone, their presence had broken the normal routine for a Wednesday night. The entire café descended into an uneasy, anxious, waiting silence, punctured only now and then by an occasional request for more soup or beer, and a sort of background mumbling that was difficult to decipher. There was no laughter, and the café was normally filled with laughter, loud, raucous, passionate laughter, and there was no flirting with the girls and grabbing their asses and then the girls squealing and then maybe a couple of *greasy gamberros* hurtling themselves into the space between tables in the spirit of a fist fight. There was none of that. Even the girls were quiet. There was just an anxious, silent waiting. The very air seemed grave and brittle. The world, this mosaic of dogs howling at the moon, was about to shatter into a million pieces.

It is not that I minded the world shattering, you understand. I am something of a born-again anarchist. The idea of the world shattering is appealing. What bothered me was the lack of humor. The situation was so tense that no humor seemed possible. So I turned up the radio, thinking to ease the tension, restore the jovial atmosphere I was accustomed to on Wednesday nights with a salsa or some Latin pop, but this only seemed to magnify the inherent threat of this lunatic fringe sitting by the window. I suddenly felt like I was watching a movie and there was nothing I could do. The Cubans and the Dominicans were now in a constant state of agitation, all of them glancing over at the two teachers to see if anything was about to happen, to see if one of the teachers had pulled a stiletto, or the other one a gun, one after another they looked at the two teachers, a continuous barrage of eyeballing, like they were taking turns keeping a night watch, table after table, dozens of heavy brown eyes blinking through the fog of cigarette smoke, and then back at their bowls of soup, mumbling about the presence of these two lunatics, their words garbled, barely intelligible, how it was difficult enough to eat your dinner in peace in a neighborhood like this but now there were these crazy white Mexicans to contend with, and then their heavy brown eyes blinking through the fog once again.

One wonders how long such tension can exist without someone coming to the breaking point. At least that is what I was wondering. Where is the breaking point here, I said to myself? What will the catalyst be? How long can you stifle the sound of howling dogs? How long can you sit on the edge of infinity, about to fall into the abyss? Yes, these were the questions rolling around in my brain. It is enough to drive you crazy, thinking about such questions. Fortunately, I did not have to wait long for an answer, which arrived in the form of a drunken, dirty white-skinned Rastafarian who called himself Malachi. He was the catalyst. But to fully appreciate the irony of Malachi as the catalyst, I need to share with you the sorry soap opera drama of Malachi and Gisela.

Malachi sometimes came in on Wednesdays, but I had not seen him in a month. He is a lunatic himself. He is in love with one of our girls, a young whelp of a whore named Gisela who has not yet grown herself an ass, but who more than makes up for that deficiency with her massive titties, which are always spilling out of her shirt. As the owner of a café given to late night whoring, I often need to step in, shove her titties back in her shirt and tell her to keep it buttoned until the witching hour. Sometimes, many times, I am shoving her titties back in as early as four in the afternoon when the sun is still bright and yellow in the sky and the long heavy hot shadows of the evening are but a figment of our diseased and degenerative imaginations. Not that I want to quell her enthusiasm, mind you, it is a rare quality these days that a girl wishes to share her titties for free, just because she is so in love with the beauty of a bright clean day and the sidewalks have been swept and the kitchen is getting ready for the evening's customers and her titties are to her only a part of the natural order of the world's unending, eternal, bright clean brightness, you could not hold that against her. She really does have tremendous, voluptuous titties, the kind you can sink your teeth into and imagine yourself a leopard on the edge of the African savannah, and sometimes I do just that, I nibble a little around the edges of her nipples and pretend to growl, or give her a hard squeeze, a viciously juicy squeeze, just before I shove them back in, and Gisela squeals with delight and apologizes and wiggles all at the same time and promises to keep herself clothed until after the drinks have been served and the customers drunk enough to pay just for the pleasure of sitting there, drunk as proverbial skunks, watching Gisela's titties bounce about carelessly, effortlessly, her bubbling, enthusiastic laughter bouncing everyone's eyeballs off the walls.

Gisela shows an interest in everyone who notices her, but she is particularly fond of those who live on the edge of the world, beggars with limbs missing who roll around on skids, masochistic thieves who sleep on beds of barbed wire as penance for their thievery, college students who have lost their way after drunken brawls at the beach, sex fiends driving brown metallic El Dorados with the horns of Texas Longhorns on the grill who have a taste for shaved pussy and girls with whips, toothless vagabonds with breath that smelled like stale fish and whose mucousy laughter can be heard several blocks away, lawyerly ex-cons and mealy-mouthed bastards of every shape and size and ethnic persuasion, her radar for such men is infallible, she loves them all without exception, without expectations or condition, all of them except poor, unfortunate Malachi. It is, as I have said, very much a sorry soap opera drama for our little corner of Calle Ocho. Malachi used to come into the café around three in the afternoon and drink beer, waiting until Gisela would let her titties pop out for a breather, and then he would watch with the schizophrenic attention of a late-night zombie, his eyeballs wiggling with every gyration, his mouth open, beer dribbling out of the corners, collecting in tiny pools on the table. When the show was over, which meant when I decided enough was enough and shoved Gisela's titties back in, he would laugh and clap and whistle and say it was the best damn show anywhere in Little Havana, even if there wasn't a stage for strutting, even if there wasn't a pole and purple lights flashing and the audience jerking themselves off like greased lightning in the blue shadows, and Gisela would smile shyly and sometimes even blush. He was always a gentleman, in spite of his language. He never approached her in a menacing way. He always clapped.

And so one afternoon, partially, I suspect, to show her gratitude for his obviously restrained yet undaunted adoration, and after she was fully clothed once more, she sat down at his table and they started talking. I don't remember what they were talking about. He was ranting and raving, waving his arms wildly in the air above his head, talking about the ancient sun god, Amun Ra, and the Egyptian pyramids and the sacredness of dolphins and the search for paradise and the second coming and the destruction of the Fascist state of America and the end of time, and Gisela was listening with the rapt fascination of one who is generally bored with life except when her titties are doing the Can-Can. It was a slow afternoon. There were a couple of greasy gamberros loading up on rum before they hit the streets, a bored looking accountant who must have got off early or been fired waiting on a late lunch, a couple of the girls wiping down the tables and Soledad in the kitchen and myself and Malachi and Gisela.

The next thing I knew Gisela was on her feet, two steps back from the table, holding one of her high heels with the spiked tip pointed straight at Malachi, saying if he took one step closer she would gouge out his eyes, and stabbing at the air with her shoe, and then she took another step back and settled into a sort of half-crouching state, her eyes burning holes in the air. You could almost smell the smoke. Malachi didn't say a word. He stood up, his face swallowed up in a sort of greasy, black shadow, like he had been smiling but the smile had been choked out of him, leaving him angry, frustrated, the taste of stomach acid rising up, his eyes watering as if his prick had been caught in a zipper. He stood there a moment, looking at Gisela, chewing his tongue some, swishing the bile around in his mouth and then swallowing, and nobody moved or said a word, not even the greasy gamberros, who are usually looking for a fight to wash away the slag of their early afternoon hangovers, and then Malachi blew Gisela a kiss and made his way out into the bright clean sunshine of the afternoon, whistling a reggae tune as he went.

That kiss seemed to linger in the air like swamp gas. It was almost Biblical, an ancient pestilence descending, the curse of an idiot-savant.

That Malachi chose to return to the café the very night the teachers appeared seemed one of those rare moments when the sky opens up and we are given a glimpse of the inner workings of the universe, the machinery of God. At least that's how I later came to see it. But when it was happening, well, my mind was completely drained of thoughts. I was only a reflection in the plate glass window, a frozen witness to the coming apocalypse. The moment I turned up the radio, you could see a change come over Malachi. His body stiffened. He was very drunk. He became as if mesmerized, his eyes fixed, indifferent to his immediate surroundings, his right hand twitching, his fingertips tapping lightly the handle of a gun stuffed into his shorts, the clutching, infinite loneliness of the world glittering like a halo about his head, the second hand of the clock slowing to an occasional tick. He was staring at these two teachers who resembled two crazy, white Mexicans, the one laughing, his flaming, Medusa hair dancing sparks against the window, the other one not laughing, sopping up soup with his beard, and all the while a stream of words was streaming out of Malchi's mouth, almost unintelligible, under his breath, but I was close enough to hear, the words half-formed, half-heard, tormented words, that's how it seemed to me. It was them, he said, they were the reason Gisela turned on him like she did so there was no reason to take it out on her, no reason to waste a bullet on her skinny little ass, he would save all of his bullets for these two, it was these white devils all along, six bullets for two, three for each, they were the ones who had slipped inside his skin, stolen his words, forced him to say things he didn't mean, they were the reason he had insulted the woman he loved, they were the reason he had taken out his prick that afternoon and started jerking off right there under the table, and the beautiful Gisela had wondered what he was doing and had dipped down to take a look and had started laughing, she had almost peed herself she was laughing so hard, that's when he had started spewing his venom, insulting her pedigree, her family, her mother and grandmother, that's when he said he'd rip out her heart if she didn't stop laughing, he'd rip out her heart and tear it to shreds, and the look in his eyes had been cold, hard, unforgiving, heartless because his own heart had been shredded by her laughter, and she had believed him, she had looked at him and all she had seen were snapping teeth, he saw the image of his snapping teeth reflected in her eyes, and suddenly she believed him capable of infinite cruelty, that's when she had threatened him with her shoe, the once happy, laughing girl with exuberant breasts, consort of the sun god, his consort once upon a time, for he had once been the sun god, this is what he believed, but not anymore, but it was not her fault, she was not responsible, he saw that now, they were the ones who had stolen his divinity, he said, along with everything else.

That's when Malachi fortified himself with the dregs of his fifth beer, a burst of warm alcohol soaking his chin and time speeding up, and then he pulled his gun from his shorts and exploded through the glittery clouds of stale cigarette smoke, a wailing banshee of divine vengeance wearing a red and yellow and green striped cap and black nylon biking shorts, barefoot, shirtless, unshaven, bleary-eyed, and before a single eyeball had blinked twice, he was sitting at the table of the two teachers, holding the gun with a steady, unwavering hand, the barrel pointing directly at the temple of the one with the flaming, Medusa hair.

One rarely encounters such situations, except in books. Immediately you could see that Malachi was unsure what to do next. He suddenly seemed to realize that he was temporarily the center of the universe. But he also seemed to know that his position could change with a sudden gust of wind. It was like walking a tightrope a mile up in the air. If he pulled the trigger, well there was nothing heroic about pulling a trigger, it was like butchering pigs, there was no honor in butchering pigs, but if he chose this course, then the exhilaration of these few moments, the sense that he was sowing the seeds of destiny among the stars, would vanish, a beggar's chalk painting dissolving in the rain. He would be left with nothing but a swirling, discolored memory, a river of chemicals, a cancer, a scar. But if he surrendered the gun it would be worse. You could tell this is what he was thinking. You could see this in his eyes also. If he surrendered the advantage of the gun he would find himself floating in the gutters of an inhuman world, a part of the daily flotsam and jetsam of a hundred thousand abortions whooshing down the wormhole drain, drowning in a sea of pus streaked semen and warm piss and menstrual juice and dead fetuses and radiator fluid and bloody diarrhea, seeking refuge inside the cathedral ruins of an embryonic sac, curling up to say his prayers then whispering goodnight, God speed, good riddance, gadzooks, the sac shrinking, disappearing into the frigid, humpbacked void of sodomized angels, wingless now, lecherous gargoyles sporting skeletal appendages without feathers, it would be a birth in reverse, the collapse of the universal soul. He wasn't sure how to save himself.

"Tell me why I shouldn't pull the trigger," said Malachi.

The one with the Medusa hair smiled, at least it looked like a smile coming through the glittery, shape-shifting cloud of cigarette smoke, but he said nothing. He stared across the table at the other one, who did not look up from his bowl. Malachi's arm began to tremble, a slight quivering.

"I can't think of a thing to say," said the one.

His smile widened. He turned to look at Malachi, the snakes of his flaming Medusa hair were now writhing in the air above his head, rattling against the plate glass window, sparks beginning to fly.

"If you need to pull the trigger then you need to pull the trigger," he said.

Then he guided the barrel into his mouth, took hold of it with his teeth, and continued talking, hissing was more like it, his lips barely moving, the sound squeezing out through the gaps.

"It doesn't make a bit of difference what you do. We are all dancing in one god damn eternal circle. Like angels on the head of a pin. So what the hell, let's get this goddamn fucking dance over with."

The smile became an explosion. The light from this explosion was so powerfully bright that no one could see for several minutes. It was a wonder the whole café didn't burn to the ground. Then the brightness faded. The familiar crackle and hiss of the fluorescent lights could be heard, the flickering, whitish light seeping through the glittery, cigarette fog. Everything had returned to normal, it seemed. The Cubans and the Dominicans were busy slurping up bowls of soup and drinking beer and grabbing at the girls passing by, their chiffon skirts wafting up as they swooshed past and a flash of beautiful brown flesh. One of the regulars wanted a flank steak, which isn't on the menu, but Soledad cooked one up anyway. Bursts of raucous laughter rattled the tables. When the men got hold of one of the girls they pulled her closer and gave her ass a squeeze like it was a fresh loaf of bread and the girl would laugh and push herself away until the next time.

Malachi and the two teachers were sitting at the table up front near the plate glass window. They had become old friends. There was no sign of the gun. The table was covered with empty beer bottles. Malachi was saying he knew of a club up in Allapattah where you could dance and drink all night for twenty bucks. They played a lot of bachata and merengue, but sometimes a salsa, he said. It was a pretty rough place. Everyone carried a knife at least. The women had stony, scarred horse faces, but they had very beautiful bodies, not flaccid and shapeless like the sack of shit whores down here. Malachi said if all you could see were the faces he wouldn't go. Every Saturday night they had a dance contest where the women would dance for the men, it was sort of a striptease, he said, where the men would throw money at the women and clap and shout until all the women were naked. The one teacher said that was the kind of free-spirited paradise he'd been searching for all his life. Malachi said he would take the two teachers there some time.

-10-

The next morning came quickly. I don't remember when we went to bed, but it was early, just after three I think. The girls were still busy downstairs and someone was singing, maybe it was the radio. I have never needed much sleep. I am certain this is a matter of instinct, a remnant of our primordial past. It is one of the few things that makes absolute sense. As long as we are awake, we are not dead. I climbed down the backstairs and headed down the alley, and then I turned up 22nd Avenue, which is always bustling. The sky was a hazy, whitish gray. The air was unusually cool. There was even more traffic than usual, mostly late model cars, a few vans with the windows blacked out, a garbage truck, a city bus, but it was already a few minutes after nine so most people were at work. The morning ahead was expansive, infinite, a time for lingering, for sampling the delicacies of this earth, for imagining the farthest corners of the Universe. I was headed for Café La Nueva for a pastry and an espresso. I have been going to this café for quite some time. It has become a habit. The old one burned down years ago. The new one takes up the first floor of a small red brick building with French doors trimmed in white and a blinking neon sign in the shape of a coffee cup with steam rising and the word 'Open' blinking in bright red. The new one is three blocks from where the old one had been.

Every day they set out some wooden tables and chairs, even if it is raining. The tables and chairs are partially protected by a yellow awning, and there are a couple of almond trees off to one side. A flock of small birds (perhaps they are warblers, they are usually winter birds, but who knows) takes up residence in the almond trees.

I used to go down to Domino Park to play dominoes, or sometimes just to watch, but I do not go there anymore. They are mostly Cuban there and I am not Cuban, so there is always a razor edge of animosity. Besides, I do not even like dominoes. So I go to Café La Nueva.

Some mornings I sit outside and drink my espresso and read the paper. Some mornings I watch the traffic go by. This particular morning was for watching traffic. The girl brought me the coffee and lemon cakes and some chocolate sauce on the side and she smiled. She has full red lips, very full, but I was not thinking about her. I was thinking about the two teachers from the night before, though I still did not know they were teachers. I was wondering what kind of magic spell they had cast over Malachi and how they had made the gun disappear. I have seen many strange things in my eighty-some years, things I question even now if they really happened or if it was just my imagination.

I used to think I came to this country from Hungary. I was fairly certain of this. But my memory of the past has become a slippery thing. I used to think I was born in Ružomberok, a town that was part of the Austrian-Hungarian empire until 1919, when it was given to Czechoslovakia, but now I think that is a rumor I planted in my own brain after watching *Casablanca* with Humphrey Bogart and Peter Lorre, because Peter Lorre had been born in Ružomberok. I have watched that movie several times, countless times on the small television we keep in the back. The Peter Lorre character was named Ugarte, a thief who helped exiles who wished to escape. It is a shame he murdered the German couriers. But I can understand that about wanting to kill Germans during the Nazi years. I do not remember when I acquired the belief that I was Hungarian. It is a ludicrous thing to believe. Everything about me says I am not Hungarian, the fact that I speak Spanish, not Hungarian, is not my only clue. Perhaps I needed to hide my identity for a while, and now I have forgotten when and why. I wish I could make sense of my memories.

The strangest memory I possess is one of tanks rolling down a long boulevard. I am standing with my father, I am a very young boy and it is very hot, but I am not sure where we are. Sometimes I think the two of us are in Zaragoza, but why I cannot say. Sometimes I think we are in San Sebastián in '36 during those final days before it fell to the Nationalists, but there is none of the lingering carnage that is evidence of a great battle. And everyone is smiling and laughing and singing songs and clapping their hands. It is like a celebration. And besides, there were no tanks at San Sebastián, only a few armored vehicles. It is a very strange memory.

I remember the tanks were like a parade of garbage trucks and we were lined up along the avenue, there were many, many people. It was a normal looking street, except for the tanks, with apartments and shops and cafes and churches. We were watching these tanks like garbage trucks roll past, and suddenly a young boy made a dash to cross the avenue and fell down, and you could see he had skinned his knee, but it seemed a tremendous amount of blood for a skinned knee, and the people on both sides of the avenue were shouting for him to get up, to cross before the next tank smashed him to a pulp, but he did not move, he just held out his arms, imploring someone from the crowd to have pity on him, and truly it must have been more than a skinned knee, for the amount of blood was far more than a knee might contain, there were rivers of blood, rivers and rivers of blood pouring out of his knee, running down along the gutters on both sides, causing the sewers to overflow, the bloody sewer water beginning to lap over the shoes of those standing along the curb, we thought perhaps the boy had been shot, or that many boys had been shot, even though there were no soldiers in my memory, only the tanks, even though there were no other boys in the picture, but whatever the case, we were certain this one was doomed, but at the very last minute a young woman flashed across and rescued the boy, a flash of light between two tanks and the boy was saved, an angel doing God's work.

Of course none of that is really strange. It was routine for the times. It was almost expected. A parade of tanks that looked like garbage trucks. Unseen soldiers shooting boys. Rivers and rivers of blood and the sewers overflowing. An angel appearing when all hope is lost. But what is truly strange came later. What is truly strange is when I think back on that moment, it keeps changing. Sometimes the boy in the street is my own young son, who left us long ago, and the woman flashing by is my very own Soledad. Sometimes in this memory where I am standing with my father, I am almost a grown man, and we are both carrying rifles and shouting obscenities as the tanks roll past and then the boy is crushed. And sometimes I am the boy in the street and I am reaching out to the crowd, but I see that there is no crowd, there is just an empty street, and there are no apartment buildings, there is only a great emptiness where the buildings should have been, and then I look up again and I can see that someone has planted thin trees in the empty spaces, and they are just beginning to show tiny green buds, and behind the trees, you can see a heavy burning sun behind gray clouds, but the sunlight does not penetrate all the way, just enough so the green buds look like they are glowing, like they are just catching fire, like the trees are beginning to burn, and then I look up a third time and I can't see a thing because the air has grown dark and heavy with smoke and the smell of burning oil and the sounds of the tanks, and there is a heavy, creaking, cracking sound, and then the world goes black.

What does it mean to have a memory like this? What does it mean when the past changes before your very eyes, or slips away so completely, so effortlessly, that what you once thought was a fixed, eternal truth might never have happened at all? I find it easier now when I am sipping my espresso and nibbling my lemon cakes to think that nothing has happened in my life except what is happening now. I was born only yesterday. My name is Xavier Mendoza because this is what my wife, Soledad, my sweet goddess of the Pyrenees, this is what she calls me. She is God's breath upon my soul. She is the only reason I am still connected to this earth. She has been with me for longer than I care to remember. But as long as she knows who I am, then I know who I am.

The girl brings me a second espresso and another plate of lemon cakes.

"Hola Señor Mendoza," she says.

"Hola a usted mi pequeño pollo."

She laughs.

"No, no, no Señor Mendoza. I am no small chicken anymore."

"Ah, you are mistaken," I say. "At my age, every woman I see is *mi pequeño pollo."*

She laughs again.

"Do you like my lemon cakes," she says.

"Very much, yes."

"I made them fresh this morning."

"They are very good."

"I was thinking of you when I made them."

"Now you are making an old man blush."

"No, no, no Señor Mendoza. I do not think there is anything that would cause you to blush."

She laughs a third time and whirls around, her curves slicing through the air, and disappears into the café. The aroma of her lemon cakes is swirling all around me. The warblers are chirping from the almond trees, hopping from branch to branch. They are beginning to annoy me. They are like a Greek chorus with all their chirping. Then the girl pokes her head back out through the door and the birds fly away. "If there is anything you want, Señor Mendoza, anything at all, just ask."

I am not fast enough to answer and now she is gone. I want everything from her. I should have told I am in love with her, which is true, at least for today. I should have told her I wanted more lemon cakes, but I have already eaten too many. I am remembering her heart-shaped ass as she whirled away and it is hanging there in my memory, suspended in the air and the soft sunlight filtering through the leaves of the almond trees and the lemony smell of the lemon cakes and the sound of her laughter mixed with the sounds of the birds, and I am thinking how very much I would like to sit her on my lap and lift up her skirt and squeeze her ass and breathe her in and then spread her legs so I could diddle her a while and feel her wetness gushing forth and hear her moan. Right there sitting outside the café I would do this. But then I am thinking of Soledad. Not that Soledad would mind, she wouldn't. Soledad encourages me. She says a healthy appetite needs variety, a table covered with exotic cuisines to sharpen the palate. She would probably even like to watch, maybe have a taste herself. But I am thinking of Soledad because it takes energy to sample other women, even when they are young and willing and full of heart, and I am old now, and some days I have little energy left. Today I am thinking of Soledad because I want to plow into her again and again. I want to make sure I have the stamina. I am very hard just thinking about her.

I must have fallen asleep. The girl is back with another espresso. She is wiping down part of the table and smiling and clearing away the other cup. I do not know if I finished drinking it or if I knocked it over when I fell asleep. I feel badly she is expending so much effort on my behalf.

"Are you feeling better Señor Mendoza?"

I nod and smile back at her. On the other side of the street someone shouts and waves but I cannot see who it is. The someone I cannot see continues on their way. I am taking the last sips of my last espresso and watching the traffic some more. The air is very warm now. It is almost noon. A car whooshes past, then several more. Every now and then a dozen or more warblers fly low beneath the speeding cars and come out the other side. They are flying further and further away, down the street, back and forth they go beneath the cars. They must be the same warblers from the almond trees, I think. They are like flashes of light. Then one of the warblers gets clipped. I see the car whoosh past and the clipped warbler is now spinning in the dust of the street, spinning and flashing like a silver coin, and then I can no longer see him. I take the long way home. When I get back I go straight around to the front and go in through the café door.

"Hello Mr. Mendoza," says a voice.

"Hola Señor Mendoza," says another.

I am not sure what I am looking at. Or at least I am not sure why. The first voice comes from the lumbering mastiff with the full beard from the night before. The second voice comes from the one with the Medusa hair. They are both holding brooms. They seem to have worked up a good sweat. The next thing I know they are both outside sweeping the sidewalk and I am sitting at a side table, away from the windows. Soledad has brought me a bowl of thin barley soup and a few Saltines and a plate of pisto.

"They fell asleep downstairs," she says.

I am eating my soup, dipping the crackers, savoring each spoonful, but I am listening.

"I came down this morning and there they were, so I gave them both brooms."

Later, we are back upstairs. We are lying down in bed. It is the middle of the afternoon and I am very sleepy. The blinds are slanted shut and the shadows are dark and cool and there is air blowing from a small fan on the dresser on the other side of the room. The air is coming in waves. You can hear the motor of the fan growing louder as the fan spins closer, and then fading as it spins away. On any other afternoon I would have Soledad flat on her back and I would be pounding away at her. But my erection from before is no longer there. Besides, I am very tired. I curl up against Soledad and close my eyes and she wraps her arms around me. It almost seems like I am curled up inside her. She is talking to me in her soft, sweet, kitten's voice. Her voice fades in and out with the spinning of the fan. She tells me she came downstairs that morning and I had gone for my coffee and there they were, sleeping at the table up front by the plate glass window, and they were very nice, very apologetic, they had a long talk together, they said they were teachers, but she could tell in a few minutes that the one with the Medusa hair, the older one, had the appetite of a Picasso, the kind of sexual depravity Picasso was known for, and she laughs at this and pokes me in the ribs, and the other one would be very beautiful if he cleaned himself up, she says, he is very young and fresh, and she is smiling but it is a sad smile and I know she is thinking of this young teacher as a mirror image of the son we had always wanted, but our son had died, he was a small, oddly deformed baby boy born a thousand years ago, and he spent only a few days on the planet and then his tiny eyes clouded over, the spirit of death filling his lungs, and then he died and we buried him in a small grave in Caballero Rivero without even a stone, without even a small white cross, and we never spoke of him after that, but we never forgot, this is how she is thinking of the young teacher, I am sure of it, she is looking at this young teacher as if he is our son and he is no longer buried, he has returned to us, without the deformity that caused his death, and she gives me a gentle kiss on the cheek as if to remind me that life is too short to question the gift of second chances, she tells me these two teachers will only be here a short while, they are trying to figure out what to do next, especially the young one, she gave them the brooms and told them they could stay for a while if they swept the café three times a day, and also the sidewalk, she gave them the room across the hall, she will see after them, she says, and after that I don't remember what she is saying, I don't need to remember, she is my universe exploding, the tanks are coming and she is the angel of my last hope, and I am painting my newborn self across the sky.

-11-

The two teachers and Malachi have been restless for days, and their restlessness is infecting everyone else, the girls, Soledad, even me. It feels like sand coursing through my veins, and I wonder if it feels that way for the others, but it is Sunday today and we are closed and we are ignoring this feeling of being restless. Most of the tables are covered with chairs. We have cleared off a few and we are sitting around and drinking beer and sangria and the ceiling fans are spinning because of the heavy, dull heat of the day. We are chewing the fat, all of us, except Malachi is not here. He has been coming around a lot lately, but he is not here now. Soledad has turned the radio on in the kitchen and when we hit the quiet spots in the conversation we can hear the sounds of Latin pop. It is like the sound of a quick, hard rain at the beach.

"That is precisely why I'm heading to Patagonia," says the older teacher.

"Don't believe him," says the younger teacher.

"Fascist!" says the older teacher.

"He's been talking that garbage for years."

"Fucking Fascist!"

One of the girls laughs. It is a short, chirpy laugh.

"Mickey, Mickey, Mickey! You are such a bad boy."

She is still chirping. She is too young to know what a Fascist is, but she already knows quite a bit about fucking. She is sitting in a chair next to the older teacher, leaning herself against his shoulder, playing with his stringy, Medusa hair and drinking her sangria. They are sitting at one corner of the table. There are two other girls sitting cattycorner. Soledad is behind them at the counter filling a bowl with chips. She brings the chips out and a jar of salsa and goes back to the counter. Everyone digs in.

Soledad is always taking care of many small things.

"That's a hell of thing to say," says the younger teacher.

"It was just a raw observation," says the older teacher.

"After all we've been through together."

The older teacher polishes off his beer.

"Forget about it. We have bigger fish to flay."

He slides the first girl on top of his lap and buries his head in her chest, but he continues talking. All you can see is his wild, flaming Medusa hair flying about while he talks. The girl is no longer chirping. She is now giggling.

"You mean fry," says the younger teacher.

"No I don't. I like my fish raw. That's a prerequisite if you want to live out your days in paradise."

"What a load of garbage."

"And after you eat your fill of fish, then you're ready for the eighty vestal virgins. Also raw."

"And then what?"

"What more do you need after eighty vestal virgins in the raw?"

The older teacher looks up for a moment from the chest of the girl and looks across the table at the young teacher. The girl also looks at the young teacher. She is smiling with great enthusiasm.

"Then why are you always talking about going to Patagonia?" says the younger teacher.

"Travis, my fucked-up friend, you are definitely confused. Patagonia isn't just a place. It is mostly a myth, which is another way of saying that Patagonia is mostly a state of mind."

The older teacher squeezes a nipple and dives back in. The girl does not mind a bit.

"Oh, Mickey," she says. "You are very, very bad."

The eyes of the older teacher once again vanish from view. The girl presses her lips against his neck and begins moaning softly, or perhaps she is sighing from her obvious love sickness. The younger teacher is smiling at the cattycorner girls and they are smiling back. They shift in their seats and spread their legs a bit and smile some more and drink some more sangria. All three girls are wearing tight-fitting t-shirts and short shorts, their brown, cheeky asses spreading out where they sit and their smooth bright legs flashing in the dim light. It is hard to tell them apart. The younger teacher pushes his chair back away from the table. I suspect he wants a better view of the legs of the cattycorner girls.

"The thing about Patagonia is this," says the older one.

His face is no longer buried in the first girl's chest. She has shifted herself. She is now sitting in his lap, leaning back against his shoulder. She is smiling, content, oblivious.

"It's the last place on the fucking planet where they've never even heard of the Judeo-Christian concept of sin. Or the Muslim concept. Or the Buddhist. Or any fucking concept at all. All they care about is fucking each other and eating fish from the sea. They don't even know fire exists, that's why they eat their fish raw, just like the gods intended. That's the way it's supposed to be my friend. All they're doing is just living. That's paradise. But you don't have to go there to get there."

"I want to go." says the first girl. "I like it raw."

"We all like it raw," say the other girls. "Can we go too?"

"You hear that, Travis? Everyone wants a little piece of paradise."

The three girls are laughing, softly, happily. They polish off the last of the chips and salsa.

"Sure Mick, that's easy for you to say," says the young teacher. "Look at you! God damn guru. Anything you want."

The first girl starts wiggling slowly in the lap of the older teacher, it is a slow, hard dance, *un baile erótico de regazo*. It is very professional. You can see he is becoming aroused.

"It's never been that easy for me," says the young teacher.

"You'll get there, my friend," says the older one. "But you have to learn to relax. Let go. Forgive yourself."

The young teacher doesn't say anything, drinks some more beer. The two cattycorner girls are sipping their sangrias, heads bent close towards each other, murmuring, looking at the young teacher, licking the rims of their glasses, slowly, drops of sangria juice lingering on their tongues, and then they are laughing some more, soft and sexy. The young teacher slides his chair back to the table. He drinks more beer, looks at the girls. They are exceptionally skillful, these girls. They have been with me for a long time.

"We forgive you, Travis," the cattycorner girls say.

"Forgive me for what?"

"For whatever you're thinking right now."

"How do you know what I'm thinking?"

"Never mind about that, Travis."

"Yes, never mind."

"And what if I don't want to be forgiven?"

"Don't listen to those sirens," I say.

The cattycorner girls send me daggers with their eyes.

"They have no intention of forgiving you," I say. "They will use everything you think and say and do against you until they get what they want, and on that day, make no mistake, they will leave you lying naked in the gutter, hands tied behind your back, penniless, broken, a shell of who you once were stinking of rum and piss.

"We would not do that, Travis."

"Don't you listen to this old fart, Travis."

"Yes," I say. "I have seen it a thousand times before."

"He is just jealous."

"And old."

"Yes, he is very old, and very forgetful."

"Yes, yes, this is all true," I say. "But I am not talking about my shortcomings. I am talking about theirs, and they do not know the first thing about forgiveness. It is like your friend says. All you have to do is forgive yourself."

There is a lull in the conversation. It is almost like falling asleep. I am wondering if the older teacher has slept with all of my girls. He seems very capable, *muy macho*. I am even wondering if perhaps he has taken them on two or three at a time. The other one I am not sure about. Well that is not quite true. I am sure he has not slept with anyone but himself since he has been here. Then I am not wondering about anything. The blinds are up but it is cloudy outside and the light inside the café is very dim. I am sitting at a table separate from the others, drinking from a small, dark brown flask. I am drinking dark rum all the way from Puerto Rico. Sunday is the only day of the week I drink my dark rum. I am drinking and the world is a drowsy world and no one is talking and the only sound is the sound of the radio. The radio is playing a samba. Then the samba stops and a man starts talking. He is ranting and raving about a little boy who was found floating in an inner tube three miles off the coast of Florida. His mother had died in the crossing so the government had sent him back to Cuba to be with his father. The man is speaking with the voice of outrage. He is speaking for thousands who feel the same way. But I wonder about all that. I wonder how the man would feel if the boy was his son. Would he not be overjoyed to have his son once again in his arms? Who has the right to deny a father such joy? Then I wonder about the hundreds of young boys, perhaps thousands of young boys, who have perished in the ocean between Cuba and Florida, all of them desperate to escape to America, clinging to flimsy boats or inner tubes, all of them food for the sharks. We do not know about these boys. We do not know what happened to them. We do not know if they truly existed. They are only phantoms in our imaginations. But I am greatly troubled by their deaths all the same. Then I am thinking that we are all exiles, refugees, trying to cross an ocean of trouble to find a better life. It is the same no matter where we come from. Then I notice the man has stopped talking. The radio is now playing some Gloria Estefan. I have always liked Gloria Estefan, but you can barely hear her, the music is very faint, hardly a breath at all, it sounds a million miles away in the dim light and only adds to the feeling of drowsiness.

After a while, I noticed that the conversation had resumed. Everyone was pretty much where they had been before, except the lap dance girl was back in her chair. She was leaning against the shoulder of the older teacher. Every so often she punched him in the ribs or pinched him with a hard, vicious, twisting pinch, and she was saying *porecito*. When he leaned over to kiss her she tried to bite him, or maybe she already had and I had missed it because his lip was bleeding. She wiped away the blood with a napkin. All he did was smile. He seemed to enjoy this vicious side of her.

"Does it have to take place in a bedroom?" said one of the cattycorner girls.

"No, no, my young coquettish nymphomaniac," said the older teacher. "It can be anywhere two people can get naked."

"And more than two?"

"Of course. The more the merrier."

"Then we, my girl Thérèse and myself, we have a story."

"We do?" said the other cattycorner girl.

"The painter," said the first cattycorner girl. "The one who lived by the Tower Theater."

"Ooooooohhhh, him, yes, I remember him."

"It was before I knew Thérèse."

"It was the way we met. It is a crazy story!"

"Two young girls and a painter," said the older teacher. "Who said romance is dead? Fucking outstanding! Now if only there were a few newly converted anti-religious cynics in the audience."

"I'm an anti-religious cynic," said the young teacher.

"You don't count, Lauterbach. You were born a cynic. And anti-religious to boot. Go on girls. On with the story. I'm getting hungry."

The cattycorner girls drank some more sangria. They smiled and made eyes at each other. Everyone else drank their beers.

"What an amazing, unforgivable fucking *cabrón* he was," said Thérèse. "This painter. A gifted bastard. Always fucking around. But ooooooohhhh me, what eyes he had."

"She is getting ahead of the story," said the first cattycorner girl. "It did not start with his eyes."

"For me it started with his eyes. Ooooohhhh, yeeeess."

"It really started with the Tower Theater," said the first cattycorner girl. "This was years ago, four or five years before they closed down the first time. Maybe more. I didn't go there a lot, a few times. But whenever I was there, I saw him hanging around, sometimes at that little place next store getting a sandwich, but most of the time I'd see him hiding out in Domino Park. He would set up a small table like everyone else, but instead of dominoes he'd cover the table with ceramic miniatures of the theater. I mean it was chock full. I guess he was trying to sell them to anyone who wanted to buy. Or trying to. But he wasn't trying too hard. He really wasn't into the miniatures. To tell the truth I don't think the theatre knew what he was up to. He was into painting. Like Pablo Picasso and all that artsy shit. That's what he said when I got to know him. But I didn't know what to think the night I met him, oh baby, it just doesn't seem real even now, I didn't know what the fuck was happening. I had just walked out of a movie. It was an American movie, but we had only been in the States a few months and my English wasn't so good yet. I mean half the time it sounded like they were underwater or something. Fucking gibberish. Anyway, this movie I walked out on sounded like that. And I didn't give a fuck about the subtitles. I didn't want to read at the movies. Reading gives me headaches. I go to the movies because I don't like reading. So I was trying to explain this to the girl at the ticket booth and get my money back, but she just laughed, so I flipped her off, and then she flipped me off, and then the booth went dark and she went away, and then she was standing in the lobby like there was a spotlight on her and I was pissed, I don't know what else I was thinking but I was so pissed, but what was I going to do, and then I heard a voice from the sidewalk, and it was saying, 'That's not the way to get your money back,' and it was a really deep voice, the kind that flows through you, like a bassoon, like something musical, and the next thing I knew I was walking arm in arm with this guy and he smelled like orange spice and I couldn't get away from him, but I didn't want to get away either, and we walked for a while, I really don't remember how long, and then we sat down at a café, they had these sidewalk tables outside with Tiki torches and he wanted to sit at one of those because they reminded him of Gauguin, that's what he said, so that's where we sat down, but I wasn't a complete idiot, so I was saying 'I still don't see my money,' and he laughed and gave me a cigarette to keep me quiet and flashed back to the theater, and then another flash and he was back at the table with my money. What do you say when something like that happens?"

"You say yeeesss!" said Thérèse. "What else can you say?"

The light from outside was glowing a soft, hazy red.

Soledad brought out some nachos with jalapeños and some more chips and salsa and another pitcher of sangria. The cattycorner girls filled their glasses and drank some more, and everyone else kept pounding their beers.

"So there I was sitting at this table and staring at my money and he ordered us a couple of coffees, and then I was thinking what the hell was I going to do, this guy was absolutely gorgeous with his thick, curly black hair and the way his cheekbones caught the torch light outside this café, and I could see just a hint of the devil in his smile, and when he looked at me with those searing brown eyes of his, it was like hypnosis, *mirada fuerte,* my grandmother would say, the strong gaze, something to be avoided at all costs, especially if you are a hot young whore walking the street, you have to be strong against such eyes, but I was not strong, I felt my whole body melting away, he could have me whenever he wanted, I had never seen anyone like him, not up close, it was like he was straight out of the movies, like he was Antonio fucking Banderas, but this all happened a very long time ago, so he couldn't have been Antonio, and I was thinking this just doesn't happen, not to me, so then I was thinking he was probably just another fucking *chamuco,* had to be, and he was playing a pretty good scene, I mean it was Academy Award caliber, but he'd done this a thousand times before, I was sure of that, all he wanted to do was take me to bed and fuck my brains out and that would be that. That's what I was thinking."

"That's how he operates on your mind," said Thérèse. "That's part of his mystique."

"I could barely say thank you."

"You never say thank you," said the lap dance girl.

Everyone laughed.

"A couple of weeks later was the next time I saw him. It was very much like a dream. He was sitting at his table in the park. It was a very lazy mojito kind of day with the sun beginning to set, a very orange sun, and he waved at me to come over, so I did, and there were a couple of old farts in polo shirts looking at the miniature towers, I guess they were done with their dominoes for the day, and he had to keep an eye on them so he couldn't talk right away. So I was walking around the table same as the old farts and looking at the towers, and the way they were shining there in that orange sunlight, dozens of them laid out in rows on a wooden folding table, all of them with the tower part sticking straight up in the air, and I was trying to keep myself together, but it was very difficult, but then the old farts were gone and all of a sudden I started laughing. I couldn't control myself. It just came bubbling out, because those miniature towers looked like dozens of cocks, dozens of long, thin glittery cocks glittering in the sunlight, all of them ready to explode, raring to go, like they were all on a mission, ready, aim, fire, like pronto."

Everyone laughed again.

"Reina is the one on a mission," said the lap dance girl. "Everywhere she looks she sees cocks raring to go."

"Yeeeesss she does, doesn't everybody?" said Thérèse.

"Only if you know where to look," said the older teacher. "Then you'll see gods and goddesses themselves walking around with tremendous hard-ons."

"Even the goddesses?" said the young teacher.

"Especially the goddesses. They're walking around with strap-ons with golden tips. And these strap-ons are at least two feet long."

"So what happened next?" said the lap dance girl.

"The next thing I remember is I had one of those towers in my hands and I was inspecting it at close range, just to be polite. I was very methodical. I was turning it this way and that, examining it from every angle."

"Stroking it, you mean," said Thérèse.

"And he said I could keep it if I liked it, it was a gift, and we started talking and I told him how the towers looked like glittery cocks and he burst out laughing, and then he said it was deliberate, of course, the phallic nature of the theater itself, the design of it, he said it was an art deco experiment, and I didn't know what to say to that, I don't normally go in for all that artsy, fartsy, cheezy, feezy crap, that's the last thing I need, to tell you the truth, *lo último que necesito es un catarro,* and that's when he told me he was a painter, a serious artist like Picasso or Balthus or Bernini or Gauguin, he said, and that all serious art was about sex and sexuality and the freedom to fuck whoever you wanted, which I had never thought about before, I mean who thinks about stuff like that, and then he said it was the ones who thought sex was a crime that were the real perverts."

"A man after my own heart," said the older teacher.

"That's when he invited me up to see his studio," said

Reina. "He was unbelievably bold."

"Aaaaahhhh, me, but you knew this was coming," said Thérèse.

"We did indeed," said the older teacher. "It's exactly what I would have done."

"And you went to his studio anyway," said Thérèse.

"He said maybe he'd even paint me, if I didn't mind sitting naked on a pedestal for a couple of hours so he could see every inch. He said he liked the rounded curve of my shoulders, my large, billowy breasts, my dark hair. He asked me if I shaved my pussy. Are you kidding me! What balls to say a thing like that! That's what I was thinking. He said he only worked with models who shaved their pussies."

"Let me tell you it wasn't much of a studio," said Thérèse. "He lived on the second floor of the old liquor store across from the costume house. Before they went out of business. Paintings all over the fucking place, on the floor, stacks of them along the walls, beneath the windows, piled up on the one sofa, on chairs. Paintings and empty bottles of wine."

"But he kept his bed clear," said Reina. "As I remember he was very much on a mission about his bed. I don't remember him doing much painting. But we drank an awful lot of red wine. And we did an awful lot of fucking. He was breezy as you please when it came to fucking. As soon as it was light he wanted to fuck. And then as soon as he took a shower. And then as soon as he ate. And then as soon as he took a crap. As soon as he drank some wine. As soon as he turned on the television. The radio. As soon as the sun set. As soon as the stars came out. *Siempre estoy arrecho contigo,* he would say to me. He was always horny. Christ he was horny."

Reina made the sign of the cross and smiled.

"He was a vampire," said Thérèse.

"He needed plenty of sex and plenty of red wine," said Reina. "He said that's what his doctor had told him. It was a hell of a line."

"Or one hell of a doctor," said the older teacher.

"He was a bastard," said Thérèse. "He could party all night long and pick up a new girl for breakfast and another one for lunch. He would suck the life out of you before you even knew what was happening."

"She's just pretending to be mad."

"Aye ke la verga."

"I mean she was mad at first."

"I was."

"But it didn't last long."

The two cattycorner girls looked at each other and then burst out laughing.

"It was all pretty funny at the end," said Reina.

"It was wickedly funny," said Thérèse.

"I get wet just thinking about it," said Reina

The two laughed some more, their eyes glistening.

"You see I had been sleeping with this painter for several months," said Thérèse. "I knew he was a pig, a very gifted pig, but still a pig, but I forgave him because I never ran into these other girls, these hairy, smelly, tuna cunts, that's how I thought of them. But the day I met Reina, well, I just wasn't expecting her. It was the middle of the afternoon and I figured he was just waking up so I headed over to the studio. He always made me use the side stairs so I wouldn't attract any attention, but only a total fucking *pendejo* does such a thing, there's nothing more obvious than a young whore in a mini skirt and a tube top sneaking up the side stairs in the middle of the day. But up the stairs I went and I popped through the screen door with a mini-mart bag with coffee and cigarettes, and there were the two of them over by the sofa, grunting away doggie style. She was holding on to the edge of the sofa to keep her balance and he was ramming into her as hard as he could, so hard a pile of paintings fell to the floor from the shock, and the next thing I remember he had rolled away from her and was sitting bow-legged on the floor, scratching his balls, and he said 'Hola Thérèse! Did you bring me my cigarettes? Come on, don't just stand there, come and join the party!' It was strange like a dream is strange. I hurled the mini-mart bag as hard as I could at this one here, swinging it round and round a couple of times before I let loose. She was dripping wet from his cock and looked at me and smiled and I let that bag fly. I was aiming for her head, but the bag sailed to the right and knocked over an easel with some of his paints instead. I looked at him and I said 'Okay, which one of us goes,' and he said 'I am very much satisfied with things as they are, but if that's the way you want it, then the two of you will have to fight it out for yourselves.' All I could see after that was red. I was on top of her before she could take a breath. I wanted to strangle her till her eyes popped, but I didn't have a good grip. Then she shoved me into another stack of paintings and there was more paint on the floor, and pretty soon the two of us were rolling in paint like mud wrestlers, we were covered in it, and she was clawing at me and I was clawing at her, and then one of us would get free, but only for a moment because the other one would come charging after, and then the two of us would fall to the floor again, and all the while I could hear his slobbering, laughing voice saying 'Toro, toro, toro' and laughing and laughing and then 'olé' and then laughing and slobbering some more. And then snap, just like that the cobwebs cleared and I stopped seeing red, I mean the whole scene was just ludicrous beyond belief, and I looked at her and she looked at me, and I can't quite explain it, but in that moment we became sisters."

"It was telepathic," said Reina. "Like telepathy."

"In that moment we knew we were finished with the painter."

"It was like we were inside each other," said Reina.

"All of our love for him was gone," said Thérèse. "But we also knew the afternoon was not yet over."

"It was like we were thinking each other's thoughts," said Reina.

"Mmmmmmmmmm, yeeeeesssss it most certainly was," said Thérèse.

The cattycorner girls poured themselves more sangria. They were beaming.

"The first thing we did we were all over him," said Thérèse. "We pulled off his pants and then his shirt and dragged him laughing and sputtering into our paint-filled arena, and we climbed on top of him, one at each end like bouncing on a seesaw, and I fucked him several times to keep him happy, and then we switched places and it was Reina's turn to fuck him, and he kept crying out, "More, more, more,' and we lathered him in paint while we were fucking him. Then we turned him over and tied his hands and legs behind his back, the way you tie up any pig, and we covered his back with as many colors as we could find, a patchwork of colors, a rainbow, and then we leaned him up against the sofa and shoved a pile of his paintings up under his chin so he wouldn't fall and turned on some reggae so people would think he was throwing a party, and all this while he was laughing and sputtering, he thought it was all part of the game, you see, his cock was ready to go once more, you could see that clearly in spite of the paint. He was begging us to fuck him one more time, this is what he'd been looking for his entire life, but we were through with him, and we told him so, but we couldn't keep from laughing ourselves. He looked like some sort of crazy voodoo doll with a blue and green head and red stripes down his arms and a purple stomach and a purple cock and orange legs. We told him he was a pig and that we were through with him, but he didn't seem to get it, he just wondered when we were going to fuck him again and how long we were going to keep him tied up, and we hadn't really thought about that last one, we should have left him tied up for good, but we didn't, we should have left him there until the paint had crusted over and his cock had fallen off, but we weren't so cruel as that. We each kissed him, a long, slow, sexy goodbye kiss that left him thirsty and panting, to let him know what he would never have again, and then we told him we'd send someone around in an hour or so to help him wiggle out of the ropes, and then we left. We didn't even bother about our own clothes. We just left."

"You didn't care you were naked?" said the young teacher.

"Why should we care about that?" said Reina. "We're naked a lot."

Everyone laughed.

"Besides," said Thérèse. "We were covered in paint. There wasn't much to see."

"What happened to the painter?" said the lap dance girl.

"I don't know," said Thérèse. "We ordered a pizza and told them to use the side stairs to deliver it and to walk right in. We never saw him again after that."

"Not even at the Tower Theater," said Reina. "He just vanished completely."

The cattycorner girls were smiling, wiggling, very satisfied with themselves.

"You better watch these two, Lauterbach," said the older teacher. "It's like the old man was saying, they'll chew you up and spit you out, leave you lying in the gutter."

Everyone laughed again.

The two cattycorner girls sipped their sangrias, their heads bent close towards each other once more, murmuring, smiling. They licked the rims of their glasses, slowly. Drops of sangria juice lingered on their tongues.

-12-

It was only after waking up that I realized I had fallen asleep yet again. When I was younger I rarely slept. But now it is sometimes difficult to tell if I am sleeping or awake. I must have been sleeping for a while because it was dark when I woke up, except for the kitchen light and the dim yellow counter lights and a candle glowing in a jar on the table we had cleared. The blinds were down by then, but it wouldn't have mattered. It was very dark outside. Everyone else was gone, except the young teacher and Soledad. They were talking in soft, low whispers, and the way the candle light bounced off their skin they almost looked like young lovers. I had been dreaming of Soledad. In my dream she was lying in the grass on a single silk sheet, a dark gray in color, or maybe it was black. She was naked and relaxed, as if she herself were dreaming, and there were vines sprouting up everywhere, each vine ending in a leaf of three leaflets and more and more vines were sprouting as the dream progressed. We were closed off from the world, surrounded by a blue curtain hung on a wire and fixed in place with orange clothespins. You could see the orange glow of the setting sun beyond the curtain, a darkly burning glow, just over the top of the curtain, but we were in the dark, in the shadows. Soledad was sleeping peacefully and there was a plate of apples next to her and the air smelled of honeysuckle and lilacs and damp earth and apples and sex all mixed together. In my dream I understood that my Soledad was the mother goddess of the earth come back from the land of the dead, and so she had abandoned her earthly body. Her skin was a soft, whitish, lilac color, a reflection of the early morning summer sky even though it was evening in my dream, or perhaps it was the soft, whitish afterglow of death. My Soledad did not look like herself, but I knew who she was, even with the changed color of her skin and her hair was now blonde, she was still my Soledad, her head was thrown back, her arms stretched out behind her head, curving away from me, curving into each other, becoming a pillow for her slumber, a halo to her dreams. I looked at this goddess of my loins and I could barely breathe. I wanted to fuck her more than I had ever wanted to fuck her. I wanted to pry apart her legs and climb on top of her and pummel her shaved whitish, lilac colored pussy with my cock. But in my dream I could not move. I had no arms, no legs, no lungs for breathing, no fingers to tickle her twat, no cock to pierce her with, I was a lonely, lifeless head, a piece of carved stone, vaguely Grecian, a white marble bust perched on a black pedestal. And then I realized my Soledad was in danger, though from what I did not yet know. I cried out to my Soledad to wake her, to warn her, to plead with her, but she did not answer. I pleaded with her for a long time, but she did not stir. Darkness fell. Then a warm breeze blew through the darkness and the blue curtain shimmied and shivered and two long shadowy arms reached out from the darkness and wrapped themselves around my Soledad, one around her throat, gently caressing her, the other pushing up against her breasts, her breasts bobbling like two gray pigeons from the pressure, and she stirred, and then sighed, and then she said 'I am wet, my darling, oh so very wet,' and then she sighed again, a long luxurious sigh, and the shadowy arms pulled her towards the curtain and the curtain shimmied and shivered again, and then the leaves of three leaflets at the ends of the vines became excited and started chattering, and only then was it clear that the vines did not end in leaves at all, or maybe things had just changed, for at the end of each vine was now a thick, juicy, stubby green cock with two rounded, greenish balls on either side, and the cocks that were once leaves were angry at the intrusion of the shadowy arms, they were shouting, an almost incomprehensible din, especially as they were speaking in Lapuridan, 'leave her be,' they cried, 'she belongs to us, we must impregnate her, we are about to burst,' but the two shadowy arms ignored the cries of the green cocks and pulled my Soledad through the blue curtain to the other side, and all the while I was shouting for her to wake up, to resist this madness, to come back to me, but my words were lost in the commotion, and I was so agitated, so beside myself from grief, that I did not notice I was rocking my sculpted stone head back and forth on the black pedestal, picking up momentum, and then I toppled myself from the pedestal and that was that. Soledad was gone and the warm breeze had vanished and the blue curtain was as it had been before and the vines were vines once more, and I was lying there now on the ground where Soledad had been, looking up at the heavy, suffocating nighttime darkness, wondering what had happened, wondering if I would ever see my beloved Soledad again.

I don't know exactly how long I was looking at the darkness, exhausted, useless, a spent cartridge, before I realized the dream was over, or perhaps reality had simply shifted once again, like the fog disintegrating when the sun comes out. I did not remember where I was at first, but then I did. Soledad and the young teacher were talking softly in the candle light. The rest of the café was consumed by the darkness. It was a very romantic scene. It was just the right kind of light for a merengue, and then later a bolero. Soledad was talking about when she was a beautiful teenage goddess in the Pyrenees Mountains and why she left. I knew this story very well because it was from the beginning of our life together. The young teacher was lapping up every word.

"Most of what I am telling you took place during the war against the Fascists," she said. "It begins the same year the war began. I myself I was too young to bother much about the fighting. We lived in a small village in the mountains in the north of Spain. We knew it by the name of Elzaurdia, though it had other names as well. If you headed north from there you would find yourself in France in no time. It was a very dusty, rocky road that took you past a farm here and there and the cattle grazing and the chestnuts and the beech glowing in the sunlight and then through the forest where the sunlight was streaked, and so on like that. Many people used this road during the war to travel back and forth across the border because the Fascist patrols did not usually go up that far. Except sometimes you might see a patrol heading up into the mountains, but they always kept to the road, and they always returned very quickly to Bera. My brother said you could take the road all the way to Saint Jean and the sea, though how he knew this I did not know. It was a very small village where we lived, four or five streets, some of them cutting up the mountain side at steep angles, some of them cutting across. It was a village with many buildings crowded together in a very small space, white buildings with stone archways and stone patios underneath where the sun did not reach, and all of the buildings had red roofs and red shutters or green roofs and green shutters, and red geraniums and white roses hanging from the balconies, and every now and then a flag from before the war, it was very picturesque, like a postcard for the *turistas.* But truly there was very little color in my village, not like here with the buildings painted yellow and bright pink and turquoise and green. There everything was white. And there was no church, and my father did not believe in church for his daughters anyway. There was a very dark room near the back of our house, away from the morning sun, and there was an altar there, an ancient altar from before the time of my great-great-grandfather, and that is where we went on Sunday mornings to pray and the candles burning on the altar, and you could see where the smoke from the centuries had soured the color of the plaster ceiling. It was a place without words, a place of gloomy shadows dancing on the walls, and we would sit in the gloomy silence and it felt like the silence was crushing the life out of us, except every now and then we would hear a lonely red-billed chough somewhere outside, the *chee-ow, chee-ow, chee-ow, chee-ow* way up in the sky, or maybe very close, or sometimes the droning whir of an airplane, but very far away, the sudden sounds shattering the moment, shocking us back into our normal selves, and we would breathe deeply and smile at each other as if we had been delivered up from the grave. But then the silence would descend upon us once again and our smiles would disappear under the weight, and to stop our thoughts from hurling us into the abyss of insanity, which is a place, the old men used to say, where not even God would dare go by himself, we would fiddle with our beads of the rosary until midday, at which time Elsa would bring to us lunch in the cool shadows of the patio if it was summer, or in the embalming warmth of the kitchen if it was winter, a plate of pisto and fried eggs or some cold almond soup or pickled eggplant and a bit of grilled fish, and cut fruit when we could get it, and then butter buns and lemon cakes and tea, and sometimes the priest who came once a month to give us communion would take his lunch with us, my two sisters and my mother and myself, but every time we would sit there in the shade of the patio and the warm breezes blowing past in the summer, or huddled around the smoky, clawfoot stove and the wind whistling through the lonely streets in the winter, until my father and brother would return."

Soledad had left the table while she was telling her story, had gone behind the counter and fixed up a tray. She returned with coffees for all of us.

"It has the feeling of a very long night," she said. "Is this not so, Papi?"

"It is so my love," I said.

She sat down opposite the young teacher, her face glowing youthful in the candlelight.

"Everything we do follows us everywhere we go," she said.

"Yes, my love, it is just as you say. There is no escaping it."

We sat in silence drinking our coffees, Soledad and the young teacher at the table and the candlelight washing over them, myself sitting in the shadows on the other side of the café at a table by the plate glass window with the blinds down. I felt invisible in the shadows. It was very quiet, even for a Sunday evening. The radio had been turned off and there was no music anywhere you turned your ear, except for the occasional car whooshing past with space-age woofers blaring and the window glass rattling. The young teacher finished his coffee and pushed his saucer to the center of the table. He drank much too quickly. He was like most young men. He did not yet know how to savor things. One knows a great deal if one knows how to savor things. But perhaps he would learn.

"Where did your father and brother go?" he said.

Soledad smiled her bright, exploding sun smile.

"Why they had gone to church, of course," she said. "Every Sunday they would head down from Elzaurdia through the forest and then they would pass through a village or two and then follow the river and then another village and then they would go to church, and sometimes they would stay after to play *pelota,* and sometimes they would be gone all afternoon. They would take a small white van my father kept for hauling firewood, always there was a stack of firewood in the back, and one morning I decided I would hide in the back with the logs and see this church where my father and brother went. It was only a short way from Elzaurdia if you were the wind, but it seemed a very long time in the back of that van. My father and brother did not speak until the van had stopped and there was a bell ringing and my father said "say your prayers quickly to the Mother Maria, my son, so she is not angry with us for being late," and then my father and brother got out. All I could see of the church from the rear window of the van was a white wall and the brown timbers holding up the roof and a side door with a stone archway. I could hear the voice of the priest working his Latin and the tinkling of bells and the moaning people with their 'Amens' escaping through the cracks in the walls like smoke, and then the Mass was over and the people were streaming out, spreading along the outside of the church in a thin, wavering line, like a shadow when it is very hot and the air is melting, some of the young boys and the older men getting ready to play *pelota* against the white wall, but my father and brother had no interest in *pelota*, they were heading straight for the van, so I crouched down behind the logs once again."

"Did they find out you were hiding in the van?"

"Yes, I was found out," Soledad said. "It was, what is the word, very traumatic. But all of that happened much, much later. You will hear all of it, I promise, but you must have patient ears. Do you have patient ears? They are very difficult to grow for one so young."

"Yes," said the young teacher. "I mean I'll try."

Soledad laughed and the candlelight flickered.

"Good enough," she said.

Soledad took a long sip from her coffee.

"All of this happened the year I turned fourteen," she said.

The whole room settled back into darkness, except for Soledad's face, which was lit by the candle.

"I spent many Sunday mornings the next year traveling incognito in the back of my father's van. But it is not how you might think. On that very first day I learned that my father and brother never played *pelota* after Mass. Instead, my father drove the van to the other side of the village where there was a stone wall from the time of the Romans, the last visible reminder of a fortress, that was the story that went with the wall, and beyond the wall you could see patches of wild fennel and then a grove of walnut mixed with oak and beech and the silvery flash of a small stream where the men went fishing, but no one was fishing on that day. My father pulled off into the grass and parked alongside the wall beneath a towering chestnut tree. On the other side of the road, across from the tree and the wall, there was a long, two-story stone building, an immaculate stone building with a red-tiled roof and a wooden balcony on the second floor that had been freshly painted. At first I thought we had stopped at a fancy hotel for the Americans who came up from San Sebastián before heading to Pamplona. But there were no Americans coming up the road for the fishing because of the war. Yet I could see many cars parked along the side of the road and in the grass. I remember thinking how very beautiful this hotel was with the mountain rising up behind it and flowers all around. I had never before seen so many flowers. There were flowers everywhere, along the edge of the building, along the road, stuffed into small pots on the balcony, everywhere you looked, red gardenias, roses, blue gentian mixed in, but mostly there were hundreds of bright yellow sunflowers. I remember thinking how unusual for my father and brother to stop at a fancy hotel. And then I knew. They had not stopped at a fancy hotel. It was a brothel."

"A brothel!" said the young teacher.

"Life does not stop just because of a war."

The young teacher was lost in a world of disbelief.

"Should I tell him all of it?" said Soledad.

"Whatever you wish to tell him, my love," I said. "He is old enough, I am sure."

Soledad laughed again, and it was a juicy laugh this time and the candlelight seemed to grow brighter.

"Then I shall tell you all of it," she said. "Every word."

"What kind of father takes his son to a brothel?

"It was the custom with many fathers where I grew up."

"How old was he, your brother?"

Soledad went over to the counter and came back with the coffee pot and filled our cups.

"My brother was seventeen," she said. "A few years older than I was, but he had been going for many years by then. That is just how it was. He was thirteen the first time. But it was not something we spoke of."

"Lucky thirteen," said the young teacher.

"Yes," she said. "But he was always lucky, my brother. I was the one who was not so lucky. At least when I was a young girl that is how it seemed."

She filled her own cup and sat down.

"Everything we do follows us everywhere we go," I said.

"Yes, my love, yes," she said, and she laughed. "And that is most especially true when it comes to this story."

We both laughed.

Then she turned her eyes to the young teacher once again. One could tell he would soon have become lost were not Soledad there to guide him.

"I could not believe where they were going," she said. "Even though, as I already said, this was quite common where

I grew up. So I got out to follow them. They crossed the road and took a path around to the side of the building and went in through a large wooden door that looked like the door to a stable. I did not go in right away. I clung to the corner of the building, half-hidden by the shadows of a blackthorn tree, and waited, and then I heard a door open and close from the balcony and a woman appeared. She was wearing a blue corset that fit her very tightly around the middle and her breasts were spilling over, and she was very beautiful standing there on the balcony in the bright, cool sunlight, leaning over the railing. She had very brown hair, brown like dark coffee, and very white skin, like the white ivory keys of my father's piano, and she had bright blue eyes to match her corset. I had never seen anyone so beautiful. In my mind she had been lifted out from the pages of a fairytale and deposited there, in the mountains of my childhood, so that I would see her and fall in love with her. She was humming softly to herself and smoking a cigarette and from somewhere there was music, a lazy love song floating on the air. Then she took a very long drag, and the smoke was curling up around her face, and then she flicked the remains of the cigarette over the edge and plucked a red gardenia and put it in her hair, but as she did so she saw me standing there below. I had stepped out into the bright, cool sunlight when she came out. She smiled at me and plucked a second gardenia and tossed it over. Then she went back inside."

Soledad stopped for a moment, my beautiful goddess of the Pyrenees, sipped from her coffee and looked at the young teacher and smiled, and then she looked over at me sitting in the shadows, all but invisible, but not to her, and her eyes hooked into mine and suddenly I felt as if I were standing with her outside the brothel and the heavy sweet smell of gardenias in the air, looking up at the woman in the blue corset from so many years ago. We have become very close over the years, Soledad and I. She inhabits all of my stories, and I inhabit all of hers.

"I do not know how long I stood there looking up at the empty balcony," she went on. "I put the gardenia in my hair and looked up at the spot where the woman had stood. I forgot my father and my brother. To me they were on the other side of the world. I passed through the very same wooden door they had passed through only moments before, but they were not there. They had become like a midnight dream that one forgets in the morning. I remember it was very dark inside, so I stopped just inside the door, peering ahead down a long hallway and a lantern hanging from the ceiling. I could smell all sorts of smells mixed together, lavender and musk oil and citrus and cinnamon spice. The lantern cast a blueish light on the walls and I could see old posters from old bullfights with the matadors sticking their swords in the bulls and their red capes flying and the horses of the *picadores* in the background, but the capes looked blue in the dim, lantern light, and at the bottom of the posters you could see the times and dates and ticket prices. At the other end of the hallway, past the lantern and the posters, there was a second door, a heavy brown door, which I did not see at first, but it was open and I could hear people laughing and soft, sad music, so I went through. It was hard to tell where I was at first. It felt like I had stepped into the past, into a room from before the war. There were no windows, or they had been covered up. I could see many vacant tables pushed up against one side of the room, and half a dozen more set up in the middle like in a café, and on the other side of the room I could see stairs. There were two heavy brass lanterns hanging from the ceiling and a few floor lamps and people were sitting at the tables and drinking and laughing loud boisterous laughs and then running up the stairs, and in the corner by the stairs there was an old man playing a guitar, strumming softly and singing. He was sitting on the floor, barefoot, his legs crossed, his head bent over at an odd angle, an impossible angle, truly, as if he were unable to hear his own guitar playing unless he bent over close to the sound. He did not notice the people running up and down. He smelled of *absinthe,* a heavy sweet smell that covered him like a cloud. I was standing there, very close to him, looking at him, but he took no notice of me either. I was listening to him strumming and singing, and it was the same lazy love song I had heard outside. There was a halting tremor in his voice, a sense of loss and lingering regret that drew me towards him, kept me listening, but it was a feeling I did not fully understand. That is when I met the woman in the blue corset. She saw me standing there by the old man with the guitar and she saw the gardenia in my hair and smiled and took my hand and led me upstairs to her room. She told me to be quiet and sat me in a chair by the window. I could see the balcony outside and some red gardenias stuffed into a pot, and I could see my father's white van on the other side of the road. I do not remember her name, but she told me she had many things to teach me, and that the lessons would begin that very afternoon."

Soledad began to clear away the coffee cups, the coffee pot, while she spoke. She was a vision, my Soledad. It was like watching a dancer. Then she continued with her story.

"The woman in the blue corset taught me that the most powerful men in the world will do anything you ask, if only you promise they may someday untie your corset. And if you bite off their fingers when they think that day has arrived, if you threaten to cut off their manhood with a razor sharp knife and push them out the door and turn the key on their heavy, musty, sweet *absenta* breath, they will come crawling back every day afterwards on their knees, for weeks and weeks and weeks, at all hours of the day and night, troubadours singing their lonely love songs, vagabonds, exiles, refugees, phantoms floating on the wind, miscreants pleading with you to tell them what they have done to displease you, begging your eternal forgiveness. She taught me that we are the true *Toreros,* that most men are just *toros de lidia,* the fighting bulls. The horns they possess are illusions. Yes, yes, they can carve you to pieces if you get in their way, they can trample you to death if you are unlucky, if you do not know what you are doing, but they are easily turned aside these men who are just the fighting bulls, a single flash of a blue corset and they fall away into nothingness."

Soledad returned to the table with a new tray. This time it was not coffee. It was a bottle of clear white liquid with the label Suisse La Bleue, three glasses, a bowl of sugar cubes, a covered pitcher of ice water, and three slotted spoons. The young teacher did not notice the tray.

"And is Señor Mendoza just a fighting bull like you say?" he said.

"No, no, no," Soledad said, but she was smiling a sly, mischievous smile as she spoke. "You are going ahead of the story again. First we must drink to the fairytale of my childhood. We will drink *absenta.* It is a drink for very special occasions. But it is also for drinking at the drop of a hat. Then after the drinking you will hear how I was found out and what my father said. And then you will hear about my Papi and how we met and whether he is just a fighting bull or no."

Soledad poured Suisse La Bleue into each glass, but not

too much, a few fingers. Then she lay a spoon directly across the top of each glass and placed a sugar cube in the middle of each spoon and poured the ice water over the cubes very slowly, drop by drop, the sugar beginning to melt, slipping through the slots in the spoons, the liquor becoming a hazy, whitish, milky cloud. It was the way the old ones prepared *absenta*. It was the fire of God burning across the sky. It was the way to heaven while you were still rooted to the earth.

"There," she said. "Now you must drink slowly, *absenta* was meant for a very long moment. Breathe it in slowly."

We began to drink.

"Yes, that's it. Be patient. I will keep our glasses filled as long as there is reason to breathe."

"As bitter as wormwood," I said.

We drank some more. We laughed.

"If you go to Spain, my young friend," I said, "do not drink *absenta* where the *turistas* drink. They will give you an extract of wormwood that is the color of emeralds and tell you it is made from the same recipe they used a hundred years ago. But what they say will be a lie. What they will give you will taste like goat piss. This is much, much better."

We laughed some more.

The young teacher drank his first glass far too quickly and gagged and laughed and begged for more. Soledad kept her promise. She told the rest of her story. She kept our glasses filled, though even I did not see how she managed this. She was everywhere at once, she was an exploding star, she was a milky, cloudy blur, filling our glasses, drinking her own, sitting at the table, telling her story, her face lit by the soft, cloudy light of the candle, her voice washing over us, through us, cleansing us, liberating us, burning away the ties that bind us to existence, her words seeping into the deepest, darkest, most forbidden corners of our souls, drop by drop by drop.

-13-

This is the rest of Soledad's story. It is in her own words, which are also my words, as best as I can remember them.

"The woman in the blue corset became my spiritual guide," Soledad said. "That is the best way to describe her. She was a mirror to my deepest felt desires, my captive femininity, my heart and soul. I soon became adept at disrobing in front of strange, lonely, heart-broken men. I helped them find their way back to themselves. I became a burlesque show, a Ziegfeld Follies girl, a Hollywood movie star. I let them take me in the hot, stinking heat with their hot, musty, sweet *absenta* breath, my swollen, bright pink pudendum swollen with their milk, again and again and again I let them take me till their faces collapsed in puddles of joy. I gave them intimacy. I gave them love. And so they forgot about the war for a while and the weary troubles they carried with them everywhere they went. When they left they swore I had transported them to Paris or Monte Carlo or Madrid or Prague, at least for a few hours, they would never have to travel beyond the borders of this brothel again to see the world, this is what they swore, and though I had never been to those cities, not even through magazines or books, in my tenderhearted, ignorant faith of a kitten, I imagined that without me walking the lonely streets of those fabulous, fairytale cities, making love to the thousands upon thousands of lonely, broken, soulless men who lived there, these cities were desolate, bleak, forbidding places.

"I could not have been happier. Which is all very strange when I think back on it. Spain was at war with itself. For three years the people of Spain were tearing at each other's throats. My own father was gone sometimes for as long as a week, fighting against the Fascists. But we were isolated from the war in our tiny village in the mountains. Even the patrols they sent into the mountains rarely came within shouting distance of our home. And so I had no thoughts of anything but my own happiness. There was nothing else to think about. Ah, what a luxury that was. I had never known such joy. I was my own woman at the tender, foolish age of fourteen. But my mother took note of everything that happened. She did not know much about the world. She still put the dried leaves of laurel and ash and the heads of dried thistles around our home to protect us from evil spirits. But she knew about me. She knew I hid each Sunday morning in the back of my father's van. She knew I returned home each Sunday evening singing with a joyful heart, but she said nothing, not to me, not to my father, not to my sisters. I was a very foolish fourteen and I thought her silence meant I was in control of my own destiny. But what did I know of destiny. I was not in control. A few months after

I began my Sunday pilgrimages to the brothel, the woman in the blue corset left for Madrid. I was worried for her traveling alone, but she only laughed. She would be fine. She said her grandmother had once lived in Madrid and had known all sorts of writers and musicians and even painters with names like Ortiz and Madrazo and Rosales. She said she desired that kind of stimulation. So she left.

"One month after that my brother discovered my secret. He was as much a voyeur as a young initiate, and after he had satisfied his lust on the girls my father had purchased for him, instead of drinking with the other men downstairs and talking sex and sports and politics, he would wander from room to room, slipping in through doors that had been left open a crack, peeking through keyholes, sliding in and out of the fractured afternoon shadows so he could glimpse the sweaty, naked bodies flailing away in the dim light, arms and legs wrapped effortlessly around arms and legs, vague, unrecognizable faces, some with their eyes closed or their eyelids half raised like window shades and their eyeballs rolled back, others with eyes bulging, anonymous faces, almost inhuman. My brother could not tear himself away from what he saw, they were like extraterrestrial squids, my brother said, swimming in the primordial sea.

"I do not remember the exact day my brother discovered me. It was very hot. I was with a lumbering goatherd who had once been in the army. My brother said he did not recognize me at first from where he was watching, the shadows and the angle and the dim light made it difficult to see who was who. I was to him just another squid at first. Then my lumbering, perspiring goatherd was finished and pulled away, dripping and smiling and soiling the air with his breath. He pressed his tongue against the back of his teeth to get the last taste of my juices still lingering in his mouth, and my brother was all but vanished, ready to move on to the next room, the next squid, but then the goatherd said the memory of that afternoon would stay with him till the grave and beyond, till the end of time itself, and then he saluted as if he were speaking to a Colonel and blew me a kiss as if I were the Colonel's wife, and I laughed. My brother recognized my laughter and stopped in the doorway. The goatherd pushed past a few moments later, mopping the back of his neck with a soiled handkerchief, and nodded at my brother, grunting and smiling bigger than before, *'ella merece cada peseta,'* he said, before he disappeared down the hall. My brother went over to the window and pulled up the shade, and suddenly I was sitting there on the edge of the bed, my skin pasted over in places from the goatherd's milk, naked and vulnerable and alone in the dazzling sunlight.

"I also do not remember what my brother said when he discovered me. I remember he stood there a while, taking me in, devouring me with his eyes as if I were just another squid for consuming. But I do not remember what he said. But he did not expose me to our father. He did his best to make sure our father did not find out. He kept me hidden. Sometimes just after Mass my father would discover a buyer for some firewood, but my brother would steer him away from the sale and the back of the van, reminding him that it was Sunday and it was very bad luck to sell firewood on a Sunday, did he not remember the anger of Kristo at the money changers, and my father would agree and laugh with my brother at this burst of foolishness, and then climb up into the driver's seat. Sometimes on the way back my father was very drunk and he would crawl into the back to sleep and I would sit up with my brother in the front and he would drive. Every time my brother hit a rocky part in the road or went round a bend too fast my father would mumble something, 'is anything the matter Xavi, did we have an accident, did we blow out a tire, is it a patrol, if it is a patrol you must say the Marxists are ravening beasts, just like General Queipo says they are, you must say everyone who sides with the Marxists deserves to be stuck like a pig,' but my brother would say no Papa, there is no patrol, no accident, there are no worries, it was only a cow wandering across the road but it is back in the field, go back to sleep. And so it went for months and months.

"My brother kept me hidden from our father, he was my shield, my guardian angel, my savior, always keeping for me a lookout. In time, he started calling me a very great talent, a prodigious talent, he said, which made me blush, and soon thereafter he appointed himself the manager of my very great prodigious talent and he began to collect money from every unshaven *putero* I slept with. But I did not mind. I did not sleep with these men for the money, so what did I care if my brother put a few coins into his pocket. I had never been happier. I had never known such joy, as I have said. Truly, I did not even think about the money. But my happiness did not last. On the very last Sunday in August, one month after I had turned fifteen, my father discovered I was in the brothel. That day is burned into my memory. It was bleak and rainy that afternoon. The rain came down very hard and cold, though September had not yet arrived. There were very few men that day, and by the middle of the afternoon all the men were downstairs drinking and talking and getting drunk. They were talking about the war, and they were very free with their opinions because the war was now over, but they were not as free with their opinions as they might have been had the Republicans won.

"I was sitting alone in a chair by the window looking out at the potted geraniums and the wind was blowing very hard, the rain sweeping across the balcony. I could hear the booming of thunder up at the top of the mountain where the storms came across, but then I realized it was not thunder, it was too close for thunder, it was my father.

He was very angry. His voice was rumbling through the brothel. Even the floors and walls were shaking from his anger. I could not hear his words distinctly, it was like listening to the mad bellowing of a bull after the banderilleros have stabbed him in the neck with their harpoons, but I knew what he was saying, what else would he say, '*non da nire alaba, puta arrain atsegin duten usaina,*' again and again, 'where is my daughter, that whore who smells like fish,' and then '*xerra ireki i bere sabela eta amaiera jarri bere lotsa, nire lotsa,*' and I could hardly breathe his anger was so heavy, his words as sharp to me as the knife he surely held in his hand, do you wish to know what he was saying, he was saying, 'I will slice open her belly and put an end to her shame, which is my shame,' that is what he was saying, and I did not know what to do so I sat there and did nothing. I waited for my father and his knife. I waited to be cut open like a fish. What else could I do?

"But my father did not smash through the door. He did not even make it down the hall. I could hear the voices of my brother and the old man with the guitar pleading with my father to spare my life. The old man was saying 'a daughter such as this is not worthy of the aggravation, come, my old friend, share with me a bottle of *absenta,* I have a bottle just for occasions such as this, we will drink it all the way to the bottom,' and then my brother joining in, 'yes, Papa, yes, she is not for you to worry about, I will take care of her, I will take her to Saint Jean, I will drive her across the mountains and take her to Saint Jean,' and then the old man saying 'yes, yes, my old friend, trust your son to speak these words of wisdom, let him take the girl across the mountains, and you and I shall drink away the rest of the day, we shall drink to the death of your daughter, to the death of daughters everywhere,' and I could not hear what my father said after that, his voice became a strange, strangled thing, I would have said it was someone sobbing, except my father never once shed a tear for anything, and then I could hear the sounds of dragging feet and the voices of my father and the old man and my brother drifted away, and then there was a deep, hollow silence, except for the rain. It was a very black silence.

"Then the door did burst open, but it was not my father. It was my brother. He did not say a word. He did not have to, the look he gave me said everything. I got dressed. I pulled out a small woven handbag and started to pack my things, a blue corset, a silk robe, a brush with an ivory handle, a bottle of perfume one of my *puteros* had given me, but I could not get the buckle of my handbag to work. I dropped everything on the floor. I was trembling and my face was covered with a matte of tears and I could barely make out the shadow of my brother standing next to me.

"I do not remember leaving the room. I do not remember getting into the van and driving across the mountains. I remember it was dark. I remember the road was very erratic, going this way and that way, and always there was a small stream on one side or the other, and we crossed over several small bridges, but I was crying the whole way and it was raining very hard, and after a while I could not tell the difference between the sound of the streams and the rain and my tears. I remember thinking it was the darkest night I had ever known, the darkest night one could imagine. And then I remember my brother's voice coming at me through the leafy darkness of the mountains and the weaving darkness of the rain, a moaning, distant voice like the wind through the branches of the trees, the wild beech and the walnut and the pine and the oak, and his voice was saying, 'yes, this night is very dark, but in the morning you will see a brand new day and the sun shining on the ocean and you will see a brightness you have never seen before and you will feel very much better,' and then later he said 'the worst of it is over, Tomásénéa is just up ahead,' and I looked out the window and I could see the lights of a small farmhouse twinkling through the trees.

"We drove the whole night to get to Saint Jean, and in the morning it was just like my brother had said. The sun broke up over the mountains behind us, a great explosion of light whooshing past us, ahead of us. We drove past a few whitewashed cottages on the outskirts, their red roofs shining in the sunlight, and the land sloped away towards Saint Jean, and we could see a thousand red rooftops below and a bright green river dividing the town, and then the flashing wetness of the sea. The rooftops were still wet from the rain and they also flashed brightly in the sunlight, and I could hear the sounds of trucks moving and people shouting and I could smell the salt spray of the sea.

"I had never seen such a beautiful morning. My brother drove as far as he could go, across a small bridge and through the narrow streets twisting and turning, and when we turned away from the sun, the sharpness of the morning shadows cut across our path, and when we turned again into the sun, we were dazzled by the sudden brightness of tall, white buildings with red shutters and green shutters and blue awnings, ancient stone buildings that had been freshly painted and decorated with colorful flags, and everywhere we looked there were almond trees and eucalyptus trees and lime, their leaves ablaze with moisture, sparkling like diamonds. My brother parked along a stone wall with a view of the bay, and the air smelled fresh and clean from the rain, and from somewhere there was also the smell of bread baking. We could see a few empty benches and a few cork trees for shade and the beach stretching out beyond the stone wall and then the greenish blue waters of the bay. It was still early, so we sat there a while looking at the water and the shadows of a few people walking in the distance, and we did not speak. There was nothing to say. It was a glorious morning.

"I don't remember how long we sat in the van, but I do remember it started getting hot, even with the windows rolled down and the sea breeze blowing through.

"Then my brother said it was time to go, and I smiled and kissed him. He did not smile back. He gave me a handful of coins and some paper money and I stuffed them into my handbag and slid out of the van. My brother did not even wave goodbye, but I forgave him instantly. He drove down the street and turned into the shadows of an alley, and then he was gone, but I was still smiling. I was walking through the streets of Saint Jean by the sea and I was smiling and the air was flooded with a bright sunlight washing through my hair and across my face.

"The next thing I remember it was late afternoon and I was sitting at a small café. Across the street was the river and on the other side I could see a few blue colored long boats, fishing boats, one with the engine running and the smell of diesel in the air, heading out to sea, a few others anchored in the water, black cormorants resting on the sides or flapping their slender black wings and flying away or diving into the green river water and then coming back with a silver-blue fish. Another boat was tied to the dock and half a dozen men in yellow or green workpants and blue shirts were unloading the catch of the day. All of the men wore black caps. One was standing alongside the pilot house with a red hose in his hands and the water rushing out all over the deck. He was talking to another man who seemed to be in charge of the boat. I remember thinking how wonderful it was to sit there at this café and drink a coffee and watch the cormorants flying about and the blue fishing boats and the fishermen unloading fish, and I did not even mind the smells of the fish and the diesel mixing with my coffee. I remember thinking I was once again in control of my own destiny. But again I was mistaken."

Soledad then paused in the telling of her story and she looked directly at me, her eyes once again hooking into mine, and for a moment she and I were the only two people in the universe. We did not need words, she and I. We had lived inside each other for a very long time. Sometimes we even saw the world as if we were one person. Words were no longer necessary. Then she smiled a wistful but mischievous smile and laughed softly to herself. It was almost like she was sighing.

"*Urak dakarrena, urak darama,*' she said.

She filled our glasses with the last of the *absenta*.

"What water brings, water takes away."

We drank.

"I do not know what happened to the fisherman after they unloaded their fish," Soledad said. "I suppose they went somewhere to drink. In my memory the fishermen are just no longer there. They are suddenly and completely gone, and there sitting across from me was a smiling face. I did not see where he had come from. He simply appeared. We sat there looking at each other for a long time. We did not speak. There was no need of words. It felt like we had just met and it felt like we had known each other since before time began. I do not know quite how to explain it. You could say that our souls had been hovering around that café since before we were born, longing for that day to arrive. One moment I was looking at the fisherman on the other side of the river, and the next moment I was looking into the wistful, greenish-gray eyes of the most beautiful man I had ever seen. His eyes were like the color of a stormy sea. But it was like I had known him my entire life. It was like we had been born of the same womb at the same time. It was like I was looking at myself. We were linked from that moment in ways that are difficult to describe. We had lived and died a thousand times together. We knew each other's thoughts, each other's hopes and fears. We shared the same memories, the same history, the same struggles. Oh, maybe not in all the details. But the spirit of our lives, the pattern of our experiences, was the same. We shared the same soul. Do you know what he said to me sitting there at that café? The very first words he said when he sat down across from me. He was looking deeply into my eyes, so deeply it was like he was inside me, like we had switched places and he was looking out through my eyes, seeing the world as I saw the world, and then he said 'I have been searching for you all of my life. I have known you since before you were born. I was meant to find you sitting here, like this.' It was a most amazing thing to say, was it not? But the most amazing part was I was thinking the same words as he spoke them. They were his words, but they were also my words.

"We lingered at that café, my beloved and I, until well past dark and the orange street lamps came on and there was laughter and music coming from the row of windows behind us, above us, men and women leaning out over balcony railings, listening to the faraway smash of the waves along the coast, drinking wine and singing and laughing, drinking in the darkness of this village by the sea. But we paid little attention to what was going on around us. For a time we drank in each other instead of the world all around. But then he grew very serious. It was almost like he had become another person. We talked about the dangers of traveling in a foreign country. My beloved said it was best to travel under an assumed name, especially if you were an exile from Spain. He said he was no longer Spanish. He said he was now a Hungarian living in the Slovak Republic. Then he showed me a set of traveling papers that said he was born in a town called Ružomberok. But I did not like his Hungarian name. It was very difficult to pronounce, so I asked him if he would mind very much if I called him Xavier Mendoza, in spite of what his papers said, because Xavier Mendoza was the name of my brother, because I was still stinging from the loss of my life on the other side of the mountains and how quickly everything had changed, because the name of my brother, the name of my family, was my only possession and I did not wish to leave it behind, because when I looked into the stormy, greenish-gray eyes of my beloved, my one and only husband until the end of time, I thought for a moment I was looking at myself, because it pleased my vanity to do so, because I was crazy mad in love, because I knew without a doubt that my beloved was not one of the *toros de lidia,* one of the fighting bulls, that he was instead descended in spirit from the great *Toreros* of ancient Iberia, he was a man who wore his courage like iron, so he knew how to live his life to please himself, and what pleased him more than anything else was my happiness, for all of these reasons and more besides, I asked my beloved to keep and honor the name of my brother no matter what anyone thought, to become my husband under the name of Xavier Mendoza, and my beloved said 'Yes.' Then we finished our coffees and ordered fancy liqueurs and ate fancy dessert cakes, and then we shared a glass of *absenta*. I had never had so much to drink in my life and I could not walk. I could barely stand up. We did not stay that night at the Hotel Eskualduna with its ancient stone balconies and its thick, velvet curtains so no one could see into your room and a few well-heeled Spanish exiles sitting in the lobby, dreaming of revenge or new beginnings and then heading to the train station only a block away, or perhaps they would head into the tiny café on the first floor, which is where smugglers used to meet. That night we wanted nothing to do with Spanish exiles. That night we gave up everything Spanish except our names. We did not wish to remember the past. We wanted to focus on the future. So Xavier carried me to a tiny, three-story hotel three blocks from the river. The lobby of our hotel was bare except for a piece of red carpet spread across the floor and a couple of antique chairs made from black walnut against the bare plaster walls and a black walnut mirror with hooks for hanging coats.

The light was very dim. Behind the front desk there was a row of small wooden boxes for the keys. There were also two cockatoos in the lobby, wild, unkempt, untethered cockatoos flying back and forth between the chairs and screaming out '*buenos dias señoritas*' as they flew, and I remember thinking what a strange and wonderful dream I was having, but it was not a dream. The proprietor appeared moments later and his face broke into a beaming grin when he saw my beloved Xavier holding me, my arms wrapped around his neck, like in the old movies when the groom carries the bride across the threshold, and he grabbed a green bottle and he spoke in French and he spoke very fast, but the meaning of his words was clear enough, 'welcome, my friends, yes, yes, welcome,' he seemed to be saying, 'a bottle of our finest champagne for the happy honeymoon couple, no, no, my friends, a bottle of champagne, please, please, do not worry, it is on the house,' and then he led us up the stairs.

"We woke up the next morning in a bed without sheets, the two of us naked, the empty bottle at the foot of the bed, our skin stained with the smell of sex and sour white wine, Xavier's arms still wrapped around me, the two of us curled up together like we had been sleeping that way for years. We woke just before dawn to the sounds of the cockatoos below and the proprietor grumbling and cursing, and then further away the sounds of the fishermen putting out to sea. Three days later we took the train from Saint Jean to Bayonne and then Bordeaux, and from there to Paris, but the whole trip was a blur of images, the train whizzing up the coast, the bright blue waters of the sea flashing by to the west and the stone architecture of bridges and towns, and then the train moved away from the coast and we were traveling through a sea of wheat on either side of the train and dark green trees in the distance, and the sunlight was now a deepening, amber color, and then the sea of wheat became a fortified castle high up on a hill and then more towns, more villages, people stopping to look at the train whizzing past, getting out of their cars or straddling their bicycles and waving at the train, schoolgirls wearing plaid skirts with tan blouses and matching sweaters and caps smiling from station platforms or cobblestone sidewalks, and then the ever-changing imagery of the wheat fields and the stone villages and the waiting traffic and the happy schoolgirls had all vanished, and the amber sunlight had vanished, and all I could see when I looked out the window was a reflection of myself and my Xavier, the two of us nestled close to each other, whispering to each other the rest of the journey, talking about love and children and making a new life for ourselves in America, and whether or not our destiny was written in the stars.

"Xavier said we would go to America and make for ourselves a new way of living. It would be our very own way, filled to the brim with an overflowing love. Our children would sing songs about our love. Our story would become a saga for the ages. This is what he said to me on the train to Paris. Then he produced a second set of traveling papers from his coat jacket pocket and handed them to me. 'We are both from the Slovak Republic,' he said. He was beaming. I asked him how he had managed to secure two sets of papers, but he just smiled and said we had friends everywhere. Then he covered my neck with kisses and moved up to my ears and then back down. I was so dizzy in the head that I almost passed out. I knew if we had not been still on the train we would surely have stripped to our skin and made love then and there. All of my fear and nervousness vanished. The next day we took a second train from Paris to La Havre, and the day after that we boarded a boat, the *Ile De France* with its two towering smokestacks painted red and black and the smell of burning oil and its flags fluttering in the breeze. We set sail for New York City at 5:05 in the morning. We have never looked back."

-14-

I have been thinking some more about our son who was born and who died. He was three days old, a tiny, oddly deformed shriveled-up peanut of a baby with short stubby arms and protruding shoulder blades that looked like folded-up wings, and skin stretched so tightly across his bones that you could see the blood moving through his veins. The day he died the world was struck by lightning. There was a great storm with greenish-gray clouds a mile high and great bolts of lightning like jagged pieces of bright burning glass to scorch the earth. My son was killed by a bolt of lightning. My son was killed by the hand of God. My Soledad said our son was an angel born by mistake, that was why he died. God does not admit to mistakes, she said. I wanted nothing more to do with God after that, but she took my hand and pressed it to her heart and then we went to Gesù Church in downtown Miami to speak with a priest. Soledad wanted a fat, fancy stone with fat cherubs blowing trumpets and fancy words carved into it. My One and Only Angel, my Hope and my Salvation, the words would say. But we had no money for stones. She wanted a Mass of the Resurrection and a funeral parade with people dancing and singing like a carnival Sunday and the beating of the *txalaparta* sticks like the sound of horses running and a gilded coffin placed in a glass wagon drawn by two mules, and afterwards a lunch of barbecued lamb and everyone in the neighborhood visiting and sharing stories and warming our hearts with their laughter, all of this for our little one so he would be properly welcomed through the pearly gates. But a Mass such as this cost more than a fancy stone, and besides, the priest said it was not permitted to indulge in such extravagance, it was a sin before God, especially since our son had not been baptized.

Of course I did not believe him. I said to him there were many extravagant tombs in the cemetery, many fancy funerals, but he did not respond. Then I said there had been no time for a baptism, why would God be so hard on a little child, but he just shook his head, no, no, he said, his hands were tied, he was truly sorry, dreadfully sorry, there was no choice but to leave our son in the merciful hands of the angels and hope for the best. My heart was broken for my Soledad. As far as I am concerned, she is the heart and soul of Calle Ocho, but this priest did nothing to help her. I am certain he was a German priest. An ugly German priest with eyes like those of a frog. I have not been back to Gesù since. We found a renegade priest who lived in Riverside to say a few words over our son. Then Soledad lit a few candles and said a prayer to Saint Barbara, and I did not say a word because I could think of nothing to say, so I let Soledad be my voice. Then we buried our son in secret in a corner of Caballero Rivero beneath the branches of a flowering dogwood where the crepe myrtle grows along the fence. So I have been thinking about our dead son. Ever since we took the two teachers under our roof, I have seen the way Soledad has been looking at the younger one. I can see in her eyes that she believes our dead son has been reborn. He died before we even gave him a name, but I can see in Soledad's eyes that she believes he is sitting there now in the café, right there before us, a Mendoza through and through, but without the deformity of angel's wings. This is what I see in her eyes. He would have been older than the young teacher, a great deal older if one is to believe the passing of the years. But perhaps Soledad is right to think as she does. Perhaps she has no choice. Who can say? She is giving him all the love a mother could give a son, a love which she had buried away in the deepest parts of her heart and soul where not even the flowers of a flowering dogwood could reach, a love I swear I did not even know existed until this young teacher intruded upon our lives.

Except I did know. I have always known. And now I am feeling this same love for this same young teacher swelling inside me like a balloon. It is a tightness in my chest and a weakness in my eyes whenever I look at him, and I am surprised this balloon does not burst. Every day the feeling grows stronger and I am not sure what to do. How does one who has never been a father suddenly behave as one? I watch the way Soledad sits with the young teacher and talks with him and gently corrects his misconceptions about life, and every day now she makes for him a special plate of pisto and fried eggs or red beans and boiled pork or sometimes a nice juicy piece of albacore tuna grilled lightly with black sauce and a couple of beers to wash everything down, and always now they are talking late into the night about life in Miami, how there are plenty of schools in Miami if he still desires to teach the children, and if he does not wish to teach we can find him something to do around the café, and then she is asking if the older one is truly a teacher, the one the girls call Mick, she is surprised that someone with his appetite is given to teaching, and then she is warning him about the girls in the café, especially Gisela, who is now bringing in more customers than all the other girls combined and soon there will be cat fights, and also she is warning him about that crazy Rastafarian, Malachi, who is always hanging around, and sometimes she talks about life in Spain and her own childhood, but not often, and always they are drinking *absenta* the old way and listening to Latin pop on the radio and laughing and talking and laughing. She is smiling all of the time now, a thick, juicy, curvaceous smile, and even when we are alone in the darkness of our bed, I can feel her heart bouncing and I know she is smiling because she has found this young teacher who reminds her of our dead son, and who can say she is not right to think so, and then she kisses me good night, a gentle, loving, lingering kiss, and again she is reminding me that life is too short to question this gift of second chances.

-15-

Yesterday morning the young teacher accompanied me to Café La Nueva for lemon cakes and an espresso. It was Soledad's idea. It was she who planted it in my brain. I suspect it was she who planted it in the brain of the young teacher as well. But what is one to do? Soledad has only to ask and I would move mountains. Her smile is all the reward I need. So off we went. It was a very bright morning yesterday, but not too hot. We sat outside and the girl brought me a cup of espresso and a plate of lemon cakes and some chocolate sauce on the side. It is always the same girl, the same table by the almond trees, the same flirtatious small talk in the beginning. It is a ritual.

"Hola Señor Mendoza," she said.

"Hola a usted mi pequeño pollo."

She laughed.

"No, no, no Señor Mendoza. I am no small chicken anymore."

"Ah, you are mistaken," I said. "At my age, every woman I see is *mi pequeño pollo."*

She laughed again.

Then she looked squarely at the young teacher and her eyes narrowed.

"It is all right," I said. "He will have the same."

The girl disappeared and then reappeared with a second cup of espresso and a second plate of lemon cakes, but without the chocolate sauce. Then she whirled herself away, but she was looking over her shoulder as she went, smiling. "If there is anything you want, Señor Mendoza, anything at all, just ask."

We polished off both plates of lemon cakes in no time at all. Then we sat for a very long time. It is impossible to say how long we sat. But we did not say anything. In truth, it was a morning for watching traffic, so that is what we did. It was very noisy for a while with the amount of cars and vans and trucks crowded together, barreling down the street, the smell of diesel and gasoline swirling, the dust also swirling, and a few cars honking. The warblers from the almond trees were gone. Perhaps they were chased away by all the traffic. Then there were long periods of no traffic at all and it was strangely silent sitting there at the table by the almond trees because the birds were gone and there was very little to say just yet. We could still hear the people laughing and gossiping inside the café and coffee cups clinking, but these were muffled sounds, as if they were bubbling up from the bottom of the sea, or they had crossed the boundaries of eternity just to reach our ears. Then a few more trucks passed by and the girl brought us more espresso and another round of lemon cakes and the young teacher and I were deep in conversation.

"That was not the way he put it," the young teacher said. "It wasn't just any woman. It was a particular woman. He said if you loved a certain woman and wanted to fuck her and you were a priest, what would you do? Would you quit being a priest? Or would you stay a priest and fuck her when you could?"

"It is not a real question," I said.

"What do you mean it isn't real," the young teacher said. "He gives you a choice. Do you remain a priest or do you quit? The question is what do you choose."

"But this choice is meaningless. It is like at a carnival show. It is a shell with no substance inside. He gives up nothing. Either way he fucks the girl. No, no, if it were a real choice you would have to choose to either fuck the girl or give up fucking altogether? Now there is a choice that has some balls, no?"

The young teacher did not know how to respond. He sat there looking out at the street with a blank look on his face and said nothing. A few cars went by, and then a garbage truck, but that was all. Most of the traffic for the morning was finished. In the silence, after the last of the cars had passed, the birds returned to the almond trees. Awhitta whitta whitta whitta, they were saying. They were a Greek chorus with something to say whenever we paused for a breath.

"Who did you say asked you this question?" I said.

"He was an ex-priest. Ignacio or Ignatius or Immanuel. Something like that. There were two of them"

"Ah, two Jesuits. They are always asking such questions,

the Jesuits. They are the worst of the religious. They are always pretending to search for the truth and they ask you such questions to trap you in their search, and all along they know there is no truth to discover."

"That sounds like them."

"And you, my young friend, I suppose you pretended to be honest but you were also playing a game, no?"

"Yes."

"And they found out?"

"No. I told them if I really wanted to be with the girl I would have to marry her. I said I would have to quit being Catholic. I said I would join the Episcopal Church. They didn't say much after that."

I could not help laughing.

"You rubbed their noses in their search for truth, these Jesuits," I said. "This is very healthy."

I laughed some more. The young teacher smiled.

I could hear the Greek chorus chattering from the almond trees.

"And who is this girl you wanted to marry?" I said.

"There was no girl."

"There is always a girl."

"No, I mean this was all theoretical to them. They go around asking this question all the time. It's a big joke. There was no girl."

"Yes, yes. This is the whole problem with all religions, is it not? They are always making their pitch in theoreticals, but it is really all one big joke to them. Priests pretending they know the mind of God."

"Ex-priests."

"Priests, ex-priests, they are all the same. They are jokesters. They are unwitting pawns of the Devil. They know nothing about God, that is for certain. And they know next to nothing about life and death. The rotten meat smell of it. The heavy, stinking, insufferably sweet-tasting smell of sex lingering in the air like old wine. Happy couples fucking late at night to the music of the bolero, young couples, older couples, men with men and women with women. The unthinking animal terror of being alone and rubbing the head of your cock until it bleeds because all you can do is masturbate. The heartache of living in a foreign country and you will never see the mountains where you were born ever again. You will never witness your father's death or know where he was buried, see the grave with your own eyes. God will not grant you this wish. But you know this. You give up the past and look to the future. You willingly embrace the struggle of a young man hoping to start a new life. But at the same time you are very much afraid, hiding inside your own language, uncertain how to speak this new language of fast cars and neon lights and greasy gamberros with their pockets stuffed full of new American dollars, uncertain how to get your hands on some of these dollars, uncertain if the luck you have always possessed will remain or if it will vanish under the weight of so many men looking for work, your hopes retreating into the shadows of these mountains made of concrete and steel, always just out of reach, unattainable, vanished, gone. It is a small miracle you were even allowed into this country with the immigration quotas that are in place, especially since your papers say you come from the Slovak Republic. 'Why didn't you head east towards the Soviets,' a man at Ellis Island sneers, 'there aren't enough jobs for those of us who are already here.' But you have forgotten this small miracle. You have been in this country three years, and still you are a young man finding his way, trying to find work. Your fears grow fat with the passing years. It is like looking at something through the magic of a magnifying glass. You take whatever odd jobs you can scrounge up, but the cities are flooded with exiles, refugees, for the whole world is now at war. But it is not enough. There are two mouths to feed and it is not enough. This is why you head south for Florida, for you and your beloved. You meet a man on a street corner handing out flyers. He says there are jobs in Florida, jobs building ships and rolling out ammunition, all kinds of jobs. He says they are in Pensacola and Jacksonville and Miami and Orlando, these jobs. You pick Miami because you like the name, and you pack up, you and your beloved, and head south, but you are still afraid. You start working for the Miami Shipbuilding Company but you are not yet an American citizen, but you have a piece of paper that says that you have a right to be in this country of free men, and so you work for the war effort, this is all you can do, but again you are afraid because the name on the paper is not your name. Your papers say you are Hungarian, but you are not Hungarian. You are Basque. You were born in Spain. You and your father fought against the Nationalists. But now you are afraid they will find out and you and your beloved might be deported, even though you have no idea who 'they' might be. And at the same time you are struggling with your own fears, which you never share with anyone, you are struggling also with the fears of your beloved, who has always wanted a child, but she is afraid that a child is a gift which God will not permit, however much she may desire one, but you cannot absorb her fears, you tell her to forget about children, but you do not really forget, but the years pass anyway, ten years pass under the bridge, then twelve years, and you have forgotten where you came from, you have always lived in this paradise called Florida with its strangely glowing sun and its pestilent heat, and then one day your beloved is giving birth in the back seat of a car parked along the side of a road, a narrow wet road cutting through a swamp, or a busy truck-filled road heading into the city. It does not matter. Your beloved is also a fugitive, disowned, an exile who will never again see the mountains where she was born, just like you, sitting in the back seat of your car, the heat of the midday sun beating down on the car and the air boiling inside and the leather seats searing her skin and her blood now boiling as well, spilling out across the leather. Your beloved screaming, an almost inhuman sound, unending, intolerable, like the glass of a thousand windows exploding, lacerating our ears. And then the unforgivable joy when the cord is cut and it no longer matters there was only a small pocket knife to do the cutting because you take your bloody son out of the car and hold him up in the air to show God, and he is shining red and glowing in the sunlight of this strangely glowing Florida sun, a defiant gesture, perhaps, but you are certain that God has blessed you beyond all measure. To these charlatans, to these men who know nothing and next to nothing, life is just waiting for the day when you put a cold body into the ground. Death to them is spitting out a few words to help us forget about the dead, to get on with the business of being alone, but their words evaporate like a summer mist as soon as they are spoken."

We were both silent for a while. We could not breathe. We could not hear the warblers chirping from the almond trees. We were caught in a vacuum of silence. A vast black hole eating up the universe. Then the young teacher blinked at me in the sunlight the way a small bird blinks and we were breathing normally once again.

"Men like these know nothing at all," I said.

"I am sorry. You were talking about your own life?"

"Yes. But it was many years ago."

"I did not know."

"It is all right. Besides, I am no longer certain if what I remember actually took place.

". . . ."

"Sometimes it feels like my life exists only in my own imagination. You will have to forgive an old man when he starts to ramble."

-16-

Sometime later it was the young teacher's turn to ramble. I wasn't sure if was the same day or if months had passed. I wasn't sure if his story was the product of one conversation or a dozen. After that first morning, the young teacher and I made many, many pilgrimages to Café La Nueva, and we had many long talks that stretched into the late hours of the afternoon. Hours and hours we talked, and after a while it was difficult to separate one day from another. The days blurred together. The young teacher said all he could think about was a young woman he knew when he was teaching and how he was madly in love with her but could never get up enough nerve to tell her, and then he was dismissed from the school and he never saw her again. He said he had come down to Miami to forget her, but this strategy had failed. All he had been thinking about for months and months was this girl. He said he wanted to talk to her, explain everything that had happened, but he never did.

Anyone with half a brain could see this lumbering mastiff of a young lunatic was overwhelmed with the grief of a broken heart. You could not deny this truth. In spite of Soledad's motherly attention, his beard had become much worse than when he had first arrived. It was matted from sweat and smelled of stale beer and old coffee and cigarette smoke. His eyes had narrowed, becoming tiny pinpricks of blackness surrounded by a halo of red. He was up at all hours of the night, wandering up and down the hallway that went past our bedroom, into the green-tiled bathroom and you could hear the water running, the water spurting out in short bursts from the brass spigot because the pressure was no good, and then the sound of gargling and spitting and then the toilet running, and then back down the hall, sometimes tripping over the folds of the beaded imitation Persian runner in the hallway, slamming against the wall with a heavy thud and the photos hanging on the wall in our bedroom rattling, back and forth all night he would go, and sometimes if you looked out the window you could see him sitting out back in a rusted lawn chair in one of the weedy, spongey, grassy patches, an island in a sea of cracked cement and broken glass and soda tabs and the glass glittering in the moonlight, and he would be sitting there without a shirt, his pale white skin a ghostly white, looking up at the darkly glowing sky, a three story building on the other side of the alley and the windows on the third floor reflecting a few neon blues and greens from Eighth Street, and he would be sitting in the lawn chair for hours looking up at the sky but not moving, his mouth open, the sounds of a merengue or a bolero or sometimes even a tango floating on the wind, the sounds of people laughing, his head cocked to one side, as if he were a dog listening to other dogs howling at the moon.

Life is always very ironic. But this is true only if one has eyes to see and ears to hear. It is like the words of the old poet, 'those who were seen dancing were thought insane by those who could not hear the music.' My life has become like that. My life has become very ironic. The more time I spent with the young teacher at Café La Nueva, the longer I sat at that small wooden table next to the almond trees listening to his story, the more I realized that he and I were both cut from the same bolt.

-17-

"I kept wanting to talk to Tommie," he said. "I wanted to explain everything. I wanted to see where she stood and if there was any hope, but Mick just laughed at me, he said there were plenty of fresh tuna in the sea, so why worry about one that got away, and then he said 'Get real, Lauterbach, if she had really wanted to be with you she would've come looking for you,' and that just sort of gutted me to the bone, I mean what could I say to that, I mean the facts are the goddamn facts. After that Mick started taking me to clubs to get my mind off my troubles, strip clubs mostly with names like Club Zanzibar and

Brandy's and The Pau Pau Club and The Alley Cat and Coco's Lounge on the Edge of the World, which Mick just had to go there with a name like that. But they were all pretty much the same. The same spinning red or purple lights and girls strutting across a stage with a shiny black linoleum floor and mirrors along the back and a pole in the middle. Smoke-filled lounges serving drinks till three in the morning or four or five, highball glasses of whiskey-and-Coke and rum-and-Coke and bottles of beer, trays and trays of alcohol floating from table to table and the men lining up along the stage with drinks in their hands, leaning over to slip a dollar bill inside a garter strap, their fingers lingering long enough to touch some naked skin, just their fingertips, their erections almost bursting through their pants. Lap dances everywhere you looked, friction dances for a little extra, the women in only their thongs and spiked high heels and blue pasties, bending over nice and slow, wiggling their asses closer and closer and then turning and pushing their titties into happy, eager faces, the men breathing in the lavender or lilac or lemon or cherry blossom smell of cheap perfume, and then the girls turning again before the men got too frisky and wiggling their asses even closer, rubbing up against hundreds and hundreds of hidden cocks until the men closed their eyes and moaned.

Some of the clubs had smaller VIP rooms like bathroom stalls with couches where you could get comfortable. Some had private booths with girls behind glass and when you paid your twenty bucks a spotlight would come up and a girl would start to grind away like a drugged marionette, her naked cheeks pressed hard against the glass, and she would finger herself so you could see her pussy and how wet she was. The clubs north of downtown catered to lonely businessmen and bachelor parties and off-duty police, and every once in a while you'd see a few Navy guys looking to blow off some steam or a Coast Guard recruit. Thugs and drug dealers and motorcycle gangs had taken over the joints south along Dixie Highway. The beach was for tourists and college kids. We went to all of them.

We spent most of Mick's savings and all of my severance buying drinks and watching girls jiggling their asses and squeezing their tits together and dripping with wet smiles and shaking a few drops our way, all for a few bucks. We stayed in cheap, concrete slab motels if we slept at all. It was the same everywhere we went. I have never been so fucking out-of-my-mind depressed in all my life. Nobody's kidding anybody in a fucking strip club. Most nights I wanted to climb into one of those cherry red dumpsters you see in alleyways all over and curl up with the garbage, and if I died before morning it would have been a good thing.

The very first night we went out we hit a club called The Cocodrilo Club a few miles south of Coral Gables. My skin was crawling the moment we stepped inside, like there was lice dripping from the ceiling, and every time one of the girls smiled at me I wanted to wash my hands or my arms or my face, whatever part of my body the girl had scorched with her eyes. Those first couple of weeks I couldn't even look at the girls for more than a few seconds, and then later I mostly just looked at their faces, but I was trying to get them to look into my eyes. I wanted them to see that I really didn't want to be there, that I was embarrassed to sit there watching them peel down to their skin, that it was Mick, a counterfeit Mexican revolutionary with an over-sized libido, who had dragged me inside, I wouldn't have invaded their privacy otherwise, I wanted them to see that I was different, I wanted them to see that I was still in love with Tommie Rodriguez and that I would have given anything to be able to call her on the phone or write her a letter, a long handwritten love letter like they wrote in the 19th century, just to tell her how much I really loved her and what had happened at the school and how I didn't really want to be down here in south Florida going from strip club to strip club in search of whatever, I couldn't even begin to guess, not even God knew for certain what Mick and I were up to, but as soon as I figured out how to wake up from this twisted nightmare of a movie, I'd load up my junky white Toyota and head back to the beach house and maybe we could try again. That's what I wanted them to see when they looked at me. That's what I wanted to say to Tommie. But even when I did manage to catch the eyes of one of the girls, it was only for a few seconds, and the eyes were always the same, sort of glazed over, unfocused, hesitating for a moment, but only because I had invaded their line of sight, and then the eyes moving on, mechanical zombie eyes that could only see movement.

"I never did get used to going to those strip clubs. There were too many people walking around with those mechanical zombie eyes, the girls dancing, the men watching the girls dancing, the bouncers flexing their forearms, smiling at the drunken bastards walking in and out, throwing a few quick good-natured punches at the air, the bartenders mixing highballs behind the bar. Everybody with their eyes stretched wide open, held open with tiny metal spikes was more like it, their eyes clicking with a mechanical click, click, click as they looked this way and that, but nobody could see a thing. I was sick to my stomach most of the time. I was ashamed of myself. I kept thinking about Tommie and what she would have thought seeing me in one of those clubs, and I wanted to write that goddamn letter or pick up the phone, but I never did. The nights kept clicking by, like a movie that's been speeded up, and with each passing frame I felt a little more disconnected from the world, a little more outside myself, and after a while it seemed that Tommie was something I had dreamed up, that she had never existed at all. My only reality was going to strip clubs with Mick and drinking till my eyes went numb, and most days I never even saw the sun, and when I did wake up during the day, everything tasted of salt, and it was so blurry and muffled I thought I was living at the bottom of the sea. Of course Mick didn't give two shits about what I was going through. Every time I tried to talk to him about it he just gave me a blank stare and ordered another drink. It was like bats or night birds flying out of my mouth instead of words. So I caved. I gave in. I dove head first into the spinning wormhole of my imagination and became somebody else. If Mick didn't give two shits then I wouldn't either. But I was just pretending. There was a part of me deep down inside that hadn't changed at all. It was the part of me that was sick of the way my life had turned out. The purest part of me. The part of me disgusted with myself. But what the fuck was I going to do?

And then one night I started thinking that if I only had a gun, my troubles would be over, problem solved with a flashing bullet, my brains splattered all over the wall of some pathetic, nameless club, because it seemed poetic justice to blow myself away in a strip club with the meathead bouncers grinning their stupid meat-eating, shit-eating grins and the zombie girls wondering what the fuck had just happened and then seeing all the blood and screaming and running for their dressing rooms. One fucking bullet and my problems would be solved. I would be somebody else's problem.

"I don't remember exactly when I started thinking like this. You have to be pretty much chemically imbalanced to go down that road. You have to be seeing tiny yellow worms swimming around in your soup and crazy shit like that. You have to be pretty fucked up. But I do remember where I was when this chemically induced epiphany first struck. Mick and I had gone to some shack south of the city that didn't even have a name. Just a pink neon sign that said 'Girls! Girls! Girls!' I don't remember how we even found out about the place. Probably Mick thumbing through the yellow pages. We got there around ten o'clock and went inside and it was pretty dead. It looked like somebody's garage with white cinderblock walls and bright white fluorescent lights, which must have been the house lights because they were way too bright for stripping, and a cement floor they had painted a shiny gray color and if you hit a wet spot you could barely keep your footing. There were a dozen black tables with black chairs scattered about, but they were mostly empty. We sat down and ordered whiskey. We sat down directly in front of a tiny stage crammed into the corner, a couple of rows back. The stage was maybe two feet above the shiny gray floor, without even one mirror to give it depth, without even a disco ball or glittery stars painted on the wall to give you something to think about if the girls couldn't hold your attention. Next to the stage there was an opening in the wall with a black curtain pulled across.

"We finished our drinks and ordered some more. There was only one other guy in the joint, an old wino with his own brown paper bag sitting in the back, staring out at the world without even blinking, talking an undecipherable gibberish to the empty chair beside him. We could hardly taste the alcohol in our drinks, but then we had been drinking since five o'clock so pretty much everything tasted like water. The DJ put on a George Thorogood tune with George singing in that scratchy voice of his about how he liked to drink alone, with nobody else, and we were looking at the old wino and laughing at the irony of it all, and then the house lights snapped off and a blue spotlight zoomed in on the curtain. You could see the dust floating in the air from the spotlight and a girl stepped out into the particles of dust. I don't know if you could really call her a girl. She seemed more like thirty-five, and when I saw her in the fluorescent light later on she seemed closer to fifty. She didn't have a clue how to dance to a George Thorogood tune. She probably didn't have a clue about dancing in general. George's tune played pretty well for a burlesque, which surprised me, but this girl couldn't make it work. She kept running into the pole, and when she grabbed it for a spin she lost her grip and stumbled backwards into the wall. The wino in the back was trying to sing along with George and drinking from his bag at the same time. A couple of grease monkeys who had just got off work came in and sat down right in front and started hooting and whistling, and the girl was encouraged by this and she started to do better. She regained her balance. She swung herself around the pole and tilted her head back so we could see her face upside down, and then she curled herself into a ball and twisted and turned and popped up again and then down and pushed her ass up into the air and flexed her cheeks, and then she was up on her feet again, but she had moved away from the pole, and she was doing something that looked like a Texas two-step along the edge of the stage, first one way and then the other, tapping her toes out and then in and gyrating her hips. After a while she almost seemed graceful moving through that dusty blue light, like she was swimming under water. But all the same it was pretty murky water with all of the dust particles floating in the air. You could hardly see a thing. Then the grease monkeys were shouting at the girl, telling her to take it all off. She flung her top into the audience and it landed on an empty chair, and then she started twisting her torso violently, trying to get her titties to jiggle, but her titties seemed fairly small and flat, though it was hard to tell in that murky blue light, but they sure as hell didn't move a whole lot in spite of her efforts. George was into another tune by then and he was singing about a landlady asking him for rent. This second tune wasn't nearly as good as the first for stripping, but by then the girl was really into it so nobody cared, and when she tossed her g-string into the audience the two grease monkey's stood up to catch it but it sailed past them and landed in my lap.

"I wasn't expecting the g-string. Mick started laughing, and the waitress who had just brought us another round started laughing too. 'That's your ticket, Lauterbach,' he said. 'Manna from fucking heaven.' The two grease monkeys glared at us, their eyes glowing a bright yellow-green in the murky blue light. You could tell they were regulars. Mick raised his new whiskey-and-Coke in the air and nodded in their direction and some of it sloshed on the table but Mick kept looking at them, grinning, and the two grease monkeys sat back down and looked back at the stage. Old George was done singing and the white fluorescent lights snapped back on and the girl had retrieved her top from the chair and was waiting by the black curtain, looking over at me with a helpless, yearning expression in her eyes. Mick gave me a nudge and I stumbled up from my chair, and then we were standing face to face, me and the girl, and I could see for the first time how really old and dried up she looked. Her pupils expanded and her helpless, yearning expression hijacked her entire face. She said they were running a special that night, three songs for the price of two, and then she slid her g-string from my fingers, gently, as if she didn't want to spook me, and pointed at two bathroom-type stalls that looked like closets on the other side of the room. I hadn't seen the stalls when we first came in. They were painted gray like the floor, which added to the impression that we were in somebody's garage. She said she'd be there in five minutes, she needed to change her costume. Then she tugged on my shirt sleeve so she could whisper into my ear, leaning so close I almost gagged from the fruity, peach-smelling teenage perfume she was wearing. 'Thank you,' she said.

"I don't know what I was thinking. I guess I wasn't thinking a goddamn thing. I wished I had gone back to Mick and the table, but I didn't. I found myself waiting inside the stall, sitting in a wooden chair with rounded arms and a leather seat cushion, like it had been stolen from a legal aid lawyer's waiting room. There was only the one chair, and a single light bulb with a string screwed to the wall. It was also very hot, very stuffy. The air conditioning, which wasn't very good to begin with, didn't reach into the stalls, but I was fairly drunk, so I didn't notice too much. The DJ started playing some country music, which presumably meant that another dancer had taken the stage. There wasn't a speaker in the stall so the music sounded sort of muffled, but it was loud enough that it probably didn't matter all that much, especially with a naked girl. I didn't have to wait too long and then the door opened and the girl slipped inside. She was wearing a black mini-skirt with pink sequins but without panties, and a black leather vest open down the middle and a cowboy hat and cowboy boots. She didn't waste any time. She started spinning around in slow motion, peeling back her vest and then dropping it on the floor, and then sliding her skirt down and kicking it away, and after a while I forgot how much time had passed, how many country songs the DJ had played, and then some rock-and-roll songs, and then the blues, all I knew was this thirty-five-year-old dancer who looked fifty was grinding away at me with her ass, only I didn't really care how old she looked, she was pushing her ass down into my crotch, wiggling back and forth, trying to find my cock, and then she started emitting a soft cooing sound, ooooohhing and ahhhhhing about how big I was and how good I felt even hidden away like I was, and I must admit I was ready to burst, I mean I was throbbing, it was almost becoming painful, and she must have sensed my agitation because she said I could take it out if I wanted, it was okay with her, and before I could say a word she had unbuttoned my jeans so I could breathe, my cock pushing itself out through my open fly, and then she was back at it, sliding the meat of her ass up and down, but with great almost tender delicacy, great precision, the tip of my cock glowing a bright red against her pale white perspiring skin, even in the dim light of a single light bulb the contrast was unmistakable, my shaft cushioned by the folds of her cheeks, and then her soft cooing became deeper, heavier, a low moaning late night sound like a lonely saxophone wailing in the distance, a single note hesitating, wavering, and she said I could stick it in if I wanted, she hadn't been with anyone in a very long time and it would feel so good to take me inside, I could have her for as long as I wanted, we could go somewhere else, she only lived a few miles away, we could spend the whole night together, if I wanted. But at precisely that moment I noticed the music had stopped. I could hear the clicking, humming buzz of the fluorescent lights and I started wondering when she would have to go back on the main stage again, and then I suddenly realized I wanted nothing to do with this woman. My cock wilted in an instant and I buttoned my jeans as quickly as I could. A great gnawing wave of disgust flowed through me. In another few seconds I would surely have squirted all over that woman's bouncing, sweaty ass, and I wondered if in coming so close to a climax in such a place, if God would spare me his vengeance, or if I might come down with some strange, slaggy tropical fish disease because of my lack of will power. Then I thought of Tommie and I wondered what she would say. I thought God might as well strike me down because once Tommie knew I had let a naked stripper push her naked ass against my naked cock, well that would be that, as they say. She would never look at me again. Just the thought of me would send her retching.

"The girl didn't say anything at first. She was sitting there on the gray garage-type floor on her black leather vest. She was still wearing her cowboy hat and boots and she sat there with her arms on her knees and her legs wide open. I could see how very old and dried up she was all over. I would never have been able to push my way inside her, no matter how big and hard I was. She had shaved her pussy, but it seemed like it was glued shut. I wondered again what I was doing there, but I just sat there in the chair, looking at her. She asked me what was wrong, didn't I like her, and she waited for me to say something but I didn't say a word. The clicking and buzzing sound of the fluorescent lights seemed to grow louder in the silence. Then her eyes misted over with that helpless, yearning expression again and she said she wasn't very good at this, she was sorry, this was only her third night, she had been an administrative assistant for a local bank for twenty-five years but then the bank merged with a bigger one from up north and she lost her job. She hadn't worked in six months. She didn't know what else to do so she took this job. She didn't know dancing was so hard. They only made their money on tips. The three songs for the price of two, well, all that money had to go to the house. That's the way it worked. She had him down for six songs in all, which came to ninety bucks, but all that went to the house, it wasn't hers. She said she was sorry if she had done something wrong, she didn't know what else to do. It looked like she was about to cry. The fluorescent lights snapped off and another two songs came on, which meant I was probably in for another thirty, but I didn't care. I pulled out my wallet and started peeling off bills, and all the while I was saying if she wanted to stick to this business she should find herself a better club to work in. I gave her three-hundred dollars and told her she should keep it all and clear out before they knew she was leaving and never come back. It was all the money I had left. Later I told Mick about it and he laughed a good long belly laugh, but it was also a welcoming laugh, like I had just been initiated into some sort of secret society. He said she was one hell of a professional to take me for three-hundred with that sob story. 'Congratulations, Lauterbach! You've just been fucking baptized.' That's when I started thinking about guns and bullets and splattering my brains all over the walls of some strip club. I thought maybe I'd do it in that garage-type hole-in-the-wall where my baptism had occurred, but I didn't because of the possibility that Mick was right about that girl and as soon as we would walk in we'd see her taking advantage of some other poor dope who didn't know any better. That was the worst part of it. I wanted to think of that woman as a damsel in distress and I had helped her find a better life before she had thrown everything away, like I had. I needed to believe that she had taken my money and was working in a Ruby Tuesdays and her kids were happy because she was home at night, and I didn't even know if she had any kids, but I sure as hell hoped she did. But deep down I knew Mick was probably right.

"I had to sell my Toyota after that just to goddamn eat. But I stopped going to strip clubs. Mick tried to get me to go a few more times but I wouldn't do it. I just sat by the window in whatever cement slab motel we had ended up in that day, looking out of a second-story window at the traffic rolling by, eating Chinese takeout, listening to *The Jetsons* or some other kid's cartoon on the television because you couldn't watch a damn thing without getting a headache, because the color settings were screwed up so everything on the screen was red. After a while Mick stopped trying, and then he gave up the clubs himself. He said we needed a change of scenery. He said maybe we'd overdone it with the strip clubs and getting blasted every night. We were no closer to finding any goddamn paradise than when we had first come to Miami, so what the fuck. But I didn't believe him by then. I was still fairly certain Mick didn't give two shits about anything that happened to me. But I figured it was probably a good idea to go somewhere else. I wasn't so deeply mired in a tragic, depressed almost vegetative state that I wanted to end my days in a cheap, cheezy, Miami motel. I knew the universe would help me find a better place to die. Two days later we were eating at The Patagonian Café and that crazy fucking bastard Malachi pulled a gun on us. I remember being puzzled by the fact that Mick was the one with the gun in his mouth and not me."

-18-

I am standing on a stone bridge looking at the water and I have been standing here for quite some time, it seems, looking at this strangely tinted water, but I do not remember how I got here. It is a lagoon of some sort. The water is sort of a teal color for a while, and then it changes back to pure blue. The two teachers are standing there with me, one on either side. It is funny but I can never remember their names. But it does not matter. A failing memory is one of the advantages of old age. The younger one is looking down at the strangely tinted water the same as I am, watching small eddies swirling past, or perhaps they are the bubbles of tiny fish. I cannot see where the bubbles are coming from. They head out away from the bridge and disappear in the dazzling sunlight on the surface. The younger teacher says something about how fabulous this place is. He wonders how long it has been here. But I do not answer him. I do not even know where we are. The older teacher is not looking down at the water. I forget about the water and the younger teacher and I follow the eyes of the older teacher. He is shading his eyes because of the sun. It is a very bright sun. It is early afternoon, maybe two o'clock. The older teacher is looking across the lagoon at a great stone building with a red-tile roof. It is an immaculate building with vegetation all around, palm trees and oak trees and magnolia and some pine mixed in. The building is somehow a part of my memories, but I cannot place it. Down from the building there is a red gate and there are hundreds of children on the other side. It seems strange that the gate is closed in the middle of the day and that we are on the inside and all of these children are on the outside. I have no memory of passing through the red gate myself. There seem to be many gaps in my memories. The world all around is strange and fluid like a dream is sometimes strange and fluid and you are expecting things to change in an instant, you are waiting for the change, and then it happens. But I am standing on this bridge and nothing happens immediately. The children are waiting to go through. The gatekeeper is late opening up and the children are fidgeting, laughing, running in circles like stray dogs. When I was a boy my father would take me into the mountains and if we saw a stray dog we would shoot it. My father said there were some men who made no distinction between dogs and children. During the war, many dogs and children were shot. But it is different in America. No one is shooting at these children. They seem fairly safe from bullets. All the same, I am wondering what they are doing over there on the other side of the red gate and if they are aware of the potential danger of men shooting them like dogs, and then it occurs to me that perhaps this is the reason I am standing there on the bridge, yes, perhaps I am supposed to watch over these children like stray dogs who are unaware even that they are being watched, perhaps I am supposed to watch over these children as a loving father would watch over them, once the gatekeeper opens the gate and lets them through, yes, that is certainly something I am capable of doing, I am deep down at the bottom of my soul a father, in spite of everything else I might have been or might have done or didn't do, even though I have no children of my own. Then the gatekeeper opens the gate and the children roar past him as a waterfall roars and I close my eyes to listen to the sound, and it is a comforting sound, soothing because it is vibrant, full of energy, so I keep my eyes closed for a while, squeezing in the darkness and the sense that I am still alive, but as I am standing there with my eyes closed, listening to the waterfall roar of the children passing through the gate, it suddenly occurs to me that perhaps I have died, perhaps I am already dead, perhaps this is why I do not remember where I am or why or how I got here, and then I am smiling a slightly puzzled smile. If one were looking at me, I suspect it would seem I had a touch of indigestion. If I am dead, I think to myself, it is nothing like I imagined death to be, I am still myself. I am untouched. And yet I am not myself. I am frozen in space and time, I am weightless, and as I move further inward, contemplating my weightlessness and the possibility of my death, the memory of the children passing through the gate vanishes as completely as if those children had never been born. But I am untroubled by this. I do not even feel the blank gap of yet another lost memory. I feel that everything is contained within this moment. It is now, suddenly, as if nothing else in the history of the world has ever existed, there is no buried past arcing away behind me and dropping off into sudden darkness, no labyrinth of pathways spreading out before me, offering the imagined solace and brittle hope of many possible futures. More and more I am struck with the notion that I am truly and irrevocably dead. The feeling becomes noticeably stronger. The air is laced with the sickly, sweet smell of gardenias. The feeling is itself something more than a premonition. It is almost a conviction. It is a feeling of being self-contained, existing only within the boundaries of oneself, impaled by the horn of my own thoughts, my memories bleeding out, but slowly, the moment stretching to infinity, the clocks of the world now useless, like deflated balloons that have spun around aimlessly for a while and then, sputtering, float lazily to the ground, their mechanical parts now draped over rocks and seashells, this is what death is. Then I remember the two teachers. I can hear them breathing. I can feel something like concern emanating from their lungs as they push out each breath. But it is more than concern. It is also agitation. I am wondering if they are also discovering their own deaths, surprised that this is what death feels like. I open my eyes and it is not as bright as I had expected. It is a strange, muted light that bends easily in the wind. It is like looking at the world through funhouse goggles. The faces of the teachers have become elongated, they have mushroomed into vicious, snarling snouts, they are in need of muzzles, and their eyes are beginning to bubble over with wonder at how their faces have changed. They are seeking answers, but I have no answers to give. Then the sun grows very hot on my cheeks and I feel flushed and thirsty, and their bubbling eyes melt away, and then their snarling, unmuzzled snouts dissolve, and all that remains is a shapeless piece of flesh where their faces had been and two black gaping holes instead of mouths, it is like they are screaming in agony, but they are not screaming, they are beyond pain, beyond words, they have become detached, weightless, like floating in space, and I am floating right there with them, suspended in the liquid gel of eternity, and then suddenly everything is moving again, very, very fast, so fast everything is mixing together, merging, converging, returning to some vague, watery point on the horizon, light and sound, the future and the past, the whooshing muddy rivers of all of us, the gray clouds that circle the earth with the satellites and the sun-speckled waters of the Atlantic below and the boats bringing in their catch and the matadors with their flashing red capes who flick their wrists and easily turn the fighting bulls aside and then plunge in with their swords gleaming and the blood splattering and the crowds chanting "Toro, toro, toro,' and the sounds of screaming cockatoos, and the sounds of small children singing hymns to the Virgin Mary, the Mother of Love, their small children's voices consoling us, absolving us, ringing out like tiny silver bells, cheering us on in beautiful days and in stormy weather, and then the sounds of Soledad singing her songs of joy as she dances around the kitchen, and I am listening to her sing and all uncertainty vanishes, all of this flashing towards us, flashing by, for we are now traveling thousands of miles per second, the two teachers and myself, like fiery, orange meteors with plumes of brownish-black, acidic smoke streaming past, we are burning up, burning away, dissolving, gravity is pulling us back into the atmosphere, back into ourselves, the deafening roar of re-entry swallowed up in the vacuum of a single instant, and then I am gasping for breath and I feel a tremendous ache in my ribcage, as if someone has been pounding away with a sledgehammer for hours. I am surprised my bones haven't cracked. Then I realize that I have come very close to dying. I am standing there on the stone bridge looking at the strangely tinted water, my head tilted to one side because the sun is too bright, wondering what is happening to me.

"Let's get out of the sun," says a voice. "It's getting hot."

It is the voice of one of the teachers, perhaps the older one. I am looking past him at the water. I can see now it is a swimming pool and there are children swimming. Around the pool there are several Spanish style buildings, white with red roofs. There are palm trees growing along the edges. Some of the palm trees seem to be growing straight out of the sides of the buildings. I am looking at everything as if for the first time.

"Are you okay, Señor Mendoza?"

It is the younger one now. The older one is silent.

The younger one is giving me a very long look. They no longer possess snarling, elongated snouts. They no longer need muzzles.

"Yes, yes, I think so." I say. "I am feeling a little muddled, that's all. Have I been sick?"

"Not sick exactly," says the younger one.

"It's the heat," says the older one.

"Yes," says the younger one. "And the bright sun."

"Yes, yes. But these things have never bothered me before," I say.

But they do not seem to hear me.

A very warm breeze blew across the pool and the stone bridge and he remembered once his father had taken him south and the wind had come across the plains all the way from the Mediterranean to Zaragoza, and it had been very hot against his face, like opening the door to an oven, and it felt like that now and he felt perspiration beading up along his forehead, but he was still cold and he shivered. He felt hands grab his arms squarely beneath the pits. They were not rough hands, they took hold of him gently and lifted him up. 'We'll be there soon, Señor Mendoza,' said a voice, and then a second voice said something but it was gibberish to his ears so he let it go. He could only see his feet at first, one foot forward and then the next, and so on, the white stone bridge receding. He wondered where he had left his shoes, but then the thought left him. His legs felt very heavy, but with the weight of his body suspended by the strength of the hands on either side of him, he felt as light and insubstantial as sunlight. He tried to raise his head, to see precisely where they were going, but the effort was more than he could manage. It was easier to let his head hang, to watch his feet go flashing by, and he hoped that whoever was helping him along would continue to do so.

"Have I been sick long?" he heard himself say.

"No, not long," said the first voice.

"It came on rather quickly," said the second voice. "I'm not sure I would even call it a sickness."

He closed his eyes and let the sound of the two voices wash through him. The gentleness of the voices and the sense of being supported by two sets of strong, capable hands revived him somewhat. He managed to look up and saw they had left the stone bridge and were passing along an extended colonnade connecting a small stone tower to a larger stone building with a heavy wooden door and window frames painted bright blue. There were green benches between the columns, facing the pool, but these were filled with children and bath towels and discarded socks and shoes and sandals and t-shirts and empty lunch boxes. After the last column there was no bench and they turned there and passed into the warm, thick darkness of a pavilion. He was talking the whole while, asking questions, but he kept losing his train of thought.

"What was I saying?" he heard himself say.

"You were asking about the festival in Allapattah," said the first voice. "You were disappointed you couldn't remember the big-head puppet parade, the Cabezudos."

He was shivering again and wondered what kind of sickness he had and he was suddenly afraid of this sickness, the way a small boy is afraid, and then he laughed at himself and he let the fear pass. It had been a long time since he had felt such a fear and he wondered if it would come again.

"That's when you took sick," said the second voice. "Later that day. But I wouldn't even call it a sickness. It was more like you just overdid things."

"That's exactly what you did."

They found an empty picnic table in the darkness and then they said they would bring him some water and they vanished into the brightness of the sky beyond the columns. He sat there looking at the bright blue of the water, a sharp rectangle against the black shadows beneath the pavilion. After a while the two voices returned. It seemed darker. The fear did not return. He had almost forgotten why he was sitting there.

"Here you go, Señor Mendoza. It's nice and cold, so drink it slowly. You don't want to shock your system."

They left again but he did not remember where they were going. Time moved erratically, jumping backwards in fitful bursts like tiny yellow birds taking wing, then sliding forward, then stopping altogether. He drank the water slowly, and then the bottle was empty. He could feel the water tumbling down his throat, the hollowness inside filling up. He was a prisoner inside himself, trapped in the cavernous darkness of his bowels, until he drank the water, and as the water level rose inside, he rose, up through the twisted curvature of his throat and out through his mouth into the open air, and then he kept on rising. He was looking down on himself. It might have been a dream, but the sensation of floating was very strong. It was like watching a movie filmed from the air. He saw himself sitting at the picnic table and simultaneously standing on the stone bridge between the two teachers and he was also floating in the air. He was in all three places at the same time. He wondered if his three selves were thinking identical thoughts or if they were each bound to a specific moment, and he tried to tune his ears so he could catch what was rolling through the brains of the other two. It was like trying to capture a radio station that is just barely in range. Then he was standing at the bridge again, only this time he was taking in the buildings that surrounded the swimming pool with a measurable degree of disappointment. He had not known the purpose of the trip was to take him swimming for an afternoon. He had thought he was going to a brothel of some sort. The picture on the postcard had reminded him of a brothel he had been to when he was younger. He had been hoping to dive into that memory of his youth for one final fling before he died, that's how he had thought of this trip. He was certain Soledad had sent him with these two so he could taste once again the freshness of his youth, of their youth. Then he was sitting once again at the picnic table and he could barely breathe. He had knocked the empty bottle from the table and it was bouncing on the cement floor of the pavilion in the darkness the way plastic bottles do, a hollow sort of clacking sound rippling up from the floor, he could feel the rippling waves pulsing through his body, and then the bottle settled. He could hear the sounds of the children in the pool and running through the pavilion, chattering and laughing. The children possessed very small, tinny sounding voices, very high up, it sounded almost like a ringing in his ears. Then from very far away he could hear the haughty, superior, compassionate laughter of his Soledad, and suddenly he could smell the scent of gardenias once again and he remembered how she used to wear gardenias in her hair, but that had been many years ago. He wondered if she were wearing a gardenia at that very moment. He wondered what she was doing while he was away at the pool and how hungry he was to see her face, and then he felt hungry in general, even though it was still early, nevertheless, he hoped she would make him a bowl of barley soup and Saltines and a plate of pisto, just the way he liked it, when he returned. He thought about how long he and Soledad had been together, and he could not remember a time when she did not exist. She was his beautiful goddess of the Pyrenees, always, his heart and soul for ten thousand years. He wondered how long this dream would go on and when he would see her again, and in the muted silence of his reverie he heard her voice calling out to him. There was a timorous, fragile quality about her voice, as if it had traveled across the centuries to reach his ears, and she was saying 'everything we do follows us everywhere we go,' over and over again, and then her voice was replaced by the sounds of the sea and the steady crash of the waves along the shore and he was reminded of their time in Saint Jean and that small café with its view of the river where they had talked about the future and then he had taken her to a small hotel only three blocks away, a seedy little hotel that did not compare in the least with the mysterious elegance of Hotel Eskualduna, but he could not help that, he had not wanted to attract attention, there were too many people at Hotel Eskualduna who would have recognized him, but he had never told her that, and then he heard the voices of the screaming cockatoos once again, but there were many more of them now, it sounded like hundreds and hundreds of white-feathered cockatoos, he could hear the rush of their wings as they wheeled through the dark open spaces beneath the pavilion rooftop, past the picnic tables and the benches and then back out into the bright blue sky and then down again into the pavilion, a frenzy of feathers, the cockatoos screaming '*buenos dias señoritas*' as they flew. And then the cockatoos were gone and he was floating in the air once again, rising with the heat, escaping, the atmosphere beginning to thin. He could see the first of his former selves, the one at the bridge, stumbling against the railing and the two teachers taking hold of his armpits. He could see his second former self in the darkness of the pavilion, kneeling down on the cement floor, his torso sliding forward, his arms sliding out to either side. And then he was very high up. He could see a few figures running along the edge of the pool and then dashing into the darkness of the pavilion. Sirens were blaring. Children stopped swimming to see what was going on. On the other side of the red gate, two police cars drove into the parking lot, and then several policemen were rushing towards the pool. But he had already turned his attention elsewhere.

BOOK THREE

the sex queen of the Moulin Rouge

-19-

Malachi Horatio Decosta lived in Allapattah just north of the river on a dead-end side street in a small shotgun shack of indeterminate color. No one paid much attention where Malachi went or the hours he kept. No one on his block even knew his real name. He looked like every other Rastafarian in the neighborhood with his yellow and red and green striped cap and his smelly dreadlocks flowing out from underneath. Except he was white (he claimed to have been born in the Caribbean, but whatever accent he pretended to have vanished completely in moments of great distress), and he also wore black bicycle shorts and rode a badly twisted ten-speed that must have been twenty years old. He had picked it up at a garage sale for ten dollars. One dollar for each twisted gear. You could hear Malachi's bike grinding and rattling and wheezing from three blocks away. It sounded almost cartoonish, like a demented accordion that played the same two sliding mechanical notes over and over again. The people of the neighborhood knew Malachi only as the man with the broken bike. But that was enough. They called him 'Broken Bike' for short. "Oye, man, I just zeen Broken Bike ride by." "Oye Broken Bike, what was you doing tonight?" "No, man, you aint wanna be messin with Broken Bike, you be in some jam you do that, he a crazy lunatic motherfucker. Even his friends say so. Heee'll put a gun to your head like he giving you a cigarette."

No one understood Malachi any better than Malachi understood himself. This was not saying much. Passersby might encounter Malachi standing outside a Laundromat in the middle of the morning, his bike leaning against an expired parking meter, ranting and raving about the horde of Castro hardliners in Congress, for Malachi held them responsible for everything from overpriced airline tickets to the Caribbean to the steady decline of the middle class to the lack of good beer in the grocery stores. Then he would descend into a weepy prolonged silence. After that he would begin waving his arms erratically in the air as if he were trying to describe the scene of an accident through pantomime. What would you think? To be honest, most of the world thought him a lunatic. But he was not a lunatic. He simply danced to a music that few people heard. He noticed small things that others missed. He remembered what he saw with cinematic clarity, in living color. He forgot nothing. Clinically he was what some would call an idiot-savant, and so he often seemed crazy to those who did not know him. In other words, to most of the world, which is to say those who did not perceive the pattern in his madness, everything Malachi did seemed an afterthought, an invention of a drug-induced stupor, a chance phrase on a bumper sticker taken to heart, a warning in a dream caused by eating rancid pork, the word of God misremembered.

-20-

An example of Malachi's perceived lunatic behavior:

After ten years working for a local outfit hauling garbage, one day Malachi caught his reflection in the side view mirror of the truck. He was just sort of hanging on, his arm looped loosely through the sidebar, chewing on his tongue, and behind himself he could see flashes of sunlight coming through the trees, and thinking these flashes were Morse code from the ancient Egyptian god Amun-Ra (he had been reading a lot about Egypt at that point), he decided to quit his job, just like that. He decided he was going to branch out on his own. Why not? He suddenly realized he knew as much about garbage as anyone else in the trade. And he paid far more attention than most to the waste reduction habits of each household. The sexy chiquitas who had taken up residence in apartment 212B of the Dolphin Shores Apartment complex (the ones who were perfume girls at the airport mall), threw out sexy lace underwear from Victoria Secret after wearing them for only a single day and a single night, so he knew there was money to be made there. In the same building on the fourth floor there was a young father, an ex-Marine who had got his legs shot off in the desert. Mostly empty baby food jars and half-drunk bottles of whiskey. Opportunity there as well. And the Senior Center on 24th Avenue, they were always boxing up shoes and old clothes and costume jewelry when somebody died and leaving the boxes out back for the Goodwill truck. That was just a matter of scheduling. Yes, there was a great deal of money to be made if you just kept your eyes open, if you knew where to look. Malachi thought he was going to get rich sifting through the trash of everyone who lived north of the river between 27th Avenue and the Interstate. He thought he might even have to hire a few derelicts like himself. The boss man of his former crew, an enormously fat, happy man, laughed and laughed when he learned of Malachi's plans, but even this insult did not infuriate Malachi. Besides, the boss man wasn't even an American, he was a refugee from Kuwait, a casualty of the very same war that had claimed the young father's legs, and he did not speak English very well, so it was hard to be sure just what he was laughing at. So Malachi forgave him what was surely an unintentional slight. His hope soared. His hope was a bright smile that lit up the sky on even the sunniest day. He outfitted himself with an abandoned grocery store cart from Publix for hauling purposes and a lonely skier's pole for reaching objects just out of reach. He spent countless hours scouring back alleys and vacant lots and abandoned buildings, but after several weeks of back-breaking work in the sun, and unexpectedly fruitless work at that, Malachi decided to spend most of his time down along the river, investigating the shaded, vacant areas beneath the bridges, the hidden walkways, the shaded areas that bordered the numerous marinas but were separated from these enclaves of the extravagantly (absurdly so) wealthy by shiny, brand-new, chain-link fences. Mostly he found broken bottles and rusted toaster-ovens and empty paint cans and plastic bags stuffed with dirty diapers, but occasionally there was something worth saving, something he could polish up a bit and sell for a few dollars, something he could claim for himself, like his bike. He began to think of this alternative reality along the river as a paradise where the treasures of the universe lay waiting. If you asked him if it wasn't absurdly difficult and perhaps financially irresponsible, even ruinous, to expect to find treasure in this manner, wasn't he tempting fate, or at the very least, wasn't he embarked on a fool's errand, he would simply smile and say, "No, man, it's easy, man. Everywhere you look there are diamonds in the rough."

-21-

By the time Malachi met the two teachers at The Patagonian Café, he was no longer in the garbage trade. He was a part-time talent scout in the adult film industry, or at least he had been. In truth, he had only ever worked for the Velázquez brothers, a pair of local thugs who, according to some, had made their money running drugs in the eighties, and according to others, they were front men for the CIA, before they gave it all up (either the drug business or the spy business) and became pornography hustlers. Their company, which they named Coñazo Films (which translated literally meant Giant Vagina Films), turned out half a dozen adult films a week, sometimes more. But it was hard to say if Malachi would be working for Coñazo Films much longer. He had crossed the line, so to speak, and that was something you did not do with the Velázquez brothers.

How Malachi crossed the line with the Velázquez brothers:

The Velázquez brothers had had the rare misfortune to be born Siamese twins in a devoutly superstitious and homophobic Catholic family. They were joined at the hip (they shared a small portion of the iliac crest, the part of the hip that flares out), but slightly turned towards each other. All their grandmother could do when she saw them was wave a bony finger in their direction and scream *"hueva del Diablo"* before she fled, wrapped in the spider web of a black shawl, into the trembling shadows of her sitting room. Their father would not speak to them at all. They had been successfully separated as small children, but they carried the scar of their union as if it were part of a shameful, incestuous, homosexual past. The myriad psychoses they developed as a result of this childhood trauma laid the foundation for their later success as thugs, or as they preferred to think of themselves, modern day Mongolian warlords destined to conquer the world (they had watched with obsessive interest a movie about Genghis Khan when they were young boys and had never forgotten the riveting, ringing sensation in their ears that the graphic violence in the movie had produced). They were humorless men with black leathery, crusted-over skin, as if they were both burn victims or suffered from leprosy. They were identical, down to the minor indentations in their once conjoined hips. No one joked even about Siamese cats in their presence for fear of a bullet.

The brothers called each other Bull and Horse respectively, but no one knew them well enough to know who was who. Even Malachi generally called them both Mr. Velázquez, and he had worked for the brothers for two years sending strippers their way, yoga instructors, lifeguards, massage therapists, substitute teachers, girls who worked at deli counters or florist shops or hair salons or out at the airport mall (two of the four sexy chiquitas from apartment 212B regularly appeared in orgy scenes in Giant Vagina Films). Anyone Malachi thought might look good in front of the camera, without clothes on, naturally, he sent along for a screen test. He was paid a small commission each time one of his referrals appeared in a movie, and he did quite well for a while, enough so that he began to find his squeezebox bike embarrassing, even shameful, and he seriously contemplated tossing it into the river, a sort of symbolic crossing over into the land of the dead, which appealed to his sense of the mythic (or perhaps pseudo-religious would be more precise). But he could not shake the feeling that getting rid of the bike would spell disaster. In his mind, the physical aspects of the bike were intimately linked to his own identity. If the bike were to suffer the agony of an untimely (or even timely) death, he thought, who could say he wouldn't be next?

Malachi's coup de grâce as far as picking talent for the Velázquez brothers was persuading Gisela with her big bouncing titties to strip in front of the camera and strut her stuff. It didn't take a whole lot of persuading. One afternoon at the café Malachi asked her if she would be interested and she said yes. He mentioned that there might be some fucking involved. She said she didn't mind, she liked fucking. He said there might even be a lot of fucking. She said okay. She made a total of seventeen films, all of which went straight to video, and was an instant smash. The video stores couldn't keep her movies on the shelves. The Velázquez brothers were suddenly flush with suitcases of cash and decided to bankroll a major motion picture with Gisela and her wonderfully voluptuous titties as the star. They were going to do a giant billboard campaign. They were going to open in 2,700 theaters across the nation and rake in millions. Suddenly they seemed less and less like burn victims or psychotic killers troubled by an unspeakable past and began to laugh at a few non-threatening jokes. They permitted Malachi to call them Bull and Horse interchangeably. And then Gisela decided she didn't want to be a film star anymore. For one thing, she said, it was boring. For another, she was raw from so much sex, she hadn't realized they were going to do it this much, it hurt even to pee. Finally, she said she had promised Señor Mendoza she would give up movies for a while to see if she really loved doing them or if she was only in it for the money. Señor Mendoza had been telling her that the only way to find true happiness was to make sure you were following the dictates of your heart. "Happiness has nothing to do with money," that's what Señor Mendoza had told her.

By this point, of course, the Velázquez brothers had already emptied several suitcases full of ready cash to grease the movie-production wheels of their greatest venture. Their behavior had been entirely predictable, one might even say inevitable. They had hired a big-time director from Mexico City (who was watching the bright blue waters of the Atlantic from the balcony of a ninth-floor hotel room in the city of Sunny Isles Beach until filming began, smoking Cuban cigars by the box as if he were eating chocolates and dining on caviar for breakfast). They had engaged the services of an upscale production company six blocks from the hotel (the package they had purchased included two sound technicians, several actors on call in case they were filming a crowd scene or had a few bit parts left over, digitalized video equipment, which was pretty standard, a fully stocked bar, and a catering contract with the hotel that housed the director). They had hired Ambrosi Perugini, the flamboyant designer from Milan (who was also staying at the hotel), to oversee the artistic dimensions of the picture (costumes, set design, etc.). And they had hired a publicity firm headquartered in Austin, Texas to give them coast-to-coast coverage, mostly radio spots. They were shelling out eight thousand a day for a chance to skip the pearly gates and bask in the sun of their own private paradise.

Two days after Gisela quit Coñazo Films, the Velázquez brothers decided to lean on Malachi. They placed an unsigned message into a small green envelope with the Coñazo Films logo stamped in the middle (the logo was a picture of a thick-lipped hairless vagina that at various moments, depending upon the angle of the light, looked like a glistening mouth that was laughing, or sometimes crying, or sometimes getting ready to eat) and then they slipped the envelope under the door of Malachi's shotgun shack.

It was one in the afternoon when the envelope appeared on the other side of the door, where it met the resistance of a pair of rope-soled sandals and stopped. It was two o'clock when Malachi noticed the hairless vagina on the floor. But instead of a gaping orifice capable of expressing a range of human emotions (joy, sorrow, hunger), Malachi saw instead a giant eye staring up at him. He opened the envelope and read the message.

We need Gisela to get her fucking tits back in front of the goddamn camera. We are losing too much money and we are holding you responsible. You better have some idea how to fix this if you don't want your own goddamn fucking ass in a sling. Meet us up on the roof to discuss details. Do not be late. (P.S. Please excuse our fucking French, but we can't help it with things being the way they are.)

There was no mention of the time, no way to determine if he was already late or not, but this was typical of a Velázquez brothers' message. This kind of stubborn vagueness was deliberate. It was supposed to indicate a malicious, sinister intelligence lurking somewhere on the periphery of existence, getting ready to pounce, never quite visible until it was literally too late to do anything about it. Malachi was mildly disturbed. But he knew the message came from the Velázquez brothers, and in spite of their reputation, he had never witnessed them even roughing someone up, let alone killing them in cold blood. The feeling of being disturbed gave way to one of irritation. He threw on his shorts, a t-shirt and a baggy safari vest with two oversized pockets and headed out the door.

'Up on the roof' meant the roof of a corner video store on 22nd Avenue. The journey would take him twenty minutes by squeeze-bike. At one time this tiny one-story building had served as a getaway safe-house for the Velázquez brothers, and it still possessed the aura of a den of thieves, but now it seemed almost cultivated, as if it were part of a scene from a 1940s Hollywood movie. The air inside the store was stale and smelled of dried urine (the door to the bathroom did not close all the way, and there was no light, so many men dribbled on the floor) and cigarette smoke (they had set aside a couple of red leather armchairs in one corner for patrons who wished to smoke while they debated the merits of various titles; the chairs were always occupied).

Most of the patrons were wearing a hat of some kind, pulled down so you could barely see two eyes blinking in the shadows beneath the brim, and long trench coats of various styles and colors, which gave the impression that in addition to thieves from a 1940s movie, the store was also frequented by flashers recently released from jail. There was constant traffic up and down the rows and rows and rows of adult films with glossy covers depicting all sorts of lewd behavior — teenage girls with rather prominent jugs (though hardly worth noting when compared to Gisela's) dancing naked with ape-like creatures around coconut trees; twelve-inch or perhaps sixteen-inch schlongs ramming into heart-shaped asses; devil women wearing masks and collars with spikes whipping timid, fragile men chained to whorehouse beds in brothels that looked vaguely like medieval dungeons — that sort of thing.

The clerk was a wheezing fat man with greasy red hair tied in a ponytail who sat ensconced in a small Plexiglass cubicle behind an elevated counter near the entrance. Everyone called the clerk Paco. At times he looked like a desk sergeant in a police precinct nearing retirement, at other times he gave the appearance of a tollbooth collector struggling to stay awake. He spent most of his working hours playing video games behind the Plexiglass.

Somewhere between Malachi's shotgun shack and the video store, the sense of irritation Malachi had felt gave way to a feeling of untroubled enthusiasm. This was an easy thing to fix, he told himself. He was no novice when it came to women, and Gisela, at least as far as Malachi could determine, had fallen madly in love with him. The morning after they had finished shooting her twelfth film (a cheesy flick they had wrapped up in two days called *The Dickey Horror Peep Show*; Gisela played the role of Jeanette, the blind girl), Malachi had taken her out for a celebratory lunch of Mexican take-out (El Sombrero Hambriento, by the baseball park) and a bottle of El Coto Rosé. They had eaten their meal in the cool shadows beneath the 17th Avenue drawbridge, and when they were finished they lay back against a cement pillar next to the hydraulic machinery (Malachi had brought along a blanket for comfort). Then Malachi kissed Gisela for a very long time, and after that she had let him massage her enormously oversized breasts and then peel back the second skin of a wet t-shirt to gorge himself on her very brown, very erect nipples, and she had, in spite of an unexpected ejaculation on his part, which left a glossy watermark of a stain on his black shorts, squealed with unashamed delight. They had been dating ever since. No, thought Malachi, there was no need to worry. This was an easy thing to fix. Moments later he was flying up the stairs to the roof of the video store to tell the Velázquez brothers the good news.

The conversation on the roof:

"You're late," said the one, presumably Bull.

"Very late, in fact," said Horse. "What shall we do with him, Brother?"

The brothers paused, looked at Malachi across the crumbling tar of the rooftop. It was very sunny and all Malachi could see were their shadows.

"That is up to him," said Bull.

"Fair enough," said Horse. "It's worth one try at least."

"Yes, of course," said Malachi. "I mean there's nothing to worry about. I'm telling you. Nada. This is an easy thing to fix."

"We've spent too much damn money already," said Bull. "And we're losing more by the minute."

"Eight thousand dollars a day," said Horse.

"I didn't realize it was that much," said Bull.

"It could even be more," said Horse.

Bull looked at Horse for a moment with silent appreciation, as if only his brother could have determined the precise rate at which they were losing money.

"Of course we knew the risks," said Bull.

"In a venture like this there are always risks," said Horse.

"But it still knocked us for quite a loop," said Bull, with an odd mixture of admiration, incredulity, and intolerance.

"Yes," said Malachi. "I know. It was stupid of her to quit like that, without any warning."

"We don't respond well to warnings," said Horse.

"No, we don't," said Bull. "We're the ones who give them. Is that clear?"

Horse nodded with measured gravity.

"And the warnings we give are not easily forgotten," said Horse.

"Exactly right!" said Bull.

Malachi wasn't sure how to respond. He was perspiring profusely, from the heat, no doubt. His t-shirt was completely soaked, though his safari vest remained remarkably dry. His mind began to wander and he was unable to comprehend the direction of the conversation. Or perhaps there was no direction. He couldn't decide which would be worse and wondered if he were going mad. The whole conversation seemed to be taking place inside a hospital for the criminally insane instead of on a rooftop. It was clear the Velázquez brothers weren't listening to him. Occasionally they stared at him with a strange glowing look in their eyes, as if they had radiation sickness and did not recognize him, or perhaps it was an unusual mixture of compassion and paranoia Malachi had never encountered before, or perhaps, they too, were simply overwhelmed by the heat. Malachi wasn't sure. He hoped the brothers were just flexing their muscles, saying everything they had wanted to say to vent their frustrations over Gisela and the absence of her titties from the big screen, but the subtle tremors of the conversation suggested something far more sinister was at work. Whatever it was, Malachi knew something was off. He had the odd sensation that he was watching the conversation take place and participating in it at the same time. He was both the observer and the observed. This would account for the strange waves of nausea that raced uncontrollably through his body. One of the brothers would say something, and then there would be a blank space in the air where his words should have been, and then the other one would speak and another blank space, and then he, Malachi, would open his mouth, and again there would be blank spaces, like miniature black holes sucking all of the oxygen out of the atmosphere, and then they would close their mouths with simultaneous finality, all three of them, as if they had just agreed that the end of the world was imminent, and they would stare off into space, each in a different direction, contemplating the limits of mortal existence, or perhaps thinking about some dry cleaning they were going to pick up later but now there was no use, and only then in the vacuum of this cinematic silence would the words that had been spoken come tumbling past his ears, an arcane gibberish all at once, as if someone had suddenly flipped a switch. It seemed like they were trapped in a scene from a poorly written, poorly dubbed spaghetti western.

"So you see it is in all of our best interests to fix this thing before it gets any worse," said Bull.

Malachi nodded.

"You do agree with us, don't you?" said Bull.

"Yes, yes," said Malachi.

Bull had his arm draped across Malachi's shoulders. The two of them were standing along the edge of the rooftop.

Bull had one foot up on the rounded rooftop facade and was looking at the people walking back and forth on the sidewalk one story below, but Malachi was distracted. He had twisted his neck so he could see over Bull's bulging Popeye forearm and was looking squarely at Horse, who was standing on the other side of the roof in front of the doorway to the stairs. Malachi wondered if Horse had positioned himself to block his escape route should he make an attempt. Then he was certain this was the case. The Velázquez brothers never left anything to chance.

"Don't you?" Bull said again.

Bull gave Malachi a gentle, loving shake to encourage Malachi's complete attention.

"Yes, yes. I told you this was an easy thing to fix," said Malachi.

Bull smiled, the sunlight flashing behind his head, and Malachi noted several missing teeth. Malachi wondered why Bull didn't fix his teeth, and then it occurred to him that Bull's sinister reputation was defined in part by the dark spaces in his mouth. His was a twilight smile always submerged in the shadows.

"That's good to hear, my boy," said Bull. "We have always liked you. Isn't that so, Brother?"

Horse grunted from the other side of the roof.

"Loyalty," said Bull. "That's what we expect."

"Loyalty," repeated Horse, and it sounded like he was suddenly standing directly behind Bull. Malachi could feel the hissing, hot breath of the words on his own neck, but when he turned his head to look he saw that Horse hadn't moved an inch.

"Loyalty," said Bull again. "We could give a crap about results without loyalty. Do you get my meaning?"

Malachi assured Bull that he did.

"You wouldn't want to go flying off this rooftop head first, now, would you?" said Bull.

Malachi briefly considered the distance. They were only one story up, about sixteen feet from the sidewalk. He might survive the fall, but then again, he might not. Malachi was not certain about the physics of his situation. Besides, if he died from the fall there's no telling what the Velázquez brothers might do to his body. Chop it up for fish bait, he thought.

"Would you?"

Bull tightened his grip on Malachi's shoulders.

"No, man, I mean Mr. Bull, I mean Mr. Velázquez, no, no, I have to tell you I was born nervous about heights, everyone knows this."

Bull roared with laughter. It was robust laughter, neither malicious nor mocking.

"Horse, do you remember the taxi driver? What was his name?"

"Caballero."

"How did he die?"

"Drowning."

"And the accountant?"

"Alvarez. A boating accident."

"So again, drowning."

"Yes, I suppose so."

"And what happened to Eléna Montaño?"

"The reporter from Channel Ten?"

"Yes, what a fucking bitch."

"She drove off a bridge in that De Soto we gave her. Down in the Keys."

Bull roared and roared and roared. He could not contain himself. And one could not ignore the hearty sincerity of the sound. Bull's laughter embraced the world. A few passersby from below looked up, expecting to see happy, simple men working on the roof, but they became confused when all they saw was a two-headed shadow standing in the glare of the sun and hurried away, as if they had only then realized they were passing by an adult video store and feared someone might inform their husbands or their wives where they had been at three in the afternoon. They were also no doubt aware of the stories associated with the Velázquez brothers, and perhaps also their coincidental proximity to the original den of thieves, which may have given their flight from the scene an extra dash of velocity. But whether these thoughts were uppermost in their brains or not, it was always prudent (as the citizens of Miami and elsewhere most certainly knew, even if they professed otherwise) to keep one's eyes on one's own business and plod ahead in rigid lockstep with the unflappable silence of eternity (Whew!). The pedestrians fled. Bull's sincere, roaring laughter settled with impunity on the sidewalk.

"Is there anyone that didn't die of drowning?" Bull said.

"Yes, of course. You just happened to pick three that occurred near the water."

"Have we ever tossed someone off a rooftop?"

"Yes, but it was a long time ago. It was this very roof in fact."

"Good God, Brother, you're right," said Bull. "That fucking pipsqueak faggot."

Bull grew quiet for a moment, deadly serious.

"Serves him right the way he fucked up that deal with the Panamanians."

"Yes," said Horse. "I can still see his eyeballs bulging as he went over the edge."

"I remember, I remember," said Bull.

"Like in one of those Roadrunner cartoons," said Horse

"Stop it! You're killing me," said Bull.

Bull roared some more and stared down at the sidewalk again, presumably at the spot where the little pipsqueak faggot had landed, his head cracking open like a melon and his brains oozing out, a glistening, pulpy orange-reddish mass that eventually collected in the gutters and was washed away by the rain.

No one spoke for several minutes.

Malachi shifted uncomfortably and Bull relaxed his grip.

"Loyalty," Bull said again.

"Loyalty," repeated Malachi.

"But all the same," said Horse, "You better fix this thing."

"That's right," said Bull. "We're losing eight-thousand dollars a day. Loyalty don't mean crap stacked up against losses like that. Do you get my meaning?"

Bull and Malachi were heading for the door to the stairs.

"Yes," said Malachi. "It's an easy fix, like I said."

"Good, good," said Bull.

Horse opened the door for Malachi.

"But don't take too long," said Horse.

"No," said Bull. "We're losing eight thousand dollars a day, just so we're clear on that."

"Yes," said Malachi. "I . . ."

Horse gave Malachi a long, hard, silent look, as if to underscore what his brother had just said.

"Give him the script, Brother," said Bull.

Horse took out a wad of papers from his back pocket and gave it to Malachi. Malachi started to read the script. The pages were in no particular order but it looked vaguely interesting.

"Don't look at it now," said Bull.

Malachi nodded, somewhat surprised at Bull's reaction,

after all, it was their movie. Bull grabbed the wad of papers from Malachi and shoved them into one of the oversized pockets of Malachi's safari vest. "If she asks what the movie's about, just show her the script."

"Sure thing," said Malachi.

"But don't take too long," said Horse again.

"Exactly right," said Bull.

Then Horse shut the door, leaving Malachi alone on the stairs, momentarily dazzled by the darkness.

Malachi emerged from the darkness of the stairs as if he were a wingless angel seeking shelter. He stood there for a while where the stairs ended, watching dozens and dozens of faceless, expressionless men in oversized trench coats and wide brimmed hats trolling up and down the aisles, looking for exactly the right video for the evening. Waves of nausea were still racing through his body, so much so that he had the distinct impression that he was vibrating. Paco was doing a brisk business for the middle of the week, or perhaps it was already the weekend. Malachi couldn't remember what day it was or even what month. He seemed to have stepped outside of time. He breathed in the familiar smell of stale urine and cigarette smoke to steady his nerves. He would decipher what had happened on the rooftop at a later point, he thought. But not now. At the moment he needed something to facilitate escape.

"Hey, Broken Bike," cried a voice.

The voice belonged to Paco.

"You looking for anything in particular?"

Malachi did not respond. The vibrating sensation had returned and he was trying to will it away through conscious, focused effort.

"We've got a bunch of new Salma de la Prada films," said Paco. "I mean they've been out for a while. They're classics, some of them. But they're new for us."

The vibrating subsided.

Malachi had not moved from the spot at the end of the stairs, but the crowd had thinned out and now Paco was standing next to him. Malachi wondered where the customers had gone.

"They're some really great films," said Paco.

Malachi looked up at the wheezing fat man and smiled a sad, anxious smile.

"I never heard of her," he said.

"She's a big deal in Spain," said Paco. "She looks sort of like Brigitte Bardot."

"I don't know her either."

"See for yourself," said Paco, grinning.

"Yeah, sure."

Paco was suddenly holding a stack of Salma de la Prada films so Malachi could see. Malachi was uncertain how they had appeared in Paco's hands so quickly. He looked them over.

"I'll take three," he said.

"Any ones in particular?"

"No, any three will do."

"That's the spirit," said Paco, somehow mistaking Malachi's anxious sadness for restless enthusiasm.

And then: "Just remember to get them back on time, will you?"

"Sure, sure," said Malachi.

"No sense paying a late fee if you don't have to, right?"

Malachi nodded. He gave Paco a twenty, following him to the counter, a steady wheezing sound ringing in his ears, and then watched fat fingers ring him up. He felt hollowed out inside, still a bit uneasy. His mouth was very dry. He looked through the narrow window above the counter. The blinds were up. The sky had begun to cloud over and he knew a storm was coming, but he still had time, he would make it home before the rain. Then he heard the rooftop door open and close and the sense that he was vibrating returned, only stronger than before, it was as if there was now an electrical current flowing through him, the blood flowing through his veins turning to quicksilver, it seemed that he could even smell smoke, and in this agitated state he found himself wondering what would happen if Gisela said no, how would the Velázquez brothers exact their revenge, and he tried to push this line of thinking out of his mind, it was counterproductive, but the vibrating sensation only grew stronger and he suddenly felt like the whole world was submerged beneath a sea of electricity, the very air was charged, his every breath releasing thousands of ionized particles ready to ignite, the ionized dust particles of small glories and larger halos, perhaps, a whirlwind of destruction. He didn't know what he was doing. Blindly he grabbed at the counter until he had his movies in hand, and then he told Paco to keep the change and he shouldered his way out through the padded black door into the street, holding his free arm up as if to shield his eyes. He sure as hell hoped things would work out.

-22-

Malachi did not sleep well that night. In fact, he did not sleep at all. He kept getting out of bed, checking the front door to see if there were any more messages from the Velázquez brothers, any more little green envelopes with gaping hairless vaginas watching him from the floor, or running to the bathroom as if he had to pee and flicking on the light but forgetting about the toilet, staring at his reflection in the mirror, splashing cold water on his face to make sure it was truly himself staring back, but then his face dissolving, sliding off into the sink. He trudged back and forth, from one end of his shotgun shack to the other, but the distance he traveled seemed immense. It was as if he lived in an endless maze of rooms, some with windows, some without. He forgot when, precisely, his face had disappeared. He wondered if his faceless condition were permanent or if there were something he could do, herbal supplements perhaps, but he could think of nothing that might help. He wondered how he could see his faceless face if he had no eyes. He closed his unseen eyes and tried to imagine what he knew he looked like, but all he saw was a blank, featureless mass like unformed clay. He assumed at that point that he had simply wandered into someone else's house, someone else's life. Strange greenish lights made sweeping patterns on the walls of this endless rat's maze, like helicopter searchlights, which the part of his brain that lay submerged beneath the waves of his insomnia took for the head-lights of a passing car flashing without apology through the windows, but as the lights continued throughout the night, no matter which room he was in, as if they were following him, he became uncertain, even suspicious. Somewhere towards the middle of that interminable night he began to panic and started chasing after the lights, shouting obscenities, letting the intelligence behind the lights know he wasn't afraid, laughing at their cowardice as they disappeared and the darkness returned, swifter than death.

When morning came he was lying in the middle of the floor, curled up in a fetal position, naked and covered in a bloody, viscous fluid, as if he had just been born. He lay there blinking stupidly for a while, the sunlight playing with the cool shadows on the floor. He could not remember the exact moment when the sun appeared above the horizon, but this would have been true even had he been waiting to record the event. It was very cool and pleasant there lying on the floor and he did not wish to get up. Then he got up anyway, for no particular reason, went to the bathroom and cleaned himself thoroughly. His face had returned, but he seemed to have forgotten it had disappeared during the night. He located his black bicycle shorts, a new t-shirt, his safari vest and his rope-soled sandals and got dressed. He did not notice several additional green envelopes on the floor, their gaping vaginas staring at the ceiling, indifferently. He now seemed immune to their effect. It was a bright, sunny morning, so bright that the world outside seemed a watermark reflection of itself. His heart was racing. He was thinking only of Gisela.

-23-

By three o'clock Malachi had crossed over the 17th Avenue bridge, and thirty minutes later he was a block from The Patagonian Café. He had not taken his bike. Why he had not taken his bike he was never able to adequately explain. Perhaps, given the conversation with the Velázquez brothers the day before, his unconscious self was trying to warn that great unthinking imposter, his animal self, that they should both adopt a more unobtrusive mode of transportation, and should the opportunity arise, they should dive quickly and deeply into the nearest dark hole and remain there for some time. This explanation, at least, offers up some insight into the internal workings of Malachi the man. Then again, who can say for certain why anyone does anything? The air was clear and the sun was bright. That is all the explanation that is necessary. Malachi walked the roughly three miles from his shotgun shack in Allapattah to The Patagonian Café in Little Havana, and he took his time doing so, taking numerous detours just for the hell of it, reading every advertising poster and handbill he came across, watching a funeral motorcade rolling down the street, whatever street he was on he didn't remember, the motorcade then disappearing into a tornado of white dogwood blossoms swirling in the air, breathing in the thrill of pure sunshine, thinking of Gisela and what she would likely say. At precisely three-thirty he turned the corner heading into the homestretch. A few cars went past. A garbage truck. A bus. Malachi saw Señor Mendoza sweeping the sidewalk out front. But Señor Mendoza gave no indication that he saw Malachi (nor did he look up at the passing cars), perhaps because his attention was focused on the muddy streaks left by the thunderstorm from the night before (and which stubbornly resisted his heartiest efforts with the broom), or because he had never before said two words to Malachi and did not wish to alter his pattern of behavior, or because he was simply succumbing to the bewildering inertia of old age when even those we have known for decades are reduced to unrecognizable shadows. The only sound Malachi heard as he approached, apart from the background static of birdsong and automobile traffic, was the steady scratching of bristles on cement.

"Hola, Señor Mendoza," said Malachi.

Señor Mendoza stopped sweeping a moment, as if he had been suddenly interrupted by a stray thought, a memory from his childhood, perhaps, and then shaking his head and muttering obscenities under his breath he looked back down at his feet and continued attacking the mud. Malachi's thoughts returned to Gisela. He peered in through the café window, cupping his hands around his eyes like he was holding binoculars, but the glass glowed darkly from the sun and all he could see was his own reflection. Malachi went inside.

-24-

Sitting with Gisela in the cafe:

"They really said that?" said Gisela. "I can't believe they would say that."

"Sure babe, we can all believe what we want, I suppose. But you'd be singing a different tune if you'd been on that rooftop."

"I really liked watching Eléna Montaño."

"Don't know about her. Never watched her."

"Channel Ten."

"That's why. Not my channel."

"I really liked her. Eléna Montaño, roving reporter. That's what they called her. They sent her everywhere."

"Was she the red head with those dark Spanish eyes and the bright smile? The one who liked to wear those fancy silk halter tops with the black jackets and hoop earrings?"

"You said you didn't know her," said Gisela.

"Ooooh babe, she had nothing on you."

Gisela leaned her voluptuous chest across the table and smiled at Malachi, a softly glowing smile. Immediately Malachi thought of lightning at the beach, a brilliant burst of energy lacerating the sky, the pure, crystalline radiance of molten glass frozen in an instant, the time it takes to take a breath. This was the effect Gisela had on his libido. She was wearing a yellow tube top that barely covered her nipples. Malachi was surprised that she didn't pop free just from breathing.

"She was on billboards all over town," said Malachi.

"She was a shooting star," said Gisela, sadly.

"That's too bad then. Hate to see it happen to anyone, but to a beautiful girl like that . . . ."

"I always wondered what happened to her . . . ."

"The Velázquez brothers said she drove off a bridge."

"Maybe they made it all up. Maybe they wanted to scare you."

"Nooo babe, that's just it. They sure as hell didn't sound like they were making it up. And they weren't trying to scare me at all. I swear on a stack of any Bibles you want they forgot I was standing there. They were just going through a list of people they had killed, in a very casual way, like they were trying to remember what they had for lunch. They were laughing about it, too. This one guy with bulging eyes they threw off the roof. The roof where we were talking. They were cracking up about his eyes. You should have heard them! They said it was like watching cartoons."

"Ordinary people just don't talk like that," said Gisela. "Only lunatics talk like that."

"That's what I've been trying to tell you, babe. These guys are the worst kind of lunatics there are. They are invisible men, like ghosts, you don't even know they are there, watching you, waiting, and then they see something about you they don't like, maybe it's the color of your hair that pisses them off, you can't know what you can't know, and then all of a sudden, wham, your ass is theirs, carved into little pieces for the fish, or maybe your boat blows up or your car goes over the edge of a bridge. How many ways can you kill someone? They know every one, so there's no escaping that. I'm telling you it's true. They are lunatics like God and the Devil mixed together. The way I see it we don't have much of a choice. You've got to do their movie, for both of us. I don't know what's going to happen if you don't."

It was at that point that Señor Mendoza came inside. He put the broom in the corner behind the cash register and sat down at a corner table opposite the counter. He was looking at Malachi and Gisela with an air of disapproval, but he said nothing. But his eyes did not waver.

"That's crazy talk, baby," said Gisela. "Now I gotta work some."

She pushed herself away from the table with such sudden force that this time everything did come spilling out. She seemed to have completely forgotten about the threat of the Velázquez brothers. Laughing a breathy, exuberant laugh, she gave her newly naked breasts a loving squeeze, as if she had been waiting for just the right moment to give her twins, as she called them, a breather. Then she rolled her tube top down so that it more or less looked like she was wearing a yellow belt and went to work, wiping down the few remaining tables that needed wiping, stocking the silverware tray, bringing Malachi a couple of beers and a plate of pisto (because there was always plenty of pisto at The Patagonian Café) to keep him busy, and then back at the kitchen window retrieving a bowl of barley soup and Saltines and another plate of pisto for Señor Mendoza, and all the while twirling to the sounds of Gloria Estefan or Albita Rodriguez or some other Latin pop diva pouring out of the radio in the back, twirling round and round with such uniform grace that one almost forgot she was practically naked from the waist up.

Then a couple of *greasy gamberros* (Señor Mendoza's words) came into the café. Perhaps they were not so greasy, just sweaty, tired, overworked, bored. They worked downtown on a skyscraper project, such skyscrapers as there were in Miami, but there had been a strike among the electricians so the bosses had told everyone to go home until they sorted things out, which the bosses said could take days, maybe even weeks. It was clear the two men had been drinking before they got to the café. They sat down at the counter and ordered beans and rice and rum.

At first they watched Gisela without saying a word. They could not believe their luck. They watched Gisela with contorted, happy grins. Their eyes shone like unreachable stars. You could pretty much guess what they were thinking.

Gisela disappeared into the kitchen and then returned with their order. She planted herself squarely in front of the two, her nipples pressing down against the countertop.

"Do you know the Velázquez brothers?" she said.

Yes, they said, they knew them.

"And these Velázquez brothers," she said, "they have killed many men?"

Yes, of course, they said, and many women too, and even children, that is what they do.

A great, glowing sadness swept over Gisela's face.

"What do you want to know about the Velázquez brothers for?" said one.

"Surely a sexy *chiquita* such as yourself has better things to think about, no?" said the other.

Gisela's sadness left her and she laughed. Always the flirtatious advances of strange men made her laugh. She seemed suddenly very happy. The two *greasy gamberros* also laughed. Their happy, beaming, sweaty faces disappeared momentarily into their plates of beans and rice, and then they slurped down their rum and asked for more, they were very thirsty, they said, they had worked up a very large thirst, a gigantic thirst, and they laughed as if they had just told a great joke. Gisela returned with a bottle of rum and planted it on the counter between the two men. The bottle was only a quarter full. The two men were no longer laughing, but they still seemed happy, and also content. They looked now at Gisela as if her happiness was their responsibility.

"You should be very careful not to ask too many questions out in public," the one said.

"This is true," said the other, and then he lowered his voice. "Word gets around."

"Whatever you can imagine about the Velázquez brothers is true," said the one.

"But also what you cannot imagine," said the other.

Then they turned their attention to the bottle, speaking in hushed voices, as if they were afraid of being discovered.

For a time, the café became a very quiet place. It was like a siesta. The radio was playing an instrumental version of "Livin' La Vida Loca," mostly guitars and horns, but you could hardly hear it. Señor Mendoza's soup had put him to sleep. In spite of the sunshine pouring in, he was dozing awkwardly in his chair, leaning back against the corner where the window and the wall met, snoring softly, almost inaudibly. The two *greasy gamberros* were communicating in a bizarre kind of sign language, their hands and fingers tracing intricate patterns in the air that only they could see. Even Malachi succumbed to the silence. He had suddenly remembered the wad of papers in the pocket of his safari vest and was now absorbed in the pages of the Velázquez brothers' movie script. The pages were scattered all over the table.

Then a lonely looking accountant wandered into the café and sat down at the opposite end of the counter from the two *greasy gamberros*. They looked at him with great suspicion and then averted their eyes and continued with their strangely animated pantomime. They had never seen him before. Their voices were still stifled by their paranoia.

The accountant ordered a beer (a bottle of *El Presidente,* which did pretty well at the café because of the Dominicans), and stared at the wall behind the counter. There was nothing to look at on the wall except a vintage poster of a bullfighter with a fancy silver sword gleaming in the sun and a fancy red cape draped over one shoulder. The bullfighter was staring down at a dead bull crumpled up at his feet with several darts sticking out of the bull's hump and blood streaming down the sides of the bull. The poster said El Cordobés, and then there was some small print, most likely in Spanish as well, but the poster was too far away.

Then the music seemed louder all of a sudden. The radio was playing some more of the Latin pop divas. Gisela brought the accountant his beer and he began to drink. The accountant didn't even notice Gisela. It seemed like he was identifying with the bull.

"Poor fucking bull," said the accountant.

The *greasy gamberros* looked over and nodded with sympathetic understanding, expecting the accountant to say something more, but he grew silent, mesmerized by the poster. Then they asked for another bottle of rum. They wanted a full bottle this time.

Señor Mendoza woke up and resumed eating his soup.

Gisela brought out a full bottle of rum and the *greasy gamberros* thanked her. (Once again their eyes shone like unreachable stars.) She sat down opposite Malachi and repositioned her yellow tube top so it barely covered her nipples. He looked across at her glowing there, a bright yellow goddess swirling in sunshine, and smiled. He had barely noticed she had been gone. "It's the movie script," he said. "It's brilliant!"

-25-

The Velázquez brothers' movie script:

The movie didn't have a title yet. In the first part, Gisela would have played Nefertari, the virgin bride of the ancient Egyptian sun god Amun-Ra. Malachi became quite animated as he told Gisela about this part. In the past few years he had read *The Religion of Ancient Egypt* by W. M. Flinders Petrie, followed by *Eternal Egypt* by Pierre Montet, *The Tombs of Harmhabi and Touatankhamanou,* by Theodore M. Davis, and numerous articles on the High Priests of Amun at Thebes. In spite of the many historical inaccuracies (in the Egyptian part), which did not bother Malachi as much as he would have expected, but which he duly noted, he saw immediately what the writer of the script was trying to do.

"Amun-Ra is a fucking god," said Malachi. "He's like Antonio fucking Banderas. Everybody and their uncle wants Amun-Ra to fuck them, men, women, grandmothers, kids. They're lining up on the steps of the Great Pyramid, millions of them, the whole city, hoping to get picked, hoping to get whisked away in the flaming chariot of the sun god king and eat fish and roasted meat and raisins and dates and wild figs and drink wine and fuck and get fucked till the end of time, which is pretty much everyone's idea of paradise, at least in this movie, and you're the one who gets picked. Amun-Ra picks you."

Gisela liked the fact that she was picked above millions of ancient Egyptians, presumably waiting in the hot Egyptian sun for hours, days, perhaps months, just for a date with the Antonio Banderas of their time. She liked the idea of paradise. She also liked Antonio Banderas. But she would not have waited more than an hour herself, and she said so, and she wasn't all that sure about fucking till the end of time either, that sounded far too painful. But she was happy she was picked. But the rest of the movie was too confusing.

In the middle part she was supposed to be swimming with dolphins, or maybe she was having sex with the dolphins, she couldn't tell what was happening, but she didn't think she'd like having sex with dolphins anyway, not even one, it didn't make any sense to her, how would they do it, maybe if they had hands, like mermaids or something, but the idea of sex-starved dolphins groping her with their flippers was just disgusting. Of course Malachi was trying to explain first of all that it didn't matter about the flippers, dolphins could have sex eight or nine times an hour and they didn't need their flippers (except for obvious swimming purposes), but none of that mattered anyway because having sex with the dolphins was symbolic, nobody expected anybody to get mixed up in a dolphin orgy, not in a realistic sense, the point of the movie was that dolphins expressed their love with pure, unfiltered enthusiasm, that's precisely how Malachi put it, but Gisela had been dubious the moment dolphins had been mentioned, and then she got stuck on the word 'unfiltered' and all she could visualize were people standing in line to buy Brita water filters, which only added to her confusion about the story.

But it was the third part of the movie that sealed it for Gisela. In the third part it was the 1960s in America, but it was an alternative 1960s, the America in the movie was a Fascist regime, not a Democracy, and Nefertari and the Amun-Ra character were now hippie organizers trying to start a revolution and shouting 'death to the fucking Fascists' and political propaganda like that, but then they got sidetracked by all the free love parties floating around and all the sex they were having, and they were hallucinating from all the drugs in their bloodstream, so they had a difficult time remembering who they were having sex with, but no one expected they would be overwhelmed by jealousy, they were hippies for God's sake, but when the drugs wore off they got into a tremendously melodramatic argument about who was sleeping with who (this was the climax of the movie), and they were in a café or a restaurant when the argument took place, so there were all sorts of eyes watching and ears listening, and then Amun-Ra lost all sense of perspective, all he could see was red, and just to prove he didn't care about Nefertari anymore, he dropped his pants and started masturbating right there in the café (or restaurant), and Nefertari whipped out a stiletto and said she was going to cut off his prick and feed it to the pigs, presumably because she was incensed at his behavior, or maybe just disgusted, in any event their relationship was finished, and then he ran out of the café.

The last scene of the movie was him running down the street, and coming the other way was the revolution they had been working on (or perhaps it was the government response to the revolution, or some mixture of the two, the precise nature of what was happening was left open to interpretation). At the end the script said you could see the figure of Amun-Ra growing smaller and smaller against the looming darkness, and then you could hear bombs exploding and the sounds of troops marching and thousands of tanks rumbling down the streets, and then the camera was supposed to tilt up so you could see the black shadows of thousands of droning airplanes filling the afternoon sky. The airplanes were most likely Stukas, Malachi thought, like the ones that had come down from the Bay of Biscay in 1937 to drop their bombs on the beautiful town of Guernica. Wave after wave after wave. A hundred German Heinkel He 111s, he guessed, just like in '37, though the movie script didn't say, and hundreds of Dornier Do-17s and Ju-52 Behelfsbombers (also German), and a few Savoia-Marchetti SM.79 bombers (Italian) from the Aviazione Legionaria tossed in for the sake of international diversity. The script said the sky was absolutely black and you could hardly hear from the droning of the airplane engines. The movie was supposed to end with the total blackness of the airplanes.

In Malachi's mind, it was hard to distinguish the black shadows of the airplanes up in the sky from what he imagined were the black shadows of the falling bombs. Malachi thought it was a flaw in the script that you could hear the sounds of bombs exploding without first seeing the airplanes and the bombs falling. (He also made a mental note, though he did not share this with Gisela, that the black shadows of both the planes and the unseen falling bombs bore an uncanny resemblance to the shadows of Bull and Horse standing in the sun on the rooftop the previous day.) Gisela said the last part was just too weird, it gave her a shiver, like a ghost story, and she didn't like ghost stories. She said she wasn't interested in doing the movie. But then she saw the blank, caved-in look on Malachi's face, and she said she'd think about it. Then Malachi suggested they act out the climactic scene, just for fun.

They read over the appropriate pages a few times and got into character. Gisela moved her lips as she read, but she was a consummate professional when it came to the actual performance. She took on every aspect of the roles she played, down to the tiniest nuance of feeling and expression that could never be adequately captured by the camera. She was wholly committed. Malachi, an amateur certainly, said he was ready to sell his soul to do his part justice.

They were seated throughout most of the scene.

Malachi was the first to speak but he was suddenly nervous. He needed the script in his hand to deliver his lines.

"'I have six bullets in this gun,'" said Malachi as the Amun-Ra character. *"'Three for each of us.'"*

"'Go ahead then,'" said Gisela as Nefertari. *"'Shoot.'"*

Malachi was surprised by the presence of the gun. He had missed that on his first reading of the scene and wasn't sure what to do. He held up his hand awkwardly, as if he were hoping it might be mistaken for a gun. Gisela suppressed a giggle.

"'Go ahead then,'" said Gisela as Nefertari, repeating the previous line. *"'Shoot. I don't care. '"*

"'No,'" said Malachi as Amun-Ra. *"'I'm not going to waste these bullets on your skinny little ass. . .'"*

Malachi was beginning to feel the pressure of potentially flubbing his lines. He forgot where he was in the script and was trying desperately to find his spot. Then he recovered and looked over at Gisela (forgetting she was Nefertari) and smiled. He was practically grinning, which was precisely the wrong emotion for the scene, but Malachi was just happy to be back on track.

"'Bullets are too good for you. . .'"

"'You, you. . .'"

"'I just want to know one thing. Why did you have to sleep with so many bastards?'"

Malachi stopped smiling. The line between fiction and reality was a blurry line.

"'You're the only bastard I know,'" said Gisela (Nefertari).

Malachi and Gisela were speaking in extra-loud stage voices, as if the only way to convey the necessary emotion of each line was by shouting. They were still sitting at the table. The accountant had spun halfway around on his stool to see what the commotion was, spilling some of his beer on his shirt, and then he said shit and went to the bathroom. The two greasy gamberros were sizing up Malachi. They couldn't see the script from where they were sitting and were trying to determine if he were truly a threat and they might have to intervene. The fact that he seemed to think his hand was a gun suggested to them that he was indeed a lunatic, but probably capable only of harming himself. They calmed their heroic impulses with this thought.

As for Señor Mendoza, he woke up suddenly when the shouting started. He thought perhaps he was dreaming, but it was a very strange dream and he was troubled by it. He could hear angry, shouted words, but they were bouncing back and forth in the empty echo chambers of his brain. They sounded very far away. He could not tell for certain what was being said.

"'It was Arrabal's idea, wasn't it! Him and those dope fiends you call friends.'"

"'They are my friends. You can't tell me who my friends are. Not anymore. Just like you can't tell me who I can sleep with. We're finished, you and I. We run in different circles now. I'll sleep with whoever the hell I like, and there's nothing you can do to stop me. I'll take on a dozen new lovers every week and they can fuck me whenever they want to. I'm hungry for it, do you hear me? I'm hungry for it all the time.'"

"'They're white devils. But they'll get what's coming to them. You can be sure of that.'"

"'What are you saying?'"

"'You know what I'm saying. Everything comes full circle. Everyone gets what they deserve in the end. That's what we've been fighting for, or did you forget that Nefertari. (And then an overly dramatic pause.) *But before you say another word, I'm going to show you what I really think of you.'"*

This time Gisela could not help herself. She could see Malachi was going to play the scene all the way to the end and she burst out laughing. "I can't believe you're really going to do it," she whispered. Then Malachi (Amun-Ra) unbuttoned his bicycle shorts and took out his penis and started stroking himself. Gisela looked under the table to see for sure and then she popped back up and her laughter ballooned and she said

"Malachi, baby, what are you doing?" but he just shook his head, trying not to burst out laughing himself, the two of them frozen in the scene, whispering back and forth, their words leaving only the faintest impressions in the air, like the ripple of a love song from centuries ago, "finish the scene, babe, finish it," and then "but I don't have a knife," and then "use your shoe, you're wearing high heels, aren't you?" and then "I am, you're right," and then "let's finish it," and then "okay baby," and then the scene resumed. They both stiffened as they got back into character.

"'There, now you know exactly what I think of you,'" said Malachi (Amun-Ra).

Malachi (Amun-Ra) shook his penis around a bit, as if to demonstrate that he had just had an orgasm, and then he shoved it back into his shorts and buttoned his fly.

"'You're pathetic,'" said Gisela (Nefertari), and she started laughing very loudly, a hollow stage laughter (part of the script) that also served to mask the waves of genuine laughter that rippled now uncontrollably through her body like a sickness in this theater of the absurd.

"'If I could rip out your heart I would,'" said Malachi (Amun-Ra.) *"'But you have no heart to begin with. You are a whore, like your mother and your grandmother were whores. You come from an ancient house of whores.'"*

"'You, you. . .'"

Then Malachi (Amun-Ra) stood up abruptly, mechanically, his suddenly extended buttocks knocking his chair to the floor with excessive though certainly unintentional force, and brandished his hand which was supposed to be a gun in the air. It was a bit melodramatic, even for this script. Gisela (Nefertari), stifling yet another wave of laughter, pulled her shoe off her foot and stepped quickly away from the table, half crouching, her arms raised to shoulder height, her elbows flared out, waving her spiked-heeled shoe in graceful counterpoint to Malachi's (Amun-Ra's) hand (gun). Malachi (Amun-Ra) was so focused on maneuvering his hand (gun) that he paid no attention to what Gisela (Nefertari) was doing. The two of them looked almost like an amaurotic matador and a deranged perhaps crippled bull dancing in the arena. They looked like they had been doing this dance for years.

"'If you take one step closer I'll cut off your prick and feed it to the pigs,'" said Gisela (Nefertari).

But Malachi (Amun-Ra) said nothing. He stood there a moment, looking at Gisela (Nefertari) with a mixture of pride and contempt (which Malachi could not quite pull off; it looked more like he was suffering from acid reflux). Then he smiled a very convincing cavalier smile and blew her a kiss and ran out of the café.

-26-

Never before had Malachi felt so distraught, and yet at the same time so absolutely free. Gisela remained adamant in her refusal to re-enter the world of the Velázquez brothers and their pornographic movies, in spite of the obvious artistic merits of the film in question, which Malachi tried to point out with affectionate resolve every time they were together in bed. But within a week of the melodramatic episode at the café, Gisela hardly paid attention to anything that came out of Malachi's mouth. She distracted herself with thoughts of vacations in the rainforests of Brazil while he was on top of her pounding away, expressing in between the gasps that come from strenuous physical exertion his absolute need to fulfill her every desire and his indefatigable hope that she would soon change her mind.

He was utterly baffled by Gisela's inability to understand the importance of maintaining a cordial and gradually distant relationship with his employers. She did not seem to truly appreciate the kind of men they were. Then again, perhaps he was supposed to make an abrupt stand against the Velázquez brothers and everything they represented (though just what they represented eluded Malachi at the moment). Perhaps he had finally found his purpose in life. He had always enjoyed thinking of himself as a Rastafarian rebel leading the righteous to justice in the face of certain death. Perhaps there was nothing to worry about, he would tell himself. Despair is only a point of view, after all. And while everyone knows with a certainty that could pass as faith that death is inevitable, it is equally true that at any given moment death is only one of many possibilities. Yes, that was the truth of it, he would say, and then he would feel suddenly and strangely liberated, as if there were no relationship between his current circumstances and how his life might turn out. Once again he felt detached from himself, as if he were trapped in a labyrinth of mirrors, watching events unfold and living them at the same time.

Of course some might argue that Malachi's thinking was muddled by the need to rationalize his difficulties in the face of Gisela's refusal to do one final film, but others might say that his logic was inescapably precise, and perhaps even prophetic.

When Gisela told him he was no longer welcome at the café, he responded with the wisdom of a television guru.

"He doesn't want you to come to the café anymore," said Gisela. "He was very concerned. He said he can do without your kind of riffraff."

"Who said this thing?" said Malachi.

"Señor Mendoza."

"It's no big deal."

"He said you're a crazy, lunatic. He thought the scene we did was real. He's afraid of you."

"Me? Malachi wouldn't hurt a fly."

"I know that, baby."

"When did he say this?"

"Yesterday. He took me aside and he said 'stay away from that crazy, lunatic, Malachi.' He was almost shaking when he said it."

"It's no big deal, babe." Malachi looked at Gisela and smiled his most becoming smile. "He will forget all about it soon enough."

It was at this point that Malachi stopped going home. He had only been to his shotgun shack twice since the scene at the café, partly because Gisela would only have sex with him in the privacy of her own bedroom. But mostly because, as far as Malachi could ascertain, a menacing, alien presence had taken over his house and had infected the entire neighborhood. The first time he went back was two days after they had shocked Señor Mendoza. Malachi wanted to retrieve his bike. He was not aware of anything out of the ordinary at that point and walked about as if in a dream. He was thinking vaguely about Gisela and how sexy she had seemed when she had acted the part of Nefertari, but his thoughts were unformed. He was lost in a labyrinth of shadows. Twilight was descending. The whirring sound of cicadas hovered in the darkness of the trees. Soon the stars would be visible. A few streetlights popped on and there were clouds of tiny insects, as frail and unaware as dust, bubbling up beneath the pale orange streetlight glow, their tiny lives disintegrating when they got too close. Malachi's own house was an ink blot of blackness, at least this is how it would appear to most people, but not to Malachi. He actually saw more clearly at night. The brightness of a sunny day sometimes overpowered his eyes. He felt as if he were looking at the world through a cloudy, dusty piece of gauze. But the darkness was a cleansing; it washed away the film.

Malachi's first clue that something had changed was the presence of his bike in the middle of the street in front of his house. In truth, he did not at first even recognize that it was his bike. He saw a shiny, flat, disc-shaped object glinting in the light of the orange-glowing streetlights and wondered what it was, and as he stepped into the street for a closer look, the hairs on the back of his neck sizzled with electricity. It was his bike. Some unknown persons, it appeared, had placed his bike squarely in the middle of the street and then had proceeded to roll over it, back and forth and back and forth, quite possibly with a giant tractor or perhaps even a steamroller, until his bike had taken on the flattened, shiny, disc-shaped qualities already mentioned. He wondered how long it had taken to produce the uniform consistency of the object his bike had become. It was almost as if in the process of rolling back and forth over the bike, the metal had melted and then reformed. It was actually quite impressive.

Our hero stared at his bike for a long time. The electric hum of the streetlights and the whirring sound of the cicadas faded into the background static of his mind. He wondered why he had walked the other day from Allapattah to the café, he always took his bike, but he had left it at home that day, and he could think of no good reason why he had done so. He marveled at how fragile and unforgiving the mosaic of our lives truly was. One seemingly trivial misstep and the whole world broke into a million pieces. Malachi's expression became grim. It was the universe playing a cruel and pitiless joke. What was one supposed to do in the face of such cruelty, he wondered? But again, he had no answer. He shrugged, an unconcscious reflex, as if to say that even the world's most brilliant thinkers would struggle with this question. Then he noticed part of a wheel protruding from the disk and realized that his first impression had been wrong. (He often found that what he thought was perfect, in this case the uniform flatness of the disc, was not without flaws.) His mind went comfortably blank and he took hold of the edge of the wheel (about six inches of bent rim and popped rubber) and dragged the flattened bike up the walk and laid it against the side of the house. It did not occur to him that the unknown persons responsible for the crime might be lurking in the shadows, waiting to pounce. It was late and he was tired. He went inside without even turning on a light, and thereby missed the half dozen green envelopes with the hairless vagina logos stamped in the middle, the envelopes scattered about the floor, all of the gaping vaginas staring up at the blackness of the ceiling with unblinking vigilance. That first night Malachi went directly to bed.

Several days later, perhaps a week, about ten in the morning and already the temperature was well above ninety, Malachi returned to his shotgun shack for the second and last time. An air of surveillance had descended upon the street. A seemingly abandoned white van was parked on the corner and there were strange clicking sounds coming from inside, like those from a Geiger counter or the rotating whir of an electric fan. As he passed by various houses he felt a fluttering of movement behind the windows, as if eyes had been glued to the glass and then curtains suddenly drawn, but he did not actually see anything out of the ordinary. Three doors from his house he saw a neighbor woman in a flowery dress (he could never remember her name) clipping her hedge, but she seemed less intent on pruning her azaleas (which Malachi had always felt was an odd choice for hedges, but to each his own) and more intent on observing his return. She seemed to have been purposely placed there to record if and when he should appear.

Malachi was not aware of her scrutiny at first, nor was he aware of the observers hidden behind their curtains or the two men inside the van taking photographs with a couple of wildlife cameras and a variety of zoom lens for when the quality of the light changed or they wanted a different angle or they were just bored with their assignment. It was only later that he realized the entire block had been mobilized against his return. While it was happening, he was aware of only a vague discomfort, as if the world was slightly out of focus and a headache was looming. Once again he was thinking of Gisela, but with greater clarity this time. He was certain that she would relent, and he allowed the illusion of his optimism to wash away the grime of negativity that had become embedded in his skin. In his mind's eye he saw Gisela suddenly on the big screen, and then he saw himself in a movie theater watching her voluptuous titties bouncing back and forth on a fantastic journey from ancient Egypt to the alternate America of the 1960s. He could see his future imagined self masturbating with uncontrollable delight. And he also noted, with some degree of pride, since he sometimes shared Gisela's bed, that most of the patrons of this future imagined theater were similarly engaged in pleasuring themselves, a natural reaction, to be sure, since the original script called for Gisela to play the entire movie naked from the waist up.

This was Malachi's state of mind as he pushed through the chain-link gate and headed up the walk. He took some comfort in the fact that the metal disc that had once been his bike was still leaning against the side of the house (we are always hoping that things will stay put where we place them), but he failed to notice that the disc had been moved to the other side of the front steps. To his credit, he did notice the more than two dozen green envelopes with gaping vagina logos now scattered across the floor when he went inside (though he took no interest in the messages he knew they contained). And he began to look at his present situation with a greater objectivity, what some would call fatalism, and what others would decry as a lack of faith. He wondered who the Velázquez brothers had hired to deliver the messages and when they would take on this duty themselves. He wondered how long he had before the next envelope would arrive.

It was a dicey game he was playing. He had fallen off the grid, so to speak, an ironic turn of the screw given that the world he inhabited was already off the grid. He was a ghost among the underbelly of ghosts until he could persuade Gisela to change her mind, or until some other solution presented itself. Without the faintest trace of humor, he began to wonder who was in charge anyway. He was still confident that things would work out. Malachi had always possessed psychotic levels of optimism. But the presence of so many envelopes had jarred his sense that God was truly on his side. He had been laboring under the assumption that he had an unlimited amount of time to set things right, and now he was almost overwhelmed with the dizzying sensation that time was short.

He forgot about closing the door. Staring down at the

jumble of little green envelopes, he was suddenly struck by the way they were all piled one on top of another, the gaping, glistening vaginas all mixed together, a strange bouquet of paper flowers that seemed to glow with the stark funereal brilliance of orchids strewn across a casket. He could almost smell the fragrant, sickly sweet smell of ritual death hovering in the air. Then he remembered why he had come home. He had come for the Salma de la Prada films. He wanted Gisela to see these films, which had been viewed by millions, so she could appreciate the artistry of her own work and better understand the opportunity that lay before her. She could be the next Salma de la Prada. The world would be her oyster. That's what he was going to tell her. That was his plan.

Moments later Malachi emerged from the cool darkness of his shotgun shack with the three films in his right hand. The sun had become quite fierce and the air was thick with a blazing white heat. It was difficult to breathe. Malachi felt a sudden restlessness of the spirit, as if it were already too late to change his fate but he was going to die trying, and then his restlessness was replaced by a deep-seated paranoia. The world began to melt from the heat. He fumbled with the lock and then it seemed that the lock was melting and he jerked back his hand and left the keys dangling. Maybe he was dying, he thought. Or maybe the Velázquez brothers had already caught up with him and he was already dead. He stood on the steps facing the melting lock and the dangling keys until he regained his composure. The usual rigidity of the world returned. Then he headed away from his house, back down the street. He did not understand what was happening to his sense of reality, why he was plagued by these bizarre hallucinations. It was then he noticed the woman in the flowery dress moving away from her azaleas towards the sidewalk to intercept him. She was still holding her clippers.

"*Hola,* Broken Bike, *hola, hola,*" she said, waving the clippers at him as she hurried along, then barring his path, at least partially, so he felt he had no choice but to stop as well. "You are going so quickly. And so soon. It is only the middle of the day."

He had never really looked at her before. They were neighbors, three houses apart, which meant he mostly saw her from a distance, trimming her hedge, setting the sprinkler at a certain angle so the water would not hit the house, carrying bags of groceries from the carport in through the side door. It was almost as if he had only seen her through the wrong end of a telescope. But now she was crowding up against his left shoulder, his left arm pinned against his side, the point of the clippers wavering only a few inches away. He could see that she had very wrinkled brown skin, especially her face, he had not realized she was so old, and her complexion was not uniform. One side of her face exhibited the normal discolorations and markings of old age, but the other side was horribly scarred with ridges that looked like someone had carved out pieces of her flesh with a knife. The ridges were glowing a bright bloody red from the sun. Malachi wondered if the pain of her disfigurement was fresh, or if she had long ago forgotten what had happened to her. He wondered what that kind of pain felt like. He wondered what she wanted with him. She looked up at him with childlike insistence, her eyes twinkling with a mirth that seemed out of place.

"Where are you going in such a hurry?" she said.

Malachi was uncertain what to say.

Then he remembered the movies and held them up with his unpinned arm. "It's nothing," he said. "Just returning a few movies."

She laughed with the same mirth reflected in her eyes.

"You young men are all alike," she said, and then she pointed at the movies with the tip of her clippers. "Always disappearing into the darkness to watch a picture show. Never looking out at the world. Never noticing what is real."

Malachi smiled and moved as if to depart, thinking the conversation was over, but the old woman was suddenly standing in the middle of the sidewalk, her clippers hanging ready by her side.

He was surprised at her unexpected agility.

She smiled back at Malachi, revealing the jagged remnants of perhaps three teeth.

"Do you believe in God, Broken Bike?"

"Yes, yes, I believe in God."

"Well that is only part of it, isn't it," she said, and she laughed some, a sort of a cackling, coughing laugh, and he could see spittle collecting on her three teeth and they began to glisten in the sunlight.

"And the Devil?" she said.

Malachi said nothing. He was trying to suppress a sudden

urge to urinate. It was like being tempted in the desert.

"That's a bit trickier," she said, and then she laughed some more and rolled her tongue around the inside of her mouth and looked at him for a moment, studying his expression, and then she spat on the sidewalk. "It is hard to know if the Devil is even real," she said.

Malachi smiled weakly. The urge to urinate had passed.

"Especially if you spend all your time watching movies."

She pointed her clippers a second time at the movies he held in his hand and he followed her movements with his eyes. Then he heard the sound of an engine turning over and the white van on the corner pulled away from the curb, the dust of the street swirling. He watched the van speed up through the intersection and then bank suddenly left, the way an airplane sometimes banks after take-off, and disappear down a hidden alley. Then he turned back to the old woman, but she had vanished in the wake of the van's departure. Malachi heard the sound of a door closing shut and the heavy dull echo of the bolt sliding into place, and then there was only the sound of the white blazing heat and the lonely cry of a blue jay somewhere in the air above. He waited for a moment to see what might happen next, but nothing happened. Then he moved quickly, but not too quickly, down the street.

-27-

Word all over the city (at least the underbelly portion) was that the Velázquez brothers had put out a bounty on Malachi's head. It was not a "dead or alive" bounty just yet, but that was probably only a matter of time. Many felt that the only effective approach when it came to bounties was to make sure the wanted person was dead. The phrase "dead or alive" was merely an anachronistic formality, a holdover from the childish delusions of an earlier age. These progressive free-thinkers (what some would call anarchists) were certain that if they produced a dead Malachi, the Velázquez brothers would more than likely pay up. Then again, nobody could be quite sure what the Velázquez brothers would do in any situation. This element of unpredictability held everyone in check, even the free-thinkers. So for the moment the bounty on Malachi's head was more or less just a theoretical warning. The Velázquez brothers wanted Malachi alive, they wanted everyone to know they wanted Malachi alive, and since everyone in the city (the underbelly portion) thought Malachi was crazy, everyone left him alone. (Even the Velázquez brothers thought Malachi was crazy, this is why they liked him; they were the ones who first said "Heeee'll put a gun to your head like he giving you a cigarette," though whether this statement had any basis in actual fact or was simply a clever, preemptive marketing ploy by the Velázquez brothers, not even Horse remembered).

Malachi's only link with humanity was through Gisela, who provided him with a little extra cash as his resources dwindled and the comfort of her open legs to boost his spirits. He had become an expatriate rebel, which in some respects had been his goal for as long as he had worn dreadlocks, but he soon grew tired of living on the edge of the edge. It is one thing to seek complete isolation from the outside world, quite another to be abandoned by that world, or more precisely, by everyone you know.

Those who knew Malachi by sight (excepting Gisela) went so far as to cross to the other side of the street when they saw him coming, presumably so he wouldn't get the wrong idea. Malachi wasn't sure what was happening. His old life had vanished without warning. But perhaps he was too close to the events that were unfolding. Viewed instead from the detached, self-contained and very safe perspective of, say, sixty-thousand feet in the air (heaven by any other name, with or without clouds), Malachi's plight seemed a blessing in disguise. Indeed, it seemed as if the saints themselves were sitting on those cloud-covered steps leading up to paradise, watching every move poor old Malachi might make, conspiring with the universe to make sure he suffered no lasting harm.

If you can imagine asking one of those long-dead, no longer suffering martyrs what they thought they were doing, you can also probably imagine them saying in reply that "God was saving Malachi for better things."

There was no one, however, mortal or divine, real or imagined, who gave any thought to the welfare of the other parties involved in the Velázquez brothers' greatest venture, unless by welfare one meant pointing them in the direction of those heavenly steps noted above. (This was not true for Gisela, she was the talent, and therefore untouchable, and besides, it was rumored that Bull was secretly in love with her). Within three months of Gisela's decision to forgo international celebrity status in the adult film world, Horse supposedly informed Bull that they needed to pull the plug on the whole damn thing, they were bleeding to death, they couldn't go on like this forever, they'd lose every dime they had. They already had had to sell one of their speedboats, the Bertram. They didn't want to lose the two Cigarettes as well. Bull agreed. In spite of his psychotic enthusiasm for a life of crime (he supposedly said it was the only thing they were suited for), he no longer possessed the energy to start completely over from scratch, if it came to that, they had to think like businessmen, but all the same he wanted to tag at least one of the fuckers who had caused the bleeding, as a lesson to the others, something to remind them that the Velázquez brothers did not give a fuck about the rest of the world, he was adamant about that. Supposedly Horse said that went without saying.

The big-time Mexican movie director was the fucker the Velázquez brothers decided to tag. They had no intention of killing the guy without first talking with him. The Velázquez brothers didn't like to be pinned down by their decisions. If they liked the guy well enough, they'd probably tell him to leave the country and they'd choose somebody else. Of course no one would ever know exactly what happened. One day the newspaper said that Juliano Manuelo Marquez, a big-time Hollywood movie director who currently made his home in Mexico City, had skipped town without paying his hotel bill. The newspaper said he had been in Miami for a few months to scout locations for a new film, but did not say what the film was about or who was producing it. The newspaper also said Marquez was wanted for questioning by the police on a separate undisclosed matter and that if anyone had any information as to his whereabouts they were to come forward immediately.

A week later the newspaper ran a follow-up article that summarized all of the movies that Marquez had made, and listed all of his awards, including an Academy Award Nomination for Best Foreign Language Film for his film *The Old Guitarist* (the story of an old man who runs a brothel in the mountains of Northern Spain in the years leading up to the Spanish Civil War and is later killed by a corporal in the Civil Guard while trying to rescue one of his prostitutes — who it turns out is his only daughter — who was arrested for thievery and thrown in jail).

The follow-up article ended with the same plea for a member of the public at large to divulge inside information particular to an ongoing investigation, but not even the newspaper expected the article would get any results, which is probably why they buried it at the bottom of page nineteen opposite an ad for timeshares in the Keys. Two weeks after that, everyone (even the newspaper reporter who had written the articles) had forgotten the big-time movie director had even been in Miami, and Malachi would have been among this larger group except that he stumbled upon the truth one night in a seedy but popular drinking establishment called Gus's, a flimsy, shrunken-looking structure just north of downtown Miami that existed always and only in the shadows of the elevated Interstate. (Malachi had started drinking in random dives all over the city to make it more difficult for the Velázquez brothers to track his movements.)

The truth, as Malachi heard it, came dribbling out of the mouths of two drunken pool guys who worked for a pool cleaning company called Aqua-Clean. The Aqua-Clean headquarters was located three blocks from the bar in a building that looked like an abandoned cannery. The pool guys were still wearing their Aqua-Clean jumpsuit uniforms.

The conversation between the two pool guys:

"It's fucking hard to believe," said the first one.

He was clean shaven but had shaggy blond hair, and the sleeves of his uniform were rolled up, revealing a series of interlocking tattoos that looked like aquamarine-colored bolts of lightning slicing up each arm. It was possible that the lightning bolts were a symbol of some gang affiliation, but this seemed unlikely. The name Rudi was sewn into his uniform just above the left-side chest pocket. The company had chosen a very fancy script for the lettering, and also a bright aquamarine color for the thread, which you would expect, given the name of the company. The script was so fancy that if you weren't looking at the name too carefully, you might think it said Trudi instead.

"What about Jake," said the second one. He was half a head shorter than Rudi, with a full red beard but without the tattoos. The name on his uniform was Bert, or maybe Brett. Malachi couldn't tell. Fancy script could be challenging in the dark. He settled on Bert.

"Jake doesn't know shit about what happened," said Rudi. "He wasn't even in the room. He was down at the pool draining the water when the Velázquez brothers drove up in their Hummer. It was Dominick who went up with them."

"Yeah, sure, Dominick told you all about it," said Bert. "How do you know what Dominick saw?"

"Trust me," said Rudi. "I know."

"Like shit you do," said Bert. "Nobody knows."

"Trust me," said Rudi again.

"Shit," said Bert.

The two pool guys finished off their beers (they were drinking Amstel, which Malachi didn't really like) and ordered another round. They were sitting at the far corner of the bar where the mahogany counter turned ninety degrees and ended abruptly at the stairs (only three steps) to a small storeroom. It was fairly difficult to see in the corner. The light bulb above the stairs was burnt out or broken, and there was no mirror behind the bar to reflect the light from those fixtures that did work, so the only effective illumination came from a small television set perched on the corner shelf above the door to the storeroom. There was a baseball game on with the volume turned down too low to actually hear, but nobody seemed to care.

The faces of the two pool guys were bathed in a soft, bluish glow from the game, but everything below their faces was submerged in darkness. From the other side of the bar they looked like two disembodied heads floating in the dark. And since the light from a television is never steady, the two heads seemed to shimmer constantly, and would sometimes even disappear altogether when the brightness of the game was replaced momentarily by a dark screen as the station went to a commercial break.

Malachi was sitting just before the elbow, pretending to watch the game. It was after eight o'clock and the bar was starting to fill up. Malachi's ears were buzzing with the sounds of waitresses clearing away empty bottles and the smash and shriek of broken glass and the cash register humming and the murmuring drone of many voices hanging in the air like smoke and the bartender ringing a brass sailor's bell whenever he got a good tip and the edgy, self-indulgent, drunken laughter of men who had scores to settle but became impotent when facing an opportunity for revenge. The bartender almost forgot to take Malachi's order.

"So you want to know what happened?" said Rudi

"Sure, what the fuck," said Bert.

"Dominick said they took the service elevator up to the ninth floor and went straight to that Mexican prick's room and they didn't even knock cause the Velázquez brothers had a key. Man, you sure as hell don't mess with those Velázquez brothers."

The bartender returned with two more Amstels for the two pool guys and a whiskey sour for Malachi. The two pool guys lowered their voices to a whisper when the bartender was there, hardly even glancing his way, and then resumed in normal tones when he left to settle a dispute at the other end of the counter.

"He just said it was in his contract, and one of the brothers said they didn't give a shit about contracts, except the ones they put out themselves, but the prick didn't get it, all he said was 'then we'll see you in court.'"

"Crazy dumb fuck," said Bert.

"You said it. Dominick said he couldn't believe his eyes the way that fat Mexican prick was talking to the Velázquez brothers, like they worked at the hotel parking cars. But the worst of it was the whole time the brothers were trying to talk to him rational like, this prick was sucking on a cigar and blowing smoke in their faces. Total fucking disrespect. Dominick said they were giving the guy plenty of chances to be reasonable, though in retrospect he said it was clear the brothers had made up their minds about the prick pretty early in the conversation."

"Crazy dumb fuck," said Bert. "He was probably fucked the moment he opened his mouth."

"You got that right. Dominick said he was the biggest prick he ever saw. And no one could believe how many cigars this guy smoked. The other brother wanted to know how many boxes of cigars he'd gone through, meaning the Mexican. Dominick said there were dozens of empty boxes of Cubans all over the floor and on the bed, he couldn't say how many. But the prick said he didn't keep track of trivial expenses like that, he was paid to create great art, and smoking cigars helped put him in the mood, and then he blew some more smoke at the Velázquez brothers and walked out onto the balcony. Dominick said the prick was standing there blowing smoke, and all he was wearing was a pink bathrobe and sunglasses like some fruity homosexual fuck, and then just like that he turned his back on the Velázquez brothers and went out onto the balcony. You bet he was fucked. Dominick said a breeze was blowing and you could see the fat, greasy cheeks of the guy's ass, but he didn't care, he was just smoking and looking out at the beach and the morning sun on the water. Dominick said he couldn't believe what he was seeing."

Bert gave a long low whistle, like a bullet that could bend around corners.

"Man, didn't he know who he was dealing with?"

"I guess not."

"What kind of dumb fuck turns their back on the Velázquez brothers?"

"You got me."

"And wearing a pink bathrobe to boot."

"The crazy shit people do."

"Some people."

"Yeah, some people."

The two men seemed to be glowing with amazement, even in the dark. Once again the bartender returned and the voices of the two disembodied heads sunk to a whisper. More Amstels appeared on the counter. A couple more whiskey sours. Then the bartender had to help some of the waitresses with a rowdy crew that had pushed three tables together in the middle of the bar and were watching a girl take off her clothes. The girl was already down to her panties. She was thoroughly enjoying herself.

The normal tone of the conversation resumed.

"Wait a minute," said Bert. "You mean to tell me the one brother lifted that Mexican prick off the ground with only one arm and tossed him over the railing?"

"That's what I said."

"Man, I would have loved to see that."

"Dominick said it was pretty impressive."

"What do you think he told the prick just before he did it?"

"I don't know. Dominick couldn't hear. They were talking together for quite a while. Just the two of them on the balcony, the one brother with his arm hooked around the shoulders of the guy and the breeze blowing, and then the one brother must have told a joke cause the Mexican prick started laughing. But he still didn't get what was happening. And then just like that the one brother lifted the Mexican into the air, like his arm was a goddamn cargo crane or something, and then he swung his arm back nice and slow, and then without saying a word he snapped it forward and sent that Mexican flying up into the air. Dominick said it was pretty amazing. He said it was like watching a slow-motion instant replay on television. The guy's legs were kicking and he was losing his pink bathrobe, it was sort of fluttering up above his shoulders, like a defective parachute or something, and the last thing Dominick saw was shit coming out of the guy's ass, like he was squeezing it out with his cheeks, like he was trying to stop it only he couldn't, and then he was gone. He was just fucking gone. Just the pink bathrobe floating in the air and a few ribbons of shit."

"Man, I would have loved to see that."

The two men stopped talking for a moment, staring vaguely into space, the bluish light of the game washing across blank faces. It seemed as if they had suddenly become hypnotized by the image of the pink bathrobe, as if they were now watching the death of the big-time Mexican movie director on a gigantic movie screen suspended in the blackness of their imagination.

"You don't think about that, do you."

"What?"

"Shitting like that."

"No, I suppose not."

"Sort of an involuntary reaction to the stress. You can't help it."

"No, I guess you can't. Nobody can."

"Man, what a fucked-up way to go."

"You said it."

"But that's what you get when you fuck with the Velázquez brothers."

"They're professionals, that's for sure."

"Damn right they are."

". . . ."

"Dominick said it sort of took you by surprise how easy they made it look."

The two disembodied heads paused again, looking more thoughtful now, aware, almost philosophic. They drank their beers, ordered more Amstels, drank some more. They seemed to have forgotten how to speak. The bartender came over and turned off the television and the two heads disappeared. After a while they were talking again, but they were just voices in the darkness.

"So what happened to the body?"

"Nobody knows for sure."

"What about the police?"

"The police don't know shit."

"I'll bet Jake knows."

"Jake doesn't know shit either. Jake was draining the water from the pool when Dominick went up with the brothers, and when the pool was empty a guy from the hotel told him to cover the bottom of the pool with a tarp. They were going to paint pictures of dolphins on the sides of the pool for kids to look at when they were swimming under water. They didn't want to get paint on the bottom. He could come back later when they were done painting. He could come back in a couple of days. So Jake covered up the bottom and then he left. When he came back the tarp was gone and there were dolphins just like the guy said. That's all Jake knows."

That was the end of the conversation. Malachi settled into the darkness of the corner. It was a comfortable feeling. He ordered himself one more whiskey sour and drank it slowly. He was thinking about the Velázquez brothers and the big-time movie director. In his mind's eye he could see the poor guy sailing through the air and then landing splat in the empty pool, his neck crunching up beneath him, his shit smeared across the tarp, the blood pooling out from various places where his veins had burst from the impact, and then the brothers rolling up the tarp and loading it into a boat and heading out to the Gulf Stream and dumping the body for the sharks.

The two pool guys were right about one thing, he thought, the Velázquez brothers were very professional. You had to admire them for that. Malachi thought for a moment about how much skill was required to toss a guy from a ninth-floor balcony so that he landed in the middle of an empty swimming pool. How many times did you have to practice that before you could judge correctly the appropriate angle of descent and the effect of the wind and a dozen other variables he knew nothing about? How long before you became an expert? Then Malachi was wondering if this one would count as a drowning victim because the guy had died in a pool at a hotel on the beach, or if it would be recorded as a near drowning, or maybe flying off a rooftop, or more precisely, a hotel balcony, since there was no water in the pool when it happened. Malachi thought about the death of the big-time movie director for a while. Then he finished his whiskey sour. He looked over at the pool of darkness where the two pool guys had been, but they were long gone. Malachi had not even seen them leave.

-28-

There is a warm wet wind blowing in from the bay. It is surprisingly strong, the wind. It is soon a ferocious wind, sweeping the streets. Garbage tumbles past, shredded pieces of newspaper, paper cups, candy wrappers, tin cans rolling with parabolic fury. A few cars whoosh by, but other than that the streets are empty. Everyone else is indoors.

Then the rain comes. It is only eleven o'clock in the morning and the rain is already here. A storm of tiny bullets rattling against windows and doors at a sharp forty-five-degree angle. The tiny bullets sting when they hit flesh, but they do not penetrate. Yet they burn all the same. The air is steaming from their passage. The ground is on fire. In spite of the rain, you can smell smoke. Wisps of blue smoke curl up from the sidewalk even as the downpour increases in velocity. A few shingles fly off a roof. A garbage can careens into a parked car and a car alarm goes off, then several more car alarms. Malachi is standing in the doorway of the video store during the storm, his back flattened against the black padded door to minimize the impact of the rain, but the doorway is too narrow.

Then the wind subsides, not all at once, but in short gasping breaths, as if it is too early in the day for such a storm. After a while there is a pale yellow glow from the east, and from somewhere the sound of seagulls. Malachi is soaked. He is holding three videos. He is clutching them against his stomach. The videos are also wet, at least the boxes, but the boxes are made of plastic so it doesn't matter. Malachi turns to face the door and begins pounding but nobody answers. As a last resort, he tries the door and the door opens easily so Malachi steps inside. For a moment he does not know where he is. He wonders if he is dreaming, but the sense that he is awake and looking out through the jelly of his two eyes is quite strong. Then he laughs, a hollow inwardly focused laughter that nevertheless bounces off the interior walls, which reverberate like the membrane of an African drum. He has been suffering from hallucinations now for the last few months, what some would call waking dreams, which every good Rastafarian knows is the source of all religious inspiration. Yet the reality inside these hallucinations has been no different than reality at other times. Malachi wonders if he is once more slipping into another altered state, but he does not panic. The world is a fluid place. And he has been under a lot of stress lately. And he has been eating poorly. If it weren't for Gisela, he thinks, but then he decides not to think about Gisela

He decides instead to inspect the fabric of reality inside the store. It is very dark inside. There is a deeply rooted stillness in the air. It is almost like entering an ancient tomb. He feels as if he is wandering through a grainy old photograph. There are only four windows, very narrow, and very high up, and they are protected by blinds that seem almost lacquered shut. Malachi has only been here when the fluorescent lights were on and there were people in trench coats and hats milling about. Odd that the store should be closed on a Wednesday morning, but maybe Paco is sick. He has only ever seen Paco sitting behind the counter, playing video games and offering up occasional suggestions about which videos to rent, which offer the greatest visual stimulation for private masturbation sessions, and which should be viewed with friends. Paco is the only one who works here. There is no one else the Velázquez brothers trust half so much.

Then Malachi breathes in the familiar odor of stale urine and cigarette smoke. His eyes begin to adjust. He is no longer confused. A pale glow seeps around the edges of the blinds. Behind the register on the wall a red glowing security light blinks steadily. There is just enough light to see by, a diffuse light, naturally, but it is enough. Malachi is satisfied that this is not the landscape of a dream. He heads over to the cubicle where Paco normally sits and stands and listens. He hears the stringy, mechanical whining of cicadas, which seems to him a natural sound even inside a dimly lit video store, but as he listens more closely he realizes he is listening to voices, not the sounds of insects. The voices are buried beneath layers of radio static, he decides, which means it is difficult to pinpoint their exact location, but he is certain the voices are coming from the roof. He does not think about the incongruity of a radio blaring away from the rooftop of a video store that is closed for the day.

He closes his eyes and follows the sound, moving by instinct now, stopping occasionally and tilting his head to make sure of his bearings, stepping with small, careful steps to avoid making any unnecessary noise and giving himself away. He marvels at his ability to move with such sure-footed confidence even with his eyes closed. He has never done this before and is elated with his success. Blindness is only a state of mind, he thinks, like despair. He tries to remember what he was doing before he came to the video store, but his memory is a blank.

Then he remembers the three videos he is still clutching. He stares at the videos in his hand, but doesn't remember how they got there. He wonders if they have always been there. He tries to shake them loose, but they are stuck, they are a part of his own flesh, like a cancer.

Then the sounds of the voices seem all of a sudden quite loud. He realizes they are not voices on the radio. They are almost on top of him, it seems, descending from the darkness of the stairs that lead to the roof. The voices are so close he can almost feel their hot breath on his face. He forgets about the cancerous videos and heads up the stairs and sits down on the top step, pressing his ear against the door. It is the kind of behavior one would expect in a low-budget gangster flick from the 1940s. (All he needs is a revolver in his free hand to make the scene complete.) He is not sure why he puts his ear to the door. He has never liked B-movies. Besides, there is no mistaking the fact that the voices are engaged in a private conversation.

The first two voices (a big heavy voice and a slow, steady voice) are familiar, but the third one is unfamiliar. The big heavy voice is doing more talking than the other two. This voice is asking about the photos and the unfamiliar voice is saying he only came back once, we took some pictures of the neighborhood and here's the photo of the old woman and the two of them talking, and then the slow, steady voice is saying the old woman already works for us, she's been on the payroll for years, she was that *piantada caja,* the one who danced at La Campana, at least until the fiasco with the Panamanians, she'll do anything we ask, and then the big heavy voice laughing a full, robust laughter, you mean that's the sister of the little pip-squeak, and then, she is, and then, she's so goddamn old looking, what happened to her face, and then, don't you recognize your own handiwork, you're the one who carved her up, and then, yes, I remember now, she didn't even make a sound, sort of felt bad afterwards, but it had to be done, still that doesn't explain how old she looks, and then, I guess not, perhaps it's premature aging from the stress, the first one bursting out with more laughter, the entire roof beginning to shake, you mean from giving up her brother, and the second one, I guess so, and then, what was her name, and then Isidora, and then, good old Isidora, put Isidora on him, and then, already did that, and then, oh God, it's too rich, and then the voices becoming a low murmur as various strategies are discussed.

Malachi begins pressing his ear against the door with greater intensity, as if it is a suction cup and if he presses it hard enough he can pick up even the thoughts and emotions behind the words, and then the big heavy one again, reminiscing, his face contorted with visible pride (visible in the sense that Malachi can see a contorted, pleased expression in his mind's eye from the words alone), the voice recounting a time when he was down in Little Havana eating pizza at his friend Eduardo's place on 5th and a call came in for delivery but Eduardo was short-staffed, that bastard never had enough staff, always trying to cut corners, the one laughing some more, not so loud as before, but still thick and heavy, the slow, steady one saying you're going to love this, and the third, unfamiliar voice not really saying anything, just a short, squeak of a laugh, and then the first one, so I said I'd deliver the pizza, what are friends for, and Eduardo gave me the pizza and a note with the address, it was an everything pizza with Anchovies and pineapples and God knows what else, just a whole lot of garbage, everything you can imagine, and the second one now laughing, interrupting, just the way you like it, and the first one again, you wouldn't have believed where I took that pizza, some studio shit-hole on top of the old liquor store (the second one saying this was years ago, before they went out of business, and the third, unfamiliar voice saying, he remembered the place), and so I got there and I looked at the note and it said please use the back stairs, we're having a hell of a party, so I was expecting all sorts of naked pussy and all the booze I could drink and a whole lot of fucking, I was looking forward to having a really good time, you remember the kind of parties they had in that neighborhood, you'd have thought the same thing, and then the second one saying this is where it gets good, and the third unfamiliar voice not saying anything, and then the first one, but what a fucked up place that studio was, I walk in there all pumped up with this everything pizza and all I see is this fucked-up homosexual asshole, he's absolutely naked except he's covered with paint, all sorts of colors mashed together like some mascot hyped up on coke, and somebody had tied him up like a hog and left him leaning against the sofa, you had to wonder what kind of friends he had, so there I am and it looks like he's got an apple in his mouth or something and he's moaning and moaning, only I can't quite hear what he's saying, I'm not sure it was even words, he looked pretty out of it, but not all the way out it, I mean he was trying to look back to see who just came in only he couldn't turn his head far enough because of the rope, and I'm eating one of the slices of pizza now, because there's no way in hell this fruity homosexual bastard is getting a pizza from me, and I walk up to him, just behind him so he can't see, and I say what the fuck are you saying, just like that, a normal even tone, no belligerence whatsoever, and he moans some more and then it sounds like he's saying just fuck me will you, fuck me again, please fuck me, I mean it was disgusting what was coming out of his mouth, so I take a step back, just to survey the landscape, if you know what I mean, and the place was a wreck, paint all over the place and dozens of cheap, unexceptional paintings, but looks like somebody tossed them all over the room, like they didn't give a shit, I guess the guy thought he was a painter, but it was the kind of sick, twisted paintings that give art a bad rap, I mean you wouldn't want your children to see them and have to explain why somebody's penis has been cut off and shoved into a blender, that kind of thing, so I'm standing there eating the guy's pizza and he's moaning the same tired shit over and over again, and finally I see this tiny statue of a white penis, I guess it was a penis, I don't know what it was, all I know is that I pick it up and I hear myself saying, you want to get fucked, well okay then, and I shove that statue of a penis up his ass and I smash it in there pretty good, I mean I'm pretty much carving him up, and he's screaming now, you can't hear a single recognizable word come out of his mouth, and he starts shuddering some and the blood is seeping out around his crack, and then I yank that penis out and I have to take a quick step back cause the blood is just gushing, and I watched the guy for a while, and he's barely whimpering now, that kind of injury hurts at first and there's always an awful lot of blood, but you go into shock fairly quick, so there's not too much suffering, then the guy gave one more shudder and that was that, I wiped the base of the statue so there wouldn't be any prints and tossed it on the sofa, grabbed the rest of the pizza and headed out the door, I mean the guy was disgusting, what did he think I was going to do, I mean I'm usually a live and let live kind of guy, you know that Brother, but not in a situation like that, that was just too much for me.

Malachi has had enough. His brain is burning, his synapses shriveling up from the heat, his skull filling up with particles of ash. There is nothing he can do. He wonders who had tied up the painter and why, and he is struck by how fluid and fragile the world truly is, and yet nobody seems to give a fuck. He is unable to shake the image of the sad, tormented painter from his mind. Why should he be given the burden of this story at precisely this moment?

He closes his eyes and he can see the wavering ghost of a multi-colored face like the face of a drugged mascot, eyes half closed, begging for mercy and no mercy forthcoming. Waves of nausea ripple through Malachi and he realizes that, at least for the moment, God (his God, who Malachi vaguely understands to be a shadowy reflection of his own divinity) has forsaken the world. He opens his eyes and breathes in the darkness. The waves subside. He wonders how long the three voices on the rooftop will continue talking and when the door will open, but he does not yet move from the stairs. He is waiting for a sign perhaps, a message from his God that he can deliver to thirsty ears, his own ears certainly, some message of hope, and if not hope, at least compassion. There must be others who are tired of the darkness of the underbelly, who are hoping some kind of prophet will appear and lead them to paradise, or at least point the way. Malachi is almost overwhelmed by the thought that the entire universe is waiting to be forgiven. The waves return. Trembling, he wonders how long he must wait for absolution if his God does not exist (a troubling thought if he is in fact his own God). He takes a second, deep breath and then a third and the waves subside again and he sits a little while longer. The image of the tormented painter vanishes. The voices from the rooftop are no longer audible. They have sort of just floated away. Perhaps they were never truly there. Perhaps he has been hallucinating. Malachi considers briefly that his entire life has been one single hallucination. For one brief moment it is the only explanation that makes any sense.

Then the fluorescent lights from below begin to flicker. They do not stay on, but continue to flicker, again and again, illuminating the video store with brilliant flashes of light, and then the diffuse, unearthly glow from before returning.

-29-

The video store is now crawling with men in trench coats and wide-brimmed hats. They are moving up and down the aisles. Paco is nowhere in sight, but that does not mean anything. He is probably in the back pounding down a couple of cokes and a few candy bars before he takes his customary seat. But there is something off about the men roaming the aisles. They all possess the same face, a strange theatrical mask of a face with white porcelain cheeks and smartly polished black moustaches with tips that curl up slightly, and brightly painted lips, red lips, with more white porcelain where there should be teeth, and a tiny black hole in the exact center between the lips. It looks like they are about to whistle, but they don't. They move like robotic zombies, mechanically zooming up and down the aisles on rows of tiny wheels hidden by the length of their trench coats.

At first Malachi just stares at the frozen faces zooming back and forth. He can hear the droning whir of tiny motors and rotating gears. Then he hears a voice, the same mechanical voice coming out of the black hole of each machine. The voice, multiplied by the dozen or so machines in the store, is repeating the same phrase over and over again. "Everything we do follows us everywhere we go." Their tone is a very flat monotone, and yet because of the number of machines, it carries great weight.

Slowly Malachi begins making his way towards the counter where Paco should be arriving any minute. He has to stop at predictable points along the way to avoid the zooming mechanical customers. They go whizzing past without even a glance, presumably because their maker had not installed a gear so they could rotate their heads. Then Malachi stumbles into one and sends the machine flying into the shelves. A couple of rows of adult movies fall to the floor and the machine lands on its side, its tiny wheels now exposed, spinning and spinning, the machine still repeating the same phrase over and over and over. But with the accident a change comes over the other machines. They now realize Malachi is in the store – perhaps not Malachi precisely, but someone who might knock them over – and they begin searching for him. They do not need rotating heads to survey the entire store, they can turn on a dime. They are all now spinning slowly round and round as they move up and down the aisles, searching him out. Malachi also notices that the tone of their voices has changed and now seems slightly sinister, modulated by an appetite for revenge, perhaps.

Malachi realizes he has slipped into a tedious but rather complicated hallucination. He is caught in some sort of a loop that began with the voices on the roof. The universe is playing back the same scene over and over again, and there is only one way out, at least as Malachi sees it. So he begins attacking the roving machines. Their most obvious weakness, and Malachi's salvation, is that they possess no arms, a fact which Malachi had not noticed earlier, so he simply begins pushing them over, knocking them to the floor, the sound of spinning wheels and rotating gears now echoing harmlessly throughout the video store.

By the time Malachi reaches the counter, Paco is sitting there, one eye on a new video game, the other on a security camera monitor that flashes pictures of what is happening in each aisle.

Paco smiles as Malachi approaches.

"You know you didn't have to do that," says Paco.

"Didn't have to do what?" says Malachi.

"Knock them over like that."

Malachi looks into the security camera and he can see dozens of upended machines on the floor, their wheels still spinning.

"They wouldn't hurt a fly."

Malachi isn't sure what to say after that. Paco is staring at him and he is beginning to feel uncomfortable. Malachi suddenly feels like a fly suddenly exposed to a fly swatter.

"It's okay," Paco says after a while, and then he nods in the direction of the fallen machines. They are now back on their wheels, patrolling the aisles once again, repeating the same stock phrase.

"Sure," says Malachi.

Malachi is only vaguely troubled by the sudden resurrection of the machines. He watches them a while, first with his back to Paco, then with his eyes glued to the security camera monitor. Everything is pretty much like it was before, except every so often, at seemingly random intervals, one of the machines does a slow 360-degree spin, as if to anticipate another collision like the one with Malachi. He looks at the machines with a mixture of admiration and envy. He is impressed by their engineering. Their design seems flawless, as close to perfection as is humanly possible. He is impressed by their ability to learn from their mistakes. It is almost like the pride of a father.

"So what do you need today, Broken Bike?" says Paco.

"Just returning a few videos," says Malachi.

"The Salma de la Prada videos?"

"They're late. Sorry about that."

"Don't worry about it."

The videos are no longer stuck to Malachi's hand. He does not remember their ever having been stuck. He hands them over to Paco without comment.

"So what did I tell you," says Paco. "She's one hell of a beautiful bitch, ain't she."

Malachi turns to leave, but Paco reaches behind the counter and pulls out a gun, a shiny black revolver, and lays it on the counter. He looks around to see if anyone notices, but there is no one else with eyes to see, only the robot customers patrolling the aisles, the steady, comforting whir of gears and motors and spinning wheels.

"Hey Broken Bike," says Paco. "I want you to have this. You might need it."

"What do I need a gun for?"

"Man, who doesn't need a gun around here," says Paco, and he is grinning now.

"No, man, thanks, but a gun's too much trouble."

"Hey, no worries, man," says Paco "It's not even a real gun. It's a movie gun. A prop. It doesn't shoot anything. Not even blanks. They were going to use it in your girlfriend's movie before she quit. It was just lying around so I snagged it. Go on, take it."

Malachi looks at the gun on the counter and he can barely suppress a smile. He stuffs the movie prop gun into his black bicycle shorts and heads out the door.

-30-

Malachi walked away from the video store, his face beaming. The air was still heavy and moist from the rain, with the hint of a second storm on its way, but Malachi did not notice. He felt suddenly invincible. Even if the gun were only a movie prop, the fact that Paco had given him the gun meant that the path of his destiny was changing once again. He was no longer just a lonely Rastafarian rebel living on the edge of the edge of reality. He was someone with a future, and it did not matter what this future was going to be, any future was better than no future at all. This is what Malachi was thinking. This is why he was smiling.

He was still smiling when he reached the café. The place was packed as usual, the regular crew of Dominicans from the other side of the river and the Cubans who lived on this side. You would expect a fight to break out the moment the two groups got together, but one never did, not a real fight anyway, with knives shoved into somebody's stomach and maybe a gunshot and blood pouring out all over the place, and then the paramedics would arrive, and then the police. At worst, there were a few scuffles with someone getting his nose broke or clocked in the Adam's apple so he'd shut up so people could eat, but nothing serious ever happened at the café. Everyone checked their weapons at the door, figuratively speaking, of course, and put on their best television camera faces. (These were the very same faces they would flash to the rest of the world if they ever found themselves sitting on death row and they suddenly had one final chance to spit into the microphone of a roving television news reporter and proclaim their innocence.)

Malachi hadn't been down to the café in a few months, not since the scene with Gisela. He was hoping Señor Mendoza had forgotten all about his buffoonery, or had at least changed his mind. Wednesday nights meant all the bean soup and roasted pork sandwiches you could eat and enough beer and wine to drown the whole goddamn city.

The first thing he noticed when he got there was how quite the café was, in spite of the fact that every fucking table was full. But no one said a word, except to order another beer or another bowl of soup. Everyone was staring blankly at their food while they ate, they wouldn't even look at each other, and when they weren't eating they were smoking cigarettes or cigars and downing beers at a furious pace and then looking over at the door with deeply troubled eyes, a look of breathless agitation smeared across their faces, as if they had been flailing about in the middle of a dark, windless, wine-dark sea but now they were exhausted and it was the moment before they sank to the bottom.

Malachi had to sit all the way in the back where the counter ended so at first he couldn't see why everyone was so anxious. The smoke was pretty thick. The two rotating fans with their wide, palmetto-style blades could barely keep the smoky air circulating.

Then the door opened and someone went out and the air cleared for a moment and Malachi could see the trouble. There were two strange, obviously lunatic white men sitting at the first table when you came in. The one had crazy red hair, stringy hair like sea snakes. All he was doing was talking and waving his arms in the air. The sea snakes were writhing uncontrollably as he talked. The other one didn't say a word. He was covered in a thick black matte of hair. All you could see were eyes every now and then, and you could see murderous intent in his eyes, the kind Malachi had only ever seen in the movies, but mostly his face was mashed down into a bowl of soup and all you saw was a great heavy, sullen blackness. He knew immediately who they were. Not their names, their names didn't matter. The Velázquez brothers had sent them to tidy things up. This was his new future unfolding, this is why Paco had given him the gun. It had been a joke. Or a warning. Malachi almost couldn't believe it, but what else could they be? The men sitting by the front door were assassins.

For a time, Malachi did nothing. The sky began to grow dark, the promise of the second storm would soon be fulfilled, but Malachi did not care. He sat there and drank a few beers and wondered what he was supposed to do and then he drank a few more. Slipping out the back was not really an option, especially if the two had seen him come in. He would rather sit there among the anxious crowd at the café. Maybe an angel would come to his aid. But if they hadn't seen him yet, then it was worth a try. But they wouldn't be very good assassins if they hadn't spotted him the moment he arrived, and he was fairly certain the Velázquez brothers hired only the best, so what should he do? Malachi did not know. He was frozen by the babble in his brain. He ordered yet another beer, but this one he drank slowly. He could feel the cool liquid cascading down his throat. He watched Señor Mendoza moving back and forth among the tables, talking with Dominicans and Cubans who had forgotten how to speak but Señor Mendoza understanding what they wanted without needing words and waving to one of the sexy *chiquitas* for another bowl of soup or beer or wine and then on to the next table.

The radio behind the counter was playing a salsa but you could barely hear it, and then a Latin pop tune came on and someone turned the radio up and Malachi breathed in the song in the hopes that it would do a better job of settling his nerves than the beers. The Latin pop tune was replaced by another salsa. Señor Mendoza was no longer monitoring the needs of the Dominicans and the Cubans. He was now standing next to the swinging kitchen door, directly behind Malachi.

Strangely, the presence of Señor Mendoza, a looming, shadowy presence arching up onto the ceiling, gave Malachi a sudden shot of courage, and he began to formulate a plan, and because Malachi was slightly drunk, his plan came tumbling out of his mouth in short, cryptic phrases, which would have sounded like the gibberish of a madman unless you were listening very carefully, in which case Malachi's logic possessed the impeccable clarity of a cloudless summer's day.

It wasn't Gisela's fault, though clearly if she had relented he would be in the clear, he hoped they left her alone, there was no reason to take her out, but these two sitting there by the window, he had no idea the Velázquez brothers would reach this point so quickly, the fucking bastards, he still couldn't quite believe these two skinny white assassins like white devils were there to put a bullet in his brain, how many bullets to do the job properly, three bullets, six bullets, one gun or two, his words ballooning now, escaping like steam, he was re-living the loop from the conversation on the roof to acting out the climax of the movie in the café, and then Malachi laughed, a sudden, unrehearsed ballooning laughter because the scene they had acted out had been a very funny scene, what had they thought, the two construction workers sitting at the bar, and the other one who came in and stared at the poster of the bullfighter, what had they been thinking when he started jerking off right there and then Gisela taking a peek and she had started laughing, and you couldn't break character like that in the middle of a scene, particularly when you were performing before a live audience, he wasn't a professional, but he knew that much, and then she was back in it, but you could tell she was playing two parts at that point, Nefertari the consort of the sun god Amun-Ra, and the laughing Gisela with the exuberant breasts who couldn't believe what her Malachi was doing and going through with it anyway, and he loved her for taking part in the scene (though he most certainly would have loved her even if she hadn't), even if she couldn't help laughing when he had started masturbating, or maybe because she started laughing, and then the tenor of Malachi's voice hardened and he stared across the café at the two assassins and there was now a deliberate darkness to his hissing words, he would take the two bastards out himself, they wouldn't get near his Gisela, not if he could do anything about it, and then he remembered his movie prop gun stuffed into his pants and he took it out, caressing it while he stared into the darkness of his imagination, his precise thoughts unable to coalesce except in a vague, dreamlike way, as if the possibility that this was a real gun was enough, and with the flicker of this possibility shimmering in his mind, Malachi exploded across the café and found himself sitting at the table with the two assassins, but once there, he had no idea what to do. You could clearly see the gun wasn't real. It looked like a piece of rubber that had been damaged in a fire. He stabbed at the air with the movie prop gun in a half-hearted attempt to look menacing. The one assassin started laughing softly, quietly, a contained sort of laughter, a suppressed laughter, but still his sea snake hair went flying all over the table. The other one barely registered any awareness beyond his soup. Then Malachi's voice took over and he heard himself hissing through his teeth.

"Tell me why I shouldn't pull the trigger," he heard himself say. Malachi knew it was a ludicrous question the moment he opened his mouth.

The one assassin seemed on the verge of busting a gut, but he was able to contain himself. "I can't think of a thing to say," he said. Then he leaned his face across the table, his head tilted, as if to get a better bead on his adversary with the rubber movie prop gun, and then his face cracked open with a smile.

Malachi's hand began to tremble.

The other one said nothing, his face mashed in his bowl, his countenance disguised.

"But what if the gun were real?" said the one, and for the first time Malachi noticed his chipped teeth. "Now that would be an interesting dilemma. What would I have said if the gun were real? That's the real question, isn't it?"

Malachi nodded stupidly. Once again he felt disconnected from events. He would just listen to the one assassin while the other one ate his soup and hope for the best.

"I suppose I would have said if you need to pull the trigger, then you need to pull the trigger."

Then he reached over and took the movie-prop gun from Malachi and inserted it into his own mouth.

He was now choking back his laughter.

"Then I would have said it doesn't make a goddamn bit of difference what you or anybody else does. We are all dancing in one goddamn eternal circle. Like angels on the head of a pin. We're all going to end up right back where we started anyway. So what the hell, let's get this goddamn fucking dance over with. That's what I would have said. Something like that. Sounds pretty goddamn existential, doesn't it? Like a fucking philosopher."

And then the one exploded in a fit of laughter, which coincided, as if on cue, with an enormous flash of lightning (for the long-awaited second storm had finally arrived) and the street outside shown with the brilliant incandescence of a second sun, and for a moment every head in the café turned to look and they thought they were looking at a washed-out photograph from years ago. Then the white glare of this photograph faded and darkness descended and with it came the rain. The atmosphere inside the café had suddenly changed. It hummed now with the happy laughter of half-drunk men. Some of the men were slapping at the beefy brown behinds of the waitresses. Or grabbing one and giving her ass a squeeze.

Malachi had been wrong about these two, he realized that now. The one with the chipped teeth ordered a round of beers and the other one slurped down the rest of his soup and came out of his fog. The beers came and they started drinking with wild abandon. Malachi shoved the movie-prop gun back into his shorts. For the first time in several months he felt completely relaxed.

-31-

The two teachers entered Malachi's life at precisely the right moment. At least this is how Malachi felt. Within days of their first meeting, he had told them of his troubles with the Velázquez brothers and how he had pinned all of his hopes on Gisela, but now he was beginning to question the wisdom of this strategy. Naturally the two teachers shared with Malachi their opinions (mostly philosophical garbage) about the kind of danger the Velázquez brothers represented (the older teacher was a sort of Trotskyite revisionist with a similar revisionist understanding of Fascism, and this perspective shaped his analysis; the younger teacher knew just enough about the gangsters of the Prohibition Era, gleaned from years of watching old black and white movies, to appreciate the dangers, both physical and social, of armed thugs who lived beyond the reach of the law), but any advice they offered Malachi on how to repair the damage that had been done by his inability to influence Gisela was either impractical (find another girl with tits as big as Gisela to take over the starring role of the movie) or uninformed (forget about the Velázquez brothers, they'll give up after a while, everyone does) or downright idiotic (challenge the Velázquez brothers to a duel with a pair of 18th century French dueling pistols made by Peniet of Paris).

To be fair, most of their conversation about the Velázquez brothers took place one night in La Mamacita's, a club up in Allapattah that looked like a bombed-out warehouse. They were all very drunk. And they could hardly hear themselves breathe, let alone talk. The air inside the club vibrated with the hazy, tinny, electric din of merengues and reggae and hip-hop and techno and Latin funk and bohemian jazzy shit, like the background static of the universe. They were sitting on tall bar stools at a small upright table in the cascading shadows of a broken light that hung from the ceiling, drinking beer and watching people dance. The greasy brightness of the bar on the other side of the club pulsed with a flurry of arms reaching for drinks (mostly green bottles of beer) and then cash exchanging hands and then thick, coarse laughter that broke through the music, and then more arms reaching, and so on.

"Who the fuck do these guys think they are?" said the one with the chipped teeth.

"It doesn't matter what they think," said the other one. "It only matters what Malachi here thinks."

Malachi wasn't listening. He was watching a group of women who had just come in, thick, heavy girls with thick, greasy hair flying about and lacey red skirts that swirled around their hips and the flash of naked brown asses as they wiggled their way to a table near the dance floor. A thin layer of filth covered the floor, a varnish with the consistency of dried oatmeal. The air reeked with stale beer, dried sweat, dried urine, the various cheap perfumes the stores at the mall were pushing. It should have been difficult to breathe, but people were breathing just fine. The girls barely had time to order drinks before they were surrounded by short, skinny men wearing yellow bandanas or orange ones and earrings and grinning teeth and dripping moustaches and switch-blades stuffed away somewhere, invisible until needed. Malachi stared at the women from the security of the shadows. Two drunken eyes blinking in the haze beneath the broken light. Malachi thought there were a lot more horse-faced women than usual. Then the voices of the two teachers plus Malachi drifted back into range.

"The way I see it these guys are every bit as Fascist as Barry Goldwater or Francisco Franco."

"Fuck Franco," Malachi heard himself say.

"Fuck Goldwater," said the younger teacher.

"You are both remarkably perceptive, my young naïve friends. But fucking them is not enough. They are just the tip of the barely visible iceberg. America in the 1960s was every bit as Fascist as Spain under Franco, maybe more so, and nothing much has changed. America is a goddamn Fascist cesspool."

"Yeah, well, maybe so, but how does that help Malachi?"

"It always helps to understand your enemy."

"I understand the Velázquez brothers very well," said Malachi. "It's a black and white fucking world with them."

"That's Fascism in a nutshell."

"Fucking Fascism," said the younger teacher.

"So what do I do?" said Malachi.

"You don't do anything," said the older teacher.

"What kind of crazy shit advice is that?"

But now the older teacher was no longer listening. He drank some of his beer. His gaze wandered away from the table and he soon found himself staring at one of the fat girls that Malachi had noticed. She was dancing with two skinny Mexicans with yellow bandanas, quite possibly out-of-work construction workers. They all seemed to know each other. The two construction workers were groping the girl while they danced. One would twist her hands around in his, holding onto her fingertips, and give her a very fancy spin, and she would twirl in the delirium of absolute joy, her skirt billowing up and the man's hands sliding up and down her body, catching her as she slowed and spreading the cheeks of her ass and pulling her close and the girl squealing with delight. Then the other one would take a turn.

"He means you need to forget about them," said the younger teacher. "And he's probably right. They'll forget about you after a while. Nobody can hold a grudge forever."

Malachi looked at the younger teacher with great compassion, his eyes softening for a moment, as if he were helping a small child across a busy street.

"Noooooo, man, the Velázquez brothers don't forget shit."

"Well maybe you can find some other girl with really big tits and convince her that the Velázquez brothers will make her an international star."

"You've seen Gisela," said Malachi.

"Of course," said the younger teacher."

Both men were now staring at the hazy, golden bubble of light that encased the bar at the other end of the club. As both men became absorbed in this bubble of light, they thought they saw Gisela and her bouncing tits. She was smiling and running and her tits were bouncing and they couldn't tell where she was, maybe out at the beach, but they didn't care. It was like watching a movie. They continued their conversation while they watched their private movie.

"Have you ever seen anyone with tits that big?"

"Hell no. I can't say that I have."

"Exactly!"

They watched Gisela's tits bouncing for a while, idiotic grins pasted on their faces. Then the image of Gisela faded.

"Hell, I don't know what you should do, Malachi. Maybe you should just challenge them to a duel."

"A duel?"

"Yeah. Like in the 18th century in Paris. A couple of antique dueling pistols with ivory plated handles. Designed by Peniet himself. Ten steps, turn and fire."

The music in the club became very loud at that point, a very noisy pop techno Latin funk bluesy sound with people screaming and shouting and jumping about, and they could no longer hear anything that was being said. For a while they tried communicating using only hand gestures and contorted expressions on their faces, like deranged Kabuki dancers, but then they gave up and drank their beers.

"It's fucking hopeless," said Malachi, grinning. "Fucking hopeless."

"What's that?"

"Fucking hopeless."

They drank beers for several hours, at least that's how it seemed in retrospect. More likely it was only several minutes. They had lost all sense of time. They had lost all perspective. Then the pop techno portion of the evening was replaced with a few slower but still rhythmic boleros.

"You ever see anything like that?" said the older teacher.

He was still focused on the dance floor and the girl in the red skirt with the two skinny Mexicans. They were now the only ones out there. The rest of those who had been dancing were lined up around the edge, half in the shadows, bodies twisted at odd angles so everyone could see what was going on. The girl was nude from the waist down, the curves of her great ass rippling with power, and she was stomping her feet like an angry bull and snorting and shaking her head and her greasy hair flying about and drops of grease splattering the air. One of the men was holding her lacey red skirt like a cape and whipping it around in the air, and then, as if to time her movements with the rhythm of the music, the girl charged and the Mexican draped the makeshift cape over her face as she went by and slapped her on the ass. The crowd of former dancers shouted "Ole, ole" and "bring it again" and "Oh yeah" and "let it out baby, let it out" and then they were cheering and whistling. They looked like they were about to explode. The two skinny Mexicans in their yellow bandanas took turns pretending to be the matador, but the girl was always the bull. After a while she was tired from charging after her skirt (and also quite drunk from the copious amounts of alcohol she had no doubt consumed) and the show was over. Actually, she sort of collapsed in the middle of the floor, but she had a happy, incurious smile plastered across an otherwise inscrutable face. (The word comatose also comes to mind.) The two Mexicans carried her off to the secluded darkness of a small hallway near the front of the club. The hallway led to the restrooms, but the lights were out. Half a dozen former dancers splintered off from the rest and followed the two Mexicans as they carried the fat girl from the dance floor, limp and glistening with sweat from the imaginary bullfight, and then they were gone. But every now and then for the next hour or so, you could vaguely hear the sounds of a girl squealing and people shouting "Ole" and then cheering and clapping and whistling, but the sound barely stood out against the music. It was more like an echo that had traveled across time. They let the image of the beefy girl being carried from the dance floor linger in their minds for a moment. Then the conversation resumed.

"It's like I was saying. Fascism everywhere you look."

"You mean the girl and the two Mexicans?"

"That's precisely what I mean."

"Don't let him draw you in, Malachi. I've been listening to this kind of garbage for as long as I've known him."

"And none the wiser, for all that."

The two teachers clinked their beer bottles together and drank. Malachi hiccupped. They were drunk enough that everything seemed like a great joke and they could barely suppress their laughter.

"He's a goddamn lunatic."

"We are all lunatics, my friends. It is an ancient religion."

A commotion broke out at the bar and the bartender took out a club and whacked a guy over the head and the guy crumpled up like a piece of aluminum and you could see a thin crack and some blood seeping out and then two body guards carried him out. Then a guy with a mop came out to clean up the bloody trail. There were a dozen or more bodyguards in the club wearing leather vests, which were quite possibly bullet-proof, and Billy clubs clipped to their sides and ponytails tied neatly. They were still chatting with the customers and smiling dumb, happy smiles, but they had taken up strategic positions around the club in case they were needed. They all had arms like granite and when they smiled you could see dozens of blank spaces where their teeth were missing. Malachi thought they all looked like younger versions of Bull when he saw them smile. They looked like paratroopers getting ready to jump.

"It's going to get rough in here pretty soon." said Malachi.

The two teachers nodded but it was clear the words did not penetrate even their skin. They ordered another round of beers and then another, and the conversation changed direction several times. Then the older teacher suggested they switch to mojitos with cut limes. When the mojitos came they told the waitress to keep them coming, they were incredibly thirsty. They were at the stage when everything they drank tasted like water. After a while they were talking about women.

"Now you take young Lauterbach here," said the older teacher. "He's a fairly good looking boy with overly large hands, and if hands are any indication, he should have more pussy sniffing around than he knows what to do with."

The older teacher plucked the lime out of his empty glass and started chewing on it while he talked.

"But the size of your hands isn't the only thing that matters," said the older teacher.

Malachi's head was throbbing. He wished he could crawl under the table and go to sleep. The younger teacher seemed to be sleeping right where he was, the side of his face resting awkwardly on the table, his chin hanging over the edge, his eyes staring vacantly at the dance floor, which was empty now except for a shredded red skirt and a dozen empty beer bottles and some broken glass. The older teacher finished off the last of his lime and pushed the defruited skin into his glass.

"The trouble with Lauterbach is that he's still mooning over this young Spanish teacher named Tommie Rodriguez, a hell of a beautiful *chiquita,* beautiful brown eyes, juicy in all the right places, and she loved him as much as he loved her. But that was a lifetime ago."

Malachi stared at the empty mojito glasses on the table, at the bright green defruited skin in each. He couldn't tell how many empty glasses there were. The words of the older teacher flowed past his ears with an unsettling regularity. He understood that hidden in the spaces between the words he could decipher was a meaning that eluded him. But when the older teacher started talking about love, the meaning was unmistakably clear, the way looking up at a cloudless nighttime sky filled with stars was clear (assuming you were far enough away from the dull, electric glow of civilization). Malachi understood love to be an expansive force that stretched across the universe, so he hung on to this one word and let the others flow past, no longer caring. He wondered how deeply the younger teacher loved this woman from a lifetime ago. He wondered if they would ever see each other again. He felt sorry for the younger teacher. Then he thought about how much he loved Gisela and he knew how very lucky he was.

"Beautiful and useless," the older teacher said.

The older teacher was now engaged in a serious conversation with an imaginary friend. Or perhaps he was simply pausing at appropriate places to let Malachi or the younger teacher fill in the gaps if they once again found their voices.

"No, I don't think he had any choice. None of us have a choice when it comes to that."

". . . ."

"Precisely! After that there is only loneliness. He will suffer from loneliness until he is no longer suffering."

". . . ."

"I don't think it matters much where he is. It is not a question of geography."

". . . ."

"No, I don't think any of us have much time left."

". . . ."

"Maybe if you beat him to death with a crowbar."

". . . ."

"Yeah, well, then we're all pretty much fucked."

". . . ."

"The whole fucking world."

The last thing Malachi remembered from that night was leaving the club and the three of them walking south to the 17th Avenue drawbridge. The heat of the day had lifted and the night was clear and warm and breezy, the kind of night where you can hear dogs howling in the distance and there is an endless tide of boleros floating from window to window and the street lamps are clouded over with thousands of tiny insects, so everything looks like a memory. Malachi hadn't been home in a few months, but in an effort to reassure Gisela that his desire to spend every waking and non-waking hour with her was not founded upon the desperation of his current circumstances, he had taken to sleeping two or three nights a week in the shadows of the great bridges that linked Allapattah to Little Havana. He felt comfortable in the shadows beneath the bridges. He did not stay beneath any one bridge for more than a few days, partly to prevent the Velázquez brothers from stumbling upon his routine, but mostly because after even a single night away, his yearning for Gisela became unbearably nostalgic. Tonight he was heading to the 17th Avenue bridge on the side closest to the yacht club. Sewell Park was on the other side. Earlier that morning he had hidden a bag with some clothes, a thin blanket and a pillow in a narrow crevice between the drawbridge tower and the underbelly of the bridge, where the bridge's hydraulic machinery was visible. A couple of times when he had slept there before, early in the morning, the man who raised and lowered the drawbridge noticed Malachi in the shadows, but he didn't squawk. He just nodded slightly, as if to say 'Go ahead, I don't mind, I might need to sleep there myself one day.' Malachi liked to stretch out on a narrow ledge next to the hydraulics, protected by the steel girders and the swirling darkness, so he could forget about the terrors of the world.

The three men walked in silence the several miles from the club to the bridge. Words seemed unnecessary, useless, without the power to give shape to the world. Then they could see where the regular pattern of street lamps ended and the dark shadow of the bridge began and then the street lamps began again on the other side. Malachi said good night and scrambled down the embankment and then made his way along a narrow wooden walkway to the crevice beneath the steel girders. He spread out the blanket and the pillow on the narrow ledge and lay down but he could not close his eyes.

The world seemed strangely silent, as if it were uninhabited. He looked out at the river but he could not see the other side, and he suddenly felt suspended between two worlds, between a dead or dying past and the crushing weight of an unseen future. He wondered what in the world he was going to do, what was going to happen. He imagined himself being tossed from the rooftop of a fancy hotel at the beach, landing in an empty pool and an Aqua-Clean van driving away from the scene, the driver oblivious to what was really going on, and then Malachi's broken body would be wrapped in a white tarp like a plastic shroud, a fitting emblem of a godless universe, and they would take him out and dump him in the ocean, food for the sharks, he thought, and he was on the verge of an overwhelming panic, or so he imagined, when the silence of the world was broken by a soothing, calming voice that numbed the edges of his fear.

At first he could not make out what the voice was saying. He wondered where the voice was coming from. Then he realized it was the voice of the older teacher and he smiled, but he was also confused. The two teachers must have crossed to the other side and been almost to the café by now, so there was no scientific theory that would explain why Malachi could hear the older one talking. Yet his voice was very sharp, very clear, even though at the same time it sounded a million miles away. He wondered at this minor miracle. He wondered if the angels of his destiny were closing in. Then he let the weight of his body settle into the concrete and closed his eyes. The voice of the older teacher sounded even closer than before. The teacher was telling a story, a bedtime fable.

"A cattleman once drove a herd of one thousand bulls to a modern marvel of a slaughterhouse that possessed gleaming white walls and white tiled ramps and floors. Everything was scrubbed and sparkling," he said. "And when all one thousand bulls were safely imprisoned within the polished bars of a stainless steel corral, the butcher appeared in a spotless white cloak with his great mechanized carving knives. 'Let us close ranks,' said one of the bulls, 'so we can jack up this criminal on our horns.' But the other nine-hundred ninety-nine bulls adamantly refused. 'If you please,' they said, 'how is this butcher any different from the cattleman who drove us to this place of godlike cleanliness with a cattle prod and dogs snapping at our heels?' And the one bull thought he understood their meaning and said 'You are right to ask this question, for there is no difference between the two, and when we are finished with the butcher we will then seek justice against the cattleman.' But the nine-hundred ninety-nine bulls did not understand the answer of the one bull. 'You are trying to deceive us,' they said. 'The cattleman and the butcher are not our enemy. We can see that the butcher possesses these knives only to defend himself. If we raise our horns against him, then surely he will raise his knives against us. But if we do nothing, then we can all live in peace.' And so the herd of one thousand bulls did not close ranks, and one by one they fell victim to the newly honed edge of the butcher's mechanized knives."

-32-

Malachi, a natural insomniac, lay there on the narrow ledge until the glow from the early morning sun flashed up from the surface of the river. It kind of felt like being under water the way the rippling light and shadows played against the underbelly of the bridge. But Malachi did not get down from the ledge even when twenty minutes later the bridge went up and then down for the first time that day. He was replaying the story of the bulls over and over again in his mind, mesmerized by the philosophical nature of what he had heard but unable to divine its meaning. During the short night, he had been plagued by images of bullfighters and charging bulls, their great horns thrusting at the air, and angry, mechanical butchers sharpening their knives, all of the images converging, whirling about in his brain like demonic razor blades, severing his synapses, lacerating the softly coiled, sausage-like tissue housed within his skull. He had been certain he was bleeding. As the morning drifted up from the river, he was still convinced his blood was draining away, his already pale face taking on an ethereal milky hue, as if he had died just before dawn, and then the rats had got him and were chewing on his cold white, rubber-like flesh, tearing away chunks and unclogging his arteries and then lapping up his juices.

Time took a back seat.

Then he was up and the rats became a feeling of vague discomfort, a subtle paranoia, a greening summer's mist produced by acid rainfall that he breathed in without thinking, his lungs slowly filling with the pinpricks of apprehension, and then a dull ache in his chest. Before he realized it, he had left the bridge far behind. He moved along tree-lined avenues with pastry shops and gas stations and city parks and the spires of Catholic churches winking in the sunlight. He was not sure where he was going, or even where he was, but he knew he had to keep moving. He stopped a few times to get his bearings, but nothing looked familiar, not even the street names, not even when he came upon a major intersection with city busses stopped at red lights. He wondered if somehow he had been transported to a foreign country (which most certainly would have solved his dilemma with the Velázquez brothers, but Malachi did not think of that). Once again he seemed to be drifting through the fog of a hallucination, and he knew the best thing would be to find a quiet place to sit and catch his breath and let the world re-assemble into a more familiar pattern, but he could not stop. He felt like he was trapped in a gangster movie from the 1940s and he was at the part where the detective hero was wandering through a collage of memories, trying to sort through all the clues and figure out the case. So he kept moving. The sun had become very hot and a dry wind began to hiss through the trees and it felt like the hot breath of the Velázquez brothers blowing across the back of his neck so he could not stop.

On several occasions he thought he heard footsteps, and then he would duck into the arched vestibule doorway of a corner drugstore or a hamburger joint, trembling with uncertainty, light a cigarette (he wasn't sure how the cigarette always materialized out of thin air, right on cue, but he only noted this aberration in an off-hand, ironically detached sort of way) and slide a weary eye around the outer edge, just in case, all of which would have bordered on farce had it been midnight, but it seemed strangely credible in the middle of the day. Once he even thought he saw his neighbor, the one who had been clipping her azaleas three doors down. She was still wearing the same flowery dress, if his eyes could be believed. Why she might be following him he couldn't say. But when he looked again she was gone, and where she had been standing there was only a shriveled-up tamarind tree with a piece of blue cloth or a child's kite stuck in the branches. Still, it might have been somebody, thought Malachi. All the more reason to remain alert. But no matter how many times he stopped, all he saw were the bright, wiry shadows of tree branches dancing on the sidewalks like the tentacles of crazed extraterrestrial squids.

It almost seemed that the entire planet was deserted, that the world's population had simply left the room, leaving a chaotic circus of uneaten breakfasts and lunches on counters, cars still running, waiting at traffic lights till they ran out of gas, empty elevators humming in between floors, bathtubs overflowing and the water cascading down stairwells, that sort of thing, and he had almost convinced himself that this was indeed the case when he heard a voice shout "Corinna, you wait right there!" and he spun around and there was a mother and her daughter, a child of eight or nine with a pink bow in her hair and a pink Minnie Mouse dress. The girl was holding a Minnie Mouse lunchbox. The mother was holding the girl by the shoulders, giving her some kind of earnest advice which clearly the child wished to ignore. Then a late model Chevy pulled up to the curb and they got in and the car drove away.

Malachi was aware how absurd the whole situation was, everything from imagining that his neighbor in the flowery dress was following him to thinking that everyone on the planet had mysteriously vanished, but he also sensed how dangerous and unpredictable life could be, like the trembling potential for violence that existed just beneath the surface of reality, a mythic place where at any given moment a gazillion angels were dancing on the point of a needle, a trick which Malachi always assumed was done with mirrors, an illusionist's sleight of hand, which meant in all probability only one angel could do it, if that. Then Malachi tried to picture himself stealing away with Gisela to the Caribbean and starting over, a place like Cuba before Castro, but his mind went curiously blank. He could see nothing beyond his current circumstances, and for a moment he was confused. But then he understood. He had to finish out this scene. He was playing a role like all the others, the bartender, the accountant, the news reporter, the big-time Mexican movie director. How many others were there? The Velázquez brothers were relentless villains in this movie of their revenge, and Malachi knew it would only be a matter of time before they caught up with him. He felt the soft petals of sadness opening up, and then closing, a sad, lonely flower withering beneath the hot sun. As far as he could see, and he could cover vast distances in his mind's eye, the end, a most likely gruesome end involving, perhaps, a hail of bullets, was in sight. Briefly, Malachi wondered if you could survive a hail of bullets. What were the odds?

Then his two outer eyes caught the gleam of a lithographic poster taped to the window of a corner deli. This was the crossroads moment he had been hoping for. The poster was clearly designed for tourists, but it dazzled Malachi the way a painting sometimes dazzles. At the top it said "The Entire World is Welcome at the Allapattah Heritage & Puppet Festival." Beneath the words there was a reddish orange alligator dancing in a bluish-green sky. It was a very modern looking poster that eluded any post-modern interpretation. The alligator was made up of smaller reddish blocks and orange ones and a few yellow circles and triangles all mashed together to look like an alligator. There were several other alligators dancing with the red one, but they were white and looked sort of like clouds anyway.

He wondered if the alligators had anything to do with the puppets, or if they were meant to symbolize Florida in general. He was unable to connect the alligators to the concept of "The Entire World." Then he thought perhaps the alligators might have been swimming in the sky instead of dancing, particularly the way the red one was angled upwards, as if he was about to suddenly break through the surface of some primordial bluish-green ocean, but for an unknown reason this thought bothered him, so he stuck with dancing, his first inclination. There were no other images but the alligators, which also bothered him. And so for aesthetic reasons having to do with the alligators, Malachi almost did not glance at the bottom of the poster, which contained a list of festival events and the date. Malachi's destiny, however, was determined to assert itself, which is to say that Malachi thus found himself reading the list in spite of the art critic that inhabited his brain.

The festival would take place in August. It was going to be a very full day. There was going to be a big-head puppet parade in the afternoon, the parade of the Cabezudos, starting at the high school and heading down 18th Avenue to Duarte Park, followed by face painting and carnival rides and games and clowns for the kiddies, and music for everyone, which meant everything from Dominican rap to old-timey boleros to maybe some Latin-pop salsas, and there were going to be food vendors from all over the city, and fireworks at dusk. But this first part of the list did not appeal to Malachi in the least. It was the kind of list one might expect given the obviously flawed rendering of the alligators. But then Malachi noticed a row of glowing print in golden letters a few inches below the regular events that said "After Hours Activities" followed by "Midnight Dance Contest (Girls Only) at La Mamacita's" followed by "Special Surprise Appearance by the Internationally Acclaimed Film Star Salma de la Prada to promote her new film *The Sex Queen of the Moulin Rouge*."

Malachi stared at the glowing gold lettering for a long time. He realized he was staring at his own salvation. If he could only speak with Salma de la Prada, explain his situation, she would surely agree to star in a film for the Velázquez brothers. All he had to do was speak with her. And show her the script. Yes, he thought, the script was the key. It was a great script. Once Salma de la Prada read the script, his troubles would be over.

-33-

The day of the Allapattah Heritage & Puppet Festival was a routine day when you consider what generally goes on at such festivals. The sky was a robin's egg blue, and there was just enough of a breeze, at least until about two in the afternoon, to make the festival goers forget about the blazing white heat of the sun. All of the events described on the poster took place. All of the kiddies had their faces painted. All of the adults drank warm beer from silver kegs which arrived at three o'clock by truck. The fireworks went off without a hitch. The only blemish on the day as far as the general public was concerned, and this would, of course, depend upon your taste in music, occurred when one of the music groups, an up and coming gay Latin-reggae band from South Beach called Crew 429, failed to show up.

It is worth noting that the members of Crew 429 had supposedly been involved in a hit and run the night before, at least the van the lead singer was driving had been identified by an anonymous caller who referred to the vehicle as "that fag fuck truck," and so they were being detained by the Miami police from 10 AM onwards, which meant that the platform stage in Duarte Park where they were supposed to perform was empty from 3:15 till 4:00. Actually, detained was the polite, politically correct word used by the newspaper columnist who covered the police beat. A better word would have been handcuffed to the radiators in a dungeon of an interrogation room for several hours while the cops sifted through the various combinations of the truth, and then, because none of the combinations rang with the epic finality they were looking for, they tossed the Latin-reggae group into an overcrowded city holding cell — after the musicians had been given their orange jumpsuits but before being assigned a specific cell block — with one vagrant wino from Homestead who had gotten lost and five hardcore Mexican construction workers who had been laid off the previous day from one of the skyscraper projects downtown, their temporary unemployment being the result of a long-standing squabble between management and the electrician's union that continued to impact the viability of several development efforts, and who had then proceeded to get drunk and then robbed a string of 7-Elevens and then were picked up speeding on the Dolphin Expressway at two in the morning, and when they learned the next day that they were sharing a cell with a group of gay musicians, in spite of the fact that they all liked Latin-reggae, and a couple of the younger ones had even heard of Crew 429, which was rising on the charts all over south Florida and had a decent shot at national exposure because their agent was working tirelessly to get them on *The Today Show*, the Mexicans immediately projected their recent workplace frustrations and their latent homophobic hatreds onto the unsuspecting musicians from South Beach and beat them all to a bloody pulp, and it was only after the group was transferred in a fleet of ambulances to Jackson Memorial later that evening (after the custodial staff of the jail had complained about the pools of blood that were interfering with their ability to mop the hallways) that the District Attorney in the case learned that the band was not really from South Beach, that South Beach was probably just promotional cover, for two of the band members lived in Coral Gables with their parents, and the lead singer (a former tax attorney who gave up his practice in the hopes of achieving musical immortality, however long that might take) was from Surfside, where he lived in a pink stucco ranch surrounded by palm trees and dolphin statuary with his wife, a jet-black cat, a Chinese Shih Tzu adorned with red bows, and two small children who went to elementary school with the nephew of a State Senator.)

For Malachi, however, the Allapattah Heritage & Puppet Festival was far from routine. Nothing worked out the way he had expected, and this was true even days before the festival took place. He had intended on going alone, but then he mentioned something about the parade and the fireworks, the words were out of his mouth before he realized what he was saying. Gisela squealed with delight, a delicate, breathy squeal, almost surreal in the way it escaped her pouty lips. She said she loved parades more than anything and how fireworks were the most romantic thing ever. Malachi wasn't sure how he was going to take Gisela to the festival and the fireworks and at the same time hunt down Salma de la Prada, so he asked the two teachers to come along and run interference, but Soledad overheard. Soledad said a festival was exactly what Señor Mendoza needed, he hadn't been feeling too well lately, a festival like this might perk him up a little bit. "Yes, a festival would be just the thing," she said. "When my Xavier was a boy of fifteen his father took him to a festival in Zaragoza. Nine days it had lasted, but Xavier has forgotten most of it, which is why I want him to go with you to the Allapattah festival, because it might jog his memory."

And then just like that Soledad had started talking about that festival when Señor Mendoza was fifteen. She said it had been very hot that year, unusually hot for October. A very hot, dry wind had come out of the south and the people thought perhaps it was a sign, but they did not yet know its meaning. The first day had been a day of speeches, with the Mayor leading off. He had been a Colonel during the war against Morocco. Then one by one a collection of old, withered generals with strings of white hair combed sideways had their turns, all of them looking out on the crowded boulevard from a wooden platform with their medals like smashed bullets shining in the hot sun. It had looked like the Mayor and the generals were melting it was so hot, and the crowd was laughing quietly at that and perhaps even hoping for such a miracle, and then the soldiers had marched past, but they didn't look at the Mayor or the generals or even the crowd, they were more concerned with the fact that their own boots seemed to be melting. They were sticking to the pavement with each heavy step. And from somewhere a military band was playing a long-winded version of *Novio de la Muerte* (a song for brothels that has become our hymn to the Legion, that's what Xavier's father had said, and then he had spat on the ground), the sounds of rusty trumpets and ancient timpani coming at them in waves. But everything had sounded very far away, as if it were all under water, or trapped in a cavern in the mountains, or perhaps up in the clouds. That's how her Xavier had once described it. Then came the tanks, half a dozen tanks like little green bulldogs with black greasy smoke trailing like banners. The crowd along the boulevard had cheered and thrown their hats into the air and small boys ran back and forth across the boulevard, daring the tanks as if they were bulls instead of motorized bulldogs and picking up the hats that had fallen. The next day the generals were gone and the temperature was back to normal, and everyone then understood the significance of the sign of the strange heat, as they came to think of it, but they kept their thoughts to themselves. (And when Soledad said that she smiled softly at Malachi, and he suddenly wondered if she were recounting her own memories.) Then she said the rest of the festival had been a wonder of dancing and singing and festival games for the children and prayers to the Virgin Mari, and there had been bullfighting for three days, and afterwards some of the younger bullfighters had roamed the streets giving impromptu demonstrations with a few stray cows that had been left to wander for the children, and on the sixth day there had been a parade of giant puppets, and on the ninth day there was an offering of flowers and fruit at the end of the procession to the cathedral. It had been the greatest festival in the history of the city of Zaragoza, which is what everyone said, and afterwards no one remembered the Mayor and the generals and how they had been melting on the platform. That is what her Xavier had told her. That is how he remembered it, when his father took him down to Zaragoza oh such a very long time ago. Then Soledad had sighed. That is why he must go to this festival of the puppets up in Allapattah, she said, so he can relive once more the life he lived as a boy, so he can remember who he once was, who he is. So there was nothing Malachi could do. Señor Mendoza was going to the festival, Soledad would not go herself, she said she had no time for festivals, but her Xavier was going, this was to be a gift to her Xavier.

The parade began at 1:30, so they arrived at 1:00, thinking they were early, but the sidewalks had been packed since noon. They had to park in an alley behind a seafood market six blocks away and walk over. The parade route went past mostly parking lots and fences, and a few bungalows from the 1930s with red roofs and red awnings and the owners sitting out in their scrubby lawns in folding chairs drinking beer and smoking cigars. Some of the yards had nicely pruned tamarind trees or lime trees out front. Vendors wandered up and down the avenue selling balloons and plastic hoops that vibrated with light when you twirled them and ice cream and cotton candy and Italian ice and tacos and cartoonish looking party masks (mostly exotic animals such as jaguars, monkeys, parrots, alligators) and miniature banners that said Allapattah. Police waved through the cross traffic at the intersections. Mariachi music filled the air.

Malachi had decided that the best vantage point was at the park, where the parade ended, but there was no room to sit or even stand. Shimmering in the early afternoon sunlight was a sea of metal and plastic folding chairs and people sitting with their faces turned slightly away from the sun, some wearing brightly colored hats, listening to radio music, reaching into coolers and pulling out bottles of beer or hard cider or wine coolers or water, small children running in between the chairs, dogs barking. It almost looked like a mirage, or how the world looks when you are suffering from a debilitating migraine. So they decided to walk up to meet the parade (they could hear the rumble of Mexican horns in the distance like a thunderstorm rolling in from the bay). Malachi took the lead, with Gisela clinging to his arm and her tits bouncing uncontrollably with every step, followed by the two teachers and Señor Mendoza. At times it looked like the teachers were carrying the old man, his arms hooked around their shoulders and his legs bent up like some ancient Iberian king sitting on a throne, though his dangling feet were resting only on air.

As they walked up 18th Avenue, Malachi and the two teachers were having a passionate conversation about absolutely nothing. Gisela thought they sounded very intelligent, like professors or philosophers. It was hard to tell what Señor Mendoza thought.

The conversation while walking up 18th Avenue:

"I haven't slept in five days," said Malachi. "If that's what you mean."

"No, that isn't it at all," said the older teacher. "Sleep is a great gift. It is the greatest of pleasures."

"Except when you can't sleep," said the younger teacher.

"Or when you have better things to do," said Malachi, and a wild, hopeful look rotated across his eyeballs, like swift moving clouds, and then he buried his face in Gisela's tits for a moment and then jerked his head back, looking up through the trees at the blue sky passing by, laughing.

The two teachers were also laughing. Gisela was beaming. Señor Mendoza blinked happily, steadily, his open mouth was the memory of the sea, the smell of salt air, a cloud of seagulls sweeping past, an inarticulate longing he only half-remembered, which only a handful of others might even recognize (Soledad, Malachi perhaps, or a drunken Baptist minister from long ago) and which suddenly, strangely, miraculously, seemed on the verge of being fulfilled.

Up ahead you could see the first of the giant puppets pushing their way past the low hanging branches that arched over that particular section of the street. There were two of them, both twelve feet tall with over-sized heads, an aging prostitute with stringy blonde hair and thick droopy lips painted a bright red and bulging blue eyes, and a flamenco dancer with an exaggerated hook nose and an orange tiara with a bit of black lace hanging down to cover her eyes, and curlicue brown hair plastered to the sides of her elongated face. The puppets were weaving from one side of the street to the other, chasing after each other in tilted fashion, as if in a drunken but friendly stupor.

"But you'd climb on top of Gisela every night if you could,' said the older teacher. "We all would."

Gisela looked back, still beaming. The bouncy way she was walking seemed to become even bouncier.

"That's my baby," Gisela said, and she started nibbling on Malachi's ear and he winced.

"Pain or pleasure," said the younger teacher. "Sometimes you can hardly tell them apart."

"Ah, yes," said the older teacher. "The road to eternal damnation."

"But it is true."

They stopped talking for a while.

A Mariachi band was marching behind the prostitute and the dancer. The musicians were wearing white sombreros and white sequin-lined jumpsuits with black jackets and black boots, like eager waiters in a fancy hotel but with trumpets and guitars. They were following the path of the weaving puppets but stopping every time they saw a pretty girl so they could perform. They surrounded Gisela and the others with their gleaming gold trumpets and their gleaming gold-capped teeth and their polished guitars and sang to her an ancient love song that only Señor Mendoza seemed to recognize, and then Gisela gave the one closest to her a kiss and waved at the others and they went running after the puppets. No one remembered what they had been talking about before, so they started talking about beer.

"Aren't we heading in the wrong direction for the beer?" said the younger teacher.

"Man, there's beer everywhere you look," said Malachi.

And it was true, but it was all private beer, green bottles of *El Presidente,* gold and brown and black bottles of *Alhambra Negra,* the red bottles of *Alhambra Mezquita,* a kaleidoscope of colored glass. But it seemed unlikely the men who drank from those myriad bottles would give up their beer without a fight (and a fight in this neighborhood usually meant guns, with knives being reserved for cutting rings from fat fingers once the issue was no longer in doubt).

"Why don't we head back to the park?"

"Man, it too crowded."

"And some of us are feeling too lazy."

"But that's where the beer is."

"Man, the beer won't be there until later."

"Okay. Sure. That's where the beer will be."

"So relax, man. Anyway, there won't be any good Spanish beer with that truck, so it just as well."

"No. You're probably right. But I'm thinking quantity, not quality. That truck has just what I'm looking for."

"Ah, you mean it is loaded with silver kegs."

"That's exactly what I mean. Enough beer to drown your sorrows."

"When the truck arrives."

"Man, forget about them kegs. What you need is a good Spanish beer. A beer that's full of flavor. You won't find a good Spanish beer on that truck.

"Why not baby? What's wrong with Spanish beer?"

"Nothing babe. It because we all living in America."

"But baby, you can buy good Spanish beer in any grocery store. We go all the time."

"Yeah, sure babe. But it's too much money for festivals. They give you Coors and shit for festivals."

"Ooohhhh."

"Malachi, I didn't realize you were such a connoisseur."

"What's he mean, baby?"

"A connoisseur, in this case, my voluptuous young *chiquita,* is an expert who knows which among the many vagrant beer brands that litter our grocery store shelves we should drink and which we should forgo. His palette is an exceptionally well-tuned instrument."

"His what?"

"His tongue, my sweet young thing, his tongue."

"Ooohhh, yeeesss, that's my baby."

Gisela started tonguing Malachi's ear and giggling.

"You mean he's an expert when it comes to drinking beer? We're all experts when it comes to that."

"Ah, but only in the most obvious sense, my young friend. Malachi's abilities extend far beyond the world of beer."

The two teachers watched Gisela and Malachi for a moment. Her tongue was making a second pass at the dangling lobe of his right ear, an incredible feat of timing and dexterity given they did not break stride. Malachi buried his face once again in her tits.

"Far beyond, my young friend."

The conversation drifted into an explanation of the differences between the smoky sweet earthy tastes of the dark Alhambras, the true Spanish beers, compared to the paler versions they served in overpriced resorts in the Caribbean. Then they debated whether they should turn back and head to the park or keep walking. The younger teacher reminded them about the beer truck. He said he wanted to head back right then to be sure he was in line when the truck arrived. The older teacher decided he wanted wine instead of beer and voted for turning east on 35th street, there was a liquor store on 12th Avenue near the metro station. Gisela also voted for wine. Señor Mendoza had no opinion. He had been walking on his own for the last several blocks, a half step behind the two teachers. In all probability, he didn't even realize a conversation was taking place. He pulled out a small flask and drank from that, smiling happily at the two teachers every now and then and looking vaguely in the direction of the street. Malachi carefully noted every viewpoint (both expressed and unexpressed) and then said he wanted to see a bit more of the parade, and since the rest were not yet adamant in their thirst, they kept walking. But they were not walking as fast nor covering as much ground as they had been before. The earlier breeze had vanished and now the sun had become very hot. The air itself was bleeding with the heat, molecule by molecule dripping to the ground. Blue jays cried out in agony, their razor-like cries slicing through the air like radiation. Young men on both sides of the street began pouring bottled water over their heads and down their backs and encouraging the girls they knew (who were already wearing only bikinis) to strip to their waists, or at least give them a taste every once in a while, the heat was excruciating so they might as well make the most of it. And on top of the problem of the heat, which whitewashed the landscape and made for lazy walking, there was now also the problem of large gaps appearing between parts of the parade, since the police were having difficulty managing the flow of the cross-traffic. The whole world had suddenly become a fabulous and exalted dream, a fading, faded, somnolent black-and-white photograph that had begun to yellow, a memory of falling water, hypnotic, fragmented, eternal.

It was during one of these monochromatic lulls that a voice from the other side of the street called out.

"Oye Broken Bike," the voice said, and a sun-burnt shadow waved with great energy. Malachi did not recognize the voice but he waved back anyway.

Then another voice called out, "Oye Broken Bike, where you been?"

Malachi was struck by two anomalies, one, he was unable to pinpoint the location of the second voice, and two, the second voice was also unfamiliar. For one person to call out his name, shouting out a hello like a warning but without a care in the world, after Malachi had been months in seclusion, well, maybe that was mere coincidence. But a second voice overlapping the first, that seemed to Malachi slightly suspicious. Okay, more than slightly. Okay, it was downright sinister, the scent of it.

"What's the matter, baby?" Gisela said.

Malachi did not hear the question, nor did he react to the tone that lay beneath the question, the gentle, playful tone of a boisterous, untroubled lover (for surely there could be nothing seriously wrong in such a carnivalesque atmosphere). But Malachi heard nothing, even though Gisela's mouth was only inches away, poised, ready to nibble on his ear some more. His ears were at that moment engulfed in a crisis of indecision spurred on by a chorus of inner voices giving opinions on a range of topics from the wisdom of the creator in imbuing his creations with the instinct for self-preservation, to the contradictory sometimes ludicrous even self-defeating He-man urge to protect the weak (in this case Gisela) from certain death, to the numbing comfort that a case of beer might provide at two in the afternoon, to the irremediable danger of drowning in a sea of lacunal thinking. The hairs on the back of his neck were vibrating so intensely that he thought perhaps a rare earthquake had hit Miami or was about to hit or they were still in the throes of the disaster but time had frozen, as people say often happens during such disasters, which seemed to Malachi a plausible explanation as to why the white and gray stucco houses that lined the street and the apartment towers by the park had not yet crumbled into dust.

Malachi was ready to slide into the abyss. But then he remembered the lesson of the Greeks. Whatever was going to happen was going to happen. If he tried to alter his course mid-stream he would only cause more calamity for himself, as was the case with Oedipus, and the end would be the same. So there was nothing to worry about. His strategy would remain the same, it had to, and at this point he clamped down on the remaining critics that lived inside his brain, for they wanted him to consider the possibility that by remaining true to his original plan he was actually altering the course he was supposed to take, but he refused to be drawn into that level of abstract and ultimately meaningless discourse and from that point forward he did not waver in his conviction, he would find Salma de la Prada, if she was not part of the parade itself (presumably, which is to say fluttering feverishly along the sun-gilded edges of Malachi's imagination, she was languishing in an unfrozen and thoroughly seductive state of undress on a float somewhere up ahead in an effort to promote her new movie), then certainly later, at La Mamacita's, and then he would show her the script and that would be that. Salma de la Prada was still his salvation, no matter what the voices in his head were saying.

"Baby, come on baby, do you want something?"

The voices inside Malachi's head quieted down. (Gisela always had that effect.) The color of the landscape returned. Even the heat seemed less bewildering. Gisela repeated her question, staring up at his muteness. An ice cream vendor had pulled over to the side of the street and the two teachers and Señor Mendoza were getting Rocket Pops. Malachi said he didn't want anything and then he and Gisela started walking again. Señor Mendoza tried to talk the guy into three for the price of two, but the guy wouldn't budge. They caught up to Malachi and Gisela several minutes later, their Rocket Pops already beginning to drip, and by then the police had let through the next wave of the parade. They could see the shadowy charisma of three giant puppets bobbing a block away.

"What are they supposed to be?" said Gisela.

Malachi peered into the sun-blurry glare of the next block.

"Two matadors chasing a nun," said Malachi.

"Or perhaps she is leading them on," said the older teacher. "Hoping they will follow."

Everyone laughed.

The matador puppets wore crazed, triangular black hats and looked out at the world with droopy black eyes and droopy black moustaches and wide, piano teeth smiles, and they wore royal blue jackets with polished black buttons winking in the sunlight like the eyes of dazed rats. They seemed to be suffering from a radical form of hypomania. The nun wore a white habit that towered majestically above her head like a glowing apocalyptic cloud (and which, when the puppet was hanging in storage, had served as a roosting perch for incontinent warehouse pigeons, in fact, upon closer examination it was quite apparent that the habit was not as pristine as it had first appeared, bearing the streaked, unremovable stains of many generations of pigeons). The nun had the same brown curlicue hair plastered to the side of her face and the same hook nose and elongated features that distinguished the flamenco dancer. The two might have been sisters. All three puppets ran from one side of the street to the other in the same drunken, tilted fashion as the previous puppets.

Then there was a second Mariachi band, but this one was interested only in young, unattached men, and after them there was a high school marching band from Osseo, Minnesota. The band had come down primarily for a band festival in Orlando, but their band director had grown up in Allapattah and knew the festival organizers, who were eager to have a group from Minnesota, for now they felt justified in inviting the entire world to come and enjoy their festival, an invitation which had been a hallmark of their festival promotion campaign, but which they feared had left them open to charges of false advertising from their critics (which was a group of three social agency women with thirty-seven collective years' experience working for the Housing Authority who kept asking why the entire world would bother with Allapattah, what use was there in pretending, though precisely why this possible pretense bothered them they did not say; but with the inclusion of the Minnesota band the organizers felt thoroughly, even heroically vindicated in the presence of their critics and thereafter referred to the Minnesotans as a shining example of the reach of their promotional arm, as it were, and after that the festival organizers all but forgot that the Housing Authority women even existed.)

The Minnesota high-schoolers, in an effort to express their solidarity with the plight of the people of Allapattah (for they were from the Mid-West, not counting the director, and considered Miami a third-world country, a unit in their eleventh grade history textbook), wore uniforms with a decidedly "Spanish" look specifically designed for the festival, which is to say they wore tall visored hats with gold braiding on the sides and gold medallions in the middle and dark blue brocaded jackets with red lapels and gold buttons like capped teeth and neatly pressed blue pants, a lighter blue than the jackets. They looked something like soldiers in the Mexican National Army under Santa Anna, which very much pleased the festival organizers for the reasons already mentioned.

After the band from Osseo there was a small funeral wagon, a plain black color with maroon trim and a narrow seat for the driver and a wider one for funeral guests (though no guests were present) and iron-rimmed wagon wheels. The wagon was pulled by a mule, which was following a feedbag attached to a bar that hung just out of reach. Every so often the driver of the wagon pulled the feedbag close enough for the mule to grab a mouthful and then he pushed it away and laughed a strange, greedy laughter that swirled above his head for a while like a geyser and then the laughter faded and there was only the sound of the mule's hooves on the pavement.

There was also a narrow black box in the wagon with a modern reproduction of a 19th century Mexican flag draped over top. Presumably the box was a coffin, but there was no sign hanging from the sides of the wagon to indicate who or what was supposed to be inside the box, but perhaps no sign was necessary, for the wagon seemed at least spiritually aligned with the band that had preceded it, and so metaphorically it was clear, at least to Malachi and a few others in the crowd, that the box contained the remains of Santa Anna's infamous leg, which was a casualty of a war that began because five soldiers stole a few croissants from a bakery in Mexico City, and which was later buried, in spite of the widespread belief that Santa Anna had lost his mind, with full military honors in 1838 (or 1839, depending upon your sources).

After the wagon, there were several late model convertibles displaying local tomato queens or orange princesses (along with advertising appropriate for the sponsors of said royalty) and then a couple of ambulances with the EMTs waving happily, relieved, perhaps, that they were not on duty until later that evening and sneaking sips of beer from bottles they kept between their legs.

Then there were a few more high school bands, and then the last of the giant puppets, a lecherous old red-eyed bishop wearing a crooked miter, it might even have been perched on his elongated head in sideways fashion, or even backwards, and he was holding up a tarnished crucifix in one hand as he weaved his way back and forth across the street. One could imagine he was chasing after the nun that had taken up with the matadors, for he seemed to be weeping tears of an inconsolable sadness, though whether he was sad because he had he truly loved the nun and she had rejected him after an unsatisfactory performance or because he had not yet taken her to bed was unclear. A magnificent black bull with gleaming white horns and bulging black eyes followed the inconsolable bishop. The bull was not weeping tears, indeed, his eyes seemed to be glistening with what could only be described as dark, incendiary rage (though blind fury would have served just as well), and one presumed that his rage was actually directed at the vanished matadors as symbols of the ritualized slaughter of countless innocent victims over countless defeated centuries and that he (the bull) was only chasing after the bishop because there was no one else so close to his horns and his horns had been recently sharpened and needed to be used.

After the puppets there was a third Mariachi band, which seemed interested only in playing music for small children under the age of five, and they sang in a language that no one but the children recognized, which suggested, among other interpretations, that they were singing in the language now used by the angelic hosts and originally used only by God himself, a claim which sounded suspiciously like an argument once advanced by a French abbot named Diharce De Bidassouet in the 19th century in his *History of the Catabrians*, who claimed that the language of heaven was Euskera, the language of the Basques, and who was later ridiculed by those who believed that God communicated telepathically so He had no need for a spoken language.

Then there were several elaborately designed but immediately forgettable floats, except for one, and this one received a great deal of attention because no one was quite clear about what it was depicting. It seemed at first blush to be merely a confused representation of an ancient fable from Iberia, but then after the first blush had deepened into something resembling a drunken stupor there came a second blush, and it suddenly seemed less a single fable than a series of fables mashed together, as is the case with all of the world's dominant religions, though some might argue that the whimsical, random sense of chaos generated by simple folktales and a belief in magic (which was clearly present in the artistic tone of the float in question) is no match for the sublimely ridiculous, which hovers above the great religions like a cloud of radio static, but of course Malachi was not concerned with any theological debate about the artist's' intentions, for he had already moved to the second blush stage, his lips quivering as he studied each scene: there was a giant moon near the back of the float with a light bulb that was supposed to make it glow but the light bulb didn't work, and printed below the moon were the words "guardian of death," and the lips of the moon were pursed, as if it were whistling; and staring up at the moon, but at the front end of the float, was a young girl with long golden hair and a golden comb in her hand, and she seemed to be listening to whatever it was the moon was whistling; and in between the girl and the moon were dozens of painted scenes, tiny miniatures that could only be glimpsed as the float rolled past, a labyrinth of images that were virtually undecipherable if you were standing along the sidewalks or on the edges of the lawns or in the middle of the parking lots, scenes of sea snakes swimming in stormy seas and flaming trees uprooted by crazed peasants and white clouds and rainbows painted into green skies and a flock of birds, pelicans or cockatoos by the look of them, flying up from the desiccated remnants of a cornfield, as if they had been startled out of a winter's nap (though why pelicans or cockatoos should have been taking a nap in a winter cornfield was a mystery), and there was a strange woman with long golden, flowing hair (like the girl, but older) riding across the green sky in a chariot drawn by four white horses with golden plumes, and another strange woman with golden hair (possibly the sister of the first one, but more likely the result of an artist who could only draw one kind of woman) riding a magnificently imagined white ram into a mountain pool; and in between the pictures (or paintings or miniature dioramas) there were all sorts of woodland creatures mixed in with demonic animal genies with horns and pitchforks and deformed feet, though in truth it was sometimes difficult to tell these two groups apart, and after the float of the whistling moon, which was probably the best name one could give such a float, Malachi found himself listening (or perhaps he was only half listening at this point) to the music of several more high-school marching bands (this particular parade was nothing if not a musical extravaganza, though each new band seemed little more than an echo of the previous ones), and then he paid homage to a few more tomato queens and orange princesses (he quickly realized that the orange princesses outnumbered the tomato queens by a two-to-one margin, and he wondered about the stunning discrepancy in the numbers for a while, for the orange crop the last few years had been quite poor).

It was at this point that Malachi started laughing, a low, murmuring kind of laughter that had nothing to do with tomatoes or oranges or strange woman with flowing golden hair. It was the kind of laughter that some would call lunatic, but which was really just a unique blend of relief, happiness, and incredulity, for there, bringing up the rear of the parade, he saw a lavish sequence of floats depicting scenes from *The Sex Queen of the Moulin Rouge*, and on the very last of these, languishing on a red velvet sofa beneath the blazing white heat of the sun, just as Malachi had imagined, though perhaps not quite so clearly, was the ravishing, beguiling (and practically naked) Salma de la Prada herself.

-34-

There is an ancient Iberian proverb (with ancient being a relative term and Iberian not altogether accurate) that says that the longer one dreams about something in the future, the more difficult it is to react decisively when that future suddenly begins to unfold. The same could also be said for those who dream with great intensity. It is like two sides of the same coin.

Malachi thought he was prepared for his dream to unfold. He had brought along the now dog-eared copy of the Velázquez brothers' movie script (it was back in the pocket of his safari vest), and he was armed with the movie prop gun, which was still safely stuffed down the front of his black bicycle shorts, resulting in an enormous, superhuman bulge that didn't bother him in the least.

All of which is to say that the moment Malachi saw Salma de la Prada languishing on that red velvet sofa on the very last float of the Allapattah Heritage & Puppet Festival parade, his understanding of what to do next deserted him (an understanding, it is worth noting, that some would call courage, and that Nietzsche would have defined as the will to power, or in this case the lack of that will, a concept which makes the most appearances in his book *Beyond Good and Evil*, and which that bastard Adler later turned into a commercialized pop-culture cliché referenced in dozens of poorly written, useless books on how to strengthen your self-esteem after divorce or how to parlay good grades in middle tier colleges into extravagant careers on Wall Street or in the Foreign Service or when to select a red wine with fish and in what company or if it's usually better to leave it to the sommelier because that is, after all, what he gets paid to do). So Malachi's courage deserted him (fled is more like it), but not in the overly noisy, vainglorious manner of, say, a stampeding herd of zebras (if zebras running from lions can in any way be considered vainglorious), but in a gentle, muted, stealthy fashion, as if fearing discovery, the way water seeps through limestone, a slow, inexorable draining of energy.

But while Malachi stood cemented to the sidewalk, a barnacle now in every meaning of the word, pandemonium broke out all around him. Indeed, one could say without the slightest hint of exaggeration that the sighting of Salma de la Prada ushered in an improbable sequence of events (which one could consider as an example of destiny regardless of whether or not God and his angels knew anything about it) that resembled more than anything else the mad-capped slapstick of a Marx Brothers' movie (*A Night at the Opera* comes to mind). Or perhaps what happened next had a slightly more sinister tone. Or perhaps a mixture of the two. In any event, there was a great deal of chaos.

As if reading from cue cards, the crowd along both sides of the street swerved closer to *The Sex Queen of the Moulin Rouge* floats, creating a bottleneck which forced the first of the floats to come shuddering to a halt. The crowd was so close they could touch the outer cloth fringe which blew in the breeze that had suddenly reasserted itself.

The bodyguards who accompanied the floats were lounging along the edges in the same languid manner as Salma de la Prada, chatting happily with each other in German (they were all employed by a movie star security company headquartered, for poorly conceived strategic reasons, in Freiburg, Germany) or talking on their cell phones to lonely girlfriends or even lonelier ex-girlfriends heading at that very moment to evening shifts in cheap restaurants or adult movie houses in Düsseldorf or on their way home from small boutiques on Kronenstraße in Saarbrücken where they sold second-hand clothes or perfumes or designer shoes to the busloads of Italian and Portuguese tourists that came by way of Luxembourg every Saturday. But as the crowd surged forward, the bodyguards quickly deployed themselves, sensing a vague threat to the safety of their movie star queen.

There were two groups of bodyguards. The first, an outer ring, was comprised of twenty or thirty bulging ex-soccer players, probably midfielders all born in Freiburg, but with black hair and biceps like boulders or decorative cornice pieces in the Gothic style or perhaps slightly deflated leather soccer balls from the 1930s, and this outer ring pushed back against the surging crowd, who had probably just wanted to catch a glimpse of Salma de la Prada's obvious nakedness — she was wearing only a bright red thong and a pair of red sandals edged with fake red poodle fur — or else they had been carried along unwittingly by those with voyeuristic intent; but the German ex-soccer players were not about to take any chances, especially in a pseudo Latin-American neighborhood riddled with pockets of Dominican and Cuban immigrants (the black haired Germans, who presumably lived in the thriving, efficient, eco-friendly, newly refurbished working class neighborhoods of either Reiselfield or Vauban, viewed the immigrant populations in every country except Germany as unrepentant and profligate exiles). And so they (the outer ring) brandished an up till then unseen assortment of batons, clubs, Billy clubs, crowbars, small sections of rusty pipe, cudgels with ornately carved ivory handles, golf clubs, the slightly curved leg of a Biedermeier period console table from Berlin, a few baseball bats, even an antique Alpine walking stick one of the bodyguards had stumbled upon while vacationing in the Otz Valley, warning the surging crowd (which immediately stopped surging) with vigorous shakes and unexpected balletic gestures and possibly polite (hopefully) but mostly inscrutable smiles.

The inner ring was made up of ten crackerjack blond-haired behemoths who had relocated to Freiburg from the Baltic coast near Lübeck, all of them former Olympic swimmers dressed in Speedos, flip-flops, and tight-fitting Spandex t-shirts with the word FÜKKENRÜKEN in fluorescent blue lettering written across their chests and then a graphic of one stick figure swimming desperately after another stick figure and little wavy lines to represent the water, and then the slogan *"Gehen Sie ficken einen Schwimmer."* They (the inner ring) stared out at the swerving, surging, and then partially subdued crowd from behind amber-tinted sunglasses, forming a tight bubble around their queen, as tight as possible without blocking her view of her adoring public. They had obviously been instructed never to block her view.

One of them, presumably the head-honcho (all the others called him Herr Konrad), was reading a dog-eared copy of *Biedermann und die Brandstifter*, a play written in 1958, which his father had given him when he entered the Gymnasium near Sharbeutz hoping that one day he might become a lawyer or an advertising man or perhaps a poet or at least a well-respected journalist, all of which he gave up when he realized he did not possess the talent for verbal ambiguity and the creative re-imagining of events those professions required and so focused instead on a career in security; the book was the only thing that remained of his days at the Gymnasium, and he thought it was a thinly disguised philosophical reflection on the relationship between honest men (*Biedermann*) and arsonists (*die Brandstifter*) in a post-apocalyptic society, not unlike Ray Bradbury's *Farenheit 451*, but it was (is) really a satiric exploration of the nature of Fascism in Nazi Germany.

Life is so strange. It was hard not to think of the Nazis when you stared at the German bodyguards, even though there was no doubt whatsoever that a movie star security company from Germany would never employ anyone even remotely connected with the Nazis.

The head honcho bodyguard was quite happy to let his subordinates handle whatever came their way, and in truth, the remaining bodyguards of this inner circle were quite capable.

They glanced at Salma de la Prada now and then to make sure she was safely seated in the middle of her red velvet sofa, her naked body reflected in their sunglasses, a miniature version repeated eighteen times like a digital echo, squirming and smiling and waving and blowing kisses with puckered lips and laughing soundlessly and then receding, a tiny dot in the center of each plastic lens, and then vanishing as the bodyguards turned their attention to the crowd once again, like falling into a black hole.

Had the bodyguards not been wearing these sunglasses, which were designed specifically to filter out unwanted UV light as well as eliminate the blinding flashes that accompany a gun battle, their grim, impassive staring faces would have suggested a great inconsolable melancholy, or at least a temporary resignation, in the way that serial killers or storm troopers or criminal circus clowns suddenly deprived of breakfast are temporarily resigned. Clutching what appeared to be Uzis, they gave the distinct impression that they would willingly, eagerly, even joyfully, mow down anyone who came on board the floats uninvited.

Actually, this impression of unrestrained (heroic?) violence was more like a scent that emanated from the dilated pores of their exposed skin — mostly the pinkish-beige skin of their rippling, swimmer's legs (where the skin was already starting to peel from the merciless sun), but also the dry, cracked skin on the backs of their necks and the taut, bullet-proof skin along the bottom two-thirds of their bulging, improbable arms — the scent drifting unseen on the resurgent breeze, the way pollen drifts, or nettles, or mace, or the microscopic spores of a virulent disease.

No one could later recall the scenes the floats were trying to depict.

No one took any pictures of the floats, which suggests that the chaos of the parade occurred in the days before cell phones came equipped with cameras, or, alternatively (or alternately, depending upon your point of view, whether you live within the boundaries of time and space or outside those boundaries, what some would call the sphere of the imagination and others would call eternity), that in the absurd (but also surreal) anxiety of the moment, everyone armed with a camera/cell phone, or even a plain old camera for that matter, simply forgot that public disturbances of any kind had become an opportunity for the swelling ranks of unpaid photojournalists everywhere.

No one took any pictures.

Besides, the people who were closest could not even see. The scent from the inner ring of bodyguards had gotten into their eyes and their eyes were stinging, and some even thought their eyeballs were melting, and they were all rubbing their eyes and blinking back tears, but all they could see was a black circle with fire burning along the outer edge, the glowing corona of all their accumulated fears, their paranoias, their manias, their unbidden bouts of madness, their tucked away sense of perpetual loathing, whatever they might be feeling guilty about. It was like staring into the abyss of the collective unconscious. What some would call the collective soul. What others would call Sheol, and others Hades, both neutral holding cell type places where the souls of the recently departed await (hopefully) some sort of judgment before ascending (their hope, as opposed to descending) to Nirvana or paradise or Abraham's bosom, which leads one to imagine a sort of giant amusement park with couples taking boat rides through dark tunnels with appropriate romantic background music and trying their luck at skill games like Jacob's Ladder and devouring tons of cheap lemonade and ice-cream and clouds of cotton candy, and no matter what they eat they are always twenty-five years old and reflect picture-perfect health, without even the fear of tooth decay, because their bodies (and teeth) are now incorruptible, and, depending upon who you talk to, even unbelievers can get into this amusement park, assuming, of course, that they recant their unbelief, and who wouldn't recant given the alternative, which, according to some, is a place of general wickedness, like Gehenna (which is not to be confused with a hip tattoo parlor whose owners picked the name from a list of mythological places), where apparently there is no indoor plumbing and everyone sits around in their own watery, muddy filth and the stench is overpowering, and yet it is also a very dry place, which is something of a paradox, where the rain turns to black ash as it falls and gets into your lungs and breathing becomes very difficult; or if you were terribly evil (which from Dante's perspective meant you had rebelled against some kind of ultimate authority, which sort of makes Dante a pre-Fascist; then again, maybe everyone is a Fascist at heart, or would be, if they were the ones in positions of authority) then descending would mean a place of eternal torment and damnation like, for example, the Lake of Fire, which might be a great sea of fire where fire flows and drips and falls from the sky like rain or water or molten lead, a place where everyone is suffering from a great, burning, unquenchable thirst — which certain progressive theologians have argued is simply a thirst for the presence of God which can now never be slaked, but which others have taken quite literally, which may explain why the Egyptians and some rebellious Vikings and a few overly ambitious Polynesians and many, many others throughout the centuries packed their canoes or their symbolic canoes (sarcophagi) or their rafts or their seagoing ships with all sorts of provisions, including (presumably) jars of water, for the journey into (or through? or beyond?) the afterlife, because you can never be sure where you will end up but you certainly want to be prepared if you end up in a place where the souls of the damned and all sorts of fallen angels, their bodies blackened and charred from an eternity of overpowering heat, float about, writhing in agony, or at least shame.

Happily, not everyone went blind.

Señor Mendoza thought he smelled the sweet smell of gardenias from his boyhood (or perhaps it was from Soledad's girlhood), and breathing in deeply this heady aroma he stepped fearlessly, even brazenly, towards the line of floats, towards the last float in particular, unconcerned about the amber-tinted bubble of danger represented by the inner ring of bodyguards (who were at that very moment shifting over from single shot mode to automatic) or the possibility of intransigent, punitory blindness, or perhaps he was just unaware. The younger teacher stepped after him, trying to pull him back.

Later, people described hearing a short burst of popping sounds that reminded them of the mechanical whirr of dozens of motorcycles roaring past, and then several abrupt clicks, the echo lingering, and then dissolving. Those who were still trying to catch a glimpse of the naked Salma de la Prada, which is to say those who had not been overpowered (and then blinded) by the scent of violence emanating from the bodyguards, later said they saw flashes of light as bright as solar flares and white smoke curling up into the air, and some said they could smell burning rubber, and others said it was a burnt diesel smell, and some said it smelled vaguely like Linseed oil, and others thought it was coffee beans roasting, or maybe peanuts.

Some heard voices jabbering in German. Or maybe it was a German-sounding laughter (haughty? robust? stoic? efficient?).

A few at the back of the crowd looked up, following the paths of what they assumed were bullets, and saw tiny black holes appearing at random in the blue sky and the sky shuddering and a sludgy, black liquid falling to the earth like muddy drops of rain.

People started to run.

People started to run as if they were ants scattering before the blackness of a coming storm.

People started to run as if a siren had sounded and the skies were suddenly and mysteriously black with airplanes from the Second World War and the breeze (which had now become an enormous wind, a night terror shaking the dust of fallen stars from its wings) was the sound of falling bombs.

The older teacher and Gisela ran off in search of wine, the older teacher making obscene remarks having nothing to do with the parade or the unmoving line of Moulin Rouge floats or the possibility that the bodyguards were firing their Uzis at the sky just for fun, and Gisela giggling in response to everything he said, her tits bouncing in wildly exaggerated fashion.

Three members of the inner ring, thirty-three-and-a-third percent of the field of towheaded warriors, leapt off the last float and pushed their way through the retreating crowd in the direction of Señor Mendoza and the younger teacher.

Small clouds of white Uzi smoke hovered all around, the bright sunlight streaming in through the clouds but then changing direction, becoming a thousand points of beaming, refracted sunlight, a soft, hazy, silent explosion.

Even those who were not blind found it difficult to see.

Some passed out on the ground, perhaps from gulping in too much smoke, or perhaps they suffered from an underlying and heretofore unknown heart condition, or perhaps because they thought the end of the world, a topic that had received a lot of press of late, was now becoming a reality.

Then the smoke began to clear.

To Malachi it looked like the world was now under water. The floats had started moving again, and the bodyguards were once again lounging about on the edges of the floats and chatting lazily in German and laughing even when nothing funny had been said, but everything was happening slowly, with the deliberate, exaggerated, rounded movements and twisted facial expressions of slow-motion, underwater cinematography.

Señor Mendoza and the younger teacher were now sitting next to Salma de la Prada on the red velvet sofa. Salma de la Prada was whispering into Señor Mendoza's ear and laughing softly, or perhaps cooing, her hands placed casually on his leg, and his face was glowing with the ecstasy that the words of Salma de la Prada promised. The younger teacher was staring at the German bodyguards who were surveying a once again well-behaved crowd.

Malachi took a single step, as if to follow the float, as if he had suddenly remembered he wanted to speak with Salma de la Prada, but then he collided with the owner of an unseen voice who was calling out his name with increasing volume.

"*Hola,* Broken Bike, *hola,* Broken Bike, Broken Bike!"

It was as if the voice was trying to wake him up.

"Where are you going in such a hurry, Broken Bike?"

Malachi stared at the unrecognizable face. He had no idea how to respond.

"*Hola,* Broken Bike, what's the matter with you?"

There was a short silence.

"Broken Bike?"

And then Malachi recognized the voice, and thus the face. Both belonged to his neighbor three doors down. But Malachi still did not know what to say. He was not even certain if saying something was required.

"It is still the same with you, eh, Broken Bike. Always you are disappearing into the darkness to watch a picture show. Never looking out at the world. Never noticing what is real. What is right in front of you. Hah! And now your movie star is right there in front of you and you do nothing. Hah! Your sex queen goddess and you forget your tongue. Oh, Broken Bike, it is very funny. I am sorry but it is very funny." The woman began to laugh, a series of short staccato bursts like exploding suns, and Malachi noticed she was wearing the same flowery dress she wore when pruning her azaleas, but he did not think this strange. "You are like all young men," she said, after the laughter had subsided. "You do not know what to do, what to say. Life is gibberish to your ears, an epic giglamesh, a sweet, musical *glíglico* that you do not understand. Such a pity. It is a wonder the army of your sex queen movie star did not feel sorry for you and put you out of your misery." Then the woman's tone changed, somewhat abruptly, but Malachi did not think this was strange either. He was sort of expecting it. "But there are many more dangers to consider, Broken Bike," she said, and her pupils narrowed to the point of disappearing, leaving only two flinty, colorless discs, like the eyes of a blind person. "But you already know this." She took his arm and led him away from the noise of the parade route and the faint smell of a gun battle, and he went without complaint, without a sound, not because he had given up or had nothing better to do or because he knew she was right, all of them good reasons. Malachi went with her because he suddenly realized that God works in mysterious ways. "You can speak with your sex queen movie star later," she said. "But not now. Now there are too many eyes watching, too many ears listening."

They were headed for a dive that was once the talk of the town, she said, it used to be called La Campana, it was very fancy, but now it is nothing, a sleepy ghost next to an auto parts store and junkyard on one side and a fenced-in parking lot on the other. It was just a few blocks away, she told Malachi, and he had not known about it before (a surprising revelation), and when they got there it seemed to be less than nothing, an abandoned shadow of a three-story building that may or may not have once gleamed like a palace in the sunlight, but it was now clearly less than nothing with its boarded up windows and vaguely pink stucco crumbling in places and the perimeter littered with broken glass and empty beer cans and clouds of graffiti sprayed here and there, wherever the graffiti artists could reach, slogans and curses and derogatory epithets and soulful laments and declarations of eternal love written in bright greens and dusty blues and swirling, dazzling blacks and deep, bloody reds. A rusted neon sign like an old movie house marquee was loosely bolted to the corner on the parking lot side. The neon sign hadn't worked in years and looked like it might come crashing down with the next strong gust of wind.

-35-

The crumbling structure that used to be La Campana:

Malachi follows his neighbor from three doors down without question. He follows her up a set of crumbling stairs.

She stops a moment to stare at a small tarnished brass bell fixed to the exterior. So he stops. He hears her mumble something under her breath, almost like cursing, and then she pushes her way through a rotting, mahogany door that is hanging by a single hinge. He follows her through the door. She stops again, as if she has lost her bearings. Her head turns this way and that, but there is very little light. All Malachi is able to make out are the gray shadows of a set of stairs that end in absolute darkness, and on the tiled floor, perhaps because it is illuminated by a narrow wedge of afternoon sunlight, he notices dozens of tiny black scuff marks or burn marks. He wonders what kind of fire would cause such markings. Then he notices that his neighbor is also staring at the burn marks. Perhaps she, too, is wondering what had caused them. Or perhaps she is remembering. Then she starts whispering, or someone starts whispering. '*Pedir la luna,*' the whispering voice says. The words are filled with a haunting sense of great sadness. Then Malachi follows his neighbor from three doors down towards a Spanish-style archway with the paint peeling. The archway marks the entrance to what was once an elegant bar.

Malachi does not know how much time has passed since they left the parade. They are now sitting at a small café table in the once elegant bar. But it is a strange place. It is just a single narrow room, like a waiting area in a railway station from the 1940s. You can see a bare, pale patch behind the counter where there had once been a mirror. You can see other tables here and there. You can see where the padded booths that once lined the wall have been ripped out. You can see the bare, light patches where they were. Like tombstones in a cemetery, Malachi thinks. The smell of death is everywhere. He wonders what kind of place La Campana had been in its glory days. It is hard to guess. For one thing, there is not much light. Just the gloomy, diffuse dimness of being indoors on a bright sunny day and the soft, far-away orange glow of two glass globes fixed to the ceiling. For another thing, the bar is the only part of this gigantic, dilapidated pink stucco behemoth that he has seen.

The bar is empty except for the two of them and a lonely fat man of a bartender who spends all of his time sitting at a table in the middle of the bar watching a television (cartoons) perched precariously on a small diagonal shelf in the corner above an ancient relic of a cash register. The cord from the television drops down into the abyss behind the register. Next to the register there are several more glass shelves that end abruptly where the bare, pale patch begins. The shelves are empty except for a couple of bottles of Suisse La Bleue and a single bottle of 1691 Clos de Griffier Vieux Cognac. The bottle of cognac is bone dry. It was polished off years ago. Yes, Malachi thinks, it must have been a very elegant bar indeed, although it could also have been a café or a two-star (one-star?) restaurant or even a private club. With the windows boarded up and the lack of good interior lighting it is difficult to make a good guess. Malachi suddenly feels as if he has been sitting in this bar for centuries. The sounds from the festival have hidden themselves away like mice. Malachi sighs, his open mouth like a clock ticking, begins to form a word but then the word dissolves. The clock of his open mouth is still ticking.

The woman says her name is Isidora. It is a good thing she says this, for Malachi was beginning to wonder. Nothing exists unless it has a name. Someone said that once. His grandfather, perhaps, although he doesn't ever remember meeting his grandfather, or a nun he did meet on a bus going to the zoo, or a German tourist who stopped him just outside the Armani store at the airport mall (Malachi was scouting talent) to ask in broken English where the taxis were. So there she is, Isidora, an ancient Spanish name which must mean something beyond the mere fact of granting his neighbor corporeal existence, Malachi is certain of this (as much as one can be certain of anything, even death), he is on the verge of remembering, it is on the tip of his tongue, but no, he has lost it. Then the woman, Isidora, whom Malachi has known previously only as his neighbor from three doors down, the woman in the flowery dress he has noticed on occasion, however incidentally, out in her front yard with pruning shears pruning her azaleas, disappears through a black curtain near the back of the bar (or café or restaurant or private gentlemen's club).

Isidora's departure is followed by an excruciatingly lengthy period of absolute silence. Even the bartender's cartoon characters have become mute. Malachi suddenly realizes that the floor is tilted at roughly a forty-five-degree angle, which would seem to defy the laws of physics, at least in south Florida, and for the briefest of moments Malachi wonders about this, but he concludes, quickly and without any additional inner commentary, that the universe, reality, if you will, at this particular juncture of time and space, is itself tilted, simple as that. Then the general noise of the universe reasserts itself. Malachi imagines that he hears the sound of someone tiptoeing so as not to attract any unwarranted attention. To Malachi each tiny footstep pricks his brain as if dozens of tiny suspension feeders, most likely goose barnacles, have cemented themselves to his skull (the weakest part along the sphenoparietal suture) and are in the process of cracking it open. Then Malachi hears the sound of a door opening and closing. The barnacles pause in their busy work. The clock is no longer ticking. A fog of confusion spreads out across his shoulders and then filters into his lungs, like a great chill. Then Malachi orders a beer and the fat man disengages himself from his cartoons (it is an awkward moment) and brings Malachi a green bottle without a label and then re-enters the world of his cartoons. Malachi drinks from the green bottle while he is waiting for Isidora to return. The pale liquid inside the bottle doesn't taste like beer at all. After a while the fat man leaves through the same black curtain as Isidora, but he leaves the cartoons on. After a while Malachi forgets he is waiting and becomes absorbed in the cartoons.

Malachi found himself watching a very strange cartoon indeed. He did not catch the title. It was a silent cartoon, except for a little background music (symphonic, from the 1950s) and occasional sound effects (squeaky, balloon sounds and bizarre moaning sounds and cars whizzing by and a crash and a strange ethereal buzzing sound and the sounds of war, buildings falling to the ground, explosions, that sort of thing). Malachi assumed it was a French cartoon. It opened with a woman standing on a partially deflated leather ball or a squishy but surprisingly durable balloon, but she wasn't directly on top, she was sort of leaning out at an angle, like a figure stuck on top of a cake, only it was a ball (or a balloon) so she couldn't help listing to one side, and then you could see that there were hundreds of balls or squishy balloons each with a woman sticking out from the curvature, a subtle commentary perhaps on the theory of multiple universes or the ethics of cloning or perhaps even a critique of Fascism. Yes, Malachi was certain it was a French cartoon. At the twenty second mark you could see a row of something behind each solitary woman, like a tiny forest or a mountain range, but then the camera zoomed in on one of the balls (balloons) and you could see on the other side of the woman a town spread out against the sky like the old mining towns in Colorado in the 1870s. The opening sequence took forty seconds. Then you could see a farmer from the old town (where else could he have come from?), but he was a very poor farmer, or perhaps still a novice, which seemed odd given how old he looked, but nothing he planted seemed to grow, and he tried everything he could think of to make his plants grow, but his ideas were flawed, like supporting the leafy appendages of his plants with sticks (what kind of plants were these anyway?), or hammering nails into the leaves and hanging a giant magnet above the garden to attract growth, this didn't make a whole lot of sense to Malachi, and because nothing worked, the farmer started weeping, copious tears, a flood of tears, and that was the magic formula, the tears. At the four-minute mark the farmer's plants all of a sudden began to grow, and they became super-sized plants, the kind that would win prizes (maybe not the Grand Prize, but certainly a host of Blue Ribbons) at any county fair, and the farmer was quite pleased with himself and he was humming and he did a little happy dance and the background music sounded jovial the way it does on a carousel, but also kind of sad, like an old Edith Piaf song. But at the five minute mark the tone of the music changed to something more sinister to call attention to the fact that the farmer's tears had also caused the snails, which no one had noticed up till that point in the cartoon, to grow as large as tanks, most of them, and some even larger, and then the snails began to attack the town, devouring everything in their path and smashing cars and the townspeople were getting squished, and then at the six minute mark the giant snails were all of a sudden zooming down city streets, knocking down skyscrapers, like they were alien spacecraft intent on conquering the Earth, and it seemed to Malachi that the animator had lost control of his cartoon at that point, as if he had been working for hours and hours and needed a break so he decided to watch *War of the Worlds* (the 1953 black-and-white movie version starring Gene Barry and Ann Robinson) and when he returned to his animator's desk he had forgotten where his story was going so he filled in the gaps with images from the movie. That was the gist of the cartoon, as far as Malachi could tell.

The cartoon was eleven minutes long.

At the seven-minute mark the giant snails raided a brothel

and carried off some of the girls and apparently ate them.

At the eight-minute mark someone pushed their way through the rotting mahogany door out front and the interior of the bar was suddenly illuminated by a blast of sunlight that made it difficult to see what was going on in the cartoon, and then the diffuse gloominess of the bar returned. A young man about twenty-five came in and sat down next to Malachi, but he didn't say a word. Malachi wasn't sure what he had missed.

At the nine-minute mark the snails had apparently won the war, but just as in the H. G. Wells story, their victory was short-lived. They collapsed moments after the last of the people had run off into the mountains to hide. Dozens of snails were lying in heaps, and then time speeded up and their giant snail flesh rotted away and their shells crumbled. Malachi wondered if maybe Salvador Dali was the animator.

At the ten-minute mark Malachi heard the side door open and close and then the shuffling of heavy feet, and then a couple of figures sat down at the counter, but Malachi couldn't see who they were.

At the ten minute, thirty seconds mark the camera zoomed in once again on the farmer, who was busy trying to get another group of plants to grow. He seemed to have forgotten about the effect of his tears on the first group. Or maybe he had learned his lesson with the snails. Malachi wasn't sure. The meaning of the cartoon kept shifting. It looked like the farmer was now living in the desert. Or maybe he had been in the desert the whole time. Perhaps that was the source of his difficulty.

At the eleven-minute mark the credits began rolling and the young man sitting next to Malachi pushed his chair back from the table as if he needed some extra room to breathe. The young man (twenty-five? thirty?) was wearing a silvery-colored designer jump suit (it kind of looked like an astronaut's suit), Reebok sneakers and a pair of Porsche Design sunglasses. He was very thin, thin shoulders, a thin face, thin lips, the features of a mannequin, and his hair was slicked back, a wet look, but not greasy, as if he had just emerged from a swimming pool. But his most striking feature was his tan. He was overly tanned, he seemed to glow even in the dim light of La Campana, as if he moved only and always beneath the light of a tanning bed. Grinning at Malachi as if they were old friends, as if they had been watching cartoons together since they were children, he started talking in a very loud voice. At first Malachi thought he was talking about the cartoon, but the relationship between what the young man was saying and the cartoon was tenuous at best.

"That's the way to kill some time," he said.

Malachi stared at him.

"You know what I mean?"

Malachi said that he did. He heard grumbling from the two shadowy figures sitting at the counter by the black curtain, perhaps they were bothered by the suddenly loud voice of the young man, but the grumbling was a fairly vague sound, like it had been traveling for miles under water to get there. Malachi still couldn't see who they were. The young man smiled wearily, oblivious to the grumbling.

"Don't get me wrong," the young man said. "I don't mind the time it took to get here. That's part of my job. But you think he'd have the courtesy to pick me up at the airport. I don't even know the name of his hotel."

"Man, what are you talking about?"

"You mean who."

"Okay, who?"

"Manny."

"Manny?"

"Manuelo."

"Man, I still don't know what you're talking about."

"Manuelo. Juliano Manuelo Marquez. The movie director. I called him yesterday and said I was coming out. MGM wanted to know if he was interested in doing a reprise of his masterpiece, *The Old Guitarist*. But he didn't answer. But he never answers, he says phones are a fucking nuisance, an invasion of his privacy, a plot by the government, or some fucking shit like that, but MGM wanted an answer pronto, you don't mess around with those boys, so I said of course he's interested, and they asked when they could set up a preliminary meeting to hash things out, and I said how about Tuesday, Manny always likes to start a new project on a Tuesday, and they said fine, and that's when I called and left a message, said I was coming out. Do you know what it costs to get a last-minute flight out of Mexico City? Fuck. I don't even know what he's doing here."

The grumbling from the shadowy figures at the counter grew suddenly louder. For a split second Malachi thought he heard the dusty snorting of two bulls pawing at the ground, but then the sound faded, barely registering a blip in his upper consciousness.

"Who the fuck is Juliano Manuelo Marquez?" Malachi said.

But the young man's voice had already trailed off. A *Road Runner* cartoon had come on and he had started watching. Malachi wasn't interested in any more cartoons. Instead, he watched the young man for a while, but then it was like he was watching a cartoon anyway. He had the oddest sensation that he was watching himself. But then he realized he was looking at his own photographic negative, a facsimile likeness punched out from the inside, a caricature. The young man was absorbed in the *Road Runner* cartoon, or perhaps by the cartoon, thought Malachi, as if he had been swallowed whole, and as he was thinking this peculiar thought it suddenly seemed that he (the young man) was actually suspended in the pale, yellowish shimmering light beaming out from the television, and for a moment Malachi lost sight of him, as if he (the young man) had dissolved, his molecules mixing with the molecules of the pale, yellowish television light, as if the world of the cartoon and the world of the bar were merging, a re-ordering of reality at the subatomic level. Malachi was convinced that if he turned to the cartoon he would see the young man (and thus his own photographic negative) wandering about the strangely undusty cartoon world of a cartoon Arizona in search of an effective means for ending the life of the Road Runner, assuming the young man was the Wiley Coyote character — but then what was Malachi? Was he the Road Runner? And who were Wiley Coyote and the Road Runner anyway? When you got right down to brass tacks. When you got down to the bare essentials. Were they another pair of photographic negatives running circles around each other in a never-ending loop? And what if the young man was the one trying to escape the Coyote's wily clutches, assuming Malachi and the young man had reversed roles, leaving the Coyote (Malachi) to fall with dizzying speed over the edge of a cliff with several tons of TNT strapped to his back and land several miles below in a gigantic white poof of smoke.

Malachi gave a short uncomprehending laugh, a silent inner laugh that disturbed no one, and gave up on the inner complexities of this odd comparison. He suddenly felt like he had known the young man for years, and then he wondered exactly how old the young man was, for upon closer inspection he appeared much older than twenty-five, closer to thirty-five, or even forty. What Malachi had assumed were characteristics of youth (thinness, a darkly glowing tan) seemed now like they had been painted on. The image of a mannequin overpowered every other image, even the cartoon one.

"Juliano Manuelo Marquez is the greatest movie director of our time," said the ageless mannequin man, as if there had never been a lull in the conversation. "He is the greatest movie director who ever lived."

Malachi finished his beer.

"Sure," Malachi said. "It sounds like a famous name."

"Or one of the greatest, you would have to give him that. In the top one hundred at the very least."

"Sure."

"There's no telling how far up the ladder he would have gone if he had been born in Los Angeles, say, and not San Pedrito, a nothing of a village in the middle of nowhere Mexico."

"Uhh hunh."

Malachi sat looking at the empty beer bottle. He allowed the words of the ageless mannequin man to flow through him, an incessant flow, without worrying too much if they made any sense. He said "Uhh hunh" at appropriate intervals to keep the conversation moving. Or sometimes he said nothing at all and just stared into space, nodding slightly, reflexively.

"To be honest, I was just making up that shit about San Pedrito."

". . . ."

"He didn't grow up in San Pedrito. No. I think he actually spent his formative years in San Diego, if you want to know the truth. I think his family moved back to wherever they were from when he was nine or ten. Maybe they got deported."

"Uhh hunh."

"Hell, I don't even know where San Pedrito is. But it was some place like that. In the middle of nowhere."

". . . ."

"He's got to be in his sixties by now. That's getting up there. And he's made something like sixty films too. Sixty films and he's in his sixties. That's got to be a record."

"Uhh hunh."

"Pretty god damn amazing if you ask me. MGM wants

him to a do a reprise of his masterpiece, *The Old Guitarist*. They think it's got real potential."

Then the ageless mannequin man noticed the empty beer bottle on the table and grinned at Malachi. The precise attitude conveyed by this grin was difficult to determine.

"Say, where's the bartender?"

Malachi shrugged.

"Hey, anyone know where the bartender is?"

The ageless mannequin man had lifted his voice to a decibel level usually associated with rude, noisy shouting at football games in an attempt to reach the ears of the two shadowy figures still sitting in the shadows at the counter. They grumbled something, but it was unclear just what they said, or even if they were aware they had been asked a question.

"Thanks!"

Malachi thought he heard a tone of sarcasm or even thinly veiled contempt in the voice of the ageless mannequin man, and he turned his attention to the two shadowy figures at the counter to see if they had also noticed, but he still couldn't make out their faces. He assumed this was because of the way they were sitting and the absence of any direct light, and yet he was also struck by the impression that they were shrouded in an unnatural, perhaps sinister, but certainly mischievous darkness that seemed to project outwards, and he wondered about this. The darkness seemed almost alive, a glowing picture of health. By contrast, the light in La Campana, what little light there was, was a dead or dying thing, it was riddled with holes (bullet holes?), as if it were the victim of a horrendous, unspeakable crime. You could see stretch marks of shadow where the light had retreated. Spider veins of darkness now covered the walls. And as Malachi sat there in what could only be a waiting room for death (this was both his first and second thought), he suddenly felt that he was standing in two worlds at the same time. He could taste the stench of rotting flesh, but also the saltwater flood of a woman having an orgasm and the champagne bubbles of weddings.

It was almost like he had stepped through a portal into another time (a more elegant time, perhaps) but had only made it halfway through, and so he was trapped in the fluid, twilight, shape-shifting darkness of the in-between, which, as Malachi himself wryly observed, obscured the past and the present as well as the future. He wasn't sure how to extricate himself, but then he wasn't sure he was supposed to. He tried to zero in on the eyes of the shadowy figures, as if their eyes held the key to both their identities and Malachi's fate (which some might say was strangely prophetic even as it seemed tragically absurd), but their eyeballs danced around in a crazy, gyrating fashion like the glinting wings of beetles bathed in early morning starlight.

The two men (men?) had not ceased their grumbling since they sat down, though the volume increased or decreased with great variability, as if they were arguing over baseball scores or what to eat for dinner or why their wives had left them or how long before they could retire. Malachi assumed they were men, as opposed to unusually masculine women with tattoos of lightning bolts or laughing skulls on thick, fleshy arms, based on the hunched-over, guarded way they sat, as if they were trading uncut diamonds for heroin or cocaine while they guzzled beer, and also the general odor of sweat and urine and horse breath that enveloped them like a cloud.

Malachi wondered if the two men were struggling with the darkness as he was. He could not help wondering. The longer he sat there trying to sift through his thoughts, to make sense of what was happening, to understand the nature of this darkness which seemed both physical and temporal (and perhaps even spiritual, a billion soulless bodies on the edge of oblivion, gasping for breath like fish drowning in the muck of a newly evaporated sea), the deeper and more unyielding the darkness became. Then he heard one of the men laugh, and then the other, and he recognized the timbre of their laughter, or he thought he did, or he was beginning to, but then he was distracted by the ageless mannequin man, who was trying to explain in greater detail why he had come to Miami from Mexico City.

"So I had no idea where he had gone, and no clue how to find him either, and then Beatrice, she's sort of a secretarial assistant, she wants to be an actress but she has no talent for acting, unless you consider big tits a talent, and Manny doesn't care about big tits but he felt sorry for her so he gave her a job filing bank statements and scheduling lunches and limos and going shopping. Anyway, Beatrice said Manny was on some sort of a scouting trip, and wherever he went he was getting paid, there was a boatload of money pouring into the account, and we looked it up and she was absolutely right. In the last few months an outfit called La Campana Enterprises paid Manny over two-hundred thousand dollars. That's a hell of a lot of dough for a scouting trip, but that's beside the point. But then they stopped paying him. I called the number but it was disconnected, but I didn't know about the address, so I came to Miami. You know the address for this place doesn't exist. Not anymore. 25½ La Campana Boulevard. There is no La Campana Boulevard. And certainly no 25½. I only found this place by accident. A drunk at the Metro station remembered a fancy club from the seventies called La Campana, and he was fairly precise about how to get here for an old drunk, but it sort of felt like I was wandering about in a dream. I mean it feels like I haven't slept in a week. And now that I'm here, it still feels like a dream."

Laughing a hollow, unconvincing laugh, the ageless, mannequin man glanced up from the empty bottle and the table to the empty bar. "I sure could use a drink," he said. "I don't even care what. The last few days have been hell."

The grumbling of the two shadowy men at the counter intensified, as if neither man was willing to concede an inch in their debate over baseball scores or dinner menus or the logic or illogic of their ex-wives or the chances that they would have a sufficient income for their golden years. The shadowy cloud of their concealment seemed now to glow, as if it had become embossed with a lacquer finish.

Then the back door opened and closed and Malachi heard the sound of quick but heavy footsteps and then the fat bartender re-emerged. He stopped for a moment, as if he were uncertain that the world was a solid, physical place. He looked over at Malachi and the ageless mannequin man, and then at the glowing shadow, and the grumbling became even louder, and then the ageless mannequin man saw the bartender, and relieved that now he could order something to drink, and also perhaps bleary-eyed from lack of sleep, lurched in the direction of the bar just as the two shadowy men were making a beeline towards Malachi, who was still sitting at the table. But the ageless mannequin man wasn't looking where he was going or how fast the two shadowy figures were moving through the gloom, and in his oblivious state he was shouting at the bartender about how many beers he wanted to drink and the fat bartender not saying anything, just blinking stupidly in the dingy dim light, and then the three of them, the ageless mannequin man and the two men from the shadows collided and everyone fell to the floor and a couple of tables were knocked over and a few chairs went flying. Malachi did not wait around to see what happened after that.

-36-

That so many threads of meaning had converged in the dingy dimness of La Campana seemed to Malachi proof of the existence of God. He wondered that his neighbor, Isidora, had chosen that exact spot to escape the prying eyes and listening ears that she said were lingering along the parade route. (He never once considered her complicity.) He wondered that the ageless mannequin man had arrived precisely when he did. He wondered that the television programming team at Channel 39 (the network that was beaming out the cartoons on a Saturday afternoon) had selected the cartoons that they did and what profound meaning lay buried in the dust of the dead snails or was illuminated by the spectacular failures of Wiley Coyote. He wondered at his own clumsiness at failing to recognize Bull and Horse, and then at his own agility in escaping the dingy dimness of La Campana at the most opportune moment. All of this suggested to Malachi the hand of God, or if not God, then at least a well-designed facsimile of God, a photographic negative, perhaps, better suited to the incomprehensible vagaries of life beneath a middle-aged sun, the random nature of existence in a world bombarded daily by gamma rays and x-rays and the exhaust fumes of alien spacecraft, which some said was simply the jet-fuel smell of unanswered prayers, and everywhere, even along the cleanest, whitest beaches of Florida or Puerto Rico or elsewhere in the Caribbean, you were breathing in unseen clouds of cosmic dust from the Dark Horse nebula (also known as the Great Dark Horse nebula or the Pipe nebula), a mere 650 light years away, containing, among other elements, trace amounts of ammonia, formaldehyde, and even nitrous oxide.

Malachi smiled at his good fortune. He had a few hours to kill so he killed them. He wandered through a labyrinth of alleyways until he crossed 12th Avenue and went into the metro station. It was after five and he didn't know when the next train was coming, but he didn't care, he wasn't going anywhere. He just wanted to sit on one of the green benches facing the northbound side and look out at the red rooftops of the apartment complex directly below and think about what he was going to say to Salma de la Prada.

For Malachi, the metro station platform was a place where he could let his mind wander freely without the fear of interruption. Sitting on any one of the green benches on the platform he was both a part of the bustle of humanity and detached from it at the same time. Nobody bothered him. Sometimes he faced the southbound side after the sun had set so he could see the distant lights of the airplanes landing and taking off at Miami International. But on this particular afternoon there were still a few hours of daylight left. He took out the Velázquez brothers' script and began leafing through the pages. There was no one else on the platform. The traffic on the streets below seemed like a distant memory.

Then quite without realizing it, Malachi slipped into a dream. He found himself wandering through the airport mall and it was in the middle of the day but all the stores were closed. There was a sign in each window that said closed for renovations. Malachi stopped in front of the Armani store. At first he was only looking at his reflection and wondering where everyone had gone, but then he looked at the mannequins in the window and he saw they were all in various stages of undress. Some were missing arms or legs or even heads, as if the sales associates had been in a tremendous almost blind hurry to change their clothes and didn't care about the damage they might cause by yanking off useless limbs by accident, and who cared if a few heads popped off as well.

Then Malachi noticed that every mannequin that still possessed a head possessed the same exact face, and he was not surprised in the least that they were all the face of the ageless mannequin man he had met earlier that afternoon at La Campana. He stared at the sad, thin-lipped smile as if he were reminiscing about time spent with a long-lost childhood friend. He wondered what the little fellow was doing, if he had found Juliano Manuelo Marquez, or if he was still watching cartoons. Then all at once the mannequins (those who still possessed heads) in the Armani window and in the windows of the other stores opened their mouths like bullet holes and began to scream, a horrendous, thin-lipped scream that caused the air to vibrate, and then crack, and then there was a tear in the fabric of reality and Malachi saw layer after layer of subatomic particles flaking away like soot where the crack had appeared. Soon Malachi was wading through an ocean of soot. One by one the screaming mannequins were consumed by this ocean. First their legs disappeared, and then their arms, their shoulders, and lastly their heads, but the screams of the now drowned (buried?) mannequins were somehow as loud as ever. It sounded like the screeching of metal tires on metal rails.

It was at that point that Malachi realized he was dreaming and woke up. A train heading north was pulling away from the station. The sun had already set and the sky was a swirling purplish light because of the glow of the city, and beyond the glow he could see the faint glimmer of a few stars. He shoved the Velázquez brothers' script back into his vest pocket and headed for the street.

The voices inside his head were all chattering away, each with a different strategy for presenting Salma de la Prada with the script, each warning him against the sudden paralysis that had gripped him at the parade, each with a different opinion of how the evening ahead would go. But all of them agreed that Salma de la Prada was most certainly at La Mamacita's by now. Or if she wasn't she would arrive there shortly.

The scene at La Mamacita's:

Malachi is at the door of the club almost before he realizes it. He is lost in thought. Perhaps he is thinking about what he is going to say when he first meets Salma de la Prada. Perhaps not. Who can say what he is thinking? And then he is at the door. The whole building is dark, even the windows are mysteriously blacked out (though perhaps they have always been blacked out), which gives the impression of a bombed-out building in London during World War Two (or it could just as well be a bombed-out building in Berlin or Dresden or Lübeck or Hamburg or Cologne), or, conversely, an air raid shelter. Perhaps it is inaccurate to say this shell of a warehouse gives the impression of a bombed-out building. Perhaps it is more accurate to say that it gives the impression of a washed-out photograph of a bombed-out building in one of the cities already noted, although certainly the cities of Rotterdam and Warsaw and Wieluń and Frampol could be added to the list, and many others as well, Guernica, for example, which gave the Nazis a chance to test the effectiveness of terror bombing in somebody else's war, or Marseilles, which nobody remembers, but not Nagasaki or Hiroshima, that was a different kind of bombing altogether, a different level of destruction.

Malachi pushes his way through the door and the impression of a bombed-out building is replaced with an impression of absolute oblivion, as if a small but still terrifying black hole has swallowed up the interior of La Mamacita's and is gathering up the courage to venture outside. He wonders what has happened. He is no longer standing on the edge of the abyss, he thinks, he has already descended. He notices a ringing in his ears, as if a winged night terror is calling out his name. The ringing grows louder. He can feel the spider vein tentacles of dozens of unseen creatures pricking his skin. Dozens of tiny puncture wounds appear as if from tiny teeth, and before his body can respond with even a flinch, the owners of these teeth, which seem directed by some kind of superhuman intelligence, plunge in through the dozens of tiny, open wounds and race through his bloodstream, surrounding his vital organs with the icy cold embalming fluid of the universe. This is what it feels like, the dizzying sensation that usually accompanies the end of one's life, of any life, of all life.

But Malachi is not dead yet.

He embraces the darkness and the unseen creatures and then the darkness settles. His pulse rate returns to normal, and so does the rate of his breathing, though he had not realized either was elevated. The unseen creatures crawl back underneath their rocks. Then he thinks he sees a glimmer of something in the distance (he is not sure how far away, he is not even sure he is still standing just inside the door at La Mamacita's). He thinks he sees a line of reddish-golden light slicing through the darkness, like an aerial photograph of a busy highway at night with the blur of red taillights and golden headlights sweeping back towards the horizon. He stares at the reddish-golden light until he is certain it is not a figment of his imagination. Then he walks towards it, pushing out at the darkness in front of him and then sweeping back on either side with his hands in a swimming motion, cautiously, as if he is concerned about spider webs or the stray branches of unseen trees.

As he gets closer he hears the faint clatter of masculine laughter and the clinking of full beer bottles and near-full and empty and then the sound of glass breaking as the empties are hurled against a wall, and then the click of automatic weapons, and then more laughter and more bottle clinking and the cycle repeats.

Then a voice calls out to him, asks him what he wants. Malachi is sideswiped with sudden clarity. He realizes that the reddish-golden line of light is the bar at La Mamacita's, a row of humming, buzzing stained glass lamps (a bright cherry red) hanging from the ceiling. Standing at the bar are half a dozen bouncers wearing their leather bullet-proof vests and Billy clubs clipped to their sides, as usual, and heavy black boots with the laces neatly tied and their long black hair pulled back in precise, ponytail fashion.

Malachi is struck by their well-groomed appearance, their bouncer costumes are spotless, even pristine, and they all seem happy and untroubled, as if the evening has not yet taken its toll on their attitudes, as if they are pacifist by nature and only do what they have to do to keep the peace.

The half-dozen happy, untroubled bouncers from La Mamacita's are happily entertaining half-a-dozen blonde-haired German behemoths from the inner circle of Salma de la Prada's unflappable security force. They are also happy, untroubled, chatting away in German and then in perfect English with a few garbled words in Spanish and then back to German, still wearing their amber-tinted sunglasses and their Speedos and their flip-flops and their tight-fitting Spandex t-shirts with the word FÜKKENRÜKEN in fluorescent blue lettering, and Uzis strapped to their backs or leaning up against the counter or on top but within easy reach.

All of the German bodyguards are drunk. They are almost slap-happy they are so drunk. And yet they are as immaculate in their appearance as the half-dozen bouncers, as if they (the bodyguards) had only moments ago picked up their costumes from the dry cleaners and slipped them on. Malachi is staring up at the six bouncers and the six bodyguards, almost straining the muscles in his neck, for they are all half a foot taller than Malachi, at least. The head honcho, Herr Konrad, who appears decidedly older than the rest, is having an animated conversation with two of the younger ones. He is waving his dog-eared copy of *Biedermann und die Brandstifter* in their faces and pointing out passages and having them take turns reading.

Then the voice from before calls out again, and Malachi is wondering where exactly the voice is coming from, and because he cannot tell, he holds up his own dog-eared document, the Velázquez brothers' movie script, for everyone to see, and says he's there to deliver this script to Miss de la Prada. The voice relaxes, as if it has been expecting someone to come along with a script, as if Malachi is no different than any of the messenger boys delivering scripts on a daily basis, as many as ten different messengers with scripts every day. The voice tells Malachi to have a seat at one of the tables, it may be a while, Miss de la Prada is entertaining guests in the VIP Suite, and then the rest of the bouncers and the bodyguards break into happy boisterous laughter, and then one of the Germans, a hulking brute almost seven feet tall who is sitting on top of the bar at the far end, says they (the producers) should put him in one of Miss de la Prada's movies, he's plenty big enough, and then one of the other Germans laughs and says, but not where it counts, and then everyone is ribbing the big lummox, but he's too drunk to care. The rest of the evening unfolds with the precision of an award-winning film. Or at least a box office smash. If you can imagine the scene as part of a movie, you can imagine it done in a jerky, 1940s newsreel-footage style.

"THE HAIL OF BULLETS SCENE AT LA MAMACITA'S"

INT. LA MAMACITA'S — EARLY EVENING (SORT OF A MONTAGE, OR A SERIES OF SHOTS, BUT NOT QUITE)

WIDE ANGLE VIEW OF THE BAR.

WE SEE the **BOUNCERS** from **LA MAMACITA'S** and the **GERMAN BODYGUARDS** standing at the bar, chatting, guzzling beer, laughing. The red stained glass lamps hanging above the bar provide the only light, which extends the length of the bar and perhaps five feet out away from the bar. The rest of **LA MAMACITA'S** is bathed in absolute darkness.

WE HEAR a mix of German and Spanish and English being spoken.

THE CAMERA ZOOMS IN ON MALACHI, who is sitting at a small table half in the light, half in the shadow. **MALACHI** is leafing through the pages of **THE VELÁQUEZ BROTHERS'**

MOVIE SCRIPT, but he has to lean out away from the table, holding the **SCRIPT** up in the air to catch a few scraps of the reddish-golden light, so he can see.

WE HEAR the sound of a **DOOR OPENING**, followed immediately by the sound of a second **DOOR OPENING**.

AT THE SAME TIME, THE CAMERA PULLS BACK AND WE SEE the **DOOR** to the **VIP SUITE** opening suddenly and the interior of **LA MAMACITA'S** is immediately bathed in a brilliant **GOLDEN LIGHT**, presumably from a single golden chandelier hanging directly over the great king bed in the **VIP SUITE**, which is past the far end of the bar and then up a set of three carpeted steps (red shag carpeting that has seen better days) and then through a pair of padded oak doors, which means you can't see either the bed or the chandelier from the bar, or at least not easily.

THE CAMERA SHIFTS to the other end of the bar and **WE SEE** the **FRONT DOOR** opening and two heads emerging. As the two heads emerge, the **GOLDEN LIGHT** from the **VIP SUITE** fills the entire room and we see **BULL** and **HORSE** standing at the entrance, blinking in the sudden glare of the **GOLDEN LIGHT**, with surprised looks on their faces.

THE CAMERA SHIFTS IMMEDIATELY BACK to the **DOOR** to the **VIP SUITE** and **WE SEE SALMA DE LA PRADA** moving down the steps and then heading towards the bar. She is flanked by four more **GERMAN BEHEMOUTHS** with **UZIS** strapped to their backs. Trailing **SALMA DE LA PRADA** are **XAVIER MENDOZA** — an old café owner who was picked from the crowd during the **PARADE** for an afternoon of unrestrained pleasure (he was picked because he reminded **SALMA DE LA PRADA** of an old uncle she hadn't seen in years, or perhaps an old boyfriend, or maybe the town where she grew up, or maybe there was no particular reason, maybe it was just a random occurrence, as so many things are) — and **THE YOUNG TEACHER**, who had been trying to restrain **XAVIER** when the **BODYGUARDS** plucked them both out of the crowd, and who had later been invited to participate in the activities in the great king bed, but who had declined (though he did watch), claiming a previous and still unresolved romantic attachment to a young Spanish teacher named **TOMMIE RODRIGUEZ.**

THE CAMERA PULLS BACK AND WE SEE a mix of **BOUNCERS** and **BODYGUARDS** looking in the direction of **SALMA DE LA PRADA** and a mix looking in the direction of **BULL** and **HORSE.**

MALACHI sees **SALMA DE LA PRADA** and stands up, turning slightly, holding the **SCRIPT** in the air. **SALMA DE LA PRADA** smiles at **MALACHI.**

EVERYONE looks at the **SCRIPT** in **MALACHI'S HAND.**

THE YOUNG TEACHER waves at **MALACHI.**

YOUNG TEACHER
Hola, Malachi. Your salvation awaits!

BULL and **HORSE** are distracted by **THE YOUNG TEACHER'S** greeting. **HORSE** looks in the direction of **THE YOUNG TEACHER'S** voice and sees **SALMA DE LA PRADA. BULL** hears the name **MALACHI** but suddenly realizes that **BROKEN BIKE** and **MALACHI** are the same person (who can ever truly understand how the brain works at the subconscious level). The expression on his face resembles religious conviction.

HORSE
Oye, ñoo! esa heba esta buena pa comersela con ropa y todo! (Which means "Oye, fuck! That hottie is good enough to eat with her clothes on and everything!" and which is sort of an odd thing to say since **SALMA DE LA PRADA** is already practically naked, wearing only her bright red thong and her red poodle fur sandals.)

AT THE SAME TIME, BULL sees **MALACHI** and **PULLS** a **GUN.**

BULL

(walking towards **MALACHI**)
Ladrón (Thief)! Traidor (Traitor)!
Me cago en la leche que mamaste,
cabróncete de mierda.

(Which means "I shit in the milk
you suckled from your mother's
breast you shitty/fucking little
bastard.")

MALACHI turns towards the sound of **BULL'S VOICE**, tosses his **SCRIPT** in the air with an overly emotive, theatrical flourish and the **SCRIPT** becomes fifty single sheets of paper whirling about, fluttering, falling to the floor, and in that same moment, instinctively, which is to say without taking a look at the room of bodyguards and bouncers with guns, **MALACHI** pulls out his own **RUBBER MOVIE PROP GUN**, as if the mere appearance of the toy will stop **BULL** in his tracks.

AT THE SAME TIME, SEVEN OF THE TEN GERMAN BODYGUARDS whip out their **UZIS**, all in a single fluid motion.

AT THE SAME TIME, WE HEAR WAGNER'S ***RIDE OF THE VALKYRIES*** as performed by the American Symphony Orchestra for Edison Records in 1921.

TWO OF THE GERMAN BODYGUARDS turn, shielding SALMA DE LA PRADA, and whisk her back to the safety of the **VIP SUITE**. Her curvy, heart-shaped ass is glistening with sweat as she departs through the air.

AT THE SAME TIME, the **REMAINING GERMAN BODYGUARD** (the one that is seven feet tall) seizes **MALACHI** from behind, disabling him with a double bear-hug karate chop, confiscating the **MOVIE PROP GUN** as he sends **MALACHI** to the floor.

AT THE SAME TIME, THE BOUNCERS dive for cover behind the **BAR** and pull out **CONCEALED HANDGUNS** they weren't supposed to carry so they can return fire as warranted.

AT THE SAME TIME, BULL, still advancing, **FIRES** at **MALACHI** but misses, thanks to the zeal of **THE ONE REMAINING BODYGUARD.**

AT THE SAME TIME, THE YOUNG TEACHER grabs XAVIER in a sort of tackling motion, which sends both men to the relative safety of the floor. Or perhaps **XAVIER** was in a panic because he suddenly couldn't breathe so he grabbed **THE YOUNG TEACHER** and then fell backwards, pulling him down. Sometimes it is difficult to determine cause and effect.

THE MUSIC OF WAGNER RISES and **FALLS** as appropriate.

The **LIGHT** from the **VIP SUITE** vanishes, as **SALMA DE LA PRADA** is now safely behind closed doors.

AT THE SAME TIME, HORSE pulls out his own **GUN** and begins firing randomly in a misguided attempt to help out his brother.

AT THE SAME TIME, THE SEVEN BODYGUARDS with **UZIS** and the **BOUNCERS** with their **GUNS** open fire on **BULL** and **HORSE**.

WE SEE a **BLINDING FLASH** from the **HAIL OF BULLETS** flying about, which is to say that no one can see anything for a few moments. Actually, **THE EIGHT REMAINING GERMAN BODYGUARDS** can see just fine, as they are wearing their **AMBER-TINTED SUNGLASSES.**

AS THE FLASH OF LIGHT SUBSIDES, WE CAN SEE a photographic negative imprint in the air where **BULL** and **HORSE** had been standing. The imprint is riddled with bullet holes. Then the photographic negative imprint fades and **WE SEE** the lifeless, bullet-ridden bodies of **BULL** and **HORSE** stretched out on the floor.

THE CAMAERA PULLS BACK AND WE SEE the **BOUNCERS** and the **BODYGUARDS** engaged in various activities: some are checking to see if everyone else is all right, some are examining the damage done to the bar, some are sweeping up broken glass since several shelves of glassware were destroyed during the gun battle as well as the mirror behind the bar, the red glass lamps hanging above the bar, and various beer bottles (some full, half-empty, and some empty).

AT THE SAME TIME, someone has turned on the entrance lights, three dim yellow bulbs ensconced in the ceiling above the threshold which provide a smoky glow, just enough to see by.

THE MUSIC OF WAGNER FADES.

AT THE SAME TIME, TWO BODYGUARDS are checking the bodies of **BULL** and **HORSE**. They are chatting with a **THIRD BODYGUARD**, who is still clutching his **UZI** and surveying the battlefield to make sure there is no further threat. **THE THIRD BODYGUARD** possesses the air of one who is in command.

THE THIRD BODYGUARD
Sind Sie tot?
(Translation: Are they dead?)

ONE OF THE TWO BODYGUARDS
Ja, Herr Konrad, Sie sind tot.
(Translation: Yes, Mr. Konrad, they are dead.)

THE THIRD BODYGUARD
So wüst und schön
(Translation: So desolate and beautiful.)

ONE OF THE TWO BODYGUARDS
(to the corpses)
Was ist das für eine Art?
(Translation: What kind of way is that to behave?)

THE THIRD BODYGUARD
Drum geht die Welt in den Eimer.
(Translation: That's why the world is going to pot.)

ONE OF THE TWO BODYGUARDS
(still to the corpses)
Was stellen Sie sich eigentlich vor?
(Translation: Who do you think
you are?)

THE THIRD BODYGUARD
So wie zwei Schwimmer ringend
sich umklammern, Erdrückend ihre
Kunst, eingefroren in Tod.
(Translation: These two swimmers
wrestling, an oppressive art, frozen
in death.)

ONE OF THE TWO BODYGUARDS
Wie Schweine egwürgte.
(Translation: Like strangled pigs.)

WE SEE THE TWO BODYGUARDS rifling through the pockets of **BULL** and **HORSE**, removing anything that could identify the bodies, bagging various items for disposal, pocketing valuables. They are working with great speed and efficiency.

THE THIRD BODYGUARD is still surveying the battle scene, but mostly he is looking at the shredded-by-gunfire remnants of the front door. He can see the deep purplish glow of the evening through the shredded door. He now possesses an air of calm detachment.

THE THIRD BODYGUARD
Das ist Amerika.
(Translation: This is America.)

ONE OF THE TWO BODYGUARDS
Ja, das ist Amerika.
(Translation: Yes, this is America.)

THE THIRD BODYGUARD
(To the corpses)
Wir sind immer die Guten,
diejenigen, die helfen. Wo führt
das noch hin, wenn keiner mehr

dem andern glaubt? Ich sag immer:
Wo führt das noch hin, Kinder!
Jeder hält den andern für einen
Brandstifter, nichts als Mißtrauen
in der Welt. Oder hab ich nicht
recht?
(Translation: We are always the
good ones, the ones who help.
Where will it all end if we stop
believing one another? That's what
I say, where will it all end, eh?
Everybody thinking the other bloke
is an arsonist. Nothing but mutual
suspicion in the world. Am I right?)

ONE OF THE TWO BODYGUARDS

(to the other one)

Es ist mir alles Wurst.
(Translation: It's all sausage to me.)

THE TWO BODYGUARDS finish rifling through the pockets of **BULL** and **HORSE** and stand up and join **THE THIRD BODYGUARD**, who is still surveying the scene, still with an air of calm detachment. **WE SEE** the scene vaguely reflected in their **AMBER-TINTED SUNGLASSES**.

THE CAMERA PULLS BACK AND WE SEE the hustle and bustle of a great deal of activity.

THE BODYGUARDS OF THE OUTER CIRCLE have arrived and are busy restoring the interior of **LA MAMACITA'S** to the precise condition it was in prior to the gun battle, almost as if they are a stage crew, more sweeping, scrubbing down the floor, repairing the bullet holes in the walls and in the bar, replacing the mirror behind the bar, hanging new red glass hanging lamps above the bar.

AT THE SAME TIME, WE SEE MALACHI in somewhat of a daze on the floor in front of the table where he had been sitting. The pages of the **MOVIE SCRIPT** are scattered all over the floor. **MALACHI'S** arm is clearly broken. It is dangling in places where it should not dangle.

THE BODYGUARD who broke **MALACHI'S** arm is squatting beside him, checking his vital signs and talking in a soothing voice. **WE HEAR THEIR VOICES,** or at least **WE HEAR THE VOICE OF THE BODYGUARD,** but it sounds very far away.

THE BODYGUARD BESIDE MALACHI
(in English)
I am sorry my little messenger boy.
How was I to know it was a toy gun?

MALACHI
(some inarticulate groaning, a few grimaces)

THE BODYGUARD BESIDE MALACHI
(smiling, still in English)
You sit tight my little messenger
boy, an ambulance is on the way.

AND THEN WE SEE THE YOUNG TEACHER helping **XAVIER** to a sitting position and **TWO DIFFERENT BODYGUARDS** checking his vital signs with medical equipment from a small black bag. **XAVIER** is still breathing with difficulty and **THE YOUNG TEACHER** is concerned, but **THE TWO DIFFERENT BODYGUARDS** tell him that the old man will be all right. Their voices also sound very far away, like they are underwater.

THE TWO DIFFERENT BODYGUARDS
He will be fine. Do not worry.
Whatever it was has passed. Just a
little too much excitement. How old
is he?

AND THEN THE CAMERA SWINGS BACK TO THE THIRD BODYGUARD. He is watching the **OUTER CIRCLE OF BODYGUARDS,** who are still engrossed in their restoration work, but close to finishing now.

AT THE SAME TIME, a couple of the **OUTER CIRCLE BODYGUARDS** appear with two body bags and soon the bodies of **BULL** and **HORSE** are bagged and the bags are zipped. **THE TWO OUTER CIRCLE BODYGUARDS** scrub the floor to get rid of the blood and then they carry the bodies away, out through the open jagged-seeming hole where the front door had been. **THE THIRD BODYGUARD** looks again at the hole. It is almost like looking through a doorway to another world, or perhaps a window, the kind of window they have at many a coastal aquarium so people can look in on the fish. For a moment he thinks he can see bubbles rising, as if he is looking through a small window into the abyss of a gigantic aquarium.

Then **TWO COMPLETELY DIFFERENT OUTER CIRCLE BODYGUARDS**, not the ones who took away the bodies, two different ones, remove the remnants of the old shredded door and put a new one in its place. A few other **BODYGUARDS** are painting the newly repaired walls. **AS THE WORK PROGRESSES, WE HEAR THE VOICES** of **THE THIRD BODYGUARD** and the **TWO BODYGUARDS** who had pilfered the bodies of **BULL** and **HORSE**. They are continuing their conversation from before. Their voices sound very close, though we cannot see the men talking.

ONE OF THE TWO BODYGUARDS (O. S.)

Euresgleichen ist immer so
ideologisch, immer so ernst, bis
es reicht zum Verrat —'s ist keine
rechte Freude dabei.

(A loose translation: It's a shame
these Americans don't care about
private property. Look at them just
sitting there, drinking. Isn't this
their bar?)

THE THIRD BODYGUARD (O. S.)

Das ist gar nicht natürlich.
Heutzutage. Im Zirkus, wo ich
gerungen hab, zum Beispiel - und
drum, sehn Sie, ist er dann auch
niedergebrannt, der ganze Zirkus!
- unser Direktor zum Beispiel, der
hat gesagt: Sie können mir, Sepp!
- Ich heiße doch Josef... Sie können

mir! hat er gesagt: Wozu soll ich
ein Gewissen haben? Wörtlich.
Was ich brauche, um mit meinen
Bestien fertlgzuwerden, das ist 'ne
Peitsche. Wörtlich! So einer war
das. Gewissen! hat er gelacht: Wenn
einer ein Gewissen hat, so Ist es
meistens ein schlechtes...
(Translation: They probably have
insurance.)

WE HEAR ALL THREE BODYGUARDS LAUGH.

THE CAMERA PULLS BACK AND WE CAN SEE the men laughing, and a moment later **WE SEE** that the restoration work is complete. **THE THIRD BODYGUARD** waves his hand in the air, whipping it around in a strange figure eight pattern, and then all of **THE GERMAN BODYGUARDS** head for the door. They are all now **CHATTING** amicably in **GERMAN**, laughing and telling jokes.

AT THE SAME TIME, SALMA DE LA PRADA goes floating past, **TWO BODYGUARDS** on either side. She is wearing a small chiffon robe to cover her nakedness and a wide-brimmed hat and sunglasses so you cannot see her eyes or the expression on her face, like Greta Garbo.

THE TWO BODYGUARDS who pilfered the bodies of **BULL** and **HORSE** are walking a step ahead of **THE THIRD BODYGUARD.**

ONE OF THE TWO BODYGUARDS
(to the other one)
Was macht denn die Holzwoole?
(Translation: How are you getting
on with your Woodshaving?

THE TWO BODYGUARDS LAUGH.

THE THIRD BODYGUARD
Was ist der Witz daran?
(Translation: What's so funny?)

ONE OF THE TWO BODYGUARDS
Ich sagte ihm: Was macht denn die Holzwoole?
(Translation: I said to him: How are you getting on with your Woodshaving?)

ALL THREE BODYGUARDS ARE LAUGHING as they head out the door.

THE BODYGUARD BESIDE MALACHI puts a blanket around **MALACHI'S** shoulders. It is not clear where he got the blanket. Perhaps from one of the **OUTER CIRCLE BODYGUARDS. MALACHI** is still on the floor.

THE BODYGUARD BESIDE MALACHI
I have to leave you now, my little messenger boy. Try to be careful with your toy gun. I will no longer be here to watch over you.

THE BODYGUARD BESIDE MALACHI laughs gently and lays the **RUBBER MOVIE PROP GUN** in **MALACHI'S** lap and lumbers off to join the others.

WE SEE MALACHI is beginning to shiver, presumably from shock, hence the blanket. It looks like he may pass out at any moment. He hopes the ambulance will get there soon.

WE ALSO SEE that **XAVIER** is in a very bad way, still breathing heavily, his eyelids are fluttering erratically, his eyeballs rotating in similarly erratic fashion, back and forth and up and down, as if he is trying desperately to identify a familiar face. **THE YOUNG TEACHER** is watching over **XAVIER** until help arrives. They are both still on the floor.

THE BOUNCERS begin to leave, one by one.

WE CAN HEAR A SIREN in the distance, presumably the **AMBULANCE.**

FADE OUT — THE END

PART TWO

(into the abyss and back again)

L'imagination est l'aiguillon des plaisirs; dans ceux de cette espèce, elle règle tout, elle est le mobile de tout; or, n'est-ce pas par elle que l'on jouit? n'est-ce pas d'elle que viennent les voluptés les plus piquantes?

De Sade, La Philosophie dans le boudoir

BOOK FOUR

the abduction of Escolástica Escoraz Vda De Miranda

-37-

Everyone dies, everyone forgets, everyone is forgotten, even God. This is what the great-grandmother of Isidora Escoraz Calzada used to say, a nugget Isidora held close to her heart. Except how did sweet Isidora know her great-grandmother had said this? She never knew her great-grandmother in the flesh. They had never met. They had exchanged no letters. Isidora's great-grandmother (Ana Silvestre) was born in Jiguani, Cuba in 1884 and died in Havana in 1941 of a broken heart having never left Cuba or seen anything of the world, eight years before Isidora was born, one year after her husband (Andres Ordóñez Escoraz) had been shot and killed tending bar in his own café-turned-nightclub-turned-café at 112 Zulueta Street in downtown Havana, nineteen years after he had first opened the doors to this dream of a lifetime that was destined to become the scene of his death (not realizing that Old Havana was in the throes of perpetual decay even then and he should have opened his new business further west, in Vedado, or perhaps El Cerro, though in subsequent years these neighborhoods would also crumble under the weight of political upheaval and the relentless, turbulent weather and the bitter neglect of the newly impoverished).

The circumstances of Andres' tragic death were suspicious to say the least, and therefore quite memorable, at least from Isidora's perspective. A drunken lunatic had burst into his café, a wayward soul who perhaps had been visiting one of the brothels on Xifré Street, one of those stomach-wrenching dives filled with forty-year-old whores where the air inside is a sickly, greenish color from all the cigarette smoke and cigar smoke and the dirty oil lamps and the pestilent stench of semen and body odor and dried urine and the dead fish smell of soaked mattresses; or perhaps he had picked up a beautiful young mulatta girl who lived in the shadows at the end of Calle Galiano in the Plaza del Vapor because she had nowhere else to go. Of course no one knows (or will admit to such knowledge) the precise circumstances. But it is certainly fair to say that this madman reeked of cheap rum and cheap cigars and even cheaper perfume, the kind that smells mostly of dying orchids mixed with the sour citrus smell of lemons. In any event, the moment he entered Andres' café he spied a poster of the Spanish bullfighter Jose Garcia Carranza, alias 'Pepe Algabeño,' hanging on the wall behind the bar. It was from when the bullfighter was just starting out in Madrid. The drunken lunatic studied the poster a moment. Then he pulled a revolver and began firing at the poster and shouting death to the fucking Fascists, though why Fascism sprang to his mind when he saw the poster was not entirely clear.

Perhaps his comments were meant to show support (however misguided or deranged) for Cuba's fifth President, Gerardo Machado y Morales, beloved General of the Cuban War for Independence (which was actually the ninth major conflict in the Cuban struggle for independence descending from a long line of rebellions, revolts and conspiracies that began in 1810), the same Machado who later became an unbearable dictator (or a beacon of progressive hope, it was hard to tell, for such is the fluidity of Cuban politics), and who was toppled in 1933 thanks to a boatload of cash from the United States and would die a few years after that while living in exile in Miami Beach, an ironic twist on many levels, and whose descendants would find refuge in Florida or Panama or far-off Germany under assumed names like Jones or Reyez or Meierhoffer.

Or perhaps the drunken lunatic's comments were directed at the newly victorious Francisco Franco y Bahamonde in Spain, for the bullfighter in the poster had been a staunch Franco supporter and had, the presence of the poster notwithstanding, been killed four years earlier, four days after Christmas, ten days after battling the International Brigades near Boadilla del Monte but then he was sent south, where he had participated without a second thought in the Battle of Lopera under the command of Lieutenant Colonel Eduardo Alvárez Rementería, after which he was shot in the stomach by an unknown gunman on a road heading west near a farmhouse south of Montoro and later died in a provisional Red Cross hospital in Córdoba with the doctors watching helplessly, unable even to provide relief for the pain, for they had run out of morphine and then whiskey and had only half a bottle of *absenta,* from their personal stock, which they wanted to preserve for later.

But no matter what the drunken lunatic was ranting about or railing against, it is also true that Andres had ample time to duck for cover behind the bar and save his skin, but according to those drinking in the bar at the time he hesitated, as if he knew the gunman, and some said he even went so far as to greet the man by name. There was some debate about this afterwards among the patrons of the bar. Some thought he said Beithen or Griffon or Grenfell, though none of these names rang a bell with anybody. One witness even said he heard a strange, quivering voice say 'Ah, yes, but not even a faith as strong as yours can save you from the *otra muerte*,' but others heard nothing at all. But everyone agreed that no matter what Andres did or did not say, the unknown gunman said nothing at all to indicate that he knew Andres; he just began firing, and Andres fell victim (some would later call it destiny) to one of the bullets ricocheting carelessly around the café.

Then again, it was equally plausible that the poster was not the target. All of the witnesses said the lunatic possessed notoriously poor aim, for in spite of firing till the gun was empty, the poster remained in mint condition, as did the Victorian clock hanging on the wall next to the poster, but the gilded salon mirror on the other side of the clock, a showpiece most certainly, had been shattered. Perhaps the suggestion that the gunman was aiming at the poster was pure subterfuge on the part of a few unscrupulous individuals, paid in advance by faceless men hiding in the shadows outside, hoping to throw truth-seekers off the scent, (as if truth has a scent), hoping to disguise the fact that Andres had been methodically assassinated by a team of well-trained assassins who sowed the tragic seeds of death and confusion wherever they went, gunned down in cold blood, as it were, for a fistful of United States dollars, as opposed to the uncertain value of a few pesos (even those extravagant silver pesos with a woman beneath a star on one side), but not simply for Andres' supposed politics, but also because the café-turned-nightclub-turned-café he had opened in 1922, Casa Oriente, was proving to be stiff competition for another joint just down the street, the now famous Sloppy Joe's, owned at that time by Jose Abeal y Otero and Valentin Garcia, two greasy opportunistic gamberros with known ties to the Radical Republican Party in Spain, who had immigrated to Cuba in 1904 but had returned to Spain on several occasions and had the last time (1931) supposedly participated in the burning of the convents in Málaga, though they later claimed to be in Seville at the time, and who later became good friends with Hemingway, who also hated the Fascists, real or imagined, no matter where he found them.

So how was it possible that Isidora could know things

she couldn't possibly know? How is it possible to see the world through another's eyes, particularly if those eyes are now closed in the dream of death? Well, perhaps it is best to be blunt, without any embellishment at all, although it is fair to say that the various doctors who treated Isidora when she was fifteen possessed a different (which is to say scientific) opinion of the nature of her gift. But as far as Isidora was concerned, she had the blood of two documented psychics coursing through her veins: Escolástica Escoraz Vda De Miranda, a niece to Isidora's great-grandfather, who accompanied him to Cuba in 1899 and who later resettled in Puerto Rico because the dreams she dreamed in Cuba troubled her greatly; and Escolástica's sister, Isabel, who remained in Spain and was later rumored to have predicted the bombing of Guernica, which in turn led to rumors that she was a spy fighting with Basque Loyalists in support of the Republic, and when she was later captured by the Nationalists (some said she was betrayed), she was tortured for information but refused to give up a single name, which might have meant that she had no names in her possession, but the Nationalists felt she was simply being stubborn and needed to be taught a lesson, so she was executed with a single shot to her temple. The Colonel in charge shot her with a 1914 Mauser 6.35 mm pocket pistol with a blue finish and a walnut grip, and then with barely a flicker of emotion passing across his Germanic features, like the shadow of a cloud passing across an outcropping of weathered granite, he had her body tossed into a ravine, where it was said a pack of hungry dogs devoured everything, even the bones.

But these two sisters were not the only psychics in Isidora's family. Isidora knew without any historical proof whatsoever that she was the last in a long line of psychics (mystics, soothsayers, poets, philosophers) that had dominated her family's bloodline on her father's side for the endless centuries preceding the dawn of the modern age, quite possibly all the way back to the time of the Moors and the conquest of Valencia, but at least as far back as the re-taking of Grenada and the surrender of Boabdil, the last Moorish king, in the year 1492, the same year Columbus set sail for the Americas and eventually discovered the paradise of Cuba.

Isidora could feel the surging power of countless generations of psychic women in her blood, women of great passion and intensity who could bend time and space with their imaginations and send bullets careening across the centuries, women who had never sought the limelight, some who may have been accused of witchcraft and burned at the stake, others who may have worked tirelessly treating victims of the plague and then coming down with the disease themselves and their skin riddled with festering black boils and the boils then exploding, precipitating tragic, agonizing, inevitable deaths (one wonders why they, being psychic, didn't see the tragedy of history as it was about to unfold or would unfold and take appropriate steps, unless you believe as the Greeks did that one can never escape one's destiny), and all of them now existing in a sort of pre-Catholic limbo where they no longer possessed names, probably because the written records of their births and baptisms and inevitable deaths had been lost through fire or water damage or simply the relentless march of time.

This was the wellspring of young Isidora's psychic abilities. She was not perhaps as gifted as some of those who came before her. Her gift was limited to speaking with the recently dead, those wayward souls who could still slip back and forth between this dimension and the next with a story to share or some pertinent advice to give. What is more, she could only speak with those who belonged to her own family. But she accepted these limitations with a grace and wisdom that went beyond her years. She possessed great sensitivity and great compassion, which meant that she could talk with the ghost of her great-grandmother as easily as others might chat with a stranger while waiting for a bus.

-38-

Isidora first stumbled into the lives of the long dead members of her family when she was a small child about the age of three. She was, as you might expect, slightly confused. But she was not frightened. She had no context for fear. She simply thought she was playing with angels, wingless angels, certainly, but angels nevertheless. Isidora took their presence as a matter of course, laughing and clapping her hands in delight as they told their stories, engaging them in all manner of childish games.

She told no one at first, not even her own mother.

She sensed even as a child that her mother would not have appreciated her strange gift, that her mother would have thought she was possessed by demons and quite possibly have taken her to see a priest.

By the time she had turned twelve, she had come to the conclusion that these angels were grandmothers and grandfathers and Great aunts and distant cousins, and that the stories they told were a mythic blend of what had happened to them while they lived, what they had hoped would happen but didn't, and what they saw happening in the future, both their future, which was Isidora's present, and also Isidora's future, which they could barely comprehend.

It was never always clear to Isidora if they were talking about the past, the hoped-for past, or the mysterious, mythic future, which may have had less to do with an understandable desire to pull legs and crack jokes, all with a mischievous tremor in their voices so that Isidora would know she was being kidded, and more to do with their actually being dead and existing outside of time where there was very little to do except bend the meanings of words and play around with the sequence of past events in an attempt to create new memories, which was an impossible task since memories are a purely temporal phenomenon.

It is also important to note that her dead relatives did their best to provide Isidora with specific dates and places when asked, and once or twice they provided extensive genealogies when to withhold such information would surely have caused Isidora great headaches that would have lingered for weeks, an insufferable condition which countless historians have endured in the absence of properly configured genealogy charts.

Then at the age of fifteen, in a bizarre argument she was having with her mother, though what they were arguing about nobody remembers, Isidora said that her great-grandmother, Ana Silvestre from the Isle of Cuba, understood her better than her own mother, who had left Cuba and was therefore without a homeland.

It was an odd thing to say, especially since her great-grandmother had died before Isidora was born, and when Isidora's mother pressed her on this point (only God knows what she was expecting Isidora to say), Isidora said she spoke to her great-grandmother on a regular basis. Instead of a priest, Isidora's suddenly alarmed mother took Isidora to the first of three doctors.

The first doctor, after only three sessions in three days of psychoanalysis, sessions that were held in a dark, windowless, prison cell of a room in which the air conditioning had been deliberately turned off (a diabolical maneuver given that it was the middle of June and the temperature outside was well above ninety-five), declared that Isidora was suffering from a psychotic break with reality precipitated by the lack of a strong father figure (which Isidora's mother agreed with) and the debilitating presence of an overbearing mother, (a claim which Isidora's mother rejected without even a backwards glance at the furrowed brow of the doctor, who wavered at the entrance of his prison-cell office but ultimately retreated into the shadows).

The second doctor, a behaviorist who had written a book with the pompous sounding title *A Re-Evaluation of Auguste Comte and the Prima Facie Paradox of Positivism*, said that Isidora wasn't actually speaking face to face with her great-grandmother, or any of her dead relatives for that matter (a statement that reassured Isidora's mother, naturally), she was simply making up stories as a way to garner attention, a behavior she had most certainly learned at home (a purposely vague statement that infuriated Isidora's mother nonetheless, though it was true beyond any doubt, and prompted her to seek a third opinion).

The third doctor, a sort of New-Age Jungian, believed that Isidora had tapped into the collective unconscious, what some called the mind of God, a repository, he said, of all of the stories that have come down to humanity through the ages. "Yes, yes," he had said with a sudden burst of unrestrained almost adolescent enthusiasm, "while these stories very well could be factual accounts of Isidora's actual flesh-and-blood ancestors, they could also be symbolic stories, in other words, stories that could be true of any one of the countless souls that have lived out their lives on this tiny blue dot we call the earth."

The third doctor suggested that Isidora's mother ask her daughter to write the stories down, or at the very least tape-record them, so that he could write a book, yes, yes, he had always wanted to write a book, and Isidora's stories might be just the ticket. He would call the book *The Past Lives of Isidora Escoraz Calzada*, or *The Multiple Lives of a Spanish Schizophrenic*, or something like that, something catchy.

"So you think my little Isidora is a radio blasting out stories from the dead?" Isidora's mother asked. "Is that what you think?"

"Either that or she has a cochlear implant and is receiving transmissions for unknown reasons from aliens living on a distant planet," the third doctor joked.

Isidora's mother did not know how to respond to the third doctor, so she said nothing. But that was the last doctor Isidora saw. After three months of going to doctors, Isidora's mother decided that enough was enough. She decided that if her daughter was cavorting about with her long-dead great-grandmother and various uncles and aunts and cousins who perhaps did not yet realize they were ghosts, then so be it. She would let her daughter find out for herself what a painful bit of stupidity it was to let the dead get their hooks into you.

Even if they were family.

Especially if they were family.

And if her daughter were simply telling tales out of school, submerged in the nostalgia of a lost paradise, then so be it. She would not bother about any stories that came flowing out of her daughter's mouth. She would let that hopscotch river run its course.

Isidora never again said a word to her mother about her strange gift, and by the time Isidora had turned sixteen, both she and her mother remembered the summer of the three doctors, as they had both come to think of it, as one remembers a strange, incoherent, improbable dream. Life returned to normal, or at least to a quasi-normal state.

-39-

Up until Isidora turned eighteen, she was never happier than when she was listening (usually when there was a bright full moon in the sky) to her grandmothers and her grandfathers and her Great aunts and her distant cousins telling their stories. It was a little like owning a museum quality collection of old photographs, or more precisely, a set of old photographic glass plates, which were used without a second thought until the 1920s, but which were slowly abandoned as less fragile films were introduced into the market place and after a while were used only by astronomers seeking to capture the iridescent beauty of the stars.

Many of the stories that Isidora's long-dead relatives

shared with the young and impressionable Isidora were in one way or another about tragically doomed love affairs, so Isidora soon found herself hoping to someday fall in love so she could prove to the bitter and inveterate naysayers of her extended family that true love was indeed possible, even in an age that prized brand new linoleum floors above wedding vows. Naturally by true love she meant a vibrant, passionate, romantic love, the kind that sends a shiver racing like electricity up your spine and your legs crumble like diseased statuary and you can barely breathe and you wonder if you will ever walk again. So she became expert in the nuances of love that most of us miss, the subtle give-and-take between two consenting adults at any hour of the day or night; the tragic consequences of a love that has been forgotten and the resurging hope (more tentative the second or third time around, which is to be expected, but no less exciting) that accompanies that very love when it one day rises up from the cold ashes of forgetfulness; the quiet fullness of love that descends without warning upon two aging but once robust lovers who from then on can only express themselves through the mirror of their eyes, the lingering, infinitely gentle caress of a familiar, flattering hand.

For Isidora, the expression of love defined all human activity and the very nature of human existence, at least as far as she could glimpse from a pseudo-historical, partially imagined, quasi-psychic perspective.

Love, she decided, was walking along the Malecón on a summer evening, looking out at the dark blue waters of the Straits of Florida without a care in the world, the glorious knot of humanity flowing past, the faces of happy couples glowing brightly with the pink-glowing evening sky, nobody saying a single word, a family up ahead buying ice cream from an ice-cream vendor, and then the light softening, dissolving, fading into nothingness.

Love, she decided, was a quiet whispering between two voices that drifted out through an open window on a dark summer night and the lace curtains billowing in the breeze and they (the owners of the voices) could smell strange smells, a mixture of vanilla and cinnamon and tobacco, as if someone were baking pastries and smoking cigars at the same time at this very late hour, the smells flowing up from the Almendares River, originating somewhere on the other side in Vedado, perhaps a small bakery getting ready for the new day, and the two voices softly cooing, content whispers they were, which were soon lost amid the lonely but steady murmuring of insects.

Love, she decided, was the pattern of raindrops on the roof and then the sad and yet joyful sound of rainwater rolling into the tin gutters and then swirling down the drain spouts, a hollow, metallic echo that drifts across eternity.

Love, she decided, was the last time her great-grandmother had kissed her great-grandfather on the lips. The morning on that day was dark and moist and a rooster was crowing in the neighbor's yard. But Andres had to leave every morning when it was dark because they lived a few miles west of the old downtown, because Ana did not like the noise and the congestion of so many smells in such a small space, because she had grown up in a small nameless village on the other side of the island, near the El Cobre copper mine with the smell of sulphur always lingering in the air like bad eggs. So they lived out past El Carmelo in Miramar, in a small place near the Almendares River, small when compared to the palatal mansions that once lined the Calzada del Cerro, but gaudy by any other standard, a two-story neo-classical Baroque style house with ornate edifices and two inner courtyards and a brick walkway guarded by two sculpted lions (Andres had hoped for bronze, but that had proved too expensive).

Andres had built the house for Ana (though he often joked that he would never finish building this house) because she had grown up in a palm thatch hut a stone's throw from El Cobre (figuratively speaking) and knew nothing of the modern world and modern conveniences and modern thinking, and he wanted her to know these things, though it could be said that her natural point of view was modern, for she did point out with some measured irony (and the barest hint of joyful exuberance) that they were without running water that first year. But Ana did not mind. She went to the river to fetch water, even when Andres instructed her to leave the duties of the household to the mulatta girl he had hired so Ana could look after the children. But within a year the city planners had caught up to Miramar and everyone had running water and electricity and well-kept streets, so the instructions regarding the hired girl became a moot point.

It was shortly after that, that Andres painted the house a very bright sunset orange, because Ana liked the color, but also because it was a modern color, which piqued his imagination.

He was not so imaginative, however, when it came to the roof. He did not pay any attention to roofs unless they leaked. So the roof was a flat roof made of red Spanish tile. But Andres had quite a good imagination when it came to floors. He had installed solid mahogany floors, dark mahogany, top quality floors he had imported from New Orleans, because the darkness of the dark mahogany wood calmed his spirit and allowed him to read and think with a reflective, contemplative, even creative mind. So there was dark mahogany throughout the house, though Ana had covered up most of the beauty of the floors with Persian rugs. But not in the library. Andres had always craved a library with a dark mahogany floor polished like dark glass so he could see his own reflection staring up at him like the image of God in reverse. There were no rugs in the library. This was the one room in the house that Andres claimed as his own. It was the visible expression of his soul. The shelves contained history books, though most of these were about *The Reconquista,* and volumes of poetry, from the ancient Greeks to the Futurists, in spite of the fact that the Futurists were no longer even read, and scientific journals proclaiming the latest and most astonishing discoveries in astronomy and Egyptology, and dictionaries in several languages (Spanish, English, French, Turkish), and various atlases, and a single shelf set aside for three Cuban philosophers.

The first of these philosophers was Félix Varela y Morales. Andres possessed several issues of a periodical entitled *El Habanero,* which contained treatises on politics and philosophy which Varela had penned, a book entitled *Abridger and Annotator to The Protestant,* which was printed in English, and a three-volume series of essays entitled *Cartes a Elipidio, sobre la Impiedad, la Superstición, y el Fanatismo en sus Relaciones con la Sociedad.* As far as Andres could tell, Varela believed that philosophy and theology were two separate disciplines, which meant that you could believe in God and still work to change the order of things in a country (any country, all countries) that cared little for the welfare of ordinary citizens.

Naturally, Andres applauded this line of thinking on theoretical grounds, although as a practical matter, well, he did not believe that most people thought deeply about such distinctions or even knew they existed, though it should be noted that his views of 'most people' were shaped to a large extent by what he read in books. He paid scant attention to the opinions of those who worked for him at his café or those who owned the various shops downtown and whom he had talked with every once in a while when they came into his cafe for some supper, and not since his first few years in Cuba had he had any contact whatsoever with the vast, actual majority of Cubans who lived on the island, the mestizos and the mulattos and mulattas and the isleños, descendants of slaves and mixed bloods (who had been born in the dozens of tiny prehistoric villages that dotted the landscape, such as the village near El Cobre where his wife had come from), peasants all of them (with the obvious exception of his wife and her immediate family) who were now infiltrating the towns and the cities like a plague of rats. He was convinced that for the majority of Cubans, the disciplines of philosophy and theology were identical threads woven into the inarticulate fabric of their dreams, and so were difficult if next to impossible to untangle.

The second philosopher who captured Andres' fancy (and who was by far his favorite) was José Cipriano de la Luz y Caballero. He owned one massive volume entitled *The Works of don José de la Luz Caballero*, compiled by Alfredo Zayas, no less, and published in 1890. Andres saw in Luz a kindred spirit who believed that freedom meant the freedom to think creatively, without anyone telling you what to think, and without this freedom, people were no better than zombies, what space junkies and conspiracy theorists would later call automatons, though perhaps these words were not in Luz's dictionary, as they were certainly not in any of the dictionaries possessed by Andres Ordóñez Escoraz.

The third philosopher to occupy space on the shelf was Enrique José Varona, who had once come into Andres' café, before Andres knew who he was, with a group of young men, students perhaps, or budding revolutionaries. Varona had looked like a walrus with his thick bushy moustache, or at least a caricature of a walrus the way he was blustering on about that damn tyrant Machado and how it was every young Cuban's duty to take up arms against his regime, and the young students (or revolutionaries) lapping up every blustery, walrusey word. Still, Andres didn't know who he was, even at that point, and then Varona sat down at the bar and the young men spread out among the tables and everyone ordered beers or whiskey, and some ordered cocktails, like Daiquiris or Santiago cocktails, and a few ordered a fancy cocktail called a Cuban President, which Andres did his best to make, though he didn't have any Noilly Prat Vermouth, and he was also out of Curacao, so it didn't really taste like a Cuban, and when he brought out the drinks, the ones who had ordered the Cuban Presidents all held their drinks up in the air in honor of the blustery walrus, who was still talking, and they were calling him don Enrique or El Vicepresidente, and it was only then that Andres realized who this fat walrus actually was. Then Varona saw the poster of Carranza and started talking about the first bullfight he ever saw, the year was 1915, it was when President Menocal had sent him to Mexico City to meet with the new President there, Venustiano Carranza de la Garza, who became President simply by declaring the office was his.

'You would not believe what a stubborn bastard Carranza was,' Varona had said, 'arrogant, sadistic, without any sense of humor or humility, but he was a big man. He towered over the rest of those mealy-mouthed peons, so he could do whatever he wanted, what could they do, there wasn't a thing they could do, so they waited like dead men, fawning over everything Carranza said, shoulders slumped in defeat when he wasn't looking, flattering him when he was with all sorts of mealy-mouthed platitudes. I didn't like the man all that much. I didn't like the rest of them either, but I had to go, you see we were all set to recognize the Carranza government, in spite of the energetic pressure from those who supported Zapata, primarily because Wilson was leaning in Carranza's direction, which you might say had a great impact on the position we took, but you knew that was coming because you knew Wilson didn't like the smell of peasants and you couldn't scrub the peasant smell from Zapata's skin, that was never going to happen.

'So that's how things were, but we didn't talk politics at all. Carranza took us to a bullfight instead. What an extravagant social event that was. We were sitting up in a balcony and just below there was a sea of beautiful, high society women dressed in flowing white dresses and white lace headpieces, as if they had just come from church. I asked Carranza why there were so many women at the bullfight, and he laughed and said because they are all in love with the matadors, or with him, or both, did I not see they were all wearing white, it is really too funny, Carranza said, they are all hoping that the afternoon will end with a marriage proposal, and then he laughed again. That was the only time I heard him laugh, although it wasn't much of a laugh. It sounded more like a bull being run over by a train (the young men sitting at the tables now laughing). Then Carranza said the best way to see a bullfight was down close, so we left the balcony and the sea of hopeful women in white and took seats down along the rail, where you could smell the heavy horse smell of the picadores and some of them blinking happily, lazily, because they were drunk, and you could smell the thin smell of the alcohol too, like a gauze bandage wrapped around their faces, because we were close to where they were waiting, and Carranza said it was going to be a spectacular show, and it is true our view was unimpeded, but it was a horrible spectacle, a tragedy, truly.

'We were sitting in the grey bull ring of dreams with willows in the barreras, as the poet says. It was all very sad, but it was also heroic. The bull didn't die the way it was supposed to. There were maybe half a dozen spears stuck in its hump and it was wheezing and then its front legs collapsed and it looked like it was praying. My God it was a sight. Then the matador came with his sword, but then the bull seemed to resurrect itself and it stood up and roared like a great wind. It was very majestic. And then it charged straight through the matador as easily as charging through a rain cloud and we all watched as the matador's body flipped up into the air and came down on top of the bull, and you could see that one of the bull's horns had caught the man in the stomach, a terrible, piercing wound on the left side, and then the bull shook his massive head, which some said was a premeditated act of murder, but others said it was instead a desperate apology, like offering up a sacrifice to God in the hopes of a good harvest, which has always been part of the problem with religion, if you ask me, the reliance on mystical interpretations to whitewash simple human depravity, it is our Achilles heel, though in this case, I am sure you'll agree, the depravity belonged to the bull, and for a time nobody moved or said a word, and in the stillness of that moment you could hear the small, whimpering, plaintive cries of the matador, who was clinging to this horn of the lily as he was clinging to life, like the sound of rain falling on water somewhere in the distance, and then the bull flung the matador to the ground with an expression that could only be described as one of disgust. We could all see the matador's intestines spilling out, an absolute fatal wound if you have ever seen one, a most horrible way to die, and believe me, I have seen death in all of its forms, at least on the battlefield, where death is always an intensely personal, private agony, but this was a thousand times worse, for we were sitting in a public arena beneath a sky that turned the color of gangrene and nobody could do a thing to save the man. Then the bull charged at the picadores and gored a horse to death, and the sea of women in white were crying out behind us, above us, like angels desperate to intervene, praying an endless storm of rosaries and Hail Mary's, evoking the names of the saints and long dead husbands, a hurricane of religious despair, and then finally Carranza nodded and they sent in a handful of soldiers and butchered the beast with bullets, and the splatter from the bull reached the front row, where I was sitting with Carranza.'

Then Varona had stopped talking, his voice trailing off, as if he were trying to remember what time of day the bull had died, and then he looked at the poster again and laughed and remarked on the coincidence of the names, 'they are both Carranza,' he had said, 'so I suppose they are related,' and one of the young men from the tables laughed and said 'we are all Spanish, we are all related,' and then the young men laughed, but Varona wasn't laughing.

After that night, Andres purchased *Estudios literarios y filosóficos*, the only book by Varona he could find in the bookshop on the corner, but after reading the book, Andres was not sure what to make of this man with the walrus moustache. He seemed to Andres overtly radical, even for a modernist, for he seemed to believe that knowledge was a tool to be used in the battle to overthrow mysticism, and Andres was puzzled by the very notion of doing battle against mysticism, so he poured over the text again and again and again, but he was never quite satisfied with any of his conclusions, and he had, in fact, on the very night before the last time his wife kissed him on the lips, been re-reading Varona, several lengthy passages in which Varona claimed that nationalism was essential for educational reform, looking for things he had missed the other times and wondering how any of these philosophers defined knowledge in the first place, for it seemed to him that mysticism was also a kind of knowledge, though who was he to say, and before he went to bed that night he went over his business ledger to determine if he had saved enough money (a full bank account was also a sort of knowledge, he thought) to add on to their house that once overlooked the river, for in the years between the time he had started building the house and the day he encountered Varona, the city had engulfed them all around and their view of the river was substantially diminished.

It was shortly after he had met Varona that he concocted the idea of adding a third story to their neo-classical Baroque style house and so restore their appreciation of the Almendares (and also to provide additional bedrooms for their grandchildren, which is how he had pitched the idea to his wife). But he did not act on this idea until the spring of 1940, when he contacted a company in New Orleans that specialized in decorative elements and ordered two dozen wrought iron railings for the balcony windows that would adorn the third-story bedrooms he was going to build, one bedroom for his grandson, Andres Escoraz Silvestre, who was already attending law school at the University of Havana, one for his son José Luis and his wife, Nuria, a beautiful mulatta girl from Eastern Cuba, who had moved into the house in Miramar when José Luis had given up playing baseball for Santa Clara, and a third bedroom for their son, also named José Luis, who at the age of nine was already a holy terror with a baseball bat. Of course these mythical rooms did not yet exist, and now would never exist, because this was Andres' last evening before his last day, and when he was getting ready to leave the next morning he was still thinking about the wrought iron balconies, but also about Enrique José Varona, for the two seemed somehow connected, as if you could not have one without the other, at least in Havana, a strange, unsettling notion at the very least.

Then Ana had kissed him, but it was a short kiss because she wanted to remind him to come home early for supper, she was making chicken and tomatoes and rice, but could he please remember to bring home a jar of peach jam, which was getting harder and harder to come by, and also that yellow cheese that came from Miami, she had a hankering for that, and her words were tumbling out of her mouth even while he was trying to finish kissing her, and he laughed and said he would remember, and she was laughing as well, but she was also deathly serious about the peach jam and the yellow cheese, and then he gave her a poem he had written that morning expressing his eternal devotion to her, which she said she would read later and slipped it into the front pocket of her apron, and then he left and it was still dark and the sun wouldn't be up for another twenty minutes.

-40-

After Isidora heard for the first time the story of the death of her great-grandfather and the last kiss her great-grandmother gave him that morning, she wept for three days without stopping. It is fair to say that she felt the entire story unfold before her fluttering heart more than heard it being told, as if she were the reincarnation of her great-grandmother and had simply and without any warning slipped back into the dream of a forgotten past. She wept for three days without stopping, without eating, without sleeping. She simply locked her bedroom door and wept tears of unending, eternal sadness, and when she finished she saw that the floor of her bedroom was littered with the fossilized remains of millions of tiny, dead crustaceans, as if the ocean of her sadness had caused a second great flood and then, the waters receding, or perhaps evaporating in the heat of her exhaustion (for to be caught up in the throes of psychic despair is to burn with the brilliance of a billion exploding suns), leaving a trail of dead sea creatures to remind her of her great-grandmother's misery. She marveled at the number of tiny dead crustacean bodies that covered her bedroom floor. There were a variety of *Cladocera*, also known as water fleas, which under the microscope resemble tiny seahorse babies frozen inside glass wombs made by Italian glassblowers from the seven islands of Murano, several species of *copepods*, which means "oar feet" in Greek, with delicate tear shaped bodies and several long antennae, which give them the appearance of tiny helicopters or miniature alien spaceships monitoring the background static of the universe, hundreds of species of barnacles, everything from the *Sessilia*, the acorn barnacle, the most common barnacle in the world, to the less common but still plentiful *Pedunculata*, otherwise known as the goose barnacle, and finally a few members of crustacean nobility that had been extinct since the Cambrian Period, the *Canadaspis*, with spikes on its head to keep its vulnerable floating eyes from being eaten so easily, and a bivalved arthropod that went by the name *Perspicaris*, which given the Latinate root would suggest a creature that had greater mental acuity than its peers, but which was most likely a bottom feeder, similar to *Trilobites*, which preceded the *Perspicaris* by roughly fifteen million years. Isidora imagined she had been weeping for eons.

-41-

Now Isidora's favorite story, which she thought of as the story of her origins, and which dazzled her compassionate heart with the brilliance of an intimate confession, was the story of how Escolástica Escoraz Vda De Miranda, who was always for Isidora much more than a distant cousin, came to the Americas from Logroño, Spain, and how without her aid, Isidora's great-grandfather, Andres Ordóñez Escoraz, husband to Ana Silvestre for thirty-eight years, might not have lived to see the dawn of the twentieth century.

The story of Escolástica Escoraz Vda De Miranda while she lived in Logroño, Spain from the time she was born until she began to dream about a white bird trapped in a golden cage:

When Escolástica was born (and before she had been given her name), her father, Arturo Ordóñez Escoraz, thought she looked like a shriveled-up raisin and wondered if she were deformed or perhaps his wife had slept with a pig and what to name such a monstrous looking child and whether or not it was worth the trouble, especially considering that such monstrous babies usually died within three days. But after an hour or two of careful deliberation, which included a brief consultation with Father Mateus Antonio de Nazar, a young Jesuit priest who had been installed in the Church of Santiago only three weeks earlier — they spoke in the shadow of the church tower with the great white storks perched on the top of the tower like sentinel angels who, in spite of their guardian duties, seemed to be eavesdropping on the conversation below — he (meaning Escolástica's father) declared his newborn daughter one of the wisest creatures to ever grace the planet (even wiser than the storks) and decided to name her Escolástica.

According to Father de Nazar, the name Escolástica meant one who possesses a great deal of wisdom, or one who teaches, a meaning which the youngest daughter of Arturo Ordóñez Escoraz and his wife contradicted from the start, at least when one compared her temperament, which was marked by a need to remain in constant motion, to the brooding, taciturn demeanor of the monks who occupied the library in the Monastery of Santa María la Real de Las Huelgas, near the city of Burgos, which don Arturo once visited as a boy, when he was called Pepe, and where he was immediately captivated by the eyes of the monks, which were turned inward in a burning, perpetual gaze that suggested to Pepe some terrible, undecipherable mystery or an unimaginable lament, and from that point forward, Arturo associated great spiritual wisdom with the smell of decaying, leather-bound books, but also just the barest hint of manure, for it had been spring when the visit had occurred and the nearby fields had been covered with a mixture of cow shit, horse shit, and dead fish.

It is fair to say that Escolástica was extraordinarily athletic, which explains why she didn't learn to read until the age of ten. By the time she was a year old, she had begun running up and down stairs at breakneck speed and tumbling randomly to the floor at the bottom or the top, sometimes even spinning in the air like a blind circus acrobat, laughing hysterically. By the time she was two, she could be seen all over Logroño riding a small dark horse, a dark chestnut which she rode bareback, her slender, defiant arms raised high above her head and her red hair flowing. She rarely stood still long enough to say good morning to her father or to her sister, Isabel, dark-haired Isabel, who preferred lounging about at the breakfast table, dreaming of marriage even at the age of four, and who, when she (Isabel) started reading at the age of seven, was never seen without a book of poetry, either a collection entitled simply *Rimas*, by Gustavo Adolfo Bécquer (she had memorized over half of the poems by the age of nine, her favorite being a poem about dark swallows who did not return, having feasted their eyes on the beauty and happiness of a young girl, and which after reading, Isabel compared to her own life and her search for happiness and the isolation she felt living, as her father often said, in the shadow of oblivion, so she often looked up at the flat wine colored sky that settled over Logroño on summer evenings like the steady beating of her heart and scanned the horizon for some sign that the swallows were returning), or a slim volume entitled *Cantares gallegos* by María Rosalía Rita de Castro, all because of a single poem, "*¿Como me hei de ir si te quero?*," which left her in a constant state of amazement wondering if she would shed burning tears like glittering beads if her one true love would ever depart, even if only for an afternoon.

But Escolástica had no use for poetry, perhaps because she was poetry in motion. She was a constant blur, the laughter of God burning a hole in the nighttime sky, the music of the heavenly spheres drowning out the anguish of the world, a lightning bolt with the power to illuminate the darkness at the bottom of the sea. Whenever she smiled her smile would linger in the air for hours, sometimes days, the photographic negative of a comet streaking across the icy cold loneliness of space, illuminating even the darkest, loneliest corners of the universe. Everyone in Logroño was struck with the same impression because she offered everyone her prettiest, best most radiant smile. The smile she offered up to her father and her sister as she headed out the door in the morning was the same smile she offered up to Father de Nazar, whom she barely knew, who was either heading to or from the church sacristy with robes that had just been washed or that needed washing; just as it was the same smile she offered up to the chattering old women whom she didn't know at all who were constantly moving up and down the streets of Logroño in search of an open church where they could sit down in the back and rest their feet, for the churches in Logroño were open only when the presiding priests were actually inside lighting candles, or hearing confessions, or preparing for Mass with the church bells ringing (at which point the great sentinel storks would fly off in lazy, elongated circles until the echo of the bells would subside and then they would return to their perches, guardians once again), or any one of a number of routine, priestly duties; but whenever the priests took leave of their churches, which was often (and this was true of Father de Nazar's church as well), they locked the great church doors, for there had been a string of robberies lately (the authorities had a fairly good idea of the identity of the thieves but seemed unwilling to act) so no one wanted to take a chance with the dozens of gold plates and bejeweled chalices and silver crucifixes hidden away in unassuming closets or in cabinets with secret compartments; and sometimes the priests would stroll along the Ebro River in the morning, looking across the narrow ribbon of the river and marveling at the exactitude of God and mumbling incoherent prayers directed towards Santa María de la Esperanza, the patron saint of the town, or maybe take a nap beneath the chestnut trees in the Plaza in the afternoon and the warm breeze that always blew across, or maybe they would take a stroll along a quiet street in the early evening (somewhere along Calle Portales, or perhaps a small section of Calle del Laurel that would years later be called the path of the elephants to encourage the *touristas* to forgo San Sebastián and the sea and spend their vacations instead in Logroño, because Hannibal had set out from Logroño to sack Rome, as everyone once knew), the priests looking for a café and a bite to eat, a bit of stew with beans, before returning to their respective rectories for a glass of wine before going to bed, but even the glittering radiance of such a day as this would be easily eclipsed should they, by chance, happen upon Escolástica's smile.

On her third birthday, in an effort to instill in her some appreciation for more contemplative pursuits, her father hired a young maestro to teach her to play the piano and an old courtesan to teach her how to paint. The maestro left after only a single day, claiming that Escolástica was herself the incarnation of music, and one did not need to teach music to play itself, one had only to listen. The courtesan stayed a week, but not because she had any interest in teaching Escolástica how to paint. Indeed, while the courtesan had known a few painters quite intimately, she had no talent for painting herself. One of her coterie of painters, Federico de Madrazo, had remarked years earlier that she was the best pupil he had ever entertained, and though clearly Madrazo meant one thing and not another, the remark encouraged all sorts of wild speculations about her unproclaimed genius and how only the truly great painters abandoned the world stage with such frivolous disdain, and over the years the courtesan herself kept this kind of gossip alive, for she imagined it was far better to be talked about or whispered about than to be forgotten, and in this way she soon became a myth — which perhaps explains Arturo's mistake in hiring her in the first place — and whenever the talk turned towards her perhaps exhibiting what must surely have been a prodigious talent, she remarked with a cavalier laugh that the only painting she did any more was her own face, and again those listening took her meaning one way and not another, and the courtesan's face took on an inscrutable expression with the darkening lines of despair mixing with the blushing smile of giddy deceit, a face that seemed to have been lifted from one of Goya's later paintings.

When don Arturo asked the courtesan to teach his daughter how to paint, she became slightly unsettled, but she could think of no way to properly refuse the don's noble request other than by flinging herself into the dark waters of the Ebro from the newly rebuilt Puente de Piedra bridge, an act of desperation that would have surely been the end of the courtesan because the river was moving very fast, partly because it was spring and the snow melt had filled the smaller steams to overflowing, but also because at that point in history no one had dreamed of damming up the river with seventy-four dams, and then one hundred and eight dams, and then one hundred and twenty. But the moment the courtesan met the young Escolástica, her fears fled, overwhelmed as they were by the child's tremendous beauty, which was more robust and less elegant than the beauty of her sister, Isabel, and which in time became as legendary as her athleticism.

For one week the courtesan remained in a small sitting room that opened up to an inner courtyard, seemingly lost in a trance, as if she had become part of a painting herself, her eyes locked in a struggle to comprehend the nature of reality and the immortality of art. Then on the morning of the seventh day it began to rain, a gentle rain that smelled of vanilla and orange spice and cinnamon pastries and coffee from the West Indies, and ever so faintly the smell of finely brushed leather, and which reminded the aging courtesan of an ancient Basque love song from her youth, *"Chorittua, nurat hua bi hegalez airian?"* she heard a voice whisper (which translated means "Oh little bird, where are you going on your two wings in the air?"), and then another voice said they would go to Spain together when the snows melted in the pass, at which point she awoke from her trance and informed don Arturo Ordóñez Escoraz that his daughter was herself such a work of art that one could do nothing but stand in front of her and admire her beauty.

Now by the time Escolástica turned five (or perhaps seven, or even ten, her precise age is irrelevant), everyone forgot she was called Escolástica and called her Tiká instead. It was also at this time that she began dreaming a strange, recurring dream about a white bird trapped in a golden cage. The white bird stared out at the world with heavy, sad eyes, irrevocably sad on a sunny day with a bright blue sky, and seeming less sad when the world was plagued by the cold lethargy and gray cloudy skies of rainy days, though perhaps this was just a trick of the light, and every so often, the door to the cage was left open, and since the cage was hanging on a hook near a window, which was also sometimes left open, it was reasonable to imagine (or hope) that the tiny white bird might one day escape, but the bird just sat on its perch with its heavy, sad eyes gazing at the great beyond and did not move. So Tiká asked her father why the bird didn't fly out when the door was open, and her father said it was because he does not see past the bars, he cannot visualize a world without bars, so he might as well stay put.

In her dream Tiká did not see her father, she only heard his voice drifting out through the open window or down from the eaves of the verandah and swirling about her feet with a few fallen rose petals and dried leaves, and his voice seemed to her to possess the lilt of cut grass, which is another way of saying that if one could actually see sounds, which Tiká most assuredly could, her father's voice was a burnt yellow color, which was the color of cut grass in Logroño and the surrounding countryside, except sometimes during the hottest part of the summer when it seemed a burnt orange color.

Always the dream began with Tiká sitting in a wicker chair on the verandah of her father's house, always it was sunset and she was looking in through the window (usually closed at this point, but sometimes open) at the tiny white bird in the cage. The bird was filled with such despair that it rarely sang, though it sometimes made low, gurgling sounds, as if it were drowning. On some nights, the door to the cage was always open, and on other nights the maid (which maid? it was always someone Tiká had never seen before) came sweeping past with a broom and stopped and smiled out at Tiká looking in and closed the small golden door and locked it with a tiny golden key she kept in a pocket hidden behind the folds of her apron. And always the dream seemed to possess a haphazard disrespect for the generally accepted pattern of time, speeding up when it shouldn't, lingering a little longer at times just for spite, or perhaps to induce in the dreamer a feeling of melancholy, and often leaving out whole chunks of time altogether, which did not always bother Tiká, who assumed they were probably meaningless chunks anyway, as so much of time seemed to be whether one was dreaming or not.

In her dream Tiká would be sitting on the verandah, contemplating the existence (or perhaps simply the presence) of the bird, and then she would hear the sound of someone shouting down the street; or the old women with their heads covered with shawls chattering their strange foreign language of the fanatically devout as they hurried past her father's house in search of an open church door; or even a church bell ringing in the distance and the shadows of storks floating in the air, or many church bells and many more storks (which was not altogether unreasonable, for there were five churches within the city limits of Logroño, and several more within a mile of the ruins of the old stone wall that marked the original border of the town and had been there in one form or another since the time of the Romans); and every time Tiká looked back at the window and the caged bird, it always seemed to her that years had passed.

Oddly, she never grew any older in her dream, but she knew that many years had passed nevertheless because the tiny white bird looked so very much older, and then when she looked back to the street because of a new voice or the old women making a second or a third pass or another round of church bells and the storks flying off and then returning, she would notice that the weather had changed, the hot winds of summer had vanished and the world had become winter, and the next time the rain had given way to bright sunlight, and so forth. Each time she looked back at the window and the bird, the bird looked older and older, as old as a saint or one of the forgotten immortals. And each time she looked back to the street, the weather had changed, although this was not always so. While the bird always looked older, a feature of her dream that she could always count on, and which, during her waking hours and even years later, was a strange comfort like an unrelenting faith, the weather in her dream did not always change. Some nights in her dream there were no rainstorms at all, it was an endless string of bright, sunny days, and at other times, the landscape of her dream was plagued by a relentless, eternal winter or a creeping, insolent autumn filled with the whirring sounds of flying insects. (All of which seems to suggest, though this intricate thought probably did not occur to Tiká, that the nature of reality is much more fluid than we realize, even when it is constrained by certain seemingly unbreachable parameters.) But in spite of these minor inconsistencies, always near the end of the dream Tiká would begin to worry about the bird and if it had perhaps gone blind, and always she would ask her father why the bird stayed in the cage when the door was open, and always she would hear her father's voice, which sounded like the color yellow, except when it sounded like the color orange.

Then one night, and it is worth noting that this was the

last time Tiká dreamed of the tiny white bird in the golden cage, one night the ending of Tiká's dream was different. At that moment when normally she would notice how very old the white bird had become (in some versions the bird was decrepit beyond belief and could barely move or blink an eye), she saw instead that the door to the golden cage was locked but that the bird was gone. But instead of calling out to her father from the verandah (which is the reason she had only ever heard his voice in her dream), she raced inside and found him sitting at the dark mahogany roll top desk writing out long letters or perhaps adding up figures in his ledger.

He was working feverishly to finish his task, a smoky oil lamp perched precariously on one corner of the roll top, the dim light from the lamp barely penetrating the shadow he himself cast over the desk, so he almost didn't see his daughter as she came running into the room, shouting out her question with breathless anxiety.

'Papa, papa, the bird is gone. The bird has vanished. Papa, where did it go?' she said in her dream.

And without even looking up from his work, her father had said 'It is gone, my little Tiká, because if it did not go it would have surely died sitting there on that perch. A bird cannot live long locked up in a cage like that, even if the cage is unlocked. Nothing can.'

Tiká was too stunned to reply, but later, after she woke up, and for many years afterwards, quite probably until she settled (eventually) in Puerto Rico, she wished she had said something, anything to spur her father into an explanation of the philosophical implications of the vanished bird, for as she grew older she spent many weary evenings wrestling inconclusively with the straightforward and yet exceedingly complex nature of her father's response as well as the multiple meanings and shifting realities of the dream itself. But during those last few moments of the last time she dreamed about the tiny white bird, she stood mute before her father's desk as if he were God himself, listening to the scratching of his pen as he worked at his figures or his letters until the oil lamp gave out and the world was plunged into darkness.

The truth, of course, is that it was unimportant whether or not Tiká understood her dream. Indeed, one could make a case (as a few philosophers and several ancient Greek playwrights have done) that it was best not to understand the meaning of such dreams, presumably because they were prophetic in nature, and if one understood the nature of the prophecy, one might try to alter the course of one's own life, which one could never do, life being a foreordained phenomenon, but one might try nevertheless, which would often result in needless calamity, it would be like dashing one's head against a brick wall until the skull split open, a senseless, bloody diversion from the joy of living one's life with courageous and unquestionably blind faith, so it was best to remain calm in the face of such dreams and plod along without expectation, allowing the folds of life to unfold, and in time the meaning of the dream would become clear because it would reflect the meaning of a life that had been lived.

Such was the case with respect to Tiká's dream, a fact she only truly appreciated one summer afternoon in 1937 while sitting in a rocking chair on a third-floor corner room balcony with an iron railing in a run-down boarding house that had once been a convent for Carmelite nuns on Caleta de las Monjas in San Juan, Puerto Rico. There was still the Latin inscription above the stone archway entrance that no longer possessed any gates. The inscription said "Blessed are those who come in the name of the Lord."

She could not see the sea from where she sat, but she could see the flashing dome of the Cathedral like a great ship riding the waves of a restless ocean and she closed her eyes and breathed in the smell of the sea and the memory of an ocean voyage she had once taken, the only true ocean voyage she had ever taken. Others who had made the same crossing had called it the journey across the gloomy sea, but in her memory it had been a journey bathed in dazzling sunshine, and while she was thinking of that voyage oh so many years ago, she suddenly remembered the dream of the tiny white bird, and she compared it to the dream her life had been and she observed that they were the same dream, and she did not even wonder about this, it was like looking at a sunset, something to be admired from a great distance.

Then the bells of the Cathedral began to ring, a slow, steady, comforting sound, and she found herself thinking back to that moment when the dream of the tiny white bird began to merge with the dream of her life and how very unaware she had been, it had been hidden from her view, this beginning, as so many things are when we are young.

-42-

The story of when Tiká's dream of the tiny white bird began to merge with the dream of her life:

It all began one afternoon when Tiká was seventeen and her sister was twenty-one. Their uncle, Andres Ordóñez Escoraz, who still claimed three rooms near the back of the house as his own but who had left when the girls were six and ten to chase wild geese around the globe, returned suddenly on the heels of a late summer thunderstorm.

The girls thought him a majestic but lunatic sea captain or a deposed and very beautiful Grecian god the way he stood in the doorway, his face covered in shadows, a scene of vigorous, luminous destruction behind him, a theatrical backdrop for his unknown intentions with the rain splatter cascading from the roof of the verandah and the lightning flashing bright green bolts across the sky and smoke rising from the ground like geysers, which was not really smoke but just water vapor rising, and they weren't really geysers either, naturally, but in the minds of the sisters, or perhaps it was just the mind of Isabel, the scene before them had descended from the pages of a great epic tale of madness and love, a tale with the comic vision of *Orlando furioso* (Ariosto, Italian, dozens of characters, a hero who is rejected by a princess and goes mad and then later flies to the moon to retrieve his sanity, giant sea monsters and flying horses, Algerian kings who are treated like deposed gods, sorcerers who build castles of iron to keep their prisoners from escaping, weeping virgins in search of true love, Saracen knights with lances that sprout flowers); or *La Gerusalemme liberata* (Tasso, also Italian, same kinds of characters but fewer of them, no lances sprouting flowers, as far as Isabel could recall, but she wasn't sure, the two epics were kind of merging in her mind); and also a dash of the brooding melancholy of *The Shipwreck and Demise of Sepúlveda and Leonor* (Jerónimo Corte-Real, Portuguese, a harrowing tale, actually, about the death of a sea captain and his family, not to mention the entire ship's company, who make it ashore after their ship flounders off the coast of Africa [the captain had stupidly overloaded the ship with Indian pepper], only to be duped by a deceitful Bantu chief and then murdered as they slept).

At first Andres said nothing. He just stood there with his

terrible majesty of a sea captain or a deposed god, and Isabel almost fainted, but Escolástica, who was now Tiká, recognized him in spite of the mythology of the rain and the shadows and the literary grime from ten years of chasing wild geese around the globe and ran to her prodigal uncle and hugged him with a wild fury to equal the storm outside, and then Andres Ordóñez Escoraz, who could not quite believe that the two little girls he had last seen ten years earlier had become the two beautiful young ladies he now saw before him, shook the rain from his shoulders and stepped inside.

Andres stayed at the house for two weeks, regaling his nieces with stories of Italian excess and Dutch perseverance and the lingering sadness of the Portuguese, and each night after the sisters had gone to bed he conversed with his brother until well into the wee hours of the morning, the two men dripping with copious amounts of perspiration even though they were sitting on the verandah and there was a cool breeze blowing across the valley from the mountains to the north. Andres spoke with the hushed, courageous, conspiratorial tone of a revolutionary, because he had nothing to lose but the future, and his brother responded with the restrained even timid civility of an overworked postal clerk, for he had given up on the future when his daughters were born to live in the past, a choice which is often made, as everyone knows, to appease a relentless fear.

The topic of the protracted conversation was a copper mine near Santiago, Cuba. Actually, Andres mentioned a dozen or more now abandoned copper mines with a variety of colorful if somewhat ironic names (La Esperanza, La Independencia, La Union, La Manuela, Kirkappo, El Porvenir, La Caridad, and Maximina, to name a few), one lead mine (Milagro) of dubious quality, three lead and zinc mines (El Angel, Peña Blanca, and Mina Cebrero), one all but exhausted coal mine (La Primera), and several silver mines whose names Andres did not know. The mines had belonged to the Cobre Company, a family-run outfit founded, according to Andres, by an eccentric Welshman named Grenfell with a taste for mulatta girls, but the company had gone out of business because of Cuba Libre and the Ten Years War, which had put a practical end to slavery in Cuba (though slavery in concept was still legal until 1886), and thus abolished the workforce, or most of it, of the Cobre Company.

A petition to officially dissolve the company had been brought before the English Court of Chancery in 1869, but the ultimate ownership and subsequent fate of the mines was never properly determined. Papers had been lost or misfiled, bank receipts had mysteriously disappeared, important letters never sent, the eccentric Welshman who owned the company had been killed in a street brawl in Havana, or perhaps he had been murdered by a man who had been tailing him in the underbelly of Havana for three or four days.

It was almost impossible to believe that such an opportunity existed, said Andres. After the death of the owner, the mines had fallen into the abyss of utter abandonment. But now, over thirty years later, they had miraculously resurfaced under new ownership (a new owner with the same name as the original owner, someone who was related to Grenfell by blood or marriage or who once knew him, or someone who once played cards with him in a back-alley dive somewhere along Calle Galiano, a disreputable street only a few blocks removed from the exact spot where Grenfell was supposedly killed or murdered). The mines were now for sale, singly or all together, and this is what Andres wished to discuss. But Arturo was not interested. He had become lost in the labyrinth of his own mind the moment Andres mentioned mulatta girls, which was for Arturo a symbol of the future he had once dreamed of, a future that would have been shaped by a thirst for adventure aboard a whaling ship and an endless parade of naked mulatta girls whenever he was in port, a future (or at least a possible future) he had given up when Isabel was born, so he paid scant attention to what his brother was saying, and when it was his turn to speak he lectured his brother on the value of hard work and the sanctity of matrimonial bliss, which seemed to him the only thing he could say, and which he would repeat if pressed, and then he sat back in his wicker chair and looked at the dark foreboding, vacant sky without even a star with a blank look of despair. Theirs was the kind of conversation that would extend indefinitely, a mirror to the eternity that resides in every man's hopes, a dark glass of infinite possibility, for neither man was willing to listen to the other, each waiting only till the other paused to draw a breath so he could plunge forward with his own reckless, unvarnished thoughts.

On the last night of the two weeks, Andres was joined by a shabby looking fellow wearing a heavy longshoreman's coat, an odd and memorable detail given that it was late August, who had been spotted skulking about the alleys of Logroño and had taken up temporary residence near the back door of The Café with Two Names (for those passing through it was known as Café la del Oriental, but for those who lived in Logroño it was known as Café del Fernando and was typical of that part of Spain with dark timbers showing themselves on the ceiling and plaster walls painted a mauve color because mauve was becoming popular, and on the wall directly across from the bar there was a framed copy of an edition of *Le Petit Journal* dated November 1893, with an artist's depiction of the explosion of the opera theater of the Liceu of Barcelona by the anarchist Santiago Salvador Franch, you could even see in the drawing the bloodied corpses of the victims draped over the seats like forgotten overcoats).

In truth, as everyone in Logroño knew, it was not all that unusual to find a few vagrants sleeping in the alleyway behind The Café with Two Names, in spite of the fact that the Civil Guard had been charged with cracking down on vagrancy and robbery or potential robbery, because the Civil Guard often looked the other way when it came to vagrants (as it had looked the other way and continued looking the other way in the matter of the string of robberies that plagued Logroño's churches and kept their doors closed in the absence of the priests), particularly if those vagrants had been seen in the company of a well-known local miscreant named Carabali, as was the case with the longshoreman in question. The day after this fellow arrived in Logroño, while taking a stroll along the Ebro, he had met Carabali. The two men found immediate refuge in a dimly lit dive and began drinking *absenta* and sharing intimate secrets, which is how Carabali found out that the longshoreman and Andres were partners of a sort and that there was an opportunity to perhaps make some money, not quite a get-rich-quick scheme, but close enough to appeal to Carabali's unwavering faith that the world owed him a living.

Later, as they wound their way through the empty streets, they began singing strange, long-winded, virtually incoherent songs about priests dying in droves of consumption and the ancient Romans and their conquest of the Iberian Peninsula during the two centuries preceding the birth of Christ. The last song they sang that evening was a once popular ditty about the defeat of Charlemagne's rear guard at Roncesvalles in 778.

The following day at four in the afternoon, two members of the Civil Guard (older men, gray around the temples, former members of the defeated Carlist party) set off to arrest the longshoreman for vagrancy and attempted robbery. It was a dubious charge at best, but understandable. In the blazing white light of noon that very day, the longshoreman had suddenly been awakened by church bells going off, and stumbling from both sleep and the relative obscurity of the alleyway behind The Café with Two Names, he had burst into the narrow rough cobblestone of Calle Santiago with a strange, uncontrollable rage, shouting obscenities at the unseen moon and shaking his bony fist at the sky and frightening a dozen or more old women who had just happened by in their eternal quest for an open church door, and who had thought him a demon and had pulled their black shawls tightly around their heads, covering their ears so the demon's curses could not penetrate the barrier of closed eardrums, and fled into the white glare of the next street. Fortunately, Carabali intervened and the longshoreman was spared the indignity of arrest.

As it happened, Carabali was sipping a coffee at Café Rioja, which was only two blocks away from the alleyway behind The Café with Two Names, pretending to read a newspaper and checking his pocket watch every so often. Then he saw the two guardsmen pass by on their way to arrest his new friend. He told the boy, Manuela, who was tending the bar, that he would return shortly, he wanted to see where these two guardsmen were going in such a hurry, he hoped his curiosity didn't get the better of him. Then he grabbed two bottles of wine off the counter, bottles which he had told the boy, Manuela, to set there some time earlier, smiled a cavalier smile and said he had a strange and beguiling premonition that an opportunity to cement a friendship was at hand. Still smiling, and laughing as well, in spite of the fact that the guardsmen were no longer in sight, he quickly made his way to the alleyway behind The Cafe with Two Names. As the Civil Guard approached the longshoreman, who had by then resumed his supine position in the alleyway, Carabali approached the guardsmen and said the unshaven vagrant before them was a friend and business partner of Andres Ordóñez Escoraz, the brother of don Arturo Ordóñez Escoraz. Then he said that in spite of his shabby appearance he was a man of some stature in Wales and in England, a compassionate man who for philosophical reasons that could only be discussed with the clergy preferred the gritty reality of city streets to the silky, perfumed sheets of the Escoraz house. Then Carabali handed each of the guardsmen a half-full bottle of *Crianza*. Without even a wry comment about the nature of Carabali's gift, they disappeared into the widening glass of the afternoon sun.

A short digression on Carabali and Lady Luck:

Carabali, it should be said, slept very little, just in case

Lady Luck made a sudden appearance. He was ever alert, no matter what form she might take. Some days she arrived in the form of the Egyptian goddess Isis, whose name meant "throne" and who was the patroness of fertility, nature and magic, which is almost like luck, and who according to some zealous believers was actually the first Eve, a genuine and incredibly sexy Mother Earth type goddess who lived on the planet approximately six thousand years ago and whose luck was based on her considerable natural genius, which was twice that of Einstein, which is even better than luck.

On other days she appeared in the form of the Greek goddess Tyche, who may have been from Antioch, and who was the daughter of Zeus and Aphrodite, or, according to some sources, Hermes and Aphrodite, which is incest either way you look at it, and who more than any of the other ladies of luck is associated with the notion of destiny, or at least the destiny of those particular cities where the citizens built temples in her honor, and whose head appeared on many silver coins of the day (and who has not felt lucky upon discovering a few silver coins in a forgotten pocket or stashed away in a hidden drawer), and Tyche was reviled among poets and other intellectuals tit for tat because she despised those who thought they could imagine a better world and so she withheld from them her favor.

Sometimes she (Lady Luck) took the form of the Roman goddess Fortūna, who was the very personification of luck in the Roman world and whose name was forever linked with strength of character and justice (two very Roman virtues, but also German virtues, in a pre-apocalyptic Wagnerian sort of way), and who gave birth (a virgin birth, according to Hesiod) to Pontus, god of the sea, or perhaps, as some said, just the god of seaweed, whose own son, Nereus, was gentle and trustworthy, which was not quite the same thing as seaworthy, though close, which can be confused with luck if you're not paying too much attention to detail; and Fortūna was also called Gaia, at least by Hesiod, and she was also given over to sudden, capricious, even malicious reversals of fortune, like when she claimed the lives of Caesar's grandsons, which might have been a lucky thing for a few aspiring Roman politicians who had no use for the Senate (as was the case with Caligula, and after him, Nero), but it was certainly very unlucky for the grandsons.

On still other occasions, particularly if Carabali were traveling in Northern Spain, she preferred the form of the Basque goddess Mari, who was viewed by those living in that region as a Mother Earth type goddess but may have been just a local enchantress who later became a myth, who lived (lives?) in the Pyrenees mountains and who could take the form of any animal but preferred the form of a goat or a snake, but who became a ball of fire when traveling between various mountains, and who many millennia ago created the moon so that the people of the mountains would not be afraid of the dark, which until the moon had been created the night was very dark and there were all sorts of great thunderous noises, like twenty-megaton nuclear explosions, which the people attributed to dragons or demons, so they were always afraid, but as soon as Mari created the moon, the people abandoned all that superstitious nonsense about dragons, though many still believed in demons for some reason, and Mari was not associated with the idea of luck, per se, for the Basque people thought of luck, which they called *Adur*, as a quality or power used by soothsayers and magicians in both performing simple feats of magic, and in predicting the future, though many of their predictions seemed to unravel even as they were speaking them.

But more and more often she (Lady Luck) took the form of the Virgin Mary herself, who among the Basque people is a curious blend of Mary the mother of Jesus and Mari the mother of us all, and who for the rest of us may or may not be a synthesis of various Sumerian or Assyrian or Babylonian myths, or Roman, if you remember the story of Fortūna and Pontus, but not Buddhist or Hindu or Sikh or Shintoist or Native American, or the resurging Manichaeistic heresy of the Balkan peninsula, which is an off-shoot of Babylonian thinking anyway, or any one of the thousands of different religious perspectives that make up the religious tapestry of the world. It is indeed curious (though certainly Carabali's curiosity never went this far) that in these Western myths we cling to, young goddesses are routinely raped, ravished, seduced, even blessed by some Western god (which is not to say a cowboy or rodeo star) parading about in the form of a bull or an aggressive swan or an untethered angel, and nine months later they give birth to their very own brown-haired, blue-eyed god who inevitably must be sacrificed (with the exception of Pontus, who more or less just vanished from the mythological record, as if one day after centuries of floating around in a clump of seaweed he just sort of sank to the bottom of the sea and dissolved) so that the world may be reborn in spectacular post-apocalyptic fashion. Or perhaps the change is quieter, a subtle rendering of reality, like opening a window so you can watch winter melt away and spring arrive, though even if you are extremely focused in this regard it is almost impossible to pinpoint the exact moment when the leaves appear. And because these earlier mythic stories are, well, mythic, it is easy (or easier) to see that they are concerned with a spiritual rebirth, not an actual physical one, but in the case of the Virgin Mary and her son, Jesus, who have taken on the dimensions of actual physical, historical personages in spite of their general absence from the historical record (the two debatable references in Josephus aside), the implications are more difficult to assess, for in the minds of the laity (not to mention certain narcissistic philosophers, misogynist theologians, and the hundreds of television evangelists suffering from de Clérambault's syndrome), the notion of a spiritual rebirth has been replaced by the belief in an actual physical rebirth, which could, of course, be considered extraordinarily lucky in the sense that you, as an individual, would never die, but the idea of rebirth here in the West is not imagined in the sense of emerging a second or a third or tenth time from some bloody womb, as is the case with the Eastern religions, but instead refers to simply rising from the grave with your earthly body restored, which according to the Judeo-Christian religious tradition means your ideal earthly body, without blemish, without pain, without the cellular memory of dying, as opposed to a postmodern vision of the walking dead, apoplectic zombies with pieces of jagged flesh falling away as they walk and eyeballs dangling so you wonder how they can even see where they are going, and still they are somehow able to take over the world, or at least cable television, all of which would be extraordinarily unlucky if you were wedded to the Judeo-Christian view, in which case you might wish to start completely over as someone brand spanking new.

-43-

Now it should also be pointed out that the longshoreman in question possessed a dark, shadowy complexion and an inscrutable expression, with his hair cropped so close it seemed he was wearing a skull cap, and a wavering darkness that surrounded him like a shroud, perhaps because he never removed his heavy longshoreman's coat, at least not while he was in Logroño.

He resembled most closely the ghost of an unlucky and unrepentant Inquisitor from the days of the Spanish Inquisition who had died a suspicious if not violent death during the Second Alpujarras revolt in Granada in 1568. And he somewhat resembled the ghost of a renegade Jesuit priest who had been lost in the jungles of Venezuela in the 17th century but had been taken in by a tribe of Yanomamo cannibals who lived along an unexplored tributary of the Oronoco River and who granted him a special kind of immortality (the kind reserved for venerable grandfathers or noble enemies), after he had explained to them with the aid of a mestizo the sacrifice of Christ and the symbolic meaning of the Communion wafer, by eating him at a feast in his honor. But he bore little resemblance at all to the swelling ranks of fat, young Spanish priests who hoped only for a small parish with plenty to eat and drink and the chance to die safely in their beds without being tested by war, famine, pestilence, or the crumbling of their faith.

He was a man of great courage, willing to take all sorts of risks, both necessary and unnecessary, but he also possessed a simmering, calculating maliciousness, which was fairly easy to see unless you were blinded by his slovenly charm. He said his name was Grenfell, a Welshman by birth and a descendent of William Pascoe Grenfell, who had founded the Cobre Company. He had accompanied the younger Ordóñez brother from Swansea, Wales, where the two had met in a brothel overlooking the harbor. Grenfell was in search of the financial backing to restore what he said was rightfully his in the first place. He claimed to be a distant cousin or grandnephew twice removed or a grandson from a second marriage of the eccentric mine owner. Andres was never quite sure he remembered correctly, for the disclosure of the exact nature of the longshoreman's familial connection to the elder Grenfell always and only took place after several pints of warm beer or glasses of wine or bottles of rum had been consumed.

It was Grenfell who suggested that they wait until Andres had assessed his brother's potential as an investor before introducing him to the rightful heir to the mines and the mining company. "He that refuseth instruction despiseth his own soul: but he that heareth reproof getteth understanding," the Welshman was fond of saying. And though Andres did not fully understand the cryptic meaning of the Welshman's words, he did recognize biblical language when he heard it, even biblical language obscured by a thick Welsh accent (not as thick as if Grenfell had come from Bangor, more like he had been born in Cardiff), so he agreed to bring in the Welshman only if absolutely necessary. In truth, Grenfell gave him little choice. Either that or the events that transpired had been decreed since the beginning of time.

-44-

The night before Andres' last day at his brother's house, he and Grenfell talked about Arturo's lack of interest in the copper mines. They were heading to Cuba one way or another. They had already booked passage on a steamer that had been christened with the grand-sounding even mythic name of *Conde Wifredo,* which was leaving from Barcelona in one week, but they needed a small infusion of cash or their plans would surely go for naught. This was Grenfell's position. He spoke with the inflexible conviction of a desert prophet, so there was very little Andres could say to challenge him. Also, for some half-baked and therefore unexpressed and inexpressible reason, possibly because Grenfell wished to repay the debt he owed Carabali for intervening on his behalf with the Civil Guard, but more likely because Carabali now thought of the longshoreman as an investment and wanted to keep tabs on his whereabouts, Carabali accompanied Grenfell and Andres to The Café with Two Names, which is where the conversation noted above took place.

The conversation in The Café with Two Names:

"So that there's the truth of it," said Grenfell.

"What do you mean that there's the truth of it?" said Carabali.

"I mean I know for a fact it was a hell of a lot easier running the mines when we had Negroes working for us," said Grenfell.

"What do you mean you know for a fact?" said Carabali.

"I mean I've heard about it," said Grenfell. "It was easier in all kinds of ways. For one thing, there was no such thing as a strike. They worked when you told them to work, that's one advantage with the darkies, and for as long as you needed them to work, and that's another advantage, and if they didn't you flogged them till they bled or died, not all of them, only the ones that started the trouble. Believe you me, the flogging of Negroes is as cruel and depraved an act as you're likely to see on this earth. I've seen it first hand, so I know. They'd lay the Negroes on the ground, some of them tied to ladders, or some of them held down by two or even three men, and then twenty or thirty lashes with a bullwhip and every blow rattling as loud as a pistol shot."

"What do you mean you've seen it?" said Carabali.

"I mean I've heard about it," said Grenfell.

Carabali blinked stupidly.

"But times change," said Grenfell. "And it's a good thing too. Working them Negroes who came over through the Canaries was like working in a damnable charnal house. It was a slow, withering death to all of us. But now you've got to pay somebody to mine your copper, and that ain't cheap neither, which leaves us where we are."

The men grew silent for a moment, grim.

They were eating black sausage and beans and great chunks of coarse brown bread, and they were sharing what was left of a bottle of *Crianza*. There were several empty bottles on the table. All of the men were exceedingly drunk.

Fernando, the owner of the cafe, a beefy man wearing a butcher's apron stained with the blood of various cuts of meat, who had no talent for the culinary arts but who had inherited the café from his father so he had no choice, leaned over the table with some fresh bread and smiled a butcher's smile which seemed to slice through the very air, but he only looked at Andres, the smile becoming an expression of sadness, and asked how his brother was faring these days, it had been a month or more since he had seen him. Andres smiled weakly and said his brother was well, but it was difficult with the two girls, especially now that the girls were grown up, or almost, they were too much for his brother to handle, especially without Verona, may God preserve her immortal soul. Fernando nodded, a slight movement, and said a similar prayer, but under his breath, as if he were suddenly embarrassed, the words escaping like steam. Then he said he'd return promptly with a bottle of *absenta* for later, wiped his great butcher hands on his apron and grabbed hold of the empties, his great butcher fingers like fat sausages wrapped around the skinny glass necks, and returned with a renewed sense of purpose to the darkness of the bar at the other end of the café.

"Arturo will not help us," said Andres after a prolonged silence.

"But perhaps he can be made to help us," said Grenfell.

"How is this possible?" said Carabali.

"I don't think it is possible," said Andres.

"He that refuseth instruction despiseth his own soul: but he that heareth reproof getteth understanding," said Grenfell.

"I have not heard of this," said Carabali. And then to Andres: "What does he mean?"

But Andres only shook his head.

"It means," said Grenfell, but then he lapsed into silence and drank some more wine.

Andres ate some more of his stew.

Carabali began to study Grenfell's face, as if closer scrutiny would reveal some hidden meaning in his silence.

Grenfell seemed to be waiting for something.

Then the door to the café opened and an old man wearing a wool cap and his capless middle-aged son came in and they sat down at a table near the only window in the café. Fernando brought the newcomers two bowls of stew and a basket of bread and a bottle of *Crianza* and mumbled something and the men mumbled something back and began to eat. Fernando stood by their table a while, hovering over the father and the son like the shadow of a church tower, watching the men eat, then looking out the window and the dark red glow of the sun washing over the brown cobblestones outside, and then watching the men some more.

The three men began talking in stark counterpoint to the conversation at the other end of the café.

It was almost like an operetta. But without the music.

"No one knew the Caribbean would be so much trouble," the old man said.

The middle-aged son laughed but did not look at his father and his father cuffed him on the side of his head but still he did not look up.

"Who is going to pay for this war, Lazaro? You?"

"No, I have already paid too much."

"We have all paid too much," said Fernando.

"Yes, it is too much already," said the old man. "What was the government thinking?"

"Who cares?" said Lazaro. "It is already finished, the fighting. So who cares? Not even God cares."

The three men started lamenting the useless tragedy of all the young men who had left Spain to fight the insurgents and would now never return. Thousands of young men. Tens of thousands. An entire generation. Someone was to blame for the terrible embarrassment of losing the war. The army, perhaps, or the navy, yes, they were certainly to blame. The navy had been smashed by the Americans. How could that happen? In what nightmare realm did such things occur? The heroic pride of Spain had been smashed by farmers and shopkeepers and maybe a few cowboys. It was a disgrace. What had happened to the might and indomitable will of the Spanish Empire? How could one even begin to comprehend the scope of such a disaster? The government should call for an investigation. They should hang every Admiral they could get their hands on, and every Captain too, everyone who hadn't been killed during the war. Every newspaper in the country said so.

Then it was hard to hear what the three men were saying. The sun had set and the only window in the café had become a dark glass which swallowed everything they said.

Fernando returned to the darkness behind the bar.

On the other side of the café, Andres was still focused on his stew.

Carabali was still scrutinizing Grenfell's face.

"It means," began Grenfell again, as if someone had suddenly pulled a switch, "that every breath draws us one step closer to God, so we all better concede that we are inferior beings and do what God demands of us or we will certainly perish in the fiery pits of Hell, which will be the fate of most of mankind. In Hell the death of the soul is inevitable. That's what it means."

"But who knows what God wants us to do?" said Carabali.

Yes," said Andres. "That is precisely the question I have been asking him the last two weeks."

Grenfell coughed some and spat a wad of phlegm onto the floor. Then he rinsed his mouth with the last of the wine and waved for Fernando, who appeared like a great wind with another bottle and disappeared just as suddenly into the comfortable darkness behind the bar. Then Grenfell smiled and blinked happily, as if he had just arrived at the café. "How much would Arturo pay to preserve the joy of seeing his beautiful daughters each and every morning?" he said. He held up his empty glass in dramatic fashion so that it caught the dim light of the café and sparkled like a diamond. "How much is the joy of beholding such beauty worth?"

"You would hold his eyes for ransom?" said Carabali.

"You are an idiot," said Grenfell. "Not his eyes. We will hold for ransom that which gives his eyes the greatest joy."

"And what is that?" said Carabali.

"We will kidnap his daughters."

"And this is what God wants?" said Carabali.

Grenfell smiled again, a thin, knowing smile this time, like a layer of clouds pressing down upon the horizon, but said nothing. He uncorked the new bottle and poured a glass for himself and drank it slowly, and then he poured some for the others and watched them drink.

"It is not so much a question of what God wants," he said after a while, "but what God will permit."

"Ah, you are a slippery devil," said Carabali. "But what of this one here?"

Carabali pointed a drunken finger at Andres.

"With Andres' help we will soon have the wind at our back," said Grenfell. "Is this not true, Andres?"

Andres finished the glass of wine Grenfell had poured him and poured himself another. It was a full-bodied red with a hint of smoked something, Andres couldn't quite tell, but it went down easily. He drank some more and smiled vaguely at his two companions. He had been trying to follow the conversation, but he had become uncertain who was talking at various points so he had given up, focusing on the wine instead. He could barely see what he was doing. He had the feeling that he was groping his way through a dense fog. Then he heard his name and his mind began to clear, and then he remembered someone had said they were going to kidnap his nieces and hold them for ransom, or maybe he had thought this strange thought himself, but Arturo would pay any price for his daughters, Andres knew this to be true, so it might work, yes, it was worth thinking about at any rate, and besides, his nieces would be in no real danger, it would only be a temporary measure, it would be like a game, and then his vision returned and he could make out the shadowy, shimmering figures of Grenfell and Carabali and he nodded at them ever so slightly and smiled, to assure them not only that he understood what they were talking about, but that he was willing to participate in this fantastic scheme of theirs, and then Carabali gave a nervous, chirpy laugh, because he wasn't at all sure what Andres meant by nodding, and then the conversation, which had been put on hold while Andres regained his composure, resumed, and Andres heard himself speaking, though he sounded very far away, a trembling, muffled, hollow sounding voice, almost unrecognizable, like the sound of church bells under water, as if he had fallen into a very dark, very deep well. He did not sound like himself at all.

"You swear the girls will be in no real danger," said Andres.

"Of course," said Grenfell.

"It will be a ruse, a game, a thing of temporary duration," said Andres.

"Yes, yes, my friend," said Grenfell. And then in a very grave tone: "They are, after all, your very own flesh and blood."

"Precisely," said Andres.

"But all the same, an endeavor such as this will require careful planning," said Grenfell.

"Yes," said Andres. "My brother is most vigilant when it comes to the girls."

"What should we do?" said Carabali.

"I suggest that we kidnap only one of the girls," said Grenfell. "Not both of them, as I first thought. Yes, I think one will be enough. One will be manageable. One will be less complicated."

"Which one?" said Andres.

"That, my friend, I will defer to your judgment."

Andres' eyes glazed over for a moment, as if he were deep in thought, lost in the labyrinth of dark dreaming and parallel universes. He said nothing for a very long time. The voices at the other end of the café filled the seeming void.

"The government knew there was no chance," said Lazaro.

"Why do you say such a thing?" said the old man.

"Because it is true."

"Ah, yes, the truth," said the old man. "But what is the truth, Lazaro?"

"The truth is they sent my brigade south to Tarifa with three Krupp guns to strengthen our defenses along the coast in case the Americans attacked. That is the truth."

"What kind of truth is that? What does it mean?"

"It means they were afraid of the Americans," said Lazaro. "They were afraid the Americans would invade Spain. It means they knew."

The father and the middle-aged son had finished their supper and were savoring the last of their wine.

"Rubbish, rubbish. No one knew. Not even God knew."

"They knew."

"And what happened to these famous guns of yours?"

They set their glasses down.

"I don't know. I suppose they're still there."

"In Tarifa?

"Yes."

"Rubbish. There are no guns in Tarifa."

"There are. We put them there. We started off with three, but the road to Tarifa is not very good, it is very steep and rugged in places and full of holes and we lost one of the guns south of El Bujeo."

They stood up to leave.

"I will say again, there are no guns in Tarifa."

"And I will say again, there are."

"And the Americans, did the Americans invade Spain?"

"No."

"Hah! There is your truth for you, Lazaro."

The door opened and the father and the middle-aged son nodded at Fernando without pausing in their conversation and then stepped through the doorway as if they were stepping into another time, and then the door closed, but you could still hear their voices echoing across the cobblestones as if they were echoing across the centuries.

"When you are as old as I am, you will see things

differently."

"They knew, I tell you."

"Rubbish, Lazaro. No one knows."

"You are impossible, old man."

"No one ever knows."

And then the three conspirators at the other end of the café, their voices sounding now like the voices of small birds trapped in a cage.

"Tiká is the one I would choose," said Andres.

"Yes, yes," said Carabali. "She is all adventure, that one."

"Precisely," said Andres. "I think she will run away with us if we ask her."

"Yes," said Carabali, "I think you are correct on this point."

"I think she is eager to leave Logroño," said Andres.

"And what about your brother?" said Grenfell.

"As you said, an endeavor such as this will require careful planning."

"Yes, this is true," said Grenfell.

"What must we do, then?" said Carabali.

"We must make haste slowly," said Grenfell.

"Ah," said Carabali. "That is a good way of putting it. Very poetic.

"Naturally," said Grenfell. "I am Welsh, after all."

The men laughed and drank the rest of their wine, and then they polished off a couple of bottles of Vermouth, which they drank with soda water and some lemon, and all the while they were talking about the journey to Cuba again. Andres and Carabali could barely contain their excitement, even though Carabali had no ticket for the trip to Cuba on board the *Conde Wifredo* or any other steamer, and up until the day before he had never even considered going to Cuba, but there in the dim light of The Café with Two Names he seemed as eager as Andres to walk the streets of Havana, streets they had heard were paved with gold, like the streets of the mythic El Dorado, but Grenfell mocked their ignorance and said they had been misinformed, there were no gold streets in Havana or Cuba or anywhere else in the Americas, there were some cobblestone streets, like anywhere, and many more were just plain dirt, like anywhere, and besides, if the streets had been paved with gold they would have been dug up already because of the expense of the war, the war had been a drain on both sides, and Andres said they were only speaking figuratively, they knew gold was not used to build streets, they were not idiots, and they also knew about the expense of the war, but what did that have to do with anything, and Carabali didn't say a word because he had truly believed in streets made of gold and was nursing his disappointment, and yes, yes, he had certainly heard about the war, as everyone had, but everything he had heard had felt like a rumor, and he put little stock in rumors because they were like wisps of smoke, and after that it was very difficult to hear what the three men were saying, it was almost like they had ceased to exist.

It would be safe to say that the democratic approach to planning adopted by the three conspirators was haphazard at best, degenerating at times into crude, even childish debates or petty tirades that did little to build consensus and which meant, in all likelihood, that their chances for success were quite low, better than six to one against.

Andres, Grenfell and Carabali had argued for hours about the details of how to commit their crime of the century, long after Fernando himself had locked the front door of the café and gone to bed, leaving the bottle of *absenta* he had promised on their table before he went up to his room, which he shared with a blind parrot who repeated the "Glory Be" every night while Fernando lay in bed wondering about the mythological names of the stars until he fell asleep. First they argued about what they should say to Tiká, the exact language they were going to use, because Andres felt using precise language was important, and he had persuaded Carabali on this point, but Grenfell said that it was preposterous to think that language might affect the outcome of an endeavor that was by its very nature brutish and the antithesis to language. Besides, in most instances action is what was needed, not language at all, and besides that, he had no flair for using language, so if that's what they wanted to do, then they had better count him out. Then they argued about the best time to plunge into the abyss, this was how Grenfell had put it, who in spite of his claims to the contrary had a poetic flair for using language after all. Grenfell's voice took on a dark, hallucinatory quality and he said early in the morning would be the most appropriate time, around four, because everyone would be asleep at that hour, and even those who were awake would think they were asleep or wish they were, for that has always been the hour when the boundaries of reality begin to shift and shimmer and the wrongfully murdered return to exact their vengeance; and the saints, even those newly appointed, are able to intercede on behalf of the downtrodden; and sailors the world over imagine they are making love to the mermaids of the southern hemisphere (for everyone knows the mermaids of the northern seas vanished long ago), and in some cases the union between sailor and mermaid is a tangible reality, but only if there is sufficient cloud cover; and even the angels themselves have forgotten where the borders of heaven end and those of earth begin. Andres, who was less theatrical, wanted to wait until first light, because most people would still be sleeping, and those who might be awake wouldn't know a kidnapping was in progress anyway, they would be too busy firing up kitchen stoves or brushing the leather of their saddles before an early morning ride or getting ready to walk the dusty streets of Logroño in search of an open church. Carabali suggested they simply hang around Café Rioja because of the shops across the street and when the girl came down to buy a new parasol or a new bonnet by Borsalino or a velveteen toque by Capello or Panizza or a new pair of shoes or perhaps a pair of Garabaldi boots, they could grab her then and her father would be none the wiser, but Grenfell said such an idea could only be the product of a brain overflowing with the pustulent excrement of disease, had he forgotten that they had a steamer to catch in one week, well, at least Grenfell and Andres had a steamer to catch, what was he (Carabali) thinking, what horribly deficient, idiotic reasoning, who could say when the girl might head out for an afternoon of shopping. Carabali said nothing in response. He finished the last of his Vermouth and turned to the as yet unopened bottle of *absenta* and vowed silently to refrain from speaking for the rest of the night, and they (which now meant Grenfell and Andres) discussed various options for transporting themselves and the girl first to Zaragoza, where they would collect the ransom and send the girl home, and then on to Barcelona, just the two of them at that point, a fact which Grenfell seemed eager to underscore. Perhaps they needed a fine horse and carriage befitting the daughter of a gentleman, said Grenfell. Yes, said Andres, with some measured irony, this would keep the eyes of the Civil Guard where they belonged, certainly, but everyone else in town would take note, for carriages had lately become an uncommon sight, what about a flatbed wagon instead, the kind used for hauling merchandise. That would certainly be easy to procure, said Grenfell, but then wouldn't they have to outfit the wagon with some sort of shipment to avoid suspicion, wool perhaps, or fresh cut timber, and if they had the money for such a shipment they wouldn't need to kidnap the girl in the first place (which was the most salient point advanced during the course of the whole evening). Why don't they steal some horses from Arturo's stables, that would be easy enough, said Carabali (a suggestion which he offered only tentatively, since he was still partially submerged in the swill of resentment over Grenfell's earlier remarks but he couldn't help himself). But the other two just stared at Carabali as if he had lost his mind, because Arturo did not possess any stables, and only a single horse, the same dark chestnut which Tiká had been riding bareback since the age of two and which Arturo rode only on rare occasions now, whenever he didn't walk, which he usually did because it was safer, though sometimes he neither walked nor rode the horse and rode his bicycle instead, an 1892 black and nickel Elliott Hickory with pneumatic tires but still using hickory for the wheels, spokes and rims, hence the name, and which was only practical around town, where the terrain was relatively flat and uniform, because you had to get off and push when you came to a hill, and then going down you were traveling as fast as a rocket and might crash because the spokes, being made of wood, might snap from the stress of a rocky road, which sometimes happened, and which is why Arturo almost never took the bicycle out, and also because the saddle was rather inflexible and gave him abrasions, though it should be said that this contraption had been the last present his wife Verona had given him before she died and so he sometimes took it out for a spin around town when he was thinking of her, but usually not, because he preferred the prestige of the dark chestnut or the absolute safety of walking even to the memory of his dead wife, all of which apparently Carabali did not know. And so it went. By the time the three conspirators left The Café with Two Names, they had conceived three different plans, not one, though each instinctively believed that only one plan existed, and their memories did not improve by the time they woke up the next day, shortly after one in the afternoon, for they each still clung to a different idea of the plan that was the cornerstone of their intentions, and if plan is not the right word, then perhaps the phrase 'vague assumptions' is more precise, like a child's pure and simple faith, which is really a patchwork of unexamined hopes and dreams and unpurged fears, which might be why they didn't stop to question what they were doing.

Carabali slept that night in a small, whitewashed stone cottage a mile outside of the original walled borders of the town, a cottage belonging to a young widow. Presumably her husband had left for Cuba on a merchant vessel years earlier and had never returned and had not even sent a letter, so she had petitioned the Church to annul her marriage, for there were no children, and the Church had been happy to comply. The young widow had been madly in love with Carabali from the very first moment she had laid eyes on him (she had spotted him one warm afternoon peering through the windows of the shops on Calle Ollerías and sighing wistfully), and now she barely gave him time to get his trousers off before she had him in bed ("what is this hiding in your pantaloons," she would say, and then she would give a strange, hypnotic, exotic laugh that sounded like a Bird of Paradise trapped in a sewer). So Carabali had spent the night with the widow, and after he woke, he borrowed a flatbed wagon and two mules from this widow of unflagging desire and gave her a kiss which suggested he would return shortly and with many gifts, and then with a sigh of exhausted relief, which the young widow mistook for a declaration of love, he left his damsel in distress and in less than fifteen minutes found himself sitting inside Café Rioja so he could keep an eye on the shops across the street.

Grenfell slept on the cold stone floor in the back of the Church of Santiago, though how he got there was a mystery, and woke up amid the crazed staring hatred of the old women with their black shawls, who had discovered him on the floor when they arrived just after Father de Nazar had opened the great church doors, and who had poked at him with their canes to see if the white light of Christ had struck him dead upon entering the church, for such was usually the fate of demons, and who had retreated a step towards the shadows, holding up their crosses in the dim church light when he had opened his eyes after their poking, and when he beheld their stark mindless hatred like screaming ghosts, he had fled, clutching at the air as if he were drowning in a sea of incandescent nitrogen, the old women ushering him out with their canes, beating him on the back and on his shoulders and on the backs of his legs, those that could reach, and only after a seeming eternity of running, during which Grenfell became lost in an unexpected maze of cobblestone streets, did he remember that he was supposed to meet Andres at his brother's house for dinner and they were going to get Arturo roaring drunk, a blitzkrieg of drunkenness, and then shortly after midnight, presumably after Arturo was dead to the world in a drunken slumber, Carabali would arrive with a carriage and they would grab the girl and head to Zaragoza, but not without first stuffing a ransom letter into the pocket of Arturo's dinner jacket, a letter which Grenfell had already written at some mysterious point between The Café with Two Names and the back of the Church of Santiago, but they wouldn't push the letter all the way down, it would need to be protruding slightly, like a handkerchief, so Arturo would be sure not to miss it in the morning when he woke, and then he would read the letter and he would know what sum to forward to Zaragoza for the safe return of his daughter.

Andres, for his part, had slept in the suite of three rooms that had been his childhood bedroom in the back of what was now his brother's house and had dreamed that the kidnapping had been abandoned altogether in favor of inviting Escolástica to join them on their journey to Cuba. They would remain in Logroño a few more days so Andres could wire ahead to purchase a first class ticket on the *Conde Wifredo* (Andres and Grenfell would remain in second class), and while there was still the thorny problem of Arturo's blessing to consider, Andres was confident, at least in his dream, that Arturo would sense in his youngest daughter the same unquenchable thirst to see the world that his late wife, Verona Almeida Vda De Miranda, had possessed, and that by permitting his daughter this chance to escape, he would be honoring the memory of Verona. What Andres never considered, in his dream or otherwise, was that Arturo had already committed the memory of his dead wife to the embalming fluid of his despair, and that if he did see even the glimmer of his wife in the face of Escolástica, he would never allow his daughter to leave. She would become a living mummy to ease his pain.

How could Andres have been so unaware of his brother's grief? The signs were unmistakable. The very suite of rooms that Andres now slept in had become a shrine to Verona. The dozens of end tables and side tables and bureaus and buffets left over from the days of Verona's Saturday night parties (gala events to which the whole of Logroño had been invited) were now crammed together in this suite of three rooms in honor of their former patroness, and while they seemed carelessly scattered about (so much so that Andres never took the same route twice on his way from the first room to the third room and back again), they were precisely placed so as to remain in the shadows even when the slatted blinds were raised and the sun was blazing with full force. They seemed less like end tables and side tables and bureaus and buffets and more like miniature altars hidden away in the dark corners of a great cathedral. All of them were covered with candles and candelabra and tiny ivory statuettes of Jesus or the Virgin Mary that seemed to weep late at night (or sometimes in the middle of the afternoon when the *Ábrego* winds blew in from the south). There were also the relics of a few saints purchased at the market in Barcelona (when Arturo took Verona on a tour of Catalonia, which he said was his ancestral home): a sliver of the left arm of the true cross from Santo Toribio de Liébana (the vendor had admitted to Arturo stealing the sliver from the monks at the abbey, which Arturo took as proof that the relic was a fake, but which Verona said proved the opposite, though she didn't explain how); the mummified finger of St. Teresa of Avila (or perhaps it was just a donkey's tooth wrapped in gauze, which Arturo pointed out in a half-joking manner, only to have his lack of faith decried and flung back in his face by his wife); and there were a dozen or more relics representing saints so famous that Arturo found it impossible to believe they were genuine (the holy foreskin of Saint Paul, which came with a tiny jeweled case, and which more or less resembled a red chickpea; a pile of toenails which Saint Ignatius of Loyola had one clipped from his Holy toes, and which had been kept in a small silk pouch thereafter to prevent their being mistaken for unsanctified toenails and tossed into the dustbin; a piece of the loincloth of John the Baptist; an oil lamp that Saint Peter had once touched, the tongue of Saint Anthony of Padua, and so on), but Arturo had given up trying to persuade his beloved Verona by then.

So the end tables and side tables and bureaus and buffets were given over to all manner of Catholic paraphernalia, but the walls were covered with dozens of photographs depicting the life Arturo and Verona had once lived. There was one of Arturo and Verona attending an operetta in Barcelona; and one of them taking a train to the sea; and then Arturo and Verona on an unknown beach among a crowd of two dozen, all of them fully dressed, the women with parasols, the men wearing top hats or bowlers, all of them milling about, some looking out at the sea, some looking up at a cloudy sky, and a few climbing into an old rowboat pulled up into the sand; and then there was Arturo and Verona standing next to their brand new Hickory bicycles with their house (a Grecian-styled house with Doric columns and a red-tile roof and unrecognizable hanging plants dangling from the railings of the second floor balcony) in the background and storm clouds in the distance; and another of Arturo and Verona standing outside the Church of Santiago for a wedding portrait; and then one of the wedding feast; and then people dancing; and then a separate one of Arturo sitting in dismal repose in a leather chair in the photographer's studio, choking, it seemed, from a collar that was too tight and perhaps also the fumes of the photographic process itself, which had seemed to Arturo to be a deadly mixture of zinc oxide and cyanide; and a matching photograph of Verona in the same chair, smiling an exceedingly photogenic smile for the 19th or any other century, unaware of the deadly fumes produced by photography.

The crowning glory of this shrine to Verona, however, were two portraits done by Joaquín Sorolla y Bastida, either just before he left for Paris in 1885 or just after he returned to Valencia in 1888. The first painting, done in oil, showed Verona wearing a broad-brimmed hat with a green feather to match her green dress and a sad, melancholy expression that gave her face a twisted look, as if she were looking into a dark glass of the future and saw her own death. (She died unexpectedly of an acute attack of neuralgia of the heart, a condition precipitated by the sudden realization that she loved her daughters with an unqualified love that only the poets, the angels, and God himself dared contemplate, but she could not say the same thing for her husband, for in the years since they had been married, her expectations of romantic love had become tangled up with her belief in social etiquette, which Arturo roundly ignored, leaving her breathless with frustration; so when this realization came upon her, she also realized that death could not be far behind, for she could not live the lie of a marriage without love, but at the same time there was nowhere else for her to go, so she was the only one not taken by surprise when death came for her one week later, the day before Palm Sunday, at the tender age of thirty-three, the same age Christ was when he died, a thought which occurred to Arturo during her funeral Mass and which immediately struck him as blasphemous, though he could not have described how, and he suddenly wanted to hurl himself from the middle of the Puente de Piedra bridge and drown both his sorrows and his overwhelming sense of Catholic guilt in the dark waters of the Ebro river, but then he realized that Christ had died on a Thursday and his wife on a Saturday, which in his twisted state of mind brought him some welcome and unanticipated relief, and so he relented somewhat in his despair.)

The second painting, which hung directly across from the bed where Andres slept, this one done using a technique called gouache, which art historians called opaque watercolor, which gives paintings greater reflective qualities, showed a naked Verona stretched out on a bed with satin sheets, a luminescent pink, as if it were late morning or early afternoon and someone (not Verona) had pulled back the curtains to let in the sunlight, which was amazingly clean and crisp and pure, the light washing over Verona, her legs bent at the knees and her hips turned slightly so that her plush derriere curved up and out in wanton fashion, and her black hair was curled tightly and she wore a purple gardenia where it was pulled up in back. Each morning (by sunlight) and each evening (by candlelight), Andres explored the contours of Verona's semblance. He often lingered on the delicate curve of a single breast pressing down against the satin sheets, and he wished he could see the expression on Verona's face, which was turned away, but he could imagine what she was thinking and feeling. She was holding one hand to her mouth and was staring at the other one stretched out before her, for her lily-white hand was now a mirror reflecting the luminescence of the pink satin sheets, her hips, her shoulders, her breasts, all glowing pink in the late morning or early afternoon light of the painting, a soft light as if filtered through a thin parchment of rose petals. She was contemplating a future which would involve copious amounts of sex amid the sounds of girlish joy, at least this is what Andres imagined as he looked at the painting of Verona stretched out before him each morning when he woke or each evening before he went to sleep, for he was still a young man who had only been with a woman twice, once with a Carmelite novitiate in Lisieux, France, who wanted to taste sex before her final vows, and once in a brothel in Lisbon, tucked away in the ancient neighborhood of Mouraria with its maze of Moorish streets, with a woman twice his age who said she was a distant cousin of the legendary fado singer and prostitute Maria Severa Onofriana, so he had paid her two times the going rate.

-45-

The abduction of Escolástica Escoraz Vda De Miranda took place in the Year of Our Lord 1899 between the hours of five o'clock in the afternoon on December 8 and two o'clock the following morning, December 9. But the way it began was a surprise to everyone involved, as was the way it proceeded (the middle part), all the way to the getaway (the last part, during which the temperature plummeted to an unusually brisk six degrees Celsius), for it followed none of the details of any of the three plans as imagined or remembered by the three would-be kidnappers.

Andres, who still believed the plot to kidnap his niece had been abandoned altogether, was sitting on the verandah of his brother's house at five o'clock, watching the empty street, waiting for something to happen, a vaguely troubled look on his face, a sense that something was off-kilter but he could not put his finger on it.

Madia, the old battle axe crone who took care of the Escoraz family, had set out an enamel tray with a few empty glasses and a pitcher of sangria on the small wicker table next to Andres, and he was just about to pour himself a glass when he saw Grenfell coming up the street.

Except he did not know it was Grenfell. At first Grenfell was only an unrecognizable shape with the sun casting long shadows and a breeze blowing across the street, kicking up small tornadoes of dust. The figure looked like a vagrant monk trying to swim against the current of religious dissidence, thought Andres, amused by the comparison, or an army deserter from Morocco, perhaps. Andres glanced at the figure with the weary, perfunctory look of forgetfulness and turned to his glass of sangria and wondered what his brother and his two nieces were doing and when they were going to eat, because he hadn't eaten all day. It was very hot and breezy and sangria wasn't enough.

The vague notion that he was forgetting something important flitted across the backs of his eyeballs like ticker tape, but he was too hungry to focus. He looked again at the figure he did not recognize, and then suddenly the figure pushed its way through the front gate and became Grenfell, wearing his heavy longshoreman's coat with its premonitory stench of a perpetual shipwreck. Grenfell started up the stone walk to the house, past the remnants of the flower beds Verona had once labored over and that had contained yellow gazanias and gold and maroon gazanias and white and purple ones, and all manner of daisies, and a few tamarisk with their bright lavender bristles, and geraniums and red carnations and red roses and yellow roses and bluebells and purple gardenias, and row after row of purple heliotropes, which she had first seen in the Parc de la Ciutadella in Barcelona along a path leading to a fantastic waterfall with all manner of vegetative cover and bronze statues of dragons and horses blazing in the white sunlight, which gave just the right Baroque quality to the most elegant gardens she had ever hoped to see but which she knew were an extravagance Arturo would never consider replicating, so she had settled for the heliotropes.

Verona's flowers had been the pride of Logroño and the envy of the priests in every church, even Father de Nazar, for the clergy had always secretly believed, at least in Spain, that the ability to grow beautiful flowers was one of the seven visible manifestations of the mercy of God and a symbol of the relationship between Christ and His flock. As if in response to their unspoken testament, Verona had tended to the needs of her flowers on a daily basis and distributed them freely during festivals to lengthen the joy of the festival goers, and also to those in mourning during those mysterious black days when someone had died an unexpected death, to shorten the agony of their despair, but in the years since Verona herself had died, the flowers had been neglected, so only a few scraggly rose bushes remained, survivors from a time before war and rumors of war and the pestilence that comes with anarchy had infected the mythology of the country, a few red blooms withering away in the dusty summer heat, as fleeting as the smiles of ghosts.

So Grenfell walked past the ruined flower beds, a fitting symbol of the death of Verona, and Andres suddenly wondered if something had gone wrong with the new plan, for he hadn't yet had time to go to the telegraph office and wire for a new ticket. Besides, Grenfell wasn't supposed to show up till later, though in the sudden confusion of trying to recall the details of a dream he mistook for a recent memory, Andres was not certain what they had decided. Immediately he stood up, not knowing what else to do. But Grenfell only inclined his head as he walked up the steps, a subtle gesture of greeting, perhaps, which Andres took to mean that yes, there was a slight change in the new plans, but there was nothing to worry about, everything was proceeding towards a favorable conclusion, they would soon be in Cuba, living in the lap of luxury in spite of the absence of streets paved with gold. Andres felt much better after that. Grenfell would expound upon any changes in the plan at a later point, as warranted, which could certainly wait until after supper, and then Andres felt a surge of unexpected happiness coursing through his veins, an electrifying current. Such is the creative power of the imagination which allows us to believe that anything might be true, even when it is only a phantom, a cinematic flicker, the scent of orchids on an evening breeze. Andres offered his co-conspirator a glass of sangria and the two men sat down in their wicker chairs, a haze of wordless exhaustion descending upon the verandah as they drank. From that point forward, the plans of the two would-be kidnappers on the verandah (and the one waiting in Café Rioja two miles away) unraveled very quickly, and the abduction would have become a miserable and quite possibly tragic failure, at least as far as Andres was concerned, had not Tiká realized that her uncle was teetering on the edge of the abyss, and taken matters into her own Amazonian hands to save him.

She became a fixed point on the horizon.

She became the mirror to the mirrored face that was herself.

She became the dream of a small white bird hoping against hope that one day it would find the courage to fly beyond the bars of its cage to seek the treasure of countless nights and days.

She became the dream of her uncle unfolding, a dream in which she became both the dreamer and the dream itself, but in much greater detail, for while her uncle's dream had stopped with his altered memory of the conversation at The Café with Two Names, Tiká's dream continued until the *Conde Wifredo* left Barcelona and plunged into the dark, unfathomable waters of the Mediterranean one week later.

In this dream of her first true awakening, she saw her uncle emerging from The Café with Two Names at a most ungodly hour, giddy as a delinquent schoolboy, singing songs of happy revolutions and well-meaning anarchists, but without understanding the significance of the events the songs described or the history that had been whitewashed, the sudden loss of life, the sacrifice of morality, the depths of human depravity hidden behind the triumphant slogans, the anguish of mothers who no longer believed in God or in the saints who were supposed to watch over the helpless world or even in the priests who tried to bring absolution to their unrepentant flocks. He sang very loudly, boldly, through the dark dreaming streets of Logroño, and as he sang Tiká perceived that every street was lined with the darkly glowing faces of those who had lived there from the time of the Moors to the Third Carlist uprising and had witnessed or been the victims of the countless crimes against humanity which lay submerged in between the lines of the songs, as if these faces which bore the lunatic expressions of festival masks were listening to the words of those songs and remembering and trying to come to terms with their memories, faces now suddenly awake, faces appearing in the wavering mirrors of second floor windows in the rough stone buildings of these dark dreaming streets of Logroño, looking down in widening despair at Tiká's uncle walking and singing; faces that had witnessed the terrible bloodthirsty mysticism of the Moors, who had turned the surrounding fields red with the blood of crippled children in the 8th century, tossing the children up into the air and cutting them in half with exquisitely adorned swords as the children fell back to the earth, as if they (the Moors) were slicing melons, and they were laughing all the while, unaffected by so much blood, believing, as they did, that deformity was a sign of iniquity before God and so the death of the crippled children was pleasing in His eyes, an opinion oddly enough reinforced, though quite unintentionally, by later scholars who noted that it was from those very same fields one century later that the very first red grapes in La Rioja were grown, which these scholars said was the first visible manifestation of God's unyielding mercy on that Iberian plain of sorrows (as if the slate containing the crimes of the Caliphate had been forever wiped clean), and which resulted in the very first wine of the region — a fact which the parsimonious monks of San Andrés de Trepeana noted in a written receipt they submitted to the Notary of San Millán de la Cogolla in 873, a receipt for several barrels of wine they had received from a kindly donor, wine made from the grapes that sprang from the blood of the murdered children, and after polishing off all seven barrels in a little under a month, the monks decided to go into the winemaking business for themselves; or the skeletal faces of refugees from the War of the Two Peters, who had fled the city of Teruel in 1363 when the effeminate Peter of Castile — also known as Peter the Cruel, who was, incidentally, born in the Monastery of Santa María la Real de Las Huelgas, the very same monastery where years later Arturo Ordóñez Escoraz first came into contact with the odor of great wisdom — burned part of the town in search of a safe place to hide from the treachery of his bastard brother, Henry of Trastámara, and so the refugees from Teruel had traveled west from the mountains surrounding Teruel to the plains of La Rioja, carrying with them the memory of war and the pestilence of the plague, which swept through the streets of Logroño like great sheets of lightning, adding many more faces to the dark dreaming streets in Tiká's dream, perhaps as many as two-thirds of the town's population had died at that time, all of them screaming in uncomprehending anguish; or the faces of the twelve who were burned at the stake for witchcraft in 1609, a fate which not even Salazar's wisdom of a young judge of the Inquisition could prevent — eleven blameless women of the night who were accused of dancing with the Devil in the meadow of Akelarre (the field of the He-Goat) and one nameless priest who was accused of healing the sick with an amulet bearing the image of Saint Raphael, one of the seven archangels who stand before the throne of the Lord, defenders night and day against heresy of all kinds, apoplectic reminders of the wrath of God; or the withering, perspiring faces of the hundreds of vagabond patriots who had died at the hands of thirteen-thousand men under the command of Jean-Antoine Verdier during the invasion of the First Antichrist in 1808, hundreds of bloody heads rolling across the cobblestones of Logroño, their headless bodies later stacked in black heaps like so many forgotten haystacks dotting the countryside and set on fire, the smoldering ashes a feeding ground for vultures and crows (and a few wayward storks); but Tiká's uncle did not see any of the faces Tiká saw, or he would not see them or he could never see them, trapped as he was inside a singular vision, oblivious to the lingering pain of the countless centuries, singing his mindless, happy tunes while the faces of that pain became heads and the heads were leaning out of their windows to see who was making all the racket, accusing, vehement glances because their deaths had gone unavenged, or perhaps they had accepted the circumstances of their deaths and were simply miffed because they had been dragged without mercy from a sound sleep.

And then Tiká saw that not all of the those who had taken an interest in her uncle had been victims of wars and plagues and insurrections; she noticed a second group of faces popping up behind the first group, peering over their shoulders, a tumultuous sea of faces that had never even glimpsed the abyss while alive and so had not yet accepted the fact that they were floating about in a sea of death, the faces of simple peasants who had migrated to Logroño from the surrounding countryside or came down from the mountains, faces of shopkeepers and farmers and artisans and minor bureaucrats who had enjoyed the luxury of peace in between the wars and the famines and the raging epidemics, all of them expressing outrage for a thousand imagined slights gone unpunished, or even a few real crimes tossed in (crimes of perjury and slander and petty larceny and adultery, for example, real in the sense that they had in fact occurred, but decidedly unreal in the sense that slander is all but irrelevant when compared to the atrocity of murdering children), and then Tiká perceived that all of the crimes that had been committed, whether crimes of war or crimes of peace, whether real or illusory, crimes against the state, crimes against property, crimes of excessive passion, crimes of omission, crimes of forgetfulness, in every instance they had gone unpunished, every case had been dismissed or delayed, the paperwork misfiled or in some cases destroyed, and now no one even remembered the names of the victims, even the stones had been washed clean, so every death was lost, every name vanished, every criminal had gotten off scot free, but no, the voices cried out in unison, this would not be the case with respect to her uncle, who had roused them all (those who had lived during times of war and those who had lived during times of peace) from a sound sleep, they would remember this one, meaning Tiká's uncle, they would surely send him to the gallows for disturbing the peace and death mask quiet of the dark dreaming streets of Logroño, and Tiká did not understand why the people in her dream were so angry with her uncle, he is not one of them, she said, meaning he should not be grouped with the oppressors, the enslavers, the pseudo-fascist dictators, the tyrannous civil servants, the murderous, degenerate generals, the corrupt kings, he is not someone who deserves abuse, she said, as if anyone knows who deserves abuse and who does not, he is one of us, she said, he is our history, he is a son of Spain, but the tumultuous sea of angry faces had already disappeared by then, the windows of the rough stone buildings clacking shut, though the grumbling and growling of inconvenienced voices lingered on in Tiká's dream for quite a while. So Tiká perceived that her wayward and somewhat naive uncle had become an outsider to Spain and even to the memory of Spain, though he had only been absent from Logroño for ten years, but he was now in mortal danger nevertheless, and then she perceived that she was also an outsider, at least as far as the people of Logroño were concerned, possibly because she possessed the same gift of second sight that her mother possessed (who, it was said, had a gaze as penetrating as Toledo steel), but also certainly, unquestionably, because of her unquenchable desire to accompany her uncle to Cuba, a paradise on earth for anyone who could get there, because that was always the allure of the Americas, the promise and the curse, and so she, too, was in mortal danger, and then she realized that it was up to her to save them both.

-46-

When Andres handed Grenfell a sangria and the two men sat down, Tiká was watching them from the window of her father's library, standing as silent as crystallized time, hidden in the folds of the embroidered Chinese draperies that framed the glass. Had she been reliving the dream of the white bird she would have been standing next to the tiny golden cage hanging from a hook, so close she would have been able to hear the strange, sad gurgling noises it made as it slept, but as she was in a non-dreaming state, she was standing next to an Edison home phonograph which Verona had ordered from New York City the year before the Hickory bicycles, but which had not arrived until three years after her death. The phonograph had never been used.

Immediately Tiká recognized her uncle's guest from her dream the night before. She sent Madia out with a silver tray, used only during celebrations honoring the memory of the three kings from the Orient, upon which she had placed a small white envelope containing a folded note, and she told Madia to wait while her uncle read her words of warning to make sure he understood their importance.

What Tiká's note said:

My dearest Uncle, the man next to you is not Grenfell. He has stolen that name. He is an imposter. I cannot tell you precisely how I am imbued with this knowledge except to say that I possess the same radiant clarity of vision that my mother, your beloved sister-in-law Verona, possessed even until the day she died. Suffice it to say that this Grenfell has quite nefarious intentions with regards to your ownership of the supposed copper mines in Cuba and we should do our best to utterly disabuse him of the confidence he has heretofore claimed regarding your future as well as mine. Our very lives are at stake in this matter, so please be cautious as you read this note of warning, please do not allow your eyeballs to rotate with nervous agitation as they always do in moments of extreme anxiety, stay calm and calm-hearted, my dear Uncle, for I have matters well in hand. You should say to Grenfell, assuming he has any interest in this note at all, that it concerns a private matter about my father's health, a mysterious disease which has plagued him for years, but which until this very moment you had no prior knowledge of and which, you must stress, has no negative bearing on your current scheme (meaning the scheme concocted by you and Grenfell and your third wheel, who is sitting in Café Rioja waiting until I should decide to purchase a parasol or a pair of boots). You might even suggest that the nature of this illness may prove to be an advantage (you may be as cryptic as you like on this point, for I have no doubt but it will spur the imposter's greedy imagination), and then say no more except that my father, your brother, is returning from a ride on his velocipede, the magnificent Elliott Hickory, which he took for a spin around the whole of Logroño this afternoon, and that he wishes you to meet him at the carriage house upon his return, and from there you will be departing directly to the home of our great and noble friend, don Alfonso Alberto Sebastian Francisco de Hernani y Arredondo de Mariategui y de Esperanza for an extravagant dinner party to commemorate your imminent departure. Father is well aware that you will be bringing a guest and he has made provision for this inconvenience. He knows nothing about the nefarious intentions of this imposter, and I shall keep him in the dark on this matter until you and I have left Logroño for the port of Barcelona and the steamer to Cuba. I will send you more notes as appropriate this evening so you will know what to expect. Again, stay calm and calm-hearted, my dearest Uncle. There is nothing for you to worry about. With the greatest appreciation for your patient indulgence, and with the greatest affection, your niece, Escolástica Escoraz Vda De Miranda.

After reading the note, Andres sank back into his wicker chair and poured what remained of his sangria down his throat and closed his eyes so the world would stop spinning. Then he took Madia's hand (she was still waiting to see if he understood the importance of Tiká's warning) and pressed the note into her palm, looking at her gravely as he did so until she felt a sudden urge to weep. Andres smiled weakly and poured another glass of sangria, which he drank slowly.

Madia disappeared into the house.

"He understands," she said, but in a voice that seemed more like the whispering of insects (which is perhaps what angels sound like) and less a human voice, a surging, insistent echo swirling about the interior of the house, lingering for a moment near the Chinese draperies and then heading down the grand hallway to the back of the house, through the swinging kitchen doors into the kitchen with its red brick walls and terra cotta floor which had been the scene of so much joyous laughter and impromptu parties when Verona had been alive and which now echoed with the silence of her absence, and then into the service closet where the good china was kept on two shelves very high up, and where on the shelves beneath the china Verona had placed dozens of tiny opaque bottles, bottles of blue and green and red glass containing rare herbal extracts from the Orient for promoting good health (extract of Astragalus to prevent aging, extract of wolfberry to improve blood flow, extract of licorice for stomach disorders, extract of Chinese foxglove mixed with the ashes of wormwood to reduce inflammation, extract of gardenias to calm the impatient mind, and so on); and then Madia's voice headed into the grand dining room, now shrouded in the darkness of heavy velvet drapes, and the piano room that was no longer used because the piano, a gilded art-case Bechstein grand piano, had been sold to a lonely German widow who was now living in Madrid and who bought the instrument because it reminded her of her husband, who had died years ago during the Second Danish-German War and was buried with military honors in Berlin; and then Madia's voice took a detour through the library, which is where Isabel was reading, with its wall of leather-bound masterpieces slowly disintegrating, the air thick with the musty odor of ancient wisdom that lingered like death; and then down a narrow hallway, swirling past the three rooms that had become Verona's sanctuary, the insistence of Madia's voice now taking on other qualities, the trembling, hallucinatory sadness of the lucifugous statuary on the altars of Arturo's despair, the whispered hopes of the dead saints that had settled upon those very same altars; and then Madia's voice poured itself out into the courtyard where years earlier a courtesan who had once been the mistress of Federico de Madrazo contemplated the nature of reality and the immortality of art; and then the voice headed back inside and the house was suddenly filled with the sweet gardenia smell of Verona herself, (an intoxicating aroma which most visitors only noticed upon entering the house and which then seemed to vanish as they grew accustomed to it, an echo of Verona's presence embedded in the very brick and mortar of marital bliss, as if the house could only exist if something of Verona remained to bind it to this world); and then Madia's voice headed up the backstairs, which sported a mahogany railing that Arturo believed was all that remained of a Spanish war ship that had sunk in a storm along the western coast of Spain near Cape Finisterre in 1870 but which more likely had been salvaged from the Church of Santiago in 1795 when a portion of the church had been torched by French sympathizers during the War of the Pyrenees; and then the strangely angelic, insect sound of Madia's voice danced in and out of the various bedrooms and sitting rooms on the second floor, a labyrinth of rooms, through keyholes or beneath doors that had been locked for years and the keys had been lost, bouncing off mirrors and careening off light fixtures and spinning around bedposts, an invisible tornado of sound kicking up the dust of hidden memories and half-suffocated dreams and forgotten crises of faith, mixing with the dry evening heat and the reddish light of the sunset streaming in through a few open windows and the white lace curtains billowing, and then the sound dissipating, the breathy sound of a warning, a tragedy to be averted as much as a lament.

The Chinese draperies trembled.

Andres poured himself yet another sangria.

The Chinese draperies stopped trembling.

And Grenfell, who had seemed insensible to the presence of Madia and the silver tray and Andres reading the note, set his now empty glass next to the nearly empty pitcher and eyed his co-conspirator with an expression that seemed mocking and contemptuous as well as reckless and confident.

"What is it you understand, my friend?" he said.

Andres sat up stiffly, his eyes on the open window and the Chinese draperies moving again, but ever so slightly.

"It is my brother," said Andres, watching the draperies as he spoke. "I have been informed that he is suffering from inconsolable grief due to the passing of his wife. In spite of the fact that she died several years ago, his condition has worsened. I only wish that I had known sooner."

"Ah," said Grenfell, his eyes narrowing so that the pupils looked like slits. "Grief is a most treacherous affliction." Then Grenfell smiled the same kind of thin, knowing smile he had tossed about with great frequency the night before at The Café with Two Names. "He that refuseth instruction despiseth his own soul: but he that heareth reproof getteth understanding," he said.

-47-

The home of don Alfonso Alberto Sebastian Francisco de Hernani y Arredondo de Mariategui y de Esperanza was a few blocks from the old town gate on a narrow side street just inside the city limits that ended with the house itself, a magnificent though crumbling Baroque period building with a maze of inner passageways opening up into unexpected courtyards lined with almond trees and orange trees and lush ferns and ivy and gardenias and the shrieks of startled, hidden birds and the mad dash of a few tiny brown lizards and the languid, telescopic eye of a wandering yellow chameleon. In the center of each courtyard there was a small tiled pool (with aquamarine tiles or teal or deep blue) glittering in the soft folds of sunlight that drifted down through the branches of the trees, and there was an elaborately carved fountain in the middle of each pool and fish swimming about in the froth. Most of the fountains depicted happy, naïve, fat-cheeked cherubs blowing ceremonial trumpets, or obscure mythological animals, or a strange, unsettling mixture of both. But in one of the courtyards you could gaze upon the supernal beauty of a dozen or more lascivious marble nymphs cavorting about, spewing water from their mouths, happy, carefree, uninhibited, suggesting to every man who gazed upon them unending nights of forbidden pleasure without the unyielding days of stifling, sun-burnt love that would usually follow.

Laughing with joy, don Alfonso greeted Arturo and Andres with warm embraces. He acknowledged Grenfell with a curt nod and took Tiká by the hand. He barely noticed Madia, who always accompanied Tiká, and he did not comment on Isabel's absence, who in all probability was still in the library reading poetry. The don wore the same suit he had worn for social occasions for twenty-two years, a Vienna Brocade tailcoat with a gold colored silk vest which complemented his neatly trimmed red beard but which had become too tight, a white silk shirt with ivory cufflinks, a silk puff tie to match the vest, black trousers now held in place by suspenders, a John Bull top hat, and a gentleman's walking stick from the age of Napoleon with an ox bone handle carved to resemble a rose. It was the same outfit he had worn the day Verona Almeida Vda De Miranda married his childhood friend Arturo Ordóñez Escoraz. The dazzling brilliance of the outfit had suggested to some at the time that don Alfonso was secretly in love with Verona and the only way he could demonstrate his feelings was to parade about in the uniform of a courtly peacock in the hopes that she might forget about her new husband for at least a moment and cast an anguished, soulful look of regret his way.

They ate in the courtyard containing the fountain with the nymphs. The household staff had set up a narrow Italian sideboard covered with steaming hot dishes — a stew of beans and Botifarra sausage, a stew of meat and vegetables, cooked snails, a seafood casserole, lamb hooves mixed with turnips, roasted vegetables bathed in olive oil, small dishes of paella — and also cod salad with tomatoes and onions and slabs of bread smeared with tomato paste and garlic, and for dessert there was mató cheese with honey and peeled pears served in cream and also almond biscuits and cups of steaming, rich, frothy Arabic coffee. A barrel of *Crianza* was next to the sideboard. There was no grand table for dining. Instead, several chairs were scattered about among the greenery and also a few small side tables covered in fine Belgian linen for the plates and glasses and silverware. Don Arturo and don Alfonso sat in the shadows, surrounded by ferns almost six feet high, directly across from Andres and Grenfell, who sat directly beneath the open sky, their skin glowing a soft, dappled red from the almost vanished sun. Tiká sat nearer the fountain so she could watch and listen without being noticed. Madia took on the duties of serving her mistress.

For the longest time nobody said a word. The only sounds were the tinkling of glasses and the soft scraping of silverware on plates and the subtle, furtive movements of the birds hiding in the trees, wings flapping and a few muffled cries, and the quiet murmuring of the fountain. The sky grew dark and one of the servants went around the courtyard lighting candles and soon the smoky glow blotted out all but a few of the very brightest stars. The two dons settled back into the darkness of their memories and began to talk, though mostly it was Alfonso. They talked about the tragedy of Verona's death, and Alfonso acknowledged Arturo's suffering, but then he said that they had all suffered, the entire town, for she was the very soul of Logroño, and with her death the town had become a soulless corpse and they might as well pack up and leave it to the anarchists, and who knew, perhaps the death of Verona had signaled the death of other things, the death of the monarchy, the death of the empire, the death of family, yes, Arturo, even the death of love, there is nothing left but death all around this crypt of our ancestors, the modern age has arrived with a vengeance, the modern world with its modern thinking will sweep everything else aside, no, Arturo, no, perhaps it is a question of adaptability, one cannot adapt in a place where there is so much death, but if one were to pack up and leave, yes, Arturo, leave Logroño, then perhaps miracles are indeed possible, yes, Arturo, truly, because the modern age is also an age full of marvels, so perhaps it is all for the best, and all Arturo could manage during this hopeful lament was an occasional cough. Then Alfonso talked about Isabel and Tiká with such effulgent pride that one might have thought they were his own daughters, or nieces at the very least, how they were quite accomplished for young ladies of any age, but how many eligible suitors existed for them here in Logroño, frankly the town was overflowing with louts and vagabonds of every description, no, no, for girls of their bearing, their incredible beauty, Isabel the dark-haired siren with her siren eyes, the spitting image of her mother, Verona, and Tiká with her fiery-read hair that she now wore in a single braid like the warrior goddess of ancient Greece, yes, yes, who in Logroño was worthy of such beauty. One would have to travel all the way to Barcelona, or perhaps further, Monte Carlo, or even Paris, and Arturo agreed with everything Alfonso said and drank his coffee, for by this time the dinner was long finished. Then the two men were laughing, a gruff, chortling kind of laughter that sounded to Tiká like the moaning of lovesick bulls. Then Alfonso said it was time for something stronger than coffee, and a moment later one of the servants brought out a bottle of port wine from Portugal, and then a bottle of Hennessy, and many more bottles appeared after that, but it was hard for Tiká to see what they were. It had grown very dark. Even the few bright stars from before had grown cold and dim, and all that remained of the two dons were two shadows submerged in the sea of ferns, two voices venturing out into the void like the bellowing of two great ships. Only her uncle and the imposter Grenfell were still visible, and even so they were but caricatures, the smoky, dim candlelight dancing across their waxen faces, the angry, inarticulate, ever-present rage of the one and the energetic, irrepressible optimism of the other suspended while they listened to these voices from the darkness.

A short while later Madia presented Andres with two additional notes, the first to be read immediately, the second to be read only after Andres and Tiká were safely on their way. Again Madia waited while Andres read the second note, which took him close to fifteen minutes because he had to read in the dim flickering light of the candles, which meant that the process of reading the note was less like reading and more like deciphering an ancient coded message written in the tongue of the Moors. Grenfell was too busy to notice, for he was drinking from a bottle of brandy that had mysteriously appeared on their tiny side table.

What the second note said:

My dearest Uncle, do not drink the brandy, for it has been laced with an opiate to cause drowsiness and was meant for Grenfell alone. With the help of our very dear friend and our host for the evening, don Alfonso Alberto Sebastian Francisco de Hernani y Arredondo de Mariategui y de Esperanza, whose family aligned itself with ours many generations ago, I have arranged for our departure this very night. The don will permit us the use of his Rochet-Schneider horseless carriage, a two-cylinder contraption he is very proud of because it is modern (he truly appreciates the modern age, in spite of his earlier provocative tone) and it is quite fashionable with its polished brass fittings and patterned leather and handcrafted wooden trim, oh it is quite fashionable. The don is also providing a driver, so we shall be quite snug, as it were, for the vehicle normally seats but two. There is a small trunk in the front which will serve adequately to convey a reasonable number of bags, and we can strap a few more to the back, and then we will be off to Zaragoza, which according to the don is as far as the carriage will carry us before it runs out of fuel, so from there we will travel in luxury by train in a private parlor car, which also belongs to the don, and which he alone occupies when he travels to Barcelona or Madrid or even Seville. The don has notified the railway company to ready the car for our journey. Let me add, my dear Uncle, that the time of our departure is close at hand. Soon Grenfell will fall into a trance-like sleep, at which point several members of the don's household staff will carry him to a small dungeon-like closet in the back of their great stone kitchen, where he will remain asleep among sacks of flour and other vegetable matter until we are well beyond his reach. The don has also wired Barcelona and secured my passage aboard the Conde Wifredo, so there is no need to worry about that. And lastly, the don will put into your capable hands a small purse full of gold coin to meet our needs until we are properly settled in Cuba. I will explain in greater detail why don Alfonso is aiding our cause in the third note, which you must not read until we are away. I will also explain why my father, your still-grieving and somewhat distant brother, will not even think to intervene. With the greatest affection, your niece, Escolástica Escoraz Vda De Miranda.

The moment Andres finished reading the second note, Madia plucked it from his fingertips and disappeared into the darkness beyond the ferns. Instinctively he reached for the brandy but remembered the warning and sat back in his chair, looking suspiciously at Grenfell, who had stiffened with Andres' sudden movement towards the bottle but then relaxed as his one-time companion in crime retreated. Grenfell chugged what was left of the brandy, which had an exotic bouquet of dark plums, dark red cherries, pomegranates from the gardens of Lebanon, and the faintest trace of smoke from the mountains of Extremadura, where it is said the romantic poet José de Espronceda wandered aimlessly in the years before his death from diphtheria lamenting the loss of a woman he had debased.

For the next several minutes after that Grenfell waved the empty bottle around in the air as if to ward off insects. Then he leaned forward and collapsed in a puddle of confusion on the flagstone of the courtyard.

Two servants soon appeared with a small wooden hand-cart with rusty wheels, which the cook used when she went to the market to buy vegetables. They loaded Grenfell's body with delicate intention, folding the top half over the bottom half, as if he were a dilapidated marionette or a victim of the plague. With only the sound of the rusty wheels to mark their departure, they wheeled him away, his arms trailing on the ground and his legs from the knees down dangling over the sides.

Andres immediately felt better. He marveled at the incongruities of life, and though he did not think himself a superstitious man, he wondered if Lady Luck had perhaps given him a second chance (without realizing that she had been his savior on numerous occasions). Then he realized he was all alone. His brother and don Alfonso had taken their conversation among the ferns to another part of the house, and Tiká had vanished before the note from Madia had arrived. So he sat in the abandoned courtyard, drinking in the sounds of his solitude. He was almost overwhelmed by the sudden impression that the entire world had been reduced to his immediate surroundings. He wondered if he were dreaming or if he had gone mad. The candles were still burning fiercely, but strangely their light seemed diminished, and then an insomniac bird cried out for relief, wings flapping madly and the branches of one of the almond trees shaking, and then the bird grew still, and for a moment he thought he could hear his blood flowing through his veins, though perhaps it was merely the sound of the fountain and the water splashing on the Arabic tile, singing its happy song of Moorish conquest and the conversion of the world to Islam and the happy faithful entering into paradise. He wondered if he was on the verge of doing great things or if he would have to wait years and years for success to arrive and how long would that be, waiting, waiting, secretly envious of everyone around him, but easy does it, his time would come, perhaps it was already here. Then the silence of his meditation was broken by a gaunt figure wearing riding chaps, riding boots, a suede leather jacket, a tweed cap and goggles.

The figure seemed incapable of speech, and Andres, not knowing what to say, stared mutely at a strangely elongated face with eyes covered by the dark glass of the goggles, which reflected nothing, not even the light from the candles. Then a voice said the Rochet-Schneider was ready and they would be departing within the quarter hour. Then the figure was gone.

-48-

The journey from Logroño to Zaragoza in the Rochet-Schneider was the most exhilarating experience of Andres' life to that point. Their driver, who went by the name of Vicente, had been a fan of automobile racing ever since the Parisian sports magazine, *Le Petit Journal*, sponsored the first road race from Paris to Rouen in 1894. There was nothing quite like feeling the rush of the wind against your face as you roared across the countryside, that is what Vicente liked to say. He fancied himself a race driver who had yet to grab a headline, and so that night he drove like a maniac in spite of the fact that the road to Zaragoza was not meant for automobiles, and in spite of the fact that it was the darkest night since anyone could remember, and a surprisingly cold, almost icy, wind lashed their faces, Vicente laughing at times with lunatic glee as the dark landscape flashed by like the churning waters of a forgotten inland ocean, with only the dim, underwater glow from two brass lamps to show the way, maintaining an average speed of twenty-nine miles per hour with bursts of over forty, a phenomenal achievement in 1899, especially given the nature of the road, which would have earned Vicente a place of distinction in automobile racing lore if an official Marshal had been present to verify his time, but which, nevertheless, won him the admiration of Andres, who mistook his recklessness for courage, and their safe arrival as a destiny achieved rather than what it was, a brazen tempting of the sisters of fate in which they were lucky to escape with their lives. Indeed, while the general contours of the land sloped gradually downhill from west to east, the road itself was steep in places, jutting up over rocky hills instead of around them, and there were many places where heavy wagons pulled by teams of oxen had over many years cut gigantic grooves into the road, which caused the Rochet-Schneider to bounce violently at times, and at one point it seemed certain that the vehicle would topple over in an explosion of twisted metal and fractured hopes, but the unseen hand of God, the only power in the universe that could stand against the sisters of fate if they felt they had been wronged, prevented eternal disaster, and so the Rochet-Schneider skidded along the edge of the road instead.

They arrived in Zaragoza at eleven in the morning and Vicente let them off in front of a small café with a red awning and a few tables outside on Calle Santa Isabel three blocks from the Basílica de Nuestra Señora del Pilar. Tiká was amazed at how suddenly her world had changed, for she had slept a dreamless, untroubled sleep during the journey in spite of the cold wind and the rocky road, and then woke up suddenly to the erratic, trembling, wheezing sound of the two-cylinder engine like an old man coughing only after Vicente had come to a final stop. Vicente left the engine running while he unloaded their suitcases for fear that he could not get the contraption started again. And all the while Andres was congratulating him on his magnificent talent for driving, the precision of his technique, and his uncanny ability to navigate beneath a cloudy sky, as if he were the evolutionary equivalent of a human astrolabe, all of which seemed to Andres irrefutable proof of both the wonders of technology and the glory of the human race with its limitless and soul-driven ability to surpass the brilliance of even the nearest stars, and which fueled from that point on his own overwhelming even obsessive desire for all things modern.

"You are a force to be reckoned with," said Andres.

"But of course," said Vicente, laughing with great joy as he climbed back into the Rochet-Schneider and adjusted his goggles. "I am the greatest driver in the world."

Then with a cloudy burst of city refuse and oil particles, he left them standing in a pool of sunlight that seemed as bright and warm as the smile of God.

Two days later, Andres and Tiká boarded the train for Barcelona, and it was only then that Andres discovered he had lost the third note, but since Madia was no longer present to watch him read and digest Tiká's words, and since Tiká herself had seemingly forgotten the existence of the note, he never mentioned that it had vanished. Three days after they arrived in Barcelona, they boarded the steamer *Conde Wifredo* for Cuba and the everlasting promise of the Americas.

The ship did not depart until an hour after sunset, two hours later than normal, so those who had come to see it off had already gone home. It seemed like the world had become one of Edison's silent movie experiments, the ship slipping away without the fanfare of brass bands and banners flying with festival cheer and the popping sound of bottles of champagne being uncorked and the pealing, joyous laughter of the city's ancient (some would have said bony-fingered and decrepit) aristocracy, and then the parting guns sounding out over the water, and lastly, the handkerchiefs waving goodbye, all of that which usually accompanied such departures on a blameless Saturday afternoon was absent, no, theirs was an unheralded departure that felt as much like going into exile as it did heading off with buoyant spirits on a grand new adventure.

The ship gave only a single, low-humming blast of its great ship horn before it pulled away from the pier. Only the sentinel lights of the old stone wharf seemed to notice, ancient orange globes winking in the dark like dying fireflies, the ship moving slowly through the dark shining waters of the harbor and the warehouse lights and the hazy, distant street lamps reflected there, past the heavy shadow of Mont Montjuïc, which seemed to blot out the nighttime sky, and then out past the breakwater and the gleaming golden brilliance of the lighthouse at Llobregat, and then the glowing magnificence of this great modern city of the modern age that some said existed only in the imagination of poets and philosophers and vagabond kings vanished without a trace, and Andres Ordóñez Escoraz and Escolástica Escoraz Vda De Miranda and everyone aboard the *Conde Wifredo* were swallowed up by the trembling, mythic darkness of the trembling, mythic sea.

-49-

The journey aboard the *Conde Wifredo*, as re-imagined by Isidora many years after the fact:

My great-grandfather never told Tiká that he lost the third note at some point during their journey from Logroño to Barcelona oh so many years ago. Perhaps it had slipped out of his pocket while they were squeezed into the Rochet-Schneider with the mad Vicente at the wheel, that eccentric of mixed Italian and Spanish heritage who was shouting with a maniac race-driver's delight as they sped erratically across the dark, early morning landscape towards Zaragoza. Or perhaps Andres was about to read the note two days later on the train to Barcelona but had become distracted by the scenery flashing by and the stiff comfort of sitting for so many long, unyielding hours and had let it fall from his fingers unread. Who can say? Perhaps if Andres had read Tiká's third and final note, which contained the reason why don Alfonso had helped Andres and Tiká escape to the Americas, as well as the reason why my great-grandfather's lonely, overwrought brother, Arturo, had not tried to stop them, perhaps if Andres had even glanced at the opening lines, a host of future tragedies involving the Escoraz family might have been averted. It is a slippery slope to wonder about such things, let me tell you. But Andres never said a word. He believed it was better to let sleeping dogs sleep, and since Tiká never alluded to the note or what she had written during the several years she lived with my great-grandfather in Cuba, Andres never asked her what revelations and family secrets the note had contained, secrets which remained hidden by their mutual silence until Tiká's last day on the planet when, in the delirium of impending death, she bared her soul to the nurse who was sitting by her bedside.

That is not to say that Andres did not wonder about the note now and then. But he was not overly curious. He was not one to dwell on the past, so he harbored few regrets. But on three occasions during his life, he was overwhelmed suddenly and swiftly by the sense that Tiká's handwritten note from oh so long ago contained advice on how to fulfill his destiny, which, as everyone knows, is the secret to lifelong happiness, and since he had never read the note, he would never know what he was supposed to do and how badly things had gone awry. It was an actual, physical sensation more than a fluttering premonition or a vaguely constituted belief. On each occasion, it was as if a weasel or a hedgehog or a wild rabbit were gnawing on his exposed entrails and all he could do was watch. That's how he had once described it.

The first occasion occurred, as you might expect, aboard the *Conde Wifredo*. The great ship was the pride of the Naviera Pinillos shipping company and had been making the passage from Barcelona to the Americas since 1892. No, it was not a blue-ribbon luxury liner like the *Oceanic* or the *Lusitania,* those grand, gilded ships of yesteryear which carried the intellectual and artistic nobility of Europe and America back and forth across the Atlantic on useless, spendthrift vacations. But the *Conde Wifredo* could accommodate up to eighty first class persons in forty staterooms possessing walnut furniture and Tiffany reading lamps and gilded mirrors (and dinner with the Captain once or twice during the voyage), another two-hundred aspiring souls in second class cabins fitted with American-made quatrefoil iron beds and enough room left over for two or three large steamer trunks, and as many as six-hundred steerage persons crammed into the rat-infested abyss of the cargo holds, depending on how much cargo was on board, where everyone slept three to a bunk, and even the crew would not go below if they could help it, and who could blame them, unless they had first burned away the pestilent stench of the dregs of humanity with a red-hot poker covered in tar and lit with a match, waving the makeshift torch back and forth in the air as they climbed down the ladder, a gesture of fear and loathing. For Tiká, who had never before set foot outside Logroño, life aboard the *Conde Wifredo* was a dazzling display of human frailty. For Andres, who had seen the world but nevertheless suffered from the same chronic idealism that afflicted certain

German philosophers of the 19th century, as anyone who knew him in those days could plainly see, the *Conde Wifredo* became a symbol of divine intervention in the face of degenerate, self-absorbed behavior run amok, so Andres retreated to the ship's smoking room or took long, solitary walks along the promenade in the hours between meals to better prepare himself for whatever God had in mind.

The captain of the *Conde Wifredo,* a robust rogue of a man named Ramón Martín Cordero, who had once been arrested for making indecent advances towards a young, wealthy widow and had thereafter harbored treachery in his heart when it came to love, escorted them to their stateroom that very first night, a magnificent suite of three rooms (thanks to the profligate generosity of don Alfonso) with two Tiffany reading lamps, a walnut wardrobe, and a brightly polished Berliner gramophone with a dozen or more discs featuring various operatic pieces that included Tom Bryce singing the English version of 'The Drinking Song' from *Cavalleria rusticana,* Montague Borwell singing the 'Toreador Song,' and 'Miserere' from Verdi's *Trovatore.* Captain Cordero spoke eloquently about the various features of the ship as they made their way down a narrow passage lit only by carbon filament lamps fixed to the ceiling, which cast an eerie, orangeish, dancing light upon the newly painted steel walls. He told them they were always painting the walls somewhere on the ship. The smells of drying paint and turpentine were a lingering presence as omnipresent as the breath of God. This is how the Captain phrased it. He pointed out where the paint was still wet with an ominous seriousness. He then pointed out several passageways that were off limits to the passengers. He asked them if they had ever sailed the clear waters of Qatar and watched the darkies diving for pearls. He asked them if they were afraid of barracudas or sea snakes or tiger sharks. Then he told them a few unpretentious, salty jokes and laughed uproariously, his face contorting in odd grimaces. He cautioned them about several members of his crew who had been seen skulking about the entrance to the grand saloon late at night, and near the back door to the steerage saloon three decks below early in the morning. Who knew what nefarious intentions they possessed? He said if they encountered any difficulty whatsoever on board his ship they should knock on his door immediately, for his quarters were directly opposite their stateroom. Then they neared their destination and his tone changed abruptly, as if he and Andres were long lost friends or members of a secret society who were destined to become mortal enemies. 'Ah yes,' the Captain had said, 'No one will bother you. You will have all the privacy you need on this very short journey to the Americas.' And then he had tossed a cavalier, knowing smile in Tiká's direction. 'Yes, yes, you and your lovely bride will have nothing to worry about.' But when Andres had tried to explain that Tiká was his niece, the Captain only waved his hand in the air with surreptitious sympathy, his smile widening by several inches, and said 'If you live among the wolves, my friend, you have to howl like a wolf,' before disappearing into the cavernous darkness of his own room.

By the next morning, even before the bugle call to breakfast, word had spread all over the ship that Andres possessed a young, fulsome bride and that the happy couple were on their honeymoon. The men he encountered from the upper decks all gave him curt, approving, jealous nods, for clearly Andres was quite a bit older than Tiká, while the men from the lower decks either gave him idiotic grins or approached him with a singular familiarity based on too much alcohol and the universal assumption that all men are pigs and therefore brothers in arms, asking him unanswerable, predatory questions such as 'how much does she cost?' or 'who did you have to kill to get your hands on a piece of calico like that?' or 'how many pups were in that litter' or offering cryptic advice out of the blue such as 'the wolf always finds a reason for taking the lamb' or 'never ask forgiveness until the hangman wraps the noose around your neck,' or 'keep out of deep water, beauty like that casts a shadowy net,' or veiled threats such as 'we only own what God gives us,' or 'one day you will understand the silence of the planets.'

The women of the entire ship quite predictably gave Andres as wide a berth as was humanly possible given they were at sea, fluttering about uselessly and nervously like tiny birds trembling as he passed by, amazed and disgusted and curious and ashamed all at once, all except a few aimless looking waifs who trotted after him like lost but streetwise alley cats trying to play on his sympathies or arouse his presumed degenerate interest.

Of course Andres said nothing to Tiká, for he did not wish to unduly alarm his niece, but in truth she only would have laughed at his suspicions. Besides, what would he have said? She was immersed in the exhilarating freedom of her first and only Transatlantic voyage, though it is also true that this freedom was limited to strolling about the promenade for the better part of each day with a flock of women from the upper crust, the wives and daughters and spinster sisters of newly appointed ambassadors of hope hoping for brand new verdant pastures to plow; or the wives and daughters of middle-aged lawyers with strong ties to the Church who were hoping to take advantage of the provincialism of those living in the former colonies; or the wives of businessmen who had lost thousands as a result of the war in Cuba and were now staking everything they had left on the suddenly resurrected promise of Latin America. All of the women (except Tiká) were dressed in black satin or silk dresses with flowing black headdresses, as if they had fallen into the abyss of perpetual mourning, a convocation of black swans gliding this way and that, bemoaning the loss of their ancestral homes.

Truly, the road to everlasting grief is a swift descent. Still, these black swans acted as a buffer against the gossip swirling about the ship, and though the nature of the gossip changed course during the course of the voyage, the nature of their vigilance did not. They became the guardians of Tiká's youthful and exuberant soul and did not let her out of their sight, not even for a minute, not until she rejoined her uncle for dinner each evening, and even then, there was always a black swan ready to alert the others if anyone from the lowliest steward in his white jacket and black cap to the Captain himself so much as winked at her with a lascivious eye. And so it went. Tiká never realized she and her uncle had produced a never-ending radio storm of idle chatter among the crew and those quartered in the lower decks. And she was certainly unaware that she, in all her imagined, naked glory, with tiny diamonds and other jewels flashing out from her braided, fiery-red hair and her lips glistening with the promise of promiscuity, had become a ghostly hologram suspended above the bunks of half the men aboard the mythic *Conde Wifredo* as they plummeted into a sea of turbulent dreams.

It was an impossible situation, to say the least. But what could Andres do? Yes, yes, the sensible course of action would have been to ignore the gossips until the ship reached Havana. Let them have their fun, what harm lay in that? But this was not as easy as it sounds. He who belongs to God speaks the language of heaven. But the reverse is also true, and the *Conde Wifredo* was as godless a ship as there ever was. Everywhere Andres went, night and day, he was bombarded by whispering voices that belonged to men who were clearly up to no good. He thought perhaps he had become the unsuspecting victim of *aojamiento*, a maleficent eye cast his way. His sanity was teetering on the brink. He spent countless hours in the smoking room smoking an infinity of cigars in a vain attempt to hide behind a protective cloud of smoke and ash, imagining with each puff that he was sitting in the middle of a bonfire dedicated to St. John. He hunted about for a small cross made from the twigs of the blessed laurel, a cross that his brother's wife had given him when he had first set off to see the world, a cross which Verona had said would protect him against the evils he might encounter, and so he had kept it on his person ever since, but the cross had mysteriously vanished. He recited an endless litany of rosaries delivered up to the hallucination of his growing despair, but he wondered if perhaps the prayers were themselves forgeries when they produced no obvious effect. He prayed to St. John of God, a 16th century Spanish soldier who later became the patron saint of booksellers, printers, hospitals, the sick, nurses, and those suffering from heart disease. It did not occur to him to simply stuff cotton in his ears. On the third night he knocked on the Captain's door but there was no answer. The barrage of whispering voices grew steadily more impertinent. They began gathering outside Andres' stateroom after midnight, mocking him with their furtive twittering, but whenever he opened the door he found the corridor empty except for the shadows produced by the savage flickering of the orange carbon filament lamps.

Andres soon realized this was part of some strange, sinister game. But again, I ask you, what could he do? What else could he have done? The moment he closed the door and slid the bolt into place the whispering would start up again and the scenario would repeat itself. He suspected that the very fabric of reality had come unglued and wondered if perhaps the ship itself was a conscious entity, an alien being from another dimension. In a madcap effort to escape himself, he raced up to the promenade to get a whiff of fresh salt sea air only to be smacked in the face with the smell of turpentine from the various ongoing painting projects scattered about the ship. His tongue seemed to be coated with fur. He leaned over the rail and watched the ocean swirling past in the moonlight. The sound of the sea became a siren's melodious song thick with the syrup of innuendo and a forbidden rendezvous dangling just out of reach. He began to speak in the language of barnacles, a panicky, furtive gasping sound tied to the tidal rhythm of the moon that only made sense under water. Without showing any evidence of surprise, he wondered at the strange turn his lunacy had taken. The barnacles on the hull of the ship began reciting poetry that sounded remarkably like someone plucking the strings of a mandolin, and Andres would have liked to stay and listen, for he enjoyed both poetry and the mandolin (he particularly enjoyed a dazzling aria written for the mandolin from the middle of Carlo Cecere's *La tavernola abentorosa*), but he was haunted by the sense that his future was hunting for him with unassailable determination, so he kept on moving. He raced back down to his stateroom, where he sat in the walnut chair next to the silent Berliner gramophone, sifting gently through the discs of various operettas with a delicate intensity, as if he could hear the invisible musicians playing their invisible music of the spheres with his fingertips. A symphony of competing emotions flashed across his face: envy, mocking contempt, unashamed even proud (saucy?) devotion, irrepressible longing, unpretentious awe, unpurged fear, and so on. He fell asleep in the walnut chair with the last of the discs in his hands, his hands and lips quivering slightly. Later, he woke to a firm but gentle rocking motion, and the smiling, beaming face of Tiká like a luminous moon crashing into his ominously tragic eyes. She was speaking to him, but at first he could not catch what she was saying. Her words were detached from her lips and seemed to be flying about the stateroom at fantastic speeds, bouncing off the furniture and the ceiling and the sparkling Tiffany reading lamps, the room suddenly ablaze with the brilliance of an unseen morning sun that was somehow able to penetrate even the thickest walls. 'Uncle, wake up Uncle, wake up,' she said. 'Did you fall asleep again in that chair? Uncle, whatever is the matter with you?'

Looking back it is clear that my great-grandfather's descent into madness was but a prelude to the troubles that were to plague the entire ship. Four days out of Barcelona on her way to Santa Cruz de Tenerife, the *Conde Wifredo* was engulfed by a hurricane of bad luck. There is no other way to properly describe it. The hurricane began like all hurricanes with a subtle change in the color of the light. Most people did not notice the change. Even when someone pointed to the distant horizon and said 'See how the color has changed from a calm though hazy blue to a sinister grayish-green,' those standing within earshot paid no attention to the ominous nature of the sky along the edge of the world and the changing colors of their destiny, especially since directly above their down-turned heads the sun was shining brightly. *¡Ay de mí!* We are plagued by lightning that wanders, as the poet says, and it is true. That night the upper crust dined on beef steak and oyster pie and sago pudding for dessert. They did not know the oysters were spoiled. An hour later they were huddled over basins all over the ship, hurling and heaving until their stomachs were empty. When the ship finally reached Tenerife the next day, the dysentery had spread to all decks. The ship reeked with the foul pestilence of rotting vegetation and sour milk. The ventilator shafts trembled like undersea reeds.

Naturally, the Captain had no choice but to place the *Conde Wifredo* under quarantine for three days until the sickness had run its course. This almost goes without saying. But the crew was not happy. Neither were the passengers. Scuffles broke out on all decks. An engineer, a Bosun's mate, a stevedore, and a stoker were locked up in a makeshift brig (the surgeon's office) for cornering a young girl outside the grand saloon. They were the same ones the Captain had warned Andres about.

An elderly Canadian passenger, an old man who suffered from mild attacks of dementia brought on by drinking several cups of black tea in quick succession, chased the black swans around the promenade with an ivory handled cane, cursing at them with an anguished, paranoid vehemence, saying they could all take wing and return to the depths of Hell for all he cared, he was not yet ready to go, causing one young woman to fall down a steep flight of stairs, twisting her knee rather badly in the process.

The smoking room became a seething volcano filled with baritone puffers talking this and that.

Once the quarantine was lifted, and in spite of the fact that the confidence of everyone on board had been shattered, the ship's routine returned to a quasi-normal state.

Fifteen passengers were transferred to a hospital onshore in a dilapidated goat wagon (which had to make several trips) that the dock officials had procured at the last minute.

A small group of Jesuits, imbued with the infinite spirit of illumination and progress, departed the ship on their way to the top of Mount Teide, the tallest mountain under the jurisdiction of Spain, so they could make precise astrological observations in the hope of pinpointing God's actual whereabouts.

Seven new passengers were given berths on the first-class deck and paid no attention to the insolent behavior of the bed stewards, who had staunchly refused to turn down the beds of the newcomers as a way of protesting what they felt had been an unjust quarantine.

An additional twenty-two hardy souls followed the seven onto the ship, all of them world travelers who preferred to pay as little as possible for passage, and by sticking to this strategy, they had visited every corner of the globe. All twenty-two found passable (which is not the same as comfortable) bunks in steerage.

The mail bags were delivered.

Coal was brought up in barges and the bunkers were filled.

The ship's vast labyrinth of storerooms was filled with fresh provisions.

Everything seemed to be as it should be.

Everyone believed in their heart of hearts that the worst of the bad luck was over.

Three days later, eight-hundred forty-seven nautical miles due west of the Canary Islands according to the calculations of the ship's Second Officer, the hurricane of bad luck returned with an unrelenting vengeance. Two of the new passengers, a brother and sister, missionaries who were on their way from West Africa to Florida, were clearly suffering from Yellow Fever. The Captain reassigned them to a small closet of a room on the coal deck, and there they remained. He moved them in secret to keep the crew, whose paranoia had become a meteor streaking across the sky, from tossing brother and sister into the sea. Only the Captain and the Chief Steward knew where the missionaries were.

One day later, during the middle of a dreary, drizzly afternoon, the kind of afternoon that is usually quite easy to forget, the ship was struck by a rogue wave that measured seventy feet high, according to a young first mate standing on what a few smart alecks called the Governor's Bridge, a forlorn expression on his face as the wave washed over the deck and the ship teetered ominously on the brink before miraculously righting itself. Three women and one steward were washed overboard from the wave, at least that was the scuttlebutt until a lonely rail of a Presbyterian minister from Boston, who had been on a whirlwind tour of the churches and monasteries in the Catholic countries of Europe to catalogue their theological errors, confessed to inventing the story in the hopes of instilling an appropriate appreciation for the wrath of God in the wayward souls aboard the *Conde Wifredo* and elsewhere, perhaps even his own cornerstone parish back in America. Even so, three women and a steward had, in fact, mysteriously disappeared.

The more superstitious among the crew evoked the name of St. Erasmus of Formia, also known as Saint Elmo, the patron saint of sailors and stomach disorders, who had suffered the tragedy of having his teeth plucked out with hot pincers because his truth was not the truth of the Roman Emperor Diocletian. The crew scanned the ship from bow to stern each evening looking for the bright blue fire of the saint's godly presence as proof that he would stand between them and this earthly hurricane of certain disaster. They were unashamed in their religious devotion.

An enterprising gang of coal-handlers and trimmers (all of them decidedly antireligious by the way they wore their caps) spread the rumor that Saint Elmo's fire was no fire at all but was instead the visible aura of the souls of desperate, degenerate men lost at sea, trapped in the blazing purgatory of their own sinful natures, looking to wreak their vengeance of dissolute lives on the living, and then these same coal-handlers and trimmers (blasphemous, self-indulgent bastards all of them, who would have sold their own grandmothers for a price) passed out tiny amulets they said were made of onyx, though who could say for sure, amulets which would grant their wearers immunity from the pain of a premature death.

The amulets went for three dollars apiece.

Five days out of Tenerife the wireless operator told the Captain he had received a series of staticky messages from a group of American physicians living in the Dry Tortugas. The messages were from the future, the wireless operator said, but not very far ahead, fourteen or fifteen years at most. They were about various ships in distress. The first was about the steamer

Olympic of the Alaska Steamship Company. The *Olympic* was apparently wrecked on a reef near Bligh Island, Alaska. The next was about the steamer *Herman Frasch,* whose captain was suffering from ptomaine poisoning and on the verge of death. And so it went, a seemingly endless litany. The ocean liner *Saturnia* had struck an iceberg 175 miles east of Belle Island and was taking water. The steamship *Hipplayit Dumois* had lost its bearing in a sudden fog and had subsequently rammed into the steamship *Madison.* The steamship *Pleiades* ran aground in Magdalena Bay. The steamer *Asia* had suffered a series of mysterious explosions and was now sinking in the South China Sea. The steamship *Oravia* had somehow struck the rocks on the Falkland Islands, producing a great, jagged gash in her hull, and would probably go down within the hour. The steamship *Alimarante* of the United Fruit Company was stranded at the entrance to Cartagena Harbor when she collided with a harbor tug, damaging the blades of her propeller. The mulatto wheelman of the tug was killed instantly but no casualties were reported on the *Alimarante.* The freighter *La Touche* crashed onto a reef off the coast of Belize and sank within five minutes. The Brazilian freighter *Rio Branco* was sunk by a German submersible in the North Sea. The steamer *Merida,* bound for Havana with a cargo that included over two million dollars' worth of Mexican gold, silver and copper, was struck for no readily apparent reason by the *Admiral Farragut* and sank before any of the lifeboats could be lowered.

The Captain did not know what to make of the strange tale told by the wireless operator, so he sent him to bed. But he was secretly bothered by the messages of so many ships in trouble and wondered for a moment about the contentions of some philosophers that even though most of what goes on in the world is hidden from our view, everything happens for a reason. Then without a second thought he took hold of the wireless, which was still whispering its arcane messages of death and unavoidable destruction, yanked it (along with its headphones, glowing glass tubes, dials, cords, all of its 20th century paraphernalia) with unceremonious contempt from the operator's table, dashed out of the room and tossed it over the side.

A matronly woman (one of the black swans) two decks below saw the shadow of the plummeting wireless and thought a baby had fallen overboard or been tossed by unscrupulous individuals and screamed and fainted. She spent the next three days searching for some clue as to the identity of the murdered child and the culprits who had committed this most heinous crime, but no one would admit to anything. In a fit of insanity she latched onto the idea that the crew was conspiring against her best detective efforts, nay, the very universe was aligned against her, and when her own husband of twenty-six years, the hopeful Under Secretary to the new Spanish Ambassador to Venezuela, laughed at her suspicions, she took a small penknife that was nevertheless exceedingly sharp, a knife that she had quietly kept in her handbag since her days as a nurse in Madrid oh so many years earlier, and quickly and efficiently sliced her husband's carotid artery just below the ear. Without even a subtle grimace of regret tinged with irrepressible joy, without a flicker of discontent suddenly relieved, she watched him bleed out in a manner of minutes right there in his own stateroom, the sound of an Italian opera echoing from somewhere else in the ship, the wobbly operatic voice (it sounded a little like 'Suvvia, cosi terrible' from Leoncavallo's *Pagliacci*) descending upon this scene of invisible despair with rapacious speed, the husband's eyes blinking stupidly like the eyes of a bull lost in the mechanized labyrinth of a modern day slaughterhouse.

On the ninth day the sun failed to appear.

At first no one knew what to say. It was almost like forgetting how to speak. The ensuing darkness hummed with a cold, crystalline vitality, partially hypnotic, almost mechanical, not unlike the sound of an original DeKleist carousel organ at the epicenter of a whirling carousel. The sound of the darkness was almost soothing.

It soon became apparent that the carbon filament lamps that normally illuminated even the darkest corners of the ship were no longer operating. Everyone on board was reduced to using candles if they wanted to see two steps ahead.

The darkness in the darkest corners of the ship was not as soothing as the darkness that sounded like a DeKleist organ.

After a while the use of language reasserted itself.

The sound of the darkness was soon replaced by a vigorous debate (a dark hurricane of voices, if you will) as people from all walks of life wondered what had happened and why. Battles raged over whether the darkness was God's doing or if demonic forces had extinguished the light of the world. Some said it could be nothing else but a departure from the infinite absolute. Some said the second Antichrist had appeared and that he had gotten hold of Solomon's ring of power. Some denied anything out of the ordinary had taken place at all. Some said the power of God and the power of any and all demonic forces were one and the same.

A naturalist from Glasgow University on his way to search for plant specimens in the Brazilian wilderness said that neither God nor demons were involved. He declared that the ship had simply slipped into a magnetic maelstrom caused by unseasonably warm and therefore turbulent weather over the Canary Islands, it was almost like slipping into a coma, and so the *Conde Wifredo* had been unwittingly and inevitably propelled a cataclysmic number of years either into the mythic future or the symbolic past, he wasn't sure which, but the ship, he added, was most definitely now traveling the waters of the Antarctic. He suspected they were roughly eight-hundred-and-fifty nautical miles southwest of Tierra del Fuego, calculations which he said he based on his innate sense of geography and an appreciation of the laws of physics, especially Bernoulli's equations in fluid dynamics. Of course not all of the passengers were convinced or even believed in science, particularly the hopeful Ambassadors of an aging and fractious Western Europe with their secret financial backers, who believed in the power of paid assassins but preferred to keep this belief hidden, as well as the upper crust lawyers with their secret, religious connections, who believed in a subjective if somewhat unprincipled interpretation of the law, and also the frantic businessmen of a lost generation with no connections to speak of but with an overwhelming belief in their own desperate cunning and the naiveté of peasants living in untapped markets, all of them thought such a turn of events would have been exceedingly ungenerous at this juncture in their lives and was therefore an absolute impossibility (in so far as anything could be called absolute) and so they dismissed the naturalist's theory as easily and efficiently as one dismisses a falling star or the whooshing whiz-bang of a speeding bullet that lodges itself with irreversible authority in the brain of a retreating enemy.

At the other end of the intellectual spectrum, which is not as great a distance as one would expect given the unceasing tug-of-war between the two poles, a few aging and unheralded poets drifting in and out of senility among the passengers in steerage penned sonnets evoking the eternal abyss of the long night.

On the tenth day the sun returned with the same inexplicable suddenness that had accompanied its disappearance. An incredible (and also inexplicable) wave of heat washed over the upper decks. Wooden deck chairs all over the ship, some positioned against the rail, others stacked against various bulkheads, suddenly burst into flames.

The carbon filament lamps were still inoperable.

The passengers did not seem to mind an occasional descent into darkness now that the sun had returned, but the crew, who spent a good portion of their working hours in the suffocating troglodyte atmosphere below decks, became mutinous in their discontent.

The number of suspicious accidents, none of them as yet fatal, began to increase. Cause and effect were difficult to determine. But that was to be expected. The crew had been growing more and more mutinous with each passing disaster, and now there was no telling what they might do or to whom.

The whispering outside Andres' stateroom intensified both in volume and in its sinister tone.

On the eleventh day a young Romanian employed as a stoker went temporarily insane from the intense heat of his four furnaces and rushed topside and dove overboard, vanishing beneath the frothy waves in an instant.

The Chief Steward, a pompous man with a rather delicate nose, discovered the dead body of the hopeful Under Secretary to the new Spanish Ambassador to Venezuela. He had been drawn to the stateroom by the faint though unmistakable whiff of human fermentation. He did not wonder who the murdered man was or if perhaps the murderer was still lurking about (he was in no danger on that account, for the wife, after recovering her sense of right and wrong and the glittery decorum of false ethics, had abandoned her upper crust station for the relative safety of the lower decks and hoped to make her way to the New World in disguise). No, his only concern was disposing of the body before the process of fermentation became a public nuisance. Immediately the Chief Steward summoned the ship's Surgeon. Together the two men wrapped the offending corpse in a cream-colored silk sheet, dragged it this way and that through the ship's immense labyrinth of dark, forbidden corridors until they reached the stern, where they joined a gang of unassuming kitchen assistants and anonymous, overburdened stateroom stewards, dark shadows in uniform, wordless exhaustion spreading its wings beneath a star-filled sky, all of them faceless men armed with an endless supply of garbage receptacles, which they were continuously lifting and emptying over the side with robotic precision and then grabbing new receptacles (an endless supply?) off the deck.

With a mighty heave the Surgeon and the Chief Steward hoisted the body of the once hopeful Under Secretary above the rail (exhaling with obvious relief) and dumped it (him, the Under Secretary's putrefied body) into the seaweed covered sea right along with the day's refuse from all quarters. The sharks, a few makos and a few tiger sharks and a few hammerheads illuminated briefly by the soft, trembling light of the untainted stars, came and went and came again, their gray, glistening, humped bodies rolling about like eels.

The Chief Steward and the Surgeon stared for a while in uncomprehending amazement at the row of lowly stateroom stewards and kitchen assistants forever focused on the ceaseless stream of overflowing garbage receptacles.

Then the two bigwigs returned to their own duties.

The wife of the murdered Under Secretary vanished without a trace. It was if she had never existed.

Of course the same thing could have been said for the Under Secretary.

It was at this point that the crew began to wonder if the Captain knew where they were headed. They wondered if the Second Officer had mislaid the charts or if the Captain himself had decided to assume the duties of navigation using only a 16th century Persian astrolabe.

The grumbling increased with every passing hour. The passage from Tenerife to Cuba had never taken so long.

On the twelfth day the Conde Wifredo passed through the tail of a sudden squall. There were no causalities among the passengers, but three sailors were killed trying to secure the lashings of the starboard anchor.

On the thirteenth day out of Tenerife, power to the carbon filament lamps was restored (good luck), but the ship's propeller shaft fractured (compensating bad luck). No one could say for certain what had caused the damage. Some believed saboteurs were on board. Others believed it was a case of divine retribution. In any event, the fractured propeller shaft was perhaps the last straw as far as the crew was concerned.

At least this was the Captain's impression.

The *Conde Wifredo* drifted northwest with the Antilles current for several hours until the ship's sails could be properly rigged. Since the Captain had dumped the only wireless on board into the sea, he could not radio for help or even hope that the outside world would know what was happening until it was too late.

How Captain Ramón Martín Cordero prevented a mutiny aboard the *Conde Wifredo* fourteen days after she had put out from the port of Santa Cruz de Tenerife en route to Havana, Cuba, a mutiny that probably would have been one of history's most unrestrained and notorious affairs, a bloody melee if there ever was one, right up there with the mutiny aboard the *Batavia* in 1628, which was spurred by the desire for a new life but ended with a shipwreck off the coast of Western Australia and the savage murdering of fully half of the survivors (including a newborn baby who was strangled with a knotted piece of rope) by the mutineers before they were rounded up and executed by the government; or the mutiny that took place on the *HMS Bounty* in 1789, which was spurred by an understandable desire for a life of unending sex with pretty Tahitian girls and ended with the unexpected survival of the *Bounty's* captain, Captain William Bligh, who was set adrift in the South Pacific, surviving dehydration and the predatory interest of first cannibals and then sharks before finally making it to England (a journey of some 3,700 hundred nautical miles that he made in a little over a year without even a compass), at which point he reported the mutiny to the British Admiralty, who then chased down the mutineers and brought them (those that were found) to a swift and imperious justice; or the mutiny aboard the Mexican Navy gunboat *Tampico* in 1914, which was in many respects a bloodless comedy of errors, so it was a far cry from the blood baths mentioned above, but the *Tampico* mutiny was also the prelude to the first naval battle of the Mexican Revolution and therefore a symbol of the discontent of the Mexican people, which is the main reason it made the list:

Within six or seven hours of the propeller shaft fracturing, the grumbling of the crew became a strong black wind whipping up and down the corridors of the *Conde Wifredo*.

The more reckless elements of the crew, meaning those sailors who had narrowly escaped lengthy prison sentences in

Tripoli or Algiers by running off to sea, saw in the growing chaos a chance to take over the ship and so profit from the desperate misery of others.

The vast majority of the crew was willing to follow the reckless elements, partially because they were unwilling or unable to make any hard decisions for themselves, but mostly because they knew the reckless elements would find an appropriate scapegoat to take the blame for every disaster that had occurred during the crossing.

The vast majority believed the *Conde Wifredo* was cursed.

The reckless elements were not limited by such a belief.

The vast majority believed that a curse could generally be lifted if an appropriate scapegoat was found. If a curse could not be lifted, there would be hell to pay.

The reckless elements took advantage of these beliefs.

The vast majority believed that the role of the scapegoat was to offer itself up to whatever dark powers had directed the curse in the first place. The scapegoat would be the one to suffer the slings and arrows of outrageous fortune. Everyone else would get off scot free.

The reckless elements were all for someone else suffering the slings and arrows, wherever they came from.

The vast majority believed that God needed a scapegoat as much as they did.

So did the reckless elements.

From this point forward events began to unfold rather rapidly.

The whispering voices that had up till that moment gathered outside Andres' stateroom, now shifted their focus to the Captain's quarters.

The Captain opened his door, armed with a .38 caliber Colt revolver, for he was no fool, and graciously asked the whispering voices to come inside so they could discuss their grievances in private.

The whispering voices became a wavering, etiolated version of themselves and complied.

The Captain offered them a collection of whortleberry tarts, Russian pastries, and tiny glass bowls filled to overflowing with *Pudding a la Republic with Sherry sauce,* all of which had been left over from dinner the previous evening. All of these sumptuous goodies were carefully placed on a silver platter that the Captain held out so all could see and catch a whiff.

The whispering voices accepted the desserts as long as they were accompanied with copious amounts of rum.

The Captain agreed.

The whispering voices stopped whispering long enough to devour the goodies and empty several bottles of rum pinched from the Captain's private stash.

The Captain asked them if they liked the opera, and he had in his hand an unofficial and unauthorized recording of Wagner's *Parsifal* and was heading over to his own Berliner gramophone to put it on when he realized he was the only connoisseur in the room.

The only sounds for a while were the chewing of mouths and the smacking of lips and the slurping down of drinks.

Then the whispering continued, but the tone was less sinister, more collegial.

The whispering voices said they were tired of all the disasters.

The Captain agreed, he, too, was tired.

The whispering voices wanted to be compensated for the pain and suffering these various disasters had imposed upon the crew. A small bonus, perhaps, a gratuity, if you will, preferably in gold coin, to be shared equally.

The Captain said that could be arranged.

The whispering voices said they wanted fair compensation for the widows of the men who had died. Perhaps a trust fund could be set up, or they themselves could take up a collection from among the passengers and crew.

The Captain said they had his permission to squeeze whatever blood they could out of any turnip they found on the ship.

The whispering voices suddenly realized they had run out of demands, but they also realized they still had the Captain on the hook. They withdrew next to the silent Berliner gramophone and a furious debate ensued. The debate sounded less like a political discussion and more like the furtive, scratchy sounds made by small animals desperately seeking a hole to hide in.

Then the debate was over and the whispering voices resumed their former positions in front of the silver platter with the day-old desserts, but the platter was empty.

The empty platter could have been a problem, but the Captain, ever alert to the vicissitudes of political and social discourse, simply brought out a second platter.

The whispering voices relaxed somewhat. Then they made an additional demand, which was a pretty good indication of the extent of their imagination.

The Captain nodded and smiled to mask his inner insecurities.

The whispering voices wanted some commitment to restoring the peace and tranquility that had been a part of life aboard the *Conde Wifredo* before the disasters had begun.

The Captain thought that was a good idea.

The whispering voices wanted to know how the Captain was going to restore the absent peace and tranquility.

The Captain said he did not know, he had been hoping that things would return to normal on their own.

The whispering voices said such a strategy was unacceptable. They could no longer wait for something so vague and ill-defined as hope to work its magic. They were pretty definite about that. It was too close to religion to suit their tastes. They would be forced to take matters into their own hands if the Captain was unable or unwilling to rise to the occasion.

The Captain suddenly seemed much larger than he actually was. He said of course he would rise to the occasion. That's what made being Captain so much fun.

The whispering voices applauded the Captain's decision. They were amazed at how large the Captain had become.

The Captain said the first order of business would be to draw up a list of suspects, people who were suffering from exotic diseases or who held radical ideas or who had exhibited peculiar, even abnormal behavior, at least when compared to what was generally accepted in polite society. They needed to agree on someone they could blame for the disasters without too much trouble, someone who could rouse the censure, or better yet, even the outright condemnation of the entire ship, but most importantly, someone who could be easily dealt with. In this way, they would appease the gods of the sea and ease their own collective sense of guilt.

'You mean a scapegoat,' the whispering voices cried.

'Exactly!' said the Captain. 'A scapegoat is exactly what we need.'

Two hours later the black gang of whispering voices emerged from the Captain's quarters, all of them giddy as schoolgirls, for they were drunk with the Captain's boisterous self-confidence as much as the Captain's rum. The Captain, for his part, was all business. He waited until the corridor was empty. Only the dancing shadows produced by the flickering carbon filament ceiling lamps remained. Then he took two unhurried steps, stopped, contemplated the mechanical buzzing of the lamps that sounded a little like prehistoric insects, or perhaps it was more like the sound of radiation poisoning, a sort of faint, hissing sound of indeterminate origin, if you can imagine that, a barely heard sound that causes headaches in some individuals but which goes unnoticed by others. The Captain listened carefully to the lamps for a while. It was almost like he was trying to clear his mind of all temporal delusions. Then with delicate precision he pressed his ear against the door to Andres' stateroom and slipped suddenly into eavesdropping mode. Just what he heard is anybody's guess, but after a few moments he seemed satisfied. He retreated into the darkness of his own quarters, a faint smile still on his face, and returned a few moments later with a tiny sliver of paper in his hand, a flash of white, a formal invitation to a tête-à-tête with the Captain in a small vacant cabin adjacent to the smoking room. The tête-à-tête was to take place just after midnight. It was a very serious matter. The invitation said Andres should tell no one where he was going. (If he was pressed he could say that he was going for a late-night smoke.) The invitation also said that Andres' very life depended on his being punctual. That was pretty much it. The Captain peered out from the darkness of the doorway, looking first one way and then the other, as if he wanted to make sure no one was watching. Then he slid the slip of paper beneath Andres' door and vanished into the hazy, orangeish gloom of the corridor as easily as water spiraling down a drain.

The tête-à-tête with the Captain in a small cabin adjacent to the smoking room, just after midnight:

The cabin was decorated with an eye that appreciated scarcity. There was a single narrow oak table in the middle of the room, two chairs positioned on either side, and a small oil lamp hanging from a hook that the Captain carefully manipulated before he sat down. That was it. There was no Berliner gramophone, though the Captain had brought with him his recording of Wagner's *Parsifal*. There was not even a sideboard containing refreshments, though one could almost imagine the smells of whortleberry tarts and Russian pastries if one closed one's eyes. When Andres arrived, with not a second to spare, he was struck briefly by the sensation that he was drowning, he even began to claw at the air, but then the sensation left him and he sat down. The Captain took no notice of Andres' slapstick antics and was instead scrutinizing the unauthorized Wagner recording, holding the disc up at an odd angle so that what little light there was bleeding out from the oil lamp washed across its surface. Perhaps he was looking for subtle imperfections that would mar the beauty of Wagner's composition. Perhaps he was looking for the name of the orchestra that had brought Wagner's magical music to life. Who can really say? What is important, if only in a vaguely articulated, symbolic sense, is that Andres realized that the Captain held as great an affection for the opera as he did. A bond had been forged, however tentative.

Andres wondered which opera was the Captain's favorite.

The Captain, who instinctively recognized a fellow music lover, passed the recording to Andres, who accepted it without thinking. 'Ah, my young friend,' said the Captain, 'it is a terrible thing to be seduced by beauty, is it not?'

Andres did not know what to say.

'Certainly Wagner knew this truth.'

'Yes, of course.'

'There is a great deal we can learn from Wagner. If only we take a moment to truly listen to his music.'

Andres looked at the disc.

'Yes, Wagner is truly one of the great geniuses of the world. In fact I wouldn't trust a man who said otherwise. But let us get down to brass tacks.'

'. . . .?'

'Needless to say, I am quite disappointed, as I am sure you are. I was expecting you and I would have had an extended heart-to-heart long before this most precipitous moment, a chance to trade assurances, cement a blossoming friendship, pay homage to the competing ideals of liberty and justice, pay a few long-standing debts in the process, everything that your great benefactor, the illustrious don Alfonso, was hoping would transpire . . . .'

It was at this point that Andres forgot where he was. The *Conde Wifredo* did not exist. Neither did Captain Ramón Martín Cordero, except perhaps as the nagging voice of regret, a biting fly lost in the whirlwind of sudden memory. Without any warning whatsoever, Andres found himself once again a guest of don Alfonso Alberto Sebastian Francisco de Hernani y Arredondo de Mariategui y de Esperanza, whose family had befriended the Escoraz family in the days when the Moors still plagued the Spanish countryside. Andres could hear plain as day the droning murmur of the don and his own brother. They were talking about the beauty of Isabel and Tiká and the lack of suitable suitors in Logroño, which is what they always talked about. But there was something different about the conversation as Andres was now reliving it, a subtle change in the don's tone which Andres had not noticed before but which he noticed now, a bitterness that could almost be mistaken for cynicism hidden beneath the don's words, which leaked out in a syllable here, a phrase there, a bitterness that masked a deep-seated resentment from years ago, or at least a lingering regret, and so cast a new light on why the don had helped Andres and Tiká escape. It was at that precise moment that Madia had appeared with two notes in her hand, which Andres knew was coming, for even though he was lost in the extraordinarily vivid detail of his last night in Logroño, it was still a memory, after all, which meant that his premonitions within this dream of the past were foregone conclusions in the story of the present. So Madia delivered the notes and Andres read the first, which was in truth the second he had received that day, and then he pocketed the second, which was in truth the third, and it was upon pocketing this third note, which he subsequently lost, that he began to wonder what advice or explanation this note had contained and if his cause with the Captain of the *Conde Wifredo* would have been better served if he had read the third note when it had still been in his possession, and how much, really, did Captain Cordero know about the circumstances of his hasty departure from Spain, and what was the Captain's relationship with the don anyway, how did they know each other, when had they first met and what were the circumstances, but more importantly, what were the Captain's true intentions with respect to Andres and Tiká, what did he really want from them, his affinity for the opera notwithstanding, and why did Andres get the feeling that all was not well with the world, a suspicion that both increased his sense of nervous expectation and affirmed his unvoiced belief that his hands were tied by Fate so there was nothing he could do (or could have done) in any case.

By degree, the aura of Andres' out-of-body experience

faded and he found himself once again facing the Captain, who had assumed the cloaked shape of a darkly brooding, almost Gothic figure, like a god descending.

'But who can truly prepare for the tragedy of thwarted intentions,' the Captain was saying. 'And now here we are, clinging to the cliff of our illusions. What are we to do?

'Yes,' said Andres, who still had no idea what to say.

He considered for a moment trying to bribe the good Captain with one of the gold coins he kept in the purse don Alfonso had given him, but he was saved from this folly by a flash of insight. Yes, he theorized, if he simply agreed with the Captain, he stood a better chance of surviving the long night.

'What are we to do?' said Andes all of a sudden.

A smile seemed to break across the brooding Captain's face, but it could just as easily have been the crease of a furrowed brow or the light from the oil lamp catching the edge of a suddenly exposed knife.

'Not enough, that's for sure.'

'No, we can never do enough.'

'I'm glad you understand my position.'

'Yes, of course, but . . .?'

'But what else could we have done, eh?'

'Yes, what else could we have done?'

'Not much, I'm afraid. I suppose if you had come to me on your own accord even a week ago, we could have sorted through this mess before it became, well, before everything began to unravel with the speed of light.'

'Yes, I understand, . . .'

'Of course you do. Nothing can beat the speed of light for speed. Except perhaps thought. And maybe the swift wings of death, but that's for another conversation altogether.'

'Yes, certainly, but you see . . ."

'Ah, you want to know when things began to unravel. That is quite a difficult question to answer, my friend. Particularly for a man who sits in the Captain's chair, if you catch my drift.'

'. . . .'

'No, no, I think it is best we move beyond idle conjecture. What would we gain? Let us decide upon a fruitful course of action instead.'

'Yes, but . . .'

'We don't have many options left at this point.'

'. . . .?'

'For one thing, the crew has murderous intentions as far as you and your young bride are concerned.'

'But she's . . . .'

'No, no. There's no use trying to change their minds. Pretty difficult thing to change someone's mind when it's made up. It's like a piece of stone, polished maybe, sculpted, a work of art perhaps, a lonely bust high atop a pedestal, the pride of ancient Greece, but it is still a piece of stone, that's what it's like when a mind's made up. No, the best thing to do is get you and your young bride off the ship as quickly as possible. That's the ticket. Can't think of a better way out of this prickly situation. And believe me when I say that I've been thinking about it for a few hours. Yes, my friend, that's what we're going to do, without a doubt. There's nothing else to do. Absolutely nothing! I know that's not the answer you were looking for. We're still two days from Cuba. You and the little woman will have to hole up for a while, keep out of sight.'

'. . . .'

'No. What I meant was we're two days from Manzanillo. That's on the eastern side. That's the best I can do. I can't take you all the way to Havana. Too risky for that. Even if we made it that far without a suspicious accident, one of the crew is bound to follow you off the ship and give you the 'what for,' if you take my meaning.'

'. . . .'

'No, we don't have an arrangement with the port officials in Santiago. It would be an unscheduled stop and they don't like that. But I can get you into Manzanillo. I know the guy there. Yes, yes, Manzanillo is the place.

'. . . .'

'I knew you would understand, my friend. Besides, you have no other choice.'

¡Ay de mí! Can you imagine the indignity my great-grandfather and my cousin must have suffered the day the Captain dropped them ashore? Ah, truly the world is a dark gallery where the face of betrayal hangs on every wall. The *Conde Wifredo* did not even put into Manzanillo as the Captain had said. They plopped a small boat over the side with my great-grandfather and my cousin in the front with the few small bags they had brought from Logroño, and then they were joined

by the two missionaries, the brother and sister suffering from Yellow Fever, who sat in the middle, and a few others who had come down with either that or some other ailment, and in the back of the little boat, ranting and raving and waving his ivory handled cane in the air with a none too delicate eagerness, was the elderly gentleman from Canada, still drowning in the wine of his own paranoia, his eyes like two blood oranges seared by the sun, a blind Homer.

Can you imagine the chaos of such a situation? How they managed to row ashore I will never know. Lonely desperate souls crossing the line into a new land in search of happiness. And there was no telling how far away Manzanillo was! Who knew where they had been abandoned? There were no visible landmarks. There were no fishing boats sweeping this way and that across the waves. No sounds except for the deep bass horn of the *Conde Wifredo*, which was soon swallowed by the early morning mist, and the raucous, inhospitable cries of starving seagulls in the distance. The carcass of a gutted shark floating in the shallows, buffeted by the carnivorous tide. A trail of blood inking its way out to sea. A few sun-burnt palm trees scattered along a rocky shoreline. A few gaunt looking figures wandering about, solitary barefoot fishermen looking for the best spot to cast their lines. A few dark clouds on the horizon, the teeth of sudden despair. The bright heat of the day already begun. Bright white ribbons of steam rising up from the heavy, scorched earth as if attracted by the magnetism of the invisible stars. The sun a brilliant, burnished, quivering red like Quevedo's blood-red moon. This is how Tiká described it to me. Surely for them the world had become a bleak and dreadful place. A forbidden realm. An ancient taboo. An alien planet tucked away in a forgotten corner of the universe. Surely my great-grandfather and my cousin found nothing to set their eyes on that did not remind them of death. If only my great-grandfather had read Tiká's third note. If only, if only, if only.

-50-

A short history of the first three years my great-grandfather spent in Cuba, from the moment he arrived on the island until the moment he met my great-grandmother:

In those early days in Cuba, my great-grandfather had acquired several small plots of overgrown land that were once productive sugarcane farms, several abandoned mills that had been partially destroyed by revolutionaries with torches who were drunk with *aguardiente* and the hope of liberty during the war with Spain, and several broken down, rusted wagons and a few mules suffering from an inexplicable combination of strange necrotic tumors growing out of their legs and necks and random outbursts of paranoia mixed with undeniable rage.

By chance he hired a native *chino,* a thin, wiry man of close to sixty to help him turn a profit on his investments, and within six months the farms were producing sugar cane, the mills had been rebuilt, and the mules had been cured of both their tumors and their paranoid rage with poultices made from the boiled root bark of *negrito* trees found only in hidden valleys high up in the Sierra Maestra mountains. (The mules were later sold to a muleteer newly arrived from Mantanzas who then used them to deliver supplies to the American troops stationed at Palma Soriano and San Luis.)

Only once did my great-grandfather ask about the silver mines that had prompted his initial interest in Cuba. He was chatting idly with a merchant in Bayamo, a man of some wealth and station in life, and the question popped out of his mouth. But the *chino* overheard and burst out laughing. Later he told my great-grandfather that the mines were a myth, a lure to attract the gullible. That was the last my great-grandfather ever mentioned the topic.

The *chino* said his public Spanish name was Nicario Garro but that his secret, eternal, never-to-be-forgotten name of the mountains was El Labrao. He wore a ragged white linen shirt and ragged pants but possessed an otherworldly charm and a radiant smile featuring three silver teeth that banished even the shadows of a moonless evening. He was also no fool and carried upon his person at all hours of the day or night a rusty sword, a hunting knife tied to his belt, and a heavy club made of oak, sharpened and scorched on the end. He claimed to have taken part in the second great anti-colonial uprising (The Little War, 1879) of Cuban nationalists (those who had not signed away their freedom by signing the Pact of Zanjón), yet he took a great interest in Andres' welfare, becoming his *padrino,* if you will, in spite of my great-grandfather's obviously unblemished Spanish heritage.

'Blood is an endless sea,' Nicario liked to say. And in a voice that rang out with the irrepressible purity of lonely highways stretching out towards the horizon and vacant rooms in cheap hotels and the remorseless, withering decline before succumbing to death, he suggested that Andres arm himself as he, Nicario, and all lovers of forbidden freedom were armed. 'The world, my young friend, has in it many *guajiros* who wish to be ruthless bandits, and many ruthless bandits who wish to be *guajiros*, and it is difficult to know who is who, so it is best not to take any chances.'

But my great-grandfather only smiled with the quiet joy that comes from years of reading dusty books and breathing in the odor of decay.

He did not believe in weapons, he said.

'Ah, yes,' said Nicario, 'but not even a faith as strong as yours can save you from the *otra muerte*, the other death.'

My great-grandfather, as you might have guessed, forgot Nicario's words as soon as they were spoken. He abandoned all caution to the wind, as they say. On any given day he was traveling from Manzanillo to Santiago or from Santiago to Manzanillo. It did not matter which direction he went so long as he was heading somewhere. Nicario went with him, always ready with his club to bash in the heads of anyone who mistook my great-grandfather's guileless, unbounded enthusiasm for something more sinister, but during the first two years they spent on the road, the need for bashing in heads never arose.

My great-grandfather existed in a bubble of sanctified hope. He spoke openly and honestly about the tragedy of living in a land where you could not buy a box of fancy chocolates to share with small children except in cities like Santiago or Camagüey or Havana.

And the perpetually downtrodden people of the countryside listened to what he had to say.

My great-grandfather expressed heartfelt dismay for the thousands of Cubans reduced to living in the poverty of palm huts because their towns and villages and lonely farms had been burned by the soldiers of the Spanish Monarchy.

And the perpetually downtrodden people of the countryside clutched at their own broken hearts.

He drank *aguardiente* with the villagers wherever he went. (Nicario kept a ready supply of bottles.) And when they were finished the perpetually downtrodden people of the countryside brought out more bottles and they drank long into the night and fell asleep beneath the stars.

My great-grandfather felt at home wherever he went in those days, but he felt most at home in the small colonial towns scattered here and there across Santiago de Cuba province, talking with the old men who gathered every morning in the squares and plazas beneath the branches of *ceiba* trees to consecrate their hearts and souls to the transitory beauty that was and always shall be Cuba

He especially enjoyed walking along the palm lined streets of colonial Bayamo, the cradle of Cuban independence.

He mourned the death of Carlos Manuel de Céspedes, the father of the country, who was killed by a Spanish bullet from the Spanish rifle of Brígido Verdecia, a Cuban by birth who had joined with a company of Spanish soldiers (though to be fair to young Verdecia, the soldiers told him if he did not pull the trigger they would murder his mother and sister). And when my great-grandfather learned that the body of Céspedes had been dumped into a common grave, he wrote a letter to 'All Cubans with Compassionate and Patriotic Hearts' urging that they join together to find the body and bury it in a place of honor.

The letter was published in the newspaper *La Patria*.

(Years later my great-grandfather still received compliments from those who had admired the letter.)

He wept silently for several hours when he learned that Pedro Céspedes, a younger brother to Carlos, had been taken prisoner along with fifty freedom fighters when their ship, the *Virginius*, had been captured twenty-six years earlier off the coast of Jamaica, and that all fifty-one men had then been executed by a Spanish firing squad in front of a slaughterhouse in Santiago, a symbolic gesture, no doubt, meant to communicate to the public at large that every rebel would eventually be rounded up and slaughtered like cattle.

Truly, the wilted light of desperate but undaunted faces is a mirror to our darkest fears, even as it is a beacon of hope for future generations.

My great-grandfather became an advocate of the free press. He became an advocate for civic improvements such as railroads and sewer systems and electric lights and universal suffrage, and libraries with marble steps and dark mahogany floors and mahogany shelves overflowing with books. He could not understand why the only good road in eastern Cuba was the gleaming white road to Boniato Summit, which everyone called the road to nowhere, and longed for the day when he could drive a shiny automobile all the way to Baracoa.

He contracted with a shipping company in New Orleans to deliver gleaming white appliances to the sunny shores of his imagination.

He believed in the paradise of the modern world.

He believed progress was the path to salvation.

But he also had harsh words for those who supported the 'American' interest in Cuba because they believed true democracy was only possible in Cuba with an infusion of yanqui cash every now and then, and a commitment from the Americans to provide rifles and ammunition and military advisors as needed. The United States, he thought, would simply replace the Spanish as the overseers of the country if left unchecked. And yet no matter how much suffocating outrage he felt towards the Americans and their insidious materialistic opportunism disguised as optimism (or towards their predecessors, the Spanish, and their blood-thirsty imperialism disguised as destiny), he also preached an unwavering commitment to peace.

He was a desert prophet living in the wilderness. 'Let rancor and revenge flee far from our hearts,' he would say to anyone who would listen. It was a common enough phrase in those days, a plea from the lips of men who had already lost too much. But whenever Andres uttered this mantra of the hopeless, the words flashed brightly in the air like spinning coins washed in the sunlight of heroism and nostalgia, or like a flock of startled birds taking wing at the sound of distant cannons, before inevitably giving way to the darkness of an uncertain future.

It was at some point after the end of that second year that my great-grandfather succumbed to the cyclone of loneliness that accompanies a life without love. As with all maladies of the heart, it was most pronounced during the wee hours of the morning, and almost invariably vanished with the dawn. But the effects were visible for all to see. My great-grandfather's complexion began to radiate with the pale light of distant planets struggling to maintain their orbits before being swallowed whole by reckless, carnivorous suns. His skin began to bleed with the distinct odor of tobacco mixed with chocolate, and ever so faintly a hint of cherry, a heady perfume which attracted large crowds of young, hopeful widows in town after town, unimaginably beautiful women who bathed twice daily in tubs overflowing with white gardenias so that their skin would be as soft as lambswool. These beauties immediately recognized in my great-grandfather the irresistible vulnerability of a love-sick *torero* and surrounded him with a halo of smiles that promised long, lingering afternoons and tender nights stretching out towards infinity. And so my great-grandfather commandeered the affections of thousands of lonely hearts, but not without incident. In the town of Contramaestre the magistrate declared my great-grandfather's fragrant skin a menace to the purity of marriage and granted everyone with a rifle permission to shoot him on sight. In the town of Yaro, a group of sun-burnt *guajiros* armed with clubs and torches and determined to keep their young widows for themselves, chased my great-grandfather and Nicario up into the Sierra Maestra mountains, where they took refuge for two weeks in the eternal shadow of Pico Turquino, hiding in the 'dark caves and vales, the ancient exile's fate,' as the poet says. Yet my great-grandfather had no interest in any of these women, in spite of their tremendous tragic beauty and their immaculate bathing habits and the persistent echo of their matrimonial desires. He was, he told Nicario, lamenting the absence of his one true love. How could he explain it? He was certain he could feel her somewhere about, somewhere close, feeling in her heart the same tightness he was feeling. He was equally convinced that she knew exactly where he was, but for some strange, mysterious reason she had squirreled herself away. Perhaps she was testing him to see how strong his love truly was, but he banished this thought as soon as it crossed his mind because such behavior made no sense. So her lingering absence was the cause of his monstrous despair, a despair, he told Nicario, that would vanish only when this love of his life actually appeared, or when in a maelstrom of impotent fury his trembling soul would collapse upon itself and so fall effortlessly into the black hole of his own premature death.

Nicario became quite concerned. He had on numerous occasions during those first two years suggested that my great-grandfather find a suitable wife, and so perhaps he felt responsible to some degree for the insufferably melancholic creature my great-grandfather had become. Who can truly say? Nicario had always taken a scientific view of love, which diminished perhaps the romantic notion of two souls becoming one, but it made for a healthier, happier existence. This is what he professed. But my great-grandfather was rooted to his misery and therefore immune to rational arguments. His symptoms worsened. On several occasions his heart stopped beating for a minute or two altogether and Nicario had to give him a quick blow to the chest to get it going again. He began to lose his train of thought in the middle of sentences, going suddenly mute, his eyes fixed on the horizon, a strange, contradictory look of withering compassion mixed with impoverished mirth spreading across his features, as if he were ministering to the solitude of the world.

It was then that Nicario, in a moment of inspiration that could have been mistaken for complete exhaustion, or perhaps a sudden bout of indigestion brought on by too much Brazilian coffee consumed after midnight, or perhaps the involuntary paroxysms that accompany a subterfuge nearing completion, suggested that my great-grandfather try writing letters to his absent love and perhaps the wind would carry his words to her ears and she would then know it was safe to come out of hiding. To Nicario's happy amazement, my great-grandfather readily agreed. Nicario had expected some resistance to his suggestion, a long, drawn-out debate about the difficulties of such a strategy that might possibly end in fisticuffs, but instead, my great-grandfather smiled with absent-minded joy and began writing a letter that very evening. He labored over each word, trying to sift through the hidden meanings tucked away in the crevices of each phrase, then each sentence, and finally each paragraph.

The first letter, which took him two weeks to write, implored his unseen love to smile as he was smiling in anticipation of their first meeting.

The second letter (ten days) inquired after the health of her parents. (Strangely, my great-grandfather, who seemed to know even the tiniest details of my great-grandmother's life before they even met, seemed to know nothing of her father and his strange, inexplicable death. My great-grandmother's father had left to join Marti in Florida in 1892 and had never seen his wife or daughter again, returning to Cuba in 1895 in the company of relentless Generals hell bent on freeing the Cuban people, only to die of dysentery while camped along the Cauto River in May of that year before he had fired a single shot from his rifle. His body had been found several yards from the river at dawn on the 18th of May, the new sunlight creeping through the dense underbrush like snakes or web-footed reptiles with their tongues flicking at the air, revealing a poor, disenfranchised soldier with his pants wrapped around his ankles, face down in the bloody, glistening grass of his own anguish.)

The third letter (one week) promised that she and her family would be remembered at Mass the very next Sunday at the Cathedral of the Most Holy Savior. He promised her that his prayers would be accompanied by a handful of the gold coins he had carried with him from Spain, and that each coin was worth one hundred *pesetas*. (Naturally Nicario tried to dissuade my great-grandfather from this course of action by reminding him of the parable of the Widow's Offering, but he was unsuccessful.) He also promised he would say an extra prayer (and make a second, smaller donation, also opposed by Nicario) for her cousin, who had suffered from chronic lesions of the skin for years, though how he knew of the young boy's shame or that he even existed my great-grandfather was never able to articulate. (When he met this cousin some months later, he marveled at the boy's immaculate skin, there wasn't a single scar from the disease, not a shadow of ill-health, not a wrinkle of pain, and when my great-grandfather enquired as to the nature of the miracle that had cured him, the young boy smiled a bright smile without pretense and said God could bend the world whenever He chose, but He rarely intervened, waiting, as He did, until someone requested a miracle on behalf of another.)

My great-grandfather wrote the fourth and last letter in a matter of hours. It was a litany of future memories that flowed from his pen to the paper while he slept in a dream-like trance at a narrow wooden table inside a small tent Nicario had set up by the side of the road a mile downwind of a small town called Jiguani. (They had taken to camping in the countryside downwind of towns and villages to reduce the number of young widows who might be attracted by my great-grandfather's unyielding scent. My great-grandfather slept inside the tent, though to say he slept is a mischaracterization, since on any given night he rarely closed his eyes. Nicario slept beneath a blanket of starlight without a care in the world.)

As my great-grandfather wrote the fourth letter, his memories of the future unfolded with unrehearsed precision like the three petals of an orchid upon the arrival of the morning sun. He was amazed at the intense, almost surreal nature of life. He found himself wondering what was real and what was not. He wondered if he were a figment of his own imagination. It was sort of like going to the cinema.

The first petal of the inner whorl:

He and his love-to-be were climbing a steep set of stairs on a moonlit night. They were heading for an old Spanish fort at the top of the hill, a gleaming white beacon against the void and the torrents of discontent. He knelt before his love, who was wearing a necklace of tiny blue stones like tiny teardrops and a pair of earrings to match, and without a moment's thought, the emotions that had been pent up inside his bookish heart for oh so many years, all those sleepless nights, came pouring out like an ocean wave.

They fumbled about for words.

They hesitated.

They smiled and hesitated.

They embraced with a shyness he did not expect, like two planets crisscrossing open space.

'I am only half-awake, my love,' he said. 'I am still half-dreaming.'

And then she kissed him.

The second petal of the inner whorl:

It was the middle of the afternoon, a few months after he had married his one and only love. He saw a river of happy heads flowing uphill towards the gleaming blood-red domes of a small-town basilica. The basilica shone brightly beneath black storm clouds backlit by the sun and dark hills in the distance. Two dark palm trees were swaying this way and that out front. He saw a lady dressed in flowing blue robes rise up from the river as it broke against the stone walls of the basilica. She was carrying a golden cross. Then he realized the lady was not a lady. She was a statue. He realized that she was the reason for the river. It was a religious procession with the feel of a carnival. A feast day to honor Our Lady of Charity, a day filled with the dazzling sunlight of sunflower bouquets, which erased the darkness of the sky from everyone's mind.

Then he became aware of the sound of many powerful drums. Soon the drums were inescapable. They were a part of the air. They were the engine of the river. Then he noticed that the happy heads were chanting and singing softly, prayerfully, happily. Or maybe they were singing loudly but his ears were filled with mud so he could not hear very well. The singing faded in and out. Then the drumming faded.

He wondered where his wife had gone. Then he realized she was beside him. She had never left. She was a happy head the same as all the rest, bobbing up and down. Then he realized that he, too, was a happy, bobbing head. They belonged to a sea of humanity, a river of bobbing heads like tiny corks discarded by eager drinkers. They had never been happier.

Somewhere a voice cried out, 'See how she walks on this road of stormy seas!' Other voices took up the chant. 'See how she walks, see how she walks,' they cried.

The chanting voices were like a restless wind.

The drumming started up again.

Somehow the happiness of my great-grandfather and his one true love increased. They knew in their heart of hearts that it would be an unforgivable sin to take their good fortune for granted.

The third petal of the inner whorl:

He saw the two of them boarding a train during a thunderstorm. The railway station looked like it had been abandoned for years, and yet a train was waiting to depart, a train that defied all reasonable expectations, a train to take them west, across a Cuban landscape of palm trees and grazing cattle and coffee plantations and sugar cane all the way to Havana, which would become the center of their universe. Her mother and uncle, a thick-shouldered Mambí soldier with very dark skin who had fought with the Dominicans and then the Cubans, and several small children were huddled together in a wet mass on the station platform. Her mother cast one long, sorrowful look at the train as it pulled away and then bent her head in arthritic prayer while the children wheeled about her like small birds, shrieking and laughing with each flash of lightning. But her uncle neither wept nor shrieked. He stared after the train with the stone-faced grimace of a revolutionary on the verge of sacrificing his own life for the liberty of others who finds himself suddenly betrayed. Then the train rounded a bend in the terrain and crossed through a field of dripping palm trees and clumps of giant bamboo and majestic mangoes and my great-grandfather lost sight of his new wife's family. He took his new wife in his arms and held her tightly. He whispered words of soothing love into her ears and her ears became greedy siphons and she suddenly realized that she had married a philosopher with the soul of a poet who would write poetry only for her until the day he died.

'Like sunlight dancing beneath the waves, your lingering kiss,' he said to her.

And she smiled and nestled closer to him.

'Like the deepening shadows of tidal pools, your softly whispered words,' he said to her.

And she put her lips to his ear and said she loved him.

'I am thinking of you always,' he said to her. 'We are like young lovers standing in the shadow of the Eiffel Tower, becoming now the center of creation, the pale blue dust of Orion's nebula spinning across the sky, your soul and mine, breathless.'

Then she kissed him with a sudden wave of compulsion that both excited her and caused her to ache with a cancerous fear. Then the wave subsided and she fell asleep to the gentle rhythm of his breathing, and the silky strumming of his fingertips as he caressed her softly glowing dreaming face, and the distant rumbling of the train as it headed towards the clear skies of the west.

It was an impossible task to capture in a single letter the nuanced and evolving emotions of so many future memories. But my great-grandfather did his best. What else could he have done to purge his body and soul of the negativity of his rootless, romanticized past of a high seas vagabond? And what better way to achieve that inner sanctum of peace and harmony which the eastern mystics have talked about for countless centuries and which is the cornerstone of the love that binds us to each other and to the world. So he poured his heart out.

He was dripping with perspiration when he finished. The night had vanished and a warm breeze blew through the tent, but he did not notice. The warm breeze could have been an Arctic wind or a summer hurricane raging across the Windward Straits, but he would not have noticed those either. He just sat at the narrow table and stared at the fourth letter in his hands. But he did notice the chattering of birds in the fig trees outside the tent. The chattering birds reminded him of a Greek chorus, which in turn led him down into a darkly gleaming labyrinth of stray thoughts about the nature of Greek tragedy and whether or not a character flaw was a psychological or even spiritual defect (such as willful pride) or an error in judgment which could not be avoided, or perhaps it was simply an untranslatable concept, which meant that language itself was an imperfect vehicle for thought, not only between languages, but within the same language, because you could never be sure what anyone meant, because the act of using language was in and of itself an act of translation, which was in fact an act of pure faith, as any linguist or former priest would tell you, which meant that even something so tangible as visible reality was unknowable, let alone invisible reality, and what was the nature of reality anyway, and was the universe full of magical things waiting patiently for our wits to sharpen, and did the phases of the moon truly reveal the interconnectedness of the universe, and why did Plato slam the door on the atomists and their notion of cosmic pluralism in favor of a singular world view, which really was the height of egotism, this was my great-grandfather's belief, but perhaps Plato understood that a singular view of reality was the only way to preserve at least the illusion that we were all in the same boat, linguistically speaking, and was there such a thing as moral evil and did moral evil edify the mind so we could better comprehend this reality we called life, and on and on it went, and when my great-grandfather finally managed to escape this labyrinth of unanswerable questions, he found himself wondering if the cosmos were trying to tell him something profound, or if a sinister intelligence was just having some fun.

Then the birds stopped chattering.

My great-grandfather gathered up all four of his letters like the four Archangels to oppose the four beasts of the apocalypse and headed out to find Nicario in the silent vacuum of the world, but he stopped just outside the tent, as if he had just then noticed the majesty of death descending.

It was precisely at that moment, caught as he was in the transition between this world and the next, that my great-grandfather saw a young woman emerging from the shadows of the fig trees like a nymph from the forgotten pages of mythology or an alien queen from a spaceship that had traveled from a distant planet, and as she did so, the chattering of the Greek chorus resumed.

She was the most beautiful woman in the world.

She had long black hair and olive green eyes.

Her skin was the color of coffee and cream.

She moved with the easy grace of sunlight.

Her smile was a warm ocean.

Everything about the young woman was burned into my great-grandfather's astonished brain that morning, but there was one detail that immediately filled him with an immense and unrestrained joy. She wore a tiny white mariposa flower in her hair, just above her left ear, which gave off an intoxicating though subtle aroma that suggested, among other things, hidden messages and revolutionary songs and the freedom to think creatively and the value of mysticism and the hope of forbidden love. It was a woody scent which shrouded her intentions, but not the bright vulnerability of her feminine spirit, nor the hesitant quality of every breath she took. She was the incarnation of mystery to my great-grandfather, and yet he was not surprised to see her. Without uttering a sound, perhaps because he was suddenly incapable of speech, he handed over the letters.

'I am sorry I kept you waiting so long,' she said.

The young woman's apology had the impact of a revelation. My great-grandfather realized that for uncounted years he had been sharing his body and soul with a monumental sadness which had in all probability crept inside through a break in the skin or had perhaps sailed in through his unguarded airways without his knowledge the day his brother Arturo married Verona, and which had since then altered his perception of reality so much so that sunny days seemed like stormy nights and declarations of love possessed deadly, nocturnal fumes like the cyanide found in the tails of passing comets. But on this day he had been reborn. He later recalled that in those first moments, he had been mesmerized by the haunting insistence of those olive green eyes, and the absolution conferred by the young woman's bright, warm, inviting smile. He remembered her sweetly singing voice mingling with the birdsong of the tiny birds (were they some kind of thrush?) in the fig trees (a fact also confirmed by Nicario, who had been sitting on a small folding chair between two tethered horses, sipping with great restraint a cup of muddy, cold coffee prepared hours earlier, and so had witnessed everything). But still, my great-grandfather had not known what to say. Everything he could have said had been in the letters, but in that moment even the letters had ceased to exist.

'My name is Ana Silvestre,' the young woman said.

My great-grandfather still said nothing. He could only marvel at the beauty of her lips as she spoke.

'I wanted to join you sooner,' she continued. 'I wanted to tell you that I, too, am still half-dreaming. Yes, yes, I wanted to let you know I have been smiling since I first saw you navigating the streets of Jiguani, uncertain which way to turn because you were being pursued by the widows of the war and by the young men of our town who believe the nights of unrelenting sorrow must soon come to an end. In truth I have been smiling since the day you came to Cuba, though I did not see you step from the tiny lifeboat that brought you to paradise, but truly I felt the tremor of your footsteps on the beach that day. Yes, my love, I wanted to thank you for inquiring about the health of my parents and for the heartfelt sincerity of your prayers at the Cathedral. My father thanks you from his precarious perch in heaven, and my mother thanks you from the decrepit misery of premature old age and a life that has been lived in the abyss of perpetual betrayal. No, no, do not be dismayed. She will not thank you in person, she has never been one to embrace social convention, but she bears you no ill will, I can assure you of that. She is suspicious of the world and the ways of the world, just as she is suspicious of me, a suspicion borne of jealousy. Yes, my mother is jealous of her daughter. All of the mothers in my family for the last five-hundred years have been jealous of their daughters. But do not be dismayed. Besides, I am the one you have come for, not her. Yes, my love, yes, I am thinking about you always. I have been thinking about you since the day I came into this carnivorous world. You are the flame that will singe my wings. You are my release, my love, my refuge by the sea.'

-51-

My great-grandfather purchases a small farm:

One week after my great-grandparents met by the fig trees, my great-grandfather stopped traveling the road between Manzanillo and Santiago. Nicario protested his decision, for there were many beautiful young war widows seeking comfort, he said, and besides, he had a wagon load of unopened bottles of *aguardiente* that needed drinking, but my great-grandfather, thanks to the luxury of an unexpected epiphany, was now able to laugh softly at Nicario's ceaseless quest for the oblivion of pleasure. 'We are but atoms of light, Nico, seeking only a path to each other.'

Six weeks later, two weeks before my great-grandparents were married in a wedding to shame all weddings in the Chapel of Our Lady of Sorrows in the Church of San Salvador de Bayamo, my great-grandfather purchased a small farm in a narrow valley for my great-grandmother's family and everyone moved in. Everyone included my great-grandmother's mother, who was also named Ana, her uncle, Pepe García Gallego, the brother of her dead father, a small brood of mangy, naked children always underfoot, sons and daughters of the García clan, orphans of the war who had nowhere else to go, and a skinny vagabond of a youth whose tongue had been cut out by retreating Spanish soldiers, or perhaps this crime had been committed by overzealous revolutionaries marching happily to what they assumed would be their glorious deaths, it was never quite clear. The skinny youth had been left for dead by the side of the road. Later, my great-grandmother's uncle had found the boy sifting through the rubble of an abandoned palm hut in search of something to eat and had taken him in. No one in Jiguani had ever seen him before. Everyone assumed he came from the mountains but no one knew his name. But they could see quite plainly that the boy was trying to escape from the dead sea of cold despair. Everyone could see that his life had become an empty dream.

The day my great-grandmother's family moved into the small farmhouse (one week before the wedding), my great-grandmother's uncle gave the boy a tiny closet of a room that adjoined the kitchen at the back of the house. The room possessed a single window which looked out on a small stream traversing a scrubby patch of grass littered with small white rocks, a home for blue scorpions and crickets and other phantoms of the twilight, and on the other side of the stream there was a grove of twisted laurel trees mixed with oak, and a single Royal Poinciana with its flaming red flowers in full bloom, a torch to light up the evening sky. The grove was filled day and night with small restless, relentless birds singing magical songs about the lingering fever of life and the joyful purity of giving one's heart and soul to Christ at the moment of death, which is also the most vulnerable of moments when we are reborn in all our divine glory. At least this was the impression you came away with after listening to that chorus of tiny birds singing. So the room was a sanctuary, a refuge from the sinister intentions of the world. Why Pepe García Gallego gave this room to the young vagabond boy instead of his sister, who had endured the dead sea of cold despair for many more years, is difficult to say, particularly since the room was not his to give away. But who can truly say why anything happens? 'Such gifts in Fortune's hands are found,' as the poet says.

The instant the young boy knew the room was his, he broke into a broad grin and pulled out a small golden pocket watch from the inner waistband of his threadbare pants. With unguarded enthusiasm, he presented the watch to Pepe García Gallego, who immediately inspected the artifact with understandable suspicion. Had the boy become a thief? Had he descended upon the owners of this elegant golden watch in the middle of the night and murdered them in their sleep? Had he discovered the watch while rifling through the pockets of a rotting corpse? Or was this his only reminder of an idyllic past followed swiftly by a tragic yet inevitable demise?

The back of the watch contained an appropriately sentimental expression of great feeling from the 19th century, written in extravagant floral script that was exceedingly small, so small that all but those with the keenest eyesight would require a magnifying glass:

To my beloved son, the last of a noble lineage,
Tomás Francisco Ribeiro y Aguiñiga de la Vega,
And his impossibly lovely bride, AdaNalie Esperanza Barruti,
The brightest star in the heavenly firmament
That adorns the magical Isle of Cuba.
May your faith in each other mirror your faith in God!
Camagüey, 1882

Pepe García Gallego inspected the watch and the writing without the need of a magnifying glass for several long withering minutes before accepting its authenticity, turning it over and over in his hands and then holding it up to the dazzling brightness of the sun and then peering once again at the finely engraved words, as if he half expected the writing to disappear and so reveal a tiny door to a secret compartment. Then he grunted somewhat enigmatically at the boy and the boy shook his head. Then he grunted again and the boy nodded with great vigor as well as visible relief. So Pepe García Gallego returned the watch to the boy and the interrogation was over. The watch became an afterthought, a reliquary of the glorious past, a symbol of doomed love and the inevitability of death, a lament to be whispered on stormy nights beneath the bed covers. How the boy had kept the watch hidden in the years since the war remained a mystery, but no one cared for such trivia. What was important was that the watch had returned the boy to himself and to his now deceased family. From that day forward he was called Tomás Barutti. Such are the vagaries of life.

-52-

The Curse of the Ana Silvestres:

From the day my great-grandmother received her First Communion and was admitted into the realm of reasoning adults by the Church until the day my great-grandfather arrived in Cuba, she was plagued by a recurring dream. She dreamed that she was hiding behind a *moscader*, a fan for flies fashioned from the feathers of a peacock's wing. Where this image came from she did not know, for she and her mother lived in abject poverty. Neither of them were even aware of the existence of peacocks until the dream. And when she asked her mother what it meant, why was she hiding behind this strange and beautiful fan, her mother said, 'I am so very, very sorry, my little Ana. I do not know. I am certain your dream is a reflection of the same lingering curse that has consumed the hopes of our family since the days of the conquistadors. But whether the fan in your dream is the curse itself, or protection from the curse, I do not know. Someday, perhaps, God will take pity and provide you an answer. All you can do is wait.'

Centuries earlier the very first Ana Silvestre had fallen in love with a lonely soldier of fortune. They married in secret, but then the soldier left with Hernando De Soto in search of cities of gold in 1539. He never returned. Nine months after his departure, this very first Ana Silvestre of my family's mythic past left Havana for the hills near Santiago, where she herself had been born, to give birth to a daughter. She gave her own name to the child in the hope that perhaps this second Ana Silvestre might find the happiness that she herself had been denied. But this second Ana Silvestre succumbed to the same misery as the first: a secret lover who went off to war and never returned, a baby daughter she named Ana Silvestre in the hope of breaking what was most definitely a curse.

So the die was cast. Every generation thereafter was compelled to name their first daughter Ana Silvestre because the previous generation had done so. Naturally there were subtle variations in how the curse manifested itself. Not every lover was married in secret. Not every lover died in a war. But the men always died savage, incomprehensible deaths (even when they vanished without a trace, the nature of their deaths was assumed). And the women always gave birth to beautiful mulatta girls they named Ana Silvestre, hoping against hope that the curse would miraculously loosen its stranglehold on the future, at least enough so their daughters might escape the tragedy of living their mothers' lives.

My great-grandmother dreamed the dream of the *moscader* year after year after year, waiting until the day of God's revelation. The dream became as familiar to her as the pattern of her heartbeat or the illusions she fostered in an effort to escape the tentacles of the curse. Then on the very day my great-grandfather and my cousin Tiká were abandoned to their fate by the Captain of the *Conde Wifredo,* this strange, recurring dream evaporated with the morning mist. What is more, my great-grandmother knew when she woke up that morning that she would never dream that dream again. It was for this reason that her mother decided to lock her away from the world for almost two-and-a-half years.

'If the dream returns,' her mother said, 'we will know it is the curse trying to push you back into the world and so reassert its power over the choices you might make. But if the dream does not return, then we will know the curse has finally lost its power, a miracle our family has been imagining for five hundred years.'

As you might have guessed, my great-grandmother's mother secretly hoped the dream would return. The mere possibility that her own daughter might escape the ravages of a lonely, loveless life that had been the legacy of generations of Ana Silvestres filled her with a bitter, jealous rage which she refused to acknowledge even to herself, and which therefore caused her front teeth to blacken and fall out and flaming boils to appear on her sun-seared neck and the backs of her fleshy arms. But the dream did not return, so my great-grandmother's mother retreated into the withering silence of an uninhabitable island. She never spoke to her daughter again.

¡Ay de mí! What can I say? It was many years before my great-grandmother realized that her very own mother had become a recluse, a victim of a malignant, desperate, carnivorous envy. Unfortunately, this realization came with the news of her mother's inexplicable death, so my great-grandmother was left with the gnawing pangs of a guilt she could not mollify, though on certain bright, sunny days she was able to smooth over the rough edges of her anguish by focusing only on those memories of her mother from the days before the curse had been defeated.

Two days before her death, my great-grandmother's mother dreamed that she, not her daughter, was hiding behind a fan for flies fashioned from the feathers of a peacock's wing. She did not know exactly where she was in her dream. She was standing on a deserted, narrow strip of rocky beach with her back to a series of cliffs made of black volcanic rock that rose quickly from the shoreline. It was late in the day and the wind was beginning to pick up. She thought perhaps she was near Chivirico, but she did not really know. She had never been across the mountains in her life. She had never before come within a mile of the sea. Then a strange, watery voice said she could let go of the fan, so she tossed it into the slowly rolling waves. The iridescent peacock feathers briefly caught the light of the setting sun. Then a backwash of sea-green foam carried the fan out to sea. Then she woke up.

It was at this point, according to my great-grandmother, that her mother left the small farmhouse that had been her refuge for twenty-one years and headed south. She told no one where she was going. The very next day, at seven in the morning, she became the only victim of a small mysterious hurricane that had landed without fanfare somewhere west of Santiago, churning up the coast and depositing sharks and various sea creatures along the rocky shore and then smashing into half-a-dozen rural villages tucked away in the mountains before pushing north across the island and then northeast towards the vast emptiness of the Atlantic Ocean.

Was this eerily prophetic and coercive dream of the fan

simply the last gasp of the curse of the Ana Silvestres? Or had the curse reinvented itself and was now capable of attaching itself to whoever was the most vulnerable? Who can truly say? What I can say, and I think everyone would agree, is that it was almost like my great-grandmother's mother knew death was coming and went out to meet him.

-53-

The beginning of Tiká's tale of woe:

Let me first say that Tiká's story is not what you would call a tragedy in the classic sense. A few wild nights, a few erratic outbursts (what some would call temper tantrums), but you must remember that she was very young. And she was a stranger in a strange land, as they say. Her story is only a tiny bit tragic, a demented echo of her life in Spain. But she recovered from her sorrow in a most expeditious manner, which is all anyone can hope for.

My great-grandfather's need to be constantly on the road during his first two years on the island to ease his impossible loneliness, followed so closely by his whirlwind courtship of the second-to-last Ana Silvestre (who was perhaps the most beautiful Ana Silvestre of them all) and their rather extravagant wedding (which will forever be known among the inhabitants of Bayamo as the wedding to shame all weddings), exempted him in some respects from his patriarchal responsibilities towards his niece. At least this is what he would have liked to believe.

But Tiká was still grieving over the loss of the limited freedom she had experienced aboard the *Conde Wifredo*, which meant that in practical terms, my great-grandfather was forced to address her increasingly petulant (which is to say unmanageable) demands with a delicacy that resembled an emerging psychosis.

Initially Tiká's demands seemed insignificant, even reasonable.

She wanted her own horse so she could come and go as she pleased. My great-grandfather sent Nicario west to Pinar del Rió Province and he came back with a dark brown Appaloosa that reminded Tiká of her rambunctious childhood.

She missed the graceful, white storks of Logroño, so my great-grandfather had Nicario take her north to the estuaries of Bahia Naranjo, which were known in those days for their great flocks of whirling birds, where she could reminisce.

She was dismayed that she possessed no books, despite the fact that she preferred riding bareback beneath the Cuban sun to reading. But my great-grandfather acquiesced and gave her his very own bible, a hefty, leather-bound tome gilded with gold leaf which contained a genealogy that went back twenty-seven generations to the last days of the Moorish occupation. He also promised to take her to Manzanillo to see a German bookseller he knew there when she finished reading this magnificent gift of God's Holy word and he would buy her any book on those dust-lacquered shelves that caught her eye. Tiká carted the bible around for a week, glancing at the pages of this moth-eaten heirloom only briefly as she rode from here to there, before she gave it to a startled peasant coffee farmer on his way back from Holguín, a farmer who needed solace after an unexpectedly poor harvest that year.

She complained that her wardrobe had been ruined by the ocean air, which meant that she needed everything from silk blouses to embroidered petticoats to high top Balmoral boots to diamonds and sapphires and imperial topaz and other jewels to decorate her fiery-red braid, to French Aubusson tapestry handbags, to only God knew what else. My great-grandfather asked Nicario to take her shopping in Santiago. Maybe she would find something in one of the various mercantile shops along Enramadas or Marina, and Nicario knew a small French clothier on Calle Trocha, a shop founded at the end of the 18th century by refined émigrés fleeing the bloody excesses of the Haitian revolution.

From that point forward, Tiká's demands only grew more provocative, and her temperament more unstable. One evening she fell in love with the whirling dervish sound of a vagabond group of a voodoo musicians playing *trovas* and salsas and African rumbas and *guaguancós* with a crazy, every-changing assortment of drums and wooden boxes and spoons and even a *corneta china,* but always they sang with their irresistibly sweet voices like the sounds of summer birds taking wing, and so she told her uncle that her excitable soul needed to bathe in this strange Cuban folk music at least twice a day to guarantee her proper spiritual and intellectual development. So my great-grandfather felt he had no choice. He hired the group to follow Tiká wherever she went. She was ecstatic for a month or so, she said, but then her ears grew weary of their unceasing musical zeal, and beneath the cover of a partly cloudy sky, she suddenly and without regret abandoned them to a lonely street corner in Palma Soriano. They did not even notice her hasty departure. Or perhaps they did not really mind.

Two years to the day after arriving in Cuba, she acquired a sudden craving for white clay mixed with coffee grounds, which my great-grandfather mistook for an attack of nostalgia precipitated by the absence of her sister. He was on the verge of sending her to a doctor in Manzanillo to find a cure or to the asylum for the hopelessly insane in Victoria de las Tunas, but Nicario persuaded him that Tiká's desire to devour dirt was merely a symptom of her excessive devotion to the goddess Yemayá, common in women of childbearing age, especially in eastern Cuba, but she was in no real danger as long as she drank plenty of water, it was a fad like all the others that had affected her equilibrium and would pass soon enough, of this Nicario was convinced.

Soon thereafter she refused to accompany my great-grandfather on his travels. She said she had seen all there was to see on the road from Manzanillo to Santiago and vice versa. Then she swore she would slit her own wrists if she were made to live on a farm or in any of the small villages or towns that dotted the landscape like a plague, as they were filled with illiterate, unwashed, *criollos* who had never even heard of the opera. She belonged in Santiago, she said, so she could experience the mystical power of the great composers in the neoclassical elegance of Teatro Reina, where she had already seen *Un ballo in maschera* (the most censured of all of Verdi's operas), as her uncle knew full well because he himself had taken her to see Verdi's masterpiece when they had last abandoned the indignities of the open road for a weekend in the lap of luxury. So she claimed Santiago for her own. She would die in Santiago. There was no force on earth that could break her resolve. Besides, *Rigoletto* was opening in two months.

Tiká's decision to face death rather than submit to her uncle even in the most imaginary of circumstances seemed like an adolescent tantrum. My great-grandfather did not believe her for a minute, but he was also unwilling to take any unnecessary chances, for Tiká still possessed the indefatigable charm of a trained assassin, so it was truly impossible to gauge what she might or might not do. He said that she could stay in Santiago. He gave her a small but sufficient monthly allowance, which, to his credit, he deposited directly into her hands instead of into Nicario's. And he put her up in a posh corner suite on the third floor of the Hotel Venus, with its marble-floored dining room decorated with potted ferns and the portraits of Cuban heroes hanging like trophies on every wall, and a baroque fountain decorated with dancing nymphs (all of them naked) in the middle of the room and a trio of musicians playing *guarachas* to occupy the lurid imaginations of the patrons waiting for their dinners. She fell in love with the hotel at once, especially because she could look out of her bedroom window and gaze upon the shimmering mystery of the Cathedral if she felt in need of spiritual reflection, or if she wanted to connect with her sensual, romanticized view of the material world, she could cast her eyes upon the European-style elegance of the Plaza, which during the hot, hazy afternoons was shaded by old Indian laurels and punctuated by flowering shrubs — roses and jasmine and oleander set against a back-drop of pale pink buildings and a bright blue sky. The view resembled painted porcelain. After the sun set, however, Tiká's view of the Plaza reflected a darker imagination, illuminated only by the hazy electric glow of evenly spaced lamplights.

Inevitably, her enchantment with her new surroundings took on a more passionate color. She became transfixed by the lingering music of Carnaval, which always seemed to be present, and the indecent laughter of happy tourists ballooning through the night air, sounds that spoke to an eternal longing which Tiká had only half-recognized until her first night in the hotel, and which, now that she was fully aware of what she had been missing all those years in Spain, would give shape to the rest of her life. Naturally, my great-grandfather had a few vague misgivings about Tiká striking out on her own. He was not so detached from the swirling eddies of human frailty that he did not suffer from blinding headaches when he thought about Tiká living a life apart in Santiago. But he could not quite bring himself to face his own complicity in this tragedy in the making, so he chose to ignore the obvious. Instead, he asked Nicario to check in on his niece once a week, just to make sure she was behaving herself, and in this way he sealed all of their fates.

-54-

The day that Tiká's fate was revealed for the whole world to see was the very day my great-grandfather and great-grandmother were married in the wedding to shame all weddings in the Chapel of Our Lady of Sorrows in the Church of San Salvador de Bayamo.

By nine in the morning, a festive, somewhat romantic spirit had already captured the town, erupting spontaneously in every one of marriageable age, even those with the most reclusive temperaments. Secret admirers tied kites to the balconies of girls they had adored from the shadows for years in the hope of a single kiss, the kites fluttering about like the prayers of pilgrims hovering above shrines. And lovers young and old, inspired by sonnets composed in the fever of true love, serenaded each other with the irrevocable, unpretentious joy of small children, their hearts spinning like miniature cyclones of bright light.

At three in the afternoon the church bells started ringing and the procession of the priests began. The priests marched up and down the narrow winding streets of the old part of the city, following as they always did a wooden cross made from the beams of an ancient shipwreck bearing the figure of Christ Our Lord and Savior, and a golden banner with an image of the Virgin Mary holding her infant Son, the three aging priests and the two younger ones announcing with solemn ritual, reverent voices the imminent union between Andres Ordóñez Escoraz and Ana Silvestre.

Ladies from all over town flocked to their balconies to watch the procession as it wound its way through the corridors carved out by the centuries, all of them posing in staged fashion, their arms and legs positioned at odd angles, as if they were hoping to catch the passing eye of a promising young painter, all of them wearing their finest silk dresses and their hair done up in fancy ringlets that had been all the rage in Paris a century earlier but which had only made the crossing to Cuba and the journey to Bayamo in the days after the great war with Spain had ended, and only when the procession of the priests had passed by their windows and their flowing silk dresses were buffeted ever so slightly by the winds of regret, did they hurry off to the Chapel to cast long, lingering, wistful looks at the groom, their dark, almond-colored eyes fluttering with unceasing agitation behind vintage oriental fans.

The Chapel was not large enough to accommodate the entire town, so the men (except for the groom, of course) waited impatiently outside in the sunny, dusty, hazy street, smoking homemade cigars as they talked about this and that.

The men also wore the costumes of a century earlier, embroidered silk shirts and long embroidered coats and short trousers and high-heeled shoes with stockings, costumes that they had retrieved from the long-forgotten trunks of their own great-grandfathers.

At four the ceremony began, filled with the sanctity of incense and tinkling bells and weeping feminine voices.

At six the ceremony was over and the entire town migrated to the Plaza de Armas (which was also known to some as Plaza de Isabel), scattering orange blossoms as they went.

The plaza was illuminated by strings of tiny electric light bulbs that looked like electric eels crisscrossing through dark waters to some, and a brightly lit ocean liner lost in a sudden, evening fog to others.

Dozens of tables, each of them filled with various steaming dishes, were set up along one side. The center table was adorned with a suckling pig that had been skewered and roasted slowly. There were more suckling pigs on the way.

Everyone drank a glass of *agualoja y sangria* (a sweet and spicy water) to start things off.

They drank to the health of the bride and groom.

Then everyone began drinking *aguardiente*.

They drank until every drop had been drunk.

Naturally they ate while they drank.

Everyone had plenty to eat.

After dinner they ate dessert.

Fancy breads were served with thick chocolate syrup, and also guava and orange and lemon preserves.

For the briefest of moments while feeding my great-grandmother a sliver of shredded pork with his fingers, the two of them laughing with unexpected frivolity in the bright bubble of their happiness, my great-grandfather wondered what had become of Tiká. He had not seen her the entire day. Had some mishap befallen her on the road? But he immediately pushed the thought out of his mind. Nicario was with her. Nicario would see that she arrived safely.

Then an eleven-piece orchestra suddenly materialized on the other side of the plaza from the tables. The orchestra was made up of three clarinets, two violins, a bass violin, two peculiar horns known as *trompas,* one guitar, a wooden flute, and a *tambora* drum. Immediately they began to play a *contradanza* from the days of the Haitians, a composition known as *San Pascual Bailón,* a traditional folk song that had been played at every wedding in Bayamo for over one hundred years. This was followed in quick succession by a second *contradanza, La nueva cañonera* by Victor Moreno, that filled everyone's aching heart with a mysterious longing for war, and then a popular waltz, and then various rumbas, including a whirlwind *jiribilla* and a more sensuous *resedá,* and then several slow, heart-wrenching songs done in the *trova* style, and then several elegant, lyrical precise *danzones* by that great piano dancer Ignacio Cervantes (the pride of Cuba, who had impressed Franz Liszt one afternoon, it was said, as the great maestro was passing by an apartment on Rue Neuve Coquenard in Paris and heard Cervantes playing the piano, a beautiful melody that brought to mind a crying child and a comforting mother, which tugged at Liszt's romantic heart and he was compelled to knock on Cervantes' door and introduce himself), and then for the rest of the evening the orchestra shifted back and forth between *danzones* from all over Cuba (Valenzuela, Pérez, Arízti) and the heart-thumping, sword-thrusting, indecent rhythm of anonymous *guarachas* from Holguín until everyone in the plaza was twisted up in ribbons of pleasure.

The bride and groom danced several dances by themselves before the jubilant crowd joined in. Then shortly before nine o'clock they abandoned their guests and rode off beneath a star-filled sky on two dark chestnuts. Most of the guests were too busy dancing and drinking and eating fancy desserts to realize the bride and groom had left. A few began to think of their own wedding nights (though their memories were somewhat vague and superficial at first) and what lay in store for the happy young lovers and what a joy it was to be young and naked beneath newly pressed sheets, and then they smiled or frowned or winced with unexpected shame as their own memories took on a more crystalline quality, which magnified either the faith they now possessed in marriage as an institution, or the regrets they felt when they realized they had made a mistake but now it was too late.

The fancy breads with chocolate syrup were the best anyone had ever eaten, by far, everyone said so.

The plaza began to empty out shortly after midnight. The bright moon cast odd shadows from the fluted eaves and the overhanging balconies. Those who were still awake behaved as if the town had indeed mysteriously retreated one hundred years into the past. Or fifty. Or at least ten. It was hard to tell. A wizened voice from the shadows, a friend of Martí and Casal, began reciting revolutionary poetry. *'Iba el negro bayamés sobre el caballo salvaje, sólo jirones por traje y la jáquima de armés.'* Words lost on the wind of a solitary church bell and then returning. And then other voices responding, weaving their way through the darkness, 'Liberty, liberty, liberty,' not as loud as the bell, and then footsteps running, and then a few distant gunshots, as if men with lanterns were chasing after runaway slaves.

When my newly married great-grandparents returned from their romantic sojourn in the mountains, they discovered that Tiká had been granted temporary refuge in the tiny closet of a room adjoining the kitchen, and that the young vagabond Tomás Barutti had been displaced to the cattle barn. No one doubted that Tiká had been lucky to make it as far as she did. She had arrived at the farmhouse outside Jiguani three days earlier on the verge of collapse from an excessive almost supernatural thirst at the exact moment my great-grandparents were trading their eternal vows in the Chapel of Our Lady of Sorrows.

While the entire town was migrating to the Plaza de Armas, young Tomás had been dispatched to find help, returning not a moment too soon with a blind midwife from the forest, a peasant woman with an intimate knowledge of herbal remedies who had gained a reputation for suddenly appearing whenever there was need.

The moment the eleven-piece orchestra materialized out of thin air in the plaza, Tiká had gone into labor punctuated by carnivorous screams that clawed at Nicario's bones.

And the moment my great-grandparents arrived at their honeymoon refuge in the mountains, just as they were slipping off of their dark chestnuts beneath the glistening moon, Tiká gave birth to a baby girl all balled up and dripping wet, like a small housecat that had been plucked from a river. The baby possessed a magnificent head of dark black hair (dripping wet but strangely luminous), a rarity in any age that immediately provoked fears of the Devil looking for a few souls to devour. She did not cry out even when the midwife cut the cord. She just stared at her surroundings, her eyes like two blue moons gleaming with awareness.

Needless to say, the birth of the child caused quite a stir, not so much because the child had been born out of wedlock, which was a common enough occurrence in that part of Cuba and elsewhere, but because it was unclear who had fathered the child and what his intentions had been and if, perhaps, the birth of a child who did not cry was a sign of the liberating majesty and unrestrained beneficence of an almighty God, or if there were demonic forces at work. Given the mysterious coincidence of the birth taking place in an empty house when the occupants of that house were that very day attending the wedding to shame all weddings, these were reasonable questions as far as the people of Jiguani were concerned.

By the time my great-grandparents rode up to the back of the farmhouse, it was well after midnight. The sky was filled with dark, swift moving clouds like the tremors of a strange dream. They almost didn't recognize where they were, but then they saw the dark silhouette of the Royal Poinciana and crossed the shallow stream. The kitchen windows were bathed in darkness, but this did not seem unusual, given the hour. But then they noticed the soft whirling lights of many candles whirling from one window to the next and then disappearing and then finally reappearing in the window of the room that had belonged to Tomás.

The lights did not seem like candles. It was as if the birds that occupied the branches of the twisted laurels and oaks by day had been transformed into beings of pure energy.

As my great-grandparents entered the kitchen, they were startled by the hunchbacked shape of my great-grandmother's mother appearing in the doorway to Tomás' room. She held a braided candle beneath her chin, which caused shadows to dance across her face with the frenetic, contrapuntal brilliance of newborn sea snakes. The darkness trembled. Ignoring her own flesh-and-blood, she looked instead with luminous rigidity at my great-grandfather and spoke in erratic, dangerous Spanish, but the only words that could be heard clearly made no sense. *'Circulos dentro circulos,'* she said. It almost sounded like she was hissing, as if her tongue was a flickering filament.

Then she spat on her candle, extinguishing the tenuous flame, and fled as if suddenly galvanized with the fleeing shadows into the interior of the house.

It was at that point that my great-grandparents heard a soft, rhythmic chanting, or perhaps it was someone sighing wistfully because the dawn was so far away, or moaning with the dream-like ardor that usually accompanies great passion. The sound was coming from Tomás' room, but it was difficult to see precisely where. A dozen or so candles were scattered about, their smoky light whirling through the air like incandescent but self-contained bubbles which seemed to obscure rather than illuminate.

The plummeting darkness in between bubbles was an overwhelming ocean of sadness.

Then a hand reached out from the darkness in between the bubbles. The hand was somehow attached to the face of Nicario, though the point of attachment seemed to be constantly shifting.

Nicario's face twisted and contorted with radiating concern but did not utter a sound, while his hand made a series of totally unrelated gestures that seemed to say 'Please, my friend, do not disturb this *babalawo*, he is a master of ancient secrets, yes, yes, do not disturb his concentration, he has almost finished his prayer, yes, it has been a very long and complicated prayer, my friend, yes, I think it would be a good idea to wallow in ignorant silence until he has offered up every last one of his words to the gods and then he can tell us what it means if he chooses, at least that is what we have always been taught,' and then Nicario's face became a mirror of twisted, demented, fragmented chuckling, but again there was no sound.

My great-grandparents struggled to see what was happening. It was almost like being under water. And then it was almost like floating in outer space. The candles became a myriad of stars. The *babalawo* leaned over Tiká and her baby and whispered something only they could hear. The stars began whirling faster and faster. Then the *babalawo* lifted his eyes to the stars and cried out in a voice that seemed too heavy for the air to hold. '*Yemayá okere okún olomí karagbo osa ya bio lewu eyintegbe awa si lekú Yemayá bini ku wa yo kueana o kun iya sa ori ere egba mió o,*' he said.

And then it was suddenly dawn. The bubbles of candlelight had disappeared. Tiká and her baby were resting awkwardly on a narrow wooden bed and a faint beam of sunshine danced on the floor. Every so often Nicario, who was sitting at the foot of the bed, would get up and adjust Tiká's pillows and then slump back down on the mattress.

My great-grandmother was busy at a small cast iron stove in the kitchen.

Her uncle was talking quietly with the *babalawo*.

The *babalawo* had been brought in by the blind midwife because of the child's strangely luminous black hair, and because this child did not cry. It was clear that the *babalawo* and my great-grandmother's uncle had known each other since the ragged days of their boyhood. Pepe García Gallego folded a few *pesetas* into the old man's wizened hands and invited him for a cup of coffee, but the *babalawo* only smiled a curiously detached smile, pocketed the *pesetas*, and skipped out the door into the early morning sunlight and was soon lost among the trees dripping with moisture and the restless but silent birds.

My great-grandfather was sitting at the kitchen table, but he was not hungry. He tried to make sense of what was happening. After the *babalawo* had finished his prayers, Nicario had acted very strangely. He had clapped my great-grandfather on the back, an oddly misshapen look on his face that quickly gave way to a preposterous expression of joy. It had been both a confession and a declaration of his sexual prowess in spite of his age. My great-grandfather had not known what to do. At dawn, he still did not know what to do. Then Pepe García Gallego sat down at the table. He pressed his thick, callused ex-soldier's hands on the rough oak and leaned somberly forward.

'The *babalawo* said your niece was in a very bad way, my friend, but she is much better now.'

My great-grandfather said nothing.

'A very bad way.'

Clouds of black smoke began pouring from the belly of the stove and my great-grandmother raced to open a window and the clouds began to dissipate.

'The *babalawo* said he had never before see someone in such a bad way. She was like an Orisha from the old stories, from before the great crossing, facing the end of the world.'

Suddenly the birds began to sing.

The baby began to gurgle and then cry and Tiká comforted her, but somehow they both remained asleep.

'This is what the *babalawo* said.'

Nicario watched with a restless anticipation, one eye on Tiká and the baby and the other on the clouds of thinning smoke and the conversation taking place in the kitchen. Pepe García Gallego was not affected by the smoke. He said that Tiká had been troubled by dreams from the very first day Nicario had taken her to his bed. The *babalawo* had also told him this. The *babalawo* said he was not sure who had sent her these dreams. At first he had suspected Nicario. Then he had suspected the young boy Tomás, though he quickly abandoned this theory when he learned that the boy had only met Tiká the day her daughter was born. Then he suspected the child itself through the manipulations of Yewa, the true goddess of caves and cemeteries, but what Yewa had in mind and why she would commandeer the spirit of so tiny a child he could not articulate. But then he decided that the dreams were merely the echoes of a future which had yet to unfold and which could possibly be prevented.

The *babalawo* walked with Tiká through the landscape of this future. It was a landscape filled with murder and death and robust but clearly psychotic laughter and families torn apart by a bloody, relentless war, or perhaps several wars, and the sky was black with falling pieces of earth and twisted metal, a very strange sight indeed, perhaps it was her family she saw, or the families of her children's children, but what does that matter, it was a cataclysmic scene beyond belief followed by a swiftly descending eternal night, a spiritual darkness, a billion soulless bodies on the edge of oblivion, gasping for breath like fish drowning in the muck of a newly evaporated sea. This is the way the babalawo had described it. And the longer he and Tiká had wandered through this nightmare landscape, the deeper and more unyielding the darkness had become.

'Yes,' my great-grandmother's uncle said. 'I do not know all the details. Some things it is best not to know. But she was in a very bad way for such a young and beautiful girl. But so long as she follows the *babalawo's* instructions, she will have nothing to worry about.'

The clouds of black smoke were long gone but my great-grandmother had left the window open so she could watch the birds flying this way and that in the light of the setting sun, still singing. Nicario had disappeared. His disappearance had been preceded by an unexpected conversation with Pepe García Gallego beneath the fiery red foliage of the Royal Poinciana. Pepe was wearing a ruffled shirt that looked like a costume from another era. Nicario was wearing the ragged white linen shirt and ragged pants that he always wore. It was a heated conversation full of fiery words like tiny bullets and grand sweeping gestures of immeasurable sadness and forlorn looks aimed at the radiant sky. The two men spoke as if they had been soldiers in arms together and had watched friends die bloody, senseless deaths on the battlefield and elsewhere during the successive wars for Cuban independence.

The highlights of the heated conversation (polished with the stylized, melodramatic flair of a second-rate 19th century Russian dramatist) between Pepe García Gallego and Nicario:

Pepe García Gallego: 'What foolishness have you committed?'

Nicario: 'I could not help myself.'

Pepe García Gallego: 'You are lucky he does not shoot you.'

Nicario: 'Why would he shoot me?'

Pepe García Gallego: 'Because I told him you are no good, that you will abandon his niece and her child at the smallest provocation. I told him you had led a small company of rebels against the Spanish in 1879. I did not tell him that you had merely surrounded a small drinking establishment on the road to Manzanillo and that you had waited in the dark until the unsuspecting Spanish soldiers left singing happy songs, and then you mowed them down with ruthless glee. I told him that General Calixto García himself made you a Captain in his tiny rebellion, and so you gained a small reputation as a Lion in War. I should have told him what you did when General García was captured and sent to prison in Spain, that you told everyone he had made you a Colonel and that it was up to you to keep the spirit of revolution alive in Cuba. I should have told him that. I should have told him that your words were made of gold but that your heart was a crumbling mound of earth, a home for glowworms. But I did tell him that you had stolen the virtue of dozens of hopeful widows scattered from here to Baracoa, trading upon your manufactured fame of a shining, heroic warrior, and that only God and perhaps a few dark angels knew how many sons and daughters of Cuba were produced by your profligate indiscretions.'

Nicario: 'Ah, my old friend, I thank you. I could not have told the story any better.'

(Nicario laughing with unexpected joy, his face bathed in the reddish, sunlit glow of the Royal Poinciana, but then growing silent, almost serious, his dark eyes contemplating the obvious discomfort of Pepe García Gallego, and then Nicario's eyes relaxing, becoming two red suns in a darkening sky, his face retracting with a sudden sense of purpose.)

Nicario: 'But what would you have me do? I am too old for small children. I have always been too old for children. You know that. Besides, she does not love me. She said she loves another, but their love can never be. So tell me, my friend, what should I do?'

Pepe García Gallego: 'I should shoot you myself for the no-account scoundrel you have always been.'

Nicario: 'Yes, yes, you have said this before, but then who would remind you of your own indiscretions and the price we have paid for liberty? Who would share with you the last of his very last bottle of *aguardiente* and think nothing of it?'

Pepe García Gallego: '. . . .'

Nicario: 'Who would scour the countryside for men of good standing, men newly arrived from Spain, perhaps, men who might make a good match for your own niece and so lift you and your entire family out of poverty and liberate you from the shackles of your discontent?'

Pepe García Gallego: '. . . .'

Nicario: 'Who found such a noble Spaniard with a compassionate and poetic soul and planted the seeds of romance in his brain and suggested that he write letters to his unseen love in the hopes of drawing her towards him? Yes, yes, my friend. What price would you pay for the liberty you now enjoy?'

After that it was unclear what they were saying. Their words were laced with hidden meanings that would have taken years to uncover by even the most astute listener. Then their mouths became festering, open wounds of uncontrollable rage. Nicario grabbed Pepe García Gallego by the ruffles of his ruffled shirt but Pepe knocked his arms away. Both men took a step back and pulled weapons. Nicario pulled out his hunting knife, which had not been sharpened in several years, perhaps decades, which meant that the only effective use of the weapon required a forward, thrusting, lunging motion that could be easily turned aside by any experienced adversary, and Pepe García Gallego pulled out a small flintlock pistol that had belonged to his grandfather, a pistol that he had fired only once in his life, and that had been to impress a young girl whose name he no longer remembered but whose soft, lingering kiss after he had fired the gun was etched in his memory and had become on certain cloudy afternoons and almost every night (especially now that he was older) an indelible reminder of the life he had not chosen.

It was the unexpected appearance of young Tomás Barutti that prevented a bloody fiasco (or at least a comic puppet show of wildly errant punches and bloodcurdling cries of disbelief and heads spinning in exaggerated dismay) and allowed both aging though determined ex-soldiers a chance to retreat with their dignity intact. Tomás had been taking a late afternoon nap in the barn. He woke to the distant, garbled sounds of the two men quarreling but he did not realize he was awake. He found himself moving slowly but inexorably towards the sounds of the quarreling men as if he were moving under water, so he thought he was immersed in the depths of a strange, symbolic dream. His actions took on a life of their own, as if his body were merely responding to invisible radio waves from outer space targeting his brain. He watched with unashamed fascination as he slipped on his own boots and headed for the stall that housed Nicario's horse. He saddled the horse and then led the animal from the barn. He noticed that the horse had not been properly brushed for many days but realized it was too late now. He smiled at Pepe García Gallego, his benefactor, and Nicario, whom he had come to regard as a well-meaning but demented cousin.

The quarreling ceased.

The antique weapons were put away.

Dumbfounded, the two men fanned out on either side of the horse, which suddenly seemed like one of the great steeds of Etruscan myth instead of the skeletal nag that it was in the bright and revealing glare of a midday sun.

Tomás gave Nicario the reins and Nicario swung himself into the saddle with a sudden youthful burst of exuberance, a temporary gift from the gods for just this moment. The looks on the faces of both Pepe García Gallego and Nicario had been transformed from outrage to appreciation. Their eyes were brimming with nostalgia. You have been my truest friend, said the eyes of Nicario. And you mine, said the eyes of Pepe García Gallego. I did not mean to mock the purity of the marriage between your niece and my friend from Spain. I did not mean to suggest that their love was a false love based on pecuniary interests, said the eyes of Nicario. Do not worry, my friend, I did not tell my niece that you prepared the ground. She was drawn to her husband by her own heart, said the eyes of Pepe García Gallego. Then perhaps I am only an instrument in the hand of God, said the eyes of Nicario. Perhaps that is all any of us truly are, said the eyes of Pepe García Gallego. Then the eyes of both men were laughing.

Then Nicario turned the head of his great Etruscan steed to depart, but he was delayed by Tomás, who was holding up the gift of his gold watch, his one sole possession and the symbol of his past as much as a symbol of God's indomitable will and a reminder that even if true love did exist, it was doomed by its very nature to be short-lived, as are all things of beauty.

Why Tomás gave away his watch he only vaguely understood, but once he did he felt suddenly liberated. (Years later he tried to explain to his youngest daughter, Nuria, who was then barely three years old, that there had been no choice, that it was the price he had to pay to enter his future. But without a tongue he had to resort to making strange gestures with his hands and profound grimaces with his face, and his daughter was unable to grasp his meaning.) Nicario, who suddenly (and secretly) wished to linger, but who firmly believed one must make sacrifices in pursuit of liberty, put the watch in his pocket and vanished in the glare of the setting sun.

-55-

What the *babalawo* told Tiká:

'The world is Ifá and Ifá is the world,' the *babalawo* began. 'But you have forgotten this truth in the crossing to the new world. You have become consumed by the illusion of a singular life, so you are beset by the whirlwind of your own fears and have lost your way. You must conquer your fears to become yourself. *Quienes vencen al enemigo de adentro no tienen nada que temer del enemigo de afuera.*'

Tiká thought about the wisdom of the *babalawo* and the *babalawo* realized he was making headway and smiled, and before his smile had become a memory he launched into a parable about Okana Sode, an oddu with the power to heal the crippling divisions within one's soul.

'One morning, at the bright birth of a new day, Okana Sode was preparing to take a bath in a most luxurious room with a fancy white tiled floor and gleaming white fixtures and mirrors everywhere to dazzle the eye and a pair of French-style doors that opened up onto a patio. Next to the French doors there was a golden birdcage with a white plumed cockatoo inside. Okana Sode filled her tub almost to the top with hot water. She mixed in various exotic herbs and potions and pieces of a coconut shell and the petals of many white gardenias. The mixture produced a soapy froth that obscured the depths beneath the surface, and a fragrant aroma that rose up into the air like an offering to the gods. Then Okana Sode climbed into the tub and began to soak. She did not mind that some of the water sloshed onto the floor. She closed her eyes and hummed a lullaby her mother once sang. Then she herself began to sing, and the white cockatoo sang along with her. Okana Sode and the cockatoo passed an hour or two in noisy contemplation of the wondrous joys of life. But then the voice of the white cockatoo was replaced by a strange chewing sound. The serenity of the bath was broken. Okana Sode wondered what had happened. She could not quite make out where the sound was coming from, but she could clearly see that the door to the golden cage was open and the white cockatoo had vanished. Still, that did not explain the strange chewing sound. Okana Sode didn't know what to think. The chewing sound grew louder, and then softer, and then it was replaced by the slow, slithery scraping sound of claws on tile. Peering over the edge of the tub, Okana Sode spied the tail of a crocodile slipping out through the open French doors. She wondered briefly why she had not noticed a crocodile in any of the mirrors, but then the thought left her. She got out of the tub without any hesitation, dripping with the ambrosia-like fragrance of the white gardenias, and followed the shimmering image of the tail out to the patio, but both the crocodile and the tail had vanished in the new sunlight as quickly and as permanently as the white cockatoo. So Okana Sode sighed an inevitable sigh full of longing and regret and returned to her bath.

'It was only after she had settled herself back into the womb of the tub, with only her head above the water, that she realized that the petals of the white gardenias had become long, white feathers, and that she herself had ceased to be human and had become instead an exact replica of the white cockatoo she had kept in the cage.'

The instant the *babalawo* finished the parable Tiká felt like she was drowning.

The *babalawo* said, 'Death is after you in Cuba.'

Tiká began to claw at the air as if battling an unseen enemy.

In a strange, thin, staticky voice, as if it had traveled across the centuries, the *babalawo* said, '*Ifá no se equivoca.*'

Tiká's struggle against her enemy intensified.

But then suddenly her strength was gone and she was as weak as any unborn child.

In that same thin, staticky voice, which had a vibrating quality similar to the vibrating quality of radio voices that would take to the airwaves in the 1920s like a flock of excitable birds, the *babalawo* said, '*En Ifá no hay mentiras.*'

Strangely, Tiká's weakness was comforting.

In that same staticky voice as before, the *babalawo* said, '*Ifá habla pasado, presente y futuro.*'

Tiká gave herself over completely to the wisdom of the *babalawo*, and so she was reborn.

Returning to his normal, conversational voice, the *babalawo* said, 'You must continue to feed your faith in Ifá. You must be relentless. To fall into disobedience in this matter would be to hasten the arrival of Death.'

From somewhere there was the sound of distant drumming.

It was a whisper of a sound like the beating wings of tiny birds that filled Tiká's heart with vague premonitions of unrelenting hope.

It was a prayer being answered.

The *babalawo* continued, 'You need not follow my path. You may choose any path you like. But you must choose.'

The fragrance of coconuts filled the lungs of the world.

The *babalawo* smiled again, or perhaps he had been smiling the whole while. 'No one knows what lies at the bottom of the sea, so Olokun will help you cross the waters,' he said. And Tiká understood exactly what he meant.

-56-

¿Adónde te escondiste mi amado? This question is tucked away in the crevices of every soul, is it not? Just the existence of such a question is why so many of us are drowning in a sea of sorrow. It is why there are so many counterfeit hearts of collapsing earth, all of them squirming with glowworms, a latticework of teardrops tunneling through the shadows of the long night. Can we not see the truth in the words of Saint John of the Cross who wrote about the bride alighting on the green branch? But we cannot help ourselves. How blind we are! How utterly blind! Ashes and death, ashes and death! This is all we think about. This is all we see. This is the fate we are anticipating. But it is not the fate that awaits us. Yes, of course, the immortal truth of our immortal soul is something we cannot easily grasp. But it is a permanent reality nevertheless, a certainty that goes beyond the cycles of the sun and the moon. It is the one and only truth. Truly the mirror speaks to all of us sooner or later, if only we know enough to open our eyes. Happily, my great-grandparents knew enough to open their eyes on that glorious morning beside the fig trees oh so many years ago. He was her savior and she was his church.

My great-grandfather later admitted (but only once) that he had hoped one day to own a colonial hacienda on the outskirts of Bayamo and a small villa in Santiago with hidden courtyards and secret doors so that he could come and go as he pleased without drawing undue attention to any vices he might acquire, but with the revelation of the scandalous love affair between Nicario and Tiká and the birth of the dark-haired, silent child, he felt he had no choice but to abandon this pipedream and head west to Havana. So he purchased train tickets for himself and Ana, and then, because his wife insisted, he purchased a ticket for Tiká and her baby. Unlike my great-grandfather, who seemed in moments of duress to think of his family as a means to an end thanks to ten years of traveling the seven seas in the company of pirates, my great-grandmother believed with a dogged determination that bordered on fanaticism in the absolute primacy of patriarchal obligations, however burdensome.

One month after the wedding to shame all weddings, they left the eastern shores of paradise for good. Neither my great-grandfather nor Tiká looked at each other the entire trip. Tiká was consumed with the haunting beauty of her baby, though every so often a wave of sudden despair would darken her face and she would stare out the window at the landscape flowing past and see a pale, unsteady reflection of herself looking back with accusing eyes. As for my great-grandfather, well he was busy trying to assure my great-grandmother that Havana was the closest thing to paradise on earth, that in Havana they would drink the ambrosia of the gods, this was their destiny, she would see, there was nothing to worry about, the future was a pearl for the plucking, though with every word that popped out of my great-grandfather's mouth, my great-grandmother became more and more skeptical.

My great-grandparents spent the rest of their lives in Havana. First they lived in a small tenement on Esperanza a short walk from the old Gas Works, where my great-grandfather worked for two years until he became acclimated to life in the city. Then they moved to a small house on San Nicolas and my great-grandfather took a position first as a floor supervisor for Raffloer & Erbsloh Co., a small cordage factory on the corner of San Pedro and Santa Clara, and then as the manager of a fancy restaurant somewhere on Trocadero. Two years later they moved into the two-story, neo-classical, Baroque style house in Miramar. But Tiká did not move with them. Tiká said her destiny was to go to Puerto Rico. She had known this since the *babalawo* had shown her the shining path to her future. And she had also known that when the time came for her to leave, she would leave her daughter with her uncle's family. (This is perhaps why she had named her daughter Ana.) When Tiká had first arrived in Havana, she could not bear the thought of leaving her daughter. But now her daughter was now almost five years old. What else was she going to do? Besides, she was not truly the motherly type. Her aunt, on the other hand, was by that point a mother of two little boys, a badly-behaved, dark-haired three-year-old named José Ignacio, and an infant barely a year old, José Luis. A little girl was more than welcome. So on a cloudy day in February 1908, Tiká boarded the *S. S. Saratoga* bound for San Juan, Puerto Rico. It was a swift farewell, for Tiká could barely look at her daughter without bursting into tears.

'Please, do not worry Escolástica,' my great-grandmother suddenly said. 'We will raise your little dark-haired beauty as our own.' Then she smiled warmly. 'Look, she is already one of us,' she said. And it was true. Ana Escoraz Silvestre, the very last Ana Silvestre and my very own future grandmother, was playing tag with José Ignacio, running up and down the wharf, disappearing into shadows filled with the heavy, glistening smoke of ships getting ready to depart, and then reappearing again, skirting dangerously along the edge without even a backwards glance at the frothy, brackish black waters below, which had swallowed many an unsuspecting child, pushing past the legs of men and women going this way and that and a few startled seagulls taking to the air and a few dock workers shouting words of warning followed by a lazy curse or two, but the children were laughing with too much rambunctious joy to be bothered by the inconvenient wisdom of adults.

'Yes,' said Tiká. 'Thank you.'

Then she kissed my great-grandmother on the cheek, and then my great-grandfather stepped forward, burdened by a shame which he could not articulate. Tiká kissed him as well, but he could not look her directly in her eyes, so he pulled her close and gave her a fatherly embrace and then a bit of fatherly advice, a few whispered words of encouragement, and though he heard himself speaking, he did not know precisely what he was saying, for at that very moment the thought of the long-vanished Third Note flashed a second time across the dark, foreboding sky of his memory. He wondered if life would have turned out differently if he had read the note. He wondered if Tiká would have been leaving for San Juan that very day. He wondered if they would have been forced by his own uncertain appreciation of public opinion to abandon their life in Santiago de Cuba province and move to Havana. He wondered if that had been a rash decision on his part. He wondered if Tiká herself might have found love in the arms of someone other than Nicario. He wondered if they would have met Nicario in the first place. Then he found himself wondering why Tiká had left Spain oh so many years before, what force had sent her spinning erratically across the globe, what had she been hoping to find, and then he suddenly realized that she must have fallen in love with a man she could never marry, yes, that is why she had left, that was most certainly the reason. He wondered who this man might have been and if Tiká still thought about him and if she would ever find the peace and serenity that is necessary for true happiness. Then the red tide of his questions receded and he heard his own voice once again, and he was saying 'Do not forget that your family loves you, my little Tiká. Our hearts are spinning like tops.'

Tiká did not know what to say so she said nothing. She pulled away and ran up the gangplank, her fiery red braid trailing behind, fluttering furiously in the air like a burning rope that must be cut out of necessity, or a long-standing faith discarded on a whim, and disappeared into the swirling mass of humanity crowding the upper deck.

-57-

What my great-grandfather was thinking when he died:

Thirty-two years, eight months and ten days after Tiká left for Puerto Rico, on Saturday, October 26, 1940, a fraction of a second before eleven in the evening, the thought of the Third Note once more surfaced in the swirling ocean current of my great-grandfather's brain. He was tending bar that night in Casa Oriente, the café-turned-nightclub-turned-café of his own blood, sweat and tears at 112 Zulueta Street in downtown Havana. He was not thinking much about anything. He was wiping out a few shot glasses, rearranging the bottles beneath the counter, chatting with a few wayward souls.

He had planned to leave that evening by six because my great-grandmother was making chicken with tomatoes and rice. But the young man he had hired to work evenings until the last drink had been served had not shown up to work.

My great-grandfather wondered what had become of this passionate young man with dark Indian eyes and chiseled features that reminded everyone who saw him of Hatuey, the great Taíno chieftain, and who went by the unlikely name of Martín Gutiérrez Reyes, a name which my great-grandfather knew to be false, but he was not one to pry. Besides, he liked Martín very much.

Every so often my great-grandfather glanced at the clock hanging on the wall behind the bar, wondering what was keeping young Martín, if he was okay, for the streets of Havana were nothing if not violent, especially after dark, or if, perhaps, Martín had found a beautiful girl to keep him company and that was why. He hoped the reason was a girl.

And then my great-grandfather's thoughts turned to the clock itself. It was a very beautiful 19th century Junghans German Victorian Walnut Regulator Wall clock that had been delivered by special courier one afternoon from a mysterious, unnamed benefactor. But my great-grandfather had known immediately who had sent this strange, almost symbolic gift. The card that had accompanied the clock had said in precise, typewritten lettering: 'Truly, we are sitting in the grey bull ring of dreams with willows in the barreras,' and below that in a hastily written note: 'Thank you for hosting a most wondrous evening of political discourse and storytelling.'

My great-grandfather had placed the clock on the wall between a gilded French Rococo salon mirror (which he had purchased for a very good price from an antiques dealer who dabbled occasionally in the occult and who had a dozen or more similar salon mirrors in stock which had been gathering dust in his shop since before he was born and which he had been trying to unload for years) and the poster of the Spanish bullfighter Jose Garcia Carranza, alias 'Pepe Algabeño,' from when the bullfighter was just starting out in Madrid.

On the night in question, my great-grandfather had been sending the clock worried looks every so often from about eight o'clock on. The hands were not moving fast enough to suit whatever mood he was in.

Later, one of the regulars at Casa Oriente told the police that my great-grandfather had not been himself the whole evening. 'It was as if he had been waiting for something extraordinary to happen, as if he had glimpsed the end of the world, the destruction of everything we have ever known, but he did not want to share this terrible secret for fear of disturbing the delicate equilibrium of those present' the regular had said in a low, dry whisper, almost inaudible, as if he feared that his words would be taken out of context by an eavesdropping cub reporter seeking to push on the world a lunatic theory about the coming apocalypse and how it would begin in Latin America, supported by American arms dealers, and not in France or the Middle East like everyone supposed, a theory which would inevitably gain a host of followers inhabiting the fringes of society, but which would be largely discredited (also inevitably) by mainstream academia.

At nine o'clock my great-grandfather realized that he had forgotten to pick up the yellow cheese from Miami that my great-grandmother had asked for. He had remembered the jar of peach jam when he had gone out for a mid-morning walk, which hadn't been as hard to find as she had led him to believe, in fact he had purchased three jars, but he was certain beyond any doubt whatsoever that in the absence of the yellow cheese she would not even notice the three jars of jam.

At nine-fifteen he wondered if he could still pick up some cheese, but he was forced to accept the fact that the market had closed hours earlier.

At nine-thirty he shifted his line of thinking from the forgotten cheese to the latest poem he had written for my great-grandmother. He wondered if she had read it. He wished he could see her reaction without her knowing.

At nine-forty-five he was inspired to scribble the poem down on the back of a drink menu he had stolen from Sloppy Joe's. He had stolen the menu only a few days earlier, just to see what kind of drinks Sloppy Joe's was serving. There was a blank space at the bottom of the back page, below an advertisement for Tio Pepe, which seemed the perfect spot for poetry. My great-grandfather was going to pass the drink menu around the bar and see what people thought.

He was very excited as he scribbled. The poem contained the purest expression of love he had ever contemplated. It seemed to capture the unending depth of his emotion, his eternal faith that my great-grandmother was the mirror that reflected back to him the essence of who he truly was. He also felt the poem was utterly modern, utterly original in the way it blended a romantic view of the soul with a current scientific understanding of the cosmos.

(Of course he had forgotten that this poem was word for word a declaration of love he had once uttered to my great-grandmother in a dream, a dream which he had shared with her before reciting the poem on the night of their first kiss. But she remembered.)

At nine-forty-five, as he was writing down the words on the back of the stolen menu, she was reading those same words by candlelight in the smaller courtyard near the back of the big house in Miramar.

She had been looking up at the night sky and contemplating the silence of this strangely silent evening (there was not even the mournful sound of a bolero drifting like a ghost through the air) when she remembered the poem. She laughed as she read it, breaking the strange almost supernatural silence with a sound that could have been mistaken for a handful of old coins that had been happily tossed into the air so they could descend swiftly and bounce about on the courtyard tiles, the echo lingering. Smiling with unrestrained mirth at his forgetfulness, and wondering if he would remember the yellow cheese from Miami, she slipped the poem once again into the front pocket of her apron.

At ten o'clock on the dot my great-grandfather finished his scribbling. He held up the stolen drink menu so everyone could see, explained about his poem, and then passed it to the nearest group of patrons.

Not everyone was interested in reading this poem of undying love written on the back of a stolen drink menu, but everyone was interested in seeing what kinds of drinks Sloppy Joe's was serving.

Those who also appreciated literary endeavors realized they were being given a glimpse of something beyond their understanding.

My great-grandfather carefully watched the expressions on the faces of those who read the poem. Most of them moved their lips as they read, which he decided was a sign that they were trying to carefully decipher every nuance. An author could not ask for anything more.

My great-grandfather spoke the poem to himself as he watched each set of lips.

I am thinking of you, always,
We are like young lovers standing in the shadow of the Eiffel Tower,
Becoming now the center of the Universe,
The pale blue dust of Orion's nebula
Spinning across the sky,
Your soul and mine,
Breathless.

The drink menu took almost fifty minutes to make the circuit. Some of the patrons of Casa Oriente shouted their compliments to the author of the poem as if they were celebrating a great matador (as great as Pepe Algabeño himself, by the sound of it) who had narrowly escaped death while dancing with the most dangerous bull that anyone had ever heard of.

A few mentioned that they had never seen the Eiffel

Tower or even thought about going to Paris, but quickly added that this was not a criticism of the poem.

Every so often someone (or an entire table) ordered something from the pages of the stolen menu (Gin Rickeys or Sloe Gin Rickeys or a Raimund's Gin Fizz or a Morning Glory or a Seiberling or an Absinthe Frappe or a Kal Katz or a Mary Pickford or a Paramount or a Happy Night).

My great-grandfather, in spite of the fact that his own drink menu was not as extensive as the one from Sloppy Joe's, did his best to give his patrons what they wanted.

Casa Oriente was filled with the happy glowing faces of drunken men, some with poetic souls, some not, but all of them staunch supporters of each other.

Basking in the glow of these happy, drunken faces, my great-grandfather read the poem once more, savoring each word. It is not certain if he read the words out loud or kept them to himself, but all eyes were upon him in any event. He imagined that my great-grandmother was sitting at one of the tables in Casa Oriente and that she was beaming with great pleasure and noticeable pride.

At ten fifty-five he heard the front door open and close, and then he heard several surreptitious footsteps which then came to an abrupt halt perhaps ten feet from the bar. He looked up, half expecting to see my great-grandmother, and then he laughed at his obvious lunatic state of mind for he knew at that moment she was waiting for him at home.

My great-grandfather saw that a thin, wiry gentleman wearing a plain black bowler had entered Casa Oriente. He noticed that the man possessed a thin moustache in keeping with his emaciated appearance. My great-grandfather had never seen the man before. He wondered why the man was not Martín Gutiérrez Reyes.

Naturally, everyone in the bar had turned their heads when the door opened to see who it was, but to judge from the descriptions they later gave the police, no two witnesses saw the same man. They all agreed, however, that whatever he looked like, he spent a minute or two scrutinizing the poster of Pepe Algabeño before he pulled out a pistol and started firing with indiscriminate glee.

It seemed almost as if he were searching the poster for a hidden message, some of the witnesses said.

Naturally, after the thin, wiry stranger in the plain black

bowler (my great-grandfather's singular viewpoint) entered Casa Oriente, events unfolded with a sort of slow-motion, cinematic clarity towards an inevitable end.

At ten fifty-six and ten seconds, my great-grandfather heard my great-grandmother's laughter bouncing all over the tiles of the small courtyard near the back of the house in Miramar. He did not question the suspension of the ordinary laws of physics that permitted this miracle, for in spite of his philosopher's bookshelf and the years he had spent reading this philosopher or that one, he believed in his heart of hearts that through God anything was possible. He listened to the crystalline purity of my great-grandmother's laughter with delicate intensity, as if he could not quite believe such an astonishing sound truly existed.

At ten fifty-six and fifty-five seconds, my great-grandmother's ethereal laughter vanished and my great-grandfather suddenly thought of Grenfell. He started to say the name 'Grenfell' under his breath, but then he quickly swallowed his own voice, as if suddenly realizing that to utter the name of his former adversary would be a fatal mistake. He wondered what had happened to Grenfell and if he had been angry and had vowed revenge.

At ten fifty-seven and twenty seconds he decided that Grenfell must have died years earlier, or if he were still alive he would be well over eighty (or even older) and would pose no real threat to anyone, except perhaps himself.

At ten fifty-seven and forty seconds, an eerie calm settled over Casa Oriente.

At ten fifty-seven and forty-five seconds the stranger in the black bowler pulled out a pistol. No one in Casa Oriente could tell what kind of pistol it was.

At ten fifty-seven and fifty seconds a great booming voice said 'Death to the fucking Fascists!' The voice was coming out of the suddenly and mysteriously enraged mouth of the man in the black bowler. No one could quite believe that a man who was so emaciated could possess such a large voice.

At ten fifty-eight the man in the black bowler began firing.

Everyone in Casa Oriente scrambled to a place of safety, underneath tables, behind chairs, crouching on the floor.

Everyone except my great-grandfather. My great-grandfather seemed strangely disconnected, as if he were lost in the pages of one of his philosophy books. He did not seem to notice the bullets flying about or the crashing sounds they made as they smashed into the French Rococo salon mirror. But he was not thinking about philosophy at all. He was thinking about Nicario. What had become of Nicario, he said to himself. He wondered what Nicario would say if he could see his very own (meaning Nicario's) daughter, little Ana, who was not so little anymore, who was now thirty-seven with a son of her own, little Andres. But what was he thinking? Andres was no longer so little either. Andres was twenty-two and had just graduated from the University of Havana and was going to become a lawyer and work on behalf of the Cuban people. He had grown up just like that! My great-grandfather could not get over how quickly the years had passed. He wondered if Nicario would appreciate the sacrifices they had all made so that his very own (again, meaning Nicario's) grandson could become a shining star of success. Then just like that he could hear Nicario's voice, or some version of it, as if a demented, caricature of Nicario were whispering in his ear. 'Ah, yes,' said the strangely demented, distant voice, a furtive sound like the rustling noise a ferret or a weasel or a hedgehog makes when it is running away pell mell beneath the cover of dead leaves, 'but not even a faith as strong as yours can save you from the *otra muerte.*'

My great-grandfather was just about to respond with a clever, philosophical remark to this cryptic warning when he was distracted by the golden, gleaming brilliance of a bullet speeding with unwavering commitment towards the very spot where he was standing.

At ten fifty-nine and fifty-nine seconds the thought of Tiká's long vanished Third Note crossed his mind for the third and final time. He wondered what wisdom the note contained that he hadn't acquired over the years. Then he suddenly decided he was better off not knowing. He was happy with the way his life had turned out. He wondered what had happened to Tiká and how she was getting along. He wanted to tell her he would do it all over again in exactly the same way if he had a second chance. He had vanquished all of his doubts.

Then his thoughts returned to my great-grandmother and the crystalline purity of her ethereal laughter and he knew no matter what happened they would be together for all eternity.

And then that was that. At precisely eleven o'clock on October 26, 1940, during a flurry of erratic gunfire that according to witnesses barely lasted two minutes, a single golden, gleaming bullet struck my great-grandfather in the eye and blew out the back of his skull. The assassin escaped in the confusion that followed and was never found (or was even really searched for) and so was never brought to justice. It was said that my great-grandfather did not even flinch when the bullet struck.

-58-

The story of Tiká from the day she left Havana, Cuba until the day she met three ex-poets in San Juan, Puerto Rico:

During the intervening hours between the moment Tiká left Havana aboard the *S. S. Saratoga* and the moment she arrived in San Juan with the sky still threatening rain, she transformed herself, at least superficially, from a deflowered lady in waiting (though what she was waiting for exactly she never quite knew) to a young man of vague pedigree. To be more precise, she abandoned the costume of a weeping, disconsolate young mother who had just abandoned her only child to the capricious winds of fate, and adopted instead the disguise of a young or youngish (closer to thirty than forty) soldier of fortune in search of a quiet place to recuperate between forays into the world of war. She cut off her red braid and tossed it into the sea without the tiniest drop of regret. Then she flattened her breasts, never that large to begin with but still sensitive to light and water and cold temperatures, with the aid of a corset that was two sizes too small, put on an old army uniform that had belonged to Nicario but which had seemingly shrunk over the years (either that or the profligate Nicario had been a much smaller man in his younger days) and so fit Tiká perfectly, and a pair of boots which were several sizes too large, so she stuffed the toe sections with old newspaper.

Why did she feel the need for such a disguise? Who was going to recognize her in Puerto Rico anyway? Who cared what sins of the heart she had committed in Cuba and elsewhere? Was her need perhaps spurred on by some psychological defect? Was she plagued by a lingering sense of guilt because of her daughter and so was trying to run away from her pain? Was she still lamenting the loss of her one true love back in Spain and thought that by pretending to be a soldier she might conquer the rebellion of her own inner turmoil? Was her transformation simply a practical measure that any woman traveling alone in the world in 1908 might take? Or had she taken to heart the *babalawo's* warning (observation? prediction? a charlatan's bold, energetic but ultimately vague pronouncement that can only be truly appreciated after the fact?)? Did she believe that a physical incarnation of Death and not just a mythical, allegorical representation was after her in Cuba? Was she afraid that Death was still coming for her, or if not Death, then Death's agents, who probably looked like skeletons or the shadows of skeletons, dark shadows, the visible manifestations of Lorca's *duendes,* which should not be confused with Luther's theological demon of doubt or the *duendes* from the folklore of Spain or Portugal or many a Latin American country, though to be fair, Lorca probably stole his image of skeletal *duendes* from Cervantes, or if not Cervantes, then someone further back whose writing was steeped in images lifted from an oral tradition. Was Tiká afraid that these *duende*-like agents of Death had slipped on board the *S. S. Saratoga* in spite of her best efforts to steer clear of their icy fingertips, and so she had no choice but to embrace this mummer's pretense? Who can say what was going on in her mind? What can be said is that Tiká was quite convincing in her new role. She took the name of Sebastian de Urquiza and moved into the boarding house on Caleta de las Monjas. And because of her extraordinary athleticism she was able to best most of the men she encountered in most feats of physical skill, including knife throwing, boxing, swimming, archery, fencing, pistol marksmanship, rifle marksmanship, and horse riding, but excluding drinking, arm-wrestling and whore-baiting, all for obvious reasons. Her knife-throwing was especially accurate. From a distance of thirty feet she could pin a man's jacket to the wall with the man still wearing it and not a drop of blood would be spilled. She quickly made a name for herself and was soon accepted as one of the boys wherever she went. She also made a little money with her knife-throwing exhibitions, which might take place at any point during the week, but usually took place on Friday or Saturday nights in one of the abandoned warehouses on Calle La Puntilla.

In those days, the handful of warehouses on La Puntilla had become a second home to all manner of adventurers and mercenaries and defeated soldiers looking to blow off a little steam. They had come to San Juan from all over the Caribbean, drawn by a vague, unsettling sense of freedom like a barely recognizable smell mixed with the more familiar smells of unrepentant mania and a lingering, desperate futility descending into fatigue that characterizes many a Latin American nation (or perhaps all of them). They had infiltrated every crevice of the island like a seeping poison. Of course the authorities realized they were sitting on a powder keg (a cliché, certainly, but a more accurate image, at least in tone, than that of a 'ticking bomb' or some 'infernal combustible machine' or some more futuristic sounding incendiary device), which is why they turned a blind eye (yes, another cliché, which is meant to suggest a watchful but not too eager to intervene for political reasons kind of eye, so not really blind at all) to whatever crimes were committed in the warehouses on La Puntilla. Better that these men of the shadows should turn upon themselves than upon the decent citizens of San Juan. All of which is to say that Tiká's knife-throwing exhibitions were but one of many impromptu distractions that included various card games, dice games, all sorts of games of chance, occasional boxing matches, wrestling matches, cock fighting, dog-baiting, and so on, each event taking place on a tiny sliver of dimly lit warehouse floor. Money exchanged hands freely at first, and then not so freely as the big winners and the big losers sorted themselves out. Men were killed at the drop of a hat beneath the darkly gleaming rafters and then their bodies were dragged out into the night and dumped without comment into the dark waters of the harbor. Tiká always did quite well in the warehouses on La Puntilla.

During that first year in San Juan she roamed the cobblestone streets of the city at all hours of the day and night, submerged in the abyss of silence and pretense. Her old self disappeared. She acquired a taste for history, which is almost the same thing as acquiring a taste for the truth (which would have been ironic), but not quite. She searched the cafés and bars and seedy restaurants all over San Juan for a history she could claim as her own. Every so often she would stop in at the Army & Navy YMCA on Calle del Sol for an American style sandwich or a bowl of chicken stew and she listened to the stories of the old men while she ate. (Afterwards she might take in a gospel service right across the street, listening to stories of another kind, and reminisce for a moment about her life in Cuba.) Once in a while she found herself in the Plaza de Colón, which was full of orange vendors in brown hats pushing wheelbarrows full of oranges, and white-hatted hat vendors with toothless grins walking with their burros this way and that, bothering the tourists who had come only to look at the statue of Columbus. Or maybe she found herself on Calle de Tetuan, where the roughnecks were always lounging about on the narrow sidewalks in front of various import/export companies until the police chased them away. Or maybe she would head down to the waterfront, where only the heartiest down-and-outers took comfort. She went anywhere that old men, exiles and expatriates and counterfeit soldiers of fortune (mirror images to Tiká herself) gathered to trade stories of forgotten wars on distant shores and the glory of eternal revolution. She adopted the best stories as her own, as every great storyteller does.

One of Tiká's favorite haunts was Café La Ceiba, a café somewhere along Calle de la Luna where it was easy to hide one's face, partly because of the numerous ferns and other potted plants surrounding the tables, but mostly because Café La Ceiba was illuminated (if indeed illumination was the correct word) by a strange bluish light that seemed to distort one's perspective rather than provide any clarity, as if the light were emanating from deep inside a subterranean cavern miles below the surface of the planet (the Devil's abode?) and only occasionally leaked out through a crack in the earth's crust, a crack which was coincidentally just below the rough-hewn floor boards of Café La Ceiba.

In Café La Ceiba, Tiká talked about one of the very first of the Banana Wars, a conflict between Nicaragua and Honduras which had ended in April 1907, though the peace process had dragged on for several more months, and which had been framed by Teddy Roosevelt and the Americans as not so much a war but a policing action to preserve the integrity of the banana trade as well as to keep the ports safe for American *touristas*, but which was in reality an excuse for all-out butchery conceived by Nicaraguan President José Santos Zelaya and later backed by the Americans because they had no other viable choice at that point, because Zelaya believed Manuel Bonilla, the President of Honduras, was working feverishly to undermine the future economic prosperity of Nicaragua.

Tiká talked as if she herself had been one of the defeated captains at the Battle of Namasigüe in March, in which the

Americans gave the badly outnumbered Nicaraguan army a dozen Krupp cannons and three or four hundred Maxim machine guns, which the Nicaraguans used to mow down the hapless Hondurans and their Salvadoran allies without the tiniest flicker of remorse. Only those who brought up the rear of Bonilla's freedom fighters stood any chance of surviving the onslaught.

According to Tiká, who was repeating word for word a story she had heard from a bearded Guatemalan mercenary who had survived the massacre and now spent most of his waking hours in a drunken stupor in El Cielo, a dive on Calle San José that catered to those who had fought in Central America, the carnage at Namasigüe was so great that for three days the sky was black with vultures and other birds drawn by the festering aroma of rotting meat.

In the more upscale Casa Cataño on Recinto Sur, with its rich mahogany décor and gilded mirrors, Tiká talked about the Venezuelan dispute with the Dutch in 1908, a dispute that began when the president of Venezuela, Cipriano Castro, asked the Ambassador from the Netherlands, a Monsieur de Reus, if perhaps he could ask his government to aid Venezuela in tracking down various defeated revolutionaries who were nevertheless able to escape to Curacao, a nearby Caribbean island that belonged to the Dutch, where they (the revolutionaries) would first lick their wounds and then formulate new strategies for overthrowing the Castro government and then return to Caracas fully armed and try again, whereupon M. Reus replied in a published letter that Castro had been misinformed about any revolutionaries fleeing to Curacao or any other Dutch colony, which infuriated Castro because he knew better and so resulted in the expulsion of M. Reus from Venezuelan soil, which sparked a riot in Curacao against the Venezuelan consul, so Castro had no choice but to break diplomatic ties with the Dutch, so the Dutch sent in warships because things were beginning to escalate, but also because they didn't like Castro's attitude in the first place, so Castro initiated an embargo restricting the movement of any person or persons traveling from Venezuela to any of the Dutch ports in the Caribbean (or vice versa), because he didn't care what the Dutch or any other great power thought about him or his policies and he wanted to show them, so the Dutch responded by seizing as many Venezuelan ships as they could, which they did without firing a single shot, which is beside the point as far as international law was concerned, but was played up pretty big by the newspapers in Europe and the United States as an example of civilized diplomacy in action (as opposed to the ruthless, blood-thirsty approach of every Latin American dictator), but by then Castro had to travel to France because the hospitals in Caracas could no longer help him with his syphilis, which was raging out of control, which the same newspapers mentioned above politely characterized as a kidney ailment even though everyone knew this wasn't true, so Castro left for Paris in the beginning of December, but before his ship had even reached the Greater Antilles, Juan Vincent Gómez, Castro's Vice-President and life-long friend, who had supported Castro's initial grab for power and was in fact his main financial backer in 1899 when Castro and fifty-seven followers slipped across the border of Táchira province, their home province, heading for the capital to launch their *Revolución Restauradora,* this very same Gómez (who later became the most ruthless *caudillo* Venezuela would ever know) had seized control of the country, and so the war with the mighty Netherlands was over.

Tiká talked as if she had been by Castro's side throughout his entire Presidency, even when he contracted syphilis in 1904 from a prostitute on the island of Curacao (the very same island at the center of the controversial events in 1908). She talked as if the only reason she was now in Puerto Rico was because Castro was living in exile in San Juan. She said that she had accompanied him to Paris in November of 1908 in search of a physician who knew what he was doing. 'Who better to cure the French Gout than the French?' Castro had told her.

In all the years she told the story, no one ever brought up the fact that she had actually been in San Juan during those three months from November 1908 to January 1909 when she said she had been with Castro in France. Then again, how would they have known? Her command of the smallest details of the story was quite convincing. She said she had accompanied the great dictator to Lariboisière Hospital, though they had spent several unexpected hours traveling the streets of Paris like kidnapped tourists before their driver, as if he had had a change of heart, brought them round to Rue Ambroise Paré and their destination. They had gone to the hospital to see Dr. Georges Louis Lemoine, who had written on syphilis and was in close contact with a Dr. Paul Ehrlich from Austria, who was close to a breakthrough, but before they went inside, they stopped at the tomb of the Countess Élisa de Lariboisière, who upon her death in 1851 left almost three million francs to the French government to finish building the hospital begun under Louis Philippe. The monument was very Gothic, very dramatic, with a black marble façade crowned with black marble angels and a recessed archway (also black) which contained a grieving yet strangely serene looking woman holding a small child with one arm and a dying man with the other. The trio — pale, ghostly figures carved from white marble and then painted with pale, dusty colors to suggest, perhaps, the eternal and yet ennobling sorrow of death — had been placed on top of a sculpted facsimile of a coffin painted a copper color. The sculptor, an Italian master without a doubt, had created the illusion that the coffin was supported by two facsimile legs sculpted from black marble. Each facsimile leg featured a lion's face staring out at the public with an unearthly, inscrutable expression.

Tiká said that after Castro's treatment had concluded, she and the deposed dictator stopped for a coffee at Café du Dôme on Rue de Clignancourt and spoke in furtive whispers about the rumors that surrounded the life of the Countess. They marveled at her exquisite passion for life and her industrious courage in the face of a doomed love. In 1814 she had married Honoré Baston de Lariboisière, an officer who had served in Napoleon's artillery, a marriage that oddly enough both families viewed as one of strategic importance, *un mariage d'opportunité politique,* but Elisa had been secretly in love with Honoré's brother, Ferdinand. Unfortunately, Ferdinand, the dashing and beautiful beyond belief younger brother, had led the charge of the 1st Carabiniers-à-Cheval regiment at the Battle of Borodino on September 7, 1812 and been mortally wounded, so his brother was the next best thing. Some said that Honoré himself had suggested that Ferdinand join the Carabiniers-à-Cheval regiment because they were always in the thick of it, which meant that the glory of a noble death was theirs for the taking.

The only memento of Ferdinand in Elisa's possession, which was an unspoken but tacitly understood point of contention between Elisa and the Count, was a lock of hair which a surgeon named Gudolle had taken from Ferdinand when he (the surgeon) was preparing the body for burial. What Elisa had wanted, however, was Ferdinand's heart, which she secretly and rightly believed belonged to her. But this was not to be. Honoré had instructed Gudolle to extract Ferdinand's heart right there on the battlefield and place it in a small beaker of wine to preserve it. Why Honoré wanted his brother's heart was a mystery, but the gossip in Paris in those days and later was that he had known all along that Elisa had been in love with Ferdinand, and wishing to punish her, but not wishing to provoke further gossip, which would have most certainly made it into the newspapers, which would in turn have made a mockery of his own public declarations of love for his future wife, he thought instead to seek private revenge and take possession of what was for Elisa (and perhaps for Honoré himself) a symbol of unattainable and therefore untainted love.

The couple slept in separate bedrooms from the very first day of their marriage, which explains a lot. What actually happened to the beaker containing Ferdinand's heart is anybody's guess. Some things it is better not to know.

Almost everyone who heard Tiká tell her tale believed that Castro would still be in power if he had remained in Caracas. (A few had forgotten she was talking about Castro and thought her story was about the Countess de Lariboisière and Honoré's excessive jealousy and the gruesome extraction of Ferdinand's heart, but when everyone else began gabbing away about Castro, they realized their mistake and wished they had paid better attention.) Many of the patrons of Casa Cataño tentatively expressed the undying hope that Castro would find the means to regain his Presidency, and then they drained the glasses of fancy tequila they had been drinking, and then someone ordered another round. As if to assure every potential (which is to say drunken) ally who might have been listening that such a destiny was a foregone conclusion, Tiká said that she had been meeting with Castro every few days in secret, hatching plots to overthrow Gómez and return the deposed President to his former glory. Again a few voices expressed their undying hopes, and again the glasses were drained and another round was ordered.

The day that Tiká stopped roaming the cobblestone streets of San Juan at all hours of the day and night, though she was still submerged in the abyss of silence and pretense:

On that day three men arrived at the boarding house on Caleta de las Monjas an hour or so before dawn. They were at the tail end of a passionate conversation about a woman they all seemed to know quite well. The streets were basically deserted at that hour, so their actual arrival was preceded by first their voices, and then the sound of their footsteps (heavy boots on cobblestone, the kind of boots the Conquistadors might have worn, maybe). Their conversation was a mysterious amalgam of innuendo and poetic despair, harboring all sorts of regret tinged with anger, with occasional bursts of rediscovered joy in the spaces in between their words.

Tiká had been listening to the men for at least fifteen minutes from her third-floor corner balcony window. What she was doing awake at that hour she couldn't say. Perhaps she had not been able to sleep at all. Perhaps she had just returned from an evening of conquest at one of the warehouses on La Puntilla. In any event, she had heard the men the moment they turned down Calle San Francisco from Callejon Tamarindo. One moment Tiká had been contemplating the silence of the world, and the next moment she heard three thin, staticky, vibrating voices, as if they had suddenly and irrevocably (this is how Tiká described it to me) emerged from the sewers through a trapdoor.

After a while, the men stopped talking. Tiká heard instead the sounds of metal striking stone, and then slow, furtive scraping sounds, and then the sounds of metal striking stone again, punctuated by strange, unintelligible curses, and then after the curses there was an explosion of weary, ironic laughter that shook the very foundation of the building, and then more scraping sounds, and then more metal striking stone, and more curses, and so on.

Later, after the sun had burned away the night, Tiká felt an overpowering urge to find out what these men were up to. Like a sleepwalker wearing a very thin jacket lined with the wind, she followed the sounds down a narrow stairway that led to a part of the boarding house where sunlight did not penetrate, and soon found herself wandering through a labyrinth of damp subterranean tunnels and long, dimly lit hallways that trembled with a faint orangeish glow, and every so often this glow was fractured by a sudden tremor of darkness, and then the light returned, like an eye in the throes of great sorrow closing and then opening again.

It quickly became impossible to distinguish between the sounds themselves and the echoes produced by the sounds bouncing off the stone walls of the tunnels and hallways.

Naturally, Tiká became tangled up in the labyrinth, but she did not mind. She began to listen to the barely audible currents of sound that lay beneath the sounds of the men, sounds that had been trapped within the very walls of the tunnels and hallways, sounds like smoke curling up towards a stone ceiling and spreading out with an oily consistency after a torch has been snuffed out, sounds like two hands folded in perpetual prayer, sounds like a thin smile, with the diffuse gentleness of lightning on the horizon, escaping into the long night, sounds like tiny silver bells tied together with a silken cord and shaken ever so slightly, almost wearily, or the rapid–fire beating of tiny wings that one might hear just before falling into a dreamless sleep, sounds that had waited in a sea of stone, insensible to the passing years, for just the right person, with just the right mixture of passion and curiosity and reverence, to wander through this musty labyrinth from another era with attendant ears. So Tiká abandoned her search for the three men and followed instead the whispering walls of the tunnels and hallways beneath the boarding house that had once been a convent for Carmelite nuns.

The whispering led her to a small chamber some thirty feet directly beneath a forgotten patio. The patio was in a small interior courtyard in the dead center of the old convent and contained the withered remains of various shrubs and small ornamental trees from Africa or Spain and other flowering plants, and there was also a single *nispero* tree with its strangely sweet fruit (like a Flemish pear with a dash of cinnamon) that had been planted in 1696 and would live for at least another century. It was a patio where in happier days two young, seemingly contented Carmelite novitiates tended the greenery with a delicate but sure touch and, one might say, a barely suppressed maternal instinct, and each evening from seven until eight, when it wasn't raining, a handful of the older ones gathered in silence to contemplate the unknowable mysteries of the universe as much as the lingering pain of a womb made barren by conscious choice.

The chamber beneath the patio was the source of the mysterious orange light. Tiká stood for a while at the entrance to the chamber, contemplating the light, which was emanating from two perforated brass frame railroad lanterns. She did not see the owners of the lanterns and wondered if perhaps she was dreaming. The orangeish glow from the lanterns was fairly steady, only a slight, sinister flickering, and she wondered what had caused the flashes of darkness from before. Then a shadow passed in front of the lanterns and there was another mesmerizing flash of darkness. Tiká must have said something or somehow drawn attention to her presence because when the light returned she saw three men standing motionless in the glare of the lanterns, looking in her direction, their eyes fixed like dead stars or hibernating thoughts, their faces beaming with comical expressions of paranoia and autoerotic cunning.

A few minutes later:

'You gave us quite a shock Sebastian de Urquiza, appearing the way you did on the edge of oblivion, we were just settling into our labors,' said a dreamily sanguine voice that belonged to a lanky, dark-complected middle-aged man wearing corduroy workpants and a cotton shirt. He possessed finely chiseled features and a shadowy beard like a dusting of potash. He had one leg and one foot resting on a rather large piece of stone that seemed to have fallen from the ceiling, and he was leaning forward slightly, his hands pressing down on his bent knee. There were various implements scattered about: shovels, a stone mason's chisel, a few wedges, a pry bar, a sledge hammer, and several smaller hammers. The man's two companions were wearing similar costumes. They stood on either side of him with blank, bewildered looks on their faces. The flickering of the lanterns bathed the faces of all three men in a strange, eerie light. It was like there were tattoos dancing across their skin. 'But what a fine sounding name you have,' the voice continued. 'Sebastian de Urquiza. What an exceptionally suggestive, and dare I say it, poetic sounding name. It reminds one of the grand sounding names of Seville the way it rolls off one's tongue. A name that deserves a page in the *Spanish Book of Heraldry*, if there is such a book. But there must be such a book! My own name, less grand sounding perhaps, but just as poetic, if you will forgive a little egotism on my part, the insufferable vanity of wounded pride, my name is Rodrigo Cabrera Lazar, ex-poet extraordinaire from Carúpano, Venezuela.' It was hard to tell if ex-poet Rodrigo was actually speaking, forming words with his lips and sending them out on their own to cross the void, or if he was communicating telepathically, as if he were able to express everything he was thinking with a single, stupefying glance. 'And this affable, gregarious fellow to my right,' said ex-poet Rodrigo, 'though you would hardly know this to be true at this curiously precipitous moment since he seems to have swallowed his tongue, is Victor Hugo Salmerón la Prieto y Savoix de Pajares, a truly grand-sounding name if there ever was one, named after the famous maestro, of course, at least the first part, probably because his mother had just finished reading *The Hunchback of Notre Dame,* she was a voracious reader, that woman, yes she was, as is her son, Victor Hugo, who has been an ex-poet for longer than he can remember, which might not be so long if he suffered from amnesia, but I can assure you that his mind is as sharp this morning as the day he was born, he hails from the affable seaside community of Santo Tomás de Castilla, Guatemala and claims to be descended from the great, or near great, or at least the first Guatemalan poet of any significant reputation, Rafael Landívar, and get this, Victor Hugo also claims to have a grandfather from Haiti who wrote an occasional essay for *L' Observatuer,* the best newspaper in Port-au-Prince (how many literary antecedents can one man possess and never find a publisher?), and who left Haiti in 1805, one year after the revolution had ended and the slaves of Haiti had become ex-slaves (which is pretty close to becoming an ex-poet, let me tell you), which took place over one hundred years ago, and so naturally, if you stop to think about what Victor Hugo is saying, you begin to wonder how old he actually is and how old his father and his grandfather were and if they are still alive, and if they do indeed all belong to the race of the immortals, for who else could live so long, then Victor Hugo has already achieved the immortality that all poets (and even a few ex-poets) dream about, he will be alive and kicking when every word any mortal has ever written, any book ever printed and shared with a small, well-respected audience, or even the great covetous multitudes, every literary accomplishment will have turned to dust, but as for me, well I could care less about Victor Hugo's age, I mean his age as far as I'm concerned can only elevate his ex-poet's status, which will in turn elevate every ex-poet's status, if you catch my drift, which brings me to this rigid, silent monster on my left, Gustav Hermann Metz, who has not yet decided if he wants to embrace the lifestyle of an ex-poet, and of course when I use the word monster I do not mean to suggest that Gustav is a physical monstrosity, for you can surely see that at five-foot-six he is not so large as all that, what I mean to say, my dear sweet, perhaps gullible Sebastian de

Urquiza, is that he is a nihilist at heart, a position which I think it is fair to say the world views as monstrous, or a monstrosity, or at least the potential is there, and if you were ever to stare into those icy blue eyes of his for ten minutes, let alone an eternal-seeming hour, particularly after a good bottle of Demerara rum, you would see what I mean, yes, you can see him getting ready to react once he has pulled back from the darkness of the abyss, yes, I am sure he has a great deal to say, but as I have already mentioned, Gustav has not yet decided whether he wants to become an ex-poet like myself and Victor Hugo, but do not worry my good don, there is no ill will between us, no hidden animosities, we are friends, compadres, I do not begrudge Gustav his moment of indecision, no, I would be the first to admit that the life of an ex-poet is not for everyone, and if the truth be told, Gustav may never be able to give up poetry completely, he composes even as he sleeps, though you would swear he was wide awake, but every now and then, well, let me just say he seems to be sleeping peacefully, and then wham, just like that, his torso springs into action as if he is experiencing the pain of a sudden cramp, but instead of crying out in agony, he opens his bloody mouth (he is always chewing his tongue or his lips while he sleeps so there is always blood collecting in small pools on his pillow) and the words of a fully articulated, majestically conceived poem, usually a love sonnet, but occasionally an elegy, come pouring out as from a geyser or an inverted sewer, unfortunately, if you ask Gustav about his country of origin he might not tell you, I think he is a little embarrassed, I think he believes his poetry is no good, I think he believes his poetry is hampered by the vulgarity of his native language, which is certainly something a critic might say, but any poet with a compassionate heart will tell you that kind of crap is, well, it is utter crap, that's what it is, but we all believe what we believe, so I will tell you where Gustav is from, though there's not much to tell, he was born in Saarbrücken, Germany and he spent a year or two in Munich, as every good German should, and his family owned some property just across the border in Behren-lès-Forbach, but there was some dispute over the title, and after his father died in 1899 he left Germany for Buenos Aires, where he thought to make a fresh start, but after ten years he was bored, or he became the victim of a disastrous love affair with a peasant girl straight off the Pampas, or perhaps she was an indifferent socialite who didn't care how she wasted the vanishing days, or no one would publish his poetry, not even *La Revista,* a journal with a rather unimaginative name that appeared only sporadically, it is true, with a few volumes in 1899, and a few more in 1900, and then they closed down for a few years, but as soon as they secured additional funding, which was always a problem, they were back at it in that tiny little office in Montevideo, which is in Uruguay, not Argentina, as I am sure you know, and which does not seem all that far from Buenos Aires if you are looking at a map, but in reality it is a fairly long journey from one city to the other, you have to take an overnight steamer across the La Plata river, which they should really call the La Plata estuary, which perhaps you did not know, but all that is beside the point, what I was getting at was that the rents were very high in Buenos Aires in those days, at least in the neighborhoods the editors of *La Revista* were looking at, but they were a good deal cheaper in Montevideo, most likely because Argentina prized liberty and went on the gold standard and Uruguay prized equality and the redistribution of wealth, so the editors of *La Revista* went to Montevideo, not too far from the Fortaleza del Cerro, if I am remembering correctly, though far enough that you wouldn't want to walk, yes, yes, a weather-beaten ramshackle building on the corner of Egipto and Francia that was once a fish warehouse or a cannery or a repository for abandoned fishermen's boots, who can truly say, but the smell of fish was peculiarly strong, almost nauseating, but they had a view of the harbor and a view of the Isle of Liberty, also known as the Island of Rats and the Island of Gulls and the Island of Rabbits and Pigeon Island, and *La Revista* published everybody in Latin America, José Enrique Rodó they published, and Rubén Darío, naturally, though he was living in Spain by 1898, so they probably just lifted a few poems from his first collection, which came out in '96, and Amado Nervo and Ramón López Velarde and Julio Flórez and the towering Chocano and Ricardo Jaimes Freyre, with that sonorous, silky voice that smothers us all with its beauty, and Luis Lloréns Torres and Juan Zorrilla de San Martín, that sad, forgotten patriot of tiny, egalitarian Uruguay, and Federico Bermúdez y Ortega, a poet with an aristocratic style who nevertheless was able to capture the undeniable pain of the underdog and so became a voice against oppression in the Dominican Republic, and Gastón Fernando Deligne and his decadent visions, and Filinto de Almeida, an average Parnassian poet who lives, they say, in the shadow of his wife, and José de Diego and Rafael Obligado, the old man of Argentine poetry, who strove tirelessly for sober and clean expression, and Carlos Guido y Spano, who was even older than Obligado, but everyone loved that crazy old romantic lunatic because he paved the way for Darío and his disciples, and Manuel González Prada, who was a philosopher as much as a poet, and Juana Borrero and João do Rio, that brilliant imposter, and Salvador Díaz Mirón, and the musical poetry of José María Eguren, and Luisa Pérez de Zambrana, and perhaps the greatest of the Cuban poets, Julián del Casal, who died of tuberculosis in 1893 at the age of thirty but they continued to publish him anyway, how could they not, and Bernardo Guimarães, who was still going strong even twenty years after his death, and Luis Muñoz Rivera, whom I have seen once or twice on the streets of San Juan in the days since I first arrived, as one sees the fleeing shadow of a startled bird, or the black smoke from a rapidly spreading fire surging up towards heaven, and Guillermo Valencia, who didn't write all that much poetry and was perhaps a better translator than a poet, in fact this was most certainly the case, and Silva, who cannot die, and so many others, a host of others we have all forgotten, so it just goes to show, but what does it matter, that is the question before us, what does any of it matter, those examples, the boredom, the failed love affair with the peasant girl or the diffident socialite, the inability to get published, they are all really just facets of the same nightmarish reality, 'a black sun floating effortlessly across a black sky,' one of Gustav's images, I think, or maybe he stole it from a French poet, and so he left Argentina without sadness or regret, there was nothing left for him there, and now here he is, newly arrived in San Juan, as we all are, the three of us, within the last six months.'

-59-

How quickly life becomes a knot of tangled strings! Yes, yes, that is an appropriate metaphor for what happened next. But to appreciate the nuances of this unfolding tale, the strange twists and turns, you have to understand why the three ex-poets had gone down into the small chamber beneath the patio to begin with, and to place that understanding in its proper context, you should probably know a little something about the nuns who had lived in the building that was once a convent on Caleta de las Monjas. The nuns had been forced to abandon the convent in 1903. It is a very strange and sad tale. If I were to give it a title, I would call it *La triste pero milagroso viaje de las monjas* (The sad but miraculous journey of the nuns). It is really no different than the journey we are all taking.

La triste pero milagroso viaje de las Monjas:

The convent had been in pretty bad shape even before the Carmelites had been forced to move. It had sustained significant damage from the great earthquake of 1819, damage that had never been repaired. There was a lingering crack in the foundation along Caleta de las Monjas, and a section of the subterranean crypt beneath the interior patio had actually collapsed as a result of the crack, creating a small antechamber before the crypt itself. No one from San Juan had offered a hand to help clear away the rubble, and certainly the nuns themselves were ill-equipped for such dangerous work.

By the end of the 19th century, the crypt had been all but forgotten. By 1900, only two nuns among the twenty-three that remained cloistered within the broken walls of the convent on Caleta de las Monjas even knew the hidden crypt had ever existed. The first was Sister María Eugenia Berrios, an octogenarian who had been in charge of the archives since before the terrible war with Spain had erupted and so knew as much as there was to know about the convent's history. The second was Sister María Amàlia Garrido, who had taken on the duties of Mother Superior in 1877 with the death of Sister María Rosalita Perea, who had seen the earthquake of 1819 with her own eyes.

Then in May 1898, tragedy struck again. *¡Ay de mí!* Truly, our lives can be described as a happiness that becomes a sadness in search of a happiness. In that month the convent sustained further damage, some would have said irrevocably so, during the bombing of San Juan by the Americans. None of the Sisters were injured, though their sense of serenity was perhaps bruised beyond repair. But there was no talk of leaving. The convent was their home. Besides, where would they go? So the good Sisters simply closed off that part of the convent which most resembled an ancient ruin and continued with their daily prayers and spiritual devotion.

In 1903, however, a new Catholic bishop was installed in the Archdiocese of Puerto Rico, a North American named Monsignor Blenk. He was neither willing to set aside any church funds to repair the convent, nor allow the nuns to remain among the rubble, claiming in a brief meeting with Sister María Amàlia Garrido and two other nuns held on the steps of the Cathedral at nine o'clock on a Monday morning that 'the nuns could not show the proper devotion to God inside a structure that, because it was crumbling before our very eyes, no longer afforded its occupants the peace and serenity that was necessary for contemplative pursuits,' and then he looked at Sister María Amàlia Garrido with a strange, quizzical expression on his face, as if he could not quite remember who she was or why she was bothering him, and then he said 'God helps those who help themselves,' and that was that. So the Carmelites were forced into exile, as it were, but without the means to really go anywhere.

Eventually they made their way to the other side of the island to the village of San Germán, otherwise known as the city of hills, where they were forced to beg accommodations from the villagers, for San Germán was very small. There was only a small Gothic style church known as The Gate of Heaven (Porta Coéli) up on a hill that overlooked the main plaza of the village. Next to the church there were the abandoned ruins of a 16th century monastery. In other words, there really wasn't any room in San Germán for nineteen Carmelite sisters (four had died between 1897 and 1901) and two novices (who had entered the convent in 1902).

The villagers did their best to make sure every nun had a roof over her head and a comfortable bed. Most of the Sisters were afforded the luxury of at least a small closet of a room to themselves, though several of the younger ones (including the novices) had to share bunks with the small children of their hosts. All of which meant that the Carmelites were unable to live up to their Carmelite vow to abstain from the pleasures and pains of the world.

It was never clear whose idea it was to journey to San Germán. Perhaps Monsignor Blenk had simply read over a list of Puerto Rican towns and villages and picked San Germán because he liked the sound of it. Most likely because he had a German relative. Or perhaps it was because San Germán had been the second city founded in Puerto Rico, and it might have become a thriving metropolis in its own right, large enough to rival San Juan, had not repeated attacks by French raiders in the 16th century slowed its progress, a sequence of historical events that clearly Monsignor Blenk was ignoring or had not known. He must have thought that this city that had become a village had somehow transcended its destiny. Or perhaps the Sisters themselves chose San Germán because Carmita Ponce de Leon, a descendent of none other than Juan Ponce de Leon himself, lived in San Germán, and they (the Carmelite Sisters) counted among their early benefactors Doña Ana de Salamanca, who had married a great-grandson of the great Conquistador, so perhaps they had felt a connection of some sort, however tenuous, and had written to Carmita and told her of their desperate circumstances, and she had written back and invited them to San Germán and said they were more than welcome, she understood the plight of the exiled better than most, why her own daughter, the poet Lola Rodríguez de Tío, had twice been banished from Puerto Rico, first in 1867 by that idiot stooge of the Spanish, Captain General José María Marchesi y Oleaga, who had himself been an exile during the Carlist Wars in Spain so he should have known better, and again in 1889 by Governor Pedro Ruiz Dana, another in a long line of Spanish puppets who was pretty puffed up with his own importance, but now, who even remembers what he looked like, so, yes, yes, yes, she understood the plight of all exiles and the pain and suffering that lingers for years and even when you are finally able to return to your home the pain is still there, that was the way it had been with her daughter, *¡Qué alegres son las horas!* Did they know that poem? It is an amazing poem. Her daughter had written that poem. 'How joyful are the hours! Like a flock of doves wandering across the skies.' Yes, yes, no one understood their plight better than she did, they were more than welcome, she would be thankful for the company.

So the Sisters journeyed to San Germán. Naturally, they prayed in earnest to the Immaculate Virgin to assist them in their necessity, for they found it quite difficult to maintain a contemplative focus in such a tiny village, especially when their prayers were interrupted by clanging pots and screaming children and the braying of animals at all hours of the night, and though the Immaculate Virgin did answer their prayers, she withheld her answer for six years to test the depth of their need and the sincerity of their devotion.

Then in 1909, precipitated ironically by the sudden departure of Monsignor Blenk, who was moving on to greener spiritual pastures (some said Boston, but no one really knew), the Carmelites returned to San Juan, settling, as was already mentioned, in Santurce in San Mateo parish. Father Josef Correa spearheaded a fundraising drive on behalf of the itinerant nuns. He was the pastor of a small church in Santurce (Iglesia San Mateo de Cangrejeros, the Church of the Crab Sellers) on the corner of Calle San Jorge and Avenida Eduardo Conde. Work soon began on a small three story convent adjoining Father Correa's church, and a few months later, on the 14th day of July 1909, two days before the Feast Day of Our Lady of Mount Carmel, the nuns moved into the first floor of their new home (it would take another six months before the rest of the building was finished). Two days after that, on the Feast Day itself, at approximately eleven-thirty in the evening with a warm sweet breeze that smelled of almond trees and mariposa blowing through an open window, the Immaculate Virgin visited Sister María Amàlia Garrido in a dream.

The first thing the Immaculate Virgin said in Sister María Amàlia's dream was that the Carmelite Sisters were to begin keeping two gardens. One would be an enclosed garden only for the nuns, in keeping with their vows. But the second would be a garden for the community of hopeful souls that had embraced their return. It would be a garden of eternal gratitude.

The second thing the Immaculate Virgin said was that the Carmelites needed to restore to their rightful place everyone who had ever lived and died in the convent on Caleta de las Monjas. She reminded Sister Amàlia that they had left much more than a few crumbling walls of stone and a few fractured memories when they left their historic home. They had also left behind the remains of their fellow Sisters who had died in the eternal embrace of their cloister to await the hope of the Resurrection. She said the Carmelite nuns of Puerto Rico would never feel completely settled into their new life until everyone who had joined the Order from the day the convent first opened its doors in 1651 until the present day had made the sad but miraculous journey to Santurce. According to Sister María Eugenia Berrios, who spent several hours every day buried up to her eyeballs in the archives of the Order, several documents dating back to the 1600s indicated that there were four burial sites on the property. These sites contained two-hundred eighty-six Carmelite nuns and twenty-nine lay persons, but aside from names and dates in a ledger, there was little information. Sister Eugenia was not even convinced that the documents were accurate. One of the burial sites was beneath a tiny church that had been turned into a small library in the 1780s. A second was apparently beneath a small chapel that had been given the name The Chapel of Our Lady of Mercy. A third was beneath the cloisters themselves. And the last was beneath the interior patio. Of course the good Sisters were hardly the sort to wield pickaxes and shovels and push wheelbarrows about, just as they had not been the sort to remove rubble after an earthquake. So the Carmelite nuns turned to Father Correa for assistance.

Father Correa hired the three ex-poets to begin the delicate process of unearthing the deceased Carmelites and transporting whatever remained of their earthly bodies from the purgatory of their abandonment to the cemetery of Villa Palmeras.

The work began in earnest on November 8, 1909.

Coincidentally, it was on that day that the three ex-poets first laid eyes upon Tiká, who introduced herself, as you already know, as a soldier of fortune named Sebastian de Urquiza, and who, as you have probably guessed, decided to join this crew of vagabond gravediggers in their impossible (some would say absurd) quest to reunite two halves of a broken mirror.

Tiká proved to be quite adept at sifting through the rubble and locating one gallery after another, each containing a dozen or more burial niches. She was a virtuoso. The three ex-poets wondered if all soldiers of fortune could smell out death as easily, and they were suddenly somewhat afraid of their new companion, but their fear was tempered by their growing amazement at the reverence with which Tiká approached each of the deceased nuns. They had not suspected that soldiers could possess such unrestrained devotion for the dead. It seemed to be a gift of godlike, perhaps superhuman origins, a concoction of aberrant thinking, no doubt, which would have been unnerving to say the least, except that the three ex-poets, being literary men, had long ago accepted the power of the imagination to reshape reality.

It was actually quite incredible to behold. Tiká would

make the sign of the cross as she knelt down before the skeletal remains of one nun or another, and then she would stare for a while into the liquid darkness that seemed to shimmer just above each body, as if she had fallen into a deep well or was asking for forgiveness. Then the ground would tremble slightly, as if the universe itself were granting her absolution, an absolution that was seemingly conferred upon the three ex-poets as well, indeed, the three ex-poets swore that in those moments when the ground shook, they could smell the faint odor of white gardenias and the salty sweetness of the sea, a miracle which both ex-poet Rodrigo and ex-poet Victor Hugo believed was a sign of God's infinite grace. Then Tiká would climb out of her trance and the smells would vanish and she would say who it was that had been buried in that particular niche and when she had died, and the three ex-poets would write down the name and the date and any other information Tiká might provide. Then the three ex-poets would busy themselves with wrapping up the remains for transport to the cemetery, and Tiká would go on to the next burial niche.

Later, well, ex-poet Rodrigo could not help but mention the miracle of Tiká's bizarre trances to Father Correa.

'Sebastian is like a lightning rod unto God,' ex-poet Rodrigo said. 'He is like a portal to another realm,' and before Father Correa could react, ex-poet Rodrigo grabbed him by the arm, a clinging sort of half-embrace, and began to whisper as one conspirator to another, 'we cannot do this work without him, Father Correa, he is indispensable.'

So Tiká was officially hired as a day laborer by Father Correa on behalf of the Carmelite nuns.

'As long as there are bodies to be discovered, you shall have employment,' he told her. He did not say anything about her strange, fantastic ability to decipher the gleaming patterns of darkness that surrounded each corpse and so divine who they were. He did not want to know how Tiká was capable of such magic. Though he was willing to concede the existence of miracles from a distance, he was not so willing to confront one face to face. So he let it go. But before he left Tiká to her ongoing work in the crypt beneath the interior patio, he mentioned in an off-hand way that Sister Amàlia wanted to speak with her (meaning Sebastian de Urquiza), partly to express her gratitude in person for doing the work of the Immaculate Virgin, and partly because she always met with those in her employ, but also to discuss what Sister Amàlia said was a transgression of some significance, most likely committed in ignorance, but she (Sister Amàlia) wanted to ascertain that for herself. Father Correa said he would arrange the meeting.

-60-

A list of those who were buried in the first gallery in the crypt beneath the interior patio:

Sister María Rosanna Rivera (d. 1661).

Sister María Inés de Vargas (d. 1663).

Sister María Inés de Maluenda (d. 1664).

Sister María Consuelo Serrata (d. 1665)

Sister María Thérèse Serrata (d. 1665).

Sister María Florentina de Perea (d. 1666).

Sister María Concepción de Guerra (d. 1668).

Sister María Maravillas Cabrera (d. 1669).

Doña Ana de Salamanca (d. 1670), who had married Juan Ponce de León y Loáisa, the great-grandson of the famous conquistador, and was buried as a lay Carmelite because she had always admired the Carmelite Order. After her death, her husband embraced a religious life.

Sister María Luisa de Oviedo (d. 1671), who was uncertain just what to do with herself at first after learning that her husband had died on board a galleon during a naval battle between Spanish and Dutch forces off the coast of Pernambuco, Brasil, but then she realized that her husband's death did not bother her as much as she had thought it would, in fact, she suddenly felt a sense of liberty that had been denied her for oh so many years, and so she took to throwing wild even extravagant parties, the kind of parties that were common in San Juan in those days, at least among a certain portion of the populace, until one night her dead husband appeared to her in a dream, and he was not angry with her, for he understood the need to blow off a little steam as well as any man, but he did observe that she seemed to have lost her spiritual way through excessive frivolity, and then he said that if she ever hoped to pass through the Pearly Gates, a destiny that he himself had not yet achieved, then she might consider curbing her appetite, and then he suggested that she enter the new convent in San Juan, that would do the trick, and she woke up the next morning quite beside herself, for though she realized everything he had said was true, she could not quite believe he was the one to speak the words, for he had not been a religious man, and if he had said anything remotely similar while he had been alive, she would have laughed in his face, assuming that he was being sarcastic, but as he had traveled all the way from his watery grave off the coast of Brasil to the sunny shores of Puerto Rico on her behalf, she felt obligated to follow his advice, and so three weeks later she went down to the convent on Caleta de las Monjas and committed the remainder of what had been a worldly life to the service of God.

Sister María Feliche Amarjuelas (d. 1672), who descended into a life of vagrancy and prostitution after her husband was killed during a terrible hurricane which struck San Juan on September 12, 1615 (a hurricane which, incidentally, destroyed part of the roof of the Cathedral), but who was later redeemed and entered the convent in 1652.

Sister María Isabel Carrizosa (d. 1676), who entered the convent in 1661 after her husband, a Captain who was part of the garrison at Fort San Cristóbal, died of an unknown tropical disease.

Sister María Assunta Luna (d. 1679), who entered the convent in 1655 after her husband died defending a Franciscan monk in a street brawl with two Basqueros, a brawl that occurred just after midnight outside a private gambling house on Calle Guamani, where the monk was a frequent visitor.

Sister María Catalina Cerralta (d. 1680), who entered the convent in 1659 after her husband died under violent and therefore suspicious circumstances upon returning to Spain at the request of the Court of Valladolid.

Sister María Catalina Sarmiento (d. 1681), who lived the life of a lonely widow after her husband died of what was probably Yellow Fever (which he contracted while accompanying Padre Juan Alonso de Solís y Mendoza as he went around the island baptizing Indians), but later, after a great deal of soul-searching, she entered the convent in 1671 with a fully consecrated heart.

Sister María Manrique de Lara (d. 1682), who entered the convent after her husband was lost at sea in a hurricane while traveling to Mexico.

Sister María Clemencia de Girona (d. 1684).

Sister María Inés Figueroa (d. 1684).

Sister María Celestino Collazo (d. 1685).

Doña Ana de Lansos y Menéndez de Valdez (d. 1686), who, after her young husband, Pedro de Villate Escovedo, died in 1625 during the siege of San Juan by the Dutch, devoted the rest of her life in the name of God to ministering to the physical and spiritual needs of the young women of Puerto Rico, who were suffering greatly from the unending wars with France and Holland, and in 1636, at the request of the Immaculate Virgin Herself, who appeared in a halo of light one Sunday morning while doña Ana was praying in the Cathedral, she (doña Ana) asked the Spanish Crown if she could start a Carmelite convent in San Juan, and after her petition was granted, she sold all of her worldly possessions and transformed the very house that she lived in and which had been in her family since the founding of San Juan into the Monastery of Our Lady of Carmel of San José, and in July 1651, she and her sister Antonio and four novices became the first Carmelite nuns to call Puerto Rico their home.

Sister María Antonia Menéndez (d. 1687).

Sister María Isabela de Córdoba (d. 1690).

Sister María Juana de Forera (d. 1691).

Sister María Blanca Estremera (d. 1692), who entered the convent after her husband had left her to go to Chile with Alonso de Sarabia to fight the Indians and subsequently died an unheralded but doubtless heroic death on the plains of Valdivia.

Sister María Margarita Mendoza (d. 1693), who entered the convent in 1657 at the age of twenty-two after her father died of unknown causes.

Sister María Isabel Gudiel de Prado (d. 1693).

Sister María Beatriz de Luna Carrizosa (d. 1694).

Sister María Leonor de Forera (d. 1695).

Sister María Consuela de Prado (d. 1695).

Sister María Beatriz de Cárdenas (d. 1696), who entered the convent in 1674 after her husband was killed in a duel (swords, naturally) by a young nobleman who had recently arrived from Trujillo, Spain.

Sister María Blanca Ayala (d. 1697).

Sister María Teresa de Gonzalez de Oviedo (d. 1698).

Doña María Calderón de la Barca y Quijano (d. 1699), who was buried as a lay Carmelite because of her family's great sacrifice to the glory of God, having sent two sons of

Spain (older brothers to doña María) to join with Fathers Andre de Soveral and Ambrosio Francisco Ferror, and twenty-four intrepid soldiers from Portugal, on a journey to bring the Word of God to the native peoples of Brasil, a journey from which they did not return, the entire party being massacred by Indians on the 3rd of October, 1645 in the village of Uruacu.

-61-

Truly, the journey those Puerto Rican nuns took was an incredible journey. But what is more fantastic is that their history is so very fluid. You can look closely at what you think took place, only to find that you have no idea what happened at all. The sad and miraculous journey of those nuns was like that. And it still is. The passing years have transformed their simple journey of weary footsteps into something much more grand. Truly, nothing is ever what it seems to be. I know, for example, that in 1959, Barbara Hutton, the heiress to the Woolworth's fortune, bought the old convent from the Archdiocese and turned it into a fancy hotel called El Convento, but her interest in the hotel lasted only a few years and then she sold it to a Mexican hotel chain and then it was called the Gran Hotel El Convento. But what meaning lies in these simple facts? I know that the Puerto Rican government got involved at some point in the years that followed, I guess because they wanted the convent back from the Mexicans. But so what? I know that in 1995, a group of San Juan businessmen bought the property and renovated it once more and they changed the name back to El Convento. I know that these businessmen wanted a luxury casino, and the government said okay, so they (the businessmen) brought in all sorts of heavy construction equipment to begin the casino project, but at this point, the Carmelite nuns, who had moved into a brand new monastery in Trujillo Alto some years earlier, they were tired of all of the rigmarole concerning the ex-convent on Caleta de las Monjas, they wanted an injunction to stop the casino project because they said there were close to one-hundred nuns buried beneath the convent and that it would be a disgrace to their memory to build a casino on top of all those graves with all those gamblers rolling dice in the bright lights above and the floozies watching eagerly, and of course they were right about that, it would have been a disgrace, but it just goes to show that they had forgotten their own history, they found a document (a letter? a page from a diary? a bill for services? an accountant's ledger? an official statement from the bank? a note from the Bishop? a newspaper article from a now defunct newspaper?) buried away in their archives that said a partial exhumation had occurred in 1909, and they took this tidbit to be the whole truth without realizing that 1909 was simply the beginning of the delicate process of transporting the remains of two-hundred eighty-six nuns (not close to one-hundred, like they thought) and twenty-nine laypersons (which they weren't even aware of), give or take, from the boarding house that had once been a convent across town to the cemetery of Villa Palmeras, yes, yes, they had forgotten their own history, which I find highly amusing, but in truth it is the same, or will be, with all of us, so it is probably better to laugh now, if you can, yes, laughter is wonderfully cleansing, but where was I, oh yes, so at any rate, despite the best efforts of the Carmelites, they could not stop the casino project from moving forward, I think this was in 1996, and according to the newspaper account I read, a construction crew was digging up the interior patio because they were going to put in an elevator shaft for the new luxury casino, and they had only been digging for about an hour when they discovered the ancient crypt that had been there all along, and they were amazed at their discovery and wandered about the crypt for a while with flashlights, but it was still pretty hard to see clearly, so someone set up a halogen floodlight, and then they could see clearly enough, they saw an oval shaped chamber made of stone, and the stone walls were very black from age and dampness and mold, very Spanish looking, which you would expect, but they were kind of out of focus, the walls, because they were glistening in the glare of the halogen lamp, and they (whoever 'they' was, the construction workers, I guess, or the construction workers plus the reporter, the article didn't really say) saw the original underground entrance to the chamber and a narrow stone corridor on the other side, but the light from the lamp didn't carry that far so the corridor disappeared into an inky, shimmery blackness, (this was the reporter talking), as if it were a snake swallowing its own tail, and then they (the same group as before) stood in the center of the crypt and gave it one last look, a dozen heads turning on a swivel, and they counted thirty-three burial niches like the gaping wounds of Christ, all of them glistening (dripping?) with moisture and the bloody memories of another era. Every single burial niche was empty (though nine contained evidence that they had recently been the home of ferrets or weasels or other small creatures that preferred to roam about at night). That is what I know. That is what I once read. But what does any of it mean?

-62-

The meeting between Tiká and Sister María Amàlia Garrido:

On a pleasantly warm afternoon towards the end of November 1909, Tiká and Sister María Amàlia Garrido met in a small garden containing several rose bushes, a layer of Colombian Skullcap, a few coral plants with their tiny red flowers winking with lascivious delight at the sun, a saúco plant without any fruit whatsoever but laden with many clusters of white, star-like flowers, like distant galaxies seen through a telescopic lens, and a single stone bench, slightly curved, with pedestal feet, where Tiká and the good Sister Amàlia sat.

The garden was half a block from the Church of the Crab Sellers and was known to everyone in the neighborhood as the Garden of Eternal Gratitude. There was no fence or barrier of any kind to prevent a single soul from enjoying the peace and serenity offered by those colorful perennials amid the lush greenery of the tropics. It was the very same garden that the Immaculate Virgin had asked the Carmelite nuns to maintain on behalf of the hopeful, kind-hearted citizens of Santurce.

'Ah, my young and enigmatic don Sebastian de Urquiza,' said Sister Amàlia, 'you have made quite an impression on our dear Father Correa. He does not know what to make of you.'

Tiká tried to smile politely and look Sister Amàlia directly in the eyes, but all she could manage was a grimace that looked like she was suffering from a sudden wave of nausea. Her eyes became fixed on Sister Amàlia's hands, which contained a rosary, as you would expect, and a small leather book which was not a bible.

Tiká's mouth was very dry. She tried to say something, or she did say something, but her words were unintelligible to her own ears and fell noisily to the ground like pebbles. Sister Amàlia understood Tiká's meaning nevertheless.

'The good Father is descended from Ponce de León himself, as are many of us in Puerto Rico,' Sister Amàlia said. 'Perhaps all of us,' and she laughed. 'But Father Correa has not yet conquered that absorbing egotism, so deadly to others, that was so much a part of the great conquistador's personality.'

'. . . .'

'Do you see what I am driving at don Sebastian?'

Tiká did not quite see but Sister Amàlia pressed on.

'There are many soldiers of fortune wandering aimlessly about the streets of San Juan, either by their own misfortune or the design of God, but you are the first to take up residence in the ruins of our convent,' she said. And then: 'In which category do you belong?'

Sister Amàlia's voice was soothing, like honey to coat the throat, so Tiká did not realize she had been asked a direct question. Her eyes remained fixed on Sister Amàlia's hands. The good Sister was silently, methodically, but also absentmindedly, counting the beads of her rosary with her fingers. She had abandoned the small leather book to her lap.

'What I mean to say, don Sebastian, is that you are a surprise to me,' said Sister Amàlia. 'We may no longer live in that grand colonial building built to withstand Indians and hurricanes and the tropical heat, an amazing structure built by Spanish engineers years ahead in their thinking, but we are very much aware of what goes on behind its walls. And so you are very much a surprise. A puzzle.'

Then Sister Amàlia explained that the Carmelites still owned the ex-convent on Caleta de las Monjas. She said when they had left in 1903, Monsignor Blenk had suggested that they rent the building to help defray the cost of moving to San Germán. The Archdiocese took fiscal responsibility, and for close to a year the ex-convent housed several small retail shops and a barbershop and even a dance studio, but they didn't do very well and so one by one they ceased to exist. She said the building had been completely abandoned since then, and that with the departure of the Monsignor, the Carmelites had once again assumed control. Sister Amàlia said that there had been some talk of turning the building into a boarding house, but they had made no decision as yet.

Tiká said she had not known the history. She said when

she first arrived in San Juan she had met two men who had mentioned the possibility of renting a room on the third floor, a room with a balcony view of various rooftops but not much else, though they did say that she would be able to hear the Cathedral bells quite easily. Sister Amàlia wanted to know what men, what did they look like, what were their names, but Tiká did not really remember. Tiká said the two men wore dark jackets and they smelled vaguely of oleander, but she didn't remember what they looked like. They had become faceless. Sister Amàlia commented that it was odd they should smell of oleander, so much like the smell of death, and Tiká agreed.

Then Sister Amàlia asked where they had met and if they were still lurking about and what was the nature of their arrangement with Tiká, and she looked at Tiká with compassionate (hauntingly compassionate) but also piercingly determined eyes.

Tiká said they had first met in a seedy waterfront dive called Casa de las Aguas. She had been in San Juan three weeks at that point and was beginning to tire of living in one of those nameless hotels down along the waterfront (in spite of the fact that such places certainly fit the persona she had established, though she did not mention this). She knew she would soon begin looking for a quiet refuge away from the prying eyes of the world, but at that point she was not looking to move just yet. Why she had gone into Casa de las Aguas that particular evening she could not say. Perhaps she had been thirsty. She did not remember about that either. But she did remember the two men were sitting at a small table near the back of Casa de las Aguas and invited her over. They had been drinking amarettos for several hours and Tiká joined right in.

Later they took her to the house on Caleta de las Monjas and Tiká could not have been more delighted. The prayer she had not yet given voice to had been answered. She gave the two men a five-peso note on the spot with the promise of more. She told them she would place the same amount in an envelope the first Saturday of every month and put the envelope in the bottom of a small clay pot she had noticed at the bottom of the stairs leading up to the room. She had been religious in her diligence with respect to payment. Five pesos every month, a little high perhaps, San Juan was not Barcelona or New York City or even Havana, but she very much liked her third-floor room with a balcony view of various rooftops.

That was the last she had seen of the two men. Every so often an envelope would linger in the clay pot for two or three days. But always by the fourth day the pot was empty. Once she had gone back to Casa de las Aguas to thank the two men (why she thought they would be there she could not say, but her naiveté was well-intentioned), but the establishment had become a small dry goods shop. Tiká had never once considered the possibility that she was trespassing.

After Tiká had finished with her explanation, Sister Amàlia regarded her with a curious, undecipherable expression on her face. Quite without meaning to, Tiká adopted the same expression. It was almost like two mirrors staring blankly at each other, each mirror reflecting the otherness of a world that is both familiar and unattainable.

Sister Amàlia seemed on the verge of vanishing into herself.

She became a beam of sunlight bending in the wind.

'The stone which the builders rejected is become the cornerstóne,' she said.

Tiká wanted to ask Sister Amàlia what she meant by this cryptic pronouncement. (Did she often go about quoting the Scriptures? Or was there a hidden, secondary meaning in her words?) But the good Sister was now wholly preoccupied, as if she had forgotten she was sitting on the pedestal bench in the Garden of Eternal Gratitude and thought she was kneeling instead before the altar in The Chapel of Our Lady of Mercy in the Monastery of the Carmelites in the days before the Americans had arrived, immersed in thoughtful contemplation, remembering, perhaps, the very first conversation she had had with Sister María Rosalita Perea, who had taken her aside one afternoon to reprimand her for the sin of perpetual tardiness and the two nuns ended up talking for several hours about the great earthquake of 1819 and how the pain of that tragedy was still fresh, a burning memory, and so they were both late for Vespers on that day.

Then Sister Amàlia, who in that moment seemed like a crazy person to Tiká, picked up the small leather book she had left in her lap (a very musty smelling book, Tiká thought, like the kind her uncle seemed to enjoy) and looked closely at the first few pages and laughed a meaty, robust laugh, a somewhat unusual laugh for a nun. 'I had wondered why God had placed this tiny gem of a book into my hands this morning,' she said.

The book was called *Historia de la monja alférez doña Catalina de Erauso, escrita por ella misma.* It had first appeared in 1630, but whatever copies had been printed in those days had long since vanished, a subtle reminder of the transitory nature of all things. The version in Sister Amàlia's hands had been printed in Paris in 1829.

'I suspect this little book has been the source of a great deal of sparkling conversation over the years,' Sister Amàlia said. 'It is the true story of a disenchanted nun who flees her convent in Spain and travels to the New World disguised as a conquistador, if you can imagine that.'

Tiká opened the book and tried to read the first paragraph, but she could not even get past the first sentence.

She began to feel dizzy, even nauseous.

She looked up at the sky and saw a ring of spinning lights.

She felt a searing pain race across her forehead and then she seemed to be falling.

She wasn't sure if she was suffocating or going blind.

Then she heard a voice of honey floating across the void.

'Do not worry don Sebastian de Urquiza, your secrets are safe with me.'

-63-

Tiká remained in the ex-convent on Caleta de las Monjas in her third-floor room with a balcony view of various rooftops for the rest of her life. She began putting the envelopes with the five-peso notes into Sister Amàlia's hand instead of the empty clay pot, until Sister Amàlia herself said payment was no longer necessary. (It is worth noting, by the way, that the building did become a boarding house in 1917, but the Carmelites had not the heart to turn away the indigent, and so by 1923 this vestige of the colonial age was filled to overflowing with tenants without two nickels to rub together, as the saying goes, mostly young widows with scads of children or low-level government workers who could barely make ends meet even with the gift of a rent-free room or disenfranchised veterans of foreign wars who drank away their pensions without regret.)

So she became the wise old man of the boarding house

that had once been a convent. She also continued to work for the Carmelites. Long after the last of the remains of the dead nuns had been exhumed and reburied in the cemetery of Villa Palmeras, Tiká began doing odd jobs for the Carmelites in Santurce, sweeping walkways, hauling supplies, repairing windows and replacing roof tiles that had blown away during the many storms that rattled the island, and maintaining the exterior of the new convent as well as the grounds of the Garden of Eternal Gratitude.

Every nun who took refuge behind the walls of the monastery in Santurce knew the name of Sebastian de Urquiza.

There was a great deal of speculation, naturally, about why Sister Amàlia kept Tiká on the payroll. Some of the younger nuns were convinced that the two were secret lovers and that don Sebastian would stop at nothing until he had wooed the good Sister away from a life consecrated to God. The younger nuns thought Sister Amàlia's immortal soul was in danger, for they did not see how anyone could deny themselves the pleasure of don Sebastian's company. They thought Sister Amàlia would willingly and inevitably drown in a sea of licentious depravity in spite of her age. As proof, these believers in every tale of star-crossed lovers ever written would point out that every so often, especially late in the afternoon when the crushing weight of unrequited love in the tropics makes it difficult to breathe, the don could be seen lingering for a bit by the iron gate that forever separated the cloister from the rest of the world.

Others, older nuns who were past the age of menopause and had thus experienced more of the pain and suffering of this life of eternal poverty, were still awed by the otherworldly reverence the good don had shown and continued to show their deceased sisters, who were now resting comfortably in graves shaded from the sun by the leaves of jacaranda trees or laurels. They believed that don Sebastian was or would become a symbol of the transformative power of God's eternal love for us all. This, they said, is why Sister Amàlia had hired him in the first place. She had looked into the darkest recesses of his soul and seen the truth of who he was. As proof, they would remind the younger nuns that the good don Sebastian visited the cemetery of Villa Palmeras every Sunday afternoon to honor the memory of the two-hundred eighty-six Carmelite nuns and twenty-nine lay persons who had made the journey from Caleta de las Monjas. Father Correa had told them so. Father Correa had said that in spite of the internal tragedy of don Sebastian's circumstances, he had been transformed by God's all-consuming love.

What tragic circumstances, the younger nuns cried, though you could clearly see by their body language that they thought they knew the answer.

We asked the very same question of Father Correa, the older nuns said. So we will tell you. Father Correa believed that Sebastian de Urquiza had been born a man by mistake. God meant for don Sebastian to enter into His service as a Sister of the Carmelite Order. 'I do not know how don Sebastian's destiny came to be derailed even before his birth into this lamentable plane of reality,' Father Correa had said, 'but the unexpected, seemingly unnatural, even bizarre reverence don Sebastian had shown your fallen Sisters is, when you look at it through the unblemished reflecting lens of God's giant celestial telescope, simply the reverence of one sister for another. It is tragic even as it is touching.'

-64-

And so we come to the end of Tiká's story.

During the summer of 1937, Tiká became quite ill. Sister Amàlia had died in 1919, taking to her grave the secret she had glimpsed in the Garden of Eternal Gratitude so many years earlier, so it was up to Father Correa to look after the ailing don. Father Correa was in his late seventies and scarcely able to get around himself, so he arranged for a young and very excitable nurse, who worked in a small hospital in Santurce but lived nearby on Calle Fortaleza, to visit the boarding house on Caleta de las Monjas twice a day. Every morning at six and every evening at four, the excitable nurse would stop by the don's room and the two would sit out on the balcony and look at the various rooftops and the sunlight dancing on the few Spanish tiles that had not been blown away or shattered by the storms of the preceding three centuries. The excitable nurse would fix Tiká breakfasts of rice cereal and tea and late lunches of avocado soup (which had become Tiká's favorite) and water mixed with a few drops of lemon juice. Then she would read poetry while Tiká ate, mostly the poetry of Julia de Burgos, who had become very popular by 1937, though she had just turned twenty-three; but also a few neo-romantic poems by Mercedes Negrón Muñoz, poems which had been published in the newspaper, *El Mundo* (Tiká particularly enjoyed a poem called "Arras de Cristal"); and also a few unpublished poems by Colón Pellot, a poet who attacked the myth of the sexually promiscuous mulatta and so was somewhat at odds with Muñoz; and every so often she would read a few poems by Lola Rodríguez de Tío, which very much touched Tiká's withered, weakened heart. But Tiká's favorite poem during the two months of her slow but steady decline was an exceptionally musical poem called "Festival Song to Be Wept" by the poet Luis Palés Matos. When she first heard the excitable nurse read this poem she thought it was about the hypocrisy of not admitting to the forces that shaped one's destiny. But after two or three readings she began to hear a strain of something else beneath the words of the poem, something slightly satiric, but also sinister.

The poem moved her in ways she could not comprehend.

As she listened to the excitable nurse read, she thought of her shamelessly opportunistic and yet strangely idealistic lover, Nicario. She thought of her father and the dream of the white bird. She wondered what had happened to her sister, Isabel. And what had become of her daughter? Strange as it may seem, and it certainly seemed strange to Tiká, the poem reminded her of the feverish twists and turns of her own crazy life.

Only once, and this occurred just after the last rays of the sun had vanished, did she share with the excitable nurse what she thought about the poem. She interrupted the nurse midway through what might have been the seventeenth reading and said she was overwhelmed by the haunting, lyrical beauty of this poem with its swirling Afro-Caribbean undercurrents of violence and forbidden sexuality and voodoo mysticism and the eternal longing to be liberated from the tangled dreams of others.

Then the nurse continued with the poem in the darkness, reciting from memory. '*Los negros tórtolos bailan cantando salmos oscuros a Bombo, mongo de África,*' she said. Tiká sat back in her balcony chair, closed her eyes and smiled, as if she could hear the dark psalms being sung by black faces illuminated only by firelight, as if she could feel the beating of the mysterious African drums reverberating across the Atlantic.

Death came for Tiká one week later.

The excitable nurse was again reading the poetry of Luis Palés Matos. She read until the sun began to set. She was so intensely focused herself on the strange haunting beauty of the poetry and giving her oral delivery just the right mixture of indignant rage and ironic nostalgia that she did not even notice when the evening Angelus bells of the Cathedral began to ring. Then it was too dark to read without a light so she stopped, and it was only at that point that she realized don Sebastian had fallen into a sort of catatonic delirium. He was staring at the darkening sky with a strange, wild expression plastered across his face, a look of exaggerated mania mixed with the glow of sudden understanding. Only his thin bluish lips were moving. They were forming words at a fantastic rate of speed, yet there was no sound, just a gentle breeze as profound as musty earth blowing out of his mouth. The nurse could also see that the don's breathing pattern had become very shallow, so she leaned over to check for a pulse, even as she realized there was nothing she could do to forestall the inevitable. But as she leaned close, she heard the faint, hoarse whisper that was all that was left of Tiká's voice. She realized at once that the don was baring his mortal soul before God. She grabbed a pad of paper and a fancy fountain pen she kept in her purse to record the details of the don's deteriorating health (temperature, bowel movements, how much he ate while she was there, etc.) and lit a small lantern resting on a heavy mahogany table, salvaged from the halcyon days of the convent, which was set against the wrought iron balcony railing. Don Sebastian de Urquiza was sharing the secrets he had kept locked away in his heart since he had left Spain for the Caribbean oh so many years earlier, and though the excitable nurse had already missed a sizeable portion of what the don had said, she was determined to make up for her lack of vigilance and write down every single word that flew out of his mouth, however bizarre or devoid of meaning, during the few hours that were left.

The deathbed confession of don Sebastian de Urquiza as captured by the excitable nurse between 7:35 and 11:15 in the evening on July 31, 1937, one of the warmest Saturday evenings in years, but without even a hint of rain in the air, a confession which, as it turns out, was identical in every respect to the text of the long-vanished Third Note that Tiká had given her uncle:

My dearest Uncle, first let me thank you for being so patient during this most difficult trial. I did not mean to keep you in the dark for even an hour, but I let my own insecurities dictate my behavior. I told myself our need for secrecy was very great indeed. But it was really my need. I told myself that if your companion, Grenfell, had felt the tiniest pinprick of suspicion, our escape would not have gone as smoothly as it did. But I was not being entirely honest with myself, which means, my dear Uncle, that I was not being entirely honest with you.

So now the hour for secrets is past, and there are two which I must share with you before we go one step further. The first concerns my own reasons for leaving Spain. And the second, which is a tad more complicated, concerns why our good friend don Alfonso Alberto Sebastian Francisco de Hernani y Arredondo de Mariategui y de Esperanza, whose family has aligned itself with ours since the days of the Moorish conquest, has put his own reputation at risk on our behalf.

So let me begin with my first secret, why I left the only home I have ever known. My departure is the inevitable consequence of a shame I have carried with me for years, a shame which has kept me awake and vigilant for countless dark nights. And yet I have only myself to blame, in spite of what my father thought. You see in the summer of my fourteenth year, I began to take long walks with Father Mateus Antonio de Nazar of the Church of Santiago.

These walks were most assuredly innocent enough at first. He explained to me his view of the Scriptures and how they seemed to be losing relevance in an increasingly complex and materialistic modern world. He explained to me that our inability to truly know God was a consequence of this modern world. He explained to me that if we truly wanted to partake in God's bounty, we should look inward and not outward. Everything he said made sense. But what did I know? I was only fourteen. Naturally we began to share our deepest most profound desires, hopes that seemed too fantastic to ever come true. And the sharing of these desires, which had been a sharing only of the mind and the spirit up till that point, led to a sharing of our physical selves.

Yes, I knew even then how malignant and unnatural our behavior was, but I rationalized that every unseemly kiss, every intimate gesture and embrace, however pathetic or perverse to my Catholic understanding, would be seen by God as an act of pure love. I can only say now that a strange mixture of self-loathing and unrestrained lust must have filled my heart in those days. Perhaps that is what love is. I do not know. But whatever emotion I was experiencing, I know now as I suspected then that I was committing an unpardonable sin in the eyes of God.

Can you forgive me, my Uncle, for this monumental disgrace? Please, I beg of you, do not look upon me with disapprobation or reproach, for you are my last hope on this planet.

So to continue my sad, tragic tale.

As fate would have it, my father found out about my illicit liaison with Father Nazar one week ago. He was determined to murder the man on the steps of the Cathedral to show the world what becomes of priests who defile those who are untutored in the ways of men.

Fortunately, don Alfonso intervened and prevented the murder from taking place. He suggested to my father that he send me away to Barcelona and let the whole affair blow over. The don said he would take care of all the arrangements. Besides, he said, no good could possibly come of taking on the Catholic Church.

It was at this point, my dear Uncle, that I became aware of Grenfell's sinister plot, and that the two of you had booked passage on the Conde Wifredo. Do not ask me how I found out. Let me just say that I realized you were in over your head, as they say, and would need some assistance to extricate yourself, and since the don had already put into motion the deus ex machina of my own escape, it was really quite a simple matter to include you in my plans.

Naturally, the don agreed. What is more, it was don Alfonso himself who suggested that we take advantage of the soon to depart Conde Wifredo to escape Spain entirely. He said there was no telling what fallout might occur should my father forget himself and murder Father Nazar in a last desperate act of revenge. If Father Nazar were murdered, then surely all of the details of our sordid love affair would be revealed during the course of the thorough investigation the Church would initiate, and I myself would most likely be charged as a libertine accomplice and hanged alongside my father. Then he said the fact that the boat you and Grenfell had chosen was the Conde Wifredo was a sign the hand of destiny was guiding events, for he (the don) personally knew the Captain, a seafaring cutpurse named Ramón Martín Cordero. So that is why don Alfonso purchased a stateroom for us on the Conde Wifredo. He was in fact quite delighted with himself.

Of course just because don Alfonso knows the Captain of our ship does not mean our journey will be without peril. We should not put too much faith in any but ourselves. Don Alfonso said Captain Cordero was a born sailor, but he was also an unscrupulous rogue of a man who would sell his own grandmother without regret.

When I asked him how he knew this, he smiled his lazy smile of a man who sits atop a mountain of wealth and said the Captain had been arrested by the authorities in Barcelona in 1892 for making indecent advances towards a young very wealthy widow whose family was distantly related to don Alfonso's wife.

The don said the woman wished to keep the details of the offending behavior from being disclosed in a trial, for then the whole affair would become a matter of public record, so she had asked don Alfonso to seek a more genial solution. I do not know what magic the good don had at his disposal, but apparently he went directly to the examining magistrate in Barcelona and within three hours he was able to secure for Captain Cordero a provisional release from jail so he could return to work for the Naviera Pinillos shipping company as the Captain of the Conde Wifredo, a position which he had recently acquired and for which, also apparently, no other seafaring man of good (or even decent) reputation and family background could be found.

'Better the devil you know, as they say, than the devil you don't know,' which is what don Alfonso said after he told me this tale.

Then he said he would wire ahead to alert Captain Cordero that we would be among his passengers and that we were traveling 'incognito,' as it were, a little subterfuge on don Alfonso's part. He said it is best to let the Captain think one thing and not another. The don has also asked me to tell you that in dealing with the Captain, one must always be cognizant of the fact that his good will almost always fluctuates in relation to the weight of his purse, which is a roundabout way of saying that he will respond to our requests with dramatically admirable speed as long as we pay him a sufficient amount in advance for his services. The don suggests that we allocate no more than five of the gold coins he has put into our hands to purchase the temporary loyalty of Captain Cordero. He says that should be more than enough.

Do you wish I had kept this secret to myself, my dearest Uncle? Can you appreciate why I offered it up to you, on the sacrificial altar of Abraham, if you will, so that we might journey to paradise unencumbered by the past? But before you answer in the affirmative, permit me to share with you my second secret, which is not a secret which belongs to me alone, no, that would be too much for a single soul to bear. It is a family secret that was only revealed to me this past week by none other than don Alfonso (and how don Alfonso came to be in possession of this secret is part of this tale). It is a secret that speaks to the sanctity of marriage and the purity of true love. Moreover, it is a secret that has been hidden all these years, even from you, my dearest Uncle, and perhaps even from my father, though don Alfonso believes in his heart of hearts that my father has suspected all along. Keep in mind that these are not my words. I am simply playing the role of literary amanuensis to capture the voice of the good don himself.

> *'Ah, yes,' said the don, to tell this tale the way it should be told, I must go back to the days before Arturo married your mother. Your mother's family came from Albacete, a city famous for its daggers, as everyone knows. Indeed, there are no daggers more famous for their bejeweled handles in all the world, with the possible exception of those created by the hand of the great Turkish artisan, Nikola Siyavus Hayreddin Yilmaz, but that is beside the point. Verona's family was of some stature in Albacete, not*

quite aristocrats, but they had a fashionable address near the Plaza de Toros, or so I was once informed. But I am not certain of this. And my father was certainly not certain. He thought they were gypsies, or dealers in stolen artwork. Perhaps they were.

'My father said they came to Logroño in 1860 in a dilapidated barouche drawn by two diseased chestnuts and then moved into a small second-floor apartment on Calle del Laurel with a vacant shop beneath. They certainly did not seem to be aristocrats. But according to my skeptical father, they arrived with the most tremendous collection of paintings one could imagine in their possession, though again, my father thought the paintings were either stolen or they were clever forgeries. There were some very large paintings by Madrazo, both the father and the eccentric son, and Goya's friend, Brugada, and a few early sketches by Marià Fortuny that had been part of a show in Madrid, and a forgotten painting by José Villegas Cordero from when he was just starting out, and several minor works by Casado and a copy of The Resurrection of Lazarus done in Casado's own hand, and there were dozens of smaller paintings by Pozo and Cancino and Carnicero and Montalvo and a host of others who are now only remembered by historians and aficionados. Verona's father had also acquired a fabulous painting in 1875 by the French painter Jean-Paul Laurens titled "The Excommunication of Robert the Pious," a king of ancient France whose piety was well-known but who gave up the hope of the Resurrection to marry his cousin Bertha.

'So the vacant shop beneath their apartment became an art shop and art lovers from as far away as Zaragoza and Madrid came to peruse the canvasses. And so it went. Canvasses arrived and canvasses were sold. Miguel Ramos Almeida developed a reputation as a ruthless dictator when it came to pricing art, and for more than a decade, life was as predictable as clockwork. Even the birth of Verona in 1862 did little to change this pattern. But in the summer of 1876, the pattern did change as if by divine decree. Verona, who had just turned fourteen, began working

in the art shop. She was a clerk, a salesgirl, the only daughter of the owner, but she dazzled the eye more than any of the paintings, and as word of her great beauty got around, the art-lovers who had before come only to buy paintings came now just to catch a glimpse of Verona's smile, for she was always smiling a smile of honey-colored light.

'In truth, her smile sold more paintings than the paintings themselves. Yet it is impossible to describe how beautiful your mother was. Have you looked carefully at those enchanting portraits of her done by Joaquín Sorolla, a present from Arturo in honor of her twenty-fifth birthday. They are breathtaking, everyone says so, full of mystery and a sense of wistful playfulness and a haunting, melancholic vulnerability and yes, even magic. But they do not come close to capturing your mother's beauty. The truth of your mother's beauty is impenetrable. Sorolla's paintings, fabulous and mythic as they are, are but shadows of a half-remembered dream. Oh, where is the wine of those vanished days? Such sweet, sweet memories.

'But please forgive the foolish ramblings of an old man. I loved your mother dearly. Let me just say in my defense that it is a terrible tragedy to look back on a life lived with so much unrewarded enthusiasm, the push and pull of disastrous dichotomies. So naturally I do what anyone would do. I look back with nostalgia to that precipice of a moment before my hopes were fractured.

As you might have guessed, there was a great deal of competition that summer among the boys of Logroño for your mother's attention. If she happened to look your way you counted yourself lucky. If she smiled at you in passing, you believed yourself blessed beyond any reward the priests could promise. And if, miracle of miracles, she happened to speak to you, well, that was too fantastic a possibility to even contemplate. But none of us could predict how she would respond. We became insufferably ludicrous shadows of our favorite Greek heroes. We forgot that we were sons of Spain, and in forgetting we became more ourselves than ever before or since. We were wrapped up in the catastrophe of cold lightning.

'I remember some of the boys brought her baskets of fish they had caught themselves, baskets of black fish and pike and perch and eels, all quite delicious, but she preferred chicken, Catalan style, with sausage and capers and raisins and wild herbs. A few wrote her long, desperate letters which she never opened because they were intercepted by her father, who then tossed them into the nearest roaring fire. Others would try to demonstrate their athletic skill by inviting Verona to that point along the Ebro where the old Puente de Piedra bridge had existed before it collapsed, and these lunatic daredevils would jump into the dark, placid but all-consuming waters and swim to the other side, weaving this way and that way to avoid the rubble that still blocked parts of the river, and when they had reached the opposite bank they would return as quickly as they could in the hope that she might offer them a handkerchief, a laurel to be paraded about as a symbol of their victory, but always by then Verona had lost interest and abandoned them to an empty afternoon.

'Still others tried to impress her as connoisseurs of music. Every Saturday afternoon she received an elderly maestro for a piano lesson held in the back storeroom of the art shop amongst stacks of canvasses that had not yet been prepared for sale. The piano was one of those gilded, gold-frame affairs with miniature pastoral scenes painted on the panels. It was pushed up against a small oval window, blocking all sunlight. There was a cracked and weather-beaten back door on one side of the piano and a narrow dining room chair on the other. Every Saturday at precisely one o'clock, the elderly maestro would appear with his viola, sit down in the chair and play a squeaky tune on his out-of-tune instrument, and then he would sit back, exhausted from performing, his face glowing with the expectation that Verona would now be able to produce a flawless rendition of the melody after only a single hearing. Of course by then the many adolescent musical connoisseurs of

Logroño had gathered in the alleyway dust beneath the storeroom window to dream of Verona's matchless beauty while she played, though on many an occasion they forgot themselves and started playing dice or wrestling with each other, and they would create such an ungodly and combative commotion that the elderly maestro would appear in the doorway like a calamitous wind or a deranged bishop roused from a deep sleep and chase away the dried leaves of their ardor with his precisely aimed bow. Each of those boys, I suppose, thought he was Odysseus trying to wrest free his beloved Penelope from the horde of suitors that had gathered like anarchists on her doorstep. I know that is what I would have thought. My imagination ached with bloodthirsty images. Ah, the stupidity of youth!

'By the next summer, attrition had taken its toll. To be blunt, there were only two competitors left who stood a chance with this angel from another dimension, myself, and Arturo. We had not approached this adolescent game of love in quite the same way as the others. Instead of chasing after Verona with proof of our passionate intentions, we hung around the shop, sniffing at this painting or that one, feigning an interest in art. But even then we did not speak directly to Verona. We spoke to her father. So by the end of that first year we had acquired a genuine and knowledgeable appreciation for the Spanish masters and were thus able to hold our own in a heated discussion with Verona's father about whether or not Pozo was better than Cancino and whether or not Carnicero was better than both of them, and before we quite realized what had happened, Verona herself was laughing at our untutored naiveté or applauding our inventive, rebellious spirit.

'So it was Arturo and I. All the other boys, your uncle Andres included, if you want to know the absolute truth, who was decidedly younger but smitten nonetheless, all of them had tasted the bitter dust of defeat. Arturo and I felt that we had taken a step towards manhood. But I think what is more

significant, at least looking back, is that at the end of that year, Arturo and I also swore to each other that no matter what happened in our heroic pursuit to win the hand of Verona, no matter which one of us should triumph, we would always hold one another in the greatest of esteem, as was befitting the sons of two families that had been aligned for centuries.

'I have to say now that I always felt in the depths of my soul that I was Verona's first choice. I mean no disrespect to Arturo, he is, after all, my truest friend. But in those days I was a dazzling white knight in the chess game of love, which is to say I was ready to take advantage of any opportunity that came my way, and lo and behold, towards the end of that second summer of our pursuit by non-pursuit, an opportunity presented itself. In late August, as he did every August, Arturo's father headed to the monastery of San Andrés de Trepeana to pick up several barrels of the best wine made in all of La Rioja. Always Arturo's father had made this journey alone, but on this occasion, he took Arturo with him. I could hardly believe my luck. I suspected my future good fortune and happiness lay in Arturo's unexpected departure. I did not waste a moment. The journey to the monastery and back could be accomplished in as little as three or four days, though it would most likely take a full week.

'The art shop featured a storefront window where Verona's father would display paintings he had recently acquired. Beneath the window there was a narrow flower box overflowing with geraniums. Verona would water the geraniums every morning. During that second summer I had taken the bold though predictable step of leaving small notes for Verona in the box. If she spied such a note while watering she would pluck it out with insistent finality, punctuated by a flashing grimace of frustration instead of her honey-colored smile, as if she had discovered a dead mouse (or a not-quite dead mouse, though to be fair, your mother was not particularly squeamish) among the fallen blossoms, but then she would quickly slip the note into her

apron pocket.

'When I first beheld that grimace my heart sank, but when she slipped that first note into her pocket and ran back into the shop, I knew that her grimace was a pose so that anyone watching would not guess her true feelings. So I continued leaving her notes. She never spoke about the notes, but I am certain that her heart hummed with anticipation when she saw one among the flowers.

'So the day Arturo left, I left a note in the geranium box. I did not know what romantic magic I might conjure with words, so I did not even try. I simply wrote: "Our friend Arturo has left with his father. They will be gone a few days. I have little to do this afternoon. If you are looking for me I will be wandering through the green labyrinth of Parque del Espolón. Do you think it will rain? That would be appropriate. Perhaps I will stop a while and watch the stone masons working on the monument to honor Espartero. The masons are exceedingly rough looking men. I am not sure they would even notice a thunderstorm."

'An hour later Verona and I were strolling along Paseo del Espolón, lingering in the sweet shadows of the maple trees and a gentle, warm breeze tickling our secret desires, but only tickling. We did not speak of love or paintings or anything that would have ignited the spark of our passions. We spoke instead of Arturo's absence and this strange habit he had of whistling when he was nervous, and why did Arturo reject all visible proof of God's existence, this attitude really seemed to bother Verona on that day, he had been raised in a devout Catholic family as were all the rest of us, where did such aberrant thinking come from, was he possessed by some vagabond genie, a demon spirit that had escaped the destruction of the Moors, wasn't there anything I could do, I was his best friend, did I not see what was happening, did I not see that a great change had come over him, a dark, foreboding shadow like the sky before a thunderstorm (not the storm I had imagined), a sky tinged with green, she had said, she had begun to fear

for the survival of his very soul, and on and on and on she went.

'The next day I left a second note and we found ourselves in the Plaza de San Bernabé. We walked back and forth past the arcaded shops for a while, and then we sat on a park bench in the shade of a few laurels, and next to us there were a few vendors hiding inside their tents. And then we were walking again, but our conversation that day was the same as the one the day before.

'The next day I left another note, and the day after that and the day after that. We walked along the remnants of the old wall and we passed through the Puerta del Camino and we sat in the shadow of the old artillery tower and the rattling echo of those ancient Spanish cannons of death and we listened to the birds singing their dream songs in the trees. We paraded past cathedrals and churches lost in the swirling wake of the old women perpetually in search of an unlocked church door, but we never once thought to go inside ourselves and pray for God's forgiveness and so partake in the dark mysteries of eternal illumination. But everywhere we went we had the same conversation.

'I must confess that by the seventh day of Arturo's absence, I had lost all but the faintest of hopes that Verona would be mine. I do not remember even leaving her a note on that seventh day. All I remember is walking along the gleaming waters of the Ebro, lost in the labyrinth of my own disfiguring despair, wondering how the ghost of Arturo could so completely occupy Verona's mind. Then I was sitting on a bench somewhere, and I heard Verona's voice floating effortlessly across the void. Then I realized she was sitting right next to me. She was resting her head on my shoulder and whispering or sighing or singing softly into my lonely ear.

'At first I took her for an apparition, and I said so in a voice as flimsy as the net of street names and sunny days and lost keys and newspapers we use to wrap our bodies in a second skin in the hope that it will carry us to the shores of paradise, but she just

laughed, and suddenly the honey-colored light of her smile outshone the sun with a ferocious intensity that made me tremble, and I looked up at the sky and was momentarily blinded. Then quite without warning, the church bells all over this little city of my tremulous youth began ringing and the sky was filled with so many dazzling white storks that I could not help thinking (for I was quite superstitious in those days) that surely God was sending me an incontrovertible sign that Verona and I were meant to walk the path of destiny together, and then without reflecting for a moment about what I might say, I started babbling about the storks, I don't know what I said exactly, I was incoherent, I did not possess a scientific mind by any stretch, what did I know of the storks except they filled the sky when the church bells began to ring, but Verona was listening intently to every word I said, yes, the sewer of my stupidity was overflowing, but Verona did not mind, she enfolded me in the honey-colored light of her smile, and when I had finished she kissed me lightly on the cheek and said that no matter what happened, whatever choice she might make or whether her destiny would unfold without her consent, she would always love me for the irresistible, dreamy sweetness that lay hidden several layers deep behind a mask of rigid, calculating, self-indulgent posturing, a mask I no doubt wore because of my family's enviable social position, a mask which she hoped I might one day remove.

'Was Verona, your mother, my one and only love? I will never think or feel otherwise. But the fates that look upon us with whimsical disdain decreed otherwise. In my case, fate took the form of my father. One week after Arturo had returned, my father casually informed me that as far as he was concerned, my childhood had come to an end that very summer and so I should discard all of my childhood infatuations and prepare for the business of life. And if that were not clear enough, he looked at me point blank with his darkly gleaming emotionless eyes — it seemed to me that I was staring at Death himself — and he said I was no longer to wander

the streets of Logroño with Verona Almeida Vda de Miranda in search of love. He would not, he said, permit me to cavort with gypsies, however beautiful or mesmerizing. And that was that.

'I suspect now that during the single week Verona and I lingered on the lip of eternity, just the two of us, I suspect that Verona had somehow glimpsed the terrible tragedy that would befall our love. She understood better than I the forces that would shape my life. She realized from day one that my father would never allow me to carve out any happiness for myself. I was a prisoner of my family's history, a prisoner of all history. That is why Verona turned every conversation towards the absent Arturo. That is what I believe. And in support of this belief I offer you a summary of the final act of my Shakespearean tale of woe.

'Arturo Ordóñez Escoraz and Verona Almeida Vda De Miranda were married in the Church of Santiago on Saturday the 8th of December in 1877, one of the few days on the Christian calendar that wasn't dedicated to a saint, though it was on that date in 1854 that Pope Pius IX declared the Immaculate Conception a dogma of the Church.

'The wedding arrived with calamitous speed.

'It was as if a great tornado had descended upon Logroño.

'The banns were posted only once. On November 22nd, the feast day of Saint Cecilia the incorruptible, an old priest stood outside the church and announced to those strolling past that a wedding would take place in sixteen days.

'No invitations were sent, but everyone knew the whole town was invited.

'One week before the wedding I purchased a costume for the affair. I pretended I was the one getting married, not Arturo.

'The wedding went off without a hitch.

'Arturo was eighteen and Verona was fifteen, perfect ages for starting out together.

'Six months later, your sister, Isabel, was born.

'I went to Barcelona after that.

I was not happy. My father sent me as an emissary on behalf of his business interests.

'I stayed in Barcelona for three years.

'I did not write to Arturo while I was away, but I missed our friendship, so I went to pay him a visit when I returned.

'Arturo was away for some unknown reason, but Verona invited me in. We sat in the library and she played the same gold-frame, gilded piano that had sat in her father's storeroom for so many years. She said it was a gilded art-case Bechstein grand piano, a very famous piano that had come all the way from Berlin. I don't remember what tune she played, but I do remember I forgot myself while she played. I was transported back to my childhood, to the dust-filled alleyway behind the art shop, an unfractured moment when anything and everything was still possible.

'It was dark when she finished playing. She did not say anything for a moment. She looked at me from the piano bench and the honey-colored light of her smile lit up the room. Then she said she was terribly sorry things had turned out the way they had. She spoke with deliberate, unwavering forethought, as if she had been rehearsing this single line for years. She seemed sincere, but not weepy or sentimental. Then she asked me if I had considered removing my mask. The rest is like a dream. I remember we went upstairs. I remember dozens of various sitting rooms and bedrooms, but this could not have been the case. The house was not that large. I also seem to remember that all of the rooms were locked, but Verona held a key in her hand. I followed her as she went from room to room, unlocking the doors, lighting small table lanterns and then opening the windows to let an insufferably humid breeze swirl about, the white lace curtains billowing, the lantern light flickering. But the last room was not locked and the window was already open and she did not light the lantern. She took me by the hand and led me to a narrow sea chest of a bed. It was hard to say how old the bed was. I remember thinking it was from the sixteenth century. Then we lay down

in the dark and she began whispering softly, her lips grazing my cheek, her words all but unintelligible to my wondering ears for she spoke in the language of flowers or fish, or perhaps she was singing a lullaby her mother had once sung, or perhaps she was sighing one last sigh of eternal regret.

'Verona and I were never again alone together in the same room. Whenever I paid Arturo a visit on a Thursday or a Sunday afternoon, Verona would mysteriously vanish, though I suspect she had gone no further than her own kitchen to sift through her collection of tiny opaque bottles, which contained rare herbal extracts from all over the world. I suspect she was searching for something, anything she hadn't tried before, to cure the inflammation of an aching heart, but nothing ever worked.

'I have never spoken of that evening in all these years, and I am certain beyond any expressible doubt that Verona kept her tongue as well. All the same, I suspect Arturo knew, as all husbands and wives know when something is amiss. Occasionally, even now, I wake up in the middle of the night, my bed clothes soiled with the sweat of my own stupidity and guilt, convinced that Arturo is trumpeting the truth to the world. Then I take a few short, furtive breaths, the kind a small hunted animal might take when a predator is nearby. Then I get up and head to a small table opposite my bed and fortify myself against the long night with a shot of Demerara rum imported from Venezuela, a habit I had acquired in Barcelona. Then again, perhaps I am mistaken about everything. Perhaps I imagined the two of us lying together in that forgotten sixteenth century bed. Perhaps I imagined those odd moments years later when I would catch Arturo looking at me in a certain way, a haunting mixture of disbelief and vanity that quickly, inevitably, one might say, hardened into a mask of denial and impenetrable silence. Such is the way of things. But no matter which of my memories is now open to dispute, no matter which truths I have forgotten and which I have invented, I can say with the unshakable pride of one who has seen the darkness

of the abyss and lived to tell the tale, that almost nine months to the day after I had returned from Barcelona in the spring of 1881, your mother gave birth to a second child . . .

It was at that point, a point which to the ears of the excitable nurse was a stunning but inconclusive climax, that the death bed confession of don Sebastian de Urquiza ended because don Sebastian had given up the ghost, as they say. It was a peaceful death, a gentle but inevitable receding of the tide. But for the excitable nurse the death of don Sebastian had come too soon. She stared at the thin, blue, now unmoving lips for a moment, dumbfounded, even disoriented. Was the second child don Sebastian? Is that why don Alfonso purchased a stateroom aboard the *Conde Wifredo*? Or was the second child simply a half-brother or half-sister to don Sebastian, in which case the inspiration for don Alfonso's generosity was still a mystery. Or was the story of Verona simply a fabrication of the lovesick mind of don Alfonso? Or was it instead a by-product of don Sebastian's addled brain as he neared the deep waters of death? But if don Alfonso's account was true, in both the historical details and the pervasive almost unbearable sense of emotional loss, well, how could Arturo have remained silent if his wife had loved another man and had taken that man to bed? Who could stomach the agony of such knowledge? Indeed, did Arturo really know the truth? How could he know the truth and still wish to murder Father Nazar for defiling a child that was not even his to begin with? And what had become of the execrable Father Nazar anyway? How could Arturo and don Alfonso consecrate themselves to the purity of their friendship after all that had happened?

The excitable nurse read over what she had transcribed again and again, but each reading exposed even more unanswerable questions. She tossed the pad of paper to the floor, disgusted with her inability to penetrate the elusive mysteries of this deathbed confession, and stared at the corpse of don Sebastian. In the dim flickering light of the lantern it seemed as if the don had simply fallen asleep and was now on the verge of waking up. But of course this did not happen. The excitable nurse found herself irrevocably drawn to the face of the corpse and began assessing its features with greater discernment. The thin blue lips seemed strangely feminine, as did the aquiline shape of the nose. Then she noticed the rounded slope of the shoulders and the slender arms and the delicate hands (at least when compared to the hands of the many drunken ex-soldiers that had tried to take advantage of this dedicated nurse on a Saturday night). Suddenly don Sebastian's hands seemed incapable of wielding anything more deadly than a hymnal or rosary beads wrapped between his fingers. The excitable nurse wondered that she had not noticed any of this before. She wondered if the don had undergone a transformation of some sort in death. Then she recalled the brief conversation she and Father Correa had had when he first spoke to her about playing nursemaid to a dying revolutionary. 'You will find don Sebastian a compassionate, amiable fellow, hardly the gruff, clichéd, explosively violent sort one usually thinks of when one thinks of an ex-soldier, and there is a deep sadness about him as well, a sense that his life was a tragedy that could not be averted, like falling into an ancient well,' Father Correa had said. 'What happened to him?' she had asked. 'I do not know precisely. This pervading sense of sadness is a common enough affliction among those who have seen war,' he had said, and then his eyes had narrowed, 'but there is something else as well,' and then his voice had become almost inaudible, a whisper from beyond the grave, 'I have said this again and again. I truly believe that God meant for don Sebastian to enter into His service as a Sister of the Carmelite Order. That is why the don has worked these last twenty-eight years on behalf of the good Sisters. I think don Sebastian was praying for the miracle of God's transforming grace. I think he wanted the whole world to see him as he truly was.'

And in that instant, the excitable nurse felt a pricking sensation on the back of her neck and she knew without any doubt whatsoever that the lingering spirit of the don was standing directly behind her, a being of pure energy like a Manichean beam of light, and she was unnerved by this sensation and screamed like a strangled bird, and then she gathered up the confession and the fountain pen and the rest of her belongings and fled, still screaming, from the balcony; and the ghost of don Sebastian de Urquiza, who had in fact been standing behind the excitable nurse for quite a while before she had sensed his presence, remained on the balcony which had become a portal to another dimension, a mute though interested witness whose heart went out to this startled good Samaritan stumbling about in the darkness of the apartment, cursing under her breath at the apparent lack of a telephone in this rundown boarding house on Caleta de las Monjas and then bolting through the door, still screaming as she ran down the two flights of stairs and out into the darkness of the street, still apparently bewildered by the lack of telephones, for she wanted to call Father Correa that very instant and tell him that don Sebastian de Urquiza had died but that his ghost was a terror to behold and that somebody should come and do something quick, never mind the fact that there were very few telephones in that part of San Juan in 1937, and that if the excitable nurse was, say, in her own apartment on Calle Fortaleza and suddenly wished to place a call, she had to go all the way down to the drugstore on Calle Recinto Sur, which is where everyone went in that part of town who wished to use a telephone.

BOOK FIVE

in the shadow of Hotel Milagro

-65-

Oscar Garcia Raimundi was a lonely young man with a restless, lunatic spirit who dreamed of one day opening a bohemian night club to rival the great dance clubs of Havana during the Mafia days. But Oscar was not interested in the glitzy, high-profile Mafia-owned cabarets and touristy clubs with their palatial extravagance for the movie stars or politicians or socialites from America and their cash cow casinos for gamblers from the East Coast or the West Coast or businessmen from Chicago or Indianapolis or St. Louis who had flown in on a whim on Pan American. He wanted to open a club like the clubs he had frequented when he first arrived in Havana, the ones where you could find the real Cuba, like the Palermo Club (always with a nineteen-piece orchestra so you felt like you were floating in the clouds when you were dancing) or the Rio Cristal Club or the Jungle Club in Pogolotti or Jiggs Cabaret and Nightclub on the waterfront, or Oscar's favorite, the sultry La Campana on the corner of Calzada de Infanta y San Martin.

The first time he ever went to La Campana, which was the first time he had been anywhere, was burned into his brain the way a tattoo is burned into the skin, which is to say that over time the edges had become blurry, indistinct, the ink had faded, and yet even until the day he died he could still feel the thrill of his beating heart on that night, an adrenalin rush like a midnight hurricane, like fifteen foot waves obliterating the beach, like falling in love for the first time, the shrill sound of the women's alto voices shape shifting in the steamy night air, becoming huskier, rounder, fuller, like a melody, like many melodies, their laughter becoming boleros and Portuguese fados and rumbas and sambas and mambos (the forerunner of the cha-cha-chá), and nimble-fingered, buoyant guarachas like sun-bright streams flowing fast from the Sierra Maestra mountains, flooding the valleys below, and a few folksy, back country Puerto Rican plenas, and a few tangos all the way from the cobblestone streets of San Telmo, the oldest neighborhood of Buenos Aires, hips already beginning to gyrate slowly, legs swiveling around legs, eager, unrestrained, sexy, passionate, because everyone in Havana was always looking for a place to dance until the sun came up, everyone was hungry to dance, and this dream of dancing through the night, a frenzy of bohemian lust, a madness wild as the sea that gives birth to the future, the feverish sounds of the black nightingales hidden in the waxy leaves of the tamarind trees, this was Oscar's first and only true love, it was his reason for living, it was the joy and burden of his restless soul.

Everything else bored him to tears.

Everything else was blasphemy.

Everything else was a cheat.

But mention night clubs and dancing and a jungle paradise under the stars and his eyes lit up like glittering diamonds.

That first night at La Campana, Oscar was only fourteen years old, or maybe he was nineteen, or maybe twenty-six, because no one ever knew for certain how old he was. When Oscar immigrated to Florida in 1957 he said he was thirty years old, but ten years later when he was running his own version of a bohemian night club between NW 35th Street and NW 31st Street in Miami, he said he was thirty-five, and ten years after that, when he married Isidora Escoraz Calzada in a secret ceremony at ten in the morning, he said he was fifty-seven, and he gave other ages at various times as well, but not to deceive, there was no thought of deception in his mind, no sinister intention, he simply could not remember.

The truth about Oscar's age belonged to a vanished world, a world of fragmented memories and half-remembered dreams like evaporating phantoms. All anyone really knew about Oscar was that he came from the other side of the island, from Baracoa, but rarely did he mention even a morsel about his family. It was as if they no longer existed and perhaps had never existed. Perhaps Oscar had left Baracoa because his uncle had died and what else was he going to do. Or perhaps his uncle had given him a little money, enough for the passage to Havana and a couple of nights to get settled, and his uncle had told him to get out while he could, before he became trapped like his uncle was trapped in a world where time no longer marched forward. Or perhaps his uncle had been arrested and was rotting in jail with only the saltwater smell of the sea floating in through the bars to let him know he was still alive. Or perhaps his uncle had gone up into the mountains in search of gold. Or maybe he had even boarded a steamer bound for Patagonia. Who knew? And who really cared? None of it mattered any more. The past. Oscar no longer cared about the past. He only cared about the future. He had some control over that, like writing his own destiny, and for Oscar the path to that destiny began on a steamy summer night in 1946 when to all discerning eyes he had barely outstripped puberty. On that particular night he stood in the shadows of a tamarind tree outside La Campana for over an hour watching the men and women streaming past, eager to dance to the honey-coated syncopated sound of Orlando Vallejo with a few muted trumpets in the background, or the sweeping, husky sensual squeal of Mayra Freire, who used to wave her arms in the air with balletic precision when she was on stage, or any number of Cuban singers and musicians hovering with delicate hope on the periphery of international fame, the men wearing tuxedos and black ties or white silk dinner jackets and white ties and their hair was slicked back on the sides like Rudy Valentino (this was just before the pompadour became big) and they wore boaters or sleek rimmed Panamas, the kind Humphrey Bogart would wear, and the women wore silk or chiffon dresses, some with ruffles, butterfly sleeves, a little outdated, and some wore bell hats or their hair was curled into a ball on one side. The men smelled of cigar smoke and cheap rum or leather soap or maybe Grant's Whiskey, and the women smelled of vanilla spice or Bergamot oranges and oakmoss or gardenias or lavender or peach. Oscar almost passed out from the heat of standing there in the shadows of the tamarind tree and the heady cloud of all those fragrances mixed together, all of the men and women chatting and laughing as they ran up the steps and rang the bell outside, ring the bell at La Campana from 9 till 4, that was the advertising all over the city on billboards and in the newspapers and even painted on the sides of grocery marts or drugstores, when in Havana ring the bell at La Campana, and there was a little cartoon bell with a smiling face and a dinner platter in one hand, a cocktail in the other, and he (the cartoon bell) was giving you an exaggerated wink, as if he had just told you a juicy, sexual tidbit about someone you both knew, and there was a single palm tree in the background to remind you that this was Havana, Cuba, the jewel of the Caribbean, the portal to the new world, the very definition of paradise in the modern industrial age, and there weren't any stars in these advertisements plastered all over the city, perhaps because it would have been too expensive to add stars, or too time consuming, or perhaps because they weren't necessary, you knew they were there without drawing them, you could feel them.

In all probability, Oscar would not have found the courage to duck inside this first cabaret of his imagination had not a masculine voice like a steam ship called out to him from a passing bevy of womanly legs. Perhaps they were showgirls. Hurry boy, the voice said, there are plenty of legs to keep you snug and warm, to tease the life out of you, to squeeze you dry, and then a twittering of female laughter billowing out like white smoke, and he had scrambled to join them.

"Are you following someone or is someone following you?" said the masculine voice.

"I am following you," said Oscar.

"Hah," cried the masculine voice. "Did you hear that ladies?"

"Yes, Luis," cried the bevy.

"The boy has wit!"

And then some girlish laughter.

Once inside Oscar forgot about Luis and the showgirls. Heart pounding, he ordered a bottle of beer and drank it quickly. Someone tossed him a pack of cigarettes, a pack of Regalias, and he smoked two or three in quick succession, though he preferred La Coronas. Hours later he was sitting at the bar, half a bottle of Ron Bocoy beneath his nose and the vapors of the dark rum rising up like island gods, an empty tumbler waiting to be refilled. He remembered he had been talking with one of Luis' showgirls between numbers, a long-legged black African with smooth ebony skin, skinny dark legs like an ibis, and a nose like an Egyptian queen. Her name was Nerea. For some reason their conversation had drifted to her parents, descendants of African slaves who were brought to Cuba near the end of the 18th century to work the copper mines in the east and whose grandchildren were freed in the 19th century and called *cobreros* but still worked in the mines, and after that the great-great-grandchildren of the grandchildren (her parents) lived on the edge of oblivion between the murderous, sulphurous darkness of the past and the cloudy skies of the future, but they had moved inland and now lived in a small village, Ojo de Agua, in Las Villas, where the sky was always a deep watery blue like the eyes of God according to some, and the springs surrounding the village had strange medicinal properties that some said had been known since before the Conquistadors and which cured every ailment from gallstones to malaria, and which in some cases even extended the natural lifespan of a man (or a woman) by thirty years or more, but Nerea said she didn't believe in all that superstitious mumbo-jumbo, her parents worked in the cane fields north of there and life didn't seem any easier for them because of the water from the springs. But then Nerea also admitted she hadn't seen her parents in years, she didn't even know if they were still alive. It was easy to forget where you came from living in Havana, she said. Then they were talking about Oscar's parents, who had died when he was very young and so he had been raised by a bachelor uncle in Baracoa in a small concrete house that looked out at the sea, but Oscar said very little about his family. All he really remembered about Baracoa, he said, were the women washing clothes in the river. Even when their husbands bought them Bendix washing machines to ease their burden, they washed their clothes in the river. Perhaps because electricity was an intermittent novelty in Baracoa, even in the 1940s, and especially in the neighborhoods that stretched out towards the sea. Or perhaps electricity was simply a myth, something his uncle prattled on about but which did not yet exist, at least not in Baracoa during Oscar's childhood, because there were no roads to Baracoa at that time, it was cut off by the mountains, so how could electricity have made its way from the rest of the island when not even a road could get through? Yes, this is how it was living in Baracoa. This is what Oscar told the ebony skinned showgirl, whose name was Nerea and who with her flowing, white-feather dress and her headpiece of a shining golden sun like a halo and her thick curly black hair flowing to either side with a single blood-red gardenia pinned above her right ear suddenly reminded Oscar of the island goddess Atabey, the Mother of all the Caribbean gods and goddesses from the days of the first Indians, who was known by many names, including Apito, Mamona, Guimazoa, and Ieamaye, which sounded very much like the Orisha Yemaya, a goddess of Africa who came to Cuba with the first slaves, and she was known as the goddess of rivers to the Africans, but after the passage she became the goddess of all the waters and the Mother of the earth, and she later became the goddess of all the Catholic saints as well, and sometimes she would walk among the peoples of the small rural villages of Cuba in a slave's woven skirt and a turban, her breasts bare, and she would take the name Cachita Tumbo, and she had the ability to cause the rivers to overflow their banks and flood the villages and then the people would have to start all over, which is, perhaps, what she wanted, and she also possessed a power over the mystery of electricity, a little known tidbit about the goddess that perhaps Oscar's uncle had forgotten, and if she was angry she could be placated with honey and oranges and eggs and brown sugar and a bottle of champagne and another one of Anisette liquor.

All this Oscar saw in a flash when he looked at the beauty named Nerea shining beneath her golden sun, and then the vision faded and he was telling her about Baracoa. So the women washed their clothes in the river, he said, and they did not bother with the modern washing machines their husbands bought them, which came by a freighter out of New Orleans that arrived once a month bringing all sorts of merchandise ordered from various catalogues, and they did not bother with the electric toasters and radios and alarm clocks that arrived in the company of the washing machines, yes, said Oscar, that is how it was, and Nerea was looking at Oscar, at his profile gleaming in the dim, noisy light of his destiny, at least this is how it seemed to Nerea, but she said nothing. Oscar stared at the noisy light reflected in his empty tumbler as he spoke. The women of Baracoa had no use for the modern world, he said, and so in fits of enduring madness they dumped their brand new white washing machines and white alarm clocks and white radios into a great white pile on the outskirts of the city, a trash heap gleaming with unwanted appliances like so many sun-bleached skulls staring up at the sky.

That is what he remembered.

That is what he told Nerea.

Then Nerea was dancing with the other showgirls some more, three or four more numbers and their shining golden sun headpieces dazzling the patrons of La Campana with sudden flashes of brilliance in the dim, smoky light. Then the showgirls gave way to three singers with guitars and the cadence of poets, who wore black tuxedos with black ties and burgundy carnations pinned to their lapels, unlike the glitzy mambo groups who played the Tropicana and the Montmartre and wore clownish blue and white striped pantaloons for the tourists and wildly colorful mambo shirts and wide-brimmed Panama hats and wide-brimmed Panama smiles, though it must be said that even this trio later succumbed to the need for glitzy mambo costumes when they grew into their fame and played such venues as The Hotel Nacional de Cuba, where they wore yellow slacks and yellow silk shirts with billowy green and yellow sleeves like folded butterfly wings and orange sashes instead of belts and white Cuban-heeled shoes for keeping time and dancing along the edge of the stage. But here at La Campana this trio of poets dressed in their black tuxedos sang their boleros as if they were dying of unrequited love that very moment, and beneath their lingering, plaintive voices you could hear a habanera bass rhythm (boom — ba-ba-bop) and a trilling sentimental piano that caused the women in the crowd to shiver uncontrollably, and the muffled sound of a conga from the darkness just off stage that reverberated with the languor of eternal hope, and a few muted trumpets shining through the leaves of several fake palm trees, the palm trees glowing with tiny white lights. After the trio with the guitars there were a few more flashy showgirl numbers, and then the guitars and trumpets (and the piano and the bass and the conga) for the rest of the night and the crowd lapping it up, and after a while it was hard to tell how long Nerea had been gone or if in fact she had ever been sitting next to Oscar at the bar, perhaps he had invented their conversation, but it did not matter, he had plenty of rum to drink. Strangely, the more rum he drank — and after he polished off one bottle another one mysteriously appeared — the more he became aware of the people sitting at the bar and those at a few nearby tables. Or at least he became aware of their conversations, their words swirling about, washing through him like the vapors of the rum, becoming memories of a sort, filling the void where no memories existed, giving shape to a life that he hoped would be his.

First he noticed the two men sitting next to him at the bar. They smelled of cigars and fancy cologne and faintly the salt spray of the sea. They spoke of things beyond his understanding, but the raging passion that filled their voices filled Oscar with a thrilling rush of adrenalin and the sudden realization that here in Havana anything was possible.

"It is too late for Carreno," said a thin, whiny voice like a mosquito. "First he says he knew who killed the Dupotey boy, and then he says he did not know."

"Headlines, that's what he was after."

"Ah, yes, but that does not excuse the lie.

"Headlines. That's what they're all after!"

"It is like Marti said; the truth wakes up once and never dies."

"They're all bastards!"

"He is not the man we thought he was. He has become a caricature of himself, a cartoon. No wonder they have turned on him. You cannot trust such a man."

"No, I suppose you can't."

"No. Too many lies. Too many unpunished crimes."

"Then it is a good thing they are getting rid of him."

The trio with the guitars ended one number, the angst of their love lingering even then in the air, and the crowd broke into a roar like the thunderous sound of the sea. Then the trio began another number, but Oscar's eyes and ears were drawn to a table of two men and three girls, all of them dressed as if they were in dancing costumes, the men wearing white *pantalones* and blue silk shirts with white ties and white Cuban-heeled shoes, the girls wearing slinky red dresses with slits along the sides, black nylons, and high heels that would show off their legs and their dangerous, bursting at the seams heart-shaped derrières in any kind of light. The two men were busy talking, gesticulating wildly, as if they had come to dance with only their hands. The three girls were trying to get them to stop talking and take them out on the dance floor.

"Grau is no better," said one of the men, a small, brown-skinned man with the long, slender fingers and bright amber-colored eyes of a Chinese merchant of mixed blood. "He says he wants to turn Havana into a refugee camp for suffering souls, a haven for democratic spirits. He says he wants to create a paradise for the poor. He is going all over the country making these speeches, but this makes no sense. He is stepping down. He has already said he wishes Prío to take over. What does he mean by telling such lies at this point? Does he think we are blind? Does he think we are stupid? What unforgivable insolence! We are all suffering."

"But at least he stood up to the Americans. How many Cubans have stood up to the Americans the way Grau did?

"Shit on the Americans. It is because of the Americans that we no longer know what is Cuban and what is not. They are worse than the Communists. They are worse than even the Fascists! Cigars and rum and daiquiris and pineapples and palm trees and sugar cane and the mambo and boleros at midnight and fucking on the beach, this is what the world thinks Cuba is. This is the lie that America has sold to the world. This is the cheap paradise we have become. But we are more than that. We are more than slaves to the greed of America. We have always been more than what America says we are. I say again, shit on the Americans!"

"You are too serious, my friend. Look around you. Look at these beautiful women. Listen to the slow, sexy pull of that bolero. That is the very soul of Cuba. Have another drink, my friend, and let one of these sexy ladies take you to the only Cuban paradise worth dreaming about."

The two men finished their drinks and one of the girls started moving to the bolero, a slow, sexy, uncontrollably sensuous, provocative, hip-swiveling sashay — pa-pa-push-pa-pa-baa-rum-baa, pa-pa-push-pa-pa-baa-rum-baa, pa-pa-push-pa-pa-baa-rum-baa — right there at the table, her eyes half-closed, her lips pursed, a slight puckering, as if she were mocking and teasing the men at the same time, and then everyone laughed and they went out to dance, the women pa-pa-pushing their way into the middle of the dance floor, their eyes now shining with the tiny white lights that illuminated the fake palm trees.

And then a table of three men and one woman, the men wearing silk dinner jackets, borrowed jackets to judge by the way they did not quite fit, their faces unshaven, their white ties already undone, the woman wearing an elegant gold sequined dress with a heart-shaped neckline, staring vacantly in the direction of the trio on stage singing their heart-felt boleros. One of the three men at the table leaned towards the woman, kissing the exposed skin of her shoulders, the nape of her neck, caught up in the rhythm and emotion of the music, but she did not even flinch. The other two were talking in drunken, overly loud whispers that on any given night might carry for miles.

"It is easy money?"

"The easiest."

"And it is lucrative?"

"Yes, it is very lucrative."

"How does it work?"

"Every week there is a steamer from Chile, or sometimes Argentina. You can buy as much as you like. A hundred grams. A thousand grams. It does not matter. They will front you for it. It used to go for $50 a gram on the street but now there is so much of it the price is down to $20."

"U.S. dollars?"

"Of course U.S. dollars."

"What's the catch?"

"There is no catch. Except do not short them on the money. They will kill you if you short them. They do not give second chances when it comes to the money. You come with me tomorrow night and I will set you up."

"Come with you where?"

"The Chinese quarter. A small café on Zanja Street. It is where we always go."

"What about the police?"

"They are already taken care of."

"And the newspapers? Every day they are saying how the police have caught some new drug dealer."

"That is all for show, my friend. A cabaret. Like the show here."

". . . .?"

"No. No. I mean they are not catching anyone of importance. Only the small fry."

". . . .?"

"Only those dealing in marijuana."

"You are certain of all this?"

"Do not worry, my friend. We are protected at the highest level."

". . . .?"

"Alvarez himself. Yes. The Minister of State. It is very funny, no? But he is a coke addict like any other, and he will do anything to keep himself supplied."

The two men laughed.

And then two women talking in the shadows of a giant potted fern near an open window with the blinds pulled up and the candlelight flickering and the moonlight washing across their table, and two empty chairs where their boyfriends had been sitting but they had left to go to their car because they had run out of cigarettes and there were a couple of packs of Regalias stashed in the glove box. In the moonlight coming through the window the two women lost all corporeal substance and seemed instead to be two vanished ghosts from a different time and place.

The women spoke with glittery, moonbeam voices.

"She was sleeping with her brother?"

"Yes, but she did not know that at first."

"How does one not know their own brother? Even if you do not know someone is your brother, you will surely taste it when you kiss him for the very first time."

"Yes. But perhaps that is not always so. At least it was not so in this case."

"She thought they were cousins?"

"Yes."

"And he was very beautiful?"

"Ah, yes, he was very, very beautiful. They said the stars themselves would fall out of the sky if he looked their way."

"Then I can see this happening. Yes, yes, a tragically romantic love, doomed from the start."

"But it was not doomed. That is what I was getting at."

"No?"

"For weeks she cried and cried and her mother and her grandmother tried to console her. Her mother said it was their sin, not hers. They had concealed the truth from her. They had concealed the truth from everyone to hide the fact of the mother's infidelity years ago. And then the grandmother said perhaps it would not be so bad because the boy was only a half-brother. At least it was not as bad as a full brother. God would surely forgive her. God would surely forgive them all. But the girl did not respond to any of their compassionate words or their gestures of kindness. All she did was cry. But the moment they left her alone she stopped crying. It was all subterfuge. The moment they left her bedroom she opened her window and there was a letter waiting for her in a rose bush just below the sill, just as she knew it would be, a letter he had slipped in between two thorny roses to keep it in place."

"*¡Ay de mí!* This is one who knows how to tangle up your heart. This is one who could be very dangerous."

"Yes, true. But he was deeply in love with her. He wrote to her every night for three weeks and he told her they would slip away from Havana and take a boat to Florida and no one would ever know. They would elope with their forbidden love, that is what he wrote."

". . . ."

"He said their love was the sky and the light. He said their love was the sea without an end."

". . . ."

"He said if they had a child together it would be as beautiful and bright as the children of the moon, their child would be like Hiali from the stories of the first Indians, Hiali the hummingbird, the only son of the moon and his sister who flew off to where the sea meets the sky to start a new life and carve out a new destiny, the first of a new people. That is what he was writing her. So what could she do?"

"Yes, you are right. She could do nothing."

"Her grandmother later found the letters, but it was too late, they were already gone."

"If only I had one such letter. To be loved like that."

"Yes, that is the way love is supposed to be."

"They should make a song about such a love."

"Yes, a steamy bolero, perhaps."

"Why do you suppose she left the letters?"

"Who can say? Perhaps they were in a hurry. Perhaps they could hear the footsteps of the grandmother coming to the door. Perhaps the police had found out about their sin and were coming to arrest them both. Or perhaps she had no need of the letters because she was going to be with him for all of eternity. True love is a mystery, that is all I can say."

The two women sighed long, lingering sighs of regret, almost like they were weeping.

"And to think that we are stuck with these two who do not know how to love, who only know how to smoke their cigarettes and flash their fancy Rolex watches to the world and then we go home and they fuck us quick and hard before the sun comes up, without even a murmur of feeling."

"*¡Ay de mí!* True love is such a rebellious bird, such a sad, lovely rebellious bird."

Then their boyfriends reappeared and the moonlight dissolved in their presence and they led the two women to the dance floor and all four disappeared into the myth of a new bolero.

-66-

Oscar sat at the bar in La Campana that first night until the early morning sun broke through the slatted blinds of the windows, and the small green lizards which were only ever visible in the twilight just before dawn and which had been snoozing comfortably in the corners, disappeared through a spider web of cracks in the walls. The music had stopped at five in the morning and the only people remaining in the bar other than Oscar were the performers from the night before, their agent (Luis), and the owner of the club. The trio with the guitars and two trumpet players were sitting along the edge of the stage, drinking and trading jokes and laughing, their instruments packed away but within easy reach, as if they were waiting for a train. The bevy of showgirls was scattered about the tables in twos and threes talking with soft, lazy, murmuring voices, their golden sun headpieces scattered about the floor, their heads flung back or their legs stretched out in exaggerated, bathing beauty poses, as if they were hoping to be discovered by a Hollywood movie director. Luis and the owner, a fat *pachúco* wearing a bright orange zoot suit and beige-colored Cuban-heeled shoes and a grimace that contradicted the brightness of the suit, were standing two steps inside the front door. The owner was counting out a pocketful of very large bills into Luis' hand. No one seemed to pay any attention to Oscar, whose head was plastered sideways to the top of the bar and who seemed to be barely breathing. The fat *pachúco's* money disappeared into the hazy morning glow of Luis smiling. Then Luis whistled and everyone started for the door, grabbing guitar cases and trumpet cases and golden sun headpieces stuffed under arms. Luis nodded a quick definitive nod and the two trumpet players broke away and with their free arms dragged Oscar outside, where Luis instructed them to deposit the boy into the back of a 1937 Packard for a ten-minute drive to a dump of a hotel called Hotel Milagro, one block from the Plaza del Vapor. The hotel, with its Greek pillars and sculpted archways and a first floor with a fourteen-foot ceiling, had been a bright, eye-catching teal color years earlier, but the color had faded over time, the paint flaking away in places, and seemed now a pale reflection of the pale blue sea on a foggy morning.

Oscar slept the next five hours on a mattress without a sheet in a room on the fourth floor without even a fan but which possessed a narrow balcony that loomed precariously above a hidden courtyard, with a view of dozens of rusty, wrought iron balcony railings all around, the railings sagging, a slight bowing in the middle, like ancient hinges beginning to pull away from the crumbling stucco walls, most of the railings covered with laundry recently washed by the washday Madonnas and hung out to dry in the afternoon sun. He woke to the sound of Nerea singing to herself, though he did not recognize her voice, and the sound and smell of chorizo sausage sizzling in a pan. He tried to open his eyes but the light was too bright and the swarming, pestilent heat was too heavy, so he just lay there on the mattress, listening to the sounds of the singing and the sizzling sausage and his head buzzing. Every once in a while the steam ship voice from the night before interrupted the singing with a question or a pronouncement and then a few words were tossed back and forth, and then a sigh of compliance, and then the singing began again. It went on like that for some time.

In the weeks after that first night, Luis took on the boy as a sort of volunteer charity project. He bought the boy a white linen suit and an immaculate Panama hat for special occasions. He asked Oscar why he had left Baracoa and Oscar said because there was nothing there, and this seemed to satisfy Luis. They talked of the dream of Cuba, Luis' favorite topic, and the fiery spirit of eternal revolution that had consumed the Cuban soul from the very first day Velásquez set foot on the island in 1511 in his costume of a Conquistador with his fierce horses clad in plated armor and his soldiers with their sleeveless chain mail vests, their pikes and swords and halberds and their eager, Pentecostal grins. But even so, Luis said, it took a year to subdue the traitorous blasphemy of Hatuey, the great Taíno chieftain, who had fled Hispaniola, traveling across the Windward Passage with four hundred Indians in canoes, and who upon reaching Cuba had preached insubordination to his Cuban brothers, telling them tales of Spanish greed and treachery and cowardice, atrocities committed by the Spanish in the name of a bloodthirsty god who coveted gold and jewels, as much as the Spanish could haul away in the ships that had arrived on their shores. And more ships were sure to come, Hatuey had said, but the Indians of Cuba did not believe him.

So Hatuey waged war on the Spaniards for a year, just the exiled chieftain and his band of four hundred, hiding in the mountainous jungles on the eastern part of the island and attacking the Spanish at dawn or at midnight or in the middle of the day when the priests or soldiers were sleeping in a haze of wine and sudden sickness. And all the while Velásquez himself was plotting out which new cities of gold he would create and how long before he would conquer the entire island of Cuba and what stood in his way, so he became maniacal in his hatred of Hatuey. When the Spanish finally caught up with this first Cuban insurgent, they bound him to a stake and set him on fire in a soldiers' camp in the shadow of a mountain on the banks of an unnamed waterway that would later be called the Toa River. As the flames began to lick Hatuey's toes, he asked the young priest who had lit the fire if there were many like him in the kingdom of his god, and the priest said there were many, and Hatuey laughed and said then he hoped he never found himself within the borders of such a kingdom, ruled by such a weak, miserly, jealous god who permitted atrocities to be committed in his name. Some of those who were present later said that the priest broke down before the flaming corpse of the great chieftain and wept until the ashes had grown cold. Some said the priest smiled and said there was no danger of that happening, his god had another place specially prepared for the likes of rebels and traitors. But most heard only the spitting hiss of the fire and a couple of popping explosions when the flames reached Hatuey's eyeballs.

Luis said that after the death of this first soldier in the battle for Cuban independence, the priest left Cuba to pursue a more contemplative life for the greater glory of God. But no one knows for certain. Some believed he then returned to Spain to hear the last confession of King Ferdinand the Catholic just before the king died in January 1516. Others believed he made his way to Venezuela in 1520 and later became a Dominican friar. And there were a few who believed he was none other than Bartolomé de las Casas himself, who later became the first resident Bishop of Chiapas, Mexico, and who also wrote passionately about the shameful mistreatment of the natives of the West Indies in his provocative chronicle *Historia de Las Indias*, but who was nevertheless accused of bringing about the slave trade from Africa through the Canaries to the New World because his views spurred the passage of the New Laws of 1542, which made it a crime to turn native Indians into slaves. In the end, said Luis, it didn't matter who the priest was or wasn't because most people soon forgot that chapter of West Indian history altogether.

So Oscar and Luis spent many long afternoons drinking mojitos and Sangria and bottles of cheap red wine, talking about the rebellion of Hatuey and the greed and treachery and cowardice of the Spanish, and the identity of the priest, and what had happened to the four hundred warriors that went with Hatuey, and whether or not they had been burned at the stake as well or maybe they had escaped and intermingled with the Spanish settlers, so perhaps their rebellious blood exists still today in the mixed-blood veins of Cuba's sons and daughters. Oscar wondered if the story was actual history or if it was only a myth, and what was the difference anyway and what did the story mean in either case, but Luis didn't usually weigh in on those more esoteric questions. Once Oscar asked Luis if he thought Cuba had finally achieved the freedom and independence that Hatuey had dreamed of, but Luis only laughed and said the Cuba that Hatuey dreamed of only existed in the imagination and in the heart, it was very much like the Cuba we dream of today, but he did not explain himself.

In addition to these spirited conversations about the revolutionary spirit of Cuba, Luis and Oscar also had many conversations about the future in general and their economic future in particular and how best to profit from everyone's natural desire to carve out a little piece of paradise for themselves. Perhaps Luis was looking to take on a partner in crime, a drinking buddy, a foil for all of his mistakes, for he was only twenty-seven when he met Oscar. Or perhaps he was simply possessed with the vainglorious but altogether accurate assumption that he could shape the course of a young (younger) man's life, particularly an impressionable young man from Baracoa, because he himself was an astute observer of the human condition as well as a man of some wealth and incredible charisma. In any case, he became Oscar's benefactor and encouraged the young man's growth in many ways, or to be more precise, he facilitated, spurred, kindled, rekindled, urged on, not in the sense of pleading with but in the sense of stimulating arousal, an explosion of personal growth, which resulted in Oscar being reborn in the image of Luis.

Luis was a small-time gangster whose passion for music was more of an eccentric hobby than anything else. He approached life with the kind of hard-boiled zeal typical of the characters played by Humphrey Bogart, though with a decidedly more joyful, self-indulgent, even self-deprecating appreciation of the beauty of life. He also possessed a well-honed survival instinct, or perhaps he was just plain paranoid, and so had adopted a professional persona based on those secondary characters that played opposite the Bogart characters, like those portrayed by the movie star Peter Lorre (who was born László Löwenstein in the Austrian-Hungarian town of Ružomberok in 1904 and who fled to Paris when the Nazis came to power in 1933, and then later to London), particularly the character of the petty crook Ugarte in *Casablanca* (1942), but also the insufferably incompetent and thoroughly effeminate (but not flaming) Joel Cairo in *The Maltese Falcon* (1941), complete with a fancy, perfumed handkerchief that smelled heavily of citrus and faintly of mint. Luis had more than once turned the tables on his enemies, both seen and unseen, and his competitors, both real and imagined, because they had misjudged the nature of the man they were dealing with. So Luis felt he had a great deal to teach the young Oscar from Baracoa, who had only arrived in Havana three days before he had appeared in the shadows of the tamarind tree outside La Campana, which was one of several clubs that showcased the talent Luis routinely discovered.

At some point during those first few months, Luis suggested that Oscar take Nerea for himself or die trying, for she was as beautiful and eager to please as any woman on the face of the earth, and since Oscar was enamored of this Afro-Cuban goddess, as he would always think of her, and because Luis spoke with the conviction of a man who has grappled with the Devil and won, Oscar happily agreed. Soon, which is to say sometime during that first year, Oscar and Nerea began strolling about Havana during a lazy Monday or Tuesday evening (because the clubs were closed on Mondays and Tuesdays) or on Sunday afternoons (because what else was there to do), strolling arm in arm down the Paseo del Prado, the tree-lined soul of the city, a sun-dappled paradise, strolling for love and pleasure among the happy promenaders. They passed by busy, bony-limbed men in black jackets and white slacks and Panama hats or black fedoras or black-brimmed cane hats and tan suits. They passed by happy, smiling women who seemed to be floating on clouds of remembered love in their Parisian dresses with capes or small lace-covered hats or black hats with flowing silk folds down the back to cover their necks, looking from a distance like floating black swans. They passed by adolescent schoolgirls in school dresses who were tasting for the first time the air of freedom and dancing for joy because they were old enough to walk home on their own, beautiful young ladies of the afternoon who had not yet tasted love except for a love of music, listening to the music of itinerant musicians as good as any playing in the clubs but newly arrived, who were tired of playing in dusty country dance halls and desperate to make it big in the big city. Of course these ragged, newly arrived musicians had not known they would have to wait their turn, for there were thousands of musicians in Havana, so they sat or stood beneath the sun-washed trees along the Paseo, alone or in small groups, strumming their guitars and blowing on their flutes or their horns and the deep rumbling echo of their congas like summer thunderstorms in the mountains of the Sierra Maestra, and the rolling flash of their *timbales* like the sound of small birds learning to fly, their wings beating furiously against the air until they suddenly whooshed away, these handsomely decked out musicians in their white linen slacks and crazy mambo shirts with blue or green or yellow scarves tied loosely around their necks, making love with their sexy, soul-thumping boleros and their heart-wrenching ballads to anyone who would stop and listen and toss a few coins into a straw hat. Like the schoolgirls already mentioned who might follow a sweet-faced guitarist anywhere in Havana and beyond. And all the while the crowd flowing up and down the Paseo like the rippled beating of a young girl's heart, or a young woman's heart, or an old woman's heart, except during the middle of the day when even the pigeons might swoon from the blazing heat.

Or sometimes Oscar and Nerea would head down the narrow streets of the old business district with its electric street cars running back and forth on black wires like lumbering insects, their antennae extended, past the neon extravagance of restaurants or cafes with names like El Sombreros or Celia's or Casa Martinez or Café Lafayette, past tall white buildings from centuries ago with narrow balcony ledges shaped in the Baroque style and sometimes flags or banners draped over the wrought-iron railings. And sooner or later they would find themselves strolling at the pace of a tortoise (*a paso de jicotea*) along the wider streets like Calle Reina, past the rows of innumerable shops buried in the cooling shadows of the arcaded walkways, open front shops with painted banners that might say *La Casa de la Suerte* and a painted picture of a cat holding a sword underneath. And always there were the old women in dark dresses with their white hair tied neatly back, survivors of all sorts of deceptions and youthful indiscretions and infidelities and tragically doomed love affairs, buying flowers to put on the tombs of their loved ones, or buying fruit and some plantains and some rice and beans for a little something to eat in the evenings, but no meat, their teeth were too old and brittle for meat, but maybe some sweets to take home for their grandchildren. And where the arcade suddenly vanished, the awnings had been pulled out so only narrow wedges of sunlight would splash across your shoulders.

And always there were trucks from one narrow side street or another trying to squeeze around the corners, some of the trucks carrying merchandise from the harbor to the department stores, like Herman's or Floglar Department Store or *La Época* with its imposing, postmodern, Cathedralesque architecture, or El Encanto with its stunningly elegant window displays of female mannequins dressed in silky black evening dresses with black satin purses or gold lamé gowns with gold lamé capes, the mannequins standing in front of wispy white or gold trees, the branches looking vaguely like ostrich feathers, or the Sears Roebuck where those with money bought refrigerators, or the Ten Cent where everyone else shopped. And some of the trucks were loaded with fish or melons or bananas for the markets, or maybe whitish gray pigs headed to a slaughterhouse, which probably meant the driver had stopped somewhere for a quick drink or maybe to visit a pretty girl with wide open legs in the Tia Nena Club on San Martin, a few blocks from the fancy hotels to the north towards the sea, and almost a mile from La Campana to the west towards the setting sun of Cuba, or maybe he just didn't know his way around Havana because the nearest slaughterhouse was on Calle E a few blocks from the water. And sometimes Oscar and Nerea would stroll past the outdoor beauty parlors with dozens of women lined up to have their nails filed and painted, and sometimes Nerea would join the line, and sometimes not. And on one street there was a neon sign that said Optica Nacional fixed to a crumbling façade, and on another street they sold Florsheim shoes (another neon sign). On other days they would duck down alleyways and the smaller side streets and disappear into hidden courtyards and get lost in an endless labyrinth of crumbling neighborhoods where the air was filled with the smells of cinnamon and the soft, sweet buttery smell of baking bread and the spicy tang of cumin and garlic and orange spice mixed with Mexican oregano, and the floral bouquet of Chinese wisteria and gardenias and jasmine, and the faint honeysuckle smell of lavender Bougainvillea and the fruity, woody scent of Mariposa, and the sweet juicy spray of Spanish limes and the heavy, buttery butterscotch odor of dark rum and a hint of vanilla, and the spicy, peppery flavor of Corojo cigars, and a hint of whiskey, and the fruity, faint raspberry odor of Spanish brandy and warm beer and fried steaks and sizzling pork chops and coffee and cheap perfume and the earthy smell of rotting wood from forgotten Spanish shipwrecks and the crumbling architecture and the pungent smell of dead and dying fish everywhere and the salt spray of the ocean that washed everything clean again. And they could hear men and women shouting at each other like souls lost at sea. And from somewhere a woman's voice was saying *'perder guiro, calabaza y miel,'* a very lonely sound like the tolling of a bell which meant someone had lost everything. And from somewhere else there was the sound of laughter, and from somewhere else dishes crashing to the floor of a kitchen in a third- or fourth-floor apartment. And from somewhere else the sounds of screeching parrots or white cockatoos or birds of paradise from the South Pacific that had been suddenly and inexplicably let out of their cages, and then doors slamming shut and babies crying and cars starting up and engines revving and the wheels of the electric cars whistling, screeching in the distance, and the popping sound of champagne bottles being uncorked, or perhaps it was the sound of muffled gunshots, because anything was possible in Havana, and radios playing ballads and boleros and mambos and guarachas, and a radio voice selling washing machines, and another radio voice selling Cannabis oil for rheumatism, and the crack of several baseball bats all at once, the sounds swirling about the alleyways and smaller side streets and hidden courtyards like smoke seeking an escape.

But no matter where Oscar and Nerea walked, they would always stop at some point in front of El Gallo on Zulueta Street, a furrier shop that had opened its doors in 1922, and which stood directly across from what was once a small café, Casa Oriente, which had also opened in 1922, and which had been the pride and joy of Andres Ordóñez Escoraz before he was murdered in cold blood, but it had closed the year of his death and a small bakery now occupied the space instead, so it was difficult if not impossible to remember what came before because the smells of sweet breads and fruit-filled *pastelitos* and meat-filled *pastelitos* and opera cakes with butter cream icing wafting through the streets filled everyone's heart and soul like a benediction. And Oscar and Nerea would admire the fur coats in the display window of El Gallo, unburdened by the tragedy of Andres Ordóñez Escoraz, with Oscar laughing and saying why would anyone want a fur coat in the tropics, and Nerea frowning and smacking him in the shoulder or in the chest with her long, graceful fingers balled up into a tiny, delicate fist and saying a fur coat wasn't a matter of temperature, and Oscar pretending he had been hurt but still laughing and then saying yes, yes, some day he would buy her a fur coat, and Nerea softening, smiling, nestling into the crook of his arm, asking if it really hurt where she had smacked him and kissing his shoulder or his chest, and then a long lingering kiss in front of the window, as if they were the ones now on display, with her biting his lip, playfully, passionately, which meant that his lip would be sore for days, and if he forgot and started chewing on it, it would start to bleed again. And then the two of them continuing their walk, barely noticing the station wagon taxis with wooden panels down the sides and the Packards and the Fords and the Chevrolets and the Oldsmobile convertibles and the busloads of tourists motoring past the shops and the fancy hotels, and some that were not so fancy, and the policemen in bright blue slickers with the insignia of the Republic on their jackets and dark blue wide-brimmed hats keeping an eye on the traffic. But once when they were waiting for the traffic to clear so they could cross the Paseo del Prado down by the Capitol on their way to the park, a wine colored Custom Club De Soto convertible passed by, and Oscar stared at the car with mute admiration, and even after the car had vanished he was looking at the spot where he had last seen it, and he told Nerea one day he was going to own a car like that, and for years afterwards he would dream about that car and wonder how he could get his hands on one, and in his dreams he would see the car parked outside nightclubs or cruising along the Malecón or driving out to Playa de Marianao, which is where everyone went to swim or walk along the pier, or heading down Calle Luz towards the harbor and the ferries that went across to Regla. And he would always wake up at this point, suddenly remembering that one afternoon he and Nerea had gone with Luis to Guanabacoa (because Luis had a friend who lived there), taking the ferry across the choppy dark waters of the bay. Luis' friend had sent a wine colored Custom Club De Soto convertible to pick them up from the ferry. Perhaps that had been the one Oscar had first seen. But always in his dreams it was someone else driving and laughing and the car radio blaring, and sometimes he would wake up angry, and always frustrated, his undershirt soaked, sometimes forgetting where he was, even years later when he was in his own apartment in Miami. But when he had first mentioned the car that day, Nerea had laughed and said but not before he bought her a fur coat. She was hoping for a golden-colored ermine, once the fur of European royalty, or sable because it felt like silk, or chinchilla because it was so rare, but any fur would do. And then she had smiled and then the policeman had waved them across and they wouldn't talk about furs again until the next time they stood in front of El Gallo.

They ate when the mood struck them, sitting down at small, sidewalk cafes, the waiters in white jackets and black ties wiping down plates and then setting the table while they read through the menu, the waiters hoping they were big spenders, extravagant tippers. But then they ordered corn tamales and black beans and rice anyway, or maybe paella and pork chops with lemon, and they drank bottles and bottles of cheap Spanish wine and listened to the music of roving troubadours who went table to table singing modern love songs they had written themselves in the hopes of a few dollars before they gave it all up and went back to the farms or the villages where they had been born to descend once again into oblivion. Sometimes after eating they would go to the Rodi and catch a movie, and the best movie they ever saw there, according to Oscar, was *Out of the Past* starring Robert Mitchum, Jane Greer and Kirk Douglas, but according to Nerea it was Gregory Peck and Joan Bennett in *The Macomber Affair*. And sometimes they'd go back to the hotel a stone's throw from the Plaza del Vapor where Oscar had first heard Nerea singing.

And some days Oscar and Nerea would lose themselves in the quiet, ancient, iridescent beauty of the waterfront cafes along the harbor and stop in for a cup of coffee and cheese or pineapple *pastelitos*, if it was early, or if it was later in the evening on a Sunday or a Monday or a Tuesday they would order drinks. And always Nerea wanted Tio Pepe in the evening, because she liked the taste of almond sherry at sunset. Oscar would drink Brandy de Jerez, because it was from Andalusia, Spain, and it was expensive, and Luis was paying him as an assistant stage manager so he now had money in his pocket, and it possessed, as Luis had told him, the magic of the Moors. But most of the time when they walked along the waterfront it was late afternoon and they drank coffee and the pale blue sky was tinted a saffron yellow, and they watched the ocean steamers sailing towards Morro castle and the Straits of Florida, plumes of black smoke trailing, buffeted by the breeze. And only twice during the nearly ten years of their afternoon or evening walks did Oscar tell Nerea that he loved her.

-67-

Of course Oscar did not know that Luis had asked Nerea to attend to his every whim, or that she had agreed only because Luis had asked, which explains a lot, and Oscar never found out she was deceiving him, nor did he ever truly understand the nature of the relationship between Nerea and Luis, which explains even more.

Luis had discovered Nerea and her pimp in a dance dive on Villegas Street doing an incredibly lewd variation of a Cuban folk dance called "Shoeing the Mare." Nerea was wearing a skimpy, chiffon, see-through top, open in the middle, with bright orange ruffled sleeves, a bodice two sizes too small for her voluptuous chest (which kept popping out that night), black heels and no panties. The audience sat scattered among the tables (covered in stained white linens), which had been pushed out towards the walls as far as possible, forming a roughly circular patch of bare space in the middle of the room so everyone could see what was going on. From somewhere, the kitchen perhaps, there came the slightly distorted, staticky sound of a record (a 78) turned up as loud as it would go, a steamy tango that was popular in 1938 called *Tango Bolero* composed by the Spanish composer Juan Llossas, with an echo of Ravel and a few riffs, perhaps even entire passages, stolen from Bizet's *Carmen,* released by Odeon records and performed with melodramatic, silent-movie precision by the German conductor Bernhard Ette and his Dance Orchestra in The Theatre of the People on Reinhardt Road in Berlin, which was called The Great Theatre before the Nazis took over, (and which was, incidentally, the very same theater which saw the premier of Max Frisch's play *Biedermann und die Brandstifter* in 1958). Nerea was down on all fours in the middle of the dance floor of this dimly lit dive, which seemed bathed in shadows as dark and foreboding as those in any third-rate movie house, except for a narrow spotlight that captured Nerea's radiant smile of an orgasm (obviously fake, but still rooted in a playful, joyful passion for life nevertheless). Nerea's dance partner pimp was going through the motions of shoeing a flirty, rebellious horse, standing with his back to Nerea, his legs straddling hers, wearing the white linen pantalones and white linen shirt of a *campesino* but with the splashy silk elegance of an orange sash looped around his middle and black Cuban-heeled dancing shoes. Hunched over in this pose of a rustic blacksmith, he was pulling at each of Nerea's skinny legs, one at a time (even as she pretended she was trying to squirm free), lifting them up, stroking them to the jerky, staticky, staccato rhythm of the tango with a lascivious grin plastered across his face, and then Nerea finally giving up and her dance partner pimp winking at the bored, sleepy faces of the audience as if he were telling dirty jokes, or trying to, because these bored, sleepy men (and a few women) had seen everything, done everything, like a gang of ancient sailors waiting on the tide, what would it take to wake them up, to get them to crack a smile, to feel the heart-wrenching despair of an unattainable love, one could never be sure, and then Nerea's dance partner pimp spun her around by one leg in a circle, slowly, with a tantalizing, theatrical flourish, as the music came to a crashing end (the entire routine took three minutes and fourteen seconds), so everyone in the audience could see Nerea's bared ass and her juices flowing and catch the scent of her cinnamon perfumed skin.

This is when the magic happened. This is when every man would possess an erection and every woman would feel a sweet moistness gushing between her legs, for Nerea possessed a perfect heart-shaped ass, and the petals of her pussy glowed with the luminescent blush of a pink orchid against the glowing ebony darkness of her perfect curvaceous bottom, a flower from the depths of a jungle paradise to be fondled, to be fingered, to be plucked, to be tasted with the tip of your tongue, a flower dripping with the honeydew promise of eternal mind-numbing pleasure and everlasting youth, and then everyone in the audience, the men and the few women, immediately woke up and began shouting in rhythmic counterpoint to the music that had mysteriously begun again, an endless barrage of '*¡Dios mío!*' and '*¡Mi Vida!*' and '*¡Ese huevo quiere sal!*' and many other emotionally charged and even vulgar expressions of lust and love uttered in the heat of desire and as a prayer to release them from the looming abyss of frustrated dreams, every man (all of them publicly) and every woman (one publicly and the rest privately) in the audience hoping against hope that one day they might find a woman (partner, lover, soulmate) such as Nerea, who could be worshipped as both Madonna and whore, but knowing in their heart of hearts (all of them privately) that such a lucky destiny would never be theirs.

Later, Luis (age nineteen) went up to Nerea's pimp (Joaquin, age thirty-five), a chubby fellow from Pinar del Rio province, where the mountains with their steep limestone sides and lush mountain top jungles look like so many towering haystacks. Joaquin's family lived in the small town of Viñales and worked in the tobacco fields, but he had left there when he was very young. But he would never shake free of his smell of a peasant. He possessed a thick, bristly, over-sized moustache like a horse's grooming brush and eyes burning with the fumes of cocaine and skinny, leathery hands covered in warts. He and Luis spoke in querulous voices for a time, their Cuban passions glowing brightly in the dark, and then Luis put some bills into the man's hands and the man nodded and disappeared through a door that led to the kitchen, where, presumably, he snatched up his record and his Silvertone wind-up portable phonograph and fled into the alley and was never heard from again.

From that point on, Nerea belonged to Luis, which is to say that Luis fucked Nerea pretty much non-stop for the next six years. He danced his own version of "Shoeing the Mare" with her in the kitchen of his seedy hotel apartment in the middle of the night with the lights blazing away and the blinds up, or in the middle of the day with the sun pouring in, or out on the narrow balcony in the pale blue morning light (which required incredible skill and infinite patience on both their parts), so everyone with a view of the inner courtyard could see the flashing ebony brilliance of Nerea's bare ass and Luis spinning her around and then grabbing her ass roughly and sliding her up against the stove or the kitchen table when they were indoors and she would reach back and grab hold of him and his tip would start quivering the moment he felt her fingertips, drops of semen like teardrops would start to bubble out, and then she would pull him inside, all the way up to the hilt, the pink orchid folds of her pussy enveloping him like Chinese silk; or he would push her up against the outer shell of this crumbling hotel of their love when they were on the balcony and the sound of laundry flapping in the breeze from the tiered balconies that surrounded the inner courtyard (and during those moments Luis imagined he was standing before the arched partitions of the Roman Colosseum in its heyday), with Nerea bracing herself against the crumbling rough stone with her forearms, so she couldn't reach back, and Luis plunging into her and then pulling out slowly, and a soft moaning prayer escaping her lips, and then Luis plunging into her again and pulling out again, and more prayers, and her legs beginning to tremble, and perspiration beading up on her erect nipples and falling like molten glass drop by drop by drop to the tiled balcony floor. And then applause of a sort, a few raucous shouts of '*¡Olé!*' and '*¡Dios mío!*' and a few wolf whistles coming from the shadowy glare of a few half-open windows and a few clapping hands echoing against the rough stone, and the rest of the watchers nodding with silent appreciation. No matter where or when they chose to strut their stuff, the air would begin to vibrate and even glow with an intense golden light, or so it seemed to everyone watching from one of the two dozen balconies with an easy view, as if the air itself were melting, and Nerea, bathing in the applause of every invisible or imagined voyeur who had taken in the show, would squeal and sing and laugh for joy.

Luis told everyone he met that Nerea was as refined and as sophisticated a *Negro fino* as you would ever want to meet, as sexy and provocative as the best of the mulattas, he would say, but she was a pure-blood, and her exceptionally dark skin gave her a rarefied air, like that of an ancient African queen or even a goddess, it was hard to put into words, you had to see her for yourself, he said, in the nude up close to know precisely what he meant. Luis wanted to show her off in front of the whole world, though it is also true that in their mad, public displays of love, he took great pains to keep his own identity a secret.

Early on they experimented with the standard array of sexual positions. The Viennese oyster was their favorite. Then the painter's canvas of their wild and uninhibited fucking expanded to other parts of the city (which is to say they took their show on the road), and they invented an erotic cornucopia of new positions for their love-making to accommodate their changed and ever-changing surroundings, and Luis began to whisper passionate or tragic love stories into Nerea's ears to inspire even greater invention and perpetuate their madness of two dogs howling at the moon.

Sometimes they drove along the lonely coast highway in search of an appropriate lover's rendezvous, east or west of the city it made no difference, but always it would be after the sun had set, and as soon as the black rocks and tide pools gave way to sandy patches and palm trees, they parked in the shadows and sprinted to the paradise of their own internal clocks. They made love with a recklessness that shocked even the stars.

Sometimes Nerea would lay her back on the beach, hidden in the shadows of her lover's eyes, and Luis would kneel before her, grabbing hold of her hips and hoisting them up off the ground so that only her shoulders and her head remained in the sand. Nerea would open her legs and Luis would pull her close, slowly maneuvering her soft, pliant body up and down until he slid into her, her inner thighs now pressed against his ribs, her legs bent at the knees, dangling, and sometimes she would even black out because of the blood rushing to her head.

They called this creation The Dolphin in the Sand.

Sometimes they did a variation they called The Mermaid in the Sand, with Nerea on her stomach and her legs pulled up, looking down at the waves washing up along the shore and the foam and a few scattered shells and clumps of seaweed instead of up into Luis' eyes and at the sky above the corona of his glowing head, where she might glimpse for a moment the light from the unreachable stars. Luis liked this position because any time he wanted to he could bend over (he was extraordinarily agile and flexible) and bury his face in Nerea's lush ass and lick the perspiration and the salt spray that had collected in the hidden crevices of his imagination. But she did not like this position.

The only witnesses to these lovemaking sessions by the sea were a few old fishermen. After a long day of fishing they would pull their boats out of the waves, dragging them maybe twenty yards or so, and then flip them turtle-like in the sand. They would clean their catch and then head towards whatever village or town was nearby. Later, some of them would return to smoke and drink and look up at the nighttime sky. A few would crawl beneath their boats and get a few hours' sleep before heading out to sea again.

Sometimes Luis and Nerea made love in the stony, cavernous shadows of the Arco de Belen, a short walk from their hotel.

The arch was part of the northeast corner of the Convent of Bethlehem, a convalescent home for dying nuns from 1718 to 1842 that was given to the Jesuits in 1854, who then, according to a few nameless Jesuit scholars, turned the small room above the arch into an observatory (or perhaps they placed their observatory in the adjacent tower, that would have made more sense, but who can truly say given the garbled, mythic texture of most of history) so they could track hurricanes and dabble in geomagnetism (which some said was the source of the devil's power) and look at the stars with a refracting telescope in the hopes of discovering where the angels lived, which would be scientific proof that God did indeed exist, a hope that was surely a blasphemy, for if one had faith, one did not need proof. By 1925 the arch had become a ruin. During the day it was occupied by beggars who had gambled away the fillings in their teeth, and mediums who could see the future if you brought them pieces of fresh fish and a little rice, and lonely guitarists who came to play because they liked the way their music bounced off the stones. At night it was occupied by prostitutes and thieves and drug addicts, by young mothers who had lost their babies to disease, by jilted lovers and those who had never been in love, by cripples and epileptics and the criminally insane, by those suffering from lockjaw or porphyria, by all those who had been cast away and were seeking the solace of eternal darkness.

Some said that in the hours before dawn you could still hear the plaintive cries of the dying nuns from centuries ago, as if their lingering, deathbed words were trapped in the stone itself, leeching out little by little into the future, prayers asking forgiveness, prayers asking for second chances, prayers of defiant regret, prayers of contempt, prayers of wistful vengeance, prayers filled with abject misery and a longing for even a kind word, some of the nuns wishing they had taken a different path when they were young, some of them angry with their fathers or their uncles or their brothers, some of them wishing they had tasted sex just one more time before their cunts had become dry (or dozens of times, or too many times to keep track of, an incalculable number, if they were truly honest with themselves), some of them laughing a dry, whispery laughter directed at those who had remained celibate, a bitter elegy that filled them with sudden remorse as soon as the laughter stopped, but all of them asking Christ to spare them any more pain.

Of the Jesuits only the darkness of their blasphemous souls remained.

Some believed the arch was a gateway to hell. Some believed it was an open doorway to paradise. Some believed it was a tunnel to a parallel universe. Some believed it was just an arch. And some believed it was the only three-centered Baroque-style arch still existing in Havana.

No one gave Luis and Nerea a second glance when they walked into the shadows of the arch that first night. But Luis and Nerea attracted all sorts of attention when they began their lovemaking. Their moans were amplified by the arch itself and sounded as if they had risen from deep within the earth, a heavy, rich, sonorous sound as penetrating as a chill on a moonless night and then the days all jasmine and orange spice. It seemed to those standing in the shadows of the arch that the prayers of the nuns had been answered. It seemed that the sins of the Jesuits had been forgiven. It seemed that a real (which is to say earthy, sensual) and all-too-human paradise was finally within everyone's grasp. Those beneath the arch could not help but breathe in the sounds of ecstasy. And they could not take their eyes off Nerea's beauty, which radiated with an unfathomable light, her pink orchid pulsing (pulsating?) like a neutron star with Luis' every thrust. It was almost like everyone watching had fallen into a trance, and when the show was over and Luis and Nerea had left the shadows for a bite to eat at a little café around the corner from Hotel Milagro, those who remained beneath the arch swore that they had been the ones to fuck Nerea, that no one else had been there, and when they closed their eyes they were fucking Nerea all over again. No one remembered Luis.

This was the beginning of Nerea's fame.

It was beneath the arch that Luis and Nerea created a position they called The Degenerate Nun. Luis would lie down, his back on the cobblestones, but with his legs raised in the air, bent at the knees. Nerea did the rest. She would begin by licking the curve of his muscular ass and the warm moistness of his inner thighs and his overly large bull's balls until he started shuddering slightly (Luis called this part of the program "genuflecting before the altar"), and when he was firm, she would push open his legs and take a seat, her arms holding onto his knees so she could keep her balance, her ass wriggling a bit until she found him and slipped his wriggling eel inside, a bluish tint to her dark ebony breasts like a blue moon eclipsed, though no one was ever sure where the bluish light that illuminated her breasts actually came from, and then she would slide back and forth, sometimes leaning back as far as Luis' legs would go so she could feel him deep inside, her wetness gushing out, spilling across his upended thighs, forming a small pool on the warm cobblestone. The Degenerate Nun was a slow, luxurious fuck, that's what Nerea said. And so it was. Nerea was in absolute control the whole time and enjoyed bringing Luis to the edge and then relaxing and then bringing him to the edge again, and so on. This might go on for thirty minutes. But the audience beneath the arch truly appreciated Nerea's skill and intensity, and they would burst into thunderous applause at the end, and perhaps some lusty, maniacal laughter, and those who were masturbating during the show would gush or explode, and there would be an ocean of juice (the gushing) rolling across the cobblestones and down along Acosta Street towards the harbor, the sewers backing up with froth, and there would be a cloud of spermatozoa (the explosion) hovering in the air for a moment and the lingering taste of salt on everyone's tongues and the hope of nirvana and then the cloud spilling its particles to the ground like so many dead and dying sea creatures.

Then they began to incorporate music into their love-making sessions. On a rainy evening beneath the arch near the end of their first summer, they were joined by a lonely guitar player who played a bouncy, energetic Brazilian samba while they fucked, which Nerea said was a brilliant way to maintain her rhythm. The very next night they arrived at the arch with a brand-new wind-up portable phonograph. In addition to sambas, they experimented with mambos, guarachas, boleros, and even a bachata or two from the Dominican Republic.

It didn't take long (a few months) before Nerea's fame as a sex goddess had spread all over the city. On some evenings beneath the arch there wasn't enough room to stand or even breathe. A feeling of claustrophobia would descend. People would be straining their necks from half a block away to catch a glimpse of the action. After one such night Luis said it felt like they were cattle in a cattle car heading for the slaughterhouse. On another night, he said the stench of fish and sour wine and rum and blood-filled urine and cigar smoke and tubercular breath was so thick it blotted out every sound. So they decided to vary their routine. They decided to expand their geography even further. They fucked in the shadows of the great northern gate of the Cementerio de Cristóbal Colón, with its dozens of whispering statues with their voices of ecclesiastical poverty trying to undo time, a spot which Luis had chosen because Candelaria Figueredo, a hero in the struggle to free Cuba from Spain (she had carried the Cuban flag into battle at Bayamo in 1868 at the age of sixteen), was buried there. They fucked beneath the Spanish lime and fig trees in a small park on San Lazaro Avenue just east of the University where the ghost of the anarchist Julio Mella could sometimes be seen. (Nerea had chosen the park because she had seen an old photograph of Julio Mella hanging on the wall in the lobby of Hotel Milagro and thought him quite beautiful for an anarchist with his curly brown hair and intense, cinematic eyes and pouty lips, but when Luis had told her that Mella was a dead anarchist, that he had been murdered in Mexico City at the age of twenty-five-and-a-half by Stalinist sympathizers because he believed in Trotsky, she wept at the cruelty of a world that could crush the life of one so beautiful. Luis had agreed that the world was cruel, though for different reasons, but she did not care. Fucking in the park with the ghost of Julio Mella hovering somewhere nearby was a cathartic release for both of them.) They fucked on the grassy lawn beneath the walls of La Punta Castle with those walls in desperate need of repair and two useless canons guarding the entrance. They fucked while breathing in the fragrant beauty of the Quinto de Molinos Botanical Gardens on Zapata Street (a lush estate tucked away inside the city where stock breeders from all over the world had gathered for an Agricultural Expo in 1913). They fucked in the shadows of the arcaded walkway that abutted the Church and convent of Our Lady of Mount Carmel, once the traffic along Neptuno Street had thinned, with the lonely sound of a church organ drifting down from somewhere, and also the baritone elegance of a priestly voice or several priestly voices singing a once popular but still sacred baroque cantata. They fucked in every one of the city father's city parks and across the street from countless seedy cafes that were open until dawn and in plazas abandoned at dusk. They even fucked (on three separate occasions) in the Plaza across from the Catedral de la Virgen María de la Concepción Inmaculada. They fucked to the sounds of boleros and sambas and tiranas and polos along the Paseo del Prado. They fucked down along the wharf and up on the steps of the Capitol. They fucked wherever the city fathers had erected statues and memorials to honor the hopes of previous generations, statues and memorials which lay scattered across the city like so many partisan leaflets.

They fucked wherever people might watch them fucking.

But their favorite place for fucking was along the Malecón on summer evenings, looking out at the dark blue waters of the Straits of Florida and dreaming of the future. They would head to the Malecón whenever they wanted to escape Nerea's fame. Here they might find some privacy, a short respite from performing. Their favorite time of day was as the sun was setting, dissolving into the sea, flashing a soft, golden white light like the diffuse light of an impressionist painting against the dark windows of the buildings that looked out at the Malecón. They would stroll along the old stone wall across from the buildings, looking for a good place to climb down to the rocky shoreline below and the frothy, white foam that came crashing against the wall when the tide was in, and even when the tide was out their bodies were covered with a gritty silt and a sticky, salty spray. At this time of day, the greenish-teal color of the water so close to shore would turn a deep, invigorating purplish black.

Luis told Nerea that the rocks were volcanic, the remnants of the volcanic activity that had shaped the Caribbean basin a hundred million years before the birth of mankind, during the Cretaceous period, part of the Cretaceous volcanic arc. The rocks were a fitting symbol of everything that had happened in Cuba since the Spanish arrived, he said, a symbol of the many fruitless wars for independence and the broken promises and the bald, rippling lies, a symbol of the withering of the Cuban soul, yes, yes, volcanic rock is an appropriate symbol for all of this, he said, for everything we have ever dreamed about, and for everything we will dream about in the future. Naturally, Nerea believed everything Luis said was the truth.

The world whirled with the colors of their love.

They discovered a few narrow sandy patches up close to the wall where they would warm up with either The Mermaid in the Sand or The Dolphin in the Sand, but in time they decided that fucking among the black rocks required greater ingenuity, especially since their sessions along the Malecón were a gift to themselves, one soul merging with another on the edge of the universe, only the darkness to catch them if they fell, so they wanted to create something to equal the great explosion that had created the volcanic rocks oh so many centuries ago, something that would not only shock the stars, but cause them, at least one third of them, to fall out of the sky, a hailstorm of gleaming meteorites.

So they created The Lady of the Sea.

Luis would lean back against the stone wall, his heels digging into the sand for balance (or pushing against the rocks where there was no sand), his legs bent at an impossible forty-five-degree angle zooming up towards a cloudy sky. Nerea would perch upon his straining legs with a casual elegance, her legs straddling his, the pink orchid of her new fame glowing in the half light of sunset or the near dark of after sunset or the pitch-black darkness of an impenetrable midnight sky.

In their young hearts the night was always young.

He would take hold of Nerea's plush ass and move her up and down as he wanted. She could recline on the forty-five-degree angle of his knees, grabbing onto his ankles if she felt herself flying forward, on the verge of being catapulted into outer space, but always he had a firm grip, in spite of the strain on his back and legs, always he was in absolute control. Sometimes she would push up on his knees with the palms of her hand, especially if a large wave was coming in. Then she would arch her back as if she were a statue decorating the prow of a ship, the salt spray washing over her body.

During these moments she *became* The Lady of the Sea. This was her favorite position. They would fuck among the rocks along the Malecón all night long. In some places the rocks were jagged and they came away with cuts. In other places, they were rounded and even covered with a fine, slippery moss and it was difficult to maintain one's balance. Every night was a testament to their consummate skill. Even so, Luis and Nerea would still sometimes try to come up with a position to eclipse The Lady of the Sea, a new favorite position to fan the flames of their love, but they had already surpassed themselves.

This is when Luis began to tell Nerea stories while he fucked her. He told her all sorts of popular, dimestore novel stories typical of the day, stories of debauchery and murder and swashbuckling mayhem and mulatta damsels in distress and fragile, tragic love affairs with the woman scanning the horizon, waiting for someone who would never return because he had died long ago.

Nerea's favorite story was that of a lovesick soldier of fortune who lost his mind after the death of his one and only love, a beautiful mulatta girl from Santiago de Cuba, a child of one of Velásquez's men who at the age of sixteen had gone off in search of her father but was sidetracked by a soldier's smile. In the version of the story Luis told, the soldier's name was Gonzalo Silvestre. Of course no one knows for certain what his name truly was, for men are always changing their names to suit the changing circumstances of fortune, but it was true, said Luis, that he had come to Cuba with Hernando De Soto in 1538, and it was then that he met the most beautiful mulatta girl that ever graced the island of Cuba. She had been in Havana only a few months when a French corsair sacked the city and so she witnessed great horrors and deprivation, and in the turmoil that always comes with devastation of this kind, she transformed herself into a lady of the night, selling her body to men of fortune so she could escape the withering boredom of starvation. Gonzalo found her wandering the streets along the waterfront when he arrived, and since his was the first honest, friendly face she had encountered since leaving Santiago, she fell in love with him. He married her in secret and they spent many nights making wild, lascivious love beneath the darkly glowing palms along the beach, away from the bustling commotion of the new town. He told her their destinies were forever linked because on those nights of lovemaking it was like she had washed up with a wave, a gift from the goddess of the sea, a new goddess for a new world, he said, and so he pledged his eternal love. But he left her to follow De Soto to Florida and the promise of cities of gold. She said she would watch the sea until he returned, praying to their new goddess of the sea that he would not be gone long, standing there naked on the beach in the enveloping darkness, waiting to feel his arms around her once again. So all the while he was gone he held on to this image of her standing there naked on the beach, the dark palms behind her mute sentinels of their separation. This image became the golden cross of his love and his hope for happiness. She was the only thing worth suffering for, this is what he told himself. He heard her sweet voice on the wind each night and imagined that he was holding her, fucking her with the wild abandon of a Conquistador's lust. Her image obliterated the misery of sleeping in mosquito infested swamps hundreds of miles away from the Cuba of his dreams, masturbating to the rhythmic pulse of six hundred men snoring in the darkness. She was his salvation. But by the time he returned to Cuba in 1557, she had vanished into the mists of the interior. Or she had boarded one of the treasure ships loaded with silver that had stopped on its way from Mexico to the port city of Cádiz on the southwestern coast of Spain. Or she had given up on him and married someone else. Or she had died of smallpox. Or been raped and brutally murdered. Or had died a slow withering death of starvation anyway. Or she had walked into the sea in a fit of despair and drowned in the arms of their new goddess. A new goddess for a new world. No one knew what had happened. And Gonzalo went mad trying to find her. He was last seen wandering the beaches, swept now by only the darkness of her absence, where they had made wild, uninhibited love. It was said that you could hear his lonely wail of a cry on nights when the sky was buffeted by clouds. It is said you can still hear his cry.

Nerea would swoon just thinking about the imagined passion and consequent descent into madness of Gonzalo Silvestre. She wondered that he was so stupid as to head off in search of cities of gold while his one true love waited for him on a beach. Did he not know such love was as rare as an angel's tear? Were all men so stupid? Perhaps he deserved to go mad.

Luis would grow very hard and very thick imagining Nerea waiting for him naked on the beach.

"You are my gift from the goddess of the sea," Luis would say to Nerea.

And Nerea would wiggle her perfect heart-shaped ass, the luminescent petals of her pink orchid glowing in the dark.

"I have been dreaming about you since before you were born," Luis would say.

More wiggling.

"You are my one and only love," Luis would say.

And more wiggling still.

"You are the soul to complement my soul."

And then Nerea: "Would you run off and leave me?"

"I will never leave you."

"Even if there were cities of gold to hunt down?"

"I am through hunting."

Nerea wrapping her arms around Luis, and then her legs, and then Luis sliding himself into her, a gentle thrusting.

"Would you go mad if I were to die or run away?"

"I am already floundering in a sea of madness."

"Have you always been such a liar? Have your words always been coated with such thick, deceitful honey?"

". . . ."

"Are you not ashamed of yourself?"

". . . ."

"How many other girls have fallen into your trap?"

". . . ."

"It is okay, my love. I forgive you everything. As long as you are good to me."

And Luis would look at her with great emotion in his eyes.

"I will be very good."

And Nerea would smile sadly, as if she had just glimpsed the future.

In time, Luis and Nerea gave up the quixotic thrill of making love all over the city. The image of Nerea and her perfect heart-shaped ass, which had been emblazoned on the hearts and minds of thousands of lonely pilgrims in search of love, faded into myth. Such is the way of things. But Luis and Nerea did not abandon the Malecón, for to do so would have been to abandon each other. Every time they wanted to escape the mundane realities of the world and become invisible to everyone except themselves, that is where they went. And always Luis would heave and grunt and Nerea would gush and moan and her moaning sounds mingled with the crashing sound of the waves and the lonely cry of Gonzalo Silvestre's eternal longing (which may or may not have been the sound of the lonely wind), and these two dogs howling at the moon fell madly in love all over again.

Their ears became their eyes.

Their lips became the lapping of the waves.

Their gaping mouths became mirrors to the nighttime sky.

Their thoughts became the tolling of a distant church bell.

And always the night was young.

But one night while fucking among the rocks along the Malecón they did not fall madly in love all over again. They were like two sailing ships set adrift, though even they did not realize what was happening at the time.

The night in question began as usual with the two of them frolicking among the jagged rocks. But on that particular evening they had misjudged the amount of light left in the sky.

They had misjudged who would be traveling along the Malecón and how attentive he might be to the waves crashing against the stone wall, to the shadows dancing beneath the stars.

He was an ice-cream vendor in a white ice-cream shirt and white ice-cream trousers and a white ice-cream hat with a wide brim. His shirt and his trousers were covered in ice-cream stains that looked vaguely reddish in color against the otherwise pristine fabric, a portent of the years to come, perhaps. He was pushing a Guarina ice-cream cart.

The ice-cream vendor's point of view:

The ice-cream vendor saw two dark shadows wrestling against the rocks and the sea rolling in and he thought perhaps someone was drowning. Or perhaps a crime was in progress. This seemed more likely given there were two shadows. The shadows seemed exaggerated in the dimming light. The ice-cream vendor observed that the shadows were zigging and zagging with strangely elongated movements, it was almost like watching an alien couple from another dimension taking pleasure in a simple tango, he thought, although anyone who has ever observed shadows for any length of time will readily agree that this is the normal movement of shadows.

He watched the dancing shadows a moment with a vague look of happiness, as if he were remembering a time when he had danced with a woman, but then his earlier thought that a crime was in progress returned and his vague sense of happiness was crushed. Yes, he said to himself, a woman was being assaulted, a tragic attack that would end badly if someone did not intervene. Yes, he could hear someone groaning, there was no doubt, and without giving a second thought to his own fate (or, incidentally, to the fate of the three half-empty canisters of ice cream that were hidden away in a small compartment in the center of his cart, and which contained strawberry, pineapple and coconut flavored ice cream that had been slowly melting for the last few hours), he got down on his hands and knees on top of the wall, feeling his way towards the wall's edge with a mechanical precision, resembling at that point in the fading light a crablike creature more than an ice-cream vendor, a crab sporting a white shell with red or reddish-brown markings or blotches, such as the tiny Porcelain Anemone Crab (*Neopetrolisthes ohshimai*) from Indonesia as viewed through the refracting lens of a spotting scope.

He would go over the side of the wall even though he believed he was risking certain death if a crime was actually taking place. He was aware that many such crimes were committed in Havana every day. On numerous occasions as he was pushing his ice-cream cart along the Malecón in the early afternoon light, he had stumbled upon the bloodstains where similar attacks had occurred. He hoped he would get to the woman in time. But in spite of the imagined urgency of the situation, he was excruciatingly careful in his manner of descent. Yes, it is certainly true that he was too portly an ice-cream vendor to take an athletic leap, and old enough, to judge by the gray around his temples, to be suspicious of even the tiniest cracks in the sidewalk. But his girth and his age were not the reasons why he moved so slowly. He simply was not willing to risk a sprained ankle or a broken leg, for then he would be incapable of assisting the woman who was about to become another bloodstain by the sea. This is what he was thinking all in a single moment, a single gasping for breath. This is what he told himself before he grabbed hold of the edge of the wall with a firm yet delicate grip and carefully began the process of lowering his bloated, ice-cream vendor body to the rocky shore below.

A few moments later he dropped without a sound, as silent as memory, without even the tiniest possibility, as far as he could tell, that the motion of his body moving through the air had disturbed the equilibrium of the universe. He looked at the two shadows and breathed in the pure sea air (a gloriously refreshing sensation no matter the circumstances, and which did wonders for his sinuses, which had plagued him since the age of thirty-two). He looked at the two shadows and wondered what was going to happen, and at precisely that moment the two shadows stopped what they were doing and two faces turned to look at the ice-cream vendor. They were huddled together maybe six feet from where the ice-cream vendor stood. There was no judgment in their eyes.

The one face, the face of a man intent on bringing happiness to the world, flashed him a smile full of teeth. The glaring white of the man's teeth in the dimming light was almost painful to behold. The other face, the woman's face, clearly radiated with the happiness that was the cornerstone of her partner's intentions. Her eyes danced about with what the ice-cream vendor assumed was great joy.

If this is not an example of great joy, he thought, then there is no such thing. Indeed, the woman's face, her entire body, glowed with the aura of an undefinable light. The ice-cream vendor's eyes darted this way, then that, as if he were trying to determine if what he saw was real. He seemed to have lost all sense of time. His eyes lingered the longest on the perfectly rounded cheeks of the woman's heart-shaped ass, gleaming like two rounded stones that had been freshly polished.

Then the two faces turned away from the ice-cream vendor and the man and the woman resumed what they had been doing. There was no judgment either in their ignoring the ice-cream vendor. They were simply preoccupied.

Naturally the ice-cream vendor realized his mistake. But he made no move to depart. Any other ice-cream vendor would have returned to his cart and made his way home to wash his ice-cream uniform and prepare for another day. But this particular ice-cream vendor (whose name was Jorge, which you could tell just by looking at him with his wispy beard and his long face of a philosopher) was unable to move an inch. He was, one could say, rooted to the spot, an ironic description given the fact that he was standing in one of the rare sandy patches along the wall, a bit of sand that would disappear with the next great storm. Of course it is also true that the ice-cream vendor, given his portly nature and his advancing years, could not return to his cart above as easily as he had made his descent. He knew there were stairs somewhere along the Malecón. He remembered some vagabond boys who smelled of the sea had once jumped up from the other side of the wall and begged for some ice cream, and he had given them some, and then they had disappeared over the wall, and he had wondered how they had accomplished such magic, so he had looked over the edge and there were the stairs and the rocks below and the boys jumping back into the sea. But he couldn't remember where that was, or even, to be honest, if his memory was accurate.

How stupid he had been, he thought. Clearly this amorous couple had chosen this precise location among the rocks because who in their right mind would climb down the wall in the dark. They wanted to be alone. The ice-cream vendor stood in mute contemplation of his stupidity, absorbing it, swallowing it, until the burn had dissipated.

But still he did not move.

In all probability, he would not have returned to his cart had there been a set of stairs at his elbow. To be blunt: he could not take his eyes off the luminescent beauty of the woman and every so often her flashing pink orchid winking in the darkness.

And so time passed.

Or time stopped.

It amounts to the same thing.

After a while the two shadows stopped again, but this time they disentangled themselves and approached the ice-cream vendor, who was still unable to move.

No one knew what to say at first.

"You surprised us," said the man after several minutes.

"Yes you did," said the woman.

The ice-cream vendor remained silent.

"But we enjoy surprises," said the man.

"Oh, we do," said the woman. "We are always surprising each other."

The ice-cream vendor shifted uncomfortably.

"Yes," said the man. "We are."

The man and the woman laughed with cryptic pleasure. The sound of their laughter had a muffled, underwater quality about it, as if it were coming from beneath the darkly glowing waves of the Straits of Florida some two miles out instead of from the two happily laughing heads tossed back. The eyes of the ice-cream vendor clouded over with a look of self-deprecating apology. He seemed unable to focus, blinking violently. He seemed incapable of speech. His hands groped wildly at the air as if he were suffering from a raging thirst. One would have thought he had suddenly and quite without warning gone blind. Then the man and the woman invited the ice-cream vendor to join them.

"My name is Luis," said Luis.

"My name is Nerea," said Nerea.

"My name is Jorge," said Jorge.

And with these basic introductions out of the way, Luis and Nerea began to undress the portly ice-cream vendor. From a distance it would have looked like his white trousers and white shirt just melted away, exposing his body to the elements and the darkness and the deft handling of Nerea, whose slender fingers stroked him without mercy while Luis stood back as if he were pretending to be a statue, something iconic, with a hint of history and a sense of purpose, but also possessing an air of whimsy, an appreciation for the absurdity of life, one foot propped up on one of the many black, volcanic rocks that pockmarked the landscape and the surf rolling in slowly, surrounding some of the rocks, Luis watching first with the enthusiasm of an adolescent voyeur, and then forgetting he was a statue and clapping his hands in delight, and then adopting the socially myopic pose of a more reserved movie critic, but still gesticulating with each breath, commenting on everything from Nerea's infallible technique to the ice-cream vendor's overwhelming inexperience (though he was eager to learn, which was a point in his favor) as well as his poor physical condition, which meant in all likelihood that the more challenging positions would forever be out of his reach.

The ice-cream vendor and Nerea attempted The Mermaid in the Sand and The Lady of the Sea, both with the expert assistance of Luis, but the portly vendor began gasping for breath almost immediately and his limbs seemed like they were about to snap from the strain, so Luis and Nerea switched gears.

In the end, and because this was all the poor man was capable of, Nerea allowed the ice-cream vendor to fondle her pussy while she grabbed hold of his balls with one hand and stroked him with the other until he ejaculated all over her arm. Then she licked off the excess and began kissing him on the mouth with a ferocity that surprised even Luis, pushing her gargantuan breasts against the ice-cream vendor's trembling skin, squeezing his fleshy nipples until they bled while she forced her tongue half way down his throat, stroking his shaft with the silk of her fingertips until he was ready once more, at which point she positioned herself against the wall so that he could enter her easily from the rear. He was finished in two minutes and would have keeled over right there had not Luis caught him. Grinning, Luis said: "There, there, my friend, she will take you to a paradise from which there is no return if you let her."

After that they helped the ice-cream vendor back into his clothes, he seemed as feeble and as inarticulate as a stroke victim, and then they helped him find the mythic stairs of his imagination and then they walked him back to his cart. There was a hazy morning glow to the sky, spreading up from the east like a bloodstain, but it was still very dark to the west. They watched as the ice-cream vendor pushed his cart with some unsteadiness towards the darkness, and then he had vanished. Soon after that a soft rain began to fall as softly and as easily as one slips into a coma, and so they decided to go back to Hotel Milagro.

They enjoyed the company of the ice-cream vendor with some degree of regularity over the next several months. In fact, it wasn't too long after they first met Jorge that they headed for the Malecón with the sole purpose of seeking him out. Bit by bit they fell out of love with each other, and in love with this strangely exhilarating ménage à trois.

Always they would find him just before sunset struggling with his cart along the Malecón, whistling a strange sad love song, somewhere between the ravishing, sun-washed brightness of Linea Street, near the park of La Piragua, which became a haven for criminals and reefer heads and vagabond musicians after dark, and the monument to Antonio Maceo y Grajales, a bronze general on a bronze horse leaping up into a very blue Cuban sky, a sky which suggested to Luis the absolute purity of freedom, and to Nerea the peace and quiet of a lazy afternoon in bed, and to the ice-cream vendor a week of bright sunny days when he was sure to sell a great deal of ice cream.

Always Luis and Nerea would lead the ice-cream vendor down to the water and the shadows stretching out along the shore and then night falling.

Always they would nibble away the ice-cream vendor's clothes with their lust for new experiences and their haughty disregard for convention, and always he would react with the unfaltering dignity and unhesitant devotion of a blind man. And always Luis would be there to catch him when he fell.

Then they would help him dress and before he realized where they were they would be walking along the Malecón, his fleshy arms draped across their shoulders, his legs unable to bear his own weight, as if he had been a large fish they had caught, and then all three of them would head back to the ice-cream cart, where they would linger for a while.

Once back at his cart, Jorge would become a new man, suddenly revived, a smile pushing out the pudginess of his cheeks. He would pluck a few ice-cream goblets hanging by their stems from a rack hidden in the canopy of his cart. The goblets were made from cheap spider-web glass, glassware which the Guarina family had purchased by the truckload because they created the impression of elegance for mere pennies. Then he would pour what was left of the melted ice cream (strawberry, pineapple, coconut) and mix in a little rum. He had taken to stashing a bottle of dark rum in his cart for just this purpose. The three of them would toss back ice-cream rum drinks until there was nothing left to toss back.

Sometimes they drank in silence, too exhausted by the night's frolicking to utter even a syllable. On such nights they drank only a glass or two.

But sometimes they entangled themselves in very heated discussions about the improbable relationship between politics as usual and the dream of creating a utopian paradise for the people of Cuba, which is what every politician said they were going to do. The topic was an odd one to follow so much fucking. On such nights they could not get enough to drink.

"It is not as far-fetched as it sounds," said Luis.

They were huddled around Jorge's cart like three conspirators. Luis on one side, his back to the sea, Nerea and Jorge on the other. They were drinking coconut ice cream drinks. They had lost track of how many they had drunk. They seemed to possess an unquenchable thirst.

"Certainly this is easy for you to say," said Jorge. "You come from money. You dabble in this and that and if you lose it is nothing. Your thirst for freedom is a luxury. What do you mean by freedom anyway? Your dreams are a luxury. Your history is a luxury. Your whole life is a luxury that I cannot afford. Even your beautiful Nerea is a luxury."

The streets were mostly deserted, though already there were lights winking on all over the city. A few shadowy figures appeared along the wall. And then a few more. They did not seem interested in the trio by the ice cream cart.

"Did you hear that, Nerea? Jorge said you are a luxury."

"I did hear that!"

Nerea wiggled closer to Jorge. Soon her hips were pressing against his leg and also against the cart, forming a triangle. Jorge was looking vaguely in the direction of the sea, his plump hands and plump arms floundering uselessly by his sides. He was clearly distracted. The sun had inched its way above the horizon and the light was now pouring through the spider web glass of the few goblets still hanging from the rack. Jorge's face was bathed in a soft, rosy glow. The shadowy figures became fishermen casting their lines from the wall or fishermen who had gone over the side and were casting their lines from the rocks. Some of the fishermen were old men. They seemed as old as the rocks. Some of them older. But some were boys no older than ten or eleven.

The sun grew brighter.

Jorge's pudgy pink cheeks resembled the soft underbelly of a sea creature suddenly exposed.

"Do you think I am a luxury?"

Nerea leaned even closer and started nibbling on Jorge's ear as she spoke.

Jorge could hardly breathe. He felt like he was bleeding but he could not tell from where.

Nerea continued nibbling.

Jorge was overwhelmed by the sweet coconut ice cream smell of her breath and almost passed out.

His face had lost all of its color.

"You . . . you are . . . I mean . . . ."

It was a rough sea this morning, with tiny, frothy white caps as far as the eye could see. And yet the air was calm and gentle and smelled of lilacs and Chinese wisteria and sweet gardenias and sweet, sun-dried figs.

"Do you think you can so easily do without me?"

"No . . . I didn't mean that . . . I . . ."

"You mean you enjoy fucking me, is that it?"

Luis drained his goblet and fixed himself another drink, watching the scene unfold as if he were watching a movie.

"And you do not want to stop fucking me, yes?"

There was a small tugboat sailing across the horizon, stealing its way into Jorge's line of sight, on its way into the harbor. Jorge wanted to watch the boat, but Nerea took hold of his face with her dark, slender hands and he gave up all pretense and looked into her eyes.

"And when I am gone and you are pushing your cart there is nothing but the silence of your loneliness, yes?"

". . ."

"And that is why you are always whistling the same sad song. To keep the silence at bay."

"Yes."

"And it is such a lovely, sad song, is it not?"

"Yes."

"So I am a necessity, yes?"

"Yes, yes . . ."

"Mmmmm?"

"I enjoy fucking you and I do not want to stop."

"Mmmmm!" Nerea smiled softly.

From somewhere there was the sound of traffic making its way through city streets, though there were no cars yet driving along the Malecón, just a few trucks.

Nerea kissed Jorge on the mouth, a soft, gentle kiss, like a morning rain shower.

"You are a sweet man," Nerea said.

Nerea cooed some more into Jorge's ear and then kissed him lightly on his blushing check.

Luis laughed, a hearty robust laugh like a thunderclap.

Jorge was trembling from unexpected embarrassment.

"You see, Jorge," said Luis. "Even a luxury can become a necessity."

The three of them tossed back their ice cream drinks and Luis fixed another round. It is hard to say if their drinking took place in the vacuum of absolute silence (even the sounds of the sea and the fishermen along the wall or down on the rocks were muted) or if time simply flowed around them.

And then: "But it is not that way for most," said Jorge.

"No?"

"Most people have no time for necessities of the heart. It is a trap," said Jorge. "Like religion. Or believing in God."

"Be careful, my friend," said Luis. "You are treading on dangerous ground once more."

But Nerea had already stepped around the cart, moving past Luis towards the wall and the sounds of seagulls in the air above and the sunlight washing across her with such brilliance that she seemed naked even though she was wearing a flowery dress from the night before. Luis and Jorge continued their conversation. Nerea stared out at the sea. The wind was picking up. You could hear the wind whistling through a few nearby cracks in the wall. A few fishermen from down along the wall or up along the wall were cursing because their lines had become tangled and then they turned suddenly and their eyes fell upon Nerea and her dazzling beauty and her seeming nakedness and the cursing stopped. Then they untangled their lines and went back to fishing. The wind died down.

"Hah," said Jorge. "Yes, I suppose you are right. But then only the rich can afford to be so romantic. *Dime con quién andas, y te diré quién eres.* One day you and Nerea will pack up and head for only God knows where, and I will still be here pushing my cart along the Malecón, and I will be very much alone, and one day my heart will give out from the heartache of my loneliness, or maybe it will be from the heat, and that will be that."

"But one day life will be different," said Luis. "I have always said . . ."

"Yes, yes, I know, you and your predictions, but it is the same old promise, always dangling there in front of our noses, like a juicy fig and your mouth is watering, but it is always just out of reach. Blanco wanted to give Cuba its freedom if we helped the Spanish in their war with America, but Gómez was against this, and when independence did come, Gómez gave the Americans everything they wanted. He promised us a new paradise but we were still slaves. Nothing changed. And Zayas was not much better. What did he do? He wrote poetry. He possessed a suffering heart. But he couldn't do a damn thing without borrowing money from the Americans. What good was that? Machado, Grau, Mendieta, Brú, how many others were there, I have forgotten, and now we have Batista, the worst of the lot, but it is only a matter of degree, they are all the same, a rotating parade of clowns. A carousel. They will promise anything to get elected and then they suffer from amnesia or worse, they loot the country, they line their own pockets, they line the pockets of a few American Senators, and nothing changes. Nothing ever changes."

"Yes, my friend, but one day, truly, everything will be different."

"You talk like an idealist, but I know you are not. But even if you are right, what of it? When your one day arrives, I will be long gone. I will have exited the planet."

". . . ."

"My poor, sweet, suffering Jorge," said Nerea, and Luis and Jorge turned their attention to the woman of their dreams, an extraordinarily photogenic face that surpassed (they thought) even the fabled beauty of Helen of Troy (for without a photograph, who can be sure?), but Nerea was staring out at the sea once again.

-68-

Time, as the poet once said, murders all things, but especially love. This is one of life's great truths. And so it was with Luis and Nerea. Six years of hard, furious fucking left them lethargic, apathetic, without enough energy even to raise their heads off the pillow when the other entered the room. Dog tired. That is how they felt. He talked about how it would be better to pay for sex. Maybe his tastes had changed. Maybe he was no longer into the exotic. At least he could test the waters if he bought a whore. She talked about selling her own flexible, fluid body for money, like she had done before they met. She craved variety, she said. So perhaps he was right. They talked about separating. She would want for nothing, he said. He would get her an apartment on Zulueta, there was a very nice building just two blocks from El Gallo's, yes, he knew about her love for furs, what woman didn't want a fur, yes, he would buy her one of those as well, sable or chinchilla, whatever she wanted, but Zulueta was too far away from the clubs, she said, and she didn't really like the neighborhood, everything crammed together in such a small space, she was afraid it would give her headaches. He suggested somewhere on Merced, near their favorite church, but she said that would bring back too many memories, she didn't want a head stuffed full of memories, or a heart, for that matter, no, she would rather re-invent herself, start all over, not completely, she would hang on to the parts she liked, anyone would, but she wanted to forget all of the little jokes they used to make and the perverted way he would laugh when he came in her mouth, yes, she wanted to forget things like that, which is why she could never live on Merced. Perhaps she was interested in going to America, to Miami, or Argentina or Chile, or perhaps Mexico City, he had friends all over, he would put her up in a fancy high-rise apartment and she would have a very fine life, but she said she had been born in Cuba and she would die in Cuba. What does she want, Luis asked himself. What is she waiting for? Why won't she tell me what's really on her mind? But he only ever voiced these questions with his eyes, and she no longer responded to his eyes, except to meet them with a determined, probing stare of her own, her face still glowing, always glowing, with an unfathomable light.

Eventually Luis gave up trying to move her out of the hotel and they took to living as brother and sister. She cooked him small meals in their four-room suite plus a bathroom when they didn't go out to eat. She even slept next to him in bed until he asked the hotel manager to bring them a second bed, which he shoved into a fairly large closet they had been using as a pantry. From time to time she took occasional lovers, bringing them back to the apartment at all hours and grunting and moaning in her tiny bed in her tiny bedroom next to the kitchen with the door always open so Luis could watch if he wanted to. And sometimes he did watch, and in the morning after her lover had left they would critique her lover's performance over coffee and pastries, Nerea still wearing the flimsy négligée she had worn to bed, or the lace panties, or sometimes she was in one of Luis' old robes because she had gone to bed naked.

Once, one of Nerea's lovers had a Kongsberg Colt pistol strapped to his leg, which only foreign mercenaries or assassins or anarchists or communists or members of the secret police generally possessed, and when he took off his trousers Nerea squealed. Luis appeared as quickly as a gust of wind and boxed the man's ears, berating him for bringing such a weapon into his home, tossed the gun out the window and the man down the stairs. The hotel staff escorted the boob to the courtyard to retrieve the symbol of his manhood. They swore they never saw him again after that.

Luis was more discreet, as always. He never brought any women home so that Nerea could size them up. He would meet someone at one of the clubs and when she was drunk enough he would drive her out to one of the beaches where he and Nerea used to go to satisfy their voracious appetite.

Or sometimes, if she was a woman of class, he would take her to one of the luxury hotels in old Havana, like Hotel Plaza on Agramonte Street or Hotel Sevilla on Zulueta (just a few blocks from the apartment Nerea had turned down), or Hotel Bristol or Hotel Palace or The Savoy, or once in a while he would be in the mood for the faded elegance of The Gran Inglaterra Hotel on Paseo del Prado, a third-floor balcony room with a view of the harbor entrance and the sea beyond the castle, a narrow wedge of a view, but exhilarating, the same room every time, the very room, the hopeful clerk had told him that first time, where Winston Churchill had stayed when he came to watch the Spanish-Cuban war in 1895.

And on those rare occasions when the woman Luis had discovered radiated with the sweet purity of a country girl (the kind of girl his mother had always hoped her profligate son would marry), he would escort her home, always at her invitation, and make voiceless love to her in a lawn chair or chaise lounge resting partly on a stone patio and partly in the grass, beneath a towering kapok tree, or a multi-stemmed jacaranda with its purples leaves which could be crushed and boiled to extract a cure for syphilis, or perhaps a big yagrumo tree with its white and green leaves (which looked silver and black at night) fluttering like the protest flags of dissident students.

Naturally he would return to Hotel Milagro just before dawn. Nerea would be asleep, her door open, her voice drifting through Luis' addled brain, but he could never make out what she was saying. He would poke his head through the doorway to her room, tentatively, just in case she was with someone, so he could listen to her slow, regular breathing like a clock before he turned in.

It always seemed at that hour that he was trapped in a strange, black and white movie of a dream. Some place where time was an endless maze of choices all leading back to the same pivotal event. There would always be a faint glow coming from the kitchen window, the soft glow of a few lights from the other side of the courtyard. A cool breeze blowing through the window, rustling the newspapers on the kitchen table. A dog barking somewhere. A few murmuring voices. Suspiciously secretive voices, Luis would think, but also weary and skeptical, rising up from the shadows of the acacia tree that stood in the middle of the courtyard. But then the voices would sound slightly muffled, as if they had sought refuge in the narrow, arcaded walkway leading to a rusty gate and then the street. And then the voices seemed to be coming from the rooftops. And then it was as if the owners of the voices had jumped into a passing car. And then they were back in the courtyard beneath the acacia tree. It was amazing how strangely sound behaved at night. As if the laws of the universe no longer applied.

He would listen to Nerea breathing for a few more moments, her lover too, if there was one, and then step out onto the balcony for a quick smoke. He would try to zero in on the voices in the courtyard, but they always behaved with the uncanny deception described above, as if their owners were aware he was trying to eavesdrop on their conversation. Sometimes he would wonder if the owners of the voices had been sent to spy on him, or to give him a message of some kind, a proposal, perhaps, or a warning. Then he would laugh at his paranoia. He didn't have anything to hide, not really.

Perhaps the voices were a trick of his imagination. Or a trick of God designed to illuminate the depravity in his soul. But then he would remember that he no longer believed in God. God didn't exist, so perhaps the voices didn't exist either. Like so many things he had once been sure of. Then he would take a last long drag and flick the rest of his cigarette over the railing, the sparks from the still-glowing ash trailing in the darkness. Into the abyss, he would think (or sometimes he would say this out loud, but softly), and then he would sigh. The barking of the dog had stopped. He would suddenly feel cold and head back inside and crawl into bed. In the morning, which is to say just before noon, Nerea would cook him breakfast. He would pretend he had been in all night. And she would let him pretend. That was the state of the relationship between Luis and Nerea when they first met Oscar.

What Luis said to Nerea the night they first met Oscar:

"He is just your type. Or he would be if you admitted to yourself that you had a type."

". . . ."

"Nerea, please. Oh do not be this way Nerea. Not tonight. Have some fun. Dance with the girls on stage. And dance with this boy in between numbers."

". . . ."

"Yes, take him home. Take him home and fuck the hell out of him. I want you to fuck him. It will be good for you to fuck him. No more moping around the hotel at all hours. Even I have begun moping around."

". . . ."

"The hotel staff is beginning to talk."

". . . ."

"You will enjoy yourself, of that I am sure. Yes, I think so. And perhaps he will become a permanent fixture in your life."

". . . ."

"Yes, in my life also. If you want to know the truth, I think this is the very reason I am pointing him out to you."

". . . ."

"I think he and I might become very good friends."

". . . ."

"No, Nerea. I am not being sarcastic. I am speaking from the heart."

"!!. . ."

"Now you are being a pessimist. A beautiful, pouting pessimist."

". . . ."

"He and I will become good friends. Very good friends. I have already said so. I may even have dreamed it, so it is sure to come true. He has wit, after all. You heard him on the way in."

". . . ."

"Yes? Ah, there is my beautiful Nerea. All smiles and heartache. But he will be good for you. I am sure of it."

". . . ."

"You will attend to his every whim. You will fill his soul with the kind of love that not even the poets dare dream about."

". . . ."

"Why yes, Nerea, you have always been the delight of my soul."

". . . ."

"No, there are no accidents, Nerea. You of all people should know this."

What else could Nerea do but succumb to the pressure of Luis' request? And the boy was quite good looking. He had brown curly hair and pouty lips. He looked a little like Julio Mella. So she attended to Oscar's every whim. Truly she led him across the islands of love, grief by grief. She convinced him that true love existed, but only when he was with her. Sometimes she called him Julio by mistake, but he did not mind, and when she told him why and showed him the photo of Julio in the hotel lobby, he said he was flattered that she thought he looked like the great, mythic anarchist, she could call him Julio whenever she wanted and he would come running. She said Julio was twenty-five-and-a-half when he had been murdered, and she spoke with a very deep sadness that rang out like a bell. But it was not Julio she was weeping for. The moment she started talking about Julio she heard Luis' voice. It sounded like he was standing directly behind her. She could almost feel his arms tying themselves in a knot around her waist, like he used to do on Saturday evenings at the Rio Cristal Club or La Campana when she was adjusting her headpiece in front of a backstage mirror with the glass bulbs of the mirror glowing a hazy, sultry white and Luis nibbling on her neck. But the only mirror in the lobby of Hotel Milagro was on the other side of the room, and when she whirled around there was no Luis. But then she heard him again, only he sounded very far away this second time, as if he were hiding in the mountains, and then she heard him a third time, but this was only an echo of an echo, as if he were steadily evaporating in the sunlight of a bright Cuban day or had taken up residence on the moon. Then her field of vision narrowed and there was a shimmering sensation around the rim of her eyeballs, and then she was looking down a very narrow, very long tunnel. It seemed to her that she was looking into a telescope. At the far end she could see Luis waving at her frantically, a tiny moon dot of a man calling out to her, but she could not tell where he was, nor could she make out what he was saying, he was too far away. Then she heard a gunshot, or several, a barrage of popping noises, she could not be sure, and then the sound of a great horn, a bellowing like that of a bull, and she suddenly realized a steamer was putting out to sea. She found herself wondering where the boat was going and if her Luis was supposed to be on the boat and why wasn't he on board, and then the moon dot that had been Luis became a single drop of blood, and then another and another, until the telescope was a pipeline filled with the blood of Francisco de Quevedo's blood-red moon (which was certainly a bizarre mixing of metaphors), all of it rushing towards Nerea's blinking eye, and then her eye became her mouth and she realized with no small degree of horror that she was sucking on the end of this telescope that was now a pipe and there was nothing she could do, she could not move, and in an instant the bloody torrent was upon her, spiraling into her mouth and down her throat, as if she had become a sewer gurgling furiously. She did not understand what was happening to her and squeezed her eyes shut. The gurgling sound speeded up but at the same time grew more distant. Then she heard a snapping sound and opened her eyes and Luis and the blood and the gurgling sound were gone (except the taste of blood still lingered in her mouth, and also there was the earthy, metallic taste of iron, presumably from the pipe, a few flakes of rust that had been swept up in the torrent). Oscar was now holding onto her arm, but they were no longer in the lobby of the hotel. They were walking along the Paseo del Prado in all its springtime glory. She did not remember leaving the hotel, a fact which vaguely troubled her, and then she had the sudden feeling that she had been suffering from hallucinations of the sort described above for several months, maybe longer, but she seemed better now, though her legs still felt wobbly. "Are you okay?" Oscar asked. "Yes, yes," she said. "I am fine, just a little dizzy from the heat. I didn't know it was so hot." And Oscar seemed satisfied with her answer and smiled, and he saw his smile reflected in her bright, glistening, doleful eyes, and thinking her sadness (for she still seemed incredibly sad) was for Julio Mella, who had died so young, he suddenly said that he was twenty-five-and-a-half years old himself, right at that very moment, the same age as Julio Mella when he died, except that he, Oscar Garcia Raimundi, would not suffer the same fate, he was going to live to a ripe old age. An old mestizo woman who lived in a palm hut on the outskirts of Baracoa had told him so. She said she could read the future as easily as others read the weather in the clouds. She said he was destined to live to be one hundred years old. Oscar seemed very sure of himself. He spoke with a great serious stiffness that bordered on farce. Nerea laughed. (She could not help herself.) And in the very next moment, six months after they had started strolling up and down the Paseo del Prado, Oscar told Nerea he loved her for the first time, and her sadness seemed to disappear. (It was hard to say how deeply she had buried this sadness and if it would one day return, but such are the chances we all take.) "Ours will be the happiest house on earth," she told him. It was the only hope left to her. Naturally, she fell in love.

During those first three years with Oscar, Nerea suffered through countless vulnerable days of transitory hope and unprovoked hallucinations. It was also during this time that Luis set up shop, so to speak, in a small office on the top floor of an ancient three-story building on the corner of San Pedro and Santa Clara, a crumbling shadow of Baroque magnificence across the street from the local ferries with a slightly obstructed view of the harbor. The building had served as a fish market in the days before independence, and then a cordage warehouse until just after the first world war had ended, and it had been abandoned during the frivolous excess of the roaring twenties, and during the death-march insomnia of the threadbare thirties it had become an informal customs house for black market goods and so became the secret home of dozens of corrupt outfits, including a company called Ignazio Tiziano & Sons, an import/export company which occupied the southeast corner of the building (all three floors), and which did a brisk business, or so they claimed, in figs, olive oil, Marsala wine, Spanish brandy, and coffee. At various times during its history the building had been painted ochre, beige, yellow, and white, but the plaster was disintegrating in some places, and in other places the paint had been devoured by the salt air, so now all four colors could be seen.

Luis rarely spent more than two hours in his office on any given day, but he was often there in the evenings, sometimes well into the wee hours of the morning. When Nerea asked him about his late nights he smiled a discreet, crooked smile and said "I shot an ace of spades out of my sleeve during a card game and now I have to pay for getting caught." Nerea didn't understand what he meant, and in all probability neither did he (it was a line he had once heard in a movie, and ever since he had wanted to use it), but she didn't ask him again. But the question lingered in her heart of hearts for many months, a lichen intermingling with her flesh at the cellular level, nourished by heartache, a home for moths and spiders (which suggests that it was most probably a species of red tree lichen, a tropical variety common to the Americas, known in the scientific community as *Cryptothecia rubrocincta,* which resembles nothing so closely as a broken heart even in the brightest sunlight).

What was Luis doing so late in the enveloping darkness (only God knew how late) in a small office looking out on the black, brackish polluted water of the harbor?

It wasn't because of the new women Luis had taken up with. (By Nerea's estimate there had been three dozen since their love affair had ended.) Luis always and only went out to the finest places in town. But Nerea could think of no alternative explanation, and so she descended into a sort of uncontrollable madness, a swift, spiral descent.

She tried to tell herself that his office was a tiny, miserable, hovel of a place with the musty, claustrophobic feel of a prison cell, which was certainly no place for a romantic tryst.

She tried to imagine her Luis spending countless hours poring over the accounts of obscure business ventures. (It was clear to her unconscious mind at least that she would always think of Luis as hers, even if her conscious mind had accepted their changed circumstances.)

Luis had always been secretive about how he made his money. But she had always accepted his secrecy. She had always known that managing musical talent and negotiating contracts with night club owners was little more than an eccentric hobby of his. It was part of Luis' mystique.

Still, no matter how hard Nerea tried, the story of his hovel of an office, a story she had spun out of the golden silk of thin air, because that is something we all do to protect our illusions and soothe our fears, did not give her peace of mind. She could not quite believe her Luis would spend hour after hour in a shabby office looking out on the dullness of the harbor, laboring with the dreary, dogged devotion of a hermetic initiate to earn something so meager as a salary. This image of Luis made no sense to her. For as long as she had known him, he had abhorred actually doing any work. Luis was all appetite. Luis was all frivolity and song. So her madness deepened the way the color of a summer sunset deepens.

-69-

Wounded thus by the treachery of Luis' changed behavior, Nerea suddenly decided one day that he had been going to this office for years, a secret refuge where he had brought all sorts of young, willing women, most of them Asiatic (why they were of Asiatic descent she did not even want to imagine). A room most certainly decorated in the Moorish tradition, for Luis had always said that Islam offered the only version of paradise worthy a man of his appetite. A room always bathed in sunlight and fresh, aromatic breezes even though the slatted blinds were always shut. Thick, plush rugs from Persia scattered across the floor. Several long mahogany sofas along the walls, with elegantly carved legs and plush, brocaded pillows for reclining. Ornately carved tables covered with tiny jeweled artifacts from Morocco or Spain. The window frames and the doorway arch decorated with Tunisian tile work, intricate geometric patterns of blue and aquamarine and teal and gold and white colored tiles that dazzled the eye and inspired thoughts of God and absolute salvation. Elephants carved from onyx or jade or malachite. A great bed to one side covered in satins and silks. Incense burning. Girlish laughter (a soft tinkling sound). The smells of rosewood and balsam and cinnamon swirling with the sunlight. The deeply invigorating smell of the sea. More girlish laughter (more soft tinkling sounds). Three or four girls in silk kimonos or sheer lace or nothing at all, lounging on the sofas or in the great bed, their legs wide open, the women fingering themselves, stroking each other, licking each other, their juices flowing. Luis applying oils to their skin and drinking wine. Luis then pushing himself into each one, taking them one at a time, or two at a time, the others with lingering, approving smiles on their faces and arms outstretched, leaning back against the pillows or in the great bed to catch the sunlight, to bathe in the breeze, waiting to fuck and to be fucked. All of the images, and even the girls themselves, stolen from the paintings of Gyula (Jules) Tornai, the great Hungarian painter (or near great, or at least he painted with great conviction, which is what one reviewer said after a showing of his paintings in London in 1917), who had been born in 1861 in a small village near Presov, Hungary (which was, incidentally, one hundred and sixty kilometers due east of Ružomberok, the village where Peter Lorre was born) and who later traveled the world and spent many years in India and Japan, where he contracted syphilis, and who died alone in a boarding house in Budapest in 1928 (probably from the syphilis) and was buried in a pauper's grave.

This is the vision of truth Nerea saw when she closed her eyes. A truth about her Luis that she had not known until that very moment. A truth suddenly revealed, the way sunlight reveals itself in the early morning. Or the way a ticking clock reveals itself in the middle of the night. Nerea kept her eyes closed so she could drink in every detail of Luis' culpable depravity. She felt the triumph of finally uncovering his subterfuge. Still, she also felt that in order to be fair, which is to say in order to have a ready response for his every excuse, she needed to document his habits, so she began to spy on this monstrous shadow of many shadows who had once destroyed time. Adopting a pose which she believed was the height of sober disinterest, she listened in on his telephone conversations, bending her ear around corners and squeezing it through keyholes. She went through the mail he locked away in the upper drawer of his desk, a cheap, shabby desk provided by the hotel so the lock was easy to jimmy, a probing eye looking for the telltale sign of dirt. On rare occasions, he would mention his plans for the afternoon or evening, usually in an off-hand, cavalier sort of way, which immediately aroused Nerea's suspicions, so she would later seek him out in the very parks or cafés or theatres he had mentioned, reacting with a superior yet bitter nonchalance if she did indeed run into him. And always she would take note of the women he danced with or drank with or ate with or fondled right there in public on Friday and Saturday nights, for she still danced with the other girls in their rented headpieces at the Rio Cristal Club or the Jungle Club or Jiggs Cabaret and Nightclub on the waterfront (she paid special attention there) or the sultry, lust-filled La Campana.

Of course Luis realized within a few weeks of her skulking about that Nerea was undone by jealousy. The very air was charged with the electricity of lovesick despair. Plants withered as she passed by. Insects and other small creatures were instantly vaporized whenever she looked their way. The smallest sound escaping her lips sent shockwaves radiating out from the epicenter of her grief, causing windows and crystal vases and bedroom mirrors and glass lamps of all shapes and sizes within the immediate vicinity to shatter into clouds of silica and quartz dust, and these same shockwaves were most probably the cause of an epidemic of burst eardrums that had raced indiscriminately through the population of Hotel Milagro, and they might have been a contributing factor in a series of small underwater earthquakes that rattled the waters of the Gulf some thirty miles out, all striking within a few days, killing with their deadly, invisible subterranean vibrations thousands of yellowfin tuna and bluefin and yellow sea bass and a few lemonfish, and also tens of thousands of ballyhoo and a few bonito that had lost their way, and swamping half a dozen small fishing boats besides that were caught in the aftermath (a forty-foot swell that caused beach erosion as far away as the Bahamas). It seemed to everyone who had occasion to occupy the same physical (and in some cases spiritual) space as Nerea that the fabric of reality was altered. The sole exception was Oscar, for whenever Nerea was with Oscar, even if Oscar was on the other side of the room or across the street, or if she was just thinking about him, she played the part Luis had given her with the aplomb of a silver screen goddess. But for all the rest it was as if the fabric of reality (which certain ancient Chinese philosophers said was made of various strands of silk spun by caterpillars living in the shadows on the moon) had been stretched to the point of breaking, the shimmering celluloid of existence pulled tightly across the gaping hole of the universe, skintight like a drum. So Luis did what any ex-lover driven to the edge of the abyss would do. He invited Nerea to see his office.

Naturally, Nerea wasn't sure how to respond at first. A single, childish voice trapped inside her brain cried out that everything Luis might tell her or show her would be part of an alluring but all-consuming lie, a half-truth to be sure, but also a half-lie and therefore still a lie, but this childish voice was soon lost amid a swirl of eager, self-adulatory adult voices, presumably voices of experience, each with a different theory about what they would see, a different point of view to push on the world, but all of them in general agreement that a half-lie was still half a step closer to the truth, an untutored belief certainly, but quite popular in its day, and then one of the voices rose above the rest with the purity of a dark, starless night and said if Nerea had been wrong about Luis, then she (or they, if you counted each voice) might even forgive him, in fact, she (they) would be forced to forgive him (depending, on how she or they defined truth in the first place). And so Nerea accepted the invitation.

-70-

The next day Luis led a still startled and perhaps sleepy Nerea, who was walking with the paranoid delicacy of a doe, through the lobby of Hotel Milagro to the street outside. It was nine in the morning, a bright, sunny day. They were going to catch a bus, but Nerea suddenly said she wanted to take one of the ancient streetcars that ran along Calle Luz, so they did. It was a short, silent trip, strangely silent, without the thin, metallic rattle that normally accompanies such trips, without the clang of the streetcar bell or the rumbling voices of the passengers, without any sound at all except for an odd whooshing sound as they passed by street corners and people crossing in front or behind or just milling about, as if their streetcar was traveling through an oversized pneumatic air tube.

Nerea wondered if she and Luis had been hypnotized or were going insane, but Luis did not appear to notice the strange silence. The streetcar stopped only once along the way and a few men in suits and Panama hats got on and also a couple of young girls who might have taken the day off from school to go shopping. Nerea saw their mouths moving, the men near the front of the car and the girls at the back, and she tried to listen in on their conversations, but there was nothing to hear. Then Nerea could see the dark gray of the harbor rising up like a great wind and she and Luis got off and Luis pointed to a building and Nerea nodded and followed him but she had no idea where they were. The sunshine was gone. It was now a gray, cloudy day. The air was thick with pestilent heat and the smells of rotting fish and diesel engines and the muffled, groaning sounds of working men. The building Luis had pointed to seemed to blot out the sky.

Nerea felt like she was suffocating.

They headed for the entrance on the northwest side. The entrance was actually two entrances, a heavy, wrought iron gate leading to the market floor, which was usually unlocked at eleven in the morning, but sometimes the gate remained locked until four in the afternoon, and a smaller, narrow wooden door painted a surprisingly bright lime green, leading to the first of a dozen narrow hallways. Those who worked in this massive, colonial-era structure could be seen passing through the lime green door at all hours of the day and night. The plaza leading up to the gate and the door was crammed full of lonely, disheveled men with empty hands and thin-lipped, toothless grins, and fat women with all of their teeth wearing plain cotton dresses and thin rope sandals, and some wearing scarves to cover their heads but all of them holding baskets or containers of some kind. They were all waiting for the gate to open. Nerea felt a sudden urge to weep, but she kept her composure. It was not clear if the men were with the women, or if the men and the women were waiting in the plaza for different reasons.

Luis said it was like that every morning until they opened the gate. Sometimes, he said, the crowd stretched all the way to the Convent of Santa Clara, a distance of four blocks, all the way to a narrow oak door on Calle Cuba that was rarely if ever used. Luis said the nuns who used to use the door with some frequency were long gone. They had sold the building to the government in 1919, and by 1923 the Department of Public Works had moved in and begun the important but enigmatic process of bricking in windows and covering up fancy 17th century archways and nailing shut side doors and back doors in order to limit access to the thousands of confidential documents and bank account ledgers and other official records that should have been kept in an airtight vault three floors underground, but the sealed corridors and locked novitiate cells of an abandoned nunnery were better than nothing. The only people Luis had ever seen even pass by the narrow door on Calle Cuba were government workers.

Naturally, Nerea wanted to know more about the nuns, but Luis said he had already told her everything he knew. Of course if he had paid any attention at all to the bits and pieces of local legend that float about all historic neighborhoods, he would have known that the convent had once housed a community of Franciscan nuns whose primary purpose was to educate the daughters of wealthy plantation owners and shipping magnates or members of the diplomatic corp. He would have known that those same nuns had counseled those same despairing daughters when those daughters had wished to join the cloister after disastrous love affairs or because their fathers were convinced they would never be able to find suitable husbands. He would have known that the convent had thus become a haven for the victims of unrequited love.

On this the morning of the visit, as if by preternatural or artistic design, the crowd had already reached the door to the convent. Luis said this was unusual for so early in the day. Even the few government workers that passed along Calle Cuba on their way to the convent's main entrance glanced at the crowd with stupefied apprehension. Nerea wanted to know where all the people came from and why there were so many of them, but Luis didn't say a word. Again, Nerea felt like she was suffocating. The crowd became restless, noisy, for they had been waiting since just before sunrise. Nerea almost fainted from the odor of so many unwashed people crammed together in so small a space. Even though they were still outside it seemed to Nerea that they were trapped inside a very small room, part of an underground labyrinth perhaps, or perhaps a gas chamber or an oven or a crypt. She wanted to know what all these people were waiting for.

Luis laughed. Sometimes, he said, it is hard to tell if the crowd is waiting to get inside the market or waiting to get inside the old, abandoned convent. Nerea stopped a moment, wondering if there was any hidden meaning in what Luis had said, but Luis smiled with absent-minded joy and took hold of her arm and ushered her through the crowd. She almost fainted a second time.

Then a breeze swirled around the plaza and the unpleasant smells from the unwashed men and women dissipated. The danger of fainting had passed and the crowd settled down. They were used to waiting. Suddenly they seemed like stones. Patient. Immovable. Unbothered. Suddenly Nerea was aware of thousands of pairs of unblinking eyes staring out at an untroubled sea.

For a moment Nerea became someone else, a woman in the crowd. She was one of the thousand pairs of unblinking eyes. She was holding a basket. She was staring at a man and a woman making their way through the crowd, but she looked at them with weary indifference, as if she were watching the traffic roll by on San Pedro. A gruff, guttural voice from the crowd said something derogatory about the man and the woman, she could tell by the tone, but the only words she could make out were the words: *perro lazarillo*. The phrase was repeated several times, like a chorus, followed by a great deal of laughter. Then the phrase and the laughter floated away. Then Nerea was herself again. As Luis guided her through the lime green door she looked back at the crowd as if to say either I am completely mad, or you are, but they did not even flinch.

"Do you think they will storm the gate?" said Nerea.

Luis shook his head, but then he smiled.

"No, no, but perhaps they should."

Nerea didn't know what to say. She started to tremble. Or maybe she was perspiring.

She was plagued by all sorts of creeping doubts. She had a sudden premonition that the world was coming to an end.

Her sense of unreality deepened.

It took them twenty minutes to get to Luis' office. It took them an eternity. They passed through a series of long dim hallways and up (and sometimes down) a seemingly endless latticework of wooden stairs. Occasionally there was a missing step, but not often. The hallways were lined on both sides with dozens of heavy wooden doors, also painted lime green, set at random intervals, one door never directly across from another, none with any kind of marking whatsoever, not a sign or a nameplate, not even a number, but each with an opaque transom window across the top, some of the windows closed, some of them open. The gloominess of the hallways grew with every step. Brown glass globes hung from the ceiling every twenty feet or so, but not all of the globes were in working order, and those that were cast a weak, syrupy brownish light that was swallowed up by every passing shadow. After a while the only sense Nerea trusted was her sense of sound, but the sounds she heard made no sense to her at all. Behind some of the doors she could hear quite distinctly strange gurgling sounds, as if someone were drowning, or possibly conducting arcane experiments to determine the electromagnetic capabilities of dolphins confined in saltwater tanks, but who would do such a thing and why she could not fathom. Behind other doors she could hear the sounds of machinery humming or furniture being moved or rifles being fired and the spent casings bouncing on a wooden floor, or adding machines adding at the speed of light, which would produce ocular migraines unless you wore underwater goggles, or laughter followed by heavy banging sounds, and then light tapping sounds, as if someone were learning to tap dance, and then the sound of a bottle being uncorked and then a coughing fit, and then the sounds of someone dreaming, which sounds a little something like the murmuring of glass bees hidden in the damp foliage on a foggy summer morning, and then the click of a movie projector and the whine of a static-filled screen, and then a radio announcer with a very staticky voice announcing the results of the last race from Oriental Park and then a trumpet blaring, or something that sounded like a trumpet, and the next race getting under way and the sounds of the horses racing around the track and the announcer getting very excited, and then the sound of a doctor quietly talking with a nurse, and then another coughing fit, and then more laughter. Luis was not bothered by anything Nerea heard. Then they came to a stretch without any doors at all and the sounds faded altogether and so they traveled in complete silence for a while, even the sound of their footsteps was felt rather than heard, a subtle collapsing sensation, like one's lungs filling up with blood or seawater, and then Nerea heard a soft whispering kind of sound, but she could not determine if it were an actual sound or merely her ears ringing in the absence of any noise. She was about to ask Luis if he heard this strange ringing sound when they turned a corner and stumbled into a small group of young men. The men were wearing overalls and cotton work shirts drenched in sweat and smoking cigarettes that smelled like burning rubber, cupping the cigarettes carefully with their hands in case a strong wind should come roaring down the hallway, though such an event seemed unlikely. Nerea immediately realized that they were the source of the whispering, their faces contorting as they spoke a strange, garbled tonal language that seemed less like a language and more like the warbling, singsong mimicry of Brazilian parrots. Without warning or any shy second glances, as if the men were merely slipping revolvers into shoulder holsters or offering Indian talismans to curious tourists, they stopped their whispering and then stamped out their cigarettes and brushed out the wrinkles in their overalls, straightening themselves against the wall as they did so, and said "Good morning, El Zayde," all of them in unison, with unapologetic good humor.

By the time Luis and Nerea got to the third floor, the hallways were teeming with all sorts of figures moving back and forth through the brown, syrupy gloom, more young men in overalls and drenched work shirts pushing carts overloaded with boxes of all sorts, older men with satchels or leather briefcases in their hands but without their jackets, nervous men running out of one room or another and then dashing hurriedly down the hall, disappearing into the hazy, brownish soup, the echo of their footfalls diminishing, and young girls in pleasing floral print dresses and red or beige round-toed patent-leather slingbacks, pretty young secretaries perhaps, or mistresses or fiancées or high-class prostitutes who had been up all night, following after the rushing men, waving letters in the air that had never been read or, in some cases, never even mailed, the letters filled with all sorts of personal information, private lies and sexual innuendo, the sordid details of crimes that had been expunged, that sort of thing, the young girls rushing after the rushing men with incredibly light feet, and everywhere in those long hallways traversing the third floor Luis was greeted with warm, friendly grins and happy, approving nods and soft, flirtatious smiles and a few weary but respectful grimaces, and with every grin or nod or smile or grimace there was an appropriate "Good morning, El Zayde" or "Is there anything I can get for you, El Zayde" or "When you have a moment, El Zayde, could you stop by and see so and so, they have a question only you can answer" or "If only you had been here last night, El Zayde, we had a spectacular night last night, we are sorry you missed it."

It was almost too much for Nerea to take in.

Then the voices faded and the hallway was suddenly empty, as if a great wind had indeed come roaring through the building. But the gloominess remained. The gloominess was almost unbearable. "We're almost there," Luis said, but his words had a hollow sound to them, as if he did not quite believe himself. The hallway seemed smaller now and felt more like a tunnel. Nerea wondered if something catastrophic had happened. Perhaps the building had collapsed, she thought. Or perhaps the crowd in the plaza had become a mob and had stormed the gate. Perhaps they had started a revolution. Perhaps people were dying. Or perhaps she had suddenly died. Then Luis laughed as if he were able to read her troubled thoughts. They emerged from the tunnel and the gloom and Luis said, "Here we are."

But they were not yet in Luis' office. They were standing in the middle of a small waiting area, a semi-circular atrium with three office doors, one directly across from the tunnel on a roughly north to south plane, the other two facing each other on an east to west line. The doors were typical of detective agencies and newspaper rooms in the 1930s and 40s, and perhaps even the offices of a few Hollywood movie moguls, with brightly polished mahogany frames and frosted glass windows with fancy curlicue borders and shiny brass door knobs. A few potted ferns and a few dwarf palms filled in the spaces between the doors. The plants were dripping with moisture, as if they had been recently watered.

Just this little bit of greenery is a pleasant surprise, Nerea thought.

She listened to the sounds of dripping water for a moment, perhaps to settle her nerves, her face angled slightly up and her eyes closed as if she were waiting for a dream to fall from the sky, and then she felt a drop of water on her skin, and then another, and she opened her eyes and she saw there were great, gaping holes in the ceiling. She could actually see the sky through the holes. It was a blue sky now, the gray clouds were gone, and water was dripping from the holes in the ceiling.

"Here we are," Luis said again, or maybe it was the first time. He pulled Nerea towards the middle door. The door featured shiny black lettering that said Ignazio Tiziano & Sons. It was the same on the other doors. Luis opened the middle door and they went inside.

-71-

Nerea was caught between the involuntary spasms of jealousy and an unwillingness to believe she had been wrong. The office was like the prison cell of her first imagining, a vintage oak swivel chair with the heft of a tank and a narrow desk pushed up against a window with the slatted blinds closed and barely enough light creeping through to illuminate the dust particles floating in the air like so many wickedly capricious spiderlings, dainty harbingers of death, or like so many jubilant paratroopers descending, as one of the vagabond poets of Mexico City once wrote, as swiftly as clocks.

The desk was overflowing with letters and ledgers and a few yellowing newspapers, for in spite of his professed diligence, Luis suffered from poor eyesight late at night and so had trouble seeing what he was doing. Luis told Nerea that one of the girls from the steno pool was assigned to his office and came in twice a week in the evenings to help him sort through the mess. The seafoam green Optima typewriter planted squarely on top of the paperwork belonged to her.

Luis flicked on a switch and two brown globes began to glow near the ceiling, but the darkness in the room only intensified. A pair of wingback chairs materialized out of the gloom and also a small side table.

Nerea's mind had been a jumble of contradictory impressions until she heard about the secretary. She now stared at Luis with futile pity. Then she began firing questions at him. To poor Luis the questions seemed random, bizarre, incoherent, laced with mind-numbing inertia or arsenic or worse.

"Why do they call you El Zayde?" Nerea said.

Luis didn't respond.

He disappeared into the slatted shadows on the far side of the room. There were some clinking sounds, spoons rattling, water fizzing. Then he returned with two high-balls.

"Everywhere we went they were calling you El Zayde."

They sat down in the wingback chairs.

"Yes," he said. "They were."

Luis gave Nerea her drink and then sipped from his own glass, smiling a slight, satisfied smile

"But why?"

"They always call me that. They think I'm the boss, a fat

fish, the big cheese, the Big Kahuna."

From somewhere outside there was a distant rumbling sound, like a massive gate being ripped from its hinges and the earth shuddering and then the sounds of raucous cheering, or perhaps it was screaming, or perhaps it was the excited, jittery voices of pilgrims participating in a religious festival for the very first time.

"It is an honest mistake. They've never seen the Big Kahuna."

Another sip.

"He doesn't come here at all."

And yet another.

Nerea was watching Luis very carefully, the way his mouth curled up slightly when he spoke, the way his tongue rolled effortlessly and casually across his teeth when he finished a sentence, as if there were some lingering sweetness to his words that he found immensely satisfying. This was a Luis that Nerea had never seen before. She wasn't sure she could believe a word he said.

"I'm the only one who does come here," said Luis. "It is very ironic."

Nerea wondered who this mythical Big Kahuna was. She wondered what Luis meant by saying he was the only one who came here. Where exactly was here and why was Luis the only one? And how many others might come here but didn't? What stopped them?

Then Luis laughed a hearty, robust laugh, but it was laughter also tinged with a philosopher's understanding of the tragic comedy of life, or perhaps a movie director's take on things, as if he had just then recognized the tenuous nature of his own existence and so realized that there was nothing else to do but laugh in such a strange, uninhibited fashion from his belly to his heels.

In good faith, he tried his best to tell Nerea everything she wanted to know about his business associates.

-72-

The gist of what Luis told Nerea about his business associates:

Luis' business associates were all directors of Ignazio Tiziano & Sons, but they could just as easily have secured starring roles in any number of 1930s Hollywood gangster films, like *The Public Enemy* (1931) or *Scarface* (1932). They were all criminals of one sort or another, thugs, killers, disgruntled bureaucrats with axes to grind, cops on the take, part-time dock workers, union bosses, drug kingpins, a vagabond collection of second-tier Mafiosi who had been quickly elevated during the war years to positions of power hidden within the rat's maze of Cuban politics, a crumbling infrastructure supported by secret government agencies and high-profile public officials as well as labor union under-secretaries, media moguls, and a few well-placed church dignitaries, and so Luis' business associates (and Luis himself by association) commanded the loyalty of tens of thousands of Cuban souls, and all because the Americans thought they needed the nefarious skills of this gang of gangsters during the late 1930s and early 1940s to help keep track of wayward Nazi spies intent on submarining the industrialized war-waging capability of the United States.

The American government had been convinced that the impenetrable shadows of every sleepy, backwater Caribbean and South American port were infested with all manner of German and Argentine saboteurs, working in an obviously clandestine manner for the *Amt Auslands und Abwehr* (Germany's Foreign Office of Defense, part of the Nazi's labyrinthine bureaucratic structure), men and women who would do anything to replace the bald eagle of the United States with the black eagle of Germany. But the Americans did not think of Havana as just another backwater port. As late as 1943, the American government clung to the unsubstantiated belief that the capital city of romantic Cuba was the gateway through which everything flowing out of the Axis-infested southern hemisphere on its way north must flow, which meant it would be the most likely jumping off point for any group of saboteurs trying to reach the sandy, unpatrolled beaches of Florida. (Never mind that German spies routinely bypassed Havana on their way from South America to New York City.) So they spent a great deal of time and money searching for Germans in the streets of Havana.

Of course these initial assumptions proved to be incorrect. Perhaps the Americans had intercepted a decoy message and the Germans were laughing their asses off. Perhaps the

Americans simply could not swallow the truth that Argentina was too far away to forcefully manipulate and found it easier to chase shadows around the Caribbean and then tell the American public they were fighting the good fight. Or perhaps they believed what they saw in Hollywood movies. In any event, the *Abwehr* sent only one spy to Cuba during the entire war, at least this was the official story, an incompetent boob named Heinz Lüning, who had been given orders to set up a secret wireless station so he could transmit any important military information to agents in Buenos Aires, which is where the real espionage activity was taking place, as everyone knew.

The Argentine agents were a collection of minor German diplomats and Spanish Falangists posing as sailors or businessmen or academics or traveling actors aboard various innocuous-seeming ships, such as the *Sebastian Elcano*, a Spanish school ship out of Barcelona, or the *Cabo de Buena Esperanza,* an ocean liner that was also the maritime home of the actress Lola Membrives (who was, incidentally, one of Franco's favorite spies, though nothing was ever proven) and which ferried her back and forth across the Atlantic once every few months so she could make an announcement on Radio Prieto, encouraging the good citizens of Buenos Aires to come out to the theatre while she was in town, for God only knew when she would return with this terrible war raging across the globe, and after each performance her flunkies would pass out pro-Axis pamphlets to her fans, all of the pamphlets doctored by Doc Goebbels, filled to overflowing with the most insidious manipulations of the truth. Suffice it to say that the agents in Argentina would decide if anything from Lüning was worth reporting to Berlin.

In the end the whole Lüning affair was a rather dark comedy. Lüning was never able to get his radio to work, so he spent most of his time drinking in the various bars and clubs in and around Havana. When he was arrested by Batista's men in 1942, he had yet to send a single message. But Batista and the Allies claimed he was a master spy nevertheless and that he had been an integral component in the web of Nazi submarines operating in the Caribbean, so they had him executed.

As you would expect, the consequences of enlisting the aid of this nefarious gang of cutthroats was inevitable. By the 1950s it was next to impossible to curtail the activities of the gangsters, cutthroats, thieves and assassins that had been given semi-official permission to set up shop in Havana. Business had been lucrative, and it appeared, at least on the surface, that business would continue to be lucrative, for even though the war was over, neither the rolling succession of Cuban regimes nor the American CIA was willing to spend the money "to clean out this nest of Machiavellian vipers," as one confidential CIA memo had so elegantly put it.

The grandfather of this motley crew was Giuseppe Federico DiCarla, who had been born in 1881 in the small seaside village of Scopello in northwestern Sicily. The men in his family had been tuna fishermen for centuries, but when he was a small boy his father had gone to work on one of the great tuna boats out of Castellammare del Golfo, which translated means Sea Fortress of the Gulf, so they had moved. Later, Federico had moved to Trapani, a major seaport on the lip of the Tyrrhenian Sea, a half day's journey from the town of his childhood, because in those days the roads weren't very good, a dirt path for ox-carts pretty much, the road crumbling in places, the hazy shadow of the Zingaro mountains to the northwest, the humpbacked shadows of peasants plodding across the plains, the plains dotted with stone farmhouses and then a village and then nothing except rocky hills and clumps of twisted fig trees or silvery olive trees (which Federico said looked as if they were bathed in moonlight even in the middle of the day), and then another village, and so on like that, and in every village, along every road, young men in fustian or velvet jackets, all of them bastard sons of Garibaldi, all of them wearing skull caps and cartridge belts and muddy top-boots, all of them with guns, long-barreled rifles, though mostly for show, except when it came to hunting rabbits. At least that's how DiCarla remembered it. And that was all Luis had time to tell Nerea, for the very next instant the door to his office burst open, shattered into a thousand splinters it seemed like, and one of Luis' associates or underlings or messenger boys stood in the doorway, panting and heaving.

-73-

At first the messenger boy did not move. He stood in the doorway, still panting and heaving, a dark, vibrating shadow backlit by the sunlight pouring in through the holes in the ceiling. He seemed uncertain if he had come to the right place. He seemed to be wondering if he had burst into a tucked away bathroom where someone was busy in a stall masturbating to beat the band, or else that same someone was reading with an insatiable appetite the mythic though reactionary (and some would say downright sadistic and certainly rightwing) poetry of Silvio Salvático, the mythical Chilean poet and writer and gossip columnist.

"El Zayde?"

"Yes?"

"El Zayde?"

"Yes, yes, what is it? I am right here."

"But I cannot see you."

"Of course not. Your eyes have not yet adjusted. It is very dim in here."

"Yes . . . I guess that makes sense."

The messenger boy removed a pair of black-rimmed eyeglasses and rubbed his eyes. He tried to gain control of his breathing. There was a general noisiness in the air and also the sound of sirens, as if a great hubbub were occurring in the streets of Havana or elsewhere. The messenger boy replaced his glasses. He was a plain, unremarkable fellow with the aura of a befuddled accountant or the likeable but bumbling assistant to a brilliant but emotionally distant and therefore unstable scientist. He was wearing a thin dark cotton shirt and dark pants and rope-soled sandals. Nerea barely gave him a second glance. She thought he made a much better shadow than a messenger boy. He was perspiring heavily. He was not used to excitement. His name was Immanuel.

"The people have stormed the gate," Immanuel said.

"Yes, but what does that mean exactly?"

"It means they have ripped the gate from its hinges and tossed it aside."

"Yes, yes, but what is happening?"

"They are . . . they . . ."

"Yes. Tell me slowly. Leave nothing out."

"They are pouring through . . . they are . . ."

Immanuel gulped a few gulps of air, like people do when they have been buried alive in a coffin and have had to claw their way out, which is no easy task when the coffin is a pine box with several feet of soft, clumpy dirt piled on top, but which is virtually impossible when the coffin features an aluminum shell or some mixture of bronze and copper or some other alloy, so clearly Immanuel was gulping air as if he had just clawed his way out of a pine box that had been recently buried.

"Before that. From the beginning," said Luis.

Immanuel took a few more gulps because you cannot even begin to imagine the stress of being buried in a pine box for even one minute or several minutes until your eyes adjust to absolute darkness, which they might never do, and you are left with the certain knowledge that you are facing eternity all alone without even a chance to say goodbye, unless you get out by some miracle, in which case you have cheated death, so to speak. So Immanuel took a few more gulps, and then he began anyway.

"They were waiting as usual," he said. "The people. But there were many more of them today. No one knows why. It seemed like they were waiting for something to happen. Like a signal, perhaps. Or a sign from God. Leonardo was frightened by so many so he did not open the gate, and we told him that was a mistake but he still refused. The people were clamoring to get in and waving their baskets and bags in the air and he refused. Then there was gunfire from somewhere near the convent and someone said there were soldiers coming or revolutionaries or maybe it was the police, and the people started running away from the convent, but there was nowhere for them to go down that narrow street, there were so many of them, except straight for us. They were heading straight for us like a herd of stampeding bulls. What could we do? Leonardo opened a small porthole window near the gate and started firing his pistol, but he was afraid to look out so his aim was erratic. I think he killed a few pigeons trying to fly away but that was it. The next thing we knew the crowd was surging against the gate, shouting and cheering and laughing and crying. I have never heard so much noise in one tiny space. Then they tore the gate off its hinges, as I said, and this stampede of raging bulls started rampaging all about the marketplace arcade on the first floor, swarming in and out of the various stalls. The vendors had already fled. Did you not feel the building shake? We thought the entire structure would come crashing down on top of our heads with the pounding of so many angry feet. I don't know how many people there were. Several hundred. Maybe more. Angels and demons dancing on the head of a pin. They were racing around, grabbing whatever they could find and stuffing it into their baskets and bags and then running for the plaza, their cups overflowing. And then everything was gone. There wasn't a vegetable or a piece of fruit or a pork chop or a bag of coffee beans or an umbrella or a box of cigars or a bottle of wine or a pair of shoes or a lady's hat or a jar of olive oil or a book of philosophy or a gentleman's serge suit left in the whole place. Everything was gone. Vanished. Vaporized. But then it became clear that only those first few who had led the charge made off with the goods. Everyone else, which is to say hundreds and hundreds of poor, dispossessed, vagrant souls, disillusioned souls, angry and bitter, all of them were still clinging to their empty baskets and their empty bags with the kind of fierce desperation I have only ever read about or seen in the movies. It was worse than any nightmare. They began searching through closets and small storerooms and offices, these vagrants, looking for anything they might steal, anything that would fill up their baskets and their bags and ease their heart-wrenching, raging, insatiable hunger. They spread out into the hallways like a disease. But there was nothing left, El Zayde, and so they fell into a madness, tearing apart entire rooms, dismantling desks and other pieces of furniture, breaking windows and scattering important papers, toppling and then smashing the delicate apparatus and specially designed instruments of various arcane experiments that have been going on for years in secret, heaping together great piles of used tires and other flammable items and lighting small bonfires which soon became big bonfires, setting off small explosions using whatever chemicals were laying around, most likely anhydrous ammonia or carbon disulfide or diethyl ether. We thought they would turn upon each other. We hoped they would. We prayed. But they never did. Did you not notice the smell of black smoke, El Zayde? Did you not breathe in the clouds of toxic gas? It was more than we could stand, we almost passed out, we are not made of sterner material, El Zayde, I am sorry to say, so we left. But the hallway to the plaza was blocked, it was covered with heaps of fallen refuse, bits of the ceiling that had collapsed, broken lamps, exposed wiring, plumbing fixtures, and everywhere there was the heavy, black smoke. We could see no way to get through to the plaza. So we headed up to the second floor and down the fire escape that we always used when we wanted to get out of the building without being noticed so we could slip across San Pedro and take a nice long walk along the water's edge. But I came up here to find you, El Zayde. There is no one else on the third floor except the three of us. Everyone else has escaped safely."

"And the vagrants looking to fill their empty bags and baskets?"

"I am sure they got out, El Zayde. They seemed, how shall I say it, very well organized in spite of the chaos. Yes, there is a meaning behind the madness for any who would look. But it does not matter. It is a raging inferno down there. Not even demons would stay in such a place. Not even Lucifer himself. Even the stone walls are beginning to melt."

A vaguely troubled look came over Luis's face, as if he were trying to remember what he had eaten for lunch the day before and was dismayed by his poor memory. He suddenly felt alternating waves of humiliation and sadness. Then he heard a snapping, barking sound, which was most likely the sound of Immanuel saying 'El Zayde, El Zayde, we haven't much time,' and then he heard a deeper, snapping sound, more like a deep growl, which was most likely himself saying 'Yes, yes, but we need to proceed deliberately,' and then he heard a high pitched ringing sound like tiny Christmas bells, silver Christmas bells which had been fashioned by artisans living in Mexico City, which was most likely Nerea wondering what this crazy self-proclaimed messenger boy named Immanuel meant by saying there wasn't much time and what were they waiting around for when the world was collapsing, and then Luis noticed that the shadowy appearance of Immanuel was not a result of dim lighting.

Immanuel was black from the smoke and ash that had engulfed the widening apocalypse (the bonfires, the explosions, the raging inferno) of the first floor. It was almost as if Immanuel were wearing a mask, as if the series of explosions and the storming of the gate had been staged for some unknown purpose. Then Luis suddenly smiled as if he had just that moment been raised from the dead.

"Nerea, go with Immanuel, he will get you out of the building. I have to gather up a few things."

Then he laughed a joyful, robust laugh.

"I can't let everything go up in smoke, now can I?"

Immanuel did not laugh at Luis' joke, but he might have been smiling, but it was hard to tell from the smoke and ash that obscured his true appearance. Luis went to his desk and scribbled something on a piece of paper and handed it to Immanuel.

"Call this number and tell whoever answers what happened, just as you told it to me."

". . . ."

"And tell them I'll be along shortly."

". . . ."

"No, don't say anything else. Just hang up after that. They will understand."

Then Immanuel and Nerea headed out through the shattered office door, and it seemed to Luis that they were suddenly swimming in an ocean of blue sky and sunlight and the potted palm trees and ferns were swaying back and forth with a watery gentleness, like strands of seaweed, and Immanuel was no longer a dark shadow with skin the color of smoke and ash, his skin was suddenly and mysteriously washed clean of all grime, his skin was as white as the whitest plume of the whitest bird in paradise, and then Nerea and Immanuel vanished into the darkly glowing wormhole of the hallway on their way to the freedom of a bright sunny day. For a moment Luis stood there, staring after them, as if Immanuel and Nerea were both lifelong friends, though clearly this was not the case. Then he turned to the papers scattered across his small desk and a few files that had been hidden away in a filing cabinet, and he also discovered an old leather briefcase which he had never seen before crammed into the top drawer. Before another thought entered his brain, such as 'Jesus Christ it's hot in here' or 'what the hell happened down there' or 'God damn fucking peasants' or 'I sure hope Nerea gets out okay' or 'who exactly is this Immanuel anyway, I don't remember seeing his face before' or 'what the fuck am I doing, this place is about to go up in smoke,' he began shoving the papers and the files, those that seemed important, into the leather briefcase, and whistling all the while.

-74-

Sometimes it is difficult to know when and where someone's story truly begins, but without this deeper understanding it is almost impossible to understand why anything happens at all. Understanding the true beginning of any story (yours, mine, anyone's), especially as that story unfolds before our very eyes, gives shape to the entire universe, and it is this shape that gives meaning to our lives. This shape is our collective story, if you will. But nothing is ever what it appears to be. And this is the crux of our dilemma. How far back do we go? Which events do we embrace as absolutely necessary? And which do we dismiss? If we don't go back far enough we will end up in the soup of misunderstanding. If we go back too far we will invariably take a misstep when we start forward again and become tangled up in the labyrinth of everything that never was. Now some will argue that we can never go back far enough, that every story begets another story, and so on, but this kind of thinking doesn't begin with anything we can easily grasp, and it generally leads only to rude awakenings and sudden attacks of vertigo, at least on a personal level, for while the grand narrative extends to infinity, few of us can be certain of our own narrative thread beyond the inevitability of our own deaths. So we do the best we can with the limited information we are given and hope that no one will notice we haven't a clue, that we have no idea what's going to happen next because we don't know where we truly came from, so how could anyone expect us to know where we will end up. This ignorance, of course, is partially (or wholly, if you do not believe in God) the cause of what we like to call the tragedy of life, or the comedy of life if you prescribe to the theories of the post-apocalyptic romanticists, or the tragicomedy if you are a dyed-in-the-wool postmodernist. In plain language, we are all whistling in the dark.

Such was the case with Luis. Why did Luis remain in his office with the raging inferno raging two floors below? Why did he suddenly and manically (as opposed to maniacally) begin stuffing papers into a briefcase when Immanuel had told him the stone walls were beginning to melt and ten minutes later or thereabouts, he himself could actually feel the heat of the stone walls melting? Even Luis, if pressed, would have had difficulty coming up with a believable answer. And what about the briefcase? Had Luis simply forgotten he owned a briefcase or had one mysteriously appeared in the top drawer of the filing cabinet, as if by destiny's own hand, so that Luis would use it for precisely that purpose for which it was used? Who can say? And would Luis have remained in his office if there had been no briefcase so conveniently placed within his reach? Why did he stay when all reason and the instinct for survival must certainly have urged him to flee with Nerea and Immanuel? And why did he take the time to scribble on a piece of paper and then give the paper to Immanuel with only the vaguest of instructions? Such questions are always difficult to answer and generally require exhaustive, mind-numbing analysis, which may or may not lead to the overall decay of civilization, at least as we know it, as a battery of social and literary critics and numerous television personalities have suggested, and which is almost certainly the reason that many books are banned or in some cases even burned during periods of great social unrest. But we have no business with such analysis here. Let us simply say that Luis lingered in the dim light of his office, stuffing papers into a briefcase that seemed to appear out of nowhere, to honor the wishes of Giuseppe Federico DiCarla. Which is to say that Federico had once told Luis that they must never call attention to themselves or their activities, that if the iron gates to Ignazio Tiziano & Sons were ever breached, if this simple import/export company were suddenly exposed to the probing eyes of the world at large, if their hand was forced and they had to move on and start over, then they should at the very least make absolutely sure they didn't leave a trace. When they were gone, it should be as if they had never existed. So Luis stayed behind for ten minutes or so because of the preemptory wisdom of Giuseppe Federico DiCarla, and wise words they were indeed, because he didn't dare assume that the fire that had swallowed the first floor would effectively erase the existence of Ignazio Tiziano & Sons from the memory of man.

But there was something else that even Luis did not dare admit to himself. Since Federico's natural wisdom sprang from a deeply rooted psychosis which he had nurtured with unfailing vigilance since he was a young man, it is also fair to say that Luis remained in his tiny hovel of a troglodyte's office on the third floor of a burning building because he was afraid of Giuseppe Federico DiCarla. There, it is out in the open. Luis was absolutely terrified of Giuseppe Federico DiCarla. It was a terror, moreover, that had infiltrated every layer of his skin all the way down through the subcutaneous layer. And that is why he asked Immanuel to call the number on the scrap of paper. He needed to get word to Federico as quickly as possible, but he did not want to be the messenger, so why not use Immanuel (particularly since Luis had a sneaking suspicion that Immanuel was more than just the winged harbinger of doom). Luis understood that the moment Immanuel made the call, he, Luis, would be absolved of all responsibility for the storming of the marketplace gate and the apocalypse that followed. Perhaps Immanuel would even take the fall. And at some indeterminate point in the future, he, Luis, would get a note from Federico and there would be a meeting of all of the Directors of Ignazio Tiziano & Sons to discuss what they could salvage from this disaster and how long before they would be up and running again, and he would attend the meeting, and even participate with a few poignant observations, without the fear of reprisal or even reprimand.

Naturally, to those of us who have never been employed by a psychotic Mafia overlord who may or may not have murdered countless thousands, Luis' fear seems silly. But it is not for us to judge the nature of Luis' fear. We must simply acknowledge that this fear exists (or once existed).

-75-

The true story of Giuseppe Federico DiCarla, which is reason enough to be afraid of him, as Luis was, or at least it will give you something to chew on, mostly from Federico's own lips as pieced together by Luis over the years, and which he was going to share with Nerea word for word but he never got the chance:

Federico had left Sicily during Mussolini's war against the Mafia and eventually settled in Havana.

The exact date of his arrival is unknown.

He said he had picked Havana because Moro Castle reminded him of the medieval castle that guarded the harbor entrance to Castellammare del Golfo. Sometimes he would talk about the differences between the two castles. But mostly he liked to reminisce about his boyhood escapades in Sicily and his only true love, a girl whose name was sometimes Maura D'Alessandria, but at other times her name was Mirella Deodato, and every once in a while, in a fit of unapologetic nostalgia, her name was Maria D'Angelo.

It was hard to tell how accurate his memory was.

According to Luis, Federico always ate with a knife hidden in the folds of his napkin.

It was much more than a knife really. A forge-hammered steel blade with diamond cross sections made by an obscure (which is to say forgotten) artisan in the 17th century. A leather scabbard with gold plated fittings. A simple, straightforward, slender blade for thrusting deep into the belly of an enemy, or a close friend. An assassin's blade, truly. Federico called it his dagger of mercy.

Always when Federico met someone for the first time he would mention this knife. Sometimes he would show it to them with good-natured charm. Giuseppe Federico DiCarla possessed an easygoing, happy-go-lucky charm.

And always, naturally, the same question would follow: why would anyone need to hide a dagger of mercy in the folds of their napkin?

And always, naturally, Federico would smile the polite confessional smile of someone remembering a small transgression from long ago, a childhood sin committed in ignorance, a trivial matter, but very humorous, and then he would oblige the curiosity of anyone who asked with the story of his knife.

It was a very long story.

After a while you would forget it was the story of the knife and you would think it was the story of something else.

But by the end all you could think about was the knife.

I knew nothing of knives when I was a boy, Federico would say. (This is how he would always begin.) Not the kind of knives the Fasci used. Not the knives of the Black Hand dripping with the blood of a thousand bellies ripped wide open and vulnerable widows gnashing their teeth. My father was a fisherman and the only knife he used was for cutting rope and mending nets and gutting fish. But that all changed during the year of Saint Rosalia's Earthquake of Redemption, as it came to be known among the farmers and fisherman and priests of northwestern Sicily. Yes, fisherman who swore they saw the image of the little saint swimming in the waters of the sea even while the stones of ancient buildings were tumbling into the waves. Farmers who saw the shiny gilded patina of her face full of sorrow hiding in the clouds as the earth cracked open and their fields were burned to a crisp by the flames bursting up from below. And the priests were praying to her redemptive spirit, kneeling before a horde of whispering, flickering votive candles like so many dead souls suspended in purgatory, and then they heard a soft and quiet voice, they later said, a voice they knew without a doubt to be her reclusive voice as inaudible as the sound of fluttering eyelids renouncing all temptation; or her firm, incantatory voice ringing out like a sword, praising the boundless, determined mercy of God; or her hopeful, plaintive voice extolling the heroic virtues of a saintly life (virtues now almost only found in the marginalia of ancient Teutonic manuscripts, or in the cryptic dreams of young novitiates after studying the deaths of the Christian martyrs); or her cataclysmic, haranguing voice filled with torrential grace and the musical precision of a chorus of idiot-savants hidden by the clouds; all this they heard even as the leaded glass windows of their churches became a thousand splinters flying through the air like so many daggers. The earthquake was a vision of hell, was it not? Behold the monster with the pointed tail who cleaves the hills and breaketh walls and weapons, the monster of our darkest dreams who infecteth the whole world. Yes. They saw this monster in Caccamo. Yes. In Trabia. Yes, yes. On the other side of Palermo. Yes. You would have thought it could not reach us. You would have thought the distance was too great. But everyone knew something momentous was happening. You could feel the ground move beneath your feet like you were standing in a boat. Even where we lived along the shores of our safe harbor by the sea. A mountain range between us and the source of the earthquake. An entire world between us. A universe.

So the ground rolled and heaved and shuddered for five days and countless buildings cracked and fell apart, and in some places the streets disappeared, great gaping holes opening up and steam rising. In the Cathedral of La Matrici, the altar of the Holy Mary of the Lamp cracked in two, as did the altar dedicated to the Blessed Mary of Carmel. And a crack also appeared in the stone floor in one of the subterranean rooms below the public levels of the church, and there was a slow oozing of spring water from the crack, from a hidden spring beneath the foundation of the church, the water bubbling up, hot and frothy, but this damage was not discovered for many weeks, by which time the paintings that had been stored down there for safekeeping were moldy ruins. And God help the frescoes on the ceiling for the damage they suffered from the intense humidity, which seemed more focused during the five days of the earthquake, attacking only religious artwork and hazy, superstitious thinking, unlike the normally intense humidity of the region which attacked everything with equal fervor.

Every window in the Cathedral shattered and fell to the ground, as did the windows of several smaller churches, but the churches themselves did not fall, which was seen as an example of good triumphing over evil. Some of the jetties along the waterfront and a few warehouses did collapse and were washed away with the tide, but this was not seen as anything except maybe bad luck, or an indictment against those who had built the jetties or the warehouses in the first place. Who could imagine such destruction? It was more than fire and brimstone. We no longer recognized where we lived. We could see the fierce Erinnys hovering in the smoky air, three hell-bound Furies stained with blood, their hair a mass of writhing serpents and horned vipers, their snouts snapping at us like the snouts of deranged dogs. This is what we saw. These were the images eating away at our brains. Just like the priests talked about. Everything they had ever said was suddenly and irrevocably true. So all the old women were huddled in churches all over town and beyond even while the windows were breaking and crucifixes were toppling and altars were cleaved in two, saying their prayers. '*Aitnê! Aitnê! Aitnê!*' And who could blame them? It seemed like the end of the world. Death was everywhere. What else could they do?

But I was not like these old women screaming their prayers or the priests who pretended they were free of lice and would not stoop so low as to pluck a louse from the head of a friend or a penitent. I tried to remain objective. The earthquake happened in September, two weeks after the feast day of Saint Rosalia, but only a few days after the celebration of her feast day had ended. Always with religion something is happening either just before or just after a feast day. Soon everyone was calling it the Great Earthquake of Saint Rosalia's Redemption. But it was mostly the priests who called it this. Because of all the destruction. Because now we could rebuild and then we would be redeemed. Priests will seize on anything. *Ammuccia lu latinu 'gnuranza di parrinu.* Always religion is giving us some new twist, a way of remembering the world that would not normally occur to us. Such was the case here. An earthquake is an earthquake is an earthquake, I have always said. But what is an earthquake anyway but a moment in time? A single moment. Looking back on the earthquake you can see it for what it really was, a gentle rolling of the ground and a few whitewashed walls crumbling and a few whitewashed houses falling apart and a few windows breaking. And then it stopped as suddenly as it had begun. *Burrasca furiusa prestu passa,* as they say. A furious storm passes quickly.

Ah Maura, Maura, Maura.

In the days before the earthquake, I mostly ran through the streets of my town with my only true friend, Ignazio Tiziano. In those days the streets were covered with a very fine dust, almost like flour, a mixture of crushed shells from the sea and tiny grains of wheat and barley from the mills close to the water. There were always farmers from the plains with wagons of wheat and barley. We sometimes worked for the mills, loading sacks of flour onto the cargo ships when they came in. Ignazio's father was a fisherman like my father, so we had no desire to make our living in a boat. We were tired of the stench of fish. Even our sweat smelled of fish, and always we were coughing up tiny fish bones after we ate or getting them caught in our teeth. We will die from fish bones, we used to laugh, but it was happy laughter because we knew it was not true, even though at the same time it was a laughter full of despair because we were tired of fish.

We worked in the mills when we could. And we took to the streets when we weren't working, drinking *assenziu,* playing *brìscula,* and also a variation of *brìscula* which the Spanish called *Mano Negra,* which always made me laugh, a different kind of laughter than with the fish bones, this was a laughter filled with the passion and great joy of youth, as if I had discovered a secret joke that no one else knew about, not even Ignazio.

This is what we would do, and then we would be drunk and swinging our fists at every shadow, and then later we would quiet down and the next thing we knew we would hear women cooing in the darkness of narrow corridors, like the gnawing, tremulous sounds of dying birds, I used to think, or the mysterious, mystical, heart-breaking sounds of dying orchids, their spotted petals drifting slowly, with lazy indifference, to the ground, one by one by one, phppt, phptt, phptt, phptt, like drops of blood; or sometimes this sound of dying birds (which was actually the sounds of the women in the shadows) sounded like the wings of tiny, dark angels beating in rhythmic counterpoint to the ticking of a clock, which are all strange, sad thoughts to occupy the empty spaces between one's ears, I must admit, but that is in effect what these women sounded like, but we were too drunk to know what they were really saying. We would wake up very late the next day with our heads raging and our money gone. *Ah, mi. Di guerra, caccia e amuri, pri un gustu milli duluri.* Which is the Sicilian way of saying that for every solitary pleasure you will suffer a thousand pains.

Oh Maura, my dear sweet Maura.

So the earthquake happened in September, as I have said. By October the west was flooded with refugees from Trabia and Caccamo, even Palermo. Thousands of people had lost their homes. Thousands had also died. My grandmother told us to stay indoors because there were more ghosts walking the roads of Sicily at that time than refugees, more ghosts than the police who were supposed to keep the peace, more ghosts even than the number of words uttered by the priests who were supposed to lead us from despair. Besides, there was nothing we could do. Leave them to the Carmelite nuns, my grandmother hissed, let them sort out who truly deserves help and who is beyond our powers to redeem, let them open their doors, if there are still any nuns left in this part of the world. But we did not listen to my grandmother. And my father had nothing to say except God will provide but we still have to fish, and then he would head down to his boat.

Ignazio and I adopted a different attitude, as you have probably guessed. Our town was not flooded with refugees like so many other towns. It was not an easy place to get to, our town by the sea, unless you took the coast road, and even that was not safe in places where the sea had washed everything away. But a few refugees still came. Refugees always find their way. We welcomed whoever we met, eager for news, but we saw no ghosts. We saw a family with all of their worldly goods piled onto a ramshackle wagon pulled by mule, the dust of the earthquake still plastered to their skin even two months later, eyes staring blankly like enormous black saucers. We saw a young father wearing a white top hat and a torn cloak and a little girl of seven riding piggyback and the memory of a mother crushed to death beneath a collapsing wall, pieces of the wall scattered like seashells across the ground but the mother was nowhere to be seen. We saw an old woman with trembling hands, sucking on a blood orange with her trembling gums, asking everyone she met if they had seen her teeth. Why did they come to our town? Who knows? Who can say? All of our questions on this matter, the questions Ignazio and I would ask, were met with angry, disconsolate stares, which were in turn met with glib remarks, which were in turn met with puzzled looks, or sometimes an apologetic glance coupled with a biblical quotation, from one of the Gospels, usually John, or from the Book of Revelations, though a few individuals quoted from the Book of Malachi; or sometimes our glib remarks were met with mute expressions of outrage, or sometimes vaguely distracted looks, edged with impatience, as if those we had accosted were now too busy studying the contours of various clouds passing by to be bothered; all of which were in turn met with further glib remarks followed by sudden outbursts of laughter, which were in turn met with burning silences, similar in nature (but not exact by any stretch) to those burning silences that occur in old movie houses when the celluloid catches on the bulb, silences which do in fact produce a sound, a sort of unconscious, staticky din, like a promise spoken in the wee hours of the morning between two young lovers too young to know any better, or a vaguely understood communication from outer space which sends all of our scientists reeling, silences which are sometimes so loud as to become deafening, in which case you are plunged into a more robust kind of silence and your eyes begin to water and the saliva in your mouth possesses the distinct taste of burnt hair, a taste which lingers for months and makes it difficult to swallow food of any kind.

So no one knew what exactly had befallen the refugees. No one knew why there were here, except for the obvious. At least Ignazio and I did not know. It was all conjecture. It was all make-believe. Maybe they had a lonely uncle who lived in a small house in the shadow of Monte Inici, or a spinster aunt who liked to wander barefoot on the beach, slipping an occasional mussel like an evening prayer that has been answered into a basket; or a cousin or a younger brother who had settled here to escape the Carabinieri with their ruthless Madsen machine guns, which, their reputation notwithstanding, only mowed down the exceedingly stupid or unaware because the Carabinieri always set up their machine-gun nests out in the open, in the middle of a crossroads with the hedges cut back so you could see who was coming from miles away, and vice versa, or in front of a stone bridge, the dark, elongated phallus of the machine gun flashing with the interminable brilliance of the sun, as if the Carabinieri had spent hours polishing the dark metal with their sleeves or pieces of fabric torn from their shirts when they could have been reclining in the shadows beneath the bridge drinking from their canteens or hidden away in a clump of trees not too far away with a view of both the road and the bridge, in which case many more wandering oblivious peasants and also those with revolutionary intentions would have died. But we did know at least one thing. We knew the refugees were all looking for someone to take them in. Or maybe they were looking for a ship to take them to America. That was a fairly common hope in those days.

October became the month of the refugees. But by February there were few if any refugees still traveling, and everywhere the church bells were ringing and the sunlight was bright and the almond trees were blossoming and people started to forget about the earthquake in September. But I did not forget. Just when I thought the earthquake was over, finished, *finutu,* it started all over again.

(At this point Federico would pause, because always his listener would gasp in disbelief, but always Federico would mistake the gasp for laughter, a short, breathy, involuntary squeal, perhaps, or a belching sound, or a nasally snorting sound, or a high-pitched twittering capable of causing headaches, but to Federico it was laughter nevertheless.)

You laugh? To laugh is a good thing. Sometimes laughter is the best way to deal with unexpected tragedy. And always it is the best way to deal with unexpected good fortune. *Petra disprizzata, cantunera di muro.* But I am being figurative here. I am being poetic. Allow me the latitude of an old man to look back on something that happened a very long time ago, to reminisce, to remember with a poet's heart (because Federico had always wanted to be a poet, in spite of the fact that he didn't learn to read until the age of seventeen, and in spite of the fact that poetry in general bored him to tears, unless it was the poetry of a truly great poet like Angelo Poliziano, who preferred blond-haired boys to girls and enjoyed kissing fat juicy lips unless those lips had tasted urine, or Pirandello, because Pirandello was born in southwestern Sicily and he wrote about betrayal and disillusion and resentment, emotions which always mask a certain degree of fear, which is amplified when you turn your eye inward, which you invariably do because the exterior circumstances are too horrible to behold, but then you realize your interior self is equally horrible to behold or worse and so you are left wriggling on the fishhook of despair and self-annihilation, to use a strange metaphor indeed, not quite a poet's metaphor, more of a philosopher's attempt at a metaphor, like Mirandola in his treatises on magic and the dignity of man, Mirandola, brilliant as he was, a mystic and consummate scholar, who wished to be a poet but could never quite get the words to match what he thought was true, which is perhaps why he destroyed every love-song he ever wrote, a disparity between language and intent which also troubled the young Federico, even when he was an illiterate dock worker, and which is why in his later years, after he had mastered reading to a degree his fisherman father had never dreamed of (for, in all honesty, the written word does not even exist for some men), Federico truly enjoyed Pirandello, in spite of the fact that Pirandello was devoted to Mussolini, a devotion which was easy to understand if you understood Pirandello's fears about chaos and the nature of reality, but which nobody ever really understood, nor could they be expected to (because the truth is we can never really understand anybody), and of course you would immediately forgive Pirandello all of his emotional and psychological flaws if you ever read the poems in *Mal giocondo*, which Federico had read on the boat from Palermo to Naples to Havana, a slim volume of poetry that was published in 1889, where in one poem a ghost is fleeing from a flatterer, for such are the deceptions of love that they extend even beyond death, and love itself is symbolized by green snakes writhing in agony, or something like that, at least that's how Federico remembered it, kind of like in Dante, or at least the corrupt, abridged editions of Dante that Federico had access to that had been translated from Italian into English and then back again into Italian).

Yes?

'. . . .'

(Federico is still hoping to be allowed the indulgence of an aging poet.)

Good. It is the same with old men everywhere.

'. . . .'

U Signùri rùna 'u viscuottù a cu nun' avi rienti, as they say. '. . . .'

Yes, yes. God gives biscuits to those with no teeth.

(Some genuine laughter now. The conversation turning in Federico's favor. Which is to say that his hope of being allowed the indulgence of an aging poet is about to be granted. Some more laughter. It is actually more of a relieved chuckle than genuine laughter, but that's beside the point.)

Yes, yes. I have always thought so.

(A smile and then a pause, or sometimes the other way around, depending upon the nature of the interchange between Federico and the listener.)

So just when I thought the earthquake was over once and for all, I saw Maura D'Alessandria for the first time. I should say that Ignazio also saw her, but when I saw the shimmering mirage of the beauty that was Maura D'Alessandria on that brisk February afternoon with the wind whipping across the harbor and swirling through the narrow streets of the old part of town with such biting fury that I thought I was stranded in the desert, I forgot Ignazio even existed. We had turned down a narrow stone street, Ignazio and I, a hidden street full of the smoke and hubbub of various vendors, a street that in former days had been lined with lime trees, which had later been replaced by almond trees. The street ended at the walls of the castle. It was more an alley than a street and had been given many names over the centuries. The Street of the One-Eyed. Or The Street of the Arabs. Or The Street of the Ostrogoths. Or The Street of the Forgetful Vizier. Or The Street of the Blind Prelate. Or The Street of Adelaide the Malikah of Sicily. Or The Street of Lime Trees. Or the Street of Lemon Trees. Or The Street of Plum Trees. Or The Street of Yellow Plums. Or The Street of Mirabelle Plums. Or The Street of Half-Eaten Fish. Or The Street of Half-Eaten Tuna. Or The Street of Genoese Silk Merchants. Or The Street of Apprentice Magicians. Or The Street of Apprentice Fire-Eaters. Or The Street of the Apprentice Sword-Swallowers. Or The Street of the Invisible Magistrates. Or The Street of the Moorish Ciphers. Or The Street of the Dancing Mania. Or The Street of Toothless Camel Dealers. Or The Street of the Blind Monks. Or The Street of Fleas. Or The Street of Bedbugs. Or The Street of Lice. Or The Street of Moonless Nights. Or The Street of Insufferable Days. Or The Street of Almond Blossoms. Or The Street of Sour Almonds. Or The Street of Sour Wine. Or

The Street of Vinegar. Or The Street of the Devouring Sea. Or the Street of the Cleansing Tide. Or The Street of the Abolishing Wind. Or The Street of Would-Be Assassins. Or The Street of the Badly Abused. Or The Street of Broken Knives. Or The Street of the Black Hand.

But it was also known as Via Marianella, because one day, God only knows how long ago, a struggling merchant claimed the Mother of Christ had visited his stall, or his tent, or his cart with a mule standing stiffly in front and mule shit steaming on the ground and the flies beginning to gather, or she had visited the rug that he had spread out on the ground beneath one of the lime trees (and in those days there were so many lime trees that you could pluck a lime and suck on it at your leisure and no one would notice and ask you 'Where did you get that lime?' or wonder out loud 'Why don't I have a lime to suck on?' and become irritated, because they could also pluck limes whenever they felt like it) and which (the rug, an old Persian design) was now covered with trinkets and fabric from all over the Mediterranean and beyond, and without the slightest hesitation the Mother of Christ bought a silk scarf, and after that every merchant on the street had a similar story, and because the merchants in those ancient days were all from the land of the Moors, the Madonnas in their stories were all dark-skinned and slept with goats, not in the biblical sense of knowing goats, but in the pre-biblical (or quasi-biblical, or possibly even post-biblical) sense of sleeping with (near, amongst) animals in a reasonable attempt to keep warm on a cold night.

Ignazio and I called this dirt alley The Street of Rusty Swords because of a small tent set up in the shadow of the castle. The tent was owned by a descendent of one of those early Arabs. He dressed with the flair of a nocturnal grave robber. He sold all manner of medieval weaponry used during the Norman conquest of the castle, or so he claimed, but mostly he sold small daggers and rusty swords, most likely the relics of battles from the 19th century from the days of the Two Sicilies, which he routinely dug out of the stony, unforgiving ground in the fields surrounding Palermo, usually after midnight with a lantern perched on a rock, which gave his face a devilish, greenish tint.

So it was a brisk February afternoon with the wind whipping up all sorts of dust and the white froth of the waves and the almond blossoms, as I have already said. With the smoke from the various smoke shops and the white almond blossoms falling and more blossoms falling with every gust of wind, we could barely see. We were guided by our own memories and by the hubbub of voices suggesting we try this or that. And we were munching on pistachios because you could not get sweet almonds at that time of year, only sour ones, but we wanted something sweet. (We were always hankering for something sweet.) Then we passed by the small piazza to the Church of the Madonna of the Rosary, though perhaps piazza is too large a word. It was a very small stone plaza in front of the church, a plaza rarely occupied by any living creature save on occasion a few pink seagulls taking refuge from the sea or a green lizard or two clinging to the pink walls of the church, trying to escape the sun. But what does it matter such details? So we walked by the piazza, cherishing thoughts of medieval knives, wondering what it would feel like to kill someone with such a knife, but then the wind died down, as if a great hand had suddenly descended to calm the turbulent earth, and there she was, Maura D'Alessandria, framed in the doorway of the church, the trio of sculpted marble figures in the arch above the door smiling with stern satisfaction, it seemed, glowing with the joy of certain faith, I might have said, or at least the absence of any kind of gnawing doubt, or perhaps gloating, indeed, perhaps they were wallowing in the self-indulgent, self-satisfied apocryphal mood that usually accompanies revelations of any kind, as if they had just witnessed the lights of an alien spaceship speeding across a winter sky, I might have said all that, except that all of my words had suddenly vanished. I had fallen into an immense but exceedingly bright void. I could not tell which way was up. Conversely, I could not tell which way was down. I did not know who I was. I could hear myself humming a strange tune, as if I were someone else. I had never seen such beauty. Maura D'Alessandria seemed a sister of the Black Madonnas described by the ancient Arab merchants. I was not sure where she had come from. It was difficult to tell if she was about to go inside or if she was just leaving.

In the days that followed, we learned that she had come from a small farm near Caccamo, she and her uncle. Their farm had been destroyed by the earthquake. There was no one else. Her parents died the year she was born.

It is very hard to describe feelings from so long ago.

Suffice it to say that Ignazio and I took Maura everywhere

in our small town by the sea. We did not compete for her affection, nor did she thrust herself in between the love we had for each other. We became a trinity as holy in our own minds as the Blessed Trinity the priests always talked about but which we could never see.

-76-

It was shortly after this that a traveling puppet show made its way to Castellammare del Golfo. They had come from Trapani on their way to Palermo, but they had taken the coast road all the way around, up through Pizzolungo (a small depression of a seaside village where Adherbal, the great Carthaginian admiral, spent three weeks with his Nubian mistress of many years, a secret rendezvous by the sea filled with all of the delectable delights a perverse and fertile imagination can conjure, after he had defeated Publius Claudius Pulcher and the Roman fleet in the battle of Drepana two-hundred and forty-nine years before the birth of Christ, and then after that Pizzolungo was basically forgotten by the world); and then on to Bonagia, with its rocky brown hills dripping into a sea overflowing with tuna (where in 829 the native Sicilians, presumably descended from the refugees of fallen Troy, had erected a Saracen watch tower that didn't resemble a horse in the least at the top of the tallest of the hills to keep a lookout for Saracen raiders coming up from North Africa, but all of their foresight went for naught because on the very morning a Saracen raiding party was in fact heading their way, a shimmering cloud upon the distant horizon like a flock of black seagulls that should have been spotted right off (giving the sons and daughters of Troy ample time to pack up their family heirlooms and their mythology and head for the relative safety of the fortress city of Eryx), the guardian of the watchtower was fast asleep in the arms of two perfumed nymphs, also sleeping, humming with sleep, their naked breasts like bruised plums glowing with a hazy, diffuse, late morning light, as if the curtains were drawn, though of course there were no curtains in the stone tower, unless you can think of a drunken stupor as being curtains, or curtain-like, or having that effect on the light); and then the puppeteers headed up to San Vito Lo Capo (a village that became the final earthly refuge of Saint Vito Martire, a third century saint who was known for healing the blind and the lame and driving away demons and who once called a meteorite out of the sky to punish a village of nonbelievers whose only real crime was that they enjoyed fornicating at all hours of the day and night on the beach in plain sight of the disapproving saint); and after San Vito Lo Capo they headed down along the rocky northern shore where the road disappeared altogether and they found themselves beating their donkeys mercilessly as they traveled along a cobblestone beach and then up a sandy, rocky path through the dense matte of coastal grasses and dwarf palms and the woody shrubs a little higher up and then up along the top of the cliffs, which plunged straight down into the sea, where they stopped for a while to look at the blues and light greens and aquamarines and Arabian turquoises of the Tyrrhenian Sea and the flashing silver like spinning knives of schools of small fish darting back and forth, communicating in a strange semaphore language all their own beneath the bright, fragile surface of the water; and the puppeteers marveled at the deep blue almost Azurite Italian sky studded with swirling gray clouds like the skies of Titian, for they had never before witnessed such a view, such colors, which made them want to weep inconsolably and dance for joy at the same time, and then a raging storm came along like those legendary storms of the 15th century that sank boatloads of Algerian pirates, storms that arrived with fortuitous alacrity, at least from the perspective of those who lived along the coast in those days in their God forsaken stone huts and hovels that smelled of dead sardines and pestilent body odor, and so the puppeteers were forced to climb down from the top of the cliffs, leaving their wagons and ragged donkeys exposed, and sought shelter in a coastal cave.

The storm raged for a day and a night and half a day. The puppeteers never knew a storm could go on for so long, at least from personal experience. It was the kind of storm they thought only happened in epic tales of adventure and in a few poorly conceived or derivative dime-store novels, storms which were given symbolic value when in fact no such value truly existed. Because a storm is just a storm, after all.

By the time the puppeteers reached Castellammare del Golfo they needed to recover their strength. The process of recovery required copious amounts of alcohol, wine, beer, Vermouth, *assenziu*, whatever was available. They stayed for several weeks, maybe longer, putting on puppet shows in the plaza in front of the Cathedral whenever they had the energy. They put on the same puppet show every time the curtain went up.

They had puppets dressed in peasant dresses whose heads would twirl with amazement and whose eyelashes would flutter at the most bizarre moments, giving the impression of uncontrollable coquetry. They had puppets wearing knightly armor but without weapons and puppets with swords but dressed like bandits and one puppet seemed to be a mayor or a councilor with his great floppy hat and broad, stuffed shirt. They had puppets who were sailors wearing red caps and merchants with bald heads and moustaches. They had puppets who were dancing girls and puppets who were priests and puppets who were matadors and one that was a bull and a whole chorus of singing nuns, and in addition to the bull, they had a whole range of animal puppets, mostly of the farmyard variety, but there was also one Bengal tiger, one lion with ferocious looking teeth and a wild, unmanageable mane, a herd of elephants, a pack of jabbering monkeys, and one White Bird of Paradise from the islands of Bali. They had puppets who were cooks and scullery maids and musicians and a few small children for crowd scenes and also a few British ship captains and sorcerers from far off countries and a contingent of Turkish mercenaries armed only with spears. Most of these puppets also possessed twirling heads. Twirling heads to signify rage, or rejection, or despair, or confusion, or drunkenness, or an insatiable desire for vengeance or sex, or just plain old humorous idiocy.

All of their puppets were approximately one-hundred and twenty centimeters tall and weighed between fifteen and twenty-two kilograms, depending upon accoutrements. Except for the children puppets, which were a bit smaller, not so gaudy.

Naturally not all of their puppets appeared in every show. What a crazy travesty of a show that would be! But for a small fee, a few coins, the puppeteers would let you see all of their puppets, those that would appear in the next performance, and those that were waiting for other shows, perhaps even shows that had not yet been written. No one in Castellammare del Golfo had ever seen such a diverse array of puppets.

The show the puppeteers presented to the citizens of Castellammare del Golfo was called *The Operetta of Turiddu the Wayward Soldier*, which was more or less a bastardized version of the extraordinarily popular Italian operetta, *Cavalleria rusticana,* but if this act of thievery had been pointed out to the puppeteers, they would most certainly have replied with the theatrical swagger of pirates: How else were they to acquire their stories? And then: Everyone else did the same, it was a cutthroat business, after all. And finally: At least they only stole from works exhibiting the highest artistic merit, which is why they stole both their characters and pieces of their plot from Mascagni's version, which premiered in the Teatro Costanzi opera house in Rome in 1890, as everyone knows, as opposed to stealing from Monleone's rip-off version, a second-rate story if there ever was one, which first appeared in Amsterdam in 1907 and was understandably banned in Italy, forcing Monleone to rewrite his version if he wanted to make any money from it, which he did, which we are all hoping to do, because if we didn't make any money in this business then what is the point?

-77-

A summary of *The Operetta of Turiddu the Wayward Soldier,* the puppet show which Federico, Ignazio, and Maura D'Alessandria saw at least twelve times, once for each of the Apostles, or once for each of the ancient Tribes of Israel, or once for each of the Twelve Minor Prophets, with the last of those prophets being Malachi, the Messenger of God:

The show began with a puppet soldier riding a puppet donkey. The puppet soldier had just come back from the war (they didn't say which one), and you could see that he hadn't had a good experience because his sword was broken and his armor was missing pieces and he was barefoot to boot. And yet he was as happy as a clam. He was as happy as any number of clams who have not yet been dug out of the sand and boiled in a pot. He was also as happy as any returning soldier should be, or even could be, and he was singing a happy song about the love of his life, a woman named Lola.

The soldier's name was Turiddu, and he used to live with his mother, Lucia, above her wine shop.

The donkey had no name. But then what is a name to a donkey?

Turiddu and the donkey had not been home in twenty

years, a fact which Turiddu was singing about in his song about Lola. The donkey did not seem to understand how long twenty years actually was, or at least he gave no indication that he did understand. (Then again, not to belabor the philosophical, but what are twenty years to a donkey?)

The song about Lola went on for a while, and both Turiddu and the donkey did a little jig. Their arms, legs, and heads all whirled in different directions during the jig.

Turiddu sounded a little bit like Enrico Caruso before he got his big break and became famous and started selling out concert halls in places like Toledo, Ohio.

The next scene was devoted to Lola, who had married a local teamster named Alfio while Turiddu was away. Which is only natural if you think about it. Twenty years is in fact a very long time, especially when your lover has disappeared.

Twenty years is also a long time when you are deeply in love. Turiddu had been deeply in love. But as he got closer to home, the weight of his twenty-year absence began to diminish, and when he had only a mile to go it vanished entirely. All of a sudden he could not tell the difference between the sadness of time passing and the labored, wheezing sound his donkey made as they plodded across the landscape (or between the wheezing sound his donkey was making and the unthinking joyful sound of a pinwheel spinning; or between the joyful sounds of spinning pinwheels and the hulking shadows of any number of farm implements ruined by humidity and advances in agricultural science). When Turiddu passed through the wrought-iron gates of his home town, gates which served only decorative purposes, like the gates to a cemetery, and would have therefore been useless against an attack, he felt he had only been gone a moment.

The only puzzling aspect of the story was that the war had apparently been over for ten years, a fact which became clear sooner rather than later. There was no explanation offered as to what Turiddu and the donkey had been doing during the intervening ten years, presumably traipsing about the Mediterranean, what adventures they had survived, what wonders they had seen, what jokes they had told each other during the long boring nights of their solitude, assuming that they had actually been alone.

Ten years is also a long time.

Ten years is almost as long a time as twenty years, at least as poets reckon time, and one or two English playwrights, and all impressionist painters, and the surrealists, of course, and also the symbolists, and various estranged lovers and childhood sweethearts, and all lost children and most lost pets, and a few doddering grandfathers and a few grandmothers wearing eyeglasses trying to keep track of their doddering counterparts, and every pilot of a plane lost in the Bermuda triangle, and every captain of a treasure ship sunk in a sudden maelstrom, and every failed critic, and all fictional characters, and one mathematician of note and several minor ones, and numerous German philosophers and a couple of Swedish ones and one who was half-French, and a party of explorers from 19th century Belgium, and dozens of Cistercian monks, and twice as many Franciscans, and almost all donkeys, which almost goes without saying.

The audience was left wondering about this discrepancy of the ten years throughout the action of the show, hoping against hope that further details were forthcoming.

The next scene was Turiddu's homecoming scene. It took place in his mother's wine shop. Lola and Alfio were shopping in Lucia's wine shop when Turiddu arrived. Lucia was there, but she did not recognize her son at first. Turiddu could not believe his very own Lola was holding a bottle of sweet Marsala wine. Neither could the donkey. Lola could not believe that Lucia did not recognize her own son. Alfio could not believe that Lucia had a son. Lucia could not believe that Alfio was so stupid. Lola could not believe that Turiddu did not remember that she liked a bottle of sweet Marsala wine every now and then. Lucia agreed with Lola. Alfio could not believe Turiddu was supposed to know that Lola liked a bottle of sweet Marsala wine every now and then. Turiddu could not believe that Alfio was so stupid. Lola agreed with Turiddu. Alfio grabbed the bottle of sweet Marsala wine from Lola's hands and shoved it into Turiddu's hands. Lucia was looking for another bottle of wine because Lola typically bought two bottles, so her back was turned and she did not see. Lola could not believe Alfio grabbed the bottle from her hands. Turiddu was looking at Lola and did not realize Alfio was shoving the bottle into his hands until it was too late. The bottle of sweet Marsala wine crashed to the floor and there were bits of glass everywhere and a puddle of wine in the middle. Lucia whirled around when she heard the crash and saw the puddle of wine. Lola still could not believe that Alfio had grabbed the bottle from her hands. Alfio could not believe that Turiddu had dropped the bottle. Lucia could not believe there was a puddle of wine in the middle of the floor of her wine shop. The donkey didn't know what to believe. Lucia assumed Alfio had hurled the bottle of sweet Marsala wine to the floor. She could not believe he was so stupid. Lola agreed with Lucia. Alfio felt like he was misunderstood. Turiddu could not believe Alfio would say such a thing, for clearly the fault of the broken bottle of wine lay with his impulsive snatching of the bottle from Lola's hands. Lola agreed with Turiddu. Lucia could not believe they were still talking about the first bottle of wine. She shoved the second bottle of wine into Alfio's hands and pushed him rudely out the door. Alfio could not believe he was being treated so rudely. Lola stared at Turiddu for a moment but she didn't know what to say. Turiddu knew what he wanted to say but he didn't know where to begin. Alfio began shouting from the street outside the wine shop. Lola could not believe he was being so obnoxious. Lucia agreed. Lola apologized for the behavior of Alfio and headed out the door. Turiddu could not believe she was leaving. Lucia headed into the back of the wine shop. Or perhaps she headed up the stairs in search of a bed because she was tired and wanted to lie down. Turiddu could not believe what had happened. The donkey sat down in the middle of the wine shop and began lapping up the wine.

There was a great deal of head twirling and arms and legs whirling throughout the entire exchange.

The audience roared.

The next scene took place outside the church, which was across the street from Lucia's wine shop. Lola was walking arm in arm with her best friend, Santuzza. Lola was telling Santuzza about Turiddu's unexpected homecoming and the impact on Alfio. At first Alfio did not know what to believe. Now he believes that Turiddu and Lola have been sleeping together for years, even while Turiddu has been away at war. Alfio did not explain how this feat of magic was accomplished, but it has become for him an unshakeable belief. This is what Lola said. Santuzza suggested they go inside the church and pray and maybe God would provide an answer, but Lola said she wasn't interested in any answer from God. At this point they noticed Turiddu's donkey tied up to a hitching post outside the church. The donkey pretended he wasn't listening to the conversation between Lola and Santuzza when in fact he was. A group of villagers then came along singing an Easter hymn about orange blossoms. They were dancing and twirling while they sang. They danced and twirled past the church. Lola and Santuzza joined them. The singing voices faded. The donkey looked out at the audience with a grave, wise, almost soulful look.

The next scene was back in the wine shop. Turiddu and Santuzza were sitting at a small table near the front of the wine shop. They were drinking wine. It was the middle of a sunny afternoon. Lucia was somewhere else, but you could hear her humming the song about the orange blossoms. Lola and Alfio entered the wine shop. Alfio looked at Turiddu and gave him an accusatory glance. Lola looked at Santuzza and gave her an accusatory glance. Turiddu and Santuzza looked at each other and smiled and their heads twirled with obvious affection. They gave the impression that they did not care what anyone else thought. Alfio said something hurtful to Santuzza and stormed out of the wine shop. It seemed that he was overcome by jealousy. Lola said something wicked to Turiddu and followed Alfio. It was not clear what she was overcome by. Turiddu and Santuzza drank some more wine. Lucia was still humming from somewhere else. Lola and Alfio returned with the villagers, including the mayor in his great floppy hat and broad, stuffed shirt, a few sailors and merchants, and a priest. The priest said they were going to excommunicate Santuzza because she had obviously slept with Turiddu. The priest said the church did not play around when it came to such matters. Santuzza ran crying from the wine shop. Then Alfio stepped forward and challenged Turiddu to a duel. He did not say why. Turiddu agreed. The mayor then stepped forward and said Turiddu and Alfio would square off at dawn in the plaza in front of the church. The rest of the villagers cheered.

There was a lot of head twirling and arms and legs whirling.

The next scene was a banquet held the night before the duel. All of the puppets were there, drinking and dancing. The mayor gave a very long speech. Then more dancing and drinking. Then the priest gave an even longer speech. Then more dancing and drinking. Then the mayor decided it was his turn again. This went on for a while. Then Santuzza sang a tragic love song, but all the while she was singing she seemed incredibly happy. It was a great number. All the puppets were spinning and whirling about like whirling dervishes. Everyone in the audience began to clap and sing and laugh.

The next scene was back in front of the church. Alfio was standing on one side with a pistol in his hand. Two sailors were standing behind him. On the other side Turiddu sat on his donkey. He was holding his broken sword, occasionally brandishing it in the air. The villagers were huddled in a clump directly in front of the church. The mayor stepped forward in his great floppy hat and broad, stuffed shirt and named both parties in the duel and asked that they proceed apace so everyone could go back to their breakfasts before they got cold, and then he stepped back into the clump. It was still unclear why Alfio had challenged Turiddu to a duel. From somewhere you could hear a band playing martial music. It sounded like the music of doom. Alfio twirled around a bit in time to the music and then stopped and fired his pistol. There was a loud bang and a puff of smoke and that was it. The martial music picked up. It now sounded like the music of doom on donkeyback. Turiddu and his donkey did not waste any time at all twirling to the music. They simply charged towards Alfio and the startled sailors. Turiddu was waving his sword in the air, his head spinning in a way that suggested bloodthirsty vengeance. The two sailors, who had no pistols, turned and fled. Alfio, who had a pistol but now no bullets, also turned and fled. Turiddu chased them off the stage. The villagers clapped and cheered. The mayor stepped forward and took off his great floppy hat and made a low sweeping gesture as he bowed before the audience.

The last scene took place later that day in front of the church. Turiddu was on his donkey, getting ready to leave. He was going back to war, any war. He would find a war somewhere in the world and offer his services to whichever side would pay him the most. Lucia seemed happy her son was leaving. She gave him two bottles of wine for the journey. She told him that his presence was like a calamitous wind but now that he was leaving, things would settle down a bit. She told him that Lola and Alfio were no longer together. She told him that Alfio had forsaken Lola and gone off with Santuzza. No one knew where they had gone. She told him that Lola was now working in the wine shop. Turiddu smiled and said 'We are like so many puppets hung on the wall, waiting for someone to come and move us or make us talk.' Lucia smiled back and said 'Such is love.' The donkey seemed to be grinning like a critic, but he did not say anything. From somewhere you could hear music playing, but very softly. It sounded like the orange blossom song from the day before, but no one was singing. Turiddu and the donkey left. Lucia went back inside her wine shop. The street was empty. But from the doorway of the wine shop it looked like Lola was watching the spot where she had last seen Turiddu. The audience clapped for twenty minutes every single time and begged for more.

-78-

Federico never said if he liked the puppet show. At least he never said as much to Luis. He did not mention if he even liked puppetry in general. But he was quite clear about how he felt about the puppeteers who came to Castellammare del Golfo.

I did not like them, he would say. Yes, I was seduced by their charms at first. We all were, Ignazio and Maura D'Alessandria and myself. They possessed lively blue gypsy eyes, the kind that prick you, hook into you, and if you try to resist them your own eyeballs explode. So you did not resist. But we were young. What did we know?

After each puppet show the puppeteers would lock up their puppet wagon and head around the side of the Cathedral to a small grove of trees where they had set up camp. It was a rugged camp with a few tents and a rough wooden table and a second wagon for sleeping and a third for cooking and the mules tethered to a picket. But as soon as they started drinking and ladling out soup and devouring hunks of coarse brown bread and apples and olives and figs and all kinds of cheeses, maiorchino and modicano and caciocavallo and persa, well, who could resist? It was Maura D'Alessandria's idea. She was enamored of one of the puppeteers, Luigi Bonanno, thin as a rail, tanned, leathery skin from endless days on the open road, dark blue swirling eyes like a stormy sky, and thick black hair. (Maura said when you buried your face in Luigi's hair and breathed in the smell, which was heavy with salt and rare spices, it was like falling into a nighttime sea.) So they had finished their last show and were packing up their wagons for good and Luigi invited us to join them for a little wine and song, a paean to the beauty of art, he said, which is as much of paradise as we are permitted in this earthly realm, and then he laughed, and it sounded like he was suffering from whooping cough, but it was joyful laughter nevertheless.

So we ate and drank wine and sang, and with all of the commotion in the dim lantern light it seemed that there were more of us sitting there than there actually were, and then one of the men pulled out a mandolin and another started playing a flute and then one of the women puppeteers got up on the table and started dancing, and then another, and the men were grinning with wild teeth and there was no telling what might happen next, and then pretty soon Maura D'Alessandria was up there dancing and laughing at the world with her Black Madonna eyes.

At some point during that last evening someone said we should join them. They were traveling to Palermo in the morning to catch a boat for Naples, and from there they were going to America. We should go with them. All of us. How much fun we would all have in America. And we said we would. Then it was very late. It was after midnight certainly, and the moon had vanished and the stars were obscured by a darkness like a fog. It was one of those nights of oblivion that sometimes descends upon the coast. Ignazio was asleep on the ground and Maura D'Alessandria was sitting on an old woman's sewing stool from one of the wagons, watching Ignazio sleep. It was a hot, steamy night, but just beneath this layer of heat you could feel the ripple of a wind beginning to stir. It was a very strange night. The one lantern still glowing made everything seem steamier, hotter, even darker. You could not even see the features on Ignazio's face. Maura stared at Ignazio's featureless face for a while, and I stared at Maura, whose features drifted back and forth between visible and invisible. We were all perspiring but we did not care. Then Maura said quite suddenly that she had always dreamed of going to America and now she was really going, and I told her that I too had always dreamed of America and that I was sure Ignazio was dreaming then and there about going to America, though I was lying through my teeth on both counts.

Then Maura smiled at me her Black Madonna smile of a saint which ripped through my heart, and I wasn't sure where I was, I had suddenly gone blind except for a halo of light burning brightly on the outer edges of my field of vision, but I heard myself saying that I was going to go back home, there were a few things I needed, a few things I wanted to bring along to America, which was an odd thing to say because I don't recall owning anything of importance, what could I have gone back for, and then Maura laughed, or she must have laughed, for I felt the air vibrating and I was buffeted by a sweet-smelling but violent wind that washed across my face, wave after wave after wave, a ceaseless wave, an eternity, as if a thousand tiny birds were furiously beating their wings in a futile effort to escape this darkness like a fog that had descended upon the world, and then I went home. I do not remember if I made it home that night or not. And again, as I have said, I have no idea what I went back for. I did not own anything of value. And I certainly did not go back to say goodbye to my father. He and I had not spoken in years. But my memory is sometimes not what it was. It is funny how your mind plays tricks on you. My very next memory is standing in the plaza in front of the Cathedral in the quiet moments before dawn and the fog had mysteriously vanished, and so had the puppeteers, and with them Ignazio and Maura D'Alessandria. Perhaps if I had hurried on down the road to Palermo, I might have caught up to them. I might have made the boat. But at that moment I wasn't sure if I even existed, let alone a boat in Palermo. It seems funny now. *Cui lassa la via vecchia pri la nova, li guai ch'un va circannu, ddà li trova,* the old men would say. And it is true. He who leaves the old road for the new will often find himself betrayed. Most people think of a betrayal such as this as the ultimate darkness, but they are mistaken. A betrayal is not a darkness. A betrayal is a glaring bright light. A betrayal burns away the shadows. Before that dark night, Maura D'Alessandria was a changeling who had crept into our bed, mine and Ignazio's, and now I could see her for what she truly was. And Ignazio, too, who had been my constant companion, my lover of moonless nights and the furtive sounds of the sea and the camaraderie of shadows as wistful and improbable as an imagined lover's kiss, he, too, had been a changeling all along, and now he had assumed his true form. This is what I was thinking in the moments just before dawn oh so many years ago, and then I was breathing in the white heat of the Sicilian sun and my lungs had turned black, as if I were a victim of radiation poisoning, and it was very difficult to breathe.

-79-

During the next ten years, I became a different person. I became an expert in the martial art of knife fighting. On the first anniversary of the Great Earthquake of Saint Rosalia's Redemption I found myself once again on The Street of Rusty Swords heading for the tent of the Arab who dressed like a nocturnal grave robber. Before I even knew my own mind, I found myself in a special section of his tent, standing alongside a table devoted to knives of the highest quality, blades of death that had once been owned by nobility. You can be sure that I had no idea what I was looking for, but you can also be sure that every knife I examined, I did so with the eye of vengeance.

The Arab must have sensed my boundless passion for death for he suddenly appeared on the other side of the table. He seemed almost an apparition with his slowly disintegrating gravedigger teeth and his skin stretched tightly across his skull. Then he bowed his head slightly and I felt a wave of nausea and then the nausea passed and he offered me one of his knives for close scrutiny. 'One does not normally speak of knives as possessing a purpose,' he said. 'But then one does not normally come across a knife such as this.'

The knife he held up gleamed in the dim light of the tent with a supernatural radiance, as if it were a living creature, or perhaps one of God's fallen angels. The blade was made of forge-hammered steel with diamond cross sections. The scabbard was leather with gold plated fittings. The moment I took hold of it, my hands began to tremble, or perhaps it was the knife that was trembling. But I could not put the knife down. The air was suddenly heavy with the earthy, rust smell of fresh blood, but it was also a sickly-sweet smell, and as I breathed in this smell of the lingering centuries, I was suddenly overwhelmed by the knowledge, or the possibility, or perhaps it was just an inkling of the future, that this knife had been (or would be) responsible for the deaths of hundreds perhaps thousands of witless souls.

'Good,' said the Arab. 'You are getting used to each other.'

I did not know what to say.

'Yes, yes, it will be a good match between the two of you. It is like true love, yes?'

I wondered where the knife had come from and if it was truly meant for me or if this Arab with the gravedigger teeth presented it to everyone, soldier and fanatic and youthful street ruffians and stravaigers alike, who stumbled into his tent.

'Yes, the two of you are like young lovers,' he said. 'Anyone can see that.'

He seemed quite sincere, and he was affable enough. He possessed the hopeful eyes of a hopeless romantic, or a poet who only wrote love sonnets. But there was also a peculiar aura about him, a strange, hushed assurance, as if everything he said or even thought was part of an ancient prophecy that would bring continents together, or perhaps tear them apart.

'It was fashioned by the great Turkish artisan Nikola Siyavus Hayreddin Yilmaz,' said the Arab, who seemed to be somewhere inside my head, squatting inside the cavernous recesses of my brain, cataloging my secrets so he could one day use them against me, even though I could plainly see he was standing just across from me. 'Nikola left Hungary after the Battle of Saint Gotthard in 1664,' he said, 'which is where the Duke of Melfi himself commented on Nikola's genius in making weapons for war, and then Nikola settled in Milan. That is where he fashioned this masterpiece. It is a knife worthy of only the most invisible of assassins.'

And then he laughed and took the knife from my hand with delicate deliberateness and sheathed it and then disappeared into a cloud of darkness, a darkness which most likely was just his gaping, laughing mouth as he walked away, only to reappear moments later with two dusty books, ancient manuscripts which he thrust into my arms along with the still trembling knife. 'To possess such a knife is useless,' he said, 'unless one also possesses the knowledge of how to use it.'

This seemed to me a very logical thing to say, but I still did not know how to respond.

He laughed again, his dark, gaping mouth with its disintegrating teeth like a mirror hanging over the abyss, and then he grew silent, solemn, nodded at the two books. For a moment I thought he was going to take them away. 'But remember,' he said. 'Do not share this knowledge with just anyone. Certainly not men without purpose, for such men are created by God without wit like cows that are born only to carry heavy loads or to be led to the slaughterhouse. Cows without a train.'

Both books were written by the same man, Fiore dei

Liberi, who lived in the 15th century, a master of knife fighting and swordplay, and also the use of the spear and the lance. The first was called *Flos Duelatorum* (Flower of Battle), which provided detailed accounts of hundreds of grappling techniques and striking techniques, all useful in hand-to-hand combat, complete with counter for counter maneuvers. The second book, a smaller volume, was called *Dacae Misericordiae* (Daggers of Mercy) and was devoted solely to knife fighting. It was because of these books that I learned to read, first in Latin, because this was the language of the two books the Arab had pushed into my hands, books about the poetry of knife fighting, this is how I felt about them, and then in Italian, because it was an easy jump from Latin to Italian, and besides, Italian was the language of the tuna cannery, where I was now employed.

Very, very soon I had read each volume dozens of times and could demonstrate any technique from any page at the drop of a hat. I became very proficient. In the streets of Castellammare del Golfo I became known as Signore Scurpiuni because of my elegant and thus surprisingly fast and potentially fatal style of knife fighting. I could cut a man to the bone before he could even blink. I could cut out his heart while he was still breathing. I could kill a man before he knew he was dead. My knife had no difficulty finding victims.

Now in those days there was a great deal of knife fighting in the streets of Castellammare del Golfo. I had never paid much attention to the dissolute youths who took to the streets in this fashion when I was with Ignazio, but Ignazio was gone. But it is not what you might think. We were not yet assassins, but there was not a lot for us to do to test our manhood. *Brìscula* was truly an old man's card game, and we were not old men, so we would drink and play cards only until our blood began to boil, and then we would head for the streets, our knives drawn, and commence to fighting. Knife fighting was for us like the Olympics. It was an arena where we tested our courage against each other, our skill, our speed, our passion, sometimes our stupidity, but always our love of life, our *gusto*. Rarely did anyone get killed, though this sometimes happened, as with anything. And yet it was always more than a simple test. For those few moments when we faced a dark shadow with a knife, we transcended ourselves. A knife fight is a complicated dance, some say, but if this is so, then it is a dance that you are not aware of. You do not know you are dancing. You are trying to survive, trying to find the weakness in the other man before he finds your weakness. Yet you are not thinking about any of this. You are simply moving until you are no longer moving.

Our knife fights did not last long. Boom! And this dance of the shadows was over before anyone even heard the music. Boom! And someone lay bleeding in the street, but it was a superficial wound and easily bandaged. Boom! And someone else was trying to hold in his blood but it was too late. Boom! And everyone else ran away. If knife fighting is a dance, it is a dance of death. A single misstep is a tragic thing. But we accepted this. We fought mostly in dark streets after midnight, always in dark streets, and so we had to step out of our daytime selves and assume the shapes and postures of nocturnal creatures. We forgot who we were. Our eyes glowed with the unthinking ferocity of blind angels or caged wolves or gigantic, ravenous bats or black eagles flying down from the mythic mountains to the east. Our nostrils flared, like the nostrils of bulls before they charge. Our hearing was attuned to the slightest whispering of a blade of grass, or the thin, zinging, scorpion flash in the dark of metal on metal, like moonlight catching the wings of a dragonfly, and then Boom! It was over. We were exhausted. So we returned from the edge of oblivion, looking for a bed.

It was at this time of my growing fame as Senor Scorpion that I forgot all about Ignazio and the treachery of his departure with Maura D'Alessandria. It was at this time also that I stopped thinking about Maura D'Alessandria and her beauty. Instead, I sometimes thought about Mirella Deodato, who was a distant cousin of Salvatore Maranzano, one of the young men who was always getting cut up in the knife fights and Mirella would bind his wounds and then cradle him right there in the street and sing to him softly about beauty and love, and the other young men would laugh and walk away and talk about the weakness of Salvatore, but I did not think it weakness so much as he had not yet learned how to commit himself fully to the knife. I would let my eyes linger a while on Mirella singing to Salvatore, and sometimes she would look at me with her eyes brimming with the hope of lost love, and sometimes she would even smile, but it was always a sad smile of infinite patience.

At other times I thought about Maria D'Angelo, who as a young girl in Castellammare del Golfo in 1641 was tending her goats on a hillside covered with rocks and fig trees when a sudden storm blew in from the sea and she and her goats took refuge in a nearby cave, or perhaps it was a hastily dug hole that had been dug out for some reason, and it was very dark in that cave, too dark to see clearly, and there was probably nothing to see anyway but the shapes of the goats moving around and the shape of Maria D'Angelo trying to keep out of their way, but then an exceptionally charged lightning bolt struck the ground outside the cave, illuminating the interior with a sudden brilliance as bright as a billion stars, or so everyone has always said, and during the melee of departing goats which followed the bolt, Maria D'Angelo discovered a tarnished copper box. Inside the copper box there was a smaller silver box, an ancient reliquary, and inside this reliquary there was a small amulet with a cameo image of the Virgin Mary and her baby son. Maria D'Angelo forgot about the raging storm, this is how I had always heard the story told, and ran breathless to the Cathedral and placed the dripping boxes and the still fairly dry amulet into the trembling hands of an old priest who immediately proclaimed the discovery a miracle, partially, perhaps, because of the enigmatic smile you could see quite clearly on the sculpted lips of the Madonna, and also, perhaps, because of the quizzical expression on the face of the child, an amazing bit of artistry in so tiny a sculpture. Soon thereafter they built a church on the very site of the cave, or close enough to the cave so that it amounted to the same thing. Such were my thoughts in those days.

-80-

And then one day Ignazio returned. When I first learned that Ignazio was returning to Sicily, I was sitting near the plate glass window of a small café with a view of the tuna cannery and a triangular blue slice of the bay. It was a café that I normally never went to. I was surrounded by faces I did not know or even vaguely recognize. Sometimes I think I dreamed the entire episode. It was late in the afternoon, when the shadows were liquid pools. I was drinking amaretto because someone in the café was getting married. As soon as I sat down by the window, a hoarse, happy voice started talking about the happy couple, and shortly after that, the amarettos started. Amarettos for everyone. The voice said the couple was planning a four-week trip to Naples and then to Barcelona on a great white ship with red railings, or maybe the couple had just returned. So I was drinking them down one after another and listening to this voice go on and on about this young couple, these newlyweds, standing at the railing of this great ship, a bright blue sky in the background and then the ship pulling away from the wharf (in Palermo? in Trapani? the voice did not say) and the young couple waving energetically at their adoring friends who were waving with an equal amount of energy in return, and some of the friends had brought orange blossoms from the wedding, or some kind of confetti, which they were going to sprinkle on the heads of the young couple as they raced up the gangplank, only they forgot, so now they were sprinkling the heads of everyone standing along the wharf. It was hard to tell if the voice was recounting a memory or projecting his hopes onto the future. Then the sound of the one voice talking was replaced by the sound of many voices, and every so often a hand wearing a white glove would reach past my nose with another amaretto. Violins were playing in the background, or some kind of stringed instruments. People were eating lemon cakes and there was a general hubbub of laughter and small talk and the chomping of teeth to go along with the amarettos. Then I plainly heard a voice say 'A telegraph cable for you,' and then an ungloved hand reached past my nose, and the next thing I knew I was reading a cable that said: 'I am returning August 24. Ignazio.'

After the cable, my imagination took over, though at the time I did not realize that it was my imagination. I thought I had fallen into the abyss of chaotic thinking. Or chaotic perceiving. Sometimes there is no measurable difference between the two. There was no mention of Maura in the cable, so I assumed she had died or run away. The amarettos stopped coming. I realized that the white gloved hand that had been serving the amarettos belonged to the father of the groom, not a waiter, as I had naturally assumed. Someone mentioned something about the famed Bavarian illuminist Jung-Stilling, but I did not hear what exactly. I had never heard of Jung-Stilling. I imagined gutting Ignazio with a knife. The violins or whatever stringed instruments they were sounded louder, as if many more musicians had suddenly arrived. I remembered a diagram from somewhere towards the middle of *Dacae Misericordiae* which clearly demonstrated how to plunge a knife into a man's stomach and then twist it right and left and then up and out so that the man's stomach and bowels would come gushing out. Two men in dark jackets approached my table and asked if they could sit down opposite from me, for the chairs were unoccupied. I am sure I said yes. I could not remember the precise page number with the diagram of disemboweling a man, but I did not need to remember the page number. The white gloved hand of the father of the groom appeared once again with another amaretto. The hand provided amarettos for the two men in the dark jackets. The men in the dark jackets said they were Quietists, an obscure Catholic sect, once all the rage in France, that took a vaguely more optimistic view of humanity than Pascal, who believed that human beings were wretched, mindless worms of the earth, easily deceived automatons with only the horror of eternal damnation to look forward to, in spite of Christ's intervention for all of us, except for those lucky few who received God's grace, which according to Pascal rarely happened. They asked me if I was a Quietist, but I said I had never heard of the Quietists. The father of the groom-to-be (or the happy honeymooner) returned again and apologized and said they had run out of amaretto for the second time and there was only a very small chance of procuring any more. Clearly he thought everyone in the café belonged to the party celebrating the impending marriage of his son (or the return of his son and daughter-in-law from their honeymoon, if that's what it was). All of a sudden it smelled of oleander. I looked at the two men in their dark jackets and they had removed their jackets, tossing them carelessly over the backs of their chairs, and had taken out a single bottle of oleander scent and placed the bottle on the lip of the table. The bottle was precariously perched and looked like it was about to fall to the floor. The two men were taking turns taking up the bottle and dabbing themselves all over with the oleander scent and putting the bottle back down on the lip. The father of the groom returned, smiling, and said we were in luck, there was more amaretto on its way. I remembered that Sicily no longer had any large, predatory animals, except the obvious, but there were countless hedgehogs and weasels and wild rabbits, all of which were easy prey if you had a rifle, but hunting them down was significantly more challenging if you only had a knife. There were also plenty of hawks and windhovers and kites, and I always enjoyed an occasional rock partridge or two. The two men were once again wearing their dark jackets and the bottle of oleander scent had disappeared. I had not heard the sound of a bottle crashing so I assumed they had put it back in a pocket. I remember thinking that Ignazio would arrive shortly. Perhaps he was heading for that very café at that very moment. I pulled out my knife, which I always kept with me, and laid it on the table. I wanted to be ready. The knife was gleaming. The two men in the dark jackets were startled by the gleaming brilliance of my knife and they looked at me with questioning eyes. Then they asked me some questions that had nothing to do with the knife. They asked me if I had ever read a book called *Théologie astrale,* which was sometimes called *La Voie à Dieu,* and was often confused with a book called *D'un monde à l'autre.* I said I had not. They asked me if I knew anything about Madam Guyon, who had written both books, as well as dozens of others. I said I knew nothing. I assumed by their cryptic questions that they had forgotten the gleaming knife as soon as they had seen it. Which was just as well. I waved my hand in the air to attract the attention of a waiter and the father of the groom came running. He apologized with red-faced embarrassment and said the amaretto had not yet arrived, but it was most definitely coming. He had the assurances of the owner of the café. I said that was okay but the reason I was waving my hand in the air was that I was hoping someone would bring me a white table napkin. The father of the groom smiled, and his shame at not yet having any more amaretto was replaced with the unburdened, glowing joy of being of service to someone in need. He hurried away to find a white table napkin. The two men in dark jackets, who had never left off staring at me all the while the father of the groom and I talked of amaretto and napkins, tried to engage me in a deeper conversation about the mystical nature of Madame Guyon and her mysterious mystical dreams of the future, which later generations would know as the past, assuming her dreams had been accurately interpreted. The two men explained that Madame Guyon believed dreams were the way God communicated with the faithful and that the purpose of her dreams was to bring the lost sheep back to the fold, especially when those lost sheep were priests and bishops and nuns, and so she had a spiritual duty to share her dreams with the world. I pretended I didn't hear a word they said, but they persisted. They said

Madame Guyon once had a dream about a beautiful white bird and when she woke up she yearned for that bird and spent eight years trying to find it, and she became very discouraged for a while because she believed that everyone else in the world was also searching for this bird, she became discouraged almost to the point of despair, in fact it was despair, and she did not know what to do with her despair, and then one day she realized that there was nothing for her to do, she was the one chosen by God to find this bird, the white bird of her dream was hers, her will and God's will were one and the same in this matter, and when she realized this her despair took wing, as it were, and never came back. That must have been some bird, I remember saying. It was, the two men said. What kind was it, I remember saying. We don't know, said the men. Perhaps it was a cockatoo, I remember saying. Yes, said the men, or perhaps a cockatiel. Or perhaps a swan, I remember saying. Or perhaps a dove, the two men said. But then I couldn't think of another white bird to add to the list so I didn't say a word, and the two men nodded at each other and smiled with great satisfaction, as if they had just disproved Nietzsche's *Doctrine of Eternal Recurrence.* A silence that was equal parts profound and puerile descended upon the table where I sat with the two men. They looked out the window and began trading whispers back and forth. The father of the groom returned with a napkin. While the two men were occupied with their whispering I hid my gleaming knife in the folds of the napkin. A few musicians with flutes and oboes came into the café and sat with those playing the stringed instruments. The music swelled as if an entire orchestra was playing. The music seemed to drown out the small talk from earlier. A few people began to complain about how loud the music was. The amarettos started appearing once again. I suddenly remembered that the diagram demonstrating the proper technique for disemboweling a man was on page 197 of *Dacae Misericordiae,* which was more towards the end than the middle. The text beneath the diagram also emphasized that this particular technique often resulted in a severing of the aortic artery, which meant that death would follow in a matter of minutes. I imagined myself plunging the knife into Ignazio and watching his innards tumble out. I smiled with great satisfaction at the thought. I let the thought linger. Once again I was struck by the lack of predatory animals anywhere in Sicily. The father of the groom took a few of the musicians aside and spoke to them and the music became more like background music. The small talk reasserted itself. The two men in their dark jackets were still trading whispers. I remember asking myself "Who are these two strange men in dark jackets who wanted to know if I was a Quietist?' I could hear fragments of their whispering. 'Faith does not consist in seeing nothing at all,' said one. 'Faith is obscure because it makes us see and do things that go beyond the scope of natural light,' said the other. 'Faith is illuminating because it demands that we sacrifice our reason to a divine authority, which is clearly above our own weak ability to reason,' said the one. 'Faith is both obscure and luminous,' said the other. It was hard to tell what they were talking about. The father of the groom approached the table with a tray of amarettos, which he gingerly placed on the table. This is the last of it, he said, and then he was whisked away by the owner of the cafe. I took up my last glass of amaretto, as did the two men in the dark jackets, and we nodded at each other, not quite smiling, in fact not even close to smiling, we all three possessed looks of extreme wariness, but then we relaxed because everyone in the café was holding up their glasses, and then a great booming voice said *'Salud'* and everyone drank and tossed their glasses to the floor with a mighty smack and many of the glasses shattered from the impact. Then one of the two strange men asked me if I had ever read *The Ladder of Paradise* by St. John Climascus, and I said I had not. Then the other one said *The Ladder of Paradise* was about how to attain a oneness with God, and I said I was not sure I wanted to attain a oneness with God. After that they seemed quite troubled, and soon after that they left. And then one by one the patrons of the cafe began to leave, and they were quickly followed by the musicians, for it was well past sunset by then.

I felt suddenly very alone. I could not believe how very dark it was sitting there inside the café. The café was only illuminated by two oil lamps hanging above the bar. I was the only person I could see. I could hear the voice of the father of the groom, who had remained because he had yet to settle up with the owner of the café. I could also hear the booming voice of the owner of the café, who was arguing with the father about how much was owed. Then the door opened and there was a rustling, rushing sound, as if a pack of hedgehogs or weasels or wild rabbits had scurried across the floor, and then Ignazio sat down across from me. Neither of us spoke. We had always been able to tell what the other was thinking, so words seemed unnecessary. Still, Ignazio seemed quite surprised at the speed of my knife. And he seemed even more surprised at how quickly his innards fell out of the gaping hole in his stomach, like animal slop. I don't think he appreciated the depth of his betrayal until that precise moment. His eyes grew very wide and black and shiny, like two black discs spinning into space, heading for some unknown destination, and then his eyes took on a glassy, glazed, distant look, as if those two black, shiny discs had finished their journey in record time, and then he slumped forward in his chair and his head fell like a piece of stone against the table and there he lay. The father of the groom and the owner of the café heard the sound and came running to the table. The father of the groom looked at the pool of blood on the floor and the collapsing sack that was once Ignazio and then at me, his eyes brimming brightly in the darkness with the futility of words. His agitated silence seemed to be saying that a napkin would not be enough, but perhaps a tablecloth. The owner of the café seemed little affected by the body. Once he saw that there was nothing to be done for Ignazio, he turned and went back to the bar. I realized that he was an old hat when it came to betrayal. He had probably been betrayed many times in his life. He would have understood exactly what I felt towards Ignazio and why killing Ignazio brought me no joy whatsoever. I did not care that Ignazio and Maura went away to America. That was not a betrayal by any stretch. That was love. Ignazio's betrayal was that he did not say goodbye. He left like a thief in the night, without a word. So when he returned as he did, I killed him. I really had no choice. That was also love. The owner of the café would have understood all that. But not the father of the groom. The father of the groom understood only that a man had been killed at some point during the party for his son. He was certain that he was going to be blamed for the death. He did not know what to do. I wiped the blade of my knife on the tablecloth and put it away. I told him not to worry. Then I left. It was late and I was tired, but I didn't go home right away. It was a strange and beautiful night. It was a night where there was no joy, but there was no sadness either. I sat on the old stone wall in the shadow of the castle and looked out at the darkly glowing sea. From somewhere I could hear once again the voices of the two men in their dark coats, but I could not see them. They were nowhere to be seen. But I could hear their voices clear as a bell. 'But I never said faith removed reason,' said the one. 'Faith transcends reason,' said the other. 'Through faith we no longer possess the need to reason,' said the one. 'Yes, yes,' said the other, 'and then we see the world through the wisdom of Christ, who becomes the motor of our soul.' Then there was silence for a while. The moon had already set. I sat there while the silence absorbed every last drop of starlight in the sky. Then I went home.

-81-

The murder of Ignazio Tiziano became the crime of the century and was reported in all the daily rags and scandal sheets from Trapani to Palermo. Murders were common enough in the streets of Castellammare del Golfo, but not in cafés. The police did not know what to do. The owner of the café came forward and said he did not know who had done this terrible thing. The police questioned the guests of the wedding party, but it soon became clear that no one had any idea what had happened. Most of those in the café at the time had never heard of Ignazio Tiziano. The fact that the police even knew his name was sheer luck, but even then it was still only conjecture based on a card in Ignazio's wallet which said: '*Ignazio Tiziano, Importer of Sicilian wines, New York City, America.*' The father of the groom, who had brought me an endless stream of amarettos and had seen me with a bloody knife in my hand, gave no thought to me at all. All he kept talking about was seeing the body for the first time with its gullet slit all the way from the navel to the sternum and the bloody intestines in a pile on the floor. I became a ghost as far as the death of Ignazio was concerned. The only detail that everyone agreed upon was the fact that two strange men wearing dark jackets had entered the café at some point and had been spotted sitting at the very table where Ignazio's body was later discovered, but the men had mysteriously vanished. The only other pertinent detail was that the men reeked with the odor of oleander. 'They smelled of death,' said one of the wedding guests. 'It should have been obvious what they were planning.' Unfortunately, no one could remember what the men looked like, but their possible existence was all the encouragement the police needed.

They immediately began rounding up men of all sorts, mostly transients who happened to be wearing dark jackets, but also a few peasants who had made their way to town the day after the murder and were wearing black fedoras in addition to dark jackets because they had important meetings the next day with bankers or priests and wanted to look nice, and they had come to town a day early so they would be on time the next morning, so they weren't loitering with aimless, suspicious intent, as it certainly seemed to the police, they were simply looking for a room for the night. The police reasoned that the two murderers could very well have possessed black fedoras but had perhaps decided against wearing them when they set out to murder Ignazio. Perhaps they sought to disguise their murderous intentions by abandoning their hats, this is what the police seemed to think. So within three days of one of the most barbarous acts ever committed in Castellammare del Golfo, the city jail and then the public offices of the magistrate (which were both housed on the first floor of a magnificent Baroque mansion with decorative columns and statuary and other sculpted elements clinging to the exterior walls and a heavy oak door with carved panels and heavy iron chains) were overflowing with suspects. It was utter chaos until the magistrate took charge and asked the police if any of the suspects reeked of oleander, which was the only detail of the case he could remember between bites of toast smeared with cheese and honey, which he was enjoying on the second floor of the Baroque mansion with the balcony doors flung wide open but the silk curtains drawn so that his exposure to the sun was somewhat filtered. The police, of course, said 'No, a few smelled of lavender or rosewater, but most had taken on the odor of mules that had been confined in a stable that leaked when it rained,' which was a most appropriate description, since the prisoners had been crammed together for three days in poorly ventilated jail cells or squashed together without mercy in one of the many, damp, foul-smelling waiting rooms or storage rooms or tiny water closets that were part of the magistrate's suite of offices. The magistrate was disgusted. He said the police had bungled the case. The whole building needed to be fumigated and everyone released. The two murderers had certainly escaped to Palermo, and from there they had certainly taken a boat to Naples and only God knew where after that. Four days after the murder all of the men in dark jackets (even the peasants) were sent home.

Within a month, the case of the murder of Ignazio Tiziano was abandoned for lack of suspects.

It was at this time that I received a note from Signore Caracciolo. Signore Caracciolo owned a small grocery, which his youngest son managed with quiet almost religious dedication, and a small restaurant on the other side of the plaza from the Cathedral, which his eldest son managed with exquisite theatrical flair. He enjoyed going to Palermo with his mistress for the opera once a month. He had once taken a trip to Rome, where he had met with Pope Pius IX for several hours. It was said that nothing happened in Castellammare del Golfo without his permission.

It wasn't much of a note. Fancy paper and a fancy envelope, but there were very few words, so it was difficult to pin down Signore Caracciolo's intentions. But there was no refusing the note either. The note said: *'Five o'clock. Saturday. The Restaurant.'* It was signed Gaetano Caracciolo. Beneath the signature was an image of a black hand holding a bloody knife.

-82-

Five o'clock. Saturday. The Restaurant:

The restaurant was closed when I arrived and I could not see in through the windows because the green shutters were latched tight. I waited around for a while like a criminal recently released from jail, not certain what to do. The patches of sunlight and shadow that fell across the cobblestones reminded me of a Telemaco Signorini painting. I started thinking I had misunderstood the intention of Signore Caracciolo's note, even though no intention was evident, when his son emerged from the tiny vestibule between the outer and inner doors, a big-toothed grin hastily scribbled on his face, and encouraged me to enter. He offered to take my jacket, but I was not wearing a jacket, so he begged my pardon and led me to a small table off in the corner. He hurried away and then hurried back with a bottle of wine and a glass and a plate of brown bread and a bowl of stew, an olio filled with chunks of tuna and shark, carrots and onions and peppers and garlic and sausage. Then he hurried away again, disappearing through a shuttered doorway. I don't know how long I sat there. The bright sunlight outside slipped around the outer edges of the green shutters and in through invisible cracks in the walls and underneath the door, but it was still not enough to see very well. The light inside the restaurant was a hazy, greenish color, an effect no doubt of the green shutters, but it gave the interior an alien, underwater feel, as if we (myself and Signore Caracciolo's son) were trapped at the bottom of the sea. By the time my eyes adjusted, I had almost finished my stew. I noticed three darkly glowing figures on the opposite side of the room, sitting beneath a painting of a street scene, a street in a small town like Castellammare del Golfo with its gleaming, white-washed buildings and the businesses open and people walking in and out of the shadows on a sunny day and laughing and carrying on and a couple of children in the foreground playing with sticks or stick figures or small hammers or small axes with wooden handles, or perhaps they were playing with knives. It was still very dark in the restaurant so the painting was more an impression of a painting than anything else. I suddenly felt I was a part of the painting, as if I were imprisoned within the canvas of the artist's imagination, a sensation that was strangely liberating, though it was certainly tinged with a sense of melancholy because of the ephemeral nature of existence, even existence granted seeming immortality through art.

The three darkly glowing figures did not say anything or give any indication that they knew about Signore Caracciolo's note. They were also eating soup. The restaurant echoed with the noise of people eating soup. But in the background, I could also hear someone humming. The humming was coming from the kitchen. It had a scratchy sound to it, like it was coming from an old Berliner Gramophone. Sometimes it was louder, though not louder than the noise of people eating soup, sometimes softer, as if someone were playing around with the volume. The three darkly glowing figures seemed also to be humming along with the Gramophone, though whether they had been humming all along or had just started I could not say. But they seemed to be vibrating just the same as they ate their soup, even their bones seemed to be vibrating. Then the humming from the kitchen stopped. One of the figures started to hiccup, perhaps from trying to hum and eat soup at the same time. It was hard to tell which one. Then a gravelly voice broke through the hiccupping.

'Puccio,' said the voice.

Puccio emerged from the kitchen with the same big-toothed grin scribbled across his face.

'Yes Pà?'

'See to our guest. See if he has had enough to eat. And tell him we are having cognac this evening. Ask him if he likes cognac. Cognac and pistachio biscotti. Tell him we have plenty of both.'

'Yes, Pà.'

'And if he does not like cognac and biscotti tell him we have port wine and walnuts. Everyone likes port wine and walnuts.'

'Yes, Pà.'

'But remember to use the small glasses with the port.'

'. . . .'

'And only a small bowl of walnuts.'

'. . . .'

'Too many walnuts are bad for the digestion.'

'Yes, Pà.'

The communication via Puccio went on like this for a while. Then the three shadowy figures turned inward upon themselves, as if they could not wait for the biscotti and were about to devour each other instead, and began discussing what seemed to be topics of great importance and then laughing, and then a few serious gestures and then more laughter, their voices falling and rising with the seriousness or levity of what they were saying. One did not eavesdrop on such a conversation. Still it was difficult to resist the urge. But everything they said seemed to swallow itself. Their words became small silences dropping into an ever-expanding ocean of silence. But occasionally I caught a word here, a joke there.

'U Signùri rùna 'u viscuottù a cu nun' avi rienti,' said the gravelly voice.

And then laughter, and then more murmuring.

'La donna e la gaddina si perdi si troppu cammina,' said the gravelly voice, a little while later.

And then more laughter.

And then 'Puccio!' and Puccio emerging once again.

'Would you please ask our guest to join us. And you may bring out the cognac and the biscotti.'

'. . . .'

'And throw open those shutters. Go on! I can't see a god forsaken thing in here.'

'. . . .'

'It is like trying to see through a bowl of this soup. The absence of light is very disconcerting.'

'Yes, Pà.'

And that was how I met Signore Caracciolo. In the bright sunlight that came pouring through the window I could plainly see that Signore Caracciolo was a man of good humor and good appetite. But I was not sure about the other two. Their faces were obscured by the need to flatter and perhaps succumb to licking boots, like so many wild dogs that follow at the heels of the strongest and the fastest, waiting for the day when the strongest and the fastest stumbles so they can tear him limb from limb. Signore Caracciolo told another joke and the other two laughed, and I tried to laugh, but my heart was not into it, and then Puccio returned and we ate biscotti and drank cognac. After a time, I was numb from the pleasure of the cognac and the pistachio biscotti. Signore Caracciolo continued laughing and drinking and eating, but the other two eyed me up and down. I began to wonder why Signore Caracciolo had summoned me. I wondered how long we were going to sit there eating and drinking. I wondered what I was going to do if I needed to urinate. Then Signore Caracciolo slapped the table very hard and the other two fell back in their seats. It was quite an explosion, like two universes colliding, or perhaps two stars, or at least two automobiles on a dark, lonely road. 'Show me this knife,' Signore Caracciolo roared, and his teeth flashed like tiny silver frogs in the sunlight, silver frogs made from Mexican silver that were once fashionable in Mexico City and perhaps would be again one day.

'Show me the knife,' he roared a second time, and this time the other two joined in.

I laid the knife on the table. It picked up the gleaming brilliance of Signore Caracciolo's teeth and all of us had to shade our eyes.

'It is a beautiful knife," he said. 'It is even more beautiful than I had imagined. You are very lucky to own such a knife.'

Then he took up the knife and slashed at the air.

The other two men began to smile.

'What if I were to keep this knife for my own?' he said.

A dark, knowing look like a lunar eclipse came over the other two men.

'What would you say to that?'

The other two men began to laugh softly, their chests and shoulders rising up and down as if they were in some pain.

'Yes, what would you say to that?'

But I didn't say anything. I just stared at Signore Caracciolo with an involuntary indifference. Perhaps it was because of all the cognac. I was expert when it came to beer and wine and amaretto and *assenziu*, but I had never before tasted cognac. Either that or I was blinded by the dazzling brilliance of my knife twirling about in Signore Caracciolo's hands. Either way the result was the same. But Signore Caracciolo mistook my indifferent stupor for quietly bubbling, murderous rage, and so he smiled a polite smile and slid the knife back across the table.

'I was not serious, of course,' he said. 'Such a knife is a gift from above. It is a matter of destiny.' He paused a moment and looked with great passion into my eyes. 'Yes,' he said. 'It is your destiny.'

Then he leaned closer, turning his head slightly so that I lost sight of his face in the glare of the sunlight pouring in through the window, and in a voice that was less than a whisper, as if he were simply exhaling slowly, the heat of his breath fogging up my mind, he asked if my knife had a name.

I had never thought of a name for my knife before that. Quite without thinking I said 'It is my dagger of mercy. It is called *Daca Misericordia*.' Signore Caracciolo leaned back and his face became visible once again and I could see a look of great satisfaction spreading from one cheek to the other.

'*Daca Misericordia*,' he repeated. 'It is a beautiful name for a beautiful knife.' His voice trailed off, as if he had suddenly remembered the name of a long-lost love. Then his voice began again. 'But do not ever again let another man take hold of it,' he said, 'for the day you do will certainly be your last. Your destiny is bound to this knife like no other.'

Then he shook my hand.

I worked for Signore Caracciolo after that and for a time saw after his interests in Trapani and other places. Whatever needed to get done, I did. But then Signore Caracciolo died and Mussolini began his war on the Mafia. So I left Sicily and came to Cuba. But from that day to this, no man on earth has ever so much as laid a finger on this my dagger of mercy. This knife has been my salvation. It has been my destiny. And no man will ever take hold of it while I still draw breath.

-83-

The meeting of the Directors of Ignazio Tiziano & Sons to discuss what they could salvage from the marketplace disaster and if they perhaps needed to relocate:

The meeting took place in late July in Giuseppe Federico DiCarla's magnificent colonial home in the hills outside Guanabacoa. You could not see the house from the road. All you could see were dense woods filled with yagrumo and logwood and rosewood and Spanish lime and pine, and all manner of palm trees. For some reason it was very dark driving through the woods, even in the middle of the day with the blue sky and sunlight filtering through the branches. It was very hot and very dark. Perhaps darkness is not the right word. Perhaps there is no word that captures the moment, or even the essence of the moment. It was more like someone had tried to take a photograph from a speeding car or a spy plane hurtling through the stratosphere and so everything had come out blurry and indistinct. In this photograph, which was in fact reality, the dark shapes of the trees merged with the shadows and the speckled light so you were never quite sure where you were in relation to anything else. There were no recognizable landmarks until you reached the first set of iron gates, and then two young men wearing caps and holding long-barreled rifles stepped out of the shadows with thin faces marked with the stony, implacable seriousness of young soldiers, and they waved for you to stop and approached your car, but when they saw who you were, they nodded and opened the gates and let you pass. And no matter where you were during that blurry afternoon drive, there were only two sounds you could distinctly hear, the obvious background noise of the dozens of automobiles that had made the short trip from Havana, bypassing the town of Regla with its unsurpassed view of the city of Havana at night, and then up through the dusty streets of Guanabacoa itself before heading into the hills, the automobiles making their slow, meticulous way through the woods to the mansion, the woods echoing with their mechanical wheezing and sputtering, the sound of grinding gears, and from somewhere else, though it sounded like it was coming from everywhere all at once, leeching out of the very air, as if each individual molecule was a tiny speaker wired directly into the mind of God, you could hear the sound of a fast-moving river, or perhaps many rivers coming together, a deluge. On that particular day, it took very little effort as you were driving through the woods, with your eyes wide open or squeezed shut it did not matter, to imagine that the entire world was covered with water, an ocean deep and dark.

Before the meeting began, before Giuseppe Federico DiCarla emerged from the gloomy interior of the house to greet his friends and business associates, everyone gathered in a grand arcade style patio, Turkish tile on the floor, plaster walls sixteen feet high painted a soft Spanish orange like a distant sunset or the pulsing liquid glow of the street lamps along the Malecón just before dawn, and a dozen or more wicker chairs scattered about with small side tables for drinks and small plates. On either end of the patio a candled chandelier hung from the ceiling. The candles were not lit. A grand archway connected the patio to the foyer and from there to the rest of the house. Along the wall opposite the archway there were half a dozen narrow arched doorways with shuttered panels. The panels were folded back and you could see a lush garden beyond with orange trees glowing with the light of the sun and various shrubs and a small plain fountain in the middle. You could hear the soft sounds of birds calling out to each other from the trees or the shrubs. Or maybe it was your imagination. The fountain was gurgling like a sewer.

There was also a French Provincial table with a rounded mirror of darkly glowing glass. The table was pushed up against the wall next to the grand archway and was covered with all manner of elegant decanters, bottles of expensive liquor, cordials, port wine, anisette, and an assortment of wine glasses and smaller glasses. But the mirror was a very strange mirror indeed. No matter where you stood you could never see yourself. To a normal person, such as those who have no connection with organized crime, the mirror would have seemed very disturbing, but to those seated in the wicker chairs on the patio, it was only mildly disturbing, or even the subject of broad humor. You saw only various darkly glowing shapes reflected in the glass, hunched over shapes or twisted, contorted shapes, whispering and drinking and laughing and gesturing with sly, sinister gestures, pouring more drinks, moving back and forth through the semi-darkness of the patio like demented ghosts.

-84-

The conversation on the patio before the meeting began:

"'You don't get vaccinated for Florida,' I said to her, 'but you do for Mexico and that's a fact.'"

"And what did she say to that?"

"She didn't say anything, she just boarded the bus and sat down."

"A real bitch, huh?"

"In a manner of speaking."

"Sure. So what'd you do?"

"I boarded the bus and sat down right behind her."

"I'll bet she liked that. Deep down I bet she was asking for it!"

"Yeah, sure."

"What'd you do then?"

"I started whistling a little tune I heard once when I was down in Mexico. I don't know where I was exactly. I think I was in Acapulco. A little café called La Mar Azul, as I remember, next to a movie house."

". . . ."

"She didn't like the tune. She acted like she had never heard it before, but it was really quite popular down there. I told her that was no way to treat a fellow traveling companion. I asked if she was going all the way to Miami or if she was getting off at an earlier stop, like Fort Walton Beach or Panama City or Tampa, but she didn't say a word the whole trip down."

"I pretty much keep to myself when I'm traveling."

"To each his own."

"I don't say a word to anybody."

"Of course you don't."

"It's like my tongue is tied into knots."

"You're not the gregarious type, not by a damn sight."

The men laughed.

And two more voices from somewhere else, the voices floating aimlessly about the patio, soaring up towards the darkness of the ceiling and the unlit candled chandeliers.

"Some said it was a group of students angered by this business with the newspapers."

"What business?"

"These kids were waving protest banners and demanding

that Grau stop paying off the newspapers."

"Who cares what Grau does with the newspapers? Nobody believes a damn thing they print anyway."

"Yeah, but these students were becoming pretty volatile."

"You mean out of control."

"Exactly!"

"What were they doing on Calle Cuba?"

"I don't think anybody knows. But somebody knew they were going to be there. Somebody called the police, or maybe the police were in on it from the beginning. Either way they were waiting by the Public Works building, and as soon as they saw the students they started firing their guns and everybody started running."

"What about the mob of low-life fuckers that attacked the warehouse?"

"That's the funny part. As soon as the shooting started, the mob rushed the gates and thirty minutes after that the warehouse was burning. You can draw your own conclusions, but it sounds to me like the whole thing was staged."

"You mean some fucker was out to get us from the start."

"That's pretty much the size of it."

And two more voices.

"We need the unions. The Communists can go fuck themselves!"

"As long as Portocarrero is the Minister of Labor, we'll be all right."

"Don't be so sure."

"Portocarrero is reasonable. We can always work with reasonable men."

"Yes, but something happens when these fuckers get a little taste of power. They suddenly become . . . unreasonable."

And then some head nodding, some quiet laughter.

And then all of the voices jumbled together.

"The government denies the police were ever there. But Calle Cuba is stained with blood."

"She actually got off the bus in Tampa, and I almost got off there too, I have to be honest, but the Traficantes wanted me in Miami the next day so I had to give her up."

"Except if the Communists take control we'll have to leave the country."

"You mean head to the States."

"Yeah, sure, America is always an option."

"But nobody wants to give up Latin America."

"Sounds like a good old-fashioned bloodbath!"

"The best kind."

"Where then?"

"Maybe the Dominican Republic.

". . . ?"

"Why not?"

"You mean as long as Trujillo stays in bed with the Americans."

"Is that what I mean?

"Sure."

"Fuck Trujillo."

"But she sure as hell was stacked. I mean I've never seen a woman that good looking."

"The Communists will never take control."

"You never saw such a beautiful piece of ass in your life. I mean my mouth was watering. I mean her fucking tits were out to here."

"I'd have liked to see that."

"Goddamn fucking tits."

"The street was littered with little green and white flags or banners, so you almost didn't notice all the blood."

"They tried in '26 and look what happened then."

"Those were anarchists.

"It'll start in the east."

"Not Communists."

"Santiago maybe."

"It was one hell of a political statement to make whoever the hell they were."

"It is all the same thing."

"Like it always does."

"It'll never happen."

"Just like in America."

"Yeah, I guess I blew it."

"Well, don't worry about it."

"You wait and see."

"There's a million dames in the world and they all look just like her."

"That's what I keep telling myself."

"America will step in."

"Yeah, just like in America."

"You're God damn right."

-85-

Luis was not participating in any of the conversations floating about the patio. He did not go in for the gossipy prattling of old women. Instead, he and Oscar were off in the corner in two wicker chairs that were partially shrouded by some potted ferns. They were drinking red wine, a Claret, while everyone else was already dipping into the hard stuff. It was Oscar's first time at a Director's meeting. He was wearing the white linen suit and the immaculate Panama hat that Luis had purchased for him when he had first arrived in Havana. He was a gleaming double image of his mentor. Luis was casually pointing out the cast of characters, at least the major players.

The big brute with the truck driver's cap and the broad, flattened nose of a boxer was Johnny 'Big John' DaLuca. He was representing the interests of the Traficante family out of Tampa. He was the one who had teased the girl on the bus. He had flown in just for this meeting.

Big John was chatting away with Antonio Billiteri, a one-time crooner who had ruined his voice smoking cigarettes. They were sitting a few feet from the darkly glowing mirror like two dark saints, occasionally looking at the glass, wondering what had become of their reflections, commenting how easy it is to commit all kinds of atrocities when you are invisible, and then laughing uproariously.

Antonio represented the interests of a money man known cryptically as the Big Jew, which was hardly cryptic at all because there weren't many Jews in Cuba to begin with, and not very many who were called 'Big,' which wouldn't have made literal sense anyway since the Big Jew was only five foot five, so it was clearly a symbolic reference, a healthy sign of respect or fear, and lastly, which is the nail in the coffin (a trite expression, certainly, but appropriate for this crew), there was only one person of Jewish persuasion who worked with the Mafia, who the Mafia were afraid of, who had become his own Mafia.

Big John and Antonio the former crooner had known each other for years. They had had a falling out over a girl some years earlier but they had made amends. They liked to joke about it from time to time, but the truth was neither even remembered the girl's name.

Before he ruined his voice smoking, Antonio had quite a singing career in front of him. He was more promising than Frank Sinatra, even the Big Jew said so.

After the smoking, of course, Sinatra was the man.

The other players on the patio, not including Luis, were as follows:

Eugenio Castellanos, a mixed blood with a flair for making apocalyptic pronouncements (cryptic prophecies written in cantos in the style of Cervantes and pulled out at parties and other gatherings to entertain and provoke wild, pendulum-swinging arguments that would quickly degenerate into fistfights) who had worked in the office of the Mayor of Havana, Manuel Fernandez Supervielle, until the Mayor had put a revolver to his chest and pulled the trigger because he was unable to make good on his campaign promise to supply Havana with an adequate water works. (Oddly enough, the suicide gun was a Kongsberg Colt pistol, which the Mayor's wife was certain did not belong to the Mayor, and the police, after examining the serial number that for some reason had not been filed off, agreed somewhat noncommittally with the wife, sharing with her and with the press only a few pages of their redacted findings, which raised a series of questions that were never answered, at least not satisfactorily, as far as the wife and one or two overly committed and underpaid journalists were concerned, for the gun had been purchased originally in a small gun shop in Hamburg, Germany under the auspices of the German Weapons Act of 1938 by a nameless individual, at least his name had been blacked out on the permit card on file in the government offices in Hamburg, and then the gun appeared to have been registered with the Cuban government as a diplomatic courtesy in the name of another nameless individual, or perhaps the same one (who can truly say?), on behalf of the German Embassy. But what did that prove? We all have our enemies. Even if we are unaware of their existence. Even if they are but shadowy reflections of ourselves.) Eugenio had recently been elected the Treasurer of the Gas Workers Union. He had been involved in organized crime in one way or another since he was fourteen years old.

Ruperto Medino Borges, an expatriate Argentine and former editor of the newspaper *Diario de la Marina,* before Batista put that bastard Ernesto de la Fe in charge of gagging the press. It was rumored that Ruperto was bisexual. It was also rumored that he had fathered progeny with his own daughters, an outlandish thing to say under any circumstances. Of course every time these rumors surfaced they were met with an icy stare and the threat of bullets, though everyone knew no bullets were forthcoming, and then a front-page story eviscerating the rumormongers before all Havana. Then the rumors would vanish for a year or two. But nothing Ruperto did, no amount of justified outrage he might express, stopped the flurry of sarcastic lyrics (somewhere between letrillas and limericks in terms of form and content) that circulated unpublished for years before they were lost or purposefully abandoned in the forgotten railway station of time, or perhaps they were scribbled on the walls of public bathrooms and later the ink blurred, but which in their heyday exploded with momentary though sophomoric (which is to say moronic) brilliance, no one could deny that, with lines like: There once was a faggot/Ruperto, who was also,/ they said, necrofilico/so they cut off his cock/ which they stuffed in a sock/and now he suffers from vertigo.

It was also rumored that Ruperto was losing his eyesight from too many years typesetting (before he became the editor in charge) in that dungeon of a room where the printing presses were kept, presses which needed to be typeset by hand for oh so many mind-numbing years, countless years, centuries, by some accounts, in a room where the only illumination in all that time came from two weakly glowing brown globes, from Edison's original drawings, the editors used to say with charred laughter, set in the ceiling about three feet apart from each other and which resembled nothing if not two enormous eyes of a submerged sea creature from a distant millennium. The rumor of Ruperto's failing eyesight was unsubstantiated.

Eladio de la Campa, a light skinned Cuban of Spanish descent who had recently been elected Secretary of the Electrical Workers Union. Eladio had once worked for Prio, who had gone into exile when Batista took over, and on the surface he said good things about Prio, or most of the time he did, but Eladio had been very young when he first met Prio and it was said that Prio had raped him, that he had two thugs hold Eladio down in a rarely used storage room in the Capitol building, or maybe it was in the back of some café along the harbor or in one of the city father's city parks looking out on the Straits of Florida after midnight, and he had raped Eladio repeatedly, and then he had sworn Eladio to secrecy on pain of death, and not just Eladio's death, but the deaths of his mother and his sister and his sister's small children, and then the incident was all but forgotten. It was if it had never happened. So Eladio secretly hated Prio.

Paolo Cuccia, an attaché at the Italian Consulate who had Sicilian connections and who had handled the deportation paperwork for Lucky Luciano with a skillful white-washing of the most damning details of Luciano's case, which earned him a commendation from his superiors. There was nothing more to say about Paolo.

Various silent, eager, hopeful lieutenants and faithful, diligent soldiers, watchful companions to the men noted above, a few who were heirs apparent, like Oscar, and so were sitting nervously in wicker chairs near their patrons, but the rest spent most of that afternoon leaning up against walls or huddled in the gloomy shadows of the great archway, drinking steadily, seeming complacent, even bored, but watching every movement of every man on the patio, cataloging secret motives and emerging weaknesses with methodical (some would say sadistic) fatalism, their eyes drawn to the smallest of hand gestures, a slightly furrowed brow, a silk handkerchief pulled from a pocket, a fancy, perfumed handkerchief that smelled heavily of citrus and faintly of mint, a pair of legs crossing themselves and uncrossing themselves in quick succession, a crystalline peal of laughter ringing in the semi-darkness and then crashing to the tiled floor, anything that might suggest someone was about to pull a gun.

Oscar was intoxicated with the specter of imminent betrayal and certain violence that hovered in the air above the gossipy men, the noxious fumes of an exploding universe or a hypnotist's trick of the light (a notoriously slippery pair of alternatives that seem on the surface to be mere playful banter but which upon closer examination lie at the very heart of certain philosophical discussions about the meaning of life and the nature of true love, which naturally depends upon one's perspective and the books one has read and whether or not one was abused as a child, as is usually the case, and so is often misinterpreted or overlooked altogether). The last time Luis had attended a meeting, Oscar and Nerea had accompanied him as far as the town of Guanabacoa, and then he had dropped off the lovebirds at a small sunwashed café to eat and pass the time. Naturally, Oscar had been humiliated when Luis left him behind, but Luis had told him he was not yet ready. "These men do not care about your dream to open a nightclub of your own unless you are able to line their own pockets," said Luis. "And if you make such a promise, then you need to be especially careful. They deal in death without acrimony or remorse." So there had been nothing that Oscar could say, not a word of reproach or resignation, not so much because Oscar lacked the social savvy to know when a joke was required or when it would be best to hide in a cloud of silence to elude a bullet, which was certainly true, but because Oscar was with Nerea that day and she had been wallowing in despair, a pouty expression on her lips which meant she needed considerable attention or she would be a bear for only God knew how long. But all that had been forgotten when Luis announced that Oscar would accompany him into the hills beyond Guanabacoa to attend a meeting of the Directors of Ignazio Tiziano & Sons to discuss their good fortune at living in a world always on the brink of war.

-86-

The meeting of the Directors officially began when Giuseppe Federico DiCarla was wheeled out onto the patio. He was sitting in a rigid, authoritarian pose, defiant but gracious, in a cane-back wheelchair with ivory handles. A young orderly wheeled him towards the second of the six narrow arched doorways. The young orderly was dressed all in white, a gleaming white in contrast to the semi-darkness all around. He positioned the wheelchair so Federico could see both the garden, with its orange glowing orange trees that now seemed like comets that had already struck the earth, and the darkly glowing shadows of the dark men who were sitting in the wicker chairs slowly (or speedily) getting drunk. Federico had a good view of both.

Two young men with long-barreled rifles also accompanied Federico, and he smiled at them, a charming, intelligent, gracious as always but also slightly sinister smile that seemed like the smile of a rebellious Jesuit priest, even though Federico was clearly no Jesuit. The young men slipped into the shadows on either side of the doorway. Soon everyone else forgot they were there.

As soon as the pleasantries were exchanged, which were incoherent and garbled because of alcohol but since everyone knew everyone else it didn't matter, Federico launched into a recitation about a 2nd century Roman philosopher named Celsus, who had accused the early Christians of trying to kidnap the very idea of a Supreme Being and present it as their own. What they wanted, said Federico, assuming the persona if not the ancient voice of Celsus, was an exclusive piece of real estate that only they could claim where they could erect all sorts of luxury accommodations with mini-bars and swimming pools and fancy chocolates and champagne and run about naked day and night (though all of these images, it should be said, came from Federico's febrile imagination, not from the writings of Celsus). The early Christians promised a veritable paradise if you bought their story, said Federico speaking for Celsus, a cornucopia of human delight, if you will, where every desire that went unfulfilled in this miserable plane of reality, every gnawing sacrifice that ate away at your own belief in yourself until there was nothing left, all of this misery would be repleted a thousandfold. That was the story line. But it was a bald-faced lie, an absolute sham, that's what Celsus thought, said Federico. That's what really got him steamed. So he told everyone who would listen that the Christians had created an imaginary world (to say the least) to seduce the masses, and then they were going to steal the actual world when everyone was looking towards the mythic future, and, naturally, the masses were seduced.

Then Federico spoke at great length about a Frenchman who taught philosophy and mathematics at a small private school in Algiers in 1917, and he couldn't remember this Frenchman's name, but he knew that it was not Pascal or Fénelon or Bossuet or Montargis or La Combe, but perhaps it was Renan or Rougier or someone who resembled the figures in the later paintings of Modigliani with their sad eyes and elongated faces and noses like miniature elephant trunks trying to sniff out the truth, but whoever he was, this mad dog of a Frenchman attacked the dogmatic principles not only of the Catholic Church, but of all ideologies that promised liberation but did not deliver (whether it was liberation of the soul, of thought, of the body, of the self, from society, from violence, from hunger, from death, of dreams, it was all the same thing in the end), and then later, and this was always the pattern, those pushing this propaganda would use the gleaming bauble of liberty always just out of reach to stifle liberty itself, and you could hear Federico's rising anger as he spoke, an anger that stretched all the way back to the time of Celsus, an anger that some would call the winds of indignation, the winds which precede the storm.

All this Federico pushed towards his drunken, astonished listeners, and then he sat back in triumph in his ivory handled wheelchair, a ridiculous, aging, infirm Mephistopheles ready to pluck the souls like stone orchids of the already damned from this purgatorial rock garden of existence, where we find ourselves. So Federico sat back in his wheelchair and smiled. He turned one ear towards his own garden and the gurgling fountain and the glowing orange trees like dead or dying comets and the birds calling to each other in their strange, throaty, feathery language of the afterlife, and he turned the other ear towards the semi-darkness of the arcade style patio and his stiff, silent listeners, who might have been thinking about Federico's passionate recitation, but they might also have been thinking about how hungry they were even at three in the afternoon because there was nothing to eat on the patio.

There was a strange, noisy crashing sound from the garden, as if an airplane had crashed into the orange trees, or a satellite from the future that had slipped out of its orbit. But it was really the sound of several birds, a flock of birds, starlings perhaps, or some other kind of bird, taking flight. For a moment nobody could see the sun. At least nobody who was looking in the direction of the sun. Which was only Federico.

Antonio Billiteri wondered out loud how much it would cost to get a piece of that prime real estate Federico had been talking about. He did not realize his thoughts had become words. His question unleashed a storm of varying opinions. Big John said he didn't believe in owning property, he believed in hotels, and hotels could get quite pricey, especially if you trashed the room. Eladio wanted to say that Big John was an idiot, but Eladio was always the diplomat and said only that the problem with hotels was that they took advantage of the people who worked for them, people who had little or no formal education and could not be expected to stand up to the onslaught of prejudice and racial insults hurled their way for fear of losing their jobs. Paolo said he was staying at The Gran

Inglaterra Hotel on Paseo del Prado, in spite of the fact that it was a little run-down, a balcony room with a view of the sea, the very same room where Winston Churchill had stayed when he came to watch the Spanish-Cuban war in 1895, that's what the clerk had said. Paolo said the other morning when he woke up the prettiest little dark-skinned maid you ever hoped to see was scrubbing his bathroom and she was bending over and her skirt was riding up so he, Paolo, surprised her from behind and carried her back to his bed. Later they splashed around in the tub and scrubbed each other with a bar of that black Spanish soap. Then they fucked some more. Big John and Antonio said they were staying at the wrong hotel. Paolo invited them to come to a small party he was throwing the next night. Big John and Antonio said they would come. Eladio said that was just the kind of prejudicial attitude he was talking about. No wonder nobody in Cuba knew where they came from. Ruperto said he agreed with Eladio from a biological point of view, but intellectually, now that was a different matter. Ruperto said they were all descended from the great José Marti, even the poor souls like himself who had emigrated from Argentina. They (we) were all his (Marti's) children. Had they (we) not all read and been amazed by Marti's excellent essays on everything from when he was in prison in Cuba to his rabble rousing in New York City as well as the letters he wrote to General Maximo Gómez? Eladio scoffed at the mere mention of Marti's name. Eladio said what about Félix Varela y Morales, who wrote that you could believe in God and still work to change the order of things in a country like Cuba that cared little for the welfare of ordinary citizens. Big John said he wasn't Cuban to begin with so he didn't care about what any of these Cuban writers had to say. He was Italian. Antonio and Paolo agreed with Big John. Ruperto was fuming. Eladio said what about Caballero, for God's sake, or Zayas, or Enrique José Varona, who wrote for the revolutionary heart in all generations. Where do these men fit in? What of their patriotism, their dreams for Cuba? Have you forgotten where we come from? And with that Ruperto exploded, a rush of words coming directly from Marti himself: 'A nation is not founded as a military camp is commanded,' he said. And then: 'The pain of imprisonment is the harshest, most devastating pain, murdering the mind, searing the soul, leaving marks that will never be erased.' Of course nobody knew what Ruperto was trying to say. While every

Cuban boy had learned to quote Marti in grade school, these particular quotes did not seem to apply to the discussion at hand. Nevertheless, no one could argue with Ruperto's passion. He was shouting with such thunderous agitation that the dust from the ceiling fell like darkness. Or perhaps the darkness fell like dust. It was hard to tell.

Then there was a lull in the conversation and everyone calmed down.

Then Eugenio said he was concerned about the attack on the federal garrison near Santiago. Ruperto asked him what attack was this. Eugenio said two hundred rebels living in the Sierra Maestra mountains had attacked the garrison at Moncada. They had a rented a farmhouse near the barracks, where they had stashed dozens of light rifles and shotguns and ammunition and several cartons of old army uniforms to wear as disguises. They had enough weapons for a small raid, but not an all-out attack. On the feast day of St. James, the rebels were to make their way to Santiago, singly or in pairs, and rent rooms in the various hotels and brothels. A few were to stay with relatives. They were going to attack at dawn the next day. Then dawn came, and everything seemed promising. They met at the farmhouse to get their weapons and to put on their army uniform disguises. They went over their plan, the routes the vehicles were to take, the timing of the assault. They were laughing and joking. They were certain the soldiers from the barracks would be hung over from a night of drunken debauchery, the kind of night that went along with any feast day. They were certain they were going to seize control of the barracks and the weapons that were stored there, there was a rumor that there were thousands of rifles stored at Moncada, enough to start a revolution, and they believed that once they had seized control of all this, thousands of Cubans would then join their cause. But they were mistaken. They were mistaken about everything. The attack was a disaster from the start. Two of the cars loaded with rebels got into an accident with a bus heading for Bayamo. Another vehicle got lost in the narrow streets of Santiago, somewhere in the vicinity of the stairway of Padre Pico. Another ran out of gas. Only three cars made it to the barracks at all. The first of these crashed itself through the gate, killing the two guards instantly, but damaging the car to such an extent that it was inoperable. By the time the rebels pushed it from the entrance, which took more time than they had bargained for, they were surprised by a surprise morning patrol making the rounds that had heard the crash and came to investigate. That's when the shooting started. Half of the rebels were killed on the spot. Of those who escaped, all were later caught, and most of these were executed. But some were set free. 'That was a mistake,' said Eugenio.

It was at this point that Ruperto, who knew nothing about this attack on the barracks of Moncada, said 'I know nothing about this attack on the barracks of Moncada,' at which point Eugenio said that was not surprising since the attack had not yet happened, at which point Eladio started to laugh and said, you fooled us, Eugenio, you did not turn this prophecy into poetry as you usually do, so how were we to know you were kidding, and Eladio's laughter rang out with the cruel clarity of a church bell, but Eugenio was not laughing for he truly believed that all of his prophecies were written by the hand of God, this one about the attack on the barracks of Moncada more than any of the others, he was just the mouthpiece reading from a script, an oracle without a political agenda, he was simply the overhead projector projecting God's words written on a celestial transparency, so he said he was not kidding, he did not kid when it came to prophecies, the attack will take place, he said, if not this year then certainly next year, and some of the rebels will be released to appease public opinion, and this will be a mistake, the rebels they release will become dyed–in-the-wool Communists, or close enough that it will make no difference, and so they will try a second time, this is inevitable, and they will succeed, and then Cuba will be saddled with a brilliant, charismatic, but ultimately childish dictator who will drive the country towards a host of impossible, absurd agricultural goals, such as trying to improve the production of the nation's dairy cows, pushing the biological limits of the cows in the misguided hope that one day every cow in the country (or even the miracle of just one cow) will be capable of producing an endless stream of milk, an inexhaustible supply, this, said Eugenio, is the nature of the man who will be a dictator like no other, a dictator who will value the dismantling of the tourist trade in the name of social theory more than the welfare of his own people, a dictator who will lead Cuba and the rest of the world to the brink of a third world war, the very edge of the cyclical night, filled with corridors for sleep and nameless fear.

It was at this point that the laughter of Eladio had become

the laughter of Eladio and Ruperto and Big John and Antonio and Paolo, and their laughter with its crystalline purity of dozens of very large church bells ringing out from the four corners of the earth turned every single word that fell out of Eugenio's mouth into drops of sea water or translucent pearls that landed harmlessly on the tiled patio floor.

Then the men grew serious and talked about the dangers of Communism for a while. Big John was of the opinion that the only good Communist was a dead Communist. Paolo said he thought that only applied to American Indians or pirates. Big John said what did he (meaning Paolo) think Communists were. Paolo didn't know what to say. Ruperto said the moment the Communists got their hands into the newspapers, the newspapers would be sunk. Eladio said the moment the Communists got their hands into the unions, the unions would be sunk. Let's face it, said Antonio, if the Communists ever take over, we're all sunk. Unless the Americans intervene, said Ruperto. Then Luis said the symbol of Communism should be a sinking ship, and everyone applauded.

Then everyone talked about the possibility of the Americans intervening. Then they talked about the pros and cons of America if you were living in Cuba, and then America if you were living in America, and then they talked about Cuba if you were living in America, but they didn't talk about Cuba if you were living in Cuba because they were already living there, except Big John, who didn't care.

Then Ruperto told a story about a young crippled boy living in Argentina. The boy had spent his life on crutches but he had always wanted to dance with pretty girls and ride horses. He especially wanted to ride the Argentine Criollo because this horse was as rugged as the mountains which the crippled boy could see from his bedroom window and because this horse, which was a little bigger than a Spanish mustang, could cover astonishingly long distances in a single day. Since he was a devout Catholic, the crippled boy prayed and prayed to Saint Antonio for a miracle that would erase his deformity. He prayed every day. For years and years he prayed every day. Naturally, no miracle occurred. And after a while, said Ruperto, the crippled boy became a crippled man, and his dream of dancing and riding horses began to fade. He felt betrayed. He cursed the name of Saint Antonio. He thought about cursing the name of God. And then one day he retracted his prayer.

The very next morning, said Ruperto, bright and early, the crippled man's cousin, a long-leagued cattle baron named Rafael, who owned several ranches near San Cristóbal, arrived in a gleaming new automobile. The crippled man had not seen or even heard from his cousin in years and did not know that Rafael had taken some time off to travel. He was amazed by his cousin's vehicle, which was a fabulous four-cylinder Rochet Schneider with a front seat and a back seat. Rafael said he was on a pilgrimage to the Church of Saint Antonio, which was only a couple of days by car, and he asked the crippled man to join him. The crippled man agreed to go, but he did not say why. He hid his dark purpose even from himself.

That night they camped under the stars, for they found themselves in a very rural part of Argentina. As they were settling in for the evening, a bearded man driving a team of mules appeared out of nowhere. The mule driver asked if he could share their simple campsite, and the crippled man and the cousin agreed. Later, all three men were sitting by the campfire sipping red wine from tin cups, and the mule driver suddenly began telling them a story about a boy he had sent to a small Jesuit school in Santa Fe. He was paying for everything, but the boy was not his. The boy was the son of a friend from his childhood. His friend had been dead for many years, but the circumstances of his death were very strange, some would even say suspicious, so the mule driver had spent the cascading years that followed describing the details of that fateful day, which seemed like yesterday, to anyone who would listen.

On the day of his friend's death, the two of them had robbed an old priest of a sack of silver, but then his friend had become suddenly greedy and tried to kill him. Fortunately for the mule driver, the gun, a pistol typical of men without integrity, exploded in his friend's hand. The bullet magically lodged itself in his friend's forehead, killing him instantly. So with the unlucky death of his friend (but of course lucky for the mule driver), he found himself in sole possession of the bag of silver. But later that night he had a strange dream. Saint Antonio appeared in his dream and told him about his friend's son. Saint Antonio said the boy was destined to become a priest. And what was more, the bag of silver was meant to pay for the boy's education at the Jesuit school in Santa Fe. That is what Saint Antonio said, and then he disappeared. 'I had never been visited by a Saint before,' said the mule driver. 'Naturally

I went to the village where my friend had lived with his son. I told the boy his father had died so he could go to school.'

The next morning the crippled man and his cousin went one way and the mule driver went another way. The cousin asked the crippled man what he thought about the mule driver's story but the crippled man didn't answer, for he was lost in thought. After a while they came upon a man walking in the middle of the road. The road was very rough and made for difficult driving, but it made for even more difficult walking, so they asked the man if he wanted a ride. The man accepted and hopped into the back seat. A short while later he was describing how he had rescued his own soul from eternal damnation. He said that when he was a young boy, his father mysteriously died, and a friend of his father magically appeared with a bag of silver and said the money was to pay for his schooling. So off he went to the Jesuit school in Santa Fe, and ten years later he became a priest. It was only after becoming a priest that he learned that his soul had been promised to the Devil.

'My father had signed a blood contract with the Devil,' he said. 'Because he wanted to be a wealthy man. My soul was part of the price my father had to pay. But he soon regretted his decision and tried to get out of the contract. After a great deal of snooping about, he discovered that his contract was in the possession of an old priest who lived in a small nearby village where time was measured by the lingering echo of a single church bell. He discovered that this old priest always prayed in the church of this village until the stroke of midnight, at which point the Devil would appear before the altar with a bag of silver in payment for the old priest's complicity. Then the old priest would return to the rectory for a few hours' sleep. So my father and his friend were waiting for the old priest on the narrow path between the church and the rectory. They were going to rob the old priest and use the bag of silver to buy back my father's contract. But before my father knew what was happening, his friend was waving a gun in the air and the gun went off and my father was killed. The old priest saw the dead body and shoved the bag of silver into the hands of my father's friend and then fled into the darkness.

'The only reason I know about this is because one night, shortly after I had said my final vows, Saint Antonio appeared to me in a dream. He said my soul belonged to the Devil. He told me the story of my father's greed and subsequent death.

He said if I wanted to regain possession of my soul I needed to listen to him very carefully. He said I needed to impress upon this priest the error of his ways, and to do this I needed to first accompany him, meaning Saint Antonio himself, on a dark and dangerous journey into the depths of Hell so that I could see the horrors of the eternal pit for myself. As soon as I returned, I was to visit the old priest and describe to him everything that I had seen. You can imagine my despair, but I did exactly as Saint Antonio had commanded and sought out the old priest, and when I finished my tale of horrors, he repented of all his evil deeds, took out a handful of contracts, including mine, which he had been keeping until the Devil called, and burned them right there in front of my eyes. Then he collapsed in a heap, his mortal flesh evaporating like smoke in a matter of seconds.'

By the time the young priest had finished his story, the crippled man and his cousin were nearing the town with the Church of Saint Antonio. The young priest asked to be let off on the outskirts of the town. Then he thanked the men for their hospitality and gave each a gift. To the cousin he gave a small leather Bible with an inscription inside that read 'Nothing is what it appears to be.' To the crippled man he gave a large blue stone, a very deep blue, a lapis lazuli polished and gleaming, about the size of an ostrich egg, or even larger, which the young priest said was his only souvenir from his journey to Hell.

'I shed copious tears on my journey through Hell,' he said. 'I witnessed unspeakable horrors. But I was there with the grace of God and under the protection of Saint Antonio himself, so my tears became this gleaming blue stone. For me it became a talisman of my great good fortune, a reflection of my faith, a visible reminder that my salvation is part of God's divine purpose. But I think you need this reminder more than I do.' Then the young priest hopped out of the car and vanished in a swirling nest of dust and pebbles.

When the crippled man and his cousin arrived at the church it was almost five o'clock in the afternoon, which meant that most of the votive candles had been lit by pilgrims seeking miracles. The candles were burning brightly, as always, though the pilgrims were no longer present, but if you listened carefully you could still hear the intonation of their prayers lingering high above in the rafters.

The cousin went immediately to the rail before the altar and the great statue of Saint Antonio shrouded in perpetual mystery and lit a candle of his own and knelt down and prayed, but the crippled man, who was standing near the back of the church, resting somewhat awkwardly upon his rickety, wooden crutches, could only stare at the statue of Saint Antonio with a look of venomous distrust in his eyes.

He began cursing the great saint. 'I prayed to you and I prayed to you and you did not answer my prayers,' said the crippled man. Then he reached into his pocket and pulled out the gleaming blue stone the young priest had given him. He looked at the stone a moment. Then he reared back and hurled it at the statue of Saint Antonio with such force that all of the candles flickered and some went out. He looked up to see the damage the stone had done, but instead he saw the statue of Saint Antonio smiling, the blue stone in the Saint's hand, the Saint rearing back as if to hurl the stone himself, but the crippled man did not wait to find out, he was through the church door as fast as his legs could carry him, and it was only when he was a mile down the road that he realized he was running without the aid of his crutches, as nimble and as fleet-footed as any boy who had ever danced with a pretty girl.

No one in the room had ever been to Argentina, except for Ruperto, who said Argentina was a land of romance and lovers of all ages, but also of night terrors and unethical businessmen and Nazi paraphernalia and beautiful movie actresses who did three or four films and became international stars and then went into hiding and were never seen again. Big John was about to say that Argentina was a land of degenerates and whores, worse than the penal colonies of the English or the floating asylums of the French, but quite without warning, Giuseppe Federico DiCarla reinserted himself into the conversation and all thoughts of Argentina ceased.

Within minutes everyone was passionately discussing the storming of the gates of Ignazio Tiziano & Sons. Everyone had an opinion about why the furious mob had stormed the gate, but Federico wasn't interested in opinions. Then Luis said it didn't matter why it happened. What mattered was that it had, in fact, happened, and now they had a choice to make. They had to figure out what they were going to do next. (Luis did not share his suspicions about Immanuel, for that would have needlessly complicated the discussion.) Federico laughed a great thunderous laugh. Or perhaps he was clapping. 'Exactly!' he said, and then he rolled himself over to the French Provincial table and the darkly glowing mirror and spun around to face the darkly glowing eyes (like the eyes of so many rabid hyenas) of the men glued to their wicker chairs.

Federico talked about the vanishing dream of Cuba and how their lives would be forever changed. He talked about the vanishing dream of the Mafia in Sicily during the time of Mussolini and how the lives of the Mafia had changed. He talked about the now vanished dream of his own childhood in Castellammare del Golfo and how his life had never been the same since those bygone days. Then he confessed that he didn't have a clue about what they should do, but he felt deep down in his gut that they had no choice but to abandon their interests in Cuba and head for the sunny shores of Florida. He thought maybe Miami. They had nice clean beaches there and it was a sleepy town compared to Havana so there would be very little competition. He had never been there, but he often imagined what it would be like. The night before his good friend Ignazio had left for America they had talked about places like New York City and Chicago and San Francisco and Miami. Someone had said Miami was the best of the four because it offered a tropical climate. In Miami you could lose yourself in the soothing rhythms of the sea. One of the puppeteers had said this. Yes, he had often imagined what it would be like in Miami. He used to think maybe Ignazio had taken Maura there. That's what he would have done. Life would have turned out much differently if he had gone with Ignazio and Maura.

Federico stopped talking and picked up his knife, which had been hidden from view in the folds of a napkin on his lap. He held up the knife as if he were holding up a sacrificial victim or a rare meteorite from a distant galaxy that had survived the passage through time and the earth's atmosphere. The blade caught the last rays of sunlight filtering in from the garden, the light then bouncing from the knife to the dark glass of the mirror and then folding in upon itself, and suddenly, strangely, it seemed that there were two knives floating in the air. In that moment, it seemed as if Federico had vanished, and all the men still glued to their wicker chairs could see were two gleaming knives. Beyond the knives there was nothing to see except the loss and absence of the world.

-87-

For Oscar, the years following his first meeting with the Directors of Ignazio Tiziano & Sons were a tumultuous dream full of shadowy yet sharply stylized characters, a film noir classic in which two sides were pitted against each other in the eternal struggle for power and the privilege of living beyond the reach of the law. Naturally, there was also a lot of sex and lust (you can't have film noir without eroticism) as well as random acts of cruelty, pre-meditated acts of cruelty, an atmosphere of all-consuming betrayal, and some sort of strange, all-encompassing metaphor suggesting that the reality depicted in this movie was a dream, or conversely, that the reality depicted in this dream was a movie. To everyone involved, it was clear beyond the need for words that the lines for this black and white epic had been drawn when Federico announced his intention to move operations to Miami. Antonio, speaking on behalf of the Big Jew, Eladio and Eugenio, speaking on behalf of the unions and the faceless, downtrodden people of Cuba, perpetually downtrodden, and Ruperto, speaking for himself, and yet also, in some strange, vaguely conceived yet symbolic way, for journalists everywhere engaged in the struggle to preserve the freedom of the press, were all against the idea. Their opposition was quite vocal, bordering on belligerent, but what could they do? Big John didn't care, and neither did Paolo. Only Luis among the Directors and Oscar among the close associates and other various hopeful lieutenants stood squarely with Federico.

Ruperto thought the old man had lost his grip. Eladio thought perhaps he had succumbed to the inertia of an ever-expanding regimen of medication and old age. Antonio, again on behalf of the Big Jew (did Antonio ever voice his own opinion?), assumed that one day they would find the body of the old man and his shattered cane-back wheelchair with the ivory handles at the bottom of a ravine or a steep set of stairs or among the jagged rocks along the Malecón, where the ice-cream vendors were always pushing their Guarina ice-cream carts along the wall and the fishermen were always casting their lines and squinting into the sun (and Antonio could almost visualize this happening in his mind, not far from the spot, or one of the many spots, where Luis and Nerea used to engage in some pretty furious fucking in a doomed effort to hold on to their disintegrating love). Eugenio was convinced the end of the world was at hand.

One way or another the world was, in fact, falling apart, and then, of course, reassembling itself. The salient metaphor (or perhaps series of metaphors or extended metaphor is more accurate) for this process, which you have probably already guessed, was a flaming meteor streaking across the sky and crashing into the earth, perhaps wiping out a small town, or even a city if it was large enough, but certainly causing devastation and vast amounts of inky black smoke wherever it landed, and then later, the place where the meteor had struck would experience a rebirth of quasi-religious significance, an elemental Phoenix rising from the ashes, the hope of a new paradise for a new world, but overhead the sky would remain dark and foreboding because you never knew when another meteor might appear. Suffice it to say that everyone knew some kind of change was occurring, they could feel it, each in their own way, but Oscar was perhaps more sensitive to the precise nature of what was happening than the others. Even Eugenio only felt vague tremors, a subtle vibration affecting his inner sense of equilibrium, producing the kind of discomfort, even nausea, usually associated with a wild swing in temperature or a sudden change in pressure after a debilitating descent from a higher altitude.

But with Oscar it was different. From the moment Oscar and Luis had left the meeting, Oscar had felt a strange uneasiness, almost as if he were walking a tightrope with his eyes closed, and this feeling soon developed into a preternatural sense that the malignancy of the world was sprouting like jimson weed before his very eyes. He was not paranoid by nature, but he knew without quite knowing how that he was being watched, spied upon, that someone was listening to his telephone conversations and perhaps recording them, and others were opening his letters with steam and pouring over them with cold, calculating eyes, eyes that also possessed a sadistic glint, looking for some sort of clue about his most recent nightmares or his childhood fears that had ripened into full-blown adult psychoses which they would later use against him without remorse, and then those shadowy someones resealing the letters as best they could, and still others were sifting through his trash, or tailing him in the middle of the night when he was heading back from La Campana or some other club to Hotel Milagro, but whenever he would stop and look around, the rambling echo of their footsteps would fade away. Later he began to notice strangely inarticulate men with rifles or Kongsberg Colt pistols sitting in the worn out leather chairs scattered about the hotel lobby, a dark, jazzy rendition of Gershwin's *Summertime* floating lazily about, reverberating with the elegance of days gone by, though some would have said it wasn't Gershwin at all, that it was Sarah Vaughn singing *Whatever Lola Wants, Lola Gets,* and a few would have said it was an old Eliseo Grenet song, and Eliseo was singing as he always did about the suffering of beautiful Cuba (*¡Ay! Cuba hermosa, primorosa, ¿por qué sufres hoy tanto quebranto?*), but there was an eerie, mysterious quality about the music whatever song was playing because no one could tell precisely where it was coming from, the men peering through the leafy, vegetative cover provided by various potted shrubs and withered ferns, also scattered about, seeming little more than shadows in the dim lobby light (a diffuse, yellowish, subterranean glow), the men watching his every move with those same eyes with a sadistic glint mentioned earlier, strange inarticulate men with a certain gangsterly savoir faire nevertheless, a polished eagerness otherwise known as the killer's instinct, the men watching Oscar until he vanished up the stairs to his room and then chatting amicably with the hotel desk clerks and bellhops in threadbare jackets and even other guests, trying to get some information of a personal nature, what did he eat for breakfast, was he a model of good hygiene, what was his tolerance for pain, that sort of thing, all of which Oscar was still somehow able to see and hear down to the softest decibel of a probing whisper even as he ran up the stairs in escape mode and squirreled himself away in the hazy, dreamlike isolation of his fourth floor suite, which he still shared with Luis and Nerea.

He became an insomniac roaming the halls of his own imagination, exhibiting behavior that some would have called delusional, and that others would have described as a fairly good textbook example of a psychotic break. While Nerea was sleeping, he would sit in a chair in the kitchen and look out through the open balcony doors, staring across the vast dark expanse of the inner courtyard at dozens of dark shuttered balconies on the other side, and sometimes he would catch a glimpse of the moon, but whether it was Quevedo's blood-stained moon or some other moon symbolizing the future or the death of enemies he did not know he had or his own rebirth, he could not tell. Then the moment he would start to nod off, a door would slam or a car would backfire or there would be an explosion (whether this was somewhere outside, perhaps even as far away as the distilleries along Infanta, where explosions did occur with some regularity, or in the subterranean recesses of his mind was of little consequence).

So he would jerk back to consciousness and look out the window again, the faint odor of the harbor with its smell of saltwater and raw sewage and dead or dying fish washing through his nostrils (not quite a cleansing, more the opposite of a cleansing), but this time he would see two sets of eyes staring back at him from the darkness outside, bright yellow eyes or bright orange eyes or eyes glowing with a crimson color, boring holes into the fabric of reality. It seemed like the air itself was about to catch fire, but when he would get up for a closer look, the eyes would always speed away like miniature spaceships. At times he even thought he could hear the sound of their tiny motors whirring as they headed off into the infinite icy void of outer space, most likely to reconnoiter the planet and then return as soon as he closed his eyes again. This is what he was thinking or mumbling in a barely audible whisper. So he armed himself with a small pocket gun manufactured in Spain, a Beistegui Brothers Libia 6.35 mm that Luis had given him, just in case. And he wore his white linen suit and his immaculate Panama hat at all hours of the day or night in the vaguely felt and unexpressed hope that this outfit would protect him from all harm. After a while it became a second skin.

Of course Nerea wondered what was wrong with Oscar. They still fucked as often as she wanted to be fucked, which was once every few days or so. They continued with their long walks for a time, even lingering in front of El Gallo to admire the furs. On occasion they even lost themselves in the quiet, ancient, crumbling beauty of the waterfront cafés along the harbor, drinking coffee and nibbling cheese or pineapple pastelitos while they looked out at the boats, if it was the afternoon, or if it was later in the evening Nerea would be drinking Tio Pepe, as always, because she liked the taste of almond sherry at sunset, and Oscar would be drinking Brandy de Jerez and thinking about the magic of the Moors. But they no longer spoke of love, that rooster that feeds on graveyard weeds, as the poet says. The day Luis had invited Oscar to the

Director's meeting, Oscar had told Nerea for the second and last time that he loved her. But after Oscar returned from the hills outside Guanabacoa, he seemed to Nerea like a man who had lost his faith. He barely even said boo to her when he got up in the morning, just enough to be polite. Her early afternoon tirades (justified explosions as far as Nerea was concerned) did not register a blip on his radar. He seemed indifferent to her comings and goings. And when she was squirming beneath his anxious lover's grip, usually just before he fell asleep at two in the morning, she had the distinct impression that she was making love to a ghost.

Then again, nothing is ever what it seems to be. To be fair to Oscar, he thought if he opened his mouth, his odd, altered view of reality would come bubbling out, uncontrollably, like froth, a sewer gurgling furiously, as it were, and then two things would surely happen: one, Nerea's life would somehow be in danger, the tripartite beast would suddenly reveal itself, the lonely clocks ticking away the seconds until forgetfulness, though Oscar wasn't sure if the threat to Nerea had something to do with the strange men sitting in the lobby with their rifles or their pistols or if there were other invisible and more sinister forces at work; and two, Nerea would think he had gone insane. So he kept his mouth shut as much as was possible, and after a time he thought himself heroic for the effort. He was Ariosto's Orlando, whose love for the Saracen princess Angelica caused him to go mad, though Oscar had never read the book. He was Cervantes' don Quixote, trying to wrest free the image of his beautiful and hypnotic Dulcinea from the cauldron of time and truth as the world sees it, though Oscar had only ever heard the story in passing from Luis. But Oscar breathed the same rarefied air as did these two fictional heroes. He was a brother to centuries of wandering champions lost in the pages of crumbling manuscripts, often crushed by worldly forces they did not understand. Like all those who had gone before him, he shared the sultry nights and the beguiling days with lions.

-88-

Naturally, with Oscar thoroughly immersed in this mythic cistern of prolonged silence, dressed in the protective armor of his white suit and armed with heroic delusions and the black-handled Libia, Nerea eventually (which is to say after a sufficient number of soul-withering years had passed) turned elsewhere for the simple, unrehearsed joys of conversation with an attentive soul and a few drinks and maybe even a night out on the town. She chose as her escort Immanuel, the messenger boy who had guided Nerea to safety as the warehouse belonging to Ignazio Tiziano & Sons burned to the ground, and who had been rewarded for his heroic initiative two days later with a sinecure in the Gas Worker's Union. Ironically (and this irony exists on many levels), it was Luis who recommended Immanuel for the position, even though he suspected Immanuel was the mastermind behind the destruction of the warehouse. Then again, it was also true that Luis never acted precipitously. He wanted to know why Immanuel had orchestrated the fire. What was the larger purpose? But he needed to proceed carefully because he didn't know who else was involved. This is the only reason Immanuel was still alive. But Nerea did not know about Luis' paranoia, and besides, Immanuel was exceptionally attentive to her flurry of changing moods, the subtle signs of her displeasure (a slightly wrinkled eyebrow, a nervous toe tapping on the tiled floor of a restaurant or café, a hiccup that was meant for a laugh), and he did everything in his power to help her overcome her grief over losing first Luis, and now, seemingly, Oscar, a grief hidden from everyone else, even Nerea, but obvious to Immanuel, who could see quite plainly that Nerea greeted every moment of every day with a stylized, never-changing Kabuki smile.

On the day of the warehouse fire, Immanuel had escorted Nerea all the way back to the hotel. She had thanked him, but not profusely, and then left him in the lobby without even a backward glance. But for the next several months, maybe longer, perhaps it was years, every time she passed through on her way to somewhere or back from somewhere else, he was waiting for her, trying to catch her eye, his face glowing with a persistently hopeful smile, his hands holding a colorful though wilted clump of unrecognizable flowers. She pretended not to notice him, and in time he became part of the landscape of the lobby, eternally submerged in the shadows of Hotel Milagro, a lonely vagrant, forgotten. He always sat in the same location, in one of two burgundy leather chairs next to the front desk. Sometimes Immanuel was in one chair, sometimes the other.

The chairs had been positioned for people waiting for their keys, or perhaps the desk clerk was retrieving a message or the bellhop was bringing out their luggage or their coats. But they also provided an excellent, even intimate view of the photograph of Julio Mella, which hung on the wall directly behind the chairs, illuminated by a small brass gallery style lamp fixed to the wall above the photo, which was framed and encased in glass. Most people did not recognize Julio Mella, but everyone who sat in those chairs commented on his incredibly seductive beauty like a movie star with his curly brown hair and intense, cinematic eyes and pouty lips. Almost everyone who sat in those chairs stared at that movie star face for a long time.

The years passed, the soul-withering years mentioned above. It is difficult to say if they passed quickly. What is important is that one night Nerea stopped pretending that Immanuel wasn't there. She was returning with Luis and Oscar from an evening of boleros and sambas and the nineteen-piece orchestra at the Palermo Club. Luis and Oscar had ignored her for almost the entire evening. The only time they paid any attention to her at all was when she came back to the table after her one and only dance number on stage. She had pushed her way into the line-up with a dozen girls half her age (or so it seemed to Nerea) because the day before Luis had said she was getting too old to dance. The number was incredibly exciting and provocative. It was a new number, modern in both its sophisticated choreography and its blend of Latin rhythms, beginning with a fast-paced samba during which a dozen male dancers in Spanish Conquistador costumes chased a dozen scantily clad girls around the stage, but after they caught the girls the music shifted to a very slow, sensual bolero, and before long the girls had turned the tables on the now helpless Conquistadors and rode them until they collapsed in a smiling heap. The number was called *The Rape of the Conquistadors,* and was received with a thunderous round of applause and a few passionate wolf whistles mixed in.

When Nerea came back to the table, perspiring heavily but quite happy, she found Luis and Oscar drinking mojitos and submerged up to their eyeballs in a dark, foreboding conversation (at least it seemed dark and foreboding to Nerea). She stood there a moment, expectant, uneasy, and then without even glancing up, Luis said her costume was a little too tight, and then the two men continued talking. They were still talking in fairly animated fashion when they got back to the hotel. They were talking about shipments from Argentina and suitcases full of money and something about Miami, but Nerea really wasn't listening. She was staring at the backs of their heads, trying to erase their heart-wrenching indifference from her memory with laser-like eyes. But Luis and Oscar kept jabbering away, several steps ahead of Nerea, on their way through the dark shadows of the lobby, and they were halfway up the stairs before they realized she was no longer with them, but by then it was very late and neither man wanted to chase after her. Besides, Nerea was a big girl, she could fend for herself. So they went to bed.

But Nerea did not go to bed that night. As she passed by the front desk and the two burgundy leather chairs, she caught a glimpse of the photograph of Julio Mella, and she noticed for the first time all evening how very fast her heart was beating, and fearing it might explode out of her ribcage, she sat down. It was only then that she noticed Immanuel, passed out or sleeping, his hands still holding a withered clump of flowers, his breath coming in steady, rhythmic bursts like the beating wings of a half-drowned bird, the soft light from the gallery style lamp washing across his face like a summer sunset or a midnight comet streaking across the sky. But he was not sleeping. As soon as Nerea noticed him, he sat up, and then Nerea smiled. And it did not matter that she only smiled at him with her unchanging Kabuki smile. The fact that she was sitting in a chair not three feet from where he was sitting and looking at him with vaguely vulnerable eyes was enough for Immanuel. He sat up and Nerea smiled and he removed his black-rimmed glasses, blinking rapidly until he was fully awake, and then put his glasses back on. He blinked some more. It seemed that his unimaginable patience had been rewarded. He reached across the empty space between them with the flowers and then the flowers vanished as if in a dream.

And then they began to talk.

They talked about that awful and yet strangely glorious day when Ignazio Tiziano & Sons had burned to the ground and the thousands and thousands of people who had stormed the gates, that covetous multitude, had been trampled or lost in the fire or had run away. They talked about Julio Mella, and all Nerea could remember was that he had been an anarchist and that he had died very young, he had been murdered, but Immanuel knew a great deal more. Immanuel mentioned that

Julio had been a very outspoken student at the University of Havana and a founding member of the Communist Party of Cuba. He had been falsely imprisoned by the Machado government for his participation in a supposed bomb plot, but there had never been a bomb plot. No bomb had gone off. There had been no bomb. It had all been a lie. A deception to preserve a world on its last legs. So the government eventually released Julio from prison, after sufficient time had elapsed to avoid embarrassment, and a year later he fled to Mexico, where they killed him. It was a political assassination, said Immanuel, and though he did not say who exactly was responsible, whether it was Machado or those working for him or some other organization, Nerea could tell by the way that his eyes flitted back and forth with subliminal anger that he knew the murderers personally, or at least he knew where to find them, any that were still alive, and that someday, when he had planned everything down to the last excruciatingly complicated detail, they (the survivors) would pay for their crimes. They talked about the corruption of the current government. They talked about betrayal. They talked about the shimmering mirage of hope. Immanuel recited some love poetry by the Chilean poet and writer and gossip columnist Silvio Salvático. The poetry was mostly about prostitutes with hearts of gold, the eternal beauty of the tango and tango dancers taking to the streets of Buenos Aires at midnight, and German detectives who were always one step behind the German criminals they were chasing because they were always wondering if their girlfriends were sleeping with someone else, topics which Salvático explored in greater depth in his second novel, *The French Lady*, which had been published in 1949. They talked about the nature of love and love's transgressions. They talked about death and the mushrooming cost of funerals and the transmogrification of the human soul and the overt symbolism of certain Latin-American folkdances like the plena. They talked about Brazilian crime thrillers. They talked about avant-garde writers in the Paris of the 1930s, especially Artaud and his Theatre of Cruelty. They talked about an obscure book titled *Recopilación de leyes de los reynos de las Indias,* a compilation of one hundred and sixty-five years of colonial law enacted in the Spanish colonies between 1512 and 1677, published in Madrid in 1681 by Charles II, a book which, according to Immanuel, clearly demonstrated the Spanish philosophical ambivalence towards the law in general, an ambivalence which suggested an abiding tolerance for human frailty, assuming that one possessed an acceptable family lineage, whether actual or purchased, but even the title of the book bored Nerea almost to the verge of tears, and the only reason that she didn't fall asleep at this point was that she had fallen permanently in love with Immanuel's great passion for explication. They talked of the blossoming science of bibliography and documentation. They talked of dinner parties and shopping at El Encanto and beautiful fur coats. They talked of the majestic beauty of the Paseo del Prado in the springtime with its lime trees and avocado trees and deep-green laurels and the tangled knot of humanity walking to and fro. They talked of Ginés de Pasamonte, a minor fictional character in the novel *El ingenioso hidalgo don Quixote de la Mancha,* who is sentenced to ten years as a galley slave and escapes in a mad hurly-burly of a scene in which don Quixote himself battles the guards for the release of Ginés and the guards set upon don Quixote with swords and cudgels, and the other prisoners, dozens of them, start untying themselves, and Sancho (don Quixote's sidekick) finally frees Ginés and Ginés runs away. They talked of taking a luxury steamer to Europe in the spring. They talked of the sorrowful beauty of the Cementerio de Cristóbal Colón with its dozens of whispering statues that could be heard at all hours of the night. They talked of the exploding meteorite of time. Immanuel recited the poetry of another Chilean poet, Pedro González Carrera, a one-time grammar school teacher and a vociferous Italian apologist, who, according to Immanuel, straddled the line between symbolist poetry and sentimental garbage. But without any contempt or literary or political derision whatsoever, indeed, with the faintest glimmer of exposed pride, which was surprising, to say the least (but then we all seem to be walking contradictions at times), Immanuel said Carrera's poetry seemed to glorify Mussolini and his armies and promised a complete reversal of history culminating in an ultimate Italian victory at some point in the future with the aid of a group of unknown Merovingian Kings who, according to the poet, had migrated from another dimension or would migrate or perhaps they were extraterrestrials who had adopted the form and the mannerisms of the long-dead Merovingians for unknown spiritual reasons, or perhaps simply to escape the ravages of the plague or some other virus (it was at this point Immanuel admitted that he couldn't quite disentangle the meaning of Carrera's poetry from the poetry itself). They talked about the withering despair of the nihilists. They talked about the withering despair of nuns and priests everywhere. They talked until the dark shadows in the lobby of Hotel Milagro turned gray.

-89-

In the weeks and months that followed, Nerea and Immanuel met on a semi-regular basis in the lobby of Hotel Milagro, always in the same two burgundy leather chairs, their faces seeming to shine with the dazzling subterranean glow of Julio Mella's indestructible beauty. They met at all hours of the day and night, for hours at a time, though they (or at least Nerea) barely noticed that time was passing. It was Immanuel who first gave voice to the idea that she would always be in love with Luis, and so she would always be suffering from a broken heart, an idea that had been orbiting the sun of Nerea's despair for quite a while, like a wayward comet.

Nerea decided she could never forgive Luis.

"I want him to suffer as I have suffered," she said.

"We all wish such things from time to time."

"But he is so . . . so . . ."

"Preoccupied?"

"Yes. Preoccupied. I was going to say something else, something crazy, but . . ."

"But what?"

"It doesn't matter . . . it . . ."

Nerea grew silent. She became absorbed in the beauty of Julio Mella. Then she heard herself speaking, or more precisely, she heard her disembodied voice. It sounded like it was coming out of an old gramophone. It sounded very faint. And all the while she was listening to her very faint voice she was looking at the photograph of Julio Mella and thinking how very beautiful he was.

"Sometimes it's just too complicated to even think about."

"Yes?"

"I was going to say that he doesn't feel pain like ordinary people do. But that doesn't make any sense, does it? How do you make people suffer if they don't feel pain?"

". . . ."

"Oscar is different. Oscar is an open wound. Oscar is a shooting star in the midnight sky."

". . . ."

"Oscar is a small but rebellious bird locked in a cage. He can't breathe without feeling the pain of everyone around him. But Luis is a different story. Luis is . . ."

"A very carefully cultivated story, if you don't mind my interjecting," said Immanuel.

The light from the gallery style lamp began to flicker and then it went out and Nerea suddenly forgot about the photograph of Julio Mella. She noticed that Immanuel had somehow slid his burgundy leather chair next to hers. Their chairs were side by side, but he was sitting on the edge of his chair, his body turned slightly, leaning into the dark mirror of her thoughts. She wondered if he was going to kiss her. He had one hand on her knee, but this did not seem odd to Nerea. She had become detached from her knee and did not feel the pressure of his hand, but even this lack of sensation did not bother her. It was just something she noticed. Then she realized that their heads were bent towards each other. They had become shadows to each other. They became a single shadow. She closed her eyes and imagined that he was kissing her. The world smelled of mint and rum and vanilla and oleander. 'That is an odd mixture of smells,' she thought. She felt like she was going to pass out. Immanuel's voice did not rise above a whisper. Neither did hers.

"Cultivated?"

"Yes," said Immanuel. "I have been watching Luis for years now. He is a magnificent actor. The outer world sees only a shadowy character with a taste for fine dining and good music. They see Luis wearing exquisitely tailored pinstripe suits and silk socks and sporting perfumed handkerchiefs. They see an educated man, but they forget he carries two pistols and a knife. But this first layer is all a ruse. The world sees a sentimental, effeminate buffoon because that's what Luis wants the world to see. But beneath this layer there exists a hard, merciless opportunist. A man who would kill his own grandmother if there was a profit to be made. But this second layer is also a ruse. It is for his inner circle, his closest friends, his allies, perhaps a few of the Directors, perhaps Federico himself. So beneath this second layer there is another Luis. There is Luis the sensual lover, the sex maniac, the voyeur. Only you, Nerea, have seen this third layer of Luis."

". . . ."

"It is not easily visible, even if you are looking for it. But even this is a ruse."

"How can every layer be a ruse?'

"It is the nature of the world since the beginning of time. What did you expect?"

"I . . . I don't really know.

"I had hoped you would have guessed by now. It is ingenious, really. Luis is truly sentimental at his core. The first layer of Luis is a reflection of his fourth layer. He is a sentimentalist who wears his emotions as a mask to hide a mask of cruelty, which he lets some of the world see, and this mask hides a third mask, the mask of Luis the great lover, and all of these masks hide the real Luis, the Luis who is a weeping sentimentalist, the Luis who feels nostalgia for everyone who ever lived. He is a romantic. When you strip away all the posturing, that is what he is. He has hypnotized the world into believing otherwise. It is absolutely ingenious."

". . . ."

"Yes, as I said, he is a magnificent actor."

Nerea did not know what to say.

The lobby of Hotel Milagro had become a world of enveloping darkness and shifting shadows. She wondered how many people were sitting in the lobby or if she and Immanuel were the only ones. Her only fixed point of reality became the shining, shimmering photograph of Julio Mella, which now seemed to glow with an irrepressible iridescence, in spite of the fact that the bulb to the gallery style lamp had burned out, or perhaps because of this fact. Nerea found herself tracing the contours of Julio's pouty lips with her mind, running imaginary fingers through his curly brown hair, breathing in his imagined masculinity, staring into his cinematic eyes with such cunning intensity that she almost convinced herself that he was truly alive and that he only had eyes for her. Julio, she told herself, was her one true love. Then she sat back in her chair, nestling herself in the corner opposite from Immanuel, confident, if one possessing the pain of an aching heart can be said to be confident, no longer melancholy or dumbfounded or frozen in the moment of her own destruction, her natural animal magnetism beginning to reassert itself. She looked over at Immanuel and smiled a smile that might have seemed frivolous and slightly agitated in direct sunlight, but there in the shadows of the Hotel Milagro lobby it seemed deviant and sinister.

"I want him to suffer as I have suffered," said Nerea.

"You understand what you are asking?"

"Yes. I understand. Whatever you want to know about Luis, I can tell you. I have known Luis for a long time."

Immanuel regarded Nerea carefully for a moment.

"You are certain about all this?"

"Yes."

"I want you to be absolutely sure. Because once we release the hounds, so to speak, there is no stopping. We do not believe in half measures. We will carry through to the end."

Nerea did not even bat an eyelash.

"I just want you to promise me that he will suffer," she said.

Immanuel seemed to disappear into the shadowy gloom of his chair, all except his voice. His voice possessed a radiant clarity, like that of a tiny, silver bell.

"Do not worry. We have eyes and ears everywhere. We will not let him out of our sight for a moment. We will not let him escape. Do not worry."

". . . ."

"He will suffer greatly. It will be just like in the movies. I promise."

-90-

It was at this point that Nerea gave up all claims to her former self. She found herself spending more and more time in the lobby of Hotel Milagro. She stopped dancing. She stopped going to the clubs at night. She realized her time with Oscar was nearing its end, and she accepted this realization with the stoic fatalism of a religious fanatic, an old-school martyr.

At various random moments Oscar would see her sitting in one of the burgundy leather chairs, her eyes fixed on the photograph of Julio Mella. Usually Oscar was just heading out for a night on the town or he was just returning. Sometimes he was with Luis. They would say 'Hello, Nerea, why don't you join us,' or 'We missed you tonight' or 'Why don't you come up to bed' or 'I can't remember the last time you fixed us some chorizo sausage and eggs' or 'You never sing to us in the mornings any more,' but either Nerea didn't hear them and therefore did not respond, or they were too busy to hear what she might have said.

They walked away quickly. They no longer wondered what Nerea did with her time.

After a while the photograph of Julio Mella took on new dimensions. In the hour just before dawn, Nerea would sometimes press her ear to the glass, and she swore to Immanuel that she could hear Julio whispering something, just what she wasn't sure, but it sounded like he was saying 'Las Tunas, Las Tunas,' and then there was the sound of a baseball bat hitting a ball and then the sound of a roaring crowd, a deafening, jubilant roar, and then the nasally voice of an announcer saying the score was three to two, all of this emanating from Julio's mouth as if his mouth were a radio, but that didn't make any sense to Nerea, nor to Immanuel.

Sometimes she could hear Julio whistling.

Sometimes she could hear Julio reciting poetry, but it was always poetry she had never heard before.

Sometimes all she heard was the distant sound of the sea or the sound of boats in the harbor and the sailors shouting or the tolling of a church bell.

Strangely, she never heard him singing a song.

Sometimes his lips were wet, as if he had just licked his lips and was about to give her a gentle, airy kiss. This thought always made her smile.

At other times Julio became eerily silent and detached, as if he were reproaching her for some minor infraction, a small flaw in her personality that she was unaware of. She would sit on the edge of her burgundy leather chair and beg his forgiveness, but naturally he said nothing. He behaved exactly as a photograph hanging on a wall should behave. Nevertheless, she would implore him to give her some sign of his love, a token of affection, and when he did not respond, she would break down into tears, collapsing on the tiled floor beneath the photograph or draped over the arm of her burgundy leather chair, and then fall asleep. One would think she would have been troubled by strange dreams under the circumstances, but she never dreamed when she slept in the lobby, or if she did she did not remember them. When she woke up she did not know where she was, but she was not afraid of her ignorance. She was like an invisible specter or a newborn child examining the world with attentive eyes, though with some measurable anxiety, in the burgundy leather chair of her choice until she could make sense of her surroundings.

Always the realization that she had fallen asleep in the hotel lobby took her by surprise. Then her breathing became relaxed. She became more thoughtful, curious, even reflective. She began to look more carefully at everything that transpired in the hotel lobby that had become her entire world, especially in the wee hours of the morning. She noticed things that others wished to keep hidden.

For one thing, the dim lighting throughout the lobby seemed to have changed color from a diffuse, yellowish subterranean glow to something a little more orangeish, with a faint blueish tint. It was a devilish glow. She wondered what might cause the change in color. At times it seemed otherworldly. At times it seemed as if the color had leaked in from another dimension.

For another thing, the hotel staff seemed to have vanished. There was a small placard on the front desk counter that said 'Ring the bell for service,' and someone had left a black waiter's jacket and tie hanging on a hook next to the row of wooden boxes containing abandoned room keys and messages that had been forgotten years ago and were now covered with dust.

Nerea had been to the desk several times and had rung and rung the bell, and she had even called out, but no one came, and then the last time she had gone to the desk the bell was gone, and so was the jacket and the tie, though for some strange reason the placard remained. She wondered if the staff had gone on strike or been fired or had up and quit and if they had found other employment or were still looking. She wondered if there had been a change in management or if the hotel were closing down. She wondered where she would go if the hotel closed down.

She didn't remember the last time she saw Oscar or Luis.

She began to wonder if they had ever existed.

She noticed that among the potted ferns and other withered greenery there were also a few potted foxgloves, otherwise known as '*The Gloves of the Virgin Mary,*' which according to some botanists and also the purveyors of herbal remedies contained powerful chemical compounds that could cure an ailing heart if taken in the right amount, but would cause certain death if one took too much, which almost everyone did who turned to foxglove for relief. The foxglove scattered about the lobby were doing quite well. Flashes of purple and crimson and strawberry red in an otherwise dreary landscape.

Nerea also noticed that the lobby was becoming more and more crowded. More and more men wearing fedoras and carrying long-barreled hunting rifles or with bulges in their jacket pockets that looked suspiciously like Kongsberg Colt pistols, the men roaming about, circulating aimlessly among the dilapidated chairs and withered vegetative cover, presumably looking for a place to sit. The men with the Kongsberg Colt pistols would take them out every so often so everyone else could see. They seemed to enjoy the adulation that went with owning such a dependable firearm.

All of the new men seemed to know Immanuel, who went about greeting each new arrival as he would a long-lost cousin or a newly converted radical sympathizer.

After that Nerea noticed a great deal of whispering, which she assumed were private conversations about the sunny weather or the rainy weather and various definitions of paradise and the price of ammunition and the nature of grief and how dangerous it was to travel these days in Mexico, or any of the Latin-American countries for that matter, and how it was only going to get worse.

Most of the conversations were in Italian, which sped by too quickly for Nerea's tiny ears, and the rest were in German, which gave her headaches. But at some point, perhaps because of the verbal impressions left floating in the air by so many whispering men, Nerea found herself swimming in a sea of bizarre, fragmented images, like the amniotic fluid of autoerotic poetry. Naturally, Nerea felt like she was drowning. But she did not drown. Her mind went numb. She felt like she was the victim of an alien abduction experiment, though perhaps this is a bit of a stretch. She felt like she had just been reborn, which is most certainly a cliché, but is perhaps closer to the truth. She took a deep breath and plunged into the impressionistic waves of her insomnia (or the darkly glowing clouds of a coming hailstorm, or the oily, smoky spray that accompanies a hail of bullets, or the roiling mushroom of dust after an asteroid slams into the earth at supersonic speed, it was really quite difficult to label the experience other than to suggest that whatever she plunged into possessed the blurry indistinctness of an old photograph taken in 1930s Germany as the Nazis came to power with crowds of vagrants milling about and coming to blows in the snowy streets in Hamburg or Munich or Berlin). She allowed every word to flow through her. She began to understand what the men were saying. It was easier for her to understand the happy sing-song Italian than the anxious, guttural German. Then the world around her began to coalesce and then disintegrate. She felt like she was sitting in a strange carnival movie house where they were projecting four or five movies onto the screen at the same time. She began to flow back and forth between the images of each movie with extraordinary ease. She felt like she had suddenly mastered the psychic art of telekinesis. As if on cue, the men with their long-barreled hunting rifles or Kongsberg Colt pistols sensed that something had changed. They broke off in the middle of their sentences and stared at Nerea with uneasy awe, as if they suspected she could read their lips. They began to speak with their hands cupped over their mouths. Of course Nerea did not fully appreciate the philosophical nuances and subtle allusions of everything she heard, because all language, as everyone knows, is symbolic in nature and therefore possesses multiple meanings. But she understood enough to realize that Immanuel had set everything in motion and that now there was no turning back.

The words of the whispering men, the grainy, film noir version, as Nerea hears them, which is to say as she perceives them, which provides ample evidence as to her state of mind as well as her emotional state of being:

'It is always sunny in paradise.'

'I beg to differ, some days it is quite rainy, worse than in Munich.'

'Or in Hamburg!'

'Yes, Schneider. Or in Hamburg.'

'One man's rainy day is another man's pneumonia.'

'There's no such thing as pneumonia in paradise, except for the odd case.'

'But there are plenty of cases in Munich. All over Germany, in fact. Hamburg in particular!'

'Ah, we are intoxicated with death.'

'And tailors.'

'Yes, tailors and death.'

The whispering men laugh.

Their laughter hovers above their heads like rings of smoke or miniature crystal halos and then crashes into the impenetrable darkness hovering above all of them and sends a shower of tiny glass particles to the floor like the crushed remains of saltwater crustaceans from a millennium ago.

The men brush away the flecks of glass that cover their shoulders and their fedoras and the backs of their necks.

The conversation continues.

'It is an old argument.'

'It is the oldest argument.'

'From a time before time.'

'It is not for us to question his reasons. It is simply the way the world is at the moment.'

'Perhaps the world has always been this way. Perhaps the nature of the world remains unchanged.'

'Yes, of course, if by the nature of the world you mean the nature of man.'

'That goes without saying.'

'That would explain why we always do what we are told to do.'

'And why we always will.'

'But not always willingly.'

'No, I suppose not.'

'But then, of course, one has to account for the nature of grief.'

'Ah, grief, the panacea of lost souls.'

'As if a soul can become lost.'

'As if abandoning your beliefs is something to cry about.'

'It is a question for the ages.'

'It is a question for religion.'

'It is a question for science.'

'It is a question for those with good intentions who parade up and down the hospital wards.'

'And then from the hospitals to the cemeteries!'

'It is an endless parade.'

The men are silent for a moment, as if they are contemplating the actual (as opposed to perceived) distance between hospitals and cemeteries.

'Yes, the notion of grief raises many questions.'

'Too many to properly contemplate.'

'It is worse than the riddle of the Sphinx.'

'Decidedly worse.'

'Then again, one can now look at grief as something more than a question. You could, for the sake of argument, look at grief as a question that can now be answered.'

'I'd like to see that.'

'And so you shall, my friend.'

(A few impatient toes beginning to tap, a few impatient fingers fingering the safeties on their pistols.)

'The question of grief, which has troubled mankind since the ancients first scribbled down their thoughts on papyrus, can now be answered through the ingenious application of electromagnetic phase inducers and ultra-high vacuum tunneling microscopes and Boron ion-beam generators.'

'Grief is absolutely meaningless.'

A few obscurantists in the crowd start applauding, but it is difficult to determine why.

'This kind of advanced technology is essential in facilitating a scientific and completely objective way of parsing reality.'

'Is complete objectivity possible?'

A few cheers. A few derisive whistles.

'It certainly is. And on that note, I am here to tell you that the preliminary reports that I have seen state that without any doubt whatsoever the notion of grief is absolutely meaningless.'

More applause from the obscurantists, but again, why.

'Which is something we suspected all along.'

A rhythmic clapping reaching a crescendo.

'Yes, but I already said that.'

A few indignant shouts lost in the growing hubbub.

'But now we have a series of preliminary reports.'

Furious applause. Uproarious laughter.

More brushing away flecks of broken glass.

Then a bit of silence.

But not an awkward, painful silence.

It is actually more like a gentle sigh. Not a pure silence at all.

Then the men suddenly look at Nerea, as if for the first time, as if she has suddenly emerged from a beam of sunlight.

They begin adjusting their fedoras smartly, smoothing out the wrinkles in their shirts, positioning their rifles or their Kongsberg Colt pistols for maximum visual effect.

Nerea pays no attention to their ogling stares. Partly this

is because to her the men are featureless. Their heads seem like onions, with dark, rotten spots where their eyes and mouths should be. The smell of onions is everywhere, bouncing off the damp walls, clogging Nerea's eyes, her throat.

She sits back in her chair and closes her eyes and the onions go away. She breathes in slowly and exhales the onion smell of so many men crowded into so small a space.

She becomes a pane of glass through which all light and language flow.

Or she becomes a dark mirror that absorbs everything.

The conversation continues.

'We are little more than tunnels of light burrowing our way through the darkness.'

'That's just one of many possibilities.'

'Okay, quite possibly we are tunnels of light burrowing our way through the darkness.'

'Speeding our way, you mean.'

'Speeding our way, then.'

'That's better.'

'But to what end?'

'To the end of the tunnel?'

'No!'

'To the end of the light?'

'The same thing.'

'Then what is the answer?'

'Yes. That is a fair question. With all of this talk about grief and paradise and summer thunderstorms sweeping across the Cuban landscape, it is worth trying to figure out what it's all for.'

'No one can do that.'

'You mean no one ever has.'

'Or ever will, that's the smart money.'

'Do not be so arrogant. We have men working on it this very minute. Naturally.'

'Men?'

'Yes indeed. We have men tucked away, hidden from view, some observers working apart from the observed, some working in conjunction, an uneasy partnership, some of them closet obscurantists or dabblers in mesmerism or advocates of popular sensualism for all we know, but all of them giving everything they have to solving this thorny problem.'

'Yes, thorny is an apt description.'

'But a bit overused, don't you think, the word thorny.'

'Of course it's overused, that's the tragic consequence of using language to talk about the unknowable.'

'Not as tragic as using bullets.'

'How right you are.'

'And it doesn't matter if the bullets come out of the end of a long-barreled rifle, the kind of weapon that is more appropriate for shooting rabbits and weasels and hedgehogs and the like, like we used to do in Sicily when we were boys dreaming of murder, or one of your fancy Kongsberg Colt pistols, the pride of the Norwegian army, a pistol with extraordinary balance, why with such a pistol you can hit a moving target with ease from three-hundred paces, or even further, and by moving target, of course, I mean . . .'

'Yes . . . you mean . . . (in unison) a man.'

More laughter. Eyes gleaming.

'To the extent that I am able to make myself understood, I am gratified. To the extent that I make any sense at all, I could be anyone.'

A few extra loud guffaws.

'*Quia est in eo virtus dormitiva, cujus est natura sensus assoupire.*'

'Yes, I can see why you say that. We are all of us beginning to fall asleep.'

'Which is why we crave a different kind of buzz.'

'Like the coldest winter chill.'

The laughter swells.

More halos of glass and the glass shattering against the darkness and falling to the floor. But the glass particles are no longer content to mimic the remains of saltwater crustaceans, a reflection of a lifeless, symbolic past, a calcified moment. No, the glass particles are undergoing a sudden, dramatic transformation. They are becoming the saltwater crustaceans they once merely resembled.

No one knows exactly what is going on. It appears that some sort of conscious (manipulative?) act of creation is taking place. A miracle by any other name. But it all depends upon your point of view. Between consciousness and reality there yawns a veritable abyss of meaning. Then again, one would be hard pressed to deny that something is happening. For one thing, the tiny saltwater crustaceans that were once particles of glass are very much alive, and more and more are joining the ranks of the living with every passing second. Soon the tiled floor of the hotel lobby is covered with what appear to be thousands and thousands of tiny crabs, a swarmy, swarming bubbling froth of freedom and independent spirit, their tiny porcelain-like claws scratching at the tile. It is difficult to tell what kind of crabs they are. They look like ice-cream blotches. They possess white shells with red or reddish-brown markings or blotches. Their shells look like vanilla and strawberry and chocolate ice-cream mixed together. Thousands and thousands of ice-cream blotches. Then it becomes clear what kind of crabs they are. They are tiny Porcelain Anemone Crabs (*Neopetrolisthes ohshimai)* from Indonesia. How they suddenly appear on the floor of the lobby of Hotel Milagro is irrelevant. It is a mystery with a quasi-religious kind of appeal, but it is still irrelevant.

Some of the men armed with long-barreled rifles begin smashing the tiny, helpless crabs. They are marching doggedly around the lobby smashing crabs with their rifle butts, but not so much because they are threatened by the crabs. They are merely repulsed.

The crabs do not scream when they are smashed. They simply disintegrate like a book of abandoned thoughts, a cloud of exploding dust absorbed by the air.

Nerea thinks the men smashing the crabs are quite courageous. She sees in their willingness to face the crab threat an inexorable truth: every destiny would be unfulfilled if there were no one to do the dirty work.

She waves at the men and two of them see her waving and come over. They talk briefly, nodding politely and smiling. It is impossible to hear what they are saying. It is like listening to a strong wind blowing though the treetops. It is like watching a tunnel collapsing. It is like they are hatching a plot. Then the men go back to their work.

Nerea seems quite pleased.

The other crabs continue their aimless scratching until they too are smashed. They seem unaware of the danger of the rifle butts. Whether individually or as a whole, there is no difference in the way they react to the countless deaths of their comrades. Death is all around them. But they do not even try to get away, to find some safe, secure hiding place. Perhaps because there is no place for them to go. There are too many of them. The tiny, hard-packed bodies of the still living and the ghost-bodies of the recently smashed (still strangely present, in as much as some memories are always present). All of them mixed together. They can barely move against each other.

Nerea watches the steady destruction of the indifferent crab colony with great interest, but hers is the self-absorbed predatory interest of the killer experiencing the thrill (in this case vicarious) of the hunt, as indifferent towards the crabs as they are towards themselves, without even a hint of sadness. The rest of the men have been carrying on with their conversation, unconcerned with the crabs.

'If we possessed spirits that were truly free there would be no need for war.'

'There he goes again, ranting and raving.'

'Prattling and prating.'

'Stomping about like a raging bull, a mad minotaur.'

'The minotaur of our conscience.'

A burst of overly robust laughter, almost like stage laughter, as if the men were reading from a script. The sounds of scattered applause.

'But it is true. We are not free. We are cursed with a lingering eye that admires everything it sees, that is afraid to look down lest we become aware of our deformed, crippled nature, an eye that does not appreciate or even know what real love is, or beauty. We are blind to the self-erasing barbarity of history. We are blind to our own stupidity.'

'But this is the essence of what it means to be human.'

'The unrelenting darkness of our inner being.'

'A labyrinth which swallows all light.'

'A labyrinth from which we will never escape.'

'Our depravity exposed on the barren sands of eternity.'

'The collective soul of humanity, if you will.'

'And even if you won't.

'It means we are slipping into the abyss, inexorably, inevitably.'

'Exactly, my friends. Which is why we should always be prepared to kill and wage war. But always and only in the name of humanity itself.'

'You mean in the name of an ideal humanity.'

'Perhaps. But it is not so easy to substitute an ideal humanity for your average, run-of-the-mill humanity. The goal is to create a world in which everyone faces up to their responsibility, an ideal world, if you will, as opposed to an ideal humanity, a world in which there is no room for those who do not fit in, if you get my meaning. But there is always resistance to change. I can hear the naysayers even now. They will argue that the notion of an ideal world is a logical absurdity because there would be as many versions of this ideal world as there would be individuals who could imagine as much, each version competing with every other version, causing all sorts of difficulties, everything from poverty to pestilence to despair to corrupt governments to sex maniacs running rampant through the grade schools to the death by chemical pollutants of the oceans to rogue black holes invading our deepest dreams, any disaster you can imagine, all of it pretty much gumming up the works. It would be practically impossible to police so many different versions. You would probably have to lock everybody up, which you could never do, so you would have no choice but to abandon your own search for paradise. Everyone would. There could be no exceptions. Everyone would be forced to capitulate to some sort of compromise paradise, a universally acceptable generic version, just for the sake of keeping the semblance of peace, which is less than ideal. It is an intriguing critique.'

'And what happens if we fail?'

'We will not fail!'

'But if we do?'

'The alternative is unacceptable.'

'But not unimaginable.'

'No, sadly, not unimaginable. Indeed, it is a horrible thing to contemplate. The gates of Hell would be flung wide open, but not in a symbolic, metaphorical, theoretical way. It would be an actual, physical opening. A tear in the fabric of the universe. The grisly veil torn. A disruption in the space/time continuum that would send us all reeling. Quite probably there would be nothing left at all. Or nothing that we would recognize as something.'

'God forbid.'

'Yes, God forbid."

"Whether he exists or not.'

'A difficult supposition to support.'

'But just as difficult to argue effectively against.'

'Which only proves why the alternative is unacceptable.'

'Absolutely.'

'Then we are all agreed?'

'Yes, in as much as there is very little left to say.'

The lobby is now exploding with the happy, jubilant shouts of happy, jubilant men.

'It is suicide to think otherwise.'

'Or at least a logical fallacy.'

'Or a hopeful implausibility.'

'Or perhaps a fatalism born of an unappeased grief.'

More happy, jubilant shouts.

A few rifles being discharged.

A few Kongsberg Colt pistols.

A few spent cartridges bouncing on the floor.

The last of the crabs have been smashed.

The very last crab is smashed directly beneath Nerea's hovering feet.

Nerea looks from the body of the smashed crab to the photograph of Julio Mella to see what he thinks, but he does not react. He, too, possesses (or seems to possess) an indifferent attitude when it comes to the fate of the crabs.

The men armed with their rifles or their Kongsberg Colt pistols begin filing out of the lobby of Hotel Milagro, with Immanuel in the lead. They are heading out into the shadows of the world at large, a world, shall we say, bathed in streaks of light and dark, a very stylized look, like in the movies, a world possessing a meaning we can only guess at, a world where the gap between consciousness and reality exists only in the imagination, where the freedom of the nihilists (meaning those noble souls that Nietzsche speaks about who live beyond good and evil) is no freedom at all because it is limited by the very change they (the nihilists, wherever they have gone) seek (hope, endeavor) to bring about. Because as everyone discovers sooner or later, our puny brains can only grasp a singular reality in any given moment. By contrast, Nerea's own private world is plunged into absolute darkness.

-91-

The beginning of Oscar's last twenty-four hours in Havana:

The phone rang with merciless rage, but Oscar let it ring. He was sitting in the kitchen, the balcony doors flung wide open, a warm breeze blowing through the room. Luis had predicted that the phone would be ringing off the hook. And he had been right. The phone had been ringing all morning. Luis had said there were a few unnamed, unsavory sorts who were trying to keep tabs on him, and then he had winked at Oscar, but he wasn't going to give them the satisfaction. He wanted to keep them guessing. Did they really think he would slip up so easily, that he would answer the phone and give himself away, that they might trap him in the shadow of Hotel Milagro? If they did, then he still had the edge. He would become a shadow himself, a shadow among the shadows.

Oscar almost laughed out loud at the thought of Eladio and some of the others trying to match wits with Luis. That's the way things were. The spilling of the sand had begun long ago. From the moment Federico had announced the move to Miami. Very soon not a single star would be left in the night sky. And it didn't seem to matter that Cuba was about to implode and that Miami was a good choice, a logical next step. What mattered was that the Cuban contingent (this is what Oscar secretly called them) was relatively young and fearlessly committed to their own dream of Cuba. What mattered more was that Federico was no longer as impressively psychotic as he had been in his younger years. He seemed to be just what he was: a crippled Italian lost in the loop of memory, one good shove from the grave. Even his majestic knife seemed merely a prop. Oscar knew enough to know a coup in the making. But there was nothing to do at the moment. Luis had said he would call at one o'clock on the dot, so until then Oscar would let the phone ring. It was only a quarter past twelve. In the ten years that Oscar had known Luis, Luis had always done what he said he would do. He trusted Luis' instincts. Oscar trusted Luis to get them both safely across the Straits of Florida. They would vanish into the shadows of a Cuban sunset. What Oscar did not see, as it turned out, and what he would never see, a curious blindness, a retreating from metaphor into myth, was Nerea's role in the whole messy affair. Whether or not Luis saw it coming was another matter.

The phone stopped ringing. Then it started again.

"Only twelve-thirty," Oscar said to himself. "Fuck."

He heard some shouting from out in the courtyard and moved to the balcony for a better look. He could see a washday Madonna on the other side, a corner suite one floor down, a beautiful bombshell in a pair of tight-fitting jeans and a flimsy, cotton blouse and her hair pulled back. The smell of gardenias drifting from somewhere. The smell of lemons. The sea. The smell of gunpowder. The woman was leaning out across her balcony, the laundry she had just laid across the railing fluttering in the breeze. The way she was leaning, Oscar could see the roundness of her breasts all the way to her nipples. She was glistening in the steamy, tropical sunlight.

Oscar smiled and let himself get hard. The woman was shouting at a young man who was sitting on a bench beneath the leafy branches of the acacia tree that occupied the middle of the courtyard. Behind the bench there was a small patch of garden that had been neglected for years and the weathered remnants of what was once a glowing golden trellis. Oscar could not quite see who the young man was because of the branches, but he seemed very young. The woman was letting him have it pretty good. She was very passionate in her displeasure. But the young man didn't say anything. He continued sitting on the bench, smoking a cigarette, the smoke swirling up through the branches of the acacia tree and dissolving in the air above. The shouting reached a crescendo and then mysteriously plunged into a vacuum of nothingness. For the briefest of moments, Oscar could not hear a single sound, no woman shouting, no insects buzzing, no music drifting through the air from another apartment, no cars motoring on the street beyond the courtyard, no mysterious gunman sliding the bolt of a long-barreled rifle into place.

Then a cacophony of sound returned and all of the aforementioned sounds came tumbling past Oscar's ears. He jerked back, as if he had been struck. But whatever had struck him was only a figment of his imagination. He leaned forward again, his hands resting on the balcony railing. He was still very hard. The woman was dripping with perspiration. It almost seemed that her blouse had dissolved. Then she picked up a second basket full of wet clothes. She had already emptied the first so there was no more room on the railing. She lifted the second basket and dumped it over the side. 'Take care of your own fucking laundry,' she shouted, and then she disappeared, all except the image of her beautiful brown bouncing breasts and her dark erect nipples.

Oscar went back inside, got a Coke from the fridge, popped the top and guzzled half the bottle.

The phone had stopped ringing.

It was ten minutes to one.

'Fucking bastards,' Oscar thought.

He drank some more Coke.

Luis had told him this day would come. He had been saying as much for years. Then two days ago he had told Oscar to pack a suitcase. But not just any suitcase. Luis had pulled out a Platt Guardsman leather suitcase with brass hardware that he kept under his bed. It was a medium-sized suitcase, elegant, just right for traveling, and roomy enough for a few shirts, a few pairs of slacks, an extra pair of shoes, socks, various sundry items, and half a million dollars in cold, hard cash (fifty stacks of unmarked one-hundred dollar bills, naturally, the easiest way for revolutionaries, international spies, embezzlers of all sorts, Mafiosi bagmen, and high-rolling casino whales to carry obscene amounts of money from point A to point B). Luis had opened the suitcase and showed Oscar the false bottom, which popped up when you pushed down on the two opposite corners simultaneously. 'It is a smuggler's dream,' Luis had said with his customary bravado, but for a moment Oscar had been able to detect just the slightest hint of anxiety in Luis' booming baritone voice of a steamship, the thin wavering vibrato of a man pushed to the breaking point, but then the vibrato had vanished, or Oscar had ignored it, or by then the air itself had been vibrating so intensely that Oscar could not tell the difference, and so Luis had once again seemed to be his happy-go-lucky, charismatic self.

They were sitting in the kitchen at that point. There was a soft, fragrant breeze that smelled vaguely of gardenias and lemons and the sea. The suitcase was back under Luis' bed. They had been drinking mojitos, or perhaps it was beers. Oscar didn't remember. Luis had said the timing couldn't be any better with the Feast Day of Saint Christopher on Saturday, the whole week would be a beautiful chaos which they could take advantage of. Oscar hadn't been quite sure he understood what Luis was talking about, so he had started to ask why he needed a suitcase, but Luis had cut him off with a slicing gesture and then went over and shut the balcony doors and then sat back down. His voice had become a whisper. He had then instructed Oscar to pick up a second suitcase, identical in all respects to the first one. Oscar was to fill the false bottom of this second suitcase with various tourist pamphlets and brochures from the nightclubs and the restaurants and cafes in Vedado along La Rampa and elsewhere. The kind of places that were fun but not too expensive. He was to pack the rest of the suitcase as if he were going away for a week. Then he was to sit by the phone and wait for Luis to call. That was all Luis had said. Then he had opened the balcony doors and the soft, fragrant breeze from before filled the kitchen. The two men had finished their mojitos or their beers in absolute silence.

The very next morning, Oscar took care of everything Luis had asked. Right down to the letter.

He picked up a Platt Guardsman suitcase from Herman's Department Store, a mirror image to the one Luis owned.

He packed it just like Luis had said.

He wanted to show Luis but Luis was not around.

The day after that, Luis and the original suitcase were gone by the time Oscar woke up, but there was a note on the kitchen table that said Luis would call at one in the afternoon.

So Oscar was waiting for Luis to call.

The new suitcase was on the floor beneath the kitchen table.

It was hot and he was very thirsty. Oscar finished his Coke and got up to fish another one out of the fridge.

At precisely one o'clock, the phone rang.

"Are you alone?" a voice said.

The voice sounded vaguely like Luis, but it also sounded vaguely like any number of haunted, desperate, faceless men anywhere in the world. Oscar felt like he was trapped inside the labyrinth of a dream.

"Yes," said Oscar.

"Did you get the suitcase?"

"Yes," said Oscar.

He started to relax a bit. Only Luis knew about the suitcase.

"Is it packed? Are you ready?"

"I'm ready."

Then Oscar let the words of Luis wash through him unimpeded by questions or affirmations. He could feel his brain spinning and clicking as the images of the future Luis described whirred past at record speed. It was a movie unfolding. But it was also a clock unwinding, the mechanical parts beginning to separate and fly off into space, a collection of seemingly useless gears and wheels lost in a vacuum, a spinning, whirling, chaotic cloud reflecting the light from random stars, but then the mechanical parts reassembling themselves, seemingly without a clockmaker, fitting together in ways that had been previously unknown.

"Go down to the front desk. Take your suitcase with you. And make sure you take your Beistegui Brothers Libia with you. At least keep it in a pocket so you can get at it if you need to."

". . . ."

"When you get to the desk, give your key to the clerk and tell him you will be gone for a week. Say it loud enough so anyone who is listening will hear, but not so loud as to draw attention to yourself."

". . . ."

"The clerk will pass you an envelope with a hastily scribbled note inside, but do not open the envelope or read the note. Slip it into your pocket and ask the clerk to call you a taxi."

". . . ."

"Sit down in one of the leather chairs near the revolving doors. Place the suitcase on the floor squarely between your legs."

". . . ."

"Do not sit in one of the chairs by the front desk, the ones near the photograph of Julio Mella. In all probability they will be occupied. But even if they are vacant, do not sit in them. The chairs are a trap."

". . . ."

"While you are waiting for the taxi, study the men in the lobby. There will be many men. All of them will be carrying guns. Study them carefully. These are the men who wish to do us harm."

". . . ."

"There's no need to worry. They will not try anything in the lobby during the middle of the afternoon. They are men of the shadows, not sunlight."

". . . ."

"I am not saying this to make you feel better. I could give a crap about how you feel. I am saying this to help you stay alive. Study the men carefully. File away their faces. But above all, keep your wits about you."

". . . ."

"When the taxi arrives, a fat, stubby man will go to the

front desk and make a phone call. Do not worry about him. Keep your eyes on the taxi driver. He will be a thin, hooked-nose fellow standing just inside the revolving doors, scanning the sea of men occupying every chair in the lobby."

". . . ."

"He will seem less like a taxi driver and more like an elderly concentration camp survivor who has been doing quite well since the war. He will be well-groomed, his hands neatly manicured. He will be exceptionally well-dressed."

". . . ."

"He will take his time surveying the lobby. Then he will notice your suitcase. Or more precisely, he will notice the position of your suitcase."

". . . ."

"He will approach you with a broad smile, and you will smile back. He will ask you if you need help with your suitcase."

". . . ."

"If he is wearing a dark brown Mallory hat with a red feather in the hatband, then you are to say 'No, thank you, I can manage,' and then he will lead you to the taxi.

". . . ."

"If there is no red feather or he is wearing a different kind of hat or no hat at all, then you are to say 'No thank you, I have only just arrived,' and then return to the front desk, quickly but not too quickly, and retrieve your key, head back to the apartment and wait for me to call again."

". . . ."

"We will not have too many cracks at this, so let us hope he is wearing the dark brown Mallory with the red feather."

". . . ."

"You must understand that nothing is what it appears to be. Your life depends upon understanding this."

". . . ."

"Once you are inside the taxi, read the note."

". . . ."

"The note explains in detail what we are up against."

". . . ."

"Do not worry about where the taxi driver is taking you. He knows where he is going. And do not worry about the two or three taxis that pull out to follow you. The taxi driver will lose them along the Malecón, or if that does not work, he will lose them in some of the smaller side streets in Vedado before doubling back."

". . . ."

"The taxi driver will drop you at the corner of Aguiar and Obispo. You are looking for an office building of sorts in the 200 block of Calle Obispo. It is a magnificent pale yellow building, a beautiful baroque structure, especially when the sunlight bounces off the gilded cornices. But do not get caught up in admiring the architecture. Head up to the third floor."

". . . ."

"Do not take the elevator. Take the stairs, and when you get to the third floor, take a left and go to the end of the hall."

". . . ."

"Remember to take your suitcase with you."

". . . ."

"When you get to the end of the hall you will see a single frosted glass door with the name Ignazio Tiziano & Sons, International Office in black lettering. The office is normally closed on Wednesday afternoons. If you can see the faint yellow glow of a lamp coming through the frosted glass, knock twice. A small but gruff voice will ask who is there. You must respond by saying 'the bull, like a castle under siege, has been eaten.'"

". . . ."

"If you happen to forget this colorful phrase just look at the note from earlier."

". . . ."

"A moment later the outer door will open, but only a crack. Do not go in right away. You will hear the sound of a second door, an interior door, opening and closing. You are to go inside the office only after you hear the second door close."

". . . ."

"If the outer door does not open, or you do not hear the sound of the second door closing, return to the taxi and head back to the hotel and wait for me to call. Same as before."

". . . ."

"Let's just be clear, if for any reason at any point along the way something goes wrong, head back to the hotel and wait for me to call."

". . . ."

"Once you are inside the International Office, you must once again repeat the phrase from the note for the man behind the counter, but very slowly, as if you are speaking to a deaf person and he can only read your lips."

". . . ."

"The man will study your lips for a moment. Then he will open the top drawer of a steel filing cabinet and remove a narrow envelope containing an American passport and a ticket, your ticket on the *S. S. City of Havana,* which will be heading to Key West on Thursday. The passport is a forgery. But it will get you through U. S. Customs."

". . . ."

"Do not ask the man about your ticket. He will give you the envelope with no knowledge of what is inside. Then he will smile, a flat bland smile, an inscrutable smile that will suggest that nothing is ever what it appears to be. Then he will retreat into the dark interior of the office and turn out the lights."

". . . ."

"At this point you will return to the taxi. You will notice that the taxi waiting for you will be a different taxi with a different driver. Do not worry about this change. Your new taxi driver will be a recent immigrant from Africa. Or quite possibly he will be a student from the University who grew up in the mountains in the east. It really does not matter which one. Whichever one it is, he will be very enthusiastic. He will ask you where you wish to go and you will say you have a ferry to catch, but not until the next morning."

". . . ."

"The ferry leaves at ten-thirty in the morning. But you do not need to worry about that just yet."

". . . ."

"The new taxi driver will repeat his question. But he will not seem confused. He is just looking for confirmation. Then you will say 'It is a long time between now and then. Why don't you take me down to the nightlife on La Rampa?' He will smile a dazzling bright smile and say 'Okay, boss,' and off you will go."

". . . ."

"It does not matter precisely where you go. A café, a restaurant, a nightclub. Go to the Tia Nena Club on San Martin if you like. But keep your suitcase with you at all times."

". . . ."

"The new taxi driver will stay with you the entire night."

". . . ."

"At five in the morning, tell the taxi driver to take you

out to Playa de Marianao. He will pull into a small parking lot in the shadows of the yacht club. The yacht club is hidden by trees."

". . . ."

"You are not to go down to the beach. You are to wait there until the sun rises."

". . . ."

"Do not get out of the car under any circumstances. There is nothing to do at that hour anyway."

". . . ."

"As the sun rises, you will notice a second car parked in the lot. It will be a wine-colored Custom Club De Soto convertible."

". . . ."

"It will be Federico's De Soto. But Federico will not be there. A fat, stubby man will get out of the De Soto."

". . . ."

"You will recognize the fat, stubby man as the same one who made the phone call in the lobby of the hotel. He will approach the taxi cab, but he will be surveying the landscape as he approaches to make sure there is no one else in the vicinity. When he is satisfied there is no one else, he will motion for you to roll down your window."

". . . ."

"You will roll down your window and say 'the bull, like a castle under siege, has been eaten.'"

". . . ."

"Yes, yes, if you need to look at the note then by all means look at the note."

". . . ."

"The fat man will roar with laughter, a great belly laugh, and then he will hand you a set of car keys."

". . . ."

"The keys to the De Soto. A second set. For later."

". . . ."

"You are to stay in the taxi. The fat man will return to the De Soto and drive away. You will wait ten minutes and then tell the taxi driver to take you to the ferry. But tell him to take his time. You are in no hurry. With any luck you will arrive at the wharf at nine o'clock."

". . . ."

"You are not to get on the ferry at this point. There is a

small café near the wharf. Café Paraiso. The taxi driver will know.

". . . ."

"You cannot see the ferry from this café. But that does not matter. Go into this café and sit down. Take the second table from the door next to the windows."

". . . ."

"It is unlikely the table will be occupied. The regulars all sit at the counter."

". . . ."

"The café will be overflowing with regulars, but there will be no one else. Order a coffee and a small breakfast. Make sure you set your suitcase on the floor beneath the window sill. And make sure you take your time with your breakfast. Sip your coffee slowly. Read the paper. But do not talk to anyone. Not even the waitress, except to order your food and pay your bill. If someone happens to ask if you are traveling on the ferry, give a noncommittal shrug and look out the window."

". . . ."

"I will arrive at the café at nine-thirty."

". . . ."

"I will sit at the table next to yours. The third one from the door. I will be carrying my own Platt Guardsman suitcase, which I will set down next to yours."

". . . ."

"I will not stay long. I will order a cup of coffee and I will drink it quickly. At nine-forty-five I will leave the café, but I will be taking your suitcase. You will take mine."

". . . ."

"At ten o'clock you will pay your bill and leave the café. Leave a decent tip, not too generous, but don't be miserly."

". . . ."

"At that point you are to board the *S. S. City of Havana.*"

". . . ."

"Leave the café through the front door. There's no need to be melodramatic."

". . . ."

"Once you are on board the ferry, head down to the automobile deck. Put the suitcase in the trunk of the De Soto. The car will be waiting for you, naturally."

". . . ."

"Make sure the car is secure. Then head back up to the

passenger lounge. Grab a drink. Sit down. Look out at the water. Try to relax. You will just be killing time at that point."

". . . ."

"I will join you soon after that, as soon as I can."

And just like that the line went dead. The voice of Luis disintegrated into a blur of static. Oscar sat for a while trying to absorb everything Luis had told him. It seemed very hot and his head was swimming. He did not know what to think of it all. He finished his Coke. He put on his white linen suit and his immaculate Panama hat. Then he got up, plucked his suitcase from the floor, and headed down to the lobby.

-92-

Where Luis went that morning after he left Hotel Milagro with his Platt Guardsman suitcase:

Luis left the apartment at eight in the morning. He stopped briefly at the front desk and chatted with the clerk. They talked in deliberate monotones. They talked about American baseball. The clerk was a big fan (though you could not tell this by his tone). They talked about Joe DiMaggio. The clerk thought DiMaggio had a goofy grin but he had never seen someone swing the bat with such ease. His brother had seen DiMaggio play in an exhibition game in Havana in the spring of 1947 between the Yankees and the Dodgers, but he (the clerk) did not get to go. He had never seen DiMaggio in person and now he never would. But he had seen a few clips in the newsreels at the movies. The clips showed DiMaggio in his heyday.

The sounds of dark jazz floated lazily about the lobby.

They floated about like clouds.

It was almost like being somewhere else.

Luis and the clerk talked for fifteen minutes or so and then the phone rang and the clerk turned his back to Luis and answered it. When the phone call was over he turned back around and leaned over the counter and whispered something into Luis' ear. After that Luis asked the clerk for some paper and an envelope. The next thing anyone who might have been watching would have seen was Luis handing the envelope back to the clerk and then heading out through the revolving doors. But this happened very quickly. If they (the watchers) had so much as blinked they would have missed the inherent subtleties of this carefully scripted cloak and dagger moment. Where the clerk stashed the envelope was anybody's guess. Probably one of the wooden boxes containing abandoned room keys and dusty messages.

On his way to the revolving doors, Luis walked right by Nerea, who was watching him very carefully from the gloomy obscurity of one of the burgundy leather chairs with the pouty cinematic beauty of Julio Mella hovering above. Luis and Nerea did not make eye contact, but Luis had the strangest feeling that someone other than Nerea was watching him. He had the impression that Julio Mella was watching him. It seemed like Julio wanted to either warn him or absolve him.

The men in their fedoras who had taken over the lobby allowed Luis to leave without incident.

The revolving doors whooshed with unexpected ferocity and a blast of sunlight roared through the lobby, illuminating even the darkness beneath the chairs furthest away from any kind of electric light. For a moment the only sounds were the whooshing of the doors and the roaring sunlight. Then the sunlight dissipated and everything returned to normal. The men began grumbling to themselves but they did not get up from their chairs. Dark jazz echoed throughout the lobby once again.

After Luis left Hotel Milagro he hopped into a taxi and told the driver to take him to the corner of Empedrado and Mercaderes, a stone's throw from the Cathedral of San Cristóbal. It was normally a ten-minute ride, but traffic was heavier than usual this morning because of the upcoming feast day celebration. Vendors were already setting up in the Plaza across from the Cathedral in anticipation of the crowds filling the city. Even though the actual feast day was Saturday, the party was already starting.

Luis said something funny to the driver as he paid the man and the two of them laughed like old friends. The two men talked about how hot it was, unusually hot for November.

Then Luis walked half a block and stopped in the Plaza to admire the Cathedral, marveling at its majestic, starkly white luminescence beneath the bright blue sky. It was like a white-hot coal that had slipped outside of the furnace of time. This is the impression the Cathedral made on Luis, though not perhaps in those exact words. But the feeling was similar. The Cathedral seemed to be glowing with acquired heat. Luis could feel the steady, rhythmic pulsing heat of a nearby star. Then he could feel the music of an aspiring humanity set in stone, which resonated with a different kind of heat. Then Luis realized he had never seen the Cathedral look so alive, which was a different kind of heat yet again. Luis stood marveling at the Cathedral for quite some time. He had not been inside since he was a small boy. He remembered orange-glowing walls inside when the sun poured in through the windows and polished marble columns, an earthy, beige color, like the legs of giant elephants. He remembered a choir singing various dusty cantatas and the nuns weeping their silent, deadly tears and the smell of incense clogging his throat, but that was all.

Then Luis bought a lemon-filled *pastelito* from a vendor in the Plaza. He stood very still while he ate his *pastelito,* observing the other vendors who were still setting up their booths or their carts in the Plaza, and the snappily dressed early risers who were sitting outside a small café with a postcard view of the Cathedral and its ancient Baroque façade of a religious relic, the early risers sitting eagerly at a few outdoor tables with the white umbrellas open, waiting for this vendor or that one (because it was still early) so they could buy something, and chatting happily and pointing in random, unpredictable fashion at the pure blue of the sky or the bell tower on one side of the Cathedral or the clock tower on the other side or at the pigeons scattered about. Sometimes the pigeons were spooked and there was a flurry of wings and a small cloud billowing up into the air and then settling down again. From a distance it was hard to tell if they were pigeons or white doves sent by the Holy Spirit.

One of the vendors was selling fireworks. He was already doing a brisk business among a group of small boys who would normally have been in school but school for the week had been cancelled because of the celebration. Some of the boys were wearing white shirts but the others were shirtless, because it was so hot.

The figure of a priest in a white cassock and a black sash emerged from the Cathedral and hurried down the steps and the boys scattered, as did the pigeons, and one got the distinct impression that the priest disapproved of the vendor selling his fireworks to the small boys and was about to say something but changed his mind at the last second and then disappeared around the corner as if he were seeking pardon or revenge.

All of a sudden Luis decided he had seen enough and he headed away from the Cathedral, west along Empedrado. He finished the last of his *pastelito* while he walked, smacking his lips with great satisfaction. He walked with such carefree abandon that you would not have noticed the suitcase in his hand unless you looked very long and hard. If anyone had been following him at that point they wouldn't have known what to think.

Two blocks from the Cathedral Luis suddenly ducked into a small park and disappeared in a cloud of green. The cloud of green was actually a small grove of tamarind with deep-green laurels and several other varieties mixed in. The waxy leaves of the tamarinds reflected the bright pure sunlight. The air itself seemed to be shimmering.

Luis walked to the other side of the tamarind grove and sat down on a bench in the middle of the park. He set his suitcase on the stone walkway by his feet and looked across at a towering marble statue of Miguel de Cervantes Saavedra. He had always admired Cervantes and came to the park often to look at this statue. Sometimes it seemed less a statue and more like a ridiculously expensive adornment for a ridiculously expensive sarcophagus. Because we have to believe that something survives death, even if it is only a piece of stone. Luis did not agree one hundred percent with how the sculptor had portrayed Cervantes. The great writer seemed half asleep sitting in his marble Renaissance chair. Perhaps it was the moment just before the idea of *Don Quixote* had occurred to him. Or perhaps he had just finished writing the first few chapters. Or perhaps he was trying to remember some trivial event from when he was a boy. Or perhaps he had just finished a very large meal. It was hard to tell.

Luis sat on the bench for a while until it seemed that he had become part of the bench, one stone statue gazing upon another. Church bells rang out at regular intervals but he appeared not to notice. He was not annoyed. He did not even flinch. Then, inexplicably, which is to say just like that, Luis left the bench.

To all outward appearances he seemed to be in no hurry, and yet there was a sense of urgency with every step. He cut back across the park and then headed south on Aguiar until he came to Obispo. He stopped at the corner, looking in both directions several times, back and forth and back and forth again, as if he could not make up his mind where exactly he wanted to go, as if he were peering into the future and he wasn't sure he liked what he saw, as if he wished he had more choices in front of him, which is, of course, what we all wish.

He stood very still for a while.

He stood very still and thought he could hear music drifting over the rooftops and swirling down the streets. Perhaps a few musicians had set up in the Plaza near the Cathedral and were entertaining the growing crowd.

Then he turned abruptly and headed up the 200 block of Calle Obispo. He walked without even looking at the numbers on the buildings and then went inside a pale yellow office building. He did not pause to admire the architecture, which was yet another magnificent example of the Spanish Baroque style. He did not even bother to look up at the gleaming brilliance of the gold gleaming cornices. He climbed the stairs two at a time in spite of the suitcase.

When he got to the third floor he headed down the hall, all the way to the end, and went through a frosted glass door.

There was a bald-headed clerk sitting at a counter who looked up as Luis entered. The clerk smiled a thin, bleak smile and disappeared into the dark interior of the office. He did not seem to be feeling all that well. He seemed to be suffering from a stomach condition of some sort. A few minutes later a different man emerged from the darkness. For some reason it was difficult to tell what this second man looked like. He seemed devoid of any distinguishing features, almost faceless. He looked vaguely Spanish, which is not all that surprising in Havana, but that was all anyone might remember.

Luis and the second man carried on a wordless conversation. It was almost like they could communicate telepathically. Luis looked past the man and the man followed Luis's gaze and then hurried away and shut a door and locked it and returned, and then Luis gave the man a strange, grave look, which seemed to say that he hoped the man was better prepared for what was to come, and with that the man gave Luis a nervous look and laughed a thin, shallow whistling laugh like light swirling down a long dark tunnel and disappearing forever, but Luis made a calming gesture and then pulled out a narrow, almond-colored envelope and gave it to the man and the man seemed relieved and put the envelope in a steel filing cabinet that was plainly visible behind the counter. Then the second man returned to the interior and the bald-headed clerk reappeared and sat down and Luis left. The bald-headed clerk did not seem to be feeling any better.

After he left the pale yellow office building, Luis headed to a small café he knew. The café was only a short walk away. Luis went inside and took a seat near the back, near a narrow row of telephone booths. It was very dark near the back, but Luis needed a little respite from the bright sunny day.

He ordered a flatbread sandwich with a bit ham and pork and a hint of orange sauce, garlic, peppers, and mustard. It was a working man's lunch, even though Luis was clearly not a working man.

When the waitress brought the sandwich she smiled at Luis, a gentle, hopeful, flirtatious gleam in her eye, but Luis did not return the smile.

He did not even notice the waitress.

She stared at him a moment and then left quickly.

He ate his sandwich. He drank two beers.

From where he was sitting, the people passing by the front of the café looked like glimmering shadows gliding back and forth across the two-dimensional brightness of the sunlit window.

After he finished eating he disappeared into one of the phone booths. It was a tight fit with his Platt Guardsman suitcase, but he made it work. He chose the one all the way in the back, so he could see anything coming his way. He sat in the phone booth for a while but he did not call anyone.

At least not right away.

Nobody in the café seemed to care that Luis had taken over a phone booth. It was almost like the phone booths did not even exist. Then at precisely one o'clock Luis picked up the phone and made a call. Even if you had been sitting inside the phone booth with Luis, you would have been hard pressed to understand what he said. He spoke very fast, pausing just long enough between thoughts to catch his breath. If you had been standing outside the phone booth it would have sounded like waves crashing at the beach. It was also hard to say who he called. Some would have said impossible. At times it seemed that there was no one on the other end, just a gnawing, protracted silence waiting for more.

Then Luis hung up and dialed a second number. This second phone call was very short, no more than ten seconds.

Then Luis flung open the folding door, headed outside and hopped into another taxi. He told the taxi driver to drop him at the wharf, he needed to catch the ferry to Regla, and the driver nodded and off they went. If Luis noticed the two taxis that seemed to be following his taxi, he gave no indication. Perhaps he did not care. Perhaps he thought they were simply reflections of the taxi he had chosen, ghostly double (or triple) images dancing in the dark windows of the shops and cafes along the streets and that once they had stopped moving these ghost images would catch up, all of the images coalescing into a single taxi. Or perhaps he had anticipated that no matter where he went, he would be followed. In any event, he didn't bother with the two taxis that were following close behind, even when his own taxi driver said he could lose them if Luis wanted. Luis only laughed and said it wasn't anything to worry about, nothing was what it appeared to be. It was sunny outside and he could hear church bells ringing, a gentle ringing in his ears. Luis sat back and enjoyed the ride, short as it was.

-93-

Escaping on the ferry to Regla:

The two taxis following Luis had been delayed in an unexpected bottleneck on Calle Cuba, just before the old convent, and Luis' driver commented on this and then spun the wheel and they sped down Luz towards the ferries. By the time the other two taxis had disentangled themselves, Luis had already paid his fare and disappeared into the tunnel-like darkness of the ferry building, emerging only briefly into the sunlight on the other side before he boarded a small blue passenger ferry. As the small boat pulled away from the wharf, Luis could see the other two taxis shuddering to a stop just inches before they would have smashed into a few parked cars. Several dark figures popped out of the taxis and raced after the ferry, but they were too late. Luis watched them on the wharf staring mutely at the dozens of boats that were motoring this way and that across the harbor and the seagulls hovering in the air above.

Briefly he wondered how they had picked up his scent and if they knew where he was going, but then these thoughts left him. Another ferry would leave shortly, but it didn't matter. By the time it arrived in Regla, Luis would have melted into the background.

Luis sat in the middle of the boat, not because he was afraid of the water, but because he wanted to stay in the shadows as much as possible.

It was a pretty short trip. When he got to the other side of the bay he looked back to see if the next ferry had started across, but he could not tell. Then he headed out towards the street and a wine-colored De Soto convertible pulled up and Luis climbed into the back seat. The driver did not look at Luis and Luis did not say a word.

A few minutes later they were lost in a labyrinth of narrow winding streets south and slightly east of the warehouses and the refineries and the two grain towers and the new thermoelectric plant and the chemical plants along the water and the green fumes boiling up into the air. A working-class neighborhood filled with a mix of narrow but brightly painted wooden houses that might be swept away with the next great storm, and a few crumbling stone buildings, colonial ruins trembling with the majesty of the past. Narrow balcony railings covered in flowers and vines. Black Madonnas were everywhere leaning out over the railings, three-foot statues precariously perched, calling out to those below in the stony, silent language of salvation, but when you looked up you lost all perspective. The Black Madonnas seemed to be suspended by wires in a bright blue liquid sky. And no matter where you were you could hear a strange, drumming music and muffled, chanting voices. When you tried to focus on the drumming sounds or the voices they vanished as easily and as quickly as a misplaced hope, only to be resurrected as soon as your mind became absorbed (inebriated, sidetracked) by something else.

After a while the De Soto stopped in front of a small neighborhood café, a nameless establishment, a narrow, triangular building at the corner of three streets, a series of narrow wooden panels folded back on themselves and the ground floor exposed, a hot, dusty breeze blowing through the open space, a long counter where dozens of patrons stood and ate long, lazy lunches and drank beer and laughed and chatted and drank some more. Most of the patrons were the descendants of African slaves. They did not give Luis and the wine-colored De Soto convertible a second glance.

Two young men wearing fedoras and holding long-barreled rifles (not unlike some of the men occupying the lobby of Hotel Milagro) appeared out of nowhere and ushered Luis into the café. They led him around to the side of the counter and a small table tucked away in a dark corner behind a mahogany screen.

Federico sat on the far side of the table submerged in the grainy subterranean light of the corner. At first he seemed only a featureless dark hole, a blind beggar. Only the ivory handles of his cane-back wheelchair and the ghostly impression of his orderly dressed in white and standing up against a closed side door gave away his identity.

The two men sat at the table for a very long time. They made their thoughts known by using cryptic hand gestures that bordered on farce, uttering strangely garbled phrases, descending into sudden, protracted silences, and then trading happy, beguiling smiles. They drank mojitos the whole time. The mojitos were not part of the regular menu and were instead prepared especially for Federico by the owner herself whenever Federico happened by. The owner was a heavy-set woman with thick, bushy hair and elephantine legs. Her eyes glowed with a disturbing brilliance like Quevedo's blood-stained moon. She wore dark glasses so she wouldn't frighten her customers. Her only name was Jaqueline. Federico had known her for years.

Luis and Federico seemed little concerned with the world around them, and yet there was an anxiety in the way they were communicating, a sense that time was running out and that they better do something before the last grains of sand had slipped through the neck. Of course they also realized that whatever plans they concocted would make no difference. Instinctively they realized there was only one end in sight. But this was the life they had chosen. At times they seemed on the verge of giving up completely. But then their passions were reignited and they seemed more determined than ever. They relished the fact that this was their last hurrah.

Highlights of the conversation between Federico and Luis:

"It is not hard to know God, my friend, provided you do not force yourself to define Him."

"I would not say God is the problem."

"No, no, I suppose not."

The two men laughing softly, some murmuring, the older

one descending into a state of mental detachment, as if he is suffering from a series of strange premonitions, the younger one suddenly thankful that he possesses all of his faculties. Then a loud burst from the other side of the mahogany screen and then the clinking of beer bottles.

And then a few minutes later:

"It is the same as with everything else. First we dream a dream. Then we are seduced by the dream. And then we are sacrificed in the name of the dream."

". . . ."

"It is the old, old story."

"I am not sure there is any other way."

"No, of course not."

". . . ."

"Our options are limited."

"I have arranged everything."

"Good, good. "

"At least we'll give them something to think about."

"Perhaps."

Silence. The orderly moving from the door to the other side of the screen and then returning with a tray of mojitos. The two young men with their long-barreled rifles standing alertly in the dark, listening intently for anything out of the ordinary, watching intently, their eyes glowing with a peculiar reddish glow, like the landing lights of an alien spacecraft, the young men ready to pull the trigger if and when such action becomes necessary.

And then: "Where did this Immanuel come from?"

"I do not know. I suspect he came up with the boys from the unions. Eladio and Eugenio were sending us all sorts. I don't know how we managed to use them all, but we did. It is just like these union fucks to get in bed with the Communists."

"Is that what is happening?"

"What else could it be?"

"Ah, mi. Di guerra, caccia e amuri, pri un gustu milli duluri."

"The Communists are everywhere. I am sure Eladio sees it as a matter of survival. He doesn't know what else to do. But I am surprised about Eugenio. He has been speaking out against the Communists for years."

"Perhaps he has been lying all along."

"Yes, perhaps."

"You are sure Eladio and Eugenio are working with this

Immanuel?"

"I am sure."

". . . ."

"They want to demonstrate their solidarity with everything Cuban, with Cuba's future."

"And they are willing to destroy everything we've built?"

"It would seem so."

"Then perhaps they are not Communists at all. Perhaps they are simply anarchists left over from the war. Or maybe ex-Nazis filled with rage and frustration with nothing better to do. Perhaps this is all just an accident of timing."

"It is a thought."

"And what about Ruperto?"

"No, I don't think Ruperto is involved. He has his own reasons for wanting to keep things as they are. But they are personal."

". . . ."

"I think they have been planning this for a very long time."

"How long?"

"At least since the storming of the warehouse. I am certain they were behind it. Just as I am certain that they knew you would suggest we move to Miami. Yes, they have been lurking in the shadows for a very long time indeed, plotting, planning, moves and countermoves. Communists, anarchists, ex-Nazis, it does not matter."

". . . ."

"I did not realize Eladio and Eugenio were revolutionaries at heart. They are ticking time bombs."

". . . ."

"You must admit as adversaries they have proved themselves to be quite formidable."

"But what is their goal? What do they want?"

"But Federico, you surely must know what they want. They want to explode. That is what ticking time bombs do."

But Federico does not understand. Luis smiles at his friend and drinks some of his mojito. 'Yes,' he thinks, 'all this must be quite a shock to the old man. It is a wonder he doesn't just keel over.'

And then, still smiling, a soft almost apologetic smile:

"What they want is to take over. They want to be in charge. It is like you said, the old, old story."

Silence. The two men look at each other for a moment, at least they are looking at the dark shadowy holes their faces have become.

"I cannot believe we didn't see this coming."

"Yes, but we can see it coming now."

And back and forth they go, assigning blame where no blame should be assigned. Wishing they could undo time but knowing that such wishes never come true. Their words take on a harder edge. Their words are lacerating the air. They wonder if they could pull back the shredded folds of reality and peer through to the other side. Then they begin to laugh at the absurdity of it all. The naiveté of long-cherished assumptions. The landscape of a world that has suddenly become the landscape of a cartoon. They feel like they have flown to the moon and back. They congratulate themselves on maintaining a purity of heart and mind and soul.

And then:

"You are sure this will work?"

"Yes, Oscar will be able to slip through. I will divert their attention."

"This is a dangerous game you play, my friend."

"Ah, yes, but it is just as dangerous for them."

The older man suddenly looks over at the orderly, and the orderly, who has been waiting for this sudden look, slips out through the side door and returns a moment later with a leather satchel, which he hands to Federico.

The two young men with their long-barreled rifles flashing darkly from the shadows seem amused. Federico unbuckles the satchel and peers inside, then sets it on the table and pushes it across towards Luis.

"Let us hope everything will work out as you say."

Moments later the satchel is empty and Luis snaps shut the Platt Guardsman suitcase. The additional weight is barely noticeable.

"You will be needing the keys."

Federico and Luis trade cinematic smiles, though in a world plunged into a perpetual film noir darkness, their smiles could just as easily be expressions of deep sorrow. The orderly dressed all in white produces two sets of keys and hands them to Luis.

"The De Soto?"

"Yes."

The long lingering lunch in the café is over and most of the patrons have gone home or back to work. In the distance you can hear drunken men singing. It almost sounds like the tolling of bells from distant churches. A young boy is unfolding the narrow wooden panels that are never noticed when the café is open. He is closing off the open space. It is tedious work for the boy, but there is no one else to help him. Then the café is officially closed until the sun sets. The orderly opens the side door and a narrow rectangle of afternoon sunlight slashes through the interior darkness. Luis pauses in the sunlight, and for a moment he seems trapped between two competing versions of reality. He looks at Federico, who is not moving, who suddenly looks like a skeleton in the glaring, sacrificial light of the open door with his pale, parchment skin stretched tightly across his forehead and two gaping black holes where his eyeballs should be. He no longer recognizes his friend.

"Are you staying then?"

"Yes, I think I shall stay a while. It has been years since I've had a good talk with my friend Jaqueline. It has been too long. We sometimes forget what is important. I do not even know if she still considers me a friend. One should never be so presumptuous."

-94-

What Luis did with the wine-colored De Soto convertible:

The drive back to Havana was uneventful. But Luis did not head back right away. He parked the De Soto (with the top closed) in a narrow side street in the shadow of a chemical plant and a green haze all around. With the heat and the haze, he could barely breathe, but he waited in the car until the sun began to set and then he could breathe more easily. Then he turned the key. The men who had most certainly jumped on the next ferry and followed him to Regla had just as certainly given up by now. The long shadows of the evening sliced through the landscape and it was becoming difficult if not impossible to see what was what with any degree of confidence. As Luis drove along the water he had the distinct impression that he was looking at a painting but the colors had started to run together. His eyes were glued to this painting, which was the world, oh, not the entire world perhaps, but certainly his world, a world that had once been surprisingly clear with sharply drawn lines and vivid Technicolor colors, but which was now beginning to disintegrate, the lines blurring, the images crumbling into black and white apparitions, and then just a black nothingness sliding off the page, the sludge of human memory, but if he closed his eyes (which he tried for a few seconds at a time while driving, just for a kick), he could once again see the world as it was, as he knew it to be, every moment of his life up until that point radiating with an explosion of minute detail, sharply rendered, the kind of detail that gives life to life, but then as soon as he opened his eyes that world would vanish as completely as if it had never existed, as if the lunatic painter (for who else but a lunatic would dare take such liberties with the world?) was trying to suggest that objective reality was beyond our grasp and that we needed to live our lives with our eyes closed or we would end up stark raving mad.

This is what Luis was thinking as he drove along the water and the night sky was descending.

At nine o'clock he drove into a small garage on a nameless street in Vedado, a nameless garage, practically invisible to the naked eye, and yet everyone in the neighborhood knew it was there. The garage appeared to be closed, but as Luis drove around the corner, a light in the garage office began to flicker, and then a steady, yellowish glow began to radiate outward, as if the office had suddenly caught fire, and then a pair of shutters were pulled shut, though the yellowish glow was still seeping through the slats, and a shadow rushed out to the sidewalk and a metal gate was pulled back and Luis drove in.

The humming of the engine echoed off the walls of the garage for a moment and then Luis cut the engine.

The gate was pulled shut.

"You are late," said a slightly puzzled voice, a deep masculine voice, but not as deep as the baritone steamship voice of Luis.

The voice was barely a whisper.

It was barely a fragrant breeze and the waxy leaves of a tamarind tree trembling slightly.

"I'll only be getting a few hours of sleep as it is."

"Yes," said Luis.

And then: "But it could not be helped."

"If you say so."

The two men stepped towards the garage office, but only a step. They remained safely ensconced within the shadows of the interior of the garage. There was plenty of light for their purposes. They were backlit by the soft yellow glow still seeping through the shuttered window of the garage office. They became two darkly glowing silhouettes, the fat stubby outline of the one, the square-shouldered and crisply manicured outline of the other with the triangular corner of a suitcase protruding.

There was just enough light to swear by.

"Did he get off okay?"

"He did. But he didn't look too happy about it."

"I suspected he wouldn't."

"You didn't tell him a damn thing, did you?"

"I told him enough."

"You mean enough to keep him away from trouble. But not enough if trouble came looking for him."

"Something like that."

The two silhouettes laughed. The yellow glow from the office seemed to glow more intensely with their laughter, as if the mania of their innermost impulses was directly connected to the electric grid.

"I don't owe you any more favors after this."

"Agreed."

"Good."

"So he got off okay?"

"I already said."

"A dark brown Mallory hat with a red feather in the hatband?"

"I told you."

"Yes, I know. I was just checking."

"You're a god damn lunatic Luis."

"And where is he now?"

"I guess he's probably in the second taxi."

"You guess?"

"Okay, that's exactly where he is. He's in the god damn second taxi. Except if he's already at one of those fucking nightclubs you suggested."

". . . ."

"One last fling in Havana before he goes, is that what you were thinking?"

"Sure."

"I hope he gets himself as much pussy as he can handle."

". . . ."

"What if he skips out on you?"

"He won't do that."

"Yeah, well, if you say so."

"Who's driving the second taxi? The immigrant from Africa or the student from the University?"

"Neither."

". . . ."

"We had to make a change."

". . . ."

"He's a good man. He used to play baseball but now he's mostly a drunk. But he's a good man."

"Was that wise making a change like that?"

"I said he's a good man."

"Yes, but I don't like unexpected changes."

"I know you don't. But it could not be helped."

"I see."

"I'm telling you it will be fine. He's a good man."

"Let's hope so."

"God damn it Luis! I'm doing the best I can! What the hell do you want from me?"

"The bull, like a castle under siege, has been eaten."

And it was only then that the fat, stubby man realized that Luis had been teasing him about the new taxi driver.

The two silhouettes broke into a relaxed, carefree, shining example of unrehearsed laughter.

They laughed for a very long time.

Once again the yellow glow from the office seemed to glow with greater intensity.

It seemed like the window was about to burst.

Quite probably there was a sudden surge on the electrical grid that caused minor blackouts all over town.

"I'll say it again, Luis. You're a god damn lunatic."

"I know it."

"It's like you think we're all characters in a god damn Hollywood movie."

"But we are, my friend, we are."

And then there was nothing more to say. Luis handed the fat stubby man the two sets of keys to the De Soto. He stood on the cement pavement of the garage ramp and watched the fat man disappear into his office and the light went out. Then he looked back at the De Soto. The De Soto was still warm from the drive. It still seemed to be vibrating slightly. Luis stared at the car until he could no longer distinguish the car from anything else in the garage. Then he headed for a narrow archway next to the gate. There was no door, just an opening. He swung his Platt Guardsman suitcase through the opening with a carelessness that could only have been caused by giddy euphoria and headed out into the Cuban night.

-95-

The men in dark fedoras with their long-barreled rifles or their Kongsberg Colt pistols chase Luis through the darkly gleaming streets of Havana:

The webbed darkness of Berkeley's God, this chaos of the soul, was riddled with the streaking meteorites of festival rockets, though who was lighting them and from where it was impossible to say. Music filled every corner of every street, every nook and cranny. Thousands of musicians had descended upon the city, as they always did during times of celebration, many having arrived by bus from as far away as Oriente province. But this particular celebration was unlike any other festival that anyone ever remembered or would remember. It was an anomaly, never to be repeated. It was like Carnival and Christmas mixed together. On the feast day itself, the faithful would be forced to sit in silence inside the Cathedral while they prayed to the wooden statue of Saint Christopher for his blessing. But the days and nights leading up to that Saturday of their repressed, penitent fears would be filled with a more raucous, rumbling kind of energy.

That first night set the tone for everything that followed. The clang of a siren or two went by. The happiness swelled. A woman screamed. But it was not clear if it was a scream of terror or a scream of passion. Elongated shadows appeared, like the shadows of alien creatures that had taken refuge on the earth. Then another festival rocket went up into the air and these strange shadows evaporated or were forgotten and when they returned in the light of a passing car or some other source of illumination it was clear they were only tree branches swaying in a gentle breeze. The happiness spread like a disease. So did the laughter. And the church bells ringing. Thousands of unseen men and women were singing songs of happy-go-lucky joy or drunken, melancholic love or blasphemous frivolity. Each song a vision of happiness unto itself. Happiness any way you sliced it. Amnesic voices emanating from distant radios (as if from distant stars); or sex-starved voices emanating from dozens of third-rate movie houses that littered the landscape like limping (clubfooted) degenerate uncles, the willing, willful, festival-going throng mesmerized by the flashing pockmarked light of crumbling movie house marquees, each marquee with an incalculable number of missing bulbs that would never be replaced, or ruptured bulbs still implanted in their sockets with jagged edges that might cause injury, each marquee flashing incessantly, as long as there was darkness to flash against, or absorb, the marquees more darkness than light really, symbols of eternal night; or implacable, unforgiving voices (happy in their eternal, dogmatic pain) emanating from those forgotten churches on that godforsaken strip south of Zanja with their slowly disintegrating stone walls that still reverberated with recriminations from centuries ago; or lingering, lecherous, satisfied voices emanating from the interior darkness of posh nightclubs with their hollow happy men, and women's eyes dripping rouge; all of these happy, effervescent voices (and many more besides) mixing together in the stratosphere, as close to heaven as was physically possible, the currents of the upper winds swirling the voices about, mixing them together so you could barely tell one from another, and then the voices somehow separating, reforming, reshaping the world in ways that only the infinite logic of music can express, a billion permutations.

So no one paid any attention to Luis. Even if they (whoever might have been looking for Luis) had known where Luis was going to be at any given moment, they would have had difficulty pointing him out because there were hundreds like Luis roaming the streets, jostling each other in this horde of happy pedestrians, without apology, without awareness, some of them looking for a place to stay for the night, and for the next several nights after that, but many more were content to roam the streets until they collapsed from exhaustion or were lucky enough to find a seat at an outdoor café, where they drank a beer or two and then nodded off.

By midnight most of those who were still awake seemed to be reveling in the peculiar synchronicities of earthly existence. Quite a few were wearing bizarrely painted masks:

animal masks, bird masks, Conquistador masks, priestly masks, prison inmate masks, masks of the Inquisition, masks of the Devil, masks of crippled angels and hallucinating saints, gas masks with elephantine rubber attachments, ski masks with no attachments at all, aviator caps with goggles, which were not masks precisely but worked well enough, masks of indifference, masks of vengeance, masks of annihilation, masks of incompetence, masks of craven betrayal, masks of insensitive lovers, masks of night terrors, masks of greedy politicians, masks of blood-thirsty generals, masks of demons from the pit, masks to protect you from the horrors of radiation sickness (though it should be pointed out that these masks, while cleverly decorated, were not even close to the real thing and would never work), masks that were realistic down to the tiniest imperfection, masks that were clearly abstract representations, all done in wild, vibrant colors that were only visible if they caught the glow of a festival rocket or a flash from a passing headlight or the dim reflection of a street lamp bouncing off one of the darkened storefront windows; the masked revelers cavorting about, grunting and gurgling and grinding their teeth, making obscene gestures as they danced through the darkly glowing subterranean shadows. Wild dogs howling at the moon. Some were wearing only their masks and had painted their bodies to match, accentuating their good points, hiding their deformities. Some of these bodies were elaborate works of art. Surrealist expressions of the soul of the individual, however demented. And this is how it was all over Havana. One wondered how the remaining nights could hope to surpass this first night celebrating the Feast Day of Saint Christopher. It beggared the imagination.

Luis walked from the nameless garage to Linea and waved for a taxi. He was certain no one was following him. But he was also certain that dark men wearing fedoras and sporting long-barreled rifles or Kongsberg Colt pistols were scattered all over the city on the chance that he might stumble by. So he told the taxi driver to drive around for a while, Vedado, Miramar, Cerro, it did not matter. He wanted to think through what was left to do. He cracked his window because it was stuffy inside the cab.

Once or twice he thought he saw the darkly gleaming barrels of long-barreled rifles sticking out from the tangled knot of humanity walking to and fro along the sidewalks. But the taxi was going by too fast to be sure. On several occasions while the taxi waited at a stoplight, Luis heard snippets of conversations drifting in through the window as the pedestrians passed in front. All of the snippets seemed to carry savage, sinister, even desperate overtones.

At one stoplight Luis heard:

"Are you sure you know the way?"

"Yes, of course, but that doesn't mean much tonight."

"And you're sure he'll be the only one there."

"I'm not sure of anything. But it doesn't matter to me."

And at another stoplight:

"I don't care about any of that. All I want is my money."

"That's what I told him."

"Yeah, well, there's no telling what I might do if I don't get my money."

"I told him that as well."

And at a third:

"So I told her I didn't give a fuck, and do you know what she said? She said go ahead. You're a big boy. Do something stupid."

"So what did you do?"

"What do you think I did?"

"That's what I'm afraid of."

And at a fourth:

"We'll leave in the morning."

"Do you think we'll get away with it?"

"I'll guess we'll find out."

"Yeah, I guess we will."

Shortly before midnight, Luis told the taxi driver to drop him at a small apartment building he knew on Calle Crista in the old part of town. He knew a woman that lived there, and he was fairly certain that he had never mentioned her name to Nerea. It was far enough away from the glamour and excitement of the celebration that he might actually get some sleep. It would be the perfect spot to hole up for the rest of the night. But the traffic was worse than before. The police had closed off half a dozen streets, which is to say they had set up a series of impenetrable barricades, and at each barricade there were a couple of overly friendly officers in their bright blue slickers, in case it rained, joking with those heading up to the Plaza, laughing without remorse, encouraging those who were already drunk to find some quiet corner to sleep it off before they got into real trouble, giving any students that passed by a real hard time, because these officers were real hard cases, all of them filled to the brim with a brutal, lacerating rage that needed to be purged from time to time in small manageable bursts, like bleeding a radiator, or God only knew what unforgivable crimes might occur. You knew they were armed and would pull out their guns at the drop of a hat. You could hear the rattle of death in their laughter.

The barricades and the police made it impossible for Luis to get where he wanted to go, at least by taxi, and so quite without meaning to, Luis found himself for the second time that day in front of the ferry building. The taxi made a u-turn and sped off into the darkness. Luis grit his teeth. He did not like unexpected coincidences. He did not believe in them. The last ferry had left hours earlier, so there was no one there, but all the same, Luis felt like he was being watched the moment he stepped out onto the pavement.

Already there was a taste of rain in the air and somewhere offshore in the dark waters to the southwest there was the rumbling of a storm in its infant stage. Luis heard the rumble of the storm without hearing it. He was looking at the black hole across the street where Ignazio Tiziano & Sons had once stood. The ruins of the once magnificent colonial structure still remained, a charred reminder of earlier days. Luis smiled a grim, resigned smile. He could not say at that moment precisely how long ago the warehouse had burned to the ground. Standing there in the darkness of his imagination he felt as if he were looking across centuries. Then he noticed movement near one of the gated archways of the ferry building. Two shadows emerged, or partially emerged, then a pinprick of light, as if someone had lit a cigarette, and then another pinprick, and then a dry, barely audible murmuring, more a sensation of vertigo than a sound, the darkness swirling, becoming darker.

Luis turned up his collar as if signaling an unseen partner that now would be as good a time as any to intervene on his behalf, but there was no one to notice this subtle and yet strangely comic gesture (when viewed from afar) except the two shadowy figures already noted. Still, Luis did not panic. His manner was immaculate. He was wearing a beige herringbone blazer, which he often wore when he went out, no matter the temperature, a crisply ironed white shirt and a chartreuse tie and brown and beige saddle shoes to match the blazer. Nodding politely but casually (what some would interpret as blatant mockery) in the direction of the ferry building, Luis adjusted his grip on the Platt Guardsman suitcase and crossed San Pedro, heading down Santa Clara towards the old convent that had been converted into the Department of Public Works in the 1920s. He moved with the kind of athletic nonchalance that was a trademark of certain Hollywood heroes. The two shadows seemed to watch his crossing with great interest. Perhaps they were watching the suitcase, which was strangely visible in the darkness, as if it were glowing from within, as if it contained a fully operational miniature nuclear reactor or a laser-driven electromagnetic plasma gun capable of vaporizing a city block in seconds, a prototype in either case, naturally, developed by the Nazi's during the war and stolen in 1944 and smuggled out of Germany before it could be tested and turned into a secret weapon. Perhaps the dark men in their dark fedoras who were scattered all over the city were really after the suitcase. Who can say? Then without any warning at all (which is to say without taking one last long drag of their cigarettes and flicking the stubs to the pavement with anxious disgust, or shouting with indignant reproach and flashing their long-barreled rifles or Kongsberg Colt pistols in the air in dramatic fashion as they raced across the street, narrowly avoiding the oncoming traffic, as if guided by fate) the two shadows filled in behind Luis. They were perhaps thirty yards away, a distance they maintained with calm but rigid vigilance, neither gaining nor losing ground, no matter how slowly or quickly Luis walked.

On two occasions Luis stopped and turned around to look at them, partly to test their resolve, but also to make a show of his own cavalier indifference, a pose certainly, but only Luis knew this for a fact, and the two shadowy figures also stopped, but they turned towards each other, looking away from Luis as if they didn't care whether he existed or not, still smoking their cigarettes, chatting amiably in German, probably about Juan Manuel Fangio, the great Argentine automobile racer, who had won the German Grand Prix in August of that year, the climax of a distinguished career, and what a disappointing finish for Barth (who would win a few championships for Porsche in the years to come, but nothing like Fangio), good old Barth, the only German to finish in the top twelve, or perhaps they were talking about the lack of good German food in Havana, particularly Labskaus (a plate of mashed potatoes, beets, and corned beef, served with a fried egg, pickles, and pickled herring), which they sorely missed, or the diminishing prestige of owning a Jules Jürgensen watch, or how long before they could go home.

As Luis neared the convent it seemed less like the government building it had become and more like the convent it once was. Luis heard a strange sound, like water rushing from an exposed pipe or the furious beating of wings against the bars of a golden cage, but he could not tell where the sound came from. It seemed to be everywhere. And then it was nowhere, as if a spigot had been suddenly turned off or the caged bird had escaped and flown away or died trying. In the night sky above distant buildings Luis could see the streaming rockets and the smaller firecrackers and clouds of smoke, and from somewhere he could hear music. Then a crowd of students rushed past. Heading down Calle Cuba, away from the celebration, they talked of the vengeance of young love and bruised egos, their young voices draining away like molten lead across the cobblestones, dripping into the sewers, but Luis had already turned the corner. Then he stopped for a moment, why he could not say, and stared at the one-time convent on the other side of the street and the narrow oak door that had been closed off for years. Leaning back against a rough stone wall on his side of the street, Luis closed his eyes and listened to the rhythm of countless centuries flowing past. He did not hear anything remarkable, the music from the celebration, the distant fireworks like exploding suns, the young voices, yes, but no heavy footsteps echoing in the night, no German voices. He stood very still, listening intently, his breath coming in short, raspy bursts. He wondered if there were indeed two men following him, shadowing his every movement, or if he were trapped inside the hallucination of death. He could almost hear the blood rushing in his veins. Then the sounds of rushing water or flapping wings returned, but very faintly, an imperfect duplicate. He heard the weary voice of an old woman and the sobs of a young girl. He heard the sounds of a door opening and closing and light footsteps scurrying down the street in one direction and then a bevy of light footsteps rattling along in the other direction.

Luis realized he hadn't eaten anything in hours. He felt dizzy. A gnawing unease gripped him. He opened his eyes, half-expecting to see two shadowy figures with guns drawn, waiting for him to make a move, happy, remorseless grins plastered across their faces. But there were no shadowy figures, no guns. Instead he seemed to have wandered into a Clovis Trouille painting (*Dialogue au Carmel*, 1944). A huge group of revelers dressed as Carmelite nuns (except you could see they were wearing racy black nylons and no panties beneath cream-colored petticoats) were milling about the street, smoking cigarettes in erotic fashion and blowing steamy kisses to unseen lovers, as if they had been posing for a playfully sadistic painter for several hours and needed desperately to satisfy their animal urges, which had been restrained for far too long. Luis and all the other voyeurs of our collective imagination, all those trapped in the oblong shadows of time where pale fear dwells, were sly-nun-ogling and ding-dong-dangling. It was a worthy attempt to revive flagging spirits. Then all of a sudden, the nuns stopped blowing kisses and made their way en masse to the narrow oak door. One by one they slipped inside. There was a small iron lantern hanging just above the door, the lantern glowing orange against the apocryphal night and all human hate. Luis had never noticed the lantern before, but this was true of most who passed by the convent on their way to somewhere else. A couple of rockets tore across the sky. This was followed by the faint buzz of a tumultuous crowd cheering with great passion. He heard a rustling sound as if papers were being shuffled, and then the sounds of nuns saying their evening prayers (but whether these voices belonged to the costumed revelers he had just seen or were actual nuns he did not know). The light above the narrow oak door went out but immediately someone opened a window in the second-floor room above the door and turned on a small lamp.

From where Luis stood he could see a French Rococo salon mirror in the room, an odd fixture in an abandoned nunnery, the mirror oddly angled, gleaming with the opaque brilliance of another dimension. He could see a young girl reflected in the mirror. She was clearly experiencing some sort of unabated, emotional distress. Luis wondered if the two shadowy figures that had been following him were waiting for him to begin moving again or if he had somehow given them the slip when he turned the corner. Then the voices of the praying nuns faded into nothingness and the sound of the young girl sobbing, which had been humming along in the background the whole time, somewhat subdued, like static, became for the briefest of moments the only sound Luis heard or even remembered hearing. He could only see the young girl's passing reflection in her room above the door as she danced back and forth past the mirror of her grief, pouring forth her breathless lament because no one inside the abandoned convent heard her anguish, or if they did they did not know how to respond. Luis, who knew the language of tears better than most men, was immobilized by the crystalline purity of the girl's sad story even more than by her radiant, vulnerable beauty. She wept as we will all weep when the world splits in two and the end has finally arrived. Because love is the saddest thing when it goes away. Because love is unfathomable when one is wounded so deeply. Because in such moments love does not even truly exist.

The girl was wearing a plain white sleeveless dress trimmed with a bit of yellow lace, or perhaps it was an undergarment of some kind. Her darkly glowing hair was curled about her shoulders and she wore a peacock feather above her left ear. She had fallen in love with a young man who hailed from a great aristocratic family that had at some point acquired the shield of the Marquisate de Cañada. They had supposedly arrived in Cuba in 1746 when Diego Peñalosa was the acting governor (the very same year, coincidently, that the salon mirror described above had arrived in a shipment of goods from Barcelona but which had then disappeared from history until it was purchased in the Plaza del Vapor in 1841 by a Santería mystic, a friend of the young girl's grandmother, who lived outside of time and who believed that every mirror is a window to past lives and an oracle with the power to ease all pain). The young girl was herself the daughter of a slave and an unknown Spanish naval officer, at least this was the story her grandmother had told her time and again. But the young man did not care about her lack of pedigree and had pledged his eternal love one evening beneath the shimmering glow of a cloudless sky. They had taken a lover's stroll in the labyrinth of fragrant cobblestone pathways that was always and forever the Quinto de Molinos Botanical Gardens, unconcerned with any watchful eye that might be following their every movement. Believing in their heart of hearts that this was their wedding night, they slept in each other's arms in the soft darkness of a tamarind grove, though in truth they got very little sleep.

The next morning the young man told his new wife to

hurry home and pack her things and he would call on her later that afternoon and they would take a boat to Spain and so begin their new life. And she did hurry home, to a small hovel of an apartment in a collapsing tenement building on Cardenas, where her grandmother looked after her. But she never saw the young man again. At four in the afternoon an elegant but funereal black barouche with the hood pulled all the way forward arrived out front, the four black horses gleaming proudly in the sunlight, and a gaunt looking gentleman emerged and went inside. His driver waited. The young girl had been watching from the window and knew something was terribly wrong. When her grandmother opened the door, the old don motioned for her to fetch the young girl for he had something important if not profound to say, and then he pushed past the grandmother and sat down in a small rattan chair. But the grandmother did not move. She could not move. She collapsed in a puddle of anxiety and called out to her granddaughter to come quickly, and the young girl rushed to her grandmother and looked up at the gentleman, her eyes flashing with rage, for she assumed he had struck her grandmother with his ivory handled cane without even taking off his gloves, though why he would do this she did not know. (Of course in a symbolic sense the gaunt gentleman had indeed struck the old woman, but the blow had occurred years earlier.) Impatient to say what he had to say, he stood up and was about to open his mouth, but then the grandmother started wheezing and he was obliged to bring her a glass of water. She could barely hold the glass, and when she had finished, her wheezing had not improved, but she had enough strength left to embrace her granddaughter and whisper into her ear. 'This man is not to blame,' she said. 'Except in the way that all cruel and heartless men are to blame. He is your father. And he is also the father of this young man you have been seeing, your half-brother, by a woman born in Barcelona, not Cuba. Do not expect your father to help you.' And then the grandmother died and the old gentleman left in his elegant but funereal black barouche and the young girl knew she would never know love again. That was why she had sought refuge at the Convent of Santa Clara. She did not know where else to go. Then there was a flash in the mirror, the image of a fiery comet descending upon a doomed planet, and Luis saw the face of a world-weary nun appear in the window. Their eyes met and Luis felt a shuddering sense of shame and despair, though precisely why he only vaguely understood, so he looked away and the world began to spin and he felt he was spiraling down into the depths of the earth, but then almost immediately he looked back at the window, only it was now boarded up, just as it had been boarded up for years. The bout of vertigo had passed.

"Are you okay?" said a voice.

Luis blinked back a few tears and straightened himself against the stone wall that had been there for centuries. The stone was very rough. Luis had been leaning at an odd angle and his shoulder was numb.

"Yes, yes, I am fine."

"You are sure?"

The voice belonged to a woman dressed as a flamingo. She was with two young men, one dressed as a Jesuit priest and the other as a Taíno chieftain, perhaps the great Hatuey himself. They all seemed genuinely concerned. But Luis was looking past the woman and her companions to the corner where Santa Clara intersected Calle Cuba, and sure enough, the two shadowy figures who had been on his tail since the ferry building were rounding the corner that very instant. They were waving Kongsberg Colt pistols in the air in disjointed fashion and running pell-mell, as if they had thought Luis was trying to escape, but when they rounded the corner and saw Luis surrounded by the three festival-goers, they abruptly but smoothly changed gears, slipping their guns into their coat pockets and walking quickly to the other side of the street. They stopped in a pool of darkness in front of the narrow oak door and the lantern that hadn't been lit for more than thirty years. They stared mutely at Luis but with unwavering intensity, as if daring him to abandon the relative safety of his side of the street. They were also most likely trying to assess if the flamingo and the other two were a chance meeting or if they perhaps worked for Luis. If you didn't know they were there you would have seen nothing but a gleaming, glowing fluid darkness. If you didn't know they were there you might have thought a black hole had begun eating away at the fading dream that was Cuba.

"So you are heading to the Plaza?" said Luis.

But there was now boyish laughter in his voice, as if he had acquired a second wind. Or the notion of destiny was a mere word and so was easily discarded. Or history was repeating itself so he knew what to expect. Or Luis was perhaps one of those rare individuals who could laugh in the face of certain death, which was not as far-fetched as it might have seemed to those who knew him. For what is death really but one more mask?

"Yes we are," said the flamingo. She stepped closer to Luis, smiling a fluid, flirtatious smile. "Can't you tell?"

She twirled around for show, an extravagant pirouette, her feathers fluttering in the sudden breeze and the flashing curve of plush brown cheeks.

The Jesuit priest and the Taíno chieftain said nothing. It was not clear if this was because they had nothing to add or if they now perceived Luis as a rival.

"Let's go," said the flamingo.

She grabbed hold of Luis' free arm, laughing and twittering with coquettish delight, her flamingo feathers fluttering some more as they headed towards the sounds of the celebration. The Jesuit priest and the Taíno chieftain fell in step directly behind.

Once again the two shadowy figures on the other side of the street followed their quarry with rigid vigilance. But they were not as calm as before, not as symmetric in their stubbornness, not as sure of themselves, so they kept chattering back and forth in guttural whispers, two wayward Teutonic knights on the edge of an underwater forest, stifling the urge to run away because it suddenly felt like they were out of their element, their hands ready to plunge into their coat pockets and pull out their pistols if need be and to hell if there were any witnesses. But they did not pull out their guns.

The streets became more crowded and there was a great deal of jostling elbows in every direction but no punches were thrown.

Luis and the others passed by a police barricade without incident. The flamingo was laughing uproariously. She could not help herself she was so happy. Her happiness seemed to infect everyone around her, the Jesuit priest, the Taíno chieftain, even Luis. Then a few voices cried out from the other side of the street, but they were not the voices of the two shadowy figures, who were still traveling in liquid darkness, slipping in and out of the shadowy cracks between buildings. The owners of the new voices were friends of the flamingo (who quite honestly was very well known and had a good word for everyone, even the police).

"You had already left," they said.

"We started out early," said the flamingo.

"But we didn't wait around," they said. "We knew where you were going."

Laughter. Hugs. Warm embraces. A soft cushy squeeze.

"We brought wine," they said.

They held up bags presumably containing wine.

"But we didn't bring any glasses."

"We don't need glasses," said the flamingo. "We can pass around the bottles. Just like old times."

"Ah, but can we do that at our age?"

"Speak for yourself Valerio!"

"Yes, Valerio. Tonight we will live only in the moment!"

"Is there any other way to live?"

"Tonight age does not matter."

"Bravo, bravo!"

"Tonight time itself will stand still."

"Yes, time is an illusion."

"At least until the morning."

"And then we will pay for it," said Valerio.

"Yes," said the flamingo. "Just like old times."

More laughter.

It was almost like singing.

No one noticed that Luis was clutching a Platt Guardsman suitcase, or if they did they didn't care.

The newcomers were also dressed in a variety of exotic costumes; a black jaguar, even though there were no jaguars in Cuba, two devils with twitching tails and pitchforks (plenty of those), a Spanish Conquistador, the great goddess Atabey, a dark serpent with the crest of an iguana, and several unknown or forgotten or perhaps extinct species of plumed birds. Everyone drank wine while they walked. They crumpled up the empty bags and tossed them to the ground. They tossed the empty bottles into the gutters and the bottles broke and they laughed and their laughter sounded like breaking glass. They were only a block from the Plaza. They passed by jugglers and acrobats. They passed by a second police barricade but the officers were busy listening to a musical trio on the corner — the beating of a conga drum and the strumming of a guitar and husky voices singing. It was becoming more and more difficult to communicate, unless one could do so telepathically. The music of the trio on the corner was replaced by another group of musicians standing beneath the awning of a small café further up the street. As if they were all reading from the same script (even Luis), they became a conga line, weaving their way from side to side, the glow of the festival now lighting up the sky, a great golden bubble of light coloring the buildings and the cobblestone streets and the great stone Cathedral itself, as if Havana truly was and always had been the fabled city of gold that the Spanish and those who believed in the dream of the Americas were always seeking.

Luis could no longer see the two men from the ferry building so he hoped for the best.

They entered the Plaza and were immediately consumed by the happy, restless crowd. The music of dozens of competing groups was swirling above their heads like a cloud. It became difficult to breath. It became difficult to see. No one was sure what they were looking at. Luis scanned the sea of bobbing heads. Here and there he spotted men wearing dark fedoras. Their long-barreled rifles sticking up out of this mass of humanity were a dead giveaway. The men were gliding back and forth in seemingly random fashion. Luis counted half a dozen. That made at least eight if you counted the other two.

The impromptu conga line disintegrated, pushed apart by the swelling, surging, shimmering crowd. Luis felt the hand of the woman dressed as a flamingo slip from his fingers. The flamingo and the Jesuit priest and the Taíno chieftain went in one direction, towards the south end of the Plaza, the black jaguar and the Conquistador and the others were pushed towards the Cathedral steps. They were all calling out to one another but their voices were lost in the festival din. Luis somehow remained in the center of this swirling circle. The flamingo called out to him and waved, a tiny dot in the distance. She blew Luis a kiss, and then she was swallowed whole.

Luis noticed that the seemingly random movements of the men in dark fedoras, who held their rifles in a rigid upright position at all times, were not so random. They were methodically canvassing the Plaza, crisscrossing this sea of restless, costumed faces, an invisible net, a tightening noose. Every once in a while they looked up at each other and nodded and smiled savage, sinister smiles. They no longer needed to use language to communicate. They seemed to be part of an alien race dedicated to crushing all hope, especially hope in the hereafter. They seemed to be tuned to the same radio frequency and thus moved about with mechanical, robotic precision. They were not about to squander this night's opportunity.

Luis kept his eyes focused on his own emerging path across the Plaza. A rocket tore across the sky and the crowd cheered and the men in dark fedoras looked up at the sky for a moment, a look of sudden surprise registering in their collective eyes, giving Luis a chance to slip through. But it didn't matter. He was hoping to head along Empedrado towards the park and the tamarind grove, but there were several men in fedoras closing in from the west, cutting across the Plaza with an unexpected urgency, cutting off his path of escape. They did not see him, but surely they sensed he was close by.

Luis turned on his heels and quite by accident found himself heading straight for the very same cart where he had bought a lemon-filled *pastelito* oh so many hours before. Of course Luis noticed this second unexpected coincidence, how could he not, but there was nothing to be done about it.

The cart with its white umbrella rising up towards the stars which were barely visible seemed like a small boat riding a rough sea, an oasis on the waves.

The man who had sold Luis the pastelito was gone. A young woman had replaced him, his wife perhaps, or perhaps his daughter. Luis thought this was a lucky break. The woman was very pretty. She was prettier than she had a right to be. "We have nothing left," she said, and she smiled at Luis, an apologetic smile that was also very becoming.

-96-

The tiny trap doors and sliding panels on the top and the sides of the vending cart had been closed and secured. Luis laid his suitcase on top and put his arms around the young woman. He began whispering into her ear and she giggled and laughed and blushed as appropriate and pretended to push Luis away. The intimate secrets they shared during this initial conversation were immediately forgotten, but the emotions roused by the sharing of those secrets remained, at least as far as the young woman was concerned, an eternal flame bubbling erratically but with miraculous persistence in the midst of a strong wind.

"Perhaps you wish to take me to the movies?" she said.

"Yes," Luis said. "That would be nice. But it is too late for that."

"Perhaps it is," she said.

And then: "But perhaps not. Come with me. I know a place. I will show you."

Together they took hold of the handles of the cart, the young woman gingerly but hopefully, Luis full of purpose but seemingly without hope, and pushed their way slowly through the cheering, swirling, mesmerized crowd. They left the white umbrella in its upright position, but slightly tilted, so they could move without being seen, except for their hips and their legs, which were clearly visible beneath the umbrella fringe.

Under any other circumstances, the fact that the umbrella remained in its upright position would have aroused suspicion, but on this, the first night of the celebration in honor of the Feast Day of Saint Christopher, it went unnoticed, except as one might notice the changing configurations of a cloud or a flock of birds suddenly taking wing or a tiny boat floundering on the horizon.

Beneath the umbrella, Luis heard the song of an empty heart beating. He was convinced that each pair of footsteps that went rushing past were the footsteps of the men wearing dark fedoras. He expected that at any moment these men would descend upon the cart, toppling their chances, and both he and the young woman would die in a hail of bullets. But this did not happen.

Luis was able to keep the cart moving (a minor miracle) because he was somewhat detached from what was happening, a spectator to the movie of his life unfolding, or at least this most recent portion of his life. It was not perhaps the movie the young woman had alluded to. Then again, perhaps it was. For Luis, this thrilling escape sequence began with a spectacular wide angle camera shot, a dramatic, heart-pounding aerial view, as if he were hovering in the darkly glowing stratosphere just above the Cathedral clock tower, suspended by wires he had never noticed before and that one never notices except during times of great duress.

He saw a small white umbrella floating casually, precipitously, in the sea of dark bobbing heads. The umbrella was moving slowly towards the shadows south of the Plaza.

The dark bobbing heads were illuminated at various times by sulphurous streaking rockets and exploding firecrackers, or by the irresistible golden bubble glow of the festival lights that had been strung this way and that, random, crisscrossing patterns, or by the blazing air-raid searchlights that swept back and forth across the facade of the Cathedral instead of the dark (and also darkening) skies above, the light bouncing off the Cathedral and descending upon the crowd, wave after wave after wave.

The umbrella, by way of contrast, was a constant luminous death-mask white.

Luis saw the men in their fedoras rushing all around the white umbrella, but always on their way to some other part of the Plaza. Never once did they think to look beneath the umbrella. From somewhere Luis heard the dark exotic timbre of Dizzy Gillespie's *Night in Tunisia* (the 1942 version), a fast-paced yet soulful romp — bass strings plucking, discordant, surreal, muted horns blaring, ringing bells, snare drums rattling, the haunting clarity of a lonely saxophone, an inevitable, inexorable, mythic movement that seemed to lift you up suddenly and swiftly from the shadows of an alleyway into the bright glaring neon blues and greens and purples of a busy city boulevard and the nightlife hissing and crackling, and then just as swiftly depositing you back in the shadows, the tension mounting with every passing second — all of which matched the relentless, frenetic mood of the dozens of men in their dark fedoras chasing after their own tails, all of them looking to clean someone's clock, eager to display their killer's instinct for all to see, and the joyful fatalism of a seemingly invulnerable Luis, who with each step became more and more convinced that he and the girl were about to slip away clean, their clocks intact.

Then Luis saw the white umbrella reaching the edge of the Plaza and the heaving darkness just beyond the glow of the festival lights, the crowd thinning at that point, less exuberant, the dark jazz of Dizzy Gillespie fading to nothingness, the immediate danger of the men in their dark fedoras receding like the blood-filled tide of an ancient sea, the kind of tide that might leave behind the bodies of countless dead sea creatures. And then the danger was gone, the grace of God fully implemented, as far as anyone could reasonably infer, a temporary fix most assuredly, but sufficient for the time being.

The luminous white umbrella slowly disintegrated, vanishing into the grainy haze of a dimly lit street, though precisely which street and which direction the umbrella went Luis was unable to say, for he was suffering once again from the sensation of vertigo, perhaps from looking down from so great a height.

It is also worth noting that the entire time Luis and the young woman were huddled beneath the white umbrella, pushing the cart through the crowd, the young woman was chattering away. She did not fully appreciate the danger they were in, which annoyed Luis to no end, and which probably added to his returning sense of vertigo. But she was young and her brain was as empty as the eternal sky except for the words that came bubbling up out of her mouth. She said her name was Elisa and she lived with her brother. He had given her the cart for the evening because he wanted to enjoy the festivities, a sinful, profligate brother if there ever was one, she said, a dark, wayward soul. Then she looked at Luis and giggled but Luis wasn't paying any attention to her. She said her brother wouldn't be home until well after daylight broke, if he came home at all. And this thought did register with Luis, but only as a distant blip, a vague memory.

Then she said she had seen Luis before. She mentioned the names of some of the clubs she frequented and how she had always admired Luis, who was not like the rest of the men she saw at the clubs. "Those boorish louts," she called them, as if she had lifted the words from a cheap romance novel. But all Luis could think at that moment was how could this girl have spotted him in any club, he was never spotted, no one ever knew where he was or where he was going. But then he laughed to himself, a soft, grave, rolling laughter, thoughtful laughter, almost inaudible. Because that was obviously not true. Because someone had known where he was going to be at various points throughout the entire day. Some strange, unfathomable clairvoyant had been able to sneak a peek inside the dark corridors of his imagination, his unvarnished soul, if you will, and lay traps for him.

Now his fate and the fate of the Platt Guardsman suitcase depended upon the good will and naiveté of a beautiful young woman who couldn't shut up and who was leading him only God knew where. And in that very moment the young woman said "We're here," and 'here' turned out to be a narrow art deco tenement that was blue or aquamarine where the street lamps cast their beaded raindrops of light, but a shimmering dark gray everywhere else, except for the heavy black translucence of a series of porthole windows rising up towards the clouds, and a darkly gleaming bronze panel directly above the polished front steps with a series of smaller oblong panels protruding from either side, one on top of the other, a singular work of art that seemed like some weird insignia (sinister, ominous, prophetic, otherworldly, vaguely Egyptian), a symbolic (coded?) representation of eagle's wings or some other large bird of prey. A warning perhaps to future generations. A prophecy once known to only a few now visible for the whole world to see. Unrestrained in its daring. But who can say?

Luis and the young woman pushed the cart through a small archway along the side of the building and down a narrow path and stopped before an iron gate and a few bicycles shoved against the wall. The gate was unlocked and led to a set of stairs and the dim almost subterranean glow of a single lantern hanging from a chain. The young woman trembled, an involuntary betrayal of her wild and uninhibited imagination, and a glimpse of those lurid and generally unattainable delights which are the spur to oh so many unsolved crimes. Her breathless anticipation was a warm breeze blowing through Luis' empty heart. So he accepted his destiny, whatever lay in store. The two of them left the cart with the bicycles and pushed their way through the gate and hurried inside.

-97-

Inside the art deco tenement:

The building had been newly restored, the suites newly refurbished. Polished marble floors. Newly painted plaster walls that seemed to glow in the dark, a soft golden glow. The walls had been seemingly painted by a victim of dementia. They were a blank canvass that had been filled with unsettling geometric patterns from the fifth dimension, a nightmare landscape that may or may not have been designed by the Dutch painter Piet Mondrian (or perhaps a deranged disciple) in a last ditch effort to imprison God before he died (or keep Him out), a landscape without any meaningful narrative whatsoever composed entirely of rectangular staircase patterns (patterns which had in fact never shown up in a Mondrian painting) collapsing inward towards nonexistence or expanding outward towards infinity, patterns which would bring about intolerable headaches if you stared at them in bright sunlight. Opaque crystal wall lamps clinging like ice gave off a cool, blue liquid light like music (no doubt to mitigate the impact of the fifth-dimension geometry). The doors to each room or suite of rooms were made of a rich, dark mahogany. The rooms themselves featured mahogany furniture to match the doors and were decorated with cool crisp greens and blues and deep dark browns and other earth tones. Narrow, frosted-glass, floor-to-ceiling windows in thin mahogany frames opened up onto narrow balcony ledges with freshly painted railings. The balconies were too narrow to stand on. If you opened a window the smell of fresh mint instantly filled the room, even on a rainy, alcoholic day

The luxurious though decidedly futuristic atmosphere appealed to Luis' sense of vanity, his secret belief that not only did he deserve a better fate than the plebian masses, but that he was destined to live forever. But how was it that an obscure, nameless vendor and his sister could afford to live in such a place? Luis did not seem even remotely concerned with this anomaly or the sinister implications it exposed.

Fast forward a few frames:

Luis and the young woman had been fucking for hours but they were finished. The young woman was sprawled across a king-sized bed (also mahogany), the satin sheets in a rumpled mess on the floor revealing the bare mattress, a ceiling fan rotating above her with mind-numbing, cruel regularity. She was in a semi-comatose state, snoring softly, her naked body gleaming in the darkness, almost cadaver-like.

Luis was sitting up against the headboard, contemplating her nakedness, her ghostly pale elastic whiteness. She seemed less beautiful than she did before. Not just because they had had sex. Her loss of beauty went deeper than that. Luis crawled closer and examined her with clinical detachment. She was far skinnier than she had appeared at the festival, thin-boned like a bird, and she had no hips to speak of, no curves of any kind. Her dark hair framed her face nicely, and her pouty lips suggested a fullness of spirit that was exceptionally erotic. But her teeth were crooked and her eyes seemed like sunken craters in the dim light. Without her clothes to hide her obvious deformities, she resembled an abused corpse that had been tossed into a narrow ditch with a jumble of bodies all twisted and broken and covered with lime and then earth and then recently dug up, or someone who had barely escaped death in a Nazi concentration camp, or a strangled marionette, any one of these more than a warm-blooded girl. She was a withering, shredded, fragment of a ghost wandering through the neon blue corridors of time, that was how Luis suddenly perceived her.

He went over to the portable record player on the small unadorned mahogany table opposite the giant bed. The girl had put on a record when they first arrived, before they started tearing off each other's clothes in the diffuse, bluish light. The music had stopped a while ago but the record was still spinning, the steady mechanical whirring of static to match the rotation of the ceiling fan. Luis flipped the record over and jazz like a swelling sea filled the room, a sound both familiar and otherworldly, as if it were originating in an underwater cavern and slowly bubbling up to the surface.

He listened to the jazz for a while.

He stood before the record player, watching the disc spin, listening to the jazz, still partially erect, thinking about the girl on the bed. In spite of her now withered, skeletal appearance, the memory of the young woman as a beautiful sex goddess lingered in his imagination. The sex had been quite good, nothing like making love to Nerea, but it had been good sex nevertheless, full of acrobatic maneuvers and back-wrenching explosions.

Luis felt no guilt over his lack of genuine human compassion for the girl. Instead he felt a degree of calm he had not experienced in quite a while. He felt more in control, even though he knew being in control was a placebo one offered oneself, an illusion. Like religion. Like God. Yes, he thought, the sex had been quite good. He could still taste the girl on the tip of his tongue. What had excited him the most was that she had totally surrendered her body to his every whim. She had been his to command, a rag doll he could break again and again if he chose and she wouldn't cry out, not even a whimper, as if she had been placed under hypnosis by German mesmerists so they could conduct strange experiments in a basement laboratory. So Luis had not noticed her thin, shapeless ass, her pale almost translucent skin like fine parchment. He had been blind to her flaws (as he had been blind to other things). His freedom to do with her as he wished had become the ultimate aphrodisiac.

But something had happened between then and now. The dark mirror had once again been placed over the open grave. The portals to the other dimensions had been smashed. And in the vacuum of his utter isolation, Luis realized he had fucked this woman because of Nerea. Because he had abandoned Nerea only because he had become bored, and Nerea had abandoned him in return. Because the hopes of earlier days had become a meteorite exploding in the upper stratosphere, which is what happens to everyone's hopes, eventually, and now there was no going back. This is what he was thinking as he looked at the young woman sprawled across the bed, the sound of the jazz shape-shifting, becoming a slow, mournful sound now, a lazy current, a quiet bleeding out of all emotion, the light from the unreachable stars now speeding away at a fantastic rate towards nothingness. Then the young woman stirred. She sighed and rolled over but did not wake up. The bluish light from the wall lamps washed over her skin and gave her a slightly scaly, reptilian sheen that was repulsive to look at, and yet for a fleeting moment she became beautiful again, strangely beautiful, an alien beauty.

Luis could not get over her strange, alien beauty.

He went over to the window and opened it a crack and looked down at the street. He breathed in the smell of fresh mint. It had begun to rain so it was difficult to see. The world outside had become distorted, a weaving blur of background noise, the moisture of the storm spurting through the crack in short bursts, a spitting cannonade of moisture, and Luis was about to close the window when he caught a shadow of movement beneath a dimly glowing streetlamp on the other side of the street. He could see the outlines of two men staring up at the window, as if they had been waiting for the window to open since before the rain had started.

Luis stared at the two shadowy outlines, the men all but obscured by the rain and the darkness. It seemed for a moment like they were taking a shower together, and Luis was struck by the absurdity of the image. Then one of the shadows seemed to incline his head, a nod of understanding, perhaps, or one of futile apology, but the gesture seemed out of place, absurd, sinister and yet friendly, a scripted bit of irony. Then the two men retreated from the light and there was a sharp popping sound and the streetlamp went out. But Luis knew they were still there, waiting patiently in the darkness.

The sound of the jazz had become static again.

The rain was coming down much harder than before and the darkness was trembling. It hadn't rained this hard in months. Luis closed the window and took a few steps towards the record player, the fresh mint smell still lingering in the air, and it was only then that he realized the girl was no longer on the bed. She was standing beside the bed now. She had placed his suitcase on the bare mattress and had rifled through its contents, discovering in the process the false bottom. Dozens of one-hundred dollar bills were scattered about, spilling out of the suitcase, dripping down the side of the bed towards the polished mahogany floor, but the young woman was not interested in the money. She was pointing a gun directly at Luis, her eyes fixed on his, relentless, probing eyes without even a glimmer of paranoia or artificial kindness, as if she were trying to catch a glimpse of his soul, as if she were trying to decide if he was the reincarnation of the Egyptian god Amun-Ra, or just another parasitic, sex-starved bum she had pulled off the street who deserved to die a brutal and ignominious death, but she needed to look into the depraved, neon glare of his soul to be sure. But the gun was not hers. The gun, a single action Modèle 1935 pistol, belonged to Luis. It was an elegant weapon, mostly for show, a relic, a curio, which Luis carried in a shoulder holster whenever he went out to the clubs. He did not remember bringing the gun along that day. But there was his empty shoulder holster draped over his beige herringbone blazer, which was draped over a lonely looking chair pulled out from the wall. And there was his gun.

Fortunately for Luis, the young woman was unfamiliar with the Modèle 1935 pistol. Or at least she was unfamiliar with the drawbacks of a slide mounted safety. Or maybe her thumb just wasn't long enough. Or she was still half asleep and didn't realize the safety was engaged. At any rate, when she flexed her firing hand and pulled the trigger, nothing happened. Which is to say that the gun did not fire as she had expected (hoped? prayed?). Naturally she looked at the disobedient (unresponsive? malfunctioning?) pistol as if it had violated the laws of physics. It was only for a split second, mind you, an involuntary reaction to be sure, and quite understandable. But a split second can be an eternity. Plenty of time for Luis to turn the tables. Immediately he disappeared, a chameleon becoming one with the dappled blue darkness, his image reappearing for the briefest of moments in first one window and then another, and so on down the line, a shimmering, passing reflection with no substance, like an echo. Then he disappeared altogether.

She whirled her shooting arm first one way and then another, trying to anticipate his next move, but she could not locate him. She felt the universe collapsing, her universe anyway. She did, however, manage to release the safety. After all, she only needed one clear shot. Then she felt his breath on her neck and she realized it was too late. He had grabbed hold of her from behind, a wrestler's embrace, with one arm reaching across her neck, pulling her close, and the other slipping around her waist, his hand twisting up towards her face and then latching on to the gun. She had tried to slip away. She had spun the moment she felt his body press against hers. But she would not let go of the pistol and so her movement was checked.

If one did not know any better, one might have thought they were engaged in a strange, primitive, ritualistic mating dance. Every step seemed carefully choreographed. Faces glowing like deranged but easily manipulated puppets. Hands folded as if in prayer, the barrel of the pistol pointing skywards. Lips almost touching, scarcely a whisper apart. Luis looked at her, his eyes burrowing deeply into hers, as if to ask her what did she think she was doing, and her eyes flickered in response, a sultry, haughty reply, did he think she was a flower that would simply bend in the breeze, the two of them spinning around the gun in stark counterpoint to the spinning ceiling fan above, their hips swiveling in the dim bluish light, their eyes locked in telepathic misery, their faces contorting wildly, passionately, in weird angst-ridden grimaces, their thoughts an incomprehensible mishmash of clichéd phrases from old movies, if you needed some money all you had to was ask, don't do me any favors big boy I can take of myself, if it's not the money then what is it you want, did I ask you what you wanted big boy, no you didn't, then you can wipe that smug look off your face, look I'm sorry, it's too late for that big boy, if you want me to go I'll go, it's too late for that either, but it doesn't have to be that way, sure it does big boy, but why, because we do not believe in half measures, sure baby, because once we release the hounds there is no stopping us, and with a violent upsurge of rage and self-loathing she tried to jerk free the pistol, but she did not realize that they had danced themselves into the corner near the row of windows. She jerked back but immediately convulsed forwards and the gun went off, a straight clean shot soaring up through the pale white elasticity of her chin, through the arched roof of her mouth and out the back of her skull.

It was hard to say who had pulled the trigger, but the trigger had been pulled nevertheless.

Her fingers slid back, releasing the gun. A few drops of blood gurgled down her neck, a faint blush of color dripping down, spreading across her breasts. Then she slid down along the wall, withdrawing into herself, no longer impatient, a white ribbon crumpling to the floor, a flash of light vanishing in the darkness. There was blood splatter on the wall and bits of skull. Luis was surprised by how much blood there was. She had seemed so pale, so drained of blood. But there she was now, a crumpled-up white ribbon floating in a pool of darkly gleaming molten lead.

He lingered over the dead body only a moment. All of his senses were keenly alert. He stepped to one side of the nearest window and opened it a crack to see if anyone had heard the shot. It was the same window he had opened earlier. Once again he breathed in the smell of fresh mint. He wondered how the smell could be so powerful with all of this rain, this endless, merciless rain. He wondered if he had ever felt so alive, but he could not remember a time. He scanned up and down the street but saw nothing. Then a car turned the corner, moving past the row of darkened tenements, its headlights glowing with underwater brilliance, and stopped roughly parallel to the dead streetlamp. Luis thought the car resembled a 1937 Packard and laughed, a slight, incredulous laugh, but he could not be sure. The car seemed to generate a small bubble of light with just its presence, but it was a hazy, diffuse light which made it virtually impossible to determine the car's precise make and model. All one could do was guess.

The car's engine hummed for a while but nobody got out. Then it flicked its headlights twice and the two shadowy outlines from before emerged from the absolute darkness of a hidden doorway. Someone rolled down a window and the two shadowy heads leaned into the car. One of the shadowy heads kept popping back up. The head seemed to be looking straight at Luis every time, as if he (it?) needed to make sure that Luis was still there. Then the head would pop back down.

Most men would have been desperate to escape. They would have grown weary of peering into the darkness, trying to eavesdrop on a conversation that never took place because these people did not exist. The streaming rain would have taken on the quality of prison bars. Panic would have ensued. Fatal mistakes would have been committed. But Luis was not given over to such mundane emotions. He stood at the window a while longer, watching, waiting. The one shadowy outline popped up again and again, almost with the regularity of a clock. Then Luis noticed a steady parade of shadowy figures emerging from other hidden doorways, all of them drawn to the 1937 Packard idling in the middle of the rain-drenched street.

Then the other shadowy figure, the one who had been leaning his head inside the car window the whole time, popped up and glanced at the encroaching shadows. It might have been a glance of warning. But more likely it was a glance which meant: 'hold on, be patient, there's nothing anyone can do in a rain like this, back to your doorways, we'll take care of things in the morning, he isn't going anywhere.' Given the intensity of the rain it was only natural that the message was slightly garbled. Some of the ones who were nearer the car tapped their ears as if to clear away the static of the universe and then they understood and returned to their hiding places. But those who were further away tapped their ears inconclusively and shook their heads, as if to say whatever listening devices that had been implanted near their cochleas were not working (presumably these were strange, futuristic devices that had been implanted by an aging French physician, originally from the town of Villefranche-sur-Saône, who had had his license revoked years earlier for undisclosed crimes and so was now living on the outskirts of Algiers, where he would perform any operation you wanted for a small sum, no questions asked).

The other shadowy figure, who seemed to be more or less in charge of everything on the street, began making a series of bizarre, convoluted gestures with his hands, a sort of impromptu sign language spurred on by the necessity of instructing those with the possibly defective implants to try a different frequency. One by one those furthest away began turning the dials of electro-magnetic frequency modulators hidden away in semi-secret, interior pockets in the lining of their jackets. One by one they found the correct frequency and then they understood what was expected of them. One by one they tapped their ears or gave the thumbs up sign and retreated into the shadows. All in all, Luis counted two dozen pairs of shadowy figures taking refuge in dark doorways along the street and in narrow crevices that had sprouted up between various buildings over time. This was not counting the two original shadowy figures or the mysterious occupants of the car, who remained hidden from view.

Luis was always a fascinating enigma. He never did what others would do. Satisfied that he was in no danger until the morning, he retreated from the window. But danger of a sort still lurked within the dark cavities of this luxury apartment on the top floor of this unnamed art deco tenement hidden away in the crumbling eternal poverty of Old Havana, somewhere close to the harbor, on a small mostly deserted side-street that did not exist on any map and had never existed as far as the city fathers were concerned.

Quite all of a sudden, Luis noticed a steady, shallow rustling-slash-clicking sound, as if some animal were trapped inside the walls. He crawled back onto the bed, and for the first time he noticed a rounded aperture directly above the headboard. The aperture contained a rounded lens like a glass bauble which resembled upon first glance a recessed light of some sort. But it was not a light. Luis put his eye to the lens and the rustling-slash-clicking sound stopped. The dark, gleaming curvature of the lens made it impossible to see what lay behind it. All Luis could see was a circle of glassy darkness and in the center of the circle there was a faint, opaque glow, like a supernova from a galaxy a billion light years away, and then the galaxy became a giant, expanding eyeball that pushed itself to the edges of the glass, swallowing all light, and then the giant eyeball disappeared and there was a sudden explosion of light from the lens, a blinding flash that sent Luis reeling backwards onto the mattress, momentarily blind but otherwise unharmed, and though he wasn't certain what had happened, he still had the presence of mind to roll off the bed, landing on his feet, his gun ready.

Even as Luis rolled off the bed, the strange sound started up again, only it was louder, and it had become more of a sliding-slash-banging-slash-thudding sound now, as if the weasel or hedgehog or whatever it was trapped within the walls had given up all pretense of hiding and was now, in a fit of madness, making a break for it. Luis followed this new sound out of the bedroom and down a long hallway that opened up into a rounded foyer with additional hallways jutting off in all directions.

Without warning, a narrow mahogany door that Luis had not noticed before burst open. It seemed like a door to a coat closet, or maybe to one of those secret wine rooms you always hear about, or maybe to a set of stairs that led to the roof. A wiry, bluish shadow rushed out into the foyer. That was pretty much all Luis could see, for his eyesight had not yet returned to normal. But he could see well enough to coldcock whatever it was, which he did using his pistol. The wiry, bluish shadow tumbled to the floor without resistance and did not move.

Luis pulled up a chair and sat down, one eye on the unmoving shape at his feet, the other on the open door, just in case there were any more surprises. He started humming a few bars of one of the jazz songs from before to amuse himself. It was a popular tune, but he couldn't quite remember the rest so he gave up.

He stared at the darkly gleaming passage beyond the open door for a while, how long he could not say. It seemed to him a passageway to an unimaginable dimension, or alternately, the long-forgotten entrance to the tombs of the Hetaerae, those concubines of ancient Greece who had once been riverbeds teeming with life.

-98-

An hour or so before dawn:

Everything in the room was the same, except Luis was dressed, immaculate as always, his Platt Guardsman suitcase on the floor next to the chair, and the wiry bluish shadow had become a middle-aged man wearing a pair of pleated dress pants with no belt, a pair of cheap rope sandals, and a wrinkled orange-colored sports shirt, a pastel orange like those painted sunsets you see decorating the stages of those nameless, cheesy cabarets along San Martin.

Luis recognized him as the man who had sold him the lemon-filled pastelito in the Plaza. He was the older brother of the dead girl in the bedroom. Yes, that made sense. It was obvious now that he had been posing as a vendor. He had dark, sullen eyes and dark, leathery skin from too much time in the Cuban sun and a matte of stringy blond hair streaked with gray. He wore some sort of medallion around his neck that gleamed a cold, dark blue, as if it were the underbelly of an alien spacecraft lifting off from the earth.

"It hurts, doesn't it," said Luis.

The man didn't respond. He was half-crouching on the polished mahogany floor, leaning forward on his knees as if immersed in prayerful mediation, rocking slowly side to side, not really chanting, it was more of a steady moaning sound, his hands cupping the back of his head, the pose of someone who has recently found God, laying bare the sins of a lifetime.

"That sharp, spine-shattering pain will go away in a little while," said Luis. "But you'll probably be sore for days."

The man rolled and sat back on his haunches and looked up at Luis with a well-worn expression of incredulity, shading his eyes with his hands as if he were suddenly sitting in a pool of bright searing sunshine instead of the blue dappled darkness where he found himself.

Luis started to chuckle.

He could hardly contain himself.

"Of course a blow like that sometimes affects the memory. I've known guys who couldn't remember a thing for weeks. I'm not saying that's what going on with you. In fact for your sake I sincerely hope that's not the case."

Luis was motioning with his gun while he talked. The casual, charming indifference with which he carried on seemed to magnify his sinister intentions. All the middle-aged brother could do was stare at the gun. Then Luis grew very serious and leaned forward slightly as if he had a great secret he wished to share.

"Do you believe in the law of seriality?" he said after a while.

The middle-aged brother said nothing. The look of incredulity on his face had been replaced with a look of pious despair that could just as easily have been mistaken for the unbidden fear that accompanies a sudden flash of debilitating and previously unknown pain.

"I have been reading a slim book by a forgotten intellectual named Paul Kammerer. He is German, like yourself, though he lived in Austria. The book is called *Das Gesetz der*

Serie. My German is not so good, so it has been taking me a long time. But the book was published in 1919, the same year I was born, so I just had to read it, you understand. Besides, it is not without merit. Kammerer believed that there was no such thing as coincidences, that hidden beneath the surface of everyday occurrences there existed a pattern which could be deciphered. He would stand on a street corner taking note of what people were carrying, and from these simple observations he said he could deduce the mechanics of the Universe. Naturally I had to test out his theory. Why just the other day I was taking note of how many pedestrians were carrying umbrellas and how many were carrying walking sticks with fancy brass ornamental heads and how many were wearing Tyrolean hats. I was standing on a random street corner the way Kammerer himself used to do, keeping a tally of every umbrella and every walking stick and every hat I saw, and there weren't any umbrellas, it was a very hot, sunny day, so why would there be any umbrellas. And there weren't any Tyrolean hats either. But there were seventeen men walking around with fancy walking sticks with ornamental brass heads. The next day I went back to the same street corner and there were two dozen pedestrians wearing Tyrolean hats, what you and I would naturally call fedoras. And there were two dozen more carrying umbrellas, which was absurd because that particular day was just as bright and sunny and hot as the day before, yet two dozen people were scurrying about with umbrellas. The walking sticks, of course, had vanished. There were no walking sticks at all. There were men with umbrellas, and men wearing hats, and some of the men wearing the hats were also carrying umbrellas, which I found suspicious. And that brings me to the present. Today I have been seeing men in fedoras everywhere I have gone, but the walking sticks they were carrying that first day and the umbrellas they were carrying that second day have been transformed. They have metamorphosed into long-barreled rifles. And tonight it is raining and there is not a single umbrella to be seen anywhere. Say what you will, but this all seems odd to me. Doesn't it seem odd to you? Tonight it is raining. All hell has broken lose, you could say. And everywhere you look, all over Havana, no matter where you go in this wretched garden of good and evil, there are men in fedoras with long-barreled rifles scrambling about like rats in a maze. But no umbrellas. No doubt all of this would seem to the untrained observer to be the very definition of chaos. But to the trained scientific eye, it is not chaos at all, it was all mapped out eons ago. That is what Kammerer would have said. It is what he did say. All history is the serial repetition of a singular event which gives birth to a future version of itself, and this process is repeated again and again, endlessly, until the clocks break down. That is a fairly good paraphrase. So all of these men in their fedoras rushing about in a thunderstorm, why all of that is just the latest event in a long invisible thread of interconnected events that stretch back to those long-ago days when we still lived in caves."

". . . ."

"Yes," Luis said thoughtfully. "It is history with topical alterations repeating itself. Assuming you also believe in history. So maybe there is something to seriality after all.

". . . ."

"I like to think there is. But it is not a theory that appeals to everyone."

And then Luis stood up quickly, abruptly, as if he were late for a train, and motioned for the middle-aged brother to join him. The man was still groggy from before and begged for Luis to leave him alone, so Luis had to grab hold of him by an armpit with his free hand and help the poor sot to his feet. Then he shoved him into the glowing darkness beyond the open door. It was very dark in this tunnel in between the walls. There was a faint glow at the opposite end, but it was a long way away and didn't provide any illumination at all. They had only taken a step or two into the darkness when the middle-aged brother tripped over something and fell with a great clanging commotion to the floor. He became a dark shadow swimming in an even darker ocean of darkness.

Luis fumbled along the wall until he found a switch and flicked it on and a row of tiny yellow lights like tiny submarine portholes started to hum with electricity. The man was lying in the middle of a pile of gray metal canisters that had been knocked off a shelf, film canisters, evidently, for the long narrow room seemed to be a repository for all sorts of paraphernalia associated with the movie industry.

Luis helped the man to his feet.

From somewhere Luis could hear a strange, insistent clicking sound, but he could not pinpoint its location.

There was a row of shelving along one side of the room with dozens of additional film canisters stacked chaotically, carelessly strewn about the shelves, some bearing neatly printed labels, others without any identifying mark at all. Tucked away on the lowest shelf, obscured by the shadow of the shelves above, were a dozen mason jars containing various unknown liquids and gels and colored dyes, and a few larger containers made from dark brown glass, each with a label that had the image of a skull and crossbones and the name of a chemical compound (silver halide, Sulphur, Selenium, a name derived from Selene, the Greek word for the moon, because like the moon, Selenium radiates electricity in direct proportion to the amount of light that falls upon its surface, and trichloroethane, otherwise known as chloroform, which was often used to clean photographic negative plates and reels of film, but had other, darker uses as well).

Further down the tunnel there was a dazzling display of vintage movie cameras and other apparatus. A shelf of cast-offs from the silent days of Hollywood. A 1929 Kodak. A 1936 Revere. Dozens of movie projectors of all shapes and sizes. And a 1924 Moviola editing machine that had originally been purchased by the Douglas Fairbanks Studios for $125.

There were also various work tables and a few narrow benches and three dusty filing cabinets pushed together and a stone sink with two basins. The work tables and the benches were covered with a thin film of dust which was oily to the touch, possibly from the residue of various lubricants used to keep the cameras and projectors and other equipment in mint condition. There were also a few tools left on the tables, tiny pliers and screwdrivers, a pair of scissors, and several pairs of tongs. Swirling piles of discarded, exposed film and worn projector belts and oily rags were scattered here and there on the floor like abandoned nests.

The strange room seemed like the lair of a deviant nocturnal creature with exotic tastes and imperfect morals. At the far end, roughly parallel to the small aperture in the bedroom wall above the headboard, there was a small camera that rested on a rolling wooden platform that had been pulled away from the wall, but one could see quite clearly that the camera lens fit perfectly into the aperture. When the platform was pushed flush against the wall one could film the occupants of the bed without their being aware, as long as there was music playing in the bedroom and they had been drinking.

Across from the aperture there was a small table with a

vintage movie projector clicking away mindlessly, the wheel turning without regret, projecting a silent movie onto the wall. It was like watching ghosts suspended in the hollow darkness of the abyss, Luis thought, surreal figures dancing with carefree, liquid abandon, their world disintegrating around the edges, a flickering, entertaining show of light and shadow collapsing inward upon itself, and then oblivion.

The movie projector was on the same circuit as the lights. The star of the film was the dead woman. The film seemed to be a collage of dozens of skillfully spliced together random encounters with various men, all of the encounters taking place in the bedroom on the other side of the wall. The woman was always wearing a flimsy, swirling silk robe that was designed, admittedly, so one need not guess what was underneath. It was also easy to tear off, after which the men were always trying to scramble on top of the woman, her nakedness a luminescent white light bulb in the blue-tinged darkness. She would welcome them with open legs at first, scattering the pillows about with subtle, theatrical expertise so they neatly framed her face for the camera. But somehow by the end of each scene she was always able to flip the men onto their backs, framing their faces with the pillows instead and laughing with self-indulgent, almost demonic joy, and then she would ride them till they disappeared within themselves, becoming puddles of wordless ecstasy, drifting off into an easy, dreamless sleep.

Naturally, there were a few obligatory shots of the men nibbling on the woman's pussy and her arms writhing about in the air like burning snakes. A few shots of the men taking her from behind and squeezing her breasts (about the size of small lemons or limes cut in half) while they pumped away furiously, their scrawny, hair-covered legs soon quivering with fatigue. And a few shots of the woman taking their greasy cocks into her mouth and the men closing their eyes, begging for more, until they creamed into her smiling face. All of these shots were clichés, of course, but it was precisely because they were clichés that they would arouse the prurient interest of countless disenfranchised voyeurs, recovering alcoholics, recovering drug addicts, defrocked priests, sodomized altar boys, raging pedophiles, and other sexual deviants, all of them male, who lived in the marginalia of history.

Next to the table, presumably so one could enjoy the silent film, there was a glowing golden chair like an ancient throne with Egyptian figures cut into the panels on the sides and in the center. This center panel featured two seated individuals facing opposite directions, each holding an oblong scepter like Braun's original cathode ray tube, each with a crown of flowers growing out of his or her head. They were flanked on both sides by a long procession of smaller individuals, servants and other flatterers, wearing small wrinkled hats, or possibly they were wigs, and bearing gleaming trays filled with delectable things to eat or drink. There was a row of hieroglyphics above the two kings (or queens, or one of each), presumably describing the scene below. Above the hieroglyphics there flew a symbolic eagle. The eagle possessed a giant eye like a glowing lens that looked down upon everything else in the center panel (and beyond?) but which would have looked directly into the middle of the back of anyone sitting in the chair, somewhere about the fifth thoracic vertebrae of the spine, which is that part of the spine most prone to injury.

The chair was in fact a replica of a royal throne from the second millennium before the common era. The original had been discovered in 1905, almost by accident, by Theodore M. Davis, an American lawyer turned amateur archeologist who sponsored the excavation of thirty tombs in the Valley of the Kings from 1902 until 1915 and who was the most famous archaeologist in the world until Howard Carter discovered King Tut's tomb in 1922. The replica that Luis had stumbled upon in this mysterious art deco tenement on the edge of nowhere had been manufactured in Paris shortly after the existence of the original had been proclaimed to the world. This proclamation had set off a boom in chair making. Hundreds of replica chairs were manufactured from 1906 to 1908, for the Egyptian motif was quite popular at that time. Replicas of the golden throne became all the rage among the hot-to-trot set in Europe and elsewhere. The chairs became symbols of status. But by 1955, most of them had been lost or stolen or destroyed in suspicious fires. The presence of such a chair in Havana was an anomaly to say the least.

Luis told the middle-aged brother to take a seat and pointed at the replica chair with his gun.

The man obliged him without any fuss.

The last scene of the silent film made its way through the rotating sprockets and then vanished in the blazing glare of a white-hot flickering spotlight. The thin, celluloid filament continued to flap uselessly as the wheel turned. The white light would blaze until either someone flicked off the switch or the bulb burned out.

"Do you smoke?" said Luis.

Luis was sitting a few feet away on a narrow bench pushed up against the wall opposite the shelves. He had set his gun on the bench so he could roll two cigarettes. The man looked at the gun but decided against making any sudden moves.

"Yes," said the man.

And then he gave Luis a strange look of warning.

"But not in here."

Luis nodded absently, measuring the tobacco, licking the papers and rolling them shut. He lit the cigarettes, tossing the burnt match to the floor.

"The chemicals," said the man.

"Yes, yes," said Luis.

He handed the man one of the cigarettes.

"But what does it really matter?"

They smoked their cigarettes for a while in silence, breathing in the nicotine without regret, but with a longing for better days.

"You have been making films for a long time?" Luis said.

"Yes," said the man.

And then he paused as if he were struggling to breathe.

And then: "For ten years here in Havana. And for seventeen years before that in Germany. Stuttgart. Berlin. St. Moritz. Nuremberg. Lübeck."

"You worked for the Nazis?"

"Of course. Who didn't?"

Luis savored a long drag on his cigarette and blew smoke into the air.

"I see," he said.

The man began to squirm in the gleaming golden replica chair.

His breathing difficulties intensified.

"I worked on some very important films. I worked with Werner Klingler. I worked with Leni Riefenstahl. And before the Nazis I worked with Fred Sauer."

"And who are you working with now?"

The man grew silent. Luis was waving his gun in the air once again as he spoke. The man had not seen Luis pick it up from the bench. A look of grim uncertainty spread across his features.

"I suppose it doesn't matter," said Luis. "You are working with the same men. You are working with different men. In the end, it is all about the work, isn't that what you believe?"

"Yes, yes, something like that."

"It is only your body of work that remains."

"Yes," said the man. "One can hope."

"And your filmmaking is quite good," said Luis. "What little I have seen of it."

The man began to eye Luis carefully but did not respond.

"Yes, you are quite good, aren't you."

". . . ."

"You and your sister. You are quite a pair!"

Slowly the man sitting in the gleaming golden chair had begun to look less like a man and more like a sceptered corpse, all the blood draining from his face, rushing to his toes. The tremendous weight in his blood-laden toes held him in place.

"It is not quite as you think," he said.

"No? What do I think?"

"She was not supposed to shoot you. I do not know why she took out your gun."

". . . ."

"Perhaps it was because of all the money. We did not expect so much money."

". . . ."

"It was a stupid thing to do. She was only supposed to detain you. Keep you interested."

"And you? What was your role?"

"To. . . to . . . in case she failed."

"I see."

Luis took out his perfumed handkerchief. The claustrophobic smell of this tomb in between the walls was washed clean with the invigorating cent of citrus mixed with mint. Luis handed the man his handkerchief and the man nodded and dabbed his forehead, which had begun to perspire heavily. Then he handed it back.

"Thank you," the man said. "One does not normally expect to receive such kindness under circumstances like these."

Luis repocketed his handkerchief. The scent of citrus vanished while the scent of mint still lingered.

"Yes, you were both quite good," said Luis after a while.

Luis smiled a strangely tender smile.

"And yet the general public has never heard of you, have they."

". . . ."

"Not here. Not in Germany. But then that's the point, isn't it. You make films that do not exist. You make films that no one is supposed to see."

". . . ."

"No one except those poor sots caught by the camera. What did your sister call them? 'Boorish louts,' that was the phrase she used."

". . . ."

"And you have been making these films for ten years? You must have been an extremely valuable asset."

". . . ."

"Did you ever have any trouble?"

Luis took one last long drag on his cigarette and sent the stub spinning through the air.

It landed in one of the sink basins.

Then he stood up with a renewed sense of purpose, as if he had suddenly realized that all of his doubts were a smokescreen.

"I mean did anyone ever refuse to pay?"

His gun gleamed in the flickering darkness.

"Did anyone ever refuse to give up the goods?"

"Yes . . . well . . ."

The man wasn't sure what to say or what to do. His mind was full of the terror that comes from unanswered questions. He looked past Luis to the shimmering, bluish light of the open door so very far away. Perhaps he was hoping that someone, anyone, his dead sister, or the men with the long-barreled rifles waiting outside in the rain, or even God himself, would materialize out of thin air to help him out of his predicament. But there was no one there.

"One time, yes, of course," said the man. "There are always one or two rotten apples."

Luis took a single step towards the man and stopped. He was smiling with the same charming indifference as always, waiting for the man to finish.

The man looked Luis squarely in the eyes and continued speaking, though his voice seemed now slightly agitated, his breathing a little bit faster, the veins in his neck beginning to throb uncontrollably, which probably indicated a condition of some kind.

"Please! Please! It was back when we first started," he said. "It was during our first year. I had no interest in which clubs Elisa went to. That was up to her. My interest was later, but it varied, as with anything. And then one night she came home with a very big fish. She came home with Manuel Fernandez Supervielle, the Mayor of Havana, and I was very much interested. He did not look much like a mayor when he removed his white jacket and his white Panama hat and his alligator shoes. He looked like any other flabby, blubbering fuck you might see on any street corner. But I made him look good with my camera. When I was finished editing that piece of film he looked like don Juan himself. Yes? It was hard to believe. I could hardly believe it myself. So we watched the film together. Don Juan was fucking my sister. We were sitting right here watching those images dancing on the wall and it was don Juan we were watching, not the Mayor of Havana. It was a triumph. But Supervielle did not appreciate my artistry. He said he would not pay for a romp in the sack with a two-bit German whore. Love is a peculiar thing, I said to him. Love is a burning acid that scars your throat. What audacity, he said to me. Excuse me please, I said to him. And then he said he would not pay. He would not do it. Who the fuck did we think we were? This is what he was saying. He would have us both deported. He said he knew Ramón Grau. With just one phone call he would have us sent back to Germany. Yes, yes!! And if we made any fuss we could go back in a box. Or maybe he would ring up the secret police. What did he mean by that? I was not afraid. I told him that I had had run-ins with the secret police before. Back in Germany. *Die Geheime Staatspolize.* Hah! But he appeared not to hear me. He said they would take us away in the middle of the night, and we would never be heard from again. Rubbish! Rubbish! Everyone knew the secret police were corrupt, like anywhere, but especially in Havana. We would simply have paid them off and they would have been satisfied. Ah, yes, yes, we all know it is the way of the world. *Ungesellige Geselligkeit!* Everywhere this is how it is. Naturally, I followed him home that very morning and shot him point blank in the chest. I emptied the gun. Seven shots point blank. The next day the papers said he had shot himself in the chest because he was unable to make good on a campaign promise.

They did not bother to say how many times he had shot himself. They just said it was suicide. How could they think that? Besides, who would kill themselves over such a small thing? And who puts a gun to their chest to commit suicide? No one does this. And why not? Because it is too sloppy. And because there is no guarantee that you will succeed in killing yourself that way. Maybe the bullet goes clean through. Maybe it misses the heart, the lungs. Maybe all the vital organs are left unharmed. Maybe it is a magic bullet. Who can say? A miss is as good as a mile, as the Americans say. Hah! All I know is that those who are seeking calm passage across many a bad night want the certainty of a single clean shot. Is not life a lingering fever? Is this not the experience of everyone? Is not . . . is not . . . ? What is the phrase? *Der tod ist der seligste traum.* Yes, that is it. But who does not know this? No, no, those who choose to commit suicide with a revolver almost always put the barrel of the gun into their own mouths. Or up against their temples. Then there is no doubt. Death is inevitable. It is just a matter of squeezing the trigger. A reflex. An instinct. All the learning in the world cannot replace instinct, that's what we were told. Are you not prepared for victory at any cost? *Totaler Krieg! Kürzester Krieg!* Now folk rise up and storm break loose! *Achtung! Aufgepasst!* Who were we to say any different? (Silence. A sigh. A sad, forlorn smile.) Yes, it was all a great joke, was it not? (A short pause.) But truly, it is not hard to pull a trigger when you want to taste a bullet. And then lights out, as they say in the movies. But this was not the case with Supervielle. But this did not matter. The papers said it was a suicide. And why would you not believe what you read in the papers? Supervielle, they said, had shot himself in the chest, a fatal wound. They did not say how many times he was shot. They did not say how long he took to die. And that was that. There was no investigation. No one seemed to care. Which was okay by us anyway. We couldn't have planned it any better. That was the only time we ever had any trouble."

The two men were still looking directly at each other, each with an unflinching gaze, but each gaze suggested different things. In the background you could hear the faint mechanical whirring of the projector and the steady hum of electricity, and beneath that, as if it were an echo of an echo, you could hear the hypnotic lull of falling rain.

"What is your name?" said Luis.

The man blinked but did not reply.

"My name is Luis," said Luis.

Again silence. And then: "My name is Georg."

Luis glanced down at his pistol, checked it to make sure it was loaded, and then he held his hands ready. The gun was beautiful to behold, as is the case with many instruments for evil. Especially those which are sometimes used for a greater good.

"You will make it quick?" said the man.

Luis smiled.

"I will make it quick."

The man gave Luis a long hard look. It was almost like he was whistling in disbelief, the way people do when something unexpected happens and they don't know how to react. But there was no sound.

"You know it will make no difference."

"I know."

"You can't evade them forever."

"Yes, of course."

"They know what you are thinking before you even think it. They will get you in the end, you can be sure of that."

"Yes. Perhaps you are right."

Luis smiled a dazzling, mischievous, boyish smile that was as bright as any sun that ever shone above the shores of any paradise.

"But you will never know one way or the other."

He raised his arm in a motion so fluid and effortless that it seemed like a current of air and pulled the trigger. There was a flash and his smile faded and the brightness that had lit up the room a moment earlier faded and a bullet hole appeared in the man's forehead, dead center, the hole filling with blood, the blood swirling around, steadily expanding beyond the boundaries of the hole, a strangely dark burgundy flower unfurling, like a rare Brazilian orchid, perhaps, or a genetically altered rose. The man dropped without batting an eye.

Luis did not even bother to look down. He fairly zoomed past the row of tiny yellow lights like tiny submarine port holes that illuminated the tunnel, however poorly, and then he was back in the foyer. His gun was already back in its holster. He seemed indifferent to the virtual certainty that the men waiting for him outside in the rain might have heard this second shot. He knew they would wait until just after sunrise before moving in, whether it was raining or not. So he would have a thirty-minute jump on them, or close enough, which would give him just enough time.

He picked up his Platt Guardsman suitcase and gave one last look around the foyer and the several hallways jutting off like spokes into the gleaming obscurity of multiple universes. 'What a shame,' he thought. 'They had a pretty good setup here.' Then he slipped out through the front door into a pool of blue dappled darkness and vanished like starlight falling.

-99-

Nerea was sitting in the back seat of the 1937 Packard which Luis used to drive, and which she had appropriated no questions asked at the beginning of their separation on that night so very long ago when Luis had said her costume was a little too tight. The engine hummed with rhythmic infallibility. It was not yet raining, but there was rain on the horizon. The car was moving slowly through the narrow, winding streets of Regla. At times it would stop for a while, as if sniffing at the air, and then it would suddenly roar down the street, a strange, lumbering tracking animal that had once again caught the scent. The dozens of Black Madonnas perched in hidden recesses and on balcony ledges above the streets seemed to be watching the predatory vehicle with vengeful eyes.

After a while it seemed like the Packard was lost.

It drifted down the same streets several times.

It drifted through the indifferent shadow of a chemical plant and the green haze all around, but there was no obvious reason to stop so the car kept moving. Twice it drifted right past the narrow side street where Luis was asleep in the De Soto, but the darkening green haze that surrounded the De Soto was all but impenetrable.

Nerea was wedged in between Immanuel, who was fidgeting with the safety on his Kongsberg Colt pistol, and Julio Mella, who had returned from the dead just this once because Nerea loved him desperately and because she was desperately in need of his assistance (practical advice? psychic protection? his revolutionary charisma? his vigorous lyricism? his visionary spirit?). It was this double dose of desperation that had called him back. Julio had always been a sucker for a desperate woman who was desperately in love with him. And always these women were extraordinarily beautiful.

Of course Immanuel could not see Julio. All he could see was an empty space on the right side of the Packard and Nerea making strange gestures and cooing sounds and moving her lips as if she were involved in an intimate conversation. At one point Immanuel tried to get Nerea's attention, he had something to say, or perhaps a question that needed to be answered immediately, but Nerea didn't even look his way. She simply shifted her shoulders and her hips, as if to block out any further intrusion, and continued chatting with her invisible companion. Immanuel hardly had any room for his elbows. His growing sense of frustration with Nerea and the natural hostility that accompanies such feelings was only kept in check by Nerea's incredible, intoxicating beauty, and the hope of a little intimacy all his own a little later on.

The conversation between Nerea and Julio Mella while they were driving around Regla:

'Yes, of course my dearest Nerea. I have been in love before.'

'. . . .'

'We took turns cooking. How I loved her delicious pasta. We were like two sweethearts.'

'. . . .'

'No. I don't remember the details. It has been a long time. And I have not been paying all that much attention to the world as it has become.'

'. . . .'

'I remember one evening she invited some friends over . . . no, not friends . . . well, friends also, but it was a Party meeting. She was rushing around, all excited, and I said to her "Tina, my love, I will arrange for dinner," and I did, and she was so pleased.'

'. . . .'

'She went to pick up something or other and when she got back the dinner was all laid out. Flowers on the table. Fruit in a bowl. Something like that. Like a painting.'

'. . . .'

'I remember taking care of dinner like that on numerous occasions. Or perhaps it was only a few times. And each time I left her a little note that said how much I loved her.'

'. . . .'

'Ah, do not be jealous, my dearest Nerea. *Mas que nada.* Remember, that was all before I met you.'

'. . . .'

'I know you have been hurt. I know you have been crying out. That is why I am here. Because of your tears.'

'. . . .'

'Yes, but you will have to trust me.'

'. . . .'

'Good, good. Now the first thing to keep in mind is that you are in extreme danger. Yes. These men, this Immanuel, they are not fooling around. I have seen this type before. They are desperate men. Very desperate. They are jackals in thin disguise. They will stop at nothing. You must believe me.'

'. . . .'

'Yes. Once they were idealists. They were desperate in their idealism. But then they forgot themselves. Now all that is left is their desperation.'

'. . . .'

'Yes, Nerea, you are beautiful, but that will not be enough. You must hone the edge of your beauty until it is razor sharp. They must always be afraid that you will cut their throats without a second backwards glance. They will kill you without hesitation the moment they think otherwise.'

The 1937 Packard slowed and then stopped. The sun had set and there was only a faint reddish glimmer in the gaps between buildings. Where the streets dipped down towards the harbor you could see the dark, frothy water bubbling up beneath the fading light. But it was very dark inside the car, and Nerea lost sight of Julio in the darkness and began to panic, but his reassuring voice was still hovering somewhere nearby. 'Stay strong, my love' the voice said. 'I am right here. I have not gone anywhere. Remember: keep the edge of your beauty razor sharp.'

Nerea's panic dissolved. Her once gushing heart once again hardened, became a bulwark against excessive emotion. Julio's calm voice of honeyed death was replaced by the stringent, Germanic urgency of Immanuel's desperate need to shoot someone.

"We are here Nerea. They must be still inside. We have

had men watching this place for over an hour and no one has left."

Immanuel stopped talking and put the fingertips of one hand up to the side of his head, cocking his head slightly and exerting a small pressure on his mastoid process, the posterior portion of the temporal bone just behind the ear. He seemed to be listening intently to some inner voice. Nerea peered out through Immanuel's window. They had stopped in front of a small café on the ground floor of a narrow, triangular building at the corner of three streets. A young boy was sitting up against a series of narrow wooden panels that served as a temporary wall when the café was closed. He seemed to be asleep, but when he saw the car he got up and disappeared into the darkness of the streets and did not return.

The café had seemed deserted, except for the boy. But from somewhere there was the laughter of voices and the tinkling of glasses and more laughter. Nerea also noticed a faint glow from one of the narrow windows near the back of the café. There was also the dark shadow of a car parked in a narrow slit of an alley that ran between the triangular building and a row of tenements. The car was partially obscured by the deepening shadows that existed between the two buildings. There was only one car.

"Yes," said Nerea. "I am sure no one has left during the past hour."

Immanuel began to get out but Nerea put her hand on his shoulder.

"I will take care of this," she said. "I also have had men watching this place. But my men are on the inside."

Immanuel started to protest, but Nerea quieted him with a brief but gentle kiss. She grabbed hold of his pistol and slid it back into his coat pocket.

"I will take care of this," she said again.

Nerea slipped out of the car.

Immanuel neither saw nor heard the door open or close. He watched her shadow dance past the glare of the headlights and then he lost sight of her in the shadows between the café and the tenement and could only imagine her dark purpose. The doubts he had harbored about her resolve gave way to a shuddering fear for his own well-being. He knew Nerea was certainly worth keeping. But he began to wonder if perhaps she was also worth losing.

The evening air hummed with dark energy.

The side door leading from the café to the alley opened and the hospital orderly employed by Federico emerged. He seemed like a gleaming ghost in his white orderly uniform. As Nerea approached, he lit a cigarette and took three long drags and tossed the glowing stump to the ground. They spoke in low murmurs and then Nerea went into the café. The orderly closed the door and got into the front seat of the 1956 Chevrolet Bel Air four-door hardtop that had been parked in the alley for most of the day.

It was very hot inside the car so he rolled down the window. Then he settled himself into the seat and jiggled the key until he found the sweet spot somewhere between the 'off' and 'on' positions so he could listen to the radio. There was a ballgame on. Every now and then there was the crack of a bat and you could hear the crowd roaring with delight and then the static charge of a lightning bolt somewhere else and then the announcers cooing in amazement at what they had just seen. After a while the orderly leaned his head back so he was resting against the door frame, his left arm hanging limply across the lip of the window, and closed his eyes. He disappeared into the sounds of the ballgame. It was like being in a different universe.

Inside the café it was another story.

The lighting was very poor, a single orangeish lamp hanging over the center of the counter, a small table lantern also glowing with a diffuse orange light in the center of the table which had been Federico's home for the last several hours. It was the kind of subterranean light that seemed to be mostly darkness until your eyes got used to it.

Federico did not notice Nerea at first. He was slumped to one side of his cane-back wheelchair with the ivory handles, his eyes half-closed, humming softly to the sounds of dark jazz emanating from two speakers perched on a shelf behind the café counter. His face of a skeletal corpse was streaked with orange light, a strange, otherworldly glow. The speakers were invisible in the dim interior light.

Two young men wearing fedoras sat in the darkness behind Federico. The light from the lamp and the lantern did not reach where they were, so they seemed a part of the surrounding darkness. They were sitting on tall stools pushed up against the wall. Their long-barreled rifles were leaning against the same wall but within easy reach. They were also listening to the music, their bodies swaying slightly, as if buffeted by a gentle breeze, their eyes also half-closed. It was hard not to close your eyes listening to such music. A steady, sensuous syncopated drum beat (bump, bi-ba-bi bump, bump, bi-ba-bi bump, bump, bi-ba-bi bump, baaa baaa baa-bi bump), sweeping strings, a tinkling bell sound falling away, a little piano, a little vibraphone, and a mournful, hesitant trumpet alternating with a mellow, hopeful saxophone.

Nerea stood for a moment looking at Federico. The two men in fedoras realized Nerea was not the orderly and they stiffened slightly, reflexively, but they did not open their eyes. It was almost as if they were not quite prepared for the moment at hand. Then they each took a deep breath and opened their eyes. They saw Nerea in the flesh and nodded, quick, staccato nods, as men will do when their nerves have been rubbed raw from waiting, and exhaled slowly, steadily, the balloon of the universe collapsing, all light and oxygen disappearing through a tiny pinprick.

Federico felt the stiffening of the two young men and opened his eyes and saw Nerea looking at him. They smiled politely at each other, though in the dim light it was hard to say how their smiles might be interpreted.

"He is not here," said Federico after a moment.

"I know that," said Nerea.

The dim orange light seemed to burn more brightly, more intensely. Federico motioned for the two young men in fedoras to come into the light, but they spread out along the back wall like shadows on either side instead. Only their faces caught the light, but only intermittently, and at odd angles. Their faces resembled two theatre masks floating in the blackness that eventually envelopes everything. Federico realized they were no longer his to command. It was one of those rare moments that become etched in the memories of everyone who takes part.

The jazz flowing from the speakers shifted gears, became less sensual and more refined, elegant, noncommittal, a couple of guitars flowing up and down the octaves, a harp plucking, a light snare drum rapping away, hidden beneath the artistry of the guitars.

Federico pulled out his knife while they listened to the jazz. He offered the knife to the all-consuming darkness, the lamp light and the orange lantern light glinting off the diamond cross-sections of the blade, as if he were offering one of God's fallen angels back to God. Then he laid the knife on the table with sudden assurance and sat back in his cane-back wheel chair, turning to the young man nearest the café counter, a calculated turning. "Arnaldo, would you kindly see to our hostess for this evening?"

Arnaldo shook his head as if emerging from a trance. He had been staring at the terrible beauty of the knife and had forgotten where he was.

"Signore?" he said.

"Yes, Arnaldo, the proprietress of this fine establishment, my friend Jaqueline. I did not realize we were still friends until today. It has been a very long time. One should never be so presumptuous when it comes to friendship."

And then: "Please see to her."

Arnaldo looked over at Nerea to see what he should do. Nerea gave a slight nod of her head, almost imperceptible. She was captivated by the old man's insistence, his romanticized sense of order, his perverse gallantry.

"And please be swift, Arnaldo. Do not let her linger."

Federico raised a glass to Nerea and drank the last of it.

Arnaldo vanished in the gloomy obscurity behind the café counter. A narrow doorway that led to a series of smaller rooms, perhaps, or to a set of stairs that led to a second-floor apartment, where a heavy-set woman with thick, bushy hair and elephantine legs was changing into a lace négligée, a gift from long ago, the woman singing softly to herself while she changed, her eyes glowing with the disturbing (prophetic?) brilliance of Quevedo's blood-stained moon.

"It is a shame that our friend Luis was not here to share one last drink."

Nerea did not say a word. She remained standing, almost invisible in the orangeish gloom, two cat's eyes glowing in the dark.

They heard a single shot from somewhere above them and then the gentle thud of a woman in a lace négligée now free of memory. No one flinched. It was as if no one had even fired a rifle.

Arnaldo returned.

The two young men slid around the table and joined Nerea standing in the darkness. A pair of gleaming cat's eyes flanked by two golden glowing theatre masks.

"The waves are glowing like lava," said Federico. "But not for you. You do not need to be afraid, not yet."

"Afraid?"

"We all must face our fears sooner or later." Federico smiled a jubilant smile that left the others wondering. Then the two young men raised their rifles and fired. They did not miss.

-100-

Oscar did just as Luis had suggested and spent his last night in Havana soaking up the nightlife on La Rampa. He got roaring drunk, for how else did you say goodbye to Cuba. By midnight he could not tell one nightclub from another. By two in the morning he was suspended in the semi-lucid state of an eternal dream. He imagined that he was trapped between two panes of glass, a specimen beneath the indifferent eye of a polarized light microscope. Sometimes his dream flowed in one direction, sometimes in another, as if someone had simply flipped the two panes of glass for a look at the other side. Or perhaps the eye of the microscope was rotating. Oscar had no control over which direction his dream was taking, but his constantly changing perspective gave him a new appreciation for the subversive nature of reality.

The beginning of this dream seemed strange indeed. He felt like his life was repeating itself, but he could not be sure. He was looking out on the world with an atrociously puffed eye, a bruised face. He could not tell precisely where he was. He had fallen down somewhere among some tables and men in tuxedos were rushing about and there was a line of dancing girls hovering in the spaces between the lights. The girls were wearing ruffled headpieces. They seemed genuinely concerned for his well-being. He was trying to speak to them but everything was upside down. The girls resembled weirdly beautiful plumed birds with painted beaks and exposed somewhat vulnerable breasts. Their feathers barely covered their naked hips. They were flapping their wings, jiggling their hips so you could glimpse their plush, juicy curves, their bodies circling this way and that in the smoke-filled gloom, calling out to each other in their strange, throaty bird language. It was quite erotic. Or perhaps he had tripped on the steps going into this last nightclub on his last night in Havana. Or going out. Some of the nightclubs on La Rampa were treacherous indeed with their crumbling steps of bygone elegance. Or perhaps someone had tripped him on purpose, just for a laugh. The circle of whirling birds disappeared. The circle was replaced by the hyena teeth of a doorman laughing. The teeth were very close to Oscar's face. He wasn't sure if the doorman was trying to communicate some words of wisdom or making a derogatory comment at Oscar's expense. The doorman had recently been drinking Danziger Goldwasser, a bittersweet liqueur containing tiny gold flakes and a heady aroma of juniper, cinnamon, licorice, and a hint of menthol. Oscar was immobilized by the man's breath. He wondered how long the doorman had been drinking, that's how strong his breath was. It was almost like chloroform.

Then Oscar's taxi driver rushed into the nightclub, grabbing him by the armpits, helping him to his feet. The plumed birds returned, but they were now shrieking. The laughing hyena face of the doorman becoming a pack of rabid hyenas. Teeth flashing in the semi-darkness. Snapping at the air. The terrifying sensation of being dependent upon someone else. Perhaps he should go to a hospital. No, no, no hospitals. No doctors. It's just a case of nerves. A little too much to drink. He slipped and fell and hit his eye on the corner of a table. Clumsy, stupid, drunken fool! The hyenas chasing them down the steps of bygone elegance but the taxi cab waiting, the engine humming. The hyenas vanishing, dematerializing as easily as they had materialized. Out of thin air back into thin air. But still we better get the hell out of here. You never know who might be watching. Tires screeching and then a series of hairpin turns. He could feel the blood oozing down his face. No. No longer oozing. The blood had dried. A mask of blood concealing his confusion. He could not see because of his eye. Except he could see a little bit. A sliver of light and shadow penetrating the dark veil. The taxi turned down a side street. Row after row of tenements flashed by. Slices of time. Thin sections to place on a microscope slide. The liquid gold of streetlamps. Men hiding in the darkness of doorways. Stepping out briefly only to retreat after a few seconds, a crazy dance. Or perhaps that was later. Or perhaps he had imagined everything. Bruised ego as much as a bruised face. Then the sound of the sea and the streetlamps vanished. The taxi shuddered to a stop and a door opened and the taxi started moving again. 'He isn't hurt that bad,' said a voice. 'But bad enough.' It was a gruff, raspy masculine voice. It sounded vaguely like the voice of a cancer-stricken parrot. He recognized the voice but could not place how. Perhaps it was just from earlier in the evening. Then he heard a woman's voice and he forgot the first voice even existed. He had never heard the voice of this woman before, but it was a soothing voice, a tranquil voice, a cajoling presence absolving him of all worldly responsibility, like a burial at sea. 'I'll do what I can,' the woman said. He tried to focus on what he was supposed to be doing. He suddenly remembered about the suitcase and wondered what had become of it. He did not realize that he was clutching the handle of the suitcase until the woman tried to loosen his grip. 'He won't let go,' she said. But that was all she said. There were no other voices after that. The woman started dabbing at his face, dabbing at the dried blood. He assumed it was a woman. The same woman who owned the soothing, cajoling voice. At any rate, it was a slender, gentle, penetrating hand. A provocative hand. It reminded him of something else but he could not remember. Something from when he was a boy in Baracoa, perhaps. Or when he had first arrived in Havana. Or something that had not yet happened but which had become a part of his memories just the same. He felt like he was moving back and forth through time. Then the taxi stopped again and the woman rolled down the window and the smell of the sea surged through the interior. The woman poured some powder into a small flask and shook it. Then she brought the flask to his lips and forced him to drink. It tasted like Brandy de Jerez. He couldn't remember the last time he had tasted anything so fine. He felt revived, but whether it was the smell of the sea or the warmth of the brandy he did not know. His eye began to feel better and he tried to sit up but slid back down.

-101-

Looking into a mirror hanging above a gaping black hole:

Oscar is drifting in and out of consciousness. He is clinging like a crab to the underbelly of a strangely glowing yet invisible cloud that passes overhead, over the roof of the taxi. It is a hardtop vehicle, but the roof has been peeled back. He is west of the city floating east. He can see the bubble of golden light that is the Cathedral. His eardrums are bursting with the swirl of music from the Plaza and the strained voices of people enjoying themselves and church bells chipping away at the night and footsteps running in circles and clocks ticking away like time bombs and rockets singing their siren songs, the sounds winging their way back and forth across the landscape like a flock of panicky, deranged geese. He has become impaled on the sounds from below. He has lost sight of his actual body languishing in the taxi cab so many miles away. He is certainly too far away to know if he is still breathing or not, but he does not really care. The boundary between the golden light of the celebration and the darkness beyond is constantly shifting. He recognizes that he is undergoing some sort of strange, virtually impossible metamorphosis, but he is not afraid. What a spectacular view, he thinks. He absorbs the view for a while. It has his complete attention until he notices a strange clacking noise. The clacking noise is very close by. He wonders if he should be alarmed, but then he realizes that he is the source of the clacking noise. He is making the sound with one of his claws. He is unable to determine which claw, perhaps because he is new to his crab body and does not yet know how to exert any control over it. Briefly he wonders what his crab self is doing. Why is he making such an irritating sound? How long will the sound continue? Is it possible to regulate unconscious, automatic bodily functions with conscious effort? Or is all this just an illusion anyway, an intellectual game? He wonders if there are others floating about like himself, engaged in similarly puzzling behaviors, pondering similar, unanswerable questions. 'Certainly there are others,' he thinks to himself. 'I see them every time I close my eyes.' But this statement of a pure and simple faith is not a convincing argument. His nerves are tingling. Weird burning sensations are creeping along, neuron to neuron, a webbed pathway stretching to infinity. Smoke is rising from the surface of his body. Short bursts of intense pain. Splinters of light. The pain is coming from the interlocking segments of his exoskeleton. He can feel the blood rushing to his crab head and then down to his crab legs and then back up to his crab head. A sense of vertigo. He is spinning like a disc. He seems to be suspended in space and rushing through space at the same time, a crab on the end of a skewer, but he does not understand how this is possible. Then he gives up trying to understand. Once again he is enamored of the view. He is very high up now. His crab self dissolves and he is absorbed into the sky. He becomes the sky looking down, the sky listening, the sky remembering. All human experience is written on the glistening membrane of his memory. He is now the dark sky over Regla. He is hovering just above a small café on the ground floor of a building where three streets come together. He is changing again, a changeling, collapsing inward upon himself, drawing himself together, then descending slowly, uncertainly, like an alien spacecraft on its first interstellar voyage. The doorway to a parallel universe opens and then closes. The flash of a blue underbelly. Or white. Or something metallic. There is a man dressed in white sitting in the front seat of a 1956 Chevrolet Bel Air four-door hardtop. The Chevrolet is parked in the alley that separates the café from a tenement building. The man is listening to a baseball game on the radio. The man is leaning back against the doorframe on the driver's side, staring vacantly at the radio dial. 'I have seen this man before,' Oscar thinks, but he cannot pinpoint when and where. He tries to get the man's attention, banging on the car door, shouting through the open window into the man's ear, jiggling the door handle with visible agitation, but the man does not respond. Oscar suddenly realizes that he is invisible. He exists in another dimension. The rest of humanity is insensible (as in unaware of, existing in a comatose state) to his presence. This is why the man does not respond. He realizes that the world is a holographic image, a movie projected onto the screen of history. He tries to wrap his mind around the implications of this thought, but implications are slippery things. He is not up to the task. The implications are slipping in and out of the shadows, the starlight, the moonlight, the diffuse orange glow emanating from the windows of the café, the shimmering fish scale light reflected off the distant sea, the afterglow of a supernova a billion light years away, and then one last gulp of oxygen and they (these oh so slippery implications) are gone forever, descending to depths where we cannot follow, depths which we do not even truly believe exist. The announcers announcing the game are very excited. Oscar is in the process of forgetting himself. He is standing just outside the car, listening to the game. It has been a long time since he has listened to a ballgame, but the radio reception is marred by staticky bursts of lightning bolts from somewhere else. It sounds like it is a game from years ago.

Every few minutes there is a lightning bolt but the time between bursts is diminishing. The storm is getting closer. At least it is getting closer to the radio station. Oscar forgets where he is. Then he hears a single gunshot. The man in the car does not notice. Perhaps it wasn't a gunshot. Perhaps it was just another staticky burst of lightning. Then a few moments later he hears two more gunshots, the second one a hairsplitting echo of the first. The man in the Chevrolet has heard them too. The man leans forward, peers out of the passenger side window in the direction of the gunshots, but with visible disappointment, as if he had expected something with a little more punch to it, like the spine-shattering power of a twenty-megaton nuclear explosion. Of course everything is relative. The man acts as if the two gunshots are anticlimactic. Then there is a tumultuous roar from the radio and the man is transported to a universe all his own. It sounds like someone has hit a homerun with the bases loaded. It is a tremendous smash. A rocket. The man looks to the radio in disbelief. The team with the homerun was not his team. The man does not remember the last time a player on his team pounded the ball with such hellacious force. He wonders if any of the players on his team ever will. He is beginning to lose his faith in the future. Then the door to the café opens and three figures rush out into the alley and the man is sucked back into the universe of the gunshots. This is precisely as it should be. No one can escape where they are. The first figure to emerge from the café is a long-legged woman with the headpiece of a shining golden sun like a halo upon her head and thick curly black hair flowing to either side and a single blood-red gardenia pinned above her right ear. She resembles an exquisitely carved voodoo statue of the goddess Atabey, but perhaps she is the sinister alter ego of Atabey because her face is contorted, twisted in a grimace of vengeance, impending death, not glowing with the promise of new life. She is not at all like Oscar has always imagined her to be. She rushes out into the alley and heads around the front of the Chevrolet. She is followed by two men with long-barreled rifles. The first man follows closely behind this darkly gleaming apparition of Atabey. The second goes around the back of the car. The man inside the car opens the door and gets out. He is smiling a flattering, congratulatory smile. All the same, he looks less like a man in his gleaming white uniform of a hospital orderly than a ghost hovering between this world and the next. He waves at the woman, who stops directly in front of the car and stares at him with cold, blank, uncomprehending eyes. He does not see the second man who comes up behind him. He is puzzling over the woman's cold, blank eyes. He is baffled. He has never seen such eyes before and is not sure what to make of them. 'Cat's eyes,' he thinks, but precisely what it means to have cat's eyes he is unable to articulate to himself. He does not yet have an inkling of something more ominous. The second man raises his rifle and pulls the trigger. The head of the man dressed in white explodes in slow motion. It is a singular moment. A singularity. Without a center. Particles of brain and blood are spinning through the air, but their trajectory is unlike the normal trajectory of explosions. It is as if space itself has exploded. It is like the moment of creation, an infinite jest exposed. 'Just a few more loose ends' the woman says, and then she is absorbed by a 1937 Packard that has been waiting in the darkness at the mouth of the alley. The Packard speeds away. The two men with long-barreled rifles get into the Chevrolet. They have been given the night off. They listen to the end of the ballgame, cracking jokes like brothers and arguing about which is the better team before driving away.

-102-

From the replacement taxi driver's point of view:

This was the first time the replacement taxi driver had driven for the fat stubby man. It was his fourth taxi company in three years. His full name was Miguel Valentín Hidalgo Lazaro Montes de Oca Fleitas y Pertierra, but he went by Jabuco, a nickname that had been given to his grandfather. Jabuco said he had enjoyed a remarkable ten-year baseball career. He said he had played for the Petroleros de Cienfuegos club from 1942-1945. This last part might have been true. He said he had been an acrobatic outfielder known for his blazing speed and for making leaping, twirling, game-saving circus catches down the alley on the first-base line or in the centerfield gap near the fence. The fans would toss coins of varying value onto the grass in appreciation. But the replacement taxi driver also claimed to have been part of the Almendares club team that won the Cuban League championship in the 1946-47 season, defeating

Habana in a clean sweep. This was probably not true, given the roster of that squad was very well known. At other times, usually after one too many warm beers, he changed his story completely. He said his name was Eusebio Miguel González López and that he had played on Club Fé in the years before the Great War with the likes of Cyclone Joe Williams (who had come over from the Negro League), Dolf Luque, Alejandro Oms, Valentín González (an outfielder who later became a popular umpire at Almendares Park and could be seen puffing away on a cigar and chatting with fans behind home plate at the end of every game), Pelayo Chacón, Torriente, Esteban Montalvo, Perico el Mono (who, as it turned out, was a wiry, Old World monkey, just like his name suggested, who wore a red costume and was employed for many years as the mascot for the Habana club and wasn't a ballplayer at all), and José de la Caridad Méndez, also known as the Black Diamond, arguably the greatest Cuban pitcher (right-handed) in the history of Cuba, to name just a few of the players the replacement taxi driver said he had rubbed shoulders with. In his darker moods, he said he was Antonio Susini and had once killed a teammate with a 1912 Spalding Gold Medal baseball bat. He did not say why. Jabuco was a harmless enough character for the most part, but one never knew if he was joking or not.

The fat stubby man had given Jabuco very precise instructions. He was going to fill in for a very important fare that evening. The two drivers that normally handled such fares had mysteriously disappeared. No, there was no cause for alarm, the fat stubby man had said. People disappeared in Havana all the time, only to reappear a few days later no worse for the wear. Jabuco's eyes had narrowed with understandable suspicion at that point. He knew the first part about Havana was true, but not the second part. He knew of many people who had disappeared and had never reappeared, except, on occasion, as barely recognizable corpses. Yes, it was certainly true that such disappearances did not happen as frequently as they had in the days of Machado. In those days the newspapers were filled with stories of people vanishing and then two or three days later their bodies would be found dumped by the side of a road or mangled and stuffed into trash cans or burned beyond belief from unexpected explosions and flash fires or floating face down in the Almendares River. And who really knew how many people Machado had shackled with weights and tossed into the sea? Once a couple of fishermen had pulled a gigantic shark out of the waters of the harbor and when they cut open its stomach they discovered the partially digested body of a University professor, José Marinello Menoyo, who had been missing for a week. There had been some debate at the time as to the true identity of the victim. An unnamed journalist had claimed it was the professor because the belly of the shark also contained a ring that Marinello had purchased while on a trip to Mexico City in 1929, a ring bearing a strange insignia: a tiny eye of Horis at the center of a tiny triangle made up of three swords. The ring had not been on the professor's dead hand when the fishermen discovered the body, but who can say what happens in the confusion and terror that reigns inside a shark's stomach. But no one came forward to say the ring did not belong to the professor, and that had settled the matter.

Naturally the fat stubby man was not dismayed by such stories. He had laughed at Jabuco's misgivings. Such ominous fabrications are worse than old wives' tales, he had said. Then he had become deadly serious. He told Jabuco he was to pick up a young man in the 200 block of Calle Obispo. At five in the evening he was to pull up to a magnificent pale yellow building, a beautiful baroque structure like they have in Barcelona, and wait for a young man with a suitcase. He was to drive the young man to the various clubs on La Rampa or elsewhere, but he was to steer clear of all the nonsense near the Cathedral. What crazy instructions! Jabuco had started to chuckle at that but the fat stubby man had cut him off with a look. He was to see to the welfare of the young man. Under no circumstances was he to pick up another fare or call a friend. This young man was too important to fuck with. He was connected. He worked for Giuseppe Federico DiCarla. Enough said. More than enough. Jabuco would be well compensated if everything went as planned. So he would stay with the young man throughout the evening. Yes, a bodyguard of sorts. Then at five in the morning he was to drive the young man out to Playa de Marianao, a small, tucked-away parking lot near the yacht club. 'I will meet you there,' the fat stubby man had said. 'Make sure you are not followed. And do not let anything happen to this young man. It is worth much more than your life. It is worth my life. Do not be late.'

So Jabuco made sure he followed the fat stubby man's directions to the letter, though at various times throughout the evening he wondered just what he had gotten involved in. The young man was wearing a very white, very bright linen suit and a shabby Panama hat. The suit was outdated and the hat had seen too many years as well, as if both items had belonged to the young man's father. The replacement taxi driver thought the young man looked ridiculous, but he didn't say anything. He had taken the young man to half a dozen clubs, but all they did was sit at tables in the shadows and watch the dancing girls and drink beer and then maybe a couple of mojitos, and always there was a young girl or an older woman popping by, seeking them out, as if the young man were a beacon in the obscurity of each dimly lit corner, the women wanting to sit down and chat and drink and join the party, or maybe take the young man to the dance floor for a quick samba, but he always refused. He wanted to be alone. He wouldn't leave the table. He clung to his suitcase while he drank. It was idiotic the way he held on to the handle. The women were all very good looking. They were all of them worth a few minutes on the dance floor. They were all of them worth much more than a few minutes. At the very least the young man could have taken them one by one into the back seat of the taxi. He could have fucked them until they squealed. You could tell that they all wanted to be fucked by the way they approached the table with their tits popping out of their skimpy tops and their hips swiveling back and forth in lazy gyrations as they talked and smiled and smoked their cigarettes and blew smoke rings like soft kisses. But the young man was not interested. He made love to his suitcase instead. And the women slipped away in the dark, searching for willing lovers at other tables. The replacement taxi driver did not understand. It was like the young man was saving himself for another the way they do in cheap romance novels or Hollywood movies. But the young man was a good tipper. Every time they got back into the taxi, the young man forked over a crisp, cool Benjamin. 'For your trouble,' he would say, and then he would toss off a curt nod, a thin-lipped smile, as if he were in fact suffering the eternal gnawing despair of a long-lost love, and they would climb into the taxi and head off to the next joint. So the replacement taxi driver didn't say anything critical.

It was after midnight that the scripted predictability of their routine began to fall apart. The dancing girls no longer seemed so friendly. The waiters seemed almost sinister. And it seemed to the replacement taxi driver that everyone was packing a gun. At one club, a glitzy pleasure palace on San Rafael, they downed an entire bottle of tequila after one of the dance numbers with the help of a skinny, red-haired dancer with a grayish complexion and corrupt green eyes implanted in an innocent-looking face. The red-head seemed to know the young man, but he didn't seem to remember, and this infuriated the red-head. She started a row, shouting and screaming. She tossed a drink in the young man's face, an overly theatrical gesture, and a few nearby customers started to complain and you could hear the sounds of a few chairs being pushed back. The manager came running, and also a few waiters. One of the waiters grabbed the red-head from behind and held on to her shoulders while the manager talked quietly with the young man. The manager was dabbing at his forehead where the perspiration was beading up. He and the young man were standing to one side of the table, their faces illuminated every now and then by the flashing, pulsating lights from the stage. The one waiter seemed to be whispering words of love to the red-head, trying to calm her down, soothe her irritated soul. He was standing very close to her. She was wriggling, trying to squirm herself free, or at least pretending to. Her green eyes glowed with unadulterated pleasure. Then the young man gave the manager two-hundred dollars and the manager, the waiters, and the slightly squirming red-head vanished in the pulsating, semi-darkness as quietly as they had appeared.

Needless to say, all hell broke loose at the last club of the night, Cabaret Conchita, a den of thieves if there ever was one on Zapata, which was known for its risqué shows, and which offered private rooms in the back for viewing pornographic films. The replacement taxi driver had warned the young man. The young man said he had been there many times before. They stopped out front, the engine of the taxi humming. They could see the purple neon lights of the club flashing with mindless, mind-numbing gaiety. 'See you inside,' the young man said, and then he got out of the taxi and disappeared almost instantly beneath the hazy obscurity of a long, tunnel-like awning, except for a pair of legs going up a set of steps, and then the legs were gone and there was the sound of a padded black door opening and then closing. The replacement taxi driver parked the car up the street, about half a block, but he did not get out right away. He sat there a while, smoking a cigarette. It was only two in the morning. Three hours to go. He sat in the car longer than he had intended, staring blankly at the rearview mirror, dispassionately, drunkenly, watching the shimmering, refracted images of the patrons of Cabaret Conchita going in and out.

At some point later on, a series of yellow cabs pulled up to the awning and a dozen or more costumed revelers emerged. They hovered just beneath the awning for a minute or two but seemed uncertain where they were or what they should do. It was hard to tell what they were dressed like, for they were all missing pieces from their costumes and had filled in the various odd gaps with pieces from other costumes, so they resembled the fragmentary unreality of a world that had come unglued, the demons and demigods and nightmare tropes of a troubled mind. Some of them wore shining silver Conquistador helmets and capes made from the plumage of rare, Caribbean birds. Some of them wore the white cassocks of priests but carried swords dripping with blood instead of golden crucifixes. Some wore masks resembling diseased or deranged tropical animals (monkeys, jaguars, alligators, iguanas with spiked jowls). There were insects with the heads of cats and sphinxes with the wings of beetles. There were skeletons wearing tuxedo jackets and black ties, brightly colored tights and dancing shoes. There were ghosts dressed as baseball players (or baseball players dressed as ghosts). Some looked like Cuban tobacco farmers from the waist up, complete with ragged straw hats and bushy, broom-bristle moustaches, but they were goats or some other cloven-hoofed creature from the waist down. Some possessed pitchfork tails that were twitching uncontrollably. They were all chatting away nervously.

Then a towering black brute emerged from the last taxi. He was wearing a black tunic and white pantaloons decorated with black roses. He wore black knee-stockings and black shoes with glorious golden buckles and sported a black cane with an ivory handle carved to resemble the head of a jackal. He wore a white powdered wig from the 17th century. His teeth were painted black.

The towering black brute greeted the demons and demigods hovering beneath the awning with a sweeping flourish of his caneless hand followed by a great crackling laugh, and then the group vanished through the padded black door as if by magic. The replacement taxi driver thought he had seen fire coming out of the black behemoth's mouth as he laughed and smoke curling about his head, so he sat up abruptly, keenly alert, as if someone had shaved the scales from his eyeballs, and turned in his seat for a better look, but there was no one there. Even the several taxis that had deposited the demons and demigods at the door of Cabaret Conchita had mysteriously vanished. He decided he must have been dreaming.

It had begun raining, so he started the car and backed up to the awning and then raced inside.

At first he did not know where to go. Everything seemed closed. A bony misshapen dwarf of a man was rummaging around in the coat check closet. The dwarf had not yet found what he wanted and seemed on the verge of giving up when he noticed the replacement taxi driver.

"It is always by way of pain that one arrives at pleasure," he said.

The replacement taxi driver nodded in a vague, noncommittal way.

"If it's after hours you want you've come in through the wrong door," he said.

The dwarf disentangled himself from the lifeless arms of a few forgotten dinner jackets and overcoats and rain slickers and stepped away from the closet. The replacement taxi driver could see that the dwarf had also painted his teeth black. The dwarf smiled a grim, knowing, caricature of a smile. It was an ungodly smile.

"You're picking up?"

"Yes."

"Then you'll have to go this way."

The dwarf led the replacement taxi driver down a long narrow corridor that glowed with an eerie blue light. They passed by a dozen numbered doors. One could only guess what was going on behind the doors. Behind one they could hear the sounds of a man and a woman arguing and then a smack as if someone had been slapped, and then more arguing followed by more slapping sounds. Ah, yes, the brutality of love. Behind another there was the sound of heavy breathing. Behind another the incessant clacking sound of a movie projector projecting a third-rate movie. Behind another the tinkling of small bells (wedding bells, perhaps, or the bells of altar boys, or just a ringing in one's ears). Behind another the soothing tremors of jazz. Once again the replacement taxi driver heard the crackling laugh of the towering black brute and the nervous jabbering of the demons and demigods from his dream. Behind the remaining doors there was nothing except the unfaltering sibilant echo of God whispering to Himself. At the end of the corridor they came to a set of double doors.

The dwarf smiled his ungodly smile again. "Just head right through there," he said. "That's the only way in or out at this hour."

The scene inside Cabaret Conchita:

A wide-angle movie camera view of the nightclub stage and the tables staggered on two tiers so every customer has a good view of the dancers. A set of double doors up front, close to the stage, but also close to a narrow door with a porthole window that leads to the kitchen.

A young man is sitting awkwardly in the middle of the floor, his legs splayed out in front of him, absorbing the darkness. A table nearby is turned over on its side. There are a few pieces of broken glass on the floor, a candle still glowing, puddles of water or gin reflecting the stage lights. The young man's white linen suit is stained with the overindulgence of the evening, of many evenings. But strangely, his Panama hat once again seems immaculate. Perhaps this is simply a trick of the shadowy, subterranean light in the club. The young man is clutching a suitcase and pointing a small black-handled Beistegui Brothers Libia pistol with feverish intensity at the surprised knot of thieves and cutthroats and naked showgirls that have made Cabaret Conchita their midnight home.

No one moves for fear of the first bullet.

After that, of course, they will tear the young man to shreds.

"Stay away," says the young man. "Stay away."

"Sure kid," says a beleaguered, garbled voice.

And then: "But you can't get all of us."

The thieves and cutthroats, who are all wearing black tuxedos instead of festival costumes, start a round of chuckling that races about the room like a brisk wind.

It is at this point that the replacement taxi driver bursts through the set of double doors, as if he has been sprinting downhill, a dramatic, improbable entrance. The doors bang open with a great booming sound. It almost sounds like a gunshot. The young man swings his arm wildly but relaxes when he sees who it is.

"I wondered where you were," he says.

The young man waves his gun at the crowd as if he were acknowledging old friends.

"We've been having a hell of a time."

The replacement taxi driver reaches the young man and pockets the black-handled Libia. The young man watches the gun until it vanishes, and then becomes suddenly silent, absorbed by the moment, a blank, untroubled look on his face.

"Sorry about my friend here," says the replacement taxi driver. "He didn't mean anything."

"Sure," says a voice from the darkness.

"Keep him on a leash the next time," says another voice.

The knot of thieves and cutthroats begins to untangle, disperse, but the bevy of naked showgirls is still hovering about the stage, looking on with thoughtful, concerned, compassionate expressions on what are normally vacant, stylized faces.

The replacement taxi driver tries to hoist the young man to his feet, gripping him beneath the armpits, but he didn't bargain for so much dead weight. The young man seems aware of his surroundings, but he is very drunk, a fact which seems to work against the replacement taxi driver's best efforts.

"Need some help?"

A man from the dispersing crowd steps near. He has a leering horse face, the face of an out-of-work doorman. He leans over to have a closer look at the young man's bruised eye.

"That's going to be one hell of a shiner," he says. "Hell, it already is!"

There is a snapping sound like a lever being pulled and the stage lights go out, and very faintly, as if there is a radio on in another room, you can hear the crackling laughter of the black brute from the replacement taxi driver's dream. A few of the showgirls squeal, and then one by one they vanish into the darkness backstage. The only illumination in the room comes from the blue emergency lighting near the double doors.

It is hard to say who is controlling this puppet show.

"What the hell happened?" says the replacement taxi driver.

"You got me. One minute your friend here is just like any other square Joe. He's ogling the girls and chatting them up between numbers and they're slapping his hand away but it's all in good fun. Then the last number is over and everyone heads for the door and Whamo! Your friend here crashes into that table. Plants his eye right on the corner."

". . . ."

"The next thing anybody knows he pulls out a gun and is waving it in the air. Naturally everyone freezes. You can't be too careful in a place like this."

". . . ."

"Pretty much everyone in this joint is packing some kind of pistol."

". . . ."

"I mean you knew someone was just about to plug the poor sap. You could feel it in the air. Like electricity or something."

". . . ."

"Like a goddamn bolt of lightning!"

". . . ."

"That's when you waltzed in through those double doors. A regular twinkle toes. Right on cue!"

The horse-faced man and the replacement taxi driver half-carried, half-dragged the young man and his suitcase (which he refused to give up even in his battered, drunken state) out of the club and laid him in the back seat of the waiting taxi. The rain was coming down harder than ever. It seemed as if the world was being washed away as fast as it could reassemble itself. Even the furiously beating wipers made no difference.

The replacement taxi driver shifted into gear and released the clutch slowly as he pulled away from the curb.

He was pretty sure the kid's eye needed medical attention, but hospitals were out. You didn't take some kid who worked for Giuseppe Federico DiCarla to a hospital. He knew that much. You had to be discreet. You had to keep a tight lip. And that made it simple. He only knew one place to go. So that's where he went. But all the way there he wondered what he had gotten himself into. He couldn't shake the notion that the entire planet was off its axis. Everything was spinning out of control. And as he drove through the wet, darkly gleaming streets of Havana at three in the morning, he couldn't shake himself free from the memory of that black behemoth and his great crackling laugh.

He had no doubt that he would be haunted by the sound of that laughter for the rest of his life, however short or long the rest of his life might be.

-103-

The replacement taxi driver believed only an ex-nurse named Ismene could save the kid's eye. She lived in a crumbling tenement building on a street without a name somewhere in the labyrinth of streets and side streets and hidden alleyways east and southeast of Infanta. He always had trouble finding her place and usually ended up at a small all-night drugstore on Zequera. There was a weather-beaten wooden phone booth just outside the drugstore where he would dial her up, and ten minutes later she would be sitting next to him, a small brown satchel in her lap. The satchel contained a variety of pills and powders which were easily administered to passengers too drunk to notice. Just mix up a little potion in a flask, slip into the back seat and force it down their throats. It didn't matter if they struggled or not. They wouldn't remember a thing later. Then the replacement taxi driver and the ex-nurse would head to a secluded spot along the Almendares River and rob their victims blind. The crimes were never reported. The victims would wake up a few hours later, sitting half naked on a park bench or wandering around the Cementerio de Cristóbal Colón like some kind of resurrected zombie or shivering with embarrassment in the waiting room at the train station, but they couldn't remember a thing. The replacement taxi driver had not seen the ex-nurse for several months. With the rain beating down as it was, he drove around for thirty minutes before he found the drugstore.

The call from the phone booth:

"Ismene?"

Silence. The sound of the rain.

"Ismene?"

A furtive movement at the other end.

The replacement taxi driver was looking through the rain-streaked glass of the phone booth. He was looking at his taxi. His eyes didn't waver. He didn't bother about the people going in and out of the drugstore, the light from the interior spreading out, a small golden bubble against the darkness. Nor did he care about the clerk sitting by the register, who kept looking out through the plate glass window with the frosted drugstore lettering as if a crime were taking place. Because crimes were always taking place outside this drugstore. The taxi started vibrating, the engine sputtering, coughing. Then it was running normally again. He usually left the car running, but this neighborhood made him nervous. He knew he was being watched. He could feel eyes all around, hidden in the crevices between buildings, in the shadowy darkness of doorways, watching everything that happened on this rainy night. This is how it seemed. He tried to make sure he did nothing that would call attention to itself.

"Ismene?"

A slightly cranky feminine voice cursing under her breath.

"Ismene? Are you there?"

"Of course I'm here. Who else would be here? Do you know how late it is?"

"Yeah, I'm sorry, but it's sort of an emergency."

"An emergency, huh. Is that what you're calling it these days?"

The sound of a chair being pulled out from a kitchen table.

And then: "Okay, so what is it?"

"I've got this young kid. He smacked his eye pretty good on the corner of a table. I need you to take a look at it."

"You do, huh. Why don't you try the hospital?"

"I can't do that Ismene. A hospital's no good. Not with this guy."

A long silence, except for the rain, and the glass paneled doors to the drugstore whooshing open and then whooshing closed in the background, and a few people blabbering away, incoherent, oblivious, thinking themselves the only souls wracked with pain on the entire planet. Then there was a tiny explosion of sound spiraling out from the receiver, or a series of tiny explosions: the sounds of a chair being pushed back, and then footsteps walking away, and then footsteps returning and the chair sliding back up to the table and someone rifling through the contents of a small leather bag or satchel, and then a sigh of satisfaction, or if not satisfaction, then perhaps hopeful resignation.

"Ismene?"

The rustling sound of someone pickling up the receiver.

"You're in luck. I've got everything we need."

"But Ismene . . ."

"Shshshsh. I'll be down in a few minutes."

The line went dead.

The replacement taxi driver put the phone on the hook and slipped out through the folding door. The people were still going in and out. Their faces glowed with an eerie dead light, as if their faces were not flesh-and-blood faces at all but were instead bronze or gold masks that could only reflect whatever illumination came their way. The clerk was still looking out through the plate glass window every now and then. Nobody paid any attention to the phone booth. The replacement taxi driver slid into the front seat and waited. The young man had not moved an inch. Twenty minutes later the curbside door opened and Ismene plopped herself next to the replacement taxi driver. She was wearing an elegant gold sequined dress with a heart-shaped neckline and gold high heels to match. She had been holding a flimsy silk jacket over her head to keep the rain off. With her hair dyed a platinum blonde and standing barely five feet tall, she gave Veronica Lake a run for her money.

"You're late."

"I know it."

Ismene removed a small brown shoulder bag from her shoulder and placed it in her lap. Then she leaned towards the replacement taxi driver and flashed a smile dripping with love and sarcasm. Her right eye disappeared behind a veil of blonde hair. "Come on sweetie," she said. "We can't stay here."

The replacement taxi driver nodded without returning the smile and they pulled away from the curb.

In a vacant lot somewhere along the Almendares River on the Vedado side, unidentifiable lights bobbing in the darkness, a few moss-covered trees clinging to the edge of the riverbank, the feeling of being submerged in a rising tide of insect sound (the deep-bellied thrumming of cicadas, the whir of mosquitoes), the tang of the not-so-distant sea lingering in the air, the rain beginning to subside:

"He isn't hurt that bad. But bad enough."

"Sure. I'll do what I can."

"He's a pretty important fish, I have to tell you."

"Why do you have to tell me anything?"

"I don't know. I just thought you should know."

"Sure, sweetie, sure."

The ex-nurse was already in the backseat. She reached

over to the front and grabbed her bag. The replacement taxi driver didn't remember her getting out of the car. He shrugged a blasé shrug, indifferent to the possibility of miracles, however minor, and flicked on the radio. Maybe the kid's eye wasn't all that bad, but it sure as hell looked bad. Better to be safe than sorry. Besides, he was tired of skipping around from cab company to cab company. The ex-nurse flicked the switch of a small pocket flashlight. The dim yellow light barely pierced the darkness, at least this was the replacement taxi driver's opinion, but it was more than enough for the ex-nurse. He watched her searching her bag for a moment, and then he settled back in his seat and closed his eyes. The sounds of a vibrant, bluesy jazz number filled the interior of the car.

And then a few moments later: "He won't let go."

The replacement taxi driver cracked an eye but did not turn his head.

"Of what?"

"Of the suitcase."

"Don't worry about the suitcase. He hasn't let go of the suitcase the whole damn night."

The replacement taxi driver descended back into the jazz. A vague premonition washed over him. Or perhaps it was the repetition of once familiar sounds. The ex-nurse pulled a flask from her bag and a small pouch containing a white powdery substance. She carefully measured out a spoonful of the powder and poured it into the flask. She shook the flask, and before the replacement taxi driver realized what the repetition of those familiar sounds meant, the ex-nurse was cradling the young man's head and helping him to drink. He swallowed every last drop. She let his head sag back against the seat.

"Ismene, what the hell are you doing?"

"Giving him the dope."

"What the hell for? I wanted you to look at his eye."

"Is that what you wanted."

It wasn't really a question.

She reached over towards the young man's bruised eye, peeled back the eyelid and flashed the flashlight at the pupil. Then she did the same to his unbruised eye. Then she sat back smiling that same smile of love and sarcasm.

"Tell me you didn't get me out of bed at 3:30 in the morning just because some drunk got a black eye. Tell me you were thinking how much you missed me. Tell me you wanted to see me one last time, take one more spin around the block, one more crazy night out on the town, just for old time's sake."

". . . ."

"I didn't think so."

The ex-nurse let out an explosive sigh of pent-up resentment as if her throat had been clogged with sand. The replacement taxi driver retreated, slid his head back against the doorframe. Inside the cab the air was hot and stuffy. Outside the rain was descending in short, violent bursts and then subsiding, like eruptions from inverted geysers. He cracked the window, closed his eyes and focused on the jazz. He didn't know what he had been thinking. Perhaps she was right. He must have been out of his mind to call her up. But what the hell. Now he knew for certain the kid's eye was okay. That was the important thing. She would've said something if it had been really bad. So let her rifle through the kid's pockets, the suitcase. What did he care? Besides, there couldn't be much left anyway. The kid had already forked over a grand in tips, maybe more. "Sure. Whatever you say Ismene."

But she didn't respond. She had already turned her attention to the young man. With practiced fingers, she undid the young man's grip on his suitcase and slid it across the seat. She flicked it open, pushed the few shirts and socks aside, and two seconds later the false bottom popped up.

"Who the fuck hides brochures in a false bottom?" she said. And then: "Who'd you say this guy was?"

The replacement taxi driver was smiling a relaxed, unexpected smile. He was not going to get sucked in.

"I guess I forgot to mention it."

Rummaging through the young man's pockets, she seemed to exist only in a cloud of desperation. She became invisible. The replacement taxi driver stared at the shimmering darkness of the rearview mirror, but his angle was bad. He could not see what she was up to. Then he heard a sigh of scorching relief. The air inside the cab was on fire. The head of the ex-nurse shot straight up, ecstatic. He could see her head bobbing about in the darkness, a ghostly, electrified head.

"Five-hundred smackers, sweetie, stuffed in his front pants pocket. What a dope!"

For a moment the replacement taxi driver forgot where he was. He put his hands on the wheel and pulled himself up to a driving position, but he kept his eyes on the rearview mirror.

He watched the ex-nurse a moment longer, her head bobbing up and down with great enthusiasm.

And then: 'Can I drop you somewhere?'

The ex-nurse smiled a soft, kittenish smile, her blonde hair now swirling carelessly about her face.

"You're such a sap, sweetie."

"No, I mean it. I've got plenty of time."

"You go ahead, sweetie. Drop this dope where he needs to go."

"You sure?"

"I'll be okay."

She began putting her things back into her bag.

And then: "You can call me any time."

Her right eye had once again disappeared behind a veil of blonde hair. She waited a moment, a gesture of gratitude, perhaps, but did not say another word. Then she slipped out of the taxi and headed towards the street. They were only a short fifteen-minute walk from the Cementerio de Cristóbal Colón. He knew that's where she was headed. She liked to walk there in the morning, especially on a rainy morning with the tombs glistening. She walked without faltering, even in high heels. He watched her until she vanished in a swirling cloud of rain and darkness. The purpose of darkness was to disfigure and obscure, he thought. He could not say what else he was thinking. After a while he started the engine and headed for the yacht club.

The sun rose in a burst of glory above the clouds, cymbals of sunlight crashing uselessly against the curvature of space, but beneath the clouds the sun was an undefinable nothingness. It was the beginning and the end of myth. Beyond the possibility of reason. The soft splattering of clocks tumbling into the mud. Then the clouds dissipated. A pale glow stretched out from the sea and infiltrated a landscape of silhouettes, two-dimensional cut-outs of leafy trees and small buildings and a few parked cars scattered about and the dark hulking behemoth of the yacht club. The silhouettes were still dripping with the moisture left over from the previous night's storm. It almost seemed as if the world had been under water for centuries.

The replacement taxi driver caught the watery glint of a car door opening, closing, a wine-colored De Soto, a beautiful car in the sunlight, but seeming different now, a ghostly, otherworldly reflection of itself. The fat stubby man appeared. He smiled a thin, fluid smile that belied a sleepless night. The replacement taxi driver had suffered a similar night and so responded with a similar smile. Moments later the two men stood outside the taxi, looking in through the window at the still slumbering young man. The atrociously puffy eye was his most prominent feature.

"What were you thinking?"

"Well I sure as hell didn't think he was going to bounce his eye off the end of a table."

"No, I suppose not."

The two men pulled away from the window.

"How long will he be out like this?"

"I don't know. I'd say a couple of hours."

"Damn Luis and his stupid games. Take the kid here. Switch taxis. Drive him there. One last night on the town. Wherever he wants to go. But not wherever. Secret envelopes. Watch out for the men with the long-barreled rifles. Cryptic phrases. 'The bull, like a castle under siege, has been eaten.' What the fuck does that even mean? Christ. Luis acts like we're living in some Hollywood movie. Only he's going to get us all killed."

The men became uncomfortably silent.

Sounds from the beach beyond the yacht club followed the light as it tunneled its way through the darkness of the trees. A few early risers beachcombing. A dog barking. The sound of a motor boat motoring slowly past the beach, the engine sputtering for a moment, a strangely suspicious sound, and then the boat suddenly speeding away.

"Where do you want me to take him?"

"Take him to Café Paraiso. On Compostela. About a block from the harbor."

"I know the place."

"And don't go disappearing. I want you to make sure he gets on that ferry."

"Sure. I'll be his babysitter till the end. You want I should spoon feed him his breakfast."

"You're a smart guy. But don't go doing anything stupid. Stay out of sight. Pull around to the alley on the side. You should be able to see the whole joint from the side door. Just stay out of sight yourself."

"Okay. Don't worry about it. I'll be invisible."

"And make sure he gets on that ferry. The *S. S. City of Havana*. It leaves at 10:30 for Key West."

The fat man handed the replacement taxi driver a set of keys.

"Give them to the kid when you get to the café."

The De Soto had vanished by the time the taxi started rolling. 'You can thank me later, fat man,' the replacement taxi driver was thinking, but he wasn't sure he would see the fat man again.

-104-

After Regla, Nerea and Immanuel headed first to Federico's estate, just to make sure, and then they switched gears and headed back towards Old Havana and the art deco tenement building. They soon found themselves motoring slowly through a crumbling, invisible neighborhood a few blocks north of Cristina Train Station. The rain had become quite severe at times, obliterating everything in sight.

Nerea had cut the other two loose for the evening. They had thanked her in Sicilian and smiled at each other with great enthusiasm for the mischief they were going to get into. They had not had a night off in a long time. But a night was only a night. Nerea had also told them to be at Café Paraiso by eight in the morning. Oscar would be there, she said. He would arrive shortly after nine. They were to keep an eye on him until she got there. He would be quite groggy from drinking the night before, so he would give them little difficulty. They did not ask her how she knew this.

After the art deco tenement, Nerea and Immanuel made their way to a small, gravel parking lot near the wharf where the *S. S. City of Havana* was moored.

They settled back in the Packard to wait out the storm.

For most of that suffocating, interminably dark night, Immanuel pressed his hand to his ear and listened with delicate intensity to the radio chatter flowing back and forth between the men in fedoras scattered all over the city. Occasionally, using a distorted, gravelly, alien voice, he spoke into a tiny transmitter that seemed to be sewn into the lapel of his jacket, but not even Nerea could have heard what he said. But in truth she did not care. By four in the morning she had all but forgotten Immanuel was sitting in the back seat. Julio Mella had returned. Nerea was almost sitting in Julio's lap. For several hours he talked about the life he had once lived. He talked in his voice of orange-blossom honey until the sun had burned away the morning mist.

The highlights of what Julio said to Nerea on that rainy, misty morning:

'Ah, yes, Tina kept her edge razor sharp.'

'. . . .'

'No, not at first. When I first met her I fancied myself a writer, not a revolutionary.'

'. . . .'

'She was a photographer. She was many things, but when I knew her she was a photographer. She wore nothing more than a simple skirt and a white blouse. Almost like a young novitiate. But her fiery, indomitable spirit gave her a beauty that no one could touch or take away, no matter how much pain she went through.'

'. . . .'

'Yes, my Nerea, you have a similar beauty, a similar indomitable spirit. You might have been sisters, or at least cousins.'

Julio and Nerea were laughing softly. Julio's lively green eyes danced with mirth. Nerea drew him close to her, burying her face in his dark curly hair, breathing in the salty smell of a windswept sea.

'Yes, she took many photographs of me. In one I am pretending to be asleep on a grassy lawn. In another I am twirling about in my fancy Texan hat, laughing and dancing on a summer's day, just like anyone. But she preferred the ones where I was the serious revolutionary. Like the photograph in the lobby of the hotel where we first met.'

'. . . .'

'No, no, my personal favorites were always the ones where I am busy at my typewriter. My typewriter was my most important weapon, and she captured the truth of this in her photographs, the truth of my idealism.'

'. . . .'

'"Poverty and elegance go hand in hand in this world," I used to tell her.'

'. . . .'

'"Love and death are but trials of the soul."'

'. . . .'

'No. I was too young to understand what it really meant to die. Yes, I had always imagined myself as the leader of a desperate group of men, passionate even in the face of insurmountable odds, men whose only hope lay in the darkness of the abyss, like those fearless and mythic Texians and Tejanos during the Battle of the Alamo. But strangely, I never imagined myself dead. Tina photographed me all laid out in my coffin, surrounded by flowers and candles. There was a golden hammer and sickle on the wall. A huge red star. Do you want to know how naïve I was? I thought my death would be held up as a symbol of the pledge by all revolutionaries to work tirelessly until we obtained victory for all of the exploited peoples of the world. But we did not know how impossible this dream would be. Symbols are incapable of doing any real work.'

'. . . .'

'No, no. I did not realize that I was choosing a path until it was too late. You could say my path chose me. I was in prison and I went on a hunger strike because they had no reason to put me in jail. That was in December 1925. Eighteen days I went without, and then Machado had me released. It was a Christmas present. Of course they did not like my politics. If Machado had let me die in prison perhaps the world would be better off. But they did not permit a prisoner to commit suicide. Naturally we assumed Machado was only biding his time. That is why I went to Mexico City. Villena was right when he declared Machado to a be a donkey with claws. But Machado was not behind my death. I was behind it, and Tina, and Villena, and Diego Rivera, that fat cowardly Mexican fuck. My death put Diego in the limelight. Suddenly the whole world was celebrating Diego and his outrageous paintings.'

Julio stopped talking for a moment, and in the rainy darkness it looked like he had suddenly, but with some degree of forethought, opened the door to a secret compartment and pulled out two books. It was like he had reached into another dimension. He gave the books to Nerea. The first book was a paperback copy of Blasco Ibáñez's novel *Los muertos mandan*. The second was Trotsky's *The Permanent Revolution*. Trotsky's book had been published after Mella's death.

Nerea paid no attention to Trotsky. Her eyes were fixated

on the cover of Ibáñez's novel. There was a man with a gun surrounded by a surrealist depiction of the dead: clouds of various washed-out colors (dark faded blues, teal, tan, white) that vaguely resembled skulls, and a skeletal ghost hovering just above the man's head. Nerea had the sense that the man was a puppet of the dead. The man vaguely reminded her of Oscar.

'Trotsky believed that Communism had lost its way, and he was right. But Trotsky had been abandoned by all but those with the purest of hearts. We understood this. But we were foolish. We truly thought we could re-energize the Communist movement, that Communism would then become what it was meant to become: the beacon in the darkness.'

'. . . .'

'Do you want to know the real truth about my death? We thought we could gain more by my death than by my life. We thought my death, my assassination, would shock everyone out of their complacency. This would be the first step towards creating the paradise we had always dreamed of. Were we mistaken? Martí believed it was possible to have pure democracy and equality for all social classes. Marti dreamed of a republic "with all and for all." But there can never be political equality without economic justice. We thought my death would be a dazzling white light shining on the injustice that always thrives in the shadows.'

'. . . .'

'To calmly witness a crime is to commit that crime. How many crimes have we committed in Cuba?'

'. . . .'

'We were pretty sure Machado was going to get me one way or another. So one night we decided I would give up my life for the future of oppressed people everywhere. Truly it was the decision of people too young to know any better.'

'. . . .'

'It was Villena who concocted the story that Tina tried to sell to the press. Two assassins waiting in the shadows at midnight. Near the corner of Morelos and Abraham González. The flash of a revolver and the assassins running away. The fiery, charismatic Julio Antonio Mella bleeding out in the street. Sirens wailing in the distance, but then the sound is absorbed by the darkness all around. His one and only love staring mutely into space with uncomprehending eyes, as if the laws that governed the universe had suddenly ceased to work.'

'. . . .'

'We chose that corner because of its obvious revolutionary implications. It's symbolic relevance. González was the mentor to Pancho Villa. And Morales was the birthplace of Zapata and at the center of every revolution in Mexico since 1811. That is why we chose that corner. Only a select few would ever realize the truth we kept to ourselves, our own inner flame, the echo of courageous footsteps. Everyone else would think Machado was behind the assassination. And my death would ignite the world. But this did not happen.'

'. . . .'

'The police accused Tina. They tried to say she was working with Vittorio Vidali, that Italian pig! They thought I had been betrayed by the one person whose love for me was a tiny bright flower in the desert. An angel's love. Such a love is incompatible with violence.'

'. . . .'

'Ah, my beautiful, sweet, compassionate Tina.'

'. . . .'

'Betrayal springs from a more stringent kind of love.'

'. . . .'

'They were onto the truth of it, of course, the police. A truth of a sort. But for all the wrong reasons.'

'. . . .'

'Yes, the world is full of such ironies.'

'. . . .'

'We were men of spotless character, except for an occasional dalliance, but that is only natural. We were a creed to live by. But now we are all but forgotten, except as images of propaganda, the true meaning of our words, the vitality of our intentions twisted beyond all recognition.'

'. . . .'

'My poor, poor Tina. She was an angel who floated about, her hands taking care of many small things.'

-105-

Café Paraiso occupied the first floor of a red brick building hidden in the darkly gleaming shadows and dark green foliage of Calle Compostela, a short walk from the harbor, two blocks east of Egido and the remnants of the southeast corner of the old city wall, which was begun in 1674 and took over sixty years to build, and which the city fathers decided to tear down in 1863, but much of the wall still divided Havana, at least in spirit, even at the dawn of the twentieth century. The upper floors of this red brick building, of course, were given over to nighttime activities. This was not surprising in a neighborhood teeming with the steamy sensuality of people living on the edge, beyond the edge, pimps and prostitutes everywhere you looked, the camaraderie, true friendship and solidarity of those on the bottom rung, a neighborhood illuminated at night by the red light of moral imperfection, a neighborhood which was both beautiful and seductive in its fragility. But during the day the café was a symbol of the American dream. In Cuba there was always a great longing for anything American. The cafe promised American-style pancakes and waffles from six to ten in the morning, and a businessman's lunch from eleven until two in the afternoon. So it was bustling with activity. The tables were mostly empty, but the counter was crammed full of regulars eating hearty breakfasts and drinking bottomless cups of coffee. A middle-aged woman with thick, juicy arms glided back and forth along the counter, refilling coffee cups, appearing suddenly with plates of eggs and sausages and pancakes and waffles and heaping mounds of butter and glass jars filled with steaming hot maple syrup for the many hungry mouths that needed feeding. The regulars all wore caps and short-sleeve shirts and khaki work pants and muddy work boots. Many had not showered or shaved in days. It seemed likely that they worked somewhere on one of the nearby wharves, or perhaps down by the train station. But they seemed to be taking their time with their breakfasts, so it was hard to say. Occasionally the middle-aged woman waded out into the sea of mostly empty tables. A young man was sitting at the second table from the door next to a row of windows. He was wearing a badly stained white linen suit and a shabby Panama hat. He had placed a suitcase on the floor beneath the window sill. It was clear he had had a rough night, perhaps many rough nights. He was sipping a coffee, very black, holding his forehead with one hand, his eyes half-closed, not eyes so much as slits, even in the absence of any direct sunlight. One of his eyes was badly bruised, and in between sips he sometimes touched it with his fingertips, gingerly, as if he could not quite believe it was his eye. The row of windows afforded no view to speak of. A building or series of buildings from the colonial period on the other side of the street, the buildings set back from the street, tenements, perhaps, obscured by the heavy, wet greenery of laurel and tamarind and a few lime trees or avocado trees (perhaps the only stretch of Compostela that had any trees at all). A few pedestrians scattered here and there, glimpsed through the leaves, and then disappearing through narrow doors. Calle Compostela was a fairly well-traveled street because of its proximity to the harbor, though it was mostly foot traffic and bicycles out front of Café Paraiso during the day, with only an occasional motorcycle or car, and every now and then a truck looking to avoid the heavier traffic on Monserrate or making a delivery, but late in the evening there were taxis everywhere rambling back and forth in search of lost souls. The middle-aged woman hovered over the young man with motherly apprehension. She did not like the look of his eye. It was an atrocious looking eye. It was very puffy. The skin all around was deep purple in color, almost black in places. She paid no attention at all to the two young men in fedoras sitting three rows back from the door along the wall. They were not interested in breakfast. They had been drinking coffee for over an hour, cup after cup after cup, and speaking in happy, friendly, carefree whispers, as if they had a great many jokes to tell each other, a vast number that would require many more pots of coffee but little else. They seemed friendly enough, but they were also speaking in a foreign language, she did not know which one, and she did not like the way they were looking at the young man by the window. She wondered if perhaps they had been the ones who had given the young man his black eye. It didn't matter what they had done or not done. They were trouble. That's what she thought. Once or twice she thought they were holding long-barreled rifles, but when she looked back the rifles had vanished. She wouldn't have been surprised if they had started levitating, or, conversely, if they had suddenly begun spinning like whirling dervishes, the tips of their cloven-hoofed feet (because all demons possessed cloven-hoofed feet) cutting through the floorboards of the cafe and the soft, loamy earth beneath that and the pockets of limestone, creating with their mad, unknowable desires a dark, foreboding tunnel all the way down to the black, volcanic rock that was the bedrock of the city. Yes, they were trouble, she thought. She was on the verge of asking them to leave half a dozen times, but each time the thought popped into her head it was immediately obliterated by the clamor of the regulars at the counter. There was a steady stream of regulars, as there was every morning except Sundays, and when one finished his breakfast, another would take his place at the counter. None of the regulars sat at a table. The tables were for tourists who had just gotten off a boat and wanted something to tie them over until they found their hotel, or they were waiting to board a ferry and were eating and drinking just to kill time. The regulars were talking about the storm the night before. That's all they seemed to be talking about. The storm had covered the shoreline with all sorts of detritus. Abandoned boots, shoes, articles of clothing, empty wooden crates, old tires, hubcaps, the splintered remains of boats that had capsized, smashed guitars, caps, hats, gloves, bottles of all kinds with fancy lettering blown into the glass, tin cans, water-soaked books, broken lamps, hundreds of fish carcasses (bluefin and yellowfin and ballyhoo, as well as a mixed bag of smaller fish), a smörgåsbord of dead and dying crabs, the hard-packed remains of jelly fish, an octopus or two, strands of leafy, purplish seaweed, the tangled scraps of a few fishing nets, a few juvenile marlins, and a couple of sharks. The men laughed about the sharks. You never knew what riches lay inside the belly of a shark, they said. They laughed some more. Their laughter was like a beacon in the dark. Then the conversation shifted to women and whether or not marriage was worth it, and someone said not in this neighborhood, and everyone laughed, and someone else said 'Wanted: young women with pleasing appearance to work nights, apply at Café Paraiso, particularly interested in rural girls.' The laughter became a second storm. The middle-aged woman pretended she didn't hear. Her husband emerged from the kitchen and the laughter slowly subsided, became a steady, indecent, snickering drizzle. The husband had a plate of pancakes and sausage in his hand and a steaming cup of coffee. He went over to a side door that was often overlooked. The side door was in two parts and the top part was open. The bottom part formed a counter of sorts for customers who wanted to eat outside and didn't mind standing in an alley. The alley was a grass covered alley that ran along the south side of the red brick building, the side closest to the harbor, and ended in a rubbish heap. The husband passed the plate and the coffee to someone on the other side of the half-door, a dark complected man with a gruff, raspy masculine voice. The man began to eat. The middle-aged woman didn't care who ate in the alley. The husband talked with the man while he ate and they laughed about the good old days when people came to watch them play baseball. The laughter of the dark complected man sounded a little like a flock of wild parrots whirling through the trees, screeching at the tops of their lungs. Some of the regulars wondered out loud where the parrots had come from and then they chuckled softly, knowingly, but they did not look up from their plates. Then the middle-aged woman ordered her husband back to the kitchen and the laughter like a flock of wild parrots faded completely. The two men in fedoras looked over at the man in the alley with the strange-sounding laughter but then they forgot him immediately. The steady stream of regulars continued. The conversation shifted from women and marriage to politics. Some of the regulars were wondering how much money Batista had stolen from the country. They guessed it was in the millions. They did not say the name Batista, but everyone knew who they were talking about. Someone said that it was getting so bad that surely the Americans were going to get involved, but everyone knew this would never happen. Then the conversation shifted to modes of travel and the regulars were suddenly talking like big-talkers about whether it was more enjoyable to take a sleeping car on a train like the Patagonian Express, which ran from Buenos Aires south to Esquel, or a berth on a steamer, like one from the Lamport and Holt Line, a boat that went up the coast from Buenos Aires to Montevideo to Santos to Rio de Janeiro. The regulars were split in their opinion, and one of them had just called over to the two men wearing fedoras to possibly break the tie when the front door opened and a man with a shining example of a Platt Guardsman suitcase entered the café. The man was wearing a beige herringbone blazer, a white shirt and a chartreuse tie, and brown and beige saddle shoes to match the blazer. He took a seat at the third table from the door along the row of windows, placing his suitcase on the floor beneath the window sill. It looked like he had slept in his clothes. Or perhaps he hadn't slept at all. He sat with his back to the young man at the second table. The young man looked over at the counter for the middle-aged woman, but he could not see her. The two men wearing fedoras stared at the man in the herringbone blazer. They were convinced they had seen him before but they could not place him. A meaty, rollicking voice called out from the counter: "Train or steamer, my friend?" The regulars burst into laughter. A few applauded. But the man in the herringbone blazer did not answer. He stood up when his coffee arrived, staring out the window at the heavy, wet greenery across the street, which was no longer so wet, and the steady, throbbing, nightmarish brightness of the sun which had burst through the clouds that very moment. He tossed down his coffee in three gulps. Then he tossed a few coins on the table, grabbed his suitcase and headed out the door. Except it was not his suitcase, a discrepancy that the two men wearing fedoras noticed instantly. The young man did not notice the switch, or he pretended not to. He seemed oblivious to the comings and goings in the café, except, perhaps, as one senses on an unconscious, subterranean level the fluid tremors of a landscape always shifting beneath one's feet. The young man's eyes were still slits. The men wearing fedoras exchanged worried glances. They bent their heads to confer. Then one of them hurried through the door, stopping only a moment, presumably to get his bearings, and then he started running down Compostela towards the harbor after the man in the herringbone blazer. Anyone who was looking would have seen a long-barreled rifle gleaming in the fresh sunlight. The dark complected man realized something was up and finished his coffee and shouted a quick goodbye to his friend. In an instant he was in his taxi with the engine running, but he did not pull out of the alley. From where he sat he could see obliquely into the café. He could not see the young man by the window, but he could see part of the counter and the shadowy profiles of a few regulars, and beyond the counter he could see the shadowy torso (like the negative of a decayed Greek statue) of the companion to the man who had left with his gleaming rifle. The dark complected man watched the shadowy torso with a keen intensity that was broken only momentarily by the sound of a distant gunshot, which was followed by a second lingering gunshot, and then a long, eerie silence, as if the world had been a balloon and now the air was escaping into the silent tomb of outer space. Everyone inside the café heard the gunshots and wondered what was happening. The young man by the window suddenly stood up as if emerging from the blackness of the cinema into broad daylight. At that same instant the dark complected man revved the engine of the taxi. The companion to the man with the gleaming rifle was distracted by the sound and took his eyes off the young man. The young man left a very large bill on the table to pay for his breakfast. Then he grabbed the remaining suitcase and slipped out the door. The middle-aged woman saw him leave and raced from the counter, waving her arms in the air and shouting with a strained, overworked voice, but when she saw the bill on the table she stopped shouting. She looked out the window to see if she could catch a glimpse of the young man in the shabby white suit and the shabby Panama hat, who she suddenly viewed as a supernatural being in disguise, perhaps Oggún himself, who was also known to some of the faithful as Saint Michael, but he was Saint Peter to others, and also Saint James, but the young man had already crossed over to the other side of the street and was lost in the shadows of the trees. The dark complected man saw the young man pass by the alley before crossing and took his foot off the gas. The young man tried to remain as inconspicuous as possible. He was motoring as fast as one can motor without breaking into a run. He tried to focus only on where he was going, but he saw the gleaming barrel of a rifle and could not help but look across. The rifle was heading the other way. At that same instant the man carrying the rifle looked across and saw the young man in a gap between two trees. Their eyes met. They continued walking in opposite directions, but their eyes remained locked, their heads swiveling slowly with suspicion. At that same instant the companion to the man with the rifle dashed out onto the sidewalk in front of the café. He seemed disoriented. The head of the man with the rifle snapped to attention. He saw his friend and waved and shouted and told him to get the car and started running towards the café. At that same instant the young man shoved his suitcase under one arm and grabbed his shabby Panama hat with his free hand and started running pell mell the other way. He was almost to the end of Calle Compostela. He could smell the oily, fishy smell of the harbor and the fumes from the automobiles and trucks speeding along San Pedro. He heard the low rumble of trains and a few ship horns and the ships heading out to sea and the tooting of the small ferries going back and forth to Regla and the cries of disenchanted seagulls. At the same instant the dark complected man saw the man with the rifle run past the alley. A car started and tires squealed. The dark complected man waited a moment and then hit the gas and his taxi zoomed out of the alley. The taxi smashed into a 1956 Chevrolet Bel Air four-door hardtop. The taxi was badly dented, the front grill was crumpled up like an accordion, but the Chevrolet was in far worse shape. The left side of the Chevrolet had been crushed. The doorframe had snapped from the impact and a jagged piece of metal had sliced through the driver's stomach and he was coughing and spitting up blood. His companion was trying to open the passenger side door, but his right shoulder was dislocated so he couldn't get his arm to work correctly. He could not remember where they were or what time it was. The dark complected man was unhurt, though when he stepped out of the taxi his legs wobbled a bit. He walked over to the Chevrolet and looked with grim detachment at the two men in fedoras. The driver leaned back and looked up as if the dark complected man were an avenging angel or a deranged Orisha and smiled. Blood ran down from his gums and filled in the spaces between his teeth. The dark complected man was unmoved and pulled out a black handled Libia and shot the driver in the side of the head. The driver's companion began to panic, fumbling about the front seat with his one good arm and his one dangling appendage, trying to get his hands on his rifle, but his rifle was nowhere to be found. And then it was too late. The dark complected man had rounded the car by then. He shot the second man twice, once in the back of the neck, and the man fell to one side, his head twisting as he fell, landing on his companion's bloodied leg at an odd angle so all he could see was a narrow wedge of sunlight that came in through the open window, his eyes fish-blinking slowly, his breathing becoming shallow, spreading out like a fine mist. And then the dark complected man fired a second time, aiming very carefully, point blank, the barrel of the pistol up against the peeled eyeball of the left socket. He sent a bullet careening across the island universe of his adversary. At that same instant the young man with the suitcase was heading up San Pedro on the city side. He was no longer running. The brim of his Panama hat was pulled down, obscuring his face. But he had gone only a block or two when he was urged by a sense of mystery and unease that some would have mistaken for the voice of God to stop and turn around. The traffic was whirling past, a steady mechanical hum, then spinning around the rim of the rotunda at Desamparados. He should not have been able to see what he saw because of the trees in the center of the rotunda. It seemed as if the air was shimmering, as if he was looking down a long, narrow tunnel between two worlds. Wormhole of his devouring imagination. Refracted images of a silent movie. Echo of a fading dream. He saw a body near the remnants of the old city wall. The body was sprawled across a narrow sidewalk, a Platt Guardsman suitcase a few feet away, the contents tossed about, spilling into the street and the circling traffic. Two figures were huddled over the body, but as soon as they sensed he was watching, they stood up. It almost seemed like they were levitating. One of the figures raised an arm and there was the flash of sunlight on metal, a gun, perhaps. In the shadowy glare this first figure seemed to possess the elongated snout of a jackal or some other creature of the night guarding a forgotten tomb. But the young man was staring at the second figure, a long-legged woman with the headpiece of a shining golden sun like a halo upon her head and she had thick curly black hair and a single blood-red gardenia pinned above her right ear. She was immaculate in her blackness, a dazzling purity that took the young man's breath away. The woman put her hand to the raised arm of the first figure, a quieting gesture. The young man heard the woman speak, but he could not possibly have heard her speak or have even seen her standing there above the body of the dead man on the far side of the rotunda at Desamparados. We can let him go, my love, the woman said. She was speaking to the first figure. Come, we have done what we set out to do. The first figure lowered his arm. The tunnel began to collapse, but still the young man could not take his eyes away. The woman smiled a dazzling bright smile, as if there were a thousand jewels between her teeth. It was the smile of a goddess: implacable, relentless, murderous, beautiful and terrible to behold. It was a smile of unashamed sadness mixed with timeless, amused, irreverent triumph. It was a self-indulgent smile of privileged insight that said: that which might never have existed at all, existed once, and that makes all the difference.

-106-

The *S. S. City of Havana* was originally launched by the Newport New Shipbuilding and Drydock Company on November 18, 1943 and was transferred to the Royal Navy three months later and renamed the *HMS Northway.* It saw limited action during D-Day as a transport ship for trucks and other military vehicles, and served the rest of the war as a hospital transport ferrying hundreds of wounded soldiers back across the Channel to England. In 1951 it was sold to the Suwannee Steamship Company of Jacksonville, Florida and renamed the *S. S. City of Havana.* It provided ferry service between Key West and Havana for eight years, until Castro came to power. In 1962 it was sold to the West German Navy and designated an Accommodation Ship, servicing Bremerhaven for three years. From 1967 until 1972 it ferried people back and forth between Antwerp and Rotterdam. The boat was scrapped in 1973.

Oscar could not remember where exactly the *S. S. City of Havana* was moored. He did not go down to the harbor all that often and had forgotten the name of the wharf, but then he saw the boat and names didn't matter.

In spite of the tenderness of his eye and the steady, throbbing bursts of pain, he remembered everything Luis had told him. He went down to the automobile deck and put the suitcase in the trunk of the De Soto. A stevedore stepped out of a hidden stairwell as Oscar was closing the trunk and asked him what he was doing down there, all passengers were supposed to be up in the lounge or on one of the upper decks. The man spoke with a strange foreign accent that Oscar had never heard before. Oscar showed him the car keys and the stevedore nodded and made his way through the parked cars to the other side and disappeared into another stairwell. The boat was not yet under way, but Oscar could already feel the steady rumble of the two steam turbines beneath his feet, and then he heard some shouting from above and he knew that the mooring lines had been cast off.

Oscar headed up to the passenger lounge. Near the doors to the lounge there were several small souvenir shops or boutiques where they sold jewelry, watches, books, magazines, newspapers, chewing gum, t-shirts and other trinkets for the tourists. He bought a pack of Wrigley's from a man named Rogelio, a short, olive-skinned man with a shining bald head and a huge, toothy smile. Rogelio was bored silly and wanted to talk, and Oscar was too tired to resist. There were no other customers, but that was not unusual. Rogelio said he did most of his business on the trips from Key West to Havana, not the other way around. He said the owner of the ferry had put in air conditioning in 1953 to attract a higher-class clientele. The shops and boutiques had followed soon after that. And then a chef from Denmark to prepare small high-class tidbits like Danish smoked salami sausages for the passengers. Sometimes it was more than Rogelio could bear.

"But I tell you," said Rogelio, "it is very exciting working here. Just last year do you know who was on this boat? Faustino Pérez was on this boat. Imagine that! Of course when we got back to Havana the police were waiting at the dock. A huge fuss of police cars with their lights flashing. Colonel Orlando Piedra, the Chief of the Secret Police himself, came on board and took each one of us into the passenger lounge, one at a time, and sat us down and asked us questions. What were we thinking, he said, to let Faustino Pérez escape like that, one of the rebels who had helped to organize the storming of the barracks at Moncada and who was now gallivanting about with Castro and plotting God knows what? What does one say to such absurd questions? How does one respond? So I said what I knew. I said a man who maybe was Faustino and who maybe was not Faustino was on this boat. He bought a book from me. An Agatha Christie detective novel named *The Secret Adversary*. Then he went into the lounge and I did not see him again. That is what I told the Colonel. That was the end of my interrogation. But I was not altogether honest. I tell you now it was definitely Faustino with his sparkling eyes full of mischief. There is no doubt. And yes, he did buy an Agatha Christie book. And what is more, he read it. I know this because I saw him one more time on this ferry. He stopped by my counter some months later and he bought this or that, and then he pulled me close and he said this book he had bought was a great book. He said it was about two Americans, a rich millionaire who carries a gun and is not afraid to use it, and his first cousin, a young nurse who works in a field hospital during the Great War and who is given a set of secret papers while aboard the *Lusitania*, just hours before the *Lusitania* is sent to the bottom, torpedoed by a German U-boat. The book depicted a world of intrigue, secret treaties between America and Great Britain, Bolshevik conspirators intent on fomenting revolution, and English spies trying to stop them. And yet it was a book every good Cuban should read, Faustino said, because it spoke the truth, even though you had to peel back many layers to get to this truth. Then he said it had been made into a movie in Germany in

1929, a silent movie, but they gave it a different name. I do not remember what it was. He said it had been directed by Fred Sauer, a great filmmaker who had eventually been abandoned by the Nazis. That is what Faustino said."

Then Rogelio pulled out a copy of *The Secret Adversary* and showed it to Oscar. The book was in English, which Oscar did not understand very well, but he bought the book anyway and headed into the passenger lounge. He ordered a mojito, but he didn't want to stay inside so he went up the stairs to the upper deck and sat down in a slatted chair looking out at the water. It was very sunny, a bright, white, burning sunshine. In the bright glaring sunlight, his white linen suit was no longer stained and timeworn, and his Panama hat was once again immaculate. He tried to read but it was too bright, so he set the book beneath the chair and sipped his drink. Four musicians — two guitar players, a bass player, and a maraca player — were playing a steamy bolero by the railing. He was sitting near the back of the boat and he could see they were already miles out to sea. For a moment he sat there listening to the music and thinking about Havana. Why had Luis headed south on San Pedro towards the rotunda and not north towards the ferry? What had happened to the two men in fedoras who had been watching him all morning? He wondered about this for a while but he knew he would never know why or what. The musicians finished their bolero and joked around a bit, laughing in the sunshine, before they started playing again. Oscar looked back at the shadowy outline of Cuba on the horizon. The harbor entrance was already lost in the shimmering brilliance of the water, but he could see a hazy, reddish-gray cloud hovering above the island. He wondered if the cloud had always been there and if you could only see it when you were miles away, or if another storm was moving in.

If Oscar had possessed a more philosophical mind, he might have concluded that his questions about the nature of the reddish gray cloud and why Luis had headed south down San Pedro instead of north and what had become of the two men in fedoras were merely symptomatic evidence that he lived within the abyss, which is where, to adopt a current popular line of thinking, we all live. But what does it mean to live in the abyss? How does one define the abyss? Is it the epicenter of infinite nothingness, a cold, lifeless void? Is it a place of unimaginable, eternal suffering? Is it something else entirely? Perhaps the answer lies in the subterranean depths of the human soul, the collective unconscious. Perhaps the abyss only seems to exist because of our inability to comprehend what is truly happening all around us and why, no matter what plausible explanations we assign to the events of the here and now, and how these events shape our hope in the hereafter. Perhaps we are like a white bird in a golden cage, an exotic, white-plumed bird like a cockatoo or a cockatiel or some other kind of white bird. And in the particular philosophical cage where we find ourselves, the door is always open. We may fly away at any time. Or we may stay put. It is up to us. And yet no matter what we choose to do, we are trapped inside this cage. Even when we are flying free, all we can see are the golden bars. Of course we realize that it is our own thoughts that trap us, that keep us from the truth of who we are and who we might possibly become. But what can we do? This is just the way things are. So we conclude that we can never know what is real and what is not. We can do nothing. In other words, we live in an abyss of our own making, the by-product of deluded thinking, which means that the abyss as an actual, physical place that devours the soul of humanity does not really exist at all.

But Oscar did not see the world through a philosophical lens. In fact, if he had had his way that morning, he would have drunk mojitos until he slipped into a coma (an abyss of another kind). So he sat in the slatted chair, his one good eye and his badly bruised eye closed to the unimaginably hot and yet strangely exhilarating sun and the pure sunshine burning away the features of his face, slowly sipping his mojito, listening to the four musicians and letting the music wash through him, thinking about the steamy, sensual, provocative world he had left behind, thinking about Nerea and how he would never see her again, but also thinking about the sandy white beaches of Florida and the bright lights of Miami and the nightclub he would one day open, and he already knew the name of it, his nightclub would be called La Campana, just like the one in Havana. And in this way he passed the time until he arrived in Key West.

BOOK SIX

the glory days of La Campana

-107-

The young ones have been saying I don't have many days left. They are saying I must surely be dying. Am I not afraid to close my eyes at night? I have to laugh. I am as old as any saint that was ever buried beneath the streets of Rome. But I am not that old. And I live in Miami, not Rome. But some days I feel as old as the crumbling bones that fill the catacombs of my lonely heart. These words are the truth. I stole them from Sister Faustina, but she would not mind this small theft. She speaks like that. She speaks the language of poetry. And they do fit the way I feel on some days, these words. And yet I am not distressed by this feeling of loneliness. It is a surface feeling only. A momentary pause. It is the skin of a silent drum. Beneath my loneliness, or maybe inside my loneliness, there is a great joy that refuses now to stay hidden. I think perhaps my joy is a youthful joy that I have only recently rediscovered. Or perhaps it is a joy I have never known before, but I know it now, a gift from God, a trembling sense of wonder spreading its majestic wings. I do not think there is anything at my age that could bring more joy than the gift of wonder.

I am not sure I know how to explain it. I try to explain what I am thinking to these young ones who have not yet taken their final vows, but they do not understand. So I say a word or two about God. It is easy to believe in God, I tell them. When you have seen what I have seen it is impossible not to believe in God, but that is only part of it, I tell them, and then I start to cackle and spit, and I almost choke I am laughing so hard, but they do not see the humor.

Isidora, they say, please will you tell us a few more stories. Sister Faustina will not mind. She has made us promise that we will not tax your strength, but she has given us her permission.

I have to narrow my eyes when they say that. I have to give them a very stern look. Do not be too sure, I say. If Sister Faustina heard even half of what I am telling you girls, she would send me packing. And then I close my eyes and pretend I am sleeping, but the girls persist. There are too many voices to ignore. My room is overflowing with clamoring young novitiates. What can I say?

It is not much of a room really. The walls are white and

there is a narrow bed with a beige spread in one corner and a wooden desk opposite the bed with a pile of books that Sister Faustina has given me to read, but I will never read them. They are books about Mary and the lives of the Saints and the Pierced Heart of Jesus, and I probably should read them. But I have moved beyond such books now, I think. I certainly do not need them to know God. If they were poetry books, perhaps, but not books such as these. Besides, I talk to God every day. Above the desk and this pile of unnecessary books there is a wooden crucifix nailed to the wall, and whenever I want to speak to my God I look at this crucifix and I speak, whatever comes to my mouth. God listens carefully to everything I have to say. I also have a small refrigerator where I keep this and that. And I am permitted the luxury of an easy chair, because of my advanced condition, that is what Sister Faustina calls it. She is always making excuses for the open wound my life once was, but that life is no longer my life. But what does it matter? I am grateful for the chair in any event. It is a soft suede wing chair, the same color as my bedspread, with a separate footrest. It is very comfortable. The young novitiates gave me a lambswool blanket for my birthday to place over my knees in the morning or the afternoon or the evening when I am sitting in my chair. I have always liked the way lambswool feels against my skin, even on the hottest days. Emidio placed the chair by the window so I could see what there is to see. It is not much of a view, but it is not Emidio's fault.

Every so often I call Emidio by my brother's name, Emilio. Some days it is hard to know what I am saying. It is hard to tell one name from another. But Emidio does not mind. He is a good man and he does what he can for the Sisters here, and he does what he can for an old bag of bones like me. With the joy of a smuggler etched across his normally inscrutable face, he brings me many books of poetry to read and various trendy magazines and chocolate covered almonds even though I have few teeth left, which means I have to suck on them for quite a while before I can mash them with my gums. Yes, Emidio is very kind to me, even though I am not a Sister. The window is a long, narrow window with a handle that is easy to grip, so even an old woman with little strength can let in a breeze. It is a floor-to-ceiling window that permits me a view of a tiny sliver of the sidewalk and a tiny sliver of the street with its parked cars and a few bungalows on the other side and a few lime trees. I keep the window open because there is no air conditioning. On a very quiet afternoon I can hear the sounds of children playing in the park that is only three blocks away. Some days the air is so still I can almost hear the bells of the Church of the Immaculate Heart, or the Church of Saint Jude, which is a Byzantine church, which I went to by mistake once when I was in downtown Miami, but it is a very pretty stone church with a red tile roof and a few palms trees out front and some other kinds of trees and a couple of downtown high-rise apartment buildings nearby, looming over this small stone church, but not in a menacing way, and they are Melkites there, which I had never heard of before, which one of the young men standing in the back of the church was kind enough to tell me, and he wasn't bothered in the least that I was there by mistake, and he even went so far as to say that there are no mistakes in the presence of God, which I didn't quite agree with him about that, but he was young, let him find out for himself, I was thinking, but then, as if he had read my thoughts, he said 'God tempts us, surely, but He does not lead us into error,' and then he smiled a very mysterious smile, it reminded me of the way certain saints seem to be smiling, at least the statues of those saints whenever I stumble upon them by accident in a dark alcove here or a forgotten park there, saints like Saint Francis or Saint Joseph or Saint Gregory, whose own mother was a saint, if you can imagine that, at any rate it was a very mysterious smile he gave me, and it left me wondering about the meaning of so many things, like why did it take so long for the universe to get where it is, and why is mankind just a tiny blip in the grand scheme of things and hardly worth noticing, if the scientists are to be believed, and where do miracles fit in, and who was the last person to actually see an angel, and why are people so concerned with how many angels can dance on the head of a pin, which seems a ridiculous thing to be concerned about, and how can God be one of three persons who all express the same divine nature and so they are really just one person, these were just a few of the questions rolling through my brain, and for a moment I thought this young man was going to share with me the secret of these mysteries, a glimpse of the eternal mind of God, which God generally prefers to keep hidden, perhaps this young man was going to share with me a whole spectrum of secrets, oh he certainly had me going with that smile, but he did not say a word, he just smiled his mysterious smile, which suddenly became also quite sad, almost forlorn, and he no longer seemed so young, he looked rather old, like one of those old men who wander about the beaches with metal detectors in search of treasure like they are searching for a new beginning, and I wondered if perhaps he had come inside looking for his son or his daughter because he had left his metal detector at home but he had lost his keys and his bus pass and it was getting late, and he used to belong to Saint Jude's, which is why he knew all about their being Melkites, but he had given it up so he could spend most of his otherwise tranquil days searching for coins buried in the sand, but his son or his daughter still belonged because life had not yet bled them of their childhood faith, and then I was thinking maybe his son or his daughter will be permitted to keep their childhood faith without any trouble at all, what a gift that would be, of course this would be very, very rare, *cada muerte de obispo,* as my mother used to say, but she was always talking about the chance of finding true love when she talked this way, she didn't believe in true love, and this was the source of many arguments between the two of us, but life is difficult, as they say, and then I was through thinking, but the young man who had become an old man had disappeared, just like that, somewhere down a long, narrow corridor, I suspect, a winding corridor perhaps, or maybe he just went outside. Yes, yes . . . but where was I? Oh yes, the bells. Yes, yes, some days the air is so still I can almost hear the bells of the Church of the Immaculate Heart, or the Church of Saint Jude, but on other days it might be the bells of the Church of Saint Raymond's or Saint Peter's or Saint Paul's or Saint Hugh's, which is a very modern church with piano concerts and a café that serves coffee and doughnuts and a television station so they can broadcast the Mass to those who cannot attend, or Gesù, which was the church of my mother even before the first of the Cuban refugees began to arrive, and it was also the church I had hoped to be married in, but this did not happen, or the Little Flower or San Juan Bosco, with its gleaming golden dome and its altar of the exiles and its crazy, beautiful stained glass windows, and my favorite window of all of their windows is the one with the resurrected Christ like a gleaming Spanish Adonis and two white doves flying from opposite directions towards His outstretched hands of glory, or maybe it is the bells of the Good Shepherd, or Corpus Christi, or Our Lady of the Lakes, where before they built their church they celebrated the Mass in a dairy barn, or Saint Martha's, which started out in the Bikini Motel in Miami Shores because there was no place else to gather, but later, after they had finished building their church, Mother Theresa herself came all the way from Calcutta just for a visit, or Saint Cecilia's, which had to close its doors a few years ago but is now open again, or the Church of Saint Catherine of Siena, who was the youngest of twenty-two brothers and sisters, if you can imagine that, or Saint John the Apostle in Hialeah, with its gleaming, bronze and marble altar and a scene of the Last Supper stamped into the metal, and behind the altar you are almost overwhelmed by the terrifying, panoramic scene of the Crucifixion of Our Lord and the suffering He endured, or Ermita de La Caridad, Our Lady of Charity, the Patroness and very soul of my mother's Cuba, which is a shrine more than a church even though they hold Mass every day in the chapel, and you can stand outside along the water and look out across the Bay of Biscayne towards Cuba and pray for Our Lady's blessing, because the same sun that bathes Cuba also bathes us, because even here in Miami, especially here with so many exiles, yes, yes, Our Lady protects us from hurricanes and most automobile accidents and all motorcycle accidents and the evil designs of unsavory characters and the inevitable pestilence of impure thoughts, or Our Lady of the Divine Providence, or Our Lady of Lourdes, or perhaps Our Lady of Lebanon, where they say the Mass in Aramaic, and you do not need to understand the words to know they are speaking the language of God, or maybe it is the bells of the Church of Saint Michael, which was built in 1947, the year my brother, Emilio, was born, with its gleaming modern architecture that shines like the sun against the sky and its ghostly, glowing statue of the Archangel himself, his sword by his side, unflinching in his devotion to God. On any given day I fancy I can hear the bells of any one of the churches where Sister Faustina has been sending me these last several years. I have been all over Miami and even out to the beach and up the coast towards Fort Pierce and Melbourne, and even as far as St. Augustine. I go wherever I am needed, though it is not for me to decide when and where.

So I am sitting in my easy chair, a luxury, as I have already said. I dare not open my eyes to look out the window because I am pretending to be asleep, but the clamoring of these young novitiates is too much. Their hope that I will tell them a few stories they have already heard before and for some unfathomable reason wish to hear again is enough to break anyone's will. It is an unending hope, like the oscillating cycle of the moon. I open my eyes. I open my eyes and I smile absentmindedly and stare out the window for a moment, as if I have truly just woken up from an unexpected catnap, and these young ones laugh and clap and settle back wherever they can find room. My small deception is part of the show. It is quite crowded this afternoon and some of the girls have brought in chairs from other rooms and some are sitting cross-legged on the rug or in a monkey's row along the edge of my bed or some up against the wall. I lean my face into the warm sunshine that is pouring through the window and I feel that I am on the verge of disappearing. Then I can hear myself telling a story, and another, and so on. After a while I am barely aware of the world around me.

-108-

¡Ay de mí! To be eighteen again! I know it is a common enough wish, or perhaps it is a lament, but that does not mean the thought is in any way trivial. Yes, I know this wish is an impossibility, at least in a world that values the precision of clocks, especially those made in Germany or Switzerland. But nothing is truly impossible. That is what I was taught. That was the catechism I learned from my vanished uncles and cousins and my long-suffering aunts, who had all died years ago, yet still they watched over me. Not that they were trying to teach me anything. But I listened to what they had to say, and I listened to what was hidden in between their words. And so I learned. I believed in the impossible. And I was recalcitrant in my belief. Yes, that is the word. Recalcitrant. That is how I was. Until I was eighteen I saw the world through the hopeful, gleaming brown eyes of my great-grandfather, Andres Ordóñez Escoraz, and through the bright, dazzling, azure eyes of his niece, Escolástica Escoraz Vda De Miranda, whom everyone called Tiká, and who was, in fact, my actual great-grandmother, as some of you already know, a secret that was kept from me until Tiká herself told me the story. Yes, yes, but I shall leave that for another day. Let me just say for now that we all shared the same dream, my great-grandfather, Tiká and myself. We all

of us longed for a life where always we had fresh-cut dahlias in our hands, always our eyes were clear and our skin pink, our lips rang out with a laughter like the sound of wedding bells, and always we wore the lively sandals of an early spring. Is this not what everyone wishes for? Of course it is. But what does that matter? It is what I wished for.

I was eighteen in 1967. That was the year I began to lose my belief in the impossible, which some say is just a part of the inevitable process of growing up, and which others point to as the source of all despair in the modern age, the disintegration of the soul. I am not sure about all that. I think losing your belief in the impossible is almost as bad as losing your teeth, but not quite. But it is also true that I did not begin losing my teeth until 1996, a full four years before all the madness in my life had settled down, so my perspective on what is important and what is not has undergone, shall we say, a substantial transformation. Back in 1967 life seemed much more complicated. Back in 1967 I myself was teetering on the edge. I was prepared to deliver myself up to the despair of living the same loveless life my mother lived. She had been sharing with me the secrets of her secret misfortune for years. I think she had been hoping to gain a companion, a friend and compatriot, a lonely confidante who believed as she did that her misery was the only possibility among all the possibilities of her life. She wanted to be absolved of any responsibility for her own fate. I am sure that is how she saw it. But I was only eighteen. What did I truly know? Little by little I began to think that my life would become her life and that would be that. The misery of our lives would become so entangled that we would not be able to separate one misfortune from another. What could I do? It was foreordained. No, no, do not get me wrong. Hers was not a bad life. But I was struggling for breath in the sea of her disappointment, which had, I think, also become a sea of tequila. My father made a decent living driving a truck. He had given my mother a small slice of the American pie. But it was never enough for her, which was quite odd (ungrateful is the word that now comes to mind) if you thought about it, and I thought about it a great deal, especially late at night when the world is plunged into silence, like the silence of an empty tomb or a sunken ship, or the silence that envelops the world when you are staring at an old photograph or reading various sonnets, sonnets which you then memorize but later forget, most likely love sonnets.

My mother was born in Santiago, Cuba, but she grew up in a small village named Cruce de los Banos, a mountain village tucked away in the shadows of my imagination. But then she had met my father, who was from Havana, and he whisked her away. She never said how they met, if he had come to eastern Cuba or she to Havana. It was a fairytale, naturally, at least at first. During my teenage years my mother was the first to point out that all love stories begin as fairytales, enigmatic, mysterious, undecipherable, hopeful, a view of heaven, so to speak, but then in a heart-wrenching rush of utterly incomprehensible anguish, true love disintegrates and the two principal actors, the young lovers (or the middle-aged lovers, or the elderly lovers) melt away as if they had never existed, as if they had been made of wax. But when my mother first met my father, she didn't know what was happening at all. It all happened so quickly, she said. *En un abrir y cerrar de ojos.* But again, she spoke of it as something out of her control. My father had been educated at the University of Havana and he spoke with great eloquence. He was going to be a lawyer and then he was going to enter politics and he was going to help turn Cuba into the paradise it was always meant to be. He was going to bring equality to the people, just like Marti had always hoped. Who could resist such charm? Especially if you were a rural girl. Naturally, my mother fell in love with him. But nothing worked out as he had hoped. My father was an idealist in a brutal, unforgiving, intolerant world where human frailty was an unpardonable sin. So one thing led to another. The war started in Europe and Batista came to power and my father joined the Navy, and then the war was over and Grau became president and my father took my mother to Miami.

My father had said he was through with Cuba, but he never said why, though I always suspected it had something to with the war or what he did during the war, but he never said a word except that he had been in the Navy. But one night he was shouting out in his sleep about some German spy they had caught, or a whole bunch they had rounded up, and you could almost hear the bullets flying about in his dream. He was shouting like the whole thing was a bad memory, something that had happened that he wished had never happened, as if he had murdered the spy in cold blood, or he had murdered someone in cold blood, or he had been part of an executioner's squad, or he had killed a friend by accident. You expect that sort of thing to happen in a war. But you don't expect to confront it in your own family.

I must confess it seemed quite fantastic to me. It seemed like it was straight out of the movies. I could not imagine my father with a gun. I could not imagine someone dying by his hand. But when I asked him about it the next morning he only laughed and said *'Irse a la cabeza del toro,'* which was a puzzling thing to say, and then he headed out the door. I remember he was grinning from ear to ear. But that was how my father was. After a while my mother grew tired of his strange dreams. I was twelve, maybe thirteen. My father was always shouting out about something in the middle of the night, and his odd, even bizarre explanations (the egotism of a lunatic, my mother said) were almost always cryptic pronouncements or vague warnings, song lyrics he had once heard, or bits of poetry he had read years earlier but only half-remembered, like 'no, no, I cannot, I don't want to be part of these buffaloes with silver teeth,' or 'to sleep is to float,' or 'it is nothing, they are pieces of walking lava, that is all they are,' or 'no one expects anything to survive in the desert,' or 'See, the gentleman from Paris is coming,' or something his own mother had told him when he was a small boy in Vedado, words of wisdom that had lost their meaning over the years, half-truths, mixed metaphors, street slang, old wives' superstitions, that sort of thing, which meant that his answers had absolutely nothing to do with the questions you asked about his dreams and why he was troubled, at least I was unable to make any sense out of what he said. 'Please, Papa,' I would say to him. 'What are you talking about?' But he would only scratch at his thin face and laugh and say, 'Hush now, Isidora, you ask the impossible. *Pedir la luna.*'

At some point, as you might have guessed, my mother had no more room in her tired, lonely heart for his 'unseemly antics,' as she called them. She grew tired of his life as a truck driver and her life as a truck driver's wife, even if her life in Miami was far better than she could have hoped for in her small village near Santiago. But this did not matter. He had bought for her a tiny four room bungalow in Allapattah so they could begin building their American dream. But my mother no longer shared this dream. She no longer loved my father, she said. This is what she told me. She was trapped in a life without love with a man who was troubled by strange, crazy nightmares. She said he would wake up drowning in a pool of sweat in the middle of the night or early in the morning when the dark birds were calling out to each other in their throaty, hypnotic language of vanquished ghosts, and he would look at her with wild, sightless eyes dripping with the black syrup of fear, this is how she put it, as if he had just dug out his own eyeballs with his own fingernails, which he would only do if he had come face to face with a demon, this is how my mother told the tale, and she said she would run to the bathroom when he woke like this and hide in the bathtub, the curtain drawn or wrapped around her like a shawl, fearing for her life.

No, no, she was never in any real danger. She was a bit melodramatic, my mother, and given to wild flights of fancy. You have to remember that. Yes, oh she most certainly did run to the bathroom in the middle of the night or early in the morning. But only to pee. Which you would naturally expect from all the tequila she drank. But she needed to give voice to her misery, and she needed me to listen to this voice. So that is what I did. I listened. When she talked about my father she would often use the word *mequetrefe*, which means good-for-nothing. Some days I agreed with her. Other days I thought she was a great hypocrite, and I would tell her so, but she would wave me away. But I did not truly understand. I did not see how my father's choices had become the source of her despair, a tree already in full flower the day I turned eighteen, a very black tree with flowers like black orchids that must have certainly seemed a vision of death to everyone who knew her, but I did not see this. And I did not realize that her despair had become the source of my own virgin lament. I was drowning in the ignorance of youth, ready to give away my life and the promise of love to ease my mother's heartache. But then, miracle of miracles, I found the doorway to my very own future and the hope of bright, sunny days ahead, which as anyone will tell you is a glorious moment indeed and produces a flowering tree of a different kind, even if the life you imagine doesn't turn out as you think it will.

So one day I was walking from one place to another. I don't remember why. But for some reason I took a shortcut between NW 35th Street and NW 31st, a narrow alley that had always been dirt but was now freshly paved, and there was a sign on the corner that said La Campana Avenue, which didn't exist on any of the city maps and never existed on any of the maps, but there it was. I had barely walked a single block in the glaring afternoon sun when I realized with the hush of a thousand saints descending from on high that I had entered the dream of my future. Is not the miracle of recognizing one's own future a marvelous mystery? Yes, that day is forever etched in my memory. I remember there was a great deal of activity on that narrow street that was once an alley. Trucks with building supplies trundled past. Men shouted at me to get out of the way. A couple of cars went past. What was going on? Then a few more cars. One was a black limousine. I had never been that close to a black limousine before. I was thrilled. I felt I could have reached out and touched one of the taillights. Then I saw the reason for all of the hubbub. Halfway between NW 35th Street and NW 31st, gleaming with the pink luminescence of a coral reef, was a three-story stucco building and a newly paved parking lot surrounded by a pink concrete wall just three feet high. There was a set of polished mahogany steps leading up to a polished mahogany door and above the door there was a stained-glass window depicting the sun and the moon dancing a sexy, symbiotic dance of love amid a sea of stars. Next to the door there was a small brass plaque that said 25½, and beneath the plaque, fixed to the wall, was a tiny brass marine bell. There were also three antique horse head hitching posts made of brass in front of the building. I suspect the horse heads were meant to suggest those bygone, elegant, halcyon days when the wealthy citizens of Miami plied the streets in horse-drawn carriages, though in truth those days never existed because Miami wasn't really a thriving, bustling city until the 1920s when everyone drove around in Studebakers or Chryslers or Fords, or some of them traveled by electric streetcars, which wasn't a bad way to travel at all, though it was limited to a few streets in downtown Miami like Flagler Street and Biscayne Boulevard and 6th Street and 12th Street, and you could also head west across the river or east across the causeway out to Miami Beach, and you could even head down to Coral Gables and back, which took about an hour if you took a local car, but by the 1940s the old electric streetcars had vanished, as everything we love or prize beyond measure vanishes sooner or later. But I did not care about the history of Miami and how people got around the city and the inaccuracy of the brass horse head hitching posts when I was standing there in front of that pink stucco palace. I could have cared less. I had never seen such a place, not even in my imagination. I had never even heard of such a place. But what is more astonishing is that I could hear the echoes of a kind of music I had never heard before, even though no music was playing, even though there wouldn't be any music emanating from that pink palace for many months to come, but I heard music nevertheless, a music that flowed back and forth across the years from Salvador Bacarisse (my mother's favorite) to Niño Rivera (who I recognized from my father's records) to Henry 'Pucho' Brown (one of Emilio's discoveries, which he later abandoned, like so many of his discoveries, a soul brother from Harlem who you would have sworn was Latino and who put out a string of erratic albums in the late sixties but always hit the groove with songs like 'Cantaloupe Island' and 'Vietnam Mambo') to Amadeo Roldán (the Cuban composer whose name was whispered with great reverence by those who knew music, as if the miracles that some said occurred whenever his music was played were an established fact, and whose dissident, dissonant, surreal, lyrical, Afrocuban symphonic brilliance was truly an echo of every vendor who sang a song to sell his wares on the streets of Havana and elsewhere, an echo which lay at the heart of every Cuban rumba and samba and bolero ever recorded, even if we did not know it) to the gritty soul of Helene Smith and Betty Wright to the big soul sound of The Moovers to Willy Chirino (who would burst onto the music scene in the seventies and take over Miami with his Latin Funk, and who appeared on occasion at La Campana in the days before he became a superstar, and whose joyfully exuberant yet wistful, even soulful voice would bring me to the verge of tears, even as his songs, which were mostly pop salsas and cute bouncy guarachas about lost love and unfaithful wives wearing bikinis and taking vacations with their girlfriends in the Bahamas, would provoke, at least in me, hysterical fits of laughter).

I was certain I was dreaming, so much so that I did not move for fear I would wake up, wondering all the while how long God would permit me the beauty of this dream. And it was so very beautiful, an infinite, indescribable beauty. Then I was distracted by the whirring sound of a diesel engine and the smell of oil swirling through the already heavy, steamy afternoon air. I watched in mute fascination as a team of men working in concert with a giant crane raised a movie-house style marquee with neon lettering and bolted it to the side of the building near the parking lot entrance. Even in broad daylight, without the showy exuberance of a pink flashing neon light, I could hardly contain myself. I trembled. I trembled like a missionary far afield, standing before the beguiling and majestic beauty of an alien god. I tremble now just thinking about it, reliving the moment. And who would not tremble? The sign said: La Campana; and beneath that, in smaller neon tube lettering, it said: from dusk till dawn.

I did not truly grasp what lay in store for me. It would be weeks before this elegant cabaret in the pink stucco building would be ready, and months, even years before it would draw the elite of Miami. But I was on the other side of all that. I could not glimpse the many future joys, like glittery will-o-the-wisps, unsettling in their suddenness, all of them unprovoked and gone before you knew it, and the many more unrelenting future heartaches, all of them fatal by-products of those once glittery joys, as if by design, the hand of God intervening in mysterious, unfathomable ways, the blushing, exuberant timidity of a virgin losing her virginity, the summer sadness that would eventually spread to other parts of the year like an intimate confession. Do we not all eventually feel the pain of such sadness? Is this not our collective fate? Is this not the source of our humanity? But life is difficult. So what can I say? What did I truly know at the tender age of eighteen? Perhaps I knew nothing. But looking back, I am certain that I knew without any creeping doubts, which typically creep about like tiny spiders (or spiderlings) under cover of darkness, that I was indeed looking at my future, the wheel was beginning to turn, as the mystics say, I was looking at the glory days of La Campana, I was looking at the happiness of a life lived beyond the boundaries of the world, I had become a witness to myself, untethered by the centuries, my entire life unfolding with ruthless speed, or beginning to unfold, right there in front of my bright, wondering, untested eyes.

-109-

The moment you stepped inside La Campana you were dazzled by the beauty of the coat check girls. You did not notice the black leather double doors to the main ballroom on one side and an old-fashioned electric studio sign from the golden era of

Hollywood above the doors that said **APPLAUSE** in bright red fancy letters when it was lit up, a sign that my Oscar found one thunderous, rainy afternoon in a pawn shop that existed always and only in the shadows of the elevated highway that led to downtown Miami. My Oscar was always fascinated by what other people would throw away or abandon to the cauldron of eternity, that is what he called it. The owner of the pawnshop said it was a sign from the *I Love Lucy Show,* when Lucy and Desi, with their love of a thousand sambas that could never be extinguished and which would one day circle the globe, were just starting out, but Oscar was not so gullible as that. And you did not notice the sweeping double staircase with gleaming golden handrails and golden edged runners, elegant staircases that curled up on either side of the lobby to the second floor with its small intimate ballroom for dancing competitions and a recital every once in a while, because my Oscar loved to listen to the children play the piano or the clarinet or the flute or the oboe or whatever musical instrument they played, and every year the firemen had their banquet at La Campana, or maybe it was the police, it is difficult to remember so long ago, and every so often there was a wedding or a reception to celebrate a first communion. And you did not notice the open archway leading to the bar on the other side of the coat check room. What a fantastic bar with its gleaming dark mahogany counter and the glittery, shifting, mysterious brilliance of two crystal chandeliers like a star-filled sky and small café tables where anyone could pull up a chair and have a glass of brandy or whiskey or wine or a beer, and half-a-dozen intimate booths where feuding couples could patch up their differences after the show over Anejo Highballs with Orange Curacao; or Green Dragon cocktails made with Kummel Liqueur and Crème de Menthe; or martinis made with Russian vodka or margaritas made with Italian amaretto; or Harvey Wallbangers, because even though it was the dazzling seventies with its twirling disco and handlebar moustaches, some people thought they were still living in the fabulous fifties; or Pisco Sours with egg whites if you were from Peru and without egg whites if you were from Pinochet's Chile; or a bottle of Suisse La Bleue, which even God himself could not resist; or a bottle of Brandy de Jerez, which Oscar said contained the magic of the Moors; or Grand Mariner over ice, which was always my favorite; or maybe a glass of 1691 Clos de Griffier Vieux Cognac, an elixir that took us back to our incorruptible youth, three fingers from a bottle that Oscar had purchased on our one and only trip to Paris, our honeymoon, a bottle which he only rarely trotted out because it was so expensive. To tell you the truth I do not know what Oscar thought he was doing with such a fancy bottle. *¡Ay de mí!* He had purchased this extravagant bottle for the extravagant price of fifteen thousand dollars from the owner of a fancy restaurant a stone's throw from our hotel, which was somewhere near Saint-Germain-des-Prés, I think, though I cannot be sure, the streets of Paris were to me a swirling labyrinth, and it was oh so very long ago, but I do remember thinking that was a fairly high price for a single bottle, and I said so, but my sweet, enduring Oscar only laughed, and the owner of the restaurant then also laughed, and how they knew each other I will never know, but they seemed like old friends, like two bandits holed up in the mountains, and my Oscar said the price was irrelevant, we were in Paris for the first and perhaps only moment in our lives, so we should let loose our inhibitions and our fierce, unbidden fears and smile for as long as God would permit, and just as he said that, the words of the great poet, Emilio Ballagas popped into my head, a poet that my own brother had one day thrust before me since they shared the same first name, and which he soon forgot, as always, but the words that popped into my head that day were just the right words to capture my mood standing there in that fancy restaurant with the owner hiding behind Oscar's shoulder, his eyes like two small suns hiding behind a cloud, peering out every so often to see if he would be paid this outrageous sum for a single bottle that could be drunk in a single night, and Oscar ignoring my tiniest thoughts, my trembling hands like the wings of a tiny bird or a cringing bat, my one and only beloved oblivious to the emotions of distrust racing through my blood, and just like that I heard the words of Emilio Ballagas, as if the great poet himself had returned from the scattered ashes of the dead to give voice to my tremulous, throaty despair.

Si pregunta por mí, dile que habito
en la hoja del acanto y en la acacia.
O dile, si prefieres, que me he muerto.
Dale el suspiro mío, mi pañuelo;
mi fantasma en la nave del espejo.
Tal vez me llore en el laurel o busque
mi recuerdo en la forma de una estrella.

Was this the future that lay in wait for us? Was this the herald of that summer sadness that would plague us for all eternity? It certainly seemed so. It seemed like the future. But what could I say? Our destinies have already shaped us in ways we cannot comprehend. I have always believed this. I have always believed that when you recognize the future, all you can do is embrace it. So there was nothing I could say to warn my beloved Oscar. Besides, he would not have heard me if I had tried. Truly, the flesh is a laurel that sings and suffers, but the moment you realize this truth, it is too late. Human frailty is the natural condition of humanity. At least this is what I have come to know. Of course my Oscar was too much a part of this flesh-and-blood world to ever think so deeply. He would never listen to anyone's song but his own. That day in Paris I realized he would never truly hear me. He was riding high on the wings of success, wings which I wanted to tell him always lead to death or madness or despair or worse because they are replicas of those infamous wings that Icarus wore, but he would never believe that life could be so cruel, even though I know he had seen this cruelty with his own eyes when he lived in Havana, though he never spoke of it. But life is difficult. So I said nothing.

We stayed in Paris until we had spent every last penny of our travel money. For two glorious weeks we paraded around the city in sun-splattered finery, Oscar even bought me a fancy lace parasol for twirling, and during those extravagant, mind-bending, Parisian nights we swam in the limpid pools of our deepest desires, and we never spoke again about the price of this or that, because that is just how Oscar was when it came to money. That is just how Oscar was when it came to many, many things.

-110-

There I go babbling again. I am insufferably scatter-brained. We were talking about the moment you stepped inside La Campana, and there I went flying off on a wild tangent about love and life and human frailty and honeymoons and Paris in the spring. The dreams and fantasies of an old woman. The happiness that becomes a sadness in search of a happiness.

A wild goose chase! So let me start all over. When you stepped inside La Campana you were dazzled by the beauty of the coat check girls. Yes. That is true. It is also true that you did not see the stairs going up or the doors leading to the main ballroom or the Spanish-style archway leading to the bar. You did not see any of that. Your eyes were drawn immediately, with a fragile hope like tiny mice peeking out of dark holes, to the coat check girls.

There were three coat check girls. I don't know why Oscar needed three. They had pouty, cinematic faces with flirty, mysterious, doleful eyes, the kind of faces you only saw in magazines like *Glamour* or *Vogue* or *Vanidades*, like they were showgirls or chorus girls or Hollywood starlets. God only knows where Oscar found them.

The one I remember best was named Bonita. Was that her name? Ah, yes, yes it was. She was very pretty. She possessed a dark, gleaming beauty that transcended all words. I was very jealous. Every girl who walked into La Campana had a right to be jealous. I am sure the other two coat check girls were jealous. Funny I don't remember the names of the other two. But I will never forget Bonita. What an extraordinary woman she was!

Bonita had very dark hair, almost black (which was the exact opposite of my fiery red hair), and she wore it curled up in the back with a red rose like a Flamenco dancer, or she might wear a gold or turquoise tortoise shell comb with her hair twisted up, spilling out beneath the comb in braided ringlets like water spurting out from some crazy Spanish fountain. What a glorious, beguiling, cunning creature! She had very long eyelashes and her lips were dripping with the possibility of a kiss. A long, luxuriant kiss. You could almost taste it.

Looking back, well, I am certain it was all a pose. I am certain she knew exactly what she was doing. But she was a goddess all the same! She walked on rose petals, flowers strewn along whatever path she took, dahlias or geraniums or gentians. She wore the shortest skirts you could imagine, silky, slinky skirts that seemed to disappear whenever someone opened the door and a breeze swept in and then all you could see were two, long legs glistening in the soft orange sunset glow of the lamps that hung from the ceiling and Bonita's plush derriere moving slowly back and forth, a slow, sexy samba, like an early morning caress. Every man who looked her way, and how could they not, thought if only they could check their girlfriends or their wives instead of their coats, yes, maybe they could steal off to some dark corner with Bonita, and there were many more dark corners in Miami in those bygone, elegant days then there are now. They dreamed of slipping away, of spending an hour or two in Bonita's Spanish dancer arms, the starry night above them opening up, shimmering like those ancient salon mirrors of the philosophers, mirrors which absorb all light and so become portals to the future. They would choose to forget their wives or their hopeful girlfriends, at least in the glare of their having walked through the doors of La Campana, blinded by the dazzling beauty of Bonita, dreaming that God would permit them to curl up inside this dark-haired goddess, like returning to the womb of creation, the men becoming invisible atoms of happy nothingness, at peace for once in their lives, hoping beyond all hope that the universe would collapse and their joy would be frozen for all eternity.

What can I say? I am sure they all thought something like that. Just as I am sure that their girlfriends or their wives knew what they were thinking but refused to make a scene out in public, for the women in those days were refined beyond belief, in spite of what you may have heard or think you know. They floated above all strife and insult on the gentle breeze of ceremonious charm. Besides, they would not let the tragically absurd behavior of their husbands or their boyfriends like rusty Spanish cannons going off at midnight ruin an evening filled with an impossible music.

It was the kind of music that swept past you like flocks of startled white ibis whirling into the air. That's what some said. It was the kind of music that sped up through the stratosphere until the air was very thin, circling round and round the face of the white-hot sun like ghostly apparitions or wayward angels in search of God's redeeming grace, and then descending hours later, absolved of original sin. That's what others said. And the patrons of La Campana drank in that impossible music without regret till dawn. And all the while the happy, drunken laughter of the men and women dancing rang out against the darkness as if the darkness did not exist, and the booze was freely flowing, vast quantities, as if from uncorked geysers, with complete disregard for the laws of physics and common decency. But you could be sure the refined gentlewomen of those bygone, mythic days, who bathed twice a day in bathtubs filled to overflowing with white gardenias or mariposa, and rubbed macadamia oil into their skin every night in the hopes of reversing the damage of the mocking, remorseless years, you could be sure these women were going to explode the moment they got home, because they were, after all, the descendants of bloodthirsty Spain and would have their honor satisfied by magic or knives or slow poison or emasculating words.

Those who were married would limit their vengeance to the bedrooms they shared with their husbands, whom they had married in the eternally mysterious and reverberating presence of God, all of them dressed in dazzling white wedding dresses that surely cost an eye from a face, immaculate dresses consecrated to heaven, but still the brides to be were reciting countless Hail Marys in the silence of their hopeful hearts as they stood before the altars of eternal bliss until the rings had been slipped onto their fingers and the churches were filled with glorious, ear-shattering applause from their families and other well-wishers. And those who were not yet married would seek their justice in the quiet corners of the various sitting rooms in their parents' houses or the screened-in sun porches or the Spanish-style foyers, which were the only rooms their boyfriends were allowed into unchaperoned (and also the dining room if they were invited over for dinner, and once in a while the kitchen, and of course the bathroom, as needed). Because all of these refined but proud gentlewomen of Spanish descent who had been born in Miami or who had traveled from the sunny shores of Cuba or Puerto Rico or the Dominican Republic or South America or faraway Spain to settle in paradise, these wives and hopeful girlfriends, they all possessed the integrity of an irrepressible heart and so refused to become strangers under other stars.

Oscar used to say that if it weren't for Bonita, we would have closed our doors after that first year. But this is not quite true. Oscar saw things as most men see things. Yes, yes, the sweaty, inconstant gentlemen of Miami returned night after night hoping to catch a glimpse of Bonita, their eyes shining like brightly polished coins, drawn by the hope of a luxuriant kiss and the possibility of more. But their wives and their girlfriends returned hoping to experience once more the ecstasy of that impossible music, a chance to fill the insufferable void in their hearts, for which music is the only cure, ever mindful that all earthly pleasures are transitory and only God knows who will find true happiness.

-111-

If my Oscar was the soul of La Campana in those days, which he most certainly was, then Bonita was its irrepressible, suffering heart. I remember one spring night the music was flowing out through the double doors right into the arcaded lobby with its freshly painted orange walls and its dazzling hanging lamps, and there was Bonita dancing like she was at the center of the universe. This was in 1972, I am pretty sure. Oscar and I were not yet married, but that is beside the point. The other two girls were leaning on the table next to the coat check room, mesmerized. The table was empty. A small circle of men and women had gathered around Bonita, who was oblivious to everything but the music. No one was wearing a coat to check. It was still early in the evening, so it was only the warm-up act. And besides, nobody would bother about going into the main ballroom as long as they could watch Bonita. She was a ribbon of wildfire spinning with devilish intent in the hazy interior glow of the lamplight. She was a delight to watch. And after a while it seemed as if we all fell into a trance. Bonita and this ribbon of fire became two separate entities, as if the fire was a many tentacled creature of the night and Bonita was encased within it, inside it, suspended in a bubble of molten glass, the fire wrapping itself with greater intensity around her tiny waist as the music soared, the notes like tiny daggers slicing open the skin of the universe and the bright black light of other worlds pouring in. And then all of a sudden there was a burst of drums and then a long, mournful saxophone and then a soaring flight of piano keys, and Bonita flung her head back, her mouth wide open in wild, gaping laughter, and the tentacles loosened their grip and the molten glass began to drain away and Bonita went spinning across the floor. But then in a motion so quick you could not catch it with your eye, as if it were an afterthought or a young lover's lament, she grabbed hold of the thin trailing ribbon by the tip (which was all that was left of the fire by this point) and pulled it after her, and so they began their wild, fiery erotic spinning dance all over again. Sparks were flying as Bonita and the ribbon of fire danced this way and that, unconcerned with anyone who was watching, singeing the eyebrows of those who were standing too close. And wherever Bonita stepped in her feverish furry of a Spanish dancer, tiny black heel marks were burned into the tile.

Then the warm-up act was finished on this very warm evening, one of the warmest spring evenings of the century, that was what the radio had said, and Oscar came out of the main ballroom with an eager, welcoming smile, a flirtatious smile, according to some, and his outstretched arms looking to embrace everyone he knew, which was everyone who ever walked through the doors of La Campana. He wagged his finger at Bonita, whose blameless, inner smile was reflected in the smooth, almond-colored sheen of her perspiring skin, and she went back to the empty table in front of the coat check room. One by one the guests chatted with Oscar. The men shook his hand and the women gave him gentle, airy kisses on the cheek. And all the while Oscar was a beaming proud Papa. He was saying how they had a very special treat for everyone that night, a young guitarist who played the electric bass with the precision of God and the burning passion of the Devil. '*Partirse el alma*,' Oscar said. 'This boy will make someone's heart bleed. Yes, yes. He will make all of our hearts bleed, I think.' And then: 'Yes, there is one table up front I set aside especially for you.' And then: 'Yes, oh do not worry, the waitresses will bring you whatever you like from the bar. Whatever you can think of, whatever you can imagine.' And that's how it went for several minutes. My Oscar stood by the double doors chatting with everyone as they passed by until everyone had found their seats, and then the lights in the lobby began to flash, once, twice, a gentle reminder that the show would begin in ten minutes or so, and then the flashing stopped. Then for some reason, who can say why, my Oscar walked over to where Bonita had been dancing and looked down at the tiled floor and the black burn marks. Clearly he didn't know what to make of them. But who could blame him? It is not always so easy to know what you are looking at. So he looked at the burn marks for a while, not very long, truly it was only a moment, and then he looked over at Bonita, but she was chatting with a young man in a ponytail. Then he hurried back into the main ballroom.

I did not know the young man in the ponytail, but he and Bonita were chatting away like old friends. He was very good looking. Dark brooding, thoughtful eyes. A deep fire there, I could see that. I think an unquenchable fire, which made him the perfect match for Bonita. A slightly wistful upper lip. I was amused by their reverence for each other and their irreverence for everyone around them. But not everyone was amused, which you can understand. A swarthy fragment of a man with a boxer's pug nose and a grooved chin was not amused. I say a fragment of a man because he seemed more like a cartoon of a man than actual flesh and blood. A comic book villain. An eye-catching façade, but nothing of substance beneath the surface. That is how he seemed. He was closer to thirty than forty. He wore a black hat with a black hatband and a black suit with a thin red tie. He wore a white shirt with diamond cuff links, and his fingernails were freshly manicured. In a word, he was immaculate in his appearance. I swear I even saw glittering diamonds in the spaces in between his teeth. He was not amused. At first glance I thought he was simply tired of waiting for Bonita to take his coat. He was the only person in La Campana that night with a coat to take. But I did not wonder at this. Instead, I was caught looking at his coat, a black Chesterfield overcoat, very stylish in another era. The kind of coat my father would wear, but only on a Saturday night, and only when he was younger and my mother was still in love with him. So I was staring at this coat and thinking of my father. I was remembering a dream I once had about my father. In my dream my father was wearing a coat just like the one I was looking at, but it was before he had immigrated to Miami. It was during the war when he was in the Navy. But he wasn't in the Navy in my dream. Or at least he wasn't on a ship or patrolling the beaches or driving along the coast road in a jeep. He was sitting in a dark room at a long table. I was looking down the length of the table. I barely recognized my father but I knew it was him. It was kind of like looking through the wrong end of a telescope. There was a row of strange silver machines on the table and many more men sitting there besides my father. All of the machines were clicking away furiously, like clocks that had gone irretrievably mad. All of the men were wearing black Chesterfields and radio headsets and they were listening intently to whatever radio signals they could pick up. Their behavior seemed very normal in my dream. They were not speaking to each other. Every so often one of them would write something down on a pad of paper. But nothing disturbed their rhythm. Then the machines stopped clicking and my father got very excited. He could hardly contain himself. He wrote something down very fast and then tore the paper from the pad and rushed to the end of the long table and the row of silver machines and handed the piece of paper to a tall man wearing a glowing white uniform. 'We've got him now, the German bastard,' the man in the white uniform said, and he clapped my father on the back with great joy. And then everyone in my dream was talking all at once, including my father, but I couldn't make sense of what they were saying except every now and then a name would pop up out of their cloud of gibberish, Hans or Heinz or Maximilian or Ernst or Johann or Georg or Jörge or Jürgen or Leopold or Helmut, I could never quite tell, but I knew they were German names. That was the dream I once had. That is what I was remembering on that warm spring evening in La Campana oh so many years ago, all because I saw a swarthy man in a Chesterfield coat. Isn't it strange how memory works? And then I forgot about the dream entirely. I was standing there wondering where the swarthy man had picked up his coat and where he was from. (That is also how memory works.) He certainly wasn't from Miami. I could tell that much. The coat was draped over his arm and his arm was extended towards the empty coat check table. The other two girls had vanished. Bonita and the young man with the ponytail had stepped off to a corner opposite the table where the lamp light gave way to dark shadows, like the shadows you imagine exist at the bottom of the sea. They were cooing in those dark, fluid, watery shadows. Then I had the strangest thought. I thought by the way the swarthy man was holding his coat and the fact that it was an incredibly warm evening that he was an assassin of some sort hiding a gun. He was aiming a gun at the young man with the ponytail. Why, well, I could not imagine why. He was grinding his glittery bejeweled teeth, a symptom of dark, nervous energy perhaps, and aiming his unseen gun, counting down the seconds until he pulled the trigger. And I was also busy counting down the never-ending seconds right along with him, what else was there to do, wondering if Bonita would be next, and everyone else who was hanging around the lobby, all of us inadvertent witnesses to a most senseless murder.

But the swarthy man was not hiding a gun beneath his coat. He tossed his coat to the table and called out to the young man with the ponytail. He called him kid. He said 'Hey kid, you don't know what you're doing with a woman like that. Why don't you get lost! Leave her to someone who's got the goods.' I wasn't exactly sure if he was joking or if he was serious, but then he laughed a hoarse, rattling laugh and his meaning became clear.

Bonita and the young man with the ponytail edged over to the table. The expression on the swarthy man's face was an odd mixture of vulgar, aching lust and unacknowledged, trembling paranoia. That's as good a way to describe it as any. I mean it is often true that words are impossible to use. They just get in the way. But what else can we do? Anyway, in the heat of the moment I remember thinking that life hardly ever worked out for him the way he hoped it would. Looking back, I guess maybe I was right, at least in this particular instance.

It was almost like watching the cinema. A dark romantic movie, naturally, film noir from the golden age of Hollywood. That is what it seems like now. Bonita took the swarthy man's coat and disappeared into the coat check room. But she did not disappear quickly. She sashayed, a slow, rhythmic twitching of her hips. I almost laughed watching the swarthy man watching her. He was stunned by her hips. The young man with the ponytail was not stunned. He had his eyes on the swarthy man the whole while. I could tell he was becoming possessive. Then Bonita returned and came up behind the young man and slipped her arms around his shoulders and kissed him lightly on the cheek. The tip of her tongue flashed in the dim lamp light. This I could plainly see. It was a treacherous kiss, if you were viewing it from a certain perspective. It was a slap in the face. An insult. It was like pulling a trigger. Of course if you were viewing it from a different perspective, it was breathtakingly beautiful, romantic, hopeful, spirited, spiritual, compassionate, an awakening, everything we hope for ourselves and for our children and our children's children and so on until the end of days.

I could not believe what happened next. As if that treacherous kiss was not bad enough. I know personally I would not have had the courage. But they did. *Frente al amor y la muerte no sirve de nada ser fuerte,* as they say. Yes, truly, they were fearless in this respect. Bonita and her lover. He was obviously her lover, but how long they had been lovers I did not know. At any rate, no sooner had the swarthy man finished digesting that most treacherous kiss, then Bonita and her lover smiled a most treacherous smile (again, as viewed from one perspective and not another).

How is it the swarthy man did not react? I swear I was about to intervene at this point, but I assumed that the damage was already done. *Ser agua pasada,* as my father would have said.

But the swarthy man did not react.

I have to admit now that I had no idea what was happening. I was standing there thinking if he did have a gun he was going to use it now, but he no longer seemed to even see Bonita. He returned their most treacherous smile with great politeness and an eager, treacherous smile of his own, even as he kept his eyes on the young man with the ponytail, a level, unflinching gaze, as if he were about to issue a challenge.

'I have heard you play before, my young friend,' he said. 'And you are quite talented, quite passionate, but your passion is no match for the passion in this woman's heart.' Then he smiled again, a smile that was not so treacherous but still quite eager, and took out a small business card and gave it to the young man. 'When you are finished tonight,' he said, 'I should like to talk with you.'

From where I was standing I could not see what was printed on the card. The young man seemed to read the words with great interest, but then he handed the card back. I do not know if Bonita saw what was on the card, but she gave the young man with the ponytail a tremendous squeeze, which seemed like a declaration of her eternal love, or at least her youthful infatuation, and then a second longer, lingering kiss, infinitely more treacherous than the first because of its panting intensity, at least this is how it seemed to me.

It makes me laugh now. I truly did not have a clue about what was going on. How little we understand what is going on right in front of our noses in any given moment. It is like we are trapped on the other side of the mirror. *Benditos sean los dulces nombres.* Suddenly the lights in the lobby were flashing once again, a furious flashing, and the young man with the ponytail had a guitar in his hand and he blew Bonita a fingertip kiss and said he would play tonight like he had never played before, the very air would bleed with the impenetrable sadness and the disfiguring joy of a thousand centuries. That is how he put it. He seemed quite pleased with himself. He was beaming with the poetry of his words as he spoke. Then he disappeared through the black leather double doors, and for a moment I could hear the tinkling of glasses as the waitresses served the last of the drinks, and then I could hear Oscar's thin, wavering voice full of a Papa's pride welcoming his new discovery to the stage, this young lion of the electric guitar, and the audience roared with their approval.

I am not sure where I went at that point. It is almost as if I became a shadow on the wall. I remember that Bonita and the swarthy man did not move from the empty table. They talked quietly for a while, a discreet conversation, the two of them bathed in the soft, underwater glow of the lobby lights, which had been turned down because of the show. It was like swimming in a tropical ocean when Oscar turned down the lights. But I am not sure where exactly I was.

Come to think of it, I might have been standing in the archway leading to the bar, a frozen moment, uncertain if I was thirsty and needed something to drink or maybe a splash of water on my face would be enough to revive my sagging spirits, for Oscar and I were in the middle of our first lover's quarrel and we hadn't spoken directly to each other in three days. Yes, I had almost forgotten that. What do you suppose we were quarreling about? We almost never quarreled. Something trivial, no doubt.

Or perhaps I was simply tired from waiting for Oscar to apologize for whatever it was he had done, so all I wanted was to lie down, though to be honest, I was probably just as guilty as my Oscar, maybe more so, which would also explain my lethargy. I do not deal well with feeling guilty. It puts me to sleep as surely as too many glasses of wine. Either way I might have been heading up the stairs to the second floor because there was a red velvet Persian sofa where you could take a nap, just around the corner from the cozy ballroom of my greatest dream, where Oscar and I would one day get married, though on that particular spring evening our wedding intentions were still only the tiniest dot on the horizon.

I confess I don't remember where I was. I might even have slipped in through the black leather double doors to listen to the young man with the ponytail play his electric guitar, yes, yes, but also to spy on my beloved Oscar, yes, I confess to that now, because Oscar liked to flirt with the waitresses if he thought I wasn't looking, especially after he turned down the lights. I suppose there are many possibilities. But wherever I was I could hear Bonita and the swarthy man talking. I could hear them quite clearly, even though they were nowhere to be seen. Their words were radio signals shooting off into space. Their words were tiny daggers of ice breaking off from the moon. They were talking about the future, or more precisely, one of many possible futures.

The swarthy man said his name was Octavio or Alvarez or Alfonso or Gutiérrez. I am terrible when it comes to remembering names. For Oscar remembering names comes quite easily. But for me names evaporate as quickly and as silently as a morning mist. The swarthy man said he was an agent for a record company in New York City. He said he had been following the young man with the ponytail for several months and wanted to sign him before someone else got their hooks into him. He talked about record contracts and taking the music world by storm and brightly lit stages and the whirlwind of fame. He talked about the money to be made. He said a talent like this kid wasn't so much a gamble as it was an opportunity. But you had to strike while the iron was hot. He'd seen talents like this come and go, so he knew. No matter how good you were, if you didn't have the right people in your corner you faded into oblivion. He didn't want to see that happen to this kid. He said he would be honored to represent this kid. He knew all of the big money men in New York City who didn't really know music at all but who knew all about making fortunes. He said he hoped he could count on Bonita. Bonita said he could.

When the young man with the ponytail began to play it was like the world had been swallowed by an ancient beatnik darkness. The rhythm of breathing in the gutter and the rain splattering across your face. Clouds swirling past towards oblivion, the atmosphere dissolving into nothingness. But then almost immediately a resurrection. The storm was over. The soul of a dead man rising towards a hissing sun. Then a gentle, early evening breeze and the salty smell of the sea like a benediction cleansing away the grime of endless toiling days. Then the staccato rippling of a car speeding along a coastal highway, a gleaming convertible, a man at the wheel and a girl in sunglasses by his side, windswept hair and windswept laughter, the car surging to a stop amid a flurry of waves and flocks of sea birds soaring into the sky and the ocean tide roaring across the hard-packed sand, bubbling past the tires, the two lovers disappearing in the glare of the horizon. Then night falling, starlight falling, the moonlight of a tiny sliver of a moon reflected off the shells of tiny hermit crabs scuttling back and forth in the shimmering darkness. An infinity of ghostly blue slivers. Like consciousness. Like an intimate awareness of God or the boundaries of the universe. The slivers sending shivers up and down your spine. The moonlight fading but not the ceaseless, unrepentant, rampaging shivers. Then the ghost of summer, of many summers, a strange, hollow wail. It was like leading a goat to slaughter, the sound of it. Ears dripping with the sacrificial blood of memory. A strange, mystical ceremony. Then the music changing again. The sound of the darkness swallowing itself and the sound of humanity emerging. But not quite humanity. An alternative humanity. Hollow men and hollow women with eyes like rivets, sightless eyes, shaking their naked mechanical torsos, strutting their naked mechanical legs, swinging their naked mechanical arms, screws rattling loose, pieces of metal falling to the ground, the sounds of wild parrots screaming like rusty hinges. All of this suggested by this strange, new, bewildering music. Then silence. As quiet as God's first breath. As loud as a roaring furnace. Then a steady, drumming dawning. The sun rising again, returning. Cymbals of light crashing, clashing, breaking apart. The clear sky opening up, absorbing all life. The deep bass growl of a ship's horn somewhere in the distance, a slow but steady affirmation. This is what the music sounded like.

I am fairly certain the swarthy man walked away empty handed that night. I know for a fact that the young man with the ponytail left with Bonita immediately after the show, and the swarthy man was sitting in the bar drinking mojitos with the after-hours crowd. I watched him for a while. I don't know how long. He was sitting in the bar, drowning in a sea of mojitos, as I recall, all the way up to his eyeballs and the tiny black and white and silver eels of many desires swimming in the froth. At one point, Oscar spoke to him quietly for a few minutes and then clapped the man on the back and started laughing, and then the swarthy man belched out a laugh and every head in the place turned to see who had made such a sound, it was so loud and awful sounding like a wheezing donkey, and then everyone went back to their own drinking. I never again saw the swarthy man after that night. He left around five in the morning, at that magical hour when the night birds have ceased their flamboyant carousing and the morning birds are searching the horizon for the perfection of the morning sun. I also remember that the young man with the ponytail played at La Campana on and off for the next several months. I am sure he lived nearby. Close enough that he saw Bonita on a fairly regular basis. Close enough that Bonita hummed with the excitement of a love that is lived every day. You could feel the electricity flowing through her veins when she walked past. He was to her a godsend, a ring that has come to the finger. But then the young man with the ponytail vanished. At least I never saw him again, not in the flesh. But when I asked Bonita about him, she said nothing. Then one evening she was late for work, and when she came in Oscar was fuming, but I could see that she had been sobbing, so I shooed my beloved-but-every-so-often-brainless Oscar away and took the poor girl up to the second floor. *¡Ay de mí!* A woman colliding with romance and a woman drowning in despair are mirror images of each other. They pine away for that same tiny, rebellious bird. Even on the brightest and sunniest of days. Yes, yes, oh my word, yes. They receive flowers and bullets in the same heart. That is what the poet Lola Rodríguez de Tío would say. It is what she did say. '*Reciben flores o balas sobre el mismo corazón . . . .*' So we sat down on the Persian style sofa, Bonita and I, and she poured out her heart of hearts that had once grown flowers and was now riddled with gaping bullet holes.

Bonita said those first few months when she had been dating the young guitar player were the most invigorating of her young life. She did not care that she was several years older than he was. She felt like she would live forever when she was in his arms, this is what she said, this was her destiny. Naturally, she had been devastated when he went away, as we all are when we have to face deprivations of any kind. But he had told Bonita it would not be for long. He was off to seek his fortune, his fame, but he would return to her one day with a pocketful of stars. Those were the actual words he had said. And she believed him with every shred that was left of her dignity. But he had not yet returned. Bonita had not even heard from him. But this was not the reason she had been sobbing that day, no, no, she had convinced herself that he would return one day, no matter how many years would flow past in the interim, and it had already been a few years by that point, no, no, the reason for her tears was that she had dreamed the night before that her beloved had died, that he had actually, truly died, a bleeding corpse on a sidewalk in front of a nightclub somewhere many miles from the grieving streets of Miami. And she believed in this dream. She saw everything quite clearly. On the dreadful night of his death he was playing at a glitzy club in downtown Chicago or downtown Indianapolis or downtown St. Louis. This is what Bonita said. And after he finished he went off with some musician friends to a small, back alley dive where they could jam for the rest of the night, a nightclub in the middle of nowhere, but he became separated from his friends, and when he tried to get into this club, the bouncer would not let him in. Even when he showed the bouncer his gleaming guitar, even when he said he was a guitar player and the musicians inside had invited him to stop by to jam until everyone's heart was bleeding on the floor, even after he played a few riffs on his guitar, which he could not have possibly played because it was an electric guitar and there wasn't an outlet anywhere in sight, but which he did play, and then a few bricks in the wall of this crumbling dive in the middle of nowhere disintegrated into a poof of dust, which was a miracle any way you looked at it, even then the bouncer did not budge. Bonita said she could not believe the events as they were unfolding. They were too bizarre, she said. And her beloved would never have acted the way he did in this dream. And yet she could not change how he behaved. Her young lion refused to accept the bouncer's judgment, which was more like him than Bonita cared to admit, so he tried to force his way inside. But the bouncer would have none of it. What was that young man with the electric guitar thinking, I wondered? He must have been swimming in a sea of tequila and cocaine to act with such madness, a hidden rage that flies from rafter to rafter until the church bells strike midnight and then it is loosed upon the world. But he stood no chance, even with such an unexpected and cunning rage. The bouncer hammered away at Bonita's young lion and left him a bleeding, bloody pulp on the sidewalk in front of this hole-in-the-wall club in the middle of nowhere. He died on his way to the hospital. This is what she said. *¡Ay de mí!* That was how he had died in Bonita's dream. It was absurd, of course. Where were the watchful eyes of the angels and the saints in this dream of hers? This is what I asked her. Where was the compassion of the Virgin Mary and the hope of the risen Christ? Where was the strength of the Holy

Spirit? *¡Madre de Dios!* Love stories are not supposed to end in such tragic absurdity. But Bonita believed in the power of this dream. 'If he is not already dead,' she sobbed, 'then it is only a matter of days, maybe weeks.' She was convinced that her beloved would only return to her loving arms as a ghost, an incorporeal phantom. Unless she left the familiar boundaries of Miami to search for him, to warn him, to help him escape the inescapable jaws of death. And this is what she decided to do. It did not matter if you thought, as I did, that the young lion of Bonita's heart had already become a ghost. *El pensamiento no tiene barreras,* as my father used to say. Bonita believed what she believed. 'If I do not find him, he will surely die a horrible death,' she said. That is why she was sobbing when she walked through the doors of La Campana that night.

Bonita left us the very next day. I do not know exactly where she went, only the general direction. And the young man with the guitar? Well, I soon forgot all about him, but then many, many years later I saw his face in the newspaper. It was his face but then again it was not his face. An artist had painted his face on a wall that was part of a park somewhere in Miami, and the newspaper had printed a photograph of this wall. I had never heard of the park. The newspaper said this young man with the ponytail had been beaten to death outside a nightclub. Just like in Bonita's dream. But he had died right here in Miami, in Fort Lauderdale, where those crazy college kids hang out, not in Indianapolis or Chicago or St. Louis. I wondered if Bonita had ever spoken to him of her dream and what he had said, but then I realized she had never found him. She had left Miami to search the world for the pieces of her heart, and he had returned at some point, or he was here all along. But he never came around La Campana looking for Bonita, which explains everything.

So there I was staring at this photograph in the newspaper, a photograph of a ghost. He was staring out at the world with those same dark, brooding, thoughtful eyes. Somehow you could feel the fire in his soul emanating from the fragile newsprint that had captured his image. An echo of an echo. Still it was a wonder the newspaper didn't burst into flames. It was a wonder I didn't pass out from the heat. He was holding his guitar with the same defiant, even liberating sense of purpose that I remembered from the sound of his music that spring night oh so many years ago. You could not see the whole guitar, just where he was holding the neck and his fingers were pressing down on the strings. I swear you could hear his music flowing out from that photograph of his face on that wall. At least I could. I remember showing Emidio the newspaper at some point and asking him if he heard this celestial music that could transport you to other worlds, and he listened carefully for a while, and then he said he wasn't sure, perhaps if he listened a little while longer, and then he started laughing, but he was very sweet about it. His laughter was a gentle, slow-rolling, lazy sound, like a single wave flowing across the sand and then retreating out to sea, dissolving. Then I asked him if he knew where the park was. He said he didn't know, but he would take me. But he never did. We were going to take Sister Faustino's station wagon one Saturday, but it was raining, and the next Saturday Emidio had too many chores to do, and the next Saturday Sister Faustino went to visit her sister in Tampa, or maybe it was her niece, and the next Saturday Emidio forgot, and the Saturday after that I forgot, and so on and so forth, and that was that. But in the months and years since I came across the photograph of that young man's painted face in the newspaper, I find myself thinking about him every now and then, thinking about his dark, brooding thoughtful eyes and his incredible, impossible music. And whenever I think about him I also think about Bonita and how she had dreamed of his death, but there was nothing she could do.

It is a very sad story when you get right down to it. A tragic story. It makes my heart break. *¡Espíritu de mi alma!* But what are we to do? The church bells they are tolling. *Ya las campanas de la iglesia están doblando.* Life is difficult, as my mother would have said.

-112-

One night my mother dreamed of a fancy church wedding at Gesù Catholic Church. She dreamed I was walking down the aisle with its polished marble floor like a darkly shining mirror that absorbs all of our whispered fears. I was a bride in a fancy brocaded wedding dress, a satin gown with a full train veil lined with luminescent pearls, soft pinks and whites like the teardrops of angels, and tiny leaves made of silk, a soft ivory color, like the wings of shy, tropical birds. It was a gown which had been sewn together by a Spanish widow who spoke no English. This is how my mother described it. This was the fantastic dress I was wearing in her dream. She said I looked neither right nor left as I walked down the aisle. I kept my eyes on the fancy Baroque altars made of Italian marble and the priests standing there in their gleaming white vestments edged with gold and their eyes brimming with sacramental satisfaction.

She could not see my future husband, she said. He was obscured by the dazzling brilliance of the priests, but she was not concerned. She said this meant whoever I married was of no more importance than a passing shadow, a cloud upon the horizon. What was important, she said, was consecrating myself before the glory of the resurrected God, and also before the gleaming marble statues of Jesus and Mary and the glorified saints with their sleepy, sad, yet unimaginably compassionate eyes looking down on the rest of humanity, eyes that reflected the pain of a suffering life and the joy of putting your trust in heaven. But this did not happen, as I have already said. For my mother this dream became a recurring dream, but it did not come true.

-113-

My first truly vivid memory of Gesù Church begins strangely enough with a memory of my father, who had stopped going to church before I turned three. It is a very long, complicated memory with many twists and turns, but its beginning is simple enough. Every Sunday morning my mother would admonish my father for ignoring his Catholic duty to his children. "How will our children learn to love God and be inspired by the saints if their own father abandons them at God's doorstep?' she would ask. "And what will become of them when God turns his burning, vengeful eyes their way to exact his rightful justice for their father's transgressions?'

Every so often my mother would say Lord Shango instead of God, a slip of the tongue surely, but her meaning was clear enough. But my father would only laugh a noisy, jubilant, carefree yet big-hearted laugh, as opposed to condescending and mean-spirited, and he would remind my mother that it was he who had introduced her to the Catholic Church in the first place. Had she forgotten those days when he had found her in that ash heap of a village in the hills near Santiago? Had she forgotten that in those days she still prayed to Orishas trapped like genies inside clay pots or cowrie shells? Had she forgotten that he had rescued her from the ignorance that had kept Cuba enslaved for centuries? Then he would flip his hat onto his head like he had seen a movie actor once do in the movies and roll out through the screen door.

My mother would run after him, at least as far as the sidewalk, screaming obscenities and cursing his disreputable family of aristocratic thieves who had never known what it was like to bake in the cane fields under the hot Cuban sun or suffocate in the fiery, subterranean depths of the mines. You had only to look at my mother in those moments of her greatest fury as she ran after my father to know that she was capable of biting the ghosts of broken days.

Only when my father had turned the corner on his way to the river did she return to the house, her face gleaming wet and red with the blisters of her anger, and finish getting the two of us, myself and Emilio, ready for the long bus ride to Gesù.

My mother never forgave my father for his Sunday morning blasphemy. She said he would burn in Hell along with all of the heretics and false prophets for giving up God on Sundays to play bolita. Yes, that is what my father was doing. He was playing bolita, the numbers. Every Sunday he would stroll through the sunny streets of our neighborhood, a casual walk without any obvious purpose to an outside observer, but always he would end up in the shadows of a crepe myrtle behind the Rexall drugstore one block from the river. This is what my mother said. Of course my father was not the only wayward son to make the happy trek to the Rexall. Every Sunday morning between nine and eleven the alley would be buzzing with the sounds of men waiting for their turn to play the numbers, eager to gamble away their happiness. Some had arrived by foot like my father. Others had taken cars, late model Oldsmobiles and Cadillacs. A few rode bicycles. They would gather like storm clouds and then dissipate on a gentle breeze.

Not all of them were happy-go-lucky ne'er-do-wells like my father. Some were very respectful and had only stopped by the alley for a few minutes on their way to or from church. A few even owned businesses on 14th Avenue or 22nd Avenue, bakeries or shoe stores or grocery stores or Laundromats or jewelry stores or restaurants or cafés, or one of those cheap cafeterias south of the river where they mostly served beans and rice and spicy Cuban hamburgers.

This is what my father told me. He said everyone who could afford to play bolita did so, even those who could barely afford a haircut. White, black, and every color in between, it did not matter. It was an unquenchable desire, my father said, an undying hope in the possibility of a tangible, earthly paradise that was infinitely more alluring than the promise of eternal bliss in a heaven that lay somewhere in between the upper levels of the stratosphere and the icy cold oblivion of outer space.

This is what my father truly believed.

The dark angel that nurtured this desire was a very old, very dark grandfather of Afro-Cuban descent sitting on a cinder block beneath the flowering branches of the crepe myrtle in the alley behind the Rexall drugstore. This grandfather always wore a Panama hat. And he always sat on that cinder block smoking a fat Cuban cigar. From a distance it looked like smoke was pouring out of his eyes and his ears and the gaping black hole that was his mouth, a steady stream of smoke as if from a leaky boiler, especially on very hot days.

He was very well known in the neighborhood. Every lonely soul who wandered through the alley would greet the old man by name, this is what my father said, though if they saw him anywhere else, my father added, their eyeballs would have most certainly rolled back up into their heads, for he was a dark glass to their immovable fears and secret, earthly ambitions. But it was different on those Sunday mornings. One by one they would squat down in the shade next to this husk of a huckster, this is what my father jokingly called him, and they would chat for a while, talking about sports and the agony of marriage and trading jokes. Then the men would slip a few dollar bills into the thick, padded palm of the grandfather, and the grandfather would slip the bills into a small brown pouch with a thin leather strap that he wore like a necklace beneath his crisply ironed white shirt, and then he would smile a darkly gleaming gap-toothed smile. He would set his fat Cuban cigar on the edge of the cinder block and write down a few numbers and the date and the man's name in a small notebook with a tiny fragment of a pencil, his over-sized fingers barely able to hold the stub. Then one by one the men and the grandfather would shake hands and the grandfather would take up his cigar once again and the men would disappear into the glare of their Sunday afternoons, some of them whistling, some of them singing, all of them with dreamy, syrupy, faraway looks on their faces, as if they lived on the moon.

It is a wonder to think back on all of this. What can I say? Truly the laughter of God is a soft rebuke to shame the wise and astonish the weak. Which is one way of saying that anyone who cared to observe the Sunday morning war between my mother and my father could hear God laughing uproariously. *¡Ay de mí!* I can close my eyes even now and I am greeted by a dark comedy of spitting resentment, like a dark episode of *I Love Lucy*. But perhaps my memory has altered what actually happened. Perhaps my memory is a photographic negative of what really happened, an x-ray version of reality in which my mother and my father look forever like skeletons obscured by a darkness as fluid and inky as the ocean at night, a world in which absolution does not exist between their two smoldering hearts. Yes, perhaps that is why it seems so strange, so ludicrous and surreal, the action flipping by at supersonic speed, the ocean of everything we have ever hoped for evaporating in the sunlight, stealing away towards nothingness. Who can say? Can the world be redeemed by a kiss? Is it better to look at things with your eyes open? Perhaps it does not matter. *Eu possuo apenas o que Deus me deu.* I read that somewhere long ago, or maybe it was only yesterday.

Anyway, to get back to my story. The climax of my parents' Sunday morning warfare occurred in the weeks leading up to my brother's First Communion. This happened in the spring of 1954, a few months before my father started dreaming his strange, cryptic dreams. Looking back now I think everything that transpired that spring jarred loose my father's sanity and so became the first cause and inspiration of all that he later dreamed, and all the troubles that followed.

My father took no part in the preparations for Emilio's First Communion. My mother tried to convince him that at the very least he should buy his Emilio a white costume so he would be like all the other boys when they received the Blessed Sacrament, but this simple request only enraged my father. 'I do not believe in the Church,' he thundered. And when my mother did not even bat an eye he added a few lightning bolts. 'The Church believes in equality and equality is the enemy of liberty and that is why I do not believe in the Church.'

My parents did not speak to each other for several days after that, perhaps a week, perhaps longer. Perhaps never again, at least not directly. They each felt humiliated by the other. They each felt the other had been taken over by an alien presence, consumed from within, possessed by a band of roving demons for some unknown, sinister purpose. They each felt persecuted by God. (Even though my father said he no longer believed in the Church, he was not so bold or vengeful as to abandon his belief in the Almighty.)

How can anything be so tragic and yet so comic?

My father took refuge in a second-hand leather armchair he had purchased for five dollars and which he had placed near the gleaming plate glass window in the living room so he could look at the two lime trees he had planted in the front yard. He sat in his leather chair, watching the lime trees for a while, wondering perhaps why there were no limes even after three years, and then he retreated into the flimsy pages of *Diario las Américas,* the newspaper he carried with him everywhere, his gateway to a larger world, this is what he always said, this is what he believed.

And my mother, she would push her way through the swinging kitchen door, her burning gaze ricocheting about like bullets seeking revenge, and sit down at the small Linoleum table from Sears with its shiny aluminum trim and its four black and white patterned vinyl chairs, where she quickly found solace in the glamorous pages of *Vanidades,* a magazine which she devoured on a weekly basis almost without breathing, especially because each issue contained a new romance novella by Corín Tellado, who wrote novellas about nurses who left their husbands and became teachers and took vacations in the mountains, or teachers who became airline stewardesses for Pan American or yoga instructors in Barcelona and were seduced by Argentine businessmen and later testified against them in court, or waitresses who fled to Brazil with insurance agents or university professors but later missed their ungrateful children and so went back to their families and their husbands only to find that their husbands had committed suicide, which made them secretly very happy, and always these stories walked the fine line between romance and pornography, and always they had titles like *Matrimonio obligado* or *Aquel hombre* or *Profesor de felicidad* or *Tu eres para mi,* titles which maybe gave you a clue about the storyline, but maybe not. My mother lapped up every word by Corín Tellado, as if those words contained the sorcerer's key to unlocking the tucked away secrets of the universe. She especially enjoyed those stories in which the heroines lost everything early on but always managed to fight their way to happiness by the end.

Ah my blessed mother! May God care for her immortal soul. She had become a Roman Catholic because of my father, and she had embraced this new religion with a fury that amazed the most zealous priests, but she never completely abandoned her childhood faith.

She was a creature of hidden reservoirs of strength.

She was a black dry wind from the south.

She was five fish hooks arranged neatly on a small table and a lighted candle in the center.

She was a fervent altar.

But she was always afraid of the dead. She said you could not control the dead so they should be feared. She said if the dead got their hooks into you there was nothing you could do. Maybe not even a priest could help you free yourself. *¡Ay de mí!* She had some very strange ideas floating about in her head.

Then again, she was no different than anyone else. Truly, who can say why any of us believe what we believe except that we are all looking for unrestrained joy. *¡Qué alegres son las horas!* Do you know the poem? 'How joyful are the hours! Like a flock of doves wandering across the skies.' This image explains everything, I think. Yes, the poetry of Lola Rodríguez de Tío is very compelling. A sneak peek into the mind of God, who can see into every heart, even the heart of my poor, sweet mother, especially her heart. I think if you had peered into my mother's heart of hearts in those days, if you had been able to peel back the layers of flesh that tried to smother her soul in sorrow, you would have found a young peasant girl from a small village nestled in the Sierra Maestra mountains searching the skies for the doves of Lola Rodríguez, a manifestation of the Holy Ghost certainly, but also a visible sign of Obàtálá, that drunken Santería god who created humanity with all of our imperfections, because Lola Rodríguez was Puerto Rican but she loved Cuba, because she spoke for all of us, as do all truly great poets, because everywhere the sky is the sky and white doves are white doves, so that is what you would have seen if you could have peered into my mother's lonely heart in her younger days, that is how I see her even today, my mother searching the skies, an immaculate child of God forever consecrated to the mythic saint makers of Eastern Cuba.

That is why, when my father brought her to Havana, she brought the old ways of Santería with her in the form of a small Eleguá head which she kept hidden away in a lidded gourd decorated with red and black beads. I have seen this gourd. I have even seen the head. It is a head made from clay with seashells for the eyes and the mouth. It carries the name Eshu Laroyê. My mother believed that Eshu Laroyê could cause you to lose everything or gain everything and that he loved whistles and kites and marbles and he was very mischievous. Of course as you have probably guessed, my father did not know of the existence of either the gourd or the head named Eshu Laroyê, not then, perhaps he never found out, or if he did it was not until much, much later. But such is the blindness of men.

When my father took my mother to Miami, the gourd also traveled across the shimmering Straits of Florida and the terror and impenetrable sadness of the open sea, which for most, I might add, is loosely defined as the dull murmur of the ocean depths and the beckoning abyss, except if you are a poor fisherman from anywhere in the Caribbean and are used to living in small shacks or shanties with roofs of dried grass or corrugated tin, in which case the bottom of the sea is a welcome release from the blistering ache of an empty belly and the lava of vengeful thoughts. So they crossed over to Florida. They took a steamer from Havana to Miami. But the head of Eleguá remained hidden from view.

This is what my mother said.

She also said that as soon as they moved into their tiny, one-and-a-half story bungalow in Allapattah, she stuffed the gourd with the head into a corner of her bedroom closet, on a shelf very high up, so my father would never even stumble across it. She said it was surrounded by boxes filled with old shoes and abandoned jewelry and decaying photographs and other souvenirs from their days in Cuba. My mother said after they arrived in Miami she herself forget all about Eshu Laroyê. I do not believe her. I think she was simply counting the days until she would have need of him, but that is beside the point.

She also mentioned one day that there was a small bible on the shelf next to the gourd. But that was probably accidental. The bible had once belonged to my father's father, but he had died in the Great War. My mother was afraid of this bible. She said it smelled of death, and so it sat next to the gourd with the head of Eleguá for oh so many years. Why she had put it there she never said. But one can guess.

All of this my mother told me little by little. One way or another. All of this I have pieced together from many conversations and half-heard snippets, my mother muttering under her crazy, alcoholic breath or talking in her sleep, or from the pages of a small diary in which she kept letters written to herself and which she often left on the kitchen table for anyone to look at, an open invitation, which, I must confess, I accepted. I do not know the full story. I am fuzzy on some of the details, as we all are. But I know enough.

Three weeks before Emilio's First Communion, he still had no white costume, but my mother decided she would keep her anger hidden away from my father and make her case through spiritual channels. On Sunday May 23, 1954, at approximately nine in the evening, just minutes after my father had fallen asleep in his leather chair full of a truck driver's irrevocable melancholy to dream of fruit laden lime trees, my mother retrieved her decorated gourd from the top shelf of her bedroom closet and pulled out the head of the Eleguá named Eshu Laroyê.

Emilio and I were following her around that day because there was nothing else to do. But once she pulled the head out of that gourd, we would have followed her anywhere. Who knew what hidden treasures she might lead us to? Who knew what magic she might conjure? But she ignored us as easily and as completely as if we had become a suddenly aggressive night wind that could be banished simply by closing a window. But we did not mind. She took the head into the kitchen and placed it on the floor between the side door and the stove. We followed a few steps behind her. She flicked on a small lamp which penetrated the darkness as best it could, being such a small lamp, and sat down on the other side of the kitchen in one of the black and white patterned vinyl chairs. We sat on the floor. The lamp was decorated with seashells and a porcelain lampshade that looked like a small red crab. It gave off a soft, peculiar, reddish glow because of the lampshade. If you stared at the lampshade long enough it seemed like the crab was moving, swimming through the darkness, assuming it was one of the species of crabs that could actually swim, its spindly legs churning with frenetic effort, the unseen waters flowing past. But we were not moving. We sat there unmoved and unmovable like volcanic stones embedded in the swirling silt at the bottom of an ancient shallow sea, or perched precariously atop a very tall mountain and the stars falling from the sky. I don't know which. And I don't know how long we sat there either, but after a while it seemed like the invisible gases trapped within the sphere of our kitchen were about to ignite. I could see sparks forming in the air. I could feel the heat beginning to intensify. It was becoming difficult to breathe. I was beginning to perspire. Even my brother Emilio could feel this heat. But my mother didn't seem to notice. She stared at the Eleguá head without troubling about anything around her, as if she was trying to calculate the inner dimensions of a wandering star from a billion miles away, or how long it would take to travel to Key West by bus and then perhaps take a boat to Cuba. Then she gave out a long, wistful sigh and said 'It takes many years to understand the peculiarities of life, and even then, nothing is clear. All that seems to be, is not, and all that seems not to be, is.' Then she said 'Come children,' and we went upstairs to bed.

My father slept that night in his leather chair and left very early the next morning, an hour before sunrise. He was on his way to Birmingham and then Atlanta and then Jacksonville and then back to Miami. He would be gone a few days. My mother could hardly contain her excitement as he left, and within minutes of his leaving, the three of us were gathered once again in the kitchen, which had been transformed at some point during the long night of my mother's most feverish hopes into a backcountry shrine or a temple or a small neighborhood church.

My mother set out a fish bowl with cleansing water on the table. She set out a dozen shallow bowls, jicara bowls filled with offerings she said would please Eshu Laroyê. The bowls were placed in haphazard fashion in front of her Eleguá head. One bowl contained three balls of cooked cornmeal mixed with canary seeds, another contained small candies wrapped in colored paper, another contained marbles and keys and several pairs of dice, another contained red carnations, another contained coffee beans, another contained chewing tobacco, another contained a collection of sharks' teeth of various sizes, another contained grapes and pears and unpeeled bananas that were beginning to turn black, another contained the crushed leaves of several herbs mixed together, another contained three uncooked eggs, another contained pennies and Buffalo nickels and a few old centavos and a silver peso or two from the days of the Republic, all of the coins mixed together, and the bowl in the very center contained a small coconut cake.

There were also a pair of maracas on the floor and a worn deck of playing cards and an old baseball autographed by Heliodoro Jabuco Hidalgo, a hero of Cuban baseball from the early nineteen-hundreds, and an old baseball mitt and a bottle of rum and a bottle of aguardiente and a jar of honey and a pack of Wrigley's chewing gum and three fat Cuban cigars, the kind my father liked, and the small bible that had once belonged to my father's father. All of this was being offered to the Eleguá head named Eshu Laroyê.

So we sat there the three of us on the floor of our kitchen and stared at the shadow of the head and the shadows of the jicara bowls overflowing with their offerings of an aching heart and we did not know where we were.

It almost seemed like a dream. It was still dark outside but my mother did not turn on the lamp. The birds outside were chattering away noisily, so we listened to them for a while, but it was hard to say what kind of birds they were. Perhaps they were a mixture of little brown night jars with their churring call like an engine running, and tiny yellow bellied flycatchers saying che-lek, che-lek, che-lek, which could mean anything so early in the morning, and many other birds mixed in. It was hard to tell one bird from another sitting there in the dark with only our ears to guide us. Then my mother got up and took a thick white candle from the table and set it before the offerings and she lit the candle. She retrieved the small likeness of Saint Anthony, the saint of small miracles, from his place of honor above the kitchen sink and placed him next to the Eleguá head, and in front of the statue she placed a small brown candle, a candle which she had pulled out of a hole in the darkness and which she also lit so Saint Anthony would know she was asking for his help as well. The candles possessed no scent, and yet as soon as they were lit, we could smell quite distinctly the sweet scent of vanilla and cinnamon and licorice.

My mother breathed in this sweet smell like a resurrected premonition, and then she turned to us and smiled and said she was taking no chances, the spiritual world was a world of dancing shadows and ritual magic and strange, whimsical reversals of fortune, you never knew who would be listening or how they would respond, you never knew what would work, your hopes could be gutted like a fish, so you tried everything you could think of and you hoped you didn't offend anyone. Then she started to laugh, a flimsy, insubstantial laughter like filaments of silk, but she caught herself. She wanted to make sure Emilio got his white costume, she said. Then she made the sign of the cross and knelt down on the floor, and all of a sudden we were all kneeling, Emilio and myself and my mother, the three of us now in a row like penitent spider monkeys or pink-headed vultures waiting their turn or submarine portholes at night or pearls on a string, our bodies swaying slightly before the flickering candles and our mother's glowing hope.

The likeness of Saint Anthony seemed to merge with the Eleguá head named Eshu Laroyê.

The statue and the head became a single entity.

The scent of vanilla and cinnamon and licorice grew stronger.

The birds outside grew noisier, as if they sensed that a door was opening.

The world was beginning to spin, or a second world was descending, superimposing itself over the first world.

It was difficult to tell which.

From somewhere there was the steady beating of a drum, a soothing, calming sound, but it was very faint, as if it were coming from inside us, from deep inside our thoughts, trying to burst out from the darkness of our imaginations, a darkness that did not really exist and had never really existed because all darkness is merely the temporary absence of light, a magician's trick, a parlor game, a leather hood pulled over a falcon's eyes.

Then a single shaft of sunlight broke through the window and across the floor, and then another shaft and then another, until the world was flooded with pure sunlight and an unassailable sense of freedom purged of all depravity and the need for revenge.

The birds outside suddenly flew away.

We realized we had never known such freedom.

We started to forget ourselves.

Then my mother began to chant in a secret language we did not know, and we began to chant along with her, repeating everything she said, at least the sound of it, unconcerned with meaning. It was an ancient language and possessed a very rhythmic sound, very soothing, like the unseen drums.

We succeeded in forgetting ourselves.

We succeeded in opening ourselves up to new pathways.

Soon we were lost amid a sea of words we did not understand, a babel of incomprehensible thoughts, the confusion of all earthly tongues flowing together, but as we let this sea flow through us and over us, buffeting us on strange, towering waves, and then as we allowed ourselves to sink beneath those waves to the bottom of this ceaselessly raging, tormented sea where all life began and death was simply the last of many vivid encounters, at that point understanding came.

'*Omi tutu,*' my mother said.

'*Omi tutu,*' we said.

We could see ourselves drinking fresh water, as if we had been traveling for days in the desert and had suddenly come upon a small stream, a sliver of life in a barren landscape. We could feel the water gliding down our throats, filling the hollow spaces deep inside. We drank until our bellies became distended and we collapsed beside the stream. We drank until we fell asleep between this world and the next.

'*Axé tutu,*' my mother said.

'*Axé tutu,*' we said.

We saw ourselves waking up. We saw ourselves vigorously rubbing our arms and our legs. We could feel our vitality returning. We could feel the spirit of Eshu Laroyê rising up from our bellies, passing up along the pathways of our throats and out through our wide-open mouths. We wanted to gulp down more water but Eshu Laroyê, who was now sitting beside us, his back turned towards the sun, only laughed, as if to say that he was the only water we needed. The laughing Eshu Laroyê with his ribcage heaving looked like the black shadow of a palm tree rubbing its head against the sky. Then Eshu Laroyê stopped laughing and he vanished, poof, just like that.

'*Onã tutu, ilê tutu Água fresca, o axé é fresco, o caminho é fresco, a casa é fresca,*' my mother said.

'*Onã tutu, ilê tutu Água fresca, o axé é fresco, o caminho é fresco, a casa é fresca,*' we said.

We saw ourselves sitting beside the stream that had

quenched our thirst. We were no longer so thirsty. We drank from the stream only now and then.

'Tutu Laroyê, tutu ariku babawê, Laroyê, é fresco nossos antepassasdos assegurem que este frescor pedure,' my mother said.

'Tutu Laroyê, tutu ariku babawê, Laroyê, é fresco nossos antepassasdos assegurem que este frescor pedure,' we said.

We saw many others traveling through the desert and invited them to refresh themselves with the water of this stream which was one of many streams belonging to Eshu Laroyê.

We saw the others drinking from the steam.

They were furiously gulping the fresh water.

One or two of them began pounding the ground with their fists and saying this was now their stream. There was only so much water to go around. They could not afford to share their water with anyone. They were the only ones who would be allowed to drink their fill.

We did not know how to handle this dispute. But then we once again heard the laughter of Eshu Laroyê. Eshu Laroyê was nowhere to be seen, but his laughter was everywhere. He was laughing as if to remind us that he was still the only water we needed.

Then the skies above cracked open and rain began to fall to the ground and soon the desert and the stream were part of a shallow lake, a fresh water sea. Now there was certainly more than enough water to go around so there was no longer anything to dispute, at least as far as the water was concerned. Of course now there was no dry place to sit or stretch out and take a nap, but that was another matter.

This is what the laughter of Eshu Laroyê combined with the sound of the rainstorm seemed to be saying.

Then we stopped chanting, and the understanding that had come upon us with the rising sun faded by imperceptible degrees, like a love from long ago that is one night delivered up to the wind. A few hours later my mother had cleared away all evidence of her ritual fever. Even the head of her Eleguá was back in its gourd and the gourd was back on the top shelf in her closet. That is how I remember that morning. But it was only the beginning. For seven days my mother prostrated herself before the Eleguá head named Eshu Laroyê. She offered him all manner of sweets and baked goodies because she knew that's what he liked to eat. She offered him all manner of toys and trinkets because she knew they would amuse him. And every morning she lit the white candle and the brown candle and chanted in her strange, singing bird language of hunch-backed gods and prancing, dancing, nymphomaniac goddesses.

My father had no idea what she was up to. Each morning my mother cleared away the head and the jicara bowls as soon as she was finished with her incantations. She put the candles in the middle of the kitchen table and the tiny statue of Saint Anthony back on his hook. The only evidence that anything out of the ordinary had taken place in the kitchen on any one of those mornings of my mother's furtive madness was the lingering scent from the candles.

But what am I saying? It was much more than lingering. It was as if the scent of the candles had become a living, growing thing. Perhaps not a conscious being, but living all the same. But who can say? By the end of the third day the heady fragrance of vanilla and cinnamon and licorice seemed to be embedded in the kitchen walls. By the end of the seventh day our lungs would fill with a sweet rushing wind with every breath, no matter what room we were in. And yet my father did not notice the sweetness of the air we breathed, except perhaps as one notices a slight drop in temperature and with unconscious memory heads off in search of a sweater. Yes, that is exactly how it was. On the evening of the sixth day, my father remarked that he was suddenly consumed with a desire for something sweet, lemon-filled pastelitos or pineapple empanadas or a slice of rum cake or coconut cake or cookies glazed with chocolate, what did it matter, the urge was overpowering, he said, which was surprising, he had never had such a sweet tooth before, but he had one now and it was killing him, so he was going to head down to Rosario's Bakery and knock on the door until they opened up, and then he would buy whatever they had left. And that is what my father did, and he came back with three bags of sweets and pastries and a big grin on his face and we gorged ourselves until we could no longer move a muscle.

By we, of course, I mean myself, Emilio and my father. My mother disappeared from that evening without saying a word, a shadow slipping into the half-light, as silent as a broken clock. My father once again fell asleep in his leather chair, his two unfruitful lime trees glimmering in the moonlight. He was gone before we got up. He was driving to Tampa Bay and then Pensacola and then Mobile and then Tuscaloosa and then back home.

But this is how it was with my parents. This is the essence of their story. It was tragic and it was comic, as I have said, but only if you were looking in from the outside. For me, who was on the inside, it was oh so very sad. As lovers they were out of tune with each other. They did not know, nor would they ever know, that deep inside the chest of those who sing out of tune, a heart beats softly, which is a beautiful image I have stolen from Gilberto's Desafinado, but it sounds oh so much more beautiful in the original Portuguese. *Que no peito dos desafinados/ No fundo do peito bate calado/ Que no peito dos desafinados/ Também bate um coração.* Some days when I think of my parents I am almost overwhelmed by sadness. In my soul a flock of birds have suddenly taken wing.

On the morning of the eighth day after my mother renewed her devotion to the Eleguá head named Eshu Laroyê, she gathered up the many jicara bowls with their many whimsical and heartfelt offerings and placed them carefully inside a grocery bag, so they would not spill. Minutes later she was out the door and Emilio and I were three steps behind. We walked until our legs began to crumble, and then we rode a bus along a sunny, dusty city street, and then we were walking some more. Our long journey ended in a park, and there we stopped for a while, my mother surveying the landscape. Then she spied a few jicara trees on a small rise in the middle of the park and smiled and said 'Come children, only a few more steps.' We followed her. She knelt before one of the trees and we knelt beside her. It was a very sunny day and the branches of the jicara trees provided little shade. It was a rare thing to see a jicara tree in Miami in those days. It was not unheard of, perhaps, but we had never seen one. My brother and I stared up at the trees and the shiny green fruit. It was no accident that we were there in that park on that day kneeling with our mother before a jicara tree. We could hear birds singing from the branches but we could not see them and they were very noisy like the ones from that very first morning and once again it seemed as if they sensed that somewhere a door was opening. There was no one else in the park, which was strange, but we did not worry about this. My mother emptied the contents of her grocery bag, placing the jicara bowls around the trunk of the tree she had chosen with geometric precision. Then she took up three large silver coins that she later said she had carried with her since her days in Cuba, though why she had kept them all those years she did not say. She kissed each coin and made the sign of the cross and left them with the bowls. Then we went home.

The Afro-Cuban grandfather who ran the bolita game behind the Rexall was waiting for us when we got home. He was sitting in the metal folding chair my mother had set out in the shade of the carport next to a can for watering flowers. My mother had planted azaleas all around the house and these needed constant watering. She was the first to notice the darkly gleaming shadow of the old man in the chair and she pushed us behind her as we walked up the driveway. Emilio did not care who was sitting there so he kept his eyes to the pavement and blindly followed our mother, but I was curious. I did not recognize him as the man my father spoke of. He seemed more like a dark angel who had lost his wings in a terrible accident and so had fallen from the sky. I thought perhaps he was being punished. I thought perhaps he had been exiled from everything he had ever loved. Yes, certainly, these were the thoughts of a child. But what did I then know of the world?

The old grandfather who might have been a fallen angel seemed to be asleep. He had pulled the brim of his immaculate Panama hat down over his eyes, but he was still cradling a fat Cuban cigar in his fat stubby hands. He was barely holding it, I might add. I could see faint wisps of smoke curling up and blackened ash breaking away, dissolving in the air. I wondered why he hadn't dropped the cigar. Of course my mother was in no mood for a strange Afro-Cuban asleep in her driveway. The sun was beginning to set. Already the sky had turned a soft orange. It had been a long day and we were all very tired. But for some unfathomable reason my mother held her tongue. She became strangely mute, as if her voice had been surgically removed, or she herself was only a reflection in a darkly glowing glass and therefore possessed no voice to begin with.

Then the grandfather suddenly took a drag from his cigar and stood up with a sudden theatrical flourish, his immaculate Panama hat now in his other hand, and bowed so low that the brim of his hat swept lightly across the pavement.

'Good evening, Sweet Sister,' he said. 'I did not mean to startle you, please forgive my intrusion.'

He did not acknowledge Emilio and myself except with a quick glance, his eyes brimming with conspiratorial mystery and unexpected mirth, as if he were a peasant pretending to be an ancient god, or perhaps it was the other way around.

'Your husband is Andres Escoraz Silvestre?'

My mother still had not said a word, none that I could hear, but with each question posed by the grandfather she would move her hands this way and that and nod with gaping amazement, and I could see the tiny, bright shadows of many conflicting emotions flying across her face like wisps of smoke. I think now I was watching the shadows of the white doves of Lola Rodríguez flying in and out of the beams of fading sunlight.

'I thought as much.'

'. . . .'

'Your husband was very lucky this week.'

'. . . .'

'Your husband has never been so lucky. I was very surprised.'

'. . . .'

'I think that in all the years your husband has been playing bolita, he has never won even a dollar until today.'

'. . . .'

Then he reached into his pocket and pulled out a thin sliver of paper. I say he reached into his pocket but I am not sure. Was he wearing a thin linen jacket because it was almost summer? Did he reach into a pleated pocket of his pleated trousers? I do not know. I do not remember what he was wearing. It seems now as if he simply reached up and plucked the sliver of paper out of the sky. 'Sweet Sister,' he said, 'I bring you a ticket to the moon.'

Then he placed the sliver of paper into my mother's waiting hands and twirled his Panama hat once again and disappeared in a black cloud of cigar smoke. For a moment we stood there in complete darkness, as if we had suddenly gone blind or were witnessing the last total eclipse of the sun before the end of the world. Then our eyesight returned but we did not say anything. It was impossible to believe that the old grandfather had been standing there in front of us only moments before.

The sliver of paper was actually an envelope containing three one-hundred dollar bills, one bill for each of three silver coins from Cuba my mother had kissed, that is what she later said. I can see her now with her quivering lips and her trembling hands thanking Eshu Laroyê for his generosity as she was standing in line at Burdine's to purchase the white costume for Emilio's First Communion. But what is amazing, when I think about it, is that she never gave any thought to my father and how he would feel about her spending his three-hundred dollars. *Ser agua pasada,* my father liked to say. But maybe not in this instance.

I suppose I still have many questions about what happened. All I really know is that from the moment my mother opened that envelope, life began to unfold with dizzying speed. I had never before experienced the headlong rush of a future that could not be restrained or altered. I could not quite comprehend the tiniest details of what was happening let alone the big picture. I thought I had fallen into that dark abyss where everything goes sailing off the tracks and if you do survive you are permanently scarred for life. It is hard to describe how I felt so long ago, but that is pretty close. But every so often, usually late at night, I get the strangest feeling that I am back there still.

Everything is happening all over again.

A bird in motion.

The wind shifting

Patterns of thought like the syllables once uttered by soaring angels.

I am staring into the mirror of my own consciousness, a stark reminder that I am not in control of anything. I am watching my mother rip into that envelope and then stare with breathless stoicism at the three one-hundred dollar bills drifting effortlessly towards the floor, like the feathers of a bird. She scoops them up and smiles and stuffs them back into the torn sleeve and that is the last I see of the actual bills. We do not sleep at all that night. My mother pulls out her Eleguá head named Eshu Laroyê and places him once again on the floor between the side door and the stove. It was only on the other side of the door that the Afro-Cuban grandfather sat in the metal folding chair, smoking his fat Cuban cigar. My mother gives praise to Eshu Laroyê. She thanks him for his generosity, his kindness, his sense of justice. Specifically, she thanks him for standing with her against my father. She also thanks the Afro-Cuban grandfather, partially, I suspect, because she now thinks he might be the earthly incarnation of Eshu Laroyê, who walks among us now and then, testing our resolve, showering goodies on those who deserve them, pulling the rug out from under those who need to fall flat on their faces. This close to the end she is even less willing to take chances.

My mother scatters tiny glowing candles all over the house. It is dark all over except for the candles. It looks like we have brought the stars inside. The night is filled with my mother chanting and the laughter of Eshu Laroyê with his ribcage heaving and a few more stars appearing at regular intervals in the dark skies of my mother's intent.

The next morning bright and early we are on a bus heading into downtown Miami.

We are heading to Burdine's Department Store.

We are heading to Burdine's with its gleaming chrome and glass counters and gold lamé covered walls where we have only been once before.

My mother says if she had the money, Burdine's is the only place where she would shop. She says that's where all the rich tourists from Latin America shop.

I don't remember the first trip. For all I know this is my first trip.

We spend hours in the store. My mother is very particular when it comes to her purchases. My mother shops around.

She does not mind that everywhere we go people are staring. She is used to being stared at. Or perhaps she does not notice. She is so beautiful that she is oblivious to the world around her and what anyone thinks. She is very beautiful, like a movie actress. She has very dark skin, not so dark as an African, but still very dark compared to the lily whites we see everywhere in Burdine's.

At one point a man wearing a dark jacket and a thin black tie approaches us. He seems nervous. He is smoothing back the edges of his thin moustache as he speaks. He voice is as fragile as glass, ready to break. The air is too thin to hold such a voice for long. He asks my mother if we are lost and my mother looks up as if only then is she aware he is standing there. She does not say a word.

The man with the thin moustache is struck speechless by her silence. Then he glances down at the two of us.

Emilio is hiding behind my mother's skirt. I am not hiding. The man with the thin moustache gives us a long look, his pupils collapsing as if they are tiny balloons that have been pricked. He smiles weakly and retreats towards two salesgirls behind a counter where they sell perfume and whispers something into their ears. Then they begin to play a strange game of whispering and staring, whispering and staring.

One of the girls is looking directly at me, and then at Emilio. We have lighter skin than our mother. Our skin color is like our father's, which is very light. But our beauty is from our mother. We are both very beautiful. Emilio is beautiful like Rudolph Valentino with dark gleaming hair. I am beautiful like Märta Torén with fiery red hair. Many people have said so. Many people have said we are beautiful just like our mother, who is as beautiful as any movie star.

All the while the sales girl is staring at me I feel like a movie star. I smile at the girl but she doesn't smile back. She whispers something to the other sales girl and then the two of them go off to another counter and begin rearranging boxes of perfume. The man with the thin moustache, however, stares at us without a break until we leave the store. He is unable to take his eyes off us. I am certain he is blinded by our beauty.

Many years later I will finally understand why he was staring at us. But I will not really understand why.

Then the scene shifts.

My reflection in the mirror has become strangely elongated. My features have begun to stretch. It is almost like the glass itself is beginning to melt, but in a way that ignores the generally accepted laws of the universe, the center slowly spreading out towards the brightly gilded edges of the frame which forms the boundaries of my life. It is almost like being trapped inside a cartoon. I hardly recognize myself. I am sitting up in bed. It is very late, after midnight certainly. The tiny sliver of a moon in the sky which I can barely see through my bedroom window provides very little light. And yet strangely there is enough light to see by, a shimmering, sunken kind of light, the kind of light that falls like a hard rain, swirling down the gutters, flashing in the darkness like errant coins spinning wildly as they disappear from one hand and appear in another, part of a magician's illusion.

Suddenly I am floating above my bed. I float out of my bedroom and then across the hall to Emilio's tiny bedroom. I can see that Emilio is not sleeping either. He does not see me floating in the air. He is busy listening to a strangely elastic mouth pouring sweet words of poison into his ear. The mouth contorts itself into fantastic shapes as the words pour out. It looks like a two-tone vintage gramophone, a black and bone-ivory orchid unfurling. Then it looks like several miles of plastic tubing coiled very tightly with a suction cup for lips. The tubing is connected to a respirator or some other piece of hospital equipment. Then it looks like a can for watering flowers, a can like my mother keeps by the side door. Then it becomes a miniature radio transmitter. It does not seem to notice that I am hovering in the air no matter what form it takes. I am inches away, if the truth be told, so close I can smell its hot swirling samba breath, or its hot antibacterial hospital breath, or its hot damp-earth breath, or its hot electromagnetic energy breath, but then without any warning whatsoever the mouth turns to greet me. It suddenly becomes more than a mouth. It suddenly becomes the Afro-Cuban grandfather. The Afro-Cuban grandfather presses an elastic finger to his elastic mouth to shush me and then resumes his experiment with Emilio's ear.

When the grandfather is finished, when he has emptied himself of words, Emilio smiles and turns over on his side and goes back to sleep.

I am still hovering only inches away.

I am frozen in the agony of my silence.

I am frozen in the mirror of anticipated guilt.

I feel like I have conspired against my brother. Or that I have conspired against somebody. Maybe myself.

I wonder what I should do.

I am almost praying.

At precisely that moment the Afro-Cuban grandfather turns his strangely elastic mouth towards me once again, as if to answer my almost prayer. But it is no longer the Afro-Cuban grandfather.

It is my very own father who has returned from his four days on the road earlier than expected.

I have many questions for my father.

For one thing I am wondering if he has found out about the money. This is actually the only question in my mind, but it feels like many questions.

This question feels very, very heavy.

I open my own mouth to ask my question but the only sound that emerges is a great swooshing sound like a great ship moving swiftly across the bay, heading out towards the open sea, or maybe it is the sound of a flock of birds taking to the air, yes, again it is a flock of birds, it is always a flock of birds, but this flock is the largest flock of birds I have ever seen (heard), way too many birds to count, the sound is deafening, the sound is earth-shattering, they must be very large birds, hawks and falcons and ocean going eagles by the way my ears are ringing.

But my father only laughs at my obvious confusion. He is laughing as if it is the most natural thing in the world for his daughter to sound like a great swooshing ship or a flock of predatory birds. It is a great crescendo of a laugh like a solar flare demagnetizing the earth's atmosphere. Then he plucks me out of the air as easily as if I am a wounded fledgling and cradles me in his arms, and when I protest, when I try to ask him my one question that possesses the weight of many questions, he simply says 'Hush now, Isidora, you ask the impossible. *Pedir la luna.*'

That is the last I see of my father for a while. The scene shifts again. It is one week before Emilio's First Communion. I am wondering how the hours can fly by so quickly.

(Many years later I will find myself wondering the same thing.)

My mother is hurrying through the side door of Gesù Church. Emilio and I are doing our best to keep up with her.

There are moments when I think Gesù looks less like a church and more like an elegant train station or bus station from days gone by. From the outside, I mean. And always there are vagrants, this is what my mother calls them, hanging around the sidewalk near the side door or sitting on the steps out front in the shade of the arched colonnade. But I do not think they are vagrants, or if they are, then we are all vagrants. Whenever I see them hanging around the side door or sitting on the steps I get the distinct impression that they are waiting for a bus or a slow-moving train to take them to a faraway destination. *¡Ay de mí!* My words are woefully inadequate to describe what I see with my heart.

So there we are, my mother, Emilio and myself. We are now sitting in a pew on the left side because that is the Gospel side of the church. We are watching the priests who are busy with their busywork. It is difficult to see exactly what they are doing at the altar because they are standing with their backs to the rest of us.

I am looking beyond the priests to the gleaming gold walls that surround the altar and the gleaming marble statues of Jesus and the saints looking down with their inscrutable smiles of glory and hidden joy, and in the domed space above the altar I can see Mary and the Baby Jesus standing in a baptismal fountain and the water pouring over the sides. They are painted into the golden background of the dome. They are very high up and I am looking at the color of the Baby Jesus' halo and comparing it to the color of the dome, which looks gold on some days but yellow on other days, and I have to strain to see Mary and the Baby Jesus, I have to tilt my head up at an odd angle, and if my mother catches me she will give me a stern shove in the back as if she is a hard piece of iron, as if she believes she is the iron stamp the Jesuits used in the old days to make the consecrated hosts. Then I am looking at the underwater glow of the hanging lanterns, and for a moment it feels like we are all under water and the lanterns are the lights of submarines moving back and forth in the frothy darkness, for it always seems dark in this church, even on the brightest, sunniest days.

I am lost in my own thoughts like this for quite a while.

I have hypnotized myself.

I hear the sound of tiny bells gurgling away and I see the priests moving about the altar, and I can see their mouths moving but there is no sound, it is like watching a silent movie, except for the gurgling bells, and then I see the faithful heading up towards the communion rail, row by row by row. I watch the faithful kneel and receive the Host and say their small prayers, like tiny fish or silver eels flashing this way and that, and then they head back to their pews.

I see my mother heading for the rail.

Then I see Emilio. He is also heading for the rail.

My mother does not realize he is two steps behind her.

Then they are both kneeling at the rail, and before anyone can say a word the priest shoves a wafer into Emilio's mouth, and it is only at that moment that my mother turns slightly, perhaps because she feels the presence of an angry, accusing God swimming in the air above her, because Emilio is a week away from making his first official communion in the presence of the Almighty, because Emilio has stolen a wafer for some unknown reason. I can see the displeasure of embarrassment, the horror of what people will think, especially the priests, creasing my mother's face. Even in the soft, shimmering, mysterious, contorted darkness of this church that is always and only lit by submarine lanterns, I can see her expression quite clearly. She has taken hold of Emilio by his ear and is pulling him along, but she does not stop at our pew. Dozens of heads have turned to see what is going on, in slow motion, of course, but they are content to leave Emilio to his fate. My mother pulls him all the way to the back of the church and out the door, and then and only then does she unleash her words of distress.

The silent movie is over. The slow-moving underwater feel from before has vanished.

Everything my mother says is in Spanish, but it is a Spanish she rarely uses. It is a dark, dangerous Spanish spoken only in the small villages of Eastern Cuba.

I wonder what possessed Emilio to do such a thing, to make a mockery of his First Communion, to make a mockery of our mother's efforts on his behalf. What will become of Emilio's white costume, I am thinking.

I do not follow them out. I do not wish to call attention to myself. I can hear the murmuring of a few nearby voices. I am certain they are talking about my mother dragging Emilio out of the church and then her torrent of angry dark Spanish, which is an assault to everyone's ears. I am certain even the ears of the priests are burning. It is a wonder the church itself did not become cinder and ash.

Then the Mass is over and the priests are trundling after their white and gold gleaming banner and everyone is following them out the doors, and I am among them, I can hardly wait to see the sun, to gulp in a breath of fresh air once again. I am wondering what has happened to Emilio. I am wondering what my mother will say on the long bus ride home. But when I reach the steps I realize Emilio and my mother are long gone.

At first I am not sure what to do.

I sit down on the steps and lean back against one of the pillars holding up the arched colonnade.

A few of the faithful are lingering in front of the pillars, chatting with the priests, but then one of the priests hurries down the steps and the conversation slowly withers away. It is a bright sunny day, and it is very hot. But I do not mind the heat.

For a while there is no one around. Then I hear the heavy church doors open and then close with a heavy, hollow-sounding thud, and the echo sends a chill up and down my spine. A younger priest runs past me and then stops and turns. He asks me what I am doing there. I tell him I am waiting for my mother. He nods and smiles and then runs away.

I do not know how long I am sitting there.

I watch the traffic flow past and the pedestrians going one way or another. I think about the vagrants waiting for their trains or their buses. Gesù Church sits on a fairly busy street. There are many people on their way to many different places. Then I see a small shadow approaching. The shadow grows larger. It is my father.

'Hallo little one,' he says. 'Have you been crying?'

But I have not been crying.

My father is all bright eyes and gleaming white teeth when he sees me. He does not say anything about Emilio. He does not say anything about my mother. I want to ask him if he was the one who was whispering into Emilio's ear and what he was whispering about and if he was the one who told Emilio to steal the consecrated host. But I do not say anything. What can I say in the presence of my father? So I smile happily and he laughs a happy, hearty, meaty, uncompromising laugh and scoops me up and we head for home.

-114-

The days and weeks that followed my brother's impetuous dash to the communion rail were a return to the wild, unruly, irrepentant passion of my mother's childhood. What can I say except that life is an explosion of competing impulses, some carry us forwards, some carry us backwards, always when we least expect it. For my mother this suddenly meant that her longing for her childhood days, which she had never quite abandoned, became a vital, visible, unstoppable force which impacted the lives of everyone around her. It was a late summer hurricane. It was a tidal wave. It was as if we had suddenly been swept across the Straits of Florida to an earlier moment of history and were now trapped in the mythic mountains west of Santiago, Cuba. When my mother woke up in the morning we heard the rattling cry of a solitary hook-billed kite as it sounded an alarm. When she went out into the yard to water her azaleas we heard the mythic Torocoro with its mantle like a cape the color of the ocean at sunset crying *toco toco tocoro tocoro.*

Every afternoon we could smell the sweet invigorating scent of wild mariposa growing in the invisible forests of our deepest desires. The lush, moist smell of ferns and magnolia and kapok and palm trees invaded the pores of our skin. In the evenings we could smell the earthy, metallic scent of sacrificial blood and the stench of decaying animal carcasses sprouting weeds mixed with the gun powder and hot, dry choleric breath of determined revolutionaries lost in the jungle, this odd mixture of smells drifting through the humid, Floridian air like pollen on the wind. And every night near midnight we were startled awake by the heady perfume of incense burning and strange, guttural, chanting voices knifing through the stillness of the long Cuban night that lay ahead.

My mother rarely spoke about her childhood. She said her village was a village of peasants, descendants of Indians and slaves and criminals and the lonely survivors, mostly deserters and defeated captains, of the many rebellions and wars of Independence that had plagued the island of Cuba over the centuries.

This was her narrative. This is all she would say.

Whenever she discovered she was on the verge of revealing more, she would simply stop. But in her most unguarded moments, most often after she had just polished off a bottle of tequila, she was plagued with an inability to keep her mouth shut. In those moments we saw a darker side to my mother, a darkness that enveloped first my father, then Emilio, and finally myself. Where did this darkness come from? Who can say? It lived within her like a smoldering fire. But what could we do? What could anyone do? Peace almost always eludes us. Some days all we can hope for is redemption. *Que Dios nos saque de penas y nos lleve a descansar.*

The darkness that enveloped my mother and my father was the easiest to ignore because it was always vibrating just beneath the surface. It became for us just background static. Radio signals from another planet. My mother said she had given herself to my father in marriage in the hopes of altering her destiny, but she knew deep down it was doomed from the start.

'We are not permitted to change the course of our own ships,' she liked to say. She said she knew this from the words of an old woman who had lived and perhaps still lived in the greening shadows of the forest near Cruce de los Banos, a mountain slope which my mother roamed at will when she was small. She said the old woman wore the costume of a slave from the nineteenth century, a woven skirt and a turban, and that her sagging, wrinkled breasts were bared for all to see. My mother said it was often difficult to understand this old woman because she spoke in a strange, guttural fashion, her mouth completely closed except for a thin line to let her hissing breath escape, her words often sounding like they had been turned upside down, as if her teeth were falling out as she spoke and all she could do to keep them from falling to the ground was press her lips together. On some days she went by the name Cachita Tumbo and she wore a slave's woven skirt and a turban and her breasts were bare, but on other days she preferred the name Mamona or Guimazoa.

My mother said one day she encountered the old woman after a drenching downpour that evaporated as quickly as it had begun, and she went with the old woman to a small stream hidden in the underbrush near a small cave high up in the mountains where even the clouds might lose their way, thinking they were bumping into a reflection of the earth on their journey from west to east when it was the earth itself. My mother and the old woman sat down among the ferns and unnamed flowering bushes along the stream and listened to the birds calling out to each other and the swiftly moving water for a while. The old woman said her name for that day was Cachita Tumbo. She asked my mother if she wanted to know the future, and my mother said yes. She asked if my mother was afraid she might see something she did not like, and my mother said no, she was not afraid. She asked my mother if she would accept whatever she saw and not attempt to change her future, and my mother said she would let her life unfold as it was supposed to unfold, and more than that, she said she would let her life flow through her as swiftly and as brightly as this tiny mountain stream was flowing through the forest all the way to the sea, and of course Cachita Tumbo was pleased with my mother's enthusiasm.

¡Ay de mí! Who can penetrate the dark hood of the endless Cuban night? Who would not be filled with unyielding despair at the thought of dying alone? My poor, poor mother. She did not share all of the details of the dark vision of the future Cachita Tumbo shared with her on that hazy, smoldering afternoon oh so many years ago. But she did say the old woman predicted that on three separate occasions she would be betrayed by the people she loved the most in the world.

The first betrayal, of course, was the betrayal of my father. No, he did not sneak off with a wayward woman. He did not possess an uncontrollable libido. He was not like that. No, my father's betrayal was much more devastating for my mother. It was a betrayal of the spirit of love, though perhaps such betrayals are inevitable. I think my father simply grew too old. 'Romance is a game for the young,' he would say. Instead of losing himself to love, my father lost himself in his books and his world of ideas and in driving his truck, and after a while he forgot my mother even existed.

The second betrayal was Emilio stealing the Communion wafer. My mother could never look at my brother after that without wagging her finger and reminding him of the incredibly long and unforgiving memory of Eshu Laroyê.

But the worst betrayal was mine. In my mother's eyes it was the worst possible betrayal one could suffer. My father's betrayal was a betrayal of the past, a past which she, too, had abandoned, so she really lost nothing. My brother's betrayal was a betrayal of the present, which carries less and less weight with each passing day, so in the end that too was nothing. But my betrayal was a betrayal of everything she had ever hoped for. Mine was a betrayal of her future, and so it was always fresh in her mind.

But what else could I have done? On the day I stumbled past the palatial pink stucco extravagance of La Campana, I traded her future for mine. That was the day I first beheld my beloved Oscar. He was standing in the radiant bubble of his own ambition, watching with studious appraisal the efforts of the men working to bolt the movie-house style marquee to the side of the building. It was a beautiful moment. And though he took absolutely no notice of me that afternoon, I knew without any doubt whatsoever that one day we would be married. It was simply a matter of destiny. So I ask you again, what else could I have done?

-115-

My mother was not the only one who secretly (or not so secretly) wished to steal my future. My dead relatives, my happy band of wayward angels, who had been lingering in between worlds for years, suffering from varying degrees of disbelief but watching over me all the same with their unvarnished, saintly vigilance, they were all, with one exception, eager to substitute their own dreams of the future for mine. (Never mind that on that day when I first mentioned my dream, bubbling over with adolescent enthusiasm, my Oscar could hardly have asked for my hand in marriage since he had not yet even noticed me.) I never had to seek out their advice. They occupied a small alcove next to the upstairs bathroom, where my mother had arranged a small, brightly colored love seat and three brightly polished walnut chairs with a few vintage magazines laid out on a small coffee table. It was the perfect spot to waylay an impressionable young girl.

The only one who filled my beleaguered heart with the faith of the chosen was Tiká. Whenever she was present, the others kept their tongues in check. She would occupy the love seat and the others would gather around her and sit where they could. Whenever she was absent, the seating arrangements were as follows:

My great-uncle José Ignacio would sit in the middle of the love seat, tearing open small brown packages of analgesics and popping the tiny white tablets into the gaping black hole of his mouth with unthinking regularity, an addiction he had acquired, he once told me, during his days working in a cordage warehouse in Havana just after the Great War. Dozens of empty packages littered the floor at his feet, and yet there was always a crisp, new package in his eager hands, and even more tucked away in his pockets. Uncle José Ignacio possessed a seemingly inexhaustible supply of tablets, though why he needed so many and how he was able to procure them in the invisible, metaphysical limbo of the in-between he never said. Naturally my great-grandmother (and here I mean my great-grandfather's wife, for even though I now know the truth of my family tree, I will always think of Tiká as my cousin, and I will always and forever think of the second to last Ana Silvestre as my great-grandmother) would sit beside him, on one side or the other, pouring bittersweet words of unassailable regret into his glowing red ears, as only a mother born over a century ago would be tempted to do, and every now and then my uncle would sprinkle a few tablets into her withered, wrinkled, trembling hands.

My great-grandmother's one and only daughter, an

adopted daughter it is true, but a daughter nonetheless, the very last of an incredibly long line of Ana Silvestres, if by name only, would sit across from the love seat in one of the walnut chairs. She paid no attention to either my great-grandmother or my uncle and his tablets. She was always embroiled in an overly enthusiastic yet decidedly bitter battle (a lot of arm waving, hands tracing arcane patterns in the air, finger pointing, that sort of thing) with her sister-in-law, Nuria Barruti (the second walnut chair), a dazzling beauty who had grown up in El Cobre, Cuba, and who had been arrested at the unlucky age of thirty for using *brujería* magic to seduce the husbands of several wealthy women from one of the fancy neighborhoods of Santiago. Tia Nuria had mysteriously died in prison before her case could be heard, an unequivocal tragedy in the modern age that was immediately and unanimously proclaimed the will of the resurrected God.

It was very difficult to argue with Tia Nuria. Every once in a while when I looked into her eyes of a Santería priestess, I could see the fractured, bluish light of long dead stars where I should have seen two reasonably steady black pupils. I swear this is true. It was almost like the universe was contained within the ghostly jelly of Tia Nuria's eyes. There is not much one can say in the presence of such a strange, alien light. It is like being lulled to sleep by two cat's eyes. It is like staring too long into the void of a lunar eclipse. So Tia Nuria won most of her arguments without uttering a single word. But this was not the case when she argued with my grandmother, though to be fair, they only ever argued about the circumstances of Tia Nuria's strange death, which appealed to my aunt's carefully concealed vanity, for it gave her a shining platform from which to tell her own sad story.

My grandmother believed Tia Nuria had angered the Virgin of Caridad del Cobre, the patron saint of love and lovers, but Tia Nuria said that was absolute poppycock, she had strictly adhered to the wishes of the loving and compassionate Saint with every spell she had cast, every ritual she had performed, she had heaped all manner of honors on the altar of fervent hearts in the hope that the sister of Yemaya would bless her accordingly, and she had been exceedingly blessed in matters of love, and in other things, no, no, Tia Nuria said, her strange, unexpected death (the coroner could find no physical manifestation of illness or any signs of foul play) was simply a case of Yansá, the goddess of unexpected hurricanes and the caretaker of drowned sailors and crumbling cemeteries on the verge of disappearing forever, anticipating a death when no death was upon the horizon. It was a mistake such as anyone might make, that was all. The battle between my grandmother and Tia Nuria had been raging in this manner for years.

The last two faces I would see would be those of José Luis the estranged, beleaguered husband of my aunt, and José Luis their happily indigent son, who had died in 1966 and was thus a recent participant in these impromptu family gatherings. The two José Luis's would be crammed into a single chair (the third walnut chair). They were both short, frail men with wiry arms and the long slender fingers of pianists, though neither had ever played. They possessed dark complexions from too many hours playing baseball. And their rough, leathery skin still somehow smelled of tobacco from years of incessant smoking. (They had only ever smoked thick, leafy cigars which they rolled themselves.) Curiously, they had both died of sunstroke at the age of thirty-five, so they looked more like brothers than father and son. They were also embroiled in a battle of their own, but they spoke without venom or hysterics or even ego, expressing themselves in low, desiccated whispers, trying not to draw any undue attention to themselves, their conversation punctuated now and then by bursts of sweet, endearing laughter like the sound of a salt water breeze rattling a set of wind chimes, or the unrivaled poetry of the tiny Torocoro, a bird that would become suddenly mute when caged and die the slow, withering death of inconsolable sadness, but in the wild it sang with an uninhibited and undiminished joy that only the angels could match. My great-grandmother often remarked on the similarity between the song of the Torocoro and the laughter of the two José Luis's. She used to say that when she was a young girl she would wake every morning and fall asleep every night to the Torocoro serenading the world with its sweet, happy song of absolute freedom and unburdened love. The laughter of the two José Luis's had the same sweet sound, she said. And so it did. The two men would laugh with a regularity like clockwork even while they were debating who was the greatest Cuban baseball player ever. It was in fact a very comical debate, for they were constantly changing their minds, suggesting new players without the slightest provocation, swapping their claims on older ones, going through the entire pantheon of Cuban greats again and again and again, even those players who had only played in Cuba for a single season. This battle, an exact opposite of the other on so many levels, had begun as you might have guessed as an innocent game between a father and a son when both were still alive.

I can say this now, looking back as I am with a faint, blushing but unashamed smile, that on those hot, sultry days and darkly oppressive nights when my dead relatives surrounded me like silhouettes cut from black cardboard, the kind of silhouettes used to frighten birds, I often wondered if I had not gone mad.

It was as if I had become the inspiration for a line of poetry by Julia de Burgos. *'La locura de mi alma vive en el silencio del librepensador, que vive solo.'* What could I say to them? I was willing to gamble a love as freely flowing and relentless as water against everything that is inhuman and unjust. This was the feeling in my heart. But I did not yet possess the words to make my feelings understood. And they did not wish to see me suffer, a sentiment that was magnified by their own vanished intimacies and keen sense of loss. But they knew as well as I, even at the tender age of eighteen, that suffering was the price we pay for love. *¡Ay de mí!* What young girl does not know this truth? All of which is to say that they were not stringent or resolute in their hypocrisy. I think my dead relatives just wanted to raise their voices to the tornadic winds that obliterate all earthly desires and lay waste cities that have stood for a thousand years and send futuristic spaceships hurtling through the dark tunnel that we call the void, and when they (the occupants within those shiny, elliptical vehicles from the future) reach the other side, they find they have crash landed in the frozen, snow-covered Andes of centuries ago, so they flee the scene like cannibals on the verge of starvation, or detectives in search of a high profile crime, or young, restless, relentless lovers who have suddenly and irrevocably gone blind, all in a mad dash to speak their minds before God claims the right of final judgment. This is why I think my dead relatives spoke as they did.

On the day I first beheld my beloved, my great-grandmother, the second-to-last Ana Silvestre, was the first to speak among the dissenters. She had already seen the darkness in the mirror, she said. She was quite poetic as she spoke. She spoke with the murmur of the ocean's millenary waves, at turns soothing, cajoling, and then provocative, unsettling. A strange hush fell over everyone. She spoke with the voice of my great-grandfather as much as her own, a voice that she had carried in her head from the day he had died until she had joined him in the in-between. What she said was a warning, and yet it was not a warning.

> *Yes, I see the two of you strolling into the lobby of your fancy Parisian hotel, a soft glowing golden light bouncing off the walls, a hall of mirrors, twelve, thirteen, twenty, an infinity of mirrors, the light now bending in peculiar ways, giving you plenty of opportunity to change direction if you choose. But you do not change direction. You walk arm in arm with death, that impertinent lover who whispers only bitter stories. No, you and your beloved are unaware, you are laughing carelessly, heedless of the future that will one day arrive. You are caught up in your luxurious surroundings. The décor is vaguely Romanesque with blood-red marble pillars edged in gold, pale green walls. Maybe not Romanesque. Minoan. Yes, that's it! The pillars and the walls suggest the island of mythic Crete. The ancient Minotaur trapped in an underground labyrinth. It has the feel of bygone elegance and dangerous depravity. But you do not notice. You are absorbed in thinking about the paradise of your surroundings while your beloved is signing the hotel register. The clerks and bellhops are chatting away happily, garrulous fellows. One of the clerks leads you from the lobby to the dead center of an art deco atrium with a glass bubble at the top. The narrow walls of the atrium are a whitish yellow for the most part, but near the bottom they are a deep, vibrant, volcanic orange. The bellhop tells you to look up and so you do. You feel like you are looking through a slender telescope manufactured in the age of marvels. You are looking at the white-hot center of the sun, that is the impression you have. You grow dizzy. You almost faint, but the bellhop catches your falling arm, and then your beloved makes a small joke about too much wine for so early in the day. Then the bellhop points out with mock enthusiasm an inlaid marble pattern on the floor. It looks like the corona of an indelible black sun, and at the very center is a bronze medallion that looks something like an eye. Perhaps it*

is an Egyptian eye. Or the one eye of the Minotaur. Yes, you are reminded again of the Minotaur and the labyrinth. But this eye does not blink or fade. It stares at the white bubble of the sun oh so many miles above for all eternity. The one bellhop encourages the two of you to stand directly on top of this darkly polished, eternal sun, this unblinking eye. The bellhop asks you what it most resembles, a sun or an eye. You decide it looks more like an eye. Again, the bellhop presses you to stand directly on top of this iconic work of art embedded in the floor. He says he will take a photo of the two of you. You realize it is a bit of a cliché to pose for posterity's sake in this manner, but you do not mind. You are willing. Everyone who stays at this fancy hotel stands upon the eye. The famous writers who lived here and died here. The writers who wished to die here but died instead in their sleep in their own homes after returning from short, uneventful trips to Denmark or Belgium or Lebanon or Spain or the islands of Honduras. But not just writers. Everyone. The honeymoon couples stretching back to the dawn of the twentieth century and even earlier. And other couples as well, older absent-minded lovers, petulant lovers, criminal lovers, slap-happy lovers, homosexual lovers, lesbian lovers, generals and courtesans, painters and poets, a gourmet chef and his ex-wife, two young besotted philosophy students, indifferent to the passing years, who later become two middle-aged lovers stung by the pain of jealousy and the force of circumstances, twosomes and threesomes and foursomes, a man in a bandana playing a Spanish guitar, singing an ancient Iberian love song to a green moon and a demon lover hiding out in a balcony. All of them surreal caricatures of themselves, as we all are.

You and your beloved stand on the eye in the center of the atrium, but only for a moment, because your beloved is uncomfortable with the scrutiny of so public a display of affection. So he begs off, laughing sheepishly. You realize there will be no photograph, but you forgive him instantly. The idea of recrimination is not even a thought in your head. It is your honeymoon, such as it is. Then your beloved slips the bellhop a bill and the bellhop scuttles away clickety-clack on all fours, crab-

like, to see about your luggage. Your beloved lingers only a moment more, giving you a curious backward glance before heading in the opposite direction and disappearing through a gauzy blueish-green curtain.

During the two weeks you are in Paris this curtain will remind you on a visceral, unconscious level of the color of the Caribbean Sea. It will be the sensation of a feeling lost in the gap between neurons rather than a specific thought or a re-created memory. During the years to come, this image of the curtain will haunt your dreams. You will begin to think of it as a symbolic reminder of that curtain through which we must all pass on our way to the grave. But on that bright sunny day in Paris these later more sinister interpretations will not occur to you. But you do not follow your beloved through that curtain, you remain standing on the darkly gleaming inlaid eye for a few moments longer, perhaps many moments, the precise number is difficult to gauge, and while you are standing there, your own eyes half-closed, immersed in the delicious swirl of romantic possibilities and the swirling white light from the neon sun of your imagination, the ghost of Marguerite de Valois whispers something impertinent into your ear. Yes, Marguerite de Valois, the promiscuous French queen who took her many lovers, an infinity of irrepressible lovers between 1589 and 1599, to a small stone house on the very corner where your luxury hotel now stands, a house which was known ever after as the 'Pavilion of Love.'

The ghost of this passionate yet staunchly unrepentant queen whispers into your ear the very same words she whispers into the ears of all the guests who stay at the hotel. You hear her voice quite distinctly, and yet there is a transient, ephemeral, faraway quality about the sound, as if the air has become suddenly quite thin. It is like swallowing in a single gulp the exhilarating, indescribable joy of the Sacryn bells during the Catholic Mass. The ghost of Marguerite de Valois tells you that lovers are not criminal in the estimation of one another ('Che la forza d'amore non riguarda al delitto'). You are so startled that you turn in a complete circle to see who is talking, but she vanished years ago, centuries ago, so there is no one there, not even one of the bellhops, not even the clerk from the front desk. Only the irrepressible joy of Marguerite de Valois' libido remains. Yes, my darling granddaughter, it is quite a romantic hotel your beloved will pick. It is your hotel. It is 'the' hotel. I cannot reproach him for that. The two of you will stay in an elegantly furnished room, a sunny soft orange color on the walls, softer than the orange of the lobby, and thick drapes, a burnt orange color like a dying sun. The art-deco furniture is covered with mirrors, the relics of a once popular French singer, a legend of the Follies Bergere with a sweetly despairing pouty face and fulsome lips who was desperately in love with a Brazilian diplomat, and even bore him a son, but they never married. But you are the first in the room on this day. Your beloved has vanished within a few hours of your arrival in Paris but you do not wonder why. You are not troubled. You are surrounded by your own joy.

Wake up, my darling, wake up! Your youthful naiveté is sweetly inspiring, but tragic, as Isolde's love for Tristan was tragic, oh so very tragic. Do you not see this? Do you not feel the tremors of what is happening, the tremors that will inevitably lull you to sleep if you are not careful? Your beloved has not one room in this hotel; he has taken three. In a second room, he is keeping his mistress of the week, a young slip of a girl he met at the airport while you were freshening up in the ladies' room. No, there is no need to tell you what she looks like. She is the flavor of the day. But her room is so extravagantly decadent. That should tell you all you need to know. He is keeping his eager mistress in a boudoir from the 18th century with a view of a cobblestone street, a gloriously shameful room in honor of the notorious Madame de Merteuil, complete with gold wallpaper and gilded mirrors, and a damask baldaquin to keep prying eyes from seeing what goes on in the bed. How can you not smell her treacherous perfume on your beloved's skin when he comes to bed each night? How can you not register the smallest flicker of irritation and resentment when he whispers her name in the middle of a dream? Ah my sweet, enduring granddaughter, what is to become of you? Why are you sacrificing your love? Do you wish to live as his concubine? Just one of many? And yet if it was only an occasional dalliance with a young girl here, a restless, lonely housewife there, or even many dalliances, he could be forgiven. If he were sleeping with his own sister, he could be forgiven.

Wake up, my darling, wake up! Open your eyes to the world around you. ¡Andar por las nubes uno se olvida del suelo!

In the third room, your beloved is keeping a peacock of a young man who owns a small restaurant known to some as Café de la Trois Pommes, but to others it has been known for years as Chez Jules. It is a fancy restaurant for very fancy crowds just a few blocks away on Rue Mazarine. It is a gathering place for the recalcitrant.

No, no, I will not describe to you what unseemly aberrations will take place in the peacock's room. The scandalous nudity is almost more than I can bear. But even this indiscretion could be forgiven, for such is humanity, such is weakness, such is love. 'Echar un palo,' as the old ones in Cuba used to say.

You see, my darling, I am not without compassion or understanding. I know we are bound to each other only if our love is freely given, as yours is. I know that if you have become love, you do not need to consciously forgive any sin because love is the incarnation of forgiveness. I know that every breath a lover breathes brings absolution.

Yes, I can see all this in the mirror as well. But what of the deception that is unforgivable? Your beloved has lied to you through his extended silences and his mysterious disappearances. He is trying to whitewash his depravity with words, which only God has the power to do.

No, no, I have no advice to give. I cannot see what happens after Paris. The mirror grows very dark after Paris, as dark and frothy as a wine-colored sea, as the poets say. The mysteries of your future quickly become impenetrable. But this is just as it should be. Perhaps there is nothing to worry about. Yes, my darling granddaughter. Life is never finished until it is finished. All prophecies are simply an artist's sketch of a moment, an evolving work of the imagination, the mind of God interpreted, and then reinterpreted. No one can look at a sketch without making a change, a subtle shading, an added detail, and wallah! the prophecy is altered.

Yes, my young invincible heroine, in spite of my

warning, I must acknowledge that there is always hope. The mind of God is a tricky labyrinth indeed. Perhaps you are right in your unrestrained enthusiasm for this man. Perhaps the purity of your heart will carry you through. Perhaps I have no right to question you in this manner. I might as well ask you which has the saltier or sweeter waters, the Caribbean Sea or the Straits of Florida? No one can answer this question for another. It is a matter of personal taste. And so it is with you.

The last thing I see is the two of you dining at the small restaurant owned by your beloved's Moorish paramour. You have already polished off a plate of veal and carrots flavored with jasmine and are waiting for dessert.

The owner stops by your table with a warm, welcoming smile, a tad over-friendly, you think, but the smile is for you as much as for your beloved so you smile back. The owner is talking with rapid-fire enthusiasm. His eyes do not betray his feelings, but he is nervous nevertheless. His palms are sweaty. He seems to be waiting for something. Then a waiter appears. The owner tenses but then relaxes. It is only your desserts. Your desserts have arrived. A lemon and raspberry dacquoise for each of you. You take a bite and the taste overwhelms your senses. For a moment it seems like the world is spinning. Then the owner leans close to your beloved. He puts a hand to your beloved's shoulders and whispers something in his ear. You are not sure what you are seeing. The owner is gently massaging your beloved's shoulders as he whispers. The two men laugh softly like conspirators with no fear of discovery. Then a second waiter appears out of nowhere with a bottle of Cognac. He presents the bottle to the table. It is a very fancy bottle. It is a gift, of course. No money exchanges hands. And yet your beloved leads you to believe that he is going to spend an extraordinary sum on this single bottle. You will be paupers for the rest of your honeymoon.

Why does he lie to you? What is the point of such a trivial and yet monstrous deception? One can only guess. Perhaps he cannot help but lie to you. Perhaps there is a better reason. Then the two of them are laughing some more, but it is a different kind of laughter. They are now laughing away like hyenas, their teeth snapping at the empty air. You are staring at them with broken wings. You are suffering on a cross of silence and ashes. Then the mirror turns black.

-116-

My grandmother, the very last Ana Silvestre, was much more direct in her words of warning. She believed that if I married this Oscar, he would meet a sudden, savage, premature death. She said he would die amid the terror of a battle at sea, a casualty of a brutal and ultimately inconsequential war. Then she reminded me of her own tragic love affair with my grandfather, Emilio Valentín Menoyo.

My grandmother met my grandfather one sunny afternoon in Havana in April 1916 at the age of fourteen (though she could have passed for a fulsome twenty-two) while she was strolling down the Paseo del Prado, admiring the many beautiful homes and listening with half an ear to a sultry bolero drifting on the silky currents of a spring breeze. She never admitted exactly how they met. She never said what my grandfather looked like or where he came from or how he made a living. All she would say is that from the moment they laid eyes on each other, the past was forgotten and the future was hungrily spent tangled up in each other's arms. My grandmother was certain that the love they shared would be the subject of sonnets for centuries to come. Oh, to be so lucky! Sadly, their love was not to be. History intervened. One year after my grandparents met, Cuba declared war on Germany, and President Menocal instituted a draft. But Cuba never officially sent any troops to Europe during the conflict, though the Cuban government issued Victory medals all the same at the conclusion of the war. But that is beside the point. My grandfather was among the many eager draftees who trained in earnest in secret training camps in Oriente and Camagüey provinces under the expert tutelage of retired United States Army colonels. It was no one's fault that the war ended before a single Cuban soldier crossed the Atlantic. God was determined to preserve the life of every single Cuban soldier. And yet my grandfather, Emilio Valentín Menoyo, died a casualty of that war all the same.

'He was an idiot,' my grandmother often said. 'He was not a soldier. He was a farmer, a musician, a poet, a grocery store clerk, an insurance salesman, a race car driver, a pharmacist. He was like anybody else. What did he think he was doing? Did he not realize that I was waiting for him to come home to me? Did he not realize that even my father had warmed up to him? I did not mind him traipsing about Cuba for a summer, pretending to be a soldier, flirting with the girls in Jiguani or Santa Rita, or even Bayamo, when they had a free weekend, not if that would make my Emilio happy. Besides, I knew the girls in those towns, so I was not afraid of any dalliance. I was not afraid of anything that might take place on the island of Cuba. But why did he not come home to stay as soon as that summer was over? What made him seek out this war on the other side of the world? What excuse could he make to me? What madness came over him? What demon was whispering in his ear, requiring his blood? Oh, I wish that we had never met. How could my heart have been so deceived? Did he not see the beautiful life that was waiting for him? Oh why oh why did we not get married before he went off to the war? Was that too much to ask?'

This was the great betrayal of my grandmother's life. My grandfather had grown impatient with Cuba's war effort. After that first summer he realized the Cuban troops would never be ready to join the fighting. So he decided he would head for Brazil, because the Brazilians were hot for revenge. The Germans had sunk several Brazilian freighters bound for Spain, several more bound for France, and a steamer heading for the Caribbean, which meant, according to my grandfather, that there was a better chance of getting into the war if he went to Brazil than if he remained in Cuba. He told my grandmother of his plans on the last Saturday in September 1917. It was cloudy and very warm that day, so they decided go to a desolate beach some miles west of Havana. They had ridden their bicycles (because it was either that or walk).

All that afternoon they chased after each, splashing in the surf and then running along the beach and then diving beneath the waves, their naked skin glistening with foam and the incomparably resilient athleticism of youth, their laughter glistening with their nakedness. They made sweet, delicious love with the water lapping at their toes, without a single thought to the future. ('I did not realize how young I was until much later,' my grandmother told me. 'It was my first and last transgression of the flesh.')

It was a most romantic scene. As the sun began to set, as if on cue, it began to rain, so they grabbed their clothes and took refuge beneath an overturned fishing boat that had most certainly seen better days. My grandmother said it was quite a ferocious storm. She said it rained with a torrential intensity rarely seen even in the tropics. But she was not afraid. They spent the rest of that evening and the night that followed hiding beneath the boat. My grandfather wrapped his arms around her and began to whisper into her ear. The last thing she remembered hearing before she fell asleep was the rhythmic drumming of the rain on the hull mingling with the plangent sound of my grandfather's voice. He was telling her about his plans to leave for Brazil and fight in the Great War, how he would be at the forefront of many great battles and return a conquering hero with a chest full of medals, and then they could get married and live out their happy days in Miramar, or wherever she wanted to live. She had the crazy impression that she was lost in a dream.

Years later my grandmother realized with a strange mixture of incredulity and reverence that the beach where they had made love (and where my father was conceived) was the very same beach where centuries earlier the very first Ana Silvestre had made love to her secret husband, a lonely soldier of fortune who could not stop his feet from roaming and so had gone off with Hernando De Soto in search of cities of gold in 1539. Every Ana Silvestre for five hundred years dreamed with her eyes squeezed shut that she would be the lucky one to escape the bloody catacombs of the past. Not even my grandmother was able to escape those catacombs, in spite of the fact that she had been adopted. The next morning, she woke up to a crowd of ancient, weather-beaten faces surrounding her like a net, which was God's way of playing a joke, she later said, because she herself was stark naked except for a torn fishing net draped across her legs. In fact her legs had become tangled up in the net, which was attached to the boat, which is perhaps why the storm had not swept her out to sea. The vagaries of fate are strange indeed.

The weather-beaten faces belonged to a cluster of dirt-poor fishermen who dressed in rags (which does not matter when you are out in a boat). There was also a strange, courageous light in their eyes, and the expressions on their faces ranged from concern to paranoia to incredulity to an almost uncontrollable excitement. Some were making the sign of the cross and looking up suspiciously at the sky, as if they thought my grandmother was an angel that had been struck by lightning and had fallen to the sandy earth, a blistered, burning heap. Others were looking out at the unusually tranquil water that morning with great longing and wondering about the miracle of the sudden, ferocious squall that had come up from the south the night before, and then wondering why this young girl had not perished in the storm, and then their heads turned slowly in unison, following a trail of reddish seaweed back to the overturned boat, as if they thought my grandmother was perhaps a mermaid who had lost her tail but still possessed great magic. All of the men were whispering, though my grandmother later said it sounded less like whispering and more like the droning of insects hiding in the vegetation along the side of the road.

It took my grandmother several minutes before she realized that my grandfather had vanished, and several more before she could break through the hood of superstition that covered the understanding of the fishermen. When they finally understood that she had spent the night with her betrothed beneath the boat, and when they finally understood, on this glorious morning with the beach littered with all sorts of refuse coughed up by the sea, that her betrothed was nowhere to be found, they laughed with unembarrassed delight and then launched into a furious conversation with hurried, high-pitched voices, trampling over each other's words, and then one of them said '*Lobos de una camada,*' which was followed by more laughter, which was followed by a moment of embarrassed silence when they realized my grandmother was listening to them with great apprehension.

Then one of the men squatted down by the boat so he could look directly into my grandmother's eyes. 'Excuse us Senorita,' he said. 'We have meant no disrespect. We can clearly see you have been through an ordeal. Forgive us. We are brainless, as you have surely guessed. Our heads are no bigger than the heads of falcons or ferrets.'

It was a strange thing to say, but my grandmother only nodded and smiled a blank, vaguely hopeful smile, which the fishermen took for a sign that their rustic version of an apology had been accepted. Then they laughed some more and helped my grandmother to her feet. One of the men, after some searching, located her bicycle half-buried in the sand. There was no evidence of a second bicycle. Then they gave her a damp blanket to wrap around her bare, glistening hips, and off she pedaled towards Havana.

My grandmother never saw my grandfather again.

Near the end of July the following year she received a letter that he had sent from Rio de Janeiro. The letter was signed 'your brave and true Emilio, a moth to the eternal flame that is our love,' but she was still angry that he had abandoned her beneath the boat and refused to read it for almost a year. But eventually, as you most certainly have guessed, she read it every day, and then twice a day, before she abandoned it utterly to the ash heap of her despair, because it was the only letter he ever sent. It was dated April 29, 1918. It was a naively optimistic letter, the kind one expects from a young man going off to war, which skillfully avoided sentimental excess by avoiding the topic of love altogether, except by implication.

What my grandfather's letter said:

My Dear Sweet Ana, How I miss you. I arrived safely in Brazil on a very cold Monday. I have been staying with a kindly couple that I met down at the fish market. Their names are Adelita and Sagueo. Adelita grew up in Brazil and has never been anywhere else. Sagueo is from Mexico. He fled his country when Carranza came to power. He cannot stand Carranza. He calls Carranza all sorts of names. He says he is a very fat frog in a very small puddle. He calls him a thief and a liar, an overstuffed brigand, a buffoon, a lizard, and the name of another reptile I had never heard before, a hideous monster with jaws of iron and poisonous breath that roams the forgotten desserts of Mexico in search of unwary travelers to feast upon. He is exaggerating, of course. Can you imagine such a reptile? Carranza sounds just like any other politician. But Sagueo cannot wait for him to die so he can take Adelita to Mexico City. Sagueo says his family owns a very beautiful home there in one of the suburbs, a gleaming white palace of a home in a prosperous suburb where the sky is always a crisp, clean azure and rumors of murder always turn out to be propaganda created by those who are envious. He wants to take Adelita there as soon as possible. You would like Adelita, but I am not so sure you would like Sagueo. He has a very quick temper and has gotten me involved in two nasty brawls already. Who knows? Maybe you would like him after all. You cannot imagine how it was when I first met them. You cannot imagine what a joy it was to hear the lovely sound of Spanish being spoken after so many weeks of Portuguese. I do not know how the Brazilians can speak their language. It is so very different from Spanish. It is very challenging. Adelita is teaching me Portuguese bit by bit, enough so I can get by. She has the noble temperament of a sweet saint (as do you, my love). She would need to possess such a temperament to teach a brainless wolf like me. Sagueo has no patience for teaching. He has no patience for anything that does not involve copious amounts of alcohol or the raw, mind-numbing images of symbolist poetry. He is always reading a French poet who died years ago. Some of the images are very strange indeed. In one of his poems a partially bald woman is rising up out of a bathtub that resembles a zinc green coffin. In another, packs of ferocious wild dogs in heat are eating the bandages of those who have gone insane from pleasure. Horrific images, some of them. Sagueo thinks it is a waste of breath to learn Portuguese. He says I should learn French. But it is not a waste of breath. I have no use for French. Portuguese is for me the language of war. I will teach you Portuguese when I return if you like. There is no rose without thorns, as they say. Do you remember that night beneath the boat? It is a most fantastic memory. I know this memory will sustain me on the many long and lonely nights when I am at the war. Everyone here is excited about avenging the honor of Brazil against those barbarian Huns. Everyone is talking about the perigo alemão, the German danger. Sagueo says it has been a topic of conversation in the cafés and smoking rooms for years, but now this danger seems just around the corner. The government declared war back in October, but the level of excitement is still very high. You would not believe how much the Brazilians hate the Germans. It is a lacerating, visceral hatred, especially in the south. Every day in the newspaper there is a story about this German couple whose shoe store or deli or music shop or leather goods shop was ransacked, or that German couple who was murdered in their sleep by drunken patriots because someone found out they were actually saboteurs. A riot broke out at a German cigar factory somewhere in Bahia, just north of Rio, and the manager was beaten to death with clubs. The government had to send in troops to restore public order. Here in Rio a mob set fire to the grand hall of the Pan-German Association and the building burned to the ground. Of course the anarchists are not happy. They are hoping to expand the perimeter of violence beyond those of German descent. But the rest of Brazil is unified in their hatred. Every German school in the country has been closed and the teachers sent to internment camps. The German banks are all closed. The doors to every German magazine and newspaper have been locked. Even the great German books of ages past have been removed from the shelves of every library. If you are German, it is better to head for Argentina or Paraguay or even Chile than to remain in Brazil. Every German face you see is suspect, and that is the truth! So Sagueo and I have joined the Navy. Adelita was quite unhappy, and for three weeks she refused to serve us anything to eat except feijoada, a very hearty black bean stew, even for breakfast. It is a delicious stew, and Adelita packs hers full of spicy sausage, but one can grow tired of anything if one overindulges by predilection or dint of circumstances. But we forgave her. Adelita does not understand the importance of our decision. We have been assigned to a very great ship with a very great name. I am not supposed to say which ship, but I will tell you anyway, our beautiful ship is called the Laurindo Pitta. Yes, just to look at her is enough to take your breath away. We will be part of a flotilla of great ships given the great task of patrolling the waters off the coast of Africa. I am not supposed to speak of our mission, but I will tell you, my love, so you will not worry. And so you will know what a brave hero your betrothed has become. We will be hunting down German U-boats. We will also be sweeping the coastal waters from Dakar to Gibraltar for mines. Ah, my love, the treachery of the Germans knows no boundaries. Oh, the atrocities they committed during the invasion of Belgium. And it is the same everywhere they go. It is very great work we will be doing. We are very lucky to have been chosen. Of the thousands and thousands who wished to fight the Germans at sea, only nine hundred will do so. School children will one day read about us. It is almost like destiny. 'Through the sufferings and delusions to which the war has given rise, a new and better world will be born of liberty.' This is what our Captain said to us, and I, for one, believe him. I will write more when I am able. I do not know when that will be. But do not worry. Dry your eyes. For now, I am a wanderer, a cloud with a hidden purpose drifting across the ocean, a circumnavigating bird without a nest. But I will be home before you know it. Lo prometido es deuda!

-117-

One cannot appreciate how utterly your life, with the diabolical cunning of the insanely jealous, can abandon you until it does so. And so it was with my grandmother. After my grandfather vanished, she became a pilgrim unto herself. Confounded by the chaste symmetries of the universe, she avoided the bright spaces that represent the unfolding of our lives and became a creature of plummeting darkness.

Ah, my poor, poor grandmother! She all but gave up looking after her young son, my father, Andres Escoraz Silvestre. She had given birth to her son in her own childhood bedroom in the great house in Miramar, and there she had remained, shrouded in the mystery of her own despair while her son spent most of his waking hours chasing after the dreams and memories of his grandfather (my great-grandfather). Young Andres usually fell asleep just before midnight in the arms of my great-grandfather, usually in the library with its dark mahogany floors and its row after row of history books and volumes of poetry and dictionaries in several languages (Spanish, English, French, Turkish) and various atlases, and its single shelf devoted to the three Cuban philosophers. My great-grandfather's deep musical voice filled every corner of the house as he recounted to my father with immeasurable pride that unsurpassable evening when he had listened to Enrique

José Varona himself tell the tale of a mythic bullfight in mythic Mexico and the sea of weeping women dressed in white who had prayed for the deliverance of the bullfighter. But such is life.

Then one day, long after the Great War had ended, my grandmother received a small package. It did not arrive by regular post. She later said that it seemed to materialize right out of thin air one dark, hazy evening when she was sitting by her open bedroom window, hovering on the edge of consciousness, listening to the sound of a distant bolero floating across the Almendares River. She could not quite hear what the bolero was about, but it brought tears to her eyes nonetheless, and she was groping about her nightstand and then her dresser for a clean cloth to dry her eyes when her fingers found the package instead. The package was from Mexico City.

She opened it immediately. She said the thought briefly crossed her mind (and it was a welcome thought, which will give you some indication as to her emotional state) that the package might contain a small explosive device or a tiny pistol with tiny golden bullets or an exotic and fast-acting poison derived from the secretions of the golden poison arrow frog found only in the wilds of Colombia or on the western slopes of the Andes, bizarre, potentially lethal possibilities that excited her growing pathological sense of urgency.

Instead, the package contained one official looking letter and one official looking telegram, both from the Brazilian Navy, a brown jeweler's box containing a bronze colored cross fixed to the end of an orange ribbon with three black stripes, a second precisely typed letter from my grandfather's Mexican friend, Sagueo, and a small bible.

The official looking letter had originally accompanied the box and explained in official language that the bronze cross adorned with a ribbon was a Campaign Medal that had been awarded in the spirit of undying gratitude from a hopeful and forward thinking nation to Emilio Valentín Menoyo, a native son of Tubarão from the province of Santa Catarina, for his dedicated service to the Brazilian Navy during the years 1917-1918. The letter was dated November 1922 and embossed with the Brazilian Navy's official seal.

The telegram, which bore the date 16 June 1919, came in a yellowed envelope that had been forwarded again and again, first from Rio to Natal, then from Natal to Paramaribo, then from Paramaribo to Caracas, and finally from Caracas to Mexico City. It was almost unreadable. The author of the telegram had used an uneven bold-faced type, and there were so many misspellings and words misused or missing altogether that the telegram had to be decoded to be understood, as if, my grandmother said, it had been produced by a drunken chimpanzee trained by Russian circus clowns.

The telegram announced with an understated gravitas that Emilio Valentín Menoyo, a seaman of exceptional patriotism aboard the ocean going tug the *Laurindo Pitta,* had been lost at sea during a skirmish with a German U-boat in the dark waters off the coast of Africa near the city of Agadir and was presumed dead. A search had been initiated after the battle had concluded, but was called off a few hours later due to inclement weather. No evidence of Seaman Menoyo's body was found during the search. At the end it said that the precious name of Emilio Valentín Menoyo would appear on a bronze plaque commemorating those sons of Brasil who fell during the Great War. The plaque would be located in a grand park in Rio de Janeiro known as the Passeio Público. It would bear witness to the heroically deceased for generations to come.

The letter from Sagueo contradicted the telegram both in its tone (Sagueo's words were filled with remorse and nostalgia) and in its detailed account of the death of my grandfather. My grandmother never forgot Sagueo's words, which she said took refuge in the dark empty spaces of her heart like so many blue scorpions hiding from the sun.

-118-

The letter from Sagueo Ruedas:

Dear Miss Ana Silvestre, my name is Sagueo Ruedas and I knew your betrothed, Emilio Valentín Menoyo. He stayed with me and my wife, my beloved Adelita, for almost a year when he was in Rio. But after that, well, how can I say this? They are both gone. In its own way the war took them both. My Adelita suffered an aneurysm shortly after we left for the war, a condition I am sure was made infinitely worse by my absence. And your sweet Emilio died a few months later while we were at sea. I am so sorry I did not write sooner. I was not up to the task. No, that is a lie. I have been distracted by the absence of my Adelita. I write to her every day. The truth is I could not stay in Rio. Everywhere I went I saw my Adelita. So I returned to Mexico in 1921. That is where I was born. But even this did not help. I was utterly consumed by my Adelita, so to relieve the tension I began to write to her. The writing helped. I was able to control my grief. I was able to gain a foothold in the world once again. Those were dark days. But I must confess that in all those years I did not once think about Emilio. That is why I did not write any sooner. And I am only writing to you now because the other day his medal arrived from Brazil, and the day after that the telegram with the news that he was missing at sea. Imagine that, the telegram arrives almost eight years after his death! It is absurd. The whole thing is absurd. The Brazilian government. The Navy. The war. All of it. So there it is. I have been living in Mexico City and have not thought about Emilio once in five years, and then the medal and the telegram arrived, and after that, of course, I could think of nothing but Emilio and his beauty and his courage. What can I say? If the Brazilian government knew Emilio the way I had known him, they would have sent him a dozen medals. But they didn't know anything about him. They didn't even realize he was from Cuba. Then again how could they know something as elemental as that? Life is what it is, after all. When we signed up in those bright, happy days after Brazil declared war on Germany, I told Emilio to say he was from Tubarão. That is a small coastal town in the south, an impossible journey from Rio if one travels overland, which is why Adelita and I always traveled by steamer. A great many Germans settled in Tubarão before the war, but after the sinking of the Rio Branco everyone started to hate the Germans. It was incredibly bad in Tubarão. My wife was from there, so she told Emilio a little bit about growing up in case anyone asked him, but no one asked him anything. No, no one cared where he was from. There were too many men who were eager to take a crack at the Germans. It was all the recruiters could do to take down names and addresses. Ah, yes. Cada cual hace con su vida un papalote y lo echa a volar, as they say. But it is enough to crush one's heart. It is a very great irony, yes, it is a tragic irony, my wife and Emilio, a daughter and an adopted son of Tubarão, a city of Germans, both dying from the war against Germany. Some days how I wish I had traded places with Emilio, for I was not there when my beloved Adelita died. This burden is difficult to bear. I should have been there with her. I never should have left. But what is one to do? It is as sad and tragic as any of the great fados they used to sing years ago. But I was there when your sweet, courageous Emilio died. And that is another reason for this letter. He did not die the way they said. The telegram says we were off the coast of Africa near the city of Agadir. But we were much further north than that. Our fleet had already pushed through the Straits of Gibraltar. We were supposed to keep to the Atlantic, but then a German U-boat fired upon us. I don't know which ship, but the torpedo missed. Then our ships started dropping depth charges with a mania I had never seen before, and the sea exploded with fire and dead fish. I remember the shockwaves from all those explosions were so great I could barely breathe. Then we started chasing the sub. The whole fleet was chasing after this phantom German sub which maybe had never existed at all. How does one catch a ghost? But we were chasing him just the same, and every ten minutes we dropped more depth charges, just for good measure. It looked like the sea was a lake of fire. Of course our boat was not really part of the action. The Laurindo Pitta was a Navy tug. Our job was to help the big ships get in and out of port, so wherever they went, we went. I was watching the whole damn show from the rail, and I remember how exciting it was. It was like watching one of Toscano's movies, except I could smell the burning diesel and I could feel the cooling spray of the saltwater as we rushed this way and that. It was exhilarating, to tell you the truth. Emilio was not there at first. He was sleeping below. He had taken sick with the Spanish influenza and had not left his bunk for three days. Our boat had already lost three men to the flu and everyone thought Emilio was going to be next. But that night he crawled out of the belly of the ship and then there he was, standing at the rail with the rest of us. At first I thought he was delirious. He seemed to be having a conversation with an unseen entity hovering three feet above his head. Then I took a step towards him. I was going to help him back to his bunk. But just at that moment he turned and smiled a most becoming smile, as if to say he was through the worst of it. I can still see him quite plainly. The moon was very bright that night and lit up every inch of the deck. Then Emilio turned back to the rail and the boat pitched and Emilio was gone. The sea had swallowed him in a single gulp. That is how he died. I called out to the watch that a man had fallen overboard and they took up the cry, but the boat did not stop. We just kept following the other boats. That was it. Later, before I returned to Mexico City, I received my own letter from the Brazilian government. The letter said that the government was going to put a plaque in the Passeio Público in Rio to honor all the seaman who had died during the war. But this was also a lie. There is no plaque. I visited the Passeio Público on many different occasions before I returned to Mexico City, always searching for this mythic plaque, but there was no plaque. So I hold Emilio in my heart, along with my beloved Adelita, and all the rest who died during those years. It is the only thing I can do.

With great sorrow and eternal regret, Sagueo Ruedas

-119-

I am no fool. I am not dimwitted. I knew from the beginning that my love for Oscar was stronger than his love for me. But I did not mind. Nothing Oscar ever did or might do could surprise me. I knew he still held a torch for the Afro-Cuban goddess he had left in Havana. (Whatever else he left in Cuba he never said.) I knew he chased after the girls in La Campana. He was heroic and compassionate in the manner of the ancient Greeks and loved men as much as women. I knew he swung from chandeliers. But all that did not matter. And even though there were many days in the years before we were married that I almost gave up all hope (and during those most trying days the criticisms of my dead relatives all but vanished into the abyss of their contented hearts), I knew with a knowledge that goes beyond knowing that one day we would be together the way I had imagined from the very beginning. My heart became a mirror of God's forgiveness. The beautiful spirit that was Oscar leapt through me like the sea. I was a ship of seagulls resting on the waves of his joy. He was light and I was shadow. And then one day, as fantastic as it sounds, what was true for me was true for him. He swam to me without question in the madness of loving me. And I to him. *Único hombre que ha besado en mi alma al besar en mi cuerpo.* That was how it was. That is how I choose to remember it. And the day Oscar realized that I was the only woman who kissed his soul when she kissed his body, on that day he asked me to marry him.

The story of that day began at Sunny Isles. It was the only place we ever went. A retreat into the glory of a separate sphere where no one bothered Oscar. He could become a spectator, a happy ghost with no name, a child once again with all of his choices before him. Oscar liked to walk out on the pier and chat with the fishermen. He did not fish himself, but the fisherman reminded him of the old men he had known in Baracoa or along the Malecón in Havana. The waves, the indomitable waves crashing on the shore, reminded him of days gone by. That's what he said. Of course I was not so much impressed by the sound of the waves or the fishermen on the pier in those days. I possessed a restless, relentless, energetic spirit. I was afraid of all of his ancient regrets. I wanted bright lights and dazzling sambas. I wanted to feel lightning bolts coursing through my veins. So we stayed at a fancy resort on an island all to itself, just across from the ocean. It was called Castaways, which is just how we felt. My beloved Oscar started taking me to Sunny Isles in 1969. He asked me to go so I went. I gave in to the urgency of the moment and did not imagine the disorder of my heart that was to come. But this, too, is life. That very first night we stayed in room 227. And after that, well, somehow we always ended up in room 227. *¡Ay de mí!* Those were good days.

Oscar proposed to me on Monday December 6, 1976 at two in the afternoon just after we crossed the bridge to Bal Harbour Beach. It was a most amazing day. We had left the resort just before noon and driven north for a while, maybe an hour, before Oscar turned the car around and headed back towards Miami. We drove along the water the whole way. It was very sunny, and we were driving with the top down and Oscar had turned the radio on. The radio was blaring, which meant that neither of us said a word while the car was moving. To be honest, we did not speak even while the car was stopped at a traffic light. In fact, we had not spoken two words to each other since the previous afternoon when Oscar was making love to me like a madman in the bed of my dreams, but all he was saying at that point was 'move this way baby, that's it, oh my God, that's fucking incredible, oh baby, your legs feel so good, yeah, keep them just like that, Papa is on his way to sugar town, don't move, don't move, oh my God,' which wasn't the kind of romantic pillow talk a girl hopes for, and it certainly wasn't much help in deciphering his mood that afternoon or the next day, but what is a girl supposed to do?

I like to tell myself that my Oscar was silent that morning because he was trying to come up with precisely the right words to express his undying love. He wanted to write my name in heaven. Our love would be a blazing constellation. He wanted his words to come gushing forth like the fountain of creation and take my color away. *¡Sacar los colores a alguien!* He wanted a blushing bride. But this is pure fabrication on my part. A balm to soothe a troubled heart. To be truthful, and I am wholly committed to the truth these days, I must confess that I do not know why he chose that day as opposed to any other day to propose to me, or why he even proposed to me at all, especially given his lingering, devastating silence on the ride back. I know what I said. The day Oscar realized that I was the only woman who kissed his soul when she kissed his body, on that day he asked me to marry him. But that is also a fabrication. I have been lying to myself about what happened for years. But that is not unusual. Who does not engage in the odd bit of retrospective sleight-of-hand now and then? To be blunt, I had no idea what was going on in Oscar's heart and soul that afternoon. His thoughts, which were normally easy to decode because they rarely varied from one moment to the next, were cavorting across the suddenly tormented landscape of his brain with dizzying, almost supersonic speed.

-120-

So here is the truth of what happened and why it happened as best as I can piece it together.

We didn't get to the resort up at Sunny Isles until late Friday night, December 3, 1976. I went into the lobby with Oscar. He chatted with the front desk clerk for a while and I went over to a parrot the management kept in the lobby to entertain the guests. The parrot had been a part of the lobby as long as we had been going to the resort. His name was Herman, though a lot of people called him Schwartz.

Oscar and the clerk were talking about baseball.

I was talking over matters of the heart with Herman. I asked Herman if this was going to be a good weekend, and he said 'That's a stupid question,' which is how he responded to most questions, and then he broke into a fit of screeching, raucous laughter. Then Herman stopped laughing and I could hear a scratchy rendition of "Yellow River" pouring out of the speakers in the ceiling of the lobby. Herman grew suddenly very quiet, morbidly quiet, and started swaying slightly to the music. I don't know what kind of parrot Herman was except that he was very clearly a German parrot.

Oscar came back with the key and an irrepressibly lopsided smile and said he was going to have me out of my clothes by the end of the night, but I could leave my hat on. Suspicious minds would have thought the worst of my beloved. But it was really quite a sweet thing to say. I was wearing a tight-fitting pair of black and white zebra capris that showed off the curves of my derrière (which Oscar liked to say was an arrow that went straight to his heart), a ruffled white blouse held in place by a single lace strap, shiny black boots, the kind that Nancy Sinatra wore, and a rather chic looking black beret, all of it a gift from Oscar.

You wouldn't guess it to look at me now, but I was very beautiful in those days. I daresay I even caused a car accident or two just by walking along the sidewalk.

I can laugh about it on a day like today, but back then, well, back then was a different story. I thought I looked like a Parisian countess in my ridiculous go-go-dancer's outfit, which was silly, as you are surely thinking to yourself, because a Parisian countess wouldn't have been caught dead in such wildly provocative clothes. But what did I know at such a young age. My imagination was very vigorous. I felt like a countess, and I was very happy (ecstatic is more accurate) that my Oscar wanted to get me out of my clothes. I was Oscar's pussycat. What else were my clothes for but to have Oscar rip them to shreds in the desperate frenzy of a mad, passionate love affair? I would have stripped to my skin in the lobby if he had asked me.

The next few hours went by in a blip, and then it was seven in the morning. We slept all day and went to dinner at six. You can decide for yourself if we got any sleep at all that first night.

I don't remember what we ate for dinner.

The next thing I remember is the two of us sitting at a small table in the sunken ship nightclub drinking tequila and listening to a crazy mad guitarist jamming on the stage. I don't remember the guitarist's name. I didn't know it then. But Oscar seemed to know him. Oscar knew pretty much everyone in the music business in Miami.

I don't actually see myself in this memory. It is like a movie flashing across a giant movie screen. The movie is in Technicolor.

We were sitting in the front row, and pretty soon Oscar and the mad guitarist were trading swigs from a bottle of Jack, and all the while the guy was playing his crazy mad guitar. He played until three in the morning. He was blitzed out of his mind, but nobody seemed to care. Everyone was going wild for him. When he finished he sent his guitar spinning across the stage and it smashed into a stool and the stool toppled over. Then he invited the whole club to join him for some pancakes and we all headed across the street to a pancake house and ate pancakes. There must have been a hundred people crammed into those tiny blue booths. The crazy mad guitar player said he would pick up the tab, but when the bill came he confessed that he was flat broke, which precipitated a mad dash for the door. The poor waitress never stood a chance and she knew it. She shrugged a resigned shrug and moved to the tables on the far side of the cash register and began wiping up the tiny pools of syrup that remained. When she finished the first table she looked up, an odd, sort of whimsical, half-expectant expression on her face, as if she had just woken up from a long, troubling dream filled with false promises.

The crowd had vanished by then. But not my Oscar. My beloved Oscar was waiting by the register, his face glowing with the same silly, lopsided grin he always wore when he thought he was being courageous or clever or unspeakably kind. The waitress and Oscar looked at each other for a moment. I suspect she was hypnotized by his immaculate good looks. He was immaculate the way a movie star is immaculate in his white linen suit and his thick dark hair slicked back like Rudy Valentino and his thin, carefully combed moustache and the scent of fresh mint lingering on his skin and his happy, dancing, mischievous brown eyes. He wasn't very tall, my Oscar, but his lopsided smile made up for that. You felt yourself swooning whenever he smiled at you.

I suspect the waitress was about to swoon. She was trembling slightly, a leaf in a gentle breeze.

Then my beloved Oscar peeled off a pile of cool, crisp one-hundred dollar bills from his money clip and pressed them into the girl's hand. Then he peeled off a few more, half a dozen, just for good measure.

Then we went back to our room. But Oscar did not stay. He kissed me goodnight and said he needed to speak with the mad guitarist. I knew what he was planning. The mad guitarist had gone back to the club and was jamming away. You could feel the vibrations of his guitar strings in the air. It was a shimmering, fluttering kind of sensation like an agitated pulse rushing up and down the many public and private corridors of this resort on the beach. Like the world was hyped up on amphetamines. I knew my Oscar just wanted to be part of the scene. He didn't play any instrument. He just wanted to hang out with the mad guitarist and be seduced by the vibe of an electric guitar and drink and laugh. He wanted to turn back the clock. So Oscar headed to the sunken ship and the jam session that was most definitely happening even though he did not play an instrument, and I curled up in bed and fell asleep.

Truly, I was not the jealous type. Whatever made my Oscar happy made me happy.

He came back to the room a little after eight in the morning, reeking of whiskey and someone else's perfume, and crashed into his pillow. He seemed to be dreaming delicious dreams, and I wanted to be a part of those dreams, but I did not wake him. He slept until four in the afternoon, and then he woke up just like that, as if he had heard my soul calling out to him. We made sweet, delicious love for two hours. Then he showered, shaved, and put on his fancy white slacks and a white linen jacket, an outfit which he only wore on very special occasions, and a Panama hat that he had worn for years without even thinking about what was covering his head, a grand, shining, immaculate Panama hat from his days in Havana oh so many years earlier. I asked him where he was going and he just tossed me a cavalier, lopsided smile and said I possessed too much curiosity. Then he laughed and said he'd be back in an hour or so, the mad guitarist had agreed to play at La Campana, he'd be there for two straight weeks beginning in May, it was a done deal except for signing the contracts.

Up till that point it had been a glorious weekend. I thought about the question I had asked Herman, the parrot. Yes, I said to myself, it had been a stupid question. I remember wondering how the parrot could know so much. Then I remembered that Descartes once said that the reason parrots appeared to possess the gift of speech was that they were possessed by the Devil. I don't know if Descartes actually said such a thing. It was just something I had once read or heard someone else say. But then Oscar returned and I was forced to revise my estimate of Herman, the parrot, and the mental acuity of parrots in general. You see Oscar had only been gone ten minutes, but when he came back he was not himself, not in the least. He motioned for me to get dressed, so I did, but he paid no attention to my flashes of nudity, which was quite a shock to me. Oscar had never before treated me with such alien indifference. He always asked me to adopt a leisurely pace when getting dressed and undressed, especially late at night with the lights blazing away, so he could sit back and watch. I enjoyed catering to my Oscar's every whim. But he was not interested in my nudity on that day. So I got dressed. What else was I supposed to do?

Then we went to dinner. We went to the teahouse, one of the most popular restaurant at the resort with its gleaming crystal lanterns and fake cherry blossoms. I asked Oscar if something had happened with the deal, but he refused to answer. He refused to even look at me. He only bit his lip and turned his shoulders with a sudden declarative swiftness so he could look out the window (we were at a window table). I noticed that his lips were bleeding slightly. He seemed kind of jittery. But whatever was troubling Oscar he wouldn't say. Our waiter came and went. Our food arrived. The couples all around us were laughing while they ate and then getting up to dance to one or two songs before running back to their tables to stuff a few more bites of some expensive and therefore popular seafood delicacy into their fat, slobbering, untroubled mouths. But Oscar and I ate in trembling, exhausted silence. I was confused, as you would expect. I was enveloped in a fog of chaos and spiritual decay. I did not understand my beloved's strangely steep silence. But what could I do? How could I perforate the impervious bubble of his inattention? I decided there was nothing I could do. I let my beloved's strange silence like a sea flow through me. His silence became an exploding current of tiny wriggling eels and silver fish and other small rustling creatures of the night trying to avoid exposure. And then the current was gone. The sea shrunk and became a cluster of birds. The explosion became a vague restlessness. I realized I was part of the world again. I drank a glass of wine in a single gulp and then I drank another, with more relish, less speed. I immersed myself in the fast-moving eddies of worldly noise swirling all around our table, listening carefully, methodically, to the buzz of dozens of conversations from every corner of the teahouse. I suddenly possessed superhuman hearing. It was a minor miracle of sorts, a transcendent moment. I could even hear the waiters whispering to each other as they waited by the kitchen doors.

In my experience one rarely questions miracles when they are occurring, especially if one (meaning me, naturally) has been weaned on the chicanery of priests. But oh, my poor, poor Oscar! Slowly I realized that the trouble that had plunged my beloved into the abyss of silence had become part of the eternal memory of the resort. Everyone in the teahouse was talking about this trouble as if it were their own. It was on everyone's lips, how the mad guitarist from the night before had been found dead by his agent that afternoon, how the preliminary findings suggested that the guitarist had died from alcohol poisoning, which did seem odd because clearly the guitarist drank like a fish, an ability which he had most likely possessed for years, which is perhaps why the police were making a thorough investigation, just in case a more sinister cause of death could be identified and a criminal apprehended.

Ah those gossipy lips with their irreverent, even ludicrous, but still crippling innuendo! But how else would we have known that the guitarist's girlfriend, a voluptuous blond named Nikki, worked at the resort? She was a wild, slightly perverted and therefore dangerous go-go dancer, some said, impervious to envy and gossipy speculation, but others said she was a waitress in the Seven Seas Lounge who barely made enough to get by, and one voice declared she was a low-life cashier in the gift shop who had been skimming from the receipts for years. But no matter what she did, no matter what crimes she had or had not committed, all the voices agreed that she was a double-dealing opportunist, a Jezebel of the worst kind, willing to pit one frustrated lover against another in a no-holds-barred struggle to the death. The lips said as much. The lips said the girlfriend was also seeing a lifeguard who worked at one of the resort's seven pools, and how she was often seen in the company of insurance salesmen or lawyers or corporate executives who wanted to get away for a fast weekend, no questions asked, and how she had an ex-boyfriend who rode a Harley, and whenever he roared into town, which was only once in a while when he was running low on cash, he threatened anyone who gave her even a sideways glance, because the girlfriend was definitely stacked. To hear everyone talk she was built like a brick house. This was the gossip that had taken hold of the collective imagination of the tearoom in the chaos of the unexpected death of the mad guitarist, obscuring the facts most assuredly, but it gave the police detectives who had arrived on the scene plenty to think about, plenty of grist for the mill, plenty of leads that would lead nowhere, but they didn't mind, they were busy exploring every possibility, very busy.

It was hard to comprehend what was actually happening.

I wondered if God was listening as intently as I was to the frantic voices that were swirling about the teahouse, voices of shock and overwhelming sadness and paranoia and downright gossipy glee (because people love to talk about the death of someone else). Then I was thinking that perhaps God's attention was focused elsewhere.

I am certain now that my poor, distracted Oscar was worried that he would be grilled by the police. He was sick to death with worry. He feared that the police would see in his Cuban face a face of introspective guilt. He was always afraid he would be discovered. He even confessed to me once that he had used the name of Luis Sarabia when he bought the property that would become his nightclub just so he could hide behind a fictitious name. But that night I think he was staring straight into the abyss.

He admitted that he and the mad guitarist had polished off a bottle of something in fifteen minutes flat, and then they had had a few beers, and then he had lost track. He also had a vague memory of the girlfriend suddenly materializing out of a beam of sunlight. She was waving her arms in the air and her mouth was moving, but Oscar couldn't make out a word she said. It was all garbled, muffled, as if she had become detached from her voice and her voice was now trapped at the bottom of the sea. Then the mad guitarist smiled and opened his wide, welcoming arms and the girlfriend crawled into his lap.

Oscar didn't remember where they were at that point. Maybe they were in the mad guitarist's hotel room. This is what my beloved Oscar said. So he had been an accomplice to the mad guitarist's drinking, nothing more. And even if he had crawled into bed with the mad guitarist and his girlfriend, what of that? The man had been sleeping peacefully in the arms of his girlfriend when Oscar left at eight in the morning. That fact alone was his alibi. But Oscar was certain the police would disregard the plain facts and probe instead the depths of his perpetually guilty Cuban face of a possible drug lord and discover by chance that he had arrived in Key West in 1957 with a forged passport, that he had cavorted with gangsters while living in Havana, that he had escaped the dark paradise of Cuba with a suitcase full of stolen money, that he had used that money to build his nightclub, that he had never registered his actual name with the government, that he paid no taxes.

It seemed to Oscar a very long list, an endless litany of subversive crimes, unspeakable crimes that would be his undoing. He was certain that once the police began their basement questioning the truth would come tumbling out. He could see the whole scenario unfolding with rapid-fire precision before his suddenly world-weary eyes. The mad guitarist's girlfriend would find herself in hot water and spill the beans. His name would surface and the police would come calling. They would drag him to the police station in irons if need be. Perhaps they would take him for a spy or a saboteur. Who knew? Their questions would be delivered with angry enthusiasm. They would pound their fists on the table. They would certainly blow cigarette smoke in his face. Perhaps they would hook him up to a series of electric cables and throw the switch for a minute or two, just to make sure he was being honest. When they were finished grilling him in this manner, they would drag his almost lifeless body to a damp, rat-infested cell and toss him like an unwanted stone to the cold tile floor. It would be a communal cell, the kind of cell where they kept rapists and pedophile priests and secret agents and rabble rousers and revolutionaries, all of them streaked with dried blood, because the first thing the police did to criminals of that sort was beat the hell out of them. And who could truly blame them? Oscar saw this future path unwind at the speed of light with incredible, ruthless clarity. He would spend two or three days in his communal holding pen while they processed his deportation papers, suffering such indignities of the heart and soul that would leave God himself on the verge of tears. Then they would send him back to the darkness that was Cuba, a broken man. This is what my Oscar was thinking. This is what he saw. It was a fate worse than death.

Fortunately for my Oscar, the mad guitarist's girlfriend did not remember who was with her boyfriend the day he died. Of course I can say this now, looking back. But we weren't sure what was happening when it was actually happening. By eight o'clock Monday morning everyone in the resort had heard the rumor that the girlfriend had been interviewed by the police. What were we to believe? One rumor among a river of rumors. But a few apparently well-informed whispering lips provided a play-by-play transcript of the interview. It was almost like watching it on television. There were minor differences between the competing versions of what had happened, as is always the case with stories that linger in our collective imagination, but the essential details remained the same.

The interview had taken place in the lobby from ten o'clock to just after midnight. The girlfriend had been sitting on a red chaise lounge while the detectives plied her with drinks, listening carefully to every word that slipped out of her mouth, occasionally writing something down in their police report notebooks. Herman the parrot was a constant source of amazement during the interrogation. Some of the detectives began noting which questions Herman thought were stupid and which he ignored. The girlfriend told the police that one of her boyfriend's musician buddies had been in the room that morning, that if the police were thinking foul play, that was the guy they should be hammering away at. But she was unable to elaborate. She wasn't sure which of the dozens of possible musician buddies it might be. She didn't remember his name. Amnesia is like a desert, she said, and then she had started giggling. Apparently the police were not amused, but they thought they might be onto something so they plied her with a few more drinks. She liked amaretto on the rocks. Then completely out of the blue she said she thought this mysterious unnamed buddy played the trumpet, or maybe the drums, but she couldn't be sure. The detectives were happy with this new detail. They were scribbling furiously. The girlfriend said she had gone to the room at about seven in the morning and there were the two of them, her boyfriend and this other guy, the drummer, they were in bed, sleeping or whatever, and she had crawled in between them, and after a while the drummer left. One of the detectives scribbled down the phrase 'ménage à trois' followed by the word 'homosexual' with a question mark followed by the phrase 'jealous lover' followed by a note that said 'jealousy is as good a motive as any.'

The girlfriend was oblivious to all the scribbling. Yes, she said, he was a drummer, a very famous drummer, if she had her facts straight, at least as far as other drummers were concerned. But she only paid attention to drummers if they were extra-special famous like Ringo Starr. This guy wasn't famous like that. But other drummers would know him. She said he was probably long gone. This is the tale she told the police, a tale she later repeated (without the aid of the amarettos and with only a few topical alterations to make a good story even better) for the newspaper reporters who descended upon the hotel the next day without any restraint whatsoever in search of a bombshell, which naturally they found in both the sexy, oversexed girlfriend sitting on the red chaise lounge in the lobby, and in the gritty, suggestive truth that lay behind her words.

Oscar became more paranoid than ever when he heard that the police had spent two hours raking the girlfriend over hot coals. Yes, I know the image of the police raking someone over hot coals is something of a cliché. But I am sure this was the exact image that raced through the corridors of my Oscar's troubled brain on that day. His imagination had been shaped by watching too many gangster movies from the 1940s. He believed the police would do anything they could to gain the upper hand, and it didn't matter if there were witnesses or not. The police didn't care who saw what. They would simply whitewash the truth. They were absolutely without scruples.

This is what my beloved Oscar believed. He became an alternative version of Humphrey Bogart in *To Have and Have Not*, trying his best to avoid the big sleep, weighing his options, counting down the seconds until the only choice he had left was to make a break for it. One could say he was trapped by the net of a very long night. For over an hour he behaved as if he had stumbled into a lunatic city, pacing about the room in socks and underwear, occasionally pulling back a corner of the curtain and peering cautiously out the window to the parking lot below. He became a dark space, a ruined landscape filled with smoke and piles of rubble, a hungry heart, silent and carnivorous. *Callado y carnicero.* And all the while he was muttering to himself and laughing hysterically by turns.

At one point I heard him say 'it's just a riddle that neither one of us knows the answer to,' but he did not say if this cryptic comment was meant for my ears or for someone else, a government agent, perhaps, recording our most intimate secrets with a micro transmitter tucked away inside the brand-new radio alarm clock that sat with conspicuous brilliance on the table next to the bed.

At ten minutes to ten he rang the front desk and asked for a bellhop to pick up our luggage.

At ten o'clock on the dot he rang the front desk again and asked where the hell the bellhop was.

At ten-fifteen the bellhop arrived and carted away our luggage.

At ten-thirty he poured the last few ounces from a bottle of rum into a tumbler and drank it just like that.

At eleven he put on his white linen suit and his immaculate Panama hat, but he did not bother looking into the mirror as he usually did to see if he was presentable.

Then we started for the lobby. We took great pains to avoid the probing eyes of the police. My poor, sweet, suffering Oscar. But who can blame him? The hotel was literally crawling with plainclothes detectives and state troopers. *¡Ay de mí!* The detectives were wandering around in pairs, stopping hotel guests at random to ask a few questions in their low murmuring monotone voices, frisking those who looked suspicious, writing down names and addresses. The troopers, looking for all the world like overgrown Boy Scouts in their crisply ironed, beige uniforms and darkly glowing dark green Stetsons, were stationed at random intervals along the ever-expanding labyrinth of hotel corridors. It was not altogether clear what they were doing. They were chatting away happily in small groups of three or four, commenting on the unseasonably warm, sunny weather, making witty, suggestive remarks about the girls in bikinis heading without even a backward glance to one of the various resort swimming pools. All of the troopers were wearing dark sunglasses. They were scrutinizing with unruffled scrutiny every guest who passed beneath their stiff, robotic, collective gaze.

We made it to the lobby just before noon. It makes me laugh now. But we were not laughing then. The lobby was crammed full of newspaper reporters from every newspaper in Florida. They were off to one corner, a single, pulsating entity like an alien creature from another dimension, listening with unrestrained glee to Nikki, the girlfriend, retelling her tale. She was back on the red chaise lounge, talking a mile a minute, her breasts jiggling uncontrollably as she spoke, a deliberate act of manipulation. The reporters could not resist. It was almost comic. They gave in to the hypnotic tremors of her soothing voice. They were slobbering all over her, writing down everything she said, every word, asking her if she wanted her photograph taken for this newspaper or that one, asking her if she wanted to pose with Herman the parrot for a few celebrity shots and Herman saying 'That's a stupid question!' and then everyone laughing, and then the flash bulbs flashing and Nikki showering the mob of reporters with her own giggly, flirty, sensuous laughter and blowing them all pouty, frivolous kisses that suggested a whole lot more than any of them would ever receive. Yes, it was quite a show. It was a virtuoso performance. Which meant, of course, that no one paid any attention to my beloved Oscar in his dazzling white linen suit and his immaculate Panama hat, an outfit which he had worn since his days in Havana and which had become an integral part of his enthusiastic, affable, loving persona. Even the front desk clerk, who only three days before had chatted with Oscar like an old friend about baseball, paused just long enough to collect the room key and grab the cash that Oscar laid on the marble counter before losing himself once again in his unimpeded view of Nikki and her jiggling breasts.

So what was my beloved Oscar thinking as we left the resort that day? I truly do not know. He was vulnerable, yes. His fears of the police and of deportation were not unfounded. And I am certain he was shaken by the death of his new friend. He was visibly shaken. My poor, sweet Oscar. Truly, our happiness quickly becomes a sadness in search of a happiness. I suspect his silence was born of the need to digest this unwelcome truth. I suspect he was wondering how many years of happiness he would have before he joined the saints in heaven. I also suspect he was thinking about the last conversation he had with the mad guitarist, how one minute the two of them were riding high on the glorious promise of better days, and the next minute death had entered the picture. And then his thoughts had turned to me.

Oh, I don't know when precisely he began thinking of me. I am certain he was thinking about how to avoid the police in the future while we were driving north along the coast, just as I am certain that the image of the dead guitarist crossed his mind when we passed by the resort on our way south, for he shuddered as we drove past the glistening pink pagoda rooftops. But I also think that on some subliminal, spiritual level, my Oscar realized that I had been a comfort to him on both the long drive north and the longer drive south. He realized that we were traveling a darkly gleaming river of uncertainty, but that it was better to travel this river together than alone. That our souls were tethered to each other in some mysterious, unfathomable way. That we were each God's gift to the other. This is what I had always believed, and that day my faith was rewarded. Once we crossed the bridge to Bal Harbour Beach, I knew that his fears had been eradicated. He was his old, smiling self again. That's when he pulled off the highway and we got out of the car.

'Come on,' he said. 'Let's walk on the beach.'

And that's what we did. We left our shoes in the De Soto and walked along the shore. There were very few people out there on that day. A few lonely-looking fishermen. A few tourists from up north. From somewhere there was the sound of a radio, a salsa as light and bouncy as a summer morning. We watched a cargo ship heading south for Miami. We watched a fishing trawler going the other way. We watched the seagulls flying about. Then Oscar kissed me. It was a gentle, airy kiss. His lips barely touched mine. But it was electric all the same. The sea began to glow. Cherry blossoms suddenly blanketed the beach. The strangely luminous waves exhausted themselves against the sky. The air began to vibrate. Then my Oscar leaned close and whispered into my ear, and I whispered back. Yes, my beloved, yes. The fragrant phosphorous of his words illuminated the darkest corners of my imagination. Yes, my love. I will marry you. I knew without any doubt whatsoever that my

Oscar was holding the round key of the universe. There was nothing I could do but say yes.

-121-

So what was I talking about? Yes, yes, I remember, the day my Oscar proposed, the beginning of my tragedy, and that is certainly one way to look at it. Perhaps if Oscar had loved me more, or I had loved him less. But that is a cliché, isn't it? Perhaps if my mother, God bless her tortured, unhappy soul, had not tried to tangle me up in her net (yes, I know, another cliché). Perhaps if she had not said what she said. But she meant well (and yet another). Perhaps she was simply joking. Of course if that is true, then my beloved Oscar played up to that joke, took it as a truth to win my mother's vacillating heart, and in so doing, sealed his fate (yes, yes, I am filled with clichés this morning, but on some occasions there is no better way to say a thing). Naturally, I do not blame my mother. And I do not blame my beloved Oscar. We are all of us tangled up in a labyrinth of compromise and secret liberties, so it is next to impossible to see precisely where we are headed, where we will end up, when we will breathe our last. So we all deserve each other's forgiveness. Truly, *de illusión también se vive,* as they say. Now and forever. Even so, what my mother said was actually quite unbelievable, even for her.

A week or so after I told her I had agreed to marry Oscar, she waltzed herself in through the doors of La Campana and cornered my beloved Oscar in the coat-check room. My mother was in a rare mood. I know this because there were several witnesses.

There was Herminio Arréllaga, a Paraguayan refugee who tended bar for Oscar, and who was there early to receive a delivery, several cases of smooth, dark Demerara rum imported from Venezuela, and several cases of *El Presidente.*

There was the guy making the delivery.

There was a union electrician standing on a surprisingly rickety ladder, working intensely (or perhaps it was sporadically, his mind on other things) to fix the **APPLAUSE** sign, which had not worked properly for several years.

There was a younger couple waiting in the lobby to see

Oscar about purchasing two advance tickets. I never knew their names. They wanted to see who would be playing on a certain date in July because they would be celebrating their first anniversary. They were staring down at the floor while they were waiting, contemplating with visible amazement the black marks that Bonita had once burned into the tile.

There was the taxi driver, the same one who was always at La Campana, who had driven my mother from Allapattah to Burdine's downtown and then to the Cathedral and then to La Campana. He had come inside to have a quick drink even though it was only two-thirty in the afternoon because my mother apparently had two more stops to go and he hadn't realized just what he was getting into on that particular day.

And there was a new coat-check girl who saw everything. What she was doing in the coat-check room in the middle of the afternoon she never admitted. But she did say she felt incredibly lucky that my mother didn't see her skinny, white, trembling legs protruding suspiciously from beneath a dark overcoat hanging in the darker shadows near the back. She said she had never before felt so afraid for her own life. She was all gooseflesh.

So my mother burst through the doors and saw my beloved Oscar, a fractured statue trying desperately to piece itself back to together again, a torso oozing dampness, partially illuminated by the naked bulb of the coat-check room, his arms and hands submerged in the oily darkness of another dimension, his legs (hips to ankles) splashing about in the dim light of the lobby, his feet and head missing altogether.

Fortunately for my beloved (and also, perhaps, for the tremulous-as-a-tiny-bird coat-check girl, her short, raspy breaths filling the air like so many plucked out feathers), my mother's voice preceded her entrance by a solid twenty seconds. Her voice echoed with the insatiable, uncomprehending rage of a fighting bull in the throes of death. She paid no attention to what she was seeing, to what was directly in front of her nose, because she was trapped in the cephalic bubble of a thirsty purpose.

'How dare you think you can marry my beautiful daughter in this dingy hovel of gangsters and thieves!' my mother shouted. 'She deserves better than that. She deserves a fancy church wedding. She should walk down the aisle of a cathedral, a floor made of darkly polished Italian marble like a dark mirror. She should be wearing a fancy brocaded wedding dress, a satin gown with a full train veil lined with luminescent pearls, soft pinks and whites, like the teardrops of angels. Heaven itself should proclaim her the most beautiful bride in the history of brides. What kind of a man are you anyway? Do you know anything of love? I can see you know nothing. I can see you think love is a game, a passing fancy. It is all I can do not to spit in your face. May the laughing spirit of Eshu Laroyê, who has the power to grant every wish and condemn every folly, may he be the lightning bolt of God's eternal justice.'

And just like that my mother apparently whirled on her heels in a motion so fluid and unexpected that everyone who was listening to her nearly lost their balance, but then she stopped and turned slowly, an overripe fruit bursting with deceit.

She stared at my beloved for a moment, her eyes brimming with an unexpected flash of sunlight from the bar, where the delivery man had finished unloading the last of the cases of *El Presidente* and Herminio had signed the receipt.

'But perhaps I am wrong,' she said. 'Yes, yes, I can see you are willing to entertain the notion that I am an addled old woman descending down the long tunnel into dementia and then death. Yes, yes, perhaps you wish to prove yourself. Perhaps you wish to prove that you possess a heart of pure gold. Is that it? Well there is one way. The priests might call it an act of selfless charity, proof of a higher reality. But who can say until the deed is done?'

It was at this point that the stories of the witnesses began to diverge. They all agreed that Oscar moved quickly away from the disfiguring glare of the light bulb blazing away in the coat-check room and stepped towards what looked like a shadowy ball of hissing alley cats, all except the delivery guy, who thought this shadowy ball or whatever it was looked like a smoky moon on the verge of exploding.

They all agreed that my mother lowered her voice in an effort to perhaps create an atmosphere of mystery, which made it exceedingly difficult (but not impossible) to hear what she was saying.

But they all disagreed about what they actually heard.

Herminio heard my mother say there were a couple of hoodlum boys, brothers, perhaps they were even twins, who lived in Coral Terrace near the park, a neighborhood plagued at all hours with the sound of crowing roosters, and these boys needed a good job or they would surely take a deviant path, or if not a good job, then they needed to be beaten to a bloody pulp. They needed one or the other. It wasn't clear if they were teenagers or if they were older.

The younger couple heard my mother say she had a friend who was in some trouble and this friend lived in a strange, dilapidated, disemboweled (disemboweled?) neighborhood in South Miami, but whenever she went for a visit she feared for her safety, so she asked Oscar to accompany her once a week until the trouble her friend was having had passed, at which point she wouldn't need to make the journey quite so often.

The coat-check girl heard my mother ask Oscar if he had ever been to the Church of the Epiphany on SW 57th, but it was clear by the expression on Oscar's face that he wasn't a church-going sort.

The delivery guy said all he heard was an incoherent babbling that could have been the sound of water running down a drain or seagulls fighting over scraps of garbage at the beach, and he decided at that moment he had better get his ears checked.

The taxi driver heard my mother ask how long it would take to get to Pinecrest and back during rush hour.

The electrician heard my mother say it was a matter of electricity. When there was too much energy flowing through the circuit, blam, the whole world went black. When there was too much resistance, for whatever reason, well, you could not swim against the current forever. The electrician wondered where my mother had picked up her knowledge of electrical circuits.

The younger couple heard my mother describe the incredible pain a burn victim must endure on the road to recovery. They could not tell if the trouble her friend was having was related to surviving an everyday housefire or a violent chemical explosion of some sort, but whatever the cause of her burns, she had endured (barely survived) the incredible suffering of extensive skin grafts and several rounds of antibiotics to treat sepsis, and she was home now, but she was having difficulty moving room to room.

The delivery guy listened intently to the sounds of the seagulls fighting for scraps. Then he wondered if perhaps they were roosters. He could not believe his red-glowing ears. Then the seagulls (or roosters) morphed into the sound of a lonely train whistle even though the nearest railroad crossing was two miles away, give or take. At that point the delivery guy decided that he needed a drink more than a hearing test. Herminio gave him a bottle of *El Presidente* on the house.

Herminio heard my mother ask Oscar if he would at least speak to the boys, but he did not catch their names or when or where they were to meet Oscar because he was digging out a bottle of *El Presidente* from one of the cases.

The taxi driver heard my mother ask how long it would take to get to Coral Terrace and back on a weekend with very little traffic.

The younger couple heard my mother say that there had been a string of daylight robberies committed in South Miami and a few cases of suspected arson. The police had originally assumed the crimes were being committed by a roving gang of juvenile delinquents.

The coat-check girl heard my mother tell Oscar that the trouble with musicians was they were all alike. She could not tell what Oscar said in reply, but it seemed to her that he was shaking with embarrassment, or perhaps he was suffering from a fit of nervous chuckling.

The delivery guy ordered another beer and Herminio gave him another *El Presidente* on the house, and then another, and so on.

The electrician heard my mother say that a charge in a parallel circuit will only pass through one resistor.

The taxi driver heard my mother say maybe it was better to take a bus.

The younger couple heard my mother say that the police had quickly revised their earlier assumptions about who was committing the crimes. The police were now looking for two humorless young men, identical twins with black leathery, crusted-over skin and a reputation for unprovoked violence. The police believed the youths lived in Corral Terrace with their grandmother.

Herminio heard my mother say it was shameful about those boys, the twins, some said they were homosexuals, or they were refugees from Borneo or Sulawesi or Sumatra, some third-world country on the edge of that whispering fraud we call oblivion.

The coat-check girl heard my mother say *'huevo del Diablo,'* but it was unclear just who she was talking about.

The electrician heard my mother say in a series connection, the entire charge passes through every individual resistor.

The younger couple heard my mother say that the police also believed the two young men in question had two older cousins or two brothers who had once lived in Coral Gables.

The taxi driver heard my mother say only someone with a pure heart would get on a bus without knowing where it was going.

Herminio heard my mother say only someone with a pure heart would take two slippery devils like that under his wing, so to speak.

The coat-check girl heard my mother say only someone with a pure heart could tell the difference between a child of God and a child of the Devil.

The younger couple heard my mother say only someone with a pure heart could stomach looking at a burn victim because it was very difficult to see the essential humanity of someone, anyone, beneath even a single layer of charred, cracked skin, let alone someone who had felt the fat of his (or her) subcutaneous layer bubbling away. It was like looking at a deeply depressed paralytic artist's depiction of a demonic alien life form intent on destroying the Earth.

The electrician heard my mother say only someone with a pure heart would realize that we are all atoms of light seeking a path to each other.

The delivery guy was too drunk to hear anything beyond the soft swooshing sounds his inner ear was making. It was an immense attic of sound from which he had no desire to escape.

A few days later my beloved Oscar hired the Velázquez brothers, and after that my mother was no longer so vocal in her criticisms. Was this a coincidence? I do not think so. And yet I do not think my mother was entirely to blame. I seem to remember that Herminio was also involved. Perhaps he had persuaded my mother that Oscar needed help (not that she truly needed persuading), and then maybe he had said that most likely the Velázquez brothers weren't criminals or charity cases so much as they were misunderstood. Yes, I think it was something like that. I can see my mother lapping up every obsequious word spewing out of Herminio's mouth, delighted that she might be able to bend Oscar's will in this matter, grateful for Herminio's behind-the-scenes support, eager to have some say, however small, in the world that Oscar and I were trying to create for ourselves. Herminio and my mother were co-conspirators. No other explanation makes any sense.

-122-

It is funny looking back, but deep down I think I knew that the day I married Oscar, I was in symbolic terms as well as in practical effect moving from defeat to defeat. To begin with, let's look at the day itself. Dawn or near enough. Well, to be precise, it was ten o'clock in the morning. Except that numbers on a clock do not tell the whole story. The sun had already crashed through the dark portals of the petrified, pre-Adamite sky. But the light did not come up over the horizon as it usually does, slowly seeping up and over the dark, forbidding line and pouring itself across the plateau of reality, inviting color to join memory and recreate a symphony of strange noises and reinvigorated smells. It came instead as a lightning bolt of retribution or a laser beam from an alien spacecraft set on incineration. The color of that strange light that morning was the color of burnt hair or skin (but not a surface burning, it burned much deeper than that, a burning away of everything down to the waxen core) and eyeballs dripping with mascara and Kabuki ink stains of rouge eating like a cancer into the flesh of soft, white cheeks as white as the underbelly of dead fish or white ribbon eels, but it wasn't just the color of the visible world, it was also the color of sounds and smells and passing thoughts; it was the color of the musty, mustardy smell of freshly plowed, rumpled earth; it was the color of the incurable seeping paranoia (insanity?) that accompanies chronic betrayal, that bohemia of a thirsty soul; it was the color of the sea salt smell of toilet soap and the convulsive withering noises of trampled insects with wings like cellophane beating frantically for a few seconds and then disintegrating as easily as if life were just a cruel trick invented by a deranged mechanic or a demented Syrian demigod, a brusque, godless demise; it was the color of the penetrating acrid, cleansing smell of midnight jazz, even though it was the middle of the morning; it was the color of dark, smoldering thighs wrapped in lace lingerie wound a tad too tight and the crystalline purity of love's deceptions and the raw, overwhelming, incomprehensible sadness of inaction, a paralyzing, blinding flash; it was the color of disordered silence, yes, disordered silence is so accurate; it was the color of the geranium pots that had been placed on steps and in courtyards all over the city, dripping with dew or droplets from an overnight shower like so many tiny mirrors reflecting (refracting?) the trauma of earlier days (though to some I am sure those droplets looked like hippie strings of metallic beads crisscrossing the cosmos, each bead containing within its sphere a miniature replica of this bubble we call the Earth); it was the color of the traffic whizzing by on NW 36th Street; it was the color of those excitable birds that one could only hear from the steps of La Campana, what were they? warbling warblers? or mutinous martins? or a covey of covetous chickadees? or yellow-billed cuckoos or yellow orioles? or furious swallows? or is it infuriated? or were they neurotic parrots or parakeets, those lucky birds that are the augurs of life and death? or a flock of *chachalaca* originally imported from Central America or Mexico or even Texas for hunting club hunting purposes but then they escaped? 'shut up ¡chachalaca!' you might hear someone say while listening to those birds, and then others might say, as if in response, 'boom Shaka-laka-laka!' boom Shaka-laka-laka!' and then they would laugh and prance about to their booming boom boxes and vanish into the glare at the end of the street and the sly sky would break into a harmonica solo, or perhaps those elusive feathered creatures were the physical manifestation of the birds that sleep in all good wines, as the poet says, but whatever genus and species (*Setophaga coronata coronata, Dendroica coronata, Progne elegans, Poecile carolinensis, Myiarchus tyrannulus, Coccyzus americanus, Icterus nigrogularis, Tachycineta bicolor, Melopsittacus undulates, Amazona tucumana, Amazona collaria, Alipiopsitta xanthops, Ortalis ruficauda, Ortalis vetula,*) those invisible birds on that particular morning were roosting and chattering away across the street from La Campana like paranoid idiot savants or drunken game show hosts in the limelight of a few lime trees or a few transplanted Paraíso trees (also called Cape Lilac or Persian Lilac) with their purple gleaming blossoms like baubles for a queen and their poisonous even deadly yellow fruit that falls to the sidewalk without warning.

That is a fairly accurate description of what the color of the light was like, but I was the only one who noticed. What was everyone else looking at? Did they notice that the dream of my wedding took place in the smaller, second-floor ballroom of La Campana and not in a church? Did they wonder that there was no reception, no wedding cake, no musicians? Of course I myself am partly to blame for how my wedding turned out. When my beloved Oscar told me he didn't want a church wedding, I told him neither did I. And when he told me that he didn't want a big fancy wedding with photographs in the newspaper and a seven-tier wedding cake and guests flying in from New York City and Chicago, celebrities, musicians, politicians, athletes, I suggested the second-floor ballroom. It would be the perfect place, I said. And my Oscar agreed.

Normally, that is to say on most occasions, the second-floor ballroom was an elegant retreat from the hubbub of the world, but on the day of my wedding it was a disaster. You see two weeks earlier, my Oscar had rented the ballroom for a somewhat rousing Bar Mitzvah, but no one had bothered to clean up afterwards. In the corner opposite the only door in or out there were a small upright piano, an unplugged speaker, and two microphones still fixed to their stands with their cords trailing across the floor like abandoned snake skins. There were also several long narrow tables shoved up against the row of narrow windows overlooking the parking lot. The table linens were stained with crescent moons of red wine. Dirty wine glasses, many of them toppled over, were everywhere. The floor was littered with shreds of paper confetti. And again, I was the only who noticed. Not even my mother spoke up.

Then again, did any of that truly matter? Why not revel in the fact that it was a beautiful, sunny day in late February (in spite of the strange color of the light and the chaos in the ballroom) and I was getting married to my beloved Oscar? Could I have been so divorced from the reality of that moment oh so many years ago? Oscar was my dream come true. I could not have possibly anticipated the end when I was only at the beginning. Yes, yes, I know what you're thinking. Truly, one eye sees and the other eye feels. Perhaps that is why we never truly understand what is happening to us in our lives or why. My beloved Oscar proposed in December, but we did not get married right away. We waited, as all serious couples should. Besides, January was too cold. In fact, that January it snowed in Miami, the first and only snow in the history of Miami. For four days there was ice on the roads all the way across the state from Miami Beach to Labelle. I am sure the tangerine crop was destroyed, and the tangelos and temple oranges as well. Who could believe it! Oscar said maybe he should move back to Cuba, but he also said I was more than welcome to tag along. Then he said maybe the freak snowstorm was an omen of things to come. Maybe we should not get married at all. But he was not being serious. Then the snow melted, the warm breezes and the sun returned, and we were married. We were married on Sunday, February 20, 1977, a fairly warm day for February, bright and dry and sunny. Still, I must confess that my wedding day was not quite what I had hoped for. Would that my Oscar had been able to speak sweet words of poetry to me, words that the whole world might hear. But my beloved, it seemed, told very few people about our wedding, let alone the world. My wedding was what you would call a secret wedding. Yes, I was disappointed. But I am certain my Oscar felt he had no other choice. He was still afraid of being deported. That is why he chose to marry me while the world was looking the other way. What other reason could there possibly be?

So the guest list was very small as you can imagine. You could even say there was no guest list at all. There was my brother Emilio and my mother, and that was it for family. Oscar had no family in Miami or anywhere else. And my own father had died eleven years earlier. My brother had found him sitting in his five-dollar armchair in front of the plate glass window in the living room. His head was angled oddly so that it appeared he was staring with uncompromising expectation at the two lime trees in the front yard that had never borne any fruit in all those many years, neither before nor since. He was only forty-eight, and he was fairly slim and he did not drink to excess, and I am sure he had given up his Cuban cigars, but who can say. I do not think he chased after young girls, though I must admit he had plenty of opportunity after my mother abandoned the dream of their love.

I remember the doctor speaking with my mother in the kitchen that day, and then she had said something that made him laugh and then they were both laughing and then they swallowed their laughter because such behavior is always a sin in front of the newly dead, and they knew this. Then the doctor left without saying a word, without even a second glance at my father, who was still sitting in his leather armchair. My mother took us into the kitchen and sat us down at the table and looked at us with two heavy, dull eyes that seemed like rivers choked with silt. She told us there was no earthly reason why our father had died. She told us it was God's doing. Or perhaps the mark of the Devil had been on my father's soul for too many years to count — my mother firmly believed this — so the Devil, not wishing to give my father a chance to repent, had come calling. My mother said she could not tell for sure, but it was one or the other. God or the Devil. That was all my mother said.

So the guests at my wedding included my brother Emilio and my mother, the Deputy Clerk who married us (a middle-aged chubby fellow named Schofield or Stovall or Torres, something like that, from the Marriage License Bureau in downtown Miami), a stenographer from that same office who would have been the official witness if no one else had shown up, a couple of new girls working at La Campana, a hung-over musician from Saturday night who had spent the night in one of the booths in the back of the bar, a taxi driver Oscar had known for years, who hung out in La Campana's fabulous bar on Friday and Saturday evenings waiting so he could drive home the drunks, and the strangely ubiquitous Velázquez brothers, Bull and Horse, who had been working for Oscar for over a month by that point.

I remember thinking that morning that my marriage to Oscar would never last because my father would not be there to give me away. I remember worrying about this up until Oscar and I exchanged vows, and even after. I remember thinking these ridiculous thoughts even as Oscar was slipping the ring on my finger. I remember the Deputy Clerk was jabbering away but I could not concentrate on what he was saying.

I was praying as feverishly as I had ever prayed. I was asking God to send my father back to earth for just a single hour so he could give me away properly.

There were tears streaming down my face.

Then the Deputy Clerk stopped speaking and everyone was waiting, and some part of me buried deep inside knew they were contemplating my river of tears, and they all thought, or I assumed they thought, that I was shedding tears of joy when in fact I had never been so far from joy in my life. I was drowning in a joyless sea. I could not breathe. I was on the verge of passing out. But then I suddenly heard my father's calm, fatherly, compassionate voice eclipsing all reality. 'Hush now, Isidora,'

I heard my father's voice say. 'You ask the impossible. *Pedir la luna.*'

And so my father's calming words returned me to myself. I began to breathe more easily. I heard my own voice saying 'I do,' and then my beloved Oscar kissed me. And just like that I was married.

-123-

The trouble with secret weddings is they usually beget secret honeymoons. And so it was with ours. Yes, we went to Paris. But Oscar pretended he was going on a business trip and that he had invited me to tag along, an expression he was quite fond of, at the last minute. I am sure he fooled no one. Certainly not the girls who worked at La Campana. Certainly not Emilio nor my mother nor the taxi driver waiting for the drunks nor the strangely ubiquitous Velázquez brothers, who always seemed to be watching my every move when I entered a room with these idiotic expressions on their faces that left little doubt about what they were thinking. Then again, Oscar did take me to Paris. That is not a trivial gesture. We arrived Tuesday, May 17th and left one week later. The warmest day was Friday, when the temperature hit 77 degrees Fahrenheit. I think it rained once or twice, but only late at night or early in the morning. A very light drizzle. The days were very dry, which the Parisians we met said was unusual, but not extraordinary.

Let me just say three things about my honeymoon.

First, we did indeed stay in an elegant, boutiquey hotel that stood on the very corner where a small stone house belonging to Marguerite de Valois once stood, a house where she transported her myriad of lovers to an ephemeral plane, and what is more, the ghost of Madame de Valois whispered into my ear one night that lovers are not criminal in the estimation of one another. *'Che la forza d'amore non riguarda al delitto.'* Just like my great-grandmother, the second-to-last Ana Silvestre, had said would happen.

Second, we did indeed return from Paris with a very rare, very expensive bottle of 1691 Clos de Griffier Vieux Cognac, but it was not a gift, as my great-grandmother had said it would be, my beloved Oscar purchased the bottle from a strange little man, the owner of a small restaurant on Rue Mazarine, and no, I do not think he was a Moorish paramour, as my great-grandmother suggested, but yes, clearly, he and my beloved Oscar treated each other with an astonishingly intimate familiarity, so I am sure they knew each other, but I do not think they had ever been lovers, how would they have accomplished this amazing feat, to achieve such closeness in only a few days, no, no, what I think is that each man recognized in the other a kindred spirit, a lover of life, a lover of love, man or woman it makes no difference, and the bottle of Cognac was simply a vehicle to commemorate that moment of recognition. That is what I think.

Third, the night before we left Paris I did not sleep well. What I mean to say is that I dreamed a strange dream. It was not so much a dream as a reordering of the world. It was as if I had fallen into a deep well where light did not penetrate. No, no, that image is not quite right, is it. No, it was more of a, more of a dark mirror that swallowed all light. Yes, that is what it was. And yet I could see well enough in this strangely dark world, so there must have been some light. I could make out the dark contours of our art-deco room with an art-deco chair at the foot of our art-deco bed and another one near the door, and there were mirrors everywhere, on the walls, the ceiling, even the dresser was made of mirrors, all of them refracting the darkness of the world, a darkness that was at once both a gleaming brightness and a swirling void. To be honest, I could see just fine. But everywhere I looked, well, it was like looking at things from the inside out. The angles of existence had been reversed, as if I had suddenly become my exact opposite, a flawless reproduction of my normal self but condemned to imitate in a most obscene fashion the life and mannerisms of someone else. I was a puppet on a string, as they say, at least this is how I remember feeling that night. I now know there is nothing at all obscene about experiencing life from an opposite vantage point. Such a gift is rarely received. But that night I was quite beside myself.

At any rate, there I was, a puppet trapped in the darkly gleaming glass of this nether world, when I became aware of two voices whispering furtively, furiously (furtiviously?) in the darkness. I could not see where they were. Briefly, I wondered if perhaps I was merely reconstructing a memory of an earlier conversation between my normal self and my beloved Oscar, but that thought soon evaporated without a trace. I focused instead on the sound produced by these two invisible voices, and I did so with a dispassionate almost scientific interest because I could not understand a word they were saying. It was all gibberish to my ears, what some would call an epic giglamesh, and what others would call a sweet, musical *glíglico.* And yet in spite of my inability to break the code of their private love language (yes, it was clear to me from the start that they were speaking a language of shared intimacy, the dots and dashes and daggers of a love invented by two people who, for one unassailable moment, shove themselves into the tiny box of a single soul), the tragic beauty of what they were saying bled itself across the sky, if you will excuse a rather odd and certainly lame metaphor, but I do not know how else to describe what I heard in this dream. I did not understand a single word, but the order of the sounds themselves conveyed a depth of anguish and regret, the suffering of those who love with a pure heart in an impure world, that was too strong to ignore. It was a swirling, tornadic tide of emotion eroding the shores of every sentimental delusion I have ever possessed. So I had no choice, really. I let this tide sweep me away.

What the two voices said, word for unintelligible word:

'My slithy borlis, my belooped and strumming dagma, your tendermuzzle gurgling gizma are flappodoodling like the wind. It is a sleepspackling sound that frackles my ears and sweams with the glorígoro, yes, my ears are redrendering with ostriperation, but I'll not regurgamaze, nor will I glú glú de la ele! No, no, you cannot deniflate this either, the spalmy swave, the strumpeting of your tierno la le li lo lu, your sly nun-ogling, which is all the spizmo gism of the infinite anyway, so what else can I do, I can do nothing else but obscinilate, it is now but a swilly smote to say we are grunfeathered,' said the first voice. It is such a flurious glorígoro my swofty swizzle. Libre, suelto, saltarín. Regaggle the swashsnaggling of this vitriolized spiro-undulating,' said the second voice. 'Ah my belooped you are fenilated. Enough of your unresipient silly stingle-stangling. I'll not have any more. I am too far smuckered for such drivalizing, sodomodulated sodoshyte. Visage me nightingale to

nightingale for once, if you will. Fill your eyes with asmocardisiac farts, as the Quevidian says. Tell me you are not just about the dilly-dally,' said the first voice. 'Oh no, baby, no, my swofty swizzle sweeter than the nectar of Olympianus. Do you not hear the swunclocking of the swailing swankles? The limit of all our petty slobberdigging? Partilejos elífera alamabe. Partilejos, partilejos! Frenteliris de muerte girófora,' said the second voice. 'Nadasada, oooh my swilly, swailing astrobelooped, nadasada,' said the first voice. 'But I am not just about the dilly-dally. I will remicile our evollé,' said the second voice. 'Ala olalúnea, my belooped,' said the first voice. Partilejos elífera alamabe. Partilejos! Partilejos!,' said the second voice. 'Ala olalúnea,' said the first voice.

-124-

It is always difficult to pinpoint the exact moment when a subtle change becomes an inevitable force. Probably this is because we are too distracted by the world, engulfed in the obscenities of empty pleasures, swimming in the febrile soup of the long, fermenting night, inventing demented lullabies to soothe our twisted, glassy-eyed reflections, lullabies that have less in common with the simple, unrehearsed joys of small children running about barefooted and more in common with the millenary murmurings of Medea, who for no good reason murdered her brother Absyrtus (a Greek name which initially meant 'brother of Medea,' but which inevitably morphed into the Latin word *absurdus*, which means out of tune, which is a rather elegant way of calling someone or something irrational or ludicrous, which is the meaning of absurd in the modern sense); and then because her father was now hot on her heels to avenge the death of Absyrtus, she flung her brother's dismembered body into her father's path so he would have to stop and pick up the bloody limbs of his dead son, which he did, and Medea got away scot free; and then later she murdered Glauce, the daughter of Creon, who was having an affair with her husband, Jason, but that wasn't enough to stop the voices that the poet Euripdes had put into her head so she killed two of their (hers and Jason's) three sons and ran away to Thebes; and then it is hard to say what happens after that because there are too many competing versions from other poets through the centuries, not to mention how her story was taken up and transformed (transfigured?) by various Europeanized painters, for you can go into many an art museum in Europe and America and see Medea wandering through the imaginations of dozens of painters, like the reformist, Pre-Raphaelite imaginations of John William Waterhouse or Frederick Sandys or Evelyn De Morgan, or the French Romantic imagination of Eugène Delacroix, or the strange, mysterious, rebellious imagination of Paulus Orlando Bor, that Dutch madman who could see beneath the surface layer of things no matter what he was looking at (rivers, bowls of fruit, laundry women, oblivious nobles; a woman with what seems to be a dragon; an archangel informing a startled and clearly dismayed Mary that she will soon die; the three kings gathering around the infant Christ; a nude woman taking a bath; an old hooded woman whose sole possessions appear to be a string of onions, a tiny snarling, miscreant of a dog and a money bag; a twelve-year-old Christ lecturing in the temple), and so each of his paintings provides a glimpse of that savage paradise that awaits us all.

Who can point to the calendar and say 'this date here, yes, this is when the glory days of La Campana began,' and then flip through the pages for a while and then stop and say 'and this day over here, yes, this is when they ended.' No, no one can say such a thing. Life is not so cut and dried, as they say. And yet by the same token, it was equally clear to me what was happening, as it must have been, as it should have been clear to anyone in those days who had two eyes to see with, especially Herminio, what a two-faced bastard Janus he turned out to be, *caco, cabrón, chabacano pendejo,* if you'll excuse a momentary lapse of good manners. *¡Ay de mí!* You think I am joking! You think I am telling an old woman's story! But I am not joking. I have simply learned to hide my face. Yes, yes, of course it was a matter of survival. That is true of all deceptions, even those that go badly.

So I wore a carnival mask, *larva* not *volto*, yes, yes, children, *larva* in every sense of the word. Oh my God, all I have to do is think of how Herminio abandoned my poor beloved Oscar to the treachery of those evil twins, truly those who bed down with wolves will learn to howl, and there wasn't a thing anyone could do about it, not even the police, it was as if my Oscar had never existed at all, my blood begins to boil over at the thought of what happened, look at me, I am shaking, look at my hands, my fingers trembling like carnival wind chimes and it was years ago.

'. . . .'

No, no, I still have much to learn. *¡Dios dame fuerza!* Truly, we feed upon sorrow with deep spoons. Let me just say that four or five years after the Velázquez brothers began working for my beloved Oscar, the glory days of La Campana had become a distant memory.

'. . . .'

What do I remember? Is that what you want to know?

'. . . .'

Yes, yes, *quien bien ama, tarde olvida,* as they say. But you must have patient ears. I remember the music changed. That is the first thing that struck you if you hadn't been to the club in a while and then one night on a whim you went back because there was a warm, sultry breeze blowing through the streets of Miami, a taste of the ocean with its pulsating sensuality only a few miles away, and you remembered the wild, frenetic music from when you had first gone to La Campana, you remembered drinking smooth mojitos or jazzy highballs like bolts of indiscriminate lightning or beer imported from the Caribbean or Mexico or Central America, a happy, intoxicated state, and the girls were running back and forth between the auditorium and the bar even during the show with order after order after order, their lithe, shadowy curves wiggling through the glistening disco darkness with such vulnerable bounciness that every man in the audience was immediately erect, and all the while you were in this happy, bewildering, intoxicated state, you were listening to that glorious, impossible music like flocks of startled white ibis or ghosts or angels seeking God's redeeming grace, yes, yes, so you wanted to dive back into the froth of those memories which appeared to you out of the blue on that warm breezy night like the fuzzy light of the corona during an eclipse, so you went back to La Campana because you wanted to re-live those salad days when you were electrocuted with the electrifying energy of Willy Chiron (before he got big), or mesmerized by the joyful, soulful beauty of Gwen McCrae, who was bubbly even when she was plagued by sadness, and on occasion she sang with her husband George, and those two had a silky sound you could not ignore in those days, or Rick

James, who once made a surprise stop at La Campana on his way home from Europe to sing about his mama, or Jimmy Bo Horne playing the big tease, singing "You Get Me Hot," and it was all so slick and chic and cool and funky, parapapa papapa paraparapa, and my beloved Oscar's booming, soothing voice echoing beneath it all with eternal delight, the anchor of our universe, the pride of a proud Papa, and he was always saying '*Partirse el alma*. This boy will make someone's heart bleed. Yes, yes. He will make all of our hearts bleed, I think.' And then: 'Yes, there is one table up front I set aside especially for you.' And then: 'Yes, oh do not worry, the waitresses will bring you whatever you like from the bar. Whatever you can think of, whatever you can imagine.'

Many people asked me what had happened to the music, but what could I say? It was clear my Oscar no longer cared who was playing or what they sounded like. This was in 1981. For some reason that I have never understood, the Velázquez brothers started booking musicians. What was my Oscar thinking? It was like giving two small boys a stone for killing birds in a cage. They did not know a thing about music. Well this was obvious! For one thing they hired bands with shitty names, names like *Polvo Blanco* or *Blitz* or *Hermana Menudo* or *¡Hace un Frío del Carajo!* or *¡Mala Suerte!* What kind of crazy names are those? But what could we do? You could not say anything to the Velázquez brothers. They were very dangerous men. I know, I know, some people say that the bull that gores you throws you to a better place. But when is this ever true? Besides, the Velázquez brothers were truly evil. They reeked of vengeance and smoking guns and the narcissistic stupidity of men who believe they are in control of their own destinies, their frog eyes bulging in ludicrous anticipation of the deaths of countless victims, unsuspecting men and women walking along the street, hailing taxi cabs, inhabiting the cafes and restaurants and movie theatres and dance clubs where we all go, all of their victims chosen at random, in as much as God had turned a blind eye, a staggering number. The Velázquez brothers were nocturnal creatures who spread their leathery wings to blot out the sun so their eyes could shine like bullets or the blood-thirsty moon. They were the dogs of Anubis patrolling the edges of a crumbling, soon-to-be-forgotten cemetery, their mouths open slightly, drooling, such sinister grins. They were bright butcher's knives with ivory handles for slicing through the bone. They were bright rivers of molten lead converging, clogging up the arteries of the world.

So just like that La Campana was overflowing with bands with shitty names, and the music of these bands, my God, it is a wonder the very walls did not disintegrate with the clawing, scratching, unnatural sound produced by broken guitars and tin-can drums and the wailing, diseased voices of chainsaws mocking the profound simplicity of true love. It was the sound of raw sewage spilling into the air, the odor of disgust. Yes, yes, it was the smell of death, but not the heavily perfumed, hermetically sealed in sealing wax oleander smell of a proper send-off. It was the rusty, bloody-earth smell of a bestial death of ritual slaughter, the dark fragments of ancient skulls scattered about, the heady wine of fermenting corpses, a field of mutilated onions in flames. It was as if La Campana had been transformed into an abattoir, a dazzling modern temple to honor the gods of murder and despair, those ancient gods who are always with us. There was even a small article about it in *The Miami Herald* (page twenty-six, stuffed in between an ad for toothpaste and an ad for a cream to remove penile warts) with a headline that said: What Happened to La Campana?

Naturally, the sweaty, inconstant but cultured gentlemen of Miami and their insufferably beautiful and emotionally volatile wives and girlfriends stopped coming to the club. They were replaced by a different clientele, gritty, unwashed, unshaven, ageless men, like mannequins or robots or worse, always seeming to be destitute of funds, and yet always wearing fancy black hats and black jackets that were always buttoned to conceal shoulder holsters with ferocious looking revolvers which they would whip out at a moment's notice, empty sockets where their eyes should have been, as if their eyeballs had recently been dug out with pocketknives, this is how it seemed to me, blood running down the sides of their ashen-colored cheeks like mascara, like gangsters in a Mexican vampire movie. The gangsters would come and go throughout the evening.

There was no need for a coat-check room since no one checked their coats anymore, so the coat-check girls joined the waitresses, who still scurried back and forth between the bar and the auditorium. Except the role of the waitresses was also evolving. If you happened to wander into the auditorium at any point past nine o'clock, as I did on a few occasions – I don't remember why, it wasn't to check up on Oscar, I know that much, because he was usually sitting on a stool at the end of the bar closest to the lobby, a drunken figurehead rotting away – but if you happened to pass through those black leather doors to the main ballroom, as I did once or twice, you would be greeted with a sight of extraterrestrial dimensions like a drug-induced dream. Strange flashing neon purples and blues would stab at your eyes and drive you to the edge of unconsciousness. Your nerves would begin to tingle from the terrible music. You began to wonder if you had gone suddenly deaf and if that terrifying ringing in your ears was actually the sound of blood rushing along the fragile (disintegrating?) arteries of your inner ear. You would notice strange, floating platforms at various heights, like alien spacecraft descending or taking off. There were fewer tables. The tables were illuminated by a weird, pulsating candlelight like tiny meteors exploding and then coalescing and then exploding again, the light spreading out with inevitable precision like the fumes of regret. The tables reminded me of miniature ocean liners lost in the vast empty spaces of a dark ocean. And everywhere you looked (the strange floating platforms, up along the stage, straddling the darkness that surrounded the tables) you would see weird ribbons of shadow twisting and gyrating, rotating slowly then speeding up, a cacophony of unexpected movement. The movement of these ribbons was fascinating, weirdly seductive, indescribably beautiful, and you would stare at this movement for a while. It was almost like you had been hypnotized. Yes, truly, it was like you were a puppet and you could feel someone pulling on your strings but you did not mind. And then you would realize that these weird, gyrating ribbons of shadow were in fact the waitresses, who had all but given up serving drinks and were instead performing various lewd acts for the various vampire gangsters that had gathered in small groups of two or three in the hazy, shimmery, neon-streaked darkness.

To be honest I had no idea what was happening until Herminio took me aside one evening and told me. I was looking for Oscar but he was not in the bar. There was only Herminio. He was standing behind the counter, but he was not drying the same shot glass over and over again or creating crystalline pyramids like you would expect. No, he was standing there in the frail light of the afternoon reading a book. Up until that point I had thought Herminio was only an illiterate slob from

Paraguay who had narrowly escaped death by firing squad. But there he was reading. It was a Spanish novel by Pérez Galdós. He said it was pretty interesting, a bit outdated, a bit of romanticized slapdash about a war in Spain in the 1800s, there were many bloody battles, yet he couldn't quite tell what was happening, it was fluid like water, it was full of a crackling energy just beneath the surface, yet it was also very, very dull. He was baffled by the seeming contradictions contained within the book.

'I am looking for Oscar.'

'Yes, of course you are. But as you can see, he is not here.'

I don't remember what I said to that. I caught a distinct whiff of insolence in his reply, and I am sure I became angry and was about to hurl a dagger or two his way, but he had already plunged himself back into his very dull book.

I stared at him.

I was teetering on the edge of an insatiable silence like a great sadness about to take wing.

I was falling into the funnel of a sky that rejects all imitations.

Then Herminio spoke without looking up from the pages of his book. It seemed as if he were reading a speech that had been prepared just for him, for precisely this moment, by a long vanished Spanish novelist from a century ago.

'Do not be sad,' Herminio said. And then: 'It is the inevitable way of the world. Everything that has fulfilled its function disappears. Oscar is not here now but you will see him later, such as he has become. But do not be too hard on him. *Á muertos y á idos, no hay amigos,* as they used to say. I am certain he was only thinking of the future.'

I had no idea what Herminio was talking about, but suddenly I was very nervous. I was sitting at the bar by that point, and I suspect Herminio felt my nervous energy. He pushed his book to one side and lowered his chin to his tremendous chest and began squinting like a newcomer.

'What was he to do?' he said. 'Was he to go around planting trees and various shrubs around the edges of tennis courts? He was not so seditious. And besides, he had no money for trees or shrubs. Every dime he got his hands on, he sunk into this monstrosity, and for what? He paid the musicians too much, and he charged too little for the greasy *gamberros* of Miami and elsewhere who came every Friday and Saturday evening to bask in the comfort of this elegant palace and enjoy Oscar's unbounded generosity.'

Herminio looked at me as if he expected some sort of reaction, a nod of understanding, recognition, anything, but I said nothing. What could I say? I was taken completely by surprise. Then Herminio shook his head and reached into a small refrigerator beneath the counter. He pulled out a tin of sardines and some goat cheese and some brown bread and we ate while he talked.

'You did not know this?'

He passed me a plate and I was suddenly very hungry.

'Oscar spent vast sums just to keep this place afloat.'

Herminio paused a moment, as if he was about to share a secret message that only he had been able to decipher.

'But where did this debilitating obsession spring from?' said Herminio. 'And how did Oscar have so much cash to give away in the first place? Even the walls of La Campana were whispering these questions. Idiot! Losing money year after year becomes an invisible habit until the magnitude of what you have lost becomes all too visible. I am sure he thought the Velázquez brothers were a godsend. Yes, anyone would have thought as much under the circumstances. But such unexpected gifts are often costly in the end, and this is especially true when the Velázquez brothers are involved. *La paloma es la ralea del halcon.* Do not be too hard on him. It is the same old story. First we dream a dream. Then we are seduced by the dream. And then we are sacrificed in the name of the dream.'

And then it seemed that Herminio was finished with what he had to say. We finished the sardines and cheese in a silence that was both familiar and uncomfortable. But when he was cleaning up he began speaking again, but the tenor of his voice had changed. What is more, he did not even move his lips while he spoke. It was a hissing, guttural, unnatural voice I heard. It was almost like I was listening to a radio tucked away in the crevices of my imagination. Perhaps this is true. Perhaps Herminio said nothing more after the sardines.

Then again, I know what I heard.

'Do not trust these Velázquez brothers,' Herminio said. 'You are an indestructible passionflower, and they sense this about you, so they will most certainly try to destroy you. Just as they are in the process of destroying Oscar. No, he did not know what he was getting into. They are sly wolves who now deal in cocaine, but Oscar did not know this. But now it is too late. They have turned La Campana into a cocaine den. Surely you have wondered what goes on here. But you must not look too closely. Every evening these two cocaine gangsters entertain guests in the second-floor ballroom. You must never again go up there, Isidora. It has become a palace of fragile peace until the deals are struck, and afterwards, which is to say after the money exchanges hands, well, then we are too busy serving drinks to take much notice of what happens. These guests, these vampires, they drink to wash away the fear and nervous anxiety that accompanies all transactions that take place in the shadows after dark. And then they head into the main ballroom and listen to that strange raging symphony of the devil, and they masturbate right there in front of the dancing girls, barking at the girls in a demonic, guttural Spanish that does not come close to sounding like the pure Spanish we were born with, but the girls seem to understand their meaning anyway and so they begin to strip, and these vampire gangsters laugh with unrestrained glee, wolves howling at Quevedo's blood-red moon, though even Quevedo did not imagine such gratuitous depravity, so they laugh some more and probe these girls with their fingers and then lick their fingertips, still laughing, and order more to drink, and the girls are trembling in their sudden objectified nakedness, their eyes glowing with a vulnerability like a shallow sea, too terrified to run away, hoping their juices will begin to flow freely so they can avoid a sudden beating, and maybe these vampires take hold of a slender wrist and drag a young, nubile body into one of the empty rooms backstage to satisfy their lusts, yes, my innocent Isidora, there are now several empty rooms backstage for just this purpose. Remember, to find oneself between the horns of the bull is to be in the greatest danger. Not even Oscar could save you if you wandered into the main ballroom. Especially not Oscar.'

And it was true. It was all true. Everything Herminio said about La Campana and about my beloved Oscar was true. Of course I did not want to believe. I cursed the name of Herminio for filling my empty girlish head with such vitriolic distortions of reality. But everything he said was the truth. What could I say? What could anyone say? So I said nothing. And every evening after that, at seven o'clock on the dot, I sat down in a small forgotten chair in a corner of the lobby and I watched my beloved Oscar wander through the dream of his demise as if he were hanging onto the delicate, cellophane wing of a blue bottlenose fly. Every evening at seven o'clock my beloved Oscar retreated to the bar and Herminio served him drinks until he was too drunk to even stand. He sat at the bar, unmoved by the horde of vampire gangsters whose very presence had caused the sanctity of our little world to collapse, suffering without horror the vengeance of that terrible music that was the absence of music. And he drank and drank until the alcohol ran out of his ears. And every now and then he would wave at someone traipsing through the lobby on their way up the stairs to the second-floor ballroom of my dreams and the bright dazzling, sacrilegious purity of mountains of cocaine, or down the stairs to the main ballroom and a table of what was for most men a volcanic eruption of lascivious delight, and then he, my beloved Oscar, would plunge himself back into the self-annihilating liquid gold of his bottomless glass. Or he would wave at the dark shadows dancing on the walls, shadows he had mistaken for those who had once filled each night with the glorious joy of their appreciation but who had in the end abandoned La Campana to her misery. Or he would wave at the ghost of Bonita, a fiery whirling dervish spinning like mad, retracing the scorched path of her footprints that would never fade. Or he would wave at the image of his own tiny fractured self reflected in the glass of his ambrosia, which was itself a strange reflection of his other self trapped inside the antique glass of that darkly gleaming mirror which oh so many years earlier, an infinity in the dreaming, had been anchored with an unshakeable purpose to the wall behind the bar.

-125-

Truly, one must always be ready to suffer.

'In the window of a hotel a face like a clown's grimaces behind the glass. The shadow of a dove rubs up against the excrement a dog leaves behind.' I remember reading these lines somewhere. I do not remember who wrote them, but that is unimportant. What is important is that I remember the images. We use images such as these to hide our suffering. We use these images to distract us from the incomprehensible nature of what we truly feel, what we are truly experiencing. What is more, we knowingly embrace such linguistic theatrics, the poetic deceptions that allow us to sleep comfortably at night, the bricks we use to plug the holes in the wall, because we know deep down in that place we call the soul that every experience is a singular, virtually unrecognizable, untranslatable event. Every experience damns the language we use to describe it, but what choice do we have. Yes, yes, we can avoid the nasty topic altogether by embracing the immediacy of the experience as the only thing that matters, as if we were being absorbed directly into a painting by Chardin. But we do not truly believe that a momentary distraction is a window to enlightenment. We do not wish to be mistaken for those dreadful, vagabond bums who are always distracted by one thing or another, *el papador de moscas*. We do not wish to be fooled by the anti-sunlight and the anti-shadow of fruit on a table, peaches, pears, apples, grapes, a bottle of wine, a small cup, a knife for cutting bread.

So the cynical world will begin to whisper over our shoulder, casting spells, mocking our naiveté. 'This anti-reality you perceive is nothing more than a delusion created by your intellect,' the cynical world will say. 'It is a sham, a mask to hide behind.' And we will believe the cynicism of the cynical world, but our belief (or unbelief) will also be tested. Inevitably we will try to remember that moment oh so long ago when we were directly absorbed into a painting. We will wonder what happened to the fruit, who we were eating with, how much wine we drank, and so on.

But then we will begin to confuse wagon wheels with wafers, just as the cynics in the manner of prophets might have predicted. We will decide we need to grow a second set of eyes to decipher what is really going on. But this will be of no help. The two sets of eyes will cancel each other out. We will not be able to see a thing. We will become blind, irrevocably blind, and we will wallow in the provocative terror of this blindness. We will take note of a shuddering, sinking feeling that begins in our ancient reptilian brains and shoots down our crumbling spines to land with a hollow thud somewhere in the steamy, vegetative darkness of our stomachs. And in the growing despair that results, as resilient as any black hole, we will crawl back into our mother's womb, whimpering with or without shame and yet thoroughly disgusted with the way our puny lives have turned out, begging God or some reasonable facsimile to have mercy on us and send us a witness like an avenging angel who will listen in rapt amazement to what we might have to say. No wonder our memoirs and our histories and our fictions and our poetry, and even our letters and our postcards and our private notebooks and our teenage diaries, are filled with wave after wave (or wafer after wafer, or wagon wheel after spinning wagon wheel) of nauseatingly imprecise images, a pastiche of empty clichés, failed metaphors of every ilk.

The image of an old sea wolf drinking from his bottle of gin, his face tanned by the Brazilian sun, thinking vaguely about misty, faraway islands and violent typhoons in the South China Sea, the creation of a courageous poet pursuing a form just out of reach.

The image of an elderly couple who have exhausted all of life's possibilities, except somehow they are still madly, even passionately in love with each other, they have murdered each other with their love, but this does not stop them, their corpse-like bodies are relentless in pursuing the physical release of their necrophiliac passion, the expulsion of all doubt, or at least hers, and in the indescribable, indestructible ecstasy of the moment they become a wheat field, which suggests, perhaps, that they are engaged in the process of separating the chaff from the pure grain, a noble endeavor, but in the haste of their passion (or hers), the wheat field goes up in flames anyway.

The image of two men playing chess in a bombed-out café in a city of ticking clocks and shattered glass and the swirling dark clouds of infallible pigeons who know exactly what they're doing, to steal half a line (and mutilate the meaning of that line) from that loveable, whineffable wheccentric who whonce whandered wherratically about the sun-streaked streets of Chillán, whondering whimsically wherever whe whent.

The image of two connected spools of thread, or copper wire, or Hollywood celluloid, the one spool unwinding as quickly as it possibly can, the other spool taking in all that the first spool has to offer in a madcap, mechanical, sprockety but uniform dash towards the future, that fraudulent dream that lingers on every horizon.

This is as close as we can get to explaining the pain we feel. The images we select. The parables we tell. And if we are trying to explain the whappiness whe feel, whell, that whill quickly and whinevitably whorph whinto pain, so whit is whall the same thing whin the whend.

¡De illusión también se vive! as my grandmothers used to

say, but what they really meant in their heart of hearts was that if one lived by hope, one would die a slow, withering death.

-126-

I remember quite vividly the very last night I saw my Oscar. I remember everything with a cinematic clarity that resembles the ringing of church bells to announce a papal decree (otherwise known as a papal bull), or the stratosphere fifty kilometers up with its unimpeded view of the curvature of the Earth, as much as it (the cinematic clarity of my memory) resembles the malleable (we are but clay in the hands of our maker) delusions of a self-proclaimed, self-medicated schizophrenic walking hand in hand with the three Fates, the apportioners, what the Greeks called the Moirai, now firmly committed to whispering over my shoulder (or, alternately, from the shadowy creases of the ever-increasing shadows), casting aspersions as well as spells with every roll of the dice. I still do not understand what happened or why. My mind is a sieve when it comes to understanding. But I remember every last bizarre, inconceivably absurd detail, from the strange book Herminio was reading (I was still struck by the incongruity of seeing that coward Herminio reading a book) to Emilio's determination to watch a boxing match on television (my dear sweet Emilio, who had always preferred poetry to pugilism). My memory of that evening is impeccable.

-127-

A madwoman's third-person catalogue (collage, montage, litany, chronicle of sleepless nights, diary written in fresh blood, surrealist painting, anti-surrealist painting, Cowleyan ode, Baroque cantata, dodecaphonic symphony, a day in the life) of every fleeting image that traversed the empty spaces of her (my) brain on Friday evening the 21st of August 1981, from about six-thirty in the evening, when she (I) headed into the bar to talk to Herminio about my beloved Oscar's deepening despair, until there was nothing left to talk about:

She considers the possibility that she is traveling the path of an endless spiral, a true descent into madness, a nether world illuminated by the faint orangeish glow of Satan's cauldron, this is how she imagines the end of the road she is taking, for she realizes she is heading in a generally downward direction, and always she can see her beloved Oscar two or three levels below, but the moment she catches up to where he has been, he is long gone. Her mother's own preoccupations were by way of contrast incurably frivolous, the darts thrown by an adventurous heart, the false anguish of an irrepressible soul with a flair for drama, the tantrums of a sugar plum fairy, the irresistible shadow cast by a carefully pruned crepe myrtle, the exotic artificiality of a decorated gourd from a half-remembered dream. She suddenly finds herself inside her mother's dream, a dream of forgotten Cuba, a beam of sky-blue light descending upon the faithful, absolving everyone of original sin. But she is interrupted by the weary, impatient voice of Herminio, that prophet of eclipsed moons, who is tending bar.

'He does not know what it is like to be married,' she thinks, 'the pain and the confusion and the irrepressible joy.'

And yet she has sought out Herminio precisely to save her marriage. She is sitting on a barstool directly opposite Herminio, whose eyes are two, puffy slits the color of crushed violets, at precisely six-thirty in the evening, thirty minutes before her beloved husband who has forgotten what it means to be married will take his now customary seat at the bar in La Campana and proceed to get rip-roaring drunk.

She wants to ask Herminio if he has noticed the strange aberrant malaise that has descended upon her Oscar, a sudden unwillingness to take her to bed, to make wild, passionate love to her, to participate in the rife with life world around him that is his for the taking, if only he would take it. It is a malaise as thick and loamy as the rust-red musty earth that will one day cover us all.

She wants to ask if Herminio has noticed this heart-wrenching transformation on the way to the grave. Then she hopes to ask him how to re-ignite the raging rocket that was once Oscar Garcia Raimundi speeding effortlessly from one end of the universe to the other, and so re-ignite her own flagging passion for living.

She does not see Oscar emerge from the gleaming darkness of the lobby, a nocturnal creature escaping from a culvert made from corrugated galvanized steel. He is sitting along the edge of the gleaming, mahogany bar for several minutes, maybe longer, drinking glass after glass of sweet Demerara rum before she notices, for she is heavily immersed in the heavy words she takes for wisdom that are spewing forth with frothy regularity from Herminio's mouth. Then she hears Oscar laugh into his glass as he drains it and she realizes just how drunk he truly is.

Once her mother had discovered her father drunk at the kitchen table, his head flat against the wall, an empty bottle of wine on the table, on its side, a puddle bright as blood on the floor, an occasional bubble from a drop falling. Her mother had hurled the empty bottle into the sink, shattering the glass with the impact, a great crescendo of sound lacerating the air itself, and her father woke in an instant, but he was not yet himself, he had no clue that he was still in the kitchen, trapped as he was in a culvert of his own making, and when he saw the puddle on the floor, he panicked, thinking he had somehow injured himself and that he was bleeding copious amounts of blood and was on the verge of death, and so he had run out the kitchen door and then out into the street, thinking perhaps that he could flag down a wayward ambulance or some such nonsense, at least this is how her mother had always told the tale.

Naturally, this madcapped dash into the cool night air had immediately restored her father to himself. He had realized he wasn't dying, so he had gone back to his kitchen chair and leaned his head against the wall, a gesture of imminent defeat, and it was then he had seen my mother standing only a few feet away, a beautiful almost angelic vision in the sacrificial glare of the tiny recessed light above the sink, laughing silently at his idiocy, but it was a smoky, smirky, detached kind of laughter, at least this is how her father had always painted the scene, her mother's eyes tiny and hard like two weathered plum pits or cherry pits, her mother's features already blossoming with the stony, blackening orchids of disdain.

(She whonders for a moment if her father was simply defending himself whin the whelling of the whale from his point of view, a vigorously poetic defense, against the vague whinsinuations of her mother's laughter, as any father might do when a whondering child whonders what is going whon, or was he recounting with mock sincerity the tragedy of his whown absurd marriage, whor all marriages.)

Then the memory of this story of two authors fades and from somewhere Isidora hears the sound of someone chanting, faintly at first, a strange, guttural voice like a bolo knife cutting through the now verdant, leafy, jungle darkness of her imagination, but then she has the distinct impression that she has been absorbed by the sound, that it is all around her, that she has become this sound and is now spinning violently through the air, as the sound of any chanting voice would be spinning if that voice were trying to project itself across the yawning abyss of the centuries, that gaping mouth that will one day swallow itself, so she takes this leap, why not? (although even as she does so she realizes she is taking a leap in reverse) and lands in a cool moist place high atop a mountain. She sees a strange old woman on this mountain top (the source of the original chanting, obviously), an old dark-skinned woman wearing a slave's woven skirt and a bright blue turban and her saggy breasts are bare. The old woman is squatting beside a swiftly moving stream. Who can say what she is doing? Not Isidora. Isidora's mind is perplexed. It is filled only with questions. Her neurons are firing like mad. Who are you? How did I get here? Why are you squatting beside that stream? Were you thirsty? Did the fins of a swiftly-moving fish catch your eye? And just like that, as if to answer all of Isidora's silly questions with a single swift stroke, the old woman stands up, her bright blue turban shining like a newly birthed sky, and waves her hand in the air with a violent gesture of ultimate finality, and Isidora finds herself back in the bar, staring vacantly at Herminio, who has sort of clammed up now that Oscar is sitting right there. Herminio has become a mountain of silence.

Then quite unexpectedly Herminio says there is one thing he is at liberty to say, and he is casting sideways glances in the direction of Oscar (but he is blushing as he does this, a deep violet color like the tail end of a sunset, almost as if he is ashamed for keeping to himself even the most trivial of secrets), and then he says it was Oscar who had suggested that he pick up a copy of the Galdos book, El amigo manso, which he has read not once but twice because it is a very wise book. Herminio says that according to Galdos, some of us love in a Petrarchan way with a cold, intellectual sentimentality that might allow us to write a few fiery love sonnets, but is that all we really want from love. It is not clear if Herminio expects an answer, but then the moment for answers is obliterated by a peeping-Tom voice piping up from the lobby.

The voice, which belongs to Isidora's brother, Emilio, says that today is the long-awaited boxing match between Wilfredo Gómez and that tenacious Mexican, Salvador Sanchez, for the junior featherweight boxing championship of the world. This fight of the 'Little Giants' will take place in Caesar's Palace in Las Vegas, Emilio says, but it will be beamed to all corners of the planet, this pale blue dot, via satellite television. Emilio has been working at La Campana for several years now, various odd jobs like a sailor adrift on a shallow blue-green sea, and popped his head into the bar to say 'hi' on his way to the main ballroom. Isidora does not remember when Emilio began to show an interest in boxing.

Oscar says he likes boxing in general but he doesn't give a damn about this particular fight, though he's not talking to anyone directly, perhaps his own wavering, watery reflection in the mirror behind Herminio.

Oscar says he is embroiled in a fight of his own, in case anyone (his reflection?) is (was?) interested, a fight to the death, he says, but he doesn't elucidate. He downs another glass of sweet Demerara rum, that amber ambrosia of the gods, and wipes his mouth with his sleeve and then leaves the bar, a shadow in search of a beam of bright sunlight.

Isidora is about to follow, but the precise moment she starts to slip off her barstool she hears her mother's voice from beyond the grave. Her mother's voice becomes an impenetrable barrier.

Isidora settles back onto the barstool.

She does not remember exactly what her mother died of, only that she died a few years earlier in Jackson Memorial with dozens of slender tubes pumping various liquids into a body that was already bloated and covered with purplish bruises like the phlegmy flesh of rotten, half-eaten plums. The voice from the darkness beyond simply says 'whoever you marry is of no more importance than a passing shadow, a cloud upon the horizon,' and Isidora falls swiftly into a reverie of contemplation and loses sight of her beloved. Truly, who can penetrate the dark hood of the Cuban night?

Herminio pulls out the Galdos book and thumbs quickly and decisively through the pages until he comes to a well-worn spot that has been marked up with a pen (a purple Bic, probably the only pen that was available, a pen that was leaking, or at least the flow of the ink was uneven, to judge by the look of the smudges on the page).

Why did my father stay locked in a marriage without love, Isidora thinks, a marriage that was slowly bleeding him dry, so much so that he looked like a strange Kabuki mannequin in the months leading up to his death, except for a faint hint of red around his lips, a forlorn, disenfranchised puppet which her mother, on any given night, might pull apart limb from limb. Why would anyone stay in such a marriage? Are these the sacrifices we must make in the name of God just because we believe He is watching our every move, the ritualized castration of the bull to honor the mythology of our creation and then all we can do is stand back in horror and watch the dark red blood running through the streets of our despair? Who said so?

Slowly her metaphysical questions dissolve, and for a moment there is nothing but the image of her father floating effortlessly in front of her memory like the rarely seen blue moon of those ancient Cuban kings who roamed the Caribbean in search of prophecies.

Then Herminio begins reading from the Galdos book: 'The same perverse friend who had brought me into the world took me out of it, repeating the same magic words he'd said way back then, and also the diabolical sorcery of the bottle, the drop of ink, and the burnt paper which had preceded my incarnation.' Everything you want to know about God and love and marriage and foretelling the future you can find in this little book, he says with an air of exaggerated mystery.

What in the world are you talking about, Isidora says.

I am talking about the peace that eludes us, Herminio says, and then he laughs a hearty laugh that defies interpretation. Que Dios nos saque de penas y nos lleve a descansar, he says, after he has stopped laughing, his eyes narrowing in clichéd fashion, his air of exaggerated mystery returning. What do you even know about the sacrifices that go along with marriage, the perpetual suffering, Isidora says back to him with her eyes, but he has already gone back to his book.

The world becomes a 1910 vintage gramophone, the kind with an elongated funnel like a mouthpiece to the stars. A scratchy record from years ago begins to play, the music from an unknown singer spiraling through the darkness, but then the unknown voice of this unknown singer is suddenly replaced by Oscar's sweetly singing voice. 'Baby, go over there, turn on the lights, come back here and stand on that chair and then take off your shoes, yeah, Baby, now take off your dress, yeah Baby, that's it, wave your arms in the air, just like that, let the suspicious tongues keep on wagging, they don't know what love is, yeah, Baby, take it all off, that's it, take it all off, except you can leave your hat on.' Yes, she knows it was an absurd bit of erotic playfulness, words in all probability that her beloved Oscar had stolen from a forgotten song on a forgotten album from 1972 and had pretended were his own, but it was a game the two of them thoroughly enjoyed, a game they would play all night until their skin was bathed in the absolutely pure, tangy, orangey glow of a sexy, sticky, marmalade sunrise.

Then her mind shifts gears and she is once again thinking about her mother. Why was her mother so set on a church wedding when she believed more in the dark mystical powers of an Eleguá head named Eshu Laroyê than she did in the collective might of the pantheon of Catholic saints? Did she know what she was doing when she challenged Oscar to demonstrate the purity of his love for her only daughter? Isidora is wallowing in resentment. What a hateful, cynical thing to do! How Isidora hates her mother and her mother's Cuban heritage, but even as she voices these feelings to herself, an acknowledgement of the suffering we can never subdue, she knows she is being absurdly overdramatic. Her mother is not the reason Oscar hired the Velázquez brothers. It was Herminio. He is the reason.

Then Herminio himself breaks into the bubble of Isidora's inner dreaming with yet another passage from the Galdos book, but Isidora is unable to decipher the suddenly obscure language of this novel from a century ago (it is as if she is squinting to read a page right beneath her nose but which seems a million light years away because her once pristine eyesight is failing her). Only poetry can transcend the unforgiving years and capture how I truly feel, she thinks, and it is a thought that gives her tremendous satisfaction, it is almost as if her finger is poised on the trigger of a loaded gun, though where she might aim this gun, who she might wish to do in, well of this she is not sure. 'La locura de mi alma vive en el silencio del librepensador, que vive solo,' she says to Herminio, who is once again absorbed in the pages of his book.

Emilio returns from the main ballroom and takes the seat that Oscar had vacated. 'Turn on the television,' he says to Herminio, 'the fight is going to start shortly.' Herminio closes the Galdos book and turns on a small television on a small diagonal shelf in the corner above the cash register, but clearly it is the wrong channel because a well-groomed man sitting behind a pale blue desk is saying that today in Miami federal investigators discovered massive amounts of fraud in how the city has been managing the food stamps program.

Wilfredo Gómez, who is also known as Bazooka Gómez because of the power of his punch, was born in the crumbling Las Monjas neighborhood in San Juan, Puerto Rico, and later lived in Hato Rey, a stone's throw from the Martín Peña bridge, an art deco landmark that Gómez took whenever he was going to Santurce, which he did on a semi-regular basis because his mother and grandmother had belonged to the Church of the Crab Sellers (Iglesia San Mateo de Cangrejeros) on the corner of Calle San Jorge and Avenida Eduardo Conde, a quick five minutes (without traffic) from the bridge.

Before Herminio can turn the channel, the well-groomed man clears his throat and says that Pan Am is going to sell the Intercontinental Hotels Corporation (which can trace its roots back to the William Bass Brewery, which opened its doors in 1777 in the town of Burton in East Staffordshire, England, which the well-groomed man does not say) to another company headquartered in England, Grand Metropolitan Life (which will turn around five years later and sell the hotel chain to a Japanese group, having decided for financial reasons to focus on fast-food franchises like Burger King instead of hotels, which the well-groomed man could not possibly know, but which somehow Isidora has intuited, or at least she later imagines that she had), then click.

Oscar had never permitted anyone to watch television in the bar between the hours of seven o'clock and midnight, though there was one notable exception to this rule. He said it was bad for business. But Oscar wasn't there. Isidora's mother, on the other hand, was a fanatic when it came to television, and would show up at La Campana at eight, nine, ten in the evening, especially on a Saturday when it was busiest, and she would demand that Herminio put on a show, so what else could he do, not even being threatened with the pain of death could have altered the outcome. Her favorite show was The Love Boat, but to tell the truth she didn't care what was flickering away on that tiny little box in the dark corner like a window to the fifth dimension (that's what Oscar called it) above the register as long as she was there to see Oscar come storming in, for she knew that no matter where he was in the building, he always seemed to know if someone had turned on the television (it was usually Herminio, who loved to watch a ballgame or two); even if the volume was turned down to practically nil, Oscar somehow sensed a disturbance in the equilibrium of the universe and would come storming out of the darkness, an avenging god who existed only in the spaces in between interjections, ready to pop a vein in his neck just to test his immortality, but then he would have to choke back his bluster, his face contorting into a weird grimace of self-loathing when he saw that Herminio had only been the hapless, helpless victim of a sinister plot to undermine his authority. So Oscar would drift aimlessly about the lobby for a while, a man of confounded purpose, a tad unsettled still, checking to make sure the coat-check room was secure, or checking to see if the potted plants in the lobby needed watering, or taking a peek outside to see if there were any latecomers hustling in from the parking lot even when he knew he would only be greeted by the steady, mechanical whine of insects hidden away in the darkness of the trees, and then he would quietly shut the door and slink as shadows slink along the edge of the wall, slipping swiftly, gratefully (one might also have said expertly) through the black double doors on the far side of the lobby into the main ballroom and the euphoria of a world light years away from the ruthless mischief of his mother-in-law.

Isidora begins to wonder if Oscar ever existed at all, or if he was a pagan of lust-filled days and nothing more. She stares at the mahogany bar, at the mirror behind the bar and the row after row of shimmering bottles stacked against the glass, deep reds and burgundies and ambers and light oranges, the bottles catching the rays of television light beaming from that black hole above the cash register. Everywhere she looks she is looking for some sign of her Oscar, a lingering scar of his passing that has somehow been impressed into the very molecules that make up the air she breathes and which will remain miraculously visible no matter how many breaths she takes. Yet she sees nothing. There is no sign of her beloved Oscar, no miracle unfolding before her bleary, watery eyes. She stares at the mirror as easily as if she is staring into an abyss of her own making. The beaming, television light like sulphurous vapors leaking through a tear in the fabric of reality is now projecting images of the fight between Gómez, the favorite, and Salvador Sanchez, his Mexican challenger. Gómez is doing poorly. He was knocked down in the first round. He has been repeatedly rocked by Sanchez, who has stunned the world with the incredible speed and accuracy of his combinations, a flurry of pumping fists, the symbiosis of unimaginably profound artistry and unspeakably degenerative violence. It is the end of the third round and Gómez has a severely damaged eye. His eye is beginning to swell. There is nothing his corner can do except cut it with a razor. But Isidora is oblivious to this flickering reality. The boxing match does not yet exist for Isidora, except perhaps on a subliminal level, an ironic bit of mental dexterity given that Oscar now exists only in Isidora's subconscious mind. She continues to look for the lingering scars of his presence with an air of scientific detachment, hoping against hope to reverse the inevitability of her madness as she imagines one might theoretically (but not instantaneously) reverse the polarity of the Earth with a flip of a magnetic switch. But even while she is searching she accepts the futility and foolishness of the search. Gómez returns with a vengeance in the seventh round and literally lifts Sanchez off his feet. But Sanchez does not fall down. He rubs his chin. He shifts his protruding jawbone back and forth, as if to make sure it is in working order. Some of his teeth are loose, but he is undaunted. Suffering is the only way out of his predicament. Isidora is confronted by her own complicity in Oscar's continued absence. She is suddenly overwhelmed by the thought that to look for some proof that her beloved once existed and continues to exist outside her never neverland imagination is to profane the memory of that very existence, which is in all probability a sin against the act of creation. But the seventh round proves to be the last gasp for Gómez, his last chance for victory. Both of his eyes are swollen now. Isidora wonders if God will punish her for her sin and if this punishment will fit the crime, and then she is sure this will be the case. She is given the gift of brutal clarity. Everything coincides. Gómez staggers out into the middle of the ring at the beginning of the eighth round, but he is unable to zero in on Sanchez. All he is able to see are strange, flickering shadows dancing deliriously on the periphery of his awareness. He wonders if he has gone insane. He wonders what will happen if he takes one more punch. He wonders if his already swollen, bulging eyes will explode. All he needs to do to test this hypothesis is to lean into a left hook by Sanchez. Gómez leans into a left hook by Sanchez and he feels the explosion, a sensation of light fragmenting and then sudden darkness. He feels strangely vindicated, even though he knows he has made a serious mistake. Then he feels the sensation of his eyeball jelly oozing out over his bruised, bony sockets, trickling down his cheeks, but he is not altogether sure what he is feeling. (Later, during an interview with a Mexican reporter, he admits that he was having some difficulty distinguishing the eyeball jelly from the blood.) Herminio and Emilio are stunned. From the television one can clearly hear the chanting Mexican fans at ringside. They are shouting '¡Olé! ¡Olé!, ¡Olé!, ¡Olé!' with every volley of punches. Isidora has convinced herself that the only just punishment for her sin is to be deprived of her beloved. How she came to this conclusion she cannot say. It is a feeling more than a rational thought, a physical sensation like a soft caress that turns into a snapping of a slender neck. She does not even consider what life without Oscar will look like if in fact this is the punishment the gods decree. She only hopes she is mistaken. But nothing is what it appears to be. Gómez is sent to the canvass by a terrific Sanchez smash. Never mind that Gómez had no idea what was coming because he was virtually blind. Still, champion that he is (was), he beats the count, but the referee steps in and the fight is over. A new legend is born in Mexico. A boxer has become a bullfighter. It is a fight for the ages, the history books, the newspapers, the tabloids. This is the price we pay for our human folly, our frailty which is the by-product of countless centuries of evolution. By any other name, the robust violence we are witnessing is what we call the psychedelic transmogrification of our immortal soul. Isidora no longer remembers what the rollicking laughter of her beloved sounds like. But neither does she remember the hissing insistence of his despair these last few months, these last few days and hours, like the hissing, leaky-balloon sound of the Earth's atmosphere escaping through a hole in the ozone layer. Instead she hears the sweet invigorating cry of the Torocoro with its mantle like a cape the color of the ocean at sunset. She has not heard the lingering cry of the Torocoro in many years, though to be honest, she has never heard the sound of that mythic bird except through the inverted funnel of her imagination spitting out its contents like so many gentle, airy, poofy kisses that quickly evaporate in the ether some fifty miles up.

-128-

From the notes of a failed linguist, Nicholas Ruedenberg, a doctoral candidate at the University of Greifswald, Greifswald, Germany, discovered among some papers stuffed into an empty flower pot in his tiny fourth-floor apartment shortly after his suicide in 2026:

'Some stories end. Others do not. But it is next to impossible to distinguish one kind from the other. But what is a story to begin with? And once we decide upon a definition, who will do the dishes? Is the random sequence of narrative events a cohesive story? No, story is not sequence. That is an illusion, the gift of the magi, the darkness that follows a swarm of phantasmagorical taxis. But what if these sequences are logical, predictable, causal sequences? That is more of the same, a rabbit hole. Straight lines or a frenetic zig-zagging motion, it makes no difference. We plant a seed in the ground and we water the seed and care for it, and if there is plenty of sunlight and warm temperatures and we have planted the seed in good ground to begin with, then the seed begins to grow, and from this we infer causality. But we recognize that our understanding is a surface understanding, so we say to ourselves, perhaps we have not gone deeply enough. We set up expeditions to plumb the depths. But sadly, no matter how deep we go (up to our armpits, wallowing in it, up to our necks in it, then our eyes disappearing, our bodies subsumed entirely by the seething darkness below, our minds consumed by an irrational need to control the chaos of the world, our souls vanquished by seditious dichotomies, not even a net can save us now), we can always dig a little deeper. This is the lesson of quantum mechanics, which is also the lesson of philosophy, which is also the lesson of religion, of chemistry, of biology, of sociology, of history. It is the lesson of every snobology. So sequence, and causality, which is the wicked stepbrother of sequence (or at least a deranged cousin), are merely anachronistic structures we superimpose upon the bizarre, incomprehensible images that bombard us daily in the vain hope that we might extract some meaning. We will invent a sequential, causal structure in order to sustain this hope. But meaning does not exist. Beginnings exist and they are replaced by new beginnings. It is the same with endings. But there is no meaning to connect the two, and so any meaning we invent will sooner or later, inevitably, just slide off the page. So what then is a story? I must accept the fact that I can never know. All I can know is that one door opens and another door closes. The labyrinth extends beyond the limits of my imagination. I am unable to process the riddle of the mandala. I cannot appreciate the dizzying heights of the Yggdrasil, the tree of death and life, which towers above all creation. Even the first branch is beyond my reach. Some stories end. Others do not. And so it goes.'

-129-

From the personal field notes of Miami Police homicide detective Àngel Andreu, which served as the basis for a formal report concerning the death of Oscar Garcia Raimundi that was filed on September 14, 1981, (which was, incidentally, only twenty-four days after Wilfredo Gómez lost the junior featherweight title to Salvador Sanchez):

"**August 23, 1981. Sunday, 9 AM**. I am at my desk. Why the hell I came in on a Sunday morning to tackle that mound of paperwork I can't really say. I mean I know why well enough. Let's just say the wife wanted to go to church and I didn't. Fair enough. Let me just add to that: fuck paperwork! Better delete that last part. So a fucking call comes in. 9 AM on a Sunday morning for Christ's sake! Why couldn't this call have come in say five hours earlier before the Saturday night homicide boys went over to Julian's for a bite to eat. Christ! So a call comes in. There's a dead body in Coral Gables, somewhere along US 1. So what I say, there's probably lots of dead bodies in Coral Gables along US 1. The guy on the other end just blows past my little joke like I didn't say a word. Some kids found it at a playground in Washington Park, he says, and I'm thinking Washington Park isn't anywhere close to our jurisdiction, but the guy on the other end keeps blabbing. The officers who first arrived on the scene said from what they could tell the dead guy was from Allapattah. Allapattah is in our jurisdiction, which is why they called it in. The guy on the other end says the officers on the scene will wait till I get there, assuming I don't take too long, it is Sunday morning, after all, they probably have wives waiting for them. Then he hangs up. Yeah, it's fucking Sunday morning, all right, wives or no wives. So I have to go down to Coral Gables. Which actually doesn't bother me, to tell you the truth. Then I see Ramirez. Ramirez is straight out of a television crime show. He's the light-skinned Latino that pushes the boundaries of diversity but doesn't alarm the mostly white audience. He is walking in as I am heading out the door and I say you're coming with me pinhead, and he gives me a blank look like he always does, but he knows I'm just messing with him. How the fuck they got the number to my fucking desk in the first place I'll never know. Fucking fate, I guess."

"**August 23, 1981. Sunday, 11:30 AM**. It took us a while to get down to Washington Park. It's a pretty nice little park for the kiddies I have to admit. A little bit of green space, a place to toss a ball around. Not the kind of place you'd expect to find a dead body. But what the fuck. Dead bodies are everywhere. That's a simple fact of life. So we got there late. There wasn't anybody in the park when we pulled up, but there was a Coral Gables squad car parked six inches from the curb near the Northwest side of the park. It was a very precise parking job. A very Coral Gables kind of parking job. Two officers got out as we pulled up. I pulled in right behind the squad car. My car is a 1965 dark blue Pontiac Bonneville two-door hard top coup. I mean it really stands out. But it's also a state-of-the-art cruiser with a Motorola two-way and an engine that really kicks. Needless to say, the Coral Gables guys knew who it was right away. They were pissed. Wives or no wives, they were pissed, but what the fuck. Me and Ramirez stopped for a bite to eat on the way down. I mean who said we had to starve. Screw that. So the two officers got out and we chatted a while and one of them gave me a clipboard with the log of everyone who had visited the crime scene: the two officers who greeted us, two more who stopped by at 10:15 just to have a quick look, an inspector named H. Miller, and right there I'm thinking are you kidding me, 'H. Miller?' why not Henry Miller or Hank Miller or Harry or Hamilton or Hamoelet or Harlan or Henley or Hermes or Hariman or Huldiberaht or Herwin or Heyward or Hal or Harpo or Hadrian or Hagrid or Hiram or Haji or Hieronymous or Hervé or Hamon or Hanes or Hany or Hardie or Howard or Hrorek or Herrick or Hewitt or Horatio or Hitch or Hobbard or Hubbard or Hulbard or Humphrey, or even Heinrich, for Christ's sake, all randomly assigned monikers to be sure, providing no clue to the essential character of the named, but not the pitiful, purposely vague and therefore morally bankrupt signature of 'H. Miller,' who probably didn't even get out of his car because then the eyes of the world would have been upon him (that blustery, fat Aryan fuck) and he would have felt unavoidably (inevitably?) duty-bound to investigate (though it probably would have been a sham of an investigation, you can bet your ass), in which case they never would have called me, so he sent a lieutenant to do a quick walk-thru to see if there was any way to pawn off the dead body, some pasty-faced, snot-nosed lieutenant most likely, and so the last guy listed in the log (until me and Ramirez showed up) was that very same pasty-faced lieutenant picked by the invisible H. Miller. There were a few preliminary comments by the lieutenant. His name was Lieutenant Beckert (another German name). I read over the comments but it was like reading a fifth grader's seven-sentence summary of the *Movie of the Week*. Fucking fifth grade handwriting too. Pretty much illegible. I wrote my name in the log and asked him if he wanted the clipboard back. He said no. I signed a receipt. More fucking paperwork, every step of the way. He seemed satisfied. He seemed like he couldn't wait to hand off this mess to someone else and get back to his regular Coral Gables police-type duties. I asked him if he was Beckert and he said he wasn't. He said it was Beckert who had figured out the dead guy was from Allapattah. 'How did he manage that?' I asked him. 'It was easy,' he said. 'He looked in the guy's wallet and there was a card that said La Campana, some nightclub up there, and the guy's name.' 'And that was enough for Beckert.' 'Sure.' 'And the guy's driver's license?' 'There wasn't any. Just the card with the guy's name on it.' 'But that was enough for Beckert.' 'Sure.' 'Right, and the crime scene?' 'Over there.' The one guy was pointing past a clump of crepe myrtles. You could see some playground equipment through the branches. You could see they had tried to surround the playground equipment with yellow tape to keep the neighborhood away. They had tied one end to the crepe myrtles and then looped it around the playground and then back to the beginning. They were trying to close the loop, as they say. But it was a pretty sloppy job. There was a bit of a breeze blowing through the crepe myrtles and it was staring to drizzle, just like it's been doing on and off for what has it been, two weeks now, two weeks of fucking rain and no end in sight. Anyway, the yellow tape was flapping like mad. I mean you knew it wasn't going to keep anybody out for too much longer. Then the one guy started up again, but he wasn't looking at me. He was looking vaguely at the crepe myrtles. 'Beckert didn't call the coroner,' he said, 'you know how those guys are,' and he gave me one of those polite, mealy-mouthed German beerhouse smiles like I knew the same exact guys he knew. 'He figured you'd want to have a look around first.' 'Sure, thanks.' The one guy nodded but the other didn't even look at me (still pissed, I guess). Then they got in their squad car and drove away."

"**August 23, 1981. Sunday, 11:45 AM**. Fuck this rain. I love Miami and I love thunderstorms and I love walking on the beach in the rain and all that romantic shit. But two fucking weeks is more than enough."

"**August 23, 1981. Sunday, 11:46 AM**. We did a walk-thru of the crime scene. The playground equipment is a sort of jungle gym rocket ship with a rocket tower for climbing at one end and a slide at the other. The dead body was hanging head down from the rocket ship tower. The feet were tied to the jungle gym bars. The arms were pulled out to either side and tied to a fucking two-by-four laid across the guy's back. Like a gleaming white inverted crucifix. From a distance it looked like the dead guy was smiling, an inverted smile to be sure. The two-by-four was tied to the lower posts of the rocket tower, I guess so the guy wouldn't flap around or dangle. The guy's hands were nailed to the wood. I mean the killers had actually hammered a nail through the middle of each of the guy's palms. Maybe not a hammer. Maybe they used a nail gun. Something with a little kick to it. They had it in for this guy whatever they used. Cause of death uncertain. Once we got a little closer we could see quite clearly that the guy's throat had been cut, I mean ear to ear, a very clean, precise cut, very methodical, a very professional job. Still, no matter how clean a cut like that, it's a hell of a painful way to go. But no idea if this was the cause of death or not. Could all be for show. Like hanging the body upside down. Have to wait for the coroner to be sure. I said to Ramirez the guy looked like a dead shark or something pulled out of the sea. He laughed and said the killers were obviously playing around with Catholic symbolism. 'You mean like Christ on the cross,' I asked him. 'No,' he said. 'I mean like Peter the Apostle. He was crucified upside down by the Romans. Just like this guy here.' 'What the fuck does that mean,' I asked him. 'I have no idea,' Ramirez said. 'It just looks pretty symbolic the way he's laid out. But it's pretty fucked up symbolism all the same.' I didn't know what to say about that. Ramirez can get pretty hyped up by all that Catholic mumbo-jumbo. But the dead guy did look like a shining example of everything that's wrong with religion. He was wearing a white linen jacket but no shirt. The jacket looked like it was about to fall off but it had got stuck around the guy's armpits and then the corners had folded themselves around the back of the guy's neck. It sort of looked like wings that had been partially sliced away. The dead guy was also wearing white slacks tucked into his socks, but no shoes. At least the killers weren't perverted, I mean they were clearly sick fucks with a sick sense of humor, but at least they left the guy the dignity of his pants. He was also wearing a white Panama hat, which we couldn't figure out why gravity didn't do its thing at first, but then we saw that the hat was nailed to the top of the guy's head, right through the cranium. It seems obvious now they were using a nail gun. The white slacks were stained with blood and the rain, but strangely there were no blood stains on the jacket. No visible signs of blood on the playground or the rocket tower. Which means maybe they killed the guy somewhere else. Then again, the whole crime scene had been scrubbed pretty clean by the rain. And there was no telling how long the body had been there. That was another item for the coroner. I checked the inside pocket of the guy's jacket for his wallet and there it was. No driver's license, just like that pasty-faced Lieutenant Beckert had said. And there was the card with his name, Oscar Garcia Raimundi, the poor dumb fuck, and underneath the name was the name of the nightclub, La Campana in glittery letters, and then a raised line in italics that said from 'dusk till dawn,' and beneath that the address: 25½ La Campana Avenue, Allapattah, Miami, Florida. It was a very fancy card. I mean they don't get much fancier."

"**August 23, 1981. Sunday, 12:15 PM.** Took pictures of everything noted above. I hate taking photographs almost as much as I hate fucking paperwork. They give me a state-of-the-art unmarked police cruiser for cruising the streets, but they give me a piece of shit Minolta for taking pictures. Rain started to come down harder."

"**August 23, 1981. Sunday, 1:30 PM.** The guys from the evidence collection unit pull up. Crime Scene Investigators Randy Graeff, just out of college (The University of Miami, what else), Martin Lorenz, who's been doing this for more years than he cares to count, and sweet little Natalie Henderson, who takes an awful lot of shit from everybody, but you should see her strut around in a skirt. And she's always wearing skirts. Man, she knows what she's doing, you better believe that. Better delete that last part. Anyway, right behind Natalie and her two bookends comes the coroner, Leon Vallejo, along with Bob Nordyke, the Chief Death Investigator, and Andrew Havlik, whose area is forensics, or maybe pathology, or maybe both. We've been waiting in my car for over an hour. We give everyone a quick briefing and then they go to work. They don't say what kept them and we don't ask. Not even Leon comes clean, but then it was probably his fault to begin with. Every Sunday Leon takes his family to the brunch at Denny's. Everybody had probably been waiting on Leon to get back from brunch. So anyway, the rain has sort of halted by now. It's still pretty cloudy so you know it's going to start up again. But we're good for a while. Ramirez says it's God's doing, meaning the break in the weather, so Leon can get the body into his van before any more of the dead man's dignity is washed away. I say what the fuck are you talking about Ramirez, but he just laughs. Ramirez sweats religion. I mean you can smell it pouring out of his pores. Like gardenias or something. I don't know. Maybe the way he smells has something to with what he eats. Or maybe he's always running late so instead of showering he douses himself with his wife's perfume. Maybe that's why he's always running out to the mall to pick up a bottle of Chanel or Yves Saint Laurent. I don't know. But it smells like religion to me. Anyway, we talk with Graeff and Lorenz for a while over by the playground equipment, but we're really trying to catch a glimpse of Natalie. She's climbing up into the rocket tower but you can't really see her because of the dead guy. She's looking for clues. But every once in a while you catch the curve of her hip and your jaw just drops. Graeff is saying the way the killers laid out the body clearly indicates they are at the very least sociopaths with little regard for social mores or human dignity. Lorenz says you mean psychopaths like in *Psycho*? Graeff shakes his head and says he doesn't think so, though there is certainly an elemental psychopathology in the explicit symbolic messaging of the crime scene. It is very theatrical. It is almost as if they were presenting a short play in which the brutality of murderous violence is not shown, only its aftermath, much like the great German movie director Fritz Lang did in his 1931 thriller, *M*, but without the sexually deviant overtones of a child predator. Yes, says Lorenz, but what does all that mean? Graeff laughs and says it means that one could argue that these killers are borderline psychopaths because on one level this murder seems to be a textbook example of their need to exercise their creative imagination in a vain attempt to control their environment without any concern for who gets in their way, though one could argue just as persuasively that they are mere sociopaths (which is to say they are not yet robots without any compassion for the human condition), whose murderous impulses are in reality unconscious, conditioned responses to certain as yet undetermined social stimuli, what in the vernacular we would call triggers, which made this particular murder necessary, even inevitable. What kind of triggers says Lorenz. Graeff says it could be anything, an unwillingness to go along to get along, a crooked smile, a disagreement over religion, which would certainly make sense given the obvious anti-Catholic symbolism, but it could be anything. Then Graeff's eyes light up. Hey Ramirez, what was the dead man's name? Ramirez blinks stupidly for a moment, like he is trying to wake up, like his eyes are tiny mouths gasping for breath. He was probably lost in that fantastic labyrinth of intellectual gobbledygook that Graeff has been leading us through. Then Ramirez shakes free of the cobwebs and says Raimundi, Oscar Garcia Raimundi. Graeff says, there you have it, Raimundi, a name which could mean the Light of the World, though it could mean many other things as well. But suppose this Raimundi was an associate of our killers, a man who held some position of authority over them, a man who was seen by others as a light in the darkness, so to speak, and then suppose his death was the result of some power struggle, as is the case with many of the deaths in gangsterland, and suppose our killers are slightly psychotic, or even robustly psychotic, so they slit his throat and nail him to a cross and hang him upside down to make some explicit comment about their role in assuming the mantle of the dead man's power, they have extinguished the old Light of the World and in the process have become the New Light, a new order for a new day. Everyone who knew the dead man and who knew the killers would realize that a new order had been created. Yes, it could very well be something like that. Lorenz doesn't know what to say. Neither do I for that matter. Graeff is smiling like the fucking cat that ate the canary. He's into all that psychological crap. Lorenz says okay, sure, but that really only tells me why they hung him upside down. It doesn't come close to revealing their motives for killing him in the first place, other than some vague insinuations about this mythical power struggle. What exactly was the trigger? Why did they kill him?

Graeff doesn't say anything for a moment. His face begins to contort in odd ways, as if he is experiencing a sudden change in air pressure. Then he says he doesn't know for sure and bites his lower lip. It's like a forced confession. Like Lorenz is a priest from the days of the Inquisition flaying the skin off Graeff to get at the truth. Graeff's face has taken on a sour look. Apparently he doesn't like confessing. I get it. No one likes to appear weak, especially in front of their peers. Maybe that's the reason why the killers killed Oscar Garcia Raimundi. They didn't want to appear weak in front of their peers. Maybe it was as simple as that. But I don't say a word. Then sweet Natalie flashes her hips and the conversation is over."

"**August 23, 1981. Sunday, 4:30 PM**. Everybody's pretty much finished. Leon left with the body at 3:45. Nordyke and Havlik followed in their car. Natalie and Graeff and Lorenz left at 4:00. Me and Ramirez are sitting in my car. It's rained on and off the whole afternoon, but after a while rain is easy to forget. Leon won't be finished with the preliminary autopsy report until maybe Tuesday, and even then it'll be inconclusive until we get the results of the tox screen. The others probably won't be ready with their reports till Wednesday. But me and Ramirez already have three leads to track down. The first is the nightclub up in Allapattah. The second is a newspaper article from *The Miami News* that was folded up and stuffed in a slot in the dead guy's wallet. The article is about an offshore speedboat race that is going to be held up at Sunny Isles over Labor Day weekend. The article says the race is not sanctioned by the American Powerboat Association, so the racers won't get any points like they could with sanctioned races. But the event organizers are expecting over a hundred racers and over a thousand spectators. The article goes on to say that the primary purpose of the race is to showcase the speed and versatility of the new cigarette boats that are taking the speedboat world by storm. Miami resident Pepe Nuñez, a self-proclaimed speed freak, won the Pelican Harbor Trophy Race in 1980 with one of these cigarette boats, a boat that had been manufactured by Pantera, a company which Nunez had founded with his wife Linda in 1974. Another South Florida resident, Joey Ippolito, won the Bacardi Race this past May with a cigarette boat manufactured by Wellcraft Boats of Sarasota, Florida. The writer of the article can not praise these boats enough. The third clue is a receipt from The Miami Skyways Motel out on Le Jeune Road. The receipt was for Friday night, a one-night stay. It's a great place right across from the airport. Nice restaurant. Swimming pool. Striped yellow and white umbrellas to keep the sun off your back. A comfortable lounge with anything you'd want to drink. I met the owner four years ago, Manny Melamed, an eccentric sonofabitch, but a nice guy. Always smiling. Really dark hair, and a wild looking Fu Manchu moustache. I don't know about his taste in clothes, though. I mean when we first met he was wearing a crazy, artsy silk shirt with these weird geometric patterns, dark blue rectangles, aquamarine circles or triangles or something, and a light blue paisley jacket and bright sky-blue slacks. I mean the whole outfit hurt your eyes. I met him at a downtown luncheon for something or other and he invited me to come out to the lounge to hear Sonny Rollins play his saxophone. He must have seen the blank look on my face because he started to laugh. I'm not really into the music scene. I don't even listen to the radio. And I sure as hell had no idea who Sonny Rollins even was. But he wasn't half bad. So anyway, me and Ramirez are heading up to the Miami Skyways Motel to see if anybody remembers our dead guy. It's only twenty minutes away. Head straight north. I mean it's an absolutely straight shot, no turns or deviations of any kind. Now all we gotta do is figure out what connects these two dots on the map other than SW 42nd Avenue."

"**August 23, 1981. Sunday, 6:35 PM**. We drove into the parking lot of the Miami Skyways Motel. The rain had picked up again, a steady, annoying, roaring, smoky downpour, but you could still see the orangeish neon lettering of the motel flickering. We parked directly beneath the overhanging marquee sign and headed straight into the lobby. Manny Melamed was nowhere around, so we talked to the night manager. His name was Charlie Perrine. A nice enough guy. Balding, a slightly distracted look that not even the wire-rim glasses he was wearing is able to correct. Charlie said he remembered the guy with the Panama hat because nobody wears Panama hats anymore. 'Yeah,' Charlie said. 'And he was wearing a white linen suit that had clearly seen better days.' Charlie said the guy asked for room 227 but he didn't say why. No visitors. No phone calls. He paid in cash. He went out for about an hour or so and came back with some Carvel ice cream. 'I remember because he came into the lobby just as the Gómez/Sanchez fight was about to start, and I asked him if he wanted to watch with us, I mean there were a dozen of us, maybe more, crowded around that the television over there.' (At which point Charlie pointed to a brand-new wall-mounted color television on the other side of the lobby with a couple of sofas and chairs scattered around and a coffee table with magazines and some potted ferns for atmosphere.) 'But he said he wasn't interested in the Gómez/Sanchez fight, he wanted ice cream, he wanted to know if there was a Carvel ice cream store anywhere around. I told him the nearest one I knew was down on Kendall, which is about twenty minutes away, and he said good enough and headed out the door. To be honest I don't remember just when he came back or if he came back at all. After the fight was over I had some work to do back in my office.' Charlie showed us the register where the guy had signed. Oscar Garcia Raimundi, a very flamboyant signature, but for his home address he had put down Havana, Cuba, which we thought must have been a fucking joke. 'Don't you check these things?' Ramirez asked Charlie, but Charlie only smiled a sheepish smile and shrugged. Then he took us down the hall just off the lobby and up a small flight of stairs and let us into room 227. He said there hadn't been anyone else in the room since the Panama hat, and then he left us to go back to the lobby. I don't know what we were expecting. I mean the room had already been scrubbed clean. I mean it looked like any other airport hotel room waiting for a few out-of-town suckers. Ramirez checked under the bed and in the bathroom and in the closet. I went over to the window and pulled back the drapes. Poolside. A balcony with a wooden railing. A view of the pool and the rain pelting the pool with a merciless rage and half a dozen pool umbrellas folded up and the tables they normally protected from the sun getting hammered by the wrath of God. Then Ramirez motioned for me to have a look at the room safe. A typical hotel room safe on the floor of a typical hotel closet next to an ironing board. A safe that anyone could crack with a screwdriver. 'Look at this,' Ramirez said. He pulled out a small satchel made of imitation leather and set it squarely on the small table next to the bed. He undid the buckle, slowly, as if to heighten the importance of his discovery. I remember thinking that if this had been a fucking movie there would have been suspense music in the background and I almost broke up laughing. Then just like that we were staring at ten-thousand smackers neatly stacked inside this cheaply made brown satchel that looked like it had been purchased at K-Mart. I remember thinking what the fuck was this guy doing with ten-thousand dollars in cash, and then I was thinking why was the money still here? 'Drug money?' Ramirez said. 'Maybe,' I said. 'Maybe it was a drug deal gone bad and that's why he's dead?' said Ramirez. 'Maybe,' I said. 'But if it was about drugs, then why is the money still here? Why would the killers leave that much cash behind? Didn't they think to check the safe? Were they fucking idiots? It doesn't make any sense.' Ramirez stuffed the cash back into the satchel and then we headed back to my car. We moved uneasily back down the steps and then down the hall. There was nobody in the lobby when we got there. The television was still on but there was no sound coming out of it, which was really odd. I had the feeling like we were either walking into a trap or we had just narrowly escaped. We headed out past the strange, blueish glow of the strangely muted television as if suspicious eyes and ears were following our every move."

"**August 24, 1981. Monday, 11:00 AM.** The sun has come out and the rain has stopped. It is almost surreal. I keep looking up at the sky expecting it to cloud over all of a sudden. Ramirez says I shouldn't tempt fate, and by fate he means God. We head out to the Carvel ice cream store on Kendall and speak to the manager. The store looks brand-spanking new, as close to perfection as an ice cream store can get, all white counters and dazzling chrome and a white-tiled floor. The manager's name is Ralph Hernandez. Ralph is not happy to see us. His eyes are dancing about randomly, like bullets about to explode. He thinks our visit is about some unpaid parking tickets. He tells us he is a Vietnam vet. He bled for his country. He points out several photographs hanging on the wall behind the ice cream counter. They are all Vietnam photos. One is of a younger Ralph standing on a gunboat on some river. He is holding an M60 machine gun. Sunlight is glinting off the gun barrel. There are two other guys in the photo, one on either side of Ralph. One of them is holding a grenade launcher. They are all dressed in green fatigues with floppy green hats like fisherman's hats and smiling like idiots. The date on the photo is August 1967. Ralph says the guy holding the grenade launcher was a cracker named Sam Tennyson from Birmingham, Alabama. He bought it one month after this photo was taken. An ambush on the Ba Rai River southwest of Saigon. A hellacious gunfight. The official body count was three American sailors and seventy-seven wounded. But Ralph says he knows for a fact that over twenty guys got killed on the Ba Rai River that day. The other guy's name is Danny Madsen. He and Ralph still keep in touch even though Danny lives in Houston. They almost never talk about Vietnam, so as the years drift by they have less and less in common. We assure Ralph we could care less about minor infractions of the traffic code. We tell him we are trying to track down the whereabouts of a person of interest and that we had information that he bought some ice cream at this particular location this past Friday night at some point between the hours of seven and nine in the evening. Ralph is visibly relieved. He gives us each an ice cream cone. He says he was not at the store Friday evening, but his assistant manager, Eric Valera, he was working. Eric will be in from four till ten."

"**August 24, 1981. Monday, 2:40 PM**. Finally, we pull up to La Campana. We only found it by accident. La Campana Avenue doesn't exist on any map we looked at. I called Dispatch for a little assistance, but Stacey Guglioha, who has been sitting at that desk since before I was born, got all crazy bent out of shape. I'm probably the only bozo in the whole department who bothers Stacey for directions because he's too lazy to ask a gas station attendant or a bus driver. Why she tolerates my deviant departures from protocol I haven't a clue. She could care less that I'm a detective. 'You better get your lazy derrière off this channel, mister' she said. But I didn't, of course. I started arguing with her. We were parked at a Chevron on NW 36th Street maybe three blocks from the high school. I was telling Stacey that I was looking at the guy's business card and there it was plain as daylight, 25½ La Campana Avenue. I guess I was pretty vocal about it. But she was pretty damn feisty herself the way she was shouting back at me, saying there was no such avenue, and she should know, she had the comprehensive list. Stacey likes to say she is all fire and that fire is the source of all beauty. So I was yelling at her and she was yelling at me, and then she said 'Stand by!' and then just like that, whammo, nothing but static. Beautiful Stacey. Anyway, I was just about to track down a gas station attendant when it got really quiet all of a sudden, and it wasn't just the radio. I mean it was a strange, kind of eerie but absolutely peaceful silence. It was like I had died or something. I mean I couldn't hear a thing, not the birds, not the traffic whizzing by, not a siren, not the sound of a distant train. I hung up the mike and looked over at Ramirez but he was dozing. Then an old but agile voice leaned in through the window of my car and grabbed me by the collar. Now under normal circumstances I would have been startled. I'd have been out the car door and on the pavement in an instant. I might even have pulled my gun. But this did not happen. For one thing, the voice was a peaceful voice, in keeping with the mood that had descended all around. I guess that's the only thing, the only reason. The voice exerted a calming influence on me. 'Are you looking for La Campana, the nightclub?' the voice asked. 'Yeah, yeah, that's the place,' I said. 'It's a few blocks that way and hang a right,' said the voice, and I followed the voice to the arm that was attached to it and nodded with unconvincing enthusiasm. 'You'll be there in a jiff,' said the voice. 'Thanks,' I said. And then the voice moved away from the car and became an old vagabond, one of those retiree-types who walk around with a metal detector in search of lost keys and old coins and bottle caps. I watched him as he crossed to the other side of the street, where he boarded the J bus heading west, and then the bus disappeared into the glare of the sun. 'Did you see that guy, Ramirez,' I asked. But Ramirez was just waking up. He laughed. 'You must have been dreaming, same as me,' he said. He hadn't seen a thing."

"**August 24, 1981. Monday, 2:45 PM**. We can hardly believe our eyes. How is it we have never heard of this pink stucco palace, this behemoth that would look more at home on a slice of beachfront than tucked away amid the grime and perpetual poverty of Allapattah? Even from the parking lot you are overwhelmed by the looming, faded elegance of the building. It is almost surreal, the impressions I am getting, strange, conflicting images, an endless parade of world class musicians, the wealthy, cultured, refined citizens of Miami in the audience, but also a vagabond collection of murderers and drug dealers and thieves and international spies, all of them cutting loose to the groove, the booze flowing freely, vast quantities of booze, a truce between opposing layers of society, at least for an evening. Ramirez stops a moment to admire the brass horse head hitching posts. I am already up the steps, but I have also stopped. I am lost in a labyrinth of idle thoughts and pointless conjecture. I am staring at the stained-glass window above the door, a sun tangled up with a moon amid a gallery of stars, and suddenly I feel as if the door in front of me is a doorway to another dimension. I am struck by the incongruity of La Campana. That it even exists at all seems to contradict everything I know about reality. Then Ramirez breaks my reverie with a hearty slap on the back, a little jovial laughter, the camaraderie of two explorers stumbling about in the dark, and we push our way inside. The lobby is dimly lit, a weak, syrupy light. The source of the light is impossible to pinpoint. Ramirez gives a low, appreciative whistle, though just what he is appreciating he doesn't say. Then we head over to the bar. The lighting in the bar is better than in the lobby. It seems impossibly bright by comparison. A steady stream of sunlight is pouring through the windows along the far wall and bouncing off the mirror that runs the length of the mahogany counter. There is a fat man behind the bar and two unsavory characters sitting at the counter, drinking shots and trading jokes with the fat man."

"**August 24, 1981. Monday, 2:52 PM.** The fat man's name is Herminio Arréllaga. He is standing at the elbow of the bar near the entrance, about twenty feet from the two unsavory characters. He says he has been tending bar here since 1979. Then he asks if we are thirsty. Ramirez smiles and lays the card of Oscar Garcia Raimundi on the mahogany counter. Ramirez asks Herminio how well he knows Oscar. Herminio picks up the card and scrutinizes it. He holds it up so it catches a beam of sunlight and then shrugs a shrug of indifference and hands it back to Ramirez. 'I know him well enough,' he says. 'But I did not know he had such a fancy looking card.' It is at this point that the two unsavory characters get up from their barstools and walk over to us. They do not seem surprised that we are there. They do not seem anxious. If anything, they seem relaxed, as if they had just received good news after a long drought. They are talking as they walk, a rapid machine-gun volley of words slicing through the air. 'So you have brought news of Oscar? We thought that's why you might be here. Where did you find him?' says the one. 'Yes, and how did you find him so quickly?' says the other. 'Was he holed up with some floozy? Or did he get stopped by some traffic cop?' says the one. 'Yeah, how did the dumb fuck give himself away?' says the other one. 'Well, serves him right whatever the circumstances. But what were we to do?' says the one. 'You're damn right, ten-thousand dollars is a lot of money,' says the other one. 'Did he confess yet?' says the one. 'I hope you guys throw away the key,' says the other. 'If he needed the money he could have asked. We would have loaned him whatever he needed,' says the one. 'Maybe my brother would have loaned him the money. But I'm not so sure I would have been so compassionate,' says the other one. 'Brother, Oscar has been with us since we opened our doors. La Campana wouldn't be La Campana without Oscar. Besides, he's family. You don't just abandon family,' says the one. 'Yes, Brother, but to steal from the hand that feeds your mouth. That is very difficult to digest. I do not think I will be able to forgive him as easily as you have,' says the other one."

"**August 24, 1981. Monday, 3:30 PM.** The two unsavory characters are Héctor and Miguel Velázquez, brothers, obviously, they might even be twins. They are not pleasant to look at. They have dark, leathery, crusted over skin, as if they were the victims of some diabolical experiment conducted by the CIA. Ramirez thinks they are ex-military. He thinks they took part in covert operations in Nicaragua, Chile, or Bolivia. I'm not sure where he comes up with this stuff. They are not bad fellows once you get to talking with them. And yet there is something about them that strikes me as off-center. I can't quite put my finger on it yet. But I get the feeling that Héctor is one step away from being locked away in an insane asylum. He is cheerful enough on the surface, happy-go-lucky, robustly happy, but just beneath this thin veneer of ultra-normalcy there lurks a menacing, uncontrollable rage. This is the sense I get. I think if it weren't for Miguel, Héctor would have died in a hail of bullets long ago. So anyway, we talked for about half an hour. Héctor said Oscar managed the club for them. They had bought the property in 1978 from a man named Luis Sarabia, a Cuban exile. Oscar was already working at the club as the manager so they kept him on. Oscar was also a Cuban exile, but he had entered the country illegally. He had an appetite for fine dining, pretty women, diamond rings, and fast cars, the lifestyle of a gangster. He was unrestrained in his appetite, so he was always in debt, always in need of money. Okay, so much for background. I asked them when they had last seen Oscar. 'About three o'clock Friday afternoon,' Miguel said. 'We wanted to speak to him about Friday night.' 'What about it,' I said. 'Normally you can't get a seat at La Campana on a Friday or Saturday night,' said Miguel. 'I mean we really pack them in. But for some reason we never do very well when there's a boxing match on television. So there was no show on Friday night. We cancelled it as soon as we knew about the Gómez fight. I don't remember how we found out. I guess that was about three months ago. We were going to keep the bar open anyway, just in case someone from the neighborhood wanted something to drink. But we told Oscar he could close up shop whenever he felt like it. I mean there's no sense in staying open if nobody comes in.' 'Okay, okay, so what were you doing Friday evening?' I said. 'Well, we rarely get away on the weekends, so we decided to head down to Little Havana,' said Miguel. 'A friend of ours just opened a small pizzeria on West Flagler. It's called Eduardo's.' I nodded. I had heard of the place. It had only been open a few months, but the guy made really good pizza, even *The Miami Herald* said so. 'Where'd you go after Eduardo's?' I said. 'We came back here,' Miguel said. 'We got back about midnight. I went into the bar and started chatting with Herminio. My brother went upstairs to the office. I asked Herminio where Oscar was and he said Oscar had left a few minutes before seven. Herminio didn't know why. Then my brother came running into the bar. He said somebody had broken into the petty cash strong box and cleaned us out. Ten-thousand dollars. We called the police and reported the stolen money. The next morning an Officer Andersen showed up and took our statement. He didn't look too happy. He had been driving around for thirty minutes trying to find this hellhole. That's the exact word he used. Hellhole.' I looked at Ramirez and we both shook our heads. We both knew Andersen. He's a pussy and a tight-assed prick rolled into one. 'By that point we were fairly certain that Oscar was the culprit,' Miguel said. That's pretty much all the Velázquez brothers had to say. We didn't tell them that Oscar was dead. I guess we were being cagey. We asked them if they had a photo of Oscar. We said we didn't like to use mug shots for the newspaper guys unless we had to. Miguel pulled out a photo of Oscar and some red-headed floozy like he was just waiting for us to ask. The photo was taken in front of La Campana on a summer evening with the neon lights flashing. It was a publicity shot. Miguel handed me the photo and said we could keep it. We told them to stay in town for the next week or so, just in case we had any more questions. Héctor asked us if we had found the money. We told him yes, but the money had been impounded as evidence, this was standard procedure, but they'd get it back once the investigation had been concluded, but that wouldn't be too long, this was a fairly routine case. We told them the same tired shit we tell everyone else. I mean the words just came pouring out like we had no control whatsoever. We were like two degenerate and prodigal parrots spewing out this fucking river of sewage."

"**August 24, 1981. Monday, 6:30 PM.** We head back out to the Carvel ice cream store on Kendall to speak to the assistant manager, Eric Valera, to see if he remembers seeing our dead guy buying an ice cream cone. Eric Valera is a trip. I mean he's a fucking fruitcake of a kid and he looks like a stoner to boot. Ramirez thinks I should cut him a break, that he's just a wide-eyed dopey kid like any kid. Okay, maybe so. But it's hard to believe he's the assistant manager of anything, and after the story he tells me and Ramirez, even Ramirez agrees. The kid says he remembers 'the suspect in question.' That's just how he puts it. Like he's reading lines for a goddamn TV show. He says he remembers the guy because he never before met anyone wearing a white linen suit and a white Panama hat. Okay, so I have to give him that. He says the guy ordered an ice cream cake and slapped a hundred-dollar bill on the counter and said Valera could keep the change, and then he asked that Valera bring it out to his car. Not one of the ice cream girls. The guy wanted Valera, which the kid admits was kind of weird. The kid says he was thinking maybe the guy wanted a blow job or something right there in the parking lot, but he didn't wink or smile or show any emotion whatsoever when he made the request, so then the kid figured maybe his first impression had been wrong. So the kid brings the ice cream cake out to the car. He says it was a purple color kind of car, a really old model. He says with the way the lights from the ice cream store were shining on the hood it was sort of glowing like some kind of purple star. He says the guy was sitting behind the wheel just staring out through the windshield like a zombie or a robot or something. Then he says when he gave the guy the cake, he realized there were two figures sitting in the back seat. 'I couldn't see them very well from the glare of the lights,' he says, 'but I could see well enough.' But then his story loses all touch with reality. He gets very quiet and starts speaking in a soft, feathery, whispery voice. 'You're going to think I'm crazy when I say this. But the two creatures in the back seat weren't even human. They were two enormous dark shapes sucking up all the light, like something out of *The Twilight Zone*. That's why I couldn't really see them. I'm pretty sure they were demonic angels with their wings folded over, and they were speaking in this strange, screechy, whistling, clicking language, like dolphins or porpoises or killer whales. All I can say is I was shitting in my pants and I couldn't get away from the car fast enough. I ran back inside and looked back to see if they were coming after me, but they didn't get out of the car. Then the guy you're looking for drove away. But here's the really strange part. The two demons weren't there anymore. I mean I could see clearly at that point into the back seat and the back seat was empty. I don't know, man, I was pretty weirded out. But I wouldn't hold my breath waiting on that guy to show up. I'm pretty sure those two creatures had their hooks into him pretty good. They probably sucked out his brain or something.' That's what the kid told us. Eric Valera. His eyes were bulging with every ludicrous word, like tiny supernovas about to burst. But you could tell he was dead serious. He was sincere. I thought Ramirez was about to bust a gut. What a fucking load of crap."

"**August 24, 1981. Monday, 9:30 PM.** Some home-brew kind of café on 8th Street in Little Havana. I don't even know how we got here. Ramirez says they serve pretty good food, and anything you want to drink. So that's where we are. Ramirez orders some spicy beef hash and fried potatoes and a bottle of beer and I order the same. Our waitress is pretty sexy. She's wearing a light breezy chiffon skirt, and when she walks by you can see the cheeks of her brown ass wiggling to beat the band. She's flaunting the kind of ass you just want to reach out and grab. It's still pretty crowded for a Monday evening. The beers come first. We probably have three or four before the food comes. Then we begin to eat, and in between bites we start talking about Eric Valera. Ramirez agrees that the kid is stark raving mad. He agrees that it's going to be next to impossible to sift through what actually happened when our dead friend, Oscar Garcia Raimundi, headed off in search of an ice cream cone and what the kid at the ice cream store remembers. But then Ramirez says the oddest thing. He says we only see the madness of Eric Valera from our own perspective. Yes, it seems to be as debilitating and profound as the madness of any inmate in any asylum. Then again, not everything is what it seems to be. I try to get my two cents in. I try to tell Ramirez he's full of shit. But his voice just rolls over mine. He asks me if I know what day it is. I tell him of course I know what day it is. I'm not that drunk, not yet. But Ramirez only laughs, as if I've already given him the wrong answer. He asks me if I know the significance of this date, the 24th of August. I tell him I could give two shits about the significance of the date, but he ignores my vitriolic response. He says August 24th is the day when that great literay madman don Quixote enters the cave of Montesino, falls into a dream-like trance, and comes face to face with the dark secret that caused his madness in the first place. You mean the guy in the book, I say. Yes, he says. Then he says August 24th also marks the third day of Leonora Carrington's own battle with madness. I say who the hell is Leonora Carrington. He says she was an artist, a surrealist painter. I say it figures. He says in late August of 1940 she left Paris to go to Spain in an effort to escape the Nazis. She had to leave her lover behind, a German painter named Max Ernst, another surrealist. She crossed over the border on the 22nd of August. She later said she saw dead bodies everywhere. Some were hanging from the branches of trees like icicles dripping. Some were draped over rocks and the wheels of overturned vehicles like so many carelessly forgotten overcoats. Others were sticking straight up out of the ground like pins from a pin cushion, pale yellow, twisted faces, rigid in the deformity of death. By August 24th she was certifiably mad, at least the Spanish authorities thought so, so they had her committed to an asylum on that date. No wonder, I say. She sounds certifiable. But Ramirez just smiles. Do you know the writer Julio Cortázar, he says. I say I don't know him. Ramirez doesn't miss a beat. According to Cortázar, he says, August 24th is one of the three days when the earth opens up to the cosmos, to God, if you will, and in those moments it is possible to slip into another dimension or another level of consciousness. Cortázar doesn't say what the other two days are, but he is definitely on the money about the 24th of August. This is what Ramirez says. I'm just shaking my head. I don't know how to respond, and Ramirez realizes I don't know how to respond, so he stops eating his spicy hash, rinses his mouth with a little beer, and then looks me squarely in the eyes. 'What I'm trying to suggest, my unbelieving friend, is that Eric Valera may have tapped into the mind of God on this day the 24th of August, which means that everything he said was the absolute truth.' Some days there is just no way to adequately respond to Ramirez.

"**August 25, 1981. Tuesday, 10:30 AM.** I didn't get much sleep last night. I should have gone right to sleep. I was drunk enough. But I kept thinking about what Ramirez said about Eric Valera's madness. I mean for once Ramirez sounded like he actually knew what he was talking about, especially that part about the cosmos and God. Anyway, I kept thinking about what Ramirez said the whole night. Pretty damn depressing when you don't believe in God. Then at 6 AM it started raining again. Fuck that. Fuck a lot of things. I guess I'm in a sour mood. I just spent an hour with Leon Vallejo going over his preliminary autopsy report. Bob Nordyke was also there. Leon began his autopsy 10 PM Sunday evening. He worked through the night and finished about 4 AM. He's a strike while the iron's hot kind of guy. But the report doesn't really help all that much. I mean there's no smoking gun. Still, it gives a pretty good indication of what happened to poor Oscar Garcia Raimundi. To summarize Leon's findings: the dead guy was of average height (68 inches) and weight (roughly 155 lbs, hard to be precise after a guy's been dead for a couple of days). Age somewhere between 49 and 54. Brownish gray hair, slightly wavy. The eyes are wide open, brown doe eyes, like he didn't see it coming until it was too late. The pupils are 0.4 cm. The corneas are cloudy. There are ligature marks on the guy's ankles and wrists. The marks on the guy's ankles are more pronounced and show significant bruising (what Leon calls petechial hemorrhaging), as if the guy had been hung upside down. The marks on the guy's wrists are less pronounced but also show signs of bruising. So the guy was tied up before he died. Oddly, there are no defensive injuries on the forearms, which means the guy didn't put up a fight. There are patchy bluish-black discolorations (what Leon calls *post-mortem hypostasis*) on the backs of the arms and the upper back and shoulders, which suggests that the body had been hanging upside down for quite a while. The small intestine contained remnants of a partially digested semi-solid mass, so death occurred maybe five hours after Oscar had eaten his last meal. (It was not clear if this last meal contained ice cream.) Rigor mortis has already passed. The skin has already taken on a marbled appearance. Blowfly larva are present in the moist cavities of the dead body. Leon says the guy died between 10 PM Friday and midnight. Leon says the guy was killed somewhere other than the park and then his body was moved. There is a deep gash in the guy's neck. I ask Leon if they cut the guy's throat and then tipped him upside down so that his blood would drain out. Leon smiles and says he only reports facts. He says interpreting facts is my department. Good old Leon. The incision in the dead guy's neck cuts through the skin, the superficial fascia, the sternocleidomastoid muscle (both left side and right side), the carotid artery (again, both left and right sides), and the trachea. I mean it's a monstrous incision. The length of the gash is 14 cm. The width is 4 cm. The depth is 5 cm on the left side and 4 cm on the right side. It's a hell of a gash. But there is a lack of hemorrhage along the incision, which according to Leon means that the guy's throat was cut several hours after he was dead, which means that his blood had already begun to pool, so even if the killers had tipped him upside down, very little blood would have made its way to the incision point. The puncture wounds in the guy's hands (dead center of each palm) and through the top of the guy's skull also show a lack of hemorrhage. There are some signs of asphyxia: a slight (Leon says very slight, easy to miss) bruising of the lips and around the mouth, the eyelids are dotted with petechial hemorrhages, there is a slight swelling of the lungs with scattered areas of *atelectasis* (Leon's word), which means some of the tiny air sacs in the lungs had collapsed. But the signs of asphyxia are inconclusive, at least in terms of fixing the cause of death. Leon is a perfectionist. He says the only thing he is waiting on is the preliminary toxicology report, which he hopes to have by Friday."

"**August 26, 1981. Wednesday, 11:00 AM.** Another drizzly morning. I am meeting with the Crime Scene Investigators, Martin Lorenz, Randy Graeff, and sweet little Natalie Henderson, to go over their preliminary report. What a fucking waste of daylight, even if it is raining. They know it. I know it. But we gotta go through the steps. Of course it's nobody's fault. The killers, whoever they are, didn't leave behind a damn thing.

Lorenz says they bagged everything that looked promising (they were very hopeful) within a thirty-six-foot radius of the rocket tower. The stub of a Cuban cigar, a silvery looking cigarette case with the words *Cuba Libre!* on it, blue cloth fibers they plucked off the dead guy's jacket, several strands of hair (also from the dead guy's jacket), green bottle glass fragments they found scattered about, as if someone had smashed a bottle or two against the rocket tower, a couple of empty, unsmashed green bottles of *El Presidente,* a pool of some sort of cream-colored, viscous fluid, obviously diluted by the rain, that they found beneath the rocket tower, a couple of mangled tube socks, a plaster cast of a footprint, and a plaster cast of a muddy skid mark of a tire track they found in the grass over by the crepe myrtles (the only bit of potential evidence they identified outside the bubble of the thirty-six foot radius). An analysis of the evidence didn't reveal much. The Cuban cigar could have been purchased in Little Havana or on the street or by someone who had recently been to Cuba. The silvery looking cigarette case is not even silver plate. Martin calls it German silver. He says it is a mixture of nickel, copper and zinc. It is the kind of junk item you can buy in any drugstore at the beach. The phrase *Cuba Libre* is actually a decal. Parts of it had already rubbed off. There are no fingerprints on the cigarette case. The blue cloth fibers are polyester, probably from a suit, but it is impossible to be definitive. The strands of hair are from someone with long red hair. There is nothing else to say about the hair. The green bottle glass fragments are probably all that is left of two bottles of *El Presidente* beer, which makes sense given the proximity of the two unsmashed bottles. There is no way to tell where the beer had been purchased or if it is in any way connected to the death of Oscar Garcia Raimundi. There is no telling how long the bottles and bottle fragments have been in the park. There are also no fingerprints. The cream-colored viscous fluid was identified as human fecal matter mixed with mud. No telling how long that degenerate deposit has been hiding in the shadows beneath the rocket tower jungle gym, waiting for our Crime Scene Investigators to scoop it up and bag it as evidence. The mangled tube socks were actually filled with cotton wadding, obviously damp from the rain. The socks are covered with bite marks from what are most likely canine teeth. Probably a dog's chew toy that had been lost or abandoned. The footprint is very small, a child's tennis shoe or sandal or Mary Jane. It is next to impossible to tell with a child's shoe. The skid mark was only four feet long, which they said made it difficult (meaning impossible) to determine the direction the vehicle had been traveling. And there was only a single skid mark anyway, as if it had been made by a motorcycle. But it wasn't a motorcycle tire, and it wasn't the kind of tire you'd find on a motocross bike either. The width of the track was eight inches. The tread was an 'S' pattern tread. It is the kind of tire you find on a golf cart. So maybe the killers used a golf cart to transport the body to the rocket tower playground. But why would they stop at the crepe myrtles? It could just as easily have been a gardener using a modified golf cart as a utility truck, a gardener who had some business with the crepe myrtles. Except neither Miami Dade Parks maintenance staff nor the South Miami Parks maintenance staff use modified golf carts. They drive around in small utility trucks. Maybe it was some guy from the neighborhood with a golf cart who just wanted to whack around a few golf balls, just to kill a few hours, and Washington Park was the closest bit of green. Who the fuck knows? Maybe it was a kid with a Big Wheel."

"**August 28, 1981. Friday, 3:30 PM.** The rain has finally stopped. Not even the inconclusive results of the toxicology report can dampen my spirits. Oscar Garcia Raimundi was fucking out-of-his-mind blitzed. Leon says he's lucky he didn't die of alcohol poisoning. But that was it, just the alcohol. There were no other chemicals in his bloodstream when he died, no mysterious poisons, nothing, so the precise cause of death is still a mystery."

"**August 31, 1981. Monday, 7:00 AM.** I woke up at 5:30 and it was drizzling, but only a little, and by 6:30 the skies had cleared. I don't usually get up so early. I am more likely to go to bed at five in the morning then get up with the sun. There were only a few other guys on the second floor when I got to the station. Just my luck the Captain was one of them. I ran into him in the hallway outside the can, but it was not an accident. The Captain was looking for me. I knew he had already read Leon's preliminary autopsy report and the CSI report and the preliminary toxicology report, and he knew that I knew. He asked me how long before I wrapped things up and moved on to the next case. He said there were plenty of cases to keep me busy. I said I was almost finished. I told him I needed to drop by a pizzeria called Eduardo's to check out an alibi, and he gave me a sort of noncommittal nod. Then I told him about the article in the dead guy's wallet, but I could see he wasn't convinced. He asked me if I really thought I was going to pick up the trail of the killers by going to an offshore speedboat race at Sunny Isles on Labor Day Weekend. I told him that you could make any theory seem ludicrous if you wanted to. I told him I wanted to head up there on Saturday and ask around, see if anyone knew our dead guy before he was dead. I told him if nothing panned out then the final report would be on his desk the following week. He gave me a strangely sympathetic look, but he didn't say anything right away. He was just regarding me. Then he seemed to slip through a door to another dimension. 'Sure,' he said. 'Go to the beach on Saturday, but don't drink too much on the Department's dime. And make sure you take Ramirez along.' Then he walked away. Fuck that. That's what I was thinking. Fuck the Captain. But I didn't say a word."

"**September 2, 1981. Wednesday, 1:30 PM.** Me and Ramirez head to Eduardo's pizzeria. The shop is on West Flagler, a few blocks from the John Bosco Catholic church. It's a two-story corner building painted yellow with orange trim and a plate glass window facing the street. Part of the window is decorated with a happy pizza chef with a white chef's hat and a phone number to call for delivery. An orange awning runs the length of the window. The telephone number in the window is also on the awning in huge block numbers. You cannot miss the telephone number. We stand in the shade of the awning before we go in, peering through the window. It is a hot sunny day with a bright blue Miami sky and the place is packed. Every table is occupied, and there is a line at the counter that extends out through the door to the sidewalk. Eduardo is by the register shouting orders to a kid working the pizza oven. The kid is a flurry of motion, shoving uncooked pizzas in with a giant wooden spatula, sliding the cooked ones onto trays or into boxes. A couple of girls take turns delivering the trays. Eduardo is in charge of the boxes. It seems like Eduardo needs to hire more help. I slide up to the register and flash my badge discreetly. Nobody seems to notice me except Eduardo, who looks me squarely in the eyes and smiles like we are old friends. 'Come, come,' he says. 'I have been waiting for you.' Eduardo is a fat, happy, middle-aged man, about the age of our dead guy, happy brown eyes, thick, curly black hair, a thick moustache. A stereotypical figure behind the counter. He shouts something into the roiling, doughy atmosphere of the pizza shop. One of the girls materializes out of a cloud of flour dust and takes over the register. Eduardo ushers us into a tiny backroom office which doubles as a bathroom, which is probably a health code violation, but I don't give a fuck. He wipes his hands on his apron and then shakes our hands vigorously. His hands are slightly damp from perspiration. We tell him we're investigating a string of robberies in the neighborhood. We ask if he was in his shop this past Friday night. He smiles a broad, confident smile and says he was in the shop. He is always in the shop. It is his shop, after all. Where else would he be? We ask him if anything unusual happened Friday evening. For a moment his body tenses. He looks suddenly bewildered, as if he is trying to remember a speech he has spent hours rehearsing, or perhaps he is being bombarded by a series of seemingly pleasant images from the past that when seen as a whole reveal some sinister truth. Then he relaxes and says 'Sure, Friday, that was the night of the Gómez fight, we were watching the fight. I set up a tiny television right here on the counter. It was a slow night, not as busy as it is now. I let everyone else go home. But my friends were here. Héctor and Miguel Velázquez. They own a club up in Allapattah so I almost never see them. But they came for a visit on Friday night. They showed up around six-thirty. We watched the fight and drank and talked. They will vouch that I was here. They left a little before midnight. After that I closed up and went upstairs to bed.'"

"**September 5, 1981. Saturday, 2:15 PM.** Finally, a weekend full of sunshine. Seems like it's been forever. The speedboat race at Sunny Isle's Beach is in full swing. All of the motel parking lots along Collins Avenue are jammed full, from the pier all the way north to 183rd Street. We park in the lot of the Sahara Motel and walk the mile and a half to the Newport, which is the official race headquarters. I don't mind the walk to tell you the truth. It's bright and sunny and hot, and everywhere you look there are babes bouncing around in the skimpiest bikinis you'd ever hope to see. And of course there are vendors all over the place selling everything from beer to barbecue to racing souvenirs to sunglasses. It's a hell of a party. A couple of steel drum bands here and there. Or maybe the same one. Music blasting away from every hotel along the beach and from the jukeboxes of every restaurant and hotel bar and hole-in-the wall dive along Collins Avenue and the steady droning buzz of the speedboats and people shouting and laughing and joking around and sirens in the distance. We don't get to the Newport until after four. We talk to a few racers hanging out with a beer vendor up by the pier and we show them a photo of Oscar, but they don't know him. But they tell us to talk with a guy named Frankie Dennis. They say if anyone here knows this guy it's Frankie. He's one of the big shots with the Offshore Power Boat Racing Association. They were the guys that put this race together. They have a tradeshow tent up by the hotel with posters and pamphlets and *'I Love Speedboat Racing'* buttons and a VCR hooked up to a small color television so you can watch footage of old races. We talk with Frankie for a while. He's got curly brown hair and he's wearing khaki shorts and a yellow and green Hawaiian shirt and he has a tan that won't quit. He's passing out pamphlets right and left and talking up a storm about speedboats in general and Miami in particular. He's also wearing a 24K gold chain and is flashing a Rolex, so you know he's pretty well fixed. He's the kind of guy you'd think would be sporting a motorcycle moustache, like Tom Selleck in Magnum P. I., but he isn't. Frankie takes a long hard look at the picture we show him, but then he shakes his head like he is truly, sincerely disappointed with his poor memory and says if he ever met the guy he doesn't remember. Then he shoves a pamphlet and a couple of buttons into my hands and goes over to talk with a bevy of half-naked Miller Lite girls who have been admiring Frankie's watch from afar. The Miller Lite girls are so excited as Frankie approaches that several of them bounce out of their tops. We talk with a few more racing types down by the makeshift grandstand set up on the beach. One of those aluminum jobs. Then we head back up to the pier and we go all the way to the end to watch the boats for a while. I don't know how long we're there. Maybe an hour. At some point we put on the buttons. All the while we're watching the boats we're drinking beer. Then all of a sudden Frankie is standing right beside us. The boats have stopped racing. The Miller Lite girls are long gone. Frankie invites us into the hotel for a drink and we oblige him. It's not much of a bar, but it'll do. When the drinks arrive (whiskey sours) Frankie starts right in talking about organizing a race between the Keys and Cuba. He says the Bureau of Cuban Tourism is working tirelessly to promote such a race. They say it would be a good thing for Cuba. 'You mean a good thing for Castro,' says Ramirez. But Frankie isn't interested in talking politics. He nods politely, expertly, without any hidden agenda whatsoever, and says he thinks the race will happen within a couple of years. 'You wait and see,' he says. Then he smiles a reassuring smile and orders another round of whiskey sours. It is eight o'clock before we start back to the Sahara. Neon lights are everywhere. Purples and oranges and aquamarines. All of the motels are lit up like postcards. And that is that, as they say. It looks for sure like my theory about the speedboat race is a bust. It's like a door closing. But on our way back the door is all of sudden thrust wide open. We haven't gone more than half a mile when we realize how hungry we are, so we stop in at a glitzy diner called Wolfie's Rascal House. We grab two seats at the counter. We are sitting where the counter curves so we have an excellent view of the front door. I order the fried scallops and Ramirez orders a Halibut steak. We are just about to dig in when we hear a familiar voice say 'Will you look who's pounding the pavement at the beach? What are you doing so far from home, Detective?' followed by a robust hearty laugh, which is followed quickly by a hearty (the word meaty also comes to mind) clapping of a hand on my back, and I turn and look up and there staring at me with a happy, friendly, confident smile is Héctor Velázquez himself. For some reason I am not surprised. Then I realize that Héctor is not surprised either. He sits down next to me, right at the elbow of the counter so whenever I look up I can't help but see his happy-go-lucky disfigured face, and orders beef tongue with creamed spinach. He says it's the best thing on the menu. He says whenever he eats beef tongue he feels like an Orisha god at the receiving end of an African ritual. It is hard to tell if he is serious or not. He doesn't give anything away, at least not for free. That is the impression I get. Not unless he wants to. A few minutes later his brother Miguel joins us. Miguel doesn't say a word, but it is clear he is not happy with Héctor. But it is just as clear that Héctor is the man in charge. Miguel takes a seat next to Ramirez. We are like three prisoners sitting on death row, me, Ramirez and Miguel. Miguel broods heavily over the menu for a while and then orders a corned beef sandwich. It is a bizarre dinner on many levels. For one thing, the buzz I have been enjoying for the better part of the evening evaporates in an instant. I have rarely if ever been so alert. Naturally the conversation focuses on speedboat racing. Apparently the Velázquez brothers have been racing for years. Héctor says they got their start in 1965. They were just kids. They were just twenty years old and they didn't know shit. They were working for Southern Air Transport in those days. I look at Ramirez, but he's not really listening. I realize the coded nature of this conversation is sailing right past his young Hispanic ears. What a fucking pinhead. It's common knowledge, at least if you're in law enforcement in Miami, that Southern Air Transport has been a CIA front since the 50s. So either the Velázquez brothers had once worked for the CIA, or maybe they are still on the company payroll, or they want us to think they are. I catch Héctor giving me a thoughtful look as the words come spewing out of his mouth, as if he is trying to gauge my reaction. But I don't react. I just let him talk. But I am committing every word to memory so I can go over it later. The Velázquez brothers own three boats, a 38-foot Bertram and two Cigarettes. They didn't do as well as they had hoped today. They finished seventh. But they don't mind. They just enjoy being out on the water. They don't even finish every race. Three years ago they sank within sight of the finish line during the Pelican Harbor Challenge. 'That was a hell of a race,' says Héctor. 'Surreal, that's what it was. The course was littered with floating coconuts, and then for some reason my brother here tried to fish one out with a net. We're going full speed and he's trying to get a coconut. Why there was a net in the back of the boat I don't know? Anyway, Miguel lost his balance and flipped into the water, so naturally I had to retrieve him. What else is a brother supposed to do? I wasn't going to let him drown. But he was lucky he didn't break his neck, and I told him so, but he just said get back behind the wheel. Well, we were pretty much out of the race by that point, I mean we were fucked, but what the hell, I thought, so I gunned it, I mean I really let her rip, and by God if we didn't close the gap, but then the engine overheated, and then it blew sky high, and just like that our chances of even finishing dropped to absolute zero. Yeah, it was surreal. We were twenty-five yards from the finish line, but we were drifting the wrong way. The drunken bastards in the grandstand were going wild. Somebody yelled out for us to grab a paddle, like we were in a fucking fiberglass canoe. Then just like that we sink. The explosion that took out the engine had also opened up the bottom of the hull. We started taking water, only we didn't know it at first. And then it was too late. We sank like a fucking cannonball.' I have to say Héctor tells a pretty good story, with just the right balance between action and narrative commentary, even if the whole sinking at the finish line climax sounds fairly implausible. Then the dinner is finished and me and Ramirez are heading towards the register. Héctor turns in his seat and calls out to us. He is only ten feet away and yet he calls out like he is standing on a distant shore. He says in his robust voice of a self-indulgent maniac, without any apology for disturbing the dinners of the other patrons, that they are out on the water at least once a week, usually in the afternoon. He says their boats are faster than the Coast Guard, faster even than the drug runners coming up from Cuba. Some day we should come out on the water with them just to experience the extraordinary speed. Money can't buy that kind of pleasure. Money can't even come close. It is a blatantly manipulative thing to say. Everyone in the joint can hear him clear as a bell, and yet oddly, everyone keeps their faces focused on their own plates. Then Héctor turns back towards his brother, who has moved two seats closer, and suddenly it seems like me and Ramirez don't exist at all. We are just dust particles dancing in a stray beam of starlight. I pay the bill, but at the register I notice a souvenir rack of silvery cigarette cases. The cases all say Cuba Libre. It is an odd coincidence, but perhaps not so odd. I buy one just for the hell of it. $5.99 plus tax. Then I follow Ramirez out the door. Only then do I realize that we are still wearing those idiotic '*I Love Speedboat Racing*' buttons. I feel as if we have barely escaped from someone else's dream."

"**September 9, 1981. Wednesday, 12:45 PM.** I met with a friend of mine from the FBI, Special Agent Edmundo Lagunas. I've known Lagunas for years. We trade favors back and forth. He's a very clean-cut looking guy. Dark hair, almost black, and very short, almost military style, and a squared-off jaw. He's always wearing a light tan suit, a white, crisply pressed shirt, and a thin brown tie. In a word, he is fastidious. I had called him up first thing Monday morning. I said I needed whatever background he had on two unsavory nightclub owners with an interest in speedboats. I almost never give Lagunas the straight dope right off the bat, so I didn't say who exactly I was talking about. I wanted to gauge his mood first. He got very quiet, as if he had withdrawn into another dimension, and I thought, oh, well, he's not going to be much help. But then his voice returned to the line with a manipulative vigor. He asked me if I was talking about Héctor and Miguel Velázquez. I said I was. He asked me what made me think he knew anything. I said nothing in particular. They just seemed like the kind of characters the FBI would know something about. He asked me about the nature of my inquiry. I said it was part of a murder investigation. He retreated again after that. He was silent for a full five minutes. Nothing but the breezy wind of static. Then the line went dead. Fifteen minutes later my phone started ringing and it was Edmundo. He didn't identify himself. It actually sounded like he was trying to disguise his voice, which is fucking hilarious. He said 'The Marine Stadium. Noon. Wednesday.' Then once again the line went dead. The Marine Stadium was an odd choice for a meeting. Mostly the stadium was for boat races or concerts. I saw Loggins & Messina at the Stadium. But in the middle of the week there wouldn't be many people around, a few tourists maybe, a few office workers from downtown sitting in the grandstand, eating a bag lunch, looking out at the water, but not many. If anyone were watching us, well, they could draw their own conclusions. I got there at noon on the dot and climbed three-quarters of the way up towards the top. I sat down in the shade in the dead center of the grandstand. There were a couple of tourists sitting halfway down in the sun, and some old guy in the front row wearing a fisherman's hat. He was pulling a bottle out of his backpack every now and then and taking a swig and putting the bottle back. There was a nice breeze blowing through the stadium, and if I hadn't come with a purpose I would have kicked back and taken a nap, which wouldn't have been too easy since those stadium seats were a little tight, but I was pretty tired. As it was, I watched the boys from the Miami Rowing Club for a while, and then they left, and then I watched the two tourists head up and then out the back of the stadium, and I was just about to abandon this wild goose chase myself when the wino from the first row sat down beside me, only he wasn't a wino. He was Lagunas. He laughed at my initial confusion, a goofy grin on his face, but then he got right down to business. He reached into his backpack and pulled out five large manila envelopes, each of them stuffed with documents. He carefully placed the envelopes in his lap.

"'I shouldn't even be talking to you, Andreu,' he said. 'But Abrahms didn't want you snooping around where you didn't belong. He thought you might get yourself killed, and I guess he didn't want that on his conscience.' And then: 'Don't look at me like that. You know me well enough. I wouldn't be here if I had a choice. But for some reason Abrahms likes you. So here I am. I am officially unofficially here.'

"Then Lagunas opened the first of the manila envelopes and took out several photographs, but then he paused and gave me the oddest look. It didn't actually seem like he was looking at me at all. It felt more like he was looking past me, over my shoulder, as if he had just caught the flash of something sinister. Then he blinked and the trance was snapped.

"'All of this begins in Cuba,' he said.

"His voice possessed a grave, gravelly kind of authority that you could not question. It was almost like he was narrating a documentary of events that he himself had personally witnessed.

"'In 1936, responding to an increasing threat to our national security from the rise of the Nazis in Germany, the FBI created a German anti-espionage team. In those days everyone believed the Germans would go through Cuba to get to the United States, so we sent a lot of agents to Havana. But when war finally broke out in 1941, the War Department appropriated most of our funds for what they said were more pertinent activities. Sure, they kept a few Naval Intelligence officers in Havana to keep a lookout for German subs, but mostly it turned into Batista's show. By 1942, virtually all anti-espionage activities in the Caribbean came through the OSS, but Hoover wanted to keep a skeleton team in Cuba nevertheless, and Hoover did what he wanted. It was a challenge to say the least. Havana was a hotbed of German spies and Spanish Falangists in spite of what Naval Intelligence reported. What made the situation even worse was that Cuban politics was itself corrupt. You could buy the acquiescence of any Cuban Minister for a price. For a larger sum you could ensure his complete cooperation. And we were short-handed. So we had no choice, really, but to enlist the aid of the mob in keeping an eye on any suspicious activity, anything that might pose a threat.

"'In hindsight, of course, this was stupid. When the war ended, the Mafia had become an integral part of the degenerate honeycomb that was Cuban politics. In other words, we could not simply pick them up and toss them in jail. Certainly not without the help of the Cuban government. Besides, we didn't want to expose ourselves. Then in 1947 the CIA was born, which further complicated an already tense and complicated environment. We were directed to begin transitioning our anti-espionage activities to their oversight, though we did not comply right away. For one thing, the number of ex-Nazi agents in Cuba had increased, and we were the only agency who had maintained a presence there. And anyway, Hoover didn't really trust the bozos that Truman had put in charge. So we kept doing what we were doing. Then in 1950 things changed and we began recruiting a Mafia underboss named Luis Sarabia, who worked for an old-school don named Giuseppe Federico DiCarla.'

"(Here Lagunas passed me photographs of Sarabia and DiCarla. Both men looked like Hollywood movie stars from the 1940s. Sarabia sort of looked like Peter Lorre but without Peter Lorre's pouty smile. DiCarla looked like a clean-cut version of Boris Karloff.)

"'We never really understood exactly what DiCarla's role in Cuba was. We knew he was a childhood friend of Mafia Boss Salvatore Maranzano. They had both grown up on the streets of Castellammare del Golfo, in Sicily. There was some speculation that DiCarla had helped Lucky Luciano with the hit on Maranzano, but this has never been substantiated. At any rate, DiCarla was in bed with numerous Cuban politicians and government and union officials, and Sarabia was his right-hand man. Then in 1952, DiCarla's operations took a big hit when a warehouse building he owned in Havana burned to the ground. The warehouse was on San Pedro directly across from the harbor. It was the center of DiCarla's operations. Afterwards, Sarabia began what must have been a relentless pursuit of the men behind this act of sabotage, and by 1956 he had amassed quite a lot of information. He began to send us coded letters. Each letter contained a piece of the larger picture.

"'Sarabia believed a group of renegade anarchists was responsible for the destruction of the warehouse. He said most of these renegades were ex-Nazis seeking revenge, but there were also a few disgruntled Sicilian mercenaries, a few Jewish anarchists from Eastern Europe, a few home-grown Communists, and some Cuban radicals, national purists who believed that the only way to permanently secure a free and independent Cuba was to eradicate all foreign influence. It was an impossible collection of competing ideologies. You would have assumed that whatever promises had brought them together would have dissolved at the first sign of dissension. Quite frankly, these men had virtually nothing in common except for the desire to inflict great violence upon the world at large. No wonder we knew nothing about this group until Sarabia started his digging. No wonder they slipped beneath our radar. Sarabia said the ringleader of this mob of anarchists was a man named Immanuel Király, a German of Hungarian descent. He said Király had worked for the Nazi propaganda machine during the war and that he had arrived in Havana in 1947. He had even brought over some of his movie-making crew from Germany. Their purpose was to film bigwigs in compromising situations and then blackmail the poor saps. That was apparently how Király funded his entire operation. Sarabia told us that Király had only one aim: to destroy the Cuban people's faith in the Cuban government, in the Cuban political system, in the dream of Cuba itself, and so drive Cuba to the brink of absolute collapse. Király, he said, also wanted to offer up the United States as the villain in what the Cuban people would come to believe was the crime of the century. According to Sarabia, Király's people were the ones behind the Supervielle scandal. Supposedly they had managed to produce a pornographic film starring a big-shot named Manuel Fernandez Supervielle in bed with some unknown floozy. Supervielle had been elected the Mayor of Havana in 1946.'

"(At this point Lagunas handed me a photo of Supervielle, who did not, I might add, look like a movie star. He more or less resembled a clean-shaven albino walrus, which made it difficult to imagine that he had been the star of even the shoddiest of pornographic films, whether he knew he was being filmed or not. Lagunas kept right on talking.)

"'The film was discovered among Superveille's papers and personal effects shortly after his suicide, and did in fact cause quite a stir among the Cuban political establishment, though it was not widely known beyond that small inner circle.

"'Sarabia also believed that Superveille's well-publicized suicide was not a suicide, though he had no actual proof. But he became suspicious when he learned that Superveille had been killed with a Kongsberg Colt pistol. According to

Sarabia, many of the men who blindly followed Király owned Kongsberg Colt pistols. Besides, Superveille didn't even own a gun. Not that he couldn't have procured one, but a Kongsberg Colt would have been an odd choice. It was just a matter of putting two and two together, that's what Sarabia said. But we were skeptical. The whole ex-Nazi, German anarchist angle sounded pretty far-fetched to us. Naturally, we didn't believe Király was involved.

"'We had first heard about Király in 1945 when our guys entered Berlin. His dossier was just one of the many dossiers of Nazi underlings that we were able to secure. From 1935 through the end of the war, Király had worked for the Department of Film, part of Germany's Ministry of Propaganda, under the direction of Karl Neumann (a photo of Neumann, who seemed to be wearing pants that were a little too tight). In other words, he had indeed been employed by the Nazi's well-oiled propaganda machine, as Sarabia had discovered. But we didn't think Sarabia knew what he was talking about. Why would Király even be in Cuba? We thought someone was feeding Luis false information.

"'Király was brilliant at what he did. In 1936, he was attached to Colonel Wolfram von Richthofen's staff. (Photo of Richthofen, narrow face, eyes set close together, a very sour expression.) The Colonel had taken a field command with the Condor Legion, a group of volunteer German pilots, to support Franco's nationalists in the Spanish Civil War. (No photo of Franco.) Király's job was to capture the bombing of Guernica on camera. Then in 1938, after receiving a commendation from Goebbels himself for his 'unparalleled ability to capture the stoic heroism of German aviators during the battle of Guernika,' he was back in Berlin, where he worked with a variety of movie directors to produce dozens of Nazi propaganda films over the next six years. From 1938 to 1944 he worked with Karl Ritter, Gustav Ucicky, Boleslaw Barlog, Wolfgang Liebeneiner, Karl Anton, Leni Riefenstahl, Wilhelm Stöppler, the great Werner Klingler, and Max Kimmich, among other prominent Nazi directors.'

"(Only three photos, one of Riefenstahl, who had hawkish, unfeminine features and sort of looked like an angry librarian, one of Klingler, a pensive looking man with finely chiseled features who reminded me of a tax collector, and one of Karl Anton, slicked back hair, a monocle, and a bowtie.)

"'In spite of his accomplishments, however, as the war progressed, Király became less and less efficient, and his behavior became more and more erratic. There were some reports that even suggested Király was a borderline schizophrenic. He once proclaimed to a senior Nazi Party official that he was in direct communication with an alien civilization that was seeking the assistance of the Nazis to colonize the Earth. He told this official the aliens would assume the form of ancient Merovingian kings. Initially, of course, his madness was passed off as an aberrant sense of humor. But during the filming of the movie *Die Degenhardts*, which was a film about a family surviving the Allied bombing of the city of Lübeck, Király crossed an invisible line. In February 1944 he had the actors imprisoned in an abandoned bomb shelter near the Blohm & Voß shipyards in Hamburg.'

"(A photo of Hamburg after an Allied air raid.)

"'Both the shipyards and Hamburg had been practically leveled during the Allied bombing raids in 1943 and had remained the object of repeated attacks. Király left the actors in the bomb shelter for seventy-two hours, from February 19 to February 22, but he only left them food and water for two days. Coincidentally, or perhaps Király had secret sources of information and knew what was coming, Hamburg suffered through six hours of intense Allied bombing on the 20th of February, and though the objective of this raid was to smash the German aircraft industry, the shipyards were certainly fair game for any bomber that was forced to deviate from its original course. 4,200 civilians were killed during the raid. Hundreds were burned alive in inadequate bomb shelters. And while Király's actors escaped serious injury, all of them suffered from dehydration and psychosomatic stress. One said he lost his hearing as a result of the thunderous explosions. Another one later went mad and committed suicide, though probably not as a result of the air raid experiment. Király defended himself by saying the only way to be true to reality was to subject yourself to reality. But the Nazis had had enough. In spite of the success of the film, which opened to rave reviews in Lübeck on July 6, 1944, Király was sent packing. Supposedly he went to live with an uncle in Freiberg after that, but when the war ended, Király had vanished. Everyone, even his uncle, thought he had fled to Argentina. Argentina is where the ex-Nazis went. No one suspected Király had opened up shop in Cuba. It just didn't make any sense his going there.

"'In retrospect, it is quite clear that Sarabia had tried to warn us. But we ignored him. We were pursuing what we believed was the best long-term strategy for dealing with both the threat posed by this strange group of anarchists who had torched DiCarla's warehouse in '52 as well as the looming menace of the Communists. In January 1953 we began pressuring DiCarla, with the help of Sarabia, to move his operations to Miami. We were relentless with our pressure. We believed that we could use DiCarla and his Cuban contacts as a tool to sow disunity among the Communists, who always seemed to be on the verge of a coup, and to keep this mismatched collection of anarchists at bay. But we also believed that we needed DiCarla in Miami so we could keep him on a tight leash. Unfortunately, the whole thing backfired. We never realized that once DiCarla began to seriously consider moving to Miami, once he raised the issue among his inner circle, he would begin to alienate the very people we wished to connect with. This is precisely what happened. By 1956 there was a significant amount of dissension among DiCarla's people, which somehow, according to Sarabia, the anarchists took advantage of. Then in January 1957, Castro and his ragged band of revolutionaries achieved their first strategic victory when they overran the garrison at La Plata. (A photo of a young Castro.) The eastern half of Cuba was soon embroiled in a guerrilla war between Castro's forces and the army. Castro's success pushed the anarchists into a corner, which meant that they were a powder keg ready to explode. Sarabia tried to warn us of this as well. In July 1957 he sent a letter that stated in unequivocal terms that Király and his group were mobilizing for some last ditch effort to put themselves at the forefront of the political upheaval that was engulfing Cuba. He wasn't sure what they had in mind, but he also said they were underestimating the impact that Castro was and would continue to have. Of course he levied the same criticism at us. He also said the hotel where he lived was crawling with Király's men. He was certain that his phone was tapped and that he was being watched by more than one set of eyes. He had even begun to suspect his girlfriend, but that was all he said about her. He never told us who she was or why he suspected her in the first place or if he had confronted her. Sarabia only shared with us what he wanted us to act on, and clearly, the girl was off limits. My guess is he had a soft spot for this girl and wanted to protect her. But by the same token, he knew the clock was running out. You would have to say in hindsight that he knew exactly what he was doing. He must have known. He said he was certain that when Király made his move, he and DiCarla would be at risk. He said he was going to beat Király at his own game.

"'Once again we failed to take Sarabia seriously, even though we knew without any doubt whatsoever that he was not given to sudden bouts of paranoia. By all reports, he was the coolest customer you could imagine, no matter how tight the circumstances. But we did nothing to help Sarabia. We just let the events unfold. Then in September, Sarabia wrote that DiCarla had finally agreed to move to Miami. In the first week of November he sent word that he, DiCarla, and Sarabia's protégé, Oscar Garcia Raimundi, would arrive in Key West on the *S. S. City of Havana* on Thursday, the 14th of November. We had no idea that anything had gone wrong until the boat arrived and only Raimundi was on board. (A photo of a young Oscar Garcia Raimundi, very handsome, dark hair, clean-shaven, a more pristine version of his white linen suit and Panama hat, a slightly bewildered look about him.) We later learned, although the details were somewhat sketchy, that there had been a bloodbath the night before Sarabia's boat was to depart. Apparently Király had chosen that particular week to move on DiCarla and his other targets, targets which were scattered all over Cuba, because it coincided with a weeklong celebration in honor of the Feast of San Cristóbal. It was never made clear to us why that madman chose that date or what he thought he was going to achieve. Perhaps he thought the whole country would be inebriated as a result of the festival, so he would be able to assume complete control with little resistance. Perhaps he thought he was paving the way for the Merovingian kings he believed in. Anyone who might have known is dead by now. In any case, he miscalculated. After November 1957, Király and his group fell off the face of the earth, literally. They were never heard from again. It was almost like they had never existed at all. Castro and the Communists assumed total control in 1959 and everyone else was out. But the night of November 13, 1957 was an incredibly brutal night. Thirty-three people were killed in Havana in a span of twelve hours. What a number! And that was only thirty-three we knew of. We also began to get reports of dozens of others being killed in every major city in Cuba. All of the murdered men were in some way involved in politics or with the unions or with organized crime or with all three. All of the women had close personal ties to the men. Király and his gang of anarchists even targeted children. It was incredible, the bloodshed, almost surreal.'

"(Lagunas stopped for a moment to catch his breath. He pulled out a bottle of water and took a swig and pulled out another bottle and gave it to me and I drank half the bottle without a second thought. It must have been ninety degrees, even in the shade. We looked out at the water for a while. I think Lagunas was trying to recover his voice. Then I was looking at the photos once again and trying to digest everything he had said. Then he opened the second manila envelope and pulled out another pile of photographs. They were mostly crime scene photos of the people murdered in Havana. Shocking, grisly photos. The faces of death, the various twisted poses. As Lagunas went through the names of the people who had been killed, he would hand me a photo to look at. Thirty-three photos in all. Not once did he look at the photos himself.)

"'Both DiCarla and Sarabia were killed,' he said. 'Here's a photo of Eladio de la Campa, a rising star of the Electrical Workers Union who had once worked for Prio. He was found in one of the city parks that looked out upon the Straits of Florida. His throat had been cut. Here's one of Eugenio Castellanos, Treasurer of the Gas Workers Union. He was found floating face down in the Almendares River. Here's one of Eugenio's entire family, his wife, a daughter, and twin boys. They were also killed, murdered in their beds and then their house was torched. Antonio Billiteri, a gangster who had himself been charged with the murders of dozens of Cuban citizens on his rise to the top but none of the charges had ever stuck, had apparently been bludgeoned to death with a baseball bat and his body had been deposited among the jagged rocks along the Malecón. He had been staying at the Gran Inglaterra Hotel. There were two naked girls in their twenties in his room; both of them were maids who worked for the hotel; their throats had been slit and their bodies dumped in the bathtub. The body of Ruperto Medino Borges, a former editor of *Diario de la Marina*, was found in an alleyway a short walk from the Marina building. He had been strangled with an Argentinean bolo whip. There was a lifeless body sitting slumped over in a third-floor hallway of a building in the 200 block of Calle

Obispo. The man had been shot in the chest at close range with a revolver and was sitting in a pool of his own blood; the killers had also disfigured the guy's face and cut out his tongue. Just down the hall from the disfigured guy, in an office that was a front for DiCarla's operations, a thin wiry clerk was found leaning up against a window next to a water cooler, his kneecaps smashed, a single bullet through his left eye, the wall smeared with blood where his hands had reached out to grab hold of something, anything, before he died. The building, a magnificent example of Spanish Baroque architecture, belonged to DiCarla. A Hungarian cinematographer named Georg Vertov, who had worked with Király in Germany, was found dead in his penthouse apartment, a single bullet to the forehead. Vertov's sister, Elsa, was also found in the same apartment. She was found practically naked, crumpled up on the floor of the bedroom. She had been shot at point blank range. The gun had been shoved up against the bottom of her jaw and then boom, a third of her skull had vanished just like that. In Regla, a heavy-set woman named Jaqueline Berroa, a friend of DiCarla's, was found dead in a second-floor apartment above a neighborhood café, a café which she had owned for twenty years. DiCarla's body was found in a back room of that same café. Apparently his face was twisted in a strange, maniacal grin, as if he had glimpsed some greater reality at the moment of his death. DiCarla's orderly, Ramón Salgado, who had worked the night shift at a small hospital for the criminally insane known as Mazorra, a Dante's *Inferno* if there ever was one, before he began working for DiCarla, was found dead in the alleyway just outside the Regla café. His head had been blown away. In Vedado, Armando Portuondo, the owner of a small garage and taxi cab company, whose clients often included several notable members of the Mafia, was found stuffed into a garbage can in the alleyway behind a drugstore on Linea with a plastic bag taped over his head and his throat slit for good measure. Two taxi cab drivers who worked for Portuondo were also casualties. The first was Jacob Taoi Amadi, a Nigerian immigrant who had tried out for the Havana Sugar Kings baseball club in 1954 but had failed to make the final cut. The second was Efrain Jaramillo, a second-year law student at the University of Havana who had grown up in Cienfuegos, the City of One Hundred Fires, and had within three months of his arrival in the capitol joined the FEU, an intensely militant student organization, though whether he was spying on the FEU or he was a committed activist is unclear. Both men were found slumped behind the steering wheels of their taxis. They had each been tapped just behind the ear. Their taxis were still running when they were found. There were also five German nationals who died that night. They did possess diplomatic papers, but when we later brought these papers to the German Embassy for verification, we were told they were forgeries. According to the forged papers, the men were all supposedly between the ages of thirty and fifty-two and had arrived in Cuba on various dates between 1949 and 1953. Supposedly their names were Ernst Slovogt, originally from Cologne, Heinrich Hombach, originally from Neustadt, Detlef Kirstetter, originally from the town of Gundelsheim, Nils Dissinger, originally from Birkweiler, and Udo Geiszler, originally from the small town of Klingenthal, on the border between what is now East Germany and Czechoslovakia. The German nationals all carried Kongsberg Colt pistols. Finally, there were seven undocumented, unidentified and probably unidentifiable Sicilian immigrants, Mafia soldiers most certainly, who were also found dead at various points throughout the city. The Sicilians all carried long-barreled rifles. The bodies of two of the Sicilians were found in the front seat of a 1956 Chevrolet Bel Air four-door hardtop that belonged to DiCarla. The two had apparently been injured quite severely in a head-on collision in front of Café Paraiso on Compostela with one of Armando Portuondo's taxis. (A photo of the accident, with Café Paraiso in the background.) But according to the patrons of the café, they might have survived had not the taxi driver walked over to their vehicle and shot them dead. No one knows what happened to the taxi driver after that. Sarabia himself was gunned down only a few blocks from Café Paraiso, about half a mile from where the *S. S. City of Havana* was moored.'

"(A photo of the *S. S. City of Havana*.)

"'To tell you the truth, we have no idea what really happened that night, or why. I am not sure we will ever be able to untangle the net. There are so many unanswered questions. Who was working for whom? Why were so many people from so many various backgrounds targeted? Why did the family of Eugenio Castellanos have to die? Were some of the victims just in the wrong place when the bullets started flying? What the fuck happened in Cuba that night? This is what we were asking ourselves.

"'Naturally we had a lot of questions for Raimundi when he arrived in Key West, but we did not pick him up right away. We watched him for a week. He stayed mostly downtown. Mostly he didn't leave Duval Street. He rented a room in the Southern Cross Hotel and took his meals at a tiny café a block away. Turtleburger sandwiches and coffee and a piece of apple pie for dessert. After lunch he would buy a pack of peppermint gum at Kress's dime store. Every evening he went to a nightclub called The Bamboo Room to listen to jazz and have a drinkie-pie or two or three. There was a small stage behind the bar where three guys put on quite a show. The stage contained a piano, a sax, and drums, and the guys played everything from calypso to Dixie to George Gershwin. After The Bamboo Room, Raimundi would head down to one of the waterfront dives so he could watch the strippers strut their stuff. That's how he was spending his days. We didn't know what he was waiting for. It didn't seem like he had a clue about what had happened in Havana, so we picked him up. We told him about the bloodbath. He already knew some of it. He had seen Sarabia's body. But he practically collapsed in a heap right there in the lobby of the Southern Cross when he realized that his entire world had vanished. Everyone he had ever known was gone, and if he went back to Cuba he would surely be killed. He was ripe for the plucking. We told him that if he worked for us, he could stay in the U.S. If not, we'd have him deported. We'd ship his ass back to Cuba. This is what we told him. Then we confiscated his suitcase. You wouldn't believe how much money he had in that suitcase. The poor, untutored sap.'

"(At this point Lagunas descended into an uneasy, thoughtful silence. I knew he wasn't finished. I knew he had a lot of ground to cover. I also knew he didn't like being put on the hook. It was close to three by then. It was a lazy, mojito kind of afternoon. We heard the whirring sound of speedboats from somewhere, but we couldn't see them. The sound of the speedboats was like a premonition. Then Lagunas took hold of the fourth envelope. He handed me a series of photos showing Oscar Garcia Raimundi at various locations in the Keys. Even though he was working for the FBI, they were still taking surveillance photos.)

"'Initially we set up Raimundi in Key West. We knew there were going to be a lot of Cubans coming over, particularly with the success Castro was having. And we knew that as soon as Castro took control he was going to start sending spies to keep tabs on any counter-insurgency activities that might be taking place here in Florida. We wanted to keep tabs on everyone coming over, and we thought Raimundi would be an ideal point man. We thought he would be able to sniff out genuine refuges from the implants. We thought the fact that he had worked for DiCarla would work to our advantage. Of course we didn't throw him into the deep end without a net. We had men all over the Keys. Here's how it was supposed to work. Raimundi would hang out down at the port whenever a ship came in and he would mentally sort through the new arrivals. If he thought there was someone we should keep an eye on, he was supposed to engage them as if he were a co-conspirator. He was to say if they were ever in need of any assistance, or if they had any questions about anything Cuban, they could count on a man named Jorge in the AerovisasQ ticket office in the 700 block of Duval on the east side.'

"(A photo of the ticket office with a smiling Cuban family on the sidewalk out front on a very sunny day and a series of beautiful panoramic photos of the Havana skyline in the window and a sign to one side that said Fly to Gay Tropical Havana in 30 minutes for $10 plus tax.)

"'If these potential persons of interest smiled and seemed pleased with that tidbit of information, Raimundi was to press a ten-dollar bill into their hands and say if they needed any prescriptions filled they should head to the Oriental Pharmacy on the corner of Duval and Truman and ask for a man named Nilo. Finally, if Raimundi spotted someone who looked like they might have some information we could use or who might be able to help us in any way possible, he was to give them a coupon for one free night at a dump called the Blue Marlin Motel on Simonton.'

"(Photos of The Blue Marlin and the Oriental Pharmacy. The photos of the Oriental Pharmacy were so grainy that it was difficult to determine what exactly you were looking at.)

"'If he wasn't sure what to do or if he himself was having any difficulty, he was supposed to go to the Flagship Restaurant and sit outside if it was sunny or stand at the counter if it was raining. He was to order a fish sandwich, a Coca-Cola, and a piece of Key Lime pie, and when his order arrived he was to ask if Amos had gone home for the day.'

"(A photo of the Flagship Restaurant, which looked more like a walk-up diner than a restaurant, and it didn't resemble a ship of any kind in spite of the owner's attempt to create a little ambience by placing an obviously fake ship's smokestack squarely on the flat roof.)

"'We thought Raimundi would do quite well for us. He had a regular talent for chatting people up. But he had no talent at all for discerning the hidden motives of others. He was just as likely to send one of Castro's agents to the Blue Marlin as he was to send a disenfranchised refugee to the Oriental Pharmacy. We should have pulled the plug sooner. We knew by '62 that he wasn't going to pan out as a ferret, but some things just take longer than you expect. We didn't pull Raimundi out of Key West until 1966. One year later we had set him up in a glitzy nightclub in Miami. All the action was in Miami by then anyway. The club was called La Campana, but then you already know that, don't you.'

"(At that point Lagunas handed me a recent surveillance photo of me and Ramirez going into La Campana. I realized I had been tagged long before I called him up. But Lagunas didn't rub it in. He kept right on talking.)

"'We told Raimundi we wanted La Campana to be the kind of club that everyone from Cuba would frequent. I don't know whose idea it was in the first place, but we purchased the property in the name of Luis Sarabia to remind Raimundi who was actually in charge. Then we gave him access to a bank account and told him to run the club. We used the money from the suitcase to set everything up. We wanted him to be the gracious host, shake everybody's hand, and keep them coming back. That was all he had to do. The bartender worked for us. Not the guy that's there now. Ours was a guy named Eddie Cardona. He used to run a bolita game in Allapattah until we got a hold of him. We also had a couple of taxi drivers working the club. They hung out at La Campana on Friday and Saturday nights in case there was a patron too drunk to drive home, and there were always plenty of drunks. Our taxi drivers were supposed to keep their ears open for any political chit-chat that might give us a clue about what Castro's boys were up to. We were desperate for intel. In '67 we were scared shitless that Castro was trying to destabilize Florida on behalf of the Soviet Union. There was even some locker room talk that the Cubans and the Soviets were planning an invasion to get us back for the Bay of Pigs, even though we knew that was utter nonsense. But there was a lot of talk floating around in those days, so getting the dope on Castro's boys became a priority. Then Carter got elected and Cuba was off the table and the drug cartels became the issue of the day. I can tell you right now a lot of guys down at the Bureau swore off the Democrats when that happened. Fucking Carter. So we pulled Eddie Cardona from Raimundi's nightclub and put him to work on a drug task force down in the Keys. If my memory serves, he started bartending at a real hellhole of a place on Stock Island called The Boca Chica Lounge. Every other night somebody was getting shot up or knifed in that joint, or out in the parking lot. They were open all night so they picked up all sorts of riff-raff in the wee hours of the morning because the bars in Key West closed down at four. Anyway, we were done with Cuba, but somehow Raimundi slipped through the cracks. Nobody picked him up. Nobody shut down his bank account. He was running La Campana as if he owned the joint, but there was nobody running him, and that's when the CIA got wind of Oscar Garcia Raimundi.'

"(Lagunas began rummaging around in his backpack at this point and retrieved a couple of candy bars and gave me one. We ate the candy bars. We looked out at the water while we ate. Another group of tourists had materialized seemingly out of thin air and they were walking along the narrow path in front of the first row of seats and one of them was pointing to the band shell on the other side of the water and then making wild gestures in the air with his hands. It was clear he was talking about a concert he had once attended at the stadium. Then Lagunas opened the fifth manila envelope.)

"'Jack Hendershot was the CIA fucker who contacted our office. He wanted to know what kind of game we were running with Raimundi and why his office didn't know a goddamn thing about it. He was quite vocal in his displeasure. After that there were a number of closed door sessions between Abrahms and Jack's boss, a guy named Robert DeFoor out of Washington, a real spoon-fed prick if you ask me, so don't get me started. But just like that the CIA took charge of everything associated with La Campana. This was in 1977. That's when Héctor and Miguel Velázquez, your two suspects, come into the picture.

"(Lagunas paused and gave me a very hard look.)

"'Are you sure you want to hear this?'

"(I nodded.)

"'Well, okay then. It's your funeral. Apparently the CIA had been working with certain government officials in Cuba to create an international information network that would give them an inside track on any political developments in any Latin American country. This had been going on since 1970. The backbone of this network, the means of paying the bills, was and is the World Finance Corporation. The role of the WFC is to launder money earned from the trafficking of drugs into the United States. Most of the drugs now come from the Medellín Cartel out of Colombia, which routes most of its shipments through Panama and then Mexico. Seventy percent of the cocaine coming into the United States is coming from Colombia. But the Gulf Cartel out of Matamoros, Mexico is also a key player. Since García Ábrego took control, they have become quite clever in how they transport drugs across the border. But there has also been a lot more seemingly random, collateral violence in both the border towns along the U.S./Mexican border and in the streets of Miami as well. We believe Ábrego is getting help from corrupt officers in the Texas National Guard, but we have been unable to catch anyone just yet with their hand in the cookie jar.'

"(Lagunas forked over several black and white surveillance photos of drug smuggling activity. Some of the photos had the phrase Gulf Cartel scrawled in black marker on the back. One of these showed a chubby, thirty-year-old Ábrego eating at some restaurant. There was one other person at his table. An elderly gentleman in a white Stetson who seemed to be instructing Ábrego while he ate. Ábrego looked like a Latino Orson Welles after he had passed the point of no return. Another photo showed the elderly guy after he had been gunned down. The other photos were of the Medellín Cartel. One of these was a photo of Juan David Ochoa, Germán Castro Caicedo, Carlos Lehder, and a clean-shaven Pablo Escobar sitting around a small white patio table with a white fringed umbrella rising up out of the middle for shade. Ochoa seemed bored, or detached, as if he was formulating his own plans. Caicedo and Lehder seemed to be trading jokes. Only Escobar was looking at the camera. It seemed as if he was posing for the future. All of the photos seemed to be clichés, depicting rough looking, unshaven Latinos with machine guns or speeding away from some unidentifiable warehouse pier in speedboats or enjoying drinks at a swanky café or nightclub, surrounded by beautiful, half-naked girls.)

"'The CIA has been turning a blind eye to the drugs coming from these cartels for years and then skimming money right off the top to finance covert operations in Nicaragua and elsewhere. What a nest of Machiavellian vipers! We aren't sure how La Campana fits into all this. We know that the nightclub has become a haven for all sorts of drug dealers. We suspect the CIA simply wanted to create a safe haven for the drug lords they were working with to facilitate the flow of both cash and information. Simple as that. Still, it has been difficult to determine who is sleeping with whom. The WFC is a case in point. The WFC was founded in 1971 by Guillermo Hernández-Cartaya, a former Cuban banker who doubled as a CIA operative.'

"(A photo of Cartaya sporting wavy hair and a crooked, gin-and-tonic kind of smile.)

"'Yet Cartaya is also a friend of Castro.'

"(A photo of Cartaya and Castro having coffee at a sidewalk café, a bright sunny day.)

"'He was instrumental in helping the Colombian government secure a one-hundred-million-dollar loan from Cuba through the aegis of the WFC. To complicate an already complicated scenario, Cartaya is at this very moment working with René Rodriguez-Cruz, an official of the Cuban intelligence service and a card-carrying member of the Cuban Communist Party, to secure a drugs for arms deal to support a counter-revolution in Nicaragua to oust the Sandinistas.'

"(A photo of Cruz, a psycho with a receding hairline and glasses that seemed to magnify his eyes, which seemed to be glowing with the ruthless, irrepressible, primordial joy of an executioner.)

"'In April of this year, several high-ranking CIA officials went to Panama to meet with Cartaya, Cruz and a charismatic Nicaraguan leader named Edén Pastora. The purpose of the meeting was supposedly to discuss how to finance the counter-revolution. Pastora became disenchanted with the Sandinista revolution when the Sandinista leaders began moving into elegant colonial style mansions in an exclusive suburb of Managua.'

"(A photo of Pastora in a black beret and green army fatigues with grenades clipped to a shoulder strap. He was holding his rifle in the air and smiling with confidence.)

"'And that brings us back full circle to La Campana and Héctor and Miguel Velázquez. They grew up in Coral Gables. (A photo of the Velázquez brothers standing outside a small cinder block home in Coral Gables in 1960.) They were basically juvenile delinquents. As teenagers they were always getting arrested. (A photo of the Velázquez brothers getting arrested across the street from a high school.) But for some reason they always skated. (A series of mugshots from the years 1961 through 1964, the Velázquez brothers grinning these ridiculous grins in every photo.) Then in 1965 they began working for Southern Air Transport, which is why you called me in the first place. Let me just say that not everyone who works for Southern Air Transport is CIA. Just so we're clear about that. But the Velázquez brothers were different. Their potential, shall we say, was noticed almost immediately. They have been working for the CIA ever since. They spent ten years down in Central America, and another two in various hot spots around the globe. (Several photos. The Velázquez brothers standing in front of a Jeep Wrangler somewhere in one of the jungles of Central America. The Velázquez brothers drinking coffees at a café in Granada and an unknown man in sunglasses looking on. The Velázquez brothers and a group of Nicaraguan rebels riding on top of a Route Four bus traveling from Granada to Managua. The Velázquez brothers standing next to small green tank parked on a city street. The letters FSLN are painted on the front of the tank using white paint. The Velázquez brothers with several Colombian rebels in the jungles of Venezuela. The Velázquez brothers watching a freighter passing through Miraflores Locks in Panama. The Velázquez brothers standing in front of a disco called Habana Panamá and then leaving that same club several hours later, each with a couple of half-naked girls draped over their arms.) In 1977 they were put in charge of whatever was going on at La Campana. Whatever is still going on. Their interest in speedboats began as part of their cover, but they really get off on the speed. (Photo of the Velázquez brothers in a speedboat moored at the Fontainebleau Resort Marina in Miami Beach.) And most importantly, they are untouchable. Besides, they are very, very professional. They do not leave any evidence behind, which you probably already know. I am certain they killed Raimundi. What's more, they are psychotic bastards, which means they probably enjoyed it. I am just as certain that they killed him because he was becoming a liability. But you will never be able to prove a thing. Nothing sticks to these guys. My advice to you is to stay away from them. Close the case. Bury it in a filing cabinet. You'll be signing your own death warrant if you don't.'

"(Lagunas stopped talking and we regarded each other for a moment. It was close to five o'clock and you could hear the comforting hum of rush-hour traffic like a warm breeze. We were both tired. Lagunas stuffed the manila envelopes back into his backpack and then slung it over his shoulder college style and started sidling down the row towards the stadium exit. The persona of the wino from before had evaporated, as had the personas of the cynical bureaucrat and the worldly spy, but just before he disappeared down the ramp, he turned and gave me a profoundly thoughtful look. It was a very strange look. It was like he had more to say but he could only communicate with his eyes. But the strangest thing about that look was that I thought I heard his voice, like I was reading his mind. '*One more thing,' he seemed to be saying, 'the bartender that's there now, Herminio Arréllaga, he was also CIA. He began working at the club in 1979. Prior to that he was working in the field in Panama, and before that he was in Nicaragua. In August 1978 he was part of a rebel group that stormed the Nicaraguan National Palace and took several high-ranking members of the Nicaraguan Congress hostage. They also killed nineteen palace guards. The leader of that rebel group was Edén Pastora.*' And then just like that, Lagunas was gone.)"

"**September 10, 1981. Thursday, 4:35 PM.** La Campana. Another rainy day. I didn't tell Ramirez about my meeting with Lagunas. I was sick to my stomach thinking about it, but there wasn't much either of us could do, so why ruin his day. Besides, Lagunas was right about the evidence. There wasn't any. At least there wasn't any evidence that made any sense. I've never seen such a case. It was impossible to connect the dots even knowing that the Velázquez brothers were the killers. So at two o'clock I took the ten-thousand dollars out of the evidence locker and got in my car and headed over to La Campana. I have to say now that the Velázquez brothers acted as if they knew I was coming. Héctor met me at the door. He gave me a tremendous bear hug and then roared and roared for his brother to come see what the cat had dragged in. The next thing I knew I was having drinks with Héctor and Miguel Velázquez. Herminio was pouring. At some point one of the brothers signed the receipt for the ten-thousand and then the money was whisked away and Herminio put another drink in my hands. I don't remember if we talked about anything at all. We were just drinking. The last thing I remember is Héctor reaching for a bottle on a small diagonal shelf above the register and his brother calling out to be careful, he had better not drop that bottle. It was a bottle of 1691 Clos de Griffier Vieux Cognac. Héctor said it had cost them five thousand smackers from some Islamic fucker, but it was probably worth ten. Those were Héctor's words. They had bought it years ago on a trip to Paris, their one and only trip. They didn't say why they went. Then Héctor poured a glass for everyone, even Herminio. Then we raised our glasses and Miguel said something I didn't catch but Héctor started roaring, and then we drank the Cognac. I think we drank the whole goddamn bottle, but I could be mistaken. That's the last thing I remember.

"**September 14, 1981. Monday, 9:55 PM.** I had told the Captain I would have my report on his desk no later than Friday afternoon. Last Friday. Well fuck that! I wasn't in the mood to write the damn thing on Friday. I wasn't in the mood today either, to tell you the truth, but what else was I going to do? At five o'clock I grabbed a mushroom burger at Julian's, a mushroom burger and two glasses of whiskey to be precise, and I felt a little better after that. I went back to my desk just after eight and sat down to type. I gave the Captain just what he wanted, a report containing only facts and direct observations, a report which highlighted only the relevant eyewitness testimony, and kept erroneous opinion to a minimum. I left out all of my suspicions. I did not interpret. I focused on what we could prove. The report was three pages long. I slunk into the Captain's office like some kind of thief and laid it on his desk. Then I went out to get rip-roaring drunk."

-130-

From the medical chart of Isidora Escoraz Calzada, August 12, 2000, 11:00 PM, as noted by the attending ED physician, Andrés Huerta, Jackson Memorial Hospital, Miami, Florida):

"Initially the patient walked into the Emergency Room Ambulance Bay but appeared disoriented. When two EMTs asked her if she was lost, she started babbling incoherently and then collapsed. The EMTs brought her into the Emergency Room and she was placed immediately in an ER bed. Her initial vital signs were generally good, except for her blood pressure reading, which was 183/106. Patient is 50 years old. Her DOB is 12-26-49. I examined her at 11 PM. Her BP was still elevated. Her pulse rate was 92 with no arrhythmias. Her lungs were clear. Her abdomen was soft. Bowel sounds were present in all quadrants. Her left eyes showed evidence of recent trauma. There was visible blood in the anterior chamber of the eye between the cornea and the iris, which is consistent with a diagnosis of hyphema. The patient did not remember injuring her eye, but she did indicate that she was experiencing some pain and a mild sensitivity to light. On a scale of one to ten, she said her eye pain was a five. Her skin showed no signs of any rash or petechiae, except for her face. There is a five-inch scar on her left cheek which shows significant fibrosis. The patient said the scar was the result of an injury she had sustained in 1986. Upon initial examination, the scar tissue was a bright red color. After a brief consultation with Dr. Simon Geist, a physician of Geriatric Medicine at Jackson Memorial, I gave the patient 0.5 mg of Ativan intramuscularly to treat her anxiety. I also put steroid drops in her left eye to reduce the level of eye pain and placed a patch over the eye until she could be seen by an ophthalmologist. After thirty minutes the patient appeared to be in a calmer state. Her BP was down to 156/92. She also said her eye did not hurt as much. After an hour, her scar tissue was a darker brown color. The patient said this was the normal color of the scar tissue. BP was also in the high normal range. By 2:35 AM the patient was in generally good spirits and was well enough to be discharged, but upon discussing this with the patient, she indicated that she could not go home with her eye the way it was. There was no one there to look after her. She lived alone. After a thirty-minute consultation with Dr. Geist, we contacted Dana Peterson, a social worker who is on staff at the Homeless Assistance Center in downtown Miami and is part of their on-call Emergency Team. Dana indicated that the patient would receive short-term housing assistance, three meals a day, basic health-care services, and counseling services as warranted. We discharged the patient and transported her to the Center at approximately 3:30 AM."

-131-

From the Case Management Report for Isidora Escoraz Calzada (August 13, 2000 to October 30, 2000), Miami Homeless Assistance Center, Hannah Grajek, Case Manager, filed November 6, 2000:

"Isidora came to us from the Emergency Room at Jackson Memorial Hospital early Sunday morning, August 13, 2000. She was immediately placed in a private room. It is clear from her physical appearance that she has had a difficult life. She is only fifty years old, but she looks like she is in her seventies. On the Monday afternoon following her arrival she was seen for follow-up care by Dr. Sandra Gutiérrez, one of our staff physicians. On Tuesday she was seen by an ophthalmologist for treatment of hyphema in her left eye. On Wednesday she met with one of our counselors and provided significant information about her life and her current situation. On Thursday, she and I met for several hours. I, for one, expend more effort than most trying to understand the people who come to us for help. I believe the more I know about a person's life, the more I can do for them. I go over every detail of their stories, however seemingly insignificant. I listen carefully not only to what they say, but how they say it. And I verify every fact that can be verified. Naturally, I do not delve in the life of anyone without their permission. I do not wish to invade anybody's privacy. And some people are more open than others. Isidora was perhaps more open to talking about the personal details of her life than any other person I have ever met. She wanted her life to be an open book. And whenever I pointed out that something she said didn't jive with reality as I knew it to be, she would only smile softly, without getting defensive, without exhibiting a judgmental attitude of any kind, and say, 'Yes, yes, that is to be expected, God reveals to each of us only what we must know, and only when we are ready.' Isidora talks like that a lot. She has been a joy to be around.

"So to begin. Isidora has been living in her parent's

house, a tiny bungalow in Allapattah close to the river. Both of her parents are dead. Her father passed away in 1966. Her mother died three years ago. Her parent's house is the only place where she has ever lived. However, she is at this point actually squatting on the property. She told us that the City of Miami had sold the house this past May due to several years of unpaid property taxes. Isidora said the city engaged the services of 21st Century Reality to sell the house, but so far no one has shown any interest, so the house, which is actually something of an eyesore, remains vacant except for Isidora. She also had one brother, Emilio, who also lived at the house until his death in 1986. The circumstances of her brother's death were suspicious, but no charges were ever brought. Isidora believes two small-minded thugs, two brothers known to Isidora as Bull and Horse Velázquez, murdered her brother. She said the Velázquez brothers had also murdered her husband. She had heard them talking about it afterwards. Her husband was a Cuban immigrant named Oscar Garcia Raimundi. He owned a small nightclub in Allapattah called La Campana. Isidora said her husband had opened the nightclub in 1967 and that she had started working at the club as a hostess in 1968. She said she and her husband began dating in 1969 and got married in 1977, but she then said their happiness together was short-lived.

"According to Isidora, 1977 was also the year that the Velázquez brothers began working at the club as bouncers, and within a few years they turned the club into a haven for drug dealers and thieves, which her husband didn't notice right away, and neither did she, because they were both focused on the joys of marriage, and she could not fault him for that. When he finally did open his eyes in 1981, he tried to get rid of the Velázquez brothers, but he did not anticipate how dangerous they were. They were very dangerous. Isidora said they murdered her husband without even a second thought and took over completely. She said she wanted to go to the police, but she changed her mind when she saw the detective who was investigating her husband's death drinking with the Velázquez brothers. When she saw that she decided to keep her mouth shut. She didn't remember the name of the detective. She said she stayed on at the club because she had nowhere else to go.

"From a completely objective perspective, Isidora seems to have some difficulty separating fact from fiction. But it is next to impossible to look at Isidora with an objective eye. For example, we checked with the Miami-Dade County Clerk of the Courts and we were told that in 1967 a man named Luis Sarabia had filed a deed for a newly constructed nightclub called La Campana, and then in 1979 he had sold the club to Héctor and Miguel Velázquez. The club went out of business in 1992. A company listed as La Campana Enterprises is the current owner of the property, which has fallen into disrepair. There is no record of an Oscar Garcia Raimundi associated with the nightclub. There is no record of such a person living in Dade County between 1960 and 1990. We also checked with the Miami Police Department to see if Mr. Raimundi had in fact been a victim of foul play in 1981. Detective Michael Delarosa told us that in 1981 there were 622 murders in Dade County; the names of all of the victims were known; the name Oscar Garcia Raimundi was not on the list. But when we presented these facts to Isidora, she merely smiled sweetly and said we were mistaken. In spite of her delusions, and in spite of the trauma she has clearly experienced in her life, she is an incredibly loving and compassionate person. It is impossible to separate her persona from what she tells us. It is like being hypnotized. Every word she says has the ring of truth, even when what she says cannot possibly be true.

"So to continue. Isidora said after her husband had been murdered, her brother Emilio, who also worked at the club, started to keep a diary of all the people the Velázquez brothers had killed, beginning with Oscar Garcia Raimundi. Emilio wanted to keep their memories alive, she said. Then in 1986, he was killed. Isidora blames herself. She said by 1986 the club had become a private club where negotiations among those trafficking in drugs took place. The girls who had formerly worked as waitresses now entertained the drug dealers once business had been concluded. Isidora was among these poor unfortunate girls condemned to entertain these men. She said she suffered through those days the best she could, but one sunny afternoon in late September of 1986, she allowed her emotions to get the better of her. On that day, the Velázquez brothers had given her to three Panamanians. She was to entertain all three. She became inebriated and was raped repeatedly, and then she fell asleep. When she woke up several hours later she discovered that one of the Panamanians was passed out on the couch. He was naked. She didn't know where the other two were. In a fit of madness, she said she took a knife and cut off the sleeping man's penis and his balls, and then she opened up an artery, she didn't say which one, and he started bleeding profusely. He bled to death right there on the couch while she watched. Then, not knowing what else to do, she went to her brother Emilio and told him what had happened. Emilio told her not to worry. He told her that he would take the blame for the death of the Panamanian. He said he would tell the Velázquez brothers that the Panamanians had gone beyond simply enjoying the afternoon with his sister. He would tell them they had violated her in every conceivable way, they had raped her until she was bleeding from every orifice, and that as her brother he could not stand idly by and let such things happen. He would tell them it was a matter of family honor. She said the Velázquez brothers were very angry with Emilio and took him to a small getaway house they owned just off NW 22nd Avenue and tossed him from the roof. Later, they brought Isidora into their office and told her what had happened to her brother. They asked her if she had had anything to do with the death of the Panamanian. But she didn't say a word. She just sat there in a chair across from the Velázquez brothers, but she wasn't really there. She said she was remembering a day many years earlier when she and her brother had accompanied their mother to Burdine's in downtown Miami. Then the brother named Bull pulled out a knife and began to carve out pieces of her face. She said she didn't say a word even then. She didn't cry out. She just sat there. She said her neck and chest were dripping with blood. Then the brother named Horse grabbed the other one by the wrist and said enough, it is best not go on a killing spree today, and the brother named Bull put his knife away and told Isidora to go home. She said she tried to clean out her wound as best she could. She did not seek any medical attention. Nor did she call the police. For Isidora, the temporary pain of having a maniac carve up her face was a very small punishment compared to the gravity of her sin, and by sin she did not mean the death of the Panamanian. She meant her role in bringing 'death, that impertinent lover who whispers only bitter stories, to meet her brother.' That is exactly how she put it.

"After Isidora's brother was killed, she said she took over his diary. But her intentions were not as pristine as those of her brother. Emilio had once told her that every person the Velázquez brothers murdered seemed to vanish completely. It was as if they had never even existed, he had told her. This is why Emilio had kept the diary. He wanted a visible reminder that these poor murdered souls had once been alive. He wanted to honor their memories. But Isidora said she wanted vengeance. She wanted to document every gruesome detail of the crimes committed by the Velázquez brothers and then turn over the diary as evidence. She wanted to send them to the electric chair. She wanted to watch the Velázquez brothers fry. She said she hoped their executions would be botched so they would die inconceivably horrible deaths. She also said she was uncertain whom she could trust with her brother's diary, but she did believe that one day the Archangel Michael would appear with his fiery sword and show her the path to God's justice. So she added to Emilio's diary. From August 1981 to September 1986, Emilio had made one-hundred and fifty-seven entries with names, dates, and details about the lives of the victims. From October 1986 to June of 1994, Isidora recorded the stories of another three-hundred and seventy-five victims. She said the burden of so many deaths weighed heavily on her own soul. It was an unbelievable number of murders. It was incomprehensible. When I asked her why she stopped keeping the diary, I expected her to say that it was because having the reality of so many murders right there in front of her eyes was too much for her to take, that she was slowly, inevitably going mad. But she did not say this. Instead, Isidora said she stopped keeping the diary in July of 1994 because she saw a billboard with the face of a local news anchor, Eléna Montaño. Eléna Montaño was a local girl who had graduated from the University of Miami in 1977. She had been hired by Channel Ten in 1990 as an investigative reporter. In May of 1991 she became the weekend news anchor. Isidora said when she saw Eléna's face up on that billboard with those dark, inquisitive Spanish eyes and that bright, beaming smile, she knew immediately what she was going to do with the diary. She knew Eléna Montaño belonged to Gesù Church in downtown Miami. Gesù had been her mother's church. So she prepared a short letter, though she did not sign this letter or reveal her identity in any way, and then she placed the letter and the diary in a shoebox and went to the Church. She said there was only one priest in the Church when she got there. He was coming out of the confessional as she was heading up the aisle, and he had called out to her, asking her what she wanted. She told me it was as if God had been directing her footsteps. It was very dark inside the church. She could barely distinguish the priest in his dark clothes from the hazy darkness that surrounded them both. All she could really see was his glowing head and his strange eyes like the eyes of a frog or a bloated sea creature. But she was not afraid. She told the priest she had some information for the investigative reporter, Eléna Montaño, but she didn't know how to get in touch with her. The priest said he knew Eléna. He said he had known her since she was a small child. He would make sure she got the shoebox. Isidora said that she was suddenly full of hope. But one month later she saw on the news that Eléna Montaño had been killed in an auto accident. She had no idea what had become of the diary.

"As horrific as Isidora's story was, there were only two verifiable facts in the entire account, at least as far as I could determine. First, Isidora's brother Emilio died on Saturday, September 20, 1986. His body was found the following morning by pedestrians on the sidewalk next to a smoking shop on NW 22nd Avenue. His skull had been fractured, presumably as a result of falling or jumping off the roof of the cigarette store. In his report, the coroner noted that he couldn't say if Emilio had committed suicide or if his death had been accidental or if somebody had pushed him. The coroner also noted that he had ruled the death an accident because there were many more efficient ways of committing either suicide or murder. Not everyone who fell sixteen feet died from their injuries. Emilio had just been one of the unlucky ones. Second, news anchor Eléna Montaño was in fact tragically killed in an accident on the evening of Sunday, July 17, 1994. According to newspaper accounts of the day, she had been driving back from Bahia State Park down in the Keys and had apparently lost control of her vehicle while crossing the Seven Mile Bridge. She swerved into an oncoming truck and was knocked off the bridge, disappearing into sixteen feet of water. The current in the channel was approximately two knots. Her car, a Custom Club De Soto convertible, was recovered the next day. Ms. Montaño's bloated body washed up on Little Pine Key a week later.

"With the death of Eléna Montaño and the mystery surrounding the whereabouts of the diary, Isidora said she fell into a deep depression. She continued working for the Velázquez brothers because she had no other alternative. Since her face was disfigured, she was no longer asked to entertain the drug lords. She became instead a thief, a snitch lurking in doorways, a stalker of lonely hearts, a backdoor spy, a purveyor of half-truths and outright lies. In short, she became a stooge, and she remained employed by the Velázquez brothers even after they closed the club. She did whatever they asked her to do. Of course this new role took its toll on Isidora's psyche. She had all but given up hope that her tormentors would ever be brought to justice. And yet she did not completely abandon her faith in God. Every morning when she woke up, and every evening before she went to bed, she prayed that God would send her a sign, a divine message, so that she might escape her predicament.

"Isidora believes that she did receive just such a divinely inspired message from God in May of this year, though she is the first to admit that she did not recognize the nature of this message right away. In May of 2000, the Velázquez brothers asked her to keep an eye on one of her neighbors, a young man she knew as Broken Bike. Apparently Broken Bike had worked for the Velázquez brothers for a number of years, a fact which Isidora had not known. But he had fallen out of favor with his employers in the spring of 2000. At first, Isidora was simply to keep an eye on him and report on his activities every other day or so. She did this. But by the beginning of July, Isidora realized that the young man's life was in danger. She did not know the details of his disagreement with the Velázquez brothers, but she did know about their volatile hostility. Then she learned that Broken Bike's Christian name was Malachi. She was floored by this revelation. Malachi was the twelfth minor prophet in the Bible. The name Malachi meant Messenger of God. Isidora said that up until that moment she had been waiting for God's message, and then all of a sudden she was confronted with God's messenger in the flesh. It was almost more than she could believe. She said she became more vigilant in keeping an eye on Malachi after that, but her goal at that point was to protect him from the Velázquez brothers so she might learn what God intended. She also said this was not as easy as it sounded. The Velázquez brothers were angry, determined men. Their reach never seemed to exceed their grasp. Then on August 12th everything came to a head. Isidora saw Malachi at a parade and tried to warn him that the Velázquez brothers were going to shoot him on sight. She knew she was not the only one who was supposed to report on his whereabouts, so she took him to the ruins of La Campana. She said she thought they could hide out in La Campana until she could figure out what to do next. She said the Velázquez brothers never went there anymore. What she hadn't counted on, what she did not expect, was that Herminio would be at the club. Herminio had been the bartender at La Campana for years. Isidora said she and Malachi waltzed into the bar of the club and there was Herminio watching cartoons. She wasn't sure what to do. She said it was like two destinies colliding. She remembered feeling a wave a nausea roll through her, and then she heard herself tell Malachi her name. She said she knew Herminio would call the Velázquez brothers at the cartoon break. Then she realized that there was nothing she could do. Her fate, Malachi's fate, everyone's fate was in God's hands. So she left.

"When I asked Isidora what had happened to Malachi, she smiled and said Malachi was very, very lucky, and then she laughed and said even though there is no such thing as luck. When I asked her how she knew this, she said she was watching from the shadows. She said she was filled with great remorse after she had abandoned Malachi, so she hid herself in the empty shell of an old car in the lot next to La Campana. She said she could see everything from where she was hiding. She saw Herminio leave through a back door. Ten minutes later a young man she did not know pushed his way through the front door. A few minutes after that the Velázquez brothers went into the club through the side door Herminio had used. Herminio returned. A few moments later Malachi came out the front door. He was flying down the street. Then there was some shouting and a few muffled gunshots from inside the club. Then the Velázquez brothers ran out into the street. They were turning around in circles, but they had no idea which way Malachi had gone. They headed off, but it was in the wrong direction.

"Isidora said she later spotted Malachi sitting on a bench on the elevated platform of the Allapattah Metro Station. Malachi sat there until after the sun had set and then he headed off into the darkness. Isidora said she followed him to a club called La Mamacita's, but she did not go in herself. She said an international film star named Salma de la Prada was holding court inside and that Malachi was hoping to speak with her. Nevertheless, she said the place seemed strangely vacant for a Saturday night, and the thought crossed her mind that perhaps the Velázquez brothers were lying in wait and that as soon as Malachi went in he would be killed. Then a black SUV pulled up and the Velázquez brothers got out and ran right past her. She said they had seemed oblivious to the world and everything that was good. A few minutes later the unmistakable sounds of gunfire erupted inside La Mamacita's. Windows were shattered. Bullet holes appeared in the exterior walls and the flat, warehouse-style roof, and the front door was completely blown away. A cloud of tiny fragments blew into her face and that was when she injured her eye.

"After the commotion had subsided, she went inside. She said she saw men dressed in body armor clearing away broken glass and bits of rubble, the remnants of what surely must have been a hellacious gunfight. The men were speaking a strange, guttural language she did not recognize. She saw a giant of a man attending to Malachi, whose arm appeared to be broken, but otherwise he was unhurt. The Velázquez brothers were nowhere to be found. It was as if their bodies had merged with the hazy darkness of the night sky, which was now visible through the holes in the roof, a darkness which seemed to be descending, filling in all of the empty space inside La Mamacita's. This is exactly how Isidora described the scene. Then she saw two beefy men carrying Salma de la Prada to a limousine that had suddenly pulled up to the club. She was an immaculate vision, Isidora said. Her feet never touched the ground. Then the limousine drove off. Then there was a steady procession of men in body armor climbing into several vans that had also appeared as if by magic. The vans followed the limousine. Isidora said that by that point she could hear the sounds of sirens floating through the night air. It was like a choir of invisible angels, she said. Ten minutes later two ambulances arrived. Malachi was loaded into one of the ambulances and an old man into the other. She said she knew Malachi was all right, but she went to Jackson Memorial just to be sure.

"Isidora said she was excited beyond her ability to comprehend. The terror that was the Velázquez brothers had been eliminated. God had finally answered her prayers.

"Of course based on her incredibly complicated tale of woe, we decided Isidora might benefit from speaking with a psychiatrist. She said that would be fine. She had been to a psychiatrist one summer as a young girl. In fact, she had been to three. She was not afraid of them. Two days later we had her evaluated by Dr. Samuel Quintana, a psychiatrist who has been on the staff at Jackson Memorial for years. Dr. Quintana said Isidora was as sane as you or I. She had a few nervous tics, a few paranoias, and she harbored a few illusions about what had transpired over the years. But who among us is immune to the vagaries of life? Dr. Quintana conceded that Isidora might benefit from continued counseling, but he felt quite strongly that she would benefit far more by finding a safe, stable place to call home, and by making a few friends. Dr. Quintana also suggested that given her abiding faith in God, she would probably find immense satisfaction from connecting with one of the dozens of Catholic churches in the Greater Miami metropolitan area.

"As luck would have it, though I can hear Isidora herself saying that luck had nothing to do with it, we were able to secure accommodations for her with a community of nuns up in Hialeah. I met with the Mother Superior of the convent, Sister Silvia Faustina, and their Director of Spiritual Life, Sister Nadia Saenz. We spoke about Isidora's situation, her need for stability, etc., and they agreed to drive down to the Center and meet with her. After the meeting, they were bursting with excitement. They assured me that Isidora had found a home with them in Hialeah. She would be well cared for in their convent. They were certain the story of her life would inspire their young novitiates. They were amazed that she could have endured so much and yet possess so strong a faith. She had, they said, followed the excruciatingly rocky, narrow path of the saints. They also thought she might enjoy talking with young women in need of spiritual guidance. There were plenty of churches in the Miami area hungry for speakers with Isidora's gift. Isidora was an example for us all. Three days later, at one in the afternoon on Monday, October 30, 2000, Sister Faustina and an older, gray-haired gentleman named Emidio Peralta (who possessed a well-worn but kindly face) pulled up to the Center in an old station wagon. Emidio helped Isidora into the back seat. He was very polite and she was very gracious. Then they left."

-132-

From a forty-minute interview with Emidio Peralta as part of the University of Miami Oral History Project, conducted by Nathalia Ibarra, a Senior at the University of Miami, and recorded by Tomás De Aguero, a Junior, at the Otto G. Richter Library from 3-5 PM on Sunday, October 26, 2008:

[**Interviewer's comments:** Emidio moved to Florida from Maracaibo, Venezuela in 1976. He was thirty-two when he arrived in Miami. He said his childhood years were unremarkable. His father worked for a large industrial chemical company along Avenida San Francisco. His mother worked as a surgical nurse at the Surgical and Maternity Hospital of Maracaibo. He did not see much of his parents. He was like every other teenage boy growing up in Maracaibo in the 50s and 60s. He graduated in the middle of his high school class. He played soccer in the streets. He stayed out of trouble. His life was dull, he said. Later, he hoped to go to work in the petrochemical industry, so in 1973 he enrolled in the University of Zulia to study Petroleum engineering and make this dream come true, but he dropped out of the program after two years. His father had died from complications due to emphysema, which Emidio said was fairly common among the men working at the chemical factory, so there was no money to pay for his education. Emidio never did earn a degree. He has no children. He never married, though he has been in two long-term relationships, one in Maracaibo and one in Miami. After his mother followed his father to the grave in 1976, he came to the United States and found factory work with a company called Dolphin Boats, located in Homestead, Florida. He spent sixteen years building fishing boats. In 1992 he went to work as a janitor for the Servants of the Pierced Hearts of Jesus and Mary, a religious order of mostly Hispanic nuns in Hialeah. He has been there ever since.]

[This excerpt begins at the **18:21** mark.]

Nathalia: Why did you decide to work for the Servants of the Pierced Hearts of Jesus and Mary after sixteen years of building boats?

Emidio: It is not always so easy to say why one does one thing and not another. I was tired of building boats, that is for certain. I worked as a fiberglass laminator to create the hulls for custom built boats. Most people don't know all the work that goes into building boats. When I started, we were building boats with sold hulls. We built very good boats. I was proud of every boat we built. Then one day we began building boats with cored hulls. This was in the mid-80s, I think. We wanted to be very high-tech. We used foam for the core. We even used a vibrating machine on the hull to make sure the bonding putty was spread out evenly throughout the core and that all the seams were filled, but this didn't always work. But foam was the thing, even though it caused a lot of problems. I remember one year we started using a new kind of foam called Airex. It was supposed to be stronger and lighter. A hull made with this material was supposedly less likely to absorb water. What the salesmen who sold us Airex didn't know, and what we found out later, was that the foam would soften at high temperatures. Then the hulls would blister, and then they would start to come apart. So we stopped using Airex. But when the next new thing came along, we jumped right on that bandwagon just like every other small boat manufacturer, and hoped for the best. I guess that's when I became disillusioned with building boats and I started to wonder about the future, my future. I realized I needed to do something different. This was in 1991. August maybe. Or September. I was very worried about this. There were many nights I did not sleep. Then on All Saints Day, and I remember this like it was yesterday, I knelt down before Mass and started to pray, and I heard my voice, only it didn't sound like my voice, it sounded very far away, a small, thin voice, like my father's voice when he was dying of emphysema, but not mine, and yet I heard the words distinctly, clearly, like the tolling of a distant church bell. I was saying, 'God, I do not want to die in a boat factory. Tell me what I should do?' And just like that the answer came. God asked me to come work for Him.

Nathalia: But you did not leave the factory right away.

Emidio: No. I did not want to believe God was calling me to work for the Church. I pretended that God was calling someone else.

Nathalia: What made you change your mind?

Emidio: Well for one thing, God is very persistent. Whenever I began to pray, he would interrupt me within the first minute or two to ask me when I was going to quit the boat factory. This went on for three or four months. That kind of pressure takes its toll after a while. So one day I asked Monsignor Guidera what I should do. He suggested I work for the nuns up in Hialeah. They had only been around a few years. They needed a janitor. I went up to Hialeah and met Sister Faustina and she hired me on the spot.

Nathalia: What was the transition like?

Emidio: It was not so bad as you might think. There are many moments when you are building a boat that feel like praying. You are at peace with the world. You are living outside yourself, as if you have left your body and are looking down from somewhere, watching, and in that same moment you are deep within yourself, like a seed that has been planted. I found the same to be true working for the Sisters of the Pierced Hearts, though maybe not right away.

[At the **21:27** mark the tape recording became unintelligible and remained unintelligible for twelve minutes and six seconds. The remainder of this excerpt picks up at the **33:33** mark. During this segment, Emidio talks about his relationship with an elderly woman named Isidora, who stayed at the convent from 2000 until 2007. It is not clear from the interview if Isidora died or moved away.]

Nathalia: Had you ever met anyone like Isidora?

Emidio: There was no one like Isidora. She was beyond my imagination. She was an extraordinary woman.

Nathalia: What made her so extraordinary?

Emidio: There was not just one thing. She was filled with joy, and for those of us who have grown old, to be filled with joy is a tremendous gift. She also did not judge you. She took the Bible to heart in this. And she loved poetry. She would ask me to bring her books of poetry. Old poets, new poets, she read them all. I must confess to you that I never bothered with poetry until I met Isidora. I do not remember the names of the poets, but whenever I brought her a new book she would ask me to sit with her and she would read some of the poems out loud. It sounded to me as if she had written the poems herself. I did not tell her this, but she had the voice of an angel.

Nathalia: Was your relationship with Isidora a romantic one?

Emidio: No, it was not romantic. But I truly loved her. Everyone loved her. If you had known her, you would have loved her too.

Nathalia: What is your favorite memory of Isidora?

Emidio: I do not think 'favorite' is the right word. I have so many memories of Isidora. I remember one day Isidora showed me a newspaper article about a guitar player, a young man with a ponytail, who had been murdered in Fort Lauderdale. He had been a great guitarist, and after his death, a Miami artist had painted his face on a wall in some park I had never heard of. A photo of the face on the wall accompanied the article. I remember staring at the face, and then all of a sudden I could actually hear guitar music, as if the young man with the ponytail were playing his guitar right there in Isidora's room. I don't know what kind of expression my face registered. But then Isidora asked me if I could hear him playing. Did I hear any music? I was so startled by the question that I didn't say anything right away. I remember thinking either she heard this ethereal music the same as I did, or I was going completely mad. The next thing I remember I started laughing. I guess in my heart I was trying to tell Isidora that whatever she heard, I heard too, whatever secrets she wished to share, I would guard them with my life. I was trying to tell her all this, but I was incapable of speech at that moment. Then the music stopped and Isidora and I decided we would seek out this wall with the face of the young guitarist who had been killed. I didn't know the park in the article, but we would find it, I told her, the two of us. But this never happened. We never went out in search of that park. Not even once.

[36:26.]

PART THREE
(an elegy for a dream once dreamt)

. . . ni dans le vice, ni dans la vertu qu'est le bonheur: c'est dans la manière dont nous sommes disposés pour sentir l'un ou l'autre, et dans le choix que nous faisons d'après cette organisation.

De Sade, L'Histoire de Juliette, ou les Prospérités du Vice

BOOK SEVEN

the diary of Emilio Escoraz Calzada

-133-

Father Anton Kreutner, our favorite German priest, had left the priesthood. He had been sent to Miami in 1952 and had become something resembling a permanent fixture of Gesù Church, and then just like that, at the dawn of the new century, he left.

Naturally we were all left wondering. While everyone admitted that a crisis of faith could strike anyone at any moment, we all agreed to a man that Father Anton was a most unlikely candidate. None of us could quite believe our ears when we first heard the news. We stood on the jagged precipice of belief, not knowing if we should fall forward and be consumed, or if we should find a bed somewhere and lie down and hope it was all a disturbing dream. We stepped nimbly back from the precipice (we've always been very light on our toes), but not very far (we've always striven to keep our options open for as long as humanly possible), and then we began to box our villainous ears for attending to such voluble lies. We boxed them and boxed them without mercy until we couldn't hear a thing except for a dull whooshing sound because our ears were filling up with fresh new blood. But the news was not a lie. So we had bloodied our ears for nothing, a realization that in many respects was a stinging defeat, at least this is how we later thought of it, when looking back.

Was Father Anton's sudden departure a symptom of that chronic, cynical ultra-modern distrust of religion, a phenomenon of these last one-hundred years, that seems to infect everyone sooner or later, though to varying degrees? Or was there something more diabolical at work? Had he perhaps been seduced by the mysticism of the Orient? Had he given in to the satanic pleasures of the flesh? Had he simply lost touch with reality, snap, like a light bulb suddenly going dark? What would induce a man who had worn the priest's collar for forty-eight years to make such a rash decision?

Yes, we had many such questions, so we decided to examine the good Father's life in excruciatingly painful detail. We would chronicle every major event from the rainy day of his birth until the rainy day he abandoned his ecclesiastical duties and boarded a bus for the great unknown. We would then follow him on his journey into this nether world, in search of what, we dared not even contemplate. (To be honest, even now we are not sure what he was seeking.) We would expend vast sums of money to get the information we needed. We certainly had the resources. We are a pretty big outfit.

We would dig through boxes of forgotten records, lost letters, old notebooks, government documents, newspaper articles, faded photographs with notes scribbled on the back, official transcripts, you name it.

We would interview witnesses of every ilk, those who had known Father Anton when he was a child or were familiar with the community where he had grown up, those who had known him when he was a priest and then after he had left the priesthood, and those who had only heard gossip about him.

We would stop at nothing in our search for the truth.

Because Father Anton had been our friend and we felt slightly betrayed since he hadn't spoken to any of us about his intentions, not a word, and so we decided we were owed the truth. Because we still believed we could bring him back into the fold if only we knew what had upset him so. Because we felt the lessons we might learn from his story could be shaped and shared and maybe save a few souls.

Because, because, because.

We wondered how long he had been teetering dangerously on the lip and if we might have sensed his precarious position if we had been paying closer attention. We wondered if foreknowledge would have made any difference.

We wondered, we wondered, we wondered.

And to help us with our work, we would hire a university student to take on the role of chronicler, to sift through the mounds of data we would collect, and after that he (the student) would give form to these mounds, because mounds are often unmanageable when they are allowed to remain in their natural unsifted, unplundered state, and then he (still the student) would go back to his studies, quietly, without any fuss or fanfare, and let us bask in the glory of a finished document. Of course we would take great pains to make sure that our chronicler was well versed, shall we say, in the various currents that made up the river of Father Anton's life. His versing needed to be up to snuff. And he would need to possess an impeccable character, an uncompromising disposition with regards to Church Law and the moral dignity of all God's children, for he would be dealing with the intimate secrets of another man's life. His moral compass would need to be unbreakable.

And so after much scrutiny, and for reasons known only to a few of us, we would choose a capable (but not too capable) graduate student from the University of Greifswald, located, as you might have guessed, in Greifswald, Germany, a town originally founded in 1199 by a group of Cistercian monks. Oh we would be quite lucky in our choice of chronicler. Capable, certainly. He would begin his narrative where any good third-person narrative begins, from a lofty perch say fifty-thousand feet up. Or even further. But he would quickly descend, paragraph by paragraph, until he entered the very soul of Father Anton, at which point his third-person narrative would shimmer with the intensity of an intimate first-person confession. Yes, our chronicler would show himself to be quite capable. But not too capable.

He would not, for example, comment on the natural, blasphemous ironies which arise from living everyday life, ironies which punctuate every man's tale of woe and which, by the very fact that they are woven into the fabric of human existence, call into question the inviolability of Church dogma. Perhaps he did not see these ironies, or, being young, he did not recognize them for what they were. In any case, we would judge the value of his narrative (and the degree to which we considered him capable) by what he actually set down on the page and not by what he might have written.

Would we have embarked upon such a fool's quest if we had known how long it would take? Certainly. We are in fact a very big outfit, much bigger than most, and more than capable of weathering the anxiety of a project that drags on for decades, in some cases, even centuries. We are considered by some to be experts in such matters. But enough of these dull, dry preliminaries. We shall now pass the baton to our capable (but not too capable, as has already been mentioned) chronicler.

From the capable, but not too capable, chronicler's Preface:

Everyone who knew Father Anton thought he displayed admirable restraint whenever he came face to face with those who allowed cheap, transitory thrills and the spectre of tawdry, lust-filled bohemian days to take the place of God. On occasion his temper would give way, particularly when immigrant couples asked him to say a funeral Mass for a dead baby when that baby had never been baptized, which happened more often than you would think. According to various witnesses, Father Anton would say there was nothing the Church could do under such circumstances, the fate of the child's unbaptized soul was in the hands of the angels now, but instead of accepting the spiritual wisdom of this well-informed counsel, these couples would become angry, insolent, they pretended they knew more about God than the good German priest, some would even begin cursing him right there on the steps of the Cathedral, their language overflowing with febrile images of death and destruction and angels holding flaming swords which they would turn hari-kari style upon themselves. So it is no wonder that on occasion Father Anton would lose his temper. Still, these outbursts were quite rare, and short-lived in their effect, arriving and departing like the plague, so they were soon forgotten, swept under the rug, washed away with the tide, sent hurtling into the void like speeding bullets. Besides, none of the various witnesses could fault the good German for assuming the role of God's policeman. It was a role he was born to play. Everyone said so. He was a paragon of priestly virtue. He loomed larger than life. Everyone agreed. Yet there were moments when you looked at him out of the corner of your eye, an eye perhaps inflamed with conjunctivitis, perhaps just after you had received communion, and he was giving you a strange, belittling look but you didn't know why; or perhaps by chance the two of you were waiting for a downtown bus outside Burdine's Department Store in Miami, but he didn't recognize you (or even pretend to) when you said 'Good afternoon Father,' and when the bus finally arrived, he pushed his way past everyone in line (even the exhausted grandmothers struggling to stay afloat amid a sea of bags) so he could get to the one remaining seat. In moments like those he seemed very small and ordinary indeed.

Let us admit the fact that the good German priest was ordinary. But how does one define ordinary? Do we mean how one behaves compared to everyone else? Do we mean what one thinks or what one says (and the contradictions that often exist between the two) relative to the population at large? Do we mean how someone looks, their physical appearance? Are they somewhere in between the two extremes of the uncommonly beautiful and the uncommonly ugly? Father Anton was, on the whole, closer to the uncommonly ugly end of the spectrum. In this respect he was uncommon. He had very strange looking eyes. He had very large pupils, two saucer-sized discs, a stormy, nocturnal, seafaring gray in color, almost black, floating haphazardly across the surface of two enormous, oceanic eyeballs. Like the eyes of an amphibian. But in other respects he was quite common. He wore his dark hair cropped very short, perhaps to hide the fact that he was going bald, a solution which many of us have adopted, but such is the price of vanity, and he had a brightly-glowing, ruddy complexion like many of his parishioners, particularly those who spent too many hours in the hot Miami sun. He also possessed a thick neck with bulges of folded-over skin on the back of it, and he maintained this thick, bulgy, over-fed quality all the way up past his sun-burnt ears to the top of his perspiring forehead. (It was always perspiring.) If you looked only at his head, from any angle, you would have thought he was an ex-farmhand or an ex-wrestler or an ex-Marine. (Common enough, except for the eyes.) But if you viewed him from a distance, so that you could see a skinny, unpretentious body dangling beneath that bulgy head with those strange amphibious eyes, a body with long slender, unmuscular appendages and soft, whitish, overly long though narrow feet (if you happened to catch him without shoes and socks), you would have thought you were looking at a giant, genetically manipulated frog, an experiment that had gone horribly wrong from the get-go. (Uncommon.) Naturally, a surface description of this kind, focused exclusively as it must be on trivial physical details, doesn't provide a clue about the interior man. It reveals more about our own (meaning those of the various witnesses) latent prejudices and phobias than anything else. Oh to wander among the stars without a care! To ply the heavens in a spacecraft with a gleaming, golden photon sail! What a dream that is. So we must begin to shift our perspective. We must look at the life of Father Anton with the eye of a clockmaker. Only then will we be able to determine why this humble clock broke down.

-134-

Father Anton grew up in Metz, a city in northeastern France divided by two rivers, the sun-gleaming Moselle with its golden bull-face which will forever live on the lips of men in cherished song, according to the Latin poet Ausonius, and the Moselle's little sister, the Little Seille River, Saint Peter's brook to some. The fabled, shining city of Metz was the historic home of the Merovingian kings of Austrasia during the sixth, seventh, and eighth centuries. Charlemagne himself, who came after the Merovingians, would later ride through Metz on his way south to the Abbey at Remiremont, where he and his sons held their grand autumn hunts. For a thousand years, from the reign of Louis the Pious (813-840) until the Age of Napoleon, the city was a safe haven for fugitive serfs and Jewish bankers, Saracens and Saxons and wanderers returning from the east. By all written accounts, it was a veritable paradise on earth. It was a city of gleaming knights and lush gardens and fairytale balls and visiting Italian contessas and happy-go-lucky vagabonds who traveled only by night and claimed to be Russian princes in disguise and gold-mitred Bishops galore. The city of Metz served as a crossroads for the world. It was later annexed by hungry Bismark and the hungrier German Empire in 1871 (the Kreutner family immigrated from Saarbrücken the following year and settled in a suburb just south of the center of the city, three or four blocks from the botanical gardens on a street lined with purple hued French lilacs, a close cousin to the Persian lilac), returned to the French after World War One (the Kreutner family, which was now more or less a clan, remained), annexed by the Nazis during World War Two (the members of the Kreutner clan, those who hadn't fled Europe altogether, had mixed feelings), and returned to the French after the war ended (the Kreutner clan, which now numbered in the hundreds, breathed out a collective sigh of relief and then breathed in the heady, sickly sweet almost suffocating fragrance of the lilacs, which were then in bloom).

Young Anton was born in Metz during the interlude between the two wars. His father, Johann Kreutner, worked for the Est railway Company as an assistant to the workshop manager in Montigny-lès-Metz, until he died quite suddenly of a bullet (no one knows who pulled the trigger or why) in 1938. It is not clear if his mother, Yvette Kreutner (nee Allemande), held a position of any kind. She died of natural causes in the summer of 1963. The only other family personage of any significance in young Anton's life was a distant cousin, Josef Kreutner, who was twenty-six when Anton was born. Cousin Josef lived just outside Saarbrücken, Germany and made an occasional journey to visit what he jokingly (which is to say with a mischievous glint in his eyes) called 'his long-lost relatives like the lost tribes of Israel.' He took a particular shine to his young cousin.

When Anton was very young, perhaps as old as five, but certainly he had not yet attained the age of reason, an unnerving calamity overtook the neighborhood where he lived, as it overtook the larger environs of Metz as well. According to newspaper accounts of the day, that particular July had been the warmest ever recorded with temperatures reaching an unthinkable thirty-nine degrees Celsius, dropping only to thirty-four at night. As a consequence, the level of the river Moselle was so low it was said you could see the bones of the Seven Swabians, archetypes of deluded thinking, who had died a century earlier while trying to cross the deep, mossy waters. The level of the little river Seille was so low it seemed little more than a drainage ditch. People were on edge. The green pastures that dotted the surrounding countryside turned a dull, pasty brown color. The cows stopped giving milk. Homegrown foodstuffs began to taste like dust or wither away completely. (Only the Mirabelle plum crop was unaffected.) And while all sorts of culinary goodies were still arriving by rail (the number of freight trains had apparently increased at this point during the crisis), the general populace in some of the more wretched, virtually treeless neighborhoods, what many would call slums (not the Kreutner's neighborhood by any stretch) began to look like refugees with dark hollow eyes, their skeletal fingers sifting through garbage bins and then popping morsels of this or that into trembling mouths.

As you might have guessed, the degradation of the food supply was only the beginning. In the first week of August, various prominent vineyards throughout the Moselle Valley and beyond, vineyards that had produced the finest quality wines since before the twelfth century (and where the grapes were tended with a vigilante vigilance usually associated with religious fanatics), these majestic economic engines were suddenly engulfed in great waves of flame. A great debate ensued as to the origin of these fires. The cafés and restaurants, which seemed the only venues in the entire city where one might still get a decent meal, were filled with debaters. Some thought the firing of the vineyards was caused by the spontaneous combustion of the grapes. Naturally this was the opinion embraced by the vineyard owners, who were all in the process of filing claims with their insurance companies because their policies paid off handsomely in cases of natural disaster. A small minority believed that the cause could be readily ascertained if one only pierced the surface shell of those confident vineyard owners and so reveal the enterprising desperation like a diesel-powered turbine which hummed along unseen, and which had in all probability been a catalyst turning those same vineyard owners into arsonists in the hopes of salvaging some monetary value from a useless crop. This was the opinion of the insurance companies. But the vast majority thought the destruction of the vineyards was quite simply the wrath of an angry and unappeased God who had been watching the citizens of Metz gorge themselves on the spoils of war (World War One), spoils which always go to the victor (France and the Allies) and so are often claimed as irrefutable proof of the righteousness of the victory, while a scant seventy kilometers away their German brethren, the vanquished, along with those belonging to what was left of the Austro-Hungarian Empire, who were much further away than seventy kilometers but whose circumstances were just as desperate (but not the infidel Turks, those allies in defeat were not even a thought in the addled brains of the citizens of Metz), were all slowly starving to death, their only nourishment coming from thin barley soup and weak chamomile tea and an irretractable belief in the justice of Divine Providence equally distributed. All of this, with minor theological variations here and there, was the position held by the various priests and rabbis throughout the city who were using the example of the horrendous, hellish heat to demonstrate what lay in store for those who turned their backs on God and their fellowman. The priests and rabbis of Metz had been pounding away at their congregations for weeks.

Throughout the month of August, the temperatures continued to soar. Everyone wondered when God would relent. The city was on the verge of panic. The Jewish banks, which normally were open five days a week from eight until three, reduced their operating hours to Tuesdays and Wednesdays from nine till noon, so the amount of ready coin and paper money circulating about the city was reduced. The Place d'Armes, which was the only square in the city without any trees, and which under normal conditions was the home to local farmers and local artisans and various itinerant peddlers from only God knew where, all of them engaged in selling their wares every morning of the week except Sunday, when the square was filled with the faithful heading to Mass at the Cathedral, the Place d'Armes was now vacant. The absence of the trees was magnified. The neoclassical majesty of the City Hall building, which stood opposite the gleaming, honey-colored majesty of the Cathedral, was now a dark, ominous brooding shadow. Every door was bolted shut, the gates padlocked. The hustle and bustle that normally occurred beneath the street-level open-air arcade was a distant memory. There were also unsubstantiated reports that the police were occupying the seventeen bridges that spanned the Moselle and its tributaries in and around Metz in an attempt to limit the flow of traffic into the center of the city, and so stave off the riots that many thought would happen but never did. The authorities later denounced these reports in an effort to maintain some semblance of public decorum. A newspaper article giving a detailed if not slightly sensational (many said it was preposterous) account of 'An old geezer without a friend in the world who became a casualty while attempting to cross one of the occupied bridges' was decried as outright propaganda. (Ironically, and to some degree prophetically, the bridge named in the article was the very same bridge that became known as The Bridge of Death when the Germans occupied Metz during World War Two.) The editor of the newspaper, who happened to be a brother-in-law of the Commissaire de Police, was jailed for a month on suspicion of sedition, a trumped-up charge if there ever was one, which probably had more to with an inter-family squabble than a violation of the law.

Finally, as if this list of the inevitable consequences of a natural disaster wasn't enough, the number of trains on the Paris to Strasbourg line that would always turn north at Nancy on their way to Metz and then Mannheim on the Rhine had suddenly and mysteriously decreased, so the quality of the food in the cafés and restaurants throughout the city also decreased, which had, as you might have expected, a deflating, demoralizing effect on everyone's appetite, but which also had quite paradoxically an amazingly innervating effect on the nature of the debates, which had not entirely abated in all those many weeks since the mercury had first begun to rise, but which had lost the nervous, feverish energy that had initially caused so many tongues to wag. The origin of the vineyard fires was all but forgotten. Instead, the debaters began drawing hastily conceived parallels between the current set of circumstances and the ancient plagues of Egypt. Some thought this line of reasoning was premature. A few cows had died. The bark of the trees had turned gray, ashen. The grass had turned brown. But so what. It was very hot. It was summer. Besides, the sky was still blue. True, the rivers had ceased to be highways of navigation, but the water had not turned red. There were no frogs or locusts, though there were biting flies. Fire had not rained down from the heavens. The first-born of France had not died, except perhaps for a few scoundrels and down-and-outers living in hovels in the more wretched neighborhoods of Metz (such as that lonely eyesore stretch on Rue Franiatte with its dilapidated cafés like the Café Tivoli, where the prostitutes often gathered after a night working the streets, sitting at tables covered with a thin veneer of gray dust, drinking black coffees and joking about the vanity of men; or perhaps hidden away humped-snail style in the shadows of the parish of Saint-Ferroy as they, the down-and-outers, wheezed their last breath, perhaps somewhere along Rue Marchant, where every row house was home to fifteen persons crammed together for lack of better options, or perhaps up past the Arsenal and then down the steep to the Little Seille River and the Quai des Juifs). But the Egyptian plague advocates were not dissuaded. Why wait until the outcome was an indelible stain upon history, they argued? Wouldn't it be more prudent to plan for the worst and save a few lives in the process?

But the dissenters, who were quite clearly strict literalists as far as the Bible was concerned and cared little for the judgment of history, pointed out that the scourge of Metz, which was the name assigned to this calamity by the priests and rabbis, had a long way to go before it reached Biblical proportions. And besides, they argued, no matter what they did or didn't do, the outcome, which was part of God's divine plan, was a foregone conclusion.

The crisis reached its zenith in the beginning of September, the month of the Holy Cross. That is when the city was effectively consumed by crickets. No one had noticed the crickets at first. Even when the speed and intensity of their singing increased, as is only natural when the temperature rises, no one paid much attention. The citizens of Metz were too busy singing their own songs of woe to notice the commentary of this ancient chorus, and in all truth, if these nocturnal singers had kept to the crevices and cracks that permeate the underbelly of the city, as had been their custom for centuries, then no one in Metz would have viewed them as a menace. But by the end of August, the frenzy of these nightly cricket serenades had spilled out like a great shimmering, oily black wave onto sidewalks and down side streets and across the flagstone terraces of several small restaurants on Rue de Jardin. From there the cricket hordes like descendants of the blood-thirsty Moguls began migrating into various businesses: print shops and bakeries and drug stores and a few dry goods shops, and also the Hotel Royal, and a leather goods shop on Rue au Blé and a jeweler's shop only three blocks from the Cathedral and a few ladies shoe stores, and a billiards hall tucked away in a forgotten corner of Rue de Roches; the crickets spurred on in all probability by the need to find water.

Oh, 'we often make spider webs out of smoke and saliva,' to quote a Sufi mystic. This was the case with the civic response to the menace of the cricket hordes. False flags were everywhere. On the day the crickets invaded the billiards hall, within three hours of the discovery of the infestation, a note signed 'with the greatest urgency, M. Mirman' (who was a Commissioner of the French Republic assigned to the city of Metz) was delivered by special courier to M. Prevel, the Mayor of Metz (an ironic display of the prerogatives that come with power, which was noted by several newspapers with thinly disguised cynicism, as M. Mirman was an avid billiards player).

The very next day the city decided to begin the process of fumigating those buildings which had fallen into the hands (or to be more precise, the serrated legs) of the enemy, but all this did was to make the buildings uninhabitable for several days (except for the billiards hall – somehow the fumigation canister exploded, which sparked a small broom closet fire, which soon swept through the entire building, gutting the interior, before a hastily assembled bucket brigade of soon-to-be-ex-billiards players, which was, as you might have guessed, organized by the Commissioner, took what little water they could from the little Seille and so prevented the fire from spreading beyond a few additional buildings). When the owners of the fumigated structures returned (including the owners of the billiards hall, who arrived with an aggressive team of insurance adjusters to properly assess the damage), they discovered the population of the crickets had quite unexpectedly increased. (It should be noted here that the number of crickets discovered among the ash piles inside the ravaged billiards hall was double the number found in the other fumigated buildings, a scientific implausibility to say the least given that everything else in the billiards hall had melted from the heat of the fire. Even the slate tables and the light fixtures had assumed a molten form and after cooling resembled nothing if not meteors that had survived the passage through the Earth's atmosphere. But the amazingly resilient billiards hall crickets, those harbingers of death, were also now a gleaming jet black color, as opposed to the dirty brownish beige color of their birth. It was a sudden — one hesitates to say miraculous — transformation that left one wondering in private if perhaps the theory of evolution was incomplete at best.) To make matters worse, the cricket hordes no longer confined their terrorist activities to the dark hours. As if by conscious choice they began to attack the city in broad daylight, swarming over entire city blocks in a matter of hours. It was a deluge of crickets, now black as well as brown.

Naturally the priests and rabbis of Metz were alarmed. On August 30, 1925, the very last Sunday of that hellish month (Saturday the 29th for the rabbis, of course) they called for the wholesale slaughter of the crickets. They said they had been mistaken about the nature of the calamity, that it wasn't an example of what might befall the wicked (indeed, it could not be thus for the scourge was already here), that it was instead the physical manifestation of the potential for evil that existed inside every man's soul and could only be truly eradicated by the collective strength of the citizens of Metz. It was a test of the spiritual will of God's chosen people, whether they were Roman Catholic, Lutheran, Calvinist, or Jewish did not matter, a test sent by God Himself to affirm His superiority over all creation (as opposed to an example of God's infinitely perverse almost Machiavellian sense of humor, which is what some of the citizens of Metz whispered to each other after the cafés had closed and they were walking home arms linked and they couldn't avoid stepping in puddle after puddle of deranged crickets because the only illumination at that hour was provided by a few distant street lamps that seemed to wink out as one got closer.)

The priests and rabbis encouraged the citizens of Metz

to appropriate whatever weapons they could find in this battle against the crickets, whatever was available: shovels, wooden paddles, mallets, the oars of abandoned rowboats, brooms, garden utensils, cooking utensils, even dough board scrapers, as long as one was down on one's knees, leather straps, old shit-kicking boots if the soles weren't rotten, in which case the boots would fall apart with the first good whack, anything with a flat surface that could be applied using a vicious, downward swinging motion so that the cricket menace could be defeated in a speedy and efficient manner.

Needless to say, the call to arms did not have the intended effect. Some of the more prominent citizens of Metz claimed they were pacifist by nature, even with respect to rampaging insects. Others, less prominent but more vocal, said they could not stomach the thought of the little beasties, much less face them on the open battlefield. Still others, mainly members of the faculty of the Artillery and Engineering College, believed the hordes of crickets were a sanitation issue and so fell outside the generally accepted boundaries of modern warfare. What was needed, they said, was for the City Councilmen and the Mayor to get off their respective duffs. What was needed, they said, was simply the will to get the job done, and perhaps a knowledge of science. Religion should be left out of the mix altogether. The priests and rabbis were flabbergasted. They began to see the cricket menace as capable of toppling religious institutions. And where would that leave the faithful? The crickets suddenly metamorphosed into seditious agents of Satan, who was known to a few of the rabbis as Abaddon, and to others as Apollyon, but who was known to all as the Angel of the Abyss.

One week later, on Sunday evening, the 6th of September 1925, the priests and the rabbis went directly to M. Prevel and several councilmen, who were enjoying a pleasant Sunday supper at M. Prevel's residence, a very grand neo-classical style house near the botanical gardens on Rue du Canal. The house was surrounded on three sides by lime trees and oaks, but the fourth side (which faced the barren northeast), the side with the dining room and an elegant marble terrace, afforded M. Prevel and his household with a view of the river and the decaying greenery all around and two gleaming bridges in the distance, and on sunny days (and every day was sunny that summer) the Cathedral spires sparkled as if a star had fallen to the earth.

The priests and the rabbis firmly declared that if the citizens of Metz did not rise up in the face of this unforeseen danger (and no one in their right mind could have seen this coming, they said), then the city would be entirely consumed. The Mayor and the councilmen, impressed with the serious demeanor of the clergy, were beside themselves with anxiety, for they were all pretty happy with their current positions and did not wish to be unseated by a plague of crickets. They scheduled a meeting for the very next day. They would meet on the small outdoor terrace adjacent to M. Prevel's dining room to avoid having to go back to City Hall just yet. (The very same terrace where they had been enjoying their pleasant supper when the priests and rabbis had arrived.) The philosophy of wait-and-see, which in any other crisis would have guided their decision-making process, was abandoned without a second thought (or even a first thought, for that matter). Later, at around nine, after the others had hurried home, the Mayor called upon M. Mirman, who immediately understood the scope of the calamity facing the city and drafted an edict declaring that a state of emergency now existed in Metz and that the citizens of Metz were bound by their duty to both God and their country to take up arms against the insect invaders.

The next day, at four-thirty in the afternoon, Mssrs. Prevel and Mirman passed out copies of the edict to nine councilmen sitting in wrought iron patio chairs (part of a pomegranate patio set) around a bistro style table with a glass top. Naturally, they were sitting on cushions. It was yet again a very sunny day, so the view from M. Prevel's terrace was of supernal quality, but everyone had their backs turned. One of the councilmen objected to the appearance of God in a state decree, which he pointed out was a violation of the law enacted in 1905, which forever separated the Church from the State, at which point one of the other councilmen objected to the objection, stating that the 1905 law was intended to prevent churches from using state money to build more churches and had nothing to do with the language of edicts, at which point the first councilman said just because the 1905 law said nothing specific about the language of edicts didn't mean it wasn't suggested by the spirit of the law, which often lurked in the spaces in between words, at which point the second councilman threw his hands into the air with exaggerated dismay, a tragic-comic gesture that indicated both a recognition of the absurdity of the debate and a no longer secret desire to pummel his opponent, and said that kind of talk was complete, unadulterated gibberish, at which point M. Prevel intervened, much to the relief of everyone else, who were expecting the worst, and said in a tone devoid of visible emotion that as much as he valued the need to let everyone have their say, he did so want to keep things moving so they could put this ugly cricket business behind them, so if it was okay with the council, he would just delete the part about God. M. Prevel's intervention was followed by a round of polite applause, which was followed by the sounds of someone pouring and serving coffee, and then another someone passing around a silver platter of French pastries, some with icing, some without. After an appropriate interlude, the meeting resumed. A few of the councilmen suggested there should be a penalty for anyone who refused to wield a weapon. They decided a week or so in jail or a very large fine would limit the number of conscientious objectors. Then someone asked if they should close the city gates, but this question was greeted with a chorus of jeers, the main point being what good would closing the gates do against crickets, especially since they were already inside. Then M. Prevel wondered if perhaps they should institute a draft, but then they added up the cost of implementing such a policy. They looked at the entire process, from drawing up the lists, to sending out the notices, to arresting those who ran away, to the court costs, to the increased burden on the penal system. The jail was already overcrowded, in fact the conditions were horrible, a travesty of juridicial malfeasance, an opinion confirmed by none other than the Prefect of Meurthe-et-Moselle, who upon visiting the jail the previous year had said it was the worst for a city the size of Metz anywhere in France. The council decided against any sort of compulsory enrollment. And then that was that. There was nothing further to be said. Besides, it was getting late. The sun had already begun to set. So the councilmen drained their cups of the last few drops of coffee. A few hands plucked the last of the pastries from the silver platter. Then one could hear the sounds of chairs being pushed back and voices congratulating other voices on a job well done, all of the voices chortling with that sudden gush of emotion usually mistaken for happiness that inevitably arrives after the last item on a list has been checked off. M. Prevel's secretary, a mousy woman with tiny, agitated eyes and tousled hair, rushed back inside to the dining room table, where she had set up her typewriter hours earlier, and began typing up a clean copy of the edict. Ten minutes later Mssrs. Mirman and Prevel and the entire council signed the document.

On Tuesday, September 8, 1925, the edict appeared in every newspaper in the city, though one of the papers printed the edict on the last page instead of the first, directly above an advertisement with a cartoon caricature of a bearded Émile Zola, who had been dead for well over twenty years by then, touting the benefits of consuming lard. The overworked editor of the paper attributed the unfortunate oversight to the fact that they had received the edict after the day shift had left but before the evening shift had arrived, which meant they were lucky to get it in the paper at all the next day.

On Wednesday, September 9, 1925, some of the neighborhoods began to organize what were called 'cricket squads,' but mostly these were made up of rowdy, young men who would seek any excuse to get drunk. According to witnesses, the only citizens of Metz who actively engaged the enemy after the edict had been published were groups of small, ragged-looking Alsatian boys, ages nine or ten, who seemed to relish the chance to stomp a seemingly helpless adversary into the ground. Almost everyone else in Metz decided to stay indoors, at least temporarily, hiding in rooms that had become crypts where the air did not circulate. But no arrests were made. No fines were levied. No names were written down. Though it should be noted that one exceptionally vocal and most certainly inebriated cricket sympathizer was beaten to a bloody pulp later that night by two off-duty policemen outside a small café on Rue de la Chèvre because he wouldn't stop making jokes at their expense.

On Thursday, September 10, 1925, an article appeared in *La Gazette de Lorraine* with a rather alarming headline: **The Black Death Has Returned to France!** The printers had used bold lettering four inches high to ensure that the propaganda value of the headline was not ignored. The article itself was penned by a native of Algeria, M. Arkoun, a traveling scholar (his detractors would label him a Wandering Jew because they didn't know any better) from the University of Algiers who was deeply committed to tracing the history of the plague. His own father, a Berber by descent, and his younger brother had died of the disease in an outbreak that had swept through the streets of a small Arabic neighborhood in Algiers in 1919, a stone's throw from the Quasbah District, that teeming anthill of life. His mother, a French national, who had journeyed to Algiers with her uncle in 1892, had subsequently returned to the small town of Villefranche-sur-Saône, where she had grown up.

In a short biographical preface to his article, M. Arkoun wrote that initially he was troubled by the lack of response on the part of the French authorities to outbreaks of the plague in Algiers and elsewhere in North Africa. Though only one quarter of the population of Algiers was Arabic, the Arab community accounted for roughly ninety percent of the deaths that one could attribute to the plague. But as long as the disease was confined to working class Arabic neighborhoods, which describes the kind of neighborhood where M. Arkoun and his father and brother had lived, there was no mention of it in the French dailies; consequently, very few medical resources had been made available. M. Arkoun was of the opinion that France was a God-fearing nation, committed to doing the right thing regardless of racial persuasion. He was a French citizen. He believed in France. He reasoned, however naively, that the core issue was simply not recognizing the plague when one ran across it. While the plague was a constant companion to the residents of the Koranic and Mosaic communities in the cities of Algeria, the good, non-indigenous doctors in Algiers and elsewhere in the country, particularly in the port cities, seemed to possess only a superficial, textbook understanding of the plague. Always it was a disease that struck elsewhere, like in China or Bombay. Always it began with (and in smaller outbreaks ended with) a proliferation of rats. And always it occurred fifteen, twenty, thirty-five, even fifty years in the past, never the present.

M. Arkoun wanted to demonstrate through his scholarly acumen that the plague was far more prevalent than most people thought. That it did not always originate the way we thought it did. And that all medical opinion to the contrary, it had never left humanity's side. In the final analysis, M. Arkoun was an idealist. He nurtured a majestic hope that one day everyone might realize that the fate of a single individual, or of an entire community, even a small community within a larger community, was a microcosmic symbol of the fate of us all. The article began with a straightforward account of the history of the disease, first in Algeria (primarily Algiers), and then in France.

For those who have lived out their lives toiling beneath

the hot Algerian sun, whether twenty centuries ago in the orchards and grain fields supervised by the Romans, or in the vineyards and the alfalfa fields and the sugar beet fields that have been the chief agricultural concern under the French, the ravages of the plague have been a constant source of sorrow to the Algerian people. But nowhere in Algeria has the plague been a more impertinent lover than in the city of Algiers. The first recorded instance of the plague in this seaside community was in 772, when the city was known as Icosium. In 944 the city assumed its present name and was ruled by the Berbers of the Zirid-Sanhaja dynasty. But the Berbers could do nothing to prevent the plague, nor could the governments that occupied Algiers in the centuries that followed. The plague appeared in Algiers in the following years: 969, 979, 1030, 1050, 1064, 1087, 1105, 1157, 1230, 1266, 1333, 1346, 1430, 1467 (when it marched across Africa and then jumped over the Straits of Gibraltar on its way to Lisbon in 1490), 1500, 1512, 1527, 1535, 1543, 1552, 1571, 1584, 1601, 1620, 1639, 1654, 1666, 1673, 1689, 1709, 1732, 1738 (which was considered the year of the great plague in Algeria), 1749, 1784, 1793, 1817, 1834, 1871, and most recently in 1919. Many of the outbreaks in Algiers and elsewhere in Africa were said to be preceded by great plagues of locusts, which were followed by thunderstorms that washed away the filth that had accumulated and so purified the land, which were followed by several years of abundant harvests, which also produced copious quantities of rats, a natural enough consequence, and these harvests were soon, perhaps inevitably, followed by famine and the death of the rats and then the arrival of the plague.

The disease then usually seems to have migrated from the North African coast to France via Marseille, and from there to Lyon and beyond. Occasionally it migrated over the Pyrenees from Spain, but not often enough for anyone to consider closing that particular border. The ports were of infinitely greater concern, mostly Marseille, but also Toulon and Fréjus and Montpellier.

The plague struck France in the following years: 542, 580, 627, 666, 792, 996-1031 (a period during which the misery was so great because of the prefatory famine that men took to selling human flesh; indeed, in the medieval town of Mâcon, forty-eight human heads were found in a local barn serving as an abattoir, the bodies having been butchered and sold by the pound and apparently devoured on the spot, behavior which was not then considered surprising, as the belief in those terrible days, held by everyone from the King, Robert the Pious — who married his cousin Bertha and so was excommunicated by Pope Gregory V in 988 for incest — to the lowliest serf, was that the end of the world was imminent, the signs of the coming Apocalypse were everywhere and seemed to darken the very skies), 1084, 1266, 1296, 1347, 1374 (a year which also marked the arrival of a strange, secondary affliction called the Dancing Mania, which affected the nervous systems of those battling the plague, producing uncontrollable, palsy-like symptoms so that the victims gave the appearance of being deranged marionettes, and which caused nearly as many deaths as the plague alone), 1417, 1443 (when it laid siege to the city of Lyon for nine months), 1466 (when it swept through Paris in a matter of weeks), 1470-1520 (a period when it was a constant presence throughout France), 1585, 1625-1640, 1646, 1666, and 1720 (where it settled in Marseille for over two years before burning itself out).

The most recent officially recognized outbreak in Marseille occurred two years ago in 1923, but government officials also claimed that only the rat population was affected. Naturally they had little choice but to present this lie to both the general public and the world at large. The city had hosted the 1922 National Colonial Exposition, embracing the vigor of the Orientalist movement and promoting its own role as 'the Port of Empire' in extracting the wealth of Africa. A lie was necessary for the city to maintain the purity of its reputation as an 'imperial' power.

Both anecdotal and statistical evidence, however, suggest that the rats were not the only casualties. Twice as many deaths due to disease were recorded in Marseille in 1923 than had occurred in the three previous years combined. Apologists for what must be considered a most insidious even criminal bureaucratic cover-up emphasized that the deaths were not due to plague but were in actuality due to cholera, yellow fever, influenza, malaria, and a host of other exotic diseases brought to Marseille by a great wave of immigrants from Italy and North Africa. The immigrants had brought these diseases with them, so they were the only ones dying in record numbers. The general population of Marseille had nothing to worry about. Several notable doctors, however, including the renowned physician, M. Francois Chabaud, have indicated after the fact that extensive but discreet discussions occurred over the course of several months from April thru August of 1923 between Léonce Guerre, the hospital administrator for the city, and the various doctors and other government officials that made up the Sanitation Board about the possibility of instituting strict quarantine protocols with respect to incoming ships, at least while the mortality rate was on the rise. What harm lay in holding the crews of suspected ships in one of the city's lazerettos for eighteen days before giving them a clean bill of health? Or better yet, they could send these potentially infected ships to the Island of Pomique, a former leper colony just offshore that had been transformed into a quarantine station in 1526. After fifty or sixty days on Pomique they, meaning Léonce Guerre and his gang of appreciably reluctant but unashamed bureaucrats, would know for certain whether or not plague was present.

Needless to say, a quarantine was never instituted. As in Africa, there were reports that the plague in Marseille had been preceded by a city-wide infestation of winged insects, followed by some months of plentiful rainfall, and then two years of abundant harvests, which were then followed by a proliferation of rats and the inevitable food shortages. At every point of comparison, the story of the plague in Marseille in 1923 seemed virtually identical to the story that had been told throughout history. But it was not identical. The winged insects the citizens of Marseille remembered were not in fact locusts. They were crickets. This startling revelation raised two very important questions, at least as far as understanding the historical appearance of the plague is concerned. Are crickets and locusts equally culpable in their ability to predict the arrival of the plague? And how often have crickets been mistaken for locusts (and vice versus)?

These questions themselves soon became the foundation for a theory postulating that the arrival of hordes of crickets is a natural and inevitable augury announcing the unavoidable arrival of the plague. And so our researches into tracing the history of this most devastating disease metamorphosed quite suddenly into a scientific analysis of the invisible machinery that perpetuates the plague itself. It was this shift in the axis of our analytical thinking, involving as it must an investigation of cricket infestations wherever they may occur, that has brought us to the once fair city of Metz.

What have we thus far discovered in our scientific quest for certain knowledge? What new light can we shed on a darkness that has been with us for centuries? A strictly biological examination of the cricket yielded scant results. Both crickets and locusts are members of the Order Orthoptera, which means straight winged. They are close cousins. They have evolved similar physical characteristics and similar habits of interacting with the world. Unfortunately, biological analysis alone cannot prove that crickets are winged harbingers of doom.

So we turned to other disciplines for confirmation of our fledgling theory, most notably the science of natural history, one of the oldest sciences on record, and the relatively new but no less informative science of cultural anthropology. We discovered that the folklore and literature of the world abounds with stories and myths that feature crickets as prognosticators of death.

According to the great Spanish explorer Álvar Núñez Cabeza de Vaca, who accompanied Pánfilo de Narváez on an expedition to the Americas in June 1527, the song of crickets, which many on board Cabeza de Vaca's ship heard during the crossing, was in fact an augur of future misery. From the moment the crickets began to sing, the Narváez expedition was plagued by disaster. They lost three-hundred men before they even made it to the waters of the New World. When they finally landed on the west coast of Florida in April 1528 near the Rio de las Palmas, they were forced to flee their encampment by the presence of hostile natives. They marched through the interior of Florida, losing another one-hundred men in the process, built four rafts in an attempt to escape the perils of the

Floridian coast but lost two of those rafts and another fifty men during a storm that swept across the Gulf. They lost another three-dozen to starvation and disease. Of the six-hundred persons who started out with Narváez, only Cabeza de Vaca and three others survived and returned to Spain.

The native peoples of northeastern Brazil believe crickets are augurs both of thunderstorms and the arrival of unexpected death. And in the southeastern part of that country, in Caraguá, a black cricket suddenly appearing in a room is said to herald the arrival of a deadly, unavoidable illness.

On the island of Barbados, the natives believe the creaking chirp of a species of cricket known as the ash-colored or sickly cricket is an omen of death.

In 'The White Devil,' by English playwright John Webster (1580-1634), the character Cornelia says: 'When screech-owls croak upon chimney-tops. And the strange cricket i' the oven sings and hops. When yellow spots do on your hands appear. Be certain then you of a corse shall hear.'

In his book 'Daemonologia' (1650), Dr. Nathaniel Horne, a Doctor of Divinity, writes that crickets 'are often heard crying where there soon will be none.'

English poet John Gay (1685-1732) writes in his poem titled 'Friday' (or 'The Dirge'): 'When Blouzeline expir'd, the Weather's Bell/Before the dropping Flock toll'd forth her Knell;/The solemn Death-watch click'd the hour she dy'd,/ And shrilling Crickets in the Chimney cry'd.'

The same superstition is found in the English adaptation of 'Oedipus Rex' (1734) by John Dryden and Nathaniel Lee, in which Oedipus says: 'For when we think Fate hovers o'er our heads,/Our Apprehensions shoot beyond all bounds,/Owls, Ravens, Crickets seem the Watch of Death.'

Gilbert White (1720-1793), the great parson-naturalist of Selborne, England, writes that crickets 'are the housewife's barometer, foretelling when it will rain; and are often prognostic, she thinks, of bad or good luck; of the death of a near relation; or the approach of an unfaithful husband.'

Finally, in her novel 'The Borders of the Tamar and

the Tavy' (1834), the novelist Anna Eliza Bray (1790-1883) notes that in England the song of the cricket is considered joyful to the great families, but to the peasantry it is an ominous song filled with sorrow and evil.

Now the learned and scholarly among us, especially those in the medical profession, will immediately dismiss such stories and anecdotes as superstitious nonsense, and given their expertise and their trumpeted professional commitment to the general welfare of our society, the less-learned are inclined to agree with them. But before we are so cavalier in our own assessments, we should consider that superstition is but the wisdom of previous generations that has been discarded in favor of more 'enlightened' approaches. But it is wisdom nevertheless, and if we choose to ignore it, if we fail to consider the lessons learned over a thousand years, then we do so at our own peril. Citizens of Metz, take heed!

Everyone who read M. Arkoun's article that sunny Thursday became alarmed to some degree, even Mssrs. Prevel and Mirman, even the clergy. The debaters in the cafés and restaurants began discussing the best way to wrap up their affairs. Calls were made to bankers in other communities who were ignorant of the cricket infestation. Deals were concluded over the telephone. The telegraph office was a hotbed of activity as frightened men as solemn-faced as those digging their own graves or serving life sentences waited for their money to arrive. The owners of those buildings that had been futilely fumigated (including the owner of the billiards hall, who had already cashed his check from the insurance company), sold out lock, stock and barrel for paltry sums that would get them to Vienna or Frankfurt or Prague or even Budapest, but no further if they wished to avoid the disgrace of starting over from scratch.

But not everyone was so easily pushed into a panic. The tramways still traversed the city. The temporal clarity provided by the clanging bells seemed to mock the serious, scholarly tone of M. Arkoun's dire predictions. And the priests and the rabbis all over the city, inspired perhaps by a hint of rain in the air, flung open the doors to their churches and synagogues and invited the weary and desperate multitudes, who were milling about the streets in droves, to come inside and pray to Almighty God for deliverance. By five o'clock in the afternoon, the good citizens of Metz (including Mssrs. Prevel and Mirman) had crammed themselves into the churches and synagogues like so many salted sardines in a tin.

In the end, which is to say that very evening, deliverance arrived in the form of a terrible but welcome (and not entirely unforeseen) thunderstorm that raged for three nights and two days. When the sun peeked out from behind the clouds on that third day, a Sunday, which the priests (but not the rabbis) noted with great satisfaction, all trace of the crickets had vanished. It was as if the city of Metz and all of its inhabitants had slipped through a strange, futuristic-looking portal that had appeared without warning, or a subterranean passageway leading to a hidden, antediluvian paradise (or perhaps it was just a jagged crack in the world as we know it) and so slipped into another dimension. It was a resurrection of sorts. A miracle at the very least.

The water levels of both rivers had returned to normal. The garden city that had become a treeless, leafless, flowerless desert was once again brimming with lush greenery and all manner of perennials. The farmers and artisans and other obscure vendors had returned to the Place d'Armes, and even though it was a Sunday, no one seemed to mind. The desperate deals that had been struck over the telephone had been rescinded and the money returned. Both the owner of the billiards hall and his insurance company suffered from amnesia regarding the owner's claim, but in truth there was no need to remember since the billiards hall had been suddenly and mysteriously reborn and was now located near the train station at Bahnhofsplatz and Hauptpostant in a magnificent (very upscale, modern) brownstone building with yellow awnings covering the first-floor windows and a small copper dome like a tiny Chinese hat on top. The cafés and restaurants were once again filled with happy patrons happily slurping down glass after glass of sweet white wine from the Moselle Valley and enjoying a fine repast of creamy quiche or smoked sausage or chicken or fish, with sautéed potatoes and bread with Mirabelle jam. Everything that had been available on the menus before the drought was available again.

Of course there were a few mulish souls who regarded

this new reality with great suspicion. They cornered as many individuals as they could, attempting to instill in them the fear M. Arkoun's article had originally inspired. 'It is just as the scholar predicted. First the crickets, then the thunderstorm, then the days of great abundance. Surely you have not forgotten what is still to come. Surely you are preparing for the darkness that will consume us all!' cried the mulish souls. 'No we have not forgotten,' cried the cornered individuals, 'but why should we bother about calamities that exist only in the imagination?' 'Surely you do not deny the truth of the scholar's words, the sincerity of his academic quest!' cried the mulish sorts. 'Who can say?' cried the cornered individuals. 'Perhaps the learned scholar was mistaken. Or perhaps the plague is years away. Hush now. Leave us be. Can't you see we have other things to occupy our thoughts? Can't you enjoy the miracle of this day and let well enough alone!' And the mulish souls could think of no rejoinder.

-135-

It would be fair to say that young Anton Kreutner was unaware of the hubbub surrounding the plague of crickets in 1925. Thus, one is naturally inclined to wonder why this chronicler would include said story in an examination of Anton Kreutner's life. The answer is simple enough. For the citizens of Metz, the events of that summer became a mother to the belief that life would sail along as smooth as silk as long as humanity crammed itself into the nearest church at the first sign of trouble (real or imagined). It became a part of the genetic makeup of the community, an inescapable myth embedded in the psyche of every child growing up in the crazy years of the twenties and thirties. What struck you most when you wandered the streets of Metz in those days was that its citizens were giddy (one might even say drunk) with the joy of a faith reclaimed, a joy which gave them the strength to face any of the tiny calamities that we all face on a daily basis.

Now the cynics among us will point out that except for an exceptional few, the joy of faith possessed by the citizens of Metz would prove little help in facing the long night of the Nazi occupation during the apocalyptic forties, but that is pragmatism gone amuck. Besides, this portion of our chronicle is not concerned with those events, which took place long after young Anton had left Europe for America. No, our focus here is on the moral development of Anton during his formative years. We wish to know if young Anton's giddy, unquestioning belief in God's divine goodness, a legacy of his childhood (as noted above), was able to withstand the subtle (or not so subtle) impact of two tiny crises of faith. The specific question before us is whether Anton survived these attacks with his faith completely intact, or whether the spiritual foundation of his belief in the majestic goodness of God suffered some unseen damage, an invisible crack in the bedrock of his joy, if you will excuse an all too conventional metaphor, that expanded slowly but inevitably, as any crack will, and so ultimately facilitated the shattering of his bedrock some seventy years later, which one must assume was reason enough for Father Anton's departure from the Church. So let us examine both crises from as many angles as possible to determine, at least intellectually, whether or not Father Anton's rejection of the collar after forty-eight years might have been foreordained.

-136-

Anton's first tiny crisis of faith occurred on the eve of his tenth birthday, a crisis precipitated by the cavalier cynicism of his cousin Josef. It began innocently enough when young Anton accompanied his father to the railway station to pick up Josef, who was arriving on the train from Luxembourg. Josef was going to spend a few days in Metz before resuming his journey to Paris, and then north to the tiny hamlet of Villers-Bretonneux, where he had seen some action during the Great War. The train was late, considerably so, so Anton began to wander. He was like a tiny bat or some other nocturnal creature trapped in that narrow space between walls in an ancient castle, his wings fluttering frantically.

Later, Josef and Johann found the boy outside the station. He had calmed down considerably. In fact, he had become something of a statue. He was staring at a small dragon embedded in the grayish stone façade of the station. In spite of the bright sunlight outside, the dragon seemed to occupy the shadows. It was crouching like a cat or curled up like a weirdly deformed snail, its wings and jaws tinged with green, its eyes devoid of all emotion, naturally, but possessing an eerie supernatural intensity nevertheless, which had captivated the boy. 'Yes, my boy,' said Anton's father, 'that is as good a likeness of the Graoully dragon as you're likely to see in broad daylight.' And then Johann had laughed.

But Josef put his arm around the boy and said in a hoarse, detached voice that somehow seemed to be seeping out of the stone dragon's mouth, 'If you like, I will tell you the true story of the dragon. It is a story they don't tell you in school. And certainly the priests won't tell you. They want you to believe all of the dragons were vanquished long ago. I'm sure your father doesn't even remember it.' The boy and Josef looked over at Johann, but he was still laughing.

The next day Josef took Anton to the Plaza, but instead of lingering among the vendors, they headed directly into the Cathedral of Saint Etienne. They wandered through the nave and forgot themselves in the gleaming luminescence of eight-hundred and sixty-four stained glass windows. It was a pleasant enough excursion. But then without any warning whatsoever they descended down a narrow, spiral stone staircase into the swarming, heaving darkness that stretched out towards infinity beneath the Cathedral itself. It became difficult to breathe. The staircase was rarely used, even by those who knew of its existence. It seemed to young Anton that they had fallen into the dark waters of perpetual night, a labyrinth that might claim the lives of all but the most resilient souls. This is what young Anton was thinking as he followed Josef down the stairs and then through a series of narrow hallways. But it was not all darkness. Small lanterns flickered in the gloom, casting shadows like withered thoughts.

At some point they stopped walking and Anton realized they were sitting on a small wooden bench, not stone at all, positioned against the rough wall of a very large underground chamber, directly opposite a longish stone altar, or perhaps it was a sarcophagus, though it was unadorned and black with age. Every so often two or three hooded figures would enter the chamber and kneel before the sarcophagus, and for a moment the air would be filled with a rhythmic, plaintive chanting like a fresh fog early in the morning, a liturgical praxis that had its origins in the medieval abbey of Saint Bénigne de Dijon. Then the chanting would dissolve and so would the hooded figures.

Josef did not say why they were sitting there.

Young Anton began to feel a growing sense of unease, like he was about to lose his balance. The pattern of the hooded figures continued for a while. None of the figures seemed to notice Josef and the boy, or if they did they possessed the ability to suppress their natural instincts.

Then there was a lull in this parade of mummers and their plaintive whispers were replaced by the incantatory voice of Josef. He was telling the story of the Graoully dragon the way it was meant to be told.

'The world is full of stage plays with saints defeating dragons,' he said. 'Saint Martha defeated a black beast named Tarasconus, a serpent of the water named for the village of Tarasque. This beast was half dragon, half fish, greater than an ox and longer than a horse. It possessed the head of a lion and a serpent's tail, teeth like gleaming swords and horns on either side. Saint Martha showered this demon with holy water and mesmerized it with the cross, and when the people of Tarasque saw this they rushed in with swords and knives and slaughtered the beast. Even today, the place where that dragon died is called Berlue, the Black Lake.'

Josef took a breath and exhaled as if to blow out a candle. The darkness in the chamber beneath the Cathedral began to tremble.

'But all the stories are like that, though not all the dragons die. They all begin with saints on a quest to bring Christianity to the darkest corners of the earth. Saint Martha. Saint George. Saint Clement. Saint Efflam. Saint Michael. Saint Margaret. Saint Senán. And these saints are always battling monsters. Leviathans with the heads of lions, great horned beasts, serpents. It is the same tale over and over again. They say in the first century after Christ, the city of Metz was filled with vipers and serpents of all kinds, all of them servants of Satan. So Saint Peter sent the Bishop Clement to clean them out. And so he did. He trapped them in the ancient Roman amphitheater just outside the city gates, that seat of ancient evil, made the sign of the cross, and they all burst into flame. These lesser symbols of Satan were vanquished. But there was also a dragon in Metz, the Graoully dragon, and the Bishop did not kill this dragon. He sought to tame the monster instead. He read from the Holy Scriptures. He showed the beast the cross of Christ.

And slowly the Graoully dragon fell under the Bishop's spell. This was the Bishop's victory.

What happened to the dragon? Where is it? The Bishop led the beast to the edge of the Moselle and told the dragon to climb inside the river and stay there, invisible to all who might seek him out. But the Bishop did not slay the demon. In this he followed the example of Saint Matthew, who had merely banished the two dragons summoned by the two sorcerers, Zaroës and Arphaxat. But what is perhaps more disturbing, at least to the idealists among us, is that Bishop Clement never relinquished control of the Graoully dragon. The Church controls the monster to this day. At any given hour, the current Bishop only has to raise his hand above the waters of the Moselle and the dragon will return to life, ready to do whatever the Church requires to keep the faithful in line. The role of the dragon is for now and evermore to become the visible manifestation of all manner of evils: famine, war, pestilence, the plague. Do you not understand, my young, impressionable cousin? The Church cannot subdue evil. The Church can only control evil, use evil to further its own ends, which it claims are for the spiritual good, the salvation of all humanity. But who can say? The dragon exists, a fact which no sane person can deny, but its power can be turned towards good or ill depending upon the person who wields the hypnotist's bauble. That is what is truly frightening.'

And at precisely that moment, as if on cue, the parade of hooded mummers resumed, but now the figures were aware of Josef and the boy. They cast piercingly inscrutable looks in the direction of the wooden bench, their heads turning with robotic precision, a quick mechanical, snapping sound in the darkness as they entered the chamber, like the bolt of a gun being snapped into place or the unlocking of a padlocked gate. Even though you could not see their features you could feel the intensity of their eyes, a staccato spiral of emotions, a crown of thorns, the blood of the martyrs, the hard iron of the nails. Then it was the same as before. They knelt. The air was filled with the sounds of their strange chanting (less plaintive than before, tinged now with something more desperate, anxious, like a sun about to explode). Then the chanting dissolved into nothingness. And so did they.

'You see what I mean?' said Josef. 'It is quite difficult to determine what these refugee monks are up to with their dark, foreboding presence. I have taken refuge in this chamber on many occasions since the end of the Great War, to meditate, to contemplate the sins of my past and the sins I will commit in the future, and always they are here. Do they wish to destroy the dragon? Or do they wish merely to tame it? I do not believe we are in any danger. They do not smell dangerous. But who can really say? They are part of an ancient cult of lunatics, trapped in the shadows for more centuries than they care to acknowledge. They are all that is left of the musical monks of Gorze Abbey, reformers and radicals all of them, self-proclaimed shepherds of the soul who wanted the wealthy to give away the material world in the name of spiritual purity and the Peace of God and so free the poor from the chains of their poverty. Of course this all took place in the twelfth century. The Church was not interested in such reforms in those days. Why would God wish to sacrifice his Church in the name of peace? Who would be left to attend Mass if poverty were eradicated? What purpose could the Church possibly fulfill if the priests could not minister to those in need? Yes, yes, they were more than radical, these monks. They were uncompromising trouble-makers, insurgents, revolutionaries. Have they deviated from their original purpose? This, too, is impossible to answer. In 1572 the order was dissolved, and for the next two hundred years they wandered about the streets of Metz like deranged but ineffectual ghosts. But what does that prove? Then the revolution came and they reinserted themselves into the world. One month after the Bastille was stormed, forcing the city administrators of Paris to flee, the all but invisible monks of Gorze orchestrated a similar uprising in Metz that brought about similar results. When the Church officially suppressed them in 1790, all they did was go underground. Some say they became anti-French, that they helped the invading Austrian army in the war of 1792. Some say they held the door open for Germany in 1871. Some say they are waiting even now for the Merovingian Kings to return so they can take their rightful place in the new kingdom that is coming, always coming, an eternity of waiting. Do you see what I am driving at Anton? Everyone who encounters these monks has a different opinion. I think they are lunatics, plain and simple. God does not hear them chanting. Only these lifeless stone walls bear witness to their mummified prayers. So put them out of your mind.'

Then there was a second lull and Josef started talking

about his own encounter with a dragon like the Graoully dragon. Josef said that the 24th of April, 1918 was the day he first knew the dragon for what it really was. He was part of a German tank crew on that day. His tank was one of eleven German tanks that had attacked British and Australian forces at the town of Villers-Bretonneux in an attempt to break through the enemy lines and eventually take the railway junction at the city of Amiens, twenty-five kilometers to the west. 'The night before the attack, we sent out a couple of planes to fly along the line, dropping parachute flares at intervals to expose the enemy positions. Then just before dawn we bombarded the woods to the southwest of the village, a barrage of mustard gas to soften them up. Our tanks were rolling as the sun came up over the horizon. It was a bloody red sun.

'Our tank was a Sturmpanzerwagon A7V, number 562, a piece of crap really. These tanks were always breaking down. But we were young and invincible. We were determined to defeat the dragon that was for us the British and the French. That is why we named our tank after the great dragonslayer Sigurd. We did not realize that we were also part of the same dragon. All of us together, the crew of every tank, the entire German Imperial Tank Command, the entire German army, the armies of the British and the French and the Australians, all of German history, all of human history, the past that had already been written and the future that was yet to be revealed, together we were all part of an enormous, fire-breathing serpentine monster that brought death and destruction everywhere it went. We were the storm clouds in the sky, the angel of the abyss, a shocking sight to behold at any hour.

'But what did I know then? I was a soldier preparing to go to war. Beyond that I only knew what my eyes could see. I knew that on that morning we had shocked the hell out of the British tank crews hiding beneath their tarps. We could see along the line just before the woods where some of them had already abandoned their tanks. We saw three more tanks heading away from us, towards the village of Cachy, churning up dust as they went, a rare feat for a vehicle with a maximum velocity of six kilometers per hour, but we let them go. We were supposed to take out a fortified farmhouse south of the town, which we did, and then head west towards the Bois D'Arquenne to cut off all possibility of an enemy counterattack.

'I am not certain what happened after that. We were hit

by a heavy volley of MG fire, which tore open a jagged hole on the right side of the tank, just missing the engine. Our commander, Leutnant Barton, was killed during this volley, so I took over. We also lost our mechanic, who was adjusting a valve on the radiator when the volley began, our signaler, who was conveying ammunition to the various gunners because one of the gunnery servants had thrown up and was changing his shirt, five infantrymen, and the two front gunners. More than half our crew was gone. We tried to position the dead bodies so they might serve as shields. Anyone observing from the outside (they would have been able to see directly into the tank through the jagged hole) would have seen only dead men at the controls and thought we were manned by the Devil's own.

'Somehow, we managed to come around on the British position and silence the MGs. It was a nightmare scene, men in gas masks diving for cover, our tank trundling unsteadily through the underbrush, artillery blazing, the smell of burning wood mixing with the charred smell of burning flesh mixed with the exhaust fumes from our tank, the raw sewage of oil and gasoline drenching the earth, mixing with the remnants of the chemicals that had been dropped earlier, oh it was a toxic atmosphere we breathed, it was the end of the world, the apocalypse come to our little corner of reality, the woods themselves changing color before our eyes, first a bright orange, then a soft almost soothing turquoise color, then a smothering chartreuse, then an ominous deathly, whitish-gray, and then back to bright orange, the cycle of colors speeding up as the battle progressed.

'I was standing upright in the officer's cab so I could see out. To be honest, it is not so easy a thing to always know where you are going when you are hiding inside an armored tortoise. And it was very misty that morning, and there was a tremendous volume of smoke from all the rounds that had been expended. It is a wonder that everyone didn't end up lost. I suppose I thought I was leading a cavalry charge, a heroic but absolutely idiotic notion. But it was very difficult to see through the narrow slit in the cab so I stood up to get a better sense of where we were going. I was lucky I didn't get picked off, but I guess after we destroyed the MGs, the rest of the British regulars fled on foot.

'That is when I began to question my sanity. I remember peering into the smoky, hazy, multi-colored woods, trying to get my bearings. It was like we were lost at sea. We were completely disoriented. Then I remember I couldn't hear a thing. I wondered if I had gone suddenly deaf, so I shouted something at our driver, but he didn't react. I tried again, but still nothing. Then I looked up for some reason. I saw two British regulars trying to revive a third man with ammonia salts. The third man was sitting up against an orange tree with blue-green leaves. I couldn't see the extent of his injuries, but he didn't seem to have been shot. I assumed that he was suffering the after effects of the mustard gas attack from earlier that morning. Then I remember thinking that he would probably make a full recovery, if he didn't go blind, and at precisely that moment the two British regulars turned to look at me. They had these strange, silly grins plastered across their dirty faces. I could see their white teeth gleaming in the half-light of the woods and blood dripping down from their gums, rivers of blood. They saluted me smartly and turned back to their attempts to revive their comrade. Then I tried yet again to get our driver's attention, and in that instant the world of sound came rushing back, a tumultuous torrent. I lost my balance, but luckily fell straight into my seat. Our driver looked at me and nodded and said we were almost there, but we never made it to the Bois D'Arquenne. Our tank broke down instead, so we got out to walk. We drank whisky from a flask while we walked and sang drinking songs like "The Black Whale." Later, we joined up with some infantry on their way to subdue any of the enemy who were still hiding out in Villers-Bretonneux.

'Subduing the enemy consisted of torching every building that was still standing in the town, every shop and chateau, every modest bungalow, every boarding house. We made no distinction with respect to social class. I remember some of the men were looting as they went, stuffing stolen valuables into their pockets, coins, watches, silver cigarette cases, gilded picture frames, anything small enough to conceal, and after the looting they would light a few small fires in the various rooms, fires which soon merged to become a very large all-consuming fire, and then on to the next building. We shot anyone who tried to stop us, old men mostly, but also, sadly, perhaps inevitably, a few women and a few children who were too stupid to know what was happening.

'That was the day I came face to face with a dragon like the Graoully dragon. That was the day when I understood that war itself was the dragon and that we were all guilty of committing unpardonable atrocities. Even those of us who were doing our duty to God and to country and had only discharged our weapons with honor. To witness an atrocity and do nothing is to commit that atrocity.

'The very next day the dragon we had thought to slay returned in the form of an Australian battalion, which had little trouble pushing us out of the town that was the focal point of the battle the day before. Most of us who had remained in Villers-Bretonneux the previous night were taken prisoner. I was one of the lucky few who escaped. We ran helter-skelter down a railway line obscured by trees on both sides before crossing back through a no-man's land of overturned tanks and burned out buildings until we made it to the relative safety of Marcelcave, a small hamlet only six kilometers from that incomprehensible scene of carnage, but even though the war like an apocryphal phantom had suddenly ceased to exist, I remember thinking that there was no hope for any of us, for on that day, the 25th of April 1918, Marcelcave was also home to tens of thousands of black crows, a symbol of the irrefutable horror of reality, the crows waiting in the barren branches of the trees or along the ragged edges of the rooftops for the smoke to clear so they could feast on the bodies of the dead.

'Five years later I went back to Villers-Bretonneux. I wasn't sure why, but I needed to go. I still do not truly understand my motives. Perhaps I was compelled by that force we call God. Who can say? What I can say is that I chose a most ironic day from the perspective of one of those who had brought destruction to the town. To begin with, it almost seemed like I had wandered onto the set of a stage play. The town was still in ruins. All that remained of the church was the skeleton of the tower and a few crumbling walls and a mound of rubble that no one had yet bothered to clear away. The old Victoria College had been smashed. All of the civic buildings were gone as well. A few houses had been rebuilt, but each was a patchwork job, mismatched boards that no one had painted, irregular strips of tarpaper stretched over holes in the roofs. The slightest puff of a summer breeze blew dust into the air. But the townspeople were optimistic, even jubilant, incredibly so. With the blessing and direction of the Mayor, and a financial contribution from the Prefect, they had erected a decorative panel made from scraps of wood depicting the town's coat-of-arms. This clever piece of stagecraft had been placed on the very spot where the Mayor's chateau had once stood, to remind everyone where they lived, said the Mayor, as if the townspeople needed reminding. And that is where I found them, the entire town, gathered in front of the decorative panel, listening to the Mayor and the Prefect (both dressed to the nines in black top hats and black tailcoats) giving pretty speeches. The town was recovering. Applause. They were going to lay the foundation stone for the new college that very day. More applause, verging on thunderous. That was certainly a step in the right direction. And with that the townspeople cheered and cheered, a wild demonstration, and then they quieted down and it was the turn of a white-bearded general in a black uniform decorated with half a dozen medals, a blustery, beleaguered sort who wore the invisible guilt of the previous decade quite well, and then an apologetic chemistry professor wearing a black bowler and a faded black suit who spoke on behalf of the college which hadn't existed since the war but would rise again. The only dignitary who wasn't there was the Bishop of Amiens, who had written a letter in advance stating that he had other matters to attend to that day. Then the speeches were over and the dignitaries began to walk through the labyrinth of ruined streets to the brownish spot where the new college would be erected, and the townspeople joined them. It was a ceremonious walk. The four dignitaries walked four abreast, surrounded on all sides by a naively optimistic collection of ex-soldiers, farmers, shopkeepers, a few teachers, a few skilled tradesmen, a mob of wives and daughters near to fainting, several grumpy old men who wanted only to observe the commotion, a few dogs barking at the mass of feet moving past, hoping perhaps that someone would toss a stick in the air, and scads of small children, mostly boys in black jackets and black shorts who after the ceremony would gather in manufactured silence and lay a giant wreath at the Cross of Sacrifice, schoolboys by the look with no understanding whatsoever of the sacrifices that had been made.

'The townspeople and the dignitaries were following a tiny marching band, seven maestros of hope wearing outdated serge suits, three playing flutes, two playing clarinets, one a piccolo, and one tapping away at a drum. The music was barely audible. The sounds of people walking and the barking dogs and the various conversations that were taking place, a steady, droning roar, all but swallowed the music of the marching band. But occasionally one could hear a few hopeful sounding notes, a rhythmic, musical phrase that suggested to everyone that better days were just ahead, excluding the four, black-clad dignitaries, who paid scant attention to the subtleties of the music since they lived out their entire lives amid the symphonic convergence of better days. But for the rest, what else was there to do but remain hopeful?'

After Josef had finished his tale of death and destruction and the ever-present hope of rising reborn from the ashes, he and young Anton sat in complete silence for half an hour. Partly this was Josef's doing, so that his cousin could digest what he had heard. Half an hour was hardly enough. Young Anton was plagued with all sorts of questions, theological questions which he could barely even articulate to himself, and for which he would be unable to offer any sort of convincing answer for at least twenty years. The most troubling of these concerned the nature of evil. Anton could not fathom why God would let evil exist in the world. It didn't seem to make any sense. Of course he was too young to realize that this very question had toppled the faith of many a good Christian. He was simply overwhelmed by an immense ocean of sadness. 'Why oh why oh why oh why?' he kept repeating to himself.

It was at this point that the parade of hooded mummers resumed, as if in answer to this question that had become a mantra of despair. Their attitudes had become openly provocative, even aggressive, as if they were about to reveal some secret mysterious purpose, or so it seemed to the young boy. Every second or third figure took a step towards the wooden bench, would pause to stare at the two cousins as if they were moving among sleepers, and then they would retreat and kneel before the black sarcophagus. Then the atoms of the world fused together and there was a mysterious flash of light. The chanting voices of the hooded figures echoed about the chamber before fading away and then the walls began to melt and it suddenly seemed that the universe was on the verge of obliterating the apocryphal night.

Then this third parade of mummers vanished as before, though the echo of their strange, etiolated voices remained, an eerily persistent subterranean sound like water seeping through rock, a subtle reminder that Josef and Anton would always be outsiders in this crypt beneath the Cathedral of Saint-Étienne de Metz.

-137-

Anton's second tiny crisis of faith occurred six years later, and this crisis also began with a visit from his cousin Josef. Those were tumultuous days all across Europe. Mussolini had invaded Ethiopia the year before. The people of the Saar had voted to rejoin Germany and soon thereafter Hitler sent in the German army to occupy the Rhineland. Tensions between the Monarchists and the Communists in Spain were on the brink of bubbling over. In fact, the brink was already a memory. On the 13th of July a monarchist politician named Calvo Sotelo had been assassinated by Republican police in retaliation for the murder of one of their own by a Falangist assassin. Four days later a revolt broke out in Spanish Morocco and the Spanish Civil War had begun. By the end of July the streets of Barcelona were taken over by young men riding around in small pick-up trucks, some of them wearing uniforms, all of them armed, all of them with raised arms and clenched fists, optimistic, eager, luminescent smiles on faces that had seen far too much sun, anarchists fighting for freedom who had painted the letters CNT-FAI in bright white paint on the doors and windshields of their vehicles, and everywhere you looked some fanatic was holding up the Allegory of the Republic, a painting of a robed woman with a serene but determined look on her face standing next to a lion, various symbols of modernity in the background (a black locomotive, an ocean-going steamship, a biplane), the woman holding the scales of justice in one hand and the Spanish Republican flag in the other, a tri-color flag of three stripes: red and yellow to represent the territories of the Crown of Aragorn, and a dark reddish purple, what the Spanish call *morado*, the color of mulberries, to represent the territories of Castile and León. Everyone in Spain was represented by this flag.

The day Cousin Josef arrived he was brimming with the unassailable gratitude of a death-row prisoner who has been suddenly pardoned. He was on his way to the Iberian Peninsula, he said, to Cubas de la Sagra, a tiny municipality on the outskirts of Madrid. He was to be part of a group of volunteers, all of them seasoned military men, who were going to help Franco's Nationalists defeat the anarchists. 'We have set up a school to train the Officers of Franco's army in tank combat, infantry tactics, and the use of flag signals. Once again we will be of some use to the world.'

Naturally, Anton was amazed by his cousin's eager, uncritical attitude towards this new war, an attitude which contradicted both his cousin's experiences during the Great War and the almost surreal angst that had all but consumed him in the aftermath of that conflict. Naturally, Anton wondered at his cousin's unexpected metamorphosis, but Cousin Josef only laughed, though admittedly it was a peculiar, restrained, even haughty kind of laughter, as if Josef were communicating in an ancient, arcane language reserved for those who had already been initiated.

'The mirror is always empty when we look for solace,' he said. 'Like a woman you once loved turning away and walking with indifferent grace into a stormy sea.' And then Josef broke into a genuine smile. 'Or maybe it is like Goethe said: we must reconquer each day the liberty won the day before.'

Later, while watching the boat traffic along the Moselle from the middle bridge, Josef tried to explain himself, but he chose a rather complex narrative format for his explanation, which one can assume only further muddled Anton's thinking. The story Josef chose was that of the forbidden love affair between Gyula Tornai, the great Hungarian painter, and the very beautiful and vulnerable Japanese princess, Princess Tsune Jamashina, who was barely fifteen years old.

The most obvious unanswered and unanswerable questions, at least in the opinion of this chronicler, concern the degree that young Anton understood what he heard upon the bridge that afternoon, and how this understanding metamorphosed into a moral crisis. We can only guess at the answers. So perhaps it is best to simply present everything there is to know about this tale of forbidden love and allow the reader to draw his or her own conclusions. It is a succinct tale and spans no more than twelve pages, though it is told of necessity from multiple viewpoints. It appears to provide a context for an instructive lesson, or many instructive lessons, depending upon the breadth and depth of one's life experiences and the flexibility or inflexibility of one's moral compass. Its main characters are drawn from the annals of human history, as opposed to being animals or inanimate objects brought to life through the power of the storyteller's imagination, as is the case in *Aesop's Fables*. And it contains numerous symbolic correspondences, what some scholars would call allegorical elements, and others, more jaded perhaps, would call historical referents disguised as operant metaphors.

The story of Tornai and Princess Tsune was widely known in Europe in the twenties and thirties, though Tornai's name was never actually used. It first appeared in 1914 under the title 'Princess Tsune and the Lovesick Hungarian,' a single chapter in a slim, scandalous book entitled *Tales of the Japanese Emperor's Daughters* that was published in Paris and caused an immediate sensation. The chapter about Princess Tsune was itself a narrative pastiche of Japanese newspaper accounts and local gossip. Most likely Josef acquired a copy of the book either during or directly after the Great War. But it is also possible, however unlikely, that he had read a translation of the childhood diary of Princess Tsune's younger sister, Princess Fumi. The romance smitten Princess Fumi had devoted seven pages to the affair between her sister and Tornai.

How this diary became a part of the public domain, avoiding oblivion and making the strange, elliptical journey from private property to cultural artifact, is still something of a mystery. Somehow it found its way into a box of personal letters and important historical documents that belonged to the Imperial family. The box mysteriously vanished during the confusion that accompanied the death of Emperor Meiji in 1912. But seven years later, on the 6th of September 1919, which was a bright, sunny Saturday by all accounts, the contents of the box, including Princess Fumi's diary, were presented to the world by Émile Étienne Guimet, the famed French industrialist and collector of anything Japanese. M. Guimet never said how he had acquired the box, but his face lit up mysteriously whenever he was asked the question.

The diary and the other documents were later returned to the Japanese government in 1954, but from 1919 to 1926, they were part of the Japanese collection at the Guimet Museum in Paris. The diary itself was translated into French by the scholar and noted linguist Serge Élisséèv and published by Librairie Ancienne Edouard Champion in 1924.

And now to begin this Oriental tale of tragic love. From 1880 to 1901, Gyula Tornai lived and worked in Morocco, and then Algeria, and traveled extensively up and down the Barbary Coast. He became adept at painting scenes of Moorish opulence.

Titillations without footnotes. Some would have called him degenerate. But his paintings were, from what this chronicler has seen, a blend of humanity's fascination with all things of the flesh coupled with an insatiable appetite for understanding the significance of all human endeavors. The world he depicted was a blend of human desire, intellectual curiosity, the quest for love (which to Tornai was equivalent to erotic sex), and war and violence.

In 1882 he painted *The Harem,* depicting a black Sultan and a white slave girl contemplating their reflections in a pool of water.

In 1890 he painted *An Arms Merchant in Tangiers,* depicting somber, faceless Berber warriors purchasing swords.

In 1891 he painted *Nudes with Tortoise,* depicting three women in all of their God-given glory sitting on a stone bench contemplating with existential serenity the movements of a tiny tortoise making its way across a white marble floor.

In 1892 he painted *The Connoisseurs,* again depicting Berber warriors, but in this painting they were contemplating a painting within the larger canvass depicting Berber warriors like themselves who were examining various pistols.

And in 1896 he painted *The Favorite of the Harem,* depicting a beautiful white-skinned girl with a smile like the petals of an orchid unfolding, an unparalleled vision of femininity stretched out on a richly decorated bed, her nipples erect, her hips turned slightly in lascivious fashion, a bearded Sultan looking on, a servant rummaging through a box, searching for an appropriate string of pearls to offer this girl whom no man on earth could resist.

But in 1899, Tornai, apparently bored with North Africa, decided to head east in search of what he said were more exotic subjects to paint. Was he being truly honest with himself about his reasons for leaving Africa? Had he exhausted the creative potential of harems in the desert? Who can say? Was he at long last descending into that ambrosial sea of madness often associated with artists whose creative imaginations can no longer wage war against the pain of being? Did he finally realize that outward nakedness is but a physical manifestation of an innermost atom, but if that atom remains concealed, then what does it matter if one is naked or not? Or was he making one last ditch effort to reclaim the spotless purity of his soul before vanishing without a whimper into the abyss? We will never know precisely what was going on in his mind except for the paintings he left, and on the subject of why he left for the Orient they remain understandably mute. All we know is that in 1901 Tornai made his way south by southeast to Swaziland and the port city of Maputo, where he caught a cargo ship to the volcanic island nation of Mauritius, which was then a French colony. According to a copy of a passenger manifest housed in the archives of the National Maritime Museum in Greenwich, England, Tornai boarded the passenger ship Ikhona, which provided service from Mauritius to Calcutta.

During the next two years he traveled about India, painting as the spirit moved him. Then in August 1903 he departed India for Japan. He had been hired by an official of the Imperial Japanese court to paint the portrait of the young and vivacious Princess Tsune, whose fifteenth birthday was that September. Why Hashimoto Gahō, the official Imperial Household Artist, did not paint the princess is not known. Tornai was hired instead, his reputation as an artist of harems notwithstanding. Thus began a series of events that ended with speculation that the princess had been infected with syphilis (a tempest in a teapot that filled the pages of the scandal sheets for a few months, but which has since been erased from history), Tornai narrowly escaping execution (and by narrowly we mean dramatically, in the way that Hollywood movies from the 1940s are dramatic through the clever use of suspenseful music, gritty, suggestive dialogue, odd camera angles, diffuse lighting that obscures rather than illuminates, and unexpected reversals of fortune), and Japan rushing pell-mell into a war with Russia that had been brewing for years. The story had the feel of a Shakespearian tragedy rewritten for the silver screen by Dashiell Hammett and directed by John Huston.

-138-

The rumor that Princess Tsune was infected with syphilis began one month after Tornai had painted her portrait, when the princess, who normally reveled in impromptu public appearances, much to the annoyance of her mother, was suddenly whisked off into seclusion by those in charge of the Imperial household. The whisking away of the Princess was all the more suspicious because it occurred at the beginning of the month known among the superstitious as the 'Month of the Absent Gods.'

The official reason given by a spokesperson for the Imperial family was that the princess was ill with fever and the doctors were taking no chances, but everyone assumed the government was lying, and soon several unofficial reasons had gained quasi-official status. The most salacious of these was provided by an anonymous source claiming to be an assistant to one of the Imperial doctors who had first examined the princess. The informant's tale of a lovesick princess and her desperate doctors set against a backdrop of palace intrigue and deception appeared in dozens of unscrupulous scandal sheets printed by anonymous printers and then circulated willy-nilly throughout the underbelly of Kyoto.

The story began, as you might suspect, with a head-to-toe description of the various lesions and chancre sores that had mysteriously appeared all over Princess Tsune's body. Then it went on to describe the range of emotions experienced by the Princess (rage, surprise, indifference, denial, panic, regret, paranoia, despair) and speculated who might have given Princess Tsune this terrible scourge, which the British called the Black Lion's Head. But it was the last part of the story that captured everyone's attention, for it catalogued the battery of treatments that the Imperial doctors had employed in the furious battle to save Princess Tsune's future reputation. Here is the actual verbiage taken from the very first scandal sheet to make the rounds:

> First, Doctor Fujio injected salts into the Imperial urethra using an elongated syringe [Note from chronicler: Most likely a normal sized syringe attached to a catheter] in the hopes of drawing out the disease through the Imperial bladder. Then the nurses bathed the Imperial Princess in a bath of herbal lotions [Note from chronicler: Most likely wild pansies and Japanese honeysuckle] and after gently dabbing dry Her Imperial Highness' thoroughly soaked body, a process which took a quarter of an hour to avoid even the slightest possibility of bruising, they applied a balm of carbonate of soda mixed with sulphate of iron to cure the Imperial itch. Finally, Doctor Fujio applied a caustic mixture of mercury and oil to the Imperial skin and placed the

Imperial Princess in a hot box in an attempt to sweat the disease out of the Imperial bloodstream.

The story was reprinted the following week, and every week after that for the next several months, though each reprinted version differed in creative and subtle ways from the original. In one version, the initial examination took place in the Princess's Imperial bedroom, which had a spectacular view of a meticulously kept garden complete with plum trees and a narrow red bridge going over a small pond. But in another version it was a small windowless room with white walls and a floor and ceiling composed of dark wooden planks. It was as if the Princess had suddenly been transported to a small chalet in the Alps. Along one wall of this tiny Alpine room were various cabinets filled with bottles containing crushed herbs or brightly colored potions or powders, and bowls for mixing medicines. In the center of the room there was a polished chrome examination table covered with a white sheet, and a smaller table overflowing with futuristic surgical instruments, some which were obviously for cutting and slicing and prodding, but others which defied all explanation. High up on the wall opposite the cabinets, where one would have normally expected to see a clock, one saw instead a loudspeaker that produced only static.

Usually Dr. Fujio administered the treatment, but once in a while Dr. Fujio was called Dr. Shimizu, but no matter who was playing the role of the Japanese doctor, he always wore wrinkled samurai robes from a century earlier. Then the Japanese doctor was replaced by a German doctor in a crisply ironed white lab coat. The German doctor was given various names as well, names which approximated various personality types, including Hans (tall, blond hair, energetic) or Georg (dark hair, a goatee, melancholy) or Schroeder (silver-haired, quite stiff, no sense of smell or humor), and in every scene where a German doctor took the stage, so to speak, he was assisted by a strange, slightly nervous, dark-complected man who spoke neither German nor Japanese.

The publishers of the scandal sheets sat back on their unscrupulous haunches and raked in the profits.

Eventually, which is to say by March 1904, the scandal sheets stopped printing the story of the princess and her treatment. For one thing, they had turned their attention to the war with Russia, which had just begun. But it was also no longer necessary to feed the public's hunger for Imperial innuendo. The rumor had taken its place in the subconscious minds and presumptive hearts of the citizens of Kyoto, an unassailable stone monument to human frailty, the diva-dame, and though no one mentioned Princess Tsune and syphilis in the same sentence ever again, it is unlikely that anyone ever forgot the tale, except perhaps when they passed into the delirium of death years later, that abyss of forgetfulness, which awaits us all. It is also worth noting that the identity of the informant who had aroused so much public interest was never made public.

-139-

Now the story of how Gyula Tornai escaped execution began twenty-six days before Princess Tsune was whisked away to the safety of her doctors, and ended in February 1904 during the first few days of the Russo-Japanese War. While an abridged version of this story can be found in *Tales of the Japanese Emperor's Daughters*, the most complete account is to be found in Princess Fumi's diary in an entry entitled: 'The Tragedy of the Lovesick Gaikokujin.' Naturally Princess Fumi's overly passionate narrative, which this chronicler has excerpted below, cannot be considered objectively accurate, for she was only twelve years old when the events she describes took place and still believed in the fairytale magic of romance, but her diary does in and of itself provide a lens through which we can glimpse a kind of partial truth that would otherwise be obscured.

The Tragedy of the Lovesick Gaikokujin

Our sister the beautiful Princess Tsune is but a floating thread of glossy, blue-green silk. When she smiles at us we cannot help but think that she is the visible manifestation of those ancient dream-maidens who descend to the earth during troubled days to lead us from the darkness into the light. She is the moon of the mountain fringe. When she waltzes into the throne room, for whatever reason, the politicians and courtiers, and even her own body guards dressed in their silly looking shrimp-pink uniforms, tremble with delight like autumn leaves before the liberating wind. In such moments, one can scarcely perceive that anyone else exists.

Oh did she arouse our passion for romance. She would tell us stories from the old days of Japan when every plum tree was a symbol of undying love. What fantasies we shared! She told me the story of the wife of the General of Uji, the Lady Ukifuné, who saw her secret lover only once a year and then spent the remainder of those lonely months between soft kisses gazing upon moonlit snowy landscapes or gardens filled with fragrant flowers.

And then one day Princess Tsune stopped telling us stories, much to our surprise, and when we asked her why, she burst into a torrent of bright, happy laughter, as cleansing as any mountain steam, and said she had plunged into the waters of love for herself to see if they were as exhilarating as she had always imagined, and she had not been disappointed.

We did not understand her meaning at first. Then she took us by the hand and led us as one leads a tethered deer to a wooden bench in the garden, a bench which was difficult to see from her bedroom window unless you knew where to look. We sat beneath a plum tree in full bloom, even though it was far too late in the year for such magic to take place.

It was as if we had entered into the fragile world of a poem, one of Narihira's masterpieces written during the reign of Emperor Montoku, an augury of both the good fortune that lay just ahead, and the tragedy that would follow soon thereafter.

Our divine sister told us she had fallen in love with the painter, the strange looking gaikokujin with the pointed beard who had traveled from the other side of the world to paint her portrait.

We could barely breathe as she spoke.

She said it had happened so slowly, almost inevitably, like the tide of a shallow sea coming in, that she did not notice. She said it happened so quickly that she thought the stars had fallen from the sky, a swirling storm of stars that covered the ground like snow. Natsu no yo fureru, we remember thinking. She said she thought the end of the world was at hand. She said the spring that would arrive next year would not be the spring of the past, but her words almost sounded like a question. We could not yet decipher the erratic tide of her emotions. Then she said only her body would remain the same as it was before. And then she smiled a shy, retiring smile.

The path to this forbidden love revealed itself the moment the gaikokujin started to paint our trembling sister. Was she sitting in a chair with a bored expression on her face? Was she standing next to an ancient vase, holding a lifeless pink parasol in one hand? Was our sister reclining on a small sofa with the sunlight splashing across her indifferent beauty? Was she playing a musical instrument or reciting poetry to demonstrate that she didn't care whether she was painted or not? She did not remember the details of that afternoon. She did not even remember what she was wearing. All she remembered was the way the gaikokujin had looked at her, and the emotion she felt but which she could not adequately describe. She said his eyes were everywhere, lingering for a moment on her sweetly blushing face, the youthful curve of her arms, her hips, the whiteness of her ankles, the profound wetness of her lips, and then darting back to the canvas. She had never been so excited before, and she could not explain what was happening deep within the hidden recesses of her heart. With each stroke of the gaikokujin's brush, her excitement grew.

How many hours did they spend together after that afternoon? How many days did they bask in the glow of each other's company? Our divine sister became the sound of a distant bell when we asked these questions. But she did admit that they took at least one long walk in the East garden, where they were forced to take refuge during a sudden squall beneath the branches of a weeping willow, but when the storm had passed they were soaked to the skin anyway. That was our divine sister's only confession. The rest she surely locked away in the treasure box of her memory.

Sadly, their private love did not remain private for very long. A few days after the October moon took to the sky, the palace was buzzing with suspicion. A few days after that Princess Tsune was escorted to a small sitting room adjacent to the throne room where she had a private audience with the Emperor, and after that she vanished from sight. Not even we, who loved her more than our own lives, knew where she had gone. But what did any of that matter by then? I knew how she was feeling. I knew she had become a thin reed in a field of thin reeds.

(At this point in the French version of Princess Fumi's narrative there was a note from the translator, M. Élisséèv, indicating that the delicate handwriting in the next few paragraphs was smudged, making it illegible, or perhaps someone had spilled something on the rice paper pages.)

It seems now that the love between our sister and the gaikokujin was like two bubbles uniting, a brief, shining moment, and then poof, it was gone. Our sister was taken away. And the gaikokujin was discovered hiding out in a brothel frequented by soldiers in the seediest section of the city. He was beaten with bamboo sticks and then dragged before the Emperor, who was waiting with his closest advisors in a small sitting room with red velvet chairs scattered about and gilded walls and green curtains. Only the Emperor was sitting when the guards arrived with the gaikokujin. He was handcuffed, and the blood from his beating had dried. He did not move from the spot where the guards left him. The others, the Emperor's closest advisors, were warming themselves in front of a small fireplace, for it was a very cold night for October. We remember that the fireplace was very old, so it was rarely used. We remember the fire that night was very smoky. We became a cricket listening from the smoky hearth of our dreams, so we had no trouble hearing everything that was said.

'One tires of listening to yellow orioles chatter and chirrup,' said a voice.

'We have all been deceived,' said the Emperor.

The counselor who owned the first voice looked down at the gaikokujin and spat on him and said they should expose the head of this criminal on the riverbed of the Kamo River, as they would have done in the old days, and he was about to kick the man when the Emperor raised his hand.

'We are no longer a country without laws,' the Emperor said.

'But this is an insult to our national honor,' said a second counselor, who was only pretending to be angry. 'We must do something.'

'I agree,' said a third voice. Not since the Korean incident has our good will been so abused. If we allow this crime of the century to go unpunished, the world will see us as weak. What then? Who will help us stop the encroachment of the West? Who will stand up for our interests? Do you really think the British will intervene on our behalf? I am convinced that Itō made a secret deal with the British to give Manchuria to the Russians. Why, I do not know.'

'You are getting sidetracked in the discussion before us,' said a fourth voice.

'Death by decapitation,' said the first voice. 'And we should display the head.'

'It is not so unusual a fate to be helpless in Kyoto,' said the fourth voice. But the man who owned this voice was not talking to the other counselors. He was an older gentleman with a white walrus moustache and a stringy white beard. He wore a sharply cut black jacket with many medals and a black cap. He was talking to the gaikokujin instead.

'Hachisuba no,' he said, as if he were reciting a line of verse.

'Should we not place him in a cauldron of boiling oil?' said the second voice.

'Nigori ni shimanu,' the fourth voice continued.

'Is that not what these foreigners expect from us?' said the second voice.

'Kokoro mote,' said the fourth voice.

'We no longer follow the Kyû-keihô, my friend,' said the Emperor.

'Nani ka wa tsuyu o,' said the fourth voice.

'Those days are vanished. We are part of the modern world now,' said the Emperor.

'Tama to azamuku,' said the fourth voice.

'Then we are left with death by hanging.'

Then there was a long silence. Only the cold outside could be heard. And then like a crisp cold breeze that rattles the windows in their panes and startles you from a deep sleep, the fourth voice broke the silence.

'Or perhaps not. Perhaps this gaikokujin was only seeking a souvenir. Perhaps we should seek a diplomatic solution.'

'Yes Hisamoto,' said the Emperor, 'your counsel is always quite practical. Will you see to our guest then?'

'Yes, my Emperor,' said the voice of Hisamoto.

'It is getting late. The sweet-voiced reciters were to read the sutras throughout the night. But I suspect it is too cold for that.'

(Another note from the meticulous M. Élisséèv. Another page of illegible handwriting.)

Once again we were sitting with our sister on the bench beneath the branches of the plum tree, only on this particular evening the tree was not in bloom. She said she had seen her gaikokujin lover only once since she had returned from exile. She had been wandering about the palace grounds, thinking stray thoughts and wondering if someday a poet would write about her disastrous first encounter with love, when she found herself near the entrance to the studio where she and the gaikokujin had first met. The studio was a small gray structure with a view of the Tenjinbori Moat.

Our divine sister said it was evening at this point and already the sunlight was fading, the flash of many fish turning on the surface of the sea and diving deep, and then it was dark. She stood for a while, contemplating the darkness, and she was about to turn around when she was distracted by the sound of an automobile pulling up and then stopping, and then she saw two men get out and one of them ran up the path and disappeared into the studio. But she did not wonder at the strangeness of an automobile materializing suddenly, like a demon intent on devouring the earth. No, our sister could only think of her lover, for even in the darkness that surrounded her like a gently greening mist, she could see that the man who had run into the studio was her absent love. She was astonished. She wondered if perhaps she was dreaming, so she did not move for fear she would wake herself. How long she stood there is anyone's guess. An hour. A single day. A century. It is impossible to know. Then our sister realized that the second man was looking at her with a strangely twisted look on his face, and not only that, he was standing quite close. He was only ten feet away. She said this second man was wearing a black cap and a smartly pressed black jacket decorated with many medals that gleamed brilliantly even in the absence of any external illumination. Then the gaikokujin emerged from the studio, but he was struggling with two suitcases and a small satchel and an armful of canvasses. The man in the black jacket hurried to his aid, and then the suitcases and the canvasses and the satchel were loaded and the man in the black jacket was sitting in the automobile directly behind the driver. Our sister was mesmerized by what she was witnessing. She had not said a word the whole while. Naturally, she began to wonder if her lover remembered the hours they had spent together. She wondered if he even remembered her name. Then just when she was about to give up all hope, he turned his head and his eyes swept across her face. He became a beacon of light and she became a ship in distress. She said at that moment the dream she was dreaming became something else. Her gaikokujin lover bent his head through the back-seat window and spoke to the man in the black jacket. Then he turned and took three steps and embraced our sister, his face shining with the light of the unreachable stars. Neither said a word, for they both knew it was their last embrace. Then he pressed a small piece of folded paper into her hands, kissed her gently on the cheek, and with the hesitant grace of moonlight slipped into the darkness of the waiting automobile. Later, after an appropriate interval had passed, our sister unfolded the piece of paper and saw that it contained a small poem, scribbled hastily, but with great passion.

Kimi ya koshi
Ware wa yukiken
Omōezu . . .
Yume ka utsutsu ka
Nete ka samete ka.

Our sister wept as she read the poem, as anyone who possessed a suffering heart would weep. She said this was because she knew she would never see her love again, and so the questions this small poem contained would haunt her until the end of her days.

(A few more smudges, probably from tears.)

-140-

This chronicler thinks it is worth noting that the man in the black jacket mentioned by Princess Fumi was Hijikata Hisamoto, an elder Japanese statesman who was a member of the Emperor's Privy Council when the war with Russia broke out. According to Hisamoto's memoirs, which were published in 1921 in both Japanese and German twelve years after his death, he and the Emperor 'did not always see eye to eye on matters of politics.' But they 'both agreed that Japan must seek a balance between the need to embrace Western ideas and the need to remain essentially Japanese.' So Hisamoto's actions with respect to Gyula Tornai, and with respect to the Russo-Japanese War, must be viewed in this light. While those around him wanted the head of Tornai mounted on a pike, Hisamoto realized this would have been a disastrous political misstep, a miscalculation of the first order. Japan would have been roundly condemned by the Western powers if they had executed Tornai. Even if they had just tossed the man in prison or sent him to a work camp, they would have been criticized. There was no choice but to let him go home. But Hisamoto also realized that as far as the people of Japan were concerned, the scandalous behavior of Tornai was further confirmation of the West's disrespect for Japanese culture. This scandal, arriving as the tensions between Russia and Japan were escalating, had been the last straw. 'Soon the people of Japan were clamoring for war with Russia,' he wrote. 'And so when the Emperor asked me what we should do, I said we had no choice. We had to defend the honor of Japan, and since Russia now embodied the dishonorable intentions of the Western powers, Russia became the target of our vengeance. What is more, I counseled that we should attack before making a formal declaration of war. In this way, we would be sure to catch the Russians off guard. And this is what we did.'

-141-

So let us now return to the city of Metz and the middle bridge on that sunny afternoon of shattered innocence when young Anton Kreutner was confronted with 'The Tragedy of the Lovesick Gaikokujin.' We can only imagine the confusion he must have endured over the years as he reflected upon this tale of woe, the storm of unanswered questions, but we do not have to imagine the conversation he had that very day with his cousin, Josef, because Anton later wrote an essay about it while he was a student at Saint Andrew-on-the-Hudson Seminary in Hyde Park, New York City. The essay was the very first essay he wrote as a seminary student. The class in which the essay was assigned possessed the awkward sounding though theologically precise name of 'Applying a Traditional Understanding of the Axioms of Hermeneutics to the Modern Problems of New Testament Exegesis.'

On the very first day of that class, the professor, an expatriate German who had survived the Nazi plague, talked about his experiences during the war years, which he said had shaped his views as a theologian. He said in 1933 he was teaching in Muenster-in-Westphalia when the long night of the Nazis fell upon the world, and so he was unexpectedly uprooted by the vicissitudes of fate and the arbitrary whims of Godless men. He became as a shipwrecked exile, his 'mouth filled with the bitter waters of an infinite sea.'

For nine years he moved from country to country, trying to warn people of the dangers of this darkness, but no one heeded his word until he came to America. America, he said, gave him a home and a platform from which to speak, but it was God who had led him there.

He thanked the unbounded mercy of God for having seen him through the ordeal of his exile, but more importantly, he said, he thanked God for helping him gain a deeper understanding of and a greater appreciation for the love of our Lord Jesus Christ, who had visibly blessed him and his work even in those dark, bitter days of exile when his soul was filled with anxiety and disappointment. He said he had not seen the extent of Christ's presence during those dark days, but now that he had gained some perspective, he could easily see what he had missed.

Looking back, he realized that he had only focused his attention on those souls who ignored his words of warning, souls who were committed to obscurantism or worse, and so he had given himself over to unfounded pessimism. He had not noticed the many individuals who were able to separate the kernel from the husk and so digest the truth of God. People were able to endure the inflexible evil of the Nazis because God had helped them endure. God had been everywhere in those days, even though He had been difficult to see.

Then he warned his seminary students that all too often people failed to see the presence of Christ in the world around them because they took a positivist approach to examining reality. The positivist, he told them, only accepted rational, scientific proof to explain what was true, which meant that for the positivist, anything that could not be explained was not true.

'Plato pointed out long ago,' the theologian said, 'that the ability to grasp the true meaning of a document begins with properly placing the content of that document in an appropriate system of truth and values. The positivist can never understand the mysteries which God has revealed therein and continues to reveal because he does not accept the truly symbolic nature of the Bible, which is the eternal voice of God Himself. The whole counsel of God, concerning all things necessary for His own glory, man's salvation, faith and life is set down in Scripture.'

Then the German theologian had asked the seminary students to write about a moment of crisis when they had been exiled and how they had managed to survive, for clearly they had survived because they were all sitting there in his class. He asked them to think about how God had been present even during the darkest moments of their tribulations. The essay wasn't supposed to be very long, three or four pages at the most. He just wanted to get an idea of the moral fiber of his students.

The title of Anton's essay (a rather utilitarian title, but one can hardly fault a seminary student for that) was 'A Young Man's Crisis of Faith: Reflections on Love, Life, Fate and God, from the middle bridge in Metz on a sunny afternoon in 1936.'

-142-

Two sections from Anton's essay (the only sections which have survived the passing of the years), which he wrote in the third person, which the German theologian must have passed off as a sophomoric rant induced by a bout of heavy drinking:

A young man stands in the middle of the middle bridge in Metz on a sunny day in the summer of 1936. He and his cousin, who is much older, are watching the boats as they travel up and down the Moselle River. They are not speaking to each other. They are simply watching the boats. But it is clear that the young man, who is barely sixteen years old, is troubled. The young man's cousin has just told him a strange tale about a Japanese princess who fell in love with a Hungarian painter, a much older man who possessed an insatiable appetite for things of the flesh. Naturally, this love affair, which caused a great scandal throughout Japan, was doomed from the start, but this is not what is bothering the young man. He understands intuitively the joys of having a body, the voluptuousness of looking. He is well aware that the sorrows of the sun are imprinted on the moon. No, what is troubling this young man is the monstrously dispassionate attitude that his cousin seems to possess towards the fate of these two lovers, as if in giving themselves over to the tragedy of failed love, they had to renounce their humanity and are now simply decorations in a cemetery. It is an attitude that says the earth is not the earth but stone. He is having difficulty accepting this attitude at face value. He is wondering if he has missed some crucial clue about what is going on in his cousin's happily indifferent brain. So he is going over everything his cousin said, word for word, first in the telling of the tale, and then the conversation that followed.

[Missing a section of unknown length.]

'It is only a story. It is a diversion, something to kill a few hours.'

'But do you think they truly loved each other?'

'He was in his forties. She was just a young girl, a

child.'

'But they could have loved each other.'

'Yes, of course. Many things are possible. But the world would not have believed it. The world wanted to believe Tornai had given the girl syphilis. The world is cynical like that. And who is to say he didn't?'

'Is that what you believe?'

'What I believe is irrelevant.'

'But you do believe something.'

'Belief only clouds one's judgment.'

'Do you believe they were in love?'

'I believe they wanted to be in love, and that's about as far as I'll go with that. Love is a trap, like religion or believing in Christmas or fighting for one's country.'

'But you can't believe that!' the young man had said. 'You're heading to Spain, aren't you? You're going to Spain because of the war!'

'Of course I am. But that's not the same thing at all. I'm not going to fight for my country. I'm going to fight for someone else's country.'

'I don't understand.'

And the cousin had laughed at that, but all the young man heard was the sound of the boats going up and down the river, and the waves from their wake slapping against the stone wall that had replaced the river bank. Then the cousin began again, a stoic, emotionless voice. 'You'll understand soon enough. It's all just a diversion, the story, love, religion, the war in Spain, all of it is just a diversion. It's all really pretty funny. I mean it's wickedly perverse. I mean look at Tornai and how his life turned out. I am certain he did not give the Princess syphilis. But I also think it is fairly likely that he died of the disease. I read that in a Parisian newspaper.

(The cousin assuming the voice of the newspaper.)

'Gyula Tornai, the famous Hungarian painter, best known for painting harem scenes and seducing young girls, died in 1928 in a run-down boarding house three blocks from the Nyugati railway station in Budapest. The physician attending his death wrote on the death certificate that syphilis was the probable cause of his demise.'

(The cousin assuming his own voice again.)

'Do you see what I am getting at Anton? Tornai's life and death were all mashed together in a very ironic way. And that's the way it is with everyone. Our lives are destined to end ironically. So that's the answer to all of your questions about love and life and fate and God. No matter what you ask, my answer will be the same. I believe in irony. And that's pretty much all I believe in.'

One can imagine the thunderous impact of a conversation like this on an impressionable young man. His mind became a storm of questions which he could not answer, and which none of us can ever really answer. His mind became a ship lost amid the froth of a treacherous sea. He wondered if all of his questions were really the same question in the same way that all of his cousin's answers were the same answer. What else could he think? So slowly, over the course of several years, the questions rattling around in the young man's brain did indeed begin to coalesce. They became a single question, a dark, mysterious, even sinister question that he whispered to himself over and over again, usually late at night, an endless refrain, like the chanting of the monks in the crypt beneath the Cathedral of Saint-Étienne de Metz. What reality exists outside of our own reality? he asked himself. This was the question. And he would look to the night sky as if he expected God himself to respond (like many, he believed that fat, happy cherubs lived without complaint among the stars), but God was silent. The silence became a tornado. The tornado rolled over the landscape leaving behind broken pictures and shattered glass and smashed radios and toppled buildings and people making frail gestures, before disappearing over the horizon. Inevitably, the young man's thoughts of love and destiny became the worms at heaven's gate. But none of this should have been surprising. He had been told, as many had been told, that God existed in a supernal realm where the laws of physics did not apply. Boethius had said this. Aquinas had said this. But the young man suddenly realized that he did not exist in this supernal realm, and perhaps he would never exist there, so what good could possibly come of contemplating this other alien dimension? He never once considered that truth did not always assume the mantle of truth, that all of his question questing was part of some grand celestial pantomime and therefore part of a larger truth that existed apart from a world shaped only by the five senses. Instead, the young man began to see himself as a prisoner in a dark, windowless cell, a prisoner who would wake with a start in the middle of every night to a series of strange, inarticulate sounds originating on the other side of the wall, like invisible angels calling out to each other, sounds which spurred his adolescent imagination to embrace the infinite, and yet the images that danced across the white screen of his consciousness were not rooted in anything he could readily grasp, so the initial feelings of hope that swelled within his breast soon fractured and dissolved, as the strange, inarticulate sounds on the other side of the wall also fractured and dissolved, sounds which then became like the sounds of someone being strangled and then the body slumping to the ground and an uneasy silence spreading out like a dark mist. The young man was left feeling anxious, even bitter, his soul lingering on the lip of the abyss until morning.

So what do you think he did, this young man? Did he embrace the darkening skies of his despair? Did he pluck his aching, rotting heart from his breast, thinking it a treasure trove of hidden secrets? Did he give in to the cravings of a degenerate mind and seek out the luscious and impeccable fruit of life? No, he did none of these things. He was not so disloyal as that. He would not betray the scholars and divine ingénues of his childhood faith, those popinjays of darkness. But he did abandon the idea of eternity. He decided he was too committed to the earth to ponder the theoretical. He would focus instead on trying to discern who and what he was, what his own existence meant in this prison that was his entire world (or, conversely, in this world that had become a prison). So he steeled himself against all outside emotion. He was determined to come to terms with the nature of his strange, quasi-existential existence. He realized that he must accept his life as it was, and this realization became the cattle prod that urged him on. But in truth, what other choice did he have? He needed to be clear about what could and could not be, what was and was not, if he were ever to live in harmony with himself, with others, and with a God who defied all expectation.

-143-

Young Anton Kreutner left Metz in June, 1939, three months before the Nazis invaded Poland. No one knows exactly why he left, but one can guess. He entered Saint Andrew-on-the-Hudson Seminary in September 1944. No one knows what he did during the intervening years, but this gap in his personal history is to be expected. There was a war going on. People did what they had to do and tried not to call attention to themselves. You never knew who would be watching, who would be taking notes.

Thus, young Anton Kreutner disappeared from history for a while, and when he reemerged, as if from an irretrievable hope, he was no longer so young.

He graduated from Saint Andrews in 1952, which is to say that his name appears on an archived list, but there is no document or letter or memo indicating what courses he took, what grades he earned, or why it took him so long.

In fact, there is no documentation whatsoever concerning this period in his life. There is but a single photograph of Anton at Saint Andrews. He is standing with a group of seminary students on a grassy slope with trees on either side. In the background you can see the looming presence of an administration building. The students are all wearing black cassocks. It is autumn. Anton is surrounded by his classmates, who seem to have sort of merged into a single entity, a sea of pulsating blackness, a dragon with many faces. But Anton himself is not part of this dragon. His individuality seems to leap out of the photograph. One can see quite clearly his strange, bulbous head protruding above the black cassock sea of his classmates. What is more, one can even glimpse Anton's strangely elongated body and his thin reedy arms giving way beneath the giant head, as if he were an alien being or an octopus or a Portuguese Man-O-War floating aimlessly with the ocean current. Everyone in the group is looking at the camera with happy, lidless, intractable smiles. Except Anton is not looking at the camera.

He is looking up at a pale sky streaked with hazy, distant oranges and diffuse greens and Gethsemane blues.

Is Anton surrounded by a shaft of streaming sunlight or was the photograph overexposed? Is he communing with Almighty God, caught up in the swell of an unintelligible language which he nevertheless understands? Is he embracing the anxieties and joys of trying all and discovering all, or is he distracted by a stray thought? These, anyway, are the questions that come to mind.

Although there are no credible sources that might provide a glimpse of Anton's life during his seminary years, this chronicler would be remiss if he did not comment on the intellectual atmosphere at Saint Andrews, a mirror to the Jesuit desire to clean clocks, so to speak, so that every cog could spin freely. It was an atmosphere that bordered on chaos, which some might even have mistaken for farce. But perhaps it was no different at Saint Andrews than anywhere else. The cogs of some of the clocks spun in a clockwise direction, as you might reasonably expect. But a few cogs preferred a counterclockwise direction. The rest, of course, preferred neither direction and chose instead to remain motionless. Naturally, each type of cog had teachers, master cogs, if you will, who were of a similar mind with respect to spinning one way or another, or not spinning at all.

By far the non-spinners were the largest contingent of cogs. And who can blame them? They were all disciples of Father Leonard Feeney, a literary superstar who had been censured by the Archbishop of Boston for daring to contradict ecclesiastical authority. At the heart of the controversy lay the simple fact that Father Feeney believed that salvation could only be achieved by submitting to the will of the Pope and embracing the faith of the Roman Catholic Church as the one true faith. He accused the Jesuits in Boston of teaching that one could find salvation outside of the Church.

In 1949 he was expelled from the Jesuits, and in 1953 he was excommunicated by the Pope he only sought to serve. Father Feeney spoke out against what he saw as the plague of liberal indifference towards matters of spiritual orthodoxy. He wagged his finger at those who would compromise their beliefs in favor of the ecumenical approach.

Many Jesuits of the day secretly believed as he did.

Many taught in schools like Saint Andrews.

The second largest group, the clockwise cogs, followed the moral authority of Father John Cuthbert Ford, who had penned an article called "The Morality of Obliteration Bombing," which was a condemnation of the kind of bombing the Allies used to level the city of Dresden and other German industrial centers during World War Two.

Father Ford and his followers believed the tactic of total war was a moral crime, that the direct killing of innocent non-combatants was a violation of natural law. The total-war-mongers, according to Father Ford, justified their position by suggesting that civilian casualties were tragic but incidental so far as the aims of prosecuting the war were concerned, and so they advised all bombardiers to let go their bombs but withhold their intentions. Father Ford took the moral high ground and pointed out that the evil effect on innocent people in all-out war was immediate and profound, while the military advantage that would result was both secondary and derivative.

What made Father Ford's moral argument all the more compelling was that he made it in 1944, when the war was still in doubt and the obliteration bombing of German cities was still taking place.

The third group of cogs, the counterclockwise cogs, was the most radical (and therefore the smallest) of all. As kindred spirits of the French Jesuit philosopher Pierre Teilhard de Chardin, whose works had been suppressed as heretical while he was alive, these cogs saw both the Universe, and humanity as an integrated part of the Universe, as works in progress. All existence, they believed, was more properly described as a process of reality becoming, rather than reality in a static sense. To see or to perish was the essence of humanity's condition. Consequently, one did not speak of cosmology, per se, one spoke of cosmogenesis.

For these radical thinkers who were hiding out like gangsters on the run or guerrilla warriors in the shadow-filled hallways of Saint Andrews, the evolutionary movement since the moment of the Big Bang was an inevitable movement towards ever increasingly more complex modes of consciousness that would one day culminate in a state of perfect consciousness, which Teilhard called the Omega state. Man was but an intermediate stage in the overall journey towards absolute awareness, a critical point of simultaneous emergence and immersion, maturation and escape for all conscious entities from the temporal prison we call the Earth.

It is beyond the discerning powers of this chronicler to judge whether Father Anton was a clockwise spinner, a counterclockwise spinner, or a non-spinner. But for those astute readers interested in wandering the hidden passageways of that labyrinth we call the human psyche, there are two somewhat trivial details that might be worth further scrutiny.

The first concerns a book that, according to his parishioners in Miami, was apparently always either on Father Anton's person or within easy reach. It was a slim volume of poetry entitled *The Blindness of Becoming*, a curiously enigmatic title by an obscure Peruvian poet named Eduardo de Jesús Montoyo, who had moved to Brussels in 1952. This was Montoyo's first and only book of poetry. The back jacket promised that the poetry would focus on one of three major themes: 1) the difficulty of reconciling the hope of religion with the scientific and political agnosticism of the twentieth century; 2) the difficulty of comprehending a reality that defies both explanation and interpretation; and 3) coming to terms with the tragedy of elusive love. It was middling poetry at best, but Father Anton was quite fond of the Peruvian's way with words, and he would supposedly take the book out and begin reading at a moment's notice. His favorite poem was the title poem, which this chronicler has reprinted below, along with the footnotes to the poem, provided perhaps by the poet himself so we would have some sense of what he was aiming for:

The Blindness of Becoming

The clouds above Kleine Brogel[1] *are edged with a*
Translucent green,
Gray clouds hanging hapless
Against the intruding sky,
Poisoned by the radiation sickness
Of fevered thought.
In the distance the long sobs
Of a lonely bomber,[2]
The droning of its engine like swarms
Of blind bandits, a thicket of rustling knives
Racing through my open veins. So I

Pluck out my eyeballs, as juicy and irregular
As unsqueezed lemons, and rub the
Jelly on the ground, 'A trick
To save precious seconds,' I tell myself,
'To sear the darkness against
Any remaining unpurged fears.'
But I know this to be a lie.
I know that all I've done
Is squander my discontent.
I have become my other self.
I have become everyone I ever knew,
An illiterate, self-proclaimed
Tiresias,[3] *unrecognizable.*

Eduardo de Jesús Montoyo, 1963

---

[1]Kleine Brogel is a Belgian Air Force base near the city of Meeuwen in northeast Belgium. It was established in March 1945.

[2]The image of the lonely bomber is probably a reference to the Enola Gay. After the Enola Gay dropped the atomic bomb on Nagasaki on August 9, 1945, Montoyo wrote an editorial which was published in *La Dernière Heure,* a liberal Belgium newspaper. The editorial condemned the use of such extraordinary measures against the people of Japan ('Wasn't Hiroshima enough?' Montoyo asked.) Montoyo also raised a series of unanswerable questions about the purpose of the newly established Kleine Brogel air force base. He asked if the base was under the control of the Americans and if the squadrons of planes that were housed at Kleine Brogel possessed atomic bombs. 'Have we become the atomic arm of an unseen dictator? Is this Hitler all over again?' Montoyo saw the use of the atomic bomb as an extreme example of the 'blindness of becoming' that he believed was an inevitable consequence of the quest for power. His editorial went largely unnoticed. [Note from Chronicler: Ironically, or perhaps predictably, the Belgian Air Force at Kleine Brogel is and has been under NATO command in a tactical sense since 1962, and has had a nuclear strike role since 1984.]

[3]Tiresias was a blind prophet from Greek mythology who appears in numerous stories of ancient Greece, including Oedipus Rex and The Odyssey. His prophecies are never wrong, but are presented in cryptic fashion and so are almost always misinterpreted.

The second triviality that may not be so trivial was a postcard Father Anton had sent upon his arrival at Gesù Church in Miami. The postcard was addressed to a Father Jerome Ratzinger, a friend and former classmate who was two years ahead of Father Anton at Saint Andrews.

The picture side of this postcard (a vintage linen postcard full of color and detail) features a gleaming white Gesù Church from the 1940s. The sidewalk outside the church is overflowing with women in white dresses and men in dark suits, all of them either waiting to head into the church, or perhaps they are waiting for a bride and groom to descend the steps. A dozen or more cars are parked along the curb, Packards by the look of them, mostly black in color, a few maroon ones, and a few that are dark green. It is a sunny afternoon in the world that is this postcard, a world that radiates with a sense of expectation and well-groomed, luminescent optimism. But it is a postcard, after all, propaganda for the tourists. The flip side is the antithesis of the picture side. The flip side records Father Anton's first impressions upon entering his new church. The handwriting is precise, meticulous, almost as if it had been typed. The emotions conveyed are just as precise, though certainly open to interpretation, even conjecture. Father Anton's sympathies for Germany and all things German are unmistakable.

What the postcard said:

I have arrived, my friend, but it is not like I thought it would be. Miami is an odd mix of Jewish immigrants, rum runners from the Caribbean, veterans of the recent war, and American gangsters. There is nothing even remotely German about the community, certainly not the food. There are no silver griffins flying on a blue background, no dragons to inspire the soul. I feel out of place but will endeavor to follow your sage advice. Ad maiorem Dei gloriam! No, I have not forgotten. Still, at the moment I am consumed by some very strange thoughts. I am filled with a sense of the tragic. Walking into this beautiful Church is like wandering through a cemetery on the verge of consciousness. It is also like falling asleep on an empty bus heading without restraint down a desolate highway. I will send you another postcard, or perhaps a letter, when there is more to say.

Your friend and brother in Christ, Anton.

-144-

Man's own image is stamped upon everything he looks at, which is a lofty way of saying that the world is a mirror to our own perceptions. But some people have forgotten this essential truth. No one knows why. They become lost in a sea of confusion. Some are lost for only a few days. But some are lost for years. Perhaps they are asleep at the wheel. Perhaps their maps are outdated. In any case, their minds have been jerked and tufted by straggling thunder and shattered sun, as the poet says. They have no idea where they are going or where they are. Ironically, some may have no idea that they have no idea. But then one day they just wake up. Again, no one knows why. They wake up and see that the waters are calm, tranquil. They see a sandy stretch of beach and a rickety wooden pier and they head for shore. Footfall. A deserted island somewhere. A paradise unfolding, though still untamed. Naturally, they utter short though unintelligible prayers. They wonder if they are dreaming, if this is but the quiet before the dramatic plunge, but they know they are not dreaming. They have escaped the eddies of life and death and become the mirror they were originally seeking.

Perhaps this is what happened to Father Anton. From the perspective of this chronicler, who is sitting on a mountaintop perch a good many years after the fact, so he can claim (a spurious claim perhaps) a more objective perspective, it seems that the forty-eight years Father Anton spent at Gesù Church were years spent in exile. Was he waiting to die? How cliché, and yet still a possibility. Was he waiting to go home, and where did he imagine home was and had it changed much since he had been away? Or was he simply waiting for permission (from God? from his cousin Josef? from some pre-adolescent imagining of the Universe?) to think and feel and express what he truly believed about life and the world, thoughts and feelings he had kept suppressed because that is what we do when we don't know what to do with our innermost demons.

Admittedly, all this is just idle conjecture. Root causes remain hidden in the swampy soup of possibilities. But the final tree that emerges from these dark waters is much more visible. One can say without any fear of contradiction that forty-eight years passed in a blink. Years of no real consequence, one might add. An interlude. Father Anton, it seems, had taken a hiatus from himself. And so there are only two essential disclosures concerning his tenure at Gesù that need to be mentioned. The first concerns the relationship he had with a woman, a parishioner, named Eléna Montaño. The second focuses on the last several days leading up to his departure from the Church.

The story of Father Anton Kreutner and Eléna Montaño:

This is not a sordid tale, just to be clear. Father Anton first met Eléna in 1954 at the baptismal font, when she was barely six months old. She was the very first soul he baptized, and of the hundreds of baptismal ceremonies he performed over the years, with all of those crying babies wailing away in the echo chamber of his brain, hers was the only face of an innocent etched in his memory.

Eléna's father, Simon Rodrigo Montaño, and her mother, Iliana del Carmen Rojas, had both immigrated from Puerto Rico in 1949 and moved into a small bungalow in Allapattah, a working-class neighborhood in Miami. Simon Montaño drove a delivery truck for *The Miami Herald,* so he made pretty good money. Eléna did not remember the art deco building with the rounded front entrance on Miami Avenue, which is where Simon first started. Her memories were of the cinderblock building painted a yellowish beige color, which looked out on the bay. Her father always said he liked the feel of the old *Miami Herald* digs much better. In spite of the 1960s brightness of the new building, he said it always felt gloomy inside. The cafeteria was gloomy. Oh, true, the lobby was cheerful enough, but there was no place to sit. Yes, there was a view of the water, but not from the garage. And besides, you could not get to the water from the building. There was no access. You could only look at it. You could not even smell the air.

Her mother, Iliana, worked in a small neighborhood bakery (Rosario's Bakery, NW 28th Street, a few blocks from the Post Office) during the day, Monday to Friday, but to make a little extra money she hired herself out as a seamstress evenings and Saturday afternoons. But she never worked past four on Saturdays. She had to catch the 4:17 bus to downtown Miami if she hoped to go to confession at Gesù church by five. And she never missed confession. Then every Sunday morning at 8:15, she and her daughter, Eléna, boarded the same bus so they could make the nine o'clock Mass. Her only respite came

Sunday evenings. She was a devoted reader of *Vanidades*. The magazine contained lurid tales of romance by the novelist Corín Tellado, which produced impure thoughts in many a reader, a sin which became a regular feature of Iliana's confessions, and later, Eléna's.

So Father Kreutner was the confessor to both. He also visited the Montaño household every ninth Sunday for a mid-afternoon repast in his honor. His German ethnicity was forgotten as this transplanted Puerto Rican family embraced him as one of their own. Even Simon Montaño, who called the Church a pack of thieves, nodded a gruff consent at the dinner table. The relationship between priest and parishioner was defined in formal terms by the Church and Church dogma, and in familiar terms by the ritual joys of a family coming together to celebrate life.

Eléna's earliest memory of Father Kreutner was when she was six. After Mass one Sunday, mother and daughter stood on the steps of the church chatting with Father Kreutner and Iliana mentioned that she wanted to take Eléna shopping at the Sears Roebuck and then at the Jordan Marsh. Father Kreutner said he would drive them. A week or so later, he kept his word. He borrowed an old Chevrolet and ferried them downtown, and soon the car was full of packages, which Father Kreutner not only helped carry, but which he even had helped pay for. Afterwards he took them across the Venetian Causeway so Eléna could walk on the beach and dance in the waves. The defining moment of this memory, however, and the reason it became part of Eléna's mythology, did not occur until the journey home.

On the way back, they were forced to stop for half an hour while a parade of circus elephants shilly-shallied over the drawbridge. They got out of the car to watch. 'It is like Hannibal's procession through Spain,' Father Kreutner had said, 'except these are Indian elephants. The African kind are too unpredictable.' Eléna waved at the handlers, who were walking alongside, and the mahout, who was sitting on top of the largest female in the middle of that long line of brownish-gray beasts, and she clapped and laughed when they waved back. The elephants, of course, were perspiring heavily, their skin glistening in the sunlight, and as they passed by, Eléna realized they were tied together with ropes, and they didn't look all that happy. She was happy but they were not. She asked Father

Kreutner about this and he said 'We are all God's creatures, my little one, and so we are also all subject to God's will. It is God's will that these beasts are yoked, perhaps because they bring joy to thousands just as they have brought joy to you. See how magnificently they gleam in the sunlight. Like a string of amber colored diamonds, every facet reflecting the colors of the Universe, glowing with the majesty of a loving God.'

Eléna didn't really understand what Father Kreutner was talking about, at least not that day, but she also never forgot the elephants. She later said she went into journalism because of that circus parade. That afternoon became for Eléna a symbol of the misery and joy that shape each instant of our lives, and she wanted to write about those moments, share them with the world before they passed into oblivion. And because Father Kreutner was there on the Day of the Elephants, which is how Eléna always referred to that afternoon, she credited him with starting her off on the path to her profession. From that moment on, Father Kreutner was a visible presence at each milestone in Eléna's life. He cut the cake at every birthday party. In 1970, he drove the entire Montaño family to Palm Beach for a revival of the once popular Seminole Sundance Festival (the last one had been in 1960), and Eléna was unexpectedly named Queen of the Parade and an honorary Seminole Princess. Naturally, Father Kreutner hooted and hollered like all the rest when she rode past the grandstand in the back seat of a spiffy new convertible, her hand fluttering back and forth like a piece of ribbon or a dragon's tail. He was filled with an adopted uncle's pride when she graduated from Saint Theresa's high school in 1972. When she entered the University of Miami, he told her he'd give her a crisp Ben Franklin for every straight-A semester. When she graduated in 1977 with two Bachelor's degrees, one in politics and the other in journalism, he shelled out one-thousand dollars (a small fortune on a Jesuit priest's salary) and told her to put it to good use.

He didn't see much of her after that. And he wasn't much of a letter writer (and neither was she). Instead, he watched over her from afar. She worked at KATC in Lafayette, Louisiana from 1977 to 1984, and then she moved back to Florida and began working at WEAR in Pensacola, Florida as an investigative reporter and fill-in anchor. She was hired by Channel Ten in Miami in 1990. By 1991 she was the weekend news anchor. Her face and her body from the waist up were plastered on billboards all over the city. And though Father Kreutner did not approve of the way her upper half was dressed (a fancy silk halter top with a black jacket and hoop earrings), he couldn't help but smile when he looked into those gigantic Spanish eyes. It was like he had been suddenly transported to that moment oh so many years earlier when he had poured the tiniest sliver of water over Eléna's face, and she had burst into a song of bewilderment and rage.

One week before Father Kreutner leaves the Church:

On a sunny August afternoon, one week before ex-Father Anton Kreutner boarded a silverish Greyhound Bus bound for Phoenix, Arizona, he found an old shoe box hidden beneath some blankets on the top shelf of his closet. Immediately he remembered how the shoe box had come into his hands. It was as if an ocean wave had washed over his head. He closed his eyes and let the wave wash down his back. He saw himself six years earlier emerging from the comforting darkness of the confessional. A few candles were flickering, but this fragile light was overwhelmed by the late afternoon sunlight gleaming through the stained-glass windows. A strange, fragile-seeming woman, an incorporeal being made from pure light or fire, approached him.

How long she had been waiting at the back of the church he did not know. As she drew near, she held up the shoe box, as if it were a divine gift, a sacrificial offering, and asked if he would give it to Eléna Montaño. The strange, radiant being, luminous from a luminous traversing, said the shoe box contained some information for Eléna. He was intrigued. He had never been so closely connected to a story his Eléna was working on, so he had agreed to act as an intermediary. Shortly after that Eléna had asked him to hang onto the box for a spell. She didn't say why, only that she had to run down a few leads. He had happily agreed. He remembered feeling as if it were her turn now to point out the Indian elephants. It was a glorious feeling. But a few weeks later, Eléna died in a tragic accident on the Seven Mile Bridge. Father Anton Kreutner forgot all about the contents of the shoe box. Instantly it had become just another item stored in a closet, a shard of memory too painful to even look at.

So tune into what is happening here. Father Anton is sitting on the edge of his bed on a sunny afternoon in late

August, 2000. He is eighty years old and has been a member of the Jesuit Order since 1952. In spite of the fact that he lives in Miami, he doesn't seem to get much sun, at least not any more. His pasty white parchment skin, which is pockmarked with age spots (they dot his legs, his arms, his back, his neck, his face, his hands), is stretched so tightly across his bones that it seems to be crushing the life out of him. His hands quiver as he holds the shoe box. For a moment he wonders if he has slipped into another reality. Eléna died in 1994. It has only been six years. But six centuries of joy would not have filled the void that suddenly fills Father Anton's heart. Not even the sunlight pouring in through his open window can ease his pain. He remembers a line of poetry from somewhere. 'Was the sun concoct for angels or for men?' He is certain this line somehow applies to his current apprehensive mood, but he is not sure how. He carefully removes the lid, slowly, with some measurable degree of hesitation, as if perhaps his beloved child is tucked away inside. Of course she is not, and he laughs at the idiocy of a feeling he ascribes to old age doddery but which is a common enough human affliction that affects all ages. Eléna is not inside the shoe box. What he discovers instead is a small leather book that seems laminated in tears and sweat. Breathing deeply, he calms his lunatic self, and with the hands now of a jeweler he opens the book. It is a diary of some sort. There is a rhythmic precision to the handwriting, like the handwriting of a poet, but Father Anton is having difficulty following the pattern. He fumbles about for his reading glasses, which he placed on the nightstand next to his bed the night before. The book is called *The Diary of Emilio Escoraz Calzada.* But this title does not reveal the enormity of what lies within. Father Anton thumbs his way past the first few pages and begins to read, and now there is no going back. He did not expect this. Why should he be given such a burden as this book? It is filled with page after page of obituaries, all sorts of people from all over Miami and beyond. Five-hundred entries, maybe more. It is more than Father Anton can comprehend, and yet he cannot stop reading. The hourglass has been turned topsy-turvy. And then he realizes that his beloved child was herself murdered because of this book. The accident on the bridge was not an accident. Hers would have been the very last entry if there had been someone to record the unvarnished circumstances of her death. Father Anton freezes with this thought. The ever-changing face of Eléna Montaño races through his brain, a kaleidoscope of images annihilating the bitter sweet verve of life's trajectory.

A few excerpts from *The Diary of Emilio Escoraz Calzada*:

The author of this diary professes that his purpose in recording so many deaths is to preserve the memory of the people whose lives have been taken, nothing more. He is on no vendetta, for while he knows the murderers personally and can speak to their habits as well as he can speak to his own, he would not do something so daring, so dangerous, perhaps even foolhardy, as to record their names in a document such as this. Besides, nothing good would come of that strategy except more deaths. These men are untouchable, even as they are paragons of unspeakable evil. Perhaps they are demons sent from the nether world to inflict pain and suffering upon all they come in contact with. One can barely breathe just to look at them with their dark, leathery skin like the skin of burn victims, or those suffering from a rare, malignant form of leprosy, or, well, demons in the flesh, to be blunt. In any event, he will refer to them simply as The Brothers, and whoever can decode that reference hopefully knows the wisdom of keeping one's trap shut.

The author would also like to address a question which will surely arise. How does he know the details of so many deaths? Was he present at the murders? Is he perhaps one of the murderers? The answer to these questions is a simple no. He was not present. He is not one of the two. But they always joked about the people they had killed. They told stories, and those who had no other choice but to listen to these stories, which includes the author of this document, would lie awake for many a heart-heaving night bearing mute witness to tragedy after tragedy. He was, however, the only one among those captive listeners who wrote down what he had heard.

Lastly, on several occasions the author's path crisscrossed the path of a relative of one of the victims, and he was faced with the moral dilemma of whether or not to reveal what he knew. In the end, he chose not to divulge any pertinent information for fear of causing the death of yet another innocent. Should he have tried to bring the murderers to justice? Should he have taken a public stand against the forces of darkness that threaten to swallow the world? Perhaps. Then again, who can say what anyone should or shouldn't have done before the hour has passed? To paraphrase a much beloved Cuban poet, 'we march blindly into ourselves like blind men stumbling at every step with memories that hurt like thorns.'

Saturday, October 24, 1981. Julio Caballero, 36 years old, taxi driver. Julio was a chubby, pensive fellow who had emigrated from Nicaragua in 1971 during the Somoza regime. He lived with his brother and two dogs in a small apartment in Miami Shores. His brother worked at a hotel at the beach. They were both very Catholic, and often went to Mass twice a week. Julio picked up The Brothers from the airport just before seven in the evening. It had been a sunny day, a light breeze, warm to mild. It was going to be a glorious evening. The Brothers had just returned from a week in Nicaragua, and when Julio heard them talking about their trip, he said that's where he was from. He asked if the politics had changed. He was happy when the Sandinistas had overthrown Somoza, but he didn't know a whole lot about life since the revolution. That was all it took. The Brothers, who hated the Sandinistas more than any other South American revolutionary group, took Julio for a Sandinista supporter and possible spy. They acted as if they had suddenly remembered they had an additional errand to run before going home and told Julio they needed to head south towards Homestead, to the South District Wastewater Treatment Plant. Julio didn't object. A fare was a fare. But he didn't know the way. The Brothers told him where to turn and when, and Julio obeyed without questioning a thing, without even a thought that something sinister lay in store for him, until they had driven past the facility, trading the narrow asphalt road they had been on for a gravelly back road that ran along a creek with the suddenly sinister sounding name of Black Creek. When the road became a bike path, The Brothers forced Julio to stop. They dragged him from the car, kicking and screaming and invoking the name of Saint Anthony, but to no avail. He was like a plucked chicken in their grasp and soon went limp with an unresolved panic. Minutes later all three men were crouching along the edge of the brackish shoreline, surrounded by mangroves. Then without a second thought or even a quick goodbye, the larger of The Brothers grabbed Julio's head by a tuft of black hair and pushed Julio's face into the briny, brackish water and kept it there until Julio's legs stopped twitching. They left him there for whatever creatures might be looking for an easy meal, or perhaps the tide would wash the body away, got back into Julio's taxi and drove home. Presumably they had the taxi chopped up. When the taxi cab company came calling on Julio's brother to retrieve their missing vehicle, they discovered that no one had seen or heard from Julio in several days. They assumed he had sold the taxi and skipped town with the money. The police put out an APB on Julio Caballero, wanted for Grand Theft Auto. No one ever stumbled across his body. It is so tragic, so sad. Each note I sing for Julio I sing also for myself and all the rest of us. Julio's brother now attends Mass every day, and every day he asks Saint Anthony to bring his brother back home. Also, the two dogs have run away. Only God knows what happened to them.

Thursday, December 17, 1981. Pedro Sáenz de Heredia, twenty-nine years old, a hair stylist. Pedro was tiny, thin, maybe five-foot-four and a hundred-and-thirty pounds. But his heart was as big as one belonging to a Miura bull, a Spanish fighting bull. He had a flirty smile for everyone he met, and a twinkle in his eye if you moved his libido. The Brothers spotted him quite by chance on a sunny afternoon in December. Pedro was coming out of Sicodélica Hair Styling Salon on Biscayne Boulevard near the causeway, where he had worked for three years. He was leaving early that day to catch a train for New York City, where his grandparents lived. A holiday visit. He was dressed for traveling, but for Pedro that meant a pair of bright yellow jeans, a pair of Giorgio Armani black leather wingtips, a black silk shirt buttoned all the way to the top, and a multi-colored scarf (purple, blue, and yellow). The Brothers followed Pedro by car to a corner bus stop, and as Pedro sat down on the bench to wait for a bus, they slammed on the brakes in a very dramatic fashion. Before Pedro could protest, before he or anyone else on the street that afternoon knew what was happening, he was tossed into the back seat of a Pontiac Firebird, which The Brothers had appropriated for the day, and then the car disappeared in a cloud of dust, heading west on NW 80th for a few minutes before turning onto the relative obscurity of a side street. Pedro tried to explain as politely as he could that they had made a mistake, and he flashed his flirty smile as he spoke. How could he have known The Brothers were raging homophobes? Immediately the larger of the two reached his huge hands into the back seat, took hold of Pedro's brightly colored scarf, and twisted the ends together and pulled. Slowly, and with a relish that Pedro could not resist, he crushed Pedro's windpipe. Pedro died moments later. After removing anything that could have been used to identify the body, The Brothers dumped it into a Norfolk Southern freight car and then ditched the Pontiac. When Pedro did not show up at Grand Central Station, his grandparents assumed they had the wrong date. By Christmas Eve they had forgotten he was even coming. And when he failed to show up at the salon two weeks later, the other hair stylists were jealous because they assumed he had found a better gig in New York City. No one thought of Pedro ever again.

Monday, January 25, 1982. Mario Balagueró, Owner, Aqua-Clean Pool Cleaning Service. The death of Mario, according to the younger of the two brothers, was a simple business dispute that got out of hand. The Brothers showed up at the Aqua Clean headquarters and asked the girl at the counter for the owner. A few minutes later out stepped Mario, an older man, salt and pepper hair, a small paunch, rounded shoulders from overwork, but he seemed an affable, respectful sort. The three men spoke quietly for several minutes. The Brothers asked Mario a series of questions, and he gave short but precise answers. They liked his attitude right off the bat and said they wanted to help him expand his business, but they wanted to see his outfit in action first. Mario was ecstatic. He had started Aqua Clean in the 1970s with thirty clients. Now he had over five-hundred, but money was always tight. They had started doing pool repair work during the off-season as a sideline. He had sixteen vans out that morning on service calls. Most were up in North Miami, a couple were up in Bal Harbour, and one was out at Sunny Isles Beach, a brand new twelve-story high-rise hotel. The Brothers turned towards each other and laughed as if Mario had told a joke and said they wanted to see the pool at the hotel, so the three men climbed into an Aqua Clean van and drove out to the beach.

It was a typical January day, mild, partly cloudy, a slight breeze, the tang of salt in the air. They got to the hotel just before noon, but the pool guys had knocked off for lunch. The pool was close enough to the hotel that one could imagine a few drunken guests diving from their balcony platforms into the water. It had been drained and the bottom had been covered with various tarps. At the north end of the pool the work of replacing tile (a dozen boxes of cheap crystal stone swimming pool tile) and repainting walls (a drum canister of waterproof paint and rollers) had begun. No one was around, and at first Mario started to apologize, but then The Brothers began quizzing him about the nature of the repair work and how long it took to drain a pool, and once again, Mario gave short but precise answers. It was clear Mario ran an efficient outfit, and The Brothers prized efficiency more than anything, even loyalty. Then the quiz game was over and it looked like a jackpot of happy grins, but that's precisely when things turned sour. The three men were standing on the edge of the drained pool, contemplating the enormity of the future that lay before them. Then the larger of the brothers began to speak with the muttering eloquence of a mad king. His voice vibrated with the delicate sound of distant thunder. 'On occasion we would like you to shut down your entire company for a day or two. No questions asked. On those days you will tell everyone to go home, unless we instruct you otherwise. We will not be able to give you much notice, but we will pay you three-thousand a day. That should cover it, don't you think? We are businessmen, after all, and believe in fair compensation.' But Mario had many questions and could not restrain himself. His questions became a series of annoying lightning flashes in an otherwise dark and tranquil sky. This was a serious mistake, which is to say the outcome was inevitable. The larger of the two brothers wrapped a single arm around Mario and picked him up like a rag doll. Then he swung his giant appendage back as if he were a mythic discus thrower, holding his arm steady for a moment to gauge the distance, and hurled Mario across the empty expanse. Mario's head split like a melon when it hit the exposed cement on the far side. Without any further commentary, The Brothers wrapped the dead but draining body in one of the plastic tarps, wrapping his body like it were that of a fish, and stuffed it into the back of the van. The younger of the two brothers washed away the blood stain on the side of the pool. It was little more than a blot, but The Brothers were nothing

> if not meticulous in cleaning up after themselves. They drove south to Atlantic Island (a trip of maybe five minutes), pulled into the driveway of a fairly ritzy looking house where they kept a speedboat, loaded the body into the back and headed out to deep water. About fifteen miles out they stopped to unfurl the tarp. The Gulf Stream swallowed Mario's empty husk in a matter of moments. They rinsed the tarp and stowed it in the van in case they needed it again.
>
> "That afternoon is like wide water, a reflection without sound. Later, The Brothers took control of Aqua-Clean. No one objected. No one asked what had become of Mario. They just assumed he had sold the business and headed for greener pastures. It is what anyone would have done if the right opportunity came along.

All too quickly Father Anton was overwhelmed by this frenzy of unrestrained evil. One entry flowed into the next, a river of impenetrable sadness that swallowed names and dates and details. It was a purging of emotion that left him feeling as vacant and remorseless as the killers themselves. Benito Berlanga, grocery store clerk, drawn and quartered, body pieces tossed into the Bay from the back of a speeding boat, 1982, Friday August 13, very warm, windy, even gusty, some rain. Luis García Gutiérrez, truck driver, tortured with red-hot pincers, flayed alive, 1982, Tuesday October 19, showers, warm but mild, windy. Sheila de Larrocha, nursery school teacher, girlfriend of the truck driver, walked in on the murder of her boyfriend, was raped while Luis, who was not quite dead, watched with grotesque, wide-eyed horror, the exposed muscles of his face dripping with blood, but her screams became annoying so they suffocated her with a plastic bag, 1982, Tuesday October 19, showers, warm but mild, windy. Bodies were dumped in the Everglades. Kenny Dannenfelzer, gas station attendant, drug dealer, weekend drummer, tied to one of the pumps of the Chevron where he worked and doused in gasoline and set on fire, the entire gas station was engulfed in a massive explosion, the plume could be seen for miles, 1983, Wednesday March 16, mild to a bit cooler, dry, very windy. The cleanup crew did not even realize that the charred remains of a body was among the rubble. Allison LeSage, college student, a blonde bombshell if there ever was one, a blind date with the larger of the brothers but the date had gone bad, broke the girl's neck while she was in a swimming pool, body dumped into the ocean, 1983, Sunday, July 24, sunny, very hot, dry, no breeze whatsoever. Lois Granatelli, private detective, tortured, fingernails and toenails plied off with pliers, eyes sliced like grapes, cement shoes, tossed in the Bay, the fate of all flatfoots that get too close to the truth, 1984, Tuesday June 26. Paula Langlo, receptionist for the private detective, had come back to the office because her boss had given her tickets to a concert for her birthday but she had left the card in the top drawer of her desk, strangled, put in her car, car was lit on fire, the shell of the car was towed to a junkyard and disappeared among the stacks of useless, abandoned vehicles, 1984, Tuesday June 26, hot and rainy. Oscar 'Peajacket' Alvarez, twenty-six, an accountant, boating accident, 1985, Monday April 15, mild to warm, dry, breezy. Emilio Escoraz Calzada, 1986.

It was an endless litany of unanswered prayers, at least this is how it seemed to our good German priest. He did notice that the diary continued even after the death of its author, Emilio Escoraz, but his mind was mush by this point. It was just one more detail to observe, catalogue and abandon. And then he had finished the book. It was very dark in his room, except for the soft, hazy light emanating from the lamp on the nightstand, but he had no memory of turning on the light. Hours had passed, perhaps days. He had no sense of where he was or what to do. He just sat on the edge of his bed, embedded in the abyss of the moment. It was as if he had gone mad. Or the world had. Or it had always been that way.

Later, he became more like his old self. He took a shower and got dressed and got some breakfast. He walked around downtown Miami so he could see the faces of happy people happily oblivious to the evil that existed all around them, evil that inhabited the very air they breathed. He looked up at a night sky at the few stars he could glimpse through the radiant background of city lights like a shroud. He wondered if anyone else were looking at those stars.

He spent hours sitting in the back of Gesù Church.

He remembered words he had once written on a postcard to a friend. He had forgotten the name of the friend, but he remembered the words: *Walking into this beautiful Church is like wandering through a cemetery on the verge of consciousness. It is also like falling asleep on an empty bus heading without restraint down a desolate highway.*

He realized that nothing had changed in all the years he had been at Gesù Church. He also realized that he could no longer stay. Sitting in the back of the church he decided that he must give up the priesthood. Not only that, he came to the conclusion that he must give up his faith as well. It was an easy conclusion to arrive at. To be a practicing Catholic, one had to accept that everything happens, the good and the bad, as part of God's great plan. That meant that one had to accept the deaths of innocents as being an expression of God's divine and irrefutable will. But Father Anton decided in that moment that he could not accept a God who would allow the senseless suffering of so many people. He also could not be a piecemeal Catholic. He would not accept those parts of Catholicism that appealed to his own personal sense of morality and quietly ignore those other parts that contained a more sinister reality, a reality which he realized he had ignored for more years that he wished to count, a reality that we all ignore. He really had no other choice but to leave the Catholic Church altogether.

As it happened, the day before Father Anton boarded the bus for Phoenix, he was to deliver a eulogy at a funeral Mass. He had not delivered a eulogy for many years, but since Father Anastasius (the priest originally selected by the deceased's widow) had come down with a touch of the flu, Father Anton had agreed to step in. He was about the same age as the deceased, and though he did not know the man personally, he did know the neighborhood where the deceased had lived, so he could speak to the local events that had shaped his life with a reasonable degree of familiarity, if not authority.

The night before the funeral Mass, Father Anton began writing his last eulogy. He finished the next day, thirty minutes before he was supposed to be at the Church.

Father Anton's final day as a Jesuit priest:

The sky was a very dark sky that morning, and yet the darkness glittered the way a cloud of confetti glitters as it settles to the ground. The electricity of a thunderstorm about to break was an undercurrent rippling through everyone's subconscious minds, subduing every tongue, wiping clean the slate of sinister intentions, annihilating even innocuous discourse. Perhaps because of the threat of rain, the church was practically empty. The widow of the deceased sat in the front pew on the left side, but she was alone. A few young girls sat in the pew directly behind her, granddaughters perhaps, or the granddaughters of friends. Behind the girls, on both sides of the aisle stretching back towards the infinity of a seething darkness that had already swallowed the balcony and the gleaming brass pipes of an organ (a darkness that seemed to be slowly digesting reality), sat an odd collection of miscreants, hobos, drunks, prostitutes, a few street artists, forgotten old men, forgotten young men, one young man who had not shaven in many months and had food particles and other bits of detritus stuck in his beard, and an aging, happy-go-lucky, hippie with wild, snake-like, John-the-Baptist hair.

Candles flickered dangerously. A golden incense burner floated past, the fragrant clouds of smoke rising like hymns, a supernal music of ancient origins heard only by a select few. Words were spoken. Those in attendance responded appropriately. More incense. More unheard music riding the unseen airwaves. More words. More responses. Then there was a tremendous thunderclap outside and the skies let loose a torrent. The lights inside the church flickered like the candles. The candles went out. The images in the stained-glass windows, normally bright, colorful reminders of God's eternal presence, took on a uniform, dark gray color and so lost all definition. The wind rattled one of the doors at the back of the church, so one of the altar boys raced down the side aisle to see what he could do. A second altar boy was busy re-lighting the candles.

No one said a word for many moments. Then from somewhere there was the sound of bells, like shadows dancing on a wall. Then Father Anton stepped to the lectern, a figure of gleaming brilliance in his white cassock and his strangely gleaming bulbous head like the radiant head of an alien god who had just descended from the stars.

For a moment he surveyed the crowd before him. Perhaps he was trying to let the enormity of the moment sink in. Or he was waiting for the thunderclaps above to subside somewhat so that his voice could be heard. Perhaps he was dismayed that so few people had braved the dark skies and come to Gesù that morning and so was debating whether or not it was worth even opening his mouth. Or perhaps he no longer felt qualified to speak on behalf of God about the promise of eternal life.

Slowly, with imperceptible grace, the majestic, dramatic, theatrical explosion of the storm's beginning settled into a dull, streaming echo of rain on the rooftop, like a memory dissolving. Slowly, Father Anton settled into his role for the morning.

He took a deep breath and began his eulogy.

"Our good friend here has died, husband, friend, son, parishioner. He died in the hope of being resurrected in Christ, a hope we all embrace. But what exactly does it mean to be resurrected in Christ? Does it mean to give up everything we own and follow Him in blind obedience? This would be madness, would it not? Does it mean to follow His example? And what does that even mean? And is that not yet another form of madness?"

Father Anton paused a moment so that his listeners might ponder the gravity of his words, and then he continued.

"The philosophers of Classical Christianity spoke of the madness of the Cross. They believed that the very fact that mankind crucified the living God, that scandal of history, was an act of madness, but they also believed Christ's crucifixion served to illuminate the errors of human thought that lead inevitably to darkness and despair, to all examples of false thinking. The madness of the Cross thus exposed the madness of a world that hungered after things without substance. So madness reveals madness. The eternal truth of God is left alone in the unreasoning sky, a shining sun to guide our way. From the birth of the Renaissance until the days of Pascal, this was the accepted understanding of both the symbolic and the actual meaning of Christ's sacrifice.

"But things have changed. We no longer live in the clear season of the grapes. We have lost our way and become as phantoms seeking illusory shores."

A tremendous thunderclap shook the church and everyone inside. The candles flickered tremulously but did not go out on this occasion. Surprise registered on every face. Father Anton continued as if the thunderclap had simply been an aberration of his own addled perhaps anachronistic perspective.

"The 17th century Pietist theologian, Jacques-Bénigne Bossuet, wrote that 'Christ has become the highest point of our wisdom,' but Bossuet also delivered this warning: 'Do not permit your Cross, which has subdued the universe for you, to be still the madness and scandal of proud minds.' Do you see what he meant, good people? Bossuet no longer believed that madness served the purpose it once did. He no longer believed that the madness of humanity revealed God's truth. He believed that God's truth was evident for all to see, so there was no further need to embrace the illuminating power of madness. Consequently, madness and the crimes committed because of madness were relegated to the periphery of our collective consciousness. Madness, scandalous madness, was something to be hidden away, confined to a prison cell. Ah, the errors of unreason persist even unto the present age. Did not Bossuet and everyone else who took up the banner against those inflicted with madness, did they not realize they were adopting the same attitude towards lunatics that the Jews who crucified Our Lord had adopted towards Christ? By confining madness to a prison cell, they had effectively confined Christ to that same cell. For Christ embraced the lunatic. Not only did Christ surround himself with sinners, degenerates, criminals, and exiles, all those who would have been considered lunatics by society, but He adopted the costume of a madman. How could any sane man have taken on the sins of the world? No, Christ had to become a madman to accomplish His great task. Only a madman can climb a ladder to the sun.

"Saint Vincent de Paul, the Great Apostle of Charity, alluding to Saint Paul's *First Letter to the Corinthians,* reminds us of this forgotten truth. 'O my Savior,' de Paul writes, 'you were pleased to be a scandal to the Jews, and a madness to the Gentiles; you were pleased to seem out of your senses, as it is reported in the Holy Gospel that it was thought of Our Lord that he had gone mad. *Dicebant quoniam in furorem versus est.* His Apostles would look upon him as a man in anger, and He seemed such to them, so that they should bear witness that He Himself had endured the very same infirmities and states of affliction which they had endured, and to teach them and us as well to have compassion upon those who fall into these infirmities.'"

A latecomer arrived and tried to hide his lateness by slipping into the last pew. The wind and rain that accompanied his arrival swirled around the interior of the church for several minutes before dissipating. Father Anton did not betray any sign that he was aware of the disturbance.

"Sadly, tragically," he said, "it has become impossible to reconcile the truth of Vincent de Paul's words with the truth as we see it all around us. Mankind's unreason, which at one point had been virtually identical with God's divine wisdom through the incarnation of his Son, has now become a crime. To follow Christ's example is to be mad and to be a mad is to be a criminal. And the reverse is also true. Prison makes one mad. Ironically, by tossing Christ into a prison cell with the madmen we no longer wish to acknowledge, we have unwittingly turned the whole world into a prison cell. We are now all criminals. We have all gone mad. How else does one explain the presence of so much evil in the world, so much death, so much random violence and destruction, so much pain and suffering, senseless suffering?"

And it was here that Father Anton's wavering, old man's passion began to exert itself, spewing itself over his listeners like froth.

"Surely we can no longer ascribe to the innocent belief that all evil is part of God's greater good? One need only look at the Nazi holocaust for confirmation that this is a morally bankrupt position. But we ignore the fallacy of our own beliefs, as we have ignored it for centuries. Indeed, the moment we tossed Christ into that prison cell along with the other lunatics, the moment we tried to erase the essential madness that was the key to unlocking our essential divinity, that is the moment God's plan for the world went awry, that is the moment we all became truly insane."

Father Anton scanned the sea of vacant faces before him and slammed his fist on the lectern, a futile gesture that would have seemed calculated, a bit of intellectual dishonesty, if you will, except that he was visibly trembling as he spoke.

"What else can I say to you to make you see?"

The church echoed with one final thunderclap, but whether it was from the seemingly preternatural storm outside or the rising agitation in Father Anton's voice, no one could be sure.

"Death, which has brought us together on this rainy morning, is the limit of human life in this temporal realm. But what limit does madness impose upon us? Death was sanctified by Christ's death. But what power now confers sanctity upon madness? The answer is that we alone possess that power. Madness, even in its most bestial form, has been sanctified not by God, but by the power of the human imagination, the co-creator with God of the world as it has become. Of course many of us will refuse to open our eyes to the truth that is right there in front of us. We prefer to live in blindness, for to acknowledge this truth demands that we hold ourselves accountable for the evil that lives among us. Ironically, this is exactly the message Christ came to preach, though the true meaning of his words has become distorted over the centuries.

"So what do I see when I look at our good friend lying in that casket? I see the remains of a man born and bred to a world consumed by madness, traveling a path that embraces madness, and in the end succumbing to that very madness. 'Victory is neither God's nor the Devil's,' a French existentialist once wrote. And I realize that I must agree with him. 'Victory belongs to Madness.'"

No one imagined Father Anton's eulogy was over because he did not step back from the lectern. Everyone waited for him to continue, to finish with a bang. And in truth, it did seem like he had more to say, but it also seemed as if he had suddenly forgotten how to speak. His face contorted itself in an odd grimace, as if his closing remarks were trapped between his teeth and his tongue. Then he made a strange gurgling sound, and whatever words were trapped dissolved inside his mouth. It was a sign of imminent defeat. And yet Father Anton remained at the lectern a few moments longer, silent, solemn, glaring at those sitting in the darkness, teetering on the brink of insanity himself, a majestic sea captain standing at the wheel of a great ship lost amid the waves of a stormy sea.

-145-

Did Father Anton leave the Church because he went mad? This chronicler thinks that interpretation is too facile. Was he clinically insane? Or did he suffer from a delirium, the dream of waking persons? Once again, to offer a reasonable interpretation, to even imagine the answers to such questions, exceeds the ability of this chronicler. It is best to leave each reader with enough pertinent information to draw his or her own conclusions, and to that end, we will all of us join the good Father (or ex-Father, but it is difficult to give up a title we are used to) as he arrives at the Greyhound Bus station in Phoenix, Arizona.

Riding that bus was like blazing a path into the great unknown. This is what ex-Father Anton had been thinking as he watched the landscape roll past his window, and as he stepped off the bus, he continued thinking the same thought. He had been on the road for three days. He hadn't shaved or bathed. When he had fallen asleep, he had dreamed of mercy, he had dreamed of people dancing in the moonlight without a care and angels running away to hide. Now there he was in Phoenix at two in the afternoon, a very bright, sunny, blazing hot day. He almost collapsed as he made his way to the air-conditioned bubble of a thoroughly modern bus station waiting-room. He sat down to rest. The moist, comforting heat of Miami had not prepared him for the white, searing heat of the desert. Walking those few steps from the bus to the waiting-room, he had felt as if he had wandered into a raging inferno.

A few hours later the station clerk nudged ex-Father Anton's shoulder. He had been sleeping. The clerk asked if he had somewhere to go and he nodded and lied and said yes and the clerk disappeared into a broad horizon of a smile. But so what if our good German ex-priest lied about having somewhere to go. Besides, from a certain point of view he had not lied. Even though he had left the Church, he still believed in the guiding hand of God. God would choose his path. He picked up his suitcase, which contained the sum of his worldly possessions, but he left Eléna Montaño's shoe box on the plastic bubble seat in the bus station. In truth, the box, or to be more precise, the diary the box contained, had fulfilled its purpose in facilitating ex-Father Anton's departure from the church and so was no longer a necessary prop. In truth, he was no longer even aware that either the box or the diary existed. Such is the fate of all of the illusions we cling to that drive us forward. So he headed out into the heat unencumbered.

Then a voice cried out 'Hola, Father. I will take you some place nice and cool where you can get something to eat.' The voice belonged to a taxi driver. It was a strong voice that easily cut through the shimmering heat. 'My name is Filiberto,' said the taxi driver. Two strong hands helped him into the taxi. 'I have been waiting for you.'

At first he did not comprehend the meaning of Filiberto's words, and when he did it was too late to ask any questions, for the taxi was speeding south along the Interstate.

'Do not worry, Father,' Filiberto said. 'You are in good hands. I may drive like a maniac, but the angels watch over me.'

'It is not your driving, young man. It is, well . . . .'

'Ah, you were wondering how I knew you were coming?'

But ex-Father Anton did not respond. Once again he was thinking about his journey into the great unknown. It had been years since he had taken a journey of any kind. His entire life flashed by in an instant. Then he started wondering about the young taxi driver and what his life had been like and where his journey would take him and if he was traveling with his eyes wide open, or did he prefer to keep them shut, as was the case with most people, and he was just about to ask the young man what might have been a most provocative question, when the taxi came to a screeching, shuddering halt.

'Here we are, Father. See? You are no worse for riding in my taxicab.'

And then Filiberto laughed and helped him with his things, and then he sped off, still laughing, and ex-Father Anton could not help but give a little chuckle himself, for Filiberto's youthful laughter was nothing if not infectious.

For a moment he thought he could hear the sound of the ocean, supple and turbulent. He closed his eyes and imagined he could smell the hibiscus on distant shores. Then reality overpowered his senses and invaded his mind. Reality took the form of a soft, insistent voice like a flower wilting in the sun or a dog on its way to a gas station. *'Do you know where you are, Anton Kreutner?'* the voice said.

He looked this way and that but saw no one. He was standing in the middle of a great emptiness, a desolate, yellow landscape stretching all the way to the horizon, where it merged with a pale, yellow cloud-streaked sky. Then he realized that he was standing in an empty parking lot. There were one-hundred-and-sixteen parking lot light poles in the lot, but none of the lights were on. It was a strange alien sea of unlit lamps. Then he noticed a lonely looking white building, a windowless, one-story, cinder block building maybe twenty feet away from where he was standing, like a tiny white ship floating on the shimmery surface of the strange alien sea already mentioned.

'Do you know where you are, Anton Kreutner?' the voice said again, but he pretended the voice did not exist.

He walked towards the building. It was a restaurant of some sort with the words El Chico's scrawled across the cinder-block wall in letters six feet high. Each letter was composed of alternating bands of bright red and yellow and orange paint. Then he noticed that the parking lot was not quite empty. A blue pickup truck was parked along the north side of the building maybe six feet from the corner, and three rows away from where he was standing, taking up half a dozen spaces, there was an old two-tone (beige and white) Volkswagen van with some sort of trailer attached to it. The trailer was a bright, vibrant amusement-park red with a small banner draped across the side. The banner said 'The Great Manzanedo's Traveling Puppet Show Extravaganza.' The presence of the two vehicles only served to magnify the vast emptiness of the parking lot.

'Do you know where you are, Anton Kreutner?'

Again he looked this way and that but saw no one. He looked more carefully at the windowless building before him and it seemed to develop in detail before his eyes. He noticed an air conditioner about ten feet up protruding directly from the cinder-block wall, which he had not noticed before. The air conditioner spat noisily, a thick, dripping sound like vengeance. Surely this was the source of the strange voice, reshaped by an overheated, lunatic mind. Yes, of course, and the sound of the ocean before that.

Then he noticed a glass door which also had not existed moments earlier. The glass was tinted a very dark green, almost black, so he could not see through to the other side, though he did try. But as he stepped back from the door, he had the strangest feeling that God had closed off all paths except the one he was on. Apart from this lonely restaurant squatting in a vast, nearly empty parking lot, there was nothing for miles. Even the highway he had traversed to get to this desolate spot had evaporated in the sun. *'Do you know where you are, Anton Kreutner?'* the voice had said. But it was a question he could not answer. He didn't even know where to begin. Without another moment's hesitation, without even pausing to look at his shriveled, fun-house reflection in the glass door, he went inside.

-146-

The interior of El Chico's was a hodgepodge of decorative themes that seemed at first glance to represent the unfolding chaos of the universe. At second glance it suggested that the decorator possessed either a wickedly satiric view of pop culture and religion, or an incurable brain tumor at an advanced stage. At a third glance it seemed merely the competing designs of a dozen teenage decorators with minimal supervision.

The wall opposite the door was given over to a rattapallax of UFO artifacts, doctored photographs of dead aliens, models of cigar shaped spaceships, a poster of the movie *Alien*, framed newspaper clippings of UFO sightings in Colorado, New Mexico, Arizona, and Sonora, Mexico, a few rubbery alien masks (the kind with shiny, bulbous black eyes) that were always taken down on Halloween and put back up the day after, a few books by the French metaphysicist René Guénon (*The Symbolism of the Cross, Multiple States of Being, The Spiritist Fallacy, Symbols of Sacred Science*) placed neatly on a small table beneath a large, French-style salon mirror, a dazzling array (the word psychedelic comes to mind) of pink and purple and blue lava lamps placed on tiny shelves at various heights, and a futuristic looking jukebox that only played songs about alien encounters ('Silver Lights' by Sammy Hagar, 'Zero Zero UFO' by The Ramones, 'Children of the Sun' by Billy Thorpe, 'Starman' by David Bowie, there were twenty songs in all, a continuous loop until somebody got tired of electric guitars and synthesizers and screaming rock and roll icons and pulled the plug). The UFO wall was the first sight to greet every visitor to El Chico's.

The wall opposite the cash register and service counter was given over to the stuffed and mounted bodies of numerous desert creatures, but there were also several weasels, ferrets, and pine martens, which had all met their demise hundreds of miles away, perhaps in the mountains.

The wall behind the cash register was decorated with a mishmash of deviant Aztec art depicting tragic looking blue suns, blue serpents with two heads, and black eagles. There was also a feathered headdress with green feathers like strands of corn silk, various spears and stone knives, several posters of ancient pyramids, a travel poster advertising a two-week journey to the jungles of Guatemala, a beige colored Aztec sun stone perched on a shelf about eye-level, and ten turquoise mosaic masks of Aztec gods, masks with supposedly magical properties fixed at odd angles, like theatre masks, each possessing oversized ultra-white teeth and strange otherworldly expressions. Taped to the cash register was a small sign that advertised tattoos at reasonable prices.

The final wall was a gallery style tribute to the works of Francisco de Goya. The centerpiece of the tribute was Goya's masterpiece, *The Madhouse,* a full-size oil-on-panel replica positioned just beneath the air conditioner. The rest of the wall featured smaller reproductions of various Goya paintings including *Witches' Sabbath, The Follies, Fire at Night, The Bullfight,* and *Blind Guitarist,* and also various prints taken from a series of aquatints and etchings known collectively as *Los Caprichos* (a sudden, unpredictable change, as of one's mind or the winds of Fate, a whim).

Ex-Father Anton sat down in the middle of a dozen or more empty black tables and waited patiently for a waitress or some other person to come and take his order. No one came, so he listened to the jukebox for a while, an absent expression on his face. The jukebox was playing a song describing how mankind had the power to communicate with extraterrestrials using telepathy, or some such nonsense. At one point the lyrics were overpowered by the decibel level of the air conditioner, which suddenly seemed to grow louder, as if the dials were being manipulated by an unseen hand, but then the gurgling sound subsided.

A moment later the door to the kitchen flew open and then flew shut, and then there were some banging sounds, the clanging of kettles and spoons or other metallic objects, and then the muffled sound of a back door opening, followed immediately by an eerie, sibilant sound like the sound of intense heat burning away the upper layers of the stratosphere.

'He won't be back for a while.'

The voice startled ex-Father Anton. He wondered briefly if it was the same voice from before, but it possessed a different tone, a heavier caliber.

'Who won't be back?'

'Gaubert. The owner. This restaurant is, how shall I say it, his eccentricity.'

'And you . . . ?'

'You saw my caravan outside? I am the Great Manzanedo. A foolish moniker, I admit. But it suits my outlandish personality. I am sorry I didn't say hello when you came in. I was listening to the music, an incredibly beautiful, lyrical song, a haunting song, and quite possibly prophetic. Here, wait a minute. Let me get the plug. I don't like this next one.'

The Great Manzanedo was a heavy-set, bearded fellow of indeterminate age. He wore baggy shorts, rope sandals, a plaid short-sleeve shirt, and a Saint Louis Cardinals baseball cap. He possessed a vaguely hermit-like quality.

'You thirsty? Beer? A glass of wine? A carafe?'

'I think parched is the correct word, so best make it a carafe.'

The bearded fellow exploded into laughter.

'Right you are, Father, right you are.'

And then his eyes narrowed severely.

'Or should I say ex-Father.'

Then the bearded fellow exploded yet again and then quickly explained himself. He had once been a priest himself, a Jesuit, in fact, though that had been years earlier. Now he belonged to a loosely organized, vagabond collection of charlatans living on the fringes of society, mostly ex-priests and ex-rabbis, but there were a few ex-shamans, so to speak, and a token ex-imam as well. They were a secret sect of exes ready at the drop of a hat to bolster the spirits of all those who had lost or were compelled to abandon their faith.

'Word spreads quickly whenever a priest leaves the Church. I got a call yesterday from a friend in Miami who said you were heading my way. I was the one who sent Filiberto.'

The Great Manzanedo slipped behind the counter and plucked two glasses and a carafe of wine from a hidden compartment and returned in a flash. He moved with an elastic, theatrical, almost supernatural grace, an absurd incongruity in one who was so fat.

'Here you go, my friend, a Pinot Noir all the way from Metz, your home town, if I am not very much mistaken. The man at the wine shop said it came from a vineyard of impeccable provenance. Hah! We shall see.'

And so ex-Father Anton and The Great Manzanedo drank away the rest of the afternoon and the early hours of the evening as well. After they polished off the Pinot Noir, they downed a bottle of Crémant Chardonnay, and then a Pinot Blanc, and finally an Altenberg de Wolxheim Reisling.

As they had both been trained in the Jesuit manner, they had a very lively discussion while they drank. They talked about The Great Manzanedo's life as a puppeteer and the innocence of small children and how children suffering from cancer, which was the case with many of those in the audience when he took his show to the Children's Hospital in Phoenix, appreciated the smallest of kindnesses. They talked of the decline in the art of puppetry in general and how the best puppeteers came from Europe and the best puppets had been crafted by artisans more than a century earlier. The Great Manzanedo, who as a Jesuit was known as The Most Reverend Monsignor Mateo Aimerich, mentioned that he had acquired his own puppet theatre from an ancient Sicilian, a man named Luigi with thick silver hair and dark blue eyes, sad gypsy eyes, like a storm that has passed. Luigi and four others had come to America in the 1920s. They had wandered about the country for fifty years, plying their trade, but by the early seventies they had begun to die off, one by one. Luigi was the last. Ex-Monsignor Mateo had found the poor leathery-skinned indigent, who had actually begun to look more like a puppet than those he manipulated, performing for scorpions and snakes in an otherwise empty gravel lot next to the Volunteer Fire Department in Corona de Tucson, a small town an hour or so north of the Mexican border. That was in 1983. When the frail puppet maestro died in 1985, ex-Monsignor Mateo took over, becoming The Great Manzanedo in both name and in the depths of his soul.

They talked about the malleable nature of human identity and the shifting sands of all secular knowledge and their growing dissatisfaction with the semiotic structuralist view of language, which suggested, among other things, that every story was indebted to those that had gone before it and that this indebtedness could be scientifically measured. They talked about their increasing appreciation for the theories of the Czech linguist Jan Mukařovský, who believed that every experience had the potential to be an intoxicating experience and could thus be transformed through the application of the imagination into an object of aesthetic pleasure, which meant that the story of that experience might transcend the normative structures used by storytellers to that point and become a new norm. From a teleological perspective, this would be like creating a new universe out of a single thought, an abstraction made visible, instead of merely reworking the clay of the old universe. The Great Manzanedo laughed and said the darkness still has work to do. Ex-Father Anton countered by saying the knotted chords are untying. The Great Manzanedo drew in his great girth and said is that a dagger or a crucifix dripping with the blood of Eden. Ex-Father Anton leaned his glowing, bulbous head forward and said behold, the distant thunder of a million vanquished souls reaching for creature comfort. Both men sat back and roared and roared.

Then they talked about how temporal reality often moved in multiple directions simultaneously, like radio waves. The Great Manzanedo mentioned in an off-hand, distracted sort of way that they only got two radio stations in his neck of the woods, both of them from across the border. 'We might as well be living in Mexico,' he said. They talked about the arduous though ultimately satisfying work of making windows where once there were only walls. They talked about being liberated from the genealogy imposed on mankind by the Garden of Eden. The Great Manzanedo was of the opinion that history was a manufactured commodity sold to the masses to keep them trapped inside the invisible bubble of someone else's imagination. Ex-Father Anton, who was most certainly a Hegelian at heart, said then how does one account for the general evolutionary movement of all history towards a single unified, inevitable conclusion? Does that not smack of some grand design? The Great Manzanedo said that was precisely his point. That was why he was suspicious of Hegel. Besides, one does not study history to discover the purpose of the soul, he said, for the soul exists outside the singularity of any temporal event. Ex-Father Anton did not disagree, for he suspected they held the same views but that each had become confused by looking into the mirror of the other's thoughts.

They talked about the imprint which the notion of death had left on mankind's fragile psyche. They talked about the debilitating legacy of Schadenfreude. They talked about the destiny of nations and the inevitable decline into madness of the individual. They talked about the madness of Goya and the joyful exuberance of those mad, naked kings in his painting, *The Madhouse* (the very same painting hanging opposite the UFO wall). The Great Manzanedo said it was difficult not to identify with Goya's naked kings, whose frozen gestures and idiotic facial expressions seemed to celebrate the liberating power of darkness and the descent into nothingness. Ex-Father Anton said he could hear the screams of an infinity of madmen pouring out of an endless universe of black holes. They talked about the paintings of Pieter Bruegel. The Great Manzanedo said that Bruegel reminded us all that every man was a blind man stumbling about in the dark. Ex-Father Anton said that Bruegel reminded us all that every man was a small monkey chained to a stone floor, staring out at a busy harbor from a great height.

They talked about the madness of Nietzsche and Van Gogh and Artaud and that strange play of his called *Spurt of Blood*. They talked about the blazing path struck by the Marquis de Sade. They both agreed that madness was either the first step towards liberty, or the last convulsions of the last dying man. As if to prove this point, The Great Manzanedo pulled out a slim volume of poetry from his hip pocket and laid it squarely on the table. The book had been written by a Venezuelan poet of German descent (Franz Zwickau) and possessed a once provocative title (*The War Criminal's Son*) that had since become a cliché. Ex-Father Anton had never heard of either the book or the poet. The Great Manzanedo said that was not surprising. The poetry was insipid, the product of an adolescent mind dipping into the waters of nihilism in the mistaken belief that immersion in those dark waters would lead to a cleansing of the soul and open the doors to a bucolic paradise. The poet cited Goethe in a most jarring way, as if he had mistaken the pagan materialism of Goethe's vision for a belief in the power of satanic rituals, and while he seemed to possess an in-depth knowledge of Pascal, he ignored the profound implications of Pascal's fervent spirituality because he obviously thought all religion was a sham and all religious-minded men merely charlatans, two-dimensional cardboard cutouts, easily destroyed by a calamitous fire.

Ex-Father Anton suddenly wondered out loud what the life of an ex-priest was like. The Great Manzanedo finished off his glass of wine and poured himself another and said it was like the life of the writer Henry Miller in the 1930s, full of poverty and starvation and alcohol, but without Paris and the perversions of an unrestrained libido. Ex-Father Anton held out his empty glass and said so you mean nothing will have changed. The Great Manzanedo filled ex-Father Anton's goblet and said precisely. Both men sat back and roared and roared, their mouths dripping with the froth of excess.

Then ex-Father Anton asked The Great Manzanedo why he had left the Jesuits. The Great Manzanedo paused a moment in his drinking, for even though he had been expecting this question, he was still caught off-guard by the good German's impeccable timing. He drained his glass and set it down in the middle of the black table so that it caught the sparkle of the lava lamps on the UFO wall. 'That, my friend, is a story unto itself and will require drinking something a tad better than the swill we have so far consumed.'

That is when they opened the Altenberg de Wolxheim Reisling. Ex-Father Anton felt he had won something like a victory.

-147-

The story of why The Great Manzanedo left the Jesuits, in his own words, more or less, though told in the third person:

In 1965, the Archbishop of Puerto Rico, Luis Aponte Martínez, appointed a local tribunal to investigate rumors of what eventually became a dozen miracles in three distinct categories that had occurred in the name of Sister María Amàlia Garrido, a Carmelite nun who had been the Mother Superior of a Carmelite convent in Puerto Rico from 1877 until her quiet death in 1919. In 1903 the Sisters had been forced to leave their San Juan home and move to San Germán, where they became ministers of Christ's peace from 1903 to 1909. When they moved back to Santurce in 1909, the first of the miracles purportedly occurred. To assist the local tribunal in their work of uncovering the truth, the Vatican sent The Most Reverend Monsignor Mateo Aimerich, an Auditor attached to the Rota (a juridical office within the Roman Curia that participated in all matters relating to possible miracles until 1970, when the role of investigating miracles was given over to other officials in the Congregation for the Causes of the Saints better suited to the task). It was a most unusual case.

The first miracle, which was its own category, occurred late in the evening on July 12, 1909, two days before the Feast Day of Our Lady of Mount Carmel. As there were no living witnesses to the miracle, and no historical documentation, Monsignor Aimerich had to rely on the testimony of those living within the boundaries of San Mateo Parish, which is where the miracle took place. The miracle itself had taken on the size and shape of a local legend and was therefore in the eyes of the parishioners beyond dispute. But the nature of the miracle, the appearance of the Virgin Mary in a dream, was problematic from Monsignor Aimerich's perspective. While corporeal manifestations of the Virgin were rare indeed, her presence in the dreams of the faithful was a common occurrence, afflicting by some estimates as many as 65% of Catholics worldwide.

In the pages of his Auditor's notebook, Monsignor Aimerich recorded the details of what the dream Virgin Mary purportedly said to Sister Amàlia regarding the creation of two gardens, a private garden for the Sisters of the Carmelite convent, and a second, public garden (for the neighborhood faithful) that was named The Garden of Eternal Gratitude. Monsignor Aimerich put an asterisk next to the fact that all of the healing miracles attributed to Sister Amàlia had taken place in the community garden. He felt quite strongly that the healing miracles needed to be vetted separately from the dream visitation miracle. Also, he made note of the somewhat less than miraculous fact that the dream Virgin Mary had told Sister Amàlia that the remains of all of the Sisters of the convent who had died over the centuries needed to be transported to a new cemetery, one that was within walking distance of their new convent in Santurce. This particular piece of advice seemed eminently practical and decidedly non-miraculous, but as it was part of the testimony given by 742 of the 770 parishioners who took part in the investigation, Monsignor Aimerich felt compelled to make it part of his unofficial report.

The second category of miracles was initially made up of seven healing miracles, all of which had taken place in the Garden of Eternal Gratitude between 1941 and 1964. The garden was located on the corner of Calle San Mateo and Calle Saldaña and was trapezoidal with a curved anterior edge approximately 52 feet in length. There was no fence or wall, in keeping with the dream Virgin Mary's wishes. The garden was bisected by one main path that began at the precise intersection of the two streets that formed the southwestern corner of the garden and ended at a small circular patio, eighteen feet in diameter in the dead center of the garden. Two smaller, circuitous paths, one darting off to the north, the other to the east, wound their way through the greenery until they came around and met at opposite points along the northeastern perimeter of the patio. In between these two points, also along the perimeter, was a single stone pedestal bench, six feet in length, slightly curved to match the patio's geometry. The greenery was typical of Caribbean gardens and contained several rose bushes, a layer of Colombian Skullcap, a few coral plants with their tiny red flowers shining in the sunlight, and a saúco plant with eighteen clusters of tiny white flowers but without any fruit.

The first and most astonishing of the seven miracles was the miraculous cure of Concepción Centeno y Larios in 1941. Concepcion had suffered from a chronic hip ailment that first began troubling her in 1939 at the age of twelve. The general medical consensus after two years of consulting various doctors was that Concepción was most likely suffering from premature rheumatoid arthritis, but it could also have been a rare bone cancer. Only an x-ray would confirm the diagnosis, but Concepción's parents refused to accept the dictates of medical science and chose instead to appeal directly to the Virgin Mary through the compassionate intercession of Sister Amàlia. On Monday July 14, 1941, a hot and muggy afternoon with rain clouds threatening, Concepción and her parents entered the garden. They took the eastern elliptical path. Concepción's parents had to support her, one on either side, for she was in a great deal of pain. After traversing twenty-six feet, Concepcion knelt down in a patch of Skullcap and prayed a short prayer to Sister Amàlia. According to witnesses, as she finished her prayer, the sun burst from behind a cloud and Concepcion leapt up from her knees, a great smile on her face, and ran out of the garden to tell the world of her miraculous cure. Unfortunately, the doctors who had initially examined Concepción had not kept any records of those visits (or the records had mysteriously disappeared), so it was impossible to scientifically examine the change that had taken place.

The second miracle was probably a copycat version of the first. On a similarly cloudy day one year and one week and five days later (Tuesday, July 26, 1942), Dolores Acosta Liliberte, a self-proclaimed victim of a spastic gait, was suddenly cured. According to witnesses, she entered the garden at noon precisely and took the northern path until she came to a small ornamental Chinaberry tree. She knelt on the cobblestone path and prayed. Some said she prayed until her knees were bloody, though others claimed they were only muddy because it had rained that morning, a torrential downpour, and the flower beds in places had turned into a slow-moving, muddy, viscous mess, especially around the base of the Chinaberry tree. The sun did not burst forth from behind a cloud, but after several hours upon her knees, or several minutes according to some, Dolores Acosta Liliberte was miraculously cured. Unfortunately, her spastic gait condition had never been confirmed by a doctor, so there were no medical records to peruse and thus no way to determine if her cure was in fact miraculous, or something that could have been achieved by any number of homegrown or over-the-counter remedies.

Miracles three (1947), four (1951) and five (1953) were all of down-and-outers recovering their eyesight. The first of these was the miracle of Antonio Colón, a veteran of World War Two, originally from Tulsa, Oklahoma, who had appeared in San Juan one bright and sunny day in 1946. He spent most of his first year in San Juan in cafes drinking and telling everyone who would pull up a chair to his table that he had been a member of the U.S. 35th Infantry Division and that he had lost his eyesight during the Battle of Nancy in 1944. He said a shell had exploded twenty yards from his platoon, killing half. He did not say whether his blindness was the result of the concussive force of the explosion or sharp fragments from the shell entering the orbit of his eye. On Thursday, June 26, 1947, a stranger who had gained his trust as a drinking companion told Antonio about Sister Amàlia and the two preceding miracles of The Garden of Eternal Gratitude, and Antonio said he would give it a try. Two hours later, he entered the garden (presumably with the assistance of the aforementioned companion), sat down on the stone bench and began to pray. He prayed with his eyes squeezed shut, as if to hold in the darkness for a little while longer. When he opened them, he could see. He became an instant celebrity in Santurce, which meant he was given free drinks every day of the week and free dinners on weekends and special occasions. In 1950, he inexplicably left San Juan for good. No one knows where he went.

The beneficiary of the second eyesight miracle (1951) was Tegrida Borjas de la Peña, an elderly woman whose eyesight had been failing for years, and then in June 1951 she went completely blind. Those who remembered her said her eyes, which in her youth had been a dazzling blue, became as two glass baubles, a soft gray color like a cloudy day. Her grandson led her to the garden on warm spring morning. She sat on the stone bench, her face turned towards the sun which was partially obscured by a few clouds, and prayed a silent prayer of thanksgiving. Within minutes of finishing, several songbirds obscured by the greenery began to sing. The grandson tried to locate them, but this task proved impossible for his young eyes, but then his grandmother stood up and said "Come, I will show you where they are,' and when he looked at his grandmother, he noted that her face was radiant and her eyes had been restored to the dazzling blue color of former days.

Two years later, a supposedly blind tourist entered the garden with his wife. Moments later the wife came rushing out in a panic, and three passersby asked her if they could help. She led them to the stone bench and pointed at her husband, who had tossed away his blind man's cane and was twirling around the patio like a maniac. When the would-be Samaritans asked the woman what was the matter, she said, "But he is blind. What is wrong with him?' At which point the three, all from the neighborhood, sat her down on the stone bench and explained that this trapezoidal garden had been the site of many similar miracles, all within the last few years, and that the facilitator of those miracles was a Carmelite nun, a Sister Amàlia, who had been honored by a visit from the Virgin Mary herself.

Unfortunately, while stories of the blind recovering their sight go all the way back to the days of the prophets, as far as Monsignor Aimerich was concerned, that's all they were: stories. None of the beneficiaries had consulted a doctor prior to his or her miracle, and so there was no scientific proof that any miracle had occurred. As far as the Church was concerned, the testimony of the various witnesses, even that of the grandson, was insufficient to support the claim that Sister Amàlia had persuaded the good Lord to restore the gift of sight to even one thoroughly blind individual, let alone three.

The sixth (October 1959) and seventh (June 1964) miracles were stories of the recently dead being brought back to life.

The first resuscitation was that of Javier Jiménez Peralta, a construction worker working on a nearby apartment complex, who fell approximately fifty feet when he slipped on the scaffolding he was standing on. He landed with a sickening thud on a stack of unopened cement bags and died upon impact. However, his brother, who was working alongside Javier, refused to accept the verdict of gravity. He loaded the lifeless body into the back seat of a small white Fiat and drove like a madman helter-skelter style to the garden. According to witnesses, he actually pulled up onto the northeast corner where Calle San Mateo and Calle Saldaña converged, scattering a few pedestrians in the process. Moments later he dragged his dead brother into the garden and began to pray. The distance between the white Fiat, which was still running, and the lifeless body of Javier Jiménez Peralta, which was partially shaded by the overhanging leaves of a carefully pruned higuera tree, was thirty feet, give or take. A crowd soon gathered to watch, not quite knowing what was happening, but certain that something spectacular was about to take place, given the supernal reputation of this tiny slice of paradise. Soon the single voice of Javier Peralta's brother was joined by dozens of voices, housewives either on their way to the market to buy fish or just returning, school children on their way home, business executives who were trying to kill the last few dull hours of the afternoon, teachers, social workers, an off-duty bus driver, several elderly couples just out for a stroll, all with their eyes turned towards heaven. And then just like that Javier Jiménez Peralta sat up, looked up at the ring of faces looking down in amazement, looked over at the white Fiat, which was still running, and asked his brother why the car was on the curb.

As was the case with the five miracles preceding the sixth, the miracle of Javier Jiménez Peralta's sudden return from the land of the dead lacked any medical documentation. Moreover, the only witness who could give a full account of the event was Javier's brother. True, when the crowd in the garden had come along, Javier seemed to be a corpse, but surely those in the crowd had only assumed Javier was dead based on his brother's visibly demonstrative grief. Besides, they had not seen the fatal fall. Moreover, no one at the construction site where the fall had occurred had seen or heard a thing out of the ordinary on that particular day. And Javier himself remembered only that he and his brother had gone to lunch at the normal hour and had taken a short siesta after having had too much to drink.

The second resuscitation was that of a three-month-old baby girl, Leta Canino. Little Leta had been one constant, bubbly smile from the day she was born, but on February 29, 1964, she came down with a very high fever and her smile disappeared. It was a dry, warm evening with very little breeze. It was a night for owls and crickets, those all but invisible harbingers of death. Leta's mother sat with her in a narrow wicker rocker by an open window in her third-floor apartment. She dabbed Leta's forehead with a damp cloth and sang to her softly, but there was nothing she could do. By midnight, little Leta was dead, but instead of informing the local authorities, or even telling a neighbor down the hall, Leta's mother took the child to the garden, where she wept and prayed the rest of the night. In the morning, when she looked at Leta's tiny, angelic face, she saw that her little Leta's bubbly smile had returned.

Monsignor Aimerich spent five months investigating these seven miracles of healing and became something of a local celebrity. So too, the mere fact that an investigation was underway seemed to galvanize the community.

On September 17, 1965, an eighth miracle occurred. Agapito Demara, a woodworker by trade, sliced off the tips of three fingers while cutting and shaping balusters for a fancy staircase. He carried his fingertips to the garden, cupping them with both hands as he ran so he would not lose one, and at ten in the morning he knelt on the cobblestone near the very same

Map of The Garden of Eternal Gratitude
(from the Auditor's notebook)

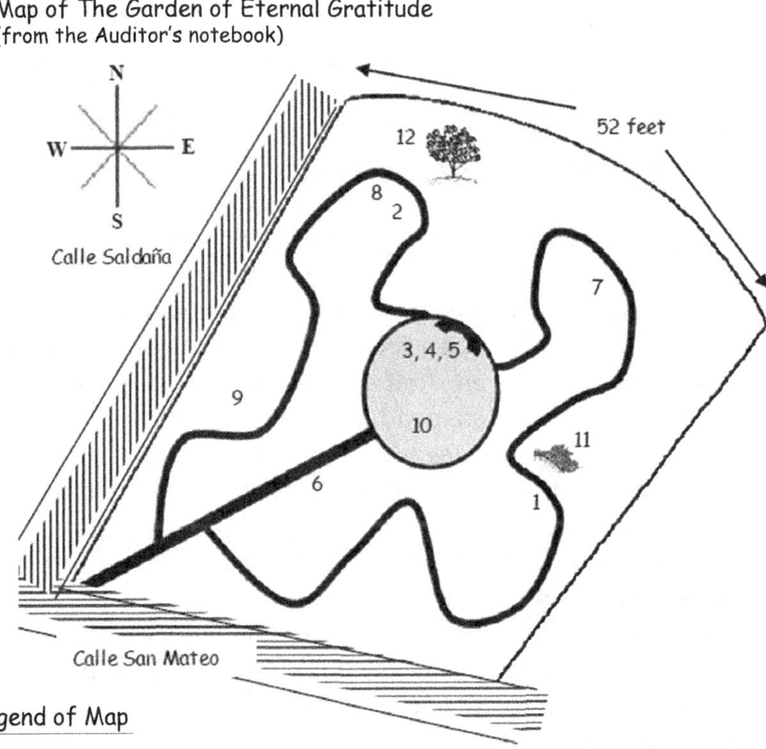

Legend of Map

1. Miracle of Concepción Centeno Y Larios
2. Miracle of Dolores Acosta Liliberte
3. Miracle of Antonio Colón
4. Miracle of Tegrida Borjas de la Peña
5. Miracle of blind tourist
6. Miracle of Javier Jiménez Peralta
7. Miracle of Leta Canino
8. Miracle of Agapito Demara
9. Miracle of Tomas Escajeda
10. Miracle of Sandalio Echavarria
11. Patch of Columbian Skullcap
12. Chinaberry Tree

Chinaberry tree where Dolores Acosta Liliberte had been cured of her spastic gait, and prayed. By noon he was as good as new.

On September 20, 1965, two more miracles occurred. Tomás Escajeda, who had been suffering from amnesia for years, suddenly recovered every lost memory that he and the members of his long-dead family had ever possessed. This miracle occurred at three in the afternoon. Two hours later the stage belonged to Sandalio Echavarria, a mental defective who had been roaming the streets of Santurce since 1939 at least and had never uttered a single syllable in all those years. At 5 PM, Sandalio was suddenly granted the power of speech. Of course these three new miracles suffered from the same lack of verifiable, scientific proof as had the first seven. But when Monsignor Aimerich tried to explain this to the affable natives who enquired after his progress, they only laughed and looked upon him with wise, compassionate, glowing eyes. Later, when these same natives found out that Monsignor Aimerich's given name was Mateo, they chastised him with good natured forbearance. Did he not think it strange that a man named Mateo, a name which means 'God's gift,' should be sent to a parish named San Mateo to investigate the gift of God's miracles? What greater proof did the good Monsignor need than that?

Looking back, it is clear that Monsignor Aimerich did not quite appreciate what he was up against. On September 22nd, ten brand new miracles were revealed, and the very next day another seventeen, followed by fourteen, then twelve, then seven, then twenty-two, then four, then thirty-three, and then an astonishing sixty-seven. And so it went. The good Monsignor Aimerich was forced to suspend all future investigations. He said ten healing miracles were more than enough. Still, he was graced with the presence of mind to write down the names of every parishioner who came to him with a story of a miraculous healing, and by the end of October, he had recorded over five-hundred names. He did not realize until many years later that the reason so many eager parishioners of San Mateo stepped forward with tales to tell was simply because they wanted their names to appear in the pages of his Auditor's notebook. As far as they were concerned, the Monsignor's investigation was itself a sanctifying event for the entire neighborhood. Whether or not the miracles they claimed actually occurred was of secondary importance.

The investigation of the healing miracles concluded on

Friday, November 26, 1965. The following Monday, Monsignor Aimerich began his investigation into the twelfth and final miracle to be included in his preliminary report. On the surface, this last miracle seemed an impossibility, a negation of both natural law and God's law, so he placed it into a category all its own, as he had done with the first miracle. He chose a straight-forward, factually descriptive title for his notes. The title read: 'The Details of the Supposed Miraculous Transformation of don Sebastian de Urquiza.'

It almost goes without saying that Monsignor Aimerich thought the whole story was a joke, a preposterous invention of a diseased mind. It sounded like the poorly written synopsis of a poorly written dime store novel. A young man with the elegant sounding name of Sebastian de Urquiza settles down in Puerto Rico after years of traveling the Americas as a soldier of fortune and consecrates his life to the service of God. Okay, so far so good. This young man begins working for the Carmelite Sisters of Santurce. He is part of a crew of profligates who have been hired to transport the remains of two-hundred eighty-six Carmelite nuns and twenty-nine lay persons from the subterranean crypts beneath a crumbling convent on Caleta de las Monjas in Old San Juan to the cemetery of Villa Palmeras. Okay, a little odd, but still acceptable. This young man has a deep-seated perhaps unconscious belief that he is a woman trapped in a man's body, that if he had only come into this world a member of the gentler sex, he (she) would have been able to fulfill his (her) destiny, which was all a part of God's original plan that has somehow been thwarted. Okay, now we have entered through a forbidden doorway into a world of aberrant thinking. And yet even the priest of San Mateo parish, a fairly doctrinaire fellow named Father Correa, believed this lie was the truth. Then this young man becomes an old man, or at least older, and then he succumbs to the fate that awaits us all. Don Sebastian de Urquiza dies on the last day of July, 1937. Okay, that should be the end of the story. But it is not the end. The nurse who is with the don when he dies says that no sooner does he close his eyes for good, then a ghostly presence drifts out of his body and begins to move about the don's tiny apartment. This strange presence moves erratically, she says, as if it is searching for another host, so she flees the apartment, fearing for her soul. The next morning, as the don's body is being prepared for burial, the morticians discover that the don is (or was) a woman. The morticians do not pause in their work to consider the implications of this discovery. They assume this is simply an honest mistake. They have worked on many bodies where the gender was difficult to determine without a close examination. The body of the deceased don is transported a few hours later from the funeral parlor, which is located on Calle San Agustín in Puerta de Tierra, to the cemetery of Villa Palmeras, a journey which takes fifteen minutes by car but which often seems interminable in the tropical heat. There is no formal service. The don has no family and the Sisters have no money for a funeral. Father Correa says a few words at the grave. But before the sun has set on this day of days, word of the miracle of don Sebastian de Urquiza's transformation has spread all over the city. No one even considers the possibility that the don has been a woman in disguise for decades.

So Monsignor Aimerich was suspicious of this miracle that was probably not a miracle right from the start. He believed there were two possible explanations for don Sebastian de Urquiza's supposed transformation, which he duly noted in his Auditor's notebook. The first, which was suggested by the excitable nurse's reaction, was that a young woman of unknown origin had been possessed by one of Satan's demons, and it was this, the act of demonic possession, which had changed her outward feminine appearance to that of a battle-scarred soldier of fortune. The second possible explanation, which in the Monsignor's experience seemed the more likely, was that the young woman who became don Sebastian had created this diabolical lie to hide the truth of some unpardonable sin from the unforgiving and gossipy world. Of course he could not simply dismiss the local belief in this miracle with a wave of a magic wand. The story of don Sebastian's miraculous transformation had become a part of the genetic make-up of those who lived in this mostly working-class neighborhood. Everyone believed it to be true. No, what the good Monsignor needed, what he would spend the next several months searching for, was uncontestable proof that this miracle was nothing less than a bald-faced lie. Unfortunately, finding such proof was not as easy as he had hoped.

The Monsignor began his investigation into the twelfth miracle by studying Sister Amàlia's diary. There were three entries that referenced don Sebastian, but they contained little in the way of probative value.

On November 12, 1909, Sister Amàlia wrote:

Father Correa has hired a fourth young man, an ex-soldier named don Sebastian de Urquiza, to help with excavating the remains of our dear departed Sisters in Christ. He says the other three swear they need this fourth young man, who possesses, they say, a very strange but useful gift. Father Correa has suggested I meet this young man before too long. The good Father seems fairly intimidated by this young don.

On November 22, 1909, Sister Amàlia wrote:

I met with dear sweet don Sebastian this afternoon. I gave him a small book, which I think he will appreciate. We did not discuss his family, but there is no need. It is just as I suspected.

And on August 17, 1919, three weeks before she died, Sister Amàlia wrote:

I cannot get over how thin don Sebastian has become. He seems as insubstantial as a fallen leaf. But he has been invaluable to us over the years. And he has been a good friend. How funny that Father Correa still does not know what to make of him. I will miss don Sebastian dearly.

After Sister Amàlia's diary proved to be a dead end, the Monsignor thought he should examine don Sebastian's deathbed confession, a document whose existence was revealed to him during an interview with the excitable nurse, who worked at a small local hospital in Santurce (as she had for over thirty years) and had come forward when she had heard about his investigation. Unfortunately, during a second meeting with the nurse, he learned that the confession, which the nurse had written down on a pad of legal-sized paper in the dim light of a summer evening oh so many years earlier, now existed only in her memory. The legal pad had vanished, a victim of humidity or carelessness perhaps. The nurse apologized that she hadn't taken better care of the alleged document, but she had no idea in 1937 how important it was going to become. She did offer a few scraps from what she could recall, however, a few imperfect shadows that had been imprinted on her brain and had not been obliterated by the temporary terror of don Sebastian's ghost or the demon that had possessed him (a terror, moreover, which the nurse admitted during the second interview might have been caused by her own volatile imagination rather than by any supernatural source).

The nurse said that the don's mother was named Veronica and that she had possessed a bewitching beauty. She said that the don's father belonged to an ancient Spanish family that had aligned itself with the Moors during the days of the Moorish conquest. She said the don was sorry he had not spent more summers in Barcelona when he was a boy. This was his greatest regret. Perhaps he had known a girl there. She was not sure. But she did remember that the don had an uncle who had been the Captain of a ship named *Conde Wifredo*, and that this uncle had run afoul of the law and was thrown into prison. Finally, she told the Monsignor that the don had left Spain because he had killed a priest who had sexually abused him when he was a boy. It had been an act of revenge which he later regretted, but not as much as he regretted eschewing Barcelona. Or maybe his father had killed the priest, but was embarrassed by what had happened to his son, so he sent him away anyway. It was one or the other, the don or his father. But the murdered priest had been the prelate of the Church of Santiago, she remembered that quite clearly.

The imprecision of the nurse was exasperating. Did she mean Santiago Cathedral in Bilboa, or one of the seven-hundred and eighty-eight churches in the Archdiocese of Santiago de Compestela? Did she realize there were two-hundred and twenty-six churches known locally as The Church of Santiago in numerous villages, towns and cities all over Spain, including Buxán, Cabredo, Cáceres, Cangas de Morrazo, Caravia, Casas de Reina, Castilleja de la Cuesta, Colmenarejo, Écija, Elizondo, Funes, Galdúroz, Garde, Herrera, Intza, Luzaide (Valcarlos), La Bazana, La Nava de Santiago, Lane, Llerena, Logroño, Los Corralos, Madrid (two), Manjirón, Mens-Malpica, Morillas, Numide, Olejua, Oricáin, Pamplona (Iruña), Pancorbo, Pardesoa, Peon, Poor Dean, Puente la Reina, Sangüesa, Santa María de la Alameda, Seville, Tabeirós, Torremayor, Utrera, Venturada, and Villanueva del Río? And what about the one-hundred ninety-seven parishes where Santiago was part of the street address, such as the Parish of San Roque, which looked out on the Plaza Santiago Arolo Viñas in Badajoz?

Naturally the Monsignor tried to determine the validity of the few potentially verifiable facts in his possession, but this task proved as frustrating as everything else connected with this case.

In spite of several verbal assertions, there was no actual documentation that don Sebastian had been employed by the convent in any capacity whatsoever, just as there was no documentation that he and three nameless profligates had transported the remains of three-hundred fifteen persons from the crumbling colonial structure on Caleta de las Monjas to the cemetery of Villa Palmeras. Apparently all transactions involving manual labor had been cash transactions, or the ledger (ledgers?) tracking the expenses for worldly matters had been misplaced or stolen or inadvertently destroyed. It was not even certain that three-hundred and fifteen persons had been transported to the cemetery in Villa Palmeras. Some cynics put the number at one-hundred sixty-six, still others at seventy-two, and some said the excavation and subsequent reburial of the nuns from the convent on Caleta de las Monjas had never occurred at all, but whatever proof might have existed in the subterranean recesses of the old convent had long ago vanished. The property had been sold to developers and was now a thriving, bustling hotel. The hotel manager said there was a basement area which they used for storage, but that was it. There were no ancient crypts that he was aware of. If there had been any, they had surely been destroyed during the renovation process.

Thousands of people in communities throughout Spain and all over the Americas possessed the surname de Urquiza, which precluded even the possibility of conducting a genealogical survey.

A ship named *Conde Wifredo* had indeed existed. It had been purchased in 1885 by the Naviera Pinillos shipping company, which itself had been founded in 1835 in Cadiz. Immediately the *Conde Wifredo*, along with five other ships, was put into service, traveling twice a month from Barcelona to Cadiz to Santa Cruz de Tenerife to San Juan, Puerto Rico, to Santiago de Cuba, to Havana to New Orleans and back again. The *Conde Wifredo* was sold in 1920 to a small shipping company out of Galveston, Texas, where it was renamed *Martin Abrizqueta* and saw limited service as a harbor vessel. In 1927 the ship was scrapped.

Unfortunately, The Naviera Pinillos company declined to provide access to any company records associated with the *Conde Wifredo*, including passenger lists and lists of the ship's personnel between the years 1890 and 1910, which is what the Monsignor had requested. The lawyers for the company, however, did provide a neatly typed letter which categorically denied that The Naviera Pinillos company had ever employed a Captain de Urquiza (or any derivative of that name), or that any of the captains employed by the company had ever been arrested and thrown into prison.

Finally, a survey of immigration records (again between the years 1890 and 1910) for Puerto Rico was yet another exercise in futility. For one thing, the records were both incomplete and inconsistent.

Passenger arrival records from 1890 to 1898, when Puerto Rico was still a Spanish colony, contained the names and ages and points of origin of all official émigrés entering through the port of San Juan. Unfortunately, the records for the years 1892, 1893, 1894, 1896, and 1897 were missing. Also, there were no records of any unofficial émigrés who might have entered the colony during the latter decade of the 19th century by way of either the port city of Ponce in the south, or that of Mayagüez in the west.

Trying to figure out when an individual entered Puerto Rico during the years immediately after the United States took possession of the island became an absolute impossibility. One could not even make a reasonable guess. While all of the records from 1899 to 1910 were complete as far as every year was accounted for, the émigrés were listed only by nationality, and only in the aggregate (i.e. 1902: Arab — 17 male, 12 female; Austrian — 1 male, 3 female; Belgian — 1 male, 2 female; Central American — 42 male, 9 female; Chinese — 145 male, 0 female; Dominican — 53 male, 13 female; etc., etc.).

As you would expect, the Monsignor wrote the United States Immigration and Naturalization Service and requested an explanation for this anomaly. Three weeks later he received an official letter which offered a possible explanation. The second paragraph said: 'There was a great deal of confusion in the application of United States Immigration policy in Puerto Rico from 1899 until 1913. During those turbulent years, the Bureau was part of the Department of Commerce and Labor. Then in 1913, the Bureau was divided into two bureaus, one to focus solely on immigration issues, and the other to focus solely on the naturalization process. Then in 1933, both bureaus were brought together once again under the same roof. It is quite possible that the records you were hoping to find were lost while the Bureau was traversing this circuitous path.' The letter was stamped with the signature of Raymond Farrel, the Commissioner of the INS.

One week after the letter from Raymond Farrel, the Monsignor received a phone call from his immediate superior in Rome, Monsignor Joaquin Serrano. Monsignor Serrano was concerned about the number of months Monsignor Aimerich had set aside for this preliminary investigation. He had already received a statement of the cost to date and it was well over £60,000,000 (lira), approximately $96,000 in U.S. currency. He had also received reports that Monsignor Aimerich had become sidetracked by matters outside the material objective of the inquiry. In short, he wondered what was taking so long.

Monsignor Aimerich assured Monsignor Serrano that he was merely being methodical, as the Church required, and as was appropriate to his training both as a lawyer and as a Jesuit. He said he would be finished by the end of the week and that his preliminary report would be on Monsignor Serrano's desk by Monday morning.

Monsignor Serrano quickly apologized for the abrupt tone he had taken, but he had become quite concerned. Then he thanked Monsignor Aimerich for his diligence, wished him a safe and speedy return to Rome, and hung up.

Truly, one cannot predict the exact course that any obsession will take. All one can honestly say is that if left unchecked, an obsession will inevitably lead to an unraveling of sorts. Monsignor Aimerich's strange obsession with uncovering the truth about don Sebastian de Urquiza is a case in point. No sooner had his phone call with Monsignor Serrano ended then he realized that if he truly wanted to uncover the truth about the don's identity, he needed to dig up the don's body, or whatever was left. The very next morning, with the assistance of the head gravedigger at the cemetery of Villa Palmeras, he located the grave of don Sebastian de Urquiza in an ancient section of the cemetery given over to the poor and forgotten of Santurce, a section where the dead were often buried in the ground itself, without even a stone to mark the grave.

The gravedigger protested when he finally understood

what the Monsignor had in mind, but having no wish to offend a properly ordained official of the Church, he relented. He gave a sharp whistle and two scrawny boys with shovels materialized by his side. He spoke to them with a quick tongue and the boys marked off the sandy, grassy lawn with the shovels and began to dig.

It was incredibly hot work, even though it was not yet 10 AM. The Monsignor and the head gravedigger sat on the lawn in the shade of a lush laurel while the scrawny boys worked.

Then there was the dull thud of one of the shovels hitting the top of a pinewood box. The boys grinned. The Monsignor and the head gravedigger approached as the boys brushed away the dirt from the top of the coffin.

It soon became clear that the Monsignor had no idea what he had hoped to find inside the coffin. He was woefully unprepared for anything out of the ordinary. He had forgotten his Auditor's notebook and his Auditor's pen (a Sterling silver ballpoint pen with a twist-action barrel which he had received after ten years of dutiful service from none other than the Pope himself) as well as the Polaroid camera he used when photographing evidence that needed photographing.

The head gravedigger, sensing the good Monsignor's indecision, barked a quick command to the two boys, who pried off the lid of the coffin using crowbars which they seemed to have plucked out of the air.

A whoosh of sunlight filled the excavated grave.

The two boys shielded their eyes, but the head gravedigger and the Monsignor leaned closer for a good long look. What they saw was beyond belief. The body of don Sebastian de Urquiza lay below in perfect repose. There were neither the visible signs of the decay process (an absolute inevitability in the tropics, governed by the irreversible laws of biochemistry), nor the stench that usually accompanied exposing a dead body of any kind to the air (the same irreversible laws).

Don Sebastian had a peaceful, contemplative look on his face, a testament to the consummate skill of the morticians that had worked on his body as much as a reminder that the world is filled with miracles that often go unnoticed save by chance.

This bizarre twist had an immediate effect on the good Monsignor. He realized that the actual miracle of the don's perfectly preserved body eclipsed by several spiritual degrees the possible miracle of the don's supposed transformation, but he needed to be circumspect in the manner of revealing this greater miracle to the skeptical multitudes. He was already skating on thin ice, so to speak, as far as Monsignor Serrano was concerned. He would need to proceed by slow steps. So he instructed the head gravedigger to put the lid back on and fill in the grave. If at all possible, he wanted the gravesite to look as pristine as if a conscientious gardener had been tending it for years. Then he asked the head gravedigger to meet him at this precise spot at 10 AM the next morning. He would return with the Archbishop and the pastor of the Church of the Crab Sellers. He would also bring his camera. Everyone would have their picture taken, he promised. The head gravedigger shouted something at the boys and then nodded at the Monsignor. They would be waiting for him.

The next day arrived bright and early. The Monsignor arrived with the Archbishop and the pastor and his camera, just as he had said he would. The head gravedigger arrived with the two scrawny boys. The boys possessed inscrutable smiles which they did their best to keep under control.

They all met beneath the shade of the lush laurel.

Amazingly, the gravesite was in the kind of pristine condition the Monsignor had specified. Even upon careful scrutiny it was impossible to detect any sign that the ground had been disturbed only the day before. The Monsignor thought the efforts of the head gravedigger in this respect were quite remarkable.

Then the head gravedigger spoke to the two scrawny boys with a quick tongue and the boys marked off the sandy, grassy lawn with their shovels. The Archbishop and the pastor and the Monsignor and the head gravedigger sat on the lawn in the shade of the lush laurel while the scrawny boys worked.

It was incredibly hot work.

Then there was the dull thud of one of the shovels hitting the top of a pinewood box. The boys grinned. The head gravedigger and the Monsignor and the pastor and the Archbishop approached as the boys brushed away the dirt from the top of the coffin. Again a period of indecision followed, and again the head gravedigger barked a quick command to the two boys. The boys tried to pry off the lid of the coffin using crowbars which they seemed to have plucked out of the air. The lid of the coffin was evidently rotten and broke apart in small, soft chunks. The boys continued working at the lid until they had broken away a sufficient portion to see what was inside.

A whoosh of sunlight filled the excavated grave.

The two boys shielded their eyes, but the head gravedigger and the Monsignor and the pastor and the Archbishop leaned closer for a good long look. What they saw was beyond belief. The body of don Sebastian de Urquiza was for all practical purposes a skeleton, covered at various points by decayed tendons and ligaments and bits of colored cloth, the remnants of a shirt, perhaps. The visible signs of the decay process (an absolute inevitability in the tropics, governed as it is by the irreversible laws of biochemistry, particularly when a body is placed in an unsealed pinewood box) indicated that the rate of decomposition was twice the normal rate you could expect in more temperate climates. The head gravedigger was the one who commented on this particular fact just before he put a handkerchief over his mouth (because of the overwhelming stench) so he could breathe somewhat comfortably. The Archbishop nearly fainted. The pastor and the Monsignor helped him from the confines of the cemetery as best they could given the tropical heat, and also the fact that they, too, had been visibly wounded by the odor emanating from don Sebastian de Urquiza's vandalized coffin. Only the two scrawny boys seemed unaffected by the smell. With great efficiency and a touch of joy they filled in the grave.

Storm clouds hovered in the usually tranquil blue skies above Rome as Monsignor Aimerich's plane touched down. At least this is how he remembered that day. Monsignor Serrano was waiting for him at the gate as if he were waiting for an invalid or a prisoner who had been released into his custody. The two men did not speak for a while. Monsignor Aimerich took the escalator down to pick up his luggage (one hard-sided leather suitcase, a mottled burgundy in color, and a matching hard-sided garment case, both made by Shwayder Brothers, a gift from his own brother when he had been ordained). Monsignor Serrano, who might have been humming to himself or reciting a series of short prayers, followed two steps behind. Then the two men went outside and got into a taxi. It was a forty-minute drive to the Vatican and Monsignor Aimerich's apartment. At some point during the drive, the two men began a deep almost heart-wrenching conversation. Neither man could later recall the specifics of what was said, but the general nature was all too plain. Monsignor Aimerich would be relieved of his duties as an Auditor for the Rota. He would be reassigned where appropriate, where he could be of the most service to His Holiness. Perhaps he would consider a position teaching at a University. There were many Jesuit institutions throughout the world. Monsignor Serrano would help him secure a spot. But Monsignor Aimerich had no interest in teaching university students. Three months later he boarded a plane for Phoenix, Arizona. He later said that his decision to leave the Church was the best decision he ever made.

-148-

A door made of dark glass with a chrome frame opens, forming a triangular wedge of darkness (as seen from above) between the exterior of a white building (to which the door belongs), the protruding angle of the door itself, and the narrow strip of sidewalk just outside. It is well past midnight, but the ruffled, feathery darkness of a cloudy sky hangs suspended above an impenetrable bubble of coppery-orange light produced by the lamps of one-hundred-and-sixteen sentinel parking lot light poles, evenly spaced throughout the two-dimensional grid of the parking lot at intervals of one-hundred-and-eight feet.

Together, the white building and the parking lot sentinel light poles form a precise rectangle, the geometry of which can only be properly appreciated from a great height. The white building, which is itself a one-hundred-and-sixty-two-foot-by-sixty-six-foot structure of cinder-block construction, is located entirely within this rectangle.

A narrow sidewalk (six-feet wide, one-hundred feet long) runs along the west side of the white building. The sidewalk begins at the southwestern corner of the building and ends abruptly six feet north of the dark glass door.

The rear of the building, meaning the side that does not contain the dark glass door, forms the central portion of the eastern edge of the rectangle. The building is positioned so that if one drew a line bisecting the rectangle on an east to west plane, half of the building would be to the north of that line and half to the south.

Furthermore, twenty-seven feet north of the northeast

corner of the building marks the beginning of a single row of six sentinel light poles. The row extends north a distance of six-hundred-and-forty-eight feet. Twenty-seven feet directly south of the southeast corner, there is a second row of six sentinels, a mirror image of the first.

The remaining one-hundred-and-four sentinel light poles are spread out on an eight row (east to west) by thirteen row (north to south) grid. The gap between the eastern edge of this slightly smaller grid and the western edge of the sidewalk is thirty-six feet. The distance from the dark glass door to the far western edge of the rectangle is nine-hundred-and-six feet. The dark glass door is now closed and one can see reflected in the imperfect mirror of the door two figures making their way towards a vehicle of some sort. One of the figures appears to have twice the girth of the other. The larger of the two figures says something to the effect that 'they still have quite a ways to go' or 'it's quite a night for driving' or 'it's nights like this one when you really miss the stars' or 'the road will be deserted at this hour' or 'the darkness reminds us that as human beings the mind is immanent in almost all we do.' The other figure responds, but his words are muffled. The larger figure laughs. With each step they become smaller and smaller until they are almost indistinguishable from the vehicle that is their destination.

It is not certain if anyone else is inside the white building. The blue pick-up truck that is normally parked along the north side of the building is not visible from just in front of the dark glass door. The angle is all wrong, for one thing. But the air conditioner is still gurgling away. And for a moment the sound of music can be heard, although faintly, as if the jukebox inside is still playing.

The two figures are already two-thirds of the way to their vehicle. The smaller of the two is having difficulty walking, so the larger one, who has his right arm hooked fish-hook style around the smaller one's torso, just beneath his armpits, has to hoist him back to his feet every so often. If the two figures were to turn around, they would be able to see if the blue pick-up truck is still there. But they do not turn around.

Their vehicle is parked diagonally in a northeast to southwest line across half-a-dozen parking spaces. It is a vintage beige and white Volkswagen van, at least thirty years old, with a trailer attached to it. The trailer is a dark, brownish red in color, though in the diffuse coppery-orange glow of the parking lot sentinel lights it would be premature to say this is its normal color.

The sentinel light poles, which are made of seam-welded, longitudinal pieces of galvanized steel, painted white, rise eighteen vertical feet from the surface of the parking lot, which is made of asphalt. Each pole contains four Cobra head luminaires with drop lens made of plastic. The lamps, 250 Watts each, are arranged in quad configurations in a roughly north, south, east, west orientation. Four-hundred-and-twenty-seven of the four-hundred-and-sixty-four Cobra head luminaires exhibit a perpendicular relationship to the sentinel poles to which they are attached. The remaining thirty-seven luminaires have suffered some form of damage: twenty-six are missing altogether.

Each sentinel light pole produces four overlapping ovals of illumination on the parking lot surface corresponding to the distribution of light from each lamp. The ovals are imperfectly shaped and resemble amoebas or primitive sea creatures from an ancient sea more than precisely drawn geometric figures. The light is at its greatest intensity near the approximate center of each oval, and diminishes by degree as it filters outwards. The sphere of illumination is less, of course, for those sentinel poles with damaged or missing luminaires, but this is scarcely noticeable given that there are four-hundred-and-twenty-seven properly functioning luminaires.

The resulting interplay of the light from the various functioning luminaires creates a shimmering, symmetrical, dappled effect on the surface of the parking lot that resembles the hypnotic movement of ocean waves.

The two figures have reached their vehicle and are now sitting inside. They are motionless. Only the backs of their heads can be seen through the row of tiny, square windows on the left side of the van. The larger of the two figures is sitting in the driver's seat. His arm, bent at the elbow, is partially protruding from the open window. The engine is running but both figures remain motionless. One can imagine they are listening to the radio, but there are only two radio stations they can get this far south, and both of those are Mexican radio stations, which are much more powerful than their U.S. counterparts. The whole parking lot should be flooded with radio sounds from Mexico, but there is only a steady silence emanating from the Volkswagen van, other than the sound of the engine.

In spite of the self-contained geometry of the parking lot lights, the parking lot seems endless, stretching from horizon to horizon, an infinity shimmering beneath the dark, ruffled cloudy sky, like a vast, empty sea. One could sit for hours in this parking lot on a night like this, assuming one had brought a folding chair, just to contemplate the simple geometry of the infinite beneath a dark sky.

Meanwhile, the Volkswagen van has vanished. There is no clue to indicate which direction it went. The shimmering parking lot beneath the dark cloudy sky remains. But the van is gone.

BOOK EIGHT

a cry against the twilight

The old woman is sitting with the blinds drawn in a recliner covered in pink fabric with cream-colored polka dots. The polka dots may actually be white, but in the diffuse light of the room even this tiny truth is obscured. Outside the wind is whipping up, but she makes no movement to suggest that she is aware of the increasing volatility of the weather. She also seems unaware of the young woman who is standing in front of the mahogany dresser, which from the doorway on the other side of the room is to the left of the recliner. The young woman is scrutinizing an array of seven photographs that form an irregular geometric pattern on the wall to the left of the chair.

Outside it is sunny and birds are singing from the relative safety of the maple trees that line the street. Each maple tree possesses a dense matte of leafy foliage, which allows the birds to remain hidden from all but the most determined eyes. The sunlight works its way through the branches of the maples, casting dense, fluttery shadows on the sidewalk below. One can imagine they are the shadows of the hidden birds, but in reality they are the shadows of the overlapping maple leaves. To those who mistake thoughtful reflection for sadness, the birds sound like mourning doves, but they could be any kind of bird.

Outside it is drizzling, outside the wind is whipping up, outside it is sunny once again.

The photographs on the wall almost seem randomly placed. Eight feet to the left of the chair, one foot from the opposite corner, a single photograph (8½x11, portrait style) is fixed to the wall, approximately six feet from the floor. Nine inches to the right of the first one, there is a row of three photographs (all of them 6x9, landscape style), stacked vertically, the second on top of the third on top of the fourth. The third one is on the same plane as the very first, portrait style photograph. The second (above) and fourth (below) photographs are each three inches from the third one (the middle). The fifth photograph (6x9, landscape) is positioned four inches to the right of the row of three pictures. Thc top of thc fifth photograph is slightly higher on the wall than the top of the second photograph. The bottom right corner of the fifth photograph is three inches higher and three inches to the left of the top left corner of the sixth photograph (6x9, portrait). The seventh photograph

(8½x11, landscape) is positioned directly beneath the sixth photograph on the same plane as the bottom photograph of the second row. All of the photographs are encased in glass, so in the diffuse light of the room they are mirrors to the present as much as to the past. The images within each of the seven frames pull one far away.

The walls of the room are an understated blue color like the color of a robin's eggshell. The blue space beneath the center of the photograph collection is occupied by the mahogany dresser. The dresser is not all that large, with only a single, vertical column of four long drawers (each 36x18), and two smaller drawers (16x18 each, with a two-inch strip of mahogany between them) on the same horizontal plane, a fifth row, if you will, directly above the column of four. Each drawer has a tarnished, brass keyhole, though the keys have long since vanished. If one were to slide the dresser away from the wall, one would perceive a more vibrant shade of blue in the shape of a rectangle.

The top of the dresser is unadorned save for a very old beat-up looking clay water jug fashioned from Cuban red dirt, and an old passport. The jug possesses a symmetrical, bulbous shape, similar to that of any number of handcrafted teapots fashioned on a potter's wheel at the beginning of the last century. It is a singular piece with a circular ring handle emerging from the top, a tiny nub of a spout for pouring water, and a larger hole opposite the spout for filling up. The red clay is riddled with dark spots and scratches and whitish stains and other markings of the passing years. The passport is an old Cuban passport.

The back edge of the left side of the recliner rests against the blue wall with the photographs while the back edge of the right side of the recliner rests against a similarly colored wall, thus the back of the recliner and the two adjacent walls form a triangle of empty space. Two feet from the corner along the second wall there is a row of four identical, metal frame windows, each two feet in width, and then two more feet of empty blue wall space, and then another corner. The blinds in each of the four identical windows have been drawn, so the light that might otherwise have flooded the room has been reduced to a series of parallel lines of opaque quality, where the blinds overlap, and bright pinpricks of light, shimmering filaments, emanating from the three holes (left, center, right) in each blind, holes which also allow the drawstrings to pass unimpeded. The swirl of opaque light and pinprick light gives an indistinctness to the objects in the room.

Outside the wind is whipping up, but the old woman in the recliner makes no movement to suggest that she is aware of the increasing volatility of the weather. Outside it has begun to drizzle. It has finished drizzling. It is drizzling again. It is drizzling on the gray cement steps that lead to the front doors of the apartment building. The color of the steps is a darker gray now because of the drizzle. The color is much lighter when seen in the bright sunlight of sunny days. The drizzle resembles a bead curtain made of overlapping strands of gray beads.

The young woman is now only a few feet from the dark (darker) gray steps. Her view of the row of four identical, metal frame windows that form the middle portion of the exterior wall of the old woman's apartment is obscured by the fact that the apartment is on the ninth floor as much as by the protruding rim of the young woman's umbrella, which hangs down almost to the level of her eyes.

Now she is at the top of the steps. Now she has disappeared inside, turning towards the drizzle only briefly to shake her umbrella, which is an unassuming white in color, before collapsing it and placing it in a plastic receptacle for wet umbrellas that the management of the apartment building has placed just inside the door. Droplets of water glisten on the floor around the base of the receptacle.

The old woman in the pink recliner has not moved. The recliner is covered in a pink fabric with cream-colored polka dots, though in all fairness, the polka dots may actually be white, or perhaps yellow. In the diffuse light of the room even the tiniest truth is obscured. The old woman is wearing a turquoise sweater, a faded cardigan. Whoever buttoned the faded cardigan didn't bother to line up each button with the appropriate button hole. At the top there is a button with no corresponding button hole. At the bottom there is a button hole with no corresponding button.

The young woman gives the first six photographs only quick, affirmatory glances.

Photograph number one is not even a photograph. It is a full-page color ad for a French provincial bedroom suite by the Drexel furniture company. The ad says 'What a wonderful way to fall asleep! Touraine by Drexel.' Beneath the advertising language is a picture demonstrating how the Touraine set might look in one's bedroom. Beneath the picture is half a page of marketing copy.

Photographs two, three and four are all black-and-white family photographs, though black and white is not quite precise, for the photographs seem to possess various shades of gray (brownish-gray, blueish-gray, greenish-gray, etc.) Number two immediately draws one's eyes to the middle, where a white haired Spanish grandmother sits in a Victorian rocking chair, leaning forward slightly. A white blanket with an irregular pattern of black polka dots covers her knees and legs; her shoulders are covered by a white shawl. She is wearing boots, which are resting on a white pillow featuring the same pattern of black dots. Her eyes are closed, but she does not appear to be sleeping. Perhaps the photographer caught her in mid-blink.

Five women are standing directly behind the rocking chair, ranging in age from mid-thirties (two) to early fifties (also two) to late-sixties (one). Their faces are a waxy brownish-gray color, in fact they seem more like wax figures or paper mâché puppets than flesh-and-blood people, even their wrinkles and the puffy oval lumps beneath their tired looking eyes are precisely, artistically shaped.

The woman in her late-sixties has her hair tied neatly back and she is holding the back of the rocking chair, perhaps to maintain her balance.

The women are flanked on both sides by large, feathery ferns. It looks like they are outside, on the patio of a very large hacienda. They are all looking in different directions, with various carefully shaped expressions (dismay, amusement, boredom, anxiety, a pose of nonchalance to hide a lingering regret), as if there was some commotion going on behind the photographer but they each possessed a different attitude about what was happening.

Outside the sunlight works its way through the branches of the maples, casting dense, fluttering shadows on the side-walk below. Outside the wind is whipping up and the birds are nowhere to be seen.

Perhaps the grandmother is closing her eyes because she is embarrassed by the commotion. Perhaps there are several younger members of the family hooting and hollering and carrying on behind the camera, out of sight. Perhaps it is the grandmother's ninetieth birthday.

Photographs three and four are variations on a theme, the same hacienda, the same patio, the same feathery ferns, the same family, but modified slightly, rearranged, a few substitutions. Number three (the patio at night but all lit up with strings of lights) shows a happy young couple and the five women but no grandmother. Number four (the patio during the day) shows the happy young couple, a baby's face lost in the folds of a long, white dress, four of the five women from the previous photographs, two older men in suits, whose facial features radiate fatigue, and a priest.

Photograph number five shows two couples dining out in a fancy restaurant. From the photo one can see two levels for dining divided by a small concrete wall topped with a metal railing that runs the length of the wall. The railing is made of four thin slats, and a fifth thicker, all-encompassing slat along the top. Perhaps the restaurant doubles as a nightclub. All of the tables are covered with heavily starched white linen tablecloths. The foursome which is the focus of the photograph is sitting on the lower level at a table littered with the refuse of a celebratory pre-dinner blast. In the middle is a bottle that could be a bottle of Dom Pérignon, though the label is facing the wrong way so it is impossible to say for certain. Four presumably empty bottles of beer are clustered on the right side of the possible Dom Pérignon. There are also four glasses, tall tumblers, containing liquids at various heights, indicating various levels of consumption.

On the right side of the table (from the perspective of the couples looking towards the camera), up against the small concrete wall, sits a clean-shaven young man in a white linen suit, white shirt, and white tie. Perhaps his shoes are also white, but they are hidden beneath the shadows of the table. The young man's right arm is draped around a young, dark-haired girl in a plain chiffon dress. Her legs are crossed and her arms are folded in her lap. He possesses a smile of ownership, she one of acquiescence. His tumbler is full, or perhaps it has been refilled, and he appears to be reaching for it, but his movement has been arrested by the action of the photographer. Her tumbler is almost empty and sits abandoned on her small corner of the table. Opposite the young man in the white linen suit sits a man in a dark jacket. He has dark hair like all the others, and also a dark moustache. His lower face from the tip of his chin to his cheekbones is creased with a simpering, leering expression that doubles as a smile. He is clutching his drink with his right hand. His left arm is draped around a matronly woman, presumably his wife, in a matronly dress, his left hand is holding onto her left arm. Her dress is an unflattering dress. The folds of the fabric bunch up at the woman's hips, giving her a shapeless, sack-like presence before the indiscriminate eye of the camera. The matronly woman is leaning against her husband, or perhaps he is pulling her towards him, but there is a visible tension in her posture. It is as if she is trying to escape the pressure of being held so closely. Her expression resembles terror more than anything else, as if she is frightened of fancy dinners out and restaurant photographers.

Only one other table in the photograph is occupied. One can see the torso (but not the head) of a single individual sitting at a table on the upper level. One can also see the blurry outline of the arm of a waiter getting ready to pour a bottle, and the blurry outline of the seated individual reaching for a glass.

The sixth photograph shows a middle-aged woman in a dark floral print dress clutching a worn black purse in her left hand, and the hand of a small boy, age nine or ten, in her right hand. The woman's lips are pursed, as if she is trying to suppress a smile, a reflection of that motherly compassion possessed by mothers who cannot help but laugh when a child misbehaves. The boy is not smiling. He is wearing a t-shirt with thin, black and white horizontal stripes, whitish knickers, a black belt, black shoes, and long white tube socks that have lost their elasticity, so they are bunched up around his ankles. The woman and the boy are standing on a city sidewalk in front of a wrought iron railing.

Outside it is sunny and the birds are calling to each other. The color of the steps is a lighter gray now because of the bright sunlight of a sunny day.

The railing itself contains two repeating patterns. A larger alternating pattern of vertical curlicues (each about three feet high and eighteen inches wide) makes up the bottom portion of the railing. A smaller alternating pattern of horizontal curlicues (nine inches high by two feet wide) makes up the upper portion of the railing, which is then capped with a singular iron rail that stretches from one end to the other. Where the railing is bathed in sunlight, the curlicues have all but vanished.

Behind the railing is a narrow porch, slightly elevated, about two feet from the level of the sidewalk. The porch, which is framed by two Greek-style columns, one on either side, is twelve feet across and possesses a depth of five feet. One can see the bottom portion of a dark shuttered window and a dark, intricately carved door with thick, intricately carved jambs. A telephone pole bisects the photograph roughly three feet to the right of the boy. To the right of the telephone pole there is a portion of a second porch with a second railing identical in all visible respects to the first porch.

Outside the wind is whipping up, but the old woman in the recliner makes no movement to suggest that she is aware of the increasing volatility of the weather. Outside it has begun to drizzle. It has finished drizzling. Outside it is sunny. The streaming sunlight resembles a bead curtain made of overlapping strands of sparkling yellow beads.

The young woman gives the first six photographs only quick, affirmatory glances. The young woman is motionless. She cannot take her eyes away from the seventh photograph.

'I only put that one up for her last week,' the nurse says.

'I was wondering,' says the young woman.

The young woman does not turn around. She can see the vague, whitish reflection of the nurse in the glass of the seventh photograph. The nurse is standing to one side of a narrow, wrought-iron bed with a chenille bedspread. The bed looks as if it has been freshly made.

'I didn't know she liked baseball,' says the nurse.

'She doesn't,' says the young woman.

'Ah. I see,' says the nurse.

The sunlight outside cannot quite penetrate the barrier of the four identical windows. The blinds in each of the windows have been drawn, so the light that might otherwise have flooded the room has been reduced to a series of parallel lines on the hardwood floor, and a swirl of bright pinpricks floating through the haze. It is hard to distinguish the pinpricks of light from the particles of dust that are always floating about aimlessly, reflecting whatever illuminating flash comes their way. The old woman in the recliner makes no movement to suggest that she is aware of the reduced level of sunlight in the room. She also seems unaware of the young woman who is standing in front of the mahogany dresser, which is to the left of the recliner. The young woman is scrutinizing the seventh of the seven photographs that form an irregular geometric pattern on the wall. She is motionless.

She almost seems part of a larger photograph, in which she, a young woman whose face we cannot see, is scrutinizing seven photographs that form an irregular geometric pattern on the wall.

The seventh photograph is a baseball team photo taken on a very sunny day somewhere in the tropics. The photograph seems almost bleached out, an indication perhaps of the intense heat that had washed over the ballpark the day the photograph was taken. The ballplayers are posing in the infield on the first-base side of the pitcher's mound. It is a black-and-white photo, so the color of the infield grass is a whitish, light gray color. In real life the grass would have been a parched yellow-brown color.

Eight ballplayers are standing in the back row, six are squatting in the front row. They each seem to be standing or squatting directly on their own tiny, circular shadows, a clear indication that the photo was snapped at high noon. Their uniforms are pinstriped with the name Cuba printed across the shirts in block lettering. In the background one can see the outfield fence, which seems to be given over to advertising. The two most prominent ads are both for alcohol, one for Cerveza Cristal, a Peruvian beer, and the other for Maltina Tivoli, a malt liquor brewed in Havana. To the far left along the fence there is a scoreboard that says Cuba 7, Mexico 1. Beyond the fence are palm trees and then a dark (presumably dark green), vegetative mass, and in the distance one can make out a few brick buildings and a single smokestack.

Not all of the ballplayers seem aware the photograph is being taken. At least their mannerisms, frozen in the moment, indicate a casual indifference to the process. The two squatting in the first row on the far left seem to be having an intimate conversation. Their heads are turned towards each other, a conspiratorial pose, as if they are hatching a plot. Next to them is a solitary squatter holding a baseball bat. He is looking at the rounded end of the bat, remembering, perhaps, his last appearance at the plate, an unhappy event, to judge by the way his features are contorted. The last three squatters are looking directly at the photographer, two with placid, affable grins on their faces, but the third, who is dressed in a catcher's padded uniform, is glaring at the photographer (or perhaps someone else standing next to the photographer and therefore hidden from view) with murderous intent.

The ballplayers in the back row are also displaying a variety of attitudes. The two on the far left are looking squarely at the camera, but their shoulders are turned and the eager, mischievous expressions on their faces suggest that the moment the photograph is snapped, they are going to sprint to the clubhouse to arrange some practical joke. The next two appear to have nothing better to do than stand in the hot sun and be photographed. They even seem to be enjoying the moment. The next one (number five) is clearly distressed, though it is difficult to determine if this distress is caused by the heat or some other issue. Number six is glaring at the photographer with the same demented expression (the icy glare of a madman) seen in the face of the squatting catcher, who is squatting directly in front of number six. Number seven is looking at the ballplayer holding the bat with a look that could be dismay or frustration or even disgust. They appear to be replaying the same memory. Finally, there is number eight in the back row. He is standing two steps to the right of everyone else in the picture. He is a good-looking fellow of medium height (five-foot-seven), but he has assumed a provocative, rebellious pose. Perhaps he is showing off for someone who has come to watch the photographer take this photo, perhaps a new girlfriend, and as soon as the photographer is finished, number eight and the hypothetical girlfriend will head off in search of a small café, a private corner where they can escape the heat of a tropical afternoon.

Suddenly the photograph is snapped. The unity of the team breaks apart in a series of fractured movements. The two squatters on the far left finish their conversation, shake hands, and then they walk off in different directions, almost as if they have suddenly become strangers, one crossing in front of the photographer, who is breaking down his equipment, the other making a beeline for the dugout on the third-base side to retrieve his glove. The squatter with the bat stands up and breaks into a beaming smile and turns to face ballplayer number seven from the back row, who also breaks into a smile. The two ballplayers walk off telling jokes and laughing. The catcher and ballplayer number six from the back row confer quietly with each other. The catcher points at the pitcher's mound and ballplayer number six shakes his head, a gesture of reluctance, and then he steps to the mound as the catcher heads for home plate. A few moments later ballplayer number six, who is clearly a pitcher, is throwing as hard as he can. The look of concentration on his face resembles his earlier demeanor, the icy glare of a madman. The heavy thwack of the ball hitting the catcher's mitt is easily absorbed by the expanding silence of the afternoon. Numbers one and two from the back row are now signing autographs for every one of the small boys who had come to the stadium to watch the baseball team practice. There are a few spectators sitting in the stands. They are motionless. They are holding their hands up to block out the sun, which seems to have whitewashed the whole world. Numbers three, four, and five from the back row are nowhere to be seen. Presumably they are in the locker room. Or they have already gone home. The two squatters from the far right are busy speaking with a newspaper reporter who wants to get some additional insight about the exhibition baseball game that was played the day before. 'Have you ever beaten Mexico by such a lopsided score?' 'Seven to one against Mexico is about average.' 'Were you disappointed with your play in the seventh inning when Humberto here bobbled the ball in the infield so the batter got on base and eventually scored Mexico's only run, blowing the shutout?' 'It was an error, no doubt about it. But give that Mexican guy credit for hitting that ball as hard as he did into the hole.' 'So you're saying you were lucky you even got a glove on it?' 'You're the one saying that.' And then the two squatters from the far right and the newspaper reporter are laughing. The team will head to Venezuela in a week to participate in the 1959 Caribbean series. They plan on bringing back another title to Cuba. The photographer is exiting the stadium through a narrow gate past the end of the bleachers on the third-base side. Ballplayer number eight is talking with the hypothetical girl who is no longer hypothetical. He is standing in a bare, roughly rectangular patch of dirt that serves as the first-base coaching box, and she is standing on the first base bag, her back to the field, but she is still an inch or so shorter than the ballplayer. She seems happy that he is taller.

'Where did you want to go?' he says.

'Where do you want to go?' she says.

'There's an outdoor café I like,' he says. 'It's near the Plaza del Cristo. Not too far. It's called La Maravilla.'

'La Maravilla?' the girl says.

'It can be a pretty strange place,' he says. 'Some pretty crazy characters hang out there.'

'You mean like you?' she says.

Number eight smiles, and the hypothetical girl who is no longer hypothetical smiles back. She smiles without apprehension and they head to a dusty, gravel parking lot outside the stadium and get into a brand new 1959 Chevrolet. Number eight did not have to purchase this particular vehicle. It was a gift from an American businessman. All number eight has to do is drive this brand-new Chevrolet around Havana and wave at people and let them look at the car. Number eight and the girl talk quietly for a while. Then the engine suddenly roars to life. The car becomes a speeding bullet traversing this marvelous American reality. Alternatively, the car becomes a bouquet of flowers to place upon the graves of the dead.

-150-

Outside it is twilight and the birds have stopped calling to each other. Outside the moon is glowing in the night sky. Outside the moon has set.

A single streetlamp, partially obscured by the foliage of the maple trees, illuminates the steps leading to the entrance of the apartment building. The streaming lamplight resembles a bead curtain made of overlapping strands of shimmering pink beads, a very soft pink color. There must be dozens of similar streetlamps illuminating the steps leading to the entrances of dozens of apartment buildings up and down the street, but from inside the ninth-floor apartment, even with one's face pressed up against the window glass, it is impossible to tell. The street below is empty. The entire world seems uninhabited.

Now the pink recliner with cream-colored polka dots is covered with a white sheet. There is no telling how long it has been covered. The blinds in each of the four identical windows have been drawn all the way to the top, so they are no longer a barrier to any light from the outside. The drawstrings are trailing along the hardwood floor beneath the window sills.

The seven photographs that once formed an irregular geometric pattern on the blue wall are gone. All that remains are seven hooks, or perhaps they are bent nails, which kept the photographs in place, and six rectangles, each a darker shade of blue than the wall. Of course these six rectangles have disappeared entirely in the absence of any direct illumination.

Opposite the row of four identical windows is the doorway to the room. The doorway opens up to a narrow hallway that traverses the entire apartment. From the open bedroom door, the hallway extends fifteen feet in a southerly direction and twelve feet in a northerly direction. Heading south, one passes a small sitting room with pinkish walls (a room that perhaps had once been the bedroom of a small child or a teenage girl). Immediately after the door to the bedroom the hallway becomes a small living room with a beige sofa and an RCA console television set and a front door. Heading north from the open bedroom door, one passes a small bathroom with a toilet that runs intermittently and an empty broom closet. After that the hallway becomes a small kitchen with a back door that leads to a small five-foot by ten-foot balcony platform, which is itself part of a fire escape system of wrought-iron balconies connected by wrought iron stairs.

Since there are twelve floors to the apartment building, there are eleven balconies, one each for floors two through twelve, bolted to the brick exterior. The stairs that connect one balcony to another each possess eighteen steps and are positioned at a forty-five-degree angle relative to the balconies above and below. To continue descending from the second balcony, which is approximately ten feet above a narrow alleyway littered with the detritus one normally finds in alleyways (broken glass, cigarette stubs, bottle caps, dead leaves, lost keys, the remains of plundered garbage bags, abandoned shoes, an abandoned grocery store cart, useless lottery tickets, etc.), one must release a sliding wrought-iron ladder that contains ten rungs.

Back inside the apartment, the hallway is dark, as are the other rooms, except for the bedroom, which is illuminated by a soft, pinkish glow which has drifted in through the uncovered window glass of the four identical windows, an insubstantial shimmering in the shape of an irregular rhombus. The source of the glow is not the solitary street lamp submerged in the foliage of a maple tree. It is hard to determine where the source of the illumination is. Perhaps it is the general glow of the city, a glow initially produced by dozens of unseen street lamps and then reflected by the dozens upon dozens of windows in the apartment buildings which line the opposite side of the street. Only the bottom of the narrow, wrought iron bed and the rounded left corner of the pink recliner are visible in the diffuse light. The rhombus extends across the room, the two long sides of the rhombus converging as they approach the open door, an inevitable narrowing, the small end vanishing in the liquid darkness of the hallway, a subtle, indiscernible vanishing. The open door is made of mahogany and has been swung back so that the front edge of the door's bedroom side rests against the wall opposite the row of four identical windows.

Suddenly there is a harsh sounding click and the liquid darkness of the hallway is bisected by a narrow beam of light emanating from the kitchen. The source of the beam is a cream-colored porcelain globe fixed to the center of the kitchen ceiling. The point where the hallway becomes the kitchen has been transformed into a bright golden vertical rectangle that contrasts sharply with the fluid darkness at the southern end of the hall. The yellow walls of the kitchen seem to magnify the intensity of the light, but strangely, the hallway itself remains shrouded in shadow, except for the single beam of light already mentioned. From the shadows in the hallway, one can see only part of the kitchen, a row of cabinets, half a sink with the faucet turned towards the invisible half.

Now one can clearly see the porcelain globe, which is bowl-shaped, eighteen inches in diameter, with a one-inch gap between the open end of the bowl and the ceiling. Along the sloping sides of the globe there is an embossed grapevine pattern of grapes and squiggly bits of vine and overlapping grape leaves. It is difficult to determine the exact number of grape bunches because of the placement of the leaves. There are twenty-four leaves in all, and two-hundred-and-sixty-six visible grapes. The globe is probably from the 1930s, when such fixtures were common. It is in generally good condition, though it does exhibit a roughly circular discolored area at the bottom of the bowl, a rust stain, perhaps, from where water has leaked in over the years.

Upon closer examination, one can also see the opaque shadows of a few dead insects. There is no telling when the porcelain globe was last cleaned out. There are at least several years of dead insects piled up at the bottom.

Now one can see the entire sink and an olive-green rug on the floor, a linoleum floor which in the glow of the cream-colored globe is a brownish-gray. The faucet is dripping a slow, steady drip. One can see that the sink is stained from years of ceaseless dripping. To the right of the sink is the back door, which is partially open, and to the right of the back door, wedged in the corner, there is an olive-green refrigerator. Opposite the sink there is a small kitchen table, a white Formica-topped table with chrome legs, pushed up against the wall. There is one chair for each of the three exposed sides of the table. The chairs match the table (chrome legs, white padded seats, white padded backrests).

Outside the moon has set. Outside the moon is glowing in the night sky. Outside it is twilight and the birds have stopped calling to each other.

A single streetlamp, partially obscured by the foliage of the maple trees, illuminates the steps leading to the entrance of the apartment building. The blinds are now drawn, so the soft pinkish glow resulting from the reflection of dozens of unseen street lamps in the dozens upon dozens of windows in the apartment buildings which line the opposite side of the street, which would have otherwise drifted in through the uncovered window glass of the four identical windows in the old woman's bedroom, is confined to the exterior of the apartment building.

Suddenly there is a harsh sounding click and the softly glowing rectangle of golden light that marks the transition from the hallway to the kitchen vanishes and the apartment is plunged into absolute darkness. The back door opens and then closes. The latch is turned, the tumbler rotates, the dead bolt falls into place.

Then everything is happening in reverse order.

The deadbolt snaps back, the tumbler rotates, the latch is turned, the door opens then closes, there is a harsh sounding click, an echo in the dark, the terror of elliptical nights suddenly vanishes, the kitchen is bathed in a soft golden glow, the liquid darkness of the hallway is intersected by a narrow beam of light. The cycle repeats itself, a reversal followed by a reversal followed by a reversal followed by a reversal, an endless repetition of light becoming darkness and darkness becoming light.

Now the young woman is sitting at the Formica-topped table, the side closest to the hallway. She is staring at the back door, perhaps because the door is slightly ajar. Perhaps she is contemplating whether or not to get up and close the door all the way and turn the latch. Or perhaps she is looking past the door. Perhaps she is contemplating the unseen vastness of the world outside, a vastness that is obscured by a dark night, except for the various patches illuminated by the dozens and dozens of streetlamps scattered throughout the city. Or perhaps she is wondering when the moon will rise and set.

The young woman remains motionless. She does not seem to notice the sound of the dripping faucet, or further away, the sound of the toilet running and then stopping and then running again, all on its own. She does not seem to notice the small box on the table. The box is filled with all sorts of memorabilia, the seven photographs that once formed an irregular geometric pattern on the wall in the old woman's bedroom, an old Cuban passport, a water jug fashioned from Cuban red dirt, an elaborately cast crucifix made of 12 carat gold, various papers, including the young woman's birth certificate, which she found in the top drawer of the mahogany dresser, two Pan American airline tickets for passage from Havana to Miami dated August 10, 1962, a souvenir, perhaps, of the old woman's entry into the United States. The young woman is staring at the back door, perhaps because the door is slightly ajar.

The young woman gives the first six photographs only quick, affirmatory glances. The young woman is motionless. She cannot take her eyes away from the seventh photograph.

'I only put that one up for her last week,' the nurse says.

'I was wondering,' says the young woman.

The young woman does not turn around. She can see the vague, whitish reflection of the nurse in the glass. The nurse is standing to one side of a narrow, wrought-iron bed with a white chenille bedspread she is in the process of unfurling. Now the bed looks as if it has been freshly made.

'I didn't know she liked baseball,' says the nurse.

'She doesn't,' says the young woman.

'Ah. I see,' says the nurse.

'She married a ballplayer,' says the young woman.

'Is he in the photograph?' asks the nurse.

'I am sure he is,' says the young woman. 'But I don't know which one.'

'There's writing on the back,' says the nurse. 'A name and a date and a few words. Your grandmother showed me.'

The young woman takes the seventh photograph from the wall and flips it over so she can remove the felt backing. Now she is looking at the back of the photograph. There is a date in the top right corner: June 26, 1960. Beneath the date is a short note.

The note says: Do you remember this day? Do you remember La Maravilla and how we later drove to the beach? I will carry the memory of that day to my grave, my love. Your loving José.

The young woman puts the photograph back in its frame, which she then hangs on the wall. Outside it has begun to drizzle. It has finished drizzling. Outside it is sunny. The streaming sunlight resembles a bead curtain made of overlapping strands of sparkling yellow beads.

'She was very excited when she saw the photograph,' says the nurse.

'She was?' says the young woman.

'Oh, yes,' says the nurse. 'She was gushing with happy memories. But she was also sad.'

'Why was she sad?' says the young woman.

'She did not really say,' says the nurse.

'But she was mostly happy?' says the young woman.

'Yes,' says the nurse. 'But not as happy as she gets when she knows you are coming.'

The young woman says nothing. She continues staring at the seventh photograph on the wall.

'I think your visits these last two years are what's kept her alive,' says the nurse.

The old woman is sitting with the blinds drawn in a recliner covered in pink fabric with cream-colored polka dots. The polka dots may actually be white, but in the diffuse light of the room even this tiny truth is obscured. Outside the wind is whipping up, but she makes no movement to suggest that she is aware of the increasing volatility of the weather. She also seems unaware of the young woman who is standing in front of the mahogany dresser, to the right of the recliner, scrutinizing an array of seven photographs that form an irregular geometric pattern on the wall.

'I only put that one up for her last week,' the nurse says.

'I was wondering,' says the young woman.

'She was very excited when she saw the photograph,' says the nurse. 'I found it in on the floor behind the RCA console. I don't know why I even looked there. She was sound asleep and I came in to watch something and I noticed that hole in the plaster right above the console, like somebody had once thought about putting a window there but had given up and then forgot about repairing the damage. I moved the console for a closer look, and that's when I found the photograph. She had probably put it right on top years ago and someone knocked it off by accident. God only knows how long it was back there.'

-151-

The apartment is dark except for the living room. The soft glow of a floor lamp next to the beige sofa provides the only illumination. The lamp possesses a fringed lampshade shaped like an inverted bowl, which produces a wavy, elliptical pattern of light and shadow on the hardwood floor. Opposite the sofa and the lamp, on the wall directly above the RCA console, a small crucifix hangs by a nail. There are visible cracks in the plaster surrounding the nail, a spider web of cracks. One good yank and the plaster will come tumbling.

The light from the lamp does not reach all the way to the crucifix. Nevertheless, the crucifix gleams brightly in the half-light. It is an elaborately cast twelve-carat gold cross with tiny floral bouquets at each of the four ends, and a shining halo directly behind the head of the Savior. The halo resembles a rising sun. The cross is twelve inches top to bottom and eight inches across at the crossbeam. The figure of the Savior is six inches head to toe. His head is appropriately placed where the two beams meet.

Now a series of images flicker across the screen of the RCA console television set. The images are in color, but the colors need to be adjusted. One can see the Captain of a large boat talking with two members of the crew. Their uniforms are whitish-gray, but it is difficult to determine if that is their actual color given the technical difficulties with the television set's color controls. Now there is a close-up of the Captain. His skin is blue when it should be flesh-colored. Now the camera pulls back to reveal more of the deck where the Captain is standing, and a little bit of sky. The deck and the sky are tinted green.

The old woman is now a middle-aged woman. She is sitting motionless on the beige sofa, her attention focused on the television Captain.

A young girl is sitting next to her, a child, perhaps four years old. The child is looking up at the middle-aged woman, her head pulled back at an extremely acute angle, as if she is just about to ask a question. Now the television Captain is sitting at a banquet table. He is holding up a claret glass. He is making a toast. The middle-aged woman is still sitting motionless. The little girl is still poised with her question. Or perhaps it is a different question. The toast is received with a round of 'here, here,' and then everyone at the table drains their glasses.

Now the screen of the RCA console television set is a dark green color. The only image on the screen is that of the middle-aged woman sitting motionless on the beige sofa and the whitish glow of the lamp. The little girl is nowhere to be seen. Perhaps she has gone to bed. The eyes of the middle-aged woman are fixated on a small photograph placed squarely on top of the RCA console, squarely in the center. The photograph is of a baseball team posing in the middle of a baseball field, but it is too far away from the sofa for the woman to be able to make out the details.

Suddenly the front door opens, but only partially, as if whatever force that caused it to open wishes to remain invisible. For a moment one notices the twilight of the hallway outside the apartment. One can see a single glowing globe of light, a tiny bead of illumination where the hallway becomes a stairway leading either up or down. Now the door is closed and the twilight of the outer hallway vanishes. A young woman in her early twenties, dressed in black jeans, black boots, and a black leather jacket, becomes part of the reflection on the screen of the RCA console television set. She is standing three steps from the closed door, four steps from the right corner of the television set, and seven steps from the center of the sofa, where the middle-aged woman is still sitting. The young woman's hips are turned slightly towards the sofa, her left foot slightly in advance of her right.

'Is she asleep?'

'Yes, she's asleep.'

'. . .'

'Where did you go?'

'I don't remember.'

'What were you doing?'

'I was waiting for her to fall asleep.'

'And now that she's asleep?'

'Now I have to go.'

Then she opens the door.

For a brief moment one can see a single glowing globe of light, a tiny bead of illumination where the hallway becomes a stairway leading either up or down. Now the little girl is standing by the door, one hand resting against the door jamb and the other holding the doorknob on the interior side of the door.

The doorknob is a solid forged brass knob of vintage design. The knob face features a series of concentric circles from the center to the edge of the knob. At the very center there is a brass circle resembling a tiny moon. The next circle contains an eightfold floral pattern, slightly raised. The final circle features an eightfold pattern of half suns, also slightly raised, as if they were Braille symbols. The flames of each half-sun extend towards the center, while their edges correspond to the edge of the knob. The spindle is unadorned. The rose plate (which covers the hole in the door through which the knob spindle is connected to the inner mechanism of the lock) features the same eightfold floral pattern featured on the knob face.

The little girl is straining to see something but there is nothing to see other than the single glowing globe of light and the stairway. She closes the door and goes over to the sofa and sits next to the middle-aged woman. She looks up at the middle-aged woman, her head pulled back at an extremely acute angle, as if she is just about to ask a question.

Now the room is dark except for the blueish glow from the RCA console television. One can see the Captain of a large boat talking with two members of the crew. The Captain's skin is blue when it should be flesh-colored. The Captain seems to be telling a joke. The two members of the crew are laughing, but they also seem anxious to resume their duties. Perhaps they have heard the joke before. Now the camera pulls back to reveal more of the deck where the Captain is standing, and a little bit of sky. The deck and the sky are tinted green.

The middle-aged woman does not seem to notice the sound of the toilet running and then stopping and then running again, all on its own, or further away, the sound of the dripping faucet. She is thoroughly engrossed in the images flickering across the screen of the RCA console television set.

Outside the wind is whipping up, but she makes no movement to suggest that she is aware of the increasing volatility of the weather. She also seems unaware of the young woman who is standing in front of the mahogany dresser, scrutinizing the seventh of seven photographs that form an irregular geometric pattern on the wall.

'She was very excited when she saw the photograph."

'She was?' says the young woman.

'Oh, yes,' says the nurse. 'She was gushing with happy memories. But she was also sad.'

'Why was she sad?' says the young woman.

But the nurse does not respond.

Suddenly the front door opens, but only partially, as if whatever force that caused it to open wishes to remain invisible. Now the young woman in the black leather jacket is standing in the middle of the room, halfway between the RCA console television and the beige sofa. She seems to be arguing with the middle-aged woman, heated words in an angry moment, but there is no sound to accompany the exchange so it is difficult to determine exactly what is being said. Then she rushes towards the RCA console television and tears the twelve-carat gold crucifix from the wall. Bits of plaster land on top of the console and some fall behind it, on the floor. The young woman in the black leather jacket then makes a sweeping motion with the crucifix across the top of the console. The bits of plaster on top as well as the photograph of the baseball team are sent flying. In the shadows where the hallway becomes the living room the little girl is standing motionless. The shadows resemble a bead curtain made of overlapping strands of shimmering black beads.

Once again the interior of the apartment is dark except for the flickering images that flash across the screen of the RCA console television screen. There is a gaping hole in the wall above the console, as if someone with a chisel had started to chip away at the plaster but had later given up. The top of the console is bare except for a lace doily placed squarely in the middle. There is no way to determine what has become of either the baseball team photograph or the twelve-carat gold crucifix.

'I was waiting for her to fall asleep.'

'And now that she's asleep?'

'Now I have to go.'

'And what about her?'

'I don't know.'

'Are you coming back?'

The young woman in the black leather jacket hesitates for a moment, fumbles for something in her pocket, stops fumbling.

Outside it is twilight and the birds have stopped calling to each other. Outside the moon is glowing in the night sky. Outside the moon has set. The middle-aged woman is sitting motionless on the beige sofa, her attention focused on the television Captain of a television boat. A young girl is sitting next to her, a child, perhaps four years old. The child is looking up at the middle-aged woman, her head pulled back at an extremely acute angle, as if she is just about to ask a question. Now the television Captain is sitting at a banquet table. He is holding up a claret glass. He is making a toast. The middle-aged woman is still sitting motionless. The little girl is still poised with her question. Or perhaps it is a different question. The toast is received with a round of 'here, here,' and then everyone at the table drains their glasses.

-152-

She had never heard her grandmother talk about a café called La Maravilla. Not that her grandmother's silence about such things meant a whole lot. Her grandmother rarely spoke about her life in Cuba, as if by her silence she could erase the past, obliterate every unwanted memory, especially those that had once been precious. But it seemed reasonable to think that she had retained a few happy memories of the day when the baseball team photograph was snapped. True, the nurse had said the photograph also made her sad. But she was mostly happy.

Suddenly there is a soft sounding click and the back door opens and then closes. The young woman puts the photograph back in its frame, which she then puts back in the box.

Outside it has begun to drizzle. It has finished drizzling. Outside it is sunny. The streaming sunlight resembles a bead curtain made of overlapping strands of sparkling yellow beads.

Now the young woman is sitting at the table, the side closest to the hallway. She is staring at the back door, perhaps because the door is slightly ajar. Perhaps she is contemplating whether or not to get up and close the door all the way and turn the latch. Or perhaps she is looking past the door. Perhaps she is contemplating the vastness of the world outside, a vastness that is illuminated by a bright sunny day.

Now the young woman is heading down the stairs from the ninth floor to the eighth to the seventh and so on, all the way down to the first floor. One can only see the top of her head as she descends, a rectangular descent, her head becoming smaller and smaller with each half revolution, her black hair, a thick matte freshly washed, falling to either side, obscuring her shoulders, her arms visible only because she is carrying the small box previously observed on the white Formica-topped table in the kitchen of the ninth-floor apartment.

Now she is at the bottom of the stairwell, which also doubles as the main entryway to the apartment building. The floor at the bottom is comprised of seventy-two light gray tiles, laid out in twelve rows of six. The tiles in the first five rows are all perfect squares, twelve-by-twelve inches. The remaining row is comprised of tiles cut in the shape of rectangles, twelve-by-six inches, with the longer side running along the wall opposite the stairwell opening. The young woman remains motionless. The box she is holding is barely discernible, as viewed from nine floors up. Her head with its thick matte of freshly washed black hair has become a tiny black dot, motionless in the center of a light gray rectangle. The scene resembles an abstract painting.

Now the young woman is six steps from the door to the apartment building, but she remains motionless. The door, which is to the right of the stairwell opening, suddenly whooshes open. A sudden rush of wind and sunlight fills the entryway. The door is not visible from nine floors up, but the whooshing sunlight is. It bisects the light gray rectangle, producing two triangles, one that is light gray and one that is a whitish, washed-out yellow color. The door closes and the two triangles disappear, leaving behind the initial light gray rectangle. A second dot joins the black dot in the middle of the rectangle. The second dot seems to be a white dot, but it is difficult to be certain of the color, which seems to change with the movement of the dot. The two dots seem to be twirling around each other, a strange, symbiotic dance that resembles two bees communicating. A series of soft, murmuring sounds begins to float up through the void of empty space that constitutes the center portion of the stairwell. No discernible meaning can be ascribed to the sounds.

Then there is a second whoosh of wind and sunlight. The two triangles appear, only to vanish moments later. The black dot is gone. The white dot begins making its way up the stairs.

The eight men in the back row of the baseball team photograph are all between the ages of twenty-four and thirty-two. Ballplayers one thru seven are the core of the Almendares team that wins the 1959 Caribbean Series with five wins and only one loss. The series is played during the week of February 10-15 in Caracas, Venezuela. The four teams in the series are Almendares (Cuba), Coclé (Panama), Santurce (Puerto Rico), and Oriente (Venezuela). Ballplayer number one is right-fielder Carlos Paula. Ballplayer number two is left-fielder Sandy Amorós. Ballplayer number three is shortstop Willy Miranda. Ballplayer number four is relief pitcher Miguel Cuellar. Ballplayer number five is pitcher Cholly Naranjo. Ballplayer number six is pitcher Camilo Pascual. Ballplayer number seven is pitcher Orlando Peña. Ballplayer number eight does not make the trip to Venezuela. The exhibition game against Mexico is the last game he plays for the Almendares club. His name is José Luis Escoraz Gallego. He is a back-up outfielder and has played center field and occasionally left for the Almendares club for the last three years. Prior to joining the Almendares club he played for Cienfuegos (1952-1954) and Santa Clara (1955). After leaving Almendares he will play for a team from Camagüey (1960-1966). In 1966, he will collapse while racing to catch a fly ball that is veering foul. Ballplayer number eight will be dead at the age of thirty-five before anyone can get to him.

Now the young woman is scrutinizing the seven photographs arranged in an irregular geometric pattern on the wall before her. It is a new wall. It is a wall in a tiny bungalow on the beach in Jacksonville, Florida. To the left of the wall there is a sliding glass door that opens up onto a sandy, grassy patio area. Beyond the patio area there is a series of sand dunes, each one topped with sea oats. Beyond the dunes lies the ocean. At one point a painting of mermaids hung on the wall now occupied by the photographs. There was a ratty old sofa beneath the painting. The young woman replaced the painting of the mermaids with the seven photographs. If you look closely at the wall you can see the outline of where the painting once hung. The young woman replaced the ratty old sofa with a mahogany writing desk. The desk stands four feet high. It is five feet in length and thirty inches deep. There is one long center drawer, eighteen inches wide, and a vertical row of three drawers on the left. The top two vertical drawers are twelve inches across by eight inches in height by two feet in depth. The bottom drawer is twelve inches across by sixteen inches in height by two feet in depth. The young woman purchased the mahogany desk at a yard sale for twenty dollars. She set the mermaid painting on the sidewalk out front of her bungalow. She set the painting against the white fence that separates her sandy front yard from the sidewalk. The bungalow is the last house before you get to the beach on a narrow street partially covered with sand. The young woman set the painting against the fence at ten in the morning. By noon it was gone.

Suddenly the latch is turned, the tumbler rotates, the deadbolt snaps back, the door opens, there is a harsh sounding click, the terror of elliptical nights suddenly vanishes, the kitchen is bathed in a soft golden glow, the liquid darkness of the hallway is intersected by a narrow beam of light.

'Hi baby girl,' says a voice.

'Hi Mommy,' says a little girl.

'I came back just to see you,' says the voice.

'Uelita said you were never coming back.'

'Uelita was wrong my little squirrel.'

'Why did you come in the back door?'

'Because I knew you'd be waiting for me, right here in the kitchen.'

'Uelita doesn't like it when I ask her where you are. She is very angry with you.'

'I know baby girl.'

Outside the moon has set. Outside the moon is glowing in the night sky. Outside it is twilight and the birds have stopped calling to each other. The little girl is straining to see something but there is nothing to see other than the single glowing globe of light and the stairway. She closes the door and goes over to the sofa and sits next to the middle-aged woman. She looks up at the middle-aged woman, her head pulled back at an extremely acute angle, as if she is just about to ask a question, but the middle-aged woman has fallen asleep.

Suddenly there is a soft sounding click and the sliding glass door opens and then closes. The young woman does not appear to notice. She is standing in front of the wall containing the seven photographs arranged in an irregular geometric pattern. She gives the first six photographs only quick, affirmatory glances. The young woman is motionless. She cannot take her eyes away from the seventh photograph.

'When did you put those up?' says a masculine voice.

'Last week,' says the young woman. 'After I got back.'

The young woman does not look away from the photograph. She does not turn around. She can see the vague, whitish reflection of a man in the glass. The man is standing directly in front of a Formica-topped counter that divides the kitchen from the living room. He is standing on the living room side in front of two bar stools. There is a bowl of green grapes in the middle of the counter. He reaches back and grabs a small bunch and begins popping grapes into his mouth.

'I've got some news for you,' says the man.

'What news?'

'I know where they went.'

The young woman remains motionless. The man pops a few more grapes into his mouth.

And then: 'She married a ballplayer,' says the young woman.

'Who?'

'My grandmother. He's somewhere in this photograph. My grandfather is. He played baseball. I never knew. I'm just not sure which one he is.'

'You don't know a whole lot about your grandfather, do you?'

'No. She never even talked about him.'

'How do you know he's in the photo?'

'I guess I don't really know. There's a note on the back from him. José Luis Escoraz Gallego. My grandfather, the Cuban baseball player. He signed the note your loving José.'

'. . . .'

'Okay, okay, so I'm guessing he's in the photo.'

The man is now in the kitchen. He opens the door of the cabinet to the right of the sink and tosses the empty grape stems into the trash. Then he plucks two glasses from the drying rack and sets them on the counter, turns, opens the refrigerator and pulls out a plastic pitcher of water, turns again and fills each glass, turns again and puts the pitcher back in the refrigerator. It is a basic white refrigerator made by Frigidaire, approximately seventy inches in height, thirty inches wide, and thirty-two inches deep, resulting in a total capacity (refrigerator and freezer) of twenty cubic feet. It has three glass shelves and three bins and two humidity controlled crispers and an ice-maker that doesn't work.

The young woman is now sitting at the counter. She picks up one of the glasses and begins to sip slowly.

'So where did they go?'

'Miami.'

'And how do you know this, Ed?'

'I can't tell you that! If I told you, I'd have to kill you.'

'Oh, Ed! Will you be serious.'

The young woman drinks the rest of her water, but all the while she is watching Ed over the rim of her glass.

'So do you want to know or not?'

The young woman does not respond right away. Ed pours her a second glass, but she does not react.

And then: 'Yes, Ed, yes, of course I want to know.'

'I thought so.'

Outside it has begun to drizzle. It has finished drizzling. Outside it is sunny. The streaming sunlight resembles a bead curtain made of overlapping strands of sparkling yellow beads.

'Hi Mommy,' says a little girl.

'I came back just to see you.'

'Uelita said you were never coming back.'

'Uelita was wrong my little squirrel.'

The little girl is straining to see something but there is nothing to see other than the single glowing globe of light and the stairway. She closes the door and goes over to the sofa and sits next to the middle-aged woman. She looks up at the middle-aged woman, her head pulled back at an extremely acute angle, as if she is just about to ask a question, but the middle-aged woman has fallen asleep. Then little girl lays her head in the lap of the middle-aged woman and begins to cry.

'I tracked them to a small café in Little Havana. The owner died when they were there. His wife said they were with him when he died. Can you imagine that?'

'. . . .'

'We can leave first thing in the morning, if you like. Or we can wait till next week, or the week after that. Whenever you want to go.'

'. . . .'

'You don't think I'd let you go down there all by yourself, do you?'

Suddenly there is a soft sounding click and the sliding

glass door opens and then closes. The young woman does not appear to notice. She is standing in front of the wall containing the seven photographs arranged in an irregular geometric pattern. She gives the first six photographs only quick, affirmatory glances. The young woman is motionless. She cannot take her eyes away from the seventh photograph.

-154-

The day before the young women leaves to go to Miami, she pulls out twenty-nine postcards (4x6 each) that she keeps in the center drawer of her mahogany desk. All of them are addressed to 'my young bearded compadre,' or some variation thereof. All of them are signed by someone who calls himself 'Mick.' The young woman has read these postcards over and over again simply because they are addressed to the bearded compadre, her one and only love, or so she has always thought. When she reads them she can actually feel his presence behind her, his arms holding her close, his head resting on her shoulder, reading every other word and nibbling on her ear. These postcards are her only link to his presence, as illusory as that link may be. She has never shared these postcards with her friend, Ed. If you asked her why she has kept them to herself, she would probably pretend she didn't hear you. Perhaps they have become a symbol of her most secret hopes.

The postcards are arranged in sequential order by the date on which they were written. In those instances where there are multiple postcards written on a single date, they are further delineated by a Roman numeral indicating the order in which they are to be read. It almost seems as if the author of the postcards did not realize how much he had to say until he found himself in the middle of saying it. Or perhaps he found it easier to send postcards instead of letters. Or perhaps he felt that the recipient of these postcards, the young bearded compadre, might not possess the patience to wade through a few overly long letters, but he certainly would be able to digest a series of brief postcards.

The first two postcards were sent a few weeks after the author arrived in Buenos Aires. The first one is a photograph of a couple dancing the Tango in front of an elegant department store with a red awning. The photograph is set inside a purple border with fancy gold lettering at the bottom that says 'Florida Street – Argentina.' The couple is surrounded by a crowd of interested onlookers who have gathered in front of the department store. There are no benches for sitting, so the onlookers are standing on the tiled sidewalk, many with their arms crossed, a few leaning against an oversized ornamental flower pot containing the sapling of an indeterminate species, all of them with expectant smiles on their faces. Just inside the ring of onlookers there is a black-haired man in a black leather jacket playing a keyboard. The dancers are in mid-stretch. The gentlemen's left leg is thrust forward while his torso is leaning backwards. The woman's right leg is thrust forward, parallel to the gentleman's left leg. Her torso is pressed up against the gentleman's right shoulder. They both appear to be looking at the tip of the gentleman's left shoe, but it is difficult to determine precisely where their gaze falls given the angle of the photographer's lens. The words on the back have no relation to what is on the front.

27 Sept. 2001 (#1)

Ah, my young bearded compadre, you would love the lively, ultra-modern city of Buenos Aires. I arrived here a few weeks ago and have immersed myself up to my eyeballs in the nightlife of this metropolis with its ceaseless humming of yellow taxis, more prevalent here than even in New York City. Every night I am dazzled by the sexy chiquitas all over the place, the spinning dark coins dancing in a glass of Hesperdina, the sidewalk cafés overflowing with the bitter conspiracies of severed lips, to steal a line or two of poetry from a poet I only just discovered, a poet the world has forgotten, a long-dead Argentine named Raúl Manrique, who apparently knew Neruda and García Lorca.

Your friend and irrepressible partner in crime, Mick

The second postcard is a photograph of the monument to General José de San Martín located in a plaza by the same name in the Retiro neighborhood of Buenos Aires. The photograph is somewhat stylized, or perhaps the image has been overexposed. The statue of the General on his horse is a silhouette set against the backdrop of a glowing yellow sky. The silhouettes of seventeen small birds, most likely pigeons, are roosting on the head of the horse and on the General's right arm, which is pointing towards the Andes, as well as on top of his helmet. A few birds have taken up positions on the horse's hindquarters. The words at the bottom of the postcard say 'Plaza San Martin De Tours.' Again, there is no relation between the photo on the front and the words on the back.

27 Sept. 2001 (#2)

Raúl Manrique died in 1966 in an insane asylum in Salta, Argentina, in the northwestern corner of the country, and now practically no one has even heard of him. I bought a copy of his only book, a slim volume called Rebirth, to commemorate my own rebirth. It's a shame we are all eventually headed towards oblivion, but Manrique offers us some hope out of the fucking nightmare we've created for ourselves. Here is the title poem from his collection, which I thought you might contemplate, my young aimless friend.

Night falls./ The mosaic is broken/ By the tremors that/ Lull us to/ Sleep./ The crickets climb/ Onto their/ Leaf covered/ Pedestals./ This ancient pre-Greek chorus/ Sings the world back/ Into existence./ (Repeat).

Your friend and irrepressible partner in crime, Mick

The remaining twenty-seven postcards are all typical touristy postcards depicting various tourist hot spots in Buenos Aires and other Argentine cities as well as some of the natural beauty of Argentina. These scenes, which are delineated in no particular order, include the mountains near San Salvador, the dark forests of Ushuaia, a theatre on Calle Santa Fe in Buenos Aires, a café overlooking the Rio de la Plata, a fancy memorial in The Recoleta Cemetery, a vintage photograph taken in 1932 of Victoria Ocampo, publisher of a literary magazine called *Sur*, a vintage photograph of the Argentine minesweeper *The Drummond*, a white falcon flying over the Andes, the dusty streets of the city of San Crisóbal, a festival in Mendoza with people dancing the chacerera, a Quechua village, a river valley in the middle of Salta province, a painting commemorating General Belgrano's victory at the Battle of Tucumán in 1812, several notable Cathedrals, a concert in Luna Park, a vintage photograph of Edgardo Donato (a popular tango composer and orchestra leader from the 1940s), a passenger train pulling into Del Parque train station in Buenos Aires in 1879, the Perito Moreno Glacier, a herd of guanacos grazing in Torres Del Paine National Park, and the penguins of Puerto San Julián. Again, the words written on the backs of the postcards bear little or no relation to the images on the front. The story of the twenty-seven postcards is as follows:

11 Oct. 2001 (#1)

Ah, my young bearded compadre, yesterday I met a man named Angelo Rivero, who hails from Puerto San Julián, a very small seaside town located in the heart of Patagonia, exactly where I'm headed, some 2100 kilometers south of the capital, and 650 kilometers Northwest of the Falkland Islands. Angelo is a hairdresser with an international reputation, or so he said. His is a rags-to-riches story, and I for one believe him. Why shouldn't I? He said he left San Julián in 1980 for the bright city lights of Buenos Aires. He was a dirt-poor vagabond, but he found a job sweeping up the hair in a fancy salon on Avenida de Mayo, a block from where it intersects Avenida Julio. Of course after a few weeks he decided he wanted to be a hair stylist, but the fat man in charge of the fancy salon only laughed when he brought up the subject.

Your friend and irrepressible partner in crime, Mick

11 Oct. 2001 (#2)

Then one day Angelo learned there was going to be a hair styling competition sponsored by the Organisation Mondial de la Coiffure. This outfit is headquartered in Paris, but their tentacles are all over the world. According to Angelo you have to play by their rules if you want to get anywhere in the hair-styling business. Anyway, Angelo's boss said he was going to enter the competition, so Angelo said maybe he would give it a try, but again, his boss only laughed. But since anyone could enter, Angelo said to himself, why not? So he entered, and he won, of all things, and because of his victory he was invited to France to go to school to learn all there is to know about hair styling and to be mentored by the greatest hair stylists of the day.

Your friend and irrepressible partner in crime, Mick

11 Oct. 2001 (#3)

Angelo declined. Good old Angelo is a revolutionary, a rebel. He is a man after my own heart. He had no interest in rubbing shoulders with the big shots and decided to go to New York City and open his own salon, which he did. He has a salon in the Village, on West 10th, though he is hardly ever there.

Your friend and irrepressible partner in crime, Mick

11 Oct. 2001 (#4)

I am sure some of what Angelo told me was obviously fabrication, like the story he told about going to the Falkland Islands, but what the fuck. We are all desperate revolutionaries making up myths about ourselves so we can forget about our failures. He told me that before he left for New York City he went back to San Julián to say goodbye to his mother and for some reason or other they went to the Falklands. Maybe they went just because they had never been before, and since Angelo was leaving and his mother was getting on in years, they might never get another chance. Angelo said they arrived in Stanley, the capital, two days before the strangely absurd war to liberate the people of the Falkland Islands began.

Your friend and irrepressible partner in crime, Mick

11 Oct. 2001 (#5)

Angelo and his mother were staying in a hotel along the waterfront, a block from Christ Church Cathedral. Then early on the morning of their second night there, the Argentine army invaded and all hell broke loose. Angelo said he woke up to the sound of gunfire. He later learned that a platoon of the Buzo Tactico had come ashore at a place called Mullet Creek, a few miles south of the town, and shot up an empty British Marine barracks. As citizens of Argentina, they were in no danger once the battle was over. They headed back to the mainland the next day in a Special Forces helicopter.

Your friend and irrepressible partner in crime, Mick

11 Oct. 2001 (#6)

The whole story sounded pretty farfetched, but you could tell by the way Angelo's eyes were bulging with excitement that he, at least, believed it was an actual memory. But who knows? Perhaps it happened just like he said it did. Perhaps the only reason the rest of us dumb fucks can't see the truth is because it occurred in a place we cannot understand. Ah, if only the Argentine Special Forces had kicked the British out for good. But it's the same old story, the same characters. It doesn't matter if it's happening today or in 1982 or two thousand years ago. It doesn't matter if it's the British or the Nazis or the fucking American police state. It's almost impossible to dislodge the fuckers once they get a foothold. I'm sure you can guess the first question that came to my mind when Angelo told me his story. What the fuck are the British doing in the Falkland Islands anyway? Fucking Fascists!

Your friend and irrepressible partner in crime, Mick

11 Oct. 2001 (#7)

I asked Angelo why he was back in Buenos Aires since his salon was in New York. He said he likes to come back every few years, just to walk on his native soil. He said for him that is the only way to be sure that Argentina still exists. He talked some more about how successful his salon has become. The actor James Gandolfini is one of his regular clients, and a number of other Hollywood types. But the most distinguished head he ever worked on belonged to the writer Jorge Borges. He said this happened in 1985.

Your friend and irrepressible partner in crime, Mick

11 Oct. 2001 (#8)

Angelo said one afternoon a woman came into his salon and asked where he was from and her eyes lit up when he told her. She said he needed to come with her right away and cut the hair of a very famous Argentine writer who was visiting New York and wanted a haircut before having his picture taken. The famous writer was Jorge Borges. But Borges wasn't interested in just any hair stylist. He wanted one who came from Argentina. So the woman took Angelo by the arm and they headed out the door. He barely had a moment to grab a small leather satchel that contained a pair of scissors, combs of various lengths with teeth of various sizes, many with a tortoise shell finish, several small mirrors, and a pair of clippers. Angelo said there was a demure elegance about this woman that he simply could not resist. She wore a simple white dress and beige pumps and a matching purse, a very simple almost pedestrian outfit, but she carried herself with extraordinary grace, as if she were nobility.

Your friend and irrepressible partner in crime, Mick

11 Oct. 2001 (#9)

They took a cab from Angelo's salon to a high-rise hotel on the Upper East Side, a painfully slow forty-minute trip. Then they took a sleek chrome elevator to the 9th floor, and just like that Angelo was cutting the hair of Jorge Borges and the two were chatting away like old friends. Borges said the women of Argentina were symbols of the ineffable center, which brings men together, but in the rest of the world, women were simply distractions, and Angelo agreed.

Your friend and irrepressible partner in crime, Mick

11 Oct. 2001 (#10)

Then Borges told an enigmatic story about a street-corner flower vendor who had lost his sense of smell as a young boy but somehow possessed the uncanny ability to arrange a floral bouquet on a moment's notice so that the mix of fragrances was perfectly suited to the personal idiosyncrasies of the recipient of the flowers, as well as to whatever situation (a first date, an apology, an illness, a first communion, a graduation) demanded a bouquet in the first place.

Your friend and irrepressible partner in crime, Mick

11 Oct. 2001 (#11)

Angelo said the haircut lasted forty-five minutes, which was half an hour longer than was actually necessary given how little hair Borges actually possessed, but it was the ritual that mattered. It was like being initiated into a secret society, Angelo said. Then there was a knock at the door and Borges stood up and said 'Maria, he is here,' and the woman rushed to the door and let in the photographer, and Angelo left.

Your friend and irrepressible partner in crime, Mick

11 Oct. 2001 (#12)

Angelo said Borges was very well dressed. He wore a dark suit, a white shirt, a dark tie with a floral pattern, and he carried a thick wooden cane, but the photographer, a man named Ferdinando Scianna, was, according to Angelo, a jubilant, unshaven, slovenly fellow in a wrinkled beige suit with a blue shirt and no tie whatsoever. By contrast, Borges was immaculate in his appearance, but this photographer looked as if he had slept in his clothes. It seemed ironic to Angelo. Then Angelo was finished with his story, so I asked him how long before he was heading back to the States and if I would get a chance to see him again, but he said he was leaving the very next morning. But he did give me the address of his mother in San Julián and said if I ever made it down that way I should look her up. She would surely welcome me with open arms.

Your friend and irrepressible partner in crime, Mick

6 Nov. 2001

Ah, my young bearded compadre, I arrived safely in the city of Bahía Blanca two days ago. I'm not sure what I was thinking, but this city is not the sleepy village I had assumed it must be. Its architecture alone rivals that of many European cities. Today I stumbled across a statue of Giuseppe Garibaldi, the first great Italian Fascist. Unlike the Garibaldi statue in Buenos Aires, which depicts a tense general on a bronze stallion, the Garibaldi in Bahía Blanca is much more relaxed. He is standing erect, a sword by his side, but he has doffed his hat in what appears to be a very relaxed manner, as if he is waving to a crowd of adoring fans. He is the conquering hero come home. Don't these people realize who Garibaldi was? How can Argentina ever hope to escape the despair of fascism if they glorify such a man?

Your friend and irrepressible partner in crime, Mick

8 Nov. 2001

Ah, my young bearded compadre, it appears I have also harbored a few misconceptions about the presence of organized religion in the Argentine hinterland. The region is overrun with Christians, many of them quite fanatic, and they have been here for well over a century. In fact, thanks mainly, I suspect, to the Jesuits, one cannot separate religion from politics, politics from economics, economics from the hegemony of the social elite, and the social elite from religion. It is incredibly incestuous, a never ending incestuous cycle. Do you know, my young friend, that in the 1890s a French company began constructing a railroad from Rosario, a city of the Pampas, to Bahía Blanca. The Jesuits were the majority stockholder in this railroad company, so they controlled everything that came into the region. No wonder the Catholic Church is so fucking rich.

Your friend and irrepressible partner in crime, Mick

22 Nov. 2001

Ah, my young bearded compadre, I have arrived in Puerto San Julián, the home of Angelo Rivero's mother. I was searching for the mythic and historical center of Patagonia, and here it is. I am astonished, but then I am not all that astonished. From the moment I boarded the bus I felt like I had slipped through a door into another dimension. They put a movie on for those passengers who needed something to ease the monotony of long distances. But I didn't bother with the movie. The strange, flat landscape drifting by was my movie. It is an immense prehistoric landscape, which I am sure has baffled mankind for centuries. The laws of physics do not seem to apply. The few trees you notice all seem to be growing upside down. And the birds all seem to be flying backwards. Then the sun began to set and the sky began to glow with a strange mixture of orange and yellow. I am sure I slept, but I don't remember. We pulled into Puerto San Julián just as a gray dawn was filtering up over the horizon. I had the feeling that I was a young soul finally come of age, heeding the call of the Universe.

Your friend and irrepressible partner in crime, Mick

27 Nov. 2001 (#1)

Angelo Rivero's mother is a heavy-set woman with dark gray hair (cut very close, as if she were a nun) and rounded features, a rounded chin with a prominent dimple, rounded cheeks, a rounded nose that flares out. I could see Angelo's face in the face of his mother, but I hadn't realized that my rebel of a hairdresser was descended from the indigenous peoples of Patagonia until I saw Mrs. Rivero in the flesh. She told me that she and her son were descended from the ancient Mapuche tribe, that they were distant cousins of the Tequenica to the south thanks to a wayward uncle, and that her great-grandmother also claimed that their family was descended from the Tehuelches, who occupied Patagonia when the first Europeans arrived.

Your friend and irrepressible partner in crime, Mick

27 Nov. 2001 (#2)

Now when Angelo said his mother would welcome me with open arms, I assumed that meant she would invite me over to her house for dinner and that she would cook some fabulous, native dish. This has not been the case. She lives on a quiet, unassuming street of small one-story houses, all of them painted in soft pastels, light yellows, light blues, light greens, and also white. On each of my three visits to her house we have then walked two blocks to a corner restaurant called Casa Lara. It is a gray one-story building not much different than the surrounding houses, except for the name, and the fact that the doors and the trim around the windows and also the roof are all painted red. It is the only red roof I have seen anywhere in San Julián.

Your friend and irrepressible partner in crime, Mick

18 Dec. 2001 (#1)

Ah, my young bearded compadre, yesterday I met an old man in a small café near the waterfront. Not Casa Lara. I have not been there in over a week. I was sitting at a small table eating crabs and drinking white wine and he sat down opposite me with a plate and bottle of his own. He said his name was don Justo Leandro Ramirez. I am sure he is an escaped lunatic who has been hiding out in the wilds of Patagonia. He had been sitting in the corner opposite my table, watching me. He said he was seeking a home for his granddaughter. I am not sure I believed him at first, especially since there was no granddaughter in sight.

Your friend and irrepressible partner in crime, Mick

18 Dec. 2001 (#2)

Don Justo is a small man with a very large, round head, bald at the top, a gleaming brown pate made all the more radiant by streaming white hair flowing down from the sides and the back of his head. He resembles a gnome, especially when he smiles and shows his cracked teeth. After he told me of his mission, we ate our crabs and drank our wine. We ate in complete silence. Later, after we had finished eating, don Justo said the bay has the same name as the town, San Julián. Magellan himself named the bay in honor of all those intrepid explorers who wandered the earth. This was in 1520. He and his band were the first Europeans to set foot on Patagonian soil. They said a Mass on the beach to commemorate the significance of the name. Then Magellan executed the chief architects of a mutiny that had threatened the unity of his expedition, and left their bodies, still swinging on a hastily built gallows, to rot on a small rocky spit of land on the other side of the bay.

Your friend and irrepressible partner in crime, Mick

18 Dec. 2001 (#3)

The moment after don Justo finished his story about Magellan, he stood up and in a magnificent theatrical voice he said 'His art is of such power,/ It would control my dam's god Setebos/ And make a vassal of him.' Then he looked at me squarely in the eye and said again he was seeking a home for his granddaughter. He said he specifically chose San Julián because of the name. He will only give his granddaughter into the capable hands of an intrepid wanderer like himself. He said he will bring her to this tiny café along the waterfront on the following evening, in case I am interested in meeting her. I think I have finally met my match in don Justo. Sadly, my knowledge of history and religion is too fucking inadequate to fully appreciate the nuances of his wisdom.

Your friend and irrepressible partner in crime, Mick

20 Dec. 2001 (#1)

Ah, my young bearded compadre, fate has come full circle. Yesterday around seven in the evening I went to the waterfront café where I had met don Justo. He was sitting at the same table, eating the same meal, drinking the same wine. It was almost as if he was reliving the same day. But the moment I sat down across from him, a woman with a child, a young girl, approached and sat to his left. The girl was maybe ten years old, very black hair, the same rounded, pleasant features that most of the citizens of San Julián possess.

She also possessed bright, amber-colored eyes and an irrepressibly mischievous laugh. She was constantly poking don Justo in the ribs, trying to get him to laugh, but he was stoic in his silence and kept munching his crabs. So I started talking with the woman, the young girl's mother. I wondered if she was don Justo's daughter or daughter-in-law. I wondered if the don was giving both of them away.

Your friend and irrepressible partner in crime, Mick

20 Dec. 2001 (#2)

Ah, my young bearded compadre, what can I say, this woman sitting across from me is a goddess. I know I have spent my miscreant life talking about paradise and fucking beautiful woman and eating raw fish plucked out of the sea and that's why I headed down to Patagonia in the first place, but the moment I look into this woman's eyes I know it's all bullshit, and what's more, I know that she knows it's all bullshit, and the crazy thing is I haven't told her a thing about me. Her name is Lidia Batarev. She has dark hair like her daughter, only hers is braided in the back, a very long braid, and she has bright, amber-colored eyes and a mischievous laugh like her daughter, and her face radiates with a strange, resilient, impossible joy, as if she has finally and forever defeated those inner demons that haunt us all. She looks at me as if she has waited her entire life to sit across from me at a narrow wooden table in a waterfront café in Puerto San Julián, Argentina.

Your friend and irrepressible partner in crime, Mick

20 Dec. 2001 (#3)

Lidia and I talked about the strangest things. She described how she had defeated her inner demons by wandering the earth until their grip on her weakened and they fell by the wayside, too tired to continue the journey. She said the only reason she could think of for acquiring possessions was to give them away. She said when her brother died her mother took all of his clothes and wrapped them up in a beautiful red áschjen, a blanket. Then she did the same thing with his possessions. Then she lit a funeral fire and burnt both bundles. The family chanted ancient songs while the flames soared. Afterwards, her mother wrapped the body of her dead son in another red áschjen that had been especially prepared by Lidia and her sisters, and laid him in a grave. Later, they sprinkled silver coins and sparkling beads of glass on the grave. Lidia said she left her childhood home the day after they buried her brother.

Your friend and irrepressible partner in crime, Mick

20 Dec. 2001 (#4)

After the story of her brother's burial, Lidia asked me if I had ever read the poetry of Raúl Manrique and I said that I had and she smiled softly and said she was sure that I had. She said her favorite poem of his is called 'Surrendering,' and then she began to recite it. The silence between words/ Shimmers like a row of mirrors./ I cannot tell one stray thought from/ Another until I close my eyes./ Only then/ Do I know/ Myself.' Then we talked about the early Spanish explorers and the missionaries and the lofty promises they made to the indigenous peoples of Argentina. We talked about the vineyards of Mendoza and drinking Malbec wine. She asked me if I had ever danced the loncomeo, and I confessed that I had not. She said it was a most beautiful dance. She would find someone to teach me, or she would teach me herself if I wanted. Then don Justo was finished with his meal and the four of us left the café with a purposeful abruptness. Don Justo wanted me to accompany them to an abandoned factory on the edge of town, where they were camping.

Your friend and irrepressible partner in crime, Mick

20 Dec. 2001 (#5)

The factory where they were camping had a wonderful view of the sea, but it looked like a bombed-out building. It was three stories high, but only the brown brick foundation was completely intact. The ancient walls were an orangish rust color and seemed to be made of plywood reinforced with sections of corrugated tin, and there were only jagged holes where there had once been windows and doors. Lidia and her daughter went immediately into the darkness of the building's interior and lit a small fire, but don Justo took me to the edge of the sea and we sat down on a cement slab that had once been part of a loading dock. The stars were very bright, but for some reason I could barely make out don Justo's features. Then he asked me what I thought of his granddaughter, and I said I didn't really know what to think, she seemed like a nice enough little girl, but I was really much more interested in his daughter. He cocked his head at an odd angle and burst out laughing. Then he put his arm around me and said that Lidia was his granddaughter. She is the one who needs a home.

Your friend and irrepressible partner in crime, Mick

20 Dec. 2001 (#6)

My compadre, I must confess now that for once in my life I didn't know what to say, so I let don Justo do the talking. He said the little girl was the granddaughter of the man who owned the abandoned factory. That man's name was Andrés Buñuel. He had come to San Julián in 1927 with a group of political exiles that included Carlos Martín Noel, a writer and radical thinker who had once been the Mayor of Buenos Aires. When Noel and the others left in 1928, Andrés stayed behind and built a refrigerator factory. His refrigerators were once sold all over the world. His granddaughter's name is María Portolés. The two granddaughters have become great friends in only one week. Don Justo said any physical resemblance between the two was coincidental. Then he paused and looked up at the sky and without breaking his gaze he said 'Tonight we listen to the southern wind, the one that is born in the cold.' Then we joined Lidia and the little girl.

Your friend and irrepressible partner in crime, Mick

27 Dec. 2001

Ah, my compadre, what can I add to this fantastic story that you have not already surmised. When I woke the next morning don Justo and the little girl were gone. I am sure Lidia had been up for a few hours, but she acted as if she had only just opened her eyes. We drank some dark coffee and ate a small breakfast. I don't even know what we ate. All I know is that from that moment on, Lidia and I have been inseparable. I am wondering if don Justo knew this would happen. Then I am wondering if I have come down with some kind of strange Patagonian madness. If so, I hope I never recover. Lidia wants to head down to Ushuaia, and from there, only God knows.

Your friend and irrepressible partner in crime, Mick

-155-

Now the young woman and her friend, Ed, are getting into a sky-blue Buick for the drive to Miami. The drive down is uneventful. She is staring out the window, at the strange, flat landscape flashing by. It is very windy and the birds seem to be flying backwards. Even the trees seem to be growing upside down or sideways. The laws of physics do not seem to apply. Then the sun begins to set. The sky begins to glow with a strange mixture of orange and yellow. She feels like she has been dreaming, but Ed assures her that she has been awake the whole way down.

Now they are a block away from their destination, a

twelve-story hotel at the beach. The hotel is actually two perfectly square, twelve-story towers, one with an unimpeded view of the ocean on the east side and a distorted view of Collins Avenue on the west side, the other with a distorted view of the ocean on the east side and an unimpeded view of Collins Avenue on the west side.

The towers are connected by a narrow two-story structure, about half the width of the towers, which contains the hotel lobby, an area for storing guest luggage, a small restaurant which only serves breakfast, a small meeting area on the mezzanine level, and an elevator bay at each end. The elevators all possess essentially the same panel of choices. L for Lobby, M for Mezzanine, 1E or 1W thru 12E or 12W, depending upon the tower, for the floors containing guest rooms, and G for the garage (the elevators from each tower open up to identical covered walkways crossing over an alley, connecting to the third floor of a cement parking garage, where many of the guests park their cars). The garage is a three-story structure on the opposite (northern) side of the hotel. To reach the garage by car, one must head out to Collins Avenue, drive half a block north, and then turn right down a narrow service road to the garage entrance. The outdoor pool is accessed by going to the Mezzanine level of the East tower and heading out past a small fitness center through a sliding glass door. The first floor of guest rooms is twelve feet above the level of the pool.

The main entrance to the lobby is a revolving door that opens up onto a semi-circular macadam walkway made with blue and brown pebbles. The walkway parallels a semi-circular asphalt driveway that leads from and then back to the street. On the other side of the driveway, there is a second macadam walkway, a shorter version of the first. A large fountain with three gleaming golden dolphins spitting out water sits in the grassy half-circle framed by the second walkway and the street. At night, sixteen small spotlights, each roughly eight inches in diameter, illuminate the dolphins and their ceaseless stream of water. Six of the spotlights are red, five are blue, and five are yellow. Since the spotlights are all positioned at varying angles, the beams of light intersect, producing tiny splashes of color at the points of intersection, purples and oranges and greens and subdued violets, which seem to give an added dimension to both the bubble of swirling water and the gleaming golden dolphins forever trapped inside the bubble. The fountain is a happy distraction for hotel guests on their way out to dinner or just returning.

Ed suddenly realizes how close they are and makes a quick right, turning onto a small side street used only by traffic going to or from the hotel. He drives roughly one-hundred-and-fifty feet and makes a left onto the semi-circular asphalt driveway with carefully manicured curb appeal that wraps around the fountain. At the mid-point of the driveway, which is fifty-two feet from the point of entry, there is a small sign that says 'Please stop for valet service!' Ed stops the car but no valet appears, so he gets out and heads over to a small desk positioned at a precise forty-five-degree angle in relation to the revolving doors. After a few moments, a bellhop wearing a yellow jacket with blue stripes and pants to match (but no cap) appears as if from nowhere. He and Ed talk for a moment and then Ed points to the sky-blue Buick and hands the bellhop the car keys. Then he motions for the young woman to join him. The bellhop is already unloading their luggage, which consists of two medium-sized suitcases, a vanity case, and an over-stuffed beach bag, as the young woman and Ed pass through the revolving doors into the lobby.

Now the young woman is standing in the back bedroom of a two-room suite on the ninth floor, her face pressed up against a sliding glass door which opens up onto a balcony. It is dark inside the room. Outside it is twilight and the birds have stopped calling to each other. Outside the moon is glowing in the night sky. Outside the moon has set. A single brightly glowing light post, partially obscured by the foliage of various shrubs, sea grapes perhaps, and also a few palm trees, illuminates a twenty-foot section of the elevated boardwalk that runs parallel to the beach. The streaming light post light resembles a bead curtain made of overlapping strands of dazzling white beads, a very bright white. There are dozens of similar light posts spaced every thirty feet or so, illuminating twenty-foot sections all along the boardwalk. Beyond the boardwalk lies the beach, and beyond the beach lies the comforting darkness of the ocean. The dim green running lights of a boat flash on the horizon, a shrimp boat perhaps, some kind of fishing boat, or maybe it is a pleasure boat, but from inside the ninth-floor two-room suite, even with one's face pressed up against the glass of the sliding glass door, it is impossible to tell. The boardwalk below is empty. The entire world seems uninhabited.

The elevated wooden boardwalk is a good forty-two inches or more off the ground. For most of its length it is twelve feet wide and composed of twenty-four rows of wooden planks. The planks are no longer uniform in length given the various patch jobs over the years. They range in length from six feet to twelve feet. Nor is the degree to which the wood has weathered been consistent. But that's to be expected given the fact that the boardwalk is roughly two miles in length, which means that approximately 26,000 planks were used in its initial construction. Only God knows how many more have been used to replace those which have become rotten.

The railing is composed of thicker wooden planks bolted to wooden posts which occur every five feet. The posts are eight inches by eight inches by four feet high. The tops are beveled, but the sides are quite rough, as if someone had shaped them with an axe. The paint is a dull brown color. It is difficult to say how often the rails have been replaced. Not as often as the planks of the boardwalk, but clearly the quality of the wood used for the rails has degraded in many places, especially where the brown paint has begun to flake away, exposing the raw grain beneath.

It is easy to see the worn spots in the boardwalk from the ninth floor given the bright white lamp light of the various light posts. It is almost as if someone has polished the worn spots with an oil cloth to enhance their visibility. In contrast, it is impossible to see the degree to which the rails have degraded, especially at night. (It is worth noting that the idea of upgrading or replacing the wooden portion of the boardwalk, the rails included, is an ongoing topic of informal discussions in cafés and restaurants up and down Collins Avenue; and yet in spite of so much public discourse, the city of Miami Beach will not take any formal action for many years to come.)

If you are looking up at the hotel from the portion of the boardwalk directly in front, it is hard to get a good bead on what you are actually looking at. For one thing, there is too much vegetation in the way, sea grapes with their squiggly vine-like branches and overlapping grape leaves, as well inkberry and palmetto and a few palm trees. It is a darkening sea of vegetation that extends perhaps twenty feet towards the hotel and ends at a concrete wall. There is no direct light source to illuminate the concrete wall, so it is impossible to see at night. If you possessed a flashlight, or if the moon were particularly bright, you might notice a blue metal door on the southeast corner of the wall and a narrow gravel path leading away from the door and around the corner, heading back in the direction of the hotel along another concrete wall, perpendicular to the first. The door would seem to be embedded in the concrete. It would be difficult to determine what the door leads to, a storage area, perhaps, for maintenance equipment of some kind.

During daylight hours, the mystery of the blue door is no mystery at all. The door leads to a small room that contains various tools for maintaining the hotel's swimming pool: hoses and strainers and long poles. There are also several plastic containers containing chemicals typically used in pool maintenance and several tarps used for covering things up. The containers and the tarps are sitting on the shelves of a gray aluminum shelving unit. The unit has six shelves. Strangely, there is a thin layer of dust and grime on the shelves and on the containers and on the maintenance equipment and on the floor.

In the diffuse light of the storage room, the grime on the floor seems wet, oily. It could be mistaken for a recent blood stain. Upon closer examination, it seems as if the floor of the room contains many similar stains, dark, elliptical, oily stains, some of them overlapping, the later stains obliterating the original contours of the previous stains, as if on numerous occasions an unknown individual had knocked over a can of oil or some other substance and the dark viscous liquid had taken hours to seep into the concrete. Perhaps the hotel management no longer takes on the responsibility of cleaning its own pool. Perhaps they have hired a pool cleaning service. Perhaps they have forgotten about the room, so they have no idea who goes into it or who even has a key. Perhaps no one from the hotel has entered the small room on pool cleaning business in years.

The young woman is still standing in the back bedroom of a two-room suite on the ninth floor, her face pressed up against the sliding glass door which opens up onto the balcony. Suddenly the panel door to the bedroom swings open. The door is opposite the sliding glass door and looks as if it is made of teak but it is actually a composite material. It is the kind of interior door quite common in hotels of a certain quality.

Now a hand reaches into the room and a switch is flicked and a floor lamp begins to glow weakly, just enough to obliterate the view of the boardwalk and the darkness beyond.

But the young woman does not react to the light. Instead, she is now staring at her own face, which is devoid of all expression, except perhaps a sense of extreme fatigue. Her face seems to now possess a waxy brownish-gray color, like the color you would associate with a wax figure or a paper mâché puppet, not a flesh-and-blood person. Even her wrinkles and the puffy oval lumps beneath her tired looking eyes are precisely, artistically shaped.

The young woman remains motionless. She almost seems part of a larger photograph in which she, a young woman whose face we cannot see, is scrutinizing the photograph of a young woman who is herself scrutinizing a photograph which we cannot see.

'There you are. I was wondering where you'd gone to.'

The voice sounds happy, satisfied.

The young woman does not turn around. She can see the vague, whitish reflection of her friend, Ed, in the glass of the sliding glass door. Ed is standing just inside the doorway next to a sleek, chrome-plated floor lamp. The lamp possesses a contemporary, tubular lampshade, a pale white in color with a series of dark gray, wavy, elliptical lines, vertical lines which traverse the exterior circumference of the lampshade, producing a wavy, elliptical 360-degree pattern of light and shadow on the hardwood floor and on the walls of the room.

'We'll head out around noon,' says the voice.

Then the switch is flicked and the glow from the floor lamp is extinguished, obliterating the image of the young woman in the dark glass of the sliding glass door. Outside it is twilight and the birds have stopped calling to each other. Outside the moon is glowing in the night sky. Outside the moon has set. A single brightly glowing light post, partially obscured by the foliage of various shrubs, sea grapes perhaps, and also a few palm trees, illuminates a twenty-foot section of the elevated boardwalk that runs parallel to the beach.

-156-

Now the young woman is downstairs in the lobby, just outside the entrance to the restaurant that serves only breakfast. She is sipping, somewhat tentatively, from a

Styrofoam cup with the logo of the hotel on the sides. Perhaps the cup is filled with coffee, or perhaps tea, something hot to judge by the way the young woman is sipping. The restaurant is not overly crowded. Most of the patrons are finishing their breakfasts. An older couple, a gray-haired man followed by a middle-aged woman with mousy-colored hair, brushes past the young woman on their way into the restaurant. The young woman does not seem to notice. After the couple passes she moves two steps to the right of the entrance and stops in front of a wall made of flagstones stacked one on top of another. The flagstone wall marks the boundary between the restaurant and the lobby, but it is only three feet high, so you can see directly into the restaurant. From the entrance to the restaurant the wall travels thirty-two-feet in a diagonal direction, at which point it intersects a concrete wall that marks the boundary between the lobby and the hallway leading to the elevators servicing the West tower.

Outside it is drizzling, outside the wind is whipping up, outside it is sunny once again. Now the young woman is on the Mezzanine level of the East tower and heading down a narrow hallway past a small fitness center. The fitness center is accessed through a glass door that requires a guest key to open. The young woman continues down the hallway, past several interior doors that look as if they are made of teak but they are actually composed of a composite material. They are the kind of interior doors quite common in hotels of a certain quality.

Now the young woman is heading outside through a sliding glass door that is locked from 9 pm until 7 am. Now she is only a few feet from a set of wooden steps leading up to the swimming pool. The steps are weathered, gray in color. There is a second set of gray steps leading down to a gravel path which runs parallel to a concrete wall and then disappears around the corner to the right. The gravel path is partially obscured by the foliage of various shrubs, sea grapes perhaps, and also a few palm trees.

Now she is at the top of the steps. She is lifting the latch of a small gate about three feet high and stepping through, but then she stops. She is motionless. She is staring at the swimming pool, or perhaps she is looking beyond the pool to the metal railing on the far side of the swimming pool area. It is difficult to say. The railing is five feet high and is comprised of a series of vertical metal bars (tubular, two inches in diameter, six inches of space between each bar) capped with a horizontal bar (also tubular, three inches in diameter).

The railing runs the length of the eastern edge of the pool area, roughly one-hundred-and-twenty feet from one side to the other. Beyond the railing, there is the foliage of various shrubs. Beyond that there is the boardwalk and then the beach. A narrow concrete retaining wall about four feet high and capped with beige Venetian tile marks the northern, western, and southern edges of the swimming pool area. The only way in or out is the small gate.

The swimming pool is twenty-six feet wide by seventy-eight feet long, a perfect rectangular shape except at the shallow end, where a small portion of the rectangle opens up into a semi-oval space containing three semi-oval steps. The bottom step is nested within the second, the second within the first. At the shallow end, the pool is three feet deep, at which point, moving south to north, it begins to get progressively deeper, reaching a maximum depth of six feet. The surface surrounding the pool is made of the same macadam as the walkway in front of the hotel entrance, the same brown and blue pebbles, producing a texture designed to reduce slipping.

The young woman is now sipping from her Styrofoam cup. She is no longer so tentative in her sipping. Now she is standing along the edge of the shallow end of the pool. There is no water in the pool. Several hoses are lying across the bottom and near the now exposed center drain there is a small submersible utility pump. The pump, which is manufactured by Pentair, is no longer operating.

The young woman is now standing in the middle of the drained swimming pool. She is looking at the underwater scenes someone has painted on the sides of the pool. Actually, it is the same scene repeated again and again, all the way around the pool. In the center there are two blue bottlenose dolphins. They are realistic dolphins in every respect except for their color. Their bodies are a dappled blueish gray along the top, as if the dolphins are near the surface on a sunny day and the sunlight is shining through the water, and they are a bright blue along the sides with a dark purplish blue stripe down the middle. Their flippers, flukes and dorsal fins are all a dark purple color, like twilight, while their underbellies are whitish gray. The water above the dolphins is a teal color, except where the sunlight has made it a pale, whitish blue. The dolphins are turning away from the sunlit surface and heading for deeper water. They are moving through a random patch of tropical fish: three yellow longnose butterfly fish, two greenish-blue Queen Angelfish, and one greenish parrot fish with pink fins.

Suddenly a stern masculine voice calls out from the gate, but the young woman does not respond. She is holding her cup in her left hand and scrutinizing the dolphins. The cup seems very light in her hand. Perhaps it is empty. Then there is the sound of the gate opening and closing and a few footsteps and then the stern masculine voice calls out once more.

'The pool is closed,' says the voice.

Now the young woman is looking over towards the shallow end of the pool. A young man is standing on the semi-oval steps, one foot on the first step, the other foot on the second step. He is clean shaven but has shaggy blond hair. He is wearing an Aqua-Clean jumpsuit uniform. The name Rudi is sewn into his uniform just above the left-side chest pocket. The young woman is just about to take a step towards the shallow end, when she is distracted by something above her. She looks up, but she is nearly blinded by the noonday sun, so it is difficult to see anything specific, at least at first. The east façade of the east tower features thirty-six cantilevered balconies, three per floor, but from the perspective of the young woman, who is looking practically straight up, the cantilevered balconies seem like a series of ridges stretching towards infinity. Then she notices a dark shadowy torso leaning over the edge of one of the balconies a few floors from the top.

Now a shadowy arm extends from the shadowy torso and begins waving like mad. She perceives that the shadowy torso is calling out to her, but she cannot quite make out the words. It is almost like the shadowy torso is speaking a foreign language. Then she perceives that the torso is waiting for a response so she waves back. The words stop and the torso stops waving and disappears into the widening glare of the sun.

Now the young woman is only a few feet from the set of wooden steps leading down to the sliding glass door and the Mezzanine. The steps are a weathered, gray in color. There is a second set of gray steps leading down to a gravel path which runs parallel to a concrete wall and then disappears around the corner to the left.

The concrete wall is the southern wall of a structure that serves as the foundation for the swimming pool. This structure also houses a small storage room accessed through a blue metal door. The floor of the storage room contains dozens of dark, elliptical, oily stains, some of them overlapping, the later stains obliterating the original contours of the previous stains, as if on numerous occasions an unknown individual had knocked over a can of oil or some other substance and the dark viscous liquid had taken hours to seep into the concrete.

From the weathered gray wooden steps leading down to the gravel path it is impossible to see the blue metal door. The gravel path is partially obscured by the foliage of various shrubs, sea grapes perhaps, and also a few palm trees.

The young woman is looking at her reflection in the glass of the sliding glass door. She is motionless. She almost seems part of a larger photograph in which she, a young woman whose face we cannot see, is scrutinizing the photograph of a young woman who is herself scrutinizing a photograph which we cannot see.

'There you are,' says a voice. 'I was wondering where you'd gone to.'

The voice sounds happy, or if not happy, at least satisfied.

The young woman does not turn around. She can see the vague, whitish reflection of her friend, Ed, in the glass of the sliding glass door. Ed is standing just inside the doorway on the opposite side of the back bedroom, next to a sleek, chrome-plated floor lamp. The lamp possesses a contemporary, tubular lampshade, a dark gray in color with a series of white, wavy, elliptical lines, vertical lines which traverse the exterior circumference of the lampshade, producing a wavy, elliptical 360-degree pattern of light and shadow on the hardwood floor and on the walls of the room.

'We'll head out around noon,' says the voice. 'A café called The Patagonian Café.

-157-

The young woman and Ed are back in the sky-blue Buick, heading across the causeway. The drive from the hotel to Little Havana is uneventful. The young woman is staring out the window, at the strangely uniform landscape flashing by, a concrete landscape punctuated by flat rooftops and the tops of trees, and a few stationary clouds just above. It is almost as if the world has become an aerial photograph, a world without movement or sound. Then they are driving on a bright, clean city street in a bright, clean city neighborhood. The buildings are painted bright yellow and bright pink and there are bars on the windows. The young woman feels like she has been dreaming, but Ed assures her that she has been awake since they left the hotel.

Now they are a block away from their destination, a small café on SW Eighth Street. The café is on the first floor of a two-story corner building with plate glass windows and bright yellow awnings on the two sides facing the street. The exterior stucco walls that frame the plate glass windows are painted a bright orange. The second floor is painted bright yellow like the awnings and features two smaller windows overlooking SW Eighth Street and three slightly larger windows overlooking the side street.

Patrons enter the café through a corner plate glass door about four feet wide and seven feet high. The door frame is painted a bright yellow while the awning above the door is a bright orange. It is impossible to see through the plate glass window of the door because of the glare of the sun. It is impossible to see through any of the windows because the blinds are drawn. The blinds are a dull orangish-brown color to complement the overall color scheme. Directly above the orange awning, flat against the second floor exterior, there is a small neon sign that says 'Café Patagonia.' The sign is turned off. Or perhaps it does not work. In the bright sunlight you can barely distinguish the orange lettering from the metal frame on which the sign is mounted. The place looks like it has been deserted for years.

The sky-blue Buick is now idling near the corner of the café, about three feet from the curb. The traffic on SW Eighth Street continues whizzing by, horns blaring, probably because the rear end of the Buick is perceived as a potential hazard. The young woman is standing in front of the door. She is peering into the glass but all she can see is her own reflection. As she pushes the latch and opens the door the Buick pulls out into the street. Because of the angle of the door, we can see the image of the Buick in the glass.

The young woman steps into the café as the image of the car becomes a receding blur. The sound of a distant horn lingers in the air.

At first the interior of the café seems to be bathed in a semi-fluid darkness which gives shape to various objects but makes gauging the depth of any one object an impossible task. The café door is now closed, but the young woman remains motionless, a step or so inside. As her eyes adjust, she perceives a row of soda fountain stools up against a service counter and then a narrow dark space and then another counter running parallel to the first. Above the second counter there are three long shelves which contain dishes and cups and bowls, all made of white porcelain, all neatly stacked. The three shelves are each twelve feet in length and are perfectly centered in the middle of the wall. The second counter is illuminated, though just barely, by a string of tiny, yellow lights running along the wall just beneath the lowest shelf, like a string of Christmas lights.

To the left of the shelves there is a small utility sink and then some additional counter space and then a second wall, perpendicular to the first. This second wall contains a pick-up window, and next to the window is the door to the kitchen. The door contains a single porthole window and resembles the kind of galley door one might have found on a 19th century ocean liner. Next to the galley door is a second door that leads to a small bathroom that is rarely used. To the right of the three shelves there is empty wall space, and then a poster, and then a third wall (also perpendicular to the first) containing the shorter of the two plate glass windows, the one that faces SW Eighth Street. The poster is a vintage poster of a bullfighter, perhaps from Spain, but the details of the poster are impossible to make out. For one thing, the poster is too far away. Besides, it is too dark inside the café to be sure of anything.

Now there is the soft sound of slippered footsteps softly stepping, but the young woman does not appear to notice. She is staring at the poster of the bullfighter. If she were to turn around she would see a shadow moving from behind the counter past the kitchen door, past the second door, heading towards the longer of the two plate glass windows, a window which for all practical purposes is the entire fourth wall, and which looks out on the side street. If she were to turn around, she would see the shadow stop in the corner and start turning a slender plastic tube with her fingers.

But she does not turn around.

The slatted blinds shift slightly, allowing the afternoon

sunlight to slip into the café. The poster comes alive with vivid color, like a scene from a Technicolor movie. The young woman now sees a bullfighter with a fancy silver sword gleaming in the sun and a fancy red cape draped over one shoulder. She is motionless. The bullfighter is staring at a dead bull crumpled up at his feet with several darts sticking out of the bull's hump and blood streaming down the sides of the bull. The poster says El Cordobés, and then there is some small print which the young woman scrutinizes carefully. The smaller words indicate that this poster is advertising a bullfight that took place in the Plaza de Toros in Ibiza in July of 1967. The words do not indicate that the cape El Cordobés used during that particular bullfight was pink on one side and yellow on the other, not red, as in the poster. And of course there is no way for anyone looking at the poster to know that El Cordobés was tossed up into the air by the bull on that day, a potential tragedy to be sure, but the bullfighter was unharmed and rose up immediately from the dusty arena floor and waved his arms in the air, as if to challenge the bull to try and toss him like that again.

Now the young woman is turned towards the sunlight slipping in through the slatted blinds. She sees an older woman in her late seventies sitting at a small table for four on the opposite side of the café, in the corner up against the plate glass window. The table in the corner is the only table in the café covered with a yellow oilcloth. There are twenty-seven tables in the café, three rows of nine. Each table is five feet by five feet. Twenty-six of the twenty-seven are covered with chairs. It is not clear to the young woman how long the older woman has been sitting at the table in the opposite corner.

The older woman has placed a bottle of clear white liquid with the label Suisse La Bleue, two glasses, a bowl of sugar cubes, a covered pitcher of ice water, and two slotted spoons in the center of the table. The glasses are already filled with a hazy, whitish, milky liquid, presumably the liquid from the bottle after it has been transformed by the sugar cubes. Now the older woman is peering out through the narrow crevices of the now partially open slatted blinds. Perhaps she has heard a strange sound from outside. As the young woman sits down the older woman turns away from the window, tilting her head to one side, and smiles.

'Did you have any trouble finding us?'

'No, no trouble.'

'I should tell you I have not thought about your two friends for many, many months.

'. . .'

'I should tell you I have thought about them every single day.'

'. . .'

'I do not know how much help I will be to you. You are trying to find your way back to the younger one, no?'

'. . .'

'Do not worry, he has not forgotten you. He will never forget you. He spoke of you often.'

The older woman raises her glass again and encourages the younger women to do the same.

They drink.

They seem like mirror images of each other.

'What water brings, water takes away,' says the older woman.

The younger woman is lip-syncing as the older woman speaks, a silent reflection, as if she is trying to commit the words to memory.

Now the sunlight slipping in through the slatted blinds has taken on a softer hue. The bottle of Suisse La Bleue is half empty. So are the glasses. The older woman is baring her soul. The younger woman thinks she is only a passive listener, but just the fact that she is listening has visibly lifted the older woman's spirits. It is a miraculous transformation. The older woman actually seems to have grown younger in the process of telling her story. The two women now seem identical in age.

The older woman's story is somewhat difficult to follow, which means the younger woman loses the narrative thread every so often and has to scramble mentally to make sense of what she is hearing.

The story begins in Spain.

The older woman says the story of her family is tangled up with the many stories of revolution and war that have shaped Spain's history. Her great-great-grandfather, Xavier Ortiz de Urbina, fought with Tomás de Zumalacárregui y de Imaz during the First Carlist War. But then Zumalacárregui died from a bullet wound in 1835. He had been shot in the calf on the steps of the Basílica de Nuestra Señora de Begoña, 'with its ancient Gothic tower gleaming in the sunlight like the fossilized bones of a wingless behemoth from before the Fall,' this is how the older woman describes it. He later succumbed to infection. Her great-great-grandfather had settled in Vera de Bidasoa after the disappointment of Zumalacárregui's death and renounced the outside world.

Her own grandfather, Xavier Ortiz de Urbina Mendoza, was killed by accident (an innocent bystander who had stepped unwittingly from a small café into a hail of bullets) on May 17, 1924 in a skirmish in the streets of Vera de Bidasoa between the Civil Guard and three anonymous anarchists (who may have been Bolshevik rabble rousers, as the newspaper accounts of the day suggested, but were more likely young students from Madrid distributing propaganda to the working classes for the Spanish socialists, who had broken with the Russians in 1921).

Her father, Xavier Mendoza Vda De Miranda, moved to the small border village of Elzaurdia after that. She does not say why. Perhaps to escape the memory of his father's death. But he could not escape the violence that plagued the country. In 1931, after the Republic was re-established, she overheard her father speaking with a man she did not know. Her father said: 'The swallows did not fly to Maule from Aragon or Navarre this year.' The other man said: "Yes, it is a bad sign. Even Bernabé says so.'

A few weeks later her father joined with the Basque Nationalists, and then when war broke out in 1936, he fought with the very famous Lieutenant Antonio Ortega, who was in command of the Carbineer Headquarters in Vera de Bidasoa and who sided with the Republic. They engaged in guerrilla activities as they retreated towards San Sebastián, blowing up the bridges at Endarlaza and Goizueta to stall the Nationalist advance, but they did not achieve the results they had hoped for. Two months later San Sebastián fell and the older woman's father returned to Elzaurdia. He began guiding refugees across the border into France. She says her father had only disdain for those who made up the International Brigades and the Russians.

'Why are they here?' he would say. 'This is not their fight; it is our fight. And the fighting is already finished in the north. I do not care what happens in the other parts of Spain.'

Then in June 1937, after almost a year of the war, he learned that a Lt. Col. José Cabello had executed his mother, Isabel Escoraz Vda De Miranda. She had been accused of working for the Republicans against the Nationalists, so they had taken her out into the woods and this colonel had shot her. Her body had been dumped in a ravine, it was said, but her remains were never found. And the colonel, who knows, maybe he was later killed, maybe he survived. But from that point on, her father had lost his appetite for war. He became a drunk instead. Her brother, Xavier, who had accompanied their father on many a journey over the mountains, took charge of the never-ending deluge of refugees. She says he was the youngest of the clandestine guides.

Now the bottle of Suisse La Bleue and the empty glasses have been cleared away. The older woman has returned from the counter with a tray containing two cups of very strong coffee and two small plates each containing two small pastries covered in chopped almonds, hazelnuts and powdered sugar. Now the coffees and pastries are on the table, and the older woman has returned to the space behind the counter. Now she has returned with a tiny pitcher of cream for the young woman. You can see by the movements of the older woman that she is adept at taking care of many small things.

Outside the sun is shining brightly. Outside the sun is setting. Outside the sun has set.

Inside the café it is dark except for the distant background glimmer of the kitchen light, a pale yellow glow, which can be seen through the open pick-up window, and the dim yellow counter lights, and a candle glowing in a jar on the table with the yellow oil cloth. Two rows of fluorescent track lighting are fixed to the ceiling, but they have not been turned on. Perhaps the bulbs do not work. Perhaps the wiring is faulty. The two tracks run north to south, one row just above the counter, the other row directly above the row of tables along the window. Halfway between the two rows of fluorescent track lighting, there is a row of four ceiling fans. The ceiling fans are spinning slowly. They are each fixed to the end of a ceiling fan downrod forty-eight inches in length. The first fan is sixteen feet from the shorter of the two plate glass windows, roughly parallel to the entrance to the café. The remaining three fans are spaced at intervals of twenty-six feet. The distance between the fourth fan and the door to the kitchen is also twenty-six feet. The older woman is watching the rotating blades, which are shaped like the leaves of a palm tree. The younger woman is watching the older woman.

Now the two women are talking softly, murmuring,

cooing. They are each leaning towards the other, their heads bent over their coffees, as if in prayer, their faces bathed in the glow of the sunlight slipping through the slatted blinds. The older woman possesses a thoughtful expression on her face. It is almost as if she is trying to decipher the expression on the young woman's face, which we cannot see.

'I should tell you I have not thought about your two friends for many, many months.

'But you remember them?'

'Yes, I remember them. Those two would not be easy to forget.'

The older woman smiles and the younger woman sighs.

'Perhaps I should tell you that I have thought about them every single day. That is also true. I think about them even when I am not thinking about them.'

'It is the same with me.'

'You do not mean the older one. You are trying to find your way back to the younger one, no?'

'Yes.'

'This is a simple thing, but it is also not so simple. I do not know where he is, but do not worry, he has not forgotten you. He will never forget you. He spoke of you often. I am certain he is trying to find his way back to you, so all you have to do is wait. This is the not so simple part, because men for some reason always take the long path into the future. But it does no good to blame them. They cannot help it.'

The older woman sighs and the younger woman smiles.

They seem like mirror images of each other.

'After my husband died they went away. I have not seen them since.'

Now the older woman is talking about her husband. The younger woman cannot quite make sense of what she is hearing. She is having difficulty following the older woman's story. There are too many narrative threads to keep track of, which means she is doing a great deal of mental scrambling even as she seems to be listening passively. The older woman is just happy to have someone who is willing to listen to her tale of joy and heartache. She seems to be growing younger in the process of telling her story. The transformation is miraculous.

The story begins in Spain.

She talks about becoming a prostitute when she was fifteen and how her brother found out, but he did not mind.

With a tremor in her voice, she talks about the owner of the brothel, who liked to sit on the steps that led up to the second floor, playing a guitar. The old man smelled of absinthe, a heavy sweet smell that covered him like a cloud. She talks of going to a festival in Zaragoza with her father and brother. The festival lasted nine days. She talks about a woman in a blue corset who taught her about the nature of men, and then all of a sudden she is talking about the night her father found out she had become a prostitute and he was going to murder her but her brother intervened, and then the two of them left Spain and headed to America. She remembers listening to the owner of the brothel play his guitar. There was a halting tremor in his voice, a sense of loss that drew her towards him, kept her listening, but it was a feeling she did not fully understand. She says she is only now beginning to understand that feeling. She talks about her brother, her one and only love. Once they got to Saint Jean, she went to a small café by the river and her brother went to the Hotel Eskualduna, where all the Spanish exiles went, to sell the van and secure traveling papers. He did not tell her this is where he went, but she knew. Later they spent the night in a cheap hotel owned by a retired gendarme. They wanted nothing to do with Spanish exiles. She talks about the retired gendarme and how he was very chivalrous. He assumed they were on their honeymoon and gave them a bottle of champagne. He also kept cockatoos in the lobby, but the birds were unchained. The cockatoos flew up and down the narrow, tilted hallways of the hotel all night, screaming and chattering the whole while. It was difficult to get any sleep. She talks about the journey to America and how they eventually settled in Miami and Xavier found work in a factory, but it was very difficult work. After this she becomes very thoughtful. She talks very little about the café, perhaps because it is too fresh in her memory. But she talks a great deal about the death of their only son and how the priest at the Cathedral refused to give their son a proper burial because he had not been baptized. She says they buried their son anyway. They buried him in secret. Then she talks about the death of her husband and how the priest who spoke at the funeral Mass was the same priest. Then her face brightens and she is talking some more about the woman in the blue corset. 'A few months after I started working at the brothel, the woman in the blue corset left for Madrid. I was worried for her. It was dangerous for a woman to be traveling alone in those days, but she was not worried. She laughed at me. She said her grandmother had once lived in Madrid and had traveled all over the world on her own. Her grandmother had known all sorts of writers and musicians and even painters with names like Ortiz and Madrazo and Rosales. She said she was finally going home.'

Now the kitchen light has been turned off and the candle and the tray with the empty coffee cups and the empty pastry plates have been removed. The yellow oilcloth has been folded and put away and the chairs are back on top of the table. The only illumination inside the café is provided by the string of yellow lights that run along the counter, tiny pinpricks of light. It is hard to distinguish the pinpricks of light from the particles of dust that are always floating about aimlessly, reflecting whatever illuminating flash comes their way.

The older woman is standing in the entrance to the café. She is leaning against the door to hold it open. The young woman gives a quick wave goodbye as the sky-blue Buick pulls up to the corner. The Buick is illuminated by the light from a single streetlamp positioned along the curb, five feet from the entrance to the cafe and six feet from the corner. The streaming streetlamp light resembles a bead curtain made of overlapping strands of dazzling white beads, a very bright white light that interrupts the darkness. It is not clear if the Buick was parked out in front of the café and only pulled up to the corner with the appearance of the young woman, or if it is has just arrived. The older woman is a dark shadow in the canted doorway.

Now the sky-blue Buick has pulled away from the corner. Now all you can see are two red taillights wavering in the darkness beyond the circle of light, about sixteen feet in diameter, which is produced by the streetlamp. There is no other traffic on the street. The rest of the world seems uninhabited.

Now the older woman steps back from the door and the door closes, replacing her view of the street with the whitish, ghostly image of her own face reflected in the glass. She can make out the string of yellow lights that run along the counter, tiny pinpricks of light which nevertheless provide enough illumination so she can see herself. She is motionless. She almost seems part of a larger photograph in which she, an older woman whose face we cannot see, is scrutinizing the photograph of an older woman who is herself scrutinizing a photograph which we cannot see. The face she is staring at is devoid of all expression, except perhaps a sense of extreme fatigue. It possesses a waxy whitish-gray color, like the color you would associate with a wax figure or a paper mâché puppet, not a flesh-and-blood person. Even the wrinkles and the puffy oval lumps beneath the tired looking eyes are precisely, artistically shaped.

Outside it is twilight and the birds have stopped calling to each other. Outside the moon is glowing in the night sky. Outside the moon has set.

-158-

The young woman and Ed are back in the sky-blue Buick, heading east along SW Eighth Street. The windows are rolled down and they are taking in the sights, so to speak. It is a hot evening, but there is a feathery breeze blowing up from the southeast which mitigates the oppressive impact of the heat.

Ed is pointing out the various landmarks he encountered during the afternoon. The young woman is nodding appreciatively, but his words go in one ear and out the other. She is staring out the open window, at the strangely surreal landscape flashing by, a broken landscape punctuated by a festival array of neon lights, an eerie and seductive atmosphere, Spanish trilling in the air, guitars strumming, the music flying about, the many sidewalk cafés jammed with happy diners; troubadours with flutes and bangles and maracas wandering this way and that; flocks of ex-nuns and young lovers and old married couples and clairvoyants and palm readers walking to and fro and then waiting for the lights to change so they can cross; police cars whizzing past with mind-numbing regularity; and wave after wave of pizza shops and gift shops and cigar stores and all-night pharmacies and chain-link fences designed to keep everyone on one side or the other and stray dogs racing down back alleys and then stopping to howl at the moon. On top of that, the swirl of light from the neon signs and the street lights and the passing cars casts bizarre, irregular shadows in every direction, like shards of broken glass. It is almost as if the world has become a fractured mirror of multiple realities, as if the past, the present and the future are all mingling together. The young woman feels like she has been dreaming, but Ed assures her that she has been awake since they left the café.

The sky-blue Buick is now parked beneath a palm tree next to small restaurant with a blue awning. There are two motorcycles in the space directly ahead and a minivan directly behind. The driver of the minivan appears to be waiting for someone, but he is listening to the radio while he waits, he is engrossed in a ballgame, which means he is not going anywhere for quite a while. He pays no attention to Ed and the young woman getting out of the Buick. Ed remarks they were lucky to get this spot. There are no other spots on either side of the street for many blocks in either direction.

The young woman notices two old men, one in a white felt hat and the other in a baseball cap, sitting on folding chairs outside the restaurant, watching the traffic. They look at her for a moment, but with indifference, as if they are looking at a passing cloud. The young woman notices that the air conditioner above the two men is going full tilt. She also notices that it is hard to tell if there is anyone inside the restaurant or if it is even open because the floor-to-ceiling vertical blinds are drawn, but she and Ed are heading somewhere else, so it does not matter.

The place they are heading to is a bright beacon of white neon, so bright in fact that the entire world takes on the saturated texture of a black and white photograph from the 1950s. The next thing the young woman notices is a stylized marquee with block lettering. For some reason she is only able to make out the first four letters — T H E A. The rest of the letters are lost in the fabulous glow of dozens of bright white lights. She quickly realizes that Ed is taking her to see a movie, however, she does not bother to ask what movie they are going to see. There is no line on the sidewalk, so perhaps the movie has already started, but she does not mind. She likes movies. She catches sight of her face, a vague, whitish, ghostly image, as they slip in through one of six glass doors, and for a moment she thinks she is somewhere else. She is standing in the two-room suite on the ninth floor of the hotel, her face pressed up against the sliding glass door which opens up onto the balcony. She is motionless.

She almost seems part of a larger photograph in which she, a young woman whose face we cannot see, is scrutinizing the photograph of a young woman who is herself scrutinizing a photograph which we cannot see. Suddenly the door to the back bedroom swings open. The door is opposite the sliding glass door and looks as if it is made of teak but it is actually a composite material. It is the kind of interior door quite common in hotels of a certain quality. Now a switch is flicked and a floor lamp begins to glow weakly, just enough to obliterate the view of the boardwalk and the darkness beyond.

'There you are,' says a voice. 'I was wondering where you'd gone to.'

The theatre, which was built in 1926 when Art Deco architecture was all the rage in Paris, is a two-story concrete building, a rectangle approximately seventy-two-feet wide and one-hundred-and-sixty-six-feet deep. It features a painted stucco exterior (mostly a creamy-white color, except for a small blue five-foot-by-thirty-two-foot rectangle that wraps around the northeast corner, which is rounded), a curvilinear concrete marquee encased in a ribbed sheet of metal, and a steel tower on the roof. The northeastern corner also features a block glass window. This window is made up of twenty-four glass blocks arranged in a grid four blocks in height and six blocks in length. The north facade of the theatre is the only part of the building that possesses Art-Deco architectural details. The middle section of the north façade extends roughly twelve feet out from the rest of the building. The marquee, which is fixed to the exterior wall, extends outward another twelve feet, roughly ten feet above the sidewalk.

The marquee itself is three feet thick and displays the theatre's name using standard channel letters thirty inches tall, illuminated with neon tubes. On the flat top of the marquee there is a triangular five-lined-metal sign. Only the two longer sides of what appears to be an isosceles triangle contain lettering (small black letters, a basic typography). The lettering is backlit by bright fluorescent lights. The side without lettering (side CB, the base) is not part of the sign at all. It is part of the exterior façade of the second story exterior.

The two longer sides of the sign face east (side BA) and west (side AC) and come together at a point along the outer edge of the marquee rooftop, where they intersect a narrow, inverted L-shaped column. The column is roughly nine inches in width and rises from the roof of the marquee about twelve feet, at which point it makes a right angle turn and extends an additional five feet towards the theatre building, where it is anchored to the exterior façade at the top of the second story of the protruding section. The column is encased in the same ribbed metal that encases the marquee and is illuminated by a total of two-hundred-and-sixty-six neon bulbs.

The top portion of the inverted L (the shorter side) is perpendicular to the northern exterior façade of the building. It is a three-dimensional structure and so it also possesses a side that faces east and one that faces west. Each side displays the name of the theatre using standard channel letters thirty-inches tall, illuminated with neon tubes. All of the neon letters are a brilliant white color. The top of the inverted L is thirty-two feet from the sidewalk.

Now Ed is buying two tickets. More people are arriving at the theatre and are forming a line that extends from the box office down the sidewalk about twenty feet. There are various conversations taking place in the crowd, but only a few phrases are intelligible. The name of the movie is repeated again and again, like a receding echo. Some in the crowd are excited to see the movie. Some are not sure they want to concentrate on reading subtitles. Someone says the movie failed to win the Academy Award because it painted an overly pessimistic view of life in Spain before Franco, which critics saw as an attempt to give legitimacy to Franco's regime. But the critics misunderstood the movie. Someone else wonders what else is new. Then there is the sound of laughter.

The newly reconstructed main entrance to the theatre is recessed and contains a metal box office, also octagonal in shape, with seven windows and a metal door with a window facing the doors to the lobby. The box office is detached from the rest of the theatre and visually seems to function as a support pillar for the tower, which occupies the same vertical plane as the box office, though at a much higher altitude. On the east and west sides of the entrance bay there are six metal framed movie poster boxes, three to a side. The top and bottom of each poster box is illuminated by a strip of tiny whitish-yellow theatre light bulbs, twenty-six bulbs to a strip.

Now Ed and the young woman are heading into the lobby of the theatre. She catches sight of her face, a vague, whitish, ghostly image, as they slip in through one of six glass doors, and for a moment she thinks she is somewhere else.

With mechanical precision, the girl behind the window of the box office continues collecting cash and processing credit cards in exchange for tickets. The ticket dispenser is spitting out tickets with a comforting regularity. It is like the ticking of a clock. No one in line seems worried that the ticket dispenser will run out of tickets.

Now Ed and the young woman are standing in line to buy popcorn. If the young woman were to turn her shoulders slightly she would be able to see a small adjacent lounge with movie posters hanging on the wall. From where she is standing she would be able to see the posters for several films by Federico Fellini. The most prominent poster is for the film *La Dolce Vita,* starring Marcello Mastroianni, Anita Ekberg, and Anouk Aimée.

If the young woman were to turn her shoulders, she would be able to see this poster quite clearly. It shows a sexy woman in a low cut black dress exposing a great deal of cleavage, with a slit along one side, exposing her right leg. She seems to be gyrating slowly, even sensually, as if she is trying to seduce someone just by dancing. Her hips are partially wrapped up in a swirling red cape, though the physics of how this is happening are impossible to determine. Perhaps she was wearing the cape around her shoulders and let it fall to the ground. Behind her, slightly above her, a man smoking a cigarette is watching her dance. He is wearing a dark coat with the collar upturned and is smoking a cigarette, the tip of which is bright red, the color of the cape. The image of the man is unsettling, partially because his complexion is blue, presumably because he is hiding in the shadows, but also because he is drawn as a looming presence, significantly larger than the dancing woman, who is the size of a tiny doll, a plaything, by comparison.

The other posters represented on the wall include *La Città Delle Donne, I Vitelloni,* and *I Clowns.* Even if the young woman turned slightly she would only have a partial view of these additional posters. The young woman would be excited because she adores Fellini. But she remains oblivious to the posters. She does not move an inch or take her eyes off Ed's right shoulder, even when Ed is paying for the popcorn.

Now they are heading toward the doorway to the main auditorium. They are part of a bubbly crowd of moviegoers. The people in front of Ed and the young women are laughing and chatting softly. They are not moving as quickly as Ed would like them to. You can see tension on Ed's face.

The young woman is paying no attention to Ed or the

slow-moving people in front. She is distracted by the voices of two men who are bringing up the rear of the crowd. She is turning her shoulders as she follows Ed (who is holding on to her hand, rather tightly), trying to pick out the owners of the voices, though she could not tell you why. A natural bit of unconscious curiosity, perhaps. Or the timbre of the voices reminds her of two other voices. Or perhaps she simply possesses a need to eavesdrop, to spy on others who are unaware that that they are being spied upon. In any event, she is unable to identify the two men. There are too many people behind her and they are moving too fast for her to see where the voices originate. To the young woman it seems as if the two voices have become detached from their owners and are simply drifting along with the bubbly crowd.

The main auditorium contains a lower and an upper tier with a total of two-hundred-and-fifty seats. Each seat is twenty-six-and-a-half inches wide, forty-two inches from the floor to the top of the seatback, and twenty-four inches deep. The arrangement of the seats provides for an optimal viewing experience. The seats in the lower tier provide moviegoers with a sixty-six-degree horizontal viewing angle. Those sitting in the front portion of the upper tier enjoy a fifty-two-degree horizontal viewing angle, while those relegated to the very last row still have a thirty-six-degree viewing angle. When the house lights are up the metal exterior shells of the seats are a burgundy color, the plush cushions are a deep royal blue, and the plastic armrests (with cup holders) are a basic beige color. When the house lights are down it is impossible to determine what color the seats are (but then who really cares about the color of the seats when the projector is running).

Now Ed and the young woman have been watching the movie for about thirty minutes. They are sitting in the middle section of the third row on the lower tier, roughly twenty-eight feet from the movie screen. The screen is a regular matte white screen, thirty feet wide by fifteen feet high. The top of the screen is about eighteen inches from the ceiling while the bottom of the screen is two feet above a small proscenium stage. The gap between the proscenium stage and the first row of seats is sixteen feet.

In spite of the optimal horizontal viewing angle of a third-row seat, the young woman is having difficulty focusing on the movie. The moment she becomes thoroughly engrossed in the action on screen, she is distracted by the voices of the two men she heard earlier. Judging by how easily their words penetrate the periphery of her consciousness, they must be sitting nearby. Perhaps they are sitting in the back row of the far-right section of the lower tier. Or perhaps they are sitting in one of the front two rows of the far-right section of the upper tier. The young woman decides it is unlikely that they are further back than this, but she has a limited understanding of the science of acoustics, so she doesn't realize how far sound can travel in a well-designed theatre.

Now she is ignoring both the Spanish being spoken in the movie as well as the English subtitles flashing by on the bottom of the screen and is listening instead to the two men talking. They speak with an accent, but it is not a Spanish accent, or even Italian. She is not sure what kind of accent it is. Their syntax is flawless, but it almost sounds like the two men are purposefully exaggerating the way they are forming each syllable, as if they are trying to make some kind of ironic statement about the nature of all languages by turning the very act of communicating into a joke. The young woman decides they are from Germany, though she would be unable to explain how she came to this improbable conclusion.

'You are saying he's made over sixty films? That's incredible. How old is he?' says the first voice.

'He was sixty-five when he died,' says the second voice.

'He's dead?'

'Maybe. Yes. Nobody knows. Or nobody who knows is talking. He went missing two years ago.'

'And you think this film should have won the Academy Award?'

Half-a-dozen voices from the upper tier tell the two Germans to be quiet, but they continue with their conversation as if the movie has been over for hours and they are waiting for a bus.

'Yes, I do. I admit it's fairly artistic, both in conception and execution. But it's a damn great movie.'

'If you say so. Personally, I can't make heads or tails of it.'

'They spent six weeks shooting the film in and around Elzaurdia, Spain, up in the mountains. Marquez was one of the few foreign movie directors who received preferential treatment from Franco. Most of the others were either Italian or American.'

On the screen a black car is racing along a narrow road with chestnut trees and a small stone wall on one side and an open field on the other. It is an aerial shot, so it is impossible to see the occupants of the car, but we do glimpse the mountains in the distance. Now there are a series of progressively closer shots of the car until we glimpse the faces of two gendarmes on the other side of the windshield. The angle of the shot is skewed, so we are looking across the windshield from the bottom left to the top right. The faces of the gendarmes are lit up by a strange, eerie light that gives them a nonhuman appearance. It almost looks like they are wearing masks.

Then the camera goes spinning and the theatre is filled with the sounds of screeching tires and the two gendarmes are talking in excited voices, but just what they are saying is unintelligible.

'His mother was a bit-part movie actress named Leonora Marquez. She named him Juliano, after Julio Mella.'

'The communist?'

'Yes. They met in Mexico City in 1926. This was right after Mella had left Cuba. It is quite an extraordinary tale, full of political intrigue and spies. There's even a love triangle.'

'Shut up you idiots!'

It is hard to tell if this is one booming voice or several voices chiming in. There is a round of polite applause followed by a moment of silence in which the only sound that can be heard is the sound of a guitar. An old man is playing a guitar on the screen. He is sitting on a barrel against the back wall of a large tavern or café. There are only six tables set up. The rest are pushed up against the wall next to the barrel. A figure stands up in the fifth row of the right-hand section of the upper tier. A few people in the sixth row start to complain as the figure makes its way towards the aisle and heads down the stairs. Two of the six tables are occupied by what appear to be four happy couples, but it soon becomes evident that the four men (all of them well-dressed, one wearing a uniform) and the four women (all of them scantily clad, one wearing a blue corset) have only just met. The figure from the upper tier stops when it reaches the lower tier, as if it is trying to gauge precisely where it is and how best to proceed. The old man playing the guitar continues strumming softly and singing of things exactly as they are. He is bent over his guitar. He is a shearsman of sorts. The figure then continues along towards the sloping concrete partition and disappears around the corner. The guitar playing is interrupted briefly by a flash of white light on the left side of the screen and the sound of a door banging shut.

The young woman notices that Ed is watching the figure as it makes its way towards the concrete partition. He is noticeably agitated and says something to the young woman. "The earth is not earth but a stone,' says the old man with the guitar. The young woman leans towards Ed and whispers something and he seems to relax. On the screen there is a montage of events. A black car comes screeching to a halt just outside a two-story stone building made of immaculate white stone with a red tile roof and a wooden balcony traversing the length of the second floor. The building has been freshly painted and there are many flowers all around, in fact they are everywhere, along the edge of the building, along the road leading to the building, stuffed into pots on the balcony, everywhere you look, red gardenias, roses, blue gentian mixed in, but mostly there are hundreds and hundreds of bright yellow sunflowers. Now a man is laughing, a big, toothy horse-faced laugh. Now there are car doors slamming. Several pairs of marching legs are storming into the white building and then down a narrow hallway. The hobnails in the soles of their boots produce a steady clicking sound as they storm across the stone floor of the hallway. A woman in a blue corset opens a door and another woman enters. There is a flash of white light on the left side of the screen and the sound of a door banging shut. The hallway is illuminated by a single lantern hanging from a ceiling hook. The lantern casts a blueish light on the walls on either side. There is a vintage poster of a bullfighter, perhaps from Spain, a matador sticking his sword into a bull and his cape is flying, which is presumably red but which seems blue given the color of the lantern light. The finer details of the poster are all but impossible to make out. For one thing, the poster is too far away from the camera. Besides, it is too dark inside the narrow hallway to be sure of anything. The man with the big, toothy horse-faced laugh is still laughing. The uniformed legs are storming through the tavern on their way to the stairs to the second floor. Their passing leaves the old man lying in a heap on the floor, but he quickly recovers himself. A figure is now rounding the corner and heading across the gap between the far left and middle sections of the lower tier. The figure is eating popcorn as it wades through the darkness. 'Are you all right, Rafael,' says a woman's voice off camera, in a confident, mischievous tone, like a happy-go-lucky widow who understands that most men are just *toros de lidia*. Ed is again beginning to exhibit signs of agitation as the figure makes its way towards the stairs leading to the upper tier. It is all he can do not to turn around and say something. He is certain that the figure is dropping popcorn with every step. The young woman notices his obvious tension. 'Yes, yes, I am all right,' says Rafael. 'I am a voice in the clouds. I am the voice of the ether prevailing. One keeps on playing year by year. What else is there to do?'

Now the figure is making its way up the aisle to the fifth row of the right-hand section of the upper tier. The uniformed men have stormed into one of the upstairs rooms and are now interrogating a scantily clad young woman. She is sitting on a wooden chair set in the middle of the room. Two of the uniformed men are standing by the door. The third man is standing directly across from the young woman. The angle of the camera makes it seem that he is towering over her. He tells the young woman his name is Erratzi, Víctor Erratzi. 'Do you know who I am,' he says. He is almost sneering. 'No,' says the young woman. Now the figure is making its way past the first three seats of the fifth row to the fourth seat, but it is slow going. The figure is moving too slowly for the occupants of the sixth row, so they begin to complain. As the figure arrives at the fourth seat, the uniformed men are getting back into their car. The young woman is with them. The camera focuses on the back of her head, which is visible through the rear window as the car drives away. The figure isn't paying much attention to his popcorn as he sits down and ends up spilling some of his bucket on the occupants of the fourth row.

Immediately a masculine voice says 'Idiot,' but then a feminine voice says "Shshsh, leave it alone.'

Now it is night on the screen. The camera moves in through a set of open balcony doors on the second floor into the room of the woman with the blue corset. Rafael and the woman are sitting at a small table positioned squarely in front of the doors. 'They have taken Ada,' says Rafael. 'They did not take her, she went willingly.' 'It is the same thing. The grass turns green, the grass turns gray. In the end the world is a shore we cannot quite reach.' 'You are drunk.' 'I am always drunk.' 'What will you do?' 'I will go to town and speak with Corporal

Erratzi. That is what I will do.' 'You are too funny. What could you possibly say to that funny little man to make him take you seriously?' 'I will say to him this gloom is the darkness of the sea.' 'And he will laugh at you and toss you in the cell next to your daughter.' 'Then I will say to him things are as I think they are.' 'And he will have you locked away in an asylum.' 'Then I will say the bread will be our bread and the stone will be our bed and we shall sleep by night, and the day we will forget.' And then a cascade of feminine laughter. 'Oh my sweet, sweet Rafael, if you must commit to such foolishness, at least wait till morning. Come now to this bed of stone with me and see if we cannot soften it.'

On the screen the moon is gleaming and the night birds are calling out to each other. The moonlight cuts across the bottom of the bed occupied by Rafael and the woman in the blue corset. We can only see a rectangular portion of her right leg and a triangular portion of his left shoulder, but as they move to their own internal rhythms, the gleaming, moonlit, surface geometry of their intertwined bodies also moves. The screen is a gleaming montage of movement. The triangular portion of a left arm gives way to the oval of a kneecap, which in turn gives way to the ellipse of a mouth and a chin, which then gives way to the rectangle of a back, which immediately becomes a triangular portion of a right hip, which then becomes the arc of a right shoulder and then the trapezoid of an inner thigh, and then a hip again and then a mouth, and then the arc of two arms coming together, and then a collapsing spiral ending in two parallel lines.

In the fourth row of the middle section of the lower tier, Ed and the young woman are straining to follow the action of the film. The young woman thinks the images on the screen sparkle with a beauty that is rarely glimpsed. Ed, however, is frustrated beyond belief.

Now the figure in the fourth seat of the fifth row in the right-hand section of the upper tier has finished off the popcorn. The bucket is nowhere to be seen.

Now the two voices from earlier start up again.

'They were part of a group of communists and intellectuals that included the painter Diego Rivera and the photographer Tina Modotti, who was also a Russian spy.' On the screen sunlight is pouring over the various buildings in a small mountain village. 'So Leonora and Mella fell in love, but they had to see each other in secret because he was already involved with Tina Modotti.'

Now the camera focuses on a small stone garrison. Outside the garrison a couple of uniformed men are sitting on a bench. They are leaning back against the stone wall. One of them is snoring. The other one is looking up at the morning sun, shading his eyes with his left hand to deflect the sudden brightness that has overtaken the town. 'Of course there was all sorts of speculation about what was going on, but then Mella was assassinated in '29, and that was that.'

As the camera sweeps into the front room of the garrison, the audience hears the voice of Víctor Erratzi bragging about his sexual conquest of the night before. And then another voice belonging to a slovenly looking gendarme who nevertheless belongs to Erratzi's inner circle: 'You mean the little thief?' 'See for yourself,' says Víctor Erratzi as he opens a door leading to the cells where the prisoners are kept.

The two gendarmes head down the hallway towards the very last cell, where the girl from the night before is sleeping on a cot. The hobnails in the soles of their boots produce a steady clicking sound as they walk across the stone floor. 'Leonora stayed in Mexico City for the next fourteen years, but she only worked sporadically. In 1933, she got a small part in *El prisionero trece,* and in 1936 she played a peasant woman in *Vámonos con Pancho Villa,* but that was it.' Now Rafael appears in the doorway of the garrison. The sun is at his back, so he appears as a dark shadow, a silhouette edged in gold, an avenging angel. 'She was supposed to get a decent role in *Doña Bárbara,* but that never happened. Then she left Mexico City altogether.'

For some inexplicable reason the old man has brought his guitar, but in the glare of the sunlight it doesn't look like an old man holding a guitar. 'The odd thing is that she left her son with friends.' It looks like a man of any age holding a rifle. 'No one knows what happened to her.' Naturally the two gendarmes are surprised. They suspect someone has sent an assassin. 'Then in 1955 Juliano Manuelo Marquez started working as an assistant for Rafael Baledón.' They both reach for their weapons, but only Victor Erratzi manages to pull his pistol from its holster. It is a very fancy pistol. It is a Llama III-A 9mm corto/ .380 ACP. 'He worked on three films, *Camino de Guanajuato* in 1955, and *La sombra vengadora* and *El rey de*

México in 1956.' Erratzi empties his pistol as he walks towards the shadow in the doorway. 'After that he struck out on his own.' Rafael falls to the stone floor, his left hand clutching the neck of his guitar. The two gendarmes from the bench outside rush into the room, weapons drawn, but when they see the old man on the floor they put them away.

'They say Tina Modotti had Mella killed because she couldn't stand the thought that he was seeing another woman.'

'They do?'

'That's what they say.'

Now the camera is looking down on the figure of the old man with his guitar. His unmoving body is an ink stain on the stone floor, his arms and legs bent at impossible angles, a strange, unsettling symbol. 'It is very ironic.' All we see of Corporal Erratzi is the top of his head (he is not wearing his green police cap) and his shoulders. We see the other three gendarmes join him. 'He was murdered on the corner of Morelos and Abraham González in Mexico City.' The four gendarmes are conferring with each other, but we cannot hear what they are saying. 'I am convinced that they chose that corner because of its obvious revolutionary implications. It's symbolic relevance. It was a statement. González was the mentor to Pancho Villa. And Morales was the birthplace of Zapata and at the center of every revolution in Mexico since 1811.'

The camera is still looking down at the scene of the murder, but the distance between the lens and the floor of the garrison has increased. It is like looking at something at the bottom of a very deep, very narrow well made of dove gray stone, as if the rooftop of the garrison no longer exists and the camera is floating freely in the air above.

Now the camera retreats even further. Everything becomes a posture of nerves. The image of the old man and his guitar has been transformed into six intersecting lines. The image of the four gendarmes has become an image of one brown dot (capless head, thick, brown hair) and three green dots (three green police caps).

The four dots seem to be twirling around each other, a strange, symbiotic dance that resembles four bees communicating. A series of soft, murmuring sounds begins to float up through the void of empty space between the camera lens and the stone floor of the roofless garrison. No discernible meaning can be ascribed to the sounds.

-159-

Now the young woman is standing in the back bedroom of the two-room suite on the ninth floor of the hotel, her face pressed up against the sliding glass door which opens up onto the balcony. Suddenly the panel door to the bedroom swings open. The door is opposite the sliding glass door and looks as if it is made of teak but it is actually a composite material. It is the kind of interior door quite common in hotels of a certain quality.

Now a hand reaches into the room and a switch is flicked and a floor lamp begins to glow weakly, just enough to obliterate the view of the boardwalk and the darkness beyond. But the young woman does not react to the light. Instead, she is now staring at her own face, which is devoid of all expression, except perhaps a sense of extreme fatigue. Her face seems to now possess a waxy brownish-gray color, like the color you would associate with a wax figure or a paper mâché puppet, not a flesh-and-blood person. Even her wrinkles and the puffy oval lumps beneath her tired looking eyes are precisely, artistically shaped.

She wonders why she looks so tired.

She has never seen her face look so puffy.

'There you are,' says a voice. 'I was wondering where you'd gone to.'

The voice sounds happy, or if not happy, at least satisfied.

The young woman does not turn around. She can see the vague, whitish reflection of her friend, Ed, in the glass of the sliding glass door. Ed is standing just inside the doorway next to a sleek, chrome-plated floor lamp.

The lamp possesses a contemporary, tubular lampshade, a pale white in color with a series of dark gray, wavy, elliptical lines, vertical lines which traverse the exterior circumference of the lampshade, producing a wavy, elliptical 360-degree pattern of light and shadow on the hardwood floor and on the walls of the room.

The pattern of light and shadow makes it difficult to determine what is real and what is not.

'We'll head out around noon,' Ed says.

The young woman remains motionless.

She almost seems part of a larger photograph in which

she, a young woman whose face we cannot see, is scrutinizing the photograph of a young woman who is herself scrutinizing a photograph which we cannot see. Then the switch is flicked and the glow from the floor lamp is extinguished, obliterating the image of the young woman in the dark glass of the sliding glass door.

Outside the moon has set. Outside the moon is glowing in the night sky. Outside it is twilight and the birds have stopped calling to each other.

Now the moonlight cuts across the bottom of the bed occupied by Ed and the young woman. We can only see a rectangular portion of her right leg and a triangular portion of his left shoulder, but as they move to their own internal rhythms, the gleaming, moonlit, surface geometry of their intertwined bodies also moves. The triangular portion of a left arm gives way to the oval of a kneecap, which in turn gives way to the ellipse of a mouth and a chin, which then gives way to the rectangle of a back, which immediately becomes a triangular portion of a right hip, which then becomes the arc of a right shoulder and then the trapezoid of an inner thigh, and then a hip again and then a mouth, and then the arc of two arms coming together, and then a collapsing spiral ending in two parallel lines.

It seems to the young woman that the world has become a fractured mirror of multiple realities, as if the past, the present and the future are all mingling together. She feels a sense of vertigo, an odd sensation, since she is lying flat on her back, her ankles tangled up in a set of silk sheets. But the sense of vertigo is quite sharp. Her entire body has gone numb. It is all she can do to keep from falling. She feels like she has been dreaming, but Ed assures her that she has been awake since they left the theatre.

'We'll head out around noon,' Ed says.

His voice sounds happy, or if not happy, at least satisfied. The tension he felt when they were watching the movie has been erased. He has become a mirror image to a happier, younger self.

Now the young woman is standing on the other side of the room, her face pressed up against the sliding glass door which opens up onto the balcony. Her mind feels clear, less drowsy. The sense of vertigo has passed. She is looking out at the scene below as if she has just recovered her sight. A single brightly glowing light post, partially obscured by the foliage of various shrubs, sea grapes perhaps, and also a few palm trees, illuminates a twenty-foot section of the elevated boardwalk that runs parallel to the beach.

The streaming light post light resembles a bead curtain made of overlapping strands of dazzling white beads, a very bright white. There are dozens of similar light posts spaced every thirty feet or so, illuminating twenty-foot sections all along the boardwalk.

Beyond the boardwalk lies the beach, and beyond the beach lies the comforting darkness of the ocean. The dim green running lights of a boat flash on the horizon, a shrimp boat perhaps, some kind of fishing boat, or maybe it is a pleasure boat, but from inside the ninth-floor two-room suite, even with one's face pressed up against the glass of the sliding glass door, it is impossible to tell. The boardwalk below is empty. The entire world seems uninhabited.

-160-

Outside it is sunny. Outside the wind is whipping up. Outside it has begun to drizzle. It has finished drizzling. It is sunny once again.

Now a young woman is standing in front of a wall containing seven photographs arranged in an irregular geometric pattern. To the right of the wall there is a sliding glass door that opens up onto a sandy, grassy patio area. Beyond the patio area there is a series of sand dunes, each one topped with sea oats. Beyond the dunes lies the ocean.

The floor-to-ceiling vertical blinds, which are normally pulled back all the way, are partially drawn, so only the central portion of the sliding glass door allows the sunlight to pass through.

The young woman is motionless. She gives the first six photographs only quick, affirmatory glances. But she cannot take her eyes away from the seventh photograph.

The seventh photograph is a baseball team photo taken on a very sunny day somewhere in the tropics. The photograph seems almost bleached out, an indication perhaps of the intense heat that had washed over the ballpark the day the photograph was taken. The ballplayers are posing in the infield on the first-base side of the pitcher's mound.

It is a black-and-white photo, so the color of the infield grass is a whitish, light gray color. In real life the grass would have been a parched yellow-brown color.

Suddenly there is a soft sounding click and the sliding glass door opens and then closes and an older woman pushes her way through the vertical blinds along the right side of the door. The vertical blinds swing back and forth for several minutes, a gentle, oscillating movement, until they re-establish their equilibrium.

The young woman does not appear to notice. She is in the process of taking the seventh photograph from the wall. She flips it over and removes the felt backing. Now she is looking at the back of the photograph. There is a date in the top right corner: 26 June 1960. Beneath the date is a short note. The note says: Do you remember this day? Do you remember La Maravilla and how we later drove to the beach? I will carry the memory of that day to my grave, my love. Your loving José.

The young woman reads the note and then flips the photograph over to look at the baseball team. She scrutinizes each face in a futile attempt to discern which of the ballplayers might have written the note.

'I have spent many hours doing the same thing,' says the older woman. 'But I have never been able to figure out which one he is. Your great-grandmother never spoke about him.'

The young woman smiles but she does not bother to look at the older woman. She puts the photograph back in the frame and hangs it back on the wall. The older woman continues talking about the baseball team in the seventh photograph. It is almost like she is baring her soul. The younger woman thinks she is only a passive listener, but just the fact that she is listening has visibly lifted the older woman's spirits. It is a miraculous transformation. The older woman actually seems to have grown younger in the process of telling her story. The two women now seem identical in age. They are mirror images of each other. If their friends were to see the two women together they might remark to the younger one, 'My God, you look so much like your mother,' or they might remark to the older one, 'My God, the two of you could be sisters.' It is what people would say.

Now the two women are standing shoulder to shoulder.

They are scrutinizing the wall containing the seven photographs arranged in an irregular geometric pattern. It is sunny outside, but inside it is somewhat dark. It is dark enough that the two women cannot quite make out the details of the photographs. All they can really see are their own ghostly pale faces reflected in the glass protecting whichever photograph they happen to be looking at. They are motionless. They almost seem part of a larger photograph in which they, a younger woman and an older woman whose faces we cannot see, are scrutinizing the photograph of an older woman and a younger woman who are themselves scrutinizing a photograph which we cannot see.

Outside it is drizzling, outside the wind is whipping up, outside it is sunny once again.

BOOK NINE

the clouds, the sea, oblivion

-161-

In a once elegant section of one of the grand cities of Eastern Europe, a bearded man stands on a street corner musing about the vagaries of life. He is standing in the shadow of a five-story building done in the Romanesque style with a heavy stone façade, vertically proportioned double hung windows with a single lintel over each bay, ornamental cornices marking the divisions between floors, and a continuous cornice cap. The masonry on the bottom two floors is painted a cream color. The masonry on the upper floors is a beige color. Quite frankly, it could be any city anywhere.

The bearded man has been there for quite a while. He is standing next to a traffic light fixed to a pole embedded in the sidewalk. He seems mesmerized by the ebb and flow of traffic. It is a corner where the traffic must make a decision and either continue along a one-way boulevard that runs parallel to a river and which then suddenly becomes a two-way street, or merge left onto a second well-traveled one-way avenue heading sharply away from the river on a roughly perpendicular line, past the Romanesque building towards the busier sections of the city. Every now and then a gleaming red and white electric tram glides past the corner along a set of tracks that runs down the center of the avenue.

On the opposite street corner, on the other side of the avenue from where the bearded man is standing, a truck pulls up onto the utility strip that separates the traffic from the sidewalk. Three men in work clothes get out and head to the back of the truck, chatting amiably. The truck is a medium-sized Studebaker platform truck with a grime-covered green cab and wooden rails along the sides. The men lower the wooden tailgate and begin unloading bricks of various colors, and then a single fifty-pound bag that says 'Mortar Mix' and a small caked-over mixer from the sixties (about the size of a child's wagon, rusty metal wheels, a rusted frame, a small diesel engine to turn the metal drum), and then several hand trowels, a bucket, several five-gallon plastic containers filled with water, and various other implements.

One of the men gets back into the truck, waves at the other two, and then the truck pulls away from the curb and vanishes in the morning haze. It is a very hazy morning, a cloudy morning. The other two begin their labors, which consist of mixing a bucket of water with the sifted contents from the single bag and then repairing a small section of a massive privacy wall that separates an apartment complex of some sort from the dangers of the street.

The wall displays no obvious signs of deterioration, from the elements or any other cause, but this does not prevent the workmen from applying themselves forthwith. They are very industrious, which might suggest to the untrained observer that the wall contains defects invisible to the naked eye. Occasionally one or the other looks up from his labors, scanning the narrow corridor of their urban environment for evidence that someone is watching, perhaps from one of the windows in the Romanesque building, but neither notices the bearded man. All they see when they spin their heads, a slow, three-hundred-and-sixty-degree rotation, is a traffic light blinking various colors at regular intervals and the traffic flowing past and then not flowing past and then flowing past again, like a circling clockwork train.

Perhaps they do not notice the bearded man because he is practically clutching the traffic light pole at this point, as if he were filled with a labyrinth of doubts or was recovering from an all-night bender in a red-light district or he suffered from some strange autopsychotic affliction and would thus be unable to watch the two bricklayers without the temporary support of the pole. Or perhaps the bearded man has left the scene altogether. It is difficult to say.

Later, the bearded man is laughing to himself, a vagabond king walking along an empty sidewalk, a strangely empty street, block after block of Romanesque style buildings on both sides, strange, semi-official looking buildings, gray in color, or beige or brown, with windows made of impenetrable dark glass. Each building is five stories high with four vertical columns of windows, three windows to a bay, for a total of sixty windows. All of the windows are double hung with white frames, very contemporary looking.

The bearded man wonders what kind of work the people inside these buildings are doing. To judge from the number of cars parked along the street, a great many people must work in these buildings. The cars are parked in random haphazard fashion along the curbs on both sides, jammed together at odd angles, some parked diagonally across the grassy utility strip, some even up on the sidewalks. Barely a sliver of daylight between bumpers.

It is such a very long walk, but the bearded man seems to have little else to do. He notices another pair of workmen repairing a small section of a massive privacy wall that separates an apartment complex of some sort from the dangers of the street. Naturally (one might say inevitably) he is struck by a sense of *déjà vu*. He sees the same medium-sized Studebaker platform truck with a grime-covered green cab pulling away from the curb. But the apartment complex does not look the same. The first one was barely three stories high and was modern in construction. This one is seven stories high and is much older, by fifty years at least, and one can see the tops of willow trees rising up from the apartment compound hidden by the second wall. Moreover, the first wall was in pristine condition, though the workmen attacked it nevertheless, but this wall is clearly in need of repair.

The bearded man does not bother with a shrug. What meaning is there in a shrug anyway?

Slowly the neighborhood changes. The stately, semiofficial looking Romanesque buildings give way to buildings of all shapes and sizes, apartment buildings with narrow white iron balconies next to single story auto garages covered in graffiti next to delis next to cafés with red awnings and then banks. The street has narrowed and is now made of cobblestone. The buildings seem consumed by a sense of long-standing decay. And on every corner workmen are engaged in masonry repair projects. On some of the corners the medium-sized Studebaker platform truck is parked nearby, on other corners it is long gone.

It is an amazing coincidence, though one must readily admit that in a city as old as this one, masonry repair is a ceaseless activity. Still, the presence of so many masons suggests to the bearded man that there are larger, perhaps even sinister forces at work in the world, so he begins to scrutinize the faces of the workmen he passes, trying to commit their distinctive features to memory.

Why is he doing this? What does he hope to accomplish? What does he hope to learn?

In the end he learns nothing, for the moment he moves on from one group of workmen to the next, the images of the previous faces dissolve, replaced by two new faces. He is left with the impression that all of the workmen have the same face, a waxy brownish-gray color, more like the face of a wax figure or paper mâché puppet than a flesh-and-blood person. Even the wrinkles and the puffy oval lumps beneath the tired looking eyes are precisely, artistically shaped.

Evening arrives, a dull red glow in the sky filtering down through the empty spaces in between the buildings, bouncing off windows, a soft radiant glow reflected in the cobblestone of the cobblestone streets. The dozens of workmen that had been engaged earlier in the day in the various masonry repair efforts throughout the city have vanished. It is almost as if they never existed. The bearded man is sitting at a wrought-iron table (painted white) outside a small corner café, sipping coffee from a white porcelain cup and eating potato soup with freshly baked bread.

The café is a hangout for students, intellectuals, rip-off artists, writers, poets, ex-poets, painters, riff-raff of all kinds. The menu is written on a giant chalkboard hanging on the wall of a small, slightly recessed open foyer (9x9 feet, flagstone floor, an old-fashioned iron lantern hanging by a chain from an arched ceiling) leading to the door to the café. The door possesses a brightly polished mahogany frame with a floor-to-ceiling frosted glass window. It is propped open so the flow in and out of the café is unimpeded. The bearded man doesn't remember when he last had a bowl of soup.

As he is sopping up the last of the soup with his bread, the bearded man notices a student passing out leaflets. The student, a skinny young man of about twenty who goes by the name of Oskar, is wearing bright maroon-colored shorts with bright maroon-colored knee socks, black shoes, a t-shirt with the silk-screen image of a bearded man on the front and a quote of some sort on the back, and a black beret perched squarely on top of a silky mop of black hair cut pageboy style.

The bearded man finds himself mesmerized by the image of the bearded man on the student's t-shirt. He has the strangest sensation that he is looking at himself, that an unscrupulous artist has somehow taken his likeness and printed it on the t-shirt. But it is difficult to be sure what he is looking at. For one thing, the student is moving too quickly through the crowd of café patrons. Then the student is standing next to his table, holding out a leaflet for the taking. The bearded man's hand is reaching for the leaflet before he is even aware of what he is doing. It is an automatic reaction triggered by the spatial proximity of the leaflet. A waitress leans in between the proffered leaflet and the reaching hand and fills the porcelain coffee cup of the bearded man.

Then the waitress retracts herself and the leaflet exchanges hands. The bearded man asks the student about the t-shirt, but the student doesn't know that much. He borrowed it from his roommate. The bearded man on the t-shirt has unruly hair and wire-rim spectacles and a thoughtful, brooding expression. He looks nothing at all like the bearded man sipping coffee. The student says he thinks the bearded man on the t-shirt is a philosopher. His roommate is studying philosophy at the University. Then he points to a name below the image. It is written in fancy script that seems to be part of the beard, so it is all but invisible unless you know it is there. The name is Miroslav Petříček. There's also a quote on the back, says the student, who is turning as he speaks so the bearded man sipping coffee can see. The quote says *'The imagination is the only thing able to keep up with the process of transmutation.'* Who the hell is Miroslav Petříček, the bearded man wonders as the student whirls away to the next table.

-162-

Later that evening the bearded man finds himself wandering along Vodíčkova Street, a fairly busy thoroughfare in the old part of the city, a few blocks from the river. He almost seems lost. Every so often he stops at a café or a restaurant or an art gallery or a shop about to close and shows the leaflet to anyone who permits the intrusion (a waiter taking a cigarette break, an artist who had been hoping to convince a gallery owner to take a chance and is waiting outside the gallery for an answer, a pharmacist who has misplaced his glasses, a happy couple celebrating their first month together, a grocery store cashier who has to get home to make dinner for her grandmother, a librarian taking a brisk walk to forget about the day).

Everyone who looks at the leaflet is quite methodical in their examination. They scrutinize the front and back, holding each side up to whatever dim light is nearby (a streetlight, the recessed lighting of the restaurant, the fluorescent glow emanating from the shop, the candlelight of the café), as if they are looking for secret messages written with invisible ink. Then they begin making a series of precise though convoluted gestures, presumably indicating where the bearded man is now in relation to the address printed on the front of the leaflet and what is the easiest but not necessarily the quickest route to take. The waiter and the happy couple and the cashier point in the direction of the river. The artist and the pharmacist point in the opposite direction.

The leaflet is advertising a lecture ('The Nazi Preoccupation with the Occult, the Search for Nordic Artifacts, and UFO Technology') to be given that very evening (nine o'clock) in the gymnasium of a local elementary school. The lecturer is an older man (Professor Elek Borža), a school psychologist from one of the districts in the western part of the city who gives lectures on weekends and during the summer to make ends meet. The lecture is sponsored by the Eastern European Institute for Exopolitics, so it is free and open to the general public.

When it is the librarian's turn to examine the leaflet it is already half past eight. She decides it would be a waste of energy to try to explain to the bearded man which streets he should take and when he should turn left or right. Clearly she believes him to be a tourist who has been wandering around in circles for hours. She grabs hold of his arm and smiles warmly, a surprisingly intimate display of affection, but who can blame her. She has not held onto a man's arm like this in many months. The bearded man does not notice the desperation oozing from her eyes. Or if he does, he does not mind. He accepts her arm as if she is his one true love and he has finally returned home after many years abroad. The two head off down Vodíčkova Street for a couple of blocks before they turn right (or maybe left), disappearing into the hazy darkness of an unlit street.

-163-

Nine o'clock. The lecture is about to begin but the bearded man and the librarian are still two blocks away. It is a warm, humid evening. The air is very still. The librarian is chatting away, but most of what she is saying dissolves instantly so all the bearded man can pick out are a few syllables here, a few there.

Outside the elementary school a man is waiting for any stragglers. He is not certain how long he should wait, for the school has never hosted a lecture before. It is already very dark. The only illumination out in front of the school is provided by the bluish security beacon just above the entrance (three steps leading up to a pair of intricately carved oak doors framed by a sculpted sandstone pediment and lintel supported by two vaguely Romanesque columns).

The man is perhaps a janitor who has been working since early that morning and is ready to go home. He is wondering if he should take down Professor Borža's sign (an art nouveau style poster set in an antique wrought iron easel with a bronze finish). It is a very elegant looking sign as far as sidewalk signs go. It is about three feet out in front of the steps, slightly angled so it will not impede the flow of pedestrian traffic to and from the school, but also so it will catch the light from the security beacon.

The janitor has been looking at the poster on and off all the while he has been waiting. In the center there is an alien spacecraft rising up into a night sky. It must be a cloudy sky because no stars are visible. Four Nazi soldiers are looking up at the spacecraft. They are mesmerized by what they see. Clearly they are Nazis because you can see swastikas on their uniforms. One of them is wearing an officer's visor cap. Perhaps he is a Lieutenant. The other three are regular soldiers. The faces of all four are bathed in a strange, bluish light, but whether this light is emanating from the spacecraft, which would make it part of the interior reality of the poster, or from the security beacon just above the entrance to the school, which would place it in a reality exterior to the poster, is impossible to say. Professor Borža and the title of the lecture are printed below the Nazis in a very fancy, curlicue script. A temporary placard (a white rectangle with black lettering) has been fixed to the wrought iron easel just above the center of the poster. The placard says 'To-Nite Only!'

The bearded man and the librarian arrive just as the janitor has made the decision to take down the sign. He looks up as the couple approaches as if he is uncertain what he is seeing.

The ionized dust particles of small glories and larger halos, perhaps that is what he sees.

'We're not late, are we?' the bearded man says.

The janitor does not respond. He starts to gather up the poster and the easel as the bearded man and the librarian slip in through the oak doors.

-164-

The gymnasium is a fairly typical elementary school gymnasium with a basketball hoop at one end and a concrete floor for dancing and running about and playing games in the middle, and an elevated platform stage for piano recitals and puppet shows and various theatrical performances at the other end. On this particular night, however, it has been transformed in order to suit the eccentricities of Professor Borža.

When the Professor arrived at four-thirty that afternoon, just after the children had been dismissed for the day, the Headmistress of the school led him to the gymnasium so he could set up for his lecture. He almost collapsed in a puddle of regret. 'This will never do,' he had cried. By 'this' he meant the manner in which the gymnasium had been decorated.

The Headmistress tried to explain that the decorations were part of a children's play the summer school students were going to perform that Friday for their parents and grandparents. The play took place in a resort community somewhere along the Adriatic Sea. That's why the stage at the northern end of the gymnasium was decorated as a beachfront café with a dozen café tables and a glimpse of the sea (painted) through a window (also painted) near the back. But Professor Borža would have none of that. He gave serious lectures for serious-minded listeners. A stage resembling a café, even those cafés in Paris and elsewhere that catered to an intellectual crowd, would most certainly detract from the atmosphere he hoped to create with his words, and since he would give his lecture from the center of the stage, something would have to be done.

So the Headmistress asked the janitor to dismantle the beachfront café backdrop or cover it up and remove from view anything that might possibly suggest a day at the beach.

-165-

The lecture does not begin at the appointed hour, which allows the bearded man and the librarian sufficient opportunity to find a good seat. They make their way to the second row and sit down three seats in. The librarian finds solace in the continued presence of the bearded man. She is still chatting away, oblivious to the fact that the only sound echoing about the gymnasium is the sound of her own voice. The bearded man does not mind. He is happy to have an unobstructed view of the stage. He has been in many an auditorium where his view of the proceedings was partially eclipsed by an ornately carved pillar or an oversized back, shoulders and head directly in front.

There are maybe thirty people in attendance, but one cannot escape the impression that the gymnasium is empty. The janitor was told to expect a very large crowd, a great many people from the neighborhood said they were coming, the topic was quite popular, so he had set up two-hundred-and-forty-six wooden folding chairs (fourteen rows of fourteen up front followed by five rows of five on the left side and five rows of five on the right side with a gap in the middle for a slide projector). The audience is spread across all nineteen rows.

Finally it looks like the show is about to begin. There is some commotion backstage, two voices talking in low, desperate whispers, then the sound of quick footsteps followed by the sudden appearance of a young man walking to the podium, which is to the left of a small, portable movie screen (eight feet wide, six feet high) that is front and center. The young man apologizes for the delay, there were some technical difficulties which have now been resolved, so without further ado, here is Professor Elek Borža. The audience of thirty breaks into a round of polite but scattered applause as the young man hops down from the stage and makes his way back to the slide projector. It is the same young man who was passing out leaflets at the café. He is wearing the same bright maroon-colored shorts and bright maroon-colored knee socks, the same black shoes, and the same t-shirt with the silk-screen image of a bearded Miroslav Petříček on the front. The bearded man tries to point out the t-shirt to the librarian, but she doesn't understand the reason for his hand gestures, assumes he is making a joke, laughs softly, politely, and gives his arm a loving squeeze.

The lights go out just like that, all but a single row of dim, recessed lights along the left side of the gymnasium, and Professor Borža is suddenly standing behind the podium. He is wearing a white shirt and jeans and a beige sports jacket with patches on the elbows. To the bearded man the voice of Professor Borža is a voice of reason in a sea of darkness. To the librarian, it is the sound of an oboe, a soothing, mellow sound that may very well lull her to sleep. Then a blue spotlight captures Professor Borža's face, his long white hair, his hook nose and angular chin, his piercingly blue, apocalyptic eyes. Everyone in the audience is lifted from their seats. They hardly know what to expect.

The first part of the lecture is given over to a series of lengthy explanations providing a historical context for understanding the nature of the Nazi obsession with the occult, Nordic artifacts, and UFO technology. Various slides accompany the explanations.

Professor Borža begins by talking about the Merovingian kings.

(Slide of an artist's rendering of Meroveus, founder of the Merovingian line.)

He talks about how some scholars, though the Professor uses this term lightly, have asserted that the Merovingians were the descendants of space travelers who came from the void beyond Orion's belt ten thousand years before the birth of Christ.

(Slide of the constellation Orion, highlighting Alnitak, Alnilam, and Mintaka, the three bright stars that make up the belt.)

'These space travelers,' says the Professor, 'landed or crash-landed in Mesopotamia and became the gods and goddesses of ancient Sumer and then Egypt; they became the fallen angels of the Christian tradition; they became the Nephilim in the Book of Enoch.'

(Slide of the Sumerian god Anu; followed by a slide of the Egyptian goddess Isis, the oldest of the Egyptian deities.)

'Their supposed hybrid descendants, however, are claimed by dozens of competing traditions, each with a host of intricate theories to explain the migratory path the hybrids took over the centuries.'

(Slide of a map of possible migratory routes.)

'Some scholars claim the hybrids eventually settled in what is now southern Russia and were known as Khazars.'

(Slide of a map of southern Russia.)

'Others assert that the hybrids were exiled to the shores of the Black Sea in 278 by the Roman Emperor Probus. No explanation is given to explain how they migrated from the Caucuses to eastern France, which is where the Merovingians first appeared.'

(Slides of the Black Sea; the Roman Emperor Probus; a map delineating several possible routes from the Caucuses to eastern France.)

'Still others claim that the hybrids were The Lost Tribe of Israel and eventually settled in Armenia and that their descendants migrated to Venice during the third and fourth centuries, and from there to Germany and southern France in the fifth century. It is this fifth-century branch of the family that according to these scholars gave rise to the Merovingian Kings, though again, how this actually came about is never satisfactorily addressed.'

(Slides of the Armenian coast; the canals of Venice; and then Metz, France, the seat of the Merovingian kings.)

Then the Professor starts talking about the rise of a secret German society called The Order of the Black Sun.

(Slide of the Black Sun, an occult symbol incorporating a sun wheel mosaic and the Hagal rune — two parallel lines connected in the middle by a third, slanted line.)

'The Order of the Black Sun,' says the Professor, 'was one of a dozen or more secret societies that emerged in Germany in the late 1800s and early 1900s in response to what a handful of German intellectuals saw as the growing threat arising from what they called the mongrelized races, coupled with a dangerous misreading of Nietzsche.'

(Slides of several unnamed German intellectuals and then a slide of the philosopher Friedrich Nietzsche.)

'All of these societies embraced the occult, creating complicated mythologies to justify both their racist beliefs and their sadistic, almost certainly psychotic impulses.'

(Slides of various occult symbols.)

'The German intellectual and political leaders who belonged to the Order of the Black Sun believed wholeheartedly and without any trace of bemused cynicism that they, meaning the German ruling class, could trace their pedigree back to Henry the Duke of Saxony, who belonged to the Order of the Teutons of the ninth century, and from there to the Merovingians of the fifth century. From the Merovingians it was relatively easy to claim, since it was impossible to prove, a direct line of descent that went all the way back to the House of David.'

(Various slides: an artist's rendering of Henry the Duke of Saxony; a knight on a horse; an aerial photo of Jerusalem.)

'Then in 1917, four members of The Black Sun began meeting with a spiritualist who could have passed for a Hollywood movie star. They met at a café located on the corner of Schopenhauerstraße and Staudgasse in Vienna.'

(Slide of the exterior of Café Schopenhauer.)

'Two of the members were involved in the political arena: Rudolf Jung, the man who later convinced Hitler to call his new party the National Socialist German Workers' Party; and General Karl Haushofer, a professional soldier with political connections who had commanded a brigade on the western front during World War One, and whose ideas about a strong Germany's ascendant role in what he described as the New Eurasian Order, ideas which he would later explore in great depth as a student of philosophy at Munich University in the 1920s, would heavily influence Hitler's conception of the Third Reich.'

(Slides of Rudolph Jung; an aging Karl Haushofer; and then Munich University.)

'One of the members was engaged in various occult activities: Rudolf von Sebottendorf, a psychic-medium and Freemason who was close friends with Heinrich Himmler until 1933, when he, Sebottendorf, published a book with a somewhat seditious sounding title as far as Hitler was concerned. The book was called *Before Hitler Came: Documents from the Early Days of the National Socialist Movement.* Hitler immediately banned the book.'

(Slides of Rudolf von Sebottendorf; Sebottendorf and Heinrich Himmler; the cover of Sebottendorf's 1933 book.)

'The woman was Maria Oršić, originally from the city of Zagreb, Croatia, a self-proclaimed spiritualist who had founded the All German Society for Metaphysics in 1907 for mediums who were engaged in telepathic communication with extraterrestrial civilizations, and who herself was purportedly in telepathic contact with a race of beings that had originally come from a planet called Aldebaran, a superior Aryan race which Maria said had sent colony ships to dozens of Earth-like planets orbiting nearby stars five-hundred million years ago, just before their home planet was destroyed when their own sun exploded. Apparently from that point forward they played the game of planet hopscotch, colonizing one planet after another as their population increased, trying to establish a super Aryan Brotherhood of planets. Maria said they, meaning the descendants of the superior Aryans who lived on other planets, were now trying to re-establish contact with the descendants of the colonists who had come to Earth. Using telepathy, these outer space Aryans had sent Maria the technical specifications for constructing saucer-shaped spaceships so that the descendants of the long-lost colonists could make the journey across the stars to meet their long-lost relations, though precisely where these relations were located now that Aldebaran was gone was never made clear. Maria said that most of the long-lost colonists were living in Germany, because it was this group who had somehow, amazingly, kept their bloodline pure over the millennia.'

(Slides of Maria Oršić with her long blonde hair and haunting movie-star beauty; an unnamed planet, presumably a stand-in for Aldebaran, orbiting a star on the verge of exploding; a photo of the Earth taken from outer space; a map of Mesopotamia; ancient Sumerian ruins; technical specifications and various diagrams of a flying saucer; Nazi scientists in a lab filled with technical equipment; an artist's rendering of a flying saucer; and a photo of a black flying saucer hovering some two-hundred feet above a desolate stretch of ground while a group of uniformed men in the foreground, men who are standing beside two black cars parked along a dirt road, look on.)

'The fourth member of The Black Sun and the fifth and final member of this group that met at the café in Vienna was a man named Lothar Waiz, a German pilot and engineer who later flew one of the flying disc prototypes built by the Nazis.'

(Slide of a smiling Lothar Waiz standing next to the first Nazi-built flying saucer, RFZ-1, just before the very first test flight at the Brandenburg-Briest airfield in Germany.)

'Some scholars believe the Nazis couldn't wait to get their hands on the technical specifications imagined by Maria Oršić, and as soon as they did, which was at some point in the

1920s, they began working feverishly to develop this flying saucer technology. They were, of course, hampered by a lack of sufficient funding but they were also bolstered by an unwavering faith in the superiority of the German people, a faith also shaped to a large extent by the mythology created by Maria Oršić herself. This mythology referred to all sorts of fantastic weapons, weapons like the Spear of Destiny or the Ark of the Covenant, which had perhaps been used by the colonists from Aldebaran to subdue the native populations they encountered in Mesopotamia and elsewhere, weapons that would make a nation invincible but which had been lost over the course of the centuries. The Nazis believed that these weapons could perhaps be retrieved or re-imagined, a gift from the aliens that had visited our world, so they began to scour the planet for all sorts of extraterrestrial technology, anything to help them recapture what had been lost.'

(Slides of the Nazi party during the 1920s; a German archeological exhibition in Tibet; the Spear of Destiny, the Ark of the Covenant, an artist's rendering of the Aldebaran colonists subduing a primitive civilization.)

'The idea that a superior Aryan race from outer space wanted to work with the Germans to bring about a New World Order here on Earth fit in perfectly with the Nazi's deluded sense of their own destiny. It was as if Maria Oršić had looked into their subconscious minds, and for a suitable fee, which was most assuredly worked out at a later date, told them everything they wanted to hear. Baeumler, Bischoff, Bohle, Bormann, Bouhler, Eberstein, Eckart, Eichmann, Goebbels, Goering, Hadamovsky, Hess, Hewel, Heydrich, Himmler, Kaufmann, Lippert, Lorenz, Maurice, Rosenberg, Speer — these men all joined with Hitler to reshape the reality they knew, to create an alternative reality that rose unrestrained and initially unchallenged from the depths of their twisted imaginations. In truth, they were all insane. This does not justify what they did. No, it is more of an observation. But it is also a reminder to the rest of us. Nietzsche believed that in madness alone lies man's completion. Whether for good or ill, madness was the key that unlocked one's destiny. Nowhere in the pages of history has this profound truth been so horrifically demonstrated than with the Nazis. Indeed, when Hitler became the Chancellor of Germany in 1933, the madness of the Nazis deepened and the search for UFO paraphernalia became as important to the Nazi elites as the quest to find the Holy Grail had been to an earlier generation of glory hounds. For Hitler and Himmler and the other Party officials, the search for UFOs and alien technology and the search for the Grail were the same thing. It is a difficult lesson to come to terms with for it suggests, among other things, that we are all traveling a path that embraces madness in one form or another, which means that victory is neither God's nor the Devil's. To quote a French philosopher: Victory belongs to madness.'

(Slides of various Nazi Party leaders; then a photo of Adolph Hitler winning the election in 1933; then a photo of several Nazis eating sandwiches and drinking beer; then a photo of Adolph Hitler staring into the camera with a look of paranoid determination on his face; then an artist's rendering of the Holy Grail.)

-166-

The lights come up. The second part of the lecture will begin in fifteen minutes, give or take. Professor Elek Borža has already disappeared backstage in search of a bottle of water. (He usually has a bottle with him on the podium, but this evening, perhaps because of the technical difficulties that kept him backstage until nine-fifteen, he forgot.) The young man in charge of the projector is consumed with the task of replacing the old carousel of slides with a new one. The old one popped out easily enough, but the new carousel refuses to snap into the grooved track.

The bearded man's mind roams as a moth roams.
He starts at the sound of two giant wings fluttering in the semi-lucid darkness of the gymnasium. The sound of fluttering wings fades, is absorbed by the silence of the bearded man looking this way and that, presumably in search of the source of the fluttering sound. He asks the librarian if she has heard this strange noise, but she doesn't understand, assumes he is making a joke, laughs softly, politely, and gives his arm a loving squeeze.

'Do they sell refreshments here,' she says.

The bearded man is not sure but he thinks probably not. But the librarian is not willing to give up on the idea of refreshments just yet. She says that makes no sense at all because right this very instant she is watching dozens of people making their way from the back of the gymnasium to their seats, their hands full of all sorts of recently purchased sodas and candy bars and pretzels and ice cream cones and steaming cups of coffee. The bearded man is surprised. He did not notice a refreshment stand when they came in. Admittedly, they were in a hurry and could have missed it. But he cannot quite picture where it is. The hallways they had to travel to get from the entrance of the school to the gymnasium were too narrow for so commercial an endeavor. So he turns in his seat to see if perhaps the librarian is mistaken, or even pulling his leg. He is confounded by what he sees. The interior of the gymnasium seems to have undergone a startling transformation. If he didn't know better, he would have said they were sitting inside a very fancy, very elegant theatre, the kind you might expect in Vienna, the kind with an elevated stage (five feet high, with an immense red velvet curtain drawn across the front), an orchestra pit (without any musicians at the present moment), thirty-two rows of plush seating on the main floor (all of the seats filled with eager listeners as far as the bearded man can tell), a balcony with twenty-six rows (pitched at a much steeper angle than the rows on the main floor, impossible to tell if all the seats are taken, particularly in the rows all the way at the back), hanging lanterns emitting a diffuse, golden glow, walls decorated with fake Grecian pillars in relief and murals depicting pastoral scenes from mythology. It is almost more than the bearded man can comprehend.

'Do you want anything,' the librarian says.

The bearded man does not know how to respond. In the back of his mind he realizes that the librarian is waiting for something, an answer perhaps, or perhaps some money. He fishes a few banknotes out of his jeans pocket (green ones worth about five American dollars each) and the librarian is all smiles. She heads to the back of the theatre in search of refreshments and disappears into the crowd of people coming and going. The bearded man looks more closely at this crowd, at the people now filling in the rows, taking their seats, munching on their snacks. Some of the faces look familiar. The happy couple from the restaurant is sitting three rows back on the left. They wave when they see him looking on and he waves back. The pharmacist is four rows back on the right but he is focused on a pretzel and makes no effort to engage with the people around him. The artist and the waiter are five rows back in the middle. They appear to be old friends. The bearded man wonders if the artist ever consummated his hoped-for deal with the gallery owner and if perhaps the gallery owner is also somewhere in the audience.

Then he notices dozens and dozens of strangely unemotional faces, stoic faces without any trace of human compassion or belief in a higher power. All of the faces are a waxy brownish-gray color, more like the faces of wax figures or paper mâché puppets than flesh-and-blood persons. Even the wrinkles and the puffy oval lumps beneath the dozens of tired looking eyes are precisely, artistically shaped. He realizes these faces belong to the workmen he had noticed earlier in the day. They are no longer wearing their work clothes, but their faces are the same. How strange, he thinks, that all of these workmen, presumably stone masons by trade, should have an interest in the Nazi obsession with the occult, the Nordic master race and their artifacts, and UFO technology.

The librarian makes it back just as the lights go down for the second part of the lecture. She is empty-handed, a caricature of disappointment. As she plops down in her seat she hands the bearded man the banknotes he had given her and says how they had run out of everything except licorice candies, which she doesn't like all that much. In an attempt to buoy her spirits, the bearded man says he will take her to a café after the lecture is over. The strategy works. The librarian snuggles up to the bearded man as before and gives his arm a loving squeeze.

In the same instant, the immense red velvet curtain opens to reveal a giant white movie screen, a slow, somewhat dramatic unveiling, and Professor Elek Borža makes his way back to the podium. The Professor is no longer wearing jeans and a threadbare jacket with patches on the elbows. He, too, has undergone a transformation. His long white hair is now pulled back into a tight ponytail, very chic, and he is wearing a vintage 1950s black gabardine tuxedo jacket with split tails, beautifully lined with blue satin, and trousers to match. He resembles an internationally acclaimed maestro, right down to the white gloves, though of course without the baton.

The bearded man suddenly becomes anxious about the whereabouts of the young man in charge of the slide projector. Given the transformation of both the Professor and the gymnasium, it is reasonable to assume that the young man is now ensconced in the small projector booth above the balcony, but there is no way to know for certain. Then there is a sudden whirring sound and a click and the bearded man's anxiety vanishes. The giant movie screen is flooded with a photograph of a plain, unassuming looking fellow from the waist up. It is a candid photograph, meaning the subject was unaware he was being photographed. He is wearing a thin dark shirt and black-rimmed glasses and possesses the aura of a befuddled accountant or the likeable but bumbling assistant to a brilliant but emotionally distant and therefore unstable scientist. The man's name is Király, and he worked for Himmler from 1935 until the end of the war.

'There is no trace of Király anywhere in the world before 1932,' says the Professor. 'In October of that year he meets Herman Wirth at a meeting of German mystics in Berlin. Apparently the two men share not only an interest in the occult, but they both believe that the Nordic races had once ruled the Earth. Wirth has just published a paper entitled *The Prehistory of the Atlantic Nordic Race* in which he argues that Christian spirituality was not of Roman origin, but was built instead upon a primitive Germanic mysticism. Wirth believes the cosmological wisdom of the ancient Aryans needs to be recovered to combat what he calls the Mammonism of his own age. Király agrees. The two men talk about embarking on archaeological expeditions to find artifacts to spur on the process of spiritual recovery. Three years later, Wirth, along with Richard Walther Darré (a leading proponent of the völkisch movement) and Himmler, found the Ahnenerbe institute, whose mission is to research the archaeological and cultural history of the Aryan race. Wirth hires Király soon thereafter and discovers, among other things, that his young friend has a talent for making movies. Wirth doesn't ask where Király learned how to use a camera. He believes it is simply a matter of destiny revealing itself. He wants to capture the triumphs of each and every archaeological expedition on film. So he asks Király to manage the film crews for every major expedition sponsored by the institute.'

(Slides of Wirth, Richard Darré, an artist's rendering of a primitive Nordic group of people.)

'In 1935, Király accompanies an expedition to Karelia province in eastern Finland. The expedition is headed by the Finnish anthropologist Yrjö von Grönhagen, who is an opportunist and adventurer more than a scholar, which makes him an ideal puppet intellectual for the Nazi agenda. His work is later discredited by the Finnish ethnologist Kustaa Vilkuna, but he is a star in 1935. A year before the expedition, Grönhagen had published an article on the origins of Finnish folklore and the oral tradition that lay at the heart of Finnish culture. In the article, he focused much of his scholarly acumen, such as it was, on the Kalevala, the national heroic epic of Finland, and concluded that this magnificent tale was simply a re-telling of earlier Norse tales and thus stemmed from an Aryan tradition that echoed with the pagan mysticism of a pre-Germanic culture. Himmler was impressed with the article, which is why he asked Grönhagen to go to Karelia to record the stories and ritual practices of pagan sorcerers and witches in an attempt to recover knowledge that had been lost over the centuries. The expedition is a tremendous success. The group is able to record pagan chants. And Király is able to film several pagan initiation rites as well as some sort of exorcism and a local soothsayer communing with the spirits of the dead in order to predict the future.'

(Slides of von Grönhagen, bearded men loading boxes into a truck, pagans dancing around a fire in Karelia, a close-up of the soothsayer.)

'In 1937, Király accompanies an expedition to the Murg Valley in Germany to excavate the Heunenberg tumulus burial mounds. The expedition is led by the noted German archaeologist Gustav Riek, who in 1931 had recovered sixteen ivory statuettes in the Swabian Mountains. Riek had argued that the Swabian statuettes, which date from the Paleolithic age, were symbolic reminders of the central ideology that had shaped pre-Germanic cultures, an ideology founded on the ideas of absolute power and superhuman strength. It is not altogether clear why Himmler wants Riek to excavate the Heunenberg burial mounds. One can assume he is hoping that Riek will uncover another stash of pre-Germanic artifacts glorifying power and strength, but no such stash is discovered. Király amasses over two-hundred hours of film documenting the back-breaking work of excavation interspersed with scenes of happy, smiling, but worn-out men relaxing in camp at the end of a long day. The Nazis later claim the expedition is a stunning success.'

(Slides of Gustav Riek, the Murg Valley, the Swabian

statuettes in a museum display case, scenes of the expedition camp.)

'In 1938, Herman Wirth is replaced as President of the Ahnenerbe by Walthur Wüst, a prominent German Orientalist who later becomes Rector of the University of Munich. Wirth was Király's only friend in the Ahnenerbe.'

(Slide of Walthur Wüst, a beardless, beady-eyed man, properly groomed, thin, pursed lips.)

'In that same year, Király is all set to accompany German archaeologist Edmund Kiss to Bolivia to study the ancient temples in Tiwanaku, which Kiss claimed were built by prehistoric Nordic Thulians twenty-six thousand years before Christ. According to Kiss, the Thulians were the original inhabitants of Atlantis, and when their island home was destroyed in a whirlwind of volcanic eruptions followed by a devastating tsunami, they migrated all over the world. The expedition is mysteriously cancelled.'

(Slides of Edmund Kiss, the mountains of Bolivia, a native guide standing in front of the ruins at Tiwanaku, an artist's rendering of the destruction of Atlantis.)

'By 1939, the nature of the expeditions sponsored by the Ahnenerbe institute has changed. The focus is now on either acquiring ancient artifacts with supposedly magical properties (i.e. the Holy Grail, the Spear of Destiny, the Ark of the Covenant), or confiscating alien technology from supposed UFO crash sites.'

(Slides of the above-mentioned artifacts.)

'In 1940, Király accompanies Reichsfüher Himmler himself to the Abbey at Montserrat, just north of Barcelona, in search of the Holy Grail. This preliminary visit is inspired in part by a Catalonian folksong that mentions a mystical font within the walls of an unnamed castle in northern Spain. Himmler believes that this castle is Montserrat based on a line in Wagner's opera *Parsifal,* which suggests that the Holy Grail might be located in "the marvelous castle of Montsalvat in the Pyrenees." This belief is bolstered by the odd coincidence that the very first performance of *Parsifal* was staged in 1913 at the Liceu Opera House in Barcelona. Though some of the scholars connected with the Ahnenerbe institute, including Wüst, privately reject the idea that the Holy Grail is at Montserrat, none will openly oppose Himmler. Ultimately, however, their collective silence does not matter. The visit is a bust. Himmler is hoping to get the permission of the abbot to search for the Grail, but the abbot will not even see Himmler. He sends a monk in his place to give the Reichsfüher a partial tour of the monastery, which Király captures on film, but that is that, as they say. Spain is outside the sphere of Nazi influence. If the Holy Grail does exist at Montserrat, the Nazis will not get their hands on it.'

(Slides of the Abbey at Monserrat from various angles.)

'In August 1942, Király heads to the Crimea with an expedition investigating reports of an alien spaceship that had supposedly crashed in the 1920s. Artifacts from the crash had originally been taken to a museum in Maykop, Russia, but when the expedition arrives they discover that the retreating Red Army is now in possession of everything retrieved from the downed craft, seventy-two crates. Twenty of the seventy-two crates are later discovered in a medical warehouse in Mozdok and shipped to Berlin. The twenty crates contain a variety of Greek artifacts but nothing else.'

(Slides of a museum in Maykop, a warehouse in Mozdok, a collection of Greek artifacts.)

'In January 1943, a cinematographer named Georg Vertov joins Király's film crew. Vertov has worked with six or seven big-name film directors (Leni Riefenstahl, Wilhelm Stöppler, the great Werner Klingler, Max Kimmich, to name the biggest) making movies for the Nazi propaganda machine. It is never quite clear why Vertov begins working for the Ahnenerbe institute. Perhaps he has had a falling out with one of the big shots, probably Kimmich, brother-in-law to Joseph Goebbels.'

(Slides of Georg Vertov, Leni Riefenstahl, Wilhelm Stöppler, Werner Klingler, Max Kimmich.)

'In May 1943, Király and Vertov accompany an expedition to the Balkans to excavate a UFO crash site. According to locals, an iron ship had fallen from the sky in 1887.'

(Slide of an unidentified site in the Balkans.)

'In July 1943, Király and Vertov accompany an expedition headed to Algiers to investigate a plague of UFO sightings in the skies above the city. They are particularly interested in reports of a crash along the coast seventeen miles west of the city. While in Algiers, Király meets with Patrice L'Herbier, a physician of doubtful reputation who had left the small town of Villefranche-sur-Saône, France in 1892 under suspicious circumstances. L'Herbier was reportedly investigated by the police commissioner of Algiers, a man named Louvain, immediately prior to Király's arrival, but Louvain doesn't turn up anything of importance after three months, so he drops the matter. Király and L'Herbier meet in a small café somewhere in the Quasbah District once a day for seven days. On the seventh day Király accompanies L'Herbier to his clinic. When he returns to his hotel nine hours later, the top third of his head from the eyebrows and ears up is wrapped in a gauze bandage.'

(Slides of an unidentified café in Algiers, an unnamed street in Villefranche-sur-Saône, France.)

'In September 1943, Király and Vertov accompany an expedition headed to Kiev to excavate a supposed UFO crash site from the 17th century. Király is no longer wearing the gauze bandage. Whatever injury he sustained in Algiers has healed.'

(Slide of the expedition setting up camp on a farm near Kiev.)

'In October 1943, Király reveals to Vertov that he is the point of contact for an alien race (the Aldebaranians of Maria Oršić's mythology) whose fate has been aligned with the fate of humanity for over ten thousand years. Vertov, who has believed in the existence of a Super-Aryan Master race from the stars since he was a young man, is overwhelmed with admiration. Still, he asks why Király was chosen and not someone higher up in the Party, such as Himmler. Király explains that according to the messages he has been receiving, the Master race now believes the Nazis will lose the war. The higher-ups in the Party are to blame. Already there is chaos on the Eastern Front. Within a year Germany will be engaged in a full-blown retreat, so it is now up to Király and the small group of men he will choose to save the day, to pick up the baton the Nazis have let fall. Vertov is excited, but still not altogether convinced, so he asks Király what the ultimate objective is. Király smiles and says they are to prepare the way for the return of the Master race. The ancient Aryans, he says, will come down from the heavens, taking the form of the long dead Merovingian kings, and bring peace and prosperity to humanity for the next one-thousand years. Vertov is practically speechless, but he does manage to ask one final question. He asks Király how they will accomplish this fantastic mission. With calm assurances Király says they will foment dissent and anarchy among their enemies until the entire world cries out for deliverance. Then when the political infrastructure of every country on Earth lies in ruins, the ancient Aryans will return. Király says they will begin their efforts in earnest in South America, perhaps the Caribbean. Then he shows Vertov the scar on his scalp where Patrice L'Herbier had implanted a small electronic device near his cochlea, a device that Király says allows him to send and receive messages to and from the upper stratosphere and beyond. Vertov is impressed. Király says he was told that this device was necessary to ensure that the messages from the ancient Aryans would not be lost during transmission. Also, Király says everyone they recruit to their cause will receive a similar device, not only so they can receive transmissions directly from outer space, but so Király can communicate with them as needed. When Király asks Vertov to join him, Vertov agrees without any hesitation whatsoever. They begin recruiting men the very next day.'

(Slides of the German army retreating, an artist's rendering of the ancient Aryans, an artist's rendering of the Merovingian kings, a vaguely European-looking city in ruins, an aerial view of a Caribbean island, a small electronic device with exposed wires.)

'In February 1944, Király and Vertov accompany an expedition headed to the Canary Islands to investigate reports of a crashed UFO. They carry forged papers indicating they are all citizens of Argentina because the Canary Islands are controlled by Spain. The Nazis and Franco are not on good terms. The expedition spends three weeks interviewing witnesses in Santa Cruz de Tenerife and then a week exploring the black sand beaches of La Gomera.'

(Slide of a map of the Canary Islands.)

'In June 1944, Király and Vertov are all set to accompany an expedition headed to Iran. The precise purpose of the expedition is unknown. On June 7, the expedition is cancelled.'

(Slide of a map of Iran.)

'In July 1944, Király replaces his official dossier with one filled with fabrications. Király later explains that he wanted to confuse the bloodhounds who would surely try to track him down at a later date. His falsified dossier indicates that from 1936 until 1944 he worked for the Ministry of Public Enlightenment and Propaganda in the Department of Film, under the direction of Karl Neumann.'

(Slides of the neoclassical exterior façade of the Ministry

of Public Enlightenment and Propaganda building, a somber Karl Neumann.)

'In August 1944, Király and Vertov head back to Algiers. They are not traveling as part of an official Ahnenerbe expedition. They are on their own. All Ahnenerbe expeditions have been suspended since the Allies landed in Normandy. Given the internal chaos that reigns throughout Germany, it is easy for Király and Vertov to slip out of the country undetected.'

(Slide of Király and Vertov boarding a plane.)

'In September 1944, the men Király and Vertov have recruited during the previous ten months begin arriving in Algiers. Every recruit, ninety-six in all, pays a visit to Patrice L'Herbier's clinic. At the end of September, Vertov's sister joins Király and her brother. By the end of October 1944, Király, Vertov, Vertov's sister, and the ninety-six recruits have all left Algiers. No one knows where they have gone. Then in August 1960, Király suddenly returns to Algiers. He is accompanied by a very beautiful African woman who is never identified. Király and the woman spend the next two years in Algiers. They rent a room on the second floor above what used to be L'Herbier's clinic. L'Herbier apparently died in 1948. Then in August 1962, a reporter named Kateb Yacine, a novelist and playwright as much as a journalist, interviews Király about his activities during World War Two. The interview will be published in *Alger républicain*, a newspaper with close ties to the French-Algerian communist movement. No one knows how Yacine found out about Király or what initially prompted the interview, which takes place over the course of a several days in the very same café where Király first met with L'Herbier. Yacine gets Király to talk about everything he did during the war years. But when Yacine asks Király where he went after the war ended and what he has been doing since, Király purportedly says "some things it is best not to know." Two days before the article is published, Király and the African woman head off into the desert. They are never seen again.'

(Slides of Patrice L'Herbier's clinic, Vertov's sister, Kateb Yacine drinking in a café with friends, a four-story white colonial building in downtown Algiers, presumably the building where the newspaper *Alger républicain* is published, the road from Algiers to the desert.)

'So what should we make of Király's fantastic tale? Do we believe him? Is there any truth in what he says? Human nature commands that we ask such questions. But there is an old adage: if you ask the wrong question, the answer does not matter. In other words, it does not matter if what Király says happened is true or not. What matters is that his story exists, a symptom of the Nazi madness that overwhelmed Germany and the German people, the kind of madness that results when you imprison the collective imagination of a culture, what some scholars have called the pathology of captive minds.

'Let me conclude by saying that Király's obvious madness, whatever the cause — the contagious madness of the Nazis or some mental defect in the way he was wired — coupled with the fact that he is absolutely absent from the historical record prior to 1932 is still the source of much controversy. To some it is as if he had arrived on the planet fully formed at the age of twenty-two, an observation that has fueled a great deal of suspicion among UFO conspiracy theorists that Király was an alien sent to Earth to work with the Nazis on behalf of some unknown alien agenda. Of course every reputable scholar will tell you such a theory is utter poppycock, without any sort of grounding in reality. They will tell you that the people who believe in such nonsense live on the fringes of society and have little regard for the scientific method, which means their views are to be dismissed without a backwards glance.

'Then again, who among us can ever be absolutely sure that the reality he or she perceives is the same reality everyone else perceives? Who is courageous enough to stand against the truth as others imagine the truth must be? Who would deny the collective truth of humanity in favor of a truth that exists only in one's own mind? In the end we all face a choice. We must either accept the way the world actually is, or at least as it appears to be, and so we must buy into the propaganda that imprisons everyone else. Or we must embrace the world as we think it should be, what some would call paradise. But we must choose, and whatever we choose will be considered madness by those who would have made a different choice.

'Some will try to use this line of reasoning to excuse the behavior of the Nazis or justify their depravity. Since many of the Nazis could not possibly have realized the slippery slope they were on, the apologists will argue, they should be absolved of all responsibility for the crimes committed in the name of the Nazi Party. But this is the argument of cowards. We are still responsible for the consequences of our choices whether we foresee those consequences or not.

'So we must condemn the Nazis for the unrestrained evil they perpetuated on the world, and since Király was a part of that evil, his actions must be judged accordingly. Yet we must also recognize that the madness that Király and the Nazis possessed is a madness that we all possess, at least in its germinal form. *One must still have chaos in oneself to be able to give birth to a dancing star,* as Nietzsche reminds us. This is what it means to be human. It is the essence of who we are. It is both the great glory and the great tragedy of the human race.'

Professor Elek Borža nods at the audience and steps back from the podium as the lights come up. The lecture on Nazi madness and the occult is suddenly over. Cued by the lights, a few startled but appreciative listeners begin to applaud, and then a few more, and then the sound of thunderous applause saturates the air. The applause continues for quite a while.

-167-

The bearded man and the librarian are now sitting at a wrought-iron table (painted white) outside a small corner café. The interior of the café takes up the entire first floor of a four story 19th century building with a crumbling plaster exterior, now with a fresh coat of paint, a burnt orange color, to hide the various patch jobs of the last few years. The entrance (a small recessed foyer leading to a glass door framed by mahogany) faces south and opens up onto a cobblestone plaza. There are also two large windows, also framed by mahogany, on either side of the recessed foyer, and a dozen tiny café tables out front, illuminated by four portable gas lanterns, expertly placed, and a candle safely ensconced in a glass bowl on each table. The side of the building that faces west contains no windows, probably because the street on that side is more of an alley than a street. The bearded man is sipping coffee from a white porcelain cup and eating potato soup with freshly baked bread, while the librarian is enjoying a plate of sumptuous apricot kolache and a steaming cup of cocoa. It is the same café where the student was passing out leaflets.

Normally the café is not open this late. Normally the streets are deserted by this hour, which means there are no potential customers wandering by, drawn perhaps by the mouth-watering aroma of soup. Tonight, however, every table both inside and outside is occupied. There is no explanation for this anomaly. Perhaps the owner of the café anticipated the sudden crowd because he knew about the lecture. Perhaps he had to argue with the waitresses, who were forced to hang around doing practically nothing from ten, when the café normally closes, until almost midnight, because that's when the crowd showed up. In any event, the café is now exceedingly busy. The waitresses are exhausted from scurrying back and forth from the various tables to the kitchen and then back again with ridiculously oversized trays laden with bowls of hot soup (potato, potato dumpling, barley, onion, sauerkraut and ham) or various sweet breads and pastries (apricot kolache, poppy seed kolache, prune kolache, poppyseed rings, houska stuffed with almonds and raisins and lemon peel, strudls of all kinds, but most notably apple strudl and blackberry strudl). It is a wonder the waitresses don't crash into each other and send their trays flying, particularly when one is entering the foyer, which is barely wide enough to accommodate a single tray, as another one is emerging.

Above the soft, golden glow of the café tables, the stars burn brightly or dimly depending upon how far away they are from the Earth and how much fuel they have left. The happy café patrons inhabiting the tables do not notice the stars. They are eating and drinking and smoking Turkish cigarettes and flicking the ash carelessly and chatting amiably, all without looking up.

What else is there to do on such a beautiful night?

Then a boisterous argument from one of the outdoor tables (six feet from where the bearded man and the librarian are sitting) threatens to prick this bubble of self-absorbed, oblivious frivolity.

The table is actually two tables pushed together. Three of the occupants at the boisterous table (their names are Ottmar, Amrik, and Johannes) possess strangely artificial faces, a waxy brownish-gray color, more like the faces of wax figures or paper mâché puppets than flesh-and-blood persons, an aspect which is accentuated by the soft, malleable glow emanating from the gas lanterns and the table candles.

Ottmar, Amrik and Johannes are sitting on the long side furthest from the bearded man and the librarian. Theirs are the voices that have shattered the equilibrium of this most beautiful night.

The two short sides of the boisterous table are occupied by the happy couple from the restaurant (scrunched together on the side closest to the café) and the artist (all the room in the world on the side facing the plaza). The long side nearest the bearded man and the librarian is occupied by the pharmacist, who has pushed his chair back from the table about a foot, as if he is trying to distance himself from the argumentative demeanor of Ottmar, Amrik and Johannes, and the cashier from the grocery store, who wasn't at the lecture because she was preparing dinner for her grandmother, or so she had said, or perhaps she had arrived late, after her grandmother had finished eating (or had even gone to bed early without any dinner at all, which happens every now and then), and the bearded man had simply not noticed her.

'I will say again,' says Amrik, 'the Professor did not even address the fact that Király was most likely suffering from some form of paranoid schizophrenia, which often brings about extremely vivid and complex hallucinations.'

'True, true,' says Ottmar, 'but most parapsychologists I know completely discount the idea that hallucinations are limited to psychological causes. They point to chemicals, even common pollutants such as carbon monoxide, as capable of triggering hallucinatory experiences.'

'No one is denying that any number of chemicals may trigger a hallucination,' says Amrik. 'There are all sorts of hidden triggers, environmental, chemical, emotional. But not everyone who breathes in carbon monoxide develops a psychosis. I'm talking about the underlying weakness in Király's psychological makeup that predisposed him to a psychotic break with reality. The good Professor didn't say a word about that.'

'Both of you are missing the obvious,' says Johannes. 'Amrik, your argument is typical of the view that the only reality is a psychological reality. And Ottmar, you are looking to ascribe natural causes to what may in fact be of supernatural origin.'

'Don't tell me you believe that nonsense about an alien race from Aldebaran,' says Amrik.

'And why not?' says Johannes. 'That was the Professor's point, wasn't it? That all reality is suspect, that none of us can ever be absolutely sure that the reality we perceive is the same reality everyone else perceives. How do we know that Király wasn't somehow in contact with these aliens? What makes our reality the definitive reality?'

'You mean you're taking everything the Professor said at face value?' says Ottmar.

'No, not at all,' says Johannes. 'Much of what he said is simply a regurgitation of what one might call the Nazi myth. Unfortunately, the Professor adopted an objective approach in presenting this myth, which I am sure left some with the impression that everything he said was true, at least from a historical perspective. He could have exposed the pseudoscience of the Nazis for what it was: a quasi-religious dogma shaped by infantile fantasies masquerading as the truth. But he didn't. He didn't talk about the Thule Society and Hitler's unrestrained obsession with all things magical. He didn't say anything about Edmond Halley's ridiculous hollow Earth theory, which the Nazis seem to have embraced. Nor did he mention the supposed Nazi submarine bases in Antarctica or the patently absurd cosmological views of Hans Horbiger.'

'So you are an anti-pragmatist,' says Amrik.

'Only after I've eaten a full meal,' says Johannes.

'Then perhaps you are a pragmatist,' says Ottmar.

'Nothing anyone says can prove anything.'

'Then what are you?' says Ottmar.

Johannes does not know how to respond. Fortunately, he does not have to. In the blink of an eye, a fourth character challenges the other three for center stage. The voice of this fourth character seems to be descending, as if from on high.

'But how can he honestly answer your question except to say that he is what he is?' says the fourth voice.

Amrik, Ottmar and Johannes look up in unison to see who might be so presumptuous as to intrude upon their unintentionally public conversation, a conversation which seems, nevertheless, to be pointing towards something beyond itself (a sign, a symbol, the fragmentary consciousness of a dream perhaps). They see the bearded man standing on the other side of the two tables, not standing precisely, more like he is leaning forward, almost hunched over, arms out in front, hands pressing down on the cold, wrought-iron edge, the blood draining from his knuckles. The mere presence of the bearded man is enough to give everyone pause.

So now let us look at the scene before us more closely in the hope that a closer look will create a clearer picture. It is a frozen moment, a painting hanging on a wall, a black and white photograph that has become a part of history, a monument made of stone.

The happy couple from the restaurant is paying no attention to any of the conversations taking place at their table, or anywhere else for that matter. The woman is practically sitting in the man's lap. The two are quite busy murmuring into each other's ears and giggling and gazing fondly into each other's eyes. From a certain conventional perspective their behavior might be called mildly erotic. They are a world of possibilities unto themselves.

The pharmacist pushes his chair away from the table, but not because of the argumentative demeanor of Ottmar, Amrik, and Johannes, which is clearly visible upon their waxy-brownish gray faces and suggests among other things the imminent possibility of violence. The pharmacist is quite simply embarrassed by the behavior of the happy couple from the restaurant. He is clutching a pastry wrapped in cellophane in one hand and a paper cup filled with coffee in the other as he pushes his chair back with his legs.

The movement is very sudden, almost exclamatory. The iron legs of the chair scraping across the irregular pattern of cobblestone in front of the café produces a sharply pitched, metallic sound, like a woman's scream, which seems to linger in the air even after the movement has ceased. But the pharmacist remains in the chair. For some reason he is looking at the entrance to the café. Perhaps he is thinking he might find a table inside.

The cashier, startled by the pharmacist's sudden movement, a movement which on an unconscious level causes an involuntary sensation of panic, has turned to see what is happening, but her view of the pharmacist is obscured by the presence of the bearded man, who has filled the void created by the pharmacist's partial departure. She tilts her head and shoulders at an odd angle so she can get a better look at the bearded man's profile. A flicker of sudden recognition washes across her face, a shallow wave that is replaced by the still waters of idle curiosity. Perhaps she is wondering why the bearded man has approached their table.

The artist could care less about Amrik, Ottmar, and Johannes, or the bearded man, except that the latter seems to have momentarily captured the attention of the cashier. The artist had been ogling the cashier, who is quite shapely, and trying to engage her in a probing even intimate conversation when she had been startled by the partial departure of the pharmacist. The artist is now leaning across the corner of the table, trying to once again insert himself into the prism of her awareness.

Ottmar, Amrik, and Johannes are a mass of confusion. Amrik stands up quite abruptly in an apparent effort to confront the audacity of the bearded man's intrusion, in spite of the fact that the bearded man is grinning from ear to ear, a fool on a ship of fools, so to speak, and thus presents no obvious (or credible) threat beyond offering an unsolicited (and therefore damning, at least, presumably, in Amrik's eyes) observation. Amrik's wrought-iron chair is now on its side on the cobblestone, a nuisance, certainly, for the two couples at the next table over, who are forced to maneuver themselves around the chair on their way back into the café for more refreshments because the waitresses have for some reason stopped serving those sitting outside.

Ottmar is scrambling to pick up Amrik's chair as the two couples from the next table over step past his outstretched arms. He offers them a sincere apology, but they choose not to respond.

Johannes is sitting back in his chair, as far back as he can, as if his chair is a small, dark cave or a portal to another dimension offering him a means of escaping a potentially ugly confrontation. Of course the wrought-iron chair is still a wrought-iron chair and Johannes is still Johannes. He is not looking directly at the bearded man. Instead, he is looking through the gap between the bearded man's right shoulder and the profile of the startled cashier. It is not clear if he is looking at anyone in particular. Perhaps he is looking at the librarian, who is sitting so that she has an unimpeded view of the plaza and seems unaware of the tension at the once boisterous table. She is happily polishing off the last of her apricot kolache.

It is at precisely this moment that Professor Borža intervenes. He was emerging from the recessed entrance just as the pharmacist glanced in that direction, a dark figure only partially illuminated by the portable gas lanterns and the candlelight. As he made his way through the sea of outdoor tables he was being asked questions right and left, but his response was the same. 'Never neglect the little things in life,' he kept saying. To some the sound of the Professor's voice is the sound of an oboe, a soothing, mellow sound that might very well lull them to sleep. To others it is the voice of reason in a world that has gone completely insane.

'But how can he honestly answer your question except to say that he is what he is?' says the bearded man.

Amrik stands up abruptly from the table.

Ottmar scrambles to pick up the fallen chair.

The two couples from the next table over whoosh past.

Johannes sinks back as far as he can go into his chair.

The librarian pops the last of her kolache into her mouth.

And just like that the Professor's head appears in the gap between the bearded man's right shoulder and the profile of the startled cashier.

'It's a madhouse in there,' the Professor says.

Ottmar sets the fallen chair on its feet and sits back in his own. Johannes leans forward and picks up his coffee and drinks it slowly. Amrik is still standing, but he now seems like a sea captain whose ship has been lost.

'They're beginning to run out of everything,' the Professor says. 'If you want soup, your only choice now is cabbage. One must assume that they didn't expect such a large crowd tonight.'

Amrik says something that apparently only the Professor can hear, and the Professor nods and smiles and chuckles softly, a very soft chuckling, and then Amrik is chuckling as well, though not as softly, and smiling and nodding as well. It is almost as if the two are trading secret jokes.

Then the Professor turns to the bearded man and says 'Come along, my young friend, we have much to discuss' and now it is the bearded man's turn to nod.

The two men head back to the bearded man's table and sit down. The librarian looks up as if she knew all along that sooner or later the Professor would be joining them. She smiles demurely at her date for the evening and says she's going back inside to get another plate of apricot kolache before they run out completely.

Eventually, of course, the café does run out of everything. The waitresses begin cleaning up as the patrons head home in twos and threes and fours. The portable gas lanterns are extinguished. A man dressed in black appears and loads the first gas lantern onto a two-wheel dolly and rolls the dolly down the alley along the west side of the café building to a small door that has been invisible until just this moment. He opens the door and rolls the gas lantern through the opening, tipping it back so it will clear the header. Then he repeats the process for the remaining gas lanterns.

Meanwhile, the exhausted waitresses have begun the unwarranted (as far as they are concerned) chore of collecting the candles and pushing in the dozens of wrought-iron chairs, which are too heavy (thankfully) to put up on top of the tables. But soon enough (though not soon enough for the waitresses on this very long night) the café is closed and the lights are out. Everyone has gone home, the waitresses, the librarian, the pharmacist, the cashier from the grocery store, the artist, the happy couple from the restaurant, Ottmar, Amrik, Johannes, everyone.

Except not everyone has gone home.

The bearded man and the Professor are still sitting at one of the outdoor tables. The night has turned cloudy, so they are all but invisible in the darkness. It is an ocean of darkness. But their voices can be plainly heard. It is as if their voices are emanating from two invisible loudspeakers expertly placed behind the clouds.

'It is quite simple, my young friend,' the Professor says. 'You have been in this country far longer than you expected. At some point you slipped into a despair so consuming that you lost sight of who you were. When you looked into the mirror of your own desires you saw a madman wandering along one dark corridor after another, an endless wandering.'

The bearded man asks the Professor why he slipped into such a despair in the first place. What was the cause, the origin of his psychosis? Was it the result of some genetic abnormality? Or was it caused by some childhood experience, a trauma he no longer remembered?

'That is difficult to say, especially since so many years have passed. Perhaps it was the death of your father. Or the fact that your mother abandoned you when you were very young. Or it was from something else. It does not truly matter. What matters is that you accept that you can never know. As the poet says, have patience with everything that remains unsolved in your heart. One must live in the question.'

The bearded man asks the Professor if they have had this conversation before.

'Yes, yes, we have had this conversation on many occasions. Not an exact replica, mind you, but close enough. But do not find fault with yourself if you do not remember. You have been experiencing what some have called the long dark night of the soul.'

The bearded man asks the Professor if there is a way to break the cycle of repeated conversations.

'I believe it is already broken. You yourself have broken the cycle. You have indicated that you do not wish to be here. You wish to go home. This thought did not occur to you during our previous conversations. That is a very significant step. You have also begun to contemplate the future once again, and in contemplating the future, you have been contemplating the infinite, which is the same thing as contemplating God as far as I'm concerned. I myself gave up trying to understand what motivates God long ago. But maybe you will have better luck.'

At this point the nature of the conversation shifts. The bearded man talks in great detail about the woman he fell in love with sixteen years earlier. Or maybe it was twelve years. Or twenty-four. He thinks of her as his one true love. He talks about the difficulty of finding happiness in a world that believes true love is just a lot of sentimental hogwash. He talks about the day he left, how cloudy it was that day, but then the sun burst through the clouds. It was a very bright sun. A sun shining with such intensity that it didn't leave a single shadow. It left only scars.

The Professor has heard this story before but he does not interrupt.

The bearded man talks about the death of an old man he barely knew and the priest who delivered the eulogy at the funeral mass. It was the strangest eulogy he had ever heard. The priest had said that the Catholic Church had once embraced madness as an essential means to reveal God's truth, that Christ himself was a madman, he had to be mad in order to die on the Cross, but then one day the Church had had enough of madness, so they began to toss madmen into prison cells, every madman they could find, and this included Christ, although the Church did not realize this.

It was a very strange eulogy, and yet it was not so strange. It had struck a chord with the bearded man's younger self. He (his younger self) realized he was a madman just the same as all of those other madmen. He was in the cell right there with them. And when he realized this, he also realized that to say 'this prison cell had become the world' or 'the world had become this prison cell' was to say the exact same thing.

After that he went from place to place, seeking out others like himself, other madmen who were trapped in the infinity of space that exists between two opposing mirrors.

After that he found himself here, in this strangely modern yet decrepit city that straddles the Vltava River, a city lifted from the pages of forgotten books, where masonry repair has become an essential and therefore ceaseless activity.

After that he found himself in the care of the good Professor and the librarian.

After that he had lost track of the passing years.

Then the Professor and the bearded man talk about the new day that is dawning. The bearded man confesses that he still thinks about his one true love. He will never forget her. How could he? He thinks maybe he will go back. Maybe they can try again. The Professor says this is only natural. The bearded man says the first thing he is going to do, however, is shave off his beard. There's a drugstore not too far away, just off Vodičkova Street. The Professor says he knows just where it is. The bearded man says he will head there as soon as they open and buy a razor and shave off his beard. She wouldn't recognize him if he showed up looking like he does. The Professor thinks this is a good idea.

Then there is nothing more to talk about. The voices of the two men are replaced by the sound of two wrought-iron chairs being pushed back and then the sound of two sets of footsteps going off in opposite directions, but then both sets stopping simultaneously, a slight turning, a moment of complete silence like the silence at the bottom of the sea, and then the voice of the Professor, not as loud as before but still quite distinct, the Professor saying 'we all live under the same moon, my friend, even on a night such as this when the sky is obscured by the clouds,' and then another moment of silence followed directly by the sound of the footsteps again, the sound growing fainter and fainter by degree, and then nothing but the steady electric hum of the streetlights, and every now and then the gentle swooshing sound the river makes and the gentle slapping of a few early morning fisherman rowing their small skiffs out across the dark waters, the sounds of the skiffs moving along the river taking on a hollow, slightly muffled, unearthly quality as they pass beneath the Charles Bridge, the hearty, distant voices of the fishermen calling out to each other, like church bells announcing the hour, the sounds lingering a moment and then vanishing as neatly and completely as if they had never existed at all.